EISENHORN
THE OMNIBUS

More tales of the Inquisition from Black Library

• EISENHORN •
Dan Abnett

XENOS
MALLEUS
HERETICUS
THE MAGOS

• RAVENOR •
Dan Abnett

RAVENOR
RAVENOR RETURNED
RAVENOR ROGUE

• BEQUIN •
Dan Abnett

PARIAH
PENITENT

• THE HORUSIAN WARS •
John French

Book 1: RESURRECTION
Book 2: INCARNATION
DIVINATION

• VAULTS OF TERRA •
Chris Wraight

Book 1: THE CARRION THRONE
Book 2: THE HOLLOW MOUNTAIN
Book 3: THE DARK CITY

• AGENT OF THE THRONE AUDIO DRAMAS •
John French

BLOOD AND LIES
TRUTH AND DREAMS
ASHES AND OATHS

INFERNO! PRESENTS: THE INQUISITION
Various authors

EISENHORN
THE OMNIBUS

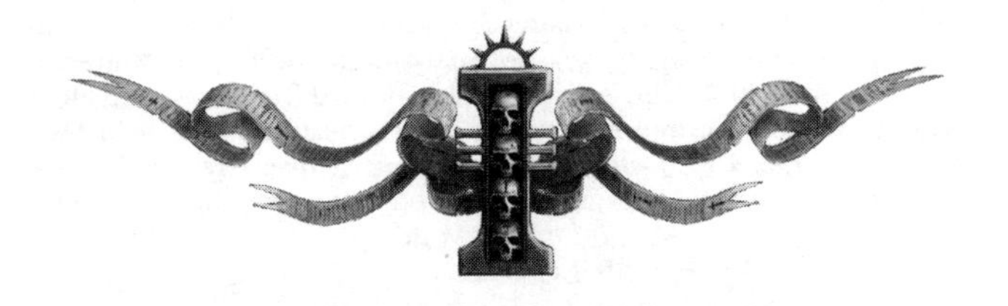

DAN ABNETT

A BLACK LIBRARY PUBLICATION

Xenos first published in 2001.
Malleus first published in 2001.
'Missing in Action' first published in *Inferno!* magazine in 2001.
Hereticus first published in 2002.
'Backcloth for a Crown Additional' first published in
Inferno! magazine in 2002.
'Regia Occulta' first published as an audio drama in 2011.
'The Keeler Image' first published digitally in 2016.
The Magos first published in 2018.
This edition published in Great Britain in 2023 by
Black Library, Games Workshop Ltd., Willow Road,
Nottingham, NG7 2WS, UK.

Represented by: Games Workshop Limited – Irish branch,
Unit 3, Lower Liffey Street, Dublin 1,
D01 K199, Ireland.

10 9 8 7 6

Produced by Games Workshop in Nottingham.
Cover illustration by Svetlana Kostina.

A CIP record for this book is available from the British Library.

ISBN 13: 978-1-78999-054-6

Printed and bound in the UK.

For more than a hundred centuries the Emperor has sat immobile on the Golden Throne of Earth. He is the Master of Mankind. By the might of His inexhaustible armies a million worlds stand against the dark.

Yet, He is a rotting carcass, the Carrion Lord of the Imperium held in life by marvels from the Dark Age of Technology and the thousand souls sacrificed each day so that His may continue to burn.

To be a man in such times is to be one amongst untold billions. It is to live in the cruellest and most bloody regime imaginable. It is to suffer an eternity of carnage and slaughter. It is to have cries of anguish and sorrow drowned by the thirsting laughter of dark gods.

This is a dark and terrible era where you will find little comfort or hope. Forget the power of technology and science. Forget the promise of progress and advancement. Forget any notion of common humanity or compassion.

There is no peace amongst the stars, for in the grim darkness of the far future, there is only war.

CONTENTS

REGIA OCCULTA

I crossed over into Jared County via the pass at Kulbrech. Air links were down, because of the Cackle, so a reluctant motorised unit of the local militia conveyed me from the capital as far as Kulbrech Town, and then only because the Jared Commissioner had been so insistent. This was – oh – 223.M41, and I was only just out on my own.

Even then, at the very dawn of my career, I was treated with a mixture of fear and suspicion. The rosette, or the title 'inquisitor,' or a combination of both, fairly focused the minds of those who met me. This attitude bores me these days. Back then, it gave me a sort of vulgar sensation of power.

Inquisitor Flammel had been killed six months before in a miserable warp transit accident, and I had been posted as a locum to cover his circuit, which was the fief worlds of the Grand Banks in the coreward reaches of the Helican sub. Circuit work is a drudge, and one acts, in the main, as an itinerant magistrate, travelling from planetary capital to planetary capital, reviewing flotsam cases gathered by the local authorities. Most are trivial and hardly Ordo business, scares conjured up by superstition and petty disputation, though I had spent eight weeks on New Bylar working through a caseload that eventually exposed a traffic in low-grade, unsanctioned psykers.

From New Bylar, I went to Ignix, the smallest and most peripheral of the fief colonies, a place locally regarded as the back end of all creation.

Ignix did not disappoint. Small, wet and whorled with ravines and meandering trenches created by an eternity of rainfall eroding its way down into the frothing seas, the planet is administratively divided into counties, each one millions of square kilometres.

Its capital is called Foothold, for it was there the first settlers made planetfall. They were miners, mineral extraction being the only profitable occupation a man can find on Ignix. Not long into their habitation, the miners of Ignix specialised and became wet miners, panning and sifting the planet's thousand thousand fast waterways, many of them temporary run-offs that surge one day and are gone the next, for precious ores.

Wet mining fortunes had built Foothold into a decent-sized but drab town. All the worthwhile minerals had been shipped off-world in return for hard cash, and the place had been constructed from the residue. The buildings were stained and grim, many of them fabricated from locally cast rockcrete or a type of melta-formed pumice brick. I was put up in an airless residentiary, and went to the courthouse every day to review the pending cases. None of them deserved my attention, or even the rubber stamp of the Ordos.

I had been there four days when the Cackle began. The name is a local one, a more appropriate description would be seasonal electrocorporeal storms. A by-product of Ignix's orbital variations and the virile behaviour of the star it circles, the storms visit each yearly cycle and blanket the northern hemisphere with a steady, florid electromagnetic display. The sky lights up. Corposant nests on rooftops and masts. Vox-links suffer. There is a continuous sound in the air, like a dry, evil chuckle, hence the name.

Some years it's mild, others it's bad. 223 was a bad year.

The Cackle was so fierce, it prevented any and all passage by air, including shuttle links from the lift harbour to starships at high anchor. Transfers on and off Ignix were suspended, and I was stuck for the duration, which turned out to be three weeks.

There was some novelty to be enjoyed at first. The flickering lights in the sky, day and night, were quite sublime, and produced certain hues that I swear I have never encountered since.

But the constant dirty chuckle became onerous and tormenting, as did the rancid, metallic sweat the charged air drew out of me. It was fuggy and close, and I quickly wearied of getting shocks from every damn metallic object I touched or used. I came to realise why the late Flammel had made Ignix a low priority on his circuit.

With the cases done with, there was little to do but wait for the Cackle to subside. I read, and studied, and struck up passing friendships with several similarly stranded travellers living in the residentiary, merchants mostly. Perhaps *friendships* is too strong a word: I knew them well enough to share a drink or a conversation or a game of regicide with, but nothing more. They understood what I was, and it made them nervous around me. For the first time in my career, that vulgar sensation of power began to feel like a burden.

Towards the end of the first week of enforced occupation, a message arrived from the commissioner of Jared County. Due to the vox-out, it was brought by a biker who had run the flooding levees and wash plains of the county limits overnight. I can only assume the commissioner had paid the man well, for he was in a poor state by the time he arrived. The Foothold administrator, an old fellow called Wagneer, brought the message slip to me and waited while I read it.

'He seems most insistent, this commissioner,' I remarked.

'Mal Zelwyn? He's a good sort, very dutiful. He knew you were in town on circuit duties, and evidently hopes you might oblige him.'

I held the slip up.

'Do you think this is genuine, administrator?' I asked.

Wagneer shrugged his sloping shoulders. 'Sounds like a hot one to me, but what do I know? I don't have rosette training.'

Zelwyn, the commissioner of Jared County, had reported a pair of killings in his township, the unimaginatively named Jared County Town. He suspected cult activity, and requested an assessment by the circuit inquisitor. I would have dismissed it except for two facts. One, I had nothing better to do, and two, Zelwyn had written:

The victims suffered deep, random cuts and slashes to the body, having been slain by a crushing head wound. Each victim was missing its left ear.

'How do I get there? Can you scare up a transport for me?' I asked.

Wagneer laughed at the idea. 'In this? All right, I'll see what I can do.'

The local militia took me overland to the pass in a Centaur, hooded against the rain and bulked out with yellow swim-bladders to allow for the fording of flash floods. The crew was not at all happy about the outing, but bit their tongues because of what and who I was. After twelve hours grinding along mud tracks and waterlogged gulches, they got me through the pass, over the iron bridge, and into Kulbrech Town.

As we crossed the old, rusting bridge, I watched the corposant crackle and dance across the posts and stanchions.

In Kulbrech Town, an odious shanty backwater, transit was arranged to carry me on the next leg of my journey. The Centaur turned back to Foothold. I went on in a cargo-8 that had seen better days.

'There's been killing, you know?' the driver mentioned, conversationally.

'I had heard something to that effect.'

The driver nodded. Tiny threads of static were playing across his knuckles as he nudged the wheel.

'Four dead,' he said.

I can honestly say that I quite admired Jared Commissioner Maldar Zelwyn. What he lacked in almost everything he made up for in sheer optimism. He showed me around Jared County Town personally, and made it clear he was tremendously proud of it.

The town straddled twelve river threads, and it seemed to be all bridges and decking and cantilevered platforms. Habs stacked up high above the steep, rain-river chutes. Water throbbed and rattled and chugged down the channels through the town on its journey from the hills to the sea. As he drove me across the New Bridge, Zelwyn proudly explained how he had seen to its construction five years earlier, for the benefit of the community. It was a large metal structure connecting the Commercia quarter to the merchantman residences, and was evidently a boon to working practices. Before the bridge, the merchants had been obliged to take taxi boats from their homes to the Commercia every day. The river it crossed was one of the largest and most powerful bisecting Jared County Town, and the New Bridge was equipped with elevating sections so it could lift to admit the passage of trade ships and other water traffic coming inshore from the coast to the warehouse docks. It was an impressive piece of engineering, lit up, as we rode across it, by the unending light-show of the Cackle. Zelwyn clearly worked hard to support and improve his community, at the back end of all creation though it was.

We drew up on the glistening wharfs of the Commercia, and got out of the bulky land car. Zelwyn was a stocky man in his late forties with thinning hair and a heavy, bushy moustache. He took a data-slate out of his overcoat pocket.

'All the victims were discovered in the Commercia district,' he told me. 'Here's a plan of the locations. It seems arbitrary to me.'

I agreed, but I didn't say so. 'Is there crime scene data? Forensic material?'

'I'm having it processed for you,' he replied.

'And you've got four now?'

'Two more since I sent my message,' he confirmed.

'Is there a pattern?'

'Apart from the way they were killed?' he asked, and shook his head. 'There's no connection between the victims, except for the area they worked in – a trolley pusher, a warehouseman, a junior mercantile clerk, and a whore. We haven't been able to connect any variables. As far as we know, they didn't know each other.'

'But you have a theory?' I asked him.

He nodded. 'The killer lives somewhere in the Commercia.'

'Because?'

'Each killing took place at a time when the New Bridge was raised. There was no crossing to the merchant district. To me, that says it must be local.'

I nodded. 'But just a regular killer, surely? Not an Ordo matter?'

'We've had our share of murders over the years, inquisitor,' Zelwyn replied. 'My office handles the cases. But this... the random mutilation, the missing ears–'

'What do you think that signifies?' I asked.

'Trophy taking?' he suggested. 'Cults do like to take trophies, I understand. Ritual, I suppose. It smacks of ritual.'

'I reckon it might.'

'Yeah, I thought so,' said Zelwyn.

'Why?'

'You wouldn't be here otherwise.'

The Cackle grew more fierce as night pushed in. When we left the Commercia, rain was beginning to fall, and sirens hooted, warning that the New Bridge was about to raise its hydraulic spans. The river was at flood tide.

I reviewed the victims in the frosty twinkle of the town morgue. Preservation methods in Jared County were not Ordo standard. The cadavers had been dumped in bulk freezer units, and came out on their gurneys caked in frost, their vulnerable tissues blackened and cold-burned.

'Sorry,' said Zelwyn, watching me work. 'I wish... our facilities could be better.'

'Forget about it,' I replied.

I used probes and skewers on the frigid bodies, sampling and measuring. The hacking wounds, some so deep they looked like claw marks, were especially ugly. They smiled like happily parted lips, their mouths full to the brim with frozen black ice.

'Cult work, then?' he asked, after a few minutes. 'Have I got a cult here I need to deal with?'

'No, a hunter,' I replied.

'A hunter?'

I nodded.

'What does that mean?'

'Trophy taking is a hunter's quirk – an ear, a finger, a lock of hair.'

'But that's ritual, isn't it?' Zelwyn asked.

'Hunters have rituals too,' I said. He looked downcast.

'Not a cult thing, then?'

'You sound disappointed.'

The Jared commissioner managed a weak smile. 'Of course not. It's just that I'd hoped I was on the money. I wanted to impress you. If this is simply some nut-job serial, I've wasted your time, and I should have known better.'

'Not to mention,' I added, wickedly, 'that if this had been cult work, I'd have dealt with it for you?'

Zelwyn shook his head.

'I'm sorry to have cost you a journey, sir,' he said.

I felt rather ashamed of my attitude. I put down the probe, wiped frosted blood off my gloved hand, and turned to face him. 'Look, I've nothing better to do. Let me help you anyway.'

'You'd do that?' he asked, rather taken aback.

'Of course. Why not?'

'Because you're... you know...'

'An inquisitor? Inquisitors don't like serial killings any more than commissioners do,' I said. 'I have certain skills, Commissioner Zelwyn. I think I can bring this animal down.'

He smiled. It was the warmest, most genuine thing I'd seen in years.

I was just trundling the last corpse back into its freezer when a militia officer came into the morgue and whispered something to Zelwyn.

He turned to look at me. I felt his pain. I mean, I actually felt it. The psyker talents that would later serve me and shape my career were still raw and unshaped in those days, but my empathetic function nevertheless resounded at his distress.

'While we were busy here...' he began.

'Talk to me, Zelwyn.'

He took a deep breath. 'While we were fussing around here, there's been another death.'

'Is the body still in situ?'

He nodded.

'Let's see it.'

We had to wait for five minutes while the New Bridge lowered its spans to let us cross into the Commercia district. Zelwyn let one of his militiamen drive us. The Jared commissioner's hands were shaking too much to be trusted.

Corposant lit up the bridge. The sky made strange colours that twisted and turned. Rain fell. The river below us rushed along, rich in sediment, towards the distant sea.

Lana Howey had worked the wharf for twelve years, and was a regular face at the drink-stops and taverns along the hem of the Commercia. She'd once been popular, a fast girl with good looks and impressive legs, but the work had taken its toll. In the months before her death, she had earned her income turning tricks for specialist customers, men who were more interested in what she was prepared to do rather than the way she looked.

Now she was dead.

Her body lay on the ground floor of a warehouse just off Commercia Main. It had been discovered by a night watchman. Slim, too slim, and wearing too much make-up, she lay naked and awkward under the over-bright portable lamps. The blood from the deep, slashing incisions had pooled under her in a slick. Her left ear was missing.

'Same as the others,' said Zelwyn, shuddering.

'No,' I said, crouching beside the body.

'No?'

'No, she's still–'

I wanted to say alive, but that would have been wrong. She wasn't alive anymore, but she was fresh, fresh compared to the freezer-burned residue Zelwyn had shown me earlier.

'The hunter again?' Zelwyn asked.

'Looks like it. The ear, you notice?'

'Why do you think it's a hunter, Inquisitor Eisenhorn?' Zelwyn asked.

'The slash wounds,' I replied. 'You see? So deep. These are the kind of deep cuts that a hunter might administer to accelerate decomposition. A kill he doesn't want, and which he wants to rot away quickly.'

Zelwyn pursed his lips. 'What are you going to do now, sir?'

'I'm going to ask you and your people to get out of this place. Withdraw to a sixty-metre perimeter.'

'Why?'

'Don't ask me that, commissioner.'

'I want to stay,' said Zelwyn.

'On your own head, then. Get your people out.'

Later on in my career, I only ever undertook auto-seances when I had a properly qualified astrotelepath to assist me. Such acts can take a toll. Back then, I was young and headstrong, and full of my own energy and will. It's a wonder I ever survived.

'Bolt the door,' I said to Zelwyn. He obliged. His men had gone. 'Do what I say and don't interrupt me,' I added.

'Right,' he said.

He stood back, near the heavy warehouse door, watching. I knelt beside the hacked corpse and sighed.

Outside, the Cackle sputtered and pulsed.

'Lana Howey?' I called softly.

I felt Zelwyn open his mouth, to ask why in the name of the Throne I was talking to a dead body. I think it was about then that he finally woke up to what was going on. I sensed fear bubbling up inside him, along with a strong desire to be outside with his men after all. He'd never seen anything like this done before.

'Lana Howey?'

The warehouse air took on the glossy, cold feel of hyper-reality. The light refined in clarity, and small details became impossibly sharp. The various odours of the place: soot, rockcrete, oil, sacking, thinners and the body itself, were suddenly more concentrated, more pronounced.

'What am I doing here?' asked the late Lana Howey.

I heard Commissioner Zelwyn groan. I felt his gnawing fear.

'Lana Howey?' I called.

'Hello, mister. What's your pleasure, then, sir?'

'Lana, my name is Gregor.'

'That's a lovely name. Gregor. You're a handsome one for sure, Gregor. What can I do for you tonight?'

'Where are you, Lana Howey?'

'I'm in the warehouse, with you, silly man. This is my place. Don't you fret. It's quiet here, discreet. You're a regular, aren't you? I know your face.'

'You've never seen me before, Lana Howey. You'll never see me again.'

'I doubt that,' she sniggered. Her chuckle was the scratchy glee of the Cackle. 'I bet you'll be back again for more, soon enough.'

'I need you to focus, Lana Howey,' I said.

'Focus? What? Why do you keep using my name, my whole name, like that? Is that your thing, mister?'

+Lana?+

I felt Zelwyn fighting back an urge to throw open the door bolts and run. I really hadn't wanted him to be here in the first place. All he could see was me kneeling beside the body. He could not see what I could see.

An after-image of the victim had appeared to me. She was wearing a cheap, revealing dress and had taken a seat on a nearby freight trunk, one leg crossed over the other. The raised foot was swinging impatiently.

+Lana? Can you hear me?+

'How do you know my name, mister?' the image asked, watching me.

+Administratum files. Lana, who was it?+

'Who was it that what? Come on, I've got punters waiting. What are you on about?'

+Lana. Please let me see. Who did this to you?+

'Who did what to me? Look, I haven't got all night,' she breathed. 'Show me some money, mister.'

I reached into my pocket and produced three crowns. The air was very cold. My breath was steaming, and so were the open wounds on the corpse in front of me. On the trunk, image Lana swung her leg.

'That'll do it,' she said. 'What do you want? Full service, all the stuff?' She stood up abruptly and reached down to pull her dress off over her head. It was only then that she seemed to notice the body on the floor.

The image stared down at it for a long time, her hands frozen in the act of bunching up her dress to drag it over and off. When she looked at me again, her eye make-up was blotted and running.

'When?' she asked.

+Not long ago.+

'Oh, Throne. What did I ever do to deserve that?'

+Nothing. Lana, I want to know who it was. Will you show me?+

She showed me.

She showed me, her voice growing steadily quieter and quieter, and when she was done, she faded altogether without any protest, casting me one last, hurt look with her make-up-stained eyes.

I took off my storm coat and laid it over the corpse.

Outside, dawn was no more than an hour away. The rain had eased off and the Cackle had dropped in intensity. Zelwyn stood by the waiting militia transports, taking repeated draws from an old hip flask. When I walked up, he offered it to me. I took a big swallow.

'Are you–?' he began

'I need a moment.' The work had drained me, not so much sapping my will as abrading my emotions.

'Can the details move in, at least?' he asked.

I nodded. Several militia officers and two coroners with a stretcher went into the warehouse at Zelwyn's nod. After a few minutes, someone brought me my coat.

I gestured to Zelwyn and walked away in the direction of the New Bridge.

'It's a good thing I stayed,' I told him. 'This turns out to be an Ordo matter after all.'

'A cult?'

'No, and not a hunter either... At least it could be either of those things, but that's not what makes it an Ordo matter. We're dealing with a regia occulta.'

'*Hidden way*,' he translated. Zelwyn was no fool, he had High Gothic.

'That's the literal translation. In the Ordo Malleus, it has a more specific meaning.'

'Go on.'

'A regia occulta is a pathway... A tunnel or portal, if you like, that links our reality with that of the warp.'

'Is it a deliberate thing?' he asked.

'Perhaps. Cults and heretics do sometimes open them deliberately. But it could be a natural occurrence. Most are. The fabric of space is thin in places, you see, and sometimes there are leaks.'

He shook his head and a sad smile appeared under his heavy moustache. 'I don't actually know much about the warp, sir,' he said.

'Nor should you, commissioner. It's forbidden lore. I'm just telling you what you need to know. There is a regia occulta in Jared County Town, and it's right here.'

We were standing at the Commercia end of the New Bridge.

* * *

It took Zelwyn just a few minutes to have the bridge and its feeder roads closed off and barricaded by the militia. Another hour, and it would have been teeming with traffic heading in for work.

'Can you tell me why this only happens when the bridge is up?' Zelwyn asked. 'I mean, surely that would block a crossing?'

'I'll do better than tell you,' I said. 'I'll show you.'

We took up a position at the Commercia end; me, Zelwyn and four men from the militia armed with powerful autorifles. At my nod, the commissioner signalled to the bridge machine room on the far bank, and the operators engaged the hydraulics. Ponderously, with a dull squeal like gates opening, the massive spans began to lift.

The Cackle fluoresced in the dawn sky over our heads. Blue ropes of fizzling corposant writhed and trickled like snakes around the iron finials of the bridge towers, and traced their way along the rising edges of the gigantic metal spans.

The hydraulics cut out when the spans were at a standard lifted position, at about forty degrees from the horizontal. We waited, looking up the steep metal slope of the span facing us. Below us, out of sight, the fast-running river gurgled and hissed.

We waited for ten minutes. Corposant gathered in increasingly heavy ribbons around the raised tips of the bridge span, as if attracted there in concentration, like lightning drawn to a conductor.

There was a dry electric crack, and we smelled ozone. One of the militiamen pointed. A whip of corposant had flicked out from the tip of one span and connected with the tip of the other, like a squiggle of electrostatic voltage crackling between two insulated orbs. It remained there, jerking and sizzling, like a bright, twisting rope tying the two halves of the raised bridge together. This feature had not been evident in the patchy disposition Lana Howey had shown me, but I suddenly felt I had discerned the key mechanism of the infernal regia occulta.

One of the militiamen started to say something, but I already knew 'it' was happening. The hairs on my neck were raised. I felt something akin to a ball of ice in my stomach, and a searing pain behind my eyes.

The killer came into view. He simply manifested out of nowhere, as if the air had parted like a curtain and let him through. He appeared high up on the span ahead of us, and began to plod down the steep slope. He did not see us at first. We heard his feet slapping heavily on the metal roadway.

Though humanoid, he wasn't human. I was the largest man in our party, and he was twice my mass and half my height again. He came wrapped in a heavy, ragged cloak of animal skins with a hood drawn up. His shoulders were very broad.

The pain behind my eyes was getting worse by the second. I could barely focus.

'Kill it,' I said.

We opened fire: four military-grade autorifles, firing reinforced rounds with fifty per cent more grain in them than standard, Zelwyn's lasgun, and my Tronsvasse assault pistol. The noise was stunning, and the muzzle flash a strobing flutter. The killer was dead in just a few seconds. Our firepower tore him apart and shredded his foul cloak, though he possessed such astonishing strength that he actually managed to walk into our fusilade a step or two, trying to shrug it off, before it overcame him.

He fell heavily, and rolled down the slope.

'He' was a mature ork warrior. Released by his spasming paws, a huge cleaver and a large metal cudgel lay on the roadway beside him. We approached slowly. Greenskins are notoriously hard to kill, and though we had blown this one wide open, I fired three more rounds into its skull to be on the safe side. Ichor, almost black in the dawn light, ran down the slope. The mangled corpse showed signs of body paint, tribal markings and lots of crude piercings and bangles. Fresh human ears were strung around its throat on a wire.

'A greenskin?' Zelwyn murmured. 'But this isn't green space. There haven't been any orks in this sub for generations.'

'It didn't come from this sub,' I said. I was finding it hard to speak or concentrate. The pain behind my eyes was even worse than before. It felt like a hot wire. 'It came from whatever random site this regia occulta connects to. This beast went hunting one day, and ended up here. We'll never know, I fancy, where... where...'

'Inquisitor? Inquisitor Eisenhorn?' I heard Zelwyn say. I felt his hand catch my arm. The pain behind my eyes had turned into full-blown psyk agony. I could barely stand, let alone speak.

And I really wanted to speak. I needed to. I needed to yell out, 'It's not over!'

The regia occulta was still open. While we had been standing there, gawping at the ork's cadaver, a second one had walked in through the hidden way.

For such a massive thing, it moved very fast. I moved like lead, transfixed by the pain the seething warp gate was lancing into my receptive mind.

I heard a feral roar, and smelled a foul animal scent. I fell, shoved aside, I think. An autorifle fired.

The ork slew the first militiaman as he landed among us, splitting the fellow straight through the crown with his jagged cleaver. The man collapsed under the force of the blow, his sectioned skull spilling open as the blade jerked back out, his heels drumming the ground. The ork caught another man by the throat, yanked him off his feet, and bit away his face.

It is awful to reflect that this unfortunate lived for at least another ten minutes.

The ork broke the back of a third militiaman with a stinging cudgel blow, before making off in great bounding leaps towards the unlit buildings of the Commercia. Zelwyn and the sole remaining militiaman fired after it. The man with the broken back lay on the ground, screaming.

'Eisenhorn?' Zelwyn yelled.

+Lower. The. Bridge.+

I didn't want to use my will on the poor fellow, but I had no choice. My mouth wouldn't work. Zelwyn wet himself as my mind intruded upon his. To his credit, he rallied and signalled the machine room.

The New Bridge slowly rattled and clanked back into place. The corposant charge between the spans shorted out and vanished as the opposite ends touched.

My mind cleared at once, the pain draining back. The regia occulta was shut.

Blood had streamed out of my nose and soaked the front of my jacket. I got up and ran towards the warehouses. The ork had vanished from sight. I had to find it, before it found anyone else. A greenskin is dangerous enough. This one was enraged, possibly wounded, and knew it was cut off and pursued by its mortal foe, man.

Zelwyn ran after me. The remaining militiaman stayed put, too shocked to move, his rifle limp in his white-knuckled hands.

'Get back, Zelwyn!' I shouted. 'Gather your militia in full force.'

'Like hell!' he yelled back. He shouted over at the units waiting behind the barricades, and they moved forwards after us. We entered the most likely venue, a warehouse stacked with mineral hoppers. Glow globes hung from the rafters, but not all of them worked. Frail daybreak glimmered through the rooflights.

'In here?' Zelwyn whispered, panting.

I held up my hand for hush. The place was quiet, except for the mocking chuckle of the Cackle. I tried to reach out with my mind, but I was drained, and no human psyker can read the greenskin mind. They are blunt to us. I took a deep breath instead, and smelled the air: mineral stink, wet rocks, and a hint, just a hint, of animal odour.

We edged forwards. I saw dark, wet spots on the rockcrete floor, leading between the piled hoppers. Unless someone had recently carried a leaky promethium drum through the place, Zelwyn had managed to wound the creature right enough. I touched one of the spots. It oozed warmth.

'It's here,' I whispered.

Zelwyn already knew that. It had come out of the shadows, nightmarishly silent for something so big, and seized him by the throat. I turned slowly.

The ork had pulled the Jared commissioner in against its massive chest like a mother hugging a baby to its breast. Its left paw entirely encircled the man's neck. Zelwyn's eyes were wide, and his face was pale. The ork raised its right hand and gently rested the massive cleaver on Zelwyn's scalp. Tiny trickles of blood ran down Zelwyn's face.

The bull-ork's yellow eyes, deep in the brow-ridged sockets, glared at me. Its heavy, flaccid lips wrinkled and twitched. Its tongue, huge and greasy, worked behind its rotting peg teeth. Each one of those teeth was the size of my palm.

The ork was not a bright beast, but it was smart enough, instinctive enough, to recognise its predicament. It was bargaining with me, a life for a life. This much I knew. Otherwise, Zelwyn would have been dead already.

I thought about taking a shot, but dared not risk hitting the commissioner. I was too spent, and it was no time to try my aim. Besides, greenskins are notoriously hard to kill. Even if I hit it, one round from a Tronsvasse would not do the trick.

All I had was my will. I couldn't impel the ork in any way, but Zelwyn was a different matter.

Without hesitation, I reached into the commissioner's panicking mind. He was still clutching his laspistol, dangling at his side. I squeezed his finger for him. The shot blew clean through the arch of the ork's slabby right foot.

The greenskin convulsed in pain, but I already had a grip on Zelwyn's motor function, and I threw him forwards. I felt his astonishment as his body acted without his permission. He flew out of the ork's briefly weakened grip so fast and hard, he careered forwards and bounced face-first off the hopper to my right.

I was already firing, my weapon braced in a two-handed grip. I emptied the assault pistol's clip into the greenskin's chest, filling the air with drenching black mist and driving the monster into the stack of mineral hoppers behind it. It smashed heavily into the metal siding, but remained on its feet.

I ejected the dead clip, and let it drop and clatter to the floor as I snapped home a reload from my coat pocket. I tore off the second clip in one go, firing into the ork's face and neck. The back of its vast skull banged repeatedly against the hopper behind it. Spray-patterns of ichor splashed out across the hopper's side.

It swayed, then took another step towards me.

'Oh, for Throne's sake,' I hissed, 'just die.'

It died. The stack of hoppers, unsettled by the repeated impacts, creaked and toppled, crushing the ork in an avalanche of rock ore, clinker and iron crates. The noise was deafening. I shielded my face. Dust billowed up, and slowly settled.

I helped the Jared commissioner to his feet. He was quaking badly. Both of us were coated with a film of rock dust. He looked at the mangled heap of wreckage, where dark, clotted ichor seeped out from under the heaps of spoil.

'Holy shit,' he murmured.

There was no way, or no way in the understanding of the Ordos, anyway, to close a regia occulta. I made it quite clear to Zelwyn that the New Bridge should never, ever be raised again, for it was that very raising, during the Cackle, that produced the unique combination of effects necessary for the regia occulta to function. He needed no persuasion. The day before I left Jared County Town, he had the machine room dismantled and the heavy gauge hydraulics uncoupled. I understand, though I cannot confirm the fact, that the New Bridge was swept away in a freak flood tide some years later. It was never replaced. The regia occulta never reoccurred in Jared County Town.

Commissioner Zelwyn, who went on to serve his community for six and a half decades, kept one of the ork cleavers on his office wall, and enjoyed telling visitors that the dried blood on its points was his.

The morning I left, he came to see me off.

'I hope I never see you again, inquisitor,' he said, shaking my hand.

'I hope so too, commissioner.'

He paused. 'I meant that in a good way,' he added.

'So did I,' I said.

* * *

I crossed over into Foothold County via the pass at Kulbrech. The reluctant motorised unit of the local militia was there to meet me, the engine of the Centaur idling. They weren't glad to see me, but I was glad to see them. The Cackle was dying away, and I would soon be gone from Ignix.

The Cackle was dying away, but it insisted on having the last laugh. Many years later, at the end of my life, the mocking elements of Ignix would return to haunt me. But this was – oh – 223.M41, and I was only just out on my own.

XENOS

BY ORDER OF HIS MOST HOLY MAJESTY
THE GOD-EMPEROR OF TERRA

SEQUESTERED INQUISITORIAL DOSSIERS
AUTHORISED PERSONS ONLY

CASE FILE 112:67B:AA6:Xad

Please enter your authority code > ● ● ● ● ● ● ● ● ● ● ● ● ● ● ●

Validating...

Thank you, Inquisitor.

You may proceed.

VERBAL TRANSCRIPT OF PICT-RECORDED DOCUMENT

LOCATION: MAGINOR DATE: 239. M41

RECOVERED FROM SERVITOR RECORDING MODULE

TRANSCRIBED BY SAVANT ELEDIX, ORDO HERETICUS INQUISITORIAL DATA-LIBRARY FACULTY, FIBOS SECUNDUS, 240. M41

[Pict-record white noise segues to] Darkness. Sounds of distant human pain. A flash of light [poss. las-fire?]. Sounds of running.

Pict-source moves, tracking, vibrating. Some stone walls, in close focus. Another flash, brighter, closer. Squeal of pain [source unknown]. An extremely bright flash [loss of picture].

[Image indistinct for 2 minutes 38 seconds; some background noise.]

A man [subject (i)] in long robes, calls out as he strides past close to the pict-source [speech unrecoverable]. Surroundings, dark stone [poss. tunnel? tomb?]. (i)'s identity unknown [partial face view only]. Pict-source moves in close behind (i), observing as (i) draws a force hammer from a thigh loop under his robe. Close up on (i)'s hands as he grips haft. Inquisitorial signet ring in plain view. (i) turns [face obscured by shadow]. (i) speaks.

VOICE (i): *Move in! Move in, in the name of all that's holy! Come on and* [words obliterated by sound-flash] *bastard monster to death!*

Further flashes of light, now clearly close las-impacts. Pict-source filters fail to block glare [white out].

[Image white out for 0 minutes 14 seconds; resolution slowly returning.]

Passing in through the high stone entrance of some considerable chamber. Grey stone, rough hewn. Pict-source pans. Bodies in doorway, and also slumped down interior steps. Massive injuries, mangled. Stones wet with blood.

VOICE OFF [(i)?]: *Where are you? Where are you? Show yourself!*

Pict-source moves in. Two human shapes move past it to left, blurred [image-stall reveals one [subject (ii)] to be male, approx 40 years, heavy-set, wearing Imperial Guard-issue body plate [no insignia or idents], significant facial scarring [old], wielding belt-fed heavy stubber; other [subject (iii)] is female, approx 25 years, svelte, skin dyed blue, tattoos and bodyglove armour of a Morituri Death Cultist initiate, wielding force blade [approx 45cm length].

Blurred shapes (ii) and (iii) move beyond pict-source. Pict-source pans round, establishing sidelong view of (ii) and (iii) engaged in rapid hand-to-hand warfare with adversaries on lower steps. Adversaries are heterogeneous mix: six humans with surgical/bionic implants, two mutants, three offensive servitors [see attached file record for stall-frame details]. (ii) fires heavy stubber [sound track distorts].

Two human adversaries pulped [backwash smoke haze renders image partially indistinct]. (iii) severs head of mutant, vaults backwards [transcriptional assumption – pict-source too slow to follow] and impales human adversary. Pict-source moves down [image jerky].

VOICE OFF: *Maneesha! To the left! To the l–*

Pict-source makes partial capture as (iii) is hit repeatedly by energy fire. (iii) convulses, explodes. Pict-source hit by blood mist [image fogs]. [Image wiped clear.] (ii) is yelling, moving ahead out of view, firing heavy stubber. Sudden crossfire laser effect [las-flare blinds pict-source optics].

[Various noise sources, indistinct voices, some screaming.]

[Image returns.] (i) is just ahead of pict-source, charging into wide, flat chamber lit by green chemical lamps [face illuminated by light for 0.3 seconds]. Subject (i) positively identified as Inquisitor Hetris Lugenbrau.

LUGENBRAU: *Quixos! Quixos! I put it all to the sword and the cleansing flame! Now you, monster! Now you, bastard!*

VOICE [unidentified]: *I am here, Lugenbrau. Kharnagar awaits.*

Lugenbrau (i) moves off-image. Pict-source pans. Image jerky. Body parts scattered on chamber floor [composite identifies subject (ii) as one of nine corpses]. Major detonation(s) nearby. Image shakes, pict-source falls sidelong.

[Image blank for 1 minute 7 seconds. Significant background noise.]

[Image returns.] Lugenbrau partly visible off frame left, engaged in combat. Afterglow-residue of force hammer blows remain burned on image for several seconds [image indistinct].

Pict-source turns to focus on Lugenbrau. Lugenbrau engaged in hand-to-hand combat with unknown foe. Movements too fast for pict-source to capture. Blur. Human figures [identity unknown, poss. adversary troops] move in from right frame. Heads of human figures explode. Figures topple.

[White out. Pict-source blanked. Duration unknown.]

[Image returns, imperfect.] Jerky shots of ground and wall. Refocus blurring. Pict-source reacquires Lugenbrau and adversary in combat [smoke fumes haze view]. Combat as before too rapid for pict-source to capture. Extensive background noise. Glowing line [believed to be blade weapon] impales Lugenbrau. Image shakes [some picture loss]. Lugenbrau immolates [image burns out].

[Pause/pict-blank of unknown duration.]

[Image returns.] Close up of face looking into pict-source. Identity unknown [subject (iv)]. (iv) is handsome, sculptural, smiling, eyes blank.

VOICE (iv): *Hello, little thing. I am Cherubael.*

Light flash.

Scream [believed to originate from pict-source].

[Image out. Recording ends.]

ONE

A COLD COMING
DEATH IN THE DORMANT VAULTS
SOME PURITANICAL REFLECTIONS

Hunting the recidivist Murdin Eyclone, I came to Hubris in the Dormant of 240.M41, as the Imperial sidereal calendar has it.

Dormant lasted eleven months of Hubris's twenty-nine month lunar year, and the only signs of life were the custodians with their lighted poles and heat-gowns, patrolling the precincts of the hibernation tombs.

Within those sulking basalt and ceramite vaults, the grandees of Hubris slept, dreaming in crypts of aching ice, awaiting Thaw, the middle season between Dormant and Vital.

Even the air was frigid. Frost encrusted the tombs, and a thick cake of ice covered the featureless land. Above, star patterns twinkled in the curious, permanent night. One of them was Hubris's sun, so far away now. Come Thaw, Hubris would spin into the warm embrace of its star again.

Then it would become a blazing globe. Now it was just a fuzz of light.

As my gun-cutter set down on the landing cross at Tomb Point, I had pulled on an internally heated bodyskin and swathes of sturdy, insulated foul weather gear, but still the perilous cold cut through me now. My eyes watered, and the tears froze on my lashes and cheeks. I remembered the details of the cultural brief my savant had prepared, and quickly lowered my frost visor, trembling as warm air began to circulate under the plastic mask.

Custodians, alerted to my arrival by astropathic hails, stood waiting for me at the base of the landing cross. Their lighted poles dipped in obeisance in the frozen night and the air steamed with the heat that bled from their cloaks. I nodded to them, showing their leader my badge of office. An ice-car awaited: a rust-coloured arrowhead twenty metres long, mounted on ski-blade runners and spiked tracks.

It carried me away from the landing cross and I left the winking signal lights and the serrated dagger-shape of my gun-cutter behind in the perpetual winter night.

The spiked tracks kicked up blizzards of rime behind us. Ahead, despite the lamps, the landscape was black and impenetrable. I rode with Lores Vibben and three custodians in a cabin lit only by the amber glow of the craft's control panel. Heating vents recessed in the leather seats breathed out warm, stale air.

A custodian handed back a data-slate to Vibben. She looked at it cursorily and passed it on to me. I realised my frost visor was still down. I raised it and began to search my pockets for my eye glasses.

With a smile, Vibben produced them from within her own swaddled, insulated garb. I nodded thanks, put them on my nose and began to read.

I was just calling up the last plates of text when the ice-car halted.

'Processional Two-Twelve,' announced one of the custodians.

We dismounted, sliding our visors down into place.

Jewels of frost-flakes fluttered in the blackness about us, sparkling as they crossed through the ice-car's lamp beams. I've heard of bitter cold. Emperor grace me I never feel it again. Biting, crippling, actually bitter to taste on the tongue. Every joint in my frame protested and creaked.

My hands and my mind were numb.

That was not good.

Processional Two-Twelve was a hibernation tomb at the west end of the great Imperial Avenue. It housed twelve thousand, one hundred and forty-two members of the Hubris ruling elite.

We approached the great monument, crunching up the black, frost-coated steps.

I halted. 'Where are the tomb's custodians?'

'Making their rounds,' I was told.

I glanced at Vibben and shook my head. She slid her hand into her fur-edged robes.

'Knowing we approach?' I urged, addressing the custodian again. 'Knowing we expect to meet them?'

'I will check,' said the custodian, the one who had circulated the slate. He pushed on up the steps, the phosphor light on his pole bobbing.

The other two seemed ill at ease.

I beckoned to Vibben, so she would follow me up after the leader.

We found him on a lower terrace, gazing at the strewn bodies of four custodians, their light poles fizzling out around them.

'H-how?' he stammered.

'Stay back,' Vibben told him and drew her weapon. Its tiny amber Armed rune glowed in the darkness.

I took out my blade, igniting it. It hummed.

The south entry of the tombs was open. Shafts of golden light shone out. All my fears were rapidly being confirmed.

We entered, Vibben sweeping the place from side to side with her handgun. The hall was narrow and high, lit by chemical glow-globes. Intruding frost was beginning to mark the polished basalt walls.

A few metres inside, another custodian lay dead in a stiffening mirror of blood. We stepped over him. To each side, hallways opened up, admitting us to the hibernation stacks. In every direction, rows and rows of ice-berths ranged down the smoothed basalt chambers.

It was like walking into the Imperium's grandest morgue.

Vibben swept soundlessly to the right and I went left.

I admit I was excited by now, eager to close and conclude a business that had lasted six years. Eyclone had evaded me for six whole years! I studied his methods every day and dreamed of him every night.

Now I could smell him.

I raised my visor.

Water was pattering from the roof. Thaw water. It was growing warmer in here. In their ice-berths, some of the dim figures were stirring.

Too early! Far too early!

Eyclone's first man came at me from the west as I crossed a trunk-junction corridor. I spun, the power sword in my hand, and cut through his neck before his ice-axe could land.

The second came from the south, the third from the east. And then more. More.

A blur.

As I fought, I heard furious shooting from the vaults away to my right. Vibben was in trouble.

I could hear her over the vox-link in our hoods: 'Eisenhorn! Eisenhorn!'

I wheeled and cut. My opponents were all dressed in heat-gowns, and carried ice-tools that made proficient weapons. Their eyes were dark and unforthcoming. Though they were fast, there was something in them that suggested they were doing this mindlessly, by order.

The power sword, an antique and graceful weapon, blessed by the Provost of Inx himself, spun in my hand. With five abrupt moves I made corpses out of them and left their blood vapour drifting in the air.

'Eisenhorn!'

I turned and ran. I splashed heavily down a corridor sluiced with melt water. More shots from ahead. A sucking cry.

I found Vibben face down across a freezer tube, frozen blood gluing her to the sub-zero plastic. Eight of Eyclone's servants lay sprawled around her. Her weapon lay just out of reach of her clawing hand, the spent cell ejected from the grip.

I am forty-two standard years old, in my prime by Imperial standards, young by those of the Inquisition. All my life, I have had a reputation for being cold, unfeeling. Some have called me heartless, ruthless, even cruel. I am not. I am not beyond emotional response or compassion. But I possess – and my masters count this as perhaps my paramount virtue – a singular force of will. Throughout my career it has served me well to draw on this facility and steel myself, unflinching, at all that this wretched galaxy can throw at me. To feel pain or fear or grief is to allow myself a luxury I cannot afford.

Lores Vibben had served with me for five and a half years. In that period she had saved my life twice. She saw herself as my aide and my bodyguard, yet in truth she was more a companion and a fellow warrior. When I recruited her from the clan-slums of Tornish, it was for her combat skills and brutal vigour. But I came to value her just as much for her sharp mind, soft wit and clear head.

I stared down at her body for a moment. I believe I may have uttered her name.

* * *

I extinguished my power sword and, sliding it into its scabbard, moved back into the shadows on the far side of the hibernation gallery. I could hear nothing except the increasingly persistent thaw-drip. Freeing my sidearm from its leather rig under my left armpit, I checked its load and opened a vox link. Eyclone was undoubtedly monitoring all traffic in and out of Processional Two-Twelve, so I used Glossia, an informal verbal cipher known only to myself and my immediate colleagues. Most inquisitors develop their own private languages for confidential communication, some more sophisticated than others. Glossia, the basics of which I had designed ten years before, was reasonably complex and had evolved, organically, with use.

'Thorn wishes aegis, rapturous beasts below.'

'Aegis, arising, the colours of space,' Betancore responded immediately and correctly.

'Rose thorn, abundant, by flame light crescent.'

A pause. 'By flame light crescent? Confirm.'

'Confirm.'

'Razor delphus pathway! Pattern ivory!'

'Pattern denied. Pattern crucible.'

'Aegis, arising.'

The link broke. He was on his way. He had taken the news of Vibben's death as hard as I expected. I trusted that would not affect his performance. Midas Betancore was a hot-blooded, impetuous man, which was partly why I liked him. And used him.

I moved out of the shadows again, my sidearm raised. A Scipio-pattern naval pistol, finished in dull chrome with inlaid ivory grips, it felt reassuringly heavy in my gloved hand. Ten rounds, every one a fat, blunt man-stopper, were spring-loaded into the slide inside the grip. I had four more armed slides just like it in my hip pocket.

I forget where I acquired the Scipio. It had been mine for a few years. One night, three years before, Vibben had prised off the ceramite grip plates with their touch-worn, machined-stamped engravings of the Imperial aquila and the Navy motto, and replaced them with ivory grips she had etched herself. A common practice on Tornish, she informed me, handing the weapon back the next day. The new grips were like crude scrimshaw, showing on each side a poorly executed human skull through which a thorny rose entwined, emerging through an eye socket, shedding cartoon droplets of blood. She'd inlaid carmine gems into the droplets to emphasise their nature. Below the skull, my name was scratched in a clumsy scroll.

I had laughed. There had been times when I'd almost been too embarrassed to draw the gang-marked weapon in a fight.

Now, now she was dead, I realise what an honour had been paid to me through that devoted work.

I made a promise to myself: I would kill Eyclone with this gun.

As a devoted member of his high majesty the God-Emperor's Inquisition, I find my philosophy bends towards that of the Amalathians. To the outside galaxy, members of our orders appear much alike: an inquisitor is an inquisitor, a being of fear and persecution. It surprises many that internally, we are riven with clashing ideologies.

I know it surprised Vibben. I spent one long afternoon trying to explain the differences. I failed.

To express it in simple terms, some inquisitors are puritans and some are radicals. Puritans believe in and enforce the traditional station of the Inquisition, working to purge our galactic community of any criminal or malevolent element: the triumvirate of evil – alien, mutant and daemon. Anything that clashes with the pure rule of mankind, the preachings of the Ministorum and the letter of Imperial Law is subject to a puritan inquisitor's attention. Hard-line, traditional, merciless... that is the puritan way.

Radicals believe that any methods are allowable if they accomplish the Inquisitorial task. Some, as I understand it, actually embrace and use forbidden resources, such as the Warp itself, as weapons against the enemies of mankind.

I have heard the arguments often enough. They appal me. Radical belief is heretical.

I am a puritan by calling and an Amalathian by choice. The ferociously strict ways of the monodominant philosophy oft-times entices me, but there is precious little subtlety in their ways and thus it is not for me.

Amalathians take our name from the conclave at Mount Amalath. Our endeavour is to maintain the status quo of the Imperium, and we work to identify and destroy any persons or agencies that might destabilise the power of the Imperium from without or within. We believe in strength through unity. Change is the greatest enemy. We believe the God-Emperor has a divine plan, and we work to sustain the Imperium in stability until that plan is made known. We deplore factions and in-fighting... Indeed, it is sometimes a painful irony that our beliefs mark us as a faction within the political helix of the Inquisition.

We are the steadfast spine of the Imperium, its antibodies, fighting disease, insanity, injury, invasion.

I can think of no better way to serve, no better way to be an inquisitor.

So you have me then, pictured. Gregor Eisenhorn, inquisitor, puritan, Amalathian, forty-two years old standard, an inquisitor for the past eighteen years. I am tall and broad at the shoulders, strong, resolute. I have already told you of my force of will, and you will have noted my prowess with a blade.

What else is there? Am I clean-shaven? Yes! My eyes are dark, my hair darker and thick. These things matter little.

Come and let me show you how I killed Eyclone.

TWO

THE DEAD AWAKE
BETANCORE'S TEMPER
ELUCIDATIONS BY AEMOS

I clung to the shadows, moving through the great tomb as silently as I knew how. A terrible sound rolled through the thawing vaults of Processional Two-Twelve. Fists and palms beating at coffin hoods. Wailing. Gurgling.

The sleepers were waking, their frigid bodies, sore with hibernation sickness, trapped in their caskets. No honour guard of trained cryogeneers waited to unlock them, to sluice their organs with warming bio-fluids or inject stimulants or massage paralysed extremities.

Thanks to Eyclone's efforts, twelve thousand one hundred and forty-two members of the planet's ruling class were being roused early into the bitter season of Dormant, and roused without the necessary medical supervision.

I had no doubt that they would all suffocate in minutes.

My mind scrolled back through the details my savant had prepared for me. There was a central control room, where I could disengage the ice-berth locks and at least free them all. But to what good? Without the resuscitation teams, they would fail and perish.

And if I hunted out the control room, Eyclone would have time to escape.

In Glossia code, I communicated this quandary to Betancore, and told him to alert the custodians. He informed me, after a pause, that crash-teams and relief crews were on their way.

But why? The question was still there. Why was Eyclone doing this?

A massed killing was nothing unusual for a follower of Chaos. But there had to be a point, above and beyond the deaths themselves.

I was pondering this as I crossed a hallway deep in the west wing of the Processional. Frantic beating sounds came from the berths all around, and a pungent mix of ice-water and bio-fluid spurted from the drain-taps and cascaded over the floor.

A shot rang out. A las-shot. It missed me by less than a hand's breadth and exploded through the headboard of an ice berth behind me. Immediately, the frantic hammering in that berth stopped, and the waters running out of its ducts were stained pink.

I fired the Scipio down the vault, startled by the noise it made.

Two more las-shots flicked down at me.

Taking cover behind a stone bulkhead, I emptied a clip down the length of the gallery, the spent shell cases smoking in the air as the pumping slide ejected them. A hot vapour of cordite blew back at me.

I swung back into cover, exchanging clips.

A few more spits of laser drizzled past me, then a voice.

'Eisenhorn? Gregor, is that you?'

Eyclone. I knew his thin voice at once. I didn't answer.

'You're dead, you know, Gregor. Dead like they all are. Dead, dead, dead. Step out and make it quick.'

He was good, I'll give him that. My legs actually twitched, actually started to walk me clear of cover into the open. Eyclone was infamous across a dozen settled systems for his mind powers and mesmeric tone. How else had he managed to get these dark-eyed fools to do his bidding?

But I have similar skills. And I have honed them well.

There is a time to use mind or voice tricks gently to draw out your target. And there are times to use them like a stub-gun at point-blank range.

It was time for the latter.

I pitched my voice, balanced my mind and yelled: 'Show yourself first!'

Eyclone didn't succumb. I didn't expect him to. Like me, he had years of resilience training. But his two gunmen were easy meat.

The first strode directly out into the middle of the gallery hallway, dropping his lasgun with a clatter. The Scipio made a hole in the middle of his forehead and blew his brains out behind him in a grotesque pink mist. The other stumbled out on his heels, realised his mistake, and began firing.

One of his las-bolts scorched the sleeve of my jacket. I squeezed the pistol's trigger and the Scipio bucked and snarled in my tight grip.

The round penetrated his head under his nose, splintered on his upper teeth and blew the sides of his skull out. He staggered and fell, dead fingers firing his lasrifle again and again, blowing the fascias out of the hibernation stalls around him. Putrid water, bio-fluid and plastic fragments poured out, and some screams became louder.

I could hear footsteps above the screams. Eyclone was running.

I ran too, across the vaults, passing gallery after gallery.

The screaming, the pounding... God-Emperor help me I will never forget that. Thousands of frantic souls waking up to face an agonising death.

Damn Eyclone. Damn him to hell and back.

Crossing the third gallery, I saw him, running parallel to me. He saw me too. He wheeled, and fired.

I ducked back as the blasts of his laspistol shrieked past.

A glimpse was all I'd had: a short, wiry man, dressed in brown heat-robes, his goatee neatly trimmed, his eyes twinkling with malice.

I fired back, but he was running again.

I ran on, glimpsed him down the next gallery and fired again.

At the next gallery, nothing. I waited, and pulled off my outer robe. It was getting hot and damp in Processional Two-Twelve.

When another minute passed and there was still no sign, I began to edge down the gallery towards his last position, gun raised. I'd got ten paces when he swung out of hiding and blazed away at me.

I would have died right there, had not the joker-gods of fate and chance played their hand.

At the moment Eyclone fired, several cryo-tubes finally gave way and yowling, naked, blistered humans staggered out into the corridor, clawing with ice-webbed hands, mewling, vomiting, blind and ice-burned. Eyclone's shots tore three of them apart and hideously wounded a fourth. Had it not been for them, those las-shots would have finished me.

Footsteps, hurried. He was running again.

I pushed on down the gallery, stepping over the blasted ruins of the sleepers who had inadvertently spared me. The wounded one, a middle-aged female, compromised and naked as she lay in the melt-water, clutched at my leg, begging for salvation. Eyclone's gunfire had all but disembowelled her.

I hesitated. A merciful headshot now would spare her everything. But I could not. Once they were awake, the hierarchy of Hubris would not understand a mercy killing. I would be trapped here for years, fighting my case through every court in their legislature.

I shook off her desperate grip and moved on.

Do you think me weak, flawed? Do you hate me for setting my Inquisitorial role above the needs of one agonised being?

If you do, I commend you. I think of that woman still, and hate the fact I left her to die slowly. But if you hate me, I know this about you... you are no inquisitor. You don't have the moral strength.

I could have finished her, and my soul might have been relieved. But that would have been an end to my work. And I always think of the thousands... millions perhaps... who would die worse deaths but for my actions.

Is that arrogance?

Perhaps... and perhaps arrogance is therefore a virtue of the Inquisition. I would gladly ignore one life in agony if I could save a hundred, a thousand, more...

Mankind must suffer so that mankind can survive. It's that simple. Ask Aemos. He knows.

Still, I dream of her and her bloody anguish. Pity me for that, at least.

I pressed on through the tomb-vaults, and after another gallery or two, progress became slow. Hundreds of sleepers had now freed themselves, the hallways were jostling with their frantic, blind pain. I skirted those I could, staying out of the way of grasping hands, stepping over some who lay twitching and helpless on the floor. The collective sounds of their braying and whimpering were almost intolerable. There was a hot, fetid stench of decay and bio-waste. Several times I had to break free of hands that seized me.

Grotesquely, the horror made it easier to track Eyclone. Every few paces, another sleeper lay dead or dying, callously gunned down by murderers in desperate flight.

I found a service door forced open at the end of the next file, and entered a deep stairwell that wound up through the edifice. Chemical globes suspended in wall brackets lit the way. From far above, I heard shots, and

I ascended, my pistol raised and braced, covering each turn of the staircase as Vibben had taught me.

I came up to what a wall-plaque told me was level eight. I could hear machine noise, industrial and heavy. Through another forced service door lay the walkways to the next galleries and a side access hatch of brushed grey adamite, which stencilled runes identified as the entrance to the main cryogenic generators. Smoke coughed and noise rolled from the hatch.

The cryogenerator chamber was vast, its roof reaching up into the pyramidal summit of Processional Two-Twelve. The rumbling equipment it contained was ancient and vast. The data-slate given to me in the ice-car had said that the cryogenerators that ran the hibernation tombs of Hubris had originally been constructed to equip the ark-fleet that carried the first colonists to the world. They had been cut and salvaged from the giant arks on arrival, and the stone tombs raised around them. A technomagos brotherhood, descended from the ark-fleet engineers, had kept the cryogenerators operating for thousands of years.

This cryogenerator was sixty metres tall and constructed from cast-iron and copper painted in matt-red lead paint. As it rose, it sprouted branches in the form of conduits and heat-exchangers that intertwined with the roof-vents. The hot air of the room vibrated with the noise of its operation. Smoke and steam wreathed the atmosphere and sweat broke out on my brow and back the moment I stepped through the hatchway.

I looked around and quickly noted where several inspection hatches had been levered away. The red paint was scored and scraped along each frame where a crowbar had been forced in, and hundreds of years of sacred unguents and lexmechanical sigil-seals applied and tended by the technomagi had been broken.

I peered in through the open covers and saw rows of copper-wound cells, vibrating rack-frames wet with black lubricant, sooty ganglions of insulated electrical routing and dripping, lagged iron pipes. Sprung-jawed clips with biting metal teeth had been attached to some of the cells, and wiring from these clips trailed back to a small and obviously new ceramite module box taped inside the hatch frame. A digital runic display on the module flashed amber.

This was where Eyclone's men had artificially triggered the revival process. That meant he had either turned and recruited local technomagi or brought in experts from off-world. Either way, this signified considerable resources.

I moved on, and clambered up a ladder frame onto a raised platform of metal grille. There was something else here, a rectangular casket measuring about a metre and a half along its longest edge. It rested on four claw-like feet and had carrying handles built into its sides. The lid was open, and dozens of cables and leads snaked out, linking it to the cryogenerator's electromechanical guts, exposed by another prised-off hatch.

I looked into the casket, but could make little sense of what I saw there: circuit boards and complex mechanical elements linked by sheaves of cable. And there was a space, a padded recess in the heart of the casket's innards, clearly waiting to receive something the size of a clenched fist. Loose cable ends and plugs were taped in place, ready to be connected. But a key component of this mysterious device was evidently missing.

My vox-link chimed in my ear. It was Betancore. I could barely hear him over the noise of the cryogenerator as he made a quick report in Glossia.

'Aegis, heavens uplift, thrice-sevenfold, a crown with stars. Infamous angel without title, to Thorn by eight. Pattern?'

I considered. I was in no mood to take any more chances. 'Thorn, pattern hawk.'

'Pattern hawk acknowledged,' he said with relish.

I saw movement from the corner of my eye about a half-second after I broke the link with Betancore: another of Eyclone's black-eyed men, running in through the main hatch with an old-model laspistol raised in his hand.

His first shot, a twinkling ball of pink light, snapped the metal handrail of the platform I stood on with an explosive ping. His second and third passed over me as I dived down, and ricocheted off the cast-iron side of the cryogenerator with scorching crackles.

I returned fire, prone, but the angle was bad. Two more las-shots came my way, one cutting sideways into the edge of the platform deck and cutting a gouge through the grille. The gunman was nearly at the foot of the ladder-frame.

Now a second gunman entered the chamber, calling out after the first, a powerful autorifle in his hands. He saw me, and began to raise the weapon, but I had a cleaner angle on him, and dropped him quickly with two rounds through the upper torso.

The other was almost below me now, and fired a shot that punched clean through the grille just next to my right foot.

I didn't hesitate. I went up and over the rail and directly down onto him. We crashed onto the chamber floor, the powerful impact throwing the Scipio out of my grasp despite my efforts to hold onto it. The man was jabbering some insane nonsense into my face and had a good grip on the front of my tunic. I had him by the throat and by the wrist of his gun-hand, forcing the laspistol away. He fired it twice into the ceiling space above.

'Enough!' I commanded, modulating my tone to emphasise my will as I drove it into his mind. 'Drop it!'

He did, meekly, as if surprised. Psyker tricks of will often baffle those who find themselves compelled by them. As he faltered, I threw a punch that connected well and left him unconscious on the floor.

As I bent to recover the Scipio, Betancore voxed me again. 'Aegis, pattern hawk, infamous angel cast down.'

'Thorn acknowledged. Resume pattern crucible.'

I pushed on after my quarry.

Eyclone made it into the upper vaults and out onto a landing platform built into the sloping side of Processional Two-Twelve. The wind was fierce. Eyclone had eight of his cult with him and they were expecting an orbital pinnace that would carry them away to safety.

They had no way of knowing that, thanks to Betancore, their means of escape was now burning in a deep impact gouge in the permafrost about eight kilometres north.

What rose above the landing platform out of the blizzard night, its down thrusters wailing, was my gun-cutter. Four hundred and fifty tonnes of armoured alloy, eighty metres from barbed nose to raked stern, landing gear still lowered like spider-legs, it rose on the blue-hot downwash of angled jets. Banks of floodlights under its beak-nose cut on and bathed the deck and the cultists in fierce white light.

Panicking, some of them fired up at it.

That was all the cue Betancore needed. His temper was hot, his mind void of anything except the fact that Vibben was dead.

The gun-turrets in the ends of the stubby wings rotated and washed the platform with withering heavy fire. Stone splintered. Bodies were reduced to sprays of liquid.

Eyclone, more intelligent than his men, had sprinted off the platform to the hatch as the gun-cutter rose into view.

And that's where he ran into me.

He opened his mouth in shock and I pushed the muzzle of Vibben's gun into it. I'm sure he wanted to say something important. I didn't care what it was.

I punched the gun so hard into his mouth the trigger guard broke his lower teeth. He tried to reach for something on his belt.

I fired.

Having emptied his brain-case and shattered it into the bargain, the round still had so much force it crossed the deck and pinked off the armoured nose of the hovering gun-cutter, just below the cockpit window.

'Sorry,' I said.

'Don't worry about it,' Betancore crackled back over the vox-link.

'Most perturbatory,' said Aemos. It was his most frequent expression. He was hunched over, peering down into the casket on the cryogenerator chamber platform. Occasionally, he reached in to tinker with something, or leaned down for a closer look. Gestures such as these made the heavy augmetic eye glasses clamped to his hooked nose make a soft dialling click as they auto-focused.

I stood at his shoulder, waiting, looking down at the back of his old, bald head. The skin was liver-spotted and thin, and a narrow crescent of white hair edged the back of his skull.

Uber Aemos was my savant, and my longest serving companion. He had come into my service in the first month of my career in the Inquisition, bequeathed to me by Inquisitor Hapshant, who was by then dying of cerebral worms. Aemos was two hundred and seventy-eight standard years old, and had provided his services as a savant to three inquisitors before me. He was alive only thanks to significant bionic augmentation to his digestive tract, liver, urinary system, hips and left leg.

In Hapshant's service he had been injured by a stub-round. Tending him, surgeons had found a chronically advanced and previously undiagnosed cancer rampant in his abdomen. Had he not been shot, he would have died within weeks. Thanks to the wound, the disease was found, excised and his body repaired with plastic, ceramite and steel prosthetics.

Aemos referred to the whole ordeal as his 'lucky suffering' and still wore the twisted plug of the stub round that had almost taken and certainly saved his life on a chain around his stringy neck.

'Aemos?'

He rose stiffly with a whine of bionics and turned to face me, shaking out the floor length green folds of his embroidered robe. His augmetic eye-wear dominated his ancient face. He sometimes reminded me of a curious insect with bulbous eyes and narrow, pinched mouth parts.

'A codifier of unique design. A series processor, similar in layout to the mind-impulse units used by the hallowed Adeptus Mechanicus to govern the linkage between human brain and god-machine.'

'You've seen such things?' I asked, a little taken aback.

'Once, in my travels. In passing. I do not pretend to have more than a cursory knowledge. I am certain, however, that the Adeptus Mechanicus would be interested in this device. It may be illicit technology or something derived from apparatus stolen from them. Either way, they would impound it.'

'Either way, they're not going to know about it. This is inquisitional evidence.'

'Quite so,' he agreed.

There were distracting noises from below us. Tomb custodians and technomagi from the cryogenerator brotherhood milled about in the chamber, supervising the mammoth and, in my opinion, futile operation to save the sleepers of Processional Two-Twelve. The whole tomb seethed with activity, and the awful screams had not yet died down.

I saw how Aemos watched the work with keen interest, making notes to himself on a data-slate strapped to his wrist. At the age of forty-two, he had contracted a meme-virus that altered his brain function for ever, driving him to collect information – any sort of information – whenever he got the chance. He was pathologically compelled to acquire knowledge, a data-addict. That made him an aggravating, easily sidetracked companion, and a perfect savant, as four inquisitors had discovered.

'Cold-bolted steel cylinders,' he mused, looking up at the heat exchangers. 'Is that to provide stress-durability in temperature change, or was it fabrication expedient? Also, what is the range of temperature change, given–'

'Aemos, please.'

'Hmm?' He looked back at me, remembering I was there.

'The casket?'

'Indeed. My apologies. A series processor... did I say that?'

'Yes. Processing what? Data?'

'I thought that at first, then I considered some mental or mental-transference process. But I doubt either now I've studied it.'

I pointed down into the casket. 'What's missing?'

'Oh, you noticed that too? This is most perturbatory. I'm still not certain, of course, but it's something angular, non-standard in shape and with its own power source.'

'You're sure?'

'There are no power inlets designed to couple to it, only power outlets. And there's something curious about the plugs. Non-standard mating. It's all non-standard.'

'Xenos?'

'No... human, just non-standard, custom made.'

'Yeah, but what for?' asked Betancore, climbing up the ladder frame to join us. He looked sour, his unruly black curls framing a dark-skinned, slender face that was usually alive with genial mischief.

'I need to make further evaluations, Midas,' said Aemos, hunching back over the casket.

Betancore stared my way. He was as tall as me, but lighter in build. His boots, breeches and tunic were made of soft black leather with red piping, the old uniform of a Glavian pilot-hunter, and over that he wore, as always, a short jacket of cerise silk with iridescent embroidery panels.

His hands were gloved in light bllek-hide, and seemed to wait ominously near the curved grips of the needle pistols holstered on his hips.

'You took a long time getting here,' I began.

'They made me take the cutter back to the landing cross at Tomb Point. Said they need the platform here for emergency flights. I had to walk back. Then I saw to Lores.'

'She died well, Betancore.'

'Maybe. Is that possible?' he added.

I made no reply. I knew how deep his foul moods could be. I knew he had been in love with Lores Vibben, or at least had decided he was in love with her. I knew things would get difficult with Betancore before they got better.

'Where is this off-worlder? This Eisenhorn?'

The demanding voice rolled up from the chamber below us. I looked down. A man had entered the cryogenerator chamber escorted by four custodians in heat-gowns, carrying light-poles aloft. He was tall, with pallid skin and greying hair, though his haughty bearing spoke of self-possession and arrogance. He wore a decorative ceremonial heat-gown of bold yellow. I didn't know who he was, but he looked like trouble to me.

Aemos and Betancore were watching him too.

'Any ideas as to who this is?' I asked Aemos.

'Well, you see, the yellow robes, like the light poles carried by the custodians, symbolises the return of the sun and thus heat and light. It denotes a high-ranking official of the Dormant Custodial Committee.'

'I got that much myself,' I muttered.

'Oh, well his name is Nissemay Carpel, and he's high custodian, so you should address him as such. He was born here, on Vital 235, fifty standard years ago, the son of a–'

'Enough! I knew we'd get there eventually.'

I walked to the rail and looked down. 'I am Eisenhorn.'

He stared up at me, barely contained wrath bulging the veins in his neck.

'Place him under arrest,' he told his men.

THREE

NISSEMAY CARPEL
A LIGHT IN ENDLESS DARKNESS
THE PONTIUS

I shot one, meaningful glance at Betancore to stay his hand, then calmly walked past him, slid down the ladder frame and approached Carpel. The custodians closed in around me, but at a distance.

'High custodian,' I nodded.

He fixed me with a steady but wary gaze and licked spittle off his thin lips. 'You will be detained until–'

'No,' I replied. 'I am an inquisitor of the God-Emperor of Mankind, Ordo Xenos. I will co-operate in any investigation you bring to bear here, fully and completely, but you will not and cannot detain me. Do you understand?'

'An... inquisitor?'

'Do you understand?' I repeated. I wasn't using my will at all, not yet. I would if I had to. But I trusted that he would have the sense to listen to me first. He could make things awkward for me, but I could make things intolerable for him.

He seemed to soften a little. As I had judged, part of his rage came from shock at this incident, shock that so many planetary nobles in his care had suffered. He was looking for somewhere to pin the blame. Now he had to temper that with the idea that he was dealing with a member of the most feared institution in the Imperium.

'Thousands are dead,' he began, a tremor in his voice. 'This desecration... the high born of Hubris, violated by a... by a–'

'A murderer, a follower of darkness, a man who, thanks to me, lies dead now under a plastic sheet on the upper landing platform. I mourn the great loss Hubris has suffered tonight, high custodian, and I wish I had been able to prevent it. But if I had not been here at all to raise the alarm... well, imagine the tragedy you would be dealing with then.'

I let that sink in.

'Not just this processional, but all the hibernation tombs... who knows what Eyclone might have wrought? Who knows what his overall ambition was?'

'Eyclone, the recidivist?'

'He did this, high custodian.'

'You will brief me on this entire event.'

'Let me prepare a report and bring it to you. You may have answers for me too. I will signal you in a few hours for an appointment to meet. I think you have plenty to deal with right now.'

We made our way out. Betancore presented the junior custodians with a formal register of evidence to be stored for my inspection. The list included the casket and the bodies of Eyclone and his men. None would be tampered with or even searched until I had looked at them. The gunman I had subdued in the cryogenerator chamber, the only one left alive, would be incarcerated pending my interrogation. Betancore made these requirements abundantly clear.

We took Vibben with us. Aemos was too frail, so Betancore and I handled the plastic-shrouded form on the gurney.

We left Processional Two-Twelve by the main vault doors into the biting cold of the constant night and carried Vibben down towards a waiting ice-car, taking her through the hundreds of rows of corpses the Custodians were laying out on the frozen ground.

My band and I had deployed onto Hubris the moment we arrived, such was the urgency of our chase. Now it looked like we would remain here for at least a week, longer if Carpel proved difficult. As we rode the ice-car back to the landing cross, I had Aemos make arrangements for our stay.

During Dormant on Hubris, while ninety-nine per cent of the planetary population hibernates, one location remains active. The custodians and the technomagi weather out the long, bitter darkness in a place called the Sun-dome.

Fifty kilometres from the vast expanse of the Dormant Plains where the hibernation tombs stand in rows, the Sun-dome sits like a dark grey blister in the ongoing winter night. It is home to fifty-nine thousand people, just a town compared with the great empty cities that slumber below the horizon line waiting for Thaw to bring their populations back.

I stared out at the Sun-dome as the gun-cutter swept us in towards it through wind-blown storms of ice. Small red marker lights winked on the surfaces of the dome and from the masts jutting from the apex.

Betancore flew, silent, concentrating. He had removed his tight-fitting gloves so that the intricate Glavian circuitry set like silver inlay into his palms and finger tips could engage with the cutter's system directly via the control stick.

Aemos sat in a rear cabin, poring over manuscripts and data-slates. Two independent multitask servitors waited for commands in the crew-bay. The ship had five in all. Two were limb-less combat units slaved directly to the gun-pods and the other, the chief servitor, a high-spec model we called Uclid, never left his duties in the engine room.

Lowink, my astropath, slumbered in his chamber, linked to the vox and pict systems, awaiting a summons.

Vibben lay shrouded on the cot in her room.

Betancore swung the cutter down towards the dome. After an exchange of telemetry, a wide blast shutter opened in the side of the dome. The light that shone out was almost unbearably bright. Betancore engaged the cockpit glare shields and flew us into the landing bay.

The inside surface of the vast dome was mirrored. A plasma-effect sun-globe burned high in the roof of the dome, bathing the town below in fierce white light. The town itself, spread out beneath us, seemed to be made of glass.

We set down on the wide bay, a twenty-hectare metal platform that overlooked the town. The surface of the platform gleamed almost white in the reflected glare. Heavy monotask servitors trundled out and towed us into a landing silo off the main pad, where pit-servitors moved in to attach fuel lines and begin fundamental servicing. Betancore didn't want anybody or anything touching the gun-cutter, so he ordered Modo and Nilquit, our two independent servitors, to take over the tasks and send the locals away. I could hear them moving around the hull, servos whirring, hydraulics hissing, exchanging machine code data bursts with each other or with Uclid in the drive chamber.

Aemos offered to find accommodation for us in the town itself, but I decided a landing berth was all we needed. The gun-cutter was large enough to provide ample facilities for our stay. We often spent weeks, or months living aboard it.

I went to Lowink's small cabin under the cockpit deck and roused him. He hadn't been with me long: my previous astropath had been killed trying to translate a warp-cipher six weeks before.

Lowink was a young man, with a fleshy, unhealthy bulk hanging from a thin skeletal frame, his body already deteriorating from the demands of a psyker's life. Greasy implant plugs dotted his shaved skull, and lined his forearms like short spines. As he came to the door, some of these plugs trailed wires, each marked with parchment labels, which led back to the communications mainbox above his cradle. Thousands of cables spilled or dangled around his tiny cabin, but he instinctively knew what each one did and could set and adjust plug-ins at a moment's notice. The room reeked of sweat and incense.

'Master,' he said. His mouth was a wet pink slit and he had one lazy, half-hooded eye that gave him a superior air quite belying his actual timidity.

'Please send a message for me, Lowink. To the Regal Akwitane.' The Regal was a rogue trader we had employed to convey the gun-cutter and ourselves to Hubris. His vessel awaited us in orbit now, ready to provide further warp-passage.

'Give Trade Master Golkwin my respects and tell him we are staying for now. He can be on his way, there is no point in him waiting. We could be here for a week or more. The usual form, polite. Tell him I thank him for his service and hope we may meet again.'

Lowink nodded. 'I will do it at once.'

'Then I'd like you to perform some other tasks. Contact the main Astropathicus Enclave here on Hubris and request a full transcript of off-world traffic for the past six weeks. Also any record of unlicensed traffic, individuals using their own astropaths. Whatever they can make available. And a little threat that it is an inquisitor requiring this data wouldn't hurt. They don't want to find themselves caught up in a major inquisition for withholding information.'

He nodded again. 'Will you be requiring an auto-seance?'

'Not yet, but I will eventually. I will give you time to prepare.'

'Will that be all, Master?'

I turned to go. 'Yes, Lowink.'

'Master...' he paused. 'Is it true that the female Vibben is dead?'

'Yes, Lowink.'

'Ah. I thought it was quiet.' He closed the door.

The comment wasn't as callous as it sounded. I knew what he meant, though my own psychic abilities were nascent and undeveloped next to his. Lores Vibben was a latent psyker, and while she had been with us, there had been a constant background sound, almost subliminal, broadcast unconsciously by her young, eager mind.

I found Betancore outside, standing under the shadow of one of the gun-cutter's stubby wings. He was gazing at the ground, smoking a lho-leaf tube. I didn't approve of narcotics, but I let it go. He'd cleaned himself up these past few years. When I'd first met him, he had been an obscura user.

'Damned bright place,' he muttered, wincing out at the abominable glare.

'A typical over reaction. They have eleven months of pitch dark, so they light their habitat to an excessive degree.'

'Do they have a night cycle?'

'I don't believe so.'

'No wonder they're so messed up. Extreme light, extreme dark, extreme mindsets. Their body clocks and natural rhythms must be all over the place.'

I nodded. Outside, I had begun to be disarmed by the notion that the night was never going to end. Now I had the same feelings about this constant noon. In his brief, Aemos had said the world was called Hubris because after spending seventy standard years getting here aboard their ark-fleet, the original colonists had found the surveys had been incorrect. Instead of enjoying a regular orbit, the world they had selected pursued this extreme pattern of darkness and light. They'd settled anyway, co-opting the cryo-generational methods that had got them here as part of their culture. A mistake, in my view.

But I wasn't here to offer a cultural critique.

'Notice anything?' I asked Betancore.

He made a casual gesture around the landing platform. 'They don't get many visitors in this season. Trade's all but dead, the world's on tick-over.'

'Which is why Eyclone thought it vulnerable.'

'Yes. Most of the ships here are local, trans-atmospheric. Some are for the custodians' use, the others are simply berthed-up over Dormant. I make three non-locals, aside from us. Two trader launches and a private cutter.'

'Ask around. See if you can find out who they belong to and what their business is.'

'Sure thing.'

'Eyclone's pinnace, the one you shot down. Did it come from here?'

He took a suck on his narc-tube and shook his head. 'Either came from orbit, or up from some private location. Lowink picked up its transmissions to Eyclone.'

'I'll ask to see those. But it could have come from orbit? Eyclone may have a starship up there?'

'Don't worry, I already thought to look. If there was one there, it's gone, and it made no signals.'

'I'd like to know how that bastard got here, and how he was intending to leave again.'

'I'll find that out,' said Betancore, crushing the tube stub under his heel. He meant it.

'What about Vibben?' he asked.

'Do you know what her wishes were? She never mentioned anything to me. Did she want her remains sent back to Tornish for burial?'

'You'd do that?'

'If that was what she wanted. Is it?'

'I don't know, Eisenhorn. She never told me either.'

'Take a look through her effects, see if she left any testament or instructions. Can you do that?'

'I'd like to do that,' he said.

I was tired by then. I spent another hour with Aemos in his cramped, data-slate-filled room, preparing a report for Carpel. I set out the basic details, reserving anything I felt he didn't need to know. I accounted for my actions. I made Aemos check them against local law, to prepare myself in case Carpel raised a prosecution. I wasn't unduly worried about him, and in truth I was bulletproof against local legislation, but I wanted to check anyway. An Amalathian prides himself on working with the structures of Imperial society, not above or beyond them. Or through them, as a monodominant might. I wanted Carpel and the senior officials of Hubris on my side, helping my investigation.

When my report was complete, I retired to my room. I paused by Vibben's door, went in, and gently placed the Scipio naval pistol between her hands on her chest, folding the shroud back afterwards. It was hers, it had done its work. It deserved to be laid to rest with her.

For the first time in six years, I did not dream about Eyclone. I dreamed of a blinding darkness, then a light that refused to go away. There was something dark about the light. Nonsense, I know, but that was how it felt. Like a revelation that actually carried some grimmer, more profound truth. There were flashes, like lightning, around the edges of my dream's horizon. I saw a handsome, blank-eyed male, not blank-eyed like one of Eyclone's drones, but vacant like an immense, star-less distance. He smiled at me.

At that time in my life, I had no idea who he was.

* * *

I went to see Carpel at noon the next day. It was always noon in the Sundome, but this was real noon by the clock. By then, Lowink, Aemos and Betancore had all dredged up new information for me.

I shaved, and dressed in black linen with high boots and a formal jacket of scaled brown hide. I wore my Inquisitorial rosette at my throat. I intended to show Carpel I meant business.

Aemos and I descended from the landing platform superstructure by caged elevator and found yellow-robed custodians waiting to escort us. Despite the rancid white light all around, they still held ignited light poles. We made short, hard shadows on the dry rockcrete of the concourse as we crossed to an open limousine. It was a massive chrome-grilled beast with pennants bearing the Hubris crest fluttering on its cowling. There were four rows of overstuffed leather benches behind the centre-set driver's cockpit.

We hummed through the streets on eight fat wheels. The boulevards were wide and, needless to say, bright. To either hand, glass-fronted buildings rose towards the blazing plasma sun-globe high above, like flowers seeking the light. Every thirty metres along every street, chemical lamps on ornate posts strained to add their own light to the brilliance.

Traffic was sparse, and there were at most a few thousand pedestrians on the streets. I noticed most wore yellow silk sashes, and that garlands of yellow flowers decorated every lamp post.

'The flowers?' I asked.

'From the hydroponic farms on east-dome seven,' one of the custodians told me.

'Signifying?'

'Mourning.'

'Same as the sashes,' Aemos whispered in confidence. 'What happened last night is a major tragedy for this world. Yellow is their holy colour. I believe the local religion is a solar belief.'

'The sun as Emperor?'

'Common enough. Extreme here, for obvious reasons.'

The custodial hall was a glass spire close to the town centre, a solar disk overlaid with the double-headed eagle of the Imperium decorating its upper faces. Nearby was the local chapel of the Ecclesiarchy, and several buildings given over to the Imperial Administratum. It amused me to see they were all built of black stone and virtually windowless. Those Imperial servants stationed here obviously had as little truck as me with the constant light.

We drew in under a glass portico and were escorted into the main hall. It was seething with people, most of them custodians in yellow robes, some local officials and technomagi, some clerks and servitors. The hall itself was of the scale of an Imperial chapel, but raised in yellow-stained glass on a frame of black cast-iron. The air was full of golden light shafting down through the glass. The carpet was vast, black, with a sun-disk woven into its centre.

'Inquisitor Eisenhorn!' declared one of my escorts through a vox-hailer. The hall fell silent, and all turned to watch us approach. High Custodian Carpel sat on a hovering lifter-throne with gilt decorations. A burning chemical light was mounted above the head of the floating chair. He swung in through the parting crowd towards me.

'High custodian,' I said with a dutiful nod.

'They are all dead,' he informed me. 'All twelve thousand, one hundred and forty-two. Processional Two-Twelve is dead. None survived the trauma.'

'Hubris has my sincere sympathies, high custodian.'

The hall exploded in pandemonium, voices screeching and shouting and clamouring.

'Your sympathies? Your damned sympathies?' Carpel screamed above the roar. 'A great part of our ruling elite die in one night, and we have your sympathies to console us?'

'That is all I can offer, high custodian.' I could feel Aemos shivering at my side, making aimless notes on his wrist slate about custom and clothing and language forms... anything to take his mind from the confrontation.

'That's hardly good enough!' spat a young man nearby. He was a local noble, young and firm enough, but his skin had a dreadful, sweaty pallor and custodians supported him as he stumbled forward.

'Who are you?' I asked.

'Vernal Maypell, heir-lord of the Dallowen Cantons!' If he expected me to fall to my knees in supplication, he was in for a disappointment.

'Because of the gravity of this event, we have roused some of our high-born early from their dormancy,' Carpel said. 'Liege Maypell's brother and two of his wives died in Processional Two-Twelve.'

So the pallor was revival sickness. I noticed that fifty or more of the congregation present were similarly wasted and ill.

I turned to Maypell.

'Liege. I repeat, you have my condolences.'

Maypell exploded with rage. 'Your arrogance astounds me, off-worlder! You bring this monster to our world, battle with him through our most sacred sanctums, a private war that slaughters our best and you–'

'Wait!' I used my will. I didn't care. Maypell stopped as if stunned and the vast hall rang silent. 'I came here to save you and deny Eyclone's plans. But for the efforts of myself and my companions, he might have destroyed more than one of your hibernation tombs. I broke none of your laws. I was careful to preserve your codes in pursuit of my work. What do you mean, I brought this monster here?'

'We have made enquiries,' answered an elderly noblewoman nearby. Like Maypell, she was ailing with revival sickness, and sat hunched on a litter carried by slaved servitors.

'What enquiries, madam?'

'This long feud with the murderer Eyclone. Five years, is it now?'

'Six, lady.'

'Six, then. You have hounded him here. Driven him. Brought him, as Liege Maypell said.'

'How?'

'We registered no off-world ship these past twenty days except yours, Eisenhorn,' Carpel said, reviewing a data-slate. 'The Regal Akwitane. That ship must have brought him as it brought you, to finish your war here and damn our lives. Did you choose Hubris because it was quiet, out of the way, a place where you might finish your feud undisturbed, in the long dark?'

I was angry by now. I concentrated to control my rage. 'Aemos?'

Beside me, he was muttering '...and what silicate dyes do they use in their stained glass manufacture? Is the structure armoured? The supports are early Imperial Gothic in style, but–'

'Aemos! The report!'

He started and handed me a data-slate from his leather case.

'Read this, Carpel. Read it thoroughly.' I pushed it at him – then snatched it away as he reached for it. 'Or should I read it aloud to all here assembled? Should I explain how I came here at the last minute when I learned Eyclone was moving to Hubris? That I learned that only by astropathic decryption of a cipher message sent by Eyclone two months ago? A cipher that killed my astropath in his efforts to translate it?'

'Inquisitor, I–' Carpel began.

I held up the data-slate report for them all, thumbing the stud that scrolled the words across the screen. 'And what about this? The evidence that Eyclone has been planning a move against your world for almost a year? And this, gathered this last night – that an unregistered starship moved in and out of your orbit to deliver Eyclone three days ago, unnoticed by your planetary overwatch and the custodian "Guardians"? Or the itemised stream of astropathic communication that your local enclave noticed but didn't bother to source or translate?'

I tossed the slate into Carpel's lap. Hundreds of eyes stared at me in shocked silence.

'You were wide open. He exploited you. Don't blame me for anything except being too late to stop him. As I said, you have my sincere condolences.'

'And next time you choose to confront an Imperial inquisitor,' I added, 'you may want to be more respectful. I'm excusing a lot because I recognise the trauma and loss you have suffered. But my patience isn't limitless... unlike my authority.'

I turned to Carpel. 'Now, high custodian, can we talk? In private, as I think I requested.'

We followed Carpel's floating throne into a side annexe leaving a hall full of murmuring shocked voices behind us. Only one of his men accompanied us, a tall, blond fellow in a dark brown uniform I didn't recognise. A bodyguard, I presumed. Carpel set his throne down on the carpet and raised a remote wand that tinted the glass plates of the room at a touch.

Reasonable light levels at last. From that alone, I knew Carpel was taking me seriously.

He waved me to a seat opposite. Aemos lurked in the shadows behind me. The man in brown stood by the windows, watching.

'What happens now?' Carpel asked.

'I expect your full co-operation as I extend my investigation.'

'But the matter is over,' said the man in brown.

I kept my gaze on Carpel. 'I want your consent for me to continue as well as your full co-operation. Eyclone may be dead, but he was just the blade-point of a long and still dangerous weapon.'

'What are you talking about?' the man in brown snapped.

Still I did not look at him. Staring at Carpel, I said, 'If he speaks again without me knowing who he is, I will throw him out of the window. And I won't open it first.'

'This is Chastener Fischig, of the Adeptus Arbites. I wanted him present.'

Now I looked at the man in brown. He was a heavy-set brute with a loop of shiny pink scar tissue under one milky eye. I'd taken him to be a young man with his clean skin and blond hair, but now I studied him, I saw he was at least my age.

'Chastener,' I nodded.

'Inquisitor,' he returned. 'My question stands.'

I sat back in my chair. 'Murdin Eyclone was a facilitator. A brilliant, devious man, one of the most dangerous I have ever hunted. Sometimes to hunt down your prey is to finish his evil. I'm sure you have experience of that.'

'You called him a "facilitator".'

'That was where his danger lay. He believed he could serve his obscene masters best by offering his considerable skills to cults and sects that needed them. He had no true allegiances. He worked to facilitate the grand schemes of others. What he was doing here on Hubris was to advance and develop someone else's plans. Now he is dead, and his scheme thwarted. We may be thankful. But my task is not done. I must work back from Eyclone, his men, from any clue he left and dig my way into whatever greater, secret darkness was employing him.'

'And for this you want the co-operation of the people of Hubris?' asked Carpel.

'The people, the authorities, you... everyone. This is the Emperor's work. Will you shrink from it?'

'No sir, I will not!' snapped Carpel.

'Excellent.'

Carpel tossed a gold solar-form badge to me. It was heavy and old, mounted on a pad of black leather.

'This will give you authority. My authority. Conduct your work thoroughly and quickly. I ask two things in return.'

'And they are?'

'You report all findings to me. And you allow the chastener to accompany you.'

'I work my own way–'

'Fischig can open doors and voiceboxes here in the Sun-dome that even that badge may not. Consider him a local guide.'

And your ears and eyes, I thought. But I knew he was under immense pressure from the nobility to produce results, so I said: 'I will be grateful for his assistance.'

'Where first?' Fischig asked, down to business at once, a hungry look on his face. They want blood, I realised. They want someone to punish for the deaths, someone they can say they caught, or at least helped to catch. They want to share in whatever successes I have so that they can look good when the rest of their population wakes up to this disaster in a few months' time.

I couldn't blame them.

'First,' I said, 'the mortuary.'

Eyclone looked as if he was asleep. His head had been wrapped in an almost comical plastic bonnet to contain the wound I had dealt him. Framed in the plastic, his face was tranquil, with just a slight bruising around the lips.

He lay on a stone plinth in the chill of the morgue below Arbites Mortuary One. His brethren lay on numbered plinths around him, those that had been recovered more or less intact. There were labelled bins of mostly liquescent material against the back wall, the remains of those that Betancore had slaughtered with the cutter's cannons.

The air in the underground vault was lit cold blue, and frost covered circulators pumped in sub-zero air directly from the ice-desert outside the Sun-dome. Fischig had provided us all with heat gowns for the visit.

I was impressed by what I saw: both the dutiful care and attention that had been used to sequester and store the bodies and by the fact that no one had touched them, according to my instructions. It seems a simple command to give, but I have lost count of the times that over-eager death-priests or surgeons have begun autopsies before I arrived.

The mortician superintendent was a haggard woman in her sixties called Tutrone. She attended us in red plastic scrubs worn over an old and threadbare heat-gown. Mortress Tutrone had a bionic implant in one eye socket, and blades and bonesaw manipulators of gleaming surgical steel built into her right hand.

'I have done as you instructed,' she told me as she led us down the spiral steps into the cold vault. 'But it is irregular. Rules state I must begin examinations, prelim examinations at least, as soon as possible.'

'I thank you for your diligence, mortress. I will be done quickly. Then you can follow protocol.'

Pulling on surgical gloves, I moved through the lines of dead – there were nearly twenty of them – dictating observations of Aemos. There was virtually nothing to be learned from the men. Some I gauged from build and coloration to be off-worlders, but they had no documents, no surgical identifiers, no clue whatsoever about their origins or identities. Even their clothing was blank... manufacturing tags and labels had been torn or burned off. I could begin a forensic investigation to identify the source of the clothing, but that would be a massive waste of resources.

On two of them, I found fresh scars that suggested subcutaneous ident markers had been surgically removed. Ident marking was not a local practice, so that at least suggested off-world. But where? Hundreds of Imperial planets routinely used such devices, and their placing and use was pretty standard. I had carried one myself for a few years, as a child, before the Black Ships selected me and it was dug out.

One of the corpses had a curious scarring on the forearms, not deep but thorough, searing the epidermis.

'Someone has used a melta-torch to remove gang tattoos,' Aemos said.

He was right. Again, it was tantalisingly incomplete.

I looked to Eyclone, where I thought my best bet lay. With the Mortress's help, I cut away his clothes, all of which were as anonymous as his followers' garb. We turned his naked corpse, looking for... well, anything.

'There!' Fischig said, leaning in. A brand mark above the left buttock.

'The Seraph of Laoacus. An old Chaos mark. Eyclone had it done to honour his then-masters twenty years ago. A previous cult, a previous employer. Nothing to do with this.'

Fischig looked at me curiously. 'You know the details of his naked flesh?'

'I have sources,' I replied. I didn't want to have to tell the tale. Eemanda, one of my first companions, brilliant, beautiful and bold. She had found that detail out for me. She had been in an asylum now for five years. The last report I had received said she had eaten away her own fingers.

'But he marks himself?' Fischig added. 'With each new cult he involves himself in, he carries their mark to show his allegiance?'

The man had a point, damn him. We looked. At least six laser scars on his body seemed likely to have been previous cult marks, burned off after he left those associations.

Behind his left ear, a skin inlay of silver was worked in the form of the Buboe Chaotica.

'This?' asked Tutrone, shaving the hair aside with her finger blades to reveal it.

'Old, as before.'

I stepped back from the body and thought hard. When I'd killed him, he had been reaching for something on his belt, or so it had seemed to me.

'His effects?'

They were laid out on a metal tray nearby. His laspistol, a compact vox-device, a pearl-inlaid box containing six obscura tubes and an igniter, a credit tile, spare cells for the gun, a plastic key. And the belt; with four buttoned pouches.

I opened them one by one: some local coins; a miniature las-knife; three bars of high-calorie rations; a steel tooth-pick; more obscura, this time in an injector vial; a small data-slate.

At the moment of death, which of these things had he been reaching for? The knife? Too slow and small to counter a man who has a naval pistol wedged into your mouth. Then again, he was desperate.

And then again, he hadn't reached for his holstered lasgun.

The data-slate, perhaps? I picked it up and activated it, but it needed a cipher to gain access. All manner of secrets might be locked inside... but why would a man reach for a data-slate in the face of certain death?

'Track marks, along the forearm,' Tutrone stated, continuing her exam.

Hardly surprising, given the narco-ware we'd recovered from him.

'No rings? No bracelets? Earrings? Piercing studs?'

'None.'

I pulled a plastic pouch from a dispenser on the surgical cart and put all his effects into it.

'You will sign for those, won't you?' Tutrone asked, looking up.

'Of course.'

'You hated him, didn't you?' Fischig said suddenly.

'What?'

He leaned back against a plinth, crossing his arms. 'You had him at your mercy, and you knew his head was full of secrets, but you emptied it with your gun. I have no compunction when it comes to killing, but I know when I'm wasting a lead. Was it rage?'

'I'm an inquisitor. I do not get angry.'

'Then what?'

I had just about enough of his snide tone. 'You don't know how dangerous this man is. I wasn't taking chances.'

'He looks safe enough to me,' Fischig smirked, looking down at the body.

'Here's something!' Tutrone called out. We all moved in.

She was working on his left hand, delicately, with her finest gauge scalpels and probes, her augmented fingers darting like a seamstress.

'The index finger of the left hand. There's unusual lividity and swelling.' She played a small scanner across it.

'The nail's ceramite. Artificial. An implant.'

'What's inside?'

'Unknown. A ghost reading. There's maybe... ah, there it is... a catch under the quick. You'd need something small to trigger it.'

She adjusted her bionic finger settings and slid out a very thin metal probe, thin like...

...a tooth pick.

'Back! Back now!' I yelled.

It was too late. Tutrone had undone the catch. The false nail sprang back and something flew out of the cavity in the finger tip. A silver worm, like a thread of necklace chain, flashed through the air.

'Where did it go?'

'I don't know, I said, pushing Tutrone and Aemos behind me. 'Did you see it?' I asked Fischig.

'Over there,' he said, pulling a short-nosed gloss-black autopistol out from his robes.

I reached for my own gun, then remembered I'd given it back to Vibben.

I snatched up a bone knife from the trolley.

The worm slithered back into the light. It was a metre long and several centimetres thick now. What foul sorcery had caused that expansion, I did not want to know. It was made of segmented metal, and the head was an eyeless cone split by a hissing mouth full of razor teeth.

Tutrone cried out as it flew at us. I pushed her down and the thing whipped across over us, hitting a corpse on a nearby plinth. There was a dreadful sucking, gnawing sound and the worm disappeared into the corpse's torso through a jagged hole.

The corpse vibrated and ruptured, filling the air with a foul mist of vapour.

The worm swished up out of it and disappeared across the floor. By then, Fischig had opened fire and blasted the shattered corpse off its plinth. The worm was long since gone.

'Touch-activated mechanism,' Aemos was murmuring to himself, 'very discreet, probably of Xenos manufacture, a guard weapon, with some mass-altering system that expands it on contact with air and/or release, hunting by sound...'

'So shut up!' I told him. I bundled him and Tutrone against the far wall. Fischig and I moved in parallel courses down through the plinth rows, weapons ready.

It reappeared. By the time I saw it, it was almost on me, thrashing forward through the air on its metallic tail. In a split second, I reflected that this was how Eyclone had wanted me to die. This was what he had intended to unleash against me on the landing platform at Processional Two-Twelve.

Rage made me deny him. I stabbed out and my extended blade jabbed directly between the gaping teeth and down the gullet. The impact knocked me back. I found I had the whole, heavy, two-metre thing thrashing on the end of my knife like a lash.

Shots banged past me. Fischig was trying to hit it.

'You'll kill me, you idiot!'

'Hold it still!'

With a metallic rasping, it was chewing down the blade and the handle towards my hand.

Tutrone came in from behind me and together we wrestled the powerful, coiling thing onto a plinth. She activated a bone-saw on her augmetic hand and sliced down through its neck with a shrill scream of spinning blades.

The body continued to thrash. She grabbed it and dropped it into an acid trough usually reserved for bio-waste. The hissing head and the knife it was still chewing away at quickly followed it.

The four of us gazed down at the thrashing remains as they disintegrated.

I looked round at Mortress Tutrone and Fischig.

'I know which one of you I'd rather have around in a fight,' I muttered.

Tutrone laughed. Fischig didn't.

'What was it?' Aemos asked me as we raced in Fischig's landspeeder through the streets to the Arbites' headquarters.

'You guessed more than I know,' I replied. 'A gift from his masters, certainly.'

'What manner of masters make a thing like that?'

'Powerful ones, Aemos. The worst kind.'

Our meeting at the Arbites' grim chambers was brief. At my request, Fischig had summoned Magus Palastemes, the head of the cryogenerator technomagi.

He took one look at the casket in the evidence room and said, 'I have no idea what it is.'

'Thank you. That will be all,' I told him. I turned to Fischig. 'Have this sent immediately to my vessel.'

'It is state's evidence–' he began.

'Who do you work for, Fischig?'

'The Emperor.'

'Then pretend I'm him and you won't be far wrong. Do it.'

Hadam Bonz was waiting for us in the interrogation room. He had been stripped naked, but Fischig assured me nothing of import had been found in his clothes.

Bonz was the gunman I had laid out in the cryogenerator chamber, the only one of Eyclone's men to have survived the night. His mouth was swollen from my blow. He had admitted nothing except his name.

Fischig, Aemos and I entered the room, a dull stone box. Bonz was shackled to a metal chair and looked terrified.

So should he, I thought.

'Tell me about Murdin Eyclone,' I said.

'Who?' The darkness had gone from his eyes now, Eyclone's spell broken. He was bewildered and confused.

'Then tell me the last thing you remember.'

'I was on Thracian Primaris. That was my home. I was a stevedore in the docks. I remember going to a bar with a friend. That is all.'

'The friend?'

'A dock master called Wyn Eddon. We got drunk, I think.'

'Did Eddon mention an Eyclone?'

'No. Look, where am I? These bastards won't say. What I am supposed to have done?'

I smiled. 'You tried to kill me for a start.'

'You?'

'I'm an Imperial inquisitor.'

At that, terror made him lose control of his body functions. He began pleading, begging, telling us all sorts of misdemeanours, none of which mattered.

I knew from the first moments that he was useless. Just a mesmerised slave, chosen for his muscle, knowing nothing. But we spent two hours with him anyway. Fischig slowly turned a wall dial near the door that vented in increasing measures of the sub-zero air outside the Sun-dome. In our heat gowns, we asked questions over and again.

When Bonz's flesh began to adhere to the metal chair, we knew there was nothing more.

'Warm him up and feed him well,' Fischig told his men as we left the cell. 'We execute him at dawn.'

I didn't ask if that meant some arbitrary time in the next cycle or real dawn, six months away, at the start of Thaw.

I didn't much care.

Fischig left us to our own devices for a while, and I ate lunch with Aemos at a public bistro almost directly under the Sun-dome. The food was sour, rehashed from freeze-dried consumables, but at least it was hot. Fountain banks projected walls of water around the edges of the bistro so that the sun-globe light made rainbows that criss-crossed the tables and aisles. On this sombre day of mourning, there were no other diners present.

Aemos was in good spirits. He chatted away, making connections I hadn't begun to see. For all his faults, he possessed a superb mind. Every hour I spent with him, I learned more techniques.

He was forking up fish and rice and reviewing his data-slate.

'Let's look at the transmission lag that Lowink detected in the messages Eyclone sent and received while on the planet.'

'They're all in cipher. Lowink hasn't unlocked them yet.'

'Yes, yes, but look at the lag. This one... eight seconds... that's from a ship in orbit... and the timeframe matches that period in which we know Eyclone's mysterious starship was here. But this... during your struggle with him last night. A lag of twelve and a half minutes. That's from another system.'

I stopped trying to macerate a lump of meat that resembled a slug and peered over. I'd never much considered the blurry side-bar that edged all astropathic message forms before.

'Twelve and a half? You're sure?'

'I had Lowink check.'

'So that gives us a reference frame?'

He smiled, pleased I was pleased. 'Three worlds in the picture. All between eleven and fifteen minutes' lag of here. Thracian Primaris, Kobalt II and Gudrun.'

Thracian Primaris was no surprise. That had been our last port of call, our last sighting of Eyclone. And, as far as we knew from the wretched Bonz, the place where he had recruited some or all of his servants.

'Kobalt's a nothing. I checked. Just an Imperial watch station. But Gudrun–'

'A primary trade world. Old culture, old families–'

'Old poisons,' he finished with a laugh, completing the proverb.

I dabbed my mouth with a napkin. 'Can we be more certain?'

'Lowink's researching for me. Once we break the cipher... I don't mean the message cipher itself, I mean the coded headers to the actual text, we'll know.'

'Gudrun...' I pondered.

My vox-link chimed in my ear. It was Betancore.

'Ever hear of a thing called the Pontius?'

'No. Why?'

'I haven't either, but Lowink's cracking some of the old transcripts. In the weeks before Eyclone arrived, someone was sending messages off the approved links to a location in the Sun-dome. They talk about the delivery of "The Pontius". It's all rather vague and indirect.'

'Do you have a location?'

'Why else do you employ us? Thaw-view 12011, on the west side of the dome, the high-rent quarter. Aristo turf.'

'Any names?'

'No, they're very exclusive and coy about such things.'

'We're on it.'

Aemos and I rose from the table. We turned to find Fischig standing there. He was wearing the full flak armour, carapace and visored helm of an Arbites now. I have to admit the effect was impressive.

'Going somewhere without me, inquisitor?'

'Going to find you, actually. Take us to Thaw-view.'

FOUR

THE SUN-DOME TOURED AT SPEED
THAW-VIEW 12011
QUESTIONING SAEMON CROTES

The wealthiest Hubrites kept winter palaces on the west perimeter of the Sun-dome. According to Chastener Fischig, they 'enjoyed both light and dark' as if that was something indulgent. They looked inwards to the lit dome and had shutters that could be opened to view the dark landscape of the winter desert. It was a spiritual thing, Aemos suggested.

Fischig shut down his terrain-following guidance as we sliced through the streets, and his heavy speeder rose up above the traffic and buildings. We hooked hard turns between glass spires and roared west.

I think he was showing off.

In the rear seating, under the roll-bars, Aemos clung on and closed his eyes with a soft groan. I rode up front with the armoured Fischig, seeing a predatory grin on his face under the visor of his Arbites helmet.

The speeder was a standard Imperial model, painted matt-brown and sporting the badges of the solar symbol and the chevrons and tail number of the local Arbites. Armoured, it turned heavily, the anti-grav straining to keep us aloft. There was a heavy bolter pintle-mounted forward of my seat. I glanced around and saw a locked rack of combat shotguns behind the rear seats.

'Give me one of those!' I yelled above the slipstream and the choppy thrum of the turbo-fans.

'What?'

'I need a weapon!'

Fischig nodded and keyed a security code into a pad built into his bulky control stick. The cage on the gun-rack popped.

'Take one!'

Aemos handed one over to me, and I began loading shells.

Thaw-view rose before us, a terrace of luxurious crystal-glass and ferrocrete dwellings built into the curve of the dome itself. We whipped low over stepped gardens, making ferns and palms shudder in our downwash.

Then Fischig keyed the fans to idle and we settled on a wide veranda deck, eight storeys up.

He leapt out, racking his shotgun.

I followed him.

'Stay here,' I told Aemos. He needed no further encouragement.

'Which one?' Fischig asked.

'12011.'

We edged along the wide, curving deck, clambering over dividing rails and trellises of climbing flowers.

12011 was glass-fronted, with wide sliding doors of mirrored window-plate.

Fischig swept up a warning hand, and took a coin from his pocket. He flipped it onto the terrace and it was atomised by nine separate las-beams.

He keyed his vox. 'Chastener Fischig to Arbites control, copy?'

'Copy, chastener.'

'Access dome central and shut down auto-defences on Thaw-view 12011. Immediate.'

A pause.

'Shut down authorised.'

He made to step forward. I halted him and tossed a coin of my own.

It bounced twice on the basalt terrace and rolled to a halt.

'I like to be sure,' I said.

We came up either side of the main picture window. Fischig tried the slider but it was locked.

He stepped back, apparently preparing to shoot the window in.

'It's arma-plex,' I told him, rapping my knuckles off the material. 'Don't be stupid.'

I pulled the plastic bag containing Eyclone's effects from my jacket and searched for the compact las-knife. Before I found it, I found the plastic key.

Slim chances but what the crud, as Inquisitor Hapshant used to say.

I slid the key into the frame lock and the window slid aside on motorised rails.

We both waited. Perfumed air and light orchestral music wafted out past us.

'Adeptus Arbites! Make yourselves known!' Fischig bellowed, his voice amplified by his helmet speaker.

They did.

Rapid gunfire, heavy calibre, blew away the terrace rail, decapitated potted shrubs and dwarf trees, cropped flower beds, and chopped down the deck's aerial mast.

'Have it your way!' bellowed Fischig and rolled in, pumping his shotgun. The blasts were deafening.

I clambered up a drain-spout onto the second level balcony, my shotgun dangling around my shoulders on its strap. Furious exchanges of fire rumbled below me.

I went in through a gauze-draped opening into the main bedrooms.

The room was over-warm and dark, dressed in red velvet with soothing, ambient music welling from hidden vox-speakers. The bed was in disarray. In one corner, on a gilt credenza, sat a portable vox-set. I padded forward and studied the responder log. Fischig's chaos down below rumbled through the floor like a distant storm.

The girl came out of a side room, a bathroom I imagine, and shrieked when she saw me. She was naked, and dived under the bedclothes for cover.

The muzzle of my shotgun tracked her.

'Who's here?'

She whimpered and shook her head.

'Inquisition,' I hissed. 'Who's here?'

She began to sob and shook her head again.

'Stay down. Get under the bed if you can.'

In the adjoining room, I heard whistling. A voice called out a name.

'Don't answer,' I told the weeping girl.

I moved slowly round to the side room door. Light shone out. There was a hint of steam and a smell of bath-oils. The whistling had stopped.

He was wary, I'll give him that. He didn't bluster out, gun blasting.

I tipped open the door with the snout of my weapon and five high velocity rounds shredded holes in the wood panel.

I fell to my belly on the floor and fired three shots in through the door gap.

'Inquisition! Throw down your weapon!'

Two more shots punched through the door.

I crawled backwards from the doorway and stood up, the gun resting in my hands.

'Come out,' I said, using my will.

A large, tattooed, naked male blundered out of the bathroom, half his face shaved and half covered with sudsy foam. A Tronsvasse Hi-Power autopistol was still in one hand.

'Put it down,' I commanded.

He hesitated, as if my will had no force. A conditioned mind, I supposed. Take no chances.

The autopistol was just pulling up to find me when I blew off his half shaved face with the shotgun and sent his body splintering back through the half-open door.

The girl was still crouched, naked, at the end of the bed, shivering. I was surprised she hadn't bolted out of cover at my command too.

I spun to face her.

'What's your name?'

'Lise B.'

'Full name!' I snapped. I wasn't concentrating on her especially, but there was something about her. An air. A *tone*.

'Alizebeth Bequin! Pleasure girl! I worked the Sun-dome these past four Dormants!'

'You're here why?'

'They paid up front! Wanted a party! Oh lords...'

Her voice trailed away and she collapsed on the bed.

'Get dressed. Stay here. I will want to talk to you.'

I moved to the door of the chamber and looked out into the unlit hall. Below, down the stairwell, gunflashes and shouts echoed up.

Seeing my shape in the doorway, a man ran towards me.

'Wylk! Wylk! They've found us! They've–'

A moment before he realised I was not Wylk, I decked him with the butt of my weapon. He fell hard.

Two solid shots raked the doorframe next to me.

I ducked back in, sliding back the grip of the shotgun.

Shots punched through the wall above the bed-head. Bequin screamed and rolled off the bed.

I blasted back, punching two more large holes in the door.

Two men slammed into the room, wild-eyed and desperate. Both were dressed in light interior clothes. One had a laspistol, the other an autorifle.

I dropped the lasgunner with one direct shot that hurled his body against the wall. The man with the autorifle opened fire, his shots chewing through one of the bed-posts.

I dived for cover as the automatic fire ripped up tufts of carpet, shattered mirrors and demolished furnishings.

Rolling, I frantically sought cover.

My would-be killer dropped face-down onto the bed. The girl pulled a long retractable knife out of the back of his neck.

'I saved your life,' she told me. 'That'll make it better for me, right?'

I told the girl to stay put in the bedroom, and from her nod I was pretty sure she would.

I stepped out into the gloomy hall. The level below had fallen silent.

'Fischig?' I voxed.

'Come down,' his reply crackled back.

A spiral stairway led down into a large, split-level lounge area. The air was thick with smoke, which coiled out of the terrace window-doors we had opened. The hard daylight of the Sun-dome streamed in, making ladder-bars of light in the drifting haze. The opposite wall of the room was a wide segmented shutter. If opened, it would reveal a view over the freezing wastes beyond the dome.

A storm of gunfire had ruined the expensive furniture and decorative fittings. Five corpses lay twisted at various points on the floor. Fischig, his visor raised, was hauling a sixth man up into a high-backed chair. The man, wounded in the right shoulder, was wailing and crying. Fischig cuffed him into place.

'Upstairs?' Fischig asked me without looking round.

'Clear,' I reported.

I walked round the room, eyeing the dead and examining items left scattered on tabletops and bureaux.

'I know some of these men,' the chastener added, unsolicited. 'Those two by the window. Locals, low-grade labourers. Long list of petty convictions on both.'

'Hired muscle.'

'Seems to be your man's way. The others are off-worlders.'

'You've found papers?'

'No, it's just a hunch. None of them have got any ID or markers, and I haven't found a cache anywhere.'

'What about this one?' I walked over to join him by the prisoner he had cuffed to the chair. The man coughed and whined, rolling his eyes. Unless he possessed unnaturally boosted strength thanks to drugs or hidden augmetics, this man wasn't muscle. He was older, spare of frame, with grizzled salt and pepper growth on his chin.

'You didn't kill this one deliberately, did you?' I asked Fischig. He smiled slightly, as if pleased that I had noticed.

'I– I have rights!' The man spat suddenly.

'You are in the custody of the Imperial Inquisition,' I told him frankly. 'You have no rights whatsoever.'

He fell silent.

'Off-worlder,' Fischig said. I raised an eyebrow. 'Accent,' Fischig explained.

I'd never have detected it myself. This was one of the reasons I used local help whenever I got the chance, even a potential troublemaker like the chastener. My work takes me from world to world, culture to culture. Slight differences in dialect or incongruities of slang regularly pass me by. But Fischig had heard it at once. And it made sense. If this was a leader rather than muscle, one of Eyclone's chosen lieutenants, then the odds were he was from off-world.

'Your name?' I asked.

'I will not answer.'

'Then I will not have that wound treated for a while.'

He shook his head. The wound was bad and he was obviously in considerable pain, but he resisted. I was even more certain he was a ringleader. He was no longer shaking or whining. He had switched in some mental conditioning, no doubt taught by Eyclone.

'Mind tricks won't help you,' I said. 'I'm much better at them than you are.'

'Go screw yourself.'

I glanced at Fischig out of courtesy. 'Brace yourself.' He stepped back.

'Tell me your name,' I said, using my will.

The man in the chair spasmed. 'Saemon Crotes!' he gasped.

'Godwyn Fischig,' spat the chastener involuntarily. He blushed and moved away, busying himself with a search.

'Very well, Saemon Crotes, where are you from?' I didn't employ any will now. In my experience, it took only one blow to loosen mental defences.

'Thracian Primaris.'

'What was your job there?'

'I was trade envoy for the Bonded Merchant Guild of Sinesias.'

I knew the name. Guild Sinesias was one of the largest mercantile companies in the sector. It had holdings on a hundred-plus planets and links to the Imperial nobility. It also, as Betancore had informed me just that morning, had a trade launch berthed at the Sun-dome landing stage.

'And what work brought you to Hubris?'

'That same work... as a trade-envoy.'

'In Dormant?'

'There is always trade to be had. Long-term contracts with the authorities on this world that require the personal touch.'

'And if I contact your guild, will it confirm this?'

'Of course.'

I walked around behind him. 'So what brought you here? To these private apartments?'

'I was a guest.'

'Of who?'

'Namber Wylk, a local trader. He invited me for a mid-Dormant feast.'

'This dwelling is registered to Namber Wylk,' Fischig put in. 'A trader, as he says, no priors. I don't know him.'

'What about Eyclone?' I asked Crotes, leaning down to stare into his eyes. There was a ripple of fear in them.

'Who?'

'Your real employer. Murdin Eyclone. Don't make me ask you again.'

'I don't know any Eyclone!' There was a ring of truth to his voice. He may well not have known Eyclone by that name.

I dragged up a chair and sat down facing him. 'There is an awful lot of your story that doesn't add up. You're found here consorting with recidivists who we can connect to a planetary conspiracy. There are charges of murder to be considered - a lot of them. We can continue this in far more intimate and comprehensive circumstances, or you can make me like you more by filling in some details now.'

'I... don't know what to tell you...'

'Whatever you know. About the Pontius, perhaps?'

A dark, stricken look crossed his face. His jaw worked for a moment, trying to form words. He quivered. Then there was a liquid pop and his head fell forward.

'Throne of Light!' Fischig cried.

'Damn it,' I growled, and bent down to lift Crotes's limp skull. He was dead. Eyclone had left failsafes in the conditioning that would trigger at certain subjects. The Pontius evidently was one of those.

'A stroke. Artificially induced.'

'So we know nothing?'

'We know a great deal? Weren't you listening? For a start we know the Pontius is the most precious secret they protect.'

'So tell me about it?'

I was about to, at least evasively, when the shutter barring the far wall to the climate extremes of the world outside the dome blew out. Hidden charges fired simultaneously. The metal sheet splayed outwards into the freezing dark. The blast-force threw both Fischig and myself to the ground.

A millisecond later, the shattered crystal in the portal blew back in at us, carried by the hurricane power of the Dormant winds outside - a blizzard of billions of razor-sharp slivers.

FIVE

COVERED TRACES
THE GLAWS OF GUDRUN
UNWELCOME COMPANIONS

Deafened by the blast, I had wit enough left to grab Fischig and roll with him out through the terrace doors as the emergency shutter clanked down from its slit in the hardwood ceiling. We lay panting and half-blind on the terrace, the hard light and warmth of the Sun-dome thawing our cold-shocked bodies.

Alarms and warning bells sounded all along the Thaw-view residences. Arbites units were already on their way.

We got up. Our clothes and simple good fortune had protected us from the worst of the glass-storm, though I had a gash straight down my left cheek that would need closing, and Fischig had a long splinter of glass embedded in his thigh between armour joints. Apart from that, we had just superficial scratches.

'Bad timing?' he asked, though he knew it wasn't.

'The charges were set off by the same spasm that killed Crotes.'

He glanced away and rebuckled one of his gauntlets, giving himself time to think. His face was a dingy grey colour, mainly through shock. But I think he was now beginning to understand the resources and capabilities of the people we worked against. Their abominable crime at Processional Two-Twelve had demonstrated the scale of their malice, but he hadn't seen that first hand. Now he was witnessing the fanatical servants of a dark cause, men who would fight without hesitation to the death. And he had seen how brutally they would cover their traces, using mental-weapons and brain-wired booby traps that spoke of vast resources and frightening sophistication.

Arbites squads moved into the dwelling and secured it while local medicae servitors patched our wounds. The clearance squads brought out the shivering girl, Bequin. She was wrapped in blankets and her face was pinched blue with cold. Under my seal and instruction, they placed her in custody. She was too cold to voice a complaint.

Fischig and I re-entered wearing heat-gowns. It would be another two or three hours before engineer teams could replace the outer shutter. From the harsh light of the terrace, we passed through three hastily hung insulation curtains into the dim, blue twilight of the apartment. The far wall was gone and we looked directly into the clear, glassy night of Hubris, a glossy grey landscape of stark shadows and backscattered light stretching away from the edge of the Sun-dome. Once more I was exposed to the piercing cold of Dormant and my blood ached.

The main room where we had questioned Crotes was a gutted cavity, blackened by soot and jewelled with glass. Hard lacquers of frost caked furniture surfaces and twisted the faces of the dead. Blood spilt by the shredding storm of glass was crusted like rubies in the dark.

We played the smoky white beams of our lamps around. I doubted we would find much now. There was a good chance any valuable documents had been set to burn or delete on the same trigger signal that had blown the shutter and killed Crotes. And it also seemed likely these people carried all truly important information internally, as memory engrams, or meme-codes, the sort of techniques usually reserved for the higher echelons of diplomatic corps, the Administratum and elite trade delegations.

That turned my mind back to Crotes's employer, the Guild Sinesias.

'It's a common enough name in this sub-sector,' Aemos told me back in the comfortable half-light of the gun-cutter in its landing platform berth. He had been researching the name 'Pontius'. 'I've turned up over half a million citizens with that forename, another two hundred thousand with it as a middle name, plus another forty or fifty thousand spelling variants.'

He waved a data-slate at me. I brushed it aside, and used a hand mirror to study the line of metal butterfly sutures in the wound in my cheek.

'What about the definite article?'

'I have over nine thousand marks with that connection,' he sighed. He began to read them from his slate list. 'The Pontius Swellwin Youth Academy, The Pontius Praxitelles Translation Bureau, The Pontius Gyvant Ropus Investment Financiary, The Pontius Spiegel Microsurgical Hospi–'

'Enough.' I sat at the codifier, typing in name groups. Flickering runes hunted and darted across the view-plate. Text extracts drifted into focus. I searched through them by eye, my finger resting on the scroll bar.

'Pontius Glaw,' I said.

He blinked and looked at me. There was a half-smile of scholarly delight on his narrow face. 'Not on my lists.'

'Because he is dead?'

'Because he's dead.'

Aemos came over and looked across my shoulder at the screen. 'But it makes a sort of sense.'

It did. A kind of illogic that had the flavour of truth. The sort of spore an inquisitor gets a nose for after a few years.

The Glaw family was old blood, a thrusting noble dynasty that had been a main player in this sub-sector for almost a millennium. The primary familial holdings and estates were on Gudrun, a world that had already come to our attention. House Glaw was also a major shareholder and investor in the Regal Bonded Merchant Guild of Sinesias, so the codifier had just revealed to me.

'Pontius Glaw…' I murmured.

Pontius Glaw had been dead for more than two hundred years. The seventh son of Oberon Glaw, one of the great patriarchs of that line, he had suffered the fate of most junior siblings in that there had been precious little for him to inherit once his older brothers had taken their turn. His eldest brother, another Oberon, had become lord of the house; the second eldest had been gifted the control of the stock-holdings; the third had taken on the captaincy of the House Militia; the fourth and fifth had married politically and entered the Administratum at high level… and so it went.

From what I remembered of Pontius Glaw's biography, required reading as a trainee, Pontius had become a dilettante, wasting his life, his robust virility, charisma and finely educated intellect in all manner of worthless pursuits. He had gambled away a significant measure of his personal fortune, then rebuilt it on the revenues of slave-trading and pit-fighting. A ruthless sliver of brutality stained his record.

And then, in his forties, with his health ruined by years of abuse, he turned to a much darker path. It has always been suspected that this turn was triggered by some chance event: an artefact or document that fell into his hands, perhaps the strange beliefs of some of the more barbaric pit-fighters he enslaved. Instinct told me the propensity had always been within him, and that he was looking for a chance to let it flourish. It is documented he was a life-long collector of rare and often prohibited books. At what point might his appetite for licentious and esoteric pornography have spilled over into the heretical and blasphemous?

Pontius Glaw became a disciple of Chaos, a devotee of the most abominable and obscene forces that haunt this galaxy. He drew a coven around him, and over a period of fifteen years committed unspeakable and increasingly brazen acts of evil.

He was slain eventually, his coven along with him, on Lamsarrote, by an Inquisitorial purge led by the great Absalom Angevin. House Glaw participated in this overthrow, desperate to be seen to distance themselves from his crimes. It is likely this alone prevented the entire family from being pulled down with him.

A monster, a notorious monster. And dead, as Aemos had been so quick to point out. Dead for more than two centuries.

But the name and the connection of facts seemed too obvious to ignore.

I wandered up to the cockpit and sat with Betancore. 'We'll need passage off-world, to Gudrun.'

'I'll arrange it. It may be a day or two.'

'As fast as you can.'

I sent word to High Custodian Carpel, informing him of some, though not all, of my findings and telling him I would shortly be leaving to continue my investigations on Gudrun. I was reading through the confidential case records of Inquisitor Angevin when two Arbites brought Bequin to my gun-cutter. I had sent orders for her to be delivered into my charge.

She stood in the crew-bay, frowning in the gloom, cuffed. She had dressed in a tawdry gown and a light cloak, but despite the cheapness of her garb and the discomfort she was in, her considerable beauty was plain to see. Good bones, a full mouth, fierce eyes and long dark hair. Yet, again, there was that air about her, that tone I had detected before. Despite her obvious physical attractions, there was something almost repellent about her. It was curious, but I was convinced I knew what it was.

She glanced round as I entered the crew-bay, her expression a mix of fear and indignation.

'I helped you!' she spat.

'You did. Though I neither asked for nor needed your help.'

She pouted. That air was stronger now, an unpleasant feeling that made me want to bundle her out of the cutter and have done with her then and there.

'The Arbites say they will charge me with murder and conspiracy.'

'The Arbites desperately want someone to pin the crimes on. You are unhappily involved in those matters, though I don't believe deliberately.'

'Damn right!' she snarled. 'This has ruined me, my life here! Just when I was getting things together...'

'Your life has been difficult?'

She fixed me with a sneer that questioned my intelligence. I'm a pleasure girl, an object, it seemed to say, lowest of the low... How difficult do you think my life has been?

I stepped forward and removed the Arbites' cuffs. She rubbed her wrists and looked at me in surprise.

'Sit down,' I told her. I was using the will.

She looked at me again, as if wondering what the funny tone was all about, and then calmly took a seat on a padded leather bench along the crew-bay's back wall.

'I can make sure the charges are dropped,' I told her. 'I have that authority. Indeed, my authority is the only reason you haven't been charged or interrogated so far.'

'Why would you do that?'

'I thought you believed I owed you?'

'Doesn't matter what I believe.' There was sullen cast to her face as she looked me up and down. I found myself intrigued. Objectively, I was looking at a girl whose looks and vivacious spirit made her undeniably desirable. Yet I... I almost wanted to shout at her, to drive her away, to get her out of my sight. I had an entirely unwarranted and instinctive loathing for her.

'Even if you clear me, I can't carry on here. They'll hound me out. I'll be marked as trouble. That'll be the end of my work. I'll have to move on again.' She stared down at the floor and muttered a curse. 'Just when I was getting it together!'

'Move on? You're not from Hubris?'

'This miserable shit-pit?'

'Where then?'

'I came here from Thracian Primaris four years ago.'

'You were born on Thracian?'

She shook her head. 'Bonaventure.'

That was half a sector away. 'How did you get from Bonaventure to Thracian?'

'By way of this and that. Here and there. I've travelled a lot. Never stayed put very long.'

'Because things get difficult?'

The sneer again. 'That's right. I'd stuck it out here longer than anywhere. Now that's all screwed up.'

'Stand up,' I snapped suddenly, using the will again.

She paused and shrugged at me. 'Make your mind up.' She got to her feet.

'I want to ask you some questions about the men who employed you at Thaw-view 12011.'

'I thought you might.'

'If you answer helpfully, I can cut you a deal.'

'What sort of deal?'

'I can take you to Gudrun. Give you a chance to make a new start. Or I can offer you employment, if you're interested.'

She smiled quizzically. It was the first positive expression I had seen on her. It made her more beautiful, but I didn't like her any better.

'Employment? You'd employ me? An inquisitor would employ me?'

'That's right. Certain services I think you can provide.'

She took two fluid steps over to me and placed her hands flat against my chest. 'I see,' she said. 'Even big bad inquisitors have needs, huh? That's fine.'

'You misunderstand,' I replied, pushing her back as politely as I could. Physical contact with her made the unnatural feeling of revulsion even stronger. 'The services I have in mind will be new to you. Not the sort of work you are accustomed to. Are you still interested?'

She set her head on one side and considered me. 'You're an odd one, all right. Are all inquisitors like you?'

'No.'

I ordered the servitor, Modo, to provide her with refreshment and left her in the crew-bay. Betancore was stood in the shadows outside the door, gazing in at her appreciatively.

'She's a fine sight,' he murmured to me as if I might not have noticed.

'You forget Vibben so quickly?'

He snapped round at me, stung. 'That was low, Eisenhorn. I was just commenting.'

'You'll like her less when you get to know her. She's an untouchable.'

'Seriously?'

'Seriously. A psychic blank. It's natural, and I haven't tested her limits. It's all I can do to be in the same room as her.'

'Such a looker too,' Betancore sighed, gazing back in at her.

'Useful to us. If she passes certain requirements, I'm going to employ her.'

He nodded. Untouchables were rare, and almost impossible to create artificially. They have a negative presence in the warp that renders them virtually immune to psychic powers, which in turn makes them potent anti-psyker weapons. The side-effect of their psychic blankness is the unpleasant disturbance that accompanies them, the waves of fear and revulsion they trigger in those they meet.

No wonder her life had been difficult and friendless.

'News?' I asked Betancore.

'Made contact with a sprint trader called the *Essene*. Master's one Tobias Maxilla. Deals in small units of luxury goods. Coming here in two days to deliver a consignment of vintage wines from Hesperus, then on to Gudrun. For a fee, he'll make room for the cutter in his hold.'

'Good work. So we'll be on Gudrun when?'

'Two weeks.'

I spent the next hour or so interviewing Bequin, but as I suspected she knew precious little about any of the men. We gave her accommodation in a small bunk-cell next to Betancore's quarters. It was scarcely more than a box, and Nilquit had to remove piles of stowed equipment to clear it, but she seemed pleased enough. When I asked her if she had any possessions she wished to collect from the Sun-dome, she simply shook her head.

I was reviewing yet more piles of data with Aemos when Fischig arrived. He was dressed in his brown serge uniform suit and carried two bulky holdalls over his shoulder, which he dropped to the deck with a declamatory thump as he stepped aboard.

'To what do I owe this visit, chastener?' I asked.

He showed me a slate bearing Carpel's official seal. 'The high custodian grants you permission to leave to pursue your inquiry. Dependent on this...'

I reviewed the slate and sighed.

'I'm coming with you,' he said.

SIX

DIVINATION BY AUTO-SEANCE
A DREAM
JOINING THE ESSENE

I lodged a formal complaint with the high custodian's office, but it was simply for show. Carpel could manufacture serious problems for me if I tried to leave without his agent. I could do that, of course. I could do as I liked. But Carpel could delay me, and I didn't know how much co-operation from the elders and administrations of Hubris I'd need later if any part of this investigation led to trial.

Besides, Carpel knew I was going on to Gudrun, and he would plainly send Fischig there under an Arbites warrant to investigate anyway. On the whole, I decided I'd rather have Chastener Fischig where I could see him.

On the afternoon before our intended departure, I had Lowink prepare for an auto-seance. I doubted whether anything further could be learned now, but I wanted to cover every avenue.

As usual, we used my quarters, with the cabin-door locked, and Betancore strictly instructed to prevent interruptions. I sat in a high-back armchair, and spent some quarter of an hour lowering my mind to a semi-trance state. This was an old technique, one of the first I had been taught when my abilities had originally been detected by the tutors of the Inquisition. On a cloth-covered table between us, Lowink laid out key evidence items: some of Eyclone's effects, some other pieces taken from Thaw-view 12011, and some from the processional. We also had the mysterious casket from the cryogenerator chamber.

Once he was satisfied I was ready, Lowink opened his mind to the warp, and filtered its raging influence through his highly trained mental architecture. This transitional moment was always a shock, and I shuddered. The temperature in the room dropped palpably, and a glass bowl on a side counter cracked spontaneously. Lowink was murmuring, his eyes rolled back, twitching and jerking slightly.

I closed my eyes, though I could still see my room. What I was seeing was a visualisation of our surroundings constructed by Lowink astropathically in the Empyrean itself. Everything shone with a pale blue light from within, and solids became translucent. The dimensions of the room shifted slightly, stretching and buckling as if they had difficulty retaining their coherence.

I took up the items on the table in turn, Lowink's projection enhancing their psychometric qualities, opening my mind's abilities to the signatures and resonances they carried in the warp.

Most were dull and blunt, with no trace of resonance. Some had wispy tendrils of auras around them, relics of passing contact with human hands and human minds. Eyclone's vox-device buzzed with the distant, unintelligible whinings of ghosts but gave up nothing.

Eyclone's pistol stung my hand like a scorpion when I touched it – and both I and Lowink gasped. I had a brief aftertaste of death. I decided not to touch it again.

His data-slate, which Aemos had yet been unable to open, was dripping with a sticky, almost gelatinous aura. The thickness of the psychic residue betokened the complex thought processes and data that had adhered to it. It gave up nothing, and I became frustrated. Lowink amplified my scrutiny and at last, as a whisper, I landed the word, or name, 'daesumnor.'

The final item for inspection was the casket. It resonated brightly with flickering bands of warp-traces. Our contact with it was necessarily brief because of the exhausting strength of its halo.

We probed, opening what seemed to be three levels of psychometric activity. One was sharp and hard, and tasted of metal. Lowink averred that this was a relic of the intellect or intellects that had crafted the casket. An undeniably brilliant but malevolent presence.

Beneath that, colder, smaller, denser, like a lightless collapsed star, lay a heavy, throbbing trace that seemed to be locked in the heart of the casket's machine core.

Around both, fluttering and swooping like birds, were the vestigial psychic agonies of the dead from Processional Two-Twelve. Their plaintive psychic noise rippled through our thoughts and sapped the emotional strength from us both. The dead souls of the processional had left their psychic fingerprints on this device that had been instrumental in their murder.

We were about to step back and end the seance when the second trace, the cold, distant, dense one, began to well up to the surface. I was intrigued at first, then stunned by its gathering force and speed. It filled my head with a nauseating, intolerable sense of hunger.

Hunger, thirst, appetite, craving...

It rose from the depths of the casket, wailing and yearning, a dark thing tearing up through the other trace energies. I glimpsed its malice and felt its consuming need.

Lowink broke the link. He slumped back in his seat, panting, his skin dotted with the stigmatic blood-spots of an astropathic augury taken far too far.

I felt it too. My mind seemed cold, colder even than the ministrations of Dormant. It seemed to take a very long time before my thoughts began to flow freely again, like water slowly thawing in an iced pipe.

I rose and poured myself a glass of amasec. I poured one for Lowink too as an afterthought. Neither of us ever came away from an auto-seance feeling good, but this was signally worse than usual.

'There was danger,' Lowink husked at last. 'Vile danger. From the casket.'

'I felt it.'

'But the whole seance was unseemly, master. As if distracted and spoiled by some... some factor...'

I sighed. I knew what he had felt. 'I can explain. The girl we have aboard is an untouchable.'

Lowink shuddered. 'Keep her away from me.'

I passed the word 'daesumnor' to Aemos in case it assisted his work on the data-slate and rested in my cabin to recover. Lowink had gone back to his tiny residence under the cockpit deck. I doubted he would be useful for much for a goodly while.

I gathered up the evidence items, re-bagged them and locked them in the cutter's strongbox, all except the casket, which was too big to fit. We kept it bagged and chained in a tarpaulin locker aft. As I hefted it up to return it to the locker, I felt the aftershock of its aura, as if we had woken something, some instinct. I considered this to be the imagination of my stung mind working overtime, but I completed the task only when I had buckled on a pair of work gloves.

Betancore joined me shortly afterwards. He had gone through Vibben's effects and found no will or instructions. Now we needed her cabin to house Fischig, so we placed her belongings and clothes in an underseat storebin in the crew-bay and together carried her wrapped body to the cot in the medical suite. I locked the door as we left.

'What will you do with her?' Betancore asked. 'There's no time to arrange a burial here now.'

'She once said she came with me to see what the stars were like. That's where we'll lay her to rest.'

Then I slept, turning fitfully despite my exhaustion. When sleep finally came, the dreams were cold and inhospitable. Murderously black, back-lit clouds rippled in fast motion across skies I didn't know, strobing with electrical flashes. Dark trees, and darker, higher walls, ranged around the edges of the dream. I felt the instinct, the hunger from the casket, lurking in some blind spot my eyes refused to find.

Carrion birds, a flock of them, swooped down from the upper reaches of the sky and took all the colour with them, staining the dream-world grey. All except for a spot of red that glittered in the colourless soil ahead of me.

With each step I took towards it, it receded. I began to run. It continued to display dream logic and moved away.

Finally, gasping for breath, I stopped running. The red spot had gone. I felt the hunger again, but now it was inside me, clawing at my belly, filling my throat with craving. The roiling clouds overhead froze suddenly, motionless, even the lightning flares stilled and captured in jagged, phosphorescent lines.

A voice spoke my name. I thought it was Vibben, but when I turned, there was nothing to see except the suggestion of a presence drifting away like smoke.

I woke. From the clock, I had been asleep only a couple of hours. My throat was raw and my mouth dry. I drained two glasses of water from the side cabinet and then fell back on the bed.

My head ached but my mind would not stop spinning. After that, no sleep came at all.

The vox-link chimed about four hours later. It was Betancore. 'The *Essene* has just made orbit,' he told me. 'We can leave whenever you like.'

The *Essene* lay slantwise above the inverted bowl of Hubris, silhouetted against the stars.

We had left the radiance of the Sun-dome into a blizzard squall. The air-frame of the cutter had vibrated wildly as Betancore lifted us out of the clutches of the ferocious, icy winds until we were riding clear over an ocean of frosty vapour.

The blizzard, a sculptural white continent, then dropped away below until we could see its tides and gusts and currents, the wide centrifugal patterns of its titanic force.

'There,' Betancore had said, with a nod to the raked front ports. Even at ninety kilometres, still rising through the thinning aeropause, he had made visual contact.

It had taken me a few more moments to find it. A bar of darkness distorting the pearly edge of the planesphere.

Another minute, and it had become a three-dimensional solid. A minute more, and I began to resolve the running lights glittering on its surface.

Yet another minute and it filled the ports. It resembled some colossal tower that had been ripped away from its earthly foundations and set adrift, tranquil, in the void.

'A beauty,' murmured Betancore, who appreciated such things. His inlaid hands flicked over the flight controls and we yawed to the correct approach vectors. The gun-cutter and the massive vessel exchanged automatic telemetry chatter. The flight deck pict-plates were alive with columns of rushing data.

'A bulk clipper, of the classic Isolde pattern, from the depot yards of Ur-Haven or Tancred. Majestic...' Aemos was muttering and annotating his idle observations into his wrist slate again.

The *Essene* was three kilometres long by my estimation, and fully seven hundred metres deep at its broadest part. Its nose was a long sleek cone like a cathedral spire made of overlapping gothic curves and barbed with bronze finials and spines. Behind that bladed front, the angular hull thickened into muscular buttresses of rusty-red plating, looped and riveted with ribs of dark steel. Crenellated tower stacks bulged from the dorsal hump. Hundred-metre masts stabbed forward from the hull like tusks and other, shorter masts projected from the flanks and underside, winking with guide lights. The rear portion of the juggernaut splayed into four heat-blackened cones, each of which was large enough to swallow a dozen gun-cutters at once.

Betancore turned us in and ran us along the flank heading aft. To us, the great vessel seemed to wallow and roll as we joined its horizontal.

A lighted dot divorced itself from the *Essene* and ran out ahead of us, flashing ultra-bright patterns of red and green lamps: a pilot drone to lead us in.

Betancore gently chased the drone and swung to port as its lights instructed. We slid neatly between two mast arrays, crossed the ribbed belly, and finally braked to station-keeping under a rectangular belly-hatch edged with black and yellow chevrons. The hatch was one of a line of six down the hull's underside, but this was the only open one. A fiery orange glow washed down over us.

Exchanging a few terse comments with Uclid in the drive room, Betancore nudged the gun-cutter upwards through the yawning hatch. I watched the edges of the hatch-mouth, two metres thick and scratched in places to the bare metal, pass by alarmingly close.

There followed a series of gentle shudders, and mechanical thumps against the cutter's outer hull. Amber light bathed the cockpit. I looked up into the glow outside, but saw little except a suggestion of dark gantries and cargo-lifting derricks.

Another shudder. Betancore threw a row of switches and there was a whine as power-feeds and autosystems wound down. He pushed back from the control deck, and began pulling on his hide gloves.

He smiled at me. 'You needn't look so worried,' he mocked.

In truth, I am most disquieted by things I have no control over. Though I have rudimentary skills, and can manage an atmospheric craft, I am no pilot, certainly not one with Midas's Glavian pedigree. That's why I employ him and that's why he makes it look so easy. But sometimes my face betrays the alarm I feel in situations where I have no ability.

Besides, I was tired. But I knew sleep wouldn't come even if I tried, and there was business to attend to anyway.

Aemos, Bequin and Lowink would stay on the cutter for now. As soon as the hull door was closed and atmosphere recirculated into the *Essene's* hold, I opened the hatch and stepped out with Fischig and Betancore.

The hold where we were docked was vaulted and immense. I reminded myself it was just one of six accommodated by this vessel. The surfaces of the walls and decking were oily black, and sodium lighting arrays bolted to the ceiling filled the place with orange tinted luminescence. The spaces above us were busy with the skeletal shapes of cranes and monotask lifters, all shut down and lifeless. Packing materials littered the open floor. The gun-cutter was held over the sealed floor hatch in a greased crib of docking pistons and hydraulic clamps.

We crossed the hold, boots ringing on the metal deck-plates. It was cold, the chill of open space still lingering.

Betancore wore his usual Glavian pilot suit and garish jacket. He was cheerful and whistled tunelessly. Fischig was impassive, oozing command in his brown Arbites uniform. He had fixed his golden sun-disk of office to the breast of his jacket.

I wore a dark sober suit of grey wool, black boots and gloves and a long navy-blue leather coat with a high collar. I had taken a stub-pistol from the weapons locker and had it in a holster rig under my left arm. My Inquisitorial rosette was buttoned away inside a pocket. Unlike Fischig, I felt no need to make a statement of authority.

A hatch clanked open on servos, and light shone out from an internal companionway. A figure stepped out to meet us.

'Welcome to the *Essene*, inquisitor,' said Tobias Maxilla.

SEVEN

WITH THE MASTER OF THE ESSENE
A FAREWELL
SCRUTINY

Maxilla was a veteran trader who had run the *Essene* down the lanes from Thracian Primaris to the Grand Banks for fifty years. He told me he'd dealt in bulk consumables at the start of his career, then begun to specialise in exotic goods when the big bonded guilds began to dominate the wholesale market.

'The *Essene*'s got speed, a sprint trader. Pays me better to carry luxury cargoes and deliver them express, even if I don't run at capacity.'

'You run this route regularly?'

'For the past few decades. It's seasonal. Sameter, Hesperus, Thracian, Hubris, Gudrun, sometimes to Messina too. When Dormant finishes on Hubris, there'll be a lot more work there.'

We sat in the luxurious surroundings of his audience suite, sipping vintage amasec from large crystal glasses. Maxilla was showing off, but that was acceptable. He had a ship and a reputation to be proud of.

'So you know these routes well?' Fischig put in.

Maxilla smiled. He was a sinewy man of indeterminate age, dressed in a full-skirted coat of red velvet with wide button-back cuffs and an extravagant black lace cravat. His smile showed teeth that were inlaid with mother of pearl. Ostentation was common among ship's masters, it was part of showing off. Forget family lineage and noble blood, one had told me once, the lineage and pedigree of starships is where the new Imperial nobility is to be found. Ship's masters were the real Imperial aristocracy.

So Maxilla seemed to think, anyway. His face was powdered with white skin-dye, and he wore a sapphire as a beauty spot on his cheek. His imposing two-horned wig was spun from silver-thread. Heavy signet rings clinked against his balloon glass as he lifted it.

'Yes, chastener, I know them well.'

'I don't think we need to start interrogating Master Maxilla yet, Fischig,' I said plainly. Betancore snorted and Maxilla chuckled. Fischig glowered into his amasec.

A servitor, its torso and head casing wrought to resemble an antique ship's figurehead, a full-breasted damsel with gilt snakes in her hair, hummed across the expensive Selgioni rug and offered us trays of delicacies. I took one out of politeness. It was a sliver of perfect ketelfish, exquisitely sautéed and wrapped in a nearly transparent leaf of pastry. Betancore helped himself to several.

'You're a Glavian?' Maxilla asked Betancore. The two promptly fell to discussing the merits of the famous Glavian longprow. I lost interest and looked around the suite. Amid the finery were a series of priceless portraits from the Sameter School, marble busts of planetary rulers, a Jokaero light-sculpture, antique weapons and mounted suits of ceremonial mirror armour from Vitria. Aemos would appreciate this, I thought. It was to be a journey of more than a week. I'd make sure he got a chance to see it.

'Do you know Gudrun?' Maxilla was asking me.

I shook my head. 'This will be my first visit. I have only been in this sub-sector a year or so.'

'A fine place, though you'll find it busy. There's a month-long festival under way to celebrate the founding of a new guard regiment. If you have the time, I recommend the Imperial Academy of Fine Arts, and the guild museums in Dorsay.'

'I may be a little occupied.'

He shrugged. 'I always make the time to do more than simply work, inquisitor. But I know your calling is rather more strenuous than mine.'

I tried to get the measure of him, but I was failing so far. He had agreed to give us passage, and for a modest fee considering what he might have demanded. I had already paid him with an Imperial bond. Most ship masters don't like to turn down a request from an inquisitor, even if they are charging. Was it just that Maxilla wanted to keep sweet with the Ordos? Or was he simply a generous man?

Or did he have something to hide?

I wondered. Truthfully, I didn't care. The other possibility was he might think this entitled him to some future favour.

If he did, he would be wrong.

The *Essene* left Hubris later that day, executed the translation to the Empyrean effortlessly, and made best speed for Gudrun. Maxilla provided quarters for us all in his state apartments, but we spent most of our time on the cutter, working. Betancore and the servitors ran an overhaul of the ship. Lowink slept. Fischig, Aemos and I worked through the paperwork on the evidence, and threw conjectures back and forth. I still held back what little I knew of the Pontius from Fischig, but it wouldn't be long before he started to make the connection himself.

Bequin kept herself to herself. She'd borrowed a set of fatigues from a work locker and I saw her about the ship, reading books she'd taken from my personal library. Poetry, mostly, and some historical and philosophical works. I didn't mind. It kept her out of my way.

On the third day of the voyage, I met Maxilla again, and we walked the upper promenade deck together. He seemed to enjoy telling me the histories and provenances of the ormolu-framed paintings displayed there. We saw the occasional servitor at work, but so far there had not been the slightest glimpse of any other living crewperson.

'Your friend, Fischig... he is an unsubtle man,' he remarked at length.

'He's no friend. And yes, he is unsubtle. Has he been asking you questions again?'

'I saw him briefly on the foredecks yesterday. He asked me if I knew a man called Eyclone. Even showed me a picture.'

'And what did you say?'

He flashed his pearly teeth at me. 'Now who's interrogating?'

'Forgive my imprudence.'

He waved a lace-cuffed hand. 'Oh, forget it! Ask anyway! Get your questions out into the open so we can clear the air!'

'Very well. What did you tell him?'

'That I did not.'

I nodded. 'Thank you for your candour.'

'But I was lying.'

I turned and looked at Maxilla sharply. He was still smiling. I had the sudden horrible notion that we had all walked into a trap and dearly wished I was carrying a weapon.

'Don't worry. I lied to him because he's an arrogant runt. But I'll give you the truth of it. I would never want to put myself in the path of an Imperial Inquisition.'

'A wise philosophy.'

Maxilla flopped down on a satin couch and smoothed the front of his coat. 'I was last on Thracian Primaris two months ago. There was talk of some cargo and I held some meetings. The usual. And that's when this Eyclone enters the frame. Didn't call himself that, of course. Bless me, I forget the name he used. But it was him. Had others with him, a sour, tight lot. One called Crotes, a trade envoy. He tried to have me believe your man was authorised by the Guild Sinesias, but that was rubbish, even though Crotes had the paperwork.'

'What did he want?'

'He was hiring to make a run, empty, to Gudrun, collect a cargo there, and bring it to Hubris.'

'The nature of the cargo?'

'We never got that far. I turned him down. It was preposterous. He was offering a decent fee, but I knew I'd make ten times that with my regular work.'

'You didn't get a contact name on Gudrun either?'

'My dear inquisitor, I'm just a shipman, not a detective.'

'Do you know who finally took his work?'

'I know who didn't.' He sat forward. 'I happen to keep up dialogues with other masters. Seems several of us turned it down, and most for the same reason.'

'Which was?'

'It felt like trouble.'

* * *

By the fifth day, my sleep patterns had begun to return to normal. Too normal, in fact, as Eyclone began to stalk my dreams again. In sleep, he came to me, taunting and threatening. I don't remember much detail, except the afterimage of his grinning face each time I woke.

In hindsight, though Eyclone was certainly in my dreams, I don't think it was his smiling face I was remembering.

The *Essene* translated back into real-space and entered the Gudrun system on the morning of the eighth day, ahead of schedule. Maxilla had boasted his ship was fast under optimum conditions and the boast hadn't been empty.

I had made arrangements with him to leave the Empyrean in the out-reach of the system, considerably short of the busy local trade lanes that most arrivals to Gudrun followed. He agreed without question. It would only be a short delay.

'Who was she?' Bequin asked me as we stood at an observation bay watching the pale shape of Vibben's shrouded body slowly turn end over end as it drifted away from the *Essene*.

'A friend. A comrade,' I replied.

'Is this how she wanted to go?' she asked.

'I don't think she wanted to go at all,' I said. Nearby, Aemos and Betancore gazed gravely out of the thick port. Aemos's expression was unreadable. Betancore's dark face was drawn and anguished.

Lowink hadn't joined us, and neither had Fischig. But as I turned, I saw Maxilla standing respectfully at the rear of the observation bay, wearing a long mourning coat of black silk and a short periwig with black ribbons. He moved forward as he saw me look.

'I hope I'm not intruding. My respects to your lost comrade.'

I nodded my thanks. He hadn't needed to make this effort, but it seemed appropriate for the ship's master to be present during a void burial.

'I'm not sure how these things are formally conducted, Maxilla,' I said, 'though I think this is what she would have asked for. I have spoken the Imperial Creed, and the Oration of the Dead.'

'Then you have done her fine service. If it is appropriate...?'

He waved forward one of his gold-plated figurehead servitors, which carried a salver of glasses and a decanter.

'It is tradition to drink a toast to the departed.'

We all took a glass.

'Lores Vibben,' I said.

A minute or so's silence followed, then we slowly dispersed. I told Maxilla we could begin our approach run to Gudrun now, and he estimated it would take two hours to reach the inner system.

Returning to the cutter, I found myself walking with Bequin. She still wore the old work-suit she had liberated, though somehow it seemed to enhance her beauty rather than stifle it.

'We're almost there,' she said.

'Indeed.'

'What will my duties be?'

I had yet to explain to her what she was or why I had recruited her. There had been ample time en route, but I had been putting it off, I suppose. I'd found time to show Aemos the finery of Maxilla's state rooms, and play regicide with Betancore. I wished I could throw off my distaste at just simply being around her.

I walked with her to the promenade deck and began to explain.

I don't know how I expected her to take it. When she took it badly and became upset, my response was barely controlled irritation. I knew it was her nature that was making me react this way and fought to find the sympathy she deserved.

She sat weeping on a shot-silk chair beneath one of the massive paintings: a hunting scene of nobles riding thoroughbred ursadons in the chase. Every now and then, she would blurt out a curse or whine a regret.

It was clear she wasn't upset that I wanted to employ her. It was simply the fundamental knowledge that she was... abnormal. A friendless, loveless life of woes and hard knocks suddenly had an explanation and that explanation was her own nature. I believe that she had always, stoically, blamed the galaxy as a whole for her troubles. Now I'd as good as kicked that emotional crutch away.

I damned myself for not thinking the consequences through. I'd robbed her of self-esteem and what little confidence she could muster. I'd shown up her lifelong efforts to find comfort, love and respect as hollow, self-destructive, self-denying futility.

I tried to talk about the work she could do for me. She wasn't much interested. In the end, I pulled up another chair and sat next to her as she worked the painful truth through her mind.

I was still sitting there when I received a vox-signal. It was Maxilla.

'I wonder if you could join me on the bridge, inquisitor? I require your assistance.'

The bridge of the *Essene* was a wide domed chamber with floors and pillars of red-black marble. Silver servitors, immaculate and intricate as sculptures, were stationed at console positions sunk into the floor, their delicate geared arms working banks of controls set into polished mahogany fascias. The air was cool and still, and the only sound was the gentle hum and whirr of the working machines.

Maxilla, still dressed in his mourning robes, sat in a massive leather throne overlooking the room from a marble dais. Articulated limbs extending from the rear of the throne suspended pict-plates and consoles in his reach, but his attention was on the massive main observation port that dominated the front of the bridge.

I strode across the floor from the entrance. Each servitor wore a mask of chased gold, fashioned into a human face of classical perfection.

'Inquisitor,' Maxilla said, rising.

'Your crew are all servitors,' I remarked.

'Yes,' he said distractedly. 'They are more reliable than pure flesh.'

I made no other comment. Maxilla's relationship with the *Essene* seemed to me akin to the way the Adeptus Mechanicus worship their god-machines. Constant involvement with such ancient instruments had convinced them of the natural inferiority of the human species.

I followed his gaze and looked at the main port. The gleaming sphere of Gudrun lay ahead, a creamy swirl of clouds stained with the lime-green phantoms of great forests under the climate cover. Clusters of black shapes thickly dotted the space between us and the planet. These were huge groups of orbiting ships, I realised. Massive dreadnoughts at high anchor, trains of great merchant ships, convoys of trade freighters streaming in under tug supervision. I had seldom seen such a wealth of orbital activity.

'Is there a problem?' I asked him.

He looked over at me, something like anxiety in his eyes. 'I have performed legal manoeuvres and entered the trade lane approach. Gudrun control has allocated me a high-anchor buoy. All relevant data is in order and my tariffs are paid. But I have just been informed that we are to be boarded and inspected.'

'This is unusual?'

'It's been ten years since anyone even suggested such a thing of my ship.'

'Explanation?'

'They say security. I told you there was a founding festival under way. You can see considerable portions of Battlefleet Scarus on station. I think the military is being over-careful of its interests here just now.'

'You mentioned my assistance.'

'The inspection launch is on its way. I feel it would facilitate matters if they were met by a ship's master and an Imperial inquisitor.'

'I can't pull strings, Maxilla.'

He laughed humourlessly and looked me in the eye. 'Of course you can! But that's not what I'm asking. With an inquisitor present, they will treat the *Essene* with more respect. I'll not have them root through this vessel mindlessly.'

I thought for a moment. This smacked of the favour I had a feeling he might call in. Worse, it stank of impropriety on his part.

'I'll agree to be present for the sake of order, provided you can assure me you have nothing to hide.'

'Inquisitor Eisenhorn, I–'

'Save your indignation for the inspection, Maxilla. Your assurance is all I require. If I assist you only to find you have some dirty secret or illicit cargo, you will have a great deal more to worry about than the Imperial Navy.'

There was a look of great disappointment on his face. Either he was a superb actor, or I had truly wounded his feelings.

'I have nothing to hide,' he hissed. 'I fancied you and I had become... if not friends then decent acquaintances at least this voyage. I have shown you hospitality and freely given information into your confidence. I am hurt that you still suspect me.'

'Suspicion is my business, Maxilla. If I have wronged you, my apologies.'

'Nothing to hide!' he repeated, almost to himself, and led me off the bridge.

A Navy pinnace, matt-grey and deep hulled, drew alongside the massive *Essene* and clamped itself to the fore starboard airgate. Maxilla and I were there to meet it, along with Fischig and two of the ship's primary servitors, spectacular creations of gold and silver machine parts.

I'd summoned Fischig on the basis that if the sight of an inquisitor would help, then an Arbites chastener would do no harm either. Betancore was instructed to keep everyone else with the cutter.

The gate-locks cycled open and the hatch jaws gaped, exhaling torrents of steam. A dozen large figures emerged through the haze. They were all dressed in the grey and black body armour of naval security, with the crest and sector-symbol of Battlefleet Scarus displayed on their chests and gold braid edging their epaulettes. All were masked in form-moulded ceramite helmets with lowered visor plates and rebreathers. They were armed with compact, short-frame autoguns.

The leader stepped forward and his men grouped behind him. They didn't form a neat echelon. Messy, I thought, casual, lacking the usual drilled discipline of the infamous naval security arm. These men were bored and going through the motions. They wanted this formality over and done too.

'Tobias Maxilla?' barked the leader, his voice distorted by his mask and vox-amplified.

'I am Maxilla,' said the ship's master, stepping forward.

'You have been notified that an inspection of your vessel is due. Furnish me with crew lists and cargo manifests. Your full co-operation is expected.'

At a nod from Maxilla, one of the servitors moved forward on silent tracks and handed the security detail's leader a data-slate with the relevant material.

He didn't look at it. 'Do you have anything you wish to volunteer before the inspection begins? It will go easier for you if you make submissions of contraband.'

I watched the exchange. There were twelve troops, hardly enough to search a ship the size of the *Essene*. Where were their servitors, their scanning units, their crowbars, multi-keys and heat-detectors?

They had no way of knowing who I was from my appearance, but why had they not remarked on the presence of an Arbites?

My vox channel was set to the cutter's. I didn't speak, but I keyed it three times. A non-verbal part of Glossia Betancore would understand.

'You haven't yet identified yourself,' I said.

The lead security trooper turned to look at me. I saw only my reflection in his tint-coated visor.

'What?'

'You haven't identified yourself or shown your warrant of practice. It is a requirement of such inspections.'

'We're naval security–' he began angrily, stepping towards me. His men faltered.

'You could be anybody.' I pulled out my Inquisitorial rosette. 'I am Gregor Eisenhorn, Imperial inquisitor. We will do this correctly or not at all.'

'You're Eisenhorn?' he said.

There was no surprise in his voice at all. A tiny thing to notice but enough for me.

The warning was already rising in my throat as their guns came up.

EIGHT

A DOZEN KILLERS
THE PROCURATOR
GRAIN MERCHANTS FROM HESPERUS

Maxilla uttered a yell of disbelief. The leader of the security detail and two of his men opened fire.

Their compact autoguns were designed for ship-board fighting and zero-gravity work: low velocity, low recoil weapons that fired blunt-nosed slugs which couldn't puncture a hull.

But they were more than capable of shredding a man.

I threw myself sideways as the first shots spanged off the deck or left ugly metal bruises on the wall. In seconds, it was utter chaos. All the security troopers were firing, some on semi-automatic. Smoke filled the air and the airgate chamber was shaking with muzzle flashes and gunfire.

One of Maxilla's servitors was decapitated and then punched into spare-part debris as it turned towards the attackers. The other tried to move to shield Maxilla, but more shots tore out its tracks and its torso.

Two shots ripped through my trailing coat, but I made it to the doorframe behind us. I yanked my stub-pistol from its holster.

Fischig had drawn his own sidearm and was blasting away as he backed towards the door. He dropped one of the troopers with a tight group of shots that sent the man flying in a puff of blood. Then Fischig was lifted off his feet by a hit to the stomach. Doubled over, he tumbled into the corner of the chamber and lay still.

Maxilla roared and raised his right hand. A beam of searing light spat from one of the ornate rings and the nearest trooper exploded, burned down to scorched bone and ragged armour in his midsection. As the smouldering ruin crashed to the deck plates, the man behind him caught Maxilla in a chasing arc of automatic fire and blasted him backwards through the glass doors of an evacsuit-bay.

The rest were charging my position. I braced and fired, placing a shot that shattered the visor of the first approaching security trooper. He fell on his face.

The stub-pistol, designed for concealment, had a four-shot clip and I had a spare magazine in my coat pocket. Seven shots remained and there were still nine of them.

At least the stubber had stopping power. The clips only held four shells because they were high-calibre solids, each the size of my thumb. The short, fat muzzle of my stubber barked again and another trooper spun sideways.

I backed down the corridor, hugging the wall. The access-way to the airgate was a wide, cable-lined passage, octagonal in cross-section and lit only by deck lights. The troopers' slow, buzzing shots hissed down the hallway at me. I fired back again, but missed my target. A salvo of rounds blew out a power relay on the wall nearby in a shower of sparks. I ducked away into shadows, and found the latch-handle of a shutter in the small of my back.

I turned, pulled it free and threw myself through it as a blizzard of shots impacted along the access-way wall.

On the other side of the shutter, I found a narrow inspection tunnel for the airgate's main docking mechanisms. The floor was metal grille, and the tight walls were thick with networks of cables and plumper hydraulic hoses. At the end, a bare metal ladder dropped down through a floor-well or up into an inspection shaft.

There was no time to climb either way. The first trooper was pushing through the shutter and raising his weapon. I shot down the length of the tunnel and blew out his chest-plate, and then jumped off the grille into the ladder well.

Five metres down, I slammed into a cage-platform. There was only red auxiliary light down here. The troopers' visors had vision amplifiers.

I was down in the guts of the vast docking clamp now, crawling between huge greased pistons and hydraulic rams the size of mature bluewood firs. Gases vented and lubricant fluids drizzled amid dangling loops of chain. The throb of heavy-duty compressors and atmosphere regulators filled the air.

I got into cover. All four red tell-tale lights on the stubber's grip were showing. I ejected the disposable plastic clip and slid the fresh one into place. Four green lights lit up in place of the red ones.

There was noise from the ladder-well. Two bulky dark shapes were moving down, backlit by the light from above.

Their visors had heat-enhancement too. That was clear the moment they both started firing at my position. I buried myself behind a piston unit but a round ricocheted off the oily metal and slammed into my right shoulder, driving me forward against the deck. My face hit the grille, and it reopened the gash in my cheek, popping out several of the butterfly clips that were just beginning to get the torn flesh to knit back together.

More shots rattled off the scant metal cover. Another ricochet hit the toe of my boot, and another punched into my arm, smashing my hand back against the wall behind me.

The impact kicked the stubber from my grip. It bounced away across the floor, just out of reach, the four green lights taunting me.

There were at least three of them out there now, moving through the confined space between machinery, firing bursts my way. I crawled on hands and knees along behind a horizontal clamp piston, low-velocity rounds pinking off the wall behind and above me.

I thought about using the will, but I had no chance of getting line of sight to try any sophisticated mind trick.

At the back end of the massive clamp, I found cover by the arrestor baffles and giant kinetic dampers that soften the impact of another ship against the docking arms. Greenish light filtered from a small control panel mounted in the wall between the dampers. The panel had a toughened plastic hood over it like a public vox-booth, and a glance showed me it was a test-reset terminal for docking array maintenance. I tried punching several icons, but the small, oval plate displayed the message Terminal locked out. Automatic safety measures were in place because a ship – the naval security troopers' pinnace – was in the docking clamp, mated to the airgate on the deck above.

I could hear scrambling above the ambient noise. The first of the troopers was clambering down the side of the clamp, following my route back to the dampers.

I took out my Inquisitorial rosette. It is a badge of office and a great deal more besides. A press of my thumb deployed the micro multi-key from its recess, and I slid it into the terminal's socket. It engaged. The screen blanked. My rosette had up to magenta level Imperial clearance. I prayed Maxilla had not encoded his entire ship with personal encryptions.

The screen flashed again. I tapped a release order into the terminal.

'Dock array in active use,' it told me in blunt green letters.

I hit override.

With a tumultuous grinding, the docking clamp disengaged. Dampers roared. Steam vented explosively. Alarms started wailing.

There was an agonised scream as the trooper on my heels was gripped and then crushed from the waist down by ten tonnes of expanding piston-sleeve.

From the deck far above, there were explosive bangs and the shriek of shearing metal. I could barely hear them above the mechanical din in the clamp chamber.

When the sighing and hissing of the massive pistons died away and the venting gases reduced to a sporadic gasp, I clambered up from behind the dampers. The entire architecture of the chamber had altered as the massive docking engines had switched from active to disengaged. Two troopers had been crushed by the heavy gear, another lay dead under a steam vent, braised in his armour by a rush of superheated steam.

I took up a fallen naval-issue autogun and retraced my steps.

By my count, there were still four loose and active. I came back along the inspection tunnel and re-entered the access-way. Warning lights strobed all along the passage and muted alarms still sounded. A figure suddenly appeared to my left. I wheeled around. It was Betancore. He was looking straight past me, one of his elegant needle pistols aimed straight at me. He fired it twice.

A distinctive stinging buzz resounded loud in my ears – and a security trooper at the far end of the passage staggered out of cover. Another shot and the man slammed over, feet out from under him.

'Came as soon as you gave the signal,' said Betancore.

'What's your tally?'

'Four, so far.'

'Then we're probably done. But stay sharp.' I smiled at myself. Telling Midas Betancore to stay sharp was like telling a dog to stay hairy.

'You're a mess,' he told me. 'What the hell happened?'

Blood ran down the side of my face from the reopened gash, I was moving awkwardly from the glancing hits to my shoulder and arm, and I was thoroughly smirched in machine oil from the docking mechanism.

'This wasn't an inspection. They were looking for me.'

'Naval security?'

'I don't think so. They lacked precision and didn't know procedure.'

'But they had kit, weapons – a Navy pinnace, Emperor damn them!'

'That's what worries me.'

We went back to the airgate. An emergency shutter had come down to seal the breach when my makeshift undocking had torn the pinnace off the side of the *Essene*. Through side ports, I could see its grey hull skewed alongside us, still attached to the clamps by one of its own docking extensors, though that was badly twisted. Its integral airgate had blown on disconnection and at least the passenger section was open to hard vacuum. If the crew had survived, they would be in the foresection, though probably helpless. Glittering debris, scraps of metal plating and sheared sections of extensor hung in the void outside.

I checked Fischig. He was alive. His Arbites uniform was heavily laced with armour, but the short-range impacts had given him internal injuries; he was unconscious and leaking blood from the mouth.

Betancore found Maxilla beyond the shattered glass doors of the evacsuit-bay. He had crawled across the floor and propped himself against a harness rack. From the chest down, his rich clothes were shredded and his legs were gone.

But then, from the chest down, he wasn't human.

'So my... bare facts are revealed to you after all, inquisitor...' he said, managing a smile. I imagined he was in pain, or shock at least. To control the sophisticated bionic lower body he had to have intricate neural linkage.

'What can I do to help you, Tobias?'

He shook his head. 'I have summoned servitors to assist me. I'll be back on my feet soon enough.'

There were many questions I wanted to ask him. Was his reconstruction the result of old injury, disease, age? Or was it, as I had a feeling, voluntary? I kept the questions to myself. They were private and didn't concern my investigation.

'I need access to your astropathic link. I need to contact battlefleet command and speed the closure of this matter. These men weren't a naval security detail.'

'I'll instruct the bridge to provide you with the access you need. You may care to extract the inspection requests from my communication log.'

That would help. I didn't think the high commanders of Battlefleet Scarus would take this lying down.

* * *

I was half-right, but only half. Within half an hour I was on the bridge of the *Essene*, surrounded by attentive servitors, reporting the incident to battlefleet command by confidential astropathic link. Before long, I was in vox dialogue with aides from the staff office of Admiral Lorpal Spatian, who requested that I secure the *Essene* at its high-anchor buoy and await the arrival of a security detail and an envoy from the battlefleet procurator.

The idea of sitting tight and waiting for more troopers to arrive didn't especially appeal.

'Deserters, sir,' Procurator Olm Madorthene told me, two hours later. He was a grizzled, narrow man with cropped grey hair and an old augmetic implant down the side of his neck under his left ear. He wore the starched white, high collared jacket, red gloves, pressed black jodhpurs and high patent leather boots of the Battlefleet Disciplinary Detachment. Madorthene had been courteous from the moment he came aboard, saluting me and tucking his gold-braided white crowned cap under his arm respectfully. His detachment of troopers were dressed and equipped identically to the ones that had boarded the *Essene* to kill us, but from the moment of their arrival I noted their greater discipline and tight order.

'Deserters?'

Madorthene seemed uneasy. He clearly disliked entanglements with an inquisitor.

'From the Guard levies. You are aware a founding is presently under way on Gudrun. By order of the Lord Militant Commander, seven hundred and fifty thousand men are being inducted into the Imperial Guard to form the 50th Gudrunite Rifles. Such is the size of the founding, and the fact that this is notably the fiftieth regiment assembled from this illustrious world, that a planet-wide celebration and associated ceremonial military events are taking place.'

'And these men deserted?'

Madorthene delicately drew me to one side as his troopers carried the corpses of the insurgents from the vicinity of the airgate and bagged them. I had set Betancore to watch over them.

'We have had trouble,' he confided quietly. 'The muster was originally to have been half a million, but the Lord Militant Commander increased the figure a week prior to the founding – he is preparing for a crusade into the Ophidian sub-sector – and, well, many found themselves conscripted with little notice. Between you and me, the great festivities are partly an attempt to draw attention from the matter. There's been some rioting in barracks at the founding area, and desertion. It's been busy for us.'

'I can well imagine. You know for certain these men are deserters from the Guard?'

He nodded and handed me a data-slate. On it was a list of twelve names, linked to file biographies and blurry holo portraits.

'They absconded from Founding Barrack 74 outside Dorsay yesterday, took uniforms and weapons from the bursary at the orbital port and stole a pinnace. No one thought to challenge a squad of naval security troopers.'

'And no one questioned their lack of credentials and flight codes?'

'Regrettably, the pinnace had been pre-loaded with a course plan and transponder codes to take it into the fleet anchorage. They would have been discovered long since had that not been the case. They were clearly looking for a non-military starship like this.'

'These are regular draftees? Infantrymen?'

'Yes.'

'Who could fly a pinnace?'

'The ringleader,' he referred back to the slate, 'one Jonno Lingaart, was a qualified orbital pilot. Worked on the ferries. As I said, a regrettable combination of events.'

I wasn't going to let this go. Madorthene wasn't lying, I was certain of that. But the information he was presenting me with was full of gaps and inconsistencies.

'What about the demand for the inspection?'

'That came from the pinnace itself. Entirely unofficial. They spotted your ship and improvised. We have sourced the inspection demand to the pinnace's vox-log.'

'No,' I said. He took a step backwards, alert to the anger that was growing in me.

'Sir?'

'I have checked the *Essene*'s communication log. It doesn't tell me the origin of the signals, but it shows the inspection demand came via astropathic link, not vox. The pinnace had no astropath.'

'That's–'

'This is the same astropathic link that allocated the *Essene* its high-anchor buoy. That's been shown as authentic enough. And these men were looking for me. Me, procurator. To kill me. They knew my name.'

He went pale and seemed unable to find a reply.

I turned away from him. 'I don't know who these men are – they may indeed have been guard draftees. But someone set them on this course to find me, someone who covered their movements, provided materials and transport, and authenticated their business with this ship. Someone either in the battlefleet or with an outrageous amount of access to its workings. No other explanation fits.'

'You're talking of... a conspiracy.'

'I am no stranger to underhand behaviour, Madorthene. Nor am I unduly perturbed by attempts on my life. I have enemies. I expect such things. This shows me my enemies are even more powerful than I suspected.'

'My lord, I–'

'What is your level of seniority, procurator?'

'I am grade one, magenta cleared, enjoying equivalency with the rank of fleet commodore. I answer directly to Lord Procurator Humbolt.' I knew this from his shoulder flashes, but I wanted to hear him tell me.

'Of course. Your superior wouldn't have trusted such a delicate matter to a junior officer. Nor did he want to show disrespect to me. I trust this matter is still held in the highest confidence?'

'Sir, yes sir! The lord procurator recognised its... delicacy. Besides, notices of any infractions are being suppressed by order of the Lord Militant Commander, so as not to foment further unrest. The details of this incident are known only to myself and my squad here, the lord procurator and his senior aides.'

'Then I'd like to keep it that way. I'd like my enemies to believe, for as long as possible, that this assassination attempt was successful. Can I rely on your co-operation, prosecutor?'

'Of course, inquisitor.'

'You will take an encrypted message back to your lord procurator from me. It will appraise him of the situation and my requirements. I will also supply you with a covert vox-link with which to contact me if any further information becomes available. Any further information, Madorthene, even if you don't believe I will find it relevant.'

He nodded keenly again. I didn't add the codicil that if I found this confidence broken I would come after him, the senior aides and the lord procurator himself like the wrath of Rogal Dorn. He could figure that out for himself.

After Madorthene and his crew had left the *Essene*, I turned to Betancore.

'What now?' he asked.

'How does it feel to be dead, Midas?'

We left the *Essene* at midnight aboard the gun-cutter. Fischig, conscious now, remained aboard Maxilla's ship, recovering from his punishing wounds in the *Essene*'s spectacularly equipped auto-infirmary.

Maxilla had agreed to keep the *Essene* at anchor for the time being. I had arranged to cover all revenues he stood to lose. I felt I might need a reliable ship at a moment's notice, and it also made sense that if the *Essene* suddenly departed, it would weaken the cover-story that we were all dead.

I talked it over with Maxilla in the bridge chamber. He sat in his great throne, sipping amasec while reconstruction servitors painstakingly restructured his lower limbs.

'I'm sorry you are now so involved, Tobias.'

'I'm not,' he said. 'This has been the most interesting run I've made in a long time.'

'You're prepared to stay until I give you word?'

'You're paying well, inquisitor!' he laughed at this. 'In truth, I am content to help you serve the Emperor. Besides, that oaf Fischig needs better care than your cutter's dingy medical suite can provide, and I can assure you I won't be running off anywhere until he's safely off my ship.'

I left the bridge, almost charmed by Maxilla's generous spirit. There could be many reasons why he assisted me so willingly – fear of the Inquisition being the chief one – but in truth, I was certain it was because he had rediscovered the pleasure of interaction with other humans. It was there in his eagerness to talk, to show off his art treasures, to help, to accommodate...

He had been alone in the company of machines for too long.

* * *

Betancore changed the transponder codes of the gun-cutter as we left the *Essene*'s hold. We kept a number of alternative craft identifiers in the codifier memory. For the past few months, and during the stop-over at Hubris, we had run as an official transport of the Inquisition, making no attempt to hide our nature.

Now we were a trade delegation from Sameter, specialising in gene-fixed cereal crops, hoping to interest Gudrun's noble estates in easy maintenance, pest-free crops now that the founding had drained their labour pool.

Betancore voxed Gudrun Control, identified us, and requested route and permission for landfall at Dorsay, the northern capital. They obliged us without hesitation. Another greedy trader in town for the festival.

We swept down through the vast elements of Battlefleet Scarus at high-anchor: rows of grotesque, swollen-bellied troop ships; massive destroyers with jutting prow-rams and proud aquila emblems; the vast battleships of the line, cold, grey orthogonal giants of space, blistered with weapon emplacements; barbed frigates, long and lean and cruel as wood-wasps; schools of fighter craft, running the picket.

Post-orbital space was seething with transports, scudding tugs, resupply launches, merchant cutters, bulky service lifters and skeletal loading platforms. Away to starboard, the mixed echelons of the merchant ships, the bulk freighters, the sleek sprint traders, the super-massive guild ships, the hybrid rogues. The *Essene* was out there somewhere.

Winking buoy lights, describing the stacks and levels of the anchor stations, filled the night, another constellation blocking out the real starfield.

Betancore nursed us down through the traffic, down into the crystal bright ionosphere, down into the opalescent ranges of the high clouds. We were heading across the crossover from night to day as the planet turned, making for Dorsay, where dawn was coming up on another day of the Festival of Founding.

NINE

AT DORSAY
MARKET FORCES
IN PURSUIT OF TANOKBREY

Dorsay wasn't waking up. It had been awake all night. Vox-horns along the old streets, avenues and canals broadcast martial themes, and streamers and pennants flew from every available surface.

I had speed-read Aemos's summation of the planet: Gudrun, capital of the Helican sub-sector, Scarus Sector, Segmentum Obscurus. Boasting a human culture for three and a half thousand years, feudally governed by powerful noble houses, whose reach and power extended across three dozen other worlds in the Helican sub-sector. Thracian Primaris, that vast, bloated hub of industry and commerce, was the most populated and productive world in the region, but Gudrun was the cultural and administrative heart. And it was reckoned the combined wealth of the noble houses rivalled the commercial worth of the output of the Thracian hives.

Seen from our approach run, Dorsay gleamed white in the dawn. It lay on the coast, around the lip of a sea-fed lagoon, straddling the mighty river Drunner. From the cutter's ports as we turned in, we could see the white specks of sailboats out in the lagoon basin. Beyond the vast white spread of the city, I could see massive stockades and emplacements established in the rolling green hills and bluffs, temporary barracks for the founding regiment.

Betancore set us down at Giova Field, the municipal port serving Dorsay. It was built on a long, narrow island in the lagoon facing the city, and the space premium meant smaller ships like ours were lowered on monotasked heavy elevators and berthed in a honeycomb of compartments drilled into the porous lava-rock of the island's heart.

Lowink stayed with the cutter. Midas, Aemos, Bequin and myself prepared to go into Dorsay. We changed into simple, anonymous clothing: dark blue robes for Aemos, plain black suits of good cloth and long leather coats for Betancore and myself, and a long gown of porcelain blue crepe with a cream-lace shawl for Alizebeth Bequin. Betancore, with some reluctance, had reopened Vibben's possessions to find clothing suitable for Bequin.

She didn't seem to mind that their former owner was dead.

Under red awnings fluttering in the dawn breeze, the island jetties were thick with passengers waiting for transport to the mainland. We queued among groups of merchants, visiting dignitaries and fleet ratings on furlough. Busking musicians and pedlars plied the captive audience.

At length, we hired one of the grav-skiffs lining up at the jetty. It was a long, speartip-shaped airboat with a glossy violet hull. Open-topped, it provided seats for six, with the steersman perched high at the aft over the bulbous anti-grav generators. It slid us across the lagoon, keeping two metres above the choppy, dappled water.

Dorsay rose before us. Now on its level, we could appreciate how majestic, how towering the city was. Rising above the water on stilts formed of vast basalt stacks and pillars, the buildings were constructed from smoothly fitted, cyclopean stone blocks, their facades limewashed, their shallow roofs dressed with verdigrised copper tiles. Gargoyles yawned at gutter ends or curled around downpipes and drain sluices. Upper storeys had balconies with railings made of tarnished copper; many balconies also had canopies. Arched stone bridges and metal stair-walks linked neighbouring buildings, sometimes across the water-filled streets themselves. Along the canal sides, stone walkways formed a water-level street for pedestrians.

And there were many of those. The place was alive with movement, colour and noise. Once we got into the city proper, our passage down the canals was slowed by other grav-skiffs, water-buses, private yawls and motor-driven boats.

Above us, at high traffic levels, speeders and atmospheric fliers buzzed back and forth. Everywhere we looked were banners celebrating Battlefleet Scarus and the Gudrunite guard regiments, especially the 50th Rifles.

Aemos chattered to himself as usual, noting the elements of Dorsay into his wrist slate, his hunger for accumulating knowledge unstinted. I watched him for a while, his nervous moves, his boyish glee at new details, his obsessive-compulsive tapping at his slate.

The keypads of that battered old slate were worn smooth.

Midas Betancore was alert and sharp as always. He sat in the front of the grav-skiff, soaking up details like Aemos. But the details he noticed would be far more pertinent and immediately useful than my old savant's.

Bequin simply sat back and smiled, the chop of the breeze fluttering her shawl. I doubted she could ever have come here under her own steam. Gudrun was the epicentre of the sub-sector culture, the big bright world she had always dreamed about and of which she yearned to be a part.

I let her have her fun. There would be hard work later.

We took a suite of rooms at the Dorsay Regency. I considered it expedient to have a base of operations on the mainland. Betancore drilled out the door frames with a hand tool and installed locator bolts with built-in flash deterrents. We also wired the internal doorways. The house servitors were given strict instructions not to enter when we were absent.

I stood on the heavy, limewashed balcony, under a faded awning of purple canvas, and listened to the March of the Adeptes as it played out, distorted, from the speaker horns that dressed the street.

The canal below was thick with traffic. I saw a skiff overladen with drunken Guardsmen, all wearing their newly issued red and gold kits. Men of the 50th Gudrunite Rifles, raising hell and risking death by drowning as they enjoyed their last hours on their homeworld. In a few days they would be packed into a troopship and bound for who knew what horror a sub-sector away.

One of them fell into the canal as they tried to stagger ashore. His comrades dredged him out, and baptised his head with the contents of a liquor bottle.

Aemos joined me, and showed me a data-slate map.

'The Regal Bonded Merchant Guild of Sinesias,' he said. 'Headquarters are five streets away.'

Guild Sinesias owned some of the most imposing premises in the commercial district of Dorsay. A spur of the Grand Canal actually fed in under the coloured glass portico of the main buildings, so that visiting traders could run their skiffs inside and disembark under cover in a tiled and carpeted reception dock.

Our grav-skiff carried us in, and we stepped out amid clusters of tall, thin, gowned traders from Messina, merchants from Sameter in ludicrously heavy hats and veils, and obese bankers from the Thracian hives.

I strode ashore and turned to offer Bequin my hand. She nodded courteously as she left the skiff. I hadn't briefed her much. The aristocratic airs and graces were her own spontaneous invention. Though I still loathed her, I admired her more with each passing moment. She was playing things perfectly.

'Your name and business here, sire, madam?' a Guild Sinesias chamberlain asked as he approached us. He was dripping in finery, gold brocaded gowns attiring every servant in the place. Augmetic implants blistered in place of his ears and he clutched a slate and stylus.

'My name is Farchaval, a merchant from Hesperus. This is Lady Farchaval. We come to tender grain contracts with the high houses of this world, and we are told Guild Sinesias will provide us the necessary brokerage.'

'Do you have a guild responser, sire?'

'Of course. My contact was Saemon Crotes.'

'Crotes?' the chamberlain paused.

'Oh, Gregor, I'm so bored,' Bequin suddenly announced. 'This is so, so very slow and dull. I want to cruise the canals again. Why can't we go back and deal with those spirited fellows at Guild Mensurae?'

'Later, my dearest,' I said, delighted and wrong-footed by her improvisation.

'You have already... visited another guild?' the chamberlain asked quickly.

'They were very nice. They brought me Solian tea,' Bequin purred.

'Let me escort you both,' the chamberlain said at once. 'Saemon Crotes is, of course, one of our most valued envoys. I will arrange an audience for you forthwith. In the meantime, please relax in this suite. I will have Solian tea sent up directly.'

'And nafar biscuits?' cooed Bequin.

'But of course, madam.'

He swept out and closed the double doors of the luxurious waiting room behind him. Bequin looked at me and giggled. I confess, I laughed out loud.

'What got into you?'

'You said we were monied merchants who expected the very best. I was just earning my salary.'

'Keep it up,' I said.

We looked around the room. Gauze-draped windows ten metres high looked out over the Grand Canal, but they were insulated to keep the noise out. Rich tapestries dressed the walls between Sameter School oils that Maxilla would have loved to own.

A burnished servitor brought in a tray of refreshments soon after that. It lowered it onto a marble-topped occasional table and trundled out.

'Solian tea!' Bequin squeaked, lifting the lid of a porcelain pot. 'And nafar biscuits!' she added with a smile, through the crumbs of the first one.

She poured me a cup and I stood by the fireplace, sipping it, striking an appropriately haughty pose.

The guild representative flew in through the doors a moment later. He was a small, spiky-haired man with flowing gowns and far too much jewellery. The Guild Sinesias brand mark was proudly displayed on his forehead.

He was, the brand indicated, property.

His name was Macheles.

'Sire Farchaval! Madam! Had I known you were visiting, I would have cancelled meets to be here. Forgive my tardiness!'

'I forgive it,' I said. 'But I'm afraid Lady Farchaval may be fast losing her patience.'

Bequin yawned on cue.

'Oh, that is not good! Not good at all!' Macheles clapped his hands and servitors trundled in.

'Provide the lady with whatever she requests!' Macheles told them.

'Ummm... vorder leaves?' she said.

'At once!' Macheles instructed.

'And a plate of birri truffles? Sautéed in wine?'

I winced.

'At once! At once!' Macheles yelped, shushing the servitors out of the room.

I stepped forward and put down my cup. 'I'll be straight with you, sir. I represent grain merchants on Hesperus, a significant cartel of grain merchants.'

I handed him my holo-dent. It was fake, of course. Betancore and Aemos had run it up, using Aemos's profound knowledge in general and his knowledge of Hesperus - gleaned from interviews with Maxilla - in particular.

Macheles seemed impressed enough by my identification.

'What sort of... size cartel are we talking about, sire?'

'The entire western continent.'

'And you offer?'

I produced a sample tube from my pocket. 'A gene-fixed strain of cereal that could be easily managed by many of your landowners now that their workforce is depleted. It is indeed a wonder.'

The servitors reappeared, delivering Bequin's delicacies.

As she munched the soft-fleshed birri, she said, 'The other guilds are bidding for this product, mister. I do hope Guild Sinesias won't miss out.'

Macheles shook the sample tube and looked at it.

'Is this,' he said, his voice dropping, 'xenos cultured?'

'Would that be a problem?' I asked.

'No, sire! Not officially. The Inquisition is of course very tight about such things. But that is precisely why we offer these discreet interviews. The entire guild buildings are buffered against trackers, intercept beams and vox-thieves.'

'I am pleased to hear it. So a xenos-cultured cereal strain would not be hard to market?'

'Naturally not. There are collective enterprises eager for assured crop yields. Especially those hot-housed by alien technology.'

'Good,' I lied. 'But I want the best return. Saemon told me that House Glaw should be the first to approach.'

'Saemon?'

'Saemon Crotes. The Guild Sinesias envoy I dealt with on Hesperus.'

'Quite so! You wish me to arrange a trade meeting with House Glaw?'

'I think that's what I said, didn't I?'

We left the Guild Sinesias dock twenty minutes later. Bequin was still licking her lips from the birri.

As soon as our skiff was clear of the building, the vox-ceiver woven into my cuff began to twitch.

'Eisenhorn.'

It was Lowink. 'I've just accepted a message from Tobias Maxilla. Do you want me to relive it?'

'Just a summary, Lowink.'

'He says the ship that took Eyclone's Gudrun-Hubris run is at anchor here. Says he's done some probing. The Rogue Trader Scaveleur. The master, one Effries Tanokbrey, is already planetside.'

'Signal Maxilla and thank him for his work, Lowink.' I said.

The identity of Eyclone's mysterious starship was now known to me.

We were taking lunch at a commercial tavern overlooking the Bridge of Carnodons when Macheles sent Sire Farchaval a private text message by vox-drone.

The drone, an oblate metal unit roughly the size of a small citrus fruit, came buzzing into the dining terrace like a pollen-insect, scudding from table to table at head-height on its tiny repeller motors until it found me. Then it hovered, chimed, and beamed its holographic cargo against the side of my crystal tumbler: the crest of Guild Sinesias, followed by a formal and obsequious text inviting Sire Farchaval and his entourage to a meeting at the Glaw estate the following afternoon. We were to meet Macheles at the guild building at four, where transport would be waiting.

The drone continued to project the message until I broke the beam with a wave of my hand and made a quick verbal assent, which it recorded. Dismissed, it bumbled away with its answer.

'How did it find us?' asked Bequin.

'A pheromonal trace,' Aemos replied. 'The guild building's master systems will have sampled you both during your visit and then it would have come searching until it matched the record in its sensors.'

Vox-drone messaging was common practice on higher tech Imperial worlds like this. It gave me an idea.

'You say the guild seemed comfortable dealing with xenos material?' Betancore was saying, raising his wine glass to sip.

I nodded. 'We'll concentrate on House Glaw for now. That's where our primary interest lies. But I'm not going to forget Sinesias. When we're done, the full weight of the Inquisition will come to bear on their dealings.'

Bequin was looking out at the fine ornamental bridge that arched over the Drunner below. 'What are those creatures?' she asked. The stone effigies of great quadruped predators decorated each span of the old crossing. The beasts were huge, with powerful, mastiff-like builds, brush tails and long snouts bristling with tusks.

'Carnodons,' Aemos said, once again delighted to be able to share his considerable knowledge. 'The heraldic animal of Gudrun. They feature in many crests and emblems hereabouts, symbolising the noble authority of the world. Rare now, of course. Hunted to near extinction. I believe only a few live wild now in the northern tundra.'

'We have a day at our disposal,' I told them, cutting through the idle talk. 'Let's use it well. Let's find this ship master, Tanokbrey.'

Betancore raised his eyebrows and was about to tell me how difficult that was going to be, until I explained my idea to him.

We used a clerical bureau on a water-street off the Ooskin Canal, and paid for a vox-drone message. I kept it simple, a brief enquiry to the master of the Rogue Trader Scaveleur concerning the possibility of off-planet passage. The cleric serving me took my text and payment without comment, and loaded the message into one of the three-dozen vox-drones that lay inert in a rack behind his seat. Then he accessed his data-files, retrieved the pheromone trace for Tanokbrey that the ship master had logged with the city administration at immigration, and installed that too.

The selected drone rose, buzzed, and floated away out of the office.

On the street outside, Betancore fired up the motor of the air-bike he had rented and made off after it.

Chances were it would lead us to our quarry. If it gave Betancore the slip, there was every reason to hope Tanokbrey would come to us. He was a commercial merchant looking for business after all.

Aemos, Bequin and I followed in a public grav-skiff, staying in vox-contact with Betancore. The canal traffic was thicker than ever, and local Arbites, as well as naval security details, were out in force. There was to be a major ceremonial cavalcade later that afternoon, and the route was being prepared. Already, crowds of spectators were gathering on the bridges and the walkways. Banners and well-wishing garlands were on display all around.

Betancore was waiting for us on a walkway in the Tersegold Quarter, a part of Dorsay famous for its taverns and clubs. I left Aemos and Bequin in the skiff.

'In there,' he said, indicating an old, bow-fronted establishment. 'I followed it inside. It delivered to the fifth table from the left. Tanokbrey is the tall man in the rose-red jacket. He has two men with him by my count.'

'Stay back and be ready,' I said.

The tavern was dark and crowded. Music and lights pulsed from the low roof, and the air was rank with the smells of sweat, smoke, hops and the unmistakable fumes of obscura.

My vox-drone was coming out through the door as I entered. It paused, delivered its message and then drifted away. A curt text informed me that the Scaveleur was not for hire.

Moving through the packed clientele, I located Tanokbrey. His rose-red jacket was of finest silk and his frizzy black hair was raked back into twists and tied with ribbons at the back of his head. He had a craggy, singularly unwelcoming face. His drinking companions were a pair of common crewmen in studded leather bodygloves.

'Master Tanokbrey?'

He looked round at me slowly and said nothing. His comrades fixed me with grim stares.

'Perhaps we could talk privately?' I suggested.

'Perhaps you could piss off.'

I sat down anyway. His men seemed astonished at my action, and stiffened. All Tanokbrey had to do was nod, I realised.

'Let me start with an easy question,' I began.

'Start by pissing off,' he replied. He was now fixing me with a caustic gaze. Without breaking eye contact, I noted that his left hand was inside his coat.

'You seem anxious. Why is that?'

No answer. His men stirred nervously.

'Something to hide?'

'I'm having a quiet drink. I don't want interruptions. Now sod off.'

'So unfriendly. Well, if these gentlemen aren't going to give us privacy, I'll press on regardless. I do hope I don't embarrass you.'

'Who the hell are you?'

Now I didn't reply. My eyes never left his. 'Your high-anchor fees are delinquent,' I said at last.

'That's a lie!'

It was, and so was what I said next. It didn't matter. The purpose was to undermine him. 'And your manifest papers are incomplete. Gudrun control may wish to impound your ship until the irregularities are cleared up.'

'Lying bastard–'

'It's an easy matter. You made a run to Hubris that is not logged, nor is any cargo list filed. How will they calculate import duties?'

His chair scraped back a centimetre or two.

'Why were you on Hubris?'

'I wasn't! Who says I was?'

'Take your pick. Saemon Crotes. Namber Wylk.'

'Don't know them. You've got the wrong man, you miserable bastard. Now frag off!'

'Murdin Eyclone, then. What about him? Didn't he hire you?'

That brought the nod at last. An imperceptible motion of his head.

The crewman beside me lunged out of his seat, a compact shock-flail snapping out of his sleeve and into his gloved hand.

'Drop it,' I willed, without even speaking.

The flail sparked as it bounced off the table top.

It was in my hand a second later. I whipped it back across its owner's face and smashed him sideways off his chair. Then I snapped it round, crushed the left ear of the other crewman and laid him full length on the floor at the foot of the table.

I sat back down, facing Tanokbrey, the flail in my hand. His face as grey and his eyes darted now with panic.

'Eyclone. Tell me about him.'

His left arm moved inside his jacket and I jabbed the flail into his shoulder. Unfortunately, I realised he was wearing armour under that silk.

He reeled from the impact, but his arm came up all the same, a short-snouted laspistol clutched in his fist.

I slammed the table into him and his shot went wild, punching through the back of a nearby ruffian. The victim toppled over, bringing another table smashing down.

Now the shot and the commotion had got the attention of the entire tavern. There was general shouting and confusion.

I didn't pay it any heed. Tanokbrey fired again through the overturned table and I dove aside, colliding with milling bodies.

The merchant was on his feet, kicking and punching his way through the mob to the exit. I could see Betancore, but the mass of bodies prevented him from blocking Tanokbrey.

'Aside!' I yelled, and the crowd parted like hatch shutters.

Tanokbrey was on the walkway outside, running for the quay at the end of the street. He turned and fired. Pedestrians screamed and ran. Someone was pushed into the canal.

Tanokbrey leapt into a grav-skiff, shot the protesting hire-driver, pushed the corpse off the steering perch, and gunned the craft away down the canal.

Betancore's air-bike was sat on its kickstand to my left. I cranked the power and swept off down the waterway in pursuit.

'Wait! Wait!' I heard Betancore yelling.

No time.

Tanokbrey's flight caused mayhem down the length of the busy canal. He drove his skiff into the jostling traffic, forcing craft to heave out of his way. Already the decorative golden filigree on the skiff's black hull was grazed and dented with a dozen glancing impacts. People on the banks and abroad on the water howled and yelled at him as he wrenched his way through. Where the street met a canal thoroughfare, he tried to extend his lead with a surge of speed. A fast-moving courier boat coming down the stream veered at the last moment, and struck the quayside with great force, sending the craft up over end, its hull shredding, its driver cartwheeling through the air.

I laced the air-bike through the disrupted traffic in Tanokbrey's wake. I wanted to gain height, and move to a level where I could coax more speed from the machine without fear of collision. But the vehicle's grav-plate had a governor unit that prevented anything more than three metres of climb. I had no time to figure out where the governor was or how to disable it. I aimed the bike between turning skiffs, water-buses heavy in the choppy canal, other darting air-bikes.

Ahead, I could hear the distant sounds of military bands.

Tanokbrey whipped out of a junction into the Grand Canal, and straight into the side of the afternoon's parade. A slow-moving river of skiffs, military barges and landspeeder escorts filled the entire width of the waterway. The craft were full of jubilant Imperial Guardsmen and officers, thundering regimental bands and battlefleet dignitaries. The air was glittering with streamers and banners, company standards, Imperial eagles and Gudrunite carnodons. One entire barge bore a massive golden carnodon sculpture to which whooping Guardsmen clung. Garlands fluttered from the barrels of a thousand brandished las-rifles. The walkways and bridges of the Grand Canal were choked with cheering civilians.

Tanokbrey's skiff smacked into the side of a troop-barge, and angry yells and jeers were loosed at him as he tried to turn. From the shore, the crowd pelted him with fruit, stones and other missiles.

Cursing back at the angry soldiers, he slammed his skiff round the rear of the barge, trying to force his way across the canal.

I was closing on him now, trying to avoid the displeasure of the mob. Hooters and sirens bayed at him from the parade boats as he jostled across their paths. A trooper from one barge leapt onto his skiff to waylay him, and Tanokbrey kicked him off into the water before he could get a good footing. That turned things even uglier. The noise of the booing and outrage was immense. The parade bunched up badly, and dozens of furious guardsmen pressed at the rails of their barges, trying to reach him.

He over-revved the skiff to get clear of them, and struck against a raft carrying a company band. Several instrument players toppled with the impact, and the proud Imperial anthem they had been playing dissolved in a cacophony of wrong notes and broken rhythms.

Enraged troopers in a smaller skiff drew alongside him, and rocked his craft dangerously as they tried to board. He pulled his handgun.

His last mistake. I pulled up short, and landed on the canal bank. There was no point in pressing the pursuit now.

Tanokbrey got off two shots into the mob. Then twenty or more freshly issued las-rifles on a neighbouring barge opened fire, smashing him and his stolen craft to pieces. The drive unit exploded, scattering hull fragments across the churning water. A curl of black smoke rose above the banners.

The young conscripts of the 50th Gudrunite Rifles had made the first kill of their military careers.

TEN

A CONFLICT OF JURISDICTION
THE HOUSE OF GLAW
STALKING SECRETS

Long after midnight, I was attempting to sleep in my bedchamber at the Dorsay Regency. Bequin and Aemos had both retired to their own rooms hours before. Reflected light from the canal outside played a series of silver ripples across the ceiling of my twilit chamber.

'Aegis, rose thorn!' Betancore's voxed whisper suddenly tapped at my ear.

'Rose thorn, reveal.'

'Spectres, invasive, spiral vine.'

I was already out of bed and into my breeches and boots, pulling my leather coat over my bare torso. I went out into the apartment lounge with my power sword in my hand.

The lights were off, but canal reflections played in here too, creating a fluttering half-light.

Betancore stood by the far wall, a needle pistol in each hand. He nodded at the main door.

They were good and they were very quiet, but we could both see slight movement against the cracks around the doors, backlit by the hall light.

A gentle vibration of the handle told me someone was springing the lock. Betancore and I dropped back against the walls either side of the doors. We closed our eyes and covered our ears. Any forcing of the door would trigger the deterrent charges, and we didn't want to wind up blind or deaf.

The door opened a crack. No flash charges roared. Our visitors had detected and neutralised the security countermeasures. They were even better than I first thought.

A slender telescopic rod extended smoothly in through the crack. An optical sensor on the end slowly began to pan around, searching the room. With a nod to Betancore, I moved forward, took hold of the rod and yanked hard. At the same moment, I ignited my power sword.

A body crashed into the doors, dragged forward by my hefty pull on the spy-stick, and came tumbling in. I leapt in to straddle the body, but despite his surprise, he writhed away with a curse, and threw a punch. I had a vague impression of a tall, thickly built man in form-fitting leather.

We flopped over together, wrestling, overturning a couch and knocking down a candle-stand. My opponent had a good grip on the wrist of my sword arm.

So I punched him in the throat with my left hand.

He collapsed, retching, onto the floor. I got up in time to hear a strong voice say, 'Put the weapons down now.'

A short, hunched figure stood in the open doorway. Betancore had both pistols trained on it, but was slowly lowering them despite himself.

The figure had used the will. I brushed the tingle aside, but it was too much for Midas. The needle pistols thumped onto the carpet.

'Now you,' the figure said, turning its silhouette towards me. 'Disarm that power-blade.'

I seldom had an opportunity to feel the effect of psyker manipulation. The technique was different from the ones I employed, and the force of will was unmistakably potent. I braced myself for the hideous strain of outright telepathic combat.

'You resist?' said the figure. A blade of mental energy stabbed into my skull, rocking me backwards. I knew at once I was fundamentally outclassed. This was an old, powerful, practiced mind.

A second stab of pain, cutting into the first. The man I had left choking was now on his knees. Another psyker. More powerful than the first, it seemed, but with far less control or technique. His attack seared through my skull and made me bark out in pain, but I blocked him as I stumbled back and stung his eager mind away with a desperate, unfocused jab.

The boiling psychic waves were rattling the windows and vibrating the furniture. Glasses shattered and Betancore fell, whimpering. The hunched figure stepped forward again, and dropped me to my knees with renewed mental assaults. I felt blood spurt from my nose. My vision swam. My grip on the sword remained tight.

Abruptly, it stopped. Roused by the disturbance, both Aemos and Bequin had burst into the room. Bequin screamed. Her psychic blankness, abruptly intruding on the telepathic maelstrom, suddenly blew the energies out, like a vacuum snuffing the heart of a fire.

The hunched figure cried out and stumbled in surprise. I drove forward, grabbed him and hurled him bodily across the chamber. He seemed frail but surprisingly heavy for such a small mass.

Betancore recovered his weapons and lit the lamps.

The man I had pulled through the doors was little more than a youth, big built with a long, shaved skull and a slit of a mouth. He was crumpled by the windows, semi-conscious. He wore a black leather bodyglove adorned with equipment harnesses. Bequin relieved him of his holstered sidearm.

The other, the hunched figure, rose slowly and painfully, ancient limbs cracking and protesting. He wore long dark robes; his thin hands were clad in black satin gloves. A number of gaudy rings protruded from the folds of the gown. He pulled back his cowl.

He was very old, his weathered, lined face wizened like a fruit stone. His throat, exposed at the gown's neckline, betrayed traces of the augmetic work that undoubtedly encased his age-twisted body.

His eyes blazed at me from their deep sockets with cold fury.

'You have made a mistake,' he said, wheezing, 'a fatal one, I have no doubt.' He produced a chunky amulet and held it up. The sigil it bore was unmistakable. 'I am Inquisitor Commodus Voke.'

I smiled. 'Well met, brother,' I said.

Commodus Voke stared at my rosette for a few lingering seconds, then looked away. I could feel the psychic throbbing of his rage.

'We have a... conflict of jurisdiction,' he managed to say, straightening his robes. His assistant, now back on his feet, stood in the corner of the chamber and gazed sullenly at me.

'Then let us resolve it,' I offered. 'Explain to me why you invade my apartments in the dead of night.'

'My work brought me to Gudrun eight months ago. An ongoing investigation, a complex matter. A rogue trader had come to my attention, one Effries Tanokbrey. I had begun to close my net around him when he was scared into flight and got himself killed. Simple cross-checking revealed that a grain merchant called Farchaval had somehow been instrumental in that incident.'

'Farchaval is my cover here on Gudrun.'

'You see fit to play-act and hide your true nature?' he said scornfully.

'We each have our methods, inquisitor,' I replied.

I'd never met the great Commodus Voke before, but his reputation preceded him. An intractable puritan in his ethic, almost leaning to the hard-line of the monodominants but for the fact of his remarkable psychic abilities. I believe something of a Thorian doctrine suited his beliefs. He had served as a noviciate with the legendary Absalom Angevin three hundred years before and since then had played a key role in some of the most thorough and relentless purges in sector history. His methods were open and direct. Stealth, co-operation and subterfuge were distasteful concepts to him. He used the full force of his status, and the fear it generated, to go where he pleased and demand anything of anyone to achieve his goals.

In my experience, the heavy-handed, terror-inspiring approach closes as many doors as it smashes open. Frankly, it didn't surprise me to learn he had already been on this planet for a full eight months.

He looked at me as if I was something he had almost stepped in. 'I am discomforted when I see inquisitors holding to the soft, cunning ways of the radical. That way heresy lies, Eisenhorn.'

That made me start. I consider myself, as I have reported, very much of the puritanical outlook. Staunch, hard-line in my own way, though flexible enough to get the job done efficiently. Yet here was Voke gauging me as a radical! And at that moment, next to him, I felt I may as well be the most extreme, dangerous Horusian, the most artful and scheming recongregator.

I tried to push past that. 'We need to share more information, inquisitor. I'll take a guess and say your investigation somehow involves the Glaw family.'

Voke said nothing and showed no response, but I felt his assistant tense psychically behind me.

'Our work is indeed clashing,' I went on. 'I, too, am interested in House Glaw.' In short, simple terms I laid out the matter of Eyclone's activities on Hubris, and drew the connection to Glaw and Gudrun by way of the mysterious Pontius.

I had his interest now. 'Pontius is just a name, Eisenhorn. Pontius Glaw on the other hand, is long dead. I served with worthy Angevin in the purge that destroyed him. I saw his corpse.'

'Yet here you are, investigating the Glaws anyway.'

He exhaled slowly, as if making his mind up. 'After Pontius Glaw's eradication, the House of Glaw made great efforts to distance itself from his heresy. But Angevin, rest his immortal soul, always suspected that the taint ran deeper and that the family was not free of corruption. It is an ancient house, and powerful. It is difficult to probe its secrets. But from time to time, over the past two hundred years, I have turned my eye to them. Fifteen months ago, prosecuting a coven on Sader VII, I uncovered traces which suggested that particular coven, and several other minor groups, were collectively being run by an all but invisible parent cult – a cult of great scope and power, old and hidden, stretching across many worlds. Some traces led to Gudrun. That Gudrun is the Glaw's ancestral home was for me, too much of a coincidence.'

'Now we make progress,' I said, sitting down in a high-backed chair and pulling on a shirt Bequin brought to me from my chamber. Aemos poured six glasses of amasec from a decanter on the dresser. Taking one as it was offered, Voke sat down opposite me. He sipped, contemplatively.

His assistant refused the glass that Aemos offered and remained standing.

'Sit down, Heldane!' Voke said. 'We have things to learn here.'

The assistant took a glass and sat in the corner.

'I hunt out a cabal controlled by a notorious facilitator,' I continued, 'a cabal set on performing an abominable crime. The trail leads to Gudrun and the Glaws. You do the same with another heretical cell–'

'Three others, in fact,' he corrected.

'Three, then. And you see the shape of a far greater organisation. From the facts as they stand, we are both approaching the same evil from opposite sides.'

He licked his lips with a tiny, pallid tongue and nodded. 'Since coming to Gudrun I have rooted out and burned two heretical cells. I am reasonably sure of the activities of another nine, three here in Dorsay alone. I have allowed them to fester as I observe them. For months, they have seemed bent on preparation for some event. Abruptly, a matter of weeks ago, their behaviour changed. This would have been around the same time as your confrontation on Hubris.'

'Eyclone's undertaking was also great, with extensive preparatory work. Yet, at the eleventh hour, something either went wrong or plans were suddenly changed. Though I defeated and destroyed him, his plans were really thwarted by the fact that the Pontius didn't arrive. What has your work revealed of House Glaw?'

'I have visited them twice in three months. On both occasions, they have made every effort to answer my questions, allowing me to search the estate and their records. I have found nothing.'

'I fear, perhaps, that is because they knew they were dealing with an inquisitor. Tomorrow, Sire Farchaval has a trade meeting with the Glaws at their estate.'

He mused on this. 'The Inquisition has a duty to stand together, firmly, against the arch-enemies of mankind. In the spirit of co-operation, I will wait and see what your dubious methods reveal. Precious little, I imagine.'

'In the spirit of co-operation, Voke, I will share all I learn with you.'

'You will do better than that. The Glaws know me, but not all of my students. Heldane will go with you.'

'I don't think so.'

'I insist. I will not have years of work ruined by another agency such as yourself running rough-shod through the matter. I require my own observer on the ground, or my co-operation will not be extended.'

He had me in a vice and he knew it. To refuse outright would simply confirm my radical, careless approach in his eyes. And I had no wish to draw battlelines against another of the Inquisition, especially a man as powerful and influential as Commodus Voke.

'Then he had better do exactly as I instruct him,' I said.

We left Dorsay for the Glaw estates the next afternoon at four. Dressed once more as wealthy but not ostentatious merchants, Bequin and I were accompanied by Aemos, Betancore and Heldane, Voke's man. Heldane, I was pleased to see, had made a reasonable job of adopting simple civilian dress. He and Betancore would pose as our bodyguard and escort, and Aemos was to take the part of a gene-biologist.

Macheles, and four other luxuriously robed envoys from the Regal Bonded Merchant Guild of Sinesias, were waiting for us at the guild headquarters. An atmospheric launch had been prepared.

The launch, a burnished dart bearing the guild crest, left the landing platform of the guild building's roof, and rose smoothly into the overcast sky. It was, Macheles informed us, to be a two-hour flight. A guild envoy circulated through the richly furnished cabin with trays of refreshment.

Macheles explained our itinerary: a formal dinner with the representatives of House Glaw that evening, an overnight stay, and then a tour of the estates the following morning. After that, negotiations if both parties were still interested.

We flew west, inland, leaving the inclement coastal weather behind and passing into a sunlit landscape of rolling pasture, low hills, and maintained forests. The snaking silver line of the Drunner winked below us. There were occasional small settlements, farmsteads, a compact market town with a tall Ecclesiarchy spire. Once in a while, we saw another air vehicle in the distance.

A dark range of hills began to fill the western skyline. Evening was beginning to discolour the clouds. The region approaching the hills rose in bluffs and headlands, a more majestic and wild landscape, thickly wooded on escarpments and deep vales.

Already, Macheles boasted, we were flying over Glaw property.

The estate itself loomed out of the dimming hills some minutes later: a three-storey main house built in the neo-gothic style, dominating a bluff and staring down across the deep valley from a hundred window eyes. The limewashed stone glowed lambently in the twilight. Adjoining the main structure were substantial wings built at different times. One led to stables and other considerable stone outbuildings along the edge of the woodland, and I presumed this to be the servants' block. The other wing edged the crown of the bluff, and was dominated by a dome that shone gold in the sinking sun. The place was huge, and no doubt labyrinthine. The population of a modest town could have been accommodated within it.

The launch settled onto a wide stone yard behind the house. At the edge of the yard, in what looked like converted coach houses, three other launches were stationed in hangars with well-equipped maintenance bays.

We disembarked into the yard. The air was cold and a night breeze was bringing spots of rain with it. The wind sighed in the stands of trees beyond the house. Heavy bars of cloud laced the evening sky above the towering hills.

Servants in dark green liveries hurried out to us, taking up our luggage and raising wide, long-handled parasols to shield us from the drizzle. A number of uniformed guards from the Glaws' house retinue flanked the yard. Haughty and confident in their long emerald stormcoats and plumed silver helmets, the guards seemed like experienced veterans to my eyes.

The servants escorted us and the guild envoys into an atrium with a black and white tiled floor and a bright, silvery cast to the light. Dozens of vast crystal chandeliers hung from the high, arched roof. More guards flanked the doorways. The Glaws' militia was clearly sizeable.

'Welcome to the House of Glaw,' a woman's voice said.

She approached us, a well-made woman of good, high stock, her powdered face bearing the proud insouciance of all nobility. She wore a regal black gown, floor length and wide in the skirt and laced with a silver overstitching, and a great twin-cusped head-dress of black mesh and pearls that tied under her chin with a wide black ribbon.

Macheles and the envoys bowed ceremoniously and the five of us made more conservative nods.

'The Lady Fabrina Glaw,' announced Macheles. She approached, green-coated servants forming a human wake behind her.

'Lady,' I said.

'Sire Farchaval. I am so pleased to meet you.'

She gave us a brief tour of the main house. I have seldom seen such extravagance and riches outside of an Imperial court – or Tobias Maxilla's staterooms. Lean hunting dogs trotted with us. She pointed out a number of ancient paintings, mostly oil portraits, but some exquisite hololithic works, as well as vivid psyk-pict miniatures. Her illustrious family... uncles, grandfathers, cousins, matriarchs, warlords. Here was Vernal Glaw in the dress uniform of the house militia. Here was Orchese Glaw entertaining the royal house of Sameter. Over there, Lutine and Gyves Glaw, brothers at the hunt.

There great Oberon himself, in the robes of an Imperial commander, one hand resting on an antique globe of Gudrun.

The envoys made appropriate noises of admiration. Fabrina herself seemed to just be going through the motions. She was acting the hostess. We were, after all, just grain merchants. This was a duty. An obligation.

I saw Aemos making surreptitious notes. I too made careful observations, especially of the house geography. In one long hallway, the stone floor was dressed by the rather worn pelts of three carnodons, skinned, spread-eagled, their massive tusked mouths and baleful eyes frozen in attitudes of rage. Even in this sad state, the size and power of these creatures spoke for themselves.

'We hunted them, but there are few left now,' Fabrina Glaw remarked, off-hand, seeing my interest. 'Old times, long passed. Life was rather more feudal then. Today, House Glaw looks entirely to the future.'

At dinner, in the massive banqueting hall, we were joined by Urisel Glaw, the commander of the house militia, and his eldest brother, Oberon, the current Lord Glaw. But the dinner was not solely in our honour. A cousin of the Glaw family and his entourage were visiting from off-world, as were several other trade delegations and a wealthy ship master called Gorgone Locke.

I was not surprised. Visiting grain traders, even ones accompanied by the prestigious Guild Sinesias, hardly merited a formal banquet. It was appropriate we should be honoured by our inclusion at a larger event. No doubt we were meant to be impressed.

I attended with Bequin and Aemos. There was no place for servants and bodyguards here, so Betancore and Heldane had been escorted to our suite and food provided for them there. That suited my approach fine.

There were five long tables in the hall, laden with roast meat, fruit and countless delicacies. Attentive butlers and serving staff moved everywhere, offering platters and topping up glasses. Stern members of the house militia in green and brocade dress uniforms and polished silver helmets stood at every corner of the chamber.

We were on the third table, with a contingent of livestock merchants from Gallinatc, a city on Gudrun's southern continent. Our status afforded us the company of Lady Fabrina, Captain Terronce from the household guard, and a talkative man named Kowitz, a House Glaw official responsible for buying produce.

Lord Oberon and his brother, Urisel, presided over the head table, with their visiting cousin, the ship master Locke and an elderly ecclesiarch called Dazzo. Kowitz was happy to tell me that Ecclesiarch Dazzo represented a missionary order from the sub-sector edgeworld Damask, which House Glaw was sponsoring.

In fact, it was difficult to shut Kowitz up. As the butlers refilled his cup, he rattled on, identifying the other parties of guests. House Glaw had interests on worlds throughout the sub-sector, and regular banquets such as this oiled the wheels and kept things moving.

Eventually, I managed to hand Kowitz off to Aemos, the only man I knew capable of out-talking him. The two fell to complex discussion of the sub-sector balance of trade.

I kept a close eye on the head table. Urisel Glaw, a bloated, thick-set man in bejewelled ceremonial battledress, was giving Gorgone Locke plenty of attention. I watched Urisel closely. There was something about the man, not the least that his wide, puffy face and slick, lacquered hair made his resemblance to portraits of his infamous ancestor Pontius uncanny. He drank unstintingly, and laughed a wet, loose laugh at the ship master's jokes. His fat, powerful fingers constantly pulled at the braided collar of his uniform jacket to ease his wide neck.

Lord Oberon was a taller, leaner man with generous, cliff-like cheekbones rising above a forked goatee. The familial characteristics of the Glaw line were plain in his physiognomy, but he was more regal and distinguished, and lacked the dissolute languor of his younger sibling. Lord Glaw spent the night chatting happily with his off-world cousin, a bumptious young cretin with a whooping laugh and flamboyant courtly manners. But his real interest seemed to lie with the quiet ecclesiarch, Dazzo.

I took note of the ship master too. Gorgone Locke was a raw-boned giant with hooded, sunken eyes. He had long red hair, tied back and beaded, and his jutting chin was peppered with silver stubble. I wondered about his ship, and his business. I would contact Maxilla and make enquiries.

The banquet lasted until past midnight. As soon as was polite, we retired to our rooms.

The Glaws had given us a suite of rooms in the west wing. Outside, the wind had got up, and was making plaintive sighs down the old chimney flues and open grates. Rain pattered against windows, and doors and shutters twitched and knocked in the drafts.

Heldane was alone in the suite's sitting room when we came back. He had several data-slates open for study on a table and looked up as we came in.

'Well?' I asked him.

He and Betancore had run sweeps of the immediate wing whilst we had been dining. He showed me the results. Most of the rooms were spy-wired with vox-thieves and a few pict-sensors, and there was a complex infrastructure of alarm systems. Heldane had set up a small jammer to blind the spy-ware in our suite.

'Comparisons,' he said, showing me an overlay of two charts on a data-slate. 'The green areas show the parts of the buildings my master gained access to during his visits.' Voke had been obliging enough to supply me with reports of his inspections.

'We can overlay in red the results of the sweeps your man and I have managed to make this evening.'

There were considerable discrepancies. Voke may have opened every door he could find, but this showed me ghost areas that he had not gained access to because he hadn't known they were there.

'These are cellars?' I asked.

'Underground rooms, certainly.' said Heldane. He had a soft, sickly voice that seemed to seep from his slit-like mouth. 'Adjoining the wine vaults.'

The drapes billowed in as an exterior window opened. Betancore, his hooded black bodyglove wet with rain, climbed inside. He pulled off his grip-gloves and boots, and unstrapped his equipment harness.

'What did you find?'

Dripping and cold, he took a glass of spirits Bequin brought him and showed me his scanner pad.

'The roof is lousy with alarms. I didn't dare probe too far, even with my jammers and sensors. There are rooms under the east wing that Inquisitor Voke didn't know about. A network of tunnels seems to link them to the west wing under the courtyard.'

I spent a few more minutes running through the details, and then went into my room to change.

I put on a heat-insulated bodyglove of matt-black plastic weave with a tight-fitting hood and supple gloves. Then I strapped a webbing harness around my torso and filled the integral pouches with a compact scope, a set of multi-keys, a folding knife, two spools of monofilament wire, a tubular torch, two jamming units and a scanner pad. I secured my vox-unit's earpiece under my hood, buckled an autopistol into the rig strapped across my chest, dropped two spare clips into a thigh pouch, and finally placed my inquisitorial rosette in my hip pocket.

This was an endeavour that risked discovery. The rosette would be my joker, to be played if it became necessary.

I went back into the sitting room and laced on the grip-gloves and grip-boots that Betancore had been using.

'If I'm not back in a hour, you can start to worry,' I told them.

Outside, blackness, rain and the assault of the wind.

The outside wall of the great house was soaked and old, the limewash crumbling in places. I had to test every move I made to make sure the overlapping teeth of the grip-pads on my hands and feet were secure.

I moved along the side of the house, feeling my way, until I was able to crouch on an outcrop of guttering. I'd taped Betancore's data-slate to my left forearm for easy reference. The tiny backlit screen showed a three-dimensional model of the building, and an inertial locator built into the slate moved the map and kept my current location centred.

Over the downpour, I heard feet crunching gravel two storeys below. I clung to the bricks and tapped off the slate so that the screen glow wouldn't give me away.

Two men from the house militia huddled in foul-weather capes passed below me, lit by the windows on the ground floor. They took shelter in a doorway porch and shortly after that I saw the flash of an igniter or match. Presently, the cloying odour of obscura drifted up to me.

They were almost directly below my perch and I didn't dare move until they were gone. I waited. My joints were going numb from the cold and from the hunched position I had been forced to adopt simply to stay on the gutter.

The rain grew still heavier and the wind swished the invisible trees of the steep woods behind the house. I could hear the men chatting. An occasional laugh.

This wouldn't do. I was losing time and the feeling in my legs.

I focused, drew in a calming breath and reached out with the will.

I found their minds, two warm traces in the cold below me. They were soft and blurred, their responses undoubtedly slowed by the opiate effects of the obscura. Difficult minds to plant strong suggestions in, but vulnerable to paranoia.

I drove in with the will, toying gently with their anxieties.

Within seconds, they started from the cover of the porch, hissing animatedly at each other, and headed off at a trot across the yard.

Relieved, I moved down the wall, bracing my weight against a jutting window ledge as I found footholds around a down-pipe bracket.

On the ground, I hugged the shadows of the west wing, and moved down the yard. Betancore's careful reconnaissance had shown up laser trips around the gatehouse, and others that extended from the edges of the border beds to the basin of a fountain in the yard. Though I could not see them, they were precisely marked on the slate, and I simply stepped over each in turn, all except the last, which ran at waist height and which I ducked under.

My goal was the launch hangars on the far side of the rear yard. The sweeps had shown up an access point to the cellar network there. Betancore had located others, but they were all in private areas of the house, or in staff sections such as the scullery, the cold store and the meat pantries.

The shutter doors of the launch hangars were closed, and the lights off within. I gripped my way up the outside stone, and up along the shallow tiled roof. At the summit of each hangar roof was a metal box-vent designed to expel exhaust fumes. With my folding knife, I prised a louvred metal panel away and slid into the duct, feet first.

The short metal funnel of the duct was open below me and I looked down at the top of a parked launch. A short drop and I was crouching on the back of the vehicle in the dim garage.

I got off the craft and went around behind it. A small wall-hatch led through into a servicing workshop, which then opened into a parts store. The ferrocrete floor was spotted with oil, and I had to move carefully in the dark to avoid knocking into obstructions such as lathes, tool-trolleys and dangling hoist chains.

I checked the slate. The access-way was at the rear of the parts store.

This door was taking itself much more seriously. A tamper-proof ceramite seal, a tumbler alarm and a keypad for entry-codes.

I sighed, though I hadn't expected this to be easy. I would need to tape a jammer to the latch to avoid tripping any alarm or access signal. Then it would be a job for the scanner to search and configure a usable code. Ten minutes' work if I was lucky. Hours if not.

I pulled off my grip gloves so I could more easily manipulate the tools, and paused. An idea struck me. My mentor, the mighty Hapshant, had lacked psychic skills of his own. A dyed in the wool monodominant, Emperor love him. But he had been a firm believer in gut-instinct. He told me a servant of the Emperor could do worse than trust a flash of instinct. In his opinion, the Emperor himself placed such feelings there.

I tapped the word 'daesumnor' into the pad. The lock cycled and the door opened.

A clean, warm, well-ventilated staircase, significantly newer than the main structures of the estate, took me down into the cellar system. There was a caged lamp every three metres down the wall. By the chart and my estimation, I was some ten metres underground, moving beneath the east wing. I removed my hood to hear better.

'Daesumnor' opened another hatch, and I entered a long hall with hatch-doors along one side. One stood open, and I could hear voices and smell smoke.

I edged along, and skirted the hatch so I could peer in.

'… secured with two weeks,' a voice was saying.

'Said that month ago!' another snorted. 'What's the matter, you trying to inflate your fee?'

The room was some kind of lounge or study. Books and slates were racked with archive-like precision in wooden stacks along the walls. Soft light glowed from pendant lamps, and also from a number of sealed, glass-topped caskets in front of the shelving. They reminded me of the protective, controlled environment units Imperial libraries used to display especially ancient and valuable texts.

The room was carpeted, and as I craned round, I could see four men sitting around a low table in throne-like armchairs. One had his back to me, but from the folds of his coat falling over the chair's arm, I was certain it was Urisel Glaw. Facing him, sitting back in his chair, was the ship master, Gorgone Locke. The other two I didn't know, but I had a feeling they'd both been at the dinner. They all had glasses of liquor and one of the unknown men was using a water-pipe to inhale obscura. Various objects lay on the table between them, some wrapped in velvet, others unwrapped and displayed. They looked like stone tablets, old relics of some sort.

'I'm just trying to explain the delay, Glaw,' Locke said. 'They're a difficult enough culture to deal with at the best of times.'

'That's why we pay you,' Glaw said with a scoffing laugh. He leaned forward and toyed with one of the tablets.

'But we won't stand much further delay. We've invested a great deal in this matter. Time, funds, resources. It's meant holding back or cancelling other enterprises, some of them very special to us.'

'You will not be disappointed, lord,' said the man with the narco-pipe. He was dressed simply in black, a slightly built, bald individual with watery blue eyes. 'The archaeoxenan provenance of these items speaks for itself. The saruthi are serious about their offer.'

Urisel started to reply and got to his feet. I ducked into cover and then moved away down the hall. Eyclone's code opened the door at the end and I crept through into a wide, circular vault. Two more hatches of regular pattern led off to either side. Ahead of me was a larger archway protected by a force screen instead of a door.

I backed into hiding alongside this opening as someone cancelled the force screen from inside. A figure stepped out, turning to raise the screen again. It was Kowitz.

I took him from behind, an arm locked around his throat to silence him, another hand pinning his right arm. He gurgled and struggled. I twisted him round and slammed his head against the doorframe.

Kowitz went limp. I dragged him in through the open force-portal. A control on the inner wall raised the screen again.

The chamber was long with a low ceiling. The climate-controlled air was dry. I realised it was a chapel of sorts, a stone-floored, rectangular nave leading to a shape that seemed to me an altar. The room was otherwise bare of features, even seats or pews. Light glowed from recessed lamps in the roof. Leaving Kowitz on the floor, I strode down the length of the chapel and took a closer look at the altar.

It was two metres high, black, fashioned from a single piece of obsidian. The glassy stone seemed to glow with an internal light. On top of it was a jewelled prayer box about thirty centimetres square. I lifted the lid carefully with the blade of my knife-tool. In a bed of velvet lay an intricate sphere. It looked like a jagged lump of quartz, the size of a clenched fist, inlaid with gold circuits and complex woven wires, like an oversized uncut gemstone in a bizarre, ornate setting.

I spun around at a sound from behind me.

Kowitz, blood dripping from his dented forehead, stood pointing a laspistol at me. His face was pale, angry, confused.

'Step away from the Pontius, scum,' he said.

ELEVEN

REVELATIONS
THE NOBLE SPORT
PACIFICATION 505

This was no place to be trapped. I dug into my reserves of concentration, and without any physical movement, struck him clean between the eyes.

A psychic goad like that, especially at close range and with a clear line of sight, should have felled him like a force hammer. Kowitz didn't even blink.

'Don't make me repeat myself,' he said, raising the weapon so it pointed at my head.

The room was psychically shielded, it had to be. Either that or something was leeching psychic energies out of the very air.

'There's been a misunderstanding, Kowitz,' I said. 'I went for a walk and must have taken a wrong turn.'

It was pretty lame, but I wanted to keep his responses engaged and his mind busy.

'I don't think so,' he hissed. He was groping behind himself with his free hand, trying to find the control panel for the entrance. There was an alarm stud on it.

I waited. At any second, he was going to glance round involuntarily to help his fumbling.

When the gesture came, I threw myself forward and down, pulling my autopistol.

He looked back with a cry and fired, but his aim was too high and the shot flared off the end wall.

From a prone stance, I punched two shots through his left collar bone, and threw him back against the force door, which crackled at the impact.

Kowitz collapsed face down on the floor and blood began to pool around him.

I reached the door control. An amber rune was flashing. The bastard had managed to press something. I hit the force door deactivator.

Nothing.

I punched 'daesumnor' into the key pad.

Nothing.

I realised I was in deep trouble.

I guessed that Kowitz had hit an alarm that locked everything out. That was what prevented me from opening the door.

Urisel Glaw and several of his house militia appeared outside the shimmering force door. I could see them peering in and shouting.

I backed from the doorway and snatched up Kowitz's laspistol. When the door opened, I would use both guns to take down anything that tried to get in.

Then something psychic, dark and monstrously powerful rushed into my mind from somewhere behind me and I blacked out.

A face was looking down at me as I came round. A handsome face with blank eyes. The face started to say something. Then it combusted and melted away, and I realised it was just a dream. And I awoke properly, into a world that was nothing but pain.

'Enough. Don't kill him,' said a voice. Another voice laughed, and a tremor of acute agony peeled through my forebrain, lungs and gut.

'Enough, I said! Locke!'

A mild, disappointed curse. The agony receded, and I was left with numbness and throbbing background pain.

I was spreadeagled, my wrists and ankles bitten by the manacles that locked me to a massive hardwood cross. They'd taken my equipment, harness, hood, earpiece, and everything else except the leggings of my bodyglove and my boots. What could only be dried blood caked my lips, mouth, chin and throat, and fresh blood still drooled from my nose.

I opened my eyes. A meaty fist was holding my Inquisitorial rosette in front of my face.

'Recognise this, Eisenhorn?'

I spat blood.

'Thought you'd wile your way in among us and then produce this crest and make us all cower in fear?'

Urisel Glaw took the rosette away and peered down into my face.

'Doesn't work that way with the House of Glaw. We're not afraid of your kind.'

'Then you... are very foolish indeed,' I said.

He slammed my head back into the cross with an open-palmed blow to my forehead.

'You think your friends are going to help you? We've rounded them all up. They're just down the cell-block yonder.'

'I'm perfectly serious,' I said. 'Others know I'm here. And you really don't want to be messing with a servant of the Inquisition, no matter how much at your mercy you think he is.'

Glaw hunched down in front of me, his hands steepled. 'Don't worry. I don't underestimate the Inquisition. I'm just not afraid of it. Now, there are some questions I'd like answers to...'

He got up and moved back. I saw the filthy stone of the cell-chamber we were in, a double-locked hatch up in one corner at the head of a flight of stone steps. Lord Oberon Glaw and the obscura pipe-smoker from the library room stood at the foot of the steps, watching intently. The ship master, Gorgone Locke, sat astride a dirty wooden bench near by. He wore some strange apparatus on his right hand, a glove of segmented metal that ended each digit with a needle-like spike.

'You've got it wrong, Glaw. It's you who will provide the answers.'

Urisel Glaw nodded to Locke, who got up and moved towards me, flexing the needle glove.

'That is a strousine neural scourge. Our friend Mr Locke is quite an expert in its application. We were delighted when he volunteered to run this interrogation.'

Locke grabbed me by the throat with his bare hand, twisted my head up and his gloved fist disappeared out of my field of view below.

A second later, and cold lances of pain threaded my lungs and heart, and my windpipe went into spasm. I began to choke.

'Educated man like you knows all about pressure points,' Locke said, conversationally. 'So do the strousii. But they like to do more than tap them – they like to burn them out. I studied with one of their sacred torturers for a year or so. This grip, for example, the one that's choking you. It's also paralysing your respiratory system, and stopping your heart.'

I could barely hear him. Blood was drumming in my ears and explosive light and colour patterns were fogging my vision.

He withdrew his glove. The pain and choking stopped.

'Just like that, I can stop your heart. Burst your brain. Blind you. So play along.'

With all the strength I could muster, I smiled and told him his sister had particularly commended my love-making skills over his.

The glove gripped my face and needles lanced into my cheeks. I blacked out again for a moment.

'...haven't killed him!' I heard Locke hiss as consciousness swam back. Dull pain oozed through my face.

'Look at him! Look at him! Where's that cocksure smile now, you little bastard?'

I didn't answer.

Locke leaned close so his brow pressed against mine and his eyes were all I could see. 'Needlework,' he snarled, his foul, obscura-flavoured breath swamping my gasping mouth. 'I just lanced a few points in your face. You'll never smile again.'

I thought about telling him I didn't see a lot to smile about, but I didn't. Instead, I lunged forward and bit into his mouth.

His scream, transmitted by our contact, shook my jaws. Blood spurted. Fists struck repeatedly and desperately against my skull and neck. His long red hair came loose and the beaded ends whipped about my head. At last, he tore away, roaring. I retched out a mouthful of blood and a good fleshy lump of his lower lip.

His gloveless hand clamped around his torn mouth, Locke stumbled back, enraged, and then hurled himself at me. He kicked hard into my belly and hip, and punched me in the cheek so forcefully, it nearly snapped my spine apart.

Then I felt the needles stab in between my ribs on my left side, and breathless agony enfolded me.

Locke was screaming obscenities into my face. Once again, pain blacked me out.

I came back in a rush of excruciating discomfort and gasping breath as Urisel wrenched Locke off me and threw him across the cell.

'I want him alive!' Urisel bawled.

'Look what he did!' Locke complained incoherently through blood and torn lips.

'You should have been more careful,' said Oberon Glaw, stepping forward. He leaned down to study me, and I gazed back into his haughty, leonine face, bearded, powerful, commanding.

'He's halfway to death,' Oberon said with annoyance. 'I told you fools I wanted answers.'

'Ask me yourself,' I gasped.

Lord Oberon raised his eyebrows and stared at me. 'What brought you to my house, inquisitor?'

'The Pontius,' I replied. It was a gamble, and I wasn't hopeful, but there was always a chance that the very word might auto-slay them as it had done Saemon Crotes in the Sun-dome on Hubris. As I suspected, it didn't.

'You came from Hubris?'

'I stopped Eyclone's work there.'

'It was aborted anyway.' Lord Oberon stepped back from me.

'What is the Pontius?' I asked, trying and failing to focus my will. The pain in my body was overpowering.

'If you don't know, I'm hardly going to tell you,' said Oberon Glaw.

He looked round at Urisel, Locke and the pipe-smoker.

'I don't think he knows anything about the true matter. But I want to be certain. Can you be trusted to work efficiently, Locke?'

Locke nodded. He approached me again, flexing the needle glove, and slid a needle into my head behind my ear.

My skull went numb. It became almost impossible to concentrate.

'My index needle is lancing right into your parieto-occipital sulcus,' Locke crooned in my ear, 'directly influencing your truth centre. You cannot lie, no matter what. What do you know of the true matter?'

'Nothing...' I stammered.

He jiggled the needle and pain ignited inside my head.

'What is your name?'

'Gregor Eisenhorn.'

'Where were you born?'

'DeKere's World.'

'Your first sexual conquest?'

'I was sixteen, a maid in the scholam...'

'Your darkest fear?'

'The man with blank eyes!'

I blurted out the last. All were true, all involuntary, but that last one surprised even me.

Locke wasn't finished. He jiggled the needle, and pierced the back of my neck with others so that my body went into paralysis and ice flowed down my veins.

'What do you know of the true matter?'

'Nothing!'

Without wanting to, I began to weep with the pain.

Gorgone Locke continued to question me for four hours... four hours that I know about. Beyond those I recall nothing.

I woke again, and found myself lying on a cold rockcrete floor. Lingering pain and fatigue filled every atom of my being. I could barely move. At that time in my life, I had never felt such an extremity of pain and despair. I had never felt so close to death.

'Lie still, Gregor... you're with friends...' That voice. Aemos.

I opened my eyes. Uber Aemos, my trusted savant, looked down at me with a soulful expression even his augmetic eyes couldn't hide. He was bruised about the face and his good robe was torn.

'Lay still, old friend,' he urged.

'You know me, Aemos,' I said, and slowly sat up. It was quite a task. Various muscle groups refused to work, and I came close to vomiting.

I looked around blearily.

I was lying on the floor of a circular rockcrete cell. There was a hatch on one side, and a cage-gated exit opposite it. Aemos was crouched near me, and Alizebeth Bequin, her gown ripped and dirty, hunched behind him, staring over at me with genuine concern. Away across the cell stood Heldane, arms folded, and behind him cowered the guilder Macheles and the four other Guild Sinesias envoys who had escorted us. All of them looked pale and hollow eyed as if they had been weeping. There was no sign of Betancore.

Aemos saw my look and said, 'Aegis insubstantial, before the deluge' in perfect Glossia.

Which meant Betancore had somehow avoided the sweep that had incarcerated all my other companions. A tiny fragment of good news.

I got up, mainly thanks to my determination and the support of Aemos and Bequin. I was still stripped down to my leggings and boots, and my torso, neck, arms and head were washed in my own blood and stippled with bruised micro-puncture wounds. Gorgone Locke had been thorough.

Gorgone Locke would pay.

'What do you know?' I asked them as my breath returned.

'We're as good as dead,' Heldane said frankly. 'No wonder my master leaves this kind of work to you suicidal radicals. I just wish I hadn't agreed to join you.'

'Thank you for that, Heldane. Anyone else want to offer something less editorial?'

Aemos smiled. 'We're in a prison cell under the west wing, to the rear, almost under the woodlands. They burst into our quarters after you'd been gone three hours and seized us at gunpoint. I memorised a careful note of the route we were taking to this place, and have mentally compared it with Midas's map, so I'm fairly sure of our location.'

'What the hell did they do to you?' Bequin asked, dabbing at wounds on my chest with a strip of cloth torn from her gown.

Wincing, I realised that was why her gown was so shredded. She had been mopping my wounds while I was unconscious. A pile of torn and blood-soaked scads of material nearby stood testament to her devotion.

'They came here an hour ago and tossed you in with us. They didn't say anything,' Heldane added.

'Are you really an inquisitor, Sire Farchaval?' Macheles asked, stepping forward.

'Yes, I am. My name is Eisenhorn.'

Macheles began to sob and his fellow envoys did the same.

'We are dead. You have taken us to our deaths!'

I felt some pity for them. Guild Sinesias was rotten to the core, and these men were corrupt, but they were only in this predicament because I had duped them.

'Shut up!' Heldane told them.

He looked round at me, and slid a tiny something from the cuff of his bodyglove. A small red capsule.

'What is it?'

'Admylladox, a ten gram dose. You look like you need it.'

'I don't use drugs,' I said.

He pushed it into my hand. 'Admylladox is a pain-killer and a mind clearer. I don't care if you do drugs or not, I want that in your system if that gate opens.'

I looked at the gate.

'Why?'

'Have you never been to a pit-fight?' he said.

The Glaws had got everything out of me they could. Now they wanted me dead. Me and my party.

And that meant sport.

The gate cranked open at what must have been dawn. Thin, grey light wafted in and was almost immediately replaced by hard, bright artificial luminescence.

House Glaw militiamen in body armour burst into our cell and drove us out through the gate with force shields and psyk-whips.

We were out in the open, blinking into the light, as the gate shut behind us.

I gazed around. A vast circular amphitheatre, enclosed by a dome high above, undoubtedly the golden dome we had seen on our approach. The floor of the pit was dank moss and earth, and lichen climbed the sheer sides of the ten-metre-high stone walls. Above the wall top, House Glaw and its guests sat in steep tiers, jeering down at us. I saw Urisel Glaw, Lord Oberon, Locke, Lady Fabrina, the ecclesiarch Dazzo, the pipe-smoking man. Terronce, the militia captain who had sat at our table during dinner, led an honour guard of nearly forty men of the retinue. All wore green armour, plumed silver helmets and all carried autoguns. More than two hundred baying members of the Glaw clan, house staff, militia and servants made up the rest of the crowd in the theatre. They'd been up all night, drinking and doing whatever other indulgence it took to turn them into hyperactive bloodthirsty hyenas by first light.

Ignoring the noise, I surveyed the compound. Breaks of trees sprouted at various places, and there were low outcrops of bare rock, giving the arena a sort of landscape.

Nearby stood a rack of rusty weapons. Macheles and his brethren had already rushed to it and taken blunt shortswords and toothless lances.

I went over and took a basket-hilted dagger and an oddly hooked scythe with a serrated inner blade.

I weighed them in my hands.

Heldane had taken a dagger and a long-hafted axe, Bequin a wicker shield and a stabbing knife. Aemos shrugged and took nothing.

The jeering and booing welled around us. Then it hushed and a chorus of gasps whispered from the auditorium.

The carnodon was six metres from nose to whipping tail. Nine hundred kilos of muscle, sinew, striped pelt and sawing tusks.

It came out from behind one of the clumps of trees, trailing a line of heavy chain behind it from its spiked collar, accelerated into a pounce and brought Macheles down.

Macheles, envoy of Guild Sinesias, screamed as he was destroyed. He screamed and shrieked far longer than seemed possible given the spurting body parts the carnodon was ripping away. It must have been my horrified imagination, but to me the screaming only stopped when he was a gnawed ribcage being shaken in the bloody moss by the vast predator.

The other envoys screamed and ran. One fainted.

'We're dead,' Heldane said again, raising his weapons.

I swallowed the capsule he had given me. It didn't make me feel much better.

Its huge bared mouth running with blood and its chain jingling, the carnodon turned on the other envoys.

Bequin shrieked.

A second carnodon sprang out of its trap towards us. It was slightly larger than the first, I noticed. It came right for me.

I stumbled and dived to my right and the feline dug its claws into the moss to arrest its pounce, overshooting and scrabbling round. Its trailing chain swished over my head. The creatures both made low, sub-sonic growls that shuddered in their cavernous throats and thumped the air.

The larger beast swung around and made for me again even as I regained my feet and leapt backwards. Heldane ran in from the side while its attention was on me, and hacked into its flank with the blade of his axe.

The carnodon issued a strangulated hiss and lashed around, hurling Voke's man across the arena, the clothing of his torso shredded by deep parallel claw marks. I jumped away and got a few of the twisted trees between it and myself.

The first carnodon had brought down another of the envoys. The shock of the impact and the crippling wounds simply silenced the man and he uttered no sound as his limp body was thrashed and worried.

The creatures were hungry, that much was evident from their prominent ribs. One factor in our favour then... when the carnodons brought down prey they were primarily interested in consuming it. The long chains secured them to ground spikes next to their traps, and allowed them free movement anywhere in the pit. Clearly the chains were measured carefully to prevent them leaping clear of the pit into the crowd.

Tail slashing back and forth, the larger predator circled the edge of the arena-bowl, its dark, deep-set eyes surveying the humans in range. Bequin had dug herself and Aemos into a corner, using her frail shield and a wall buttress as cover for them both, but the ruthless crowd were pelting them with coins and bottles and pieces of food to drive them out. They wanted sport. They wanted blood.

The circling carnodon, barking vapours of breath and spittle from its dripping snout, came round and began to accelerate towards Bequin and Aemos. Its pouncing mass alone would kill them, I was certain. I ran out from cover to intercept it side on, and the crowd whooped and stamped.

It faltered in its run up as it became aware of me rushing it from the flank, and started to turn as I cut in with the scythe. The old hook planed matted fur from its shoulder blade and left a long red scratch down its ribs. It turned hard to face me. A paw lashed out, jabbing. I jumped back, swung again, hoping to at least hit the huge paw, for its reach was far longer than mine. Then it threw itself forward, a throbbing roar welling from its throat.

I simply dropped on my back, stealing its chance to knock me down and shatter my bones. Then it was on me and over me, a paw crushing and slicing my chest, its head down, mouth open, reaching to bite off my face. Frantically, I thrust with my weapons, blind, and kicked up at its more vulnerable underside.

The weight was off me abruptly. The carnodon jerked away, making a terrible low moaning. My dagger was no longer in my hand.

The pommel was jutting down out of the beast's chin. The blade transfixed its mouth, pinning it closed. It pawed and tore at the weapon, trying to dislodge it, shaking its massive head like a horse bothered by a fly.

I got up. Blood ran from the fresh gashes on my chest. Heldane suddenly crossed my field of vision, his shredded tunic fluttering behind him. His axe came down square onto the great carnivore's back, cutting through the backbone with a loud crack. The carnodon went into spasms, thrashing and clawing, rolling in the dirt. Heldane brought the axe down again and stove in its skull.

The audience shook the pit with their howling. Missiles rained down on us. Heldane turned and looked at me with a murderous grin of triumph.

Then the huge weight of the other carnodon hit him from behind and flattened him face down into the arena floor.

It had finished with the other envoys, all except the one who had fainted, who still lay where he had fallen. It tore into the helpless Heldane, ripping his scalp, rending the flesh off his back.

With a guttural cry, I ran at it, caught it behind the ear with my scythe, and pulled. The curved blade hooked into the meat and I succeeded in yanking its head back for a second. Then a well-aimed bottle struck me on the side of the head and knocked me over. I lost my grip on the scythe.

The creature turned, leaving Heldane a mangled wreck, face down in the bloody soil. I scrambled back, kicking at it.

'Eisenhorn!' Bequin yelled, running forward on the other side. She threw her knife over the creature's back and I caught it neatly. Disturbed by her cry, the beast swung about and lashed at her, tearing the wicker shield into hanks of raffia and knocking her down.

I threw myself astride its back and thumped the dagger down repeatedly into its neck. The dagger barely seemed to bite into the thick hide.

It writhed, trying to throw me off. I saw the scythe dangling from its scalp behind the ear, grabbed it, and hooked the blade under its spiked collar.

The creature was frenzied now, pulling hard at its chain. I pushed the tooth of the dagger in through a link in the chain and down into its shoulder blade, then levered the weapon over with all the force I could muster.

The link twisted open. The chain parted.

The carnodon ran forward a few paces, bellowed, and lunged.

Effortlessly, it leapt up the side of the pit into the shrieking crowd. I was still attached to it by the scythe, the handle of which I clutched frantically. As we landed in the seating, I was thrown clear, and crashed down onto the frantic fleeing audience.

The beast was berserk. It tore into the crowd, hurling limp, mangled forms and gouts of blood into the air. The pandemonium shook the dome.

I got up, pushing away the individuals who fell and stumbled into me in their efforts to escape. Gunfire ripped out across the amphitheatre. In the higher stands, I could see the militia scrambling down, firing at the carnodon as Terronce and other men hustled towards the safety of a side exit. The militia's shots were hitting people in the crowd.

I jumped across the backs of several seats, and punched aside two servants who grabbed at me. On the steps of the seating tiers just above me, two household guards ran down, raising their autoguns to shoot at the creature loose in the crowd.

I felled one with a psychic lance powered by rage and adrenaline, and snatched his weapon from his hands. Before his companion could turn, I had blown him down the steps and over the rail into the pit with a short burst of gunfire.

I looked up at the seating where the Glaw nobles and their guests had been. Lord Glaw, Locke and the pipe-smoker had already disappeared and the guards were half-carrying Lady Fabrina and the ecclesiarch away. But Urisel Glaw was still there, bellowing at his men over the bloody tumult. He saw me.

'The Inquisition will show you no mercy,' I yelled at him, though I doubted he could hear.

Urisel stared down at me for a moment, then shouted some more oath-laden orders and turned his attention to the carnodon. It had ploughed beyond the common seating now and was disembowelling a member of the house militia. Multiple bloody gunshot wounds showed in its striped pelt.

Urisel snatched a hunting rifle that one of the men fetched for him. He took careful aim at the carnodon and fired.

The massive weapon roared and the huge bulk of the creature flipped over, its chest blasted open. Its falling bulk crushed the legs of a guard.

The crowd continued to flee, but the uproar decreased enough for me to notice that a series of bells had begun to ring. Metal bells, electrically triggered. From deeper in the vast mansion, other alarms sounded. Urisel lowered his rifle and gestured to some of his men to discover the meaning of the alarm. Those in the crowd not too far intoxicated or mindless with fear looked anxiously around.

There were distant, inexplicable sounds. I didn't wonder much about them. Urisel took aim again, at me this time.

I dived over and a section of wooden seats exploded.

I clambered up. Urisel was reloading the wide-bore hunting iron, and Terronce was heading down towards me, followed by other men.

Terronce fired. I aimed high and blew his head and his plumed silver helmet apart with another tight burst.

Urisel was about to fire again. He drew the hunting piece to his shoulder and found me in the crowd.

There was an abrupt, sizzling series of buzzing shots from somewhere behind me. Three of the militia guards at the pit rail juddered and fell, and Urisel Glaw was thrown backwards, his hunting rifle roaring as it fired wildly up into the dome. The crowd began to mob frantically again in a second, and the remaining soldiers swung their aim up, hunting for this new shooter.

I swept around and saw him at once. Midas Betancore, crouched up on the tiled slope of awning above the pit seating on the opposite side of the arena. His needle guns, one clutched in each hand, spat again, peppering the front stands with lethal shots. Members of the household and several more guards tumbled. One guard pitched over the rail and fell into the pit. Further along the front rail, the crowd's panic to get clear of the carnage turned into a stampede. The rail snapped and half a dozen pages and kitchen staff spilled down the side of the pit wall. One clung to a broken rail-end for a second before sliding off and dropping.

The remaining guards had found Midas now, and were firing up at the tiled awning with their autoguns. Tile chips exploded out in a haze of dust, but Midas was moving, sure-footed, along the terracotta shelf. Holstering his weapons, he slid down its length, grabbed the edge with both hands and executed a superb swing that carried him round and under the lip and into the emptying stands.

The guards tracked him, firing wildly, cutting down members of the screaming crowd.

I ran down to the rail. 'Cover! Cover!' I yelled down to Bequin and Aemos below. They were busy trying to drag Heldane's bloody form to the comparative safety of the pit wall. I ran to the nearby body of a guard and grabbed some more magazine clips from his harness.

A few shots whipped my way, but most were aimed across the pit at Midas. I took cover behind some seats and some of the carnodon's victims, and opened fire up at the stands, aiming short bursts at the militia. Return fire chopped my way and gobbets of wood and flesh sprayed up from my makeshift cover. Midas was moving again, his guns buzzing.

The alarms were still ringing, and now, behind them and the frenzy of the fleeing crowd, I could hear gunfire and the dull rumble of explosions.

Most of the arena had emptied now, except for the last handful of house guards trading gunfire across the pit with the stealthy Midas. The sounds of explosive fighting outside in the grounds and house were getting ever louder.

I reached the banks of seats where the masters of the house had sat. The Glaws and their honoured guests were now long gone. Urisel's hunting rifle lay on the ground, and blood flecked the seat. Midas had at least winged him with a needle round.

I pushed past the end of the seats and down into the stairwell, the autogun braced at my hip. The bodies of two staff members trampled in the press lay broken there.

Urisel Glaw had not gone far, bleeding badly from his shoulder wound. He heard me coming and staggered around, firing a small stub-pistol down the gloomy tunnel. Then he disappeared from view.

Gun-butt raised under my arm, I moved forward, searching the darkness of the dank stone tunnel. An opening to the left looked down into a stairwell that entered the cell bay below. To the right was a hatch that allowed access to the main house.

I pushed the hatch open with the barrel of the autogun.

Urisel came out of the cell-bay stairway, howling, and slammed into me from behind.

I hit the door frame face first, and the autogun fired off three shots as it twisted out of my grip.

Without even trying to turn, I doubled over and reached behind me, grabbing a fold of dress uniform cloth, and jerked Urisel Glaw around into the wall. He cried out.

I threw a left-handed punch that sent him reeling, then a right that smashed his teeth. He enveloped me in a bear hug and we stumbled back a few paces before I braced, kicked his legs out and jabbed a knuckle punch into his sternum.

The fight seemed to be out of him. I choked him with a clawing hand and cracked his skull back against the tunnel wall.

'There will be no redemption for you, sinner,' I spat into his bloody face, 'or your foul house! Use your last breaths wisely and unfold your truths to me, or the Inquisition will teach you pain that Gorgone Locke has yet to imagine!'

'You–' he gurgled through blood and spittle and flecks of shattered teeth, 'you cannot even begin to imagine the Imperial misery House Glaw will wreak. Our power is too great. We will pitch the bastard Emperor from his golden throne and make him grovel and feed upon excrement. The worlds of the Imperium will blister and burn before Oberon and Pontius. Exalted will be the Great Darkness of Slaanesh–'

I cared little for his heretical ramblings, but the mention of that daemon-blasphemy turned my stomach and chilled my heart. I knocked him down, and looked around for something with which to bind his wrists.

Beyond the tunnel, the House of Glaw shook as if caught in a war zone.

Midas Betancore appeared at the mouth of the tunnel, and saw me lashing Urisel Glaw to a heating pipe with lengths of awning cord. He holstered his needle pistols and walked down to join me. I heard him activate his vox-link and report his position. A curt response crackled back.

'What's going on?' I asked him.

'A Battlefleet Scarus naval action,' he replied smugly.

He'd been out in the dark when Glaw's men came to seize Aemos, Bequin and Heldane. I was, by then, two hours overdue, and he'd slipped away from our apartment to look for signs of me. The militia had fanned out through the estate searching for him, but Midas was the sort of man who wouldn't be found if he didn't want it to happen. He had avoided the hunting parties, broke into the house's communication annexe and sent a brief but comprehensive report in code directly to Commodus Voke in Dorsay.

Voke's response had been immediate and authoritarian. The Glaw family had forcibly detained a servant of the Imperial Inquisition and his associates. That was all the excuse Voke had needed.

His demands, which brooked no refusal, swept clean over the heads of Fleet Admiral Spatian and his officio, and went straight to the Lord Militant Commander himself. The Lord Militant had mobilised a detachment of naval security troopers into Voke's remit within half an hour.

As an inquisitor, I know I have the right and authority to demand such supportive responses myself, even from a Lord High Militant. And I have done, on a very few occasions. But I was still impressed by the respect and fear the old inquisitor conjured in men of such supreme rank.

A confident move like this was characteristic of Voke, characteristic of his crushing, heavy methods. He'd wanted the slightest reason to come down upon House Glaw with the proverbial wrath of Macharius, and I had given it to him.

My capture, at least. Part of me was certain this show of influence and authority was Commodus Voke's way of establishing himself as alpha male, inquisitorially speaking.

I didn't care. I was glad of it, in truth. The bloodshed in the arena might have broken us out, but without the assault, we'd have never made it out of the Glaw estate and the clutches of the militia alive.

The operation was coded 'Pacification 505,' 505 being the topographical signifier for House Glaw. The troops had run in before dawn in four armoured dropships, hugging the rolling terrain of the inland bluffs to avoid the more than competent sensor system of House Glaw.

The ships held off behind the neighbouring hills as the sun rose, about the time we were languishing in the cell, to allow a forward team of naval security troopers to run ahead on foot and cut holes, electronically, in the perimeter defences of the great house. By then, they were in range of Betancore's personal vox set, and he had fed them logistic information and an insider's view of the militia's deployment.

At approximately the same moment when the first carnodon had lunged up out of its trap, the dropships had spurred forward from behind a long finger of copse and came powering up the vale towards the house. The Imperial Light Intruder Frigate *Defence of Stalinvast*, retasked by Admiral Spatian on the Lord Militant's instruction to hold geosynchronous orbit above target/Glaw/505, had obliterated the launch hangars behind the yard with pinpoint strikes from its lance batteries.

Two dropships, rocketing smoke charges and antipersonnel grenades, had settled in front of the main house, blowing out all the windows. Forty black-armoured troopers from naval security had then made an assault landing and struck at the main facade. Bewildered, more than seventy men of the house militia had attempted to repel them.

The other two dropships circled behind the house and spilled their troops into a landing yard still lit by the blazing ruins of the launch block. Within three minutes a running gun battle was shuddering down the halls and corridors of House Glaw. The alarms were ringing soundly by then.

House Glaw owned close on four hundred fighting men in its retinue, not to mention another nine hundred staff, many of whom took up weapons. Glaw Militia were all trained men, veterans, well armoured in green ballistic cloth and silver helmets, well equipped with autoguns, heavy stubbers and grenades. An army, by most standards. I know more than one commander in the Imperial Guard who has taken cities, whole planets indeed, with such a number. And they had the advantage of home soil. They knew the layout, the strengths, the weaknesses, of the old estate.

Naval security took them apart. The elite of Battlefleet Scarus, armed with matt-black hell-guns and iron discipline, they conquered and purged the great house room by room.

Some pockets of resistance were heavy. The troopers lost three men in a virtually point-blank firefight around the kitchen area. A suicide run by two Glaw soldiers laden with tube charges vaporised another four and took twenty metres off the end of the east wing

Twenty-two minutes after the assault began, the militia had lost nearly three hundred men.

Numerous householders and low-ranking staff fled into the woods and valleys behind the house. A few made good their escape. Most were rounded up, and more than thirty killed by the tightening circle of Imperial Guard cordoning the estate. These men, two thousand of them, were recruits from the founding, Gudrunite riflemen roused from the barracks and shipped inland to experience a surprise taste of combat before ever leaving their birthworld.

The bloody resistance of the Glaw militia was mainly intended to give their nobles time to flee. The Glaws' off-world cousin and his retinue were cornered by the Gudrunite Rifles on the back path behind the house, arrested, and then massacred when they tried to fight their way out. Other traders and guests from the dinner surrendered to the enclosing forces.

Several orbital craft broke from the tree cover behind the main attack, launching from secret hangars in the woods behind the house. One was hammered out of the air by a trooper with a rocket launcher. Another two made it five kilometres down the valley before they were incinerated from above by the watchful *Defence of Stalinvast.*

Another, a fast and heavily armoured model, evaded the cover sweep and headed west. The *Defence of Stalinvast* launched a trio of fighters after it, and they eventually brought it down in the open sea after a lengthy chase. Only weeks of forensic recovery might reveal who had been aboard any of those craft, and there was no guarantee that an answer would be forthcoming even then. Smart money was on the likes of Lord Glaw, Lady Fabrina, Gorgone Locke, Dazzo the Ecclesiarch and the nameless pipe-smoking man. Certainly, none of those persons were among the anguished scum rounded up by the Guard or by naval security.

Ninety minutes after it had begun, Pacification 505 was signalled as 'achieved' by Major Joam Joakells of naval security.

Only then did the launch carrying Commodus Voke move in.

TWELVE

IN THE RUINS OF THE GREAT HOUSE
MURMURINGS
UPRISING

It was noon, but the night storm had persisted, and the fitful rain washed the colour out of the sky and doused the burning sections of House Glaw. A terrible, blackened ruin, it stood on the hilltop, its windows burned out, its roofs ragged, tiled lengths of beam, billowing grey and white smoke.

I sat in the yard, leaning back against the mudguard of an Imperial Guard troop carrier, sipping occasionally from a cut-glass decanter of amasec. My head was bowed. I needed medical attention and painkillers, a psychic restorative, a good meal, neural surgery to the hundreds of wounds Locke had inflicted, a bath, clean clothes...

More than anything else, I needed a bed.

Troops marched past, crunching their boots in time on the wet stone. Orders sang back and forth. Occasionally, a fighter ship made a pass overhead and vibrated my diaphragm with the throb of its afterburner.

My head swam. Fragments gathered and conflated in my unconscious and spilled over. Each time, I shook myself awake. The blank-eyed man was there, in the back of my head. I didn't want to think about him, and saw no place in this event for him, but his image lingered. Once, I was certain, he was standing across the yard from me, by the scullery door, smiling at me. I blinked him away.

I was still caked in blood, sweat and filth. Pain and fatigue clung to me like a shroud. A corporal from the naval security detail had recovered our confiscated possessions from Urisel Glaw's apartment, and I had pulled on a shirt and my button-sleeved leather coat. The trooper had handed me my Inquisitorial rosette, and I clutched it now, like a totem.

Eager men of the 50th Gudrunite Rifles jostled Glaw House staff through the yard. The prisoners had their hands behind their heads, and some were weeping.

Somebody slid down next to me on the cold flagstones and leaned back against the greasy track assembly of the carrier.

'Long night,' Midas said.

I passed the decanter to him, and he took a long swig.

'Where's Aemos? The girl?'

'Last I saw, the savant was bustling around somewhere, making notes. I haven't seen Alizebeth since we freed them from the pit.'

I nodded.

'You're half-dead, Gregor. Let me call up a launch and get you to Dorsay.'

'We're not done here,' I said.

Procurator Madorthene saluted me as he approached. He wasn't wearing his starchy white dress uniform now. In the coal-black armour of naval security, he looked bigger and more commanding.

'We've made a body exam,' he said.

'Oberon Glaw?'

'No trace.'

'Gorgone Locke? The churchman Dazzo?'

He shook his head.

I offered him the decanter with a sigh. To my surprise, he took it, sat down with us and drank a mouthful.

'They're all probably cinders in the craft that tried to escape,' he said. 'But I'll tell you this. Before it torched the two boats running the valley, the *Defence of Stalinvast* was sure it read no life signs.'

'Decoys,' said Betancore.

'The Glavian is right, for my money,' he said. Then he shrugged. 'But good armour can rob away signals. We may never know.'

'We'll know, Madorthene,' I promised him.

He took another tug on the decanter, handed it back to me and rose, brushing down his seamless armour.

'I'm glad naval security could serve you here, Inquisitor Eisenhorn. I hope it's restored your faith in the battlefleet.'

I looked up at him with a weak nod. 'I'm impressed you came to oversee yourself, procurator.'

'Are you kidding? After what happened on the *Essene*, the admiral would have had my head!'

He walked away. I liked him. An honest man doing his best amid the conflicting political interests of battlefleet command and the Inquisition. In later years, I would come to value Olm Madorthene's honesty and discretion immeasurably.

A fragile hunched figure clomped across the yard and stood over me.

'Now whose methods seem wise?' Commodus Voke asked, with a sneer.

'You tell me,' I replied, getting up.

Voke had brought a staff of nearly fifty with him, all clad in black robes, many with augmetic implants. They stripped the noble house of every shred of evidence they could find. Crates of papers, books, slates, artefacts and pict-tiles were carried out to waiting transports.

I was in no mood to argue. Pain and fatigue made my senses swim. Let Voke use his vast retinue and resources to do the painstaking work of recovery.

'Much has been deleted, dumped or burned,' a dour-faced savant called Klysis reported to Voke, as I walked with my fellow inquisitor into the shattered house. 'Much else is encrypted.'

We progressed into the basement system, and I led Voke to the force-shielded chamber where Glaw had trapped me. Kowitz's blood still marked the floor. The artefact from the altar plinth was gone.

'He referred to it as the Pontius,' I told Voke. The room no longer showed signs of being psychically shielded, so logic said the psyker-effects had been generated by the Pontius itself. As had the mental attack that had felled me, I was sure.

I leaned against the chamber wall and patiently told Voke the key points I had learned. 'Eyclone's mission to Hubris, involving the Pontius, was clearly important to them, but Oberon Glaw told me explicitly that said endeavour had been aborted... cancelled because something more vital had come into play. They referred to it as the true matter.'

'It would explain why your foe Eyclone was abandoned,' he mused. 'After all his preparations, the Glaws failed to deliver the Pontius as they had promised.'

'That fits. Dazzo and the shipmaster Locke were clearly deeply involved in this true matter. We need to establish more facts about them. I'm certain the work that concerned them touched on some archeoxenon material. They mentioned the "saruthi".'

'A xenos breed, outlying the sub-sector,' said Voke's savant. 'Little is known of them and contact is forbidden. The Inquisition holds several investigations pending, but their space is uncharted, and while they keep themselves to themselves, more urgent matters have caused investigations to be postponed.'

'But a rogue like Locke may well have established lines of contact with them.'

Klysis and Voke both nodded. 'It will bear further research,' Voke said. 'Ordo Xenos must begin a survey of the saruthi. But for now, the matter is closed.'

'How do you reason that?' I asked with a contemptuous laugh.

Voke fixed me with his beady eyes. 'House Glaw is destroyed, its principal members and co-conspirators are slain. With them are lost the items precious to their cause. Whatever they were planning is finished.'

I didn't even begin to argue with the old man. Voke was sure of his facts. His main failing, in my opinion.

He was wrong, of course. The first hint came ten days later. I had returned to Dorsay with my colleagues, and had spent some time in the care of the Imperial Hospice on the Grand Canal where my many wounds and injuries were treated. Most of the cuts and gashes were superficial, and would heal in time. Locke's work on me had left deeper scars. Multiple neural injuries afflicted my system, many of which would never repair. Augmeticists from the battlefleet's Officio Medicalis conducted micro-surgery on shredded nerve transmitters in my spine, thorax, brainstem and throat. They implanted more than sixty sections of artificial nerve fibre and ganglions. I had lost a good deal of sensitivity in my palette and oesophagus, and the reflexes on the left side of my body were dulled. My face they could do nothing with. Neural systems there had been utterly scourged. Locke's promise had been lasting. I would never smile again, nor make much of any expression. My face, impassive, was now just a mask of flesh.

Aemos visited me every day, and brought more and more data-slates and old books to my private room in the Hospice. He had established a working relationship with Voke's savants (Klysis was but one of seventeen employed by Commodus Voke), and was sifting data as it was passed to him. We tried to source information concerning the Glaws' confederates, but there was damnably little, even with Voke's platoon of savants hard at work. Locke was a shadowy, almost mythical figure, his name and reputation well known throughout the Helican sub-sector, but nothing could be found about his origin, career, associates or even the name of his vessel. Dazzo also drew a blank.

The Ecclesiarchy had no record of a churchman of that name. But I remembered what Kowitz had told me during the banquet, that Dazzo had links to a missionary order sponsored by the Glaws on the edgeworld Damask. Damask was a real place, right enough, a harsh frontier planet at the very limit of the Helican sub-sector territory, one of a hundred worthless, seldom-visited places. Astrogeographically, it lay just a few months passage spinward of the uncharted regions of the mysterious saruthi.

Lowink accompanied Aemos on one of his visits as soon as I was strong enough, and extracted from my mind a likeness of the pipe-smoking man, which he realised psychometrically on an unexposed pict-plate. The image, a little blurred, was good enough, and it was copied and circulated through all branches of the investigating authorities. But no one could identify him.

Lowink recovered an image of the Pontius too, by the same means. This baffled all who viewed it, except Aemos who immediately confirmed that the strange artefact was precisely the correct size and dimensions to fit into the cavity in Eyclone's casket, the one recovered from Processional Two-Twelve. As we had conjectured, this was what Eyclone had been awaiting, what the mass-murder in the Hubris ice tomb had been for.

'Urisel Glaw referred to Pontius as if he was still alive,' I said to Aemos. 'Certainly something with great psychic force felled me in the chamber where the Pontius was secured. Could he be alive, in some sense, some part of him, perhaps some psychic essence, captured in that device?'

Aemos nodded. 'It is not beyond the highest Imperial technologies to maintain a sentience after great physical injury or even death. But for such technologies to be within the grasp of even a mighty family like the Glaws...'

'You told me it resembled something of the mysteries of the Adeptus Mechanicus.'

'I did,' he pondered. 'It is most perturbatory. Could the foul crime of Hubris have been some effort to siphon vulnerable life energies into this artefact? To give the Pontius a massive jolt of power?'

On the third morning, Fischig visited. His own injuries were healed, and he seemed annoyed to have missed the episode at Glaw House. He brought with him a priceless antique slate, a collection of inspirational verse composed by Juris Sathascine, curate-confessor of one of Macharius's generals. It was a gift from Maxilla, from his private collection.

Delayed by the excitement of the Glaw incident, the founding resumed. The new Imperial guardsmen were shipped to troop transports in the orbiting fleet and the final ceremonies were carried out. The Lord Militant Commander was now anxious to begin his expedition into the troubled Ophidian sub-sector, and felt enough time and manpower had been spent on this little local matter.

On the tenth day, it didn't look so much like a local matter any more. Via astropathic link, news came of incidents throughout the sub-sector: a rash of bombings on Thracian Primaris; the seizure and destruction of a passenger vessel bound for Hesperus; a hive decimated by a viral toxin on Messina.

That evening, a brief, bright star suddenly ignited in the sky over Dorsay. The *Ultima Victrix*, a four hundred thousand tonne ironclad, had exploded at anchor. The blast had crippled four ships nearby.

An hour later, it became clear the incident had grown signally worse. Exactly how was not clear, even to battlefleet intelligence, but the explosion had been identified in error as a sign of an enemy attack by several components of the fleet. A frigate wing commanded by a captain called Estrum had moved to engage, and several destroyers from the advance phalanx had mistaken them for fleet intruders and opened fire. For twenty-seven hideous minutes, Battlefleet Scarus waged war against itself through the anchor lines of Navy vessels and troop ships. Six ships were lost. Eventually, apparently heedless of countermands, Estrum broke off and, with a mobile group of fifteen vessels, went to warp to outrun 'the enemy.' Admiral Spatian gave chase with a flotilla of eight heavy cruisers. The remaining fleet elements struggled to regain control and handle the wanton destruction.

The Lord High Militant, I learned, had a fit of rage so extreme he had to be sedated by his private physician.

'That doesn't just *happen*,' Betancore said. We sat in my private room, by the tall windows, looking out across the city. Ghost-flares of energy and explosion, one trailing down in the sky like a falling star, marked the night.

'Imperial battlefleets are among the most ordered and disciplined organisations in space. Confusion like that doesn't just happen.'

'Like deserters don't just get a hold of a ship and uniforms and know the name of the man whose ship they chance to board, you mean? Our unseen foe is making his influence felt. Voke talked about a parent cult, overseeing many small cells and cabals. He reckoned the Glaws were the masters of this conspiracy. I'm not so sure. There could be a yet higher authority at work.'

Urisel Glaw was held in the Imperial Basilica. He had undergone hours of intense interrogation and torture since his capture. And he had given up nothing.

I went to him that night. Voke and his interrogators were still at work, now with a sense of urgency.

They held him in what could only be described as a dungeon, ninety metres below the massive grey stone fortress. All the other prisoners taken during the raid on House Glaw were sequestered here too. In order to contain and interrogate them all, Voke had co-opted local Arbites, soldiers of the Gudrun standing army, and officials of the Ministorum. They worked in concert with his own extensive staff.

Arriving by air launch, I was met by a tall, grey-haired man in a long maroon coat attended by two armed servitors. I knew him at once. Inquisitor Titus Endor and I were of similar ages and had both studied under Hapshant.

'You are recovered, Gregor?' he asked, shaking my hand.

'Well enough to continue my work. I didn't expect to see you here, Titus.'

'Voke's reports on the Glaw case have concerned our order's sub-sector officio. Lord Inquisitor Rorken has declared the need for a full disclosure. Voke's inability to get anything out of Urisel Glaw has annoyed him. I've been diverted to assist. And not just me. Schongard is here too, and Molitor is on his way.'

I sighed. Endor, a fellow Amalathian, I could work with, though there is a proverb about too many inquisitors. Schongard was a rabid monodominant, and a liability in my view, and Konrad Molitor was the sort of radical I felt had no place in the order at all.

'This is unusual,' I said.

'It's all down to connections,' Endor remarked. 'What has come to light through your work here, and Voke's, is a massive puzzle that itself connects dozens of separate cases and investigations. I burned a heretic on Mariam two weeks ago, and in his effects found documents linking him to the Glaws. Schongard is pursuing blasphemous texts that he is certain first came into the sub-sector in the cargoes of Guild Sinesias traders. Molitor... well, who knows what he's doing, but it no doubt connects.'

'Sometimes,' I told him, 'I think we work against each other. This comes out and, look! We all hold pieces to the same mystery. How might we have taken this enemy and his structure apart a month ago, two months, if we had exchanged information?'

Endor laughed. 'Are you questioning the working practices of the most lauded Inquisition, Gregor? Working practices laid down centuries ago? Are you questioning the motives of fellow members of our convocation?'

I knew he was joking, but my manner remained serious. 'I'm decrying a system where we don't even trust each other.'

We descended, under escort, into the depths of the prison block.

'What of Glaw?'

'Gives up nothing,' said Endor. 'What he's endured so far would have broken and cracked most men, or at least had them begging for death or trying to kill themselves. He persists, almost in good humour, almost arrogant, as if he expects to live.'

'He's right. We'll never sign his death notice while he has secrets.'

Voke's men were at work on Glaw in a foul-smelling, red-painted cell. Glaw was a ruin, kept alive by expertise that matched the skill used to torture him.

To unlock an answer from the mind of the heretic is the greatest duty of an inquisitor, and I will not shrink from any means, but this way was futile. Left to me, the physical torture would have stopped days before. One look showed that Urisel Glaw was resolved not to talk.

I would have left him alone, for weeks perhaps. Despite his agonies, our constant attention betrayed our desperation, and that gave him all the strength he needed to endure. Silence and isolation would have broken him.

Inquisitor Schongard stepped back from the table where Glaw was strapped and pulled off soiled surgical gloves. He was a broad man with thin brown hair and a chilling mask of black metal surgically fixed to his face. No one knew if this mask covered some grievous injury or was simply an affectation. Dark, unhealthy, bloodshot eyes regarded Endor and myself through the oblong slits in the metal.

'Brothers,' he whispered. His phlegmy voice never wavered from that low, hushed level. 'His resistance is quite the doughtiest I have seen. Voke and I agree that some monumental work has been done to his mind, allowing him to block out the manipulations. Psychic probes have been tried, but found wanting.'

'Perhaps we should have the Astropathicus provide us with one of their primary class adepts,' said Voke from behind me.

'I don't think there's a mind block there at all,' I said. 'You would see traces of the conditioning. He'd most likely be screaming for us to stop now because he knows he cannot tell us the answer.'

'Nonsense,' whispered Schongard. 'No raw mind could withstand this.'

'I sometimes doubt whether my fellows know anything about human nature at all,' I said, mildly. 'This man is a fiend. This man is nobility. He has seen into the darkness we so fear, and he knows what power feels like. The promise of what lies at stake for him and his collaborators is enough to steel him.'

I crossed to the table and looked down into Glaw's lidless eyes. Blood bubbled at his flayed lips as he smiled at me.

'He promised the overthrow of worlds, the annihilation of billions. He boasted of it. What the Glaws are after is so great, that none of this matters. Isn't that right, Urisel?'

He gurgled.

'This is just a hardship,' I said, turning away from the heretic in disdain. 'He keeps going because he knows that what awaits him will make this all worthwhile.'

Voke snorted. 'What could be so?'

'Eisenhorn sounds convincing to me,' said Endor. 'Glaw will protect his secrets no matter what we do, for those secrets will repay him a thousand fold.'

Schongard's masked face shook dubiously. 'I am with brother Voke. What reward could be worth the prolonged ministrations of the Inquisition's finest fleshsmiths?'

I didn't answer. I didn't know the answer, in truth, but I had some notion of the scale.

And the thought of it froze my soul.

* * *

If I had harboured any doubts that the Glaws' authority had survived, they were dispelled in the course of the next week. Campaigns of explosive, toxic and psychic sabotage plagued the worlds of the sub-sector, as if all the secret, dark cells of evil hidden away within Imperial society were revealing themselves, risking discovery as they turned on their local populations, as if orchestrated by some ruling power. The likes of Lord Glaw and his accomplices had either escaped destruction or they were but part of an invisible ruling elite that now mobilised all the hidden offspring cabals on a double-dozen worlds into revolt.

'There is another explanation,' Titus Endor said to me as we attended mass in the Imperial Cathedral of Dorsay. 'For all their power and influence, the Glaws were not the summit of their conspiratorial pyramid. There were yet others above them.'

It was possible, but I had seen the Glaws' arrogance first hand. They were not ones to bow to another master. Not a human master, anyway.

The unrest had broken out on Gudrun too by then. A bombing campaign had stricken one town in the south, and an agricultural settlement in the west had been exterminated by a neural toxin released into its water supply. Battlefleet Scarus was still struggling to recover from the self-inflicted blow against it, and Admiral Spatian had returned from his mission to reassemble the panicked fleet units empty handed. Captain Estrum's mobile group had simply vanished. I had exchanged messages with Madorthene, who told me that no one in battlefleet command now doubted that the destruction of the Ultima Victrix and the subsequent mayhem had been anything other than sabotage. Our enemy's reach extended into the battlefleet itself.

Then two massive hives of Thracian Primaris rose in open revolt. Thousands of workers, tainted by the corrupt touch of Chaos, took to the streets, burning, looting and executing. They displayed the obscene badges of Chaos openly.

The Lord Militant's plans for a crusade into the Ophidian sub-sector were now indefinitely postponed. Battlefleet Scarus left anchor and made best speed to suppress the Thracian uprising.

But that was only the first. Open revolt exploded through the suburbs of Sameter's capital city and, a day later, a civil war erupted on Hesperus. In both cases, the stain of Chaos was there.

This miserable, shocking period is referred to in Imperial histories as the Helican Schism. It lasted eight months, and millions died in open warfare across those three worlds, not to mention hundreds of lesser incidents on other planets, including Gudrun. The Lord Militant got his holy crusade, though I am sure he hardly expected to be waging it against the population of his own sub-sector.

The authorities, and even my worthy fellow inquisitors, seemed stunned to the point of inactivity by this unprecedented outbreak. The archenemy of mankind often acted openly and brutally, but this seemed to defy logic. Why, after what may have been centuries of careful, secret establishment, had the hidden cults risen as one, exposing themselves to the wrath of the Imperial military?

I believed the answer was the 'true matter'. Urisel Glaw's almost gleeful resistance to our methods convinced me. The archenemy was embarked upon something so momentous that it was prepared to sacrifice all of its secret forces throughout the sub-sector to keep the Imperium occupied.

I believed, with all conviction, that it would be better for planets to burn than for that 'true matter' to be accomplished.

Which is why I went to Damask.

THIRTEEN

DAMASK
NORTH QUALM
SANCTUM

Under a leaden, rusty sky, the ball-tree forests followed the wind.

They looked like thick herds of bulbous livestock, surging across the rolling sweeps of scree, and the jostling, clattering noise they made sounded like hooves.

But they were trees: pustular, fronded globes of cellulose swelled by lighter-than-air gases generated from decomposition processes deep inside them. They drifted in the wind and dragged heavy, trailing root systems behind them. Occasionally, the pressure of one ball-tree against another caused a gas-globe to vent with a moaning squeal forced out through fibrous sphincters. Plumes of gas wafted above the tree herd.

I climbed to the top of a low plateau, where the bluish flint and gravel were caked in yellowish lichens. A couple of solitary ball-trees, small juveniles, scudded across the hill's flat summit. In the centre of the plateau's top stood a rockcrete pylon marker, commemorating the original landing place of the first settlers who had come to Damask. The elements had all but worn away the inscription. Standing by the marker, I slowly turned and took in the landscape. Black flint hills to the west, thick ball-tree forests in the wide river valley to the north, leagues of thorn-woods to the east, near to where we had set down, and grumbling, fire-topped volcanoes to the south, far away, sooting the sky with threads of sulphurous brown smoke. Clouds of small air-grazers circled over the forests, preparing to roost for the night. A surly, scarred moon was rising, distorted by the thick amber atmosphere.

'Eisenhorn,' Midas called over the vox.

I walked back down the plateau slope, buttoning my leather coat against the evening breeze. Midas and Fischig waited by the landspeeder that they had spent the past two hours unstowing and reassembling from the gun-cutter's hold. It was an old, unarmed model and it hadn't been used for three years. Midas was closing an engine cowling.

'You've got it working, then,' I said.

Midas shrugged. 'It's a piece of crap. I had to get Uclid to strip in new relays. All manner of cabling had perished.'

Fischig looked particularly unimpressed with the vehicle.

I seldom had a use for it. On most worlds, local transport was available. I hadn't expected Damask to be so... unpopulated.

Records said there were at least five colony settlements, but there had been no sign of any from orbit, and no response to vox or astropathical messages. Had the human population of Damask withered and died in the past five years since records were filed?

We'd left Aemos, Bequin and Lowink with the cutter, which had put down on the shores of a wide river basin. We'd carefully disguised it with camouflage netting. Midas had chosen a landing site within speeder range of some of the colony locations, yet far enough out to avoid being seen by anybody at those locations as we made descent. Tobias Maxilla awaited our pleasure aboard the *Essene* in high orbit above.

Midas fired up the speeder's misfiring engines and we moved off overland from the hidden cutter towards the last recorded position of the closest human settlement.

Tumble-brush scudded around the speeder, and we rode through scarpland where root-anchored trees spread aloft branches blistering with gas-sacks so that the whole plant seemed to strain against the soil and gravity in the wind. Grazers, little bat-like mammals with membranous wings, fluttered around. Larger gliders, immense headless creatures that were all flat wingspan and fluked tail, turned silently on the thermals high above us. The landscape was jagged, broken and had the bluish cast of flint. The air was dark and noxious, and we used rebreather masks from time to time.

We followed the frothy, brackish river waters for twenty kilometres and then left the wide flood banks and juddered up through rocky scarps, sculptural deserts formed by elementally shattered flint outcrops, brakes of dusty yellow fern, and seas of lichen trembling in the gusting wind. The ugly moon rose higher, though there was still daylight left.

Midas had to slew the speeder to a halt at one place where a group of much larger grazers broke across the trail, panicked by the sound of the engines. They were dove-grey giants with steep, humped backs, trunk-like snouts and long attenuated legs ending in massive pads. Their legs seemed too slender and long to support such bulks, but like the local plant life, I suspected the swollen torsos of these animals contained supporting bladders of gas.

They snorted and clattered away into the fern thickets. The speeder had stalled. Midas got out and cussed at the rotors of the turbo-fan for a few minutes until the mechanism chuckled back into life. As we waited, Fischig and I stretched our legs. He climbed up onto an igneous boulder and fiddled with the straps of his rebreather as he watched the hot blue streaks of a meteor storm slice the gloomy sky on the western horizon.

I gazed across the fern thickets. Air-grazers chirruped and darted in the hushing leaves. The wind had changed, and a forest-herd of ball-trees scudded in through the edges of the ferns, squeaking and rasping as the wind drove their globes and root-systems through the grounded plants.

We pushed on another ten kilometres, coming down into a rift valley where the ground became thick, sedimentary soil, black and wet. The vegetation here was richer and more rubbery: bulb snakelocks and bright, spiky marsh lilies, clubmoss, horsetail, tousled maidenhair, lofty cycads festooned with epiphytic bromeliads and skeins of ground-draping gnetophytes. Clouds of tiny insects billowed in the damper glades and along seeping watercourses, and large, hornet-like hunters with scintillating wings buzzed through the damp air like jewelled daggers.

'There,' said Fischig, his eyes sharp. We stopped and dismounted. A muddy expanse near the track had once been a cultivated field, and the rusty carcasses of two tilling machines lay half-buried in the sucking soil.

A little further on, we passed a marker stone struck from flint. 'Gillan's Acre' it read in Low Gothic.

We'd passed the township itself before we realised, and turned back. It was nothing but the stumps of a few walls covered with wispy weed-growth and rampant gnetophytes. Until at least five years before, this had been a community of eight hundred. A scan showed metal fragments and portions of broken machinery buried under the soil.

Fischig found the marker screened by sticky cycads at the north end of the town plot. It had been fashioned from local fibre-wood, a carved symbol that was unmistakably one of the filthy and unnerving glyphs of Chaos.

'A statement? A warning?' Fischig wondered aloud.

'Burn it immediately,' I told him.

The vox-link warbled. It was Maxilla, from orbit.

'I've been sectioning the landscape as you requested, inquisitor,' he reported. 'The atmosphere is hindering my scans, but I'm getting there. I just ran a sweep of the volcanic region south of you. It's hard to tell because it's active, but I think there are signs of structures and operating machines.'

He pin-pointed the site to the speeder's navigation system. Another seventy kilometres, roughly the location of another possible settlement listed on our maps.

'That's quite a distance, and the light is failing,' Midas said.

'Let's get back to the cutter. We'll head south at dawn.'

In the night, as we slept, something approached the shrouded cutter and set off the motion alarms. We went out, armed, to look for intruders, but there was no sign. And no sign of drifting ball-trees either.

At dawn, we headed south. The volcanic region, its smouldering peaks rising before us, was thickly forested with fern and thorn-scrub. It was hot too, as stinking, heated gas leaked into the glades from the volcanic vents that laced the rocky earth. A half-hour into the sulphurous forests we were sweating heavily and using our rebreathers almost constantly.

Below the peak of one of the largest cones, the landspeeder's rudimentary scanners detected signs of activity as we rode up a long slope of tumbled, desiccated rock. Fischig, Midas and I dismounted from the speeder and clambered up a flinty outcrop to get a better view with our scopes.

In the shadow of the cone was a large settlement... old stone and wood-built structures, mostly ruined, as well as newer, modular habitats made of ceramite. There was machinery down there, generators and other heavy systems at work under tarpaulin canopies. Tall, angled screens of reinforced flak-board had been erected on scaffolding rigs to shield the place from ash-fall. Three speeders and two heavy eight-wheelers were drawn up outside the main habitat units. A few figures moved around the place, too distant to resolve clearly.

'The last survey showed no signs of active vulcanism in this region,' Midas reminded me, echoing an observation Aemos had made on our arrival.

'See there,' I said, indicating a portion of the settlement that ran into the slope of the largest cone. 'Those old buildings are partially buried in solidified ash. The original settlement predates the activity.'

Midas pulled a map-slate from his pocket and whirred through the index. 'North Qualm,' he said. 'One of the settler habitats, a mining town.'

We watched for fifteen or twenty minutes, long enough to feel the ground shudder and see a gout of white hot liquid fire spit from one of the cones. Alarms sounded in the settlement below, but were quickly stifled. A rain of wet ash and glowing embers fluttered down across the township and settled like black snow on the flak-board screens.

'Why would they persist in working this site with the constant threat of eruption?' Fischig growled.

'Let's take a closer look,' I suggested.

Covering the speeder with foliage, we set off down the forested valley. The ground between the feathery ferns and hard, dry thorn-trees was thick with fungal growth, some of it brightly covered and glossy. Though we worked carefully, we couldn't help kicking up puffs of spores and soredia.

I was wearing my button-sleeve black coat, Fischig his brown body armour, his helmet hooked on his belt, and Midas wore his regular outfit, though he had replaced his cerise jacket with a short, dark-blue work coat. All of us melted into the forest shadows.

I still wasn't sure why Fischig had come along. After Gudrun, the remit given him by Lord Custodian Carpel seemed done with, but he had refused to return to Hubris. It seemed he trusted my instinct that the matter was far from done with.

We crossed a low stream bed, steaming with hot, pungent water that bubbled up from the vents, and came silently up along the north edge of the settlement. Now the judder of generators could be made out, the distant growl of rock-drills. Guards in khaki drill fatigues worn under spiked and blackened segments of metal body armour wandered the length of an earthwork wall that had been banked up at the edge of the trees, running great bull-cygnids on long chains. The canines were meaty brutes with lolling tongues and beards of spittle. The guards that pulled on their chains carried newly stamped, short-form lasguns on shoulder slings. Their faces were masked behind heavy black rebreathers. Workgangs, some stripped to their leggings in the heat, toiled to sluice the smouldering ash from the flak-board screens with hoses and bucket chains.

Midas pointed out where the edges of the settlement had been ringed with motion detectors and antipersonnel mines. All had been deactivated.

The constant tremors had rendered both useless as defences. But there was no mistaking the aura I had felt since we had first begun to approach. A psychic veil utterly enclosed North Qualm.

I took out my scope and played it around the settlement. More guards, many more, and dozens of filth-caked workers, lounging by the entrance to one particularly large modular shed. Several supervisors moved back and forth among the resting work gangs, holding brief conversations and making notations on data-slates. Eight workers emerged from the shed carrying long, stretcher-like trays with high sides covered with clear-plastic wraps. I zoomed the magnification of the scope to get a closer look at the faces of the supervisors. I didn't recognise any of them. They were all dour, scholarly men in grey rainproof overalls.

Something vast suddenly crossed my field of vision. By the time I had reacted and adjusted the magnification, it had passed out of sight into the works shed. I had a brief memory of bright, almost gaudy metal and a shimmering, flowing robe.

'What the hell was that?' I hissed.

Midas looked at me, lowering his scope, actual fear on his face. Fischig also looked disturbed.

'A giant, a horned giant in jewelled metal,' Midas said. 'He came striding out of the modular hab to the left and went straight into the shed. God-Emperor, but it was huge!'

Fischig agreed with a nod. 'A monster,' he said.

The cones above roared again, and a rain of withering ash fluttered down across the settlement. We shrank back into the thorn-trees. Guard activity seemed to increase.

'Rosethorn,' my vox piped.

'Now is not a good time,' I hissed.

It was Maxilla. He sent one final word and cut off. 'Sanctum.'

'Sanctum' was a Glossia codeword that I had given Maxilla before we had left the *Essene*. I wanted him in close orbit, providing us with extraction cover and overhead sensor advantages, but knew that he would have to melt away the moment any other traffic entered the system. 'Sanctum' meant that he had detected a ship or ships emerging from the immaterium into real-space, and was withdrawing to a concealment orbit behind the local star.

Which meant that all of us on the planet were on our own.

Midas caught my sleeve and pointed down at the settlement. The giant had reappeared and stood in plain view at the mouth of the shed. He was well over two metres tall, wrapped in a cloak that seemed to be made of smoke and silk, and his ornately decorated armour and horned helmet were a shocking mixture of chased gold, acidic yellow, glossy purple, and the red of fresh, oxygenated blood. In his ancient armour, the monster looked like he had stood immobile in that spot for a thousand years. Just a glance at him inspired terror and revulsion, involuntary feelings of dread that I could barely repress.

A Space Marine, from the corrupted and damned Adeptus Astartes. A Chaos Marine.

FOURTEEN

A TALE OF REPRESSION
ROGUE
RETURN TO THE FLAME HILLS

'We've not been idle,' Bequin told me with a smirk when we returned to the gun-cutter. It was noon, and river basin was filling with bumping clusters of ball-trees driven off the flint plains by the wind. They drifted over the shingle and splashed trailing roots into the water.

Bequin was dressed in work fatigues, a rebreather slung around her neck, and she carried an autopistol. As Midas and Fischig stowed the speeder under the netting, she led me into the crew-bay and waved the weapon in the direction of a thin, filthy man chained to a cargo-loop with cuff restraints. His hair was matted and his clothes, an assemblage of patched rags, were stiff with caked mud. He looked at me with fierce eyes through a shaggy fringe of wet hair.

'There were three of them, maybe more,' Bequin told me. 'Came to take a look at us using the ball-trees as moving cover. The others fled, but I brought him down.'

'How?' I asked.

She gave me that look which told me not to keep underestimating her.

'Our intruders from last night?' I wondered aloud. Bequin shrugged.

I walked over to face the captive. 'What's your name?'

'He doesn't say much,' Bequin advised. I told her to move away.

'Name?' I asked again.

Nothing. I paused, collected my mind and then sent a gentle probe into the shady recesses of his skull.

'Tymas Rhizor,' he stammered.

Good. Another gentle push at his slowly yielding mind. The levels of fear and caution were palpable.

'Of Gillan His Acre, Goddes land.'

I switched to speech, without the psychic urge now. 'Gillan's Acre? You mean Gillan's Acre?'

'Seythee Gillan His Acre?'

'Gillan's Acre?'

He nodded. 'Theesey truth.'

'Proto-Gothic, with generational nuance shift,' Aemos said, coming near. 'Damask was colonised something over five hundred years ago, and was isolated for a lengthy period. The population may not have flourished, but the language has perpetuated vestiges of older linguaforms.'

'So this man is likely to be a native, a settler?'

Aemos nodded. I saw our captive was looking from my face to Aemos's, trying to follow our conversation.

'You were born here, on Damask?'

He frowned.

'Born here?'

'Ayeam of Gillan His Acre. Yitt be Goddes land afoor the working.'

I looked round at Aemos. This would take forever. 'I can manage,' Aemos said. 'Ask away.'

'Ask him what happened to Gillan's Acre.'

'Preyathee, howcame bye lossen Gillan His Acre?'

His story was painfully simple, and shaped by the ignorance of a man whose kind had worked the poor soil of a lonely edgeworld for generations. The families, as he called them, presumably the clan groups of the original settlers, had worked the land for as long as his memory and the memory of his elders went. There were five farming communities, and two quarries or mines, which provided building materials and fossil fuel in exchange for a share of the crops. They were devout people, dedicated to the nurture of 'Goddes land...' God's land, though there was no doubt that by 'God' they meant the God-Emperor. As little as four years ago, after the time of the last survey from which records we worked, there had been upwards of nine thousand settlers living in the communities of Damask.

Then the mission came. Rhizor reckoned this to have been three years before. A ship brought a small order of ecclesiarchs here from Messina. They intended to establish a retreat and spiritually educate the neglected settlers. There had been thirty priests. He recognised the name Dazzo. 'Arch-prieste Dazzo,' he called him. Other off-worlders came too, not priests like Dazzo and his brethren, but men who worked with them. From the way he described them, they sounded like geological surveyors or mining engineers. They concentrated their attentions on the quarries at North Qualm. After about a year, the activity increased. More ships came and went. Settlers, mostly strong males, were recruited from the farm communities to work the mines, often brutally. The ecclesiarchs didn't seem to mind. As their populations drained, the farming settlements began to fail and die off. No help was given to sustain them. A disease, probably an off-world import, killed many. Then the volcanic activity began, suddenly, without warning. Everyone in the farmsteads was rounded up and pressed into service at the pits as if some great urgency was now driving the task. Rhizor and many like him toiled until they dropped, and later managed to escape, living like animals in the thorn forests.

So Dazzo and his mission had come to Damask, enslaved the population into a workforce, and were now hell-bent on mining out something from the territory around North Qualm. It seemed likely to me that the vulcanism had been triggered by incautious mining work.

I reached into his mind again... he trembled in fear as he felt the psychic touch... and showed him an image of Dazzo. Eagerly, he confirmed his identity. Then Locke, another face he knew and regarded with ill-concealed hatred. Locke had been chief among the men who had pressed the farmers into service. His cruelty had left a lasting mark. I showed him the faces of Urisel and Oberon Glaw, neither of which were known to him. At last, I visualised an image of the pipe-smoking man.

'Malahite,' he announced, recognising him at once. According to Rhizor, the obscura addict with the watery blue eyes was Girolamo Malahite, chief of the surveyors and engineers.

Fischig, who had joined us during the conversation, asked about the fibre-wood marker we had found at Gillan's Acre. Rhizor wrinkled his face with grief. That had marked the mass grave where the off-worlders had buried all those who had resisted.

Midas called me to the cockpit. I told Aemos to feed Rhizor and question him further.

Midas sat in the leather pilot's throne, his lap draped with spools of scroll paper stamped out of the electric press.

'No wonder Maxilla hid,' he said by way of an opening. 'Look here.'

The scrolls were a transcription log of the astropathic and vox traffic Midas had been able to monitor from the ships in orbit. He slid a gloved finger down the jumbled columns of figures and text.

'I make out at least twelve vessels up there, maybe more. It's difficult to say an accurate figure. These here, for example, may be two ships in dialog or the same ship repeating itself.'

'Coding?'

'That's the interesting bit. It's all standard Imperial, the Navy code called Textcept.'

'That's common enough.'

He nodded. 'And look here, the question and answer pattern indicates a capital ship checking that its fleet components have all arrived in realspace. It's a typical Imperial structure. Military... one of ours.'

'A friendly fleet.'

'Not friendly, perhaps. Look at the command identifier here... that name translates as Estrum.'

'The missing captain.'

'The missing captain... perhaps not that missing after all. Perhaps... rogue. The whole incident at Gudrun anchorage, the mistaken recognition, the "panic"... could have been an excuse to withdraw ships loyal to him.'

'But he's still broadcasting in standard Imperial code-form.'

'If his officers alone are party to the deceit, he won't want to alert the crews.'

An hour later, a large launch with fighter escort broke from the fleet and swung down to the surface of Damask. The transport set down at North Qualm, and the fighters circled the area twice before returning to their base ship. From the cutter, we could hear the booming roar of their thrusters rolling around the plateaux and valleys. Midas quickly switched the cutter's systems to minimum operation so they wouldn't make a chance detection of our instrumentation.

Aemos talked with Rhizor for most of the afternoon, and he seemed calmer and more willing to help once food had been given to him. As the light began to fail and evening approached, Aemos came to find me.

'If you want a way back in, that man might be able to help you.'

'Go on.'

'He knows the mines and the excavations. He worked there for a goodly while. I've spoken to him at length, and he seems certain he could show you to a cave network that links with the mining structure.'

We set out after dark in the speeder. Fischig drove, using the terrain scanner to see rather than the lamps. That made progress slower but more discreet. I sat next to him, and Bequin rode in the back with Rhizor. There had been some debate about which of us should go, but I had made the final selection. The speeder could hold four, and though Midas was the most able combatant in my group, more able than even the chastener in my view, I wanted him at the helm of the cutter, ready to respond. Besides, Bequin had uses of her own that I considered vital to our endeavour.

It took a long time to make the trek back to the North Qualm region, and we didn't arrive until well into the second half of the night. Clouds had masked the sky, hiding the moon and stars, and the only light was the flare of the volcanic hills, underlighting the low clouds with a fluctuating red haze. The air was thick with sulphurous smoke.

We left the speeder concealed in a hollow, its position flagged by a marker tag, and headed west around the outreaches of the area, the 'flame hills' as Rhizor called them.

Nocturnal creatures chattered and fluted in the darkness. Something larger and more distant howled. Pressing through the thorn-scrub, we became aware of the harsh artificial lighting bathing the entire settlement. The volcanoes rumbled.

It took Rhizor a little time to find what he was looking for: a series of small, shallow pools, half-filled with geothermally heated water. The syrupy surfaces of the pools seethed and bubbled, and the site was plagued with insects drawn by the heat. Rhizor splashed cautiously into the largest pool, and worked his way around a massive boulder that was swathed in bright orange lichen. Behind it, masked by thorn and cycad, was a narrow cavity. This, he said, as best as I could understand him, was the route by which he had escaped from the slave-gangs.

We checked weapons and equipment and prepared to enter. I had opened the weapons locker on the cutter and provided us with as much efficient firepower as we could comfortably manage. I had my powersword, an autopistol in a rig under my coat, and a las-carbine with a lamp pack taped under the muzzle. Other items of equipment filled the pack on my back. Bequin had kept her autopistol, and taken a flat-bladed knife, and she too had a lamp.

I'd given Fischig an old but well-maintained heavy stubber, which seemed to please him enormously. He had his Arbites pistol, and a satchel full of spare ammo drums for the stubber. Rhizor had refused a weapon. I was certain he would leave us once we were safely en route anyway.

The cavity allowed us to enter single file. I led the way, with Rhizor behind me, then Bequin, and Fischig brought up the rear. It was damnably hot in the narrow rock passage, and the sulphurous gases forced us to wear our rebreathers. Rhizor had no breather, but tied a swathe of cloth around his nose and mouth. This was the practice the slaves had used when working the mines.

The passage wound back and forth, and climbed for a while as it coiled into the hill. In places, it was so steep we had to climb up the ragged floor of the burrow. Twice we had to remove our equipment packs to ease through constricted sections.

After an hour, I began to feel the oppressive throb of the psychic veil shrouding North Qualm. As we penetrated it, I listened out for the sound of alarms or activity, but none came. Though she didn't know it, Bequin was already doing her job by creating a dead spot that allowed us to press on invisibly. I made sure none of us strayed too far from her aura of influence.

The lava flues were crawling with lifeforms adjusted to existence in the hot, chemical-rich environment: blind, toad-like hunters, transparent beetles, albino molluscs and spiders that looked like they were fashioned from white gold. A fat, pallid centipede as long as my arm spurred its way over the baked rock at one junction.

Every few minutes the earth trembled. Loose rock and dust showered down from the roof, and warm, reeking gases blew back along the winding rock halls.

The passage widened, and showed signs of excavation. Thorn-wood props supported the ceiling, and marker boards with numbers chalked on them were nailed to every sixth post. Rhizor tried to explain where we were. He did his best, and I was able to ascertain we were in a section of mine that had been worked and then abandoned. He said other things too, but the meaning was beyond me. He led us to the end of one working, a low, propped tunnel, and I shone my light into a cavity that had been dug out of the loose shale and grit. Bequin knelt and brushed grit off the floor with her hand. She exposed old tiles, made of a dull, metallic substance I couldn't identify. The tiles were perfectly fitted, despite the fact that they were irregular octagons. They were strangely unsymmetrical, with some edges overlong. Yet they all fitted almost seamlessly. We could not begin to account for it, and the pattern they made was intensely uncomfortable.

At the rear of the cavity, ancient stonework had been exposed. I was no expert, but the stone, a hard pale material glittering with flecks of mica, didn't look local. There was evidence that parts of it had been cut away with rock drills and cutting beams.

'This is old,' said Fischig. He ran his hand across the riven stone facing, 'but the damage is new.'

'The wheel-graves,' Alizebeth Bequin said suddenly. I looked over at her.

'On Bonaventure,' she explained, remembering her homeworld. 'There were famous old sites in the western hills, made by races before man. They were arranged in radiating circles, like wheels. I used to go there, when I was a child. They had been decorated once, I suppose, but the surfaces had been cut away. Ransacked by later hands. It reminds me of this.'

'There are many who make a trade in archaeological plunder,' said Fischig. 'And if it's xenos artefacts, the penalty is high.'

I'd overheard Glaw and his allies mention archeoxenon materials. If this was such a site, connected in some way to the as yet mysterious saruthi, it accounted for the way they persisted in working it despite the volcano.

What had they taken from here? What was it worth to them? What was it worth to the saruthi?

We retraced our steps back to the main seam, passing three more abandoned cavities. Each one had shown signs of the old stonework, and each had been robbed like the first.

We came to the end of the seam, and a metal ladder rose up through scaffolding to an opening in the rock ten metres up.

We climbed up into another tunnel, and at once heard the rattle of rock drills. The atmosphere was clearer here, and we were able to remove our rebreathers. Cold air, from the surface, I guessed, breezed down the tunnel. With extreme caution, we passed along, crossing the mouth of a gigantic cavern that had probably been a magmatic reservoir. The walls were polished and fused by heat. Crouching low, we looked in, and saw work gangs of men and women, undoubtedly Rhizor's kinfolk, forming basket chains to clear rock debris from the workface. There were at least a dozen of the bestial guards in their black, spiked armour. One walked the workline and administered encouragement with an electro-lash.

I peered in more intently, and tried to make sense of the main working. Two Damaskite slaves worked with rock drills, cutting back the crust of wall, exposing a wide stretch of the old stone facing. Other slaves, most of them women, laboured closely on the exposed section with small picks, awls and brushes, revealing carvings of intricate design.

A relay of shouts ran down the guard line, and we hid ourselves in the tunnel shadows. From up ahead, lamps bobbed and wove, and a party of men came down the tunnel from the surface into the cavern. Three were guards, two grey-shrouded supervisors with data-slates. The others were Gorgone Locke and the pipe-smoker Girolamo Malahite.

As I suspected, members of the Glaw cabal had escaped House Glaw alive. Estrum's rogue fleet had no doubt played a part in that salvation.

Locke was dressed in a leather robe with armoured panels woven into it. His mouth still showed the wound I had inflicted there. His mood was sullen.

Malahite was dressed in black as I had seen him before. He stood, studying data-slates, conferring with the dig supervisors and the leader of the guard team before moving to look at the exposed stretch of achaeoxenon material. The slave workers shrank back out of his way.

He exchanged a few words with the men around him, and the guard leader hurried off, returning with a bulky rocksaw. The tool trailed cables and tubes behind it, back to a socket junction at the mouth of the cavern, where it linked to a system of power and water supply lines running back up the tunnel to the generators and pumps at the surface.

The saw whined into life, pumping a sheen of water over its blade to keep it clean and cool. The guard leader carefully sliced the blade into the rock, the saw keening as it bit. In a few seconds, he had cut a slice of the carvings free. As far as I could tell, the carvings were made on individual stone blocks, and he was slicing the sculpted faces off the stones. He cut two more, and they were passed with reverence to Malahite, who studied them and then handed them on to be wrapped in plastic and placed in wooden carriers. The slices looked very much like the old stone tablets I had seen in that private study under House Glaw.

There was a loud crack. The guard leader had cut another tablet away, but it had broken into fragments. He dropped the saw and began to collect up the fragments frantically as those around him cursed and shouted. Locke moved in.

He kicked the man hard and dropped him to the ground, then kicked him repeatedly as he lay there, trying to shield his face, begging for mercy. Malahite gathered up the fragments.

'You were told to be careful, you useless bastard!' Locke was growling.

'It can be repaired,' Malahite told the ship master. 'I can fuse it together.'

Locke wasn't listening. He kicked the man again, then dragged him up and threw him against the wall. He cursed at him some more and the man whimpered, pleading apologies.

Locke turned away from the battered wretch. Then he picked up the revving saw, swung back, and dismembered the guard leader.

It was inhuman. The agonised screams filled the chamber. All the slaves wailed and moaned, and even the guards looked away in distaste. Locke laid in with murderous glee, covering himself in blood.

Then he tossed the smoking saw onto the ground at his feet, and turned to another of the guards. He pointed to the saw.

'Make sure you do a better job,' he snarled.

With huge reluctance, the guard picked up the saw and set to work.

Locke, Malahite and their party left after another ten minutes, followed by a work gang carrying the wooden crates full of cut tablets. We waited a few minutes, then followed them up the tunnel.

There was daylight ahead, scarce and thin. The tunnel came up into what I guessed was the large modular shed I had seen from my reconnaissance. Workers milled around on rest breaks, and guards and the grey-robed overseers wandered back and forth. Dig equipment and tools were piled up in the poorly lit shed. Fischig found a door at the back of the shed behind equipment boxes and broke the lock. The four of us were able to slip out of the shed from the rear into the settlement without having to pass through the main mine entrance and thus be seen.

We were now in a back lane of North Qualm, with the volcano slopes behind us. Rotting and abandoned buildings stood close all around, and flurries of ash and soot blew down over us. We kept close to the walls, holding back out of sight when anybody passed.

Behind the next jumble of ruins lay a cleared area partly masked by more flak-board screens, designed to keep the ash out. Two launches sat on the scorched ground: a large Imperial Navy transport and a smaller, older shuttle. A thicker layer of ash coated the older shuttle's hull.

Figures moved around the entry ramps of both ships. Guards and workers were moving the wooden stretchers of excavated artefacts up into the belly hold of the Navy launch. I could see Locke and Malahite standing nearby with several of the supervisors and three battlefleet officers in shipboard fatigues. One, a lean man with a receding chin and bulging eyes, wore the ribbons and insignia of a captain. Our rogue, Estrum. As I watched, the ecclesiarch Dazzo emerged from a nearby building and crossed to them, holding the hem of his rich gown up out of the ash.

Shouting suddenly boomed across the yard. An angry human voice followed by a deeper, more savage sound that set the hairs on my neck up.

Lord Oberon Glaw, dressed in a cloak and body armour, slammed out of the building Dazzo had emerged from, striding across the landing yard. A second later, the huge, ghastly bulk of the Chaos Space Marine followed him, raging and cursing.

Glaw wheeled and faced the giant monster, resuming his argument at the top of his voice. For all his size, the lord of House Glaw was dwarfed by the vividly armoured blasphemy. The Traitor Marine had removed his helmet: his face was a white, powdered, lifeless mask of hate, with smears of gold dust and purple skin paint around the hollow eyes and a dry, lipless mouth full of pearl-inlaid teeth. His only vaguely human face seemed to have been sutured onto his skull, the exposed parts of which were machined gold. There was a terrible stink of cloying perfume and organic corruption. I could not imagine the courage – or insanity – that it took to face down a Chaos Space Marine in a furious argument.

The wind was against us, and all we could hear was the violent snarl of the voices instead of actual words. Dazzo and Malahite quickly crossed to Glaw's side, and most of the other guards and workers present cowered back.

The wind changed a little.

'...will not deny me any longer, you human filth!' The awful voice of the Traitor Marine could suddenly be heard.

'You will show me respect, Mandragore! Respect!' Glaw yelled back, his voice powerful but seemingly frail against the roar of the Chaos warrior.

The Marine bellowed something else that ended in '...slay you all and finish this work myself! My masters await, and they await the perfect completion of this task! They will not idle their time while you vermin dawdle and slacken!'

'You will abide by our pact! You will keep to our agreement!'

I realised I had almost become hypnotised. Staring at the monstrous, raging figure, drawn to him by his power and sheer horror, my eyes had lingered too long on the obscene runic carvings that edged the joints of his armour, the insane sigils that decorated his chest plate. I was entranced, captivated by the golden chains that dressed his luridly painted armour, the gems and exquisite filigree covering his armour plate, the translucent silk of his cloak, and the words, the alien, abominable words, inscribed upon his form, twitching and seething with secrets older then time... secrets, promises, lies...

I forced myself not to look. Soul-destroying madness lay in the marks and brands of Chaos if one looked too long.

Mandragore shrieked in fury and raised a massive gloved fist, spiked with rusty blades, to smash Lord Glaw.

The blow didn't fall. I started, as if slapped, as a burst of psychic power rippled across the concourse.

Mandragore stepped back a pace. Dazzo moved towards him. Smaller than Glaw or Locke, Dazzo seemed even more insignificant next to the monster, but with each step he took, the Chaos Marine moved backwards.

He didn't speak, but I could hear his voice in my head. The presence and the words were so foul I barely managed not to vomit.

'Mandragore Carrion, son of Fulgrim, worthy of Slaanesh, champion of the Emperor's Children, killer of the living, defiler of the dead, keeper of secrets - your presence here honours us, and we celebrate our pact with your fellowship... but you will not seek to harm us. Never raise your hand to us again. Never.'

Dazzo was simply the most potent psyker I had ever encountered. With his mind alone, he had forced down one of the vilest of the traitors, a Space Marine sworn to the corrupt service of Chaos.

Mandragore turned away, and strode off across the compound. I saw now how Lord Glaw wilted from the confrontation, his bravado spent. Many of the workers present were weeping with the trauma of the exchange, and two of the guards were throwing up.

Shaking, I looked round at my companions. Fischig was ashen-faced and trembling, his eyes closed. Rhizor had curled up in a ball in the ashy mud, his back against the wall.

Bequin had vanished.

FIFTEEN

EXPOSED IN THE MIDST OF THE FOE
AN ILL-MATCHED WAR
FLIGHT

I had a second to realise that wherever Bequin had gone, it had left us exposed, outside the veil of her untouchable aura. I heard a cry, a strangled warning from the old ecclesiarch that was immediately accompanied by the hoot of sirens.

In the landing yard, guards were racing towards us. Dazzo was pointing directly at the section of ruin that concealed us. Locke pulled a laspistol from his robe. Angry voices, the raucous bark of cygnids.

'Fischig!' I cried. 'Fischig! Move or we're dead!'

He blinked, still pale, as if he didn't recognise his own name.

I slapped him hard around the side of his head.

'Move, chastener!' I yelled.

The first of the guards had reached the ruins, and one was kicking his way in through a boarded-up door. I saw his staring face looking out of a dirty black visor. He raised his lasgun.

I swung the powerful carbine up and laced him and the doorway with a spray of laser shots. Stone and wood debris spat and flew from the multiple impacts.

Las-shots whined in through gaps in the stone work and exploded against the outside wall.

Fischig's heavy stubber chattered into life. He played the sweep of blazing tracer shots down the dark cavities of the ruin to our left, tearing apart two more guards who were forcing their way in.

More guards, to my right, fired their weapons. My las-carbine crackled on full auto, a blur of high-pitched whines, as I raked the narrow entrance and dropped another three.

Still firing, Fischig backed into the depths of the ruin.

'Come on!' he snarled. I backed with him, our weapons laying down a storm of explosive metal and piercing energy that rippled across the ruin walls, scattering debris, spraying ash dust and bursting bodies.

Rhizor, his mind utterly gone with terror, lay on the ground. I grabbed him by the scruff of his rags and dragged him after us. He fought at me, despairing.

A large figure came leaping in though the window space in the wall through which we had observed the dealings in the yard. It was Locke. He rolled as he landed, his laspistol retching shots.

One shot clipped my left shoulder. Another three slammed into Rhizor's back and he toppled into me, knocking me flat.

Fischig saw Locke, and swung round, his finger not lifting from the stubber's blunt trigger. The rapidly cycling mechanism of the heavy weapon made a high, grinding metallic noise overlaid with the frenetic blasts of the shots.

The scant cover around Locke disintegrated, and he cried out as he threw himself behind a section of wall. He fired as he moved, and Fischig grunted in pain as a las-shot punched into his side.

'Eisenhorn! You bastard!' Locke bellowed. I pulled myself out from under Rhizor's corpse, sad that that ragged slave had paid such a price for assisting an inquisitor. Another crime on the shoulders of Gorgone Locke.

Damning the ship master's name, I pulled a frag grenade from my pack, and tossed it in Locke's direction. Then Fischig and I moved as fast as we could out through the rear of the smoke-filled ruin.

The grenade blew out the back of the structure. I hoped to the Emperor it had torn Locke limb from limb.

Coughing and spitting, Fischig and I came out into a ditch that ran behind the ruined dwellings of North Qualm and the newer modular buildings. Angled over us were the large flak-board baffles of the ash-screens.

Las-shots chipped and whacked into the screens and wailed down the dim ditch. Guards tumbled into the ditch twenty metres away, rabidly howling cygnids pouring in with them.

Fischig made the ditch his killing field, and emptied his second drum of ammunition down the length, pulverising guard and canine alike. We hurried in the opposite direction as he struggled to clamp in a fresh drum.

Guards were shooting at us through the ruins, blowing chunks from the mouldering stonework. We ran on, chased by the furious salvos.

The ditch ran out into a small yard where an eight-wheeler truck was parked. We exchanged shots with three guards who rounded the corner into the yard and dropped them, but a fourth appeared, loosing a trio of cygnids from their leashes. Baying, they pounded across the yard. I killed one with my carbine, but the truck blocked any shots at the others. The big vehicle rocked as one leapt up into its frame. A moment later, it was leaping over onto us. I put a las-round through its skull as it came down, its muscled bulk just missing me. The other came out from under the truck, filthy with axle grease, and leapt at Fischig. It knocked him over, its huge jaws locked around his armoured forearm.

I drew my powersword and thrust the crackling blade through its body.

More shots, thumping into the truck.

'Get up!' I told Fischig as we rolled the canine's dead weight off him.

The entire compound closing around us, we sprinted to the rear of a modular shed and broke the door in.

It was an equipment store, stacked with spare blades for rock drills, spools of cable, lamp-cells, and all manner of other mining equipment. We moved low between the piles of equipment, hearing shouts and running footsteps outside.

I paused, changing cells in my carbine, and keyed my vox-link.

'Thorn wishes aegis, rapturous beasts below.'

'Aegis, arising, the colours of space,' came the response immediately.

'Razor delphus pathway,' I instructed. 'Pattern ivory!'

'Pattern confirm. In six. Aegis, arising.'

Guards burst into the back of the shed, and Fischig blew them back out through the prefab wall with a wild burst of shots.

I looked around, and saw a stack of black metal boxes raised on a pallet in the corner of the shed. The paper labels were old and faded, but I prised off the lid of one box and confirmed their contents.

'Get ready to move,' I said, arming my second grenade.

'Oh shit!' said Fischig, seeing what I was doing. He was already half out the door as I placed the grenade on the top of the boxes.

We came out firing, met by a dozen or more guards who were sectioning the street looking for us. Most were pit guards in their black, ugly armour, but three were naval security troops in black cloth fatigues, no doubt part of the traitor captain's contingent.

We fired as we ran. The grenade was on a ten-second fuse. The fact that we ran through the midst of them caught them unawares. None of them was able to get a clean shot off.

Fischig and I dived headlong over a crumbling section of wall that had once surrounded North Qualm's market yard.

The grenade went off. And so did the stack of mining explosives it had been sitting on.

The shockwave concussion flattened every wall for thirty metres. The upwards force of the blast, driving before it a blistering fireball, lifted the whole modular shed twenty metres into the air and sent the shredded remains of the structure crashing down onto neighbouring buildings.

Scraps of metal, cinders and shreds of burning flak-board rained down on Fischig and myself. There was a dazed silence broken only by the warble of alarms, cries of the injured and desperate shouting. The air was fogged by ash dust. Pulling on our rebreathers, we stumbled through the murk.

I felt a jab of pain in my head. Deep, insidious, burning. Dazzo was reaching out with his terrifyingly potent mind, looking for us.

We stumbled through the smoke down an aisle between modular sheds whose windows had been blown out in the detonation.

The pain grew more intense.

'Eisenhorn. You cannot hide. Show yourself.'

I gasped as the pain took deeper hold.

Suddenly, it eased.

'Fischig! In here!'

I pushed him into an old stone outbuilding. I guessed it had once been a wash-house in North Qualm's more rural heyday.

Bequin was cowering in a corner, filthy, tearful. The sight of the Child of the Emperor Mandragore had sent her fleeing in blind panic. Like me, she had made the mistake of looking at the runes and marks on his foul, dazzling armour. Unlike me, she hadn't had the sense to look away.

She couldn't speak. She barely registered us. But we were back inside her muzzling aura and out of Dazzo's clutches for the moment.

'What now?' asked Fischig. 'They'll regroup quickly enough.'

'Midas is coming. We have to get back to the landing yard. It's the only area big enough for him to set down in.'

Fischig looked at me as if I was mad. 'He's going to fly into this? He'll be killed! And even if he does pick us up, they'll launch interceptors from the fleet. They'll launch them the moment he powers up for take off!'

'It'll be tight,' I admitted.

We dragged Bequin with us and moved out of the derelict wash-house. Outside, the settlement was still swathed in ash lifted by the blast. Fierce fires glowed in the smoke. Voices screamed orders and cygnids bayed. There was a deeper, furious bellowing too. I had a nasty feeling it was the Chaos Marine.

'Thorn attending aegis, main yard area,' I voxed.

'Aegis, main yard in three, the heavens falling.' So, they were on to him. The fleet had launched ships after the cutter.

We ran now. The smoke was slowly clearing.

A guard gang moved past us and we were forced to double back around. More guards blocked the next street.

'Through the buildings!' said Fischig.

We were behind a modular building, one of the newest and largest that Dazzo's unholy mission had set up. There was no door, but we scrambled up onto the low roof, pulling Bequin with us, and entered through a skylight.

The room we dropped into was carpeted and well furnished, an office or private study for one of the senior supervisors. There were racks of data-slates, and piles of charts and storage tiles. Several large travel trunks had been piled in one corner, with a cloak and two overcoats draped over them. One of the new arrivals from the launch had left these things here and not yet unpacked them.

'Come on!' hissed Fischig, checking the door that led out of the office into the rest of the building.

'Wait!' I said. I cut the locks off the trunks with my powersword and threw the lids back. In the first, clothes, slates, a boxed lasgun, ornate and inlaid with the name Oberon. Other miscellaneous effects.

'Come on!' Fischig repeated, frantic.

'Aegis, main yard in two,' crackled the vox.

'Eisenhorn? What are you playing at?' Fischig demanded.

'These are Glaw's things!' I said, searching the trunk.

'So what? What are you looking for?'

'I don't know.' I turned to the second trunk. More clothes, some crude and unpleasant religious icons.

Fischig grabbed me by the shoulder. 'With respect, inquisitor, that would suggest this isn't the time to be doing it!'

'We have to get out of here, we have to get the hell out of here,' Bequin murmured, her eyes darting back and forth at every sound from outside.

'There'll be something... an edge, a clue... something we can use when we get out of here...'

'We'll be lucky to escape with our lives!'

'Yes!' I stared up at him. 'Yes, we will – and if we do, we'll want to continue our struggle against Glaw, won't we?'

He threw his hands up in despair.

'Please... please...' Bequin murmured.

'Aegis, main yard in one,' crackled the vox.

The third trunk. A wrapped set of stainless steel surgical tools whose purpose I didn't even want to imagine. A small dice and counter game in a hardwood box. Clothes, more damn clothes!

With something solid wrapped in them.

I took it out.

'Satisfied?' asked Fischig.

I would have smiled if Locke had left me able.

'Go!' I said.

Beyond the stateroom was an outer annexe. More luggage trunks stood on the grilled floor, as well as wooden boxes draped in plastic.

'Don't even think about it!' Fischig snapped, seeing me look at the trunks.

'Aegis, on site!' The vox-burst was partly drowned out by the vibrating roar of a powerful aircraft passing low and fast overhead. There was a chatter of small arms, the whip of las-rifles.

I led the way out of the annexe, through a hatchway that opened onto the landing yard. Figures milled around, mainly slave-guards and naval troopers, looking skywards and firing at the looming gun-cutter that banked overhead. On the far side of the yard, by the lowered ramp of the Navy launch, Malahite saw us and shouted out. The men swung around, firing. Shots crackled around us.

Then I saw Mandragore, over to the right of the yard, charging towards us with a baleful howl.

'Back inside! Inside!' I yelled and the three of us tumbled back in through the door.

The outer wall of the building didn't stop the Chaos-beast. Neither did the hatch. Ceramite and steel shod fists tore the lightweight metal apart, twisted adamite support beams, punctured plastic panels like paper. Mandragore's baying wail preceded him, shaking us to the core.

Bequin screamed.

The vilely misnamed Child of the Emperor exploded through the end wall of the annexe, white lips drawn back around pearl teeth as he hurled out noise from his augmented torso. The boltgun in his fist was enormous.

'Not a step closer!' I yelled. With one hand, I held the primed grenade up so he could see it.

He laughed, a deep, booming chuckle of contempt.

'I mean it,' I added and kicked the crate at my feet. It was laden with plastic wrapped tablets from the mine.

'One second fuse. Another step and all this will be gone.'

He faltered. Lord Glaw and several guards appeared through the shredded wall behind him.

'For pity's sake, do as he says!' Glaw barked.

With a growl, Mandragore lowered his boltgun.

'Back off, Glaw! Back right off and take them with you!'

'You can't hope to escape, inquisitor,' said Glaw.

'Back off!'

Glaw waved his men back and retreated. Mandragore backed out slowly, a growling hiss rising from his throat.

'Grab the crate!' I told Fischig. He slung his stubber over his shoulder and did as he was told.

We edged out into the smoky daylight. Fischig and I were side by side, and I held the grenade over the crate he was carrying. Bequin cowered behind us.

In the yard, Glaw was ordering his men back. There were forty or more troops: guards, naval troopers, supervisors. I saw Dazzo, Malahite and the rogue captain Estrum among them. Mandragore did not back off as far as the others. He stayed to the right of us, his shimmering cloak drifting in the breeze, his armour gleaming. The growl continued to purr in his throat.

'Midas,' I said into my link, 'set down, hatch open.'

'Understood,' he replied. 'Be advised there are three Navy interceptors inbound. Arrival in three.'

The gun-cutter swung in over the yard, casting a wide shadow, its thrusters lifting clouds of ash. As it came in to rest on its bulky hydraulic landing skids, the cargo ramp under the cockpit whined and lowered.

Slowly, we moved around until the cutter and the ramp were behind us. The assembled enemy watched us intently, weapons raised.

'A stand-off, inquisitor,' said Glaw.

'Get your men to lower their weapons. Even the ones I can't see. Don't even consider dropping me. Midas... train the wing cannons on myself and the chastener. If anything happens to us, open fire.'

'Confirm.'

The powerful cannons in the wing mounts traversed to target us.

'Shoot us and the crate is vaporised.'

'Weapons down!' Glaw yelled, and the troops obeyed.

'Now call off those interceptors. Order them right back to their carrier.'

'I–'

'Now!'

Glaw looked round at Estrum, who started to speak into a vox link.

'The interceptors have aborted their run,' Midas told me. 'They're turning back.'

'Very good,' I told Glaw.

'What now?' he asked.

What now indeed? We had the upper hand for a moment: they didn't dare shoot or rush us, and Bequin was blocking Dazzo and any other psyker they had.

'An answer or two,' I suggested.

'Eisenhorn!' Fischig hissed.

'An answer?' laughed Glaw. Some of his men laughed too, and Mandragore rumbled a snigger. I noticed Dazzo and Malahite were both unamused.

'This material is archaeoxenon, from an old saruthi site,' I said, lifting one of the ancient, unsymmetrical tablets from the crate in Fischig's grasp with my free hand. 'It clearly has value to you, because it must have value to the saruthi. You're recovering it for them in return for what?'

'I'm not about to tell you anything,' Glaw said. 'I'm not even going to confirm your suppositions.'

I shrugged. 'It was worth trying.'

'My question remains,' said Glaw. 'What now?'

'We leave,' I told him. 'Unmolested.'

'So leave,' he said, with a mild, dismissive hand gesture. 'Put down the crate and leave.'

'This crate is the only thing that's stopping you from obliterating us. It comes with us, as insurance.'

'No!' Dazzo cried, pushing forward. 'Unacceptable! We would lose it forever!' He looked at Glaw. 'This man is our blood foe. We could never recover the artefacts. Even if we agreed to safe passage, he would not honour a deal and leave them for our recovery.'

'Of course not,' I said. 'Just as you would not honour any deal struck with me. It is a sad but true fact that no commitment or agreement of honour can be made between us. Which is why this crate comes with me. We have no other surety.'

'We're not here to offer you surety, flesh-blister,' Mandragore said sonorously. 'Only death. Or if you're unlucky, pain and death.'

'You should keep him out of the negotiations,' I told Glaw with a sideways nod at Mandragore. 'We are leaving with the crate, because you will destroy us otherwise.'

'No,' said Glaw. He stepped forward, pulling a lasgun from his coat. 'You are tripping on your own smooth logic, inquisitor. If we are to lose those artefacts for ever, I'd rather it was here, with your deaths as consolation. If you try to leave with the crate, we will fire anyway and damn the consequences. Set them down and I will give you ten heartbeats to leave.'

I could tell it was no bluff. They would go only so far to protect their trinkets. And they were not fools. They knew I would never return these items. Ten heartbeats. If we tried to board with the crate, they would fire at once. If we set it down... they would fire, but perhaps more hesitantly for fear of hitting the crate. And the cutter's guns were still a point in our favour.

'Back up to the ramp,' I whispered to Bequin and Fischig. 'Throw the crate down when I say.'

'Are you sure?'

'Do as I say. Midas?'

'Ready drive, ready cannons.'

'Now!'

The crate crashed over in the dust. The cutter's engines shrieked into power. They didn't wait ten heartbeats. The three of us were on the ramp, and the ramp was swinging shut under us, and the cutter was lifting around us. A fusillade of weapons fire hammered off the hull. The cutter's cannons roared.

The cutter swung hard about, and we tumbled as the deck pitched. Fischig cried out and fell on the ramp, spilling half out of the gently closing entryway. I grabbed him and hauled him inside before his dangling legs could be severed by the vicing ramp or shot by the enemy below.

We were away. I could tell by the angle of the deck and the vibration of the ship's frame that Midas was accelerating hard and keeping low, letting the landscape shield us from the ground fire. Alarm lights flashed in the crew-bay, indicating damage.

'Strap yourself in!' I yelled at Aemos, who was attempting to rise to assist us. 'Fischig, get Bequin in a harness! Yourself too!'

The chastener pulled the terrified girl across the deck and into a seat. I clambered forward, along the companionway, and up into the cockpit.

Midas was pulling on the controls, taking us higher. The blotchy landscape of Damask flickered past beneath us. I dropped into the seat beside him.

'How close?'

'The fighters have peeled back, on a direct intercept course. They have altitude in their favour.'

'How close?'

'Six minutes to intercept. Damn!'

'What?'

He pointed to the main tactical screen. Behind the smaller bright cursors, larger shapes were moving against the three-dimensional magnetic map of the planet's magnetosphere. 'Their fleet's moving too. The capital ships. And that's two more fighter wings launched.'

'They don't want us to get away, do they?' he added.

'With what we know?'

'They won't let us out of the system alive, will they?'

'Midas, I think I've told you the answer to that.'

He grinned, white teeth contrasting sharply with his dark skin in the cabin's half-light.

'We're going to have some fun, then,' he decided. His bare hands, sparkling with the inlay of Glavian bio-circuits, darted across the controls, adjusting our course.

'Ideas?' I asked.

'A few possibles. Let me massage the data.'

'What?'

'Trust me, Gregor, if we've even a shred of hope of getting out of the Damask system alive, it'll be through skill and subtlety. Shut up and let me compute their speeds and intercept vectors.'

'We took damage from the ground fire,' I persisted. That hopelessness was seeping into me again, the feeling of having no ability to influence the situation.

'Minor, just minor,' he said distractedly. 'The servitors have got it covered.'

He made a course change. From the screen, I saw this brought us around almost side on to the chasing fleet components, drastically reducing their time to intercept and firing range.

'What are you doing?'

'Playing the percentages. Playing safe.'

The bright globe of Damask was dropping away beneath us, and we were driving out into planetary space beyond the highest orbit points at full thrust.

'See?' he said. Another light had appeared on the tactical screen, moving around ahead of us.

'Standard Imperial battlefleet dispersal. There's always a picket ship positioned on the blind side of the subject world. If we'd kept straight on we'd have flown right into its fire-field.'

Lights flashed out in the void beyond the cockpit windows. The picket ship, a medium frigate, was firing anyway, running interference, driving us on.

'It's launched fighters,' Midas reported in a sing-song voice. 'Range in two. Chasers have range in four.'

So matter-of-fact.

I looked at the power levels. Every one of the cutter's powerful thrusters was red-lining.

'Midas...'

'Sit back. There it is.'

'What is?'

The small moon was suddenly filling our front ports as we veered around. It didn't look that small. It looked like we were about to smash into it.

I blurted out a curse.

'Relax, dammit!' he assured me, then added, 'Range in one.'

We dived towards the scarred, pocked lime-green rock that filled our vision at full thrust. Nose guns beginning to flash; six interceptors of the Battlefleet Scarus elite fighter school followed us in.

SIXTEEN

VOID DUEL
BETANCORE'S LAST STAND
TRACES

The moon was called Obol, the smallest and innermost of Damask's fourteen satellites. It was a dented, irregular nugget of nickel, zinc and selenium, six hundred kilometres across at its widest dimension. Lacking atmosphere and riddled with cavities and gorges, it shone with a lambent green glow in the light of the star, rugged terrain features and craters thrown into stark relief.

I was forcing my mind to calm, forcing my pulse rate down. The old mind skills Hapshant had trained me in.

I focused on the data-file for Obol that I had punched up on the screen - nickel, zinc, selenium, smallest of fourteen - not because I wanted to know but because the facts would act as psychopomps, little fetishes of detail to occupy my mind and steal it away from the hazard.

I looked up from the glowing text bar. A jagged crater, vast enough to swallow Dorsay city and its lagoon whole yawned up at us.

'Brace yourselves,' Midas told us all.

Just a kilometre above, he executed his move. By then, we were deeply committed to Obol's gravity and diving at full thrust. There was no question of performing a landing, or even a conventional turn.

But Midas had been flying ships since he was young, schooled in the pilot academies of Glavia. By way of his inlaid circuitry, he understood the nuances of flight, power and manoeuvre better than me, and better than most professional pilots in the Imperium. He had also tested the capabilities of the gun-cutter almost to destruction, and knew exactly what it could and couldn't do.

What worried me most was what he hoped it might do.

He cut the drive, fired all the landing thrusters, and pulled the nose around so that the cutter began to corkscrew. The view whirled before my eyes and I was flung around in my harness.

The spin seemed uncontrolled. But it was measured and perfect. With the landing jets driving us up away from the vertical, we fluttered, like a leaf, using the corkscrew motion to rob the vessel of downward momentum. Ninety metres from the dust of the crater floor, we flattened out, burning jets hard, white hot, and then arced around as Midas cut the main drive in again.

The ground leapt away under us, and we hugged across it, climbing in a savage jerk to skip over the crater lip.

From the tactical display, I saw all six fighters had dropped back to six minutes behind us. None wanted to try duplicating that move. They were diving in more conventional, slower arcs.

Midas hugged the moon, slicing us low around bluffs and buttes, down deep dry valleys hidden from the sun, across wide dust plains that had never seen a footprint. At one point, we flew between two massive cliffs of striated rock.

'They're breaking,' Midas said, leaning us to port.

They were. Four dropped into dogged pursuit, chasing us low over the landscape. The other two had broken and were heading anti-clockwise around the blindside of Obol.

'Contact?'

'We'll meet them head on in eight minutes,' said Midas. He was smiling.

He pulled a hard starboard turn down a rift valley the topographer screen had only just illuminated.

Then he slowed down to what seemed a painful, easy velocity, and banked the gun cutter around a butte that glistened green and yellow in the hard sunlight.

'What are you doing?'

'Wait... wait...'

The tactical screen showed that our four chasers had swept beyond the rift valley.

'This low to the terrain, it'll take them a moment to figure out we're no longer ahead of them.'

'What now?'

He gunned the engines and threw us out over a dust bowl after the pursuit ships.

'Mouse becomes cat,' he said.

Within seconds, a bright blob on the weapons array had been covered with red crosshairs.

Ahead of us, through a landscape of giant rocks and towering mesas that whipped by at a distressing speed, I saw the flare of afterburners.

'Scratch one,' said Midas, firing the wing cannons.

The engine flare far ahead flashed and then turned into an expanding ball of burning gases which swept past us in jagged streaks.

I was pulled back into my seat as we jinked painfully down another valley. There was another flash, of sunlight off metal, a kilometre ahead.

'And two,' said Midas.

The read-out on the autoloaders notched up red tags as drums expended. The flash blossomed with light, and then again more brightly as it spun and struck the valley wall.

Something blindingly brilliant went off to our right, and the cabin rocked, alarms squealing.

'Smart boy, too close,' said Midas, hauling on the stick to avoid an incoming cliff.

One of the fighters had gauged our feint and come around across us.

'Where's the other? Where's the other?' Midas murmured.

We had firepower on our side, firepower and Midas. The fighters were Lightnings, small, fast and dextrous, less than a quarter our size. For all intents and purposes, the gun-cutter was a transport, but its drive and weapon enhancements and its vertical thrust capability made it a formidable fighting ship when it came to a skirmish close down over terrain like this.

Something hit us hard, and we went over in a dizzying fall. Midas cursed and drew us back round in a tight turn. An Imperial fighter, just a blur of silver, crossed our field of vision.

Midas turned us again, and went after it. It ducked and turned down the deep gorges of the moon, flying by instruments alone in the cold shadows.

The gun-sensors picked up its heat trail. Midas fired on it.

He missed.

It tried to turn in a loop to come round at us. Midas fired again.

Another miss.

It came right at us. I could see the tracer jewels of its shots ripping at us. Head to head. In a steep, deep gorge.

No room for manoeuvre. No room for error.

'Goodbye,' said Midas, thumbing the fire stud.

An explosion lit the deep gulf and we flew right through the flame wash.

'Had enough yet?' Midas asked me.

I didn't reply. I was too busy gripping my armrests.

'I have,' he said. 'Time for phase two. There's another hunter right around us, and the blindsiders will be coming up in ninety seconds. A little theatrics now. Uclid?'

The chief servitor warbled a response.

We went into a dive, hard. A display told me we were venting a trail of engine gases.

'Damage?' I asked.

'Play acting,' he told me.

The dark canyon floor rushed up to meet us.

'Jettison, Uclid,' Midas ordered.

There was a thump and a bang. The cutter rocked. Behind us, something flared.

'What was that?'

'Two tonnes of spares, trash and expendable supplies. Plus all the grenades from your weapons store.'

He banked us around hard, and we zoomed into a darker cavity, a wide, deep cave in the canyon base. The walls and roof seemed dangerously close.

Six hundred metres into the cave, Midas turned the cutter to the left, cutting the thrust, floodlights piercing the gloom and reflecting off the jagged cavity.

Another hundred metres, and we settled into the dust on our landing struts. Midas cut power, cut the lights, cut everything except the most rudimentary life support.

'Nobody make a sound,' he said.

* * *

The wait, which lasted for sixty-six hours, was neither comfortable nor pleasant. We wore heat gowns and sat in the gloom as, above us, the heretic fleet scoured Obol and its immediate zone for traces of us. Eight times in the first ten hours our passive sensors registered vehicle movement and scanning in the gorge where we had faked our destruction. The deception was apparently convincing.

But we bided our time. There was no telling how persistent they would be, or how patient. Midas thought it likely they might be playing the same trick as us, lying up quiet and waiting until we betrayed ourselves by movement or signal.

After forty hours, Lowink was confident he had overheard astropathic traffic exchanges indicating a fleet departure, shortly followed by a tremor in the fabric of the fathomless immaterium. But still we waited. Waited for the one thing that I would take as convincing.

Just after the turn of the sixty-sixth hour, it came. An astropathic signal in Glossia: 'Nunc dimittis.'

We lofted from the darkness of Obol into the starlight. Everyone on the ship, myself included, I freely admit, was suddenly talking too loud and too much as we moved around, basking in the bright cabin lights and the restored heating systems. The silent, cold wait had been like a penance.

The *Essene*, slow and majestic, moved in to meet us. Once the heretic fleet had left the system, Maxilla had emerged from hiding in the star's corona and sent his signal.

As soon as we were docked, I went straight to the bridge where Maxilla greeted me like a brother.

'Are we all alive?' he asked.

'In one piece, though it was close.'

'I'm sorry I had to desert you, but you saw the size of that battlegroup.'

I nodded. 'I'm hoping you can tell me where it went.'

'Naturally,' he replied. His astronavigators had not been idle. The chief of them emerged from their annexe at the side of the domed bridge and hummed across the red-black marble of the floor to join us. Like all of his crew, it was essentially mechanical. Its organic, human component – my guess was no more than a brain and some key organs – supported both physically and biologically in a polished silver servitor sculpted in the form of a griffin, its draconian neck swept back so its beaked visage stared down at us. It floated on anti-grav plates built into its eagle wings.

It paused before us, and projected a holographic chart from its open beak. The star map was complex, and incomprehensible to the unschooled eye, but I made out some detail.

'The Navigators have analysed the warp-wake of the departing fleet and made a number of algorithmic computations. The heretics are moving out of the Helican sub-sector, out of Imperial space itself, into the forbidden stellar territories of a breed I believe are known as the saruthi.'

'I had guessed as much. But that in itself is a considerable area, more than a dozen systems. We need specifics.'

'Here,' said Maxilla, indicating a point on the shimmering three dimensional chart with one gloved hand. 'The charts have it as KCX-1288. Under optimal conditions, it's thirty weeks away from here.'

'And what is the margin for error on this calculation?'

'No greater than point zero six. The warp-wake of the fleet was quite considerable. They may of course break the journey and re-route, but we will be watching for changes in their wake.'

'Of course,' he added, 'They will presume us to be following. Even if they think you're dead, they'll know you had to have had a starship that brought you here. One they couldn't find.'

The thought had crossed my mind too. Glaw and his conspirators must at least now be expecting pursuit, or expecting someone to inform on their whereabouts and destination. They would now be trusting on vigilance, their considerable massed firepower, and their headstart.

I already had Lowink busy preparing an emergency communiqué to send back to Gudrun and Inquisition command.

'What do you know of the saruthi and their territory?'

'Nothing,' he said. 'I've never travelled there.'

I thought this a curiously brief answer for a man so usually talkative.

'So,' he said at length, 'apart from our knowledge of where they're going, have we any other advantages?'

'We have.' I took from my coat pocket the item that had rested there ever since I had liberated it from Glaw's travelling trunk in North Qualm. Maxilla regarded it with frank perplexity.

'This,' I told him, 'is the Pontius.'

We used a large, empty hold in the depths of the *Essene*. Some of Maxilla's servitors arranged lighting and powerfeeds. My own servitors – Modo and Nilquit – carried the claw-footed casket in and set in on the cold steel floor.

I stood watching, my hands buried deep in my overcoat pockets against the cold of the chamber. Aemos hunched over the casket and, with Nilquit's aid, began to connect cables. I looked over at Bequin. She stood next to Fischig, and was bundled up in a heavy red gown with a grey shawl, and there was an expression of grim reluctance on her face. She'd found it all fun at first, a game, even in the face of danger at House Glaw. But Damask had changed things for her. The monster Mandragore. She knew it wasn't a game anymore. She'd seen things that many – perhaps even most – citizens of the Imperium never see. Most lives are spent on safe worlds far from the touch of war and horror, and the obscenities that lurk out there in the darkest parts of the void are myths or rumours... if that.

But now she knew. Perhaps it had changed her mind. Perhaps she didn't want to be here any more. Perhaps she was now regretting jumping so eagerly for the offer I'd made her.

I didn't ask her. She'd tell me if she had to. We were all too committed now.

'Eisenhorn?' Aemos reached out his hands and I placed the cool hard ball of the Pontius in them. With almost priestly care, he fitted it into place.

I ordered everyone back out of the hold, even the servitors, everyone except Bequin and Aemos. Fischig closed the hold door behind him.

Aemos looked at me and I nodded assent. He made the final connection and then backed away from the casket as hurriedly as his old and augmetised limbs could manage.

At first, nothing. Small tell-tale lights winked along the edge of the casket – Eyclone's casket – and the internal wiring glowed.

Then I felt a change in air-pressure. Bequin looked at me sharply, feeling it too.

The metal walls of the hold began to sweat. Beads of moisture popped and dribbled down the wall plating.

There was a faint crackling sound, like the gentle crisping of paper in flames. It spread, growing louder. Frost was forming on the casket, on the floor around it, spreading out across the hold's decking, up the walls, across the ceiling. A glittering thickness of diamond frost coated the interior of the hold in less than ten seconds. Our breath steamed in the air and we brushed jewels of ice-dust off our clothes and eyelashes.

'Pontius Glaw,' I said.

There was no answer, but after a moment or two, a series of animal grunts and barks mewled from the vox-speakers built into the casket.

'Glaw,' I repeated.

'What–' said an artificial voice.

Bequin stiffened.

'What have you woken me to?'

'What is the last thing you remember, Glaw?'

'Promises... promises...' the voice said, coming and going as if drifting away from the microphone and then back. 'Where is Urisel?'

'What promises were made to you, Glaw?'

'Life...' it murmured. 'Where is Urisel?' There was a tone now, an anger or an impatience. 'Where is he?'

I began to frame another question, but there was a sudden flash of activity, a crackle of electronic synapses firing across the crystal surface of the ball. It had lashed out with its mind, with its potent psychic powers. If Bequin had not been here, cancelling it out, no doubt Aemos and I would have been dead.

'Temper, temper...' I said. I took a step towards the casket. 'I am Eisenhorn, Imperial inquisitor. You are my prisoner and you only enjoy cognitive function because I allow it. You will answer my questions.'

'I... will... not.'

I shrugged. 'Aemos, disconnect this menace and prepare it for disintegration!'

'Wait! Wait!' the voice was pleading despite its colourless artificiality.

I knelt down in front of the casket. 'I know that your life and intellect were preserved in this device, Pontius Glaw. I know you have waited for two centuries, trapped in a bodiless state, desperate to be made whole again. That is what your family promised you, wasn't it?'

'Urisel promised... he said it be so... the methods were prepared...'

'To sacrifice the nobility of Hubris so that their life energies might be siphoned off into you through this casket. To give you the power to create a body for yourself.'

'He promised!' The stress fell on the second word, anguished and deep.

'Urisel and the others abandoned you, Pontius. They abandoned the Hubris project at the last minute in favour of something else. They are now all in the custody of the Inquisition.'

'Nooooo...' The word turned into a hiss that died away. 'They would not...'

'I'm sure they wouldn't... unless it was something so vital, so unmissable that they had no choice. You'd know what that would be, wouldn't you?'

Silence.

'What would be more important to them than you, Pontius Glaw?'

Silence.

'Pontius?'

'They are not caught.'

'What? Who are not?'

'My brethren. My kin... If you had them, you would not be asking these questions. They are free and you are desperate.'

'Not at all. You know how it is... so many lies, so many conflicting stories. Your pitiful family trying to sell each other out in exchange for freedom. I came to you for the truth.'

'No. Credible but no.'

'You know what it is, Pontius.'

'No.'

'You know what it is. They woke you from time to time to keep you informed, woke you from the oblivion that surrounds you in that globe. Beneath House Glaw, for example, in that chapel they built to contain you. I saw you there. You subdued me with your power.'

'I would do so again,' it said, traces of fire once more flickering along the golden filaments and woven circuits that encased the jagged, quartz-like lump.

'You know what it is. They told you.'

'No.'

I reached down and grasped a sheaf of wires. 'You're lying,' I said and yanked the wires out.

A brief moan rolled from the vox-speakers and faded. The lights on the casket went out. Air temperature and pressure began to climb again. The frost began to dissolve.

'Not much then,' said Bequin.

'We're just beginning,' I replied. 'We've got thirty weeks.'

SEVENTEEN

DISCOURSES
SPECULATION ON AN UNSYMMETRICAL THEME
BETRAYAL

I went to the hold each day with Bequin and Aemos and we repeated the procedure. For the next few days, he refused even to answer. After about a week, he began to goad us and abuse us with threats and obscenities. Every few days, he tried to lash out psychically, thwarted each time by Bequin's untouchable presence.

All the while, the *Essene* plunged through the immaterium towards the distant stargroup.

In the fourth week, I changed tactics, and entered into discussion with him on any subject that occurred to me. I didn't ask a single question concerning the 'true matter'. He refused to engage for the first few days, but I remained cordial and greeted him patiently each session. At last, discourses began: on astral navigation, high ecclesiarch music, architecture, stellar demographics, antique weapons, fine wines...

He could not help himself. The isolation of his condition made him crave such contacts with a real, vibrant world. He longed to taste and read and see and live again. Within two weeks he needed no encouragement to talk. I was no friend, and he was still wary, and keen to insult on any occasion, but he clearly welcomed our conversations. When, deliberately, I missed a day, he complained sullenly, as if wounded or let down.

For my part, I had the chance to realise how dangerous Glaw was. His mind was brilliant: charming, witty, incisive, and formidably knowledgeable. It was a pleasure to talk to him and learn from him. It was a salutary reminder of the quality of mind that Chaos can steal. The greatest of us, the brightest, the most urbane and learned, can fall prey.

One day in the tenth week, I entered the chamber with Bequin and Aemos as usual and we woke him. But an uncommon sensation troubled me.

'What is this?' I said. It seemed to me the casket was not quite in the same place as usual. 'Have you been in here, Aemos?' I asked. 'Even to make standard checks?'

'No,' he assured me. The hold was locked as a matter of course after each session.

'My imagination then,' I decided.

Our discourses continued, pleasantly, each morning for an hour or so. We often discussed Imperial policies and ethics, subjects on which he was astonishingly well-read. He never strayed, never allowed himself to profess a belief or concept that might be deemed counter to the strictures of the Imperium, as if he recognised that such an admission would perforce end our entente. On occasions, I gave him openings to do so, conversational gambits that would allow him space and opportunity to criticise or denounce the way of the God-Emperor and the rule of Terra. He resisted, though at times I felt he was desperate to voice his own, contrary beliefs. But his need for activity and contact was paramount. He would not risk losing our interaction.

He could quote, extensively, chapter and verse from Imperial texts, philosophies, poetry, ecclesiarchal lore. His scholarship rivalled Aemos's. But just as he refrained from condemning himself with heretical utterances, he also refrained from actually professing loyalty to the Golden Throne. He conducted our conversations in a subjective, uninvolved way. He did not attempt to dissemble and play the part of the loyal citizen. I appreciated that this represented his respect for me. He did not insult my intelligence by lying.

More often still than politics and ethics, we talked of history. Again, in this area, his learning was tremendous, but there was also, for the first time, an eagerness, a hunger. He never asked directly, but it was clear he longed to know in detail about the events that had taken place in the two hundred and twelve years since his death. His family had clearly told him little. He made leading remarks to draw answers out of me. I gave him some, and sometimes volunteered accounts of major events, political changes and Imperial gains. I had decided beforehand not to make any mention of Imperial defeats or losses, to avoid giving him anything he might relish. The picture that Pontius Glaw got from me was of an Imperium stronger and more healthy than ever before.

Even so, it delighted him. Precious glimpses of a galaxy he had long been divorced from.

The rest of that long transit time was spent in preparation and study, daily regimes of weapons practice and combat training. Fischig ran hand-to-hand sessions each afternoon, and set himself to honing Bequin's natural dexterity and speed. I pressed weights in a makeshift gymnasium, and ran tens of kilometres each day around the empty halls and corridors of the *Essene*. Slowly, I brought myself back to peak fitness.

I worked my mind too. A disciplined regime of psychic exercises, some conducted with Lowink's help.

Aemos and I studied extensively. We worked through all the archive data we had to hand, researching the saruthi. It added little to our knowledge.

The extent of their territories was known, but virtually nothing beyond that. There had only been a handful of officially recorded contacts in the past two thousand years. I wondered how much was known about them by the rogue traders who sailed beyond the Imperial veil, men like Gorgone Locke.

All we knew with any certainty was that the saruthi were an old xenos culture – insular, secretive, lying outside the bounds of the Imperium. They were technically resourceful, mature and well-established. We knew nothing of their culture-type, beliefs, language… not even their physical appearance.

'We can at least conjecture they have some religious beliefs or values,' Aemos told me. 'Or, at the very least, they hold certain relics of their past in high regard for some symbolic or sacred purpose. Our foes only excavated that material on Damask because they knew it had value to the saruthi.'

'Holy items? Icons?'

He shrugged. 'Or ancestor spirits – or simply a desire to recover and repatriate cultural materials from their past.'

'And we know their territory was once bigger. Extending as far as Damask, even if that was but a distant outpost,' said Lowink.

We sat around an inlaid table in one of Maxilla's staterooms, the polished table top smothered in open books, scrolls, data-slates and record tiles.

'And Bonaventure,' I said. 'The wheel-graves. Bequin remarked that the site at North Qualm reminded her of those on her birthworld.'

'Perhaps,' said Aemos. 'But I am no archaexenon expert. The wheel-graves of Bonaventure are classified as "of unknown xenos manufacture" in all the texts I can find. They are but one among hundreds of unidentified relic sites in the Helican sub-sector. All traces of a long-vanished, or at least long-shrunk, saruthi civilisation… or the remnants of many miscellaneous forerunner species that roamed this part of space before man ever came this way.'

I set down a data-slate and picked up the item that lay in the centre of the table, wrapped in felt. It was the single ancient tablet that had escaped Damask with us. I had taken it from the crate during the stand-off, and it had still been in my hand when we had thrown ourselves aboard the gun-cutter. Like the stonework dug-out in the flame hill mine, it was made of a hard pale material glittering with flecks of mica that we all agreed was not indigenous to Damask. And it was octagonal, but not regularly so, being peculiarly long on two edges. The back of it was burned and scored where it had been cut away. The reverse showed a bas-relief symbol, a five-pointed star sigil. But it, too, was irregular: the radiating spars of the star were of unmatched length and they protruded at a variety of angles.

'Most perturbatory,' said Aemos, looking at it for the umpteenth time. 'Symmetry – at least, basic symmetry – is a virtual constant in the galaxy. All species – even the most obscene xenos kinds like the tyranid – have some order of it.'

'There's something wrong with the angles,' agreed Lowink, furrowing his unhealthy, socket-pocked brow. I knew what he meant. It was as if the angles in the star symbol made up more than three hundred and sixty degrees, though that of course was unthinkable.

* * *

'Who has been in here?' I asked at the start of my next session with Pontius. I glanced around the frost-caked chamber. Bequin shrugged, blowing on her hands. Aemos also looked puzzled.

'The casket has been moved again. Just slightly. Who has been in here?'

'No one,' Pontius remarked, his artificial voice colourless.

'I was not directing the question at you, Pontius. For I doubt you would tell me the truth.'

'You wound me, Gregor,' he answered softly.

'Are you sure it's not your imagination?' Aemos asked. 'You said before–'

'Perhaps.' I frowned. 'I just feel something is... changed.'

I dined with Maxilla most evenings during the long voyage, sometimes in company with the others, sometimes alone. One evening in the twenty-fifth week, only Maxilla and I sat at the stateroom table, as the gilt servitors brought in our meal.

'Tobias,' I said at length, 'tell me about the saruthi.'

He paused, and set his food-laden fork back down on his salver.

'What would you have me tell you?'

'Why you claimed to know nothing of them when I told you we were heading into their territory.'

'Because such places are forbidden. Because you are an inquisitor, and it does not do to admit transgressions to one such as you.'

I toyed with the lip of my half-empty glass. 'You have aided me eagerly and generously up to now, Tobias. I suspected your motives at first, a detail for which I have apologised. I see now you are as keen to serve the Emperor of Mankind as I. It troubles me that you would withhold information now.'

He bared his pearl-inlaid teeth and dabbed at his lips with the corner of his napkin. 'It does more than trouble me, Gregor. It has plagued me, a crisis of conscience.'

'It is time to speak then.' I refilled both of our glasses with vintage from the decanter. 'Imperial knowledge of the saruthi is scant, and as you say, forbidden. I am more than aware that rogue traders know a great deal more about the outside systems and their species than we do. You are no rogue, but you are of the merchant elite. I think it unlikely that you have never come across any information pertaining to this xenos breed.'

He sighed. 'As a young man, over ninety years ago, I travelled into saruthi space. I was a junior crewman aboard a rogue trader called the *Promethean*. The master was Vaden Awl, long dead I imagine. Now there was a true rogue. He was sure he could strike a trading deal with these unknowns, or at least rob them blind of treasures.'

'And did he?'

'No. Remember, I was junior crew. I never left the bowels of the ship, or went to the surface of any worlds. All I knew was the miserable duration of the voyage. The senior crewmembers were tight-lipped. It took them, as I understand it, a long time to find the saruthi at all, and then they were less than forthcoming. The third officer, a man I knew reasonably well, confided to me that the saruthi played tricks on Awl's trade envoys, hid from them, tormented them.

'Tormented how?'

'Their worlds were eerie, disarming, uncomfortable – something about the angles, the officer said.'

'The angles?'

He laughed sourly and shrugged. 'As if something ill and twisted had infected their dimensions. We came back empty-handed after a year. Many of the crew quit and left the *Promethean* on our return, especially when Awl, who was a sick and driven man by then, declared he was going back to try again. I quit then too, but only because I couldn't face another year below decks.'

'And Awl?'

'He went back. I presume so, anyway. A few years later I heard his ship had been taken in the Borealis Reach by eldar renegades. That's the sum of it. You can perhaps see why I was unwilling to tell you these things before... because there is nothing useful to tell. Except to incriminate myself by admitting I had gone beyond.'

I nodded. 'In future, do not hold information back from me.'

'I will not.'

'And if you "remember" anything else...'

'I will tell you at once.'

'Tobias,' I paused. 'You say the voyage of the *Promethean* was long and fruitless, and the crewmembers were tormented by the beings they eventually encountered. Do you not have misgivings about returning there?'

'Of course.' He smiled a thin smile. 'But I am bound to serve you as an agent of the Emperor, and I will do so without question. Besides, part of me is curious.'

'Curious?'

'I want to see these saruthi with my own eyes.'

I should mention the dreams.

They did not over-trouble me during the voyage, but still they lingered, every few days or so. I seldom dreamed specifically of the blank-eyed, handsome man, but he lurked obliquely in other dreams, a bystander, looking on, observing, never speaking.

The lightning flashes escorted him, closer in each dream.

At ship-dawn of the third day of the twenty-ninth week, I rose silently and left my quarters, heading down towards the hold area where Pontius was secured. It was a good four hours until our daily conversation was due to start.

I climbed into a service duct adjoining the hold space, and crawled down until I reached a circulation grille that looking down into the hold itself.

There was frost on the grille.

Below, a figure crouched by the casket, huddled in robes, lit only by a hand-lamp. The overhead lights were not on.

Pontius was awake. The frost told me that much, and I could see the tiny flashes of firing synapses and hear the low hiss of his voice.

'Tell me of the Border Wars, the ones you mentioned last time. Imperial losses were great, you said?'

'I tell you much and you tell me little back,' replied the figure. 'That was not our agreement. I said I would secretly help you if you helped me. Power, Pontius, information. If you want me to act as your emissary, I need a show of trust. How can I communicate your will to your allies, if I know nothing of the "true matter"?'

A pause.

'What is this about?' the figure asked. 'What is at stake, what thing of great value?'

Another pause.

'You should go before they discover you. Eisenhorn is becoming suspicious.'

'Tell me, Pontius. We're nearly there, just a few days to go. Tell me so I can help you.'

'I... will tell you. The Necroteuch. That is what we are after, Alizebeth.'

EIGHTEEN

KCX-1288 BY THE LIGHT OF THE QUILL-STAR
INTO THE WOUND
THE WRONGNESS

On the first day of the thirty-first week, just under a day outside Maxilla's estimate, the *Essene* burst back into realspace deep inside the system designated KCX-1288. Almost at once we were in danger.

The local star was a vast, swollen fireball pulsing and retching out its last few millions years of life. Distended and no longer spherical, it glowed with a malevolent pink fire beneath a cooling crust of black shreds and tatters that looked like rot infecting its granular skin. Firestorms swirled and blistered across its enlarged surface and vomited gouts of stellar matter out into the system. An immense column of excreting gas and matter plumed away from the behemoth star, almost a light year long. It looked like a huge, luminous quill stabbed into the soft ball of that sun.

From the moment of our arrival at the translation point, sirens and alarms began shrilling on the bridge. External radiation levels were almost immeasurable, and we shuddered and rocked through waves of searing star debris. The entire system was lousy with drifting radioactive banks, ash clouds, flares and the splinters of matter they projected, and magnetic anomalies. Our shields were full on and already we were taking damage.

Maxilla said nothing, but furrowed his brow in concentration as he steered the juddering ship in through the treacherous course, negotiating the gravity pools and radioactive undertows.

'It's falling apart,' said Aemos, awed, gazing at the main projection screen and the furiously scrolling bars of data that flickered across it. 'The whole damn system is in a state of collapse.'

'Any sign of them?' I called to Maxilla.

'We must be right on their tail. They were half a day ahead of us, no more. Damn this interference. Wait–'

'What?'

He said something I couldn't hear over the cacophony.

'Say again!'

Maxilla cancelled the screaming sirens. The juddering and shaking continued, and now we could hear the groaning and creaking of the *Essene*'s hull under stress. He pointed to the pict-plate that overviewed the *Essene*'s sensor operations.

'I'm picking up their drive-wake and gravitational displacement, but in these conditions it's getting really hard to read them with accuracy. There–' He tapped a gloved finger on the plate. 'That's undoubtedly a drive-wake, but how do you explain it?'

I shook my head. I'm no mariner.

'They've split,' said Midas, looking over our shoulders. 'The main portion has fallen back, maybe out of the system itself to a safe distance, and a smaller, core group has continued on in. Maybe five ships, six at most.'

'That's how I read it too,' Maxilla agreed. 'A fleet division. I'd guess they didn't want to risk sending their biggest ships into this maelstrom.'

'I can see why,' murmured Bequin, gazing at the seething turmoil on the main display.

'Forget about the ones that have withdrawn. Follow the lead group in,' I said.

'I would advise–' Maxilla began.

'Do it!'

With the aid of his navigational servitors, he adjusted the *Essene*'s trajectory and set on after the drive-wake of the smaller group, driving in system.

'There! There, look!' Maxilla called out suddenly, adjusting a secondary display unit to magnify and enhance an image. It was distant, but we could see the burst-open hulk of an Imperial cruiser drifting in a halo of slowly dissipating energy.

'Definitely one of Estrum's ships. Holed by meteor storms. They ran into trouble the moment they pressed on.'

The *Essene* shook again.

'What about us?' I asked.

Maxilla conferred with Betancore. There was a particularly violent shudder and the main lights went out for a second.

'We need shelter,' Maxilla told me frankly.

As far as the *Essene*'s bewildered and over-taxed sensors could establish, there were fifteen planets in the system, as well as millions of planetoid fragments, mostly ragged embers of wasted rock and venting energy. Our quarry's drive wake led directly to the third largest, one of the inner worlds. It was a scabby, ruined, semi-shattered ball with lingering swathes of swirling bluish atmosphere. Craters covered its northern hemisphere; some impacts had been so large that they had torn open the mantle and exposed the livid red core beneath, like a skull cracked with devastating wounds. Even as we watched, we saw scatters of light dot and blossom across the surface as meteors struck and incinerated continents far below.

We tore in through the convulsing fabric of space, past moons of blood and striated mackerel clouds of dust. A vast sheet of stellar fire swept out at us, throwing the ship wildly off course and hurling silver lumps of rock and ice against our shields.

'Madness!' cried Fischig. 'They wouldn't have come here! It's death!'

Maxilla looked at me, as if hoping I'd agree with the chastener and call us off for the sake of the *Essene*. 'You are sure of their traces?'

Maxilla, his hands flexing on the controls, swallowed and nodded.

'Get us down there, into whatever shelter the planet's bulk can give us. At least let's confirm their corpses before we leave.'

Descent took twenty minutes, none of them smooth and none of them guaranteeing a sequel. I wanted to use the time to get Lowink or Maxilla's astropaths to check on the approach of the task force from Gudrun that had set out, on my instructions thirty weeks ago, to rendezvous with us here.

But it was impossible. The stellar distortion rendered astrotelepathy blind.

I cursed.

We went in steeply, down towards the dark side of the wounded planet. Blooms of fire consumed crater-pocked landmasses in the darkness below and ammoniacal storms raged in oceanic measures. Even here, with the planet between us and the convulsing sun, the ride was hard and rough. We saw, for a second as we passed, another ship ruin, another of Estrum's fleet splintered and destroyed. A death world; a death system.

'Our enemies must have made a mistake,' said Aemos, holding on to the edge of a console to steady himself. 'The saruthi can't be here. If they ever inhabited this system, they must have long since abandoned it.'

'Yet,' I countered, 'the heretic fleet's advance group presses on with great determination and purpose.'

The *Essene* continued to descend, closer than it would normally come to a planetary body. Only ribbons of atmosphere remained, and Maxilla clung to the ragged surface, passing barely ten kilometres above the bare rock. Drizzles of shooting stars rained past us.

'What's that?' I asked.

Maxilla adjusted his sensors and the resolution of the display. A huge wound in the planet's crust yawned before us, a thousand kilometres wide; a cliff-like lip of impact-raised rock with a vast cavity beneath.

'The sensors can't resolve it. Is that meteor damage?'

'Perhaps, from an angled strike,' said Aemos.

'Did they go past or in?' I asked.

'In?' barked Maxilla, incredulously.

'In! Did they go in?'

Aemos was leaning over the servitor at the sensor station. 'The drive wake ebbs and disappears here. Either they were vaporised en masse at this point or they indeed went inside.'

I looked at Maxilla. The *Essene* bucked again, thrown by a gravity pool, and the bridge lights went out briefly for a second time.

'This is a star-going ship,' he said softly, 'not built for surface landing.'

'I know that,' I replied. 'But neither were theirs. They have more information than we do... and they have gone inside.'

Shaking his head, Maxilla turned the *Essene* down towards the vast wound.

The rift cavity was dark, and limitless according to the sensors, though in my opinion, the sensors were no better than useless now. A dull red glow suffused the darkness far below us. The violent shaking had stopped, but still the hull creaked and protested at the gravitational stress.

We had the sudden impression of moving through some structure, then another, then a third. The display revealed the fourth before we passed under it: an angular hoop or arch eighty kilometres across. Beyond it, more in the series, towering around us as we progressed, as if we were passing down the middle of a giant rib-cage.

'They're octagonal,' said Aemos.

'And irregular,' I added.

No two of the rib-arches were the same, but they displayed the same form and lack of symmetry as their companions – the shape we now instantly associated with the saruthi.

'These can't be natural,' said Maxilla.

We continued in under the cyclopean spans, passing through a dozen, then a dozen more.

'Light sources ahead,' a servitor announced.

A dull, greenish glow fogged into being far away down the avenue of octagonal arches.

'Do we continue?' asked Maxilla.

I nodded. 'Send a marker drone back to the surface.'

A moment later, the rear display showed a small servitor drone struggling back up the vast channel towards the surface, running lights winking.

We ran on past the last arch. There was another judder.

Then we were riding clear into light, smooth, pale, green light.

There seemed to be no roof or ceiling to whatever we were in, though inside the planetary cavity we undoubtedly were. Just hazy green light, and below, a carpet of wispy cloud.

All turbulence stopped. We were like a ship becalmed.

The atmosphere in this place – logic battled to make us remember we were inside the crust of a planet – was thin and inert, a vaguely ammoniacal vapour. None of us could explain the source of the pervasive luminescence or the fact that the *Essene* sat comfortably at grav anchor in the serene quiet. As Maxilla had pointed out, it was not a trans-atmospheric vessel and it should have been impossible to stabilise it this close to a planetary body without severe stress damage.

From its system registers, the *Essene* seemed happy enough, happy to have ridden out the vile stellar storms of KCX-1288 into this safe harbour.

Apart from minor impact damage, only two of the ship's systems were inoperative. The sensors were blind and giving back nothing but odd, dead echoes. And every chronometer on the ship had stopped, except two that were running backwards.

Betancore and Maxilla studied the imperfect returns of the sensor arrays and concluded land of some sort lay beneath us, under the cloudbank. We estimated that it was six kilometres straight down, though in this vague, hazy rift it was difficult to say.

If Glaw's heretics were here, they had left no trace. But with our sensors so badly occluded, their advance fleet could be anchored just on the other side of the clouds.

We dropped to the cloudbank from the *Essene* in the gun-cutter shortly afterwards. All of us had buckled on hard-armour vacuum suits from Maxilla's lockers. Lowink, Fischig, Aemos and I shambled about the crew bay, getting used to the heavy plate and bulky quilting of the suits.

Bequin was in the cockpit with Betancore, watching him take us down. The pair of them wore borrowed vacuum suits too, and she was pinning up her hair so it would not interfere with the helmet seal.

'Good hunting, inquisitor,' crackled Maxilla from the *Essene* above us.

'He'll be down there, won't he?' asked Bequin, and I knew she was referring to Mandragore.

'It's likely. Him... and whatever this is all about.'

'Well, you heard what Pontius said,' she replied.

How could I not have? The Necroteuch. One doesn't hear a word like that and forget it. It had taken her weeks to gain the confidence of our bodiless prisoner, to play the part of a disaffected traitor. I hadn't been sure she was up to it, but she had performed with patience and a finely gauged measure of play-acting. It had been a risk, letting her slip in to see Pontius alone. She had assured me she could do it and she had not been wrong.

The Necroteuch. If Pontius Glaw was telling the truth, our enterprise had even greater urgency now. I had wondered what could be so precious, so important as to galvanise our enemies so, make them risk so much. I had my answer. Legend said the last extant copy of that abominable work had been destroyed millennia before. Except that by some means, in antique ages past, a copy had come into the hands of the saruthi race. And now they were preparing to trade it back to Glaw's Imperial heretics.

We came down through the clouds and saw the land below, a wide, rolling expanse of dust sweeping down to what seemed to be a sea. Liquid frothed and broke along a curved shoreline a hundred kilometres long. Everything was a shade of pale green, bathed by the radiance that glowed through the wispy clouds. There was a misty softness to it all, a lack of sharp focus. It seemed endless, toneless, slow. There was a calm, ethereal feel that was at once soothing and unnerving. Even the lapping sea seemed languid. It reminded me of the seacoast at Tralito, on Caelun Two, where I had spent a summer recuperating from injuries years before. Endless leagues of mica dunes, the slow sea, the balmy, hazy air.

'How big?' I asked Midas.

'Is what?' he asked.

'This... place.'

He pointed to the instruments. 'Can't say. A hundred kilometres, two... three... a thousand.'

'You must have something!'

He looked round at me with a smile that had worry in it. 'Systems say it's endless. Which is, of course, impossible. So I think the instruments are out. I'm not trusting them, anyway.'

'Then what are you flying by?'

'My eye – or the seat of my pants. Whichever you find most reassuring.'

We followed the slow curve of the endless bay for about ten minutes. At last, details emerged to break up the uniform anonymity.

A row of arches, octagonal, jutting from the sand a few hundred metres back from the waterline, ran parallel to the water. They were each about fifty metres broad, in everything but scale the twins of the arches Maxilla had guided the *Essene* through. They extended away as far as we could see in the green haze.

'Set us down.'

We sat the gun-cutter on the soft dusty-sand half a kilometre from the shore, clamped on our helmets and ventured out.

The radiance was greater than I had expected – the cutter's ports had been tinted – and we slid down brown-glass over-visors against the glare.

I hate vacuum suits. The sense of being muffled and constrained, the ponderous movement, the sound of my own breath in my ears, the sporadic click of the intercom. The suit shut out all sounds from outside, except the crunch of my feet on the fine, dry sand.

We shuffled down to the water's edge in a wide file. All of us except Aemos carried weapons.

It looked like a sea. Green water, showing white at the breakers.

'Liquid ammonia,' Aemos said, his voice a low crackle over the vox.

There was something strange about it.

'Do you see it?' he asked me.

'What?'

'The waves are moving out from the shore.'

I looked again. It was so obvious, I had missed it. The liquid wasn't rushing in and breaking, it was sucking away from the shore and rolling back into itself.

It was chilling. So simple. So wrong. My confidence withered. I wanted to strip off the claustrophobic suit and cry out. And I would have, except for the stark red warning lights on the atmosphere reader built into my suit's bulky left cuff.

What was it Maxilla had said? The saruthi had tormented the men of the *Promethean*? I didn't know for a moment if the unnatural behaviour of the sea was their doing – how could it have been? But I understood how insidious, distressing torment might have played upon them.

Fischig and Betancore had approached the first of the arches. I looked across and saw them dwarfed by the unsymmetrical structure. The next in the line was three hundred metres away, and they seemed regularly spaced. Each one, as far as I could see, was irregular in a different way, though the size and proportions were identical.

Bequin was kneeling on the shoreline, brushing the sand aside gently with her gauntlet. She had found what was perhaps the most distressing detail so far.

Under the sand, a few centimetres down, the ground was tiled. Tesselated, irregular octagonal tiles, just like the ones she had found on the floor of the mine working at North Qualm. Once more, they fitted perfectly, impossibly, despite their shape.

The more of them she uncovered, the more she brushed the sand away.

'Stop it,' I said. 'For our sanity, I don't think it's worth trying to discover if they cover the entire beach.'

'Can all of this... be artificial?' she asked.

'It can't be,' said Aemos. 'Perhaps the tiles and the arches are part of some old structure, long abandoned, that has since been flooded and covered with the dust... due to... to...'

He didn't sound at all convincing.

I crossed to Fischig and Betancore and stood with them gazing up at the first arch. It was wrought from that odd, unknown metal we had seen on Damask.

'What do we do know?' Fischig asked.

'Well, I hate to state the obvious,' said Aemos from down the beach, 'but the last row of these we found formed a deliberate pathway that led the *Essene* in here. Should we assume this serves the same purpose?'

I stepped forward, through the broad, towering shape of the first arch. 'Come on,' I said.

We walked for what I estimated was perhaps twenty minutes. Estimated. All of our chronometers were dead. After the first few minutes we began to hear a distant, repetitive boom; a low, almost sub-sonic peal like thunder that rolled out from somewhere far away over the sea. Or seemed to. It came every half minute or so. There were long intervals of silence, and just when we'd thought we'd heard the last, another boom would come. Like the crunch of our own footsteps, we could hear it through the suits, even with our vox circuits switched off.

I voxed to Maxilla. 'Can you hear that?'

There was a crackle, and no immediate reply. Then a sudden burst of transmission. Maxilla's voice: '...as you instruct, Gregor, but it's not going to be easy. Say again... what did you say about Fischig?'

'Maxilla! Repeat!' I began, but his voice continued over the top, incoherent. It wasn't a reply. I was just picking up his voice. I felt my spine go cold.

More static.

'Tell Alizebeth, I agree with that! Ha!'

It went dead.

I looked back at the others. Their pale faces gazed out of the tinted brown faceplates like ghosts.

'What... was that?' I murmured.

'An echo?' Aemos whispered. 'Some kind of transmission anomaly caused by the atmosphere and the–'

'It's not a conversation I've ever had.'

Another boom of thunder rolled across the dry, softly lit shore.

* * *

After my estimated twenty minutes, we passed through what was suddenly the last arch. We all stopped. Ahead of us, the land rose more steeply, into hills and low ridges. The terrain there was darker, inhospitable. The overall radiance had dulled, and the sky was a deep green, oozing into blackness over the hills.

'There... there were more in the row!' Fischig exclaimed. 'More arches!'

He was right. The octagonal colonnade had disappeared as we passed through the last arch. I stepped back through, imagining perhaps that from the other side the arches might reappear. They didn't. The booming continued.

We set off towards the hills. Bursts of static hissed through our vox units.

'Transmissions,' said Lowink. He fiddled with his vox-channels. 'I can't tune them in, but they're chatter. Military. Back and forth.'

Our quarry, perhaps.

'Look!' said Betancore, pointing behind us. Beyond the shore and the retreating line of arches, three ominous dark shapes hung under the clouds, out over the sea. Two Imperial frigates and an old, non-standard merchantman, floating at grav-anchor.

'How did we not see them when we passed?'

'I don't know, Midas. I'm not sure of anything anymore.'

When I turned back to the rest of the group, I saw Aemos unclasping his helmet.

'Aemos!'

'Calm yourself,' he said, uncovering his wizened old head. With the wide locking collar of the suit around him, he looked like a tortoise, pushing its gnarled head from its shell. He raised his left arm and showed me the atmosphere reader. The lights were green.

'Human-perfect atmosphere,' he said. 'A little cold and sterile, but human-perfect.'

We all unclasped our helmets and pulled them off. The chilly air bit my face, but it was good to be free of the suits. There was no scent to the air, none at all. Not salt or ammonia or dust.

We helped each other fasten our helmets to our shoulder packs. The booming was duller and more distant now it didn't have our hollow helmets to resonate through. We could hear each other's footsteps, each other's breathing, the suck and lap of the ocean. I could suddenly smell Bequin's perfume. It was reassuring.

I led the group on, and we climbed slowly into the rising land. Now free of the helmet, I understood our ponderous progress was a result of more than our heavy suits. It was somehow difficult to gauge distance and depth. We stumbled every now and then. The whole place was profoundly wrong.

We came upon them very suddenly. The sudden resumption of the vox-traffic was our only warning. Our speakers burst into life simultaneously.

'Run! Move up! Segment two!'

'Where are you? Where are you?'

'Cover to the left! That's an order! Cover to the left!'

'They're behind me! They're behind me and I c–'

A fierce hiss of static.

Ahead, coming down the ridges and slopes of the dark rise, we saw soldiers. Imperial Guard, wearing red and gold combat armour. Gudrunite riflemen.

'Cover!' I ordered, and we dropped down into the shelter of the rising dunes, readying weapons.

There were sixty or more of them, hurrying down the upper slopes towards us in a wide straggle, running. There was no order to it. They were fleeing. An officer in their midst was waving his arms and shouting, but they were ignoring him. Many had lost helmets or rifles.

A second later, their pursuers came over the rise and fell upon them from behind. Three black, armoured speeders in the livery of Navy security, and a following line of thirty troopers in their distinctive black armour, ordered, disciplined, marching in a spaced line, firing their hell-guns into the backs of the fleeing conscripts. The landspeeders swept in low, drizzling the slopes with cannon fire. The shots threw up plumes of dust, and the mangled bodies of men. A second later and all three landspeeders passed over us at what seemed like head-height, overshooting across the ammonia sea and banking round to follow in on another pass.

Some of the Gudrunites were firing back, and I saw one trooper topple and fall. But there was no co-ordination, no control.

'What the hell! Do we stay hidden?' gasped Bequin.

'They'll see us soon enough,' said Fischig, sliding open the feed slit of his heavy stubber's box magazine.

The odds were terrible, and ever since the incident on the *Essene*, I'd had a morbid loathing of the black-clad troopers.

But still...

I pulled out my heavy autopistol and tossed it to Aemos, freeing my las-carbine from the fastener lugs on my pack. Bequin drew her own weapons, a pair of laspistols. Lowink and Midas had their firearms – a las-carbine and a Glavian needle-rifle respectively – already braced in their hands.

'Look to the troops,' I told Fischig, Lowink and Bequin. 'Do what you can, Aemos. Midas – the fliers are down to us.'

We bellied forward through the dunes, and then came up firing. Fischig's big gun smashed into the lip of the high ridge, kicking up dust, before he found range and demolished three of the stalking troopers.

Lowink's carbine cracked out, and Aemos fired the autopistol hesitantly.

Bequin was amazing. She'd used her time well during the thirty-week passage, and Midas had clearly instructed her carefully. A laspistol in each hand, she whooped out a battle-cry of sorts and placed careful shots that dropped two more of the troopers.

The troopers balked in their ruthless advance, realising the situation had suddenly changed. The scattering Gudrunites also wavered, and some of them, the officer included, turned and began to confront the killers. I had been counting on this. We couldn't take them alone. I had trusted that our sudden intervention might galvanise the Guardsmen.

Still, many ran.

A fierce firefight erupted along the ridge between the halted troopers and those Gudrunites below who were turning to fight. Lowink. Fischig, Aemos and Bequin moved forward in support.

The landspeeders swept back, hammering the shore with shells.

Betancore dropped to one knee, raised his exotic weapon and fired. The long barrel pulsed and made a sound like a whispered shriek. Explosive splinters tore through the nearest speeder as it crossed down over us and it blew apart in the air.

Burning wreckage scattered across the sand.

I chased a second with my carbine. It was turning to present on us, and the turn made it slow. My shots missed or deflected from the armour. As its heavy cannon began to fire, pulverising the sand in a stitching row towards me, I shot the pilot through the face plate.

Still firing, it plunged suddenly and hit the beach fifty metres behind me. It bounced, shredding apart, struck again and crashed into the breakers in a spray of debris that threw up thousands of mis-matched splashes.

The third speeder turned in and made another pass, killing six more of the fleeing Gudrunites, who presented easy targets on the sand. Midas had his weapon trained on it and fired as it passed over, missing. He fired again, striking its rear end as it burned away.

It kept going. Over the beach. Out to sea. I have no idea what he hit – the crew, the control systems – but it just kept going, on and on, until it disappeared from sight.

We pressed up the slope, in among the Gudrunites now. They were dirty and dishevelled to a man, none older than twenty-five. Seeing us and the damage we had wrought, they cheered, perhaps imagining we were part of some greater rescue force.

On the upper ridge, the last few troopers were crumpling. Fischig charged them, his stubber wailing, and a dozen Gudrunites went with him, eager to turn on their tormentors.

The ridge fight lasted another two minutes. Fischig lost two of the Gudrunites with him, but made certain none of the troopers survived. Law enforcement, I remember thinking, had robbed the military of a fine soldier in Chastener Fischig.

I sought out the Gudrunite officer as his men collapsed, weary with exhaustion and relief. Some were weeping. All of them looked scared. Smoke from the battle drifted down the ridge in the windless air.

The officer, a sergeant, was no older than his men. He had attempted to grow a beard, but his facial hair wasn't really up to it. He saluted me even before I had shown him my badge of office. Then he fell on his knees.

'Get up.'

He did.

'Inquisitor Eisenhorn. And you are...?'

'Sergeant Enil Jeruss, second battalion, 50th Gudrunite Rifles. Sir, is the fleet here? Have they found us?'

I held up my hand to quieten him down.

'Appraise me, quickly and briefly.'

'We wanted no part of it. We were mustered to the frigate *Exalted*, waiting to ship out. When we ran from Gudrun high anchor, the captain told us all Gudrun had fallen and we were relocating.'

'The captain?'

'Captain Estrum, sir.'

'And then?'

'Thirty weeks in transit to get here. The moment we arrived, we knew something was wrong. We protested, demanded to know what was happening. They called it dereliction and sent dozens to the firing squads. We were given a chance to follow orders or die.'

'Not much of a chance.'

He shook his head. 'No, sir. That's why I tried to get the men out. We broke and ran, once we'd got in there, once they were busy. They came after us to hunt us down.'

'In where?'

He gestured back over the ridge. 'The darkness.'

'Tell me what you saw,' I said.

NINETEEN

JERUSS MAKES HIS REPORT
AT THE PLATEAU
THE TRUE MATTER

'I don't even know what world we're on,' Sergeant Jeruss said. 'They never told us. The ride in was rough, though.'

'It has no name, as far as I know. Go on.'

'They deployed us from the ships along this beach as an escort detail for the main party.'

'How many men?'

'Over a hundred naval security troopers, and three hundred or so of us guard.'

'Vehicles?'

'Speeders like you saw, and a pair of heavier personnel carriers for some crates of cargo and the main party.'

'What do you know of them?'

Jeruss shrugged. 'Of the cargo, nothing. In the main party was the captain, and Lord Glaw of Gudrun. He's a worthy nobleman from my homeworld.'

'I know him. Who else?'

'Some others too: a merchant, an ecclesiarch, and a great and terrible warrior that they tried to keep away from us regular troops.'

Mandragore, no doubt. And Dazzo and Locke. The core of Oberon Glaw's cabal.

'Then what?'

Jeruss pointed up the slopes in the dark, forbidding uplands. 'We advanced into that. It seemed to me they knew where they were going. Things changed as we went further in. It got darker and warmer. And it was hard to negotiate the way, as if–'

'As if what?'

'We couldn't judge distances. Sometimes it was like wading through hot wax, sometimes we could barely slow ourselves down. Some of the men panicked. We found polygons, like these on the beach.'

It was his word for the hoop-like arches.

'There were rows of them, aisles, marching away into the uplands. They were so irregular they disturbed the mind. They seemed to vary, to change.'

'What do you mean "irregular"?'

'I went to no officer school, sir, but I am educated. I understand simple geometry. The angles of the polygons did not add up, yet they were there.'

Chilled, I recalled Maxilla's mention of the 'unwholesome' angles, and thought too of the marking on the tile I had taken from Damask.

'We followed some of these rows, passing through polygons on occasions. The ecclesiarch and the merchant seemed to be leading us. And there was another man, a tech-priest type.'

'Slim build? Blue eyes?'

'Yes.'

'His name is Malahite. He played a part in choosing your path?'

'Yes, they deferred to him on several occasions. Finally, we came to a plateau. A great raised, wide space, overlooked by jagged peaks of rock. The plateau was artificial. Tiled with smooth stones that–'

He tried to make a shape with his index fingers and thumbs but shrugged and gave up.

'More impossible polygons?'

He laughed nervously. 'Yes. The plateau was vast. We waited there, the men grouped around the outside of the space, the main party and the vehicles in the centre.'

'And then?'

'We waited what seemed like hours, but it was impossible to tell because our chronometers had all stopped. Then there was some kind of dispute. Lord Glaw was arguing with some of the others. I saw this as a chance. I got the men ready. Nearly ninety of us, ready and eager to trust to chance and flee. All eyes were on the shouting match. The big warrior – God-Emperor save me! – he was shouting by then. I think the sound of his voice was what decided us. We slipped away in twos and threes, from the back of the ranks, down the sides of the plateau, and ran back the way we'd come.'

'And they discovered your escape?'

'Eventually. And came hunting for us. The rest you know.'

I waited a few moments for him to collect himself, and gathered the men around. There were about thirty riflemen left, all of them scared, and another three or four wounded. Aemos did what he could for them.

I rose and addressed them all. 'In defying your officers and leaders, you have served the Emperor. The men who brought you here are Imperial heretics, and their enterprise is criminal. My purpose here is to stop them. I intend to press on at once on that mission. I cannot vouch for the safety of any who follow me, but I count it as a mark of honour to the Emperor himself that you will. He needs our service here, now. If you take seriously the oaths you made to the Imperium when you became Guardsmen, then you will not hesitate. There is no more vital battle in which you might give your lives.'

Wild, frightened faces stared back at me. There was a murmur of agreement, but these were young inexperienced men, some no more than boys, who had been thrown into the deep waters of madness.

'Steel yourselves, and know that the Emperor is with you and for you in this. I don't exaggerate when I say the future rests in our hands.'

More voluble assent now. These men weren't cowards. They just needed a purpose and a sense that they were fighting for a worthy cause.

I whispered briefly to Fischig and he immediately stepped up and raised his voice to the Imperial creed, and the song of allegiance, hymns that every child in the Imperium knew. The Gudrunites joined in lustily. It centred and focused their determination.

Still, the booming came along the shore.

With Betancore's help, I stripped arms and equipment from the fallen. There were enough weapons to make sure every man had a lasrifle or a hell-gun. We also managed to assemble three intact naval trooper uniforms, mixing and matching from the dead.

I stripped off my bulky vacuum suit and began to put on the polished black combat armour of a naval security trooper. Midas attempted to do the same, but his build was too slim for the heavy rig. The troopers were, to a man, large brutes.

We dressed Fischig in the armour instead, and then, so as not to waste the third set, chose a heavy-set Gudrunite from Jeruss's group, a corporal named Twane.

'What's the Gudrunite command channel?' I asked Jeruss as I adjusted the helmet vox set.

'Beta-phi-beta.'

'And of the men you left in there at the plateau, how many others might side with us?'

'All the Gudrunites, I would say. Sergeant Creddon's unit, certainly.'

'Your job will be to rally them to us when we get inside. I'll give the word.'

He nodded.

We left the wounded on the shore, as comfortable as we could make them, and advanced into the dark uplands.

As Jeruss had told me, it quickly became darker and warmer. The sleek black body armour I was now wearing had an integral cooling system, but it didn't seem to help. And the wrongness still afflicted us. It was difficult to walk without stumbling in places.

We came upon the first of the arches, and Jeruss led us through, though we would have been able to follow the course without difficulty. Footsteps and the tracks of heavy vehicles had left deep prints and ruts in the soft dusty soil.

We were advancing up a cluster of hills, dark and uninviting with a glowering sky above. There were many rows of arches, some overlapping. We became disoriented. It seemed on occasions that as we passed through one arch, we came out through another in a different row. The tracks never wavered or broke, but we seemed to blink between one aisle of hoops and another. And the angles of the joints in the arches were – as Jeruss had said – geometrically incorrect.

'I think,' Aemos said quietly to me as we walked onwards, 'the lack of symmetry is in every particular and every dimension.'

'Meaning?'

'The three we can see and the fourth – time. Dimensions have been stretched and warped. Perhaps accidentally. Perhaps to torment us. Perhaps for some other purpose. But I think that is why things are so twisted and wrong.'

We came at last upon the place Jeruss had called the plateau. It was a flat-topped mound nearly a kilometre across, smoothly tiled with octagonal tesserae that mocked logic. The sides sloped down to the dusty soil and all around, the site was ringed by ragged brown peaks and crags. Above, the sky was dark and flecked with stars.

On our side of the plateau, a semi-circle of several hundred men sat huddled around the rim, waiting. I could feel their tension. More than half of them were Gudrunites; the others were troopers. Smaller groups of soldiers stood in ordered ranks further towards the centre of the plateau, escorting two Navy troop carriers in which figures sat, and a pair of empty landspeeders. A pile of crates had been removed from the carriers and piled on the tiled ground.

On the far side of the plateau, a row of arches led away into the surrounding rocks.

We lay in cover and waited, watching.

After an interminable period, there was movement on the far side and figures emerged from the arches. Even at a distance, I could tell they were Dazzo and Malahite, with four naval troopers in escort. They came out briskly, signalling to the main group at the vehicles. All the troops around the rim got to their feet.

Other shapes now appeared through the arches. They were impossible to define at first; grey, reflective shapes that had no human form or intelligible movement.

I took out my scope, and trained it on them, carefully resolving the magnification.

And I saw the saruthi for the first time.

There were nine of them, as far as I could tell. They made me think of arachnids, or crustaceans, but neither comparison was entirely accurate. From their flat, grey bodies extended five supporting limbs, jointed in such a way so that the main mid-limb joint was raised higher than the horizontal torso. There was no symmetry to the arrangement of limbs, or to the way in which they moved. Their scuttling pace was irregular and without repetition of order. It was disturbing merely to watch them walk. Each limb ended in a calliper of polished silver, a metal stilt clasped in the digits of each limb, lifting them a further metre or so off the ground. The metal spikes of the stilts made a clacking, tapping sound on the hard tiles that I could hear despite the distance. Their heads were oblate shapes rising on thick, boneless columns from the tops of their bodies. They had long skulls and lacked obvious mouths or eyes, though several flaring, nostril-like openings showed on their snouts. There was no symmetry to the arrangement of these openings either, nor to the shape of the skulls, and their necks sprouted off-centre from their backs.

They were loathsome, filthy things. Each creature was twice the mass of a man, with gleaming grey flesh.

Shouts and noises of alarm came from some of the waiting men. Several turned and fled from the plateau, scrabbling, wailing.

The nine saruthi clicked their way out into the open from the hoop, fanning out until they formed a semi-circular line facing Dazzo and Malahite. I saw Oberon Glaw, Gorgone Locke, Estrum and the monstrous form of Mandragore descend from the vehicles to join their comrades.

I confess that I was, by then, as afraid as those with me. I have seen horror, and horror itself does not terrify me. Nor indeed was there anything horrific about these beings. Alien, yes, and as a puritan that was alarming. But objectively, they were impressive, striking creatures; assured, almost majestic.

My fear stemmed from a deeper, gut instinct. As with this world we had entered, there was a wrongness to them, to their shape, their movement, their design. Each scuttling limb, each swaying head, betrayed an unholy nature. I could not have believed how reassuring symmetry could be, and how distressing might be its lack. They were warped things, warped from any civilised sense of grace, any human understanding of aesthetics. Their bodies and limbs were so irregular, they didn't even seem to make sense as if, like the tiles and the arches, their angles didn't add up correctly.

Fear, then, swayed me. I looked around at my companions, and saw fear on their gazing faces too; fear, revulsion, disbelief.

Aemos saved my life and sanity. He and he alone stared in wonder at the saruthi, a perplexed smile of intellectual delight on his ancient face.

'Most perturbatory,' I heard him murmur.

That simple detail made me laugh. My confidence returned, and with it, my resolve. I waved Fischig and the soldier, Twane, over to me, and then made certain that Bequin, Midas and Jeruss were sufficiently in control of their faculties to be left in charge. Jeruss and Twane needed some fierce cajoling. Bequin was already prepared, her weapons drawn. The sight of Mandragore had fired her will.

'Wait for my signal,' I told Midas. To Fischig I said, 'Keep an eye on our friend here,' meaning Twane.

The three of us crept down from cover and approached the edge of the plateau. The men were all on their feet, murmuring, alarmed, looking at the meeting taking place at the centre of the platform. Naval security officers scolded the Gudrunites and kept them in line, but I could tell they were uneasy too.

We came up the slope and melted into the watching crowd. Gudrunites got out of our way – three more naval oppressors with blank visors and low-strapped hell-guns.

We came almost to the front of the crowd. A trooper near me growled, 'I didn't sign up for this!' as he stared at the saruthi two hundred metres away.

'Pull yourself together!' I snapped to him and he looked at me sharply.

'It isn't right!' he murmured.

'We'll see, won't we?' I said, patting my hell-gun. 'If Estrum and these others have led us into a nightmare, they'll see how Scarus Fleet's troopers account for themselves!'

He nodded and readied his own weapon.

Twane, Fischig and I moved forward again. No one paid us any heed. Indeed, many troopers were moving forward to flank the vehicles now.

I looked again at the meeting. Oberon Glaw, his long robes spilling down from upraised arms, was greeting the saruthi with words I couldn't hear. It went on a while.

Finally, he half turned and gestured towards the waiting crates. His voice reached me.

'And in good faith we have brought the properties as agreed.'

Locke moved back from the group. 'Attend me!' he ordered to the naval troopers around him. I moved forward at once, and so did Fischig. In a second, we were part of a team of more than a dozen troopers carrying the first of the crates forward. I was right next to Locke, my black-gloved hands clutching the carrying handle next to his brawny fists.

We set the crates down in front of the saruthi and withdrew a few paces. Locke remained and opened a crate lid as one of the saruthi clattered forward.

I saw them now, close to. It was no better. Their grey skin was covered with whorled pores, and the nostrils on their snouts flared and clenched. I could see that each of their limbs ended in what looked abominably like a human hand, grey skinned, gripping the cross-bar of each silver stilt.

The saruthi that had moved forward set two of his stilts down on the tiles and reached into the open crate with flickering fingers. It searched by touch for a moment, and then withdrew its hands empty. Its eyeless skull swayed slightly on its neck. Then it raised those free hands high, clasped together, as a man might raise his hands over his head in victory.

The long, rubber-jointed fingers of each hand – and I cannot say for sure how many digits each hand had or even if they each had the same number – twisted and clenched around each other and formed a shape. A visage. A human face. Eyes, a nose, a wide mouth. Perfect, impossible, chilling.

The raised effigy of a face seemed to study us. Then the mouth moved.

'Your bond you have with truth made, being man.'

There was a hush of alarm in the crowd at my back. The voice was dull and tuneless, without inflection, but the finger-mouth puppeted the speech with awful precision.

'Then we may trade?' Glaw stammered.

The hands parted and the face vanished. The creature took up its stilts again and scuttled backwards. Its kin also moved back, away from the arch.

More creatures emerged, more saruthi identical to those who had already appeared, flanking other things. There seemed to be four of them, with body structures similar to the aliens, but they were bloated and misshapen. Their rugose flesh was white and sickly and blotched with marks that seemed like disease. Instead of stilts, their limbs were fitted with heavy, metal hooves, linked all around by wires that acted like shackles. These pallid, wretched things – slaves of the saruthi I had no doubt – moaned as they moved, filling the air with a sickly whining. The waiting saruthi jabbed at them with the points of their stilts as they clattered past onto the plateau.

Between them, on their backs, the four slave-things carried a trapezoidal casket of black metal, covered with irregularly spaced wart-like protuberances. They came to a halt and sank down onto their bellies.

Dazzo and Malahite moved forward, approaching the casket bearers. A stilted saruthi scuttled around beside them, reached a long limb over to extend his silver calliper, and pressed the point against one of the protuberances.

The casket opened on invisible hinges, like the petals of a malformed flower. I think I had expected light to radiate out, or some other show of power.

There was none. Malahite stepped forward between the kneeling limbs of the slave-things and reached out, but Dazzo pushed him back with a curse and a slap of psychic power that sent him sprawling.

A ripple of response ran through the saruthi, making them scuttle on the spot.

Now Dazzo reached into the casket. He took out a tiny oblong, no bigger than a boltgun's magazine, and held it in trembling hands, gazing at it.

A book. Ancient parchment encased in a sleeve of black saruthi metal, closed with a clasp.

'Well, ecclesiarch?' Glaw growled. 'We need confirmation.'

Dazzo unclasped the cover and turned the first antique page.

'The true matter is ours,' he stammered, and fell to his knees.

The Necroteuch. They had the Necroteuch.

It was now or never, I thought.

TWENTY

MY ALLY, CONFUSION
THE WRATH OF MANDRAGORE
AGAINST OBERON

I bellowed, 'Look out! They're attacking!' and slammed myself hard into the two troopers by my side. As we went over in a clumsy, thrashing heap, I fired my hell-gun wildly for good measure.

Tension among the humans gathered around the plateau was intense. The saruthi, I firmly believe, had deliberately used their devices and environment to foment that tension, perhaps intending to weaken and cow the humans they found themselves dealing with. If so, they had done too good a job. Gudrunites and troopers alike were at snapping point, their minds and spirits rattled by their location and by what they had seen. A warning voice and a few shots was all it took to spill the tension over.

All around me, men yelled out and weapons crackled. Assuming an attack on their high-born leaders, the troopers still firmly loyal to Glaw and Estrum surged forward, firing on the saruthi with their assault guns. Others wavered in confusion and lashed out at those around them. The Gudrunites around the rim of the plateau turned their guns on their oppressors, or fired at the vehicles.

From the rim of the plateau, Midas and Bequin led our rearguard in a charge, weapons blazing.

In a second, the air was full of shouts and screams, gunfire and skittering las-bolts. Total confusion reigned.

I could hear Jeruss on the guard vox channel rallying his comrades, calling for them to turn on the Navy personnel. The naval security combat channel was riven with orders and countermands, squeals of rage and bellowed curses. I heard Oberon Glaw screaming for order, and the baying howl of Mandragore behind it all.

'Fischig! Twane! Sow confusion! Make for the target!'

Disguised like me, the pair moved forward. The mayhem was too dense and frenzied for there to be any sense of opposing sides. Guards fought naval troopers, or even each other, and indiscriminate fire whipped in all directions.

I shot down a trooper who ran past me, and another nearby who turned in dismay. Past them, I saw the tall, spare form of the rogue captain, Estrum, gazing at me through the smoke wash with incredulity. His eyes bulged more than ever. 'What the hell are you doing, trooper?' he managed to bark, his pronounced Adam's apple bobbing furiously.

'Performing the ministry of the sacred Inquisition,' I told him and shot him through the head.

The saruthi had been thrown into a state of great agitation. I have no way of knowing what emotions they were experiencing, if they experienced any at all. But they reacted as if horrified by the turn of events, distressed and appalled. Hell-gun fire from troopers who were convinced that the aliens were the aggressors blasted into two of them. One burst open and collapsed onto the tiles in a spreading pool of grey ichor and gristle. The other lost a limb and began to drag itself towards the arches with its remaining stilts.

Over the tumult of gunfire and human voices, the saruthi began to wail. Whether it was a threat, a warning, a call of distress, or an order to retreat I could not tell. They scuttled maniacally, their alien shriek shaking the air.

Two clattered forward suddenly, towards the bewildered trooper escort. Electric-blue discharges fizzled around the saruthi's swaying heads and then spat raking beams of ice-bright energy at their attackers. Two troopers were vaporised, their constituent matter boiling away in searing flashes of light.

I caught sight of Mandragore. The brute had already killed one trooper in an attempt to curtail the mindless wildfire, but now the saruthi had fired on them, the troopers clearly felt justified in their action and redoubled their efforts. An alien beam sliced into Mandragore's arm, and rage consumed him. He attacked the saruthi himself, wielding a massive chain-axe.

I hoped they'd kill him.

I pushed through a jumble of bodies and came out on the other side of the parked vehicles. Ahead I saw Dazzo, still kneeling by the ghastly white slave-beasts as if in a trance. The unholy prize was clenched in his hands.

I ran at him.

Fischig, his helmet missing, appeared alongside me. His borrowed black armour was awash with blood.

'Twane!' he bawled over his shoulder, and the disguised Gudrunite appeared, running after us, firing from the hip. Grenades were now exploding amid the mindless fighting. Bodies and chips of octagonal tiling were hurled into the air. One of the troop carriers was on fire.

The three of us were closest by far to the accursed 'true matter'. A saruthi came ploughing forward, spurring the jostling, frenzied slave-things aside with its stilt-spikes as it made for Dazzo.

With a juddering blow from one stilt, it knocked the kneeling man over and sent the Necroteuch scattering from his hands.

Malahite, on his hands and knees by the slave-things, let out a cry and dived after it. The saruthi jittered around to stop him just as Fischig and Twane blew it apart with hell-gun shots. Stringy grey fluid splashed across the tessellated tiles.

Another saruthi, its skull crackling with electrical power, blasted its kin's murderers. Twane convulsed and exploded in a drizzle of matter. By his side, Fischig was thrown over by the blinding detonation, his armour ripped open.

There was no time to help him. Clutching the book, Malahite was running away across the plateau, away from the straggled, brutal warfare. I severed his left leg at the knee with a round from my hell-gun and he dropped onto his face. When I reached him, he was clawing forward, daubed in blood, reaching for the fallen book.

'Leave it!' I snapped, pulling off my helmet and pointing the hell-gun down at him one handed. He saw my face and cursed. I knelt and picked up the little volume. Even through my armoured gloves, I could feel its heat. For a second, a long hypnotised second, it was all I knew. I understood why Dazzo had remained kneeling there for so long after he first grasped it. The content of the book, that ancient lore, was alive somehow, fidgeting, rustling, calling to me.

Calling me by name.

It knew me. It beckoned to me, telling me to open it and experience its wonders. I didn't even think to resist. What it was showing me was so wondrous, so sublime, so beautiful... the stars themselves, and behind the stars, the mechanisms of reality, the intricate and oh-so perfect workings of a transcendent natural force we misguidedly and dismissively called Chaos.

I undid the wire-like claps that kept the book shut...

Abruptly, a rough, foul psychic force burst into my mind, breaking the spell. I began to turn, to look away from the opening book. That half-turn was just enough to stop me dying.

I was felled by a monumental blow to the shoulder. As I dropped, the book spun helplessly from my yearning hand. The tiles underneath me were awash with blood.

My blood.

I rolled over as the next blow came. The screaming teeth of the chain axe missed me by a hair's breadth and shattered the bloody tiles.

Mandragore, bastard child of the Emperor.

I scrambled backwards in blind panic. The stinking Chaos warrior was right on me, his lurid armour flecked with human blood and alien ichor. My dazed half-turn at the last moment had spoiled his first blow, but still the back plate of my naval trooper combat armour was shredded; the left shoulder guard was completely ripped away. The glancing shoulder wound was savage and deep. Blood gouted through torn flesh and armour, cascading down my left arm. Writhing backwards, I found my hands slipping on the blood-washed octagons.

I lashed out with my mind. It was no match for his fearsome psychic capacity, but it was enough to put him off his swing. The shrieking chain-blade of the axe sawed through the air over my ducking head.

My fallen hell-gun was out of reach, and I doubted it would have made a dent in the monster anyway. His baying face, its sutured-on skin stretching around the gaping jaws of his skull, was all I could see.

My left arm was numb and useless. I threw myself to my feet, pulling my sword from my webbing.

The device is a fine weapon, of the old kind. It has no material blade like other, cruder models I have seen. It is a hilt, twenty centimetres long, inlaid and wound with silver thread, enclosing a fusion cell that generates a metre-long blade of coherent light. The Provost of Inx himself blessed it for me, charging it to 'protect our brother Eisenhorn always from the spawn of damnation.'

I prayed now that he hadn't been wasting his breath.

I ignited the blade and fended away the next axe swing. Sparks and metal shrapnel flew from the clash, and the beast's huge strength nearly struck it from my hand. I jumped back a pace or two from the next whistling bow. My head was swimming. Was it the loss of blood or the after-effects of that seductive book?

Mandragore was incandescent with fury now. I was proving to be annoyingly difficult to slay – for a mere mortal.

I had a dread feeling it wouldn't last.

He rushed me again, towering over me, and I managed to deflect the force of the chain-axe. But immediately he brought the butt of the weapon's long haft around and struck me in the chest, sending me flying. I actually left the ground and cleared several metres.

I landed hard on my injured shoulder. The pain rendered me insensible for a second. That was all he needed.

He crossed the blood-flecked tiles to me in two strides, the axe rising in the air as his growl rose in pitch. With a flailing motion, I kicked the Necroteuch towards him. It struck the toe of one great boot.

'Don't forget what you came for, abomination!' I rasped out.

Mandragore Carrion – son of Fulgrim, worthy of Slaanesh, champion of the Emperor's Children, killer of the living, defiler of the dead, keeper of secrets – paused. With a hacking laugh, his soulless eyes never leaving me, he stooped for the book.

'You counsel well, inquisitor, for... a...'

His fingers were around the Necroteuch, the metal-shod digits dwarfing it. His voice trailed away. Triumph faded from his hideous face; rage drained away; blood-lust dimmed. His mask of skin hung slack from its sutures. The light in his blood-rimmed eyes dulled.

The Necroteuch sang through every fibre and shred of corrupted being, stealing from him all sense of the outside world.

I stood, unsteadily, flexed my grip on the power sword, and sheared his head from his shoulders.

Before it had even struck the ground, the spinning skull combusted and blazed white hot, dripping liquid flame onto the tiles. The fireball bounced and rolled, rocked over, and consumed itself in a ferocious, dirty fire that swiftly left nothing behind but blackened shards of skull in a smouldering scorch mark.

The body remained standing, burning from within the torso, shooting long tongues of sickly green flame up out of the neck cavity. A column of filthy black smoke rose into the still air. The gaudy robes and cloak quickly caught, and thick flames enfolded the headless, metal ruin.

At the last moment, I struck off Mandragore's fist with the sword's bright blade, and the Necroteuch it clutched fell clear of the flames. I felt as though it was pleading with me to take it up again, to immerse myself again in the wonders it contained.

Such wonders. I bent down, torn by duty. The thing should be destroyed, but it held such secrets! Could not the Inquisition, and the Imperium as a whole, benefit from the infinite truths it contained? Had I even the right to destroy something so priceless?

The puritan part of me had no doubt. But another part abhorred the idea of wasting it. Knowledge is knowledge, surely? Evil stems from how knowledge is used. And such knowledge was here…

Perhaps if I read a page or two, I could make a better decision.

I shook my head to cast away the insidious thoughts. The noise of the battle came rushing back. I looked back across the plateau, beyond Mandragore's upright, burning corpse and the sprawled body of Malahite. The last few pockets of fighting were playing out, and the great tiled platform was littered with dead and debris. Both carrier vehicles were ablaze. The saruthi had gone, taking even their corpses with them. It seemed to me the Gudrunites had overwhelmed the troopers by sheer numbers. Few figures were still standing, and I could see none of my companions.

His regal cloak torn and his face bloodied, Oberon Glaw strode towards me, a laspistol clenched in his right hand.

'Throw that down, Glaw. It's over.'

'For you, yes.' He raised the weapon. A munitions canister on one of the burning carriers ignited and blew the armoured vehicle apart in a stunning conflagration. Flung out by the blast, broken armour plating and sections of track whizzed through the air like missiles. A chunk of trans-axle impaled Lord Glaw through the back of the head. He fell without a sound.

I grabbed a piece of smoking hull plate, and scooped the Necroteuch up on it. I would heed no more of its soft enticements. I let it slide off the makeshift scoop into Mandragore's upright corpse, so that it fell down through the open neck of the blazing armour into the furnace of the torso.

The flames turned red, then darker still. The blaze grew more intense. Something without a mouth screamed.

I limped away from the pyre. Malahite was alive and awake, calling out, 'Locke, please! Please!' in a hoarse voice.

Across the plateau, one of the naval speeders lifted into the air. Gorgone Locke was at the controls, with Dazzo slumped in the seat beside him. In moments, the racing speeder was disappearing over the ragged peaks, away from the plateau, towards the endless beach.

Midas, Bequin, Aemos and Lowink had survived the ordeal and the battle, though all had minor injuries. Two dozen Gudrunites were also still alive, including Jeruss.

Aemos wanted to see to my wound, but I had bound it tight to stanch the flow of blood and I wanted to waste no more time.

'I think it would be prudent to get out of here,' I told them.

Fischig lay on a makeshift stretcher. The saruthi weapon that had obliterated

Twane had cost him an arm and half of his face. Mercifully, he was unconscious. Two Gudrunites bore him up.

'It pains me to say this, but we're taking him too,' I told Midas and Jeruss, indicating the collapsed Malahite.

'Are you sure?' Betancore asked.

'The Inquisition will want to plunder his brain.'

Our ragged, battered party left the dark uplands and retraced our steps to the hazy levels of the beach. The booming had increased in volume and frequency and the sky was growing dark.

'It is as if,' said Aemos ominously, 'this place is coming to an end.'

'We don't want to be here when that happens,' I said.

From the beach, we could see the two Imperial frigates and the merchantman had departed. A wind, thick with an afterburn of ammonia, was picking up. Their vacuum suits more or less intact, Midas and Lowink went ahead to recover the gun-cutter.

My vox link crackled. Maxilla's voice suddenly sang out.

'Eisenhorn? For pity's sake, are you there? Are you there? Three ships just left, moving right past me! Conditions are worsening. I cannot stay here much longer. Respond! Please respond!'

'Maxilla! This is Eisenhorn! Can you hear me? We need you to move in and pick us up. We have injuries... Fischig and several others. This whole environment may be collapsing. Repeat, I need you to move the *Essene* in to my location and pick us up!'

A moment or two of static. Then his answer.

'As you instruct, Gregor, but it's not going to be easy. Say again, what did you say about Fischig?'

'He's hurt, Maxilla! Come and get us!'

'Hurry!' Bequin shouted over my shoulder. 'We don't want to be here any more!'

More static. 'Tell Alizebeth, I agree with that! Ha!'

The echoes, delays and dislocations were catching up with themselves. The wrongness was righting itself and, I thought with irony, that made things no better for us.

TWENTY-ONE

A GATHERING OF PEERS
LORD RORKEN CONTEMPLATES
MALAHITE'S SECRETS

Two days later, aboard the *Essene* at anchor beyond the treacherous reaches of system KCX-1288, we made our rendezvous with the Imperial taskforce outbound from Gudrun.

We'd made good our escape from the world of the plateau in less than two hours. As Aemos had predicted, the place seemed to unravel around us, as if that apparently timeless realm of the sea, the beach and the uplands had been nothing but an ingenious construct, a space engineered by the saruthi to accommodate the meeting with their human 'guests.' As we rode the gun-cutter back to the waiting *Essene*, the hazy radiance had begun to dim and atmospheric pressure dropped. We were beset by turbulence, and natural gravity began to reassert its influence. The impossible cavity had begun to decompose. By the time Maxilla was running the *Essene* down the dark corridor of arches as fast as he dared, the inner space where we had confronted the aliens was nothing but a dark maelstrom of ammonia and arsenical vapours. Our chronometers and horologiums had begun to run properly again.

We left the fractured planet behind, braving flares and gravity storms as we made a dash for the outer system. Forty minutes after leaving that place, rear-aligned sensors could find no trace of the 'wound,' as if it had collapsed, or had never been there to begin with.

How the saruthi came and went I had no idea, and Aemos was little help. We had seen no sign of other vessels or other points of egress from the planet's crust.

'Do they live within the planet?' I asked Aemos as we stood at an observation platform, looking back at the retreating star through glare-dimmed ports.

'I fancy not. Their technologies are beyond my ken, but I feel that they might have arrived on the plateau through those archways from another world, into a place they had built for the meeting.'

Such a concept defied my imaginings. Aemos was suggesting interstellar teleportation.

Outside the system, there had been little trace of the heretical fleet. As far as Maxilla was able to tell from drive and warp wakes, the three ships, no doubt bearing Locke and Dazzo, had rejoined their attentive flotilla and moved away almost at once into the immaterium.

Other warp indicators informed us that the taskforce was approaching, no more than two days away. We dropped grav-anchor, saw to our wounds, and waited.

Thirty weeks before, as we departed Damask, I had sent my request for assistance to Gudrun via Lowink astropathically. I had outlined as much of the situation as possible, providing what detail and conjecture I could, and had hoped the Lord Militant would send a military expedition to support me. I did not demand, as the likes of Commodus Voke were wont to do. I was sure the urgency and importance of my communiqué would speak for itself.

Eleven ships loomed out of the empyrean before us in battle formation: six Imperial frigates running out in the van, fighter wings riding out ahead of them in formation. Behind this spearhead of warships came the battleships *Vulpecula* and *Saint Scythus*, each three times the size of the frigates, each a bristling ogre of a vessel. To the rear was an ominous trio of cruisers, black ships of the Imperial Inquisition. This was no military expedition. This was an Inquisitorial taskforce.

We exchanged hails, identified ourselves and were escorted into the fleet pack by an honour guard of Thunderhawks. Shuttles transferred our wounded, including the still unconscious Fischig and the prisoner Malahite, to medicae faculties aboard the Saint Scythus. An hour later, at the request of Admiral Spatian, I also crossed by shuttle to the battleship. They were awaiting my report.

My left arm bound and tightly slung in a surgical brace, I wore a suit of black and my button-sleeved leather coat, my rosette pinned at my throat. Aemos, in sober green robes, accompanied me.

In the echoing vault of the *Saint Scythus*'s docking bay, Procurator Olm Madorthene and a detail of Navy stormtroopers waited to greet us. Madorthene wore the impressive white dress uniform in which I had first seen him, and the men's blue armour was rich with gold braid and ceremonial decoration.

Madorthene greeted me with a salute and we strode as a group towards the elevators that would carry us up into the command levels of the ship.

'How goes the uprising?' I asked.

'Well enough, inquisitor. We understand the Lord Militant has declared the Helican Schism over and quashed, though pacification wars are still raging across Thracian.'

'Losses?'

'Considerable. Mainly to the population and materials of the world affected, though some fleet and guard units have taken a beating. Lord Glaw's treason has cost the Imperium dear.'

'Lord Glaw's treason has cost him his life. His body rots on a nameless world in the system behind us.'

He nodded. 'Your master will be pleased.'
'My master?'

Lord Inquisitor Phlebas Alessandro Rorken sat in a marble throne at the far end of a chapel-like audience hall two decks beneath the main bridge of the *Saint Scythus*. I had met him twice before, and felt no more confident now for those experiences. He wore simple robes of crimson over black clothing and gloves, and no other decoration except for a gold signet ring of office on one knuckle. The austere simplicity of his garb seemed to accentuate his authority. His noble skull was shaved except for a forked goatee. His eyes, deep set and wise, glittered with intelligence.

Around him was his entourage. Ten Inquisitorial novices of interrogator rank or below, upheld banners, sacred flamer weapons, caskets of scrolls and slates, gleaming tools of torture on red satin cushions, or open hymnals. Flanking them were four bodyguards in red cloaks with double-handed broadswords held stiffly upright before their faces. Their armour was ornate, and the full visors had been fashioned and painted into the likenesses of four apostolic saints: Olios, Jerido, Manezzer and Kadmon. The masks were flat-eyed and expressionless and almost naive, lifted exactly from representations on illuminated manuscripts of old. A huddle of dark-robed savants waited nearby, and a dozen cherub servitors in the form of podgy three-year-olds with golden locks and the spiteful faces of gargoyles circled around, scolding and mocking, on grav-assisted golden wings.

'Approach, Eisenhorn,' Lord Rorken said, his soft voice carrying down the chamber effortlessly. 'Approach all.'

At his words, other figures emerged from anterooms along the sides of the hall, and took their seats to either hand. One was Admiral Spatian, an ancient, skeletal giant in white dress uniform, attended by several of his senior staff. The others were inquisitors. Titus Endor, in his maroon coat, unescorted save for a hunched female savant. He cast me an encouraging nod as I passed by. Commodus Voke, wizened and shuffling, helped onto his seat by a tall man in black. The man's head was bald and hairless apart from a few sickly clumps. His scalp, neck and face were livid with scar-tissue from injuries and surgery. It was Heldane. His encounter with the carnodon had not improved his looks. Like Endor, Voke nodded to me, but there was no friendship in it.

Next to him, Inquisitor Schongard, stocky and squat, the black metal mask obscuring everything but his raddled eyes. He took his seat and was flanked by two lean, supple females, members of some death-cult by the look of them, both nearly naked save for extensive body art, barbed hoods and harnesses strung with blades.

Opposite Schongard sat Konrad Molitor, an ultra-radical member of the Ordos I had little love or respect for. Molitor was a fit, athletic man dressed from head to toe in a tight weave-armour bodyglove of yellow and black check with a polished silver cuirass strapped around his torso. His black hair was close-trimmed and tonsured and he affected the air of a warrior monk from the First Crusade. Behind him stood three robed and hooded acolytes, one carrying Molitor's ornate powersword, another a silver chalice and paten, and the third a reliquary box and a smoking censer. Molitor's pupils were bright yellow and his gaze never wavered from me.

Last to take his seat, at Lord Rorken's right hand, was a giant in black power armour, a Space Marine of the Deathwatch, the dedicated unit of the Ordo Xenos. The Deathwatch was one of the Chambers Militant, Chapters founded exclusively for the Inquisition, obscure and secret even by the standards of the blessed Adeptus Astartes. At my approach, the warrior removed his helmet and set it on his armoured knee, revealing a slab-jawed, pale face and cropped grey hair. His thin mouth was curled in a frown.

Servitors brought a seat for me, and I took my place facing the Lord Inquisitor. Aemos stood at my side, silent for once.

'We have read your preliminary report, Brother Eisenhorn. Quite a tale it is. Of great moment.' Lord Rorken savoured the last word. 'You pursued Glaw's heretic fleet to this Emperor-forsaken outer world, certain that they planned to trade with a xenos breed. That trade, you stated, was for an item whose very nature would threaten the safety and sanctity of our society.'

'I reported correctly, lord brother.'

'We have known you always to be earnest and truthful, brother. We did not doubt your words. After all, are we not here in... unusual force?'

He gestured around and there was some laughter, most of it forced, most of it from Voke and Molitor.

'And what was this item?'

'The aliens possessed a single copy of a profane and forbidden work we know as the Necroteuch.'

The reaction was immediate. Voices rose all around, in surprise, alarm or disbelief. I heard Voke, Molitor and Schongard all calling out questions and scorn. The assembled retainers, novices and acolytes around us whispered or gabbled furiously. The cherubs wailed and fluttered into hiding behind Lord Rorken's throne. Rorken himself studied me dubiously. I saw that even the grim Space Marine looked questioningly at the inquisitor.

Lord Rorken raised his hand and the hubbub died away.

'Is that confirmed, Brother Eisenhorn?'

'Lord, it is. I saw it with my own eyes and felt its evil. It was the Necroteuch. As far as I have learned, the xenos breed – known as the saruthi – came upon a lost copy thousands of years ago, and through recently established lines of communication with the Glaw cabal, agreed to exchange it for certain artefacts of their own culture.'

'Preposterous!' spat Commodus Voke. 'The Necroteuch is a myth, and a wretched one at that! These twisted alien filth have fabricated this as a lure for the gullible heretics!'

I looked over at Voke and repeated, 'I saw it with my own eyes and felt its evil. It was the Necroteuch.'

Admiral Spatian looked up at Lord Rorken. 'This thing, this book – is it so valuable that these heretics would throw the entire sub-sector into schism to cover their attempts to retrieve it?'

'It is priceless!' cut in Molitor from across the chamber. 'Beyond worth!

If the legends of it are even fractionally true, it contains lore surpassing our understanding! They would not think twice of burning worlds to get it, or of sacrificing their entire resources to acquire the power it would bring them.'

'It has always been plain,' Endor said softly, 'that the stakes in this matter have been astonishingly high. Though I am shocked by Brother Gregor's news, I am not surprised. Only an icon as potent as the Necroteuch could have set this bloodshed in motion.'

'But the Necroteuch! Such a thing!' Schongard hissed.

'Were they successful, Inquisitor Eisenhorn?' the Space Marine asked suddenly, staring directly at me.

'No, brother-captain, they were not. The effort was desperate and close run, but my force was able to spoil their contact with the xenos saruthi. The aliens were driven off, and most of the heretics' advance guard, including Lord Glaw and a blasphemous child of the Emperor allied to his cause, were slain.'

'I read of this Mandragore in your report,' said the Space Marine. 'His presence was fundamental in the decision for my unit to accompany this force.'

'The Emperor's Children, Terra damn their souls, clearly wanted the book for themselves. They had sent Mandragore to assist Glaw in its recovery. That beings such as they took it seriously confirms the truth of my story, I believe.'

The noble Space Marine nodded. 'And Mandragore is dead, you say?'

'I killed him myself.'

The Deathwatch warrior sat back slightly, his brows rising gently in surprise.

'Some heretics escaped your purge?' Schongard asked.

'Two key conspirators, brother. The trader, Gorgone Locke, who I believe was instrumental in forging the original contact between the saruthi and Glaw's cabal. And an ecclesiarch named Dazzo, who I would see as the spiritual force behind their enterprise. They fled from the fight, rejoined the waiting elements of their fleet, and left this system.'

'Destination?' asked Spatian.

'It is still being plotted, admiral.'

'And how many ships? That bastard traitor Estrum ran with fifteen.'

'He lost at least two frigates in that star system. A non-standard merchant ship that I believe belongs to Locke is with them.'

'Have they taken to their heels and run defeated, or have they some further agenda?' Lord Rorken asked.

'I have further research to make before I can answer that, lord.'

Spatian stood and looked towards the Lord Inquisitor. 'Even if they're running, we can't permit them to escape. They must be hounded down and annihilated. Permission to retask the battle-pack and prepare to pursue.'

'Permission granted, admiral.'

Then Molitor spoke up. 'No one has asked the most important question of our heroic Brother Eisenhorn,' he said, stressing the word 'heroic' in a way that did not flatter. 'What happened to the Necroteuch?'

I turned to face him. 'I did what any of us would have done, Brother Molitor. I burned it.'

* * *

Uproar followed. Molitor was on his feet, accusing me of nothing short of heresy at the top of his reedy voice. Schongard raised his own serpentine tones in support of the accusations, while Endor and Voke shouted them down. The retinues howled and bickered across the floor. Both the Deathwatch captain and I remained seated and silent.

Lord Rorken rose. 'Enough!' He turned to the glowering Molitor. 'State your objection, Brother Molitor, quickly and simply.'

Molitor nodded, and licked his lips, his yellow eyes darting around the room. 'Eisenhorn must suffer our sternest censure for this act of vandalism! The Necroteuch may be a foul and proscribed work, but we are the Inquisition, lord. By what right did he simply destroy it? Such a thing should have been sequestered and brought before our most learned savants for study! To obliterate it out of hand robs us of knowledge, of wisdom, of secrets unimaginable! The contents of the Necroteuch might have given us insight into the archenemy of mankind, incalculable insight! How might it have strengthened us and armed us for the ceaseless fight? Eisenhorn has disgraced the very heart of our sacred Inquisition!'

'Brother Schongard?'

'My lord, I agree. It was a desperate and rash action by Eisenhorn. Carefully handled, the Necroteuch would have provided us with all measure of advantageous knowledge. Its arcane secrets would have been weapons against the foe. I may applaud his rigorous efforts in thwarting Glaw and his conspirators, but this erasure of occult lore earns only my opprobrium.'

'Brother Voke? What s–' Lord Rorken began, but I cut him off.

'Is this a court, my lord? Am I on trial?'

'No, brother, you are not. But the magnitude of your actions must be analysed and considered. Brother Voke?'

Voke rose. 'Eisenhorn was right. The Necroteuch was an abomination. It would have been heresy to permit its continued existence!'

'Brother Endor?'

Titus did not rise. He turned in his seat and looked down the hall at Konrad Molitor. 'Gregor Eisenhorn has my full support. From your moaning, Molitor, I wonder what kind of man I am listening to. A radical, certainly. An inquisitor? I have my doubts.'

Molitor leapt up again, raging. 'You knave! You whoreson bastard knave! How dare you?'

'Very easily,' replied Endor, leaning back and folding his arms. 'And you, Schongard, you are no better. Shame on you! What secrets did you both think we could learn, except perhaps how to pollute our minds and boil away our sanity? The Necroteuch has been forbidden since before our foundation. We need not know what's in it to accept that prohibition! All we need is the precious knowledge that it should be destroyed, unread, on sight. Tell me, do you need to actually contract Uhlren's Pox yourself to know that it is fatal?'

Lord Rorken smiled at this. He glanced at the Space Marine. 'Brother-Captain Cynewolf?'

The captain made a modest shrug. 'I command kill-teams charged with the extermination of aliens, mutants and heretics, lord. The ethics of scholarship and book-learning I leave to the savants. For whatever it's worth, though, I would have burned it without a second thought.'

There was a long silence. Sometimes I was almost glad no one could tell when I was smiling.

Lord Rorken sat back. 'The objections of my brothers are noted. I myself commend Eisenhorn. Given the extremity of his situation, he made the best decision.'

'Thank you, my lord.'

'Let us retire now and consider this matter. I want to hear proposals for our next course of action in four hours.'

'What now?' Titus Endor asked as we sat in his private suite aboard the *Saint Scythus*. A female servitor brought us glasses of vintage amasec, matured in nalwood casks.

'The remnants must be purged,' I said. 'Dazzo and the rest of the heretic fleet. They may have been cheated of their prize, and they may be running now. Perhaps they'll run for years. But they have the resources of a battlegroup at their disposal, and the will to use it. I will recommend we hunt them down and finish this sorry matter once and for all.'

Aemos entered the chamber, made a respectful nod to Endor, and handed me a data-slate.

'The admiral's astronavigators have finished plotting the course of the heretic fleet. It matches the estimations Maxilla has just sent me.'

I scanned the data. 'Do you have a chart, Titus?'

He nodded and engaged the functions of a glass-topped cogitator unit. The surface glowed, and he entered the reference codes from the slate.

'So... they're not running back into Imperial space. No surprise. Nor out to the lawless distances of the Halo Stars.'

'Their course takes them here: 56-Izar. Ten weeks away.'

'In saruthi territory.'

'Right in the heart of saruthi territory.'

Lord Inquisitor Rorken nodded gravely. 'As you say, brother, this business may be less finished than we thought.'

'They cannot hope to count the saruthi as allies, or believe they would give them safe haven. The entente between Glaw's forces and the xenos breed was fragile and tenuous to say the least, and what peace existed between them was ruined by the violence. Dazzo must have some other reason to head there.'

Lord Rorken paced the floor of his state chamber, brooding, toying with the signet ring of office on his gloved finger. His flock of cherubs roosted uneasily along the backs of armchairs and couches around the room. Twitching their gargoyle heads from one side to another, they watched me keenly as I stood waiting for a reply. 'My imagination runs wild, Eisenhorn,' he said at last.

'I intend to question the archeoxenologist, Malahite, directly. I am sure he can furnish us with additional intelligence. Just as I am sure he lacks the capacity to resist displayed by his aristo master Urisel.'

Rorken stopped pacing and clapped his gloved hands together with a decisive smack. Startled, the cherubs flew up into the air and began mobbing around the high ceiling. 'Course will be laid for 56-Izar at once,' said Lord Rorken, ignoring their lisping squawk. 'Bring me your findings without delay.'

Naval security had imprisoned Girolamo Malahite in the secure wing of the battleship's medicae facility. The injury I had given him had been treated, but no effort had been made to equip him with a prosthetic limb. I was looking forward to opening his secrets.

I passed through the coldly lit infirmary, and checked on Fischig. He was still unconscious, though a physician told me his condition was stable. The chastener lay on a plastic-tented cot, wired into wheezing life-supporting pumps and gurgling circulators, his damaged form masked by dressings, anointing charms and metal bone-clamps.

From the infirmary, I passed down an unheated main companionway, showed my identification to the duty guards, and entered the forbidding secure wing. I was at a second checkpoint, at the entrance to the gloomy cell block itself, when I heard screaming ringing from a cell beyond.

I pushed past the guards and, with them at my heels, reached the greasy iron shutters of the cell.

'Open it!' I barked, and one of the guards fumbled with his ring of electronic keys. 'Quickly, man!'

The cell shutter whirred open and locked into its open setting. Konrad Molitor and his three hooded acolytes turned to face me, outraged at the interruption. Their surgically gloved hands were wet with pink froth.

Behind them, Girolamo Malahite lay whimpering on a horizontal metal cage strung on chains from the ceiling. He was naked, and almost every centimetre of skin had been peeled from his flesh.

'Fetch surgeons and physicians. And summon Lord Rorken. Now!' I told the cell guards. 'Would you care to explain what you are doing here?' I said to Molitor.

He would, I think, have preferred not to answer me, and his trio of retainers looked set to grapple with me and hurl me from the cell.

But the muzzle of my autopistol was pressed flat against Konrad Molitor's perspiring brow and none of them dared move.

'I am conducting an interview with the prisoner...' he began.

'Malahite is my prisoner.'

'He is in the custody of the Inquisition, Brother Eisenhorn...'

'He is my prisoner, Molitor! Inquisitorial protocol permits me the right to question him first!'

Molitor tried to back away, but I kept the pressure of the gun firm against his cranium. There was no mistaking the fury in his eyes at this treatment, but he contained it, realising provocation was the last thing I needed.

'I, I was concerned for your health, brother,' he began, trying to mollify, 'the injuries you have suffered, your fatigue. Malahite had to be interrogated with all speed, and thought I would ease your burden by commencing the–'

'Commencing? You've all but killed him! I don't believe your excuse for a moment, Molitor. If you'd truly intended to help me, you would have asked permission. You wanted his secrets for yourself.'

'A damn lie!' he spat.

I cocked the pistol with my thumb. In the confines of the iron cell, the click was loud and threatening. 'Indeed? Then share what you have learned so far.'

He hesitated. 'He proved resilient. We have learned little from him.'

Boots clattered down the cell bay outside and the guards returned with two green-robed fleet surgeons and a quartet of medicae orderlies.

'Throne of Terra!' one of the surgeons cried, seeing the ruined man on the rack.

'Do what you can, doctor. Stabilise him.'

The physicians hurried to work, calling for tools, apparatus and cold dressings. Malahite whimpered again.

'Threatening an Imperial inquisitor with deadly force is a capital crime,' said one of the hooded acolytes, edging forward.

'Lord Rorken will be displeased,' said another.

'Put away your weapon and our master will co-operate,' the third added.

'Tell your sycophants to be silent,' I told Molitor.

'Please, Inquisitor Eisenhorn.' The third acolyte spoke again, his soft voice issuing from the shadows of his cowl. 'This is an unfortunate mistake. We will make reparations. Put away your weapon.'

The voice was strangely confident, and in speaking for Molitor, displayed surprising authority. But no more than Aemos or Midas would have done for me should the situation have been reversed.

'Take your assistants and get out, Molitor. We will continue this once I have spoken with Lord Rorken.'

The four of them left swiftly, and I holstered my weapon.

The chief physician came over to me, shaking his head. 'This man is dead, sir.'

At Lord Rorken's request, the warship's senior ecclesiarch provided a great chapel amidships for our use. I think the shipboard curia was impressed by the Lord Inquisitor's fury.

We had little time to repair the damage done by the incident, even though the medicae had placed Malahite's lamentable corpse in a stasis field.

Lord Rorken wanted to conduct the matter himself, but realised he was duty bound to offer me the opportunity first. To have denied me would have compounded Molitor's insult, even if Rorken was Lord Inquisitor.

I told Rorken I welcomed the task, adding that my working knowledge of the entire case made me the best candidate.

We assembled in the chapel. It was a long hall of fluted columns and mosaic flooring. Stained glass windows depicting the triumphs of the

Emperor were backlit by the empyrean vortex outside the ship. The chamber rumbled with the through-deck vibration of the *Saint Scythus*'s churning drive.

The facing ranks of pews and the raised stalls to either side were filling with Inquisitorial staff and ecclesiarchs. All my 'brothers' were in attendance, even Molitor, who I knew would not be able to stay away.

I walked with Lowink down the length of the nave to the raised plinth where Malahite lay in stasis. Astropaths, nearly thirty of them, drawn from the ship's complement and the Inquisitorial delegation, had assembled behind it. Hooded, misshapen, some borne along on wheeled mechanical frames or carried on litters by dour servitors, they hissed and murmured among themselves. Lowink went to brief them. He seemed to relish this moment of superiority over astropaths who normally outranked him. Lowink had not the power to manage this rite alone; his resources were enough for only the simplest psychometric audits. But his knowledge of my abilities and practices made him vital in orchestrating their efforts.

I looked at Malahite, flayed and pathetic in the shimmering envelope of stasis. Grotesquely, he reminded me of the God-Emperor himself, resting for eternity in the great stasis field of the golden throne, preserved until the end of time from the death Horus had tried to bestow upon him.

Lowink nodded to me. The astropathic choir was ready.

I looked around and found Endor's face in the congregation. He had placed himself near Molitor and had promised to watch the bastard closely for me. Schongard sat near the back, disassociating himself from his fellow radical's transgression.

I saw Brother-Captain Cynewolf and two of his awe-inspiring fellow Space Marines take their place behind the altar screen. All of them were in full armour and carried storm bolters. They weren't here for the show. They were here as a safeguard.

'Proceed, brother,' Lord Rorken said from his raised seat.

The choir began to nurse the folds of the warp apart with their swelling adoration. Psychic cold swept through the vault, and some in the congregation moaned, either in fear or with involuntary empathic vibration.

Commodus Voke, helped from his seat by the baleful Heldane, shuffled forward to join me. As a concession to Lord Rorken for allowing me this honour, I had agreed that the veteran inquisitor could partake of the auto-seance at my side. The risk was great, after all. Two minds were better than one, and in truth, it would be good to have the old reptile's mental power at close hand.

'Lower the stasis field,' I said. The moaning of the astropaths grew louder. As the translucent field died away, Voke and I reached out ungloved hands and touched the oozing, skinless face.

The veil of the warp drew back. I looked as if down a pillar of smoke, ghost white, which rushed up around me. In my ears, the harrowing screams of infinity and the billion billion souls castaway therein.

* * *

Blue light, streaked with storm-fires. A sound that mingled seismic rumbling and the ethereal plainsong of long decayed temples. A smell of woodsmoke, incense, saltwater, blood…

A cosmic emptiness so massive and ever-lasting, my mind numbed as I raced across it. It was gone in a blink, just fast enough to prevent the sheer scale taking my sanity with it.

Another blink. Flares of red. Colliding galaxies, catching fire. Souls like comets furrowing the immaterium. Voices of god-monsters calling from behind the flimsy backdrop of space.

Blink. Oceanic blackness. Another snatch of plainsong.

Blink. Stellar nurseries, fulsome with embryonic suns.

Blink. Cold light, eons old.

Blink.

'Gregor?'

I looked around and saw Commodus Voke. I had not recognised his voice at first. It seemed to have been softened, as if the event had humbled him. We stood on a slope of green shale, under a pair of suns that radiated enormous heat. Desiccated mountains lined the horizon, looming like fortresses.

We moved across the clinking shale towards the sound of the excavator. An ancient monotask, its pistons slimy with oil, dug into the side of a rock face with shovel-bladed limbs. It gouted steam and smoke from its boiler stack and excreted rock waste down a rear conveyor belt into heaps of glittering spoil.

We moved past it, and past other excavations in the rock face where smaller servitors brushed and polished fragments from the exposed strata and laid them carefully on find-trays.

Malahite stood watching them work. He was younger here, youthful almost, tanned and fit by the suns and the work. He wore shorts and loose fatigues, his skin streaked with dust.

'I thought you'd come,' he said.

'Will you co-operate?' I asked him.

'I've little time to talk,' he said, bending down to examine items that a servitor had just placed on a tray. 'There's work to do. A great deal to uncover before the rains come in a week or so.'

He knew who we were, but still he could not quite divorce himself from the reality around him.

'There's plenty of time to talk.'

Malahite straightened up. 'I suppose you're right. Do you know where this is?'

'No.'

He paused. 'A fringe world. Now I come to think of it, I've forgotten its name myself. I am happiest here, I think. This is where it starts for me. My first great recovery, the dig that makes my name and reputation as an archaeoxenologist.'

'It is later events we wish to speak of,' said Voke.

Malahite nodded, untied his bandanna and wiped the sweat from his cheeks. 'But this is where it begins. I will be celebrated for these finds, feted in high circles. Invited by the noble and famous House of Glaw to dine with them and enter their service as a prospector. Urisel Glaw himself will recruit me, and offer me a lucrative stipend to work for him.'

'And where will that lead?' I asked. 'Tell us about the saruthi.'

He bristled and turned away. 'Why? What can you offer me? Nothing! You have destroyed me!'

'We have means, Malahite. Things can be easier for you. The House of Glaw has doomed you to an unthinkable fate.'

He caught my eye, curious intent. 'You can save me? Even now?'

'Yes.'

He paused and then picked up one of the trays. It was suddenly full of the chipped octagonal tiles from the Damask site. 'They had an empire, you know,' he said, sorting through the tiles, showing some to us. The pieces meant nothing. 'The history is here, inscribed pictographically. Our eyes do not read it though. The saruthi have no optical or auditory functions. Smell and taste, the two combined in fact, are their primary senses. They can detect the flavours of reality, even those of dimensional space. The angles of time.'

'How?'

He shrugged. 'The Necroteuch. It warped them. Their empire was small, no more than forty worlds, and very old by the time the book came into their possession. Carried by humans, fleeing persecution on Terra in the very earliest days. Thanks to their taste-based sensory apparatus, they derived from the Necroteuch more than a simple human eye could read. From that first taste, the profound lore of the Necroteuch passed through their culture like wildfire, like a pathogen, transforming and twisting, investing them with great power. It led to war, civil war, which collapsed their empire, leaving worlds burned out or abandoned, contracting their territory to the far-flung fragment we know today.'

'They are corrupted – as a species, I mean?' asked Voke.

Malahite nodded. 'Oh, there's no saving them, inquisitor. They are precisely the sort of xenos filth you people teach us to fear and despise. I have encountered several alien races in my career, and found most to be utterly undeserving of the hatred that the Inquisition and the church reserves for anything that is not human. You are blinkered fools. You would kill everything because it is not like you. But in this case, you are right. The contagion of the Necroteuch has overwhelmed the saruthi. Never mind that they are xenos, they are a Chaos breed.'

He shivered, as if a chill wind was picking up but the suns continued to beat relentlessly.

'What are their resources, their military capability?'

'I have no idea,' he said, shivering again. 'They abandoned their spaceship technology centuries ago. They had no further need of it. As I said, the Necroteuch had warped their sensory abilities. They became able to undo the angles of space and time, to move through dimensions. From world to world. They mastered the art of constructing spaces in four dimensions, environments that existed only at specific time-points.'

'Like the one where the trade was meant to take place.'

'Yes. KCX-1288 was once part of their empire, ravaged in their civil war. They chose it for the meeting because it was remote from their main population centres. They built the tetrascape inside specifically for us.'

'Tetrascape?'

'Forgive me. I coined the term. I thought I might use it in a learned paper one day. A tailored, four-dimensional environment. In that particular case, engineered with a human climate. We were their guests, you see.'

'How was the deal arranged?'

'Locke, the rogue trader. He was on a retainer to the House of Glaw, had been for years. A mercenary roaming the stars at the behest of the Glaws. He ventured into saruthi territory, and eventually made contact. Then he discovered the existence of the Necroteuch, and knew what it would be worth to his masters.'

'And they agreed to trade?' I was becoming impatient. Time, surely, was running out.

He shuddered again. 'It's cold,' he said. 'Isn't it? Getting colder.'

'They agreed to trade? Come on, Malahite! We can't help you if you delay.'

'Yes... yes, they agreed. In exchange for the return of artefacts and treasures from worlds they had abandoned and no longer had access to.'

'Wasn't the Necroteuch precious to them?'

'It was in their souls, in their minds, woven into their genetic code by then. The book itself was incidental.'

'And you were employed to excavate the materials that the Glaws intended to trade?'

'Of course. I was promised such power, you know...'

His voice tailed off. Beyond the distant mountains, the sky was growing dark. A strengthening breeze scattered loose shale around our feet.

'The rains?' he said. 'Surely not this early.'

'Concentrate, Malahite, or you'll slip away! The Necroteuch is destroyed, the trade prevented, and House Glaw is shattered and defeated! So why are Locke and Dazzo leading their fleet into saruthi territory?'

'What's that?' he asked sharply, holding up a hand for quiet. It was indeed colder now, and chasing clouds obscured the suns. A distant, plaintive threnody was just audible.

'What are they doing?' Voke spat.

He looked at us as if we were stupid. 'Repairing the damage you've done to their cause! The high and mighty masters of the Glaw cabal have masters of their own to please! Masters whose wrath defies thought! They must assuage them for the loss of the Necroteuch!'

I looked across at Voke. 'You mean the Children of the Emperor?' I asked Malahite.

'Of course I do! The Glaws couldn't do all this alone, even with their power and influence. They made a pact with that foul Legion for support and security, in return promising to share the Necroteuch with them. And now that's gone, the Children of the Emperor will be most displeased.'

'And how do they hope to avoid this displeasure and make amends?' Voke asked. Like me, he was becoming alarmed by the stain in the sky and the sound in the wind.

'By obtaining another Necroteuch,' I said, realising, answering for Malahite.

The archeoxenologist clapped his hands and smiled. 'Brains, at last! Just when I was giving up hope for you. Well done!'

'There is another?' asked Voke with a stammer.

'The saruthi happily traded back their human copy because they had their own,' I said, cursing myself for not seeing the obvious sense before.

'Well done again! Indeed they have, inquisitor.' Malahite was gleeful and smiling, though he was clearly shivering now, and desperate for warmth. 'It's a xenos transcription, of course, composed in their, I'd say language, but perhaps flavour is a better word. However, the arcane knowledge it contains is still the same. Dazzo and his masters will have the Necroteuch, despite the set-backs you have caused.'

Lightning flashed, and the wind lifted walls of dust and storms of shale particles around us.

'Our time is up,' Voke cried to me.

'How true,' said Malahite. 'And now, your promise. I have answered you fully. Are you men of your word?'

'We can't save you from death, Malahite,' Voke told him. 'But the abominations you have chosen to align yourself with are coming to consume your soul. We can at least be merciful and extinguish your spirit now, before they arrive.'

Malahite grinned, flecks of shale clicking off his exposed teeth. 'Damn your offer, Commodus Voke. And damn you both.'

'Move, Voke!' I cried. Malahite had simply been keeping us talking, padding his story out. He knew damn well we had nothing much to offer him except a swift end. That didn't interest him. He wanted revenge. That was his price for speaking. He wanted to make sure we were still here, when the end came, to die with him.

The desert behind him ruptured upwards, throwing rock and dust into the cyclonic gale. A column of blood exploded out of the ground like a geyser, half a kilometre wide and a dozen high. It rose like a gigantic tree, swirling with pustular flesh, sinew, muscle, ragged tissue and a million staring eyes that coated it like glistening foam.

Branch-like tendrils of bone and tissue whipped out from the swirling, semi-fluid behemoth and tore Malahite apart.

It was the most complete, most devastating fate I have ever seen a man suffer. But he was still smiling, triumphantly, as it happened.

TWENTY-TWO

IN THE MOUTH OF THE WARP
A MANDATE TO PURGE
56-IZAR

The psychically manifested memory of the fringe world and its excavation site blurred away, shattering like an image in a broken mirror. But the towering daemon-form remained, keening in the lethal darkness, driving the tempest of damnation down upon us.

I felt Voke lash out with his mind against the thing, but it was a futile gesture, like a man exhaling into the face of a hurricane.

'Back!' I yelled, my voice lost and distant even to me.

I saw him falling into the void at my side, reaching for me. I yelled his name again, holding out my hand. He cried out an answer I couldn't hear.

Instead, I heard shouting, screaming and the blast of gunfire.

I sprawled painfully onto the cold paved floor of the chapel, soaked with blood and plasmic-residue, gasping for air, my heart bursting. The noises now were all around me, deafening and clear.

I rolled.

Panic was emptying the chapel. Priests and novices alike, acolytes and retainers, all were fleeing, wailing, overturning pews. Lord Rorken was on his feet, his face pale, and his devoted bodyguard, with their saintly masks, were charging forward, their broadswords whirring as they described masterful figures of eight.

I saw Voke, unconscious, nearby. Like me, he was saturated with inhuman gore and the drooling liquor of the immaterium.

I couldn't find my balance, and there was a dullness in my head. I retched clots of blood. I knew I was damned. Damned by the warp, ruined and stained. I had strayed too close too long.

The astropaths were staggering backwards, frantic, shrieking. Some were already dead, and others were convulsing or haemorrhaging. As I looked up, two exploded simultaneously, like blood-filled blisters. Arcs of warp-energy flashed among them, frying minds, fusing bones and boiling body fluid.

Malahite's corpse had gone. In its place on the plinth, crouched a thrashing, screeching horror of smoke and rotting bone. The astropaths had broken the link, having staunchly sustained it long enough for Voke and I to escape. But something had come back with us.

It had no form, but suggested many, as a shadow on a wall or a cloud in the sky might flicker and resemble many things in a passing moment. Inside its fluttering robes of smoke, starlight shone and teeth flashed.

The first of Rorken's bodyguards was on it, slicing with his sword. The razor-keen blade, engraved with votive blessings and curial sacraments, passed harmlessly through wispy, ethereal fog.

In response, a long, attenuated claw of jointed bone, like a scythe with human teeth growing from the blade edge, lashed out and chopped through his torso and his holy blade, bisecting both.

I fumbled for a weapon, any damn weapon.

There was a cacophony of gunfire.

Storm bolters blasting, the three Deathwatch Marines advanced towards the horror. Their black armour was rimed with psychic frost. Over his vox-speaker, Cynewolf could be heard, admonishing the foe and barking tactical instructions to his comrades.

Their Chapter-wrought bolters continued to boom in unison until the unremitting fire had blasted the thing from the warp backwards in a scrambling, shrieking smear of blackness and bone limbs. It fell back off the plinth into the retreating astropaths, crushing dead and living alike.

Brother-Captain Cynewolf moved ahead of his companions, faster than seemed to me possible for such a heavily armoured form. Tossing aside his spent bolter, he drew his chainsword and hacked again and again into the writhing mass, driving it backwards into the adulatory stalls, which splintered like tinder wood.

Lord Rorken strode past me, wielding a ceremonial silver flamer he had snatched from one of his attendants. The acolyte ran behind, struggling to hold on to the gold-inlaid fuel tanks and keep pace with his master.

Rorken's voice sang out above the mayhem. 'Spirit of noxious immateria, be gone from hence, for as the Emperor of Mankind, manifold be his blessings, watches over me, so I will not fear the shadow of the warp...'

Holy fire spurted from the Lord Inquisitor's weapon and washed across the warp-spawned thing. Lord Rorken was chanting the rite of banishment at the top of his lungs.

Endor pulled me to my feet and we both lent our voices to the words.

There was a tremor that seemed to vibrate the entire ship.

Then nothing remained of the vile creature except a layer of ash and the devastation it had wrought.

As penance for the act of transgression that had led to this warp-invasion, Konrad Molitor was charged with rededicating and reconsecrating the violated chapel. The work, overseen by the arch-priests of the curia and the techno-adepts of the Glorious Omnissiah, took all of the first six weeks of our ten-week transit time to 56-Izar. Molitor took his duties seriously, dressed himself in a filthy sackcloth shirt of contrition, and had his retainers scourge him with withes and psychic awls between ceremonies.

I thought he got off lightly.

* * *

I spent a month recovering from the physiological trauma of the auto-seance in one of the battleship's state apartments. The psychological damage I suffered during that event lasted for years after. I still dream of that geyser of blood, clothed in myriad eyes, filling the sky. You don't forget a thing like that. They say memory softens with time, but that particular memory never has. Even today, I console myself that to have forgotten would have been worse. That would have been denial, and denial of such visions eventually opens the doors of insanity.

I lay upon the apartment's wide bed all month, propped up with bolsters and pillows. Physicians attended me regularly, as did members of Lord Rorken's staff, dressed in their finery. They tested my health, my mind, my recovering strength. I knew what they were looking for. A taint of the warp. There was none, I was sure, but they couldn't take my word for it, of course. We had come close, Voke and I, close to the precipice, close to the edge of irreconcilable damnation. Another few seconds...

Aemos stayed with me, bringing me books and slates to divert me. Sometimes he read aloud, from histories, sermons or stories. Sometimes he played music spools on the old, horn-speakered celiaphone, cranking the handle by hand. We listened to the light orchestral preludes of Daminias Bartelmew, the rousing symphonies of Hanz Solveig, the devotional chants of the Ongres Cloisterhood. He warbled along with operettas by Guinglas until I pleaded with him to stop, and mimed the conductor's role when the Macharius Requiem played, dancing around the room on his augmetic legs in such a preposterous, sprightly fashion it made me laugh aloud.

'It's good to hear that, Gregor,' he said, blowing dust off a new spool before fitting it into the celiaphone.

I was going to answer, but the strident war-hymns of the Mordian Regimental Choir cut me off.

Midas visited me, and spent time playing regicide or plucking his Glavian lyre. I took these recitals as a particular compliment. He'd been dragging the lyre around for years, ever since I had first met him, and had never played in my hearing, despite my requests.

He was a master, his circuit-inlaid fingers reading and playing the coded strings as expertly as they did flight controls.

On his third visit, after a trio of jaunty Glavian dances, he set his turtle-backed instrument down against the arm of his chair and said 'Lowink is dead.'

I closed my eyes and nodded. I had suspected as much.

'Aemos didn't want to tell you yet, given your condition, but I thought it was wrong to keep it from you.'

'Was it quick?'

'His body survived the seance invasion, but with no mind to speak of. He died a week later. Just faded away.'

'Thank you, Midas. It is best I know. Now play again, so I can lose myself in your tunes.'

* * *

Strangely, I came to enjoy Bequin's visits most. She would bustle in, tidying around me, tut-tutting at the state of my water jug or the collapse of my bolsters. Then she would read aloud, usually from books and slates Aemos had left, and often from works that he had already declaimed for my edification. She read them better, with more colour and phlegm. The voice she put on to do Sebastian Thor made me laugh so hard my ribs hurt. When she got to reading Kerloff's Narrative of the Horus War, her impersonation of the Emperor was almost heretical.

I taught her regicide. She lost the first few games, mesmerised by the pieces, the complex board and the still more complex moves and strategies. It was all too 'tactical' for her, she announced. There was no 'incentive'. So we started to play for coins. Then she got the gist and started to win. Every time.

When Midas visited me next, he said sourly, 'Have you been teaching that girl to play?'

Towards the end of my third week of recuperation, Bequin arrived in my apartment and declared, 'I have brought a visitor.'

The ruined side of Godwyn Fischig's face had been rebuilt with augmetic muscle and metal, and shrouded with a demi-visage mask of white ceramite. His lost arm had also been replaced, with a powerful metal prosthetic. He was clad in a simple, black jacket and breeches.

He sat at my bedside, and wished me a speedy recovery.

'Your courage has not been forgotten, Godwyn,' I said. 'When this undertaking is over, you may wish to return to your duties on Hubris, but I would welcome your presence on my staff, if you choose so.'

'Nissemay Carpel be damned,' he said. 'The high custodian of the Dormant Vaults may call for me, but I know where I want to be. This life has purpose. I would stay here in it.'

Fischig remained at my side for hours, long into the night, by ship-time. We talked, and joked occasionally, and then played regicide with Bequin looking on. At first, his problems in manipulating the pieces with his unfamiliar new limb afforded us plenty of amusement. Only when he had beaten me in three straight games did he admit that Bequin, in her infinite wisdom, had been coaching him for the past few weeks.

I had one last visitor, a day or two before I was finally able to walk and go about my business uninterrupted by periods of fatigue. Heldane wheeled him in on a wire-spoked carrier chair.

Voke was shrunken and ill. He could only speak by way of a vox-enhancer. I was sure he would be dead in a matter of months.

'You saved me, Eisenhorn,' he husked, haltingly, through the vox augmetic.

'The astropaths made it possible for us to live,' I corrected.

Voke shook his gnarled, sunken head. 'No... I was lost in a realm of damnation, and you pulled me back. Your voice. I heard you call my name and it was enough. Without that, without that voice, I would have succumbed to the warp.'

I shrugged. What could I say?

'We are not alike, Gregor Eisenhorn,' he continued, tremulously. 'Our concept of inquisition is wildly at variance. But still I salute your bravery and your dedication. You have proven yourself in my eyes. Different ways, different means, is that not the true ethic of our order? I will die peacefully – and soon, I think – knowing men such as you maintain the fight.'

I was honoured. Whatever I thought of his modus operandi, I knew our purposes pointed in the same direction.

With a weak gesture he beckoned Heldane forward. The man's raw, damaged head was no prettier than when I had last seen it.

'I want you to trust Heldane. Of all my students, he is the best. I intend to recommend his elevation to the level of high interrogator, and from there, inquisitional rank beckons. If I die, look to him for my sake. I have no doubt the Inquisition will benefit from his presence.'

I promised Voke I would do so, and this seemed to please Heldane. I didn't like the man much, but he had been resilient and unfaltering in the face of savage death, and there was no doubting his ability or dedication.

Voke took my hand in his sweaty claw and rasped 'Thank you, brother.'

As it turned out, Commodus Voke lived on for another one hundred and three years. He proved nigh on impossible to kill. When Golesh Constantine Pheppos Heldane was finally elected to the rank of inquisitor, it was all Voke's doing.

The sins of the father, as they say.

Invasion training began three weeks off 56-Izar. Initially, Admiral Spatian's plan was for a fleet action, a simple annihilation of any targets from orbit. But Lord Rorken and the Deathwatch insisted that a physical invasion was required. The recovery and destruction of the xenos Necroteuch had to be authenticated, or we would never know for sure that it was truly gone. Only after that objective was achieved could extreme destructive sanction be unleashed on 56-Izar.

All that could be learned from my associates and the surviving Gudrunites concerning the saruthi tetrascapes – ironically, we were using Malahite's term by then – was collated during a scrupulously searching series of interviews conducted by naval tacticians and Brytnoth, the Deathwatch's revered librarian and strategist.

The collected information was profiled by the fleet's cogitators, and simulations created to acclimatise the ground forces. To my eyes, the simulations conveyed nothing of the wrongness we had experienced on the world of the plateau.

Brytnoth himself conducted my interviews, accompanied by Olm Madorthene. Shaven-headed, a giant of a man even without his armour, Brytnoth was nevertheless cordial and attentive, addressing me with respect and listening with genuine interest to my replies. I tried to do verbal justice to my memories of the experience, and additionally related the theories that Malahite had expounded during that fateful seance.

Eschewing the luxury of a servitor scribe or clerk, Brytnoth made his own notes as he listened. I found myself engrossed watching the warrior's paw working the dwarfed stylus almost delicately across the note-slate.

We sat in my apartments for the sessions, which often lasted hours. Bequin brought in regular trays of hot mead or leaf infusions, and Brytnoth actually extended his little finger as he lifted the porcelain cups by the handle. He was to me the embodiment of war in peacetime, a vast power bound into genteel behaviour, striving to prevent his awesome strength from breaking loose. He would lift the cup, small finger extended, consult his notes and ask another question before sipping.

The fact that small finger was the size and shape of an Arbites' truncheon was beside the point.

'What I'm trying to establish, brother inquisitor, is whether the environments of the saruthi xenos will hinder our forces or deprive them of optimum combat efficiency.'

'You can be sure of that, brother librarian.' I poured some more Olicet tea from the silver pot. 'My comrades were disoriented for the entire duration of the mission, and the Gudrunite riflemen had broken because of the place more than anything else. There is a wrongness that quite disarms the senses. It had been conjectured by some that this is a deliberate effect used by the saruthi to undermine sentients used to three physical dimensions, but the traitor Malahite made more sense in my opinion. The wrongness is a by-product of the saruthi's preferred environments. We can expect the effect to be the norm on any homeworld of theirs.'

Brytnoth nodded and noted again.

'I'm sure your Chapter's experience and specialised sensor equipment will be a match for it,' put in Madorthene. 'Myself, I'm worried about the Guard. They'll be the mainstay of this action.'

'They've all seen the preliminary briefing simulations,' Brytnoth murmured.

'With respect, I have too and they hardly do justice to the places we will find ourselves in.' I looked across the table into Brytnoth's face. His rugged features were sunken and colourless, the common trait of one who spends most of his life hidden within a combat helmet. His hooded eyes regarded me with interest. What wars, what victories, had those eyes witnessed, I wondered. What defeats?

'What do you suggest?' Brytnoth asked.

'Adverse cross-training,' I replied. I'd thought about it long and hard. 'Olm here knows I'm no military man, brother-librarian, but that's the way it seems to me. Make the troops practise overburden and off-balance. Blindfold them in some exercises, cuff them in others, alter gravity in the training vaults. Make the weighted packs they carry off centre and awkward. Switch light levels without warning. Crank the temperature and air pressure up and down. Simply make it hard for them. Train them to run, cover, shoot and reload in off-putting extremes. Make them learn all their essential combat procedures so well they can do them anywhere, under any circumstances. When they hit the ground at 56-Izar, let the fight be all they worry about. Everything else should be instinctive.'

Madorthene smiled confidently. 'The infantry forces at our disposal are primarily Navy troopers and Mirepoix light elite from the Imperial Guard, seasoned soldiers all, unlike the poor Gudrunite foundees you had to nursemaid, Gregor. We'll put them through the hoops and raise their game for the big push. They've got the combat hours and the balls to do it.'

'Don't stint,' I warned Madorthene. 'And those foundees you refer to - Sergeant Jeruss and his men. I want them with me when I go in.'

'Gregor! We can give you a crack squad of Mirepoix who–'

'I want the Gudrunite survivors.'

'Why?' asked Brytnoth.

'Because whatever their combat inexperience, they've seen a tetrascape. Those are the men I want at my side.'

Madorthene and Brytnoth exchanged glances, and the procurator shrugged. 'As you wish.'

'As for the others, like I said, don't stint on the training regime.'

'We won't!' he chuckled, mock-outraged at the idea. 'The drill masters will work the regiments so hard, they'll yearn for real battle.'

'I'm serious,' I said. 'Every man that deploys on to 56-Izar - the venerated Deathwatch included, Emperor bless them - should be ready to lose control of his senses, his judgment, his fortitude and even his basic mental faculties. They're going to be hit hard, but in an insidious way. I don't care if every man jack of them forgets his own mother's name and wets himself, they must still know how to hold a line, fire and reload, adore the Emperor and respond to orders.'

'Succinctly put,' Brytnoth said. 'I will, of course, temper your proposals before I put them to my battle-brothers.'

'I don't care what you tell them,' I chuckled, 'as long as you don't let on who it came from.'

'Your anonymity is assured.' He smiled. A wonder, that. I consider myself one of the very few mortals to have made a Librarian of the Adeptus Astartes smile. To have seen a Librarian of the Adeptus Astartes smile even.

Brytnoth pushed his slate and stylus aside and looked over at me with curiosity. 'Mandragore,' he said.

'The bastard child of the Emperor? What of him?'

'I'm told you killed him yourself. In single combat. Quite a feat for one such as you - and I mean no disrespect.'

'No disrespect is taken.'

'How did you do it?' he asked frankly.

I told him. I kept it simple. Brytnoth made no reaction but Madorthene was quietly agog.

'Brother-Captain Cynewolf will be fascinated,' Brytnoth said. 'I promised him I'd find out the details. He was dying to ask you about it, but he didn't dare.'

Now that was funny.

We prepared ourselves for the approaching war. It was going to be arduous, and, unlike most campaigns, not divided into two sides. I observed training sessions, impressed by the efforts and the discipline. I even had the terrifying pleasure of watching Captain Cynewolf's kill-team conduct a target-decoy hunt through the hold levels.

We were ready. Ready as we'd ever be.

In the ninth week of transit, Lord Inquisitor Rorken and Admiral Spatian issued a joint declaration, officially enforced by will of the Ecclesiarchy. A Mandate To Purge 56-Izar, as the term and parameters are understood in the Imperial codes. That was the seal on the action. There was no turning back now. We were heading through the immaterium at high warp to invade and, if necessary, destroy the saruthi world.

Through my weeks of convalescence, I dreamed little. But on the last night before our arrival at 56-Izar, the blank-eyed, handsome man returned to stalk the landscape of my dreams.

He was talking to me, but I couldn't hear his words, nor understand his purpose. He led me through drafty halls in a ruined palace, and then departed silently into the dream wilds beyond, leaving me alone, naked, in a ruin that tottered and crumbled down onto me.

The saruthi were in my dreams too. They rose through the brick debris of the collapsed palace effortlessly, finding angles and pathways that I could not see. The multiple nostrils on their swaying heads flared as they got the taste of me. Their skulls coruscated with energy...

I woke, soaked with night-sweat, more out of my wide bed than in it. Dislodged bolsters were scattered over the floor.

The vox-link on my night stand was beeping.

'Inquisitor Eisenhorn?'

'Sorry to wake you,' said Madorthene. 'But I thought you'd want to know. The fleet exited the immaterium twenty-six minutes ago. We are entering invasion orbit of 56-Izar.'

TWENTY-THREE

INVADING THE INVASION
BENT ANGLES
IN THE GARDENS OF THE SARUTHI

The war had already begun.

56-Izar hung like a pearl in space, milky white and gleaming. Vivid flashes and slower blossoms of destruction underlit its translucent skin of cloud. The heretic fleet had arrived two days ahead of us, and had begun its assault of the planet.

I kept thinking of it as Estrum's fleet, but it wasn't of course. I'd made certain of that. This was Locke's battle fleet now, I was sure.

The thirteen ships had blockaded 56-Izar in a non-standard but effective conquest pattern. Serial waves of their fighter-bombers, interceptors and dropships rained down on the planet and the orbiting heavies bombarded the surface with their entire batteries.

They detected our battle-pack the moment we came out of warp. Their picket ships, the heavy destroyers *Nebuchadnezzar* and *Fournier,* wheeled round to protect their hindquarters. Admiral Spatian held our battle-pack off orbit and chased the frigates *Defence of Stalinvast, Emperor's Hammer* and *Will of Iron* straight in to clear the way.

On their heels, he sent out the massed fighter squadrons of the expeditionary force, and diverted the battleship *Vulpecula* to engage the enemy flagship, a heavy cruiser named the *Leoncour.*

The *Emperor's Hammer* and the *Will of Iron* pincered and torched the *Nebuchadnezzar* after a brief but fierce exchange. The explosion lit the void. The *Defence of Stalinvast* and the *Fournier* locked each other tightly in a longer, slower dance of warships, and eventually slammed together, squeezing boarding parties and naval security units into each other's hulls.

The locked ships tumbled away, in an embrace of death.

The *Vulpecula* raced forward and misjudged the *Leoncour*'s evasion, suffering a trio of broadsides. Coming about, spilling debris into the gulf, the Imperial battleship raised its guns and hammered the *Leoncour* so hard and so furiously that the enemy flagship broke up and blew out like a dying sun.

Limping, the *Vulpecula* turned slowly and began its long-range harrying of the enemy ships closer to the target world's atmosphere. Spatian committed the rest of his group then, ranging them forward in a three-pronged division, of which the central and largest was headed by the majestic *Saint Scythus.*

Distances closed. The near-space of 56-Izar was awash with fire patterns and the streaking comets of missiles. Now the ferocious, high-velocity small ship phase began as waves of interceptors and light bombers from both fleets met and buzzed around each other like rival swarms of insects. The tiny lights whirled and danced in the void, faster and more numerous than the unaided eye could follow. Even the tactical displays overwhelmed the senses: pict-plates flickering with thousands of type markers and flashing cursors, spinning, overlaying, vanishing and reappearing.

The heretics had seeded a buffer zone behind their deployment with mines, and the *Emperor's Hammer*, spurring forward in a fleet intruder role, suffered heavy damage and was forced to break away. Heretic interceptors fell upon the stricken ship like carrion flies on a dying beast.

The *Will of Iron* moved past the *Emperor's Hammer* and began to sweep a path through the mine zone with its specialised clearing devices. Triggered by probing force cones, the floating weapons began to detonate in their thousands.

Spatian's intent was to cut a wedge into the enemy's wide formation and bring at least some of his ships within range of the planet's surface. Once that bridging objective was achieved he could begin to unleash the planetary assault, confident of providing the dropships with some covering fire.

The *Saint Scythus* was first to secure such a position. Its main guns mercilessly disposed of the heretic cruiser *Scutum* and forced the carrier frigate *Glory of Algol* into a desperate retreat.

Hundreds of dropships rushed like a blizzard out of the battleship and the two frigates and the Inquisitorial black ship that had moved in behind it.

Most of the dropships were the grey landing boats of the Imperial Guard, jets firing as they hammered down into the cloudy atmosphere of 56-Izar. But scattered among them were a handful of scarab-black landing craft and drop-pods of the Deathwatch.

The counter-invasion had begun.

Within the first hour of the war, we managed to land more than two-thirds of our one hundred and twenty thousand Mirepoix Light Elite Infantry on the surface of 56-Izar, almost half of the motorised armour brigades, and all sixty Adeptus Astartes warriors of the Deathwatch.

Sensor sweeps showed 56-Izar to be a bland, unremarkable world beneath its heavy veil of atmosphere. Vast, low continents of inorganic ooze punctured by ranges of crystalline upland and surrounded by inert chemical oceans. The only signs of advanced life – of life of any kind, indeed – were a string of city-sized structures arranged in a chain along the equatorial region of the main continent. The nature and composition of these structures was virtually impossible to read from orbit. The heretics had concentrated their invasion efforts on the three largest structures, and Admiral Spatian was targeting these areas, judging that the enemy would not be wasting time invading unviable sites.

Losses were high. The approaches were thick with enemy interceptors, micro-mines and the fire of surface to air defences. All of this was human warfare. There was no sign or hint of any saruthi participation at all.

Behind the main landing force came the Inquisitorial squads, five specialised assault units designed to follow the military in through the opening they made and oversee the primary objectives: the capture or destruction of the heretic conspirators and the obliteration of any further Necroteuch material. I had control of one squad; the others were led by Endor, Schongard, Molitor and Lord Inquisitor Rorken himself. Voke was too ill to command a squad, and his emissary, Heldane, accompanied Endor's party.

My own force, designated Purge Two, was made up of twenty Gudrunite riflemen, Bequin, Midas and a Deathwatch Space Marine called Guilar. A member of the Adeptus Astartes had been seconded to each inquisitor. Fischig had demanded to accompany me, but he was still weak from his injuries and surgery and I had turned him down with a heavy heart. He remained on the battleship with Aemos, who was, by any standards, a non-combatant.

Our transport, an Imperial Guard dropship, left the *Saint Scythus* directly behind the force designated Purge One, in Lord Rorken's lander. We rode out the vibrating, shuddering descent strapped into the g-chairs of the troop bay.

Jeruss's men sang as we dropped. Their standard-issue Gudrunite uniforms had been augmented with fresh body armour from the fleet stores, and they had sewn Inquisitorial emblems onto their sleeves next to the regimental badge of the 50th Gudrunite Rifles. They were in good humour, eager and determined, encouraged, I believe, by the faith I had shown in selecting them. Madorthene had confided to me that they had scored consistently above average in the adverse training program. They joked and boasted and rang out Imperial battle hymns like veterans. Their experiences since the founding at Dorsay had baptised them very quickly indeed.

Bequin had also been transmuted by experience in the months since I had first met her on Hubris. A hard, serious woman had replaced the scatty, selfish pleasure-girl from the Sun-dome, as if she had at last found a calling that suited her. She had certainly thrown herself into her new life with dedication and vigour. I considered the changes a distinct improvement. Many are called to the service of our beloved Emperor, and many are found wanting. Despite the ordeals, Alizebeth Bequin had proved herself. If there was a point at which her transformation could be identified, it was the plateau. The sight of Mandragore's corpse had exorcised her fears.

Dressed in a black, armoured bodyglove and a long black velvet coat, she sat in the seat next to me, scrupulously checking her las-carbine. The chastener had trained her well. Her gloved hands made swift, professional movements over the weapon. Only the trim of black feathers around her coat's collar betrayed a vestige of the painted, frocked and decorated girl of old.

Midas sat the other side of me, ill at ease. He made a lousy passenger and I knew he wanted to be up in the dropship's cockpit instead of the Navy pilot. He wore his cerise jacket, despite the objections of the dour Guilar, who considered its brash colour 'unsuitable for combat'. His needle pistols were holstered, and his long Glavian rifle rested across his knees.

I wore brown leather body armour and my button-sleeve coat for the assault, a trade off between protection and mobility. The symbols of my office were proudly displayed on my chest above my sash. Librarian Brytnoth, in a gesture that honoured me, had sent a bolt pistol for my personal use. It was a compact, hand-crafted model with a casing of matt-green steel. The rectangular-pattern magazines slid into the handgrip, and I had one locked in place and another eight in the loops of my belt.

After eight minutes of violent descent, we levelled out and the vibrations diminished. Guilar, seated next to the ramp-hatch, made the sign of the aquila in the air and locked his helmet into place.

'Twenty seconds!' the pilot announced over the cabin vox.

We soared down free of the clouds and into the fire and darkness of the near-surface warzone, moving at full burn towards one of the orbitally identified city structures. The site was ringed by a series of what seemed to be colossal lakes or reservoirs, and the liquid they contained was ablaze, with raging walls of fire reaching up thousands of metres. Night-black smoke fanned from the fires and blocked the immediate daylight, and the world below was amber-lit by the seething flames and the crossfire of weapons.

The dropship shook as the braking jets fired, and we lurched around in a drunken yaw before settling. Guilar thumped a wall-stud and the ramp-doors opened with a yowl of metal on metal. Cold air and smoke blew into the cabin.

We came out onto a wide, glistening flat of white mud that squelched wetly under our running, jumping boots. The mudflats lay between two of the burning lakes, and we could feel the heat of the immense fires on our faces. The coiling flames reflected in dazzling patterns off the wet mud.

Burning debris from a crashed lander littered the white flats, as well as the charred bodies of several Mirepoix. Las-fire cut the air above us. A kilometre ahead there were the familiar shapes of raised, hoop-like arches, 'tetragates' as they had been dubbed by the fleet's tech-priests, some shattered and broken by the assault. Beyond them rose the pearl-white flanks of a great edifice, the target structure, curved and segmented like a gigantic sea-shell, spotted with a thousand tiny scorch marks and blast-scars.

We advanced behind Guilar. The air smelled of fuel-vapour and another rich scent, like liquorice, that I couldn't readily identify.

'Purge Two, deploying on surface at chart mark seven,' I reported over the vox.

'Understood, Purge Two. Purge One and Purge Four report safe landing and deployment.'

So Rorken and Molitor's groups were down. No word yet of Endor or Schongard.

As we pushed past the first of the shattered hoops, Guilar faltered, pausing to shake his helmeted head. I could feel the wrongness already, the insidious twisting of the saruthi environment. It seemed likely the effect was being accentuated by the broken tetragates. These silent devices projected and sustained the saruthi tetrascapes, and they were now faulty and incomplete.

The Gudrunites noticed it too, but seemed unfazed.

'Take point!' I told Jeruss, and Guilar looked at me sharply.

'You need time to get used to this, Brother Guilar. Don't argue.'

Jeruss and three Gudrunites moved into the vanguard. Even they were having trouble, shambling awkwardly as if intoxicated. The angles of space and time were truly bent and twisted here.

Behind us, thrusters retched and our dropship rose off the gleaming mud, its ramp and landing struts folding up into its belly. It was barely sixty metres up when a missile struck it amidships and blew out its mainframe. The burning cockpit section tumbled away from the airburst and fell into a lake of fire. Metal debris from the destroyed main section peppered the white mud below.

But for the grace of the God-Emperor, we could all have been aboard it.

Moving at an unsteady trot, we came to the saruthi edifice. Its great, luminous form was the size of an Imperial hive and its foundations ran down beneath the white mud. I tried to get a sense of the structure, but it was no good and I quickly gave up rather than risk disorientation. It was like an ammonite with its polished segments and perfect curves, but my human eyes could not read its true shape. The overlaps and edges did not meet as one would expect, and conjured distracting optical illusions when any attempt was made to follow them from one point to another.

We reached the foot of it. There were no doors or entrances, and those who had come before us had tried to blast their way through the lustrous surface, only to find it apparently solid within.

I moved my squad back from the barrier and we retraced our approach down the line of the tetragates. Those nearest to the structure were still intact.

As I had anticipated, we stepped through the last one and were immediately inside the edifice, as if we had passed through the pearly walls.

Inside, there was a low radiance shed by some source inside the walls. It was warm, and the smell of liquorice was more pungent and intense. The floor, translucent and pearly, was concave and flowed up into the curve of the walls.

We moved forward, weapons ready. The corridor – and I use that word in the loosest sense – seemed to describe a spiral, like the inner form of a great conch or the canals of a human ear, but at no time did we feel anything but upright.

Opening into a horn-like cone, the spiral gave out into a huge, almost spherical chamber. It was impossible to estimate its true size, or define its true shape. It seemed to be some kind of ornamental garden or even farm. Silver walkways, suspended invisibly by gravity or some other force, ran between curving tanks of liquid that formed beds for huge, multi-coloured cycads and other bulbous, primitive plants. The fleshy growths towered around us, dripping with moisture and swathed in creepers and climbing succulents. Ropes of vine and beards of flowering foliage hung from invisible fixtures in the air above the beds. There were insects in here, flitting between the swollen bell-shapes, crescents and columns of the gigantic vegetation. One landed on my sleeve and I swatted it, noticing with revulsion that it had five legs, three wings and no symmetry.

We followed the silver path. It passed through a tetragate, and at once we found ourselves in another garden chamber, similarly filled with glossy, abundant plant life thriving in sculptural tanks. The tallest growths in here - giant yellowish horsetails streaked with orange veins - rose eighty or ninety metres above the floating pathway.

Guilar called a word of alarm, and his storm bolter began to fire, raking across this second chamber from the silver path on which we walked. The shots burst gourd-like plants in fibrous bursts of sap and hacked shreds of leaf and tendril into the air.

Return fire came at us. Las-fire and the crack of autorifles. Through the sickly growths of this indoor jungle, the soldiers of the heretics moved against us.

TWENTY-FOUR

PURGE TWO ENGAGES
A SILENT REVOLUTION
DAZZO'S TRIUMPH

They came through the plant growth, along the silver paths, blasting, men clad in the stained uniforms of the 50th Gudrunite Rifles and the black armour of the naval security detail. Two of the Gudrunites in my squad toppled and fell from the path, their corpses disappearing into the oily waters of the tanks below. But most of the enemy gunfire was going wild.

Purge Two countered, lasguns barking. I moved to the front of the group and began firing my bolt pistol. There was precious little room for manoeuvre on the silver walkway, and even less cover.

My first shot went wide, so wide I wondered if the bolter was misaligned. Then I remembered the devious nature of the saruthi tetrascape and compensated. Two shots, two satisfying hits. Bequin and Midas both had the trick of it too, and Jeruss's boys were learning.

Guilar made a lot of noise, ripping through the gardens with his storm bolter. But it seemed to me he was still discomforted by the environment.

It was a salutary moment. To see one of the god-like warriors I have regarded with great awe ever since the day, thirty years ago, when I watched the White Scars take Almanadae, become fallible. For all his power, courage, superhuman vigour and advanced weapons, he was achieving nothing, whereas Yeltun, the youngest of the Gudrun boys, had made three kills already.

Was it arrogance? Overconfidence in his own abilities?

'Guilar! Brother Guilar! Adjust your fire!'

I heard him curse something about insolence, and move ahead down the path, detonating plant bulks with his shots.

'Why doesn't the bastard listen?' Midas complained, sighting his Glavian rifle and decapitating a heretic trooper at one hundred metres.

'Close up!' I ordered. 'Jeruss! Frag them!'

Jeruss and three others began to lob frag grenades over the thickets. Explosive flashes blew water ooze and vegetable matter up from the tanks, and the air became foggy with plant fibre and sappy moisture.

There was an abrupt change in tone in the enemy fire. The boom of a bolter rang out over the crack and snipe of the laser weapons.

I looked down the silver path in time to see Guilar jerk backwards as multiple bolter rounds struck his chest plate. With a cry of rage rather than pain, he went over, off the path, into the bubbling water of the tank behind us and vanished.

Thrusting the heretic foot soldiers out of the way, his killer came down the pathway towards us.

'Oh no!' Bequin cried. 'Please-by-the-Golden-Throne-no!'

Another of the Emperor's Children, the brother if not the twin of foul Mandragore. His scintillating cloak blew out behind him, and his steel-shod hooves shook the path. He was bellowing like a bull auroch. His bolter spat and the Gudrunite beside me burst apart.

The Children of the Emperor, shadowy sponsors of this entire enterprise, were here to protect their investment. Had they come, unbidden, after Mandragore's death? Had Dazzo or Locke summoned them?

I fired the bolter at him, joining the fusillade of desperate weapons blasts that Purge Two levelled in a frantic attempt to slow him down. Fear made the men forget the best of their training, and many of the shots were wild. He didn't seem to feel those few that struck his armour.

'Purge Two! This is Purge Two! The Children of the Emperor are here!' I yelled into my vox. I knew I would be dead in an instant. It was imperative that Fleet Command knew of this dire development.

A black shape burst up from the dark water, cascading froth and ooze in all directions. Brother Guilar slammed into the Chaos Marine, wrenching him over, and they both fell thrashing into the adjacent tank. Something, probably the heretic's bolter, fired repeatedly underwater and the side of the tank below the floating path splintered out in a rush of liquid. The soupy water flooded out, draining away into the gullies between the garden structures. As the fluid level dropped, the titanic combatants emerged, blackened with mire, wrestling and trading inhuman blows among the tangled roots and feeder tubes of the tank's murky bottom.

Ceramite-cased fists pounded into armour plates. Chips of plasteel flew from the impacts. The Chaos Marine's vast paws clawed at Guilar, tearing at his visor and shoulder guards. Guilar drove him backwards, his feet churning in the shallow, thick water. They slammed in the bole of a cycad. The enemy grappled, getting a better grip, stabbing a jagged gauntlet spike through the armpit seal of the Deathwatch's imperator armour. Guilar staggered, and as he fell back, a massive backhanded slap knocked him over and tore his helmet off.

The Chaos Marine landed on the sprawling Guilar, tearing at his throat, driving fists like boulders into his face.

There was a bang of weapon discharge and a flash. His face destroyed and his collapsed skull burning from the inside, the Chaos filth fell back into the swamp water.

Guilar rose, unsteady, his storm bolter in his hand, blood pouring from the wounds in his face and neck.

It was a formidable victory. Jeruss and his men cheered and whooped and then renewed their advance on the remaining heretics. The enemy, resolve lost, pulled back and vanished into the dense thickets of the gardens.

Dripping, Guilar climbed back onto the path and looked down at me.
'I'm glad you're still with us, Brother Guilar,' I said.

We traced the paths on through the gardens of the saruthi, unopposed. The enemy dead we passed – floating in the tanks or sprawled on the pathways – had signs of branding on their faces. Chaos marks, burned into the skin by evil rather than heat. Admiral Spatian had hoped that some of the heretic forces, especially the Gudrunite Imperial Guard, might yet be restored to the Imperial cause. Like Jeruss and his men, most had been unwilling pawns caught up in Estrum's treason, and the fleet tacticians had presented models of victory wherein Locke and Dazzo found the bulk of their ground forces turning against them.

Such a hope was dashed. The minds of these good men had been burned away and poisoned by Chaos. The heretics had enforced the loyalty of their stolen armies.

Via tetragates we advanced, passing through six more garden spheres, then on into wide, tiled courtyards and halls of asymmetrical pillars whose function we could not imagine. Twice, we had brief skirmishes with heretic forces, driving them back into the warped cavities of the edifice. More often, we could hear ferocious war, full-blown battles that seemed right at hand but of which there was no visual or physical trace.

Contact with fleet command was fragmentary. Purge One – Lord Rorken's party – was locked in combat somewhere, and nothing had been heard of Molitor's Purge Four. Schongard's group, Purge Five, was lost somewhere in the tetrascape. Plaintive calls for aid came from them at irregular intervals, piteous half-sane ramblings about 'impossible spaces' and 'spirals of madness.'

From Titus Endor we heard nothing.

The main surface war still raged. Mirepoix commanders reported gains along the fire lakes that edged the target edifices, one of which was reportedly beginning to implode as if great harm had been done to it internally.

In a vault of smooth, polished beige that seemed to us to have no ceiling, we found our first saruthi. They were dead, a dozen of them, their grey bulks split and mauled, silver stilts torn off. Through the next gate lay a spiral room littered with a hundred more. Moving among the grey dead, their pallid limbs dripping with ichor, were several of the white slave beasts that had carried the Necroteuch onto the plateau. They seemed to me to have broken free as many dragged their wire restraints. Some had taken up silver stilts and were stabbing them slowly and repeatedly into the corpses of their grey masters.

I wondered if the pitiful white things were a separate race enslaved by the saruthi, or a bastardised, mutant caste kept in servitude. The invasion, it seemed, had freed them to turn on their owners and butcher them. Such is the price of slavery, sooner or later.

The slave-things offered us no threat. They didn't even appear to notice the humans moving amongst them. With silent, methodical determination, they mutilated the bodies of the saruthi.

In another chamber, an oval dish with tessellated tiles and a strangely warm atmosphere, living saruthi milled aimlessly in their hundreds. Some had lost stilts and were limping, others lay in trembling masses, their skulls flopped back on their bodies. The smell of liquorice, or whatever it was, reeked here. As we watched, white slave-things lumbered into the chamber through another tetragate and began to twist apart and maul the saruthi, one by one, with the calm, methodical motions of insects. The saruthi offered no resistance.

This story was repeated in other chambers and curving halls. saruthi lay dead or meandering without purpose, freed slaves finding them by touch and dismembering them.

I wonder, even now, as to the meaning of these alien scenes. Had the saruthi given up, resigned to their doom, or had some other circumstance stolen their will to live and resist? Not even the tech-priests or the xenobiologists could provide an answer. There is, ultimately, only the fact of their alien nature; abstract, inscrutable and beyond the capacity of the human mind to fathom.

When we found the archpriest Dazzo, he was close to death.

A battle of titanic proportions had taken place in the tetrascape where he lay. Thousands of dead lay on the tiled floor: Mirepoix infantry and heretic troops alike. Two Children of the Emperor and three Deathwatch were among the fallen. The tetrascape, by far the largest of any we had seen in the edifice, reached away beyond the curve of all human dimensions, and the jumbled corpses covered the endless floor into infinity.

Dazzo lay at the foot of an asymmetrical block that rose from the tiles like a standing stone. His body was torn by gunshot wounds. Heldane sat nearby, his back to the great block, guarding the archpriest with an autopistol. Heldane's torso was smirched in blood and his breathing was laboured.

He saw us approach through the tetragate and lowered the gun weakly.

'What happened here, Heldane?'

'A battle,' he said, wheezing. 'We came upon it as it was raging. When Inquisitor Endor saw this wretch, he drove us into the fight to reach him. It was a blur after that.'

'Where's Endor?' I asked, looking around, hoping I would not see his corpse among the dead.

'Gone… gone after Locke.'

'Which way?'

He pointed weakly to a tetragate on the far side of the sea of bodies.

'Does Locke have the Necroteuch? The saruthi Necroteuch, I mean?'

'No,' Heldane said. 'But he has the primer.'

'The what?'

'Dazzo got it out of this thing somehow,' he said, slapping the stone block that supported him. 'A language primer. A translation tool. Without it, the saruthi version of the text is unreadable to us.'

'How in the Emperor's name did he do that?' Guilar asked.

'With his mind,' Heldane said. 'Can't you feel that after-burn of the psychic effort?'

I found that I could. The mental taste of a mind almost burned out. The raised block was clearly another part of the saruthi's mysterious technology, perhaps the equivalent of an Imperial cogitator, perhaps something more sentient, even something alive. Dazzo, whose psychic abilities I already knew to be monstrous, had identified it and psychically assaulted it, forcing it to give up its secrets. An extraordinary feat of the mind, a triumph of will.

'A polyhedron,' Heldane added. 'Irregular, small, made of pearl, it seemed to me. It just came out of the block into his hands. Materialised. I saw it happening as I fought my way to them. But the effort destroyed his mind. Endor cut him down. He hadn't the strength to resist.'

'How do you know it was this... primer?' asked Bequin.

'I read it in his dying mind. Like I said, there is no resistance left there. See for yourself.'

I crossed over to Dazzo and knelt next to him. Ragged breathing sucked in and out of his bloody mouth. I drove my mind into his, pushing aside pathetic strands of denial, and confirmed Heldane's story. With inhuman willpower, Dazzo had wrenched the language primer from the saruthi technology, and with it the whereabouts of the xenos Necroteuch. Dying, he had passed both to Locke to finish the task.

'Gregor!' Midas hissed. I turned. Far away, across the curve of the tetrascape, heretic troops were advancing through the dead. They began firing at us.

Guilar and the Gudrunites fired back, taking what cover they could to resist.

'Brother Guilar, I need you to hold these bastards at bay.'

'Where are you going, inquisitor?' he asked, sliding a fresh clip into his storm bolter.

'After Locke and Endor, to do what I can.'

TWENTY-FIVE

XENOS NECROTEUCH
ENDGAME
THE BLANK-EYED MAN

We left the firefight behind us and plunged through the tetragate. Bequin, Midas and I, racing as fast as we could through the disorienting spirals and imbricating segments of the dying saruthi edifice.

As we ran, I reported the situation to fleet command, but had no reply or way of knowing if they'd understood me. Then I tried Titus Endor, but the vox was dead.

Moving at speed, the place became even more of a four-dimensional maze, but I had in my mind now the engram I had taken from Dazzo, the memory trace of the route to the xenos Necroteuch he had ripped from the block.

By my estimation - and it could hardly be trusted - we were approaching the heart of the edifice. Perhaps not the physical or geographic heart, but that part of the dimensional construct buried most deeply in the interlocking lamina of warped space and time.

There were more saruthi here, skittering and clicking around on their silver limb-braces without purpose or response. The smell of liquorice filled the warm, glowing tunnels and tiled chambers.

We heard screaming ahead of us, and the thump of gunfire.

'Titus? Titus! It's Eisenhorn! Do you read?'

The vox coughed into life. 'Gregor! For the love of the Emperor! I need–'

It broke again. More shots.

We hurried through a tetragate and almost at once had to dive for cover as las-fire flurried around us. The chamber we had entered was by no means the largest we had found in the place, but it was singular. Dark, and gloomy, it lacked the radiance that shone from the walls and floors elsewhere. The lustrous material that composed the rest of the edifice was here grey and dissected, as if dead.

Another block, like the one Heldane had been propped up against but many times the size, rose from the ashy floor, streaked with oily, greenish matter that ran down its flanks and pooled at the base. An asymmetrical shelf jutted from it, just above the height of an average human, and a blue octahedron sat upon it, glowing internally.

The xenos Necroteuch. Dazzo's engram immediately confirmed it.

The chamber stank with its evil, the liquorice smell, so rich and cloying it made us gag. Behind and above the main pillar, warped sculptures of metal, bone and other organic materials grew from the walls and curving roof. Vicious hooks on filthy chains dangled from these outgrowths. This was not saruthi handiwork but a touch of pure Chaos, spawned by the Necroteuch, infecting the xenos fabric of its sanctum.

Smaller pillars, irregular and unmatched, dotted the floor around the main block. In between them, a gunfight was raging. The three of us ran from the exposure of the lit tetragate and found shelter behind the nearest of the smaller blocks. Las-shots wove in and out of the stone shapes, ricocheting and rebounding.

'Titus!'

'Gregor!' He was twenty metres away, a third of the way into the chamber, huddled behind a block and firing his laspistol at figures closer to the Necroteuch's resting place.

I glimpsed Locke, and eight or nine heretic troopers.

I looked to either side of me at Bequin and Midas. 'Choose your targets,' I told them. We began to fire in support of Endor, dropping at least one of the heretics. As they reeled from the salvo, Endor leapt up and ran forward. A las-shot clipped him and blew him back against a stone upright.

I ran forward myself, firing my bolt pistol which I had braced in both hands. I blew chunks from the blocks ahead of me, and hit at least one of the enemy gunners. I reached Endor.

He was wounded in the chest. It would be fatal if we couldn't get him clear quickly. I pulled him into cover, and waited while Bequin ran up through the rows to my side.

'Pressure, here!' I said, showing her, my hands wet with my old friend's blood. She did as she was told.

I became aware of thunderous noises from beyond the chamber. The place shook. More thunder rolled and a section of the curved ceiling suddenly splintered and collapsed, cascading wreckage down, allowing cold exterior light to shaft in. A second later, three more holes ruptured and burst through the roof, and from outside I could hear the muffled hammering of bombardment.

'Midas!'

He was already moving up to my left, ditching his needle rifle for the pistols in the tight confines. Lethal Glavian needles hissed through the air. The ground continued to shake. A further section of roof came down.

Leaving Endor with Bequin, I ducked from pillar to pillar, braving the deluge of shots. Midas and I switched to our earpiece links and Glossia.

'Thorn ushers Aegis, a tempest sinister.'

'Aegis attending, tempest in three.'

I counted the three beats and ran forward as Midas hurled his frag grenade to my left before opening fire with both pistols.

The flash and bang of the blast obscured the bombardment outside for a moment. A heretic was flung upwards, limbs flailing, and glanced brokenly off a pillar before hitting the ground.

Midas's 'tempest' of covering confusion had allowed me to get within ten metres of Locke. I could no longer see him, however. Keeping my grip on my bolt pistol, I drew my power sword in my left hand and came around the block.

Locke and one of his men had chosen the exact same moment to plough forward into me. We broke from cover and came face to face in the narrow gap between pillars. My pistol's first shot missed the lunging Locke and tore the left arm off his accomplice. Before the wailing man had even hit the ground, Locke's laspistol had put a round through the meat of my right arm. A long-bladed dagger flashed forward in his other hand. We slammed into each other. I tried to sweep my power sword around, but it struck something and Locke side-stepped. The basket hilt of his dagger smashed into my face and knocked me over onto my back. With a grin that he knew I could never copy, he raised his laspistol to fire down into my brain.

Two tonnes of xenos-quarried stone pillar, sliced through at hip-height by my power blade, crushed him into the flaking ground.

I rose.

Gorgone Locke was still alive. His belly and pelvis were smashed under the fallen pillar and his arms were pinned. He gazed up at me through blinking, bewildered eyes.

'Gorgone Locke, in the eyes of the Holy Inquisition, you are thrice damned by action, association and belief,' I said, beginning the catechism of abolition.

'N-no...' he whispered.

As I completed the exclamation, I cut the mark of heresy into the flesh of his brow with the tip of my sword. By the time I had finished, he was dead from his crush injuries.

The shattering chamber still shook. On their long chains, the hooks swung. Dust and fragments dribbled down from the tears in the roof, falling through the bars of cold light. I reached down and found the pearl polyhedron in Locke's blood-soaked coat. The primer. I slipped it into my pocket and turned to see Midas approaching.

'The last of his rats have fled,' he said, holstering his pistols. He looked down at the dead ship master. 'So perish all heretics, eh?'

I reached up with on hand to take the xenos Necroteuch from its shelf – and found myself unable to move. Some enormous psychic force froze me rigid.

'So perish all heretics indeed,' said a voice. 'Turn him so he can see me.'

Involuntarily, I swung round, my hand still raised in the act of reaching out. I saw Midas, also paralysed and rigid, his dark features locked in a rictus of dismay.

Konrad Molitor, my brother inquisitor, was standing before me, smiling. His three hooded servants were at his side.

'Such valour, Gregor. Such dedication. I thought you'd be the one to find the prize.'

I tried to answer, but my mouth refused to obey me. Spittle bubbled between my clenched teeth.

Molitor looked around at his cowled companions. 'Let him speak,' he said.

The psychic constraints on my voice slackened. Speech was still an effort. 'W-what are you d-doing, Molitor?'

'Recovering the priceless Necroteuch, of course. We really, really can't have you destroying another copy now, can we?'

'W-we?'

'There are many who believe mankind will benefit more from the study of this artefact than from its destruction. I have come to safeguard those interests.'

'R-rorken will n-never allow... y-you will b-burn for–'

'My estimable Lord Brother Rorken will never know. Feel how this place quakes. See how the roof splinters and collapses? Ten minutes ago, I signalled to the fleet that the primary objective was achieved. I gave the code for Sanction Extremis. They believe the Necroteuch had been found and safely disposed of. Our forces are withdrawing, with all haste. The batteries of the fleet have begun to level these xenos places. No one will know that the divine Necroteuch has been carried off safely. Not a shred of evidence will survive the bombardment. Not a shred of evidence... nor any voice of dissent.'

His yellow-pupilled eyes regarded me. 'How brave of you to give your life in the assault on 56-Izar. Your name will be remembered on the roll of honour. I assure you, I'll see to that myself.'

'B-b-b-bastard...' I fought with my mind to break free, but it was impossible. This was not Molitor's hold on me. One of his retainers, or all three in concert, supremely powerful.

'Fetch it for me,' Molitor said to one of his men, gesturing to the Necroteuch with a wave of his checked sleeve. 'We would be well to leave promptly.'

The hammering bombardment was now a perpetual shaking roar. The robed figure slid forward and took down the blue octahedron, cupping it in elegant, long-nailed fingers. He seemed to study it, and looked round at Molitor.

'It is useless,' he said.

'What?'

'Unreadable. Locked within an impenetrable xenos language code.'

Molitor stammered. 'No! Impossible! Break the code!'

'Would that I could. It is beyond even my ability.'

'There must be a means of translation!'

The hooded man holding the Necroteuch looked round at me.

'He has a primer. The only primer. He's trying not to think about it, but I can see it in his mind. Look in his coat pocket.'

The smile returned to Molitor's face. He came close to me, reaching out a hand towards my coat. 'Devious to the last, Gregor. You whoreson wretch.'

A las-round blew his hand off at the wrist.

Molitor screamed and stumbled back, clutching his smoking stump.

Bequin, her face pursed grimly, her las-carbine at her shoulder and aimed at his heart, appeared beside me.

'Kill them! Kill them!' Molitor screamed. I felt the immediate pressure of the psychic vice tightening to finish me. Then I reeled away, freed. The psychic blank of Bequin's untouchable nature shielded me now she was at my side. The servant holding the Necroteuch took a step backwards in surprise.

Molitor, frantic with pain and anger, saw that his powerful psychic was thwarted somehow and yelled 'Albaara! T'harth!'

Code words. Trigger words. The pair of servants who had remained by his side sprang forward, their robes shredding away.

Arco-flagellants. Heretics reprogrammed and rebuilt with augmetics and bionics to serve as murderous slaves. The trigger words woke them from their calming states of bliss and plunged them into maniacal rages.

Out of their robes, they were foul, hunched things, encrusted with crude surgical implants and sacred charms. Their hands were lashing clutches of electrowhips, their eyes dull, bulbous orbits under the rims of the tarnished pacifier helmets bolted to their skulls.

Midas, Bequin and I fired our weapons together, raking them with punishment as they charged forward. The damage they suffered was immense, but still they came on, their bodies pumped with intoxicating adrenal fluid, pain-blockers and frenzy-inducing chemical stimulants. They didn't feel what we were doing to them.

One was just an arm's length from me when my desperate rain of bolts finally defeated it. A shot exploded the armoured matrix of chemical dispensers on its shoulder, spraying fluid into the air. In a second, it fell convulsing to the ground at our feet as the damage robbed it of its drug-source and left nothing but agony behind.

The other barely felt the punctures of Midas's too subtle needles. Frantically, we split to either side, out of its path. Braying and thrashing its whip-limbs, it pounded after Midas, who ducked left and right between pillars, trying to evade it. Only his Glavian-bred grace and speed kept him out of its inexorably advancing grip.

He knew he had seconds left. Bequin and I were moving, but there was precious little we could do.

Midas pulled off his pouch of grenades, priming one as he twisted and side-stepped between the pillars, scarcely avoiding a withering lash of flexible metal whips that scored gouges in the stone.

Midas feinted left and then threw himself directly at the beast, snagging the strap of his pouch around its neck as he vaulted over its shoulder head first.

The grenades detonated in one stunning flash and atomised the ravening man-beast. Caught in the shockwave, Midas was thrown into a pillar and dropped unconscious.

'Eisenhorn! Eisenhorn!' Molitor was wailing as he and his remaining servant hunted for me. His voice was cracking with pain and fury.

'Stay at my side,' I told Bequin as we ran deeper into the chamber. 'That psychic can't touch me while I'm close to you.'

Half the ceiling and a significant part of the wall blew in. For a second the air was solid with billowing orange fire.

Deafened, our skins scorched by the blast, Bequin and I were back on our feet in a moment. The chamber was open to the sky now, and cold white light poured in, heavy with smoke.

'Come on!'

Together we scrambled towards the blast-damaged wall, picking our way up the smouldering slope of broken stone and whatever material the saruthi used for construction. This material was fused and bubbling, like plastic or flesh.

We headed for the light.

We emerged high on the curving upper face of the saruthi edifice. It was cold, and the wind that came across the segmented ridges of the polished white roof was brisk and full of the odours of smoke, fyceline and promethium.

We were at a dizzying height. The pearly flanks of the vast structure arced away to a ground far below and the surface was hard and polished like ice. Bequin slipped, and I managed to grab her before she slid away down the curve.

From up here, high in the alien sky, we could see across the lakes of fire and the vast smoke banks that roiled away for hundreds of kilometres. We could see flocks of troopships soaring up and away through the smoke cover towards the parent ships in orbit. On the flats of white mud far beneath us, Imperial troops ran to waiting dropships, discarding packs and helmets and even weapons in their haste to leave. Tanks and armoured carriers wallowed and puffed through the wet mud and up onto the tongue-like ramps of heavy lifters. Shells and las-fire flickered across the lakes and mud as the remaining heretic forces fought on heedless.

Lances and forks of dazzling energy bit down from the clouds, murdering the landscape. Obeying Molitor's instructions to the letter, Admiral Spatian was levelling the area. All five of us inquisitors, along with Cynewolf and key Deathwatch and selected officers of the invasion force, had been given the code words to unleash this doom. Molitor had sealed our fate. Once given, Sanction Extremis could not be revoked, even if my vox had been working instead of crippled by the electromagnetic bursts that accompanied every orbital strike. As per the battle plans, Spatian was systematically wasting the invasion site as fast as possible, even at the cost of his own retreating ground forces.

Another saruthi edifice, twenty kilometres away, died. Shaped in a form that suggested a nautilus shell, its opalescent curves were cracked and split by blue-hot heavy lasers. The die-straight beams came down through the clouds from ships so far up they were invisible, and tore through the edifice like testamental judgment. Waves of fighter-bombers swept in, sowing payloads of munitions that bloomed in rippling seas of explosions. Guided warheads, sleek like airborne sharks, whined overhead on the last stage of their first and final journey from starship to target.

The edifice ruptured and blew out. Light-shock lit the hemisphere. A towering column of white ash-smoke rose, folding into a fifteen-kilometre torus-shaped cloud.

The sight was stunning, shocking. Bequin and I gazed at it. A few heartbeats later it was repeated behind us, forty kilometres distant, as another saruthi edifice was annihilated.

The edifice on whose smoothly curving upper surfaces we now stood was undoubtedly going to go the same way soon. Even now, I knew, the co-ordinates were being loaded into the fleet's gunnery servitors.

We ran along the lip of another curved segment. Afterburners red against the black smoke, more dropships came in, heading towards cheering, gesticulating huddles of Mirepoix infantry out on the flats. I was astounded at the selfless courage of the dropship crews. Spatian's bombardment wasn't waiting for them to move in and pull out. They were risking everything to make the surface run and retrieve as many troopers as they could.

'Gregor!' Bequin shouted in my ear.

I turned. Down the shell-form span of the roof behind us, Molitor and his henchman had appeared out of the blast hole. Unsteady, they scrambled up after us.

A las-shot whined past me, kissing the pearly surface and leaving a burn-scar.

'The primer, you whoreson bastard! Give me the primer!' Molitor yelled.

I gave him a full clip of bolt rounds instead.

The first of the thundering tracer shots splintered chunks out of the edifice roof. Then I hit and exploded his left thigh, his belly and his throat.

Konrad Molitor bucked and twitched as the rounds tore through him, and then fell. His mauled body slid down the curve of the roof and disappeared, leaving a smear of blood behind it.

His henchman advanced, heedless of the shots, throwing off his hooded robe.

He was naked beneath it. Tall, well muscled, with a golden cast to his skin. His face was handsome and tiny residual horns sprouted from his skull.

His eyes were blank.

My prophetic dreams were made flesh.

Terror seized me, turned my heart inside out.

TWENTY-SIX

CHERUBAEL
THE BRINK
EXTERMINATUS

The blank-eyed man – though in truth he was not a man, but a daemon in human form – strode up the shining curve towards me. The glowing octahedron of the saruthi's unholy text was clasped in one nimble hand.

'I would like the primer now please, Gregor.'

'What *are* you?'

'This is no place for introductions.' He gestured about himself. Lances of annihilation blasted down into the mud-flats nearby.

'Humour me...' I managed.

'Very well. My name is Cherubael. Now, that primer. Time is ticking away.'

'Time will always tick away,' I said. 'Who made you?'

'Made me?' The blank-eyed man smiled at me duplicitously.

'You're... a *daemonhost*. A conjured thing. Tell me who made you and who commanded you and Molitor to come after this prize... and I might give you the primer.'

He laughed and licked his thin lips with a glossy forked tongue.

'Let us both be abundantly clear about this, *Gregor*. You will give me the primer. Either you will hand me the primer now, or I will come over to you and take it. And break every bone in your body. And defile that girl at your side. And break every bone in her body too. And then drag your jiggling carcasses down into the chamber below and string you both up on the hooks, and burn out your agony centres as I wait for the bombardment to flatten this place.'

He paused.

'Your choice.'

'You've been in my dreams for a long while now. Why is that?' I pressed.

'You are gifted, Gregor. And time is not the arrow that humans like to think it is. A second in the warp would show you that. Why, a second in the four-dimensional habitats of the saruthi should have proved it too. Your dreams were just nightmares of something yet to happen.'

'Who made you?' My voice was insistent. His answer was the one I least expected, and it left me all but stunned.

'The Holy Inquisition made me, Gregor. A brother of yours made me. Now, for the last time, give me that–'

The daemonhost swung around suddenly as voices called out from lower down the roof. Brother-Captain Cynewolf was clambering up out of the blast hole, flanked by Midas and another Deathwatcher carrying the limp form of Titus Endor.

Cynewolf raised his storm bolter and fired at the blank-eyed man.

Cherubael reached out and caught the glowing shells, plucking them out of the air.

'Go home, Astartes bastard!' he yelled down the sloping roof at Cynewolf. 'This has nothing to do with you!'

The fiend came up the ridge until he was facing me. I could see the tiny arcs of power darting across his glowing skin. I could smell the stink of corruption.

Eye to eye now.

He held out his hand, palm up, fingernails long and polished like claws.

'Clever of you to find an untouchable to cancel me out.' He looked over at Bequin. 'How did you manage that?'

'Fate, like time, is not linear, Cherubael. Surely you know that. I found Bequin in the same way that the dreams of you found me.'

He nodded. 'I like you, Gregor Eisenhorn. So very challenging and stimulating – for a human. I wish we had leisure to discourse and break bread... But we haven't!' he snapped suddenly. 'Give me the primer!'

I took out the polyhedron. His smile broadened.

I dropped the artefact onto the silky roof and, before it could slide away, crushed it under the heel of my boot.

The daemonhost took a step backwards, gazing down at the crunched dust.

He looked up at me again with his blank eyes. 'You are a man of singular dedication, Gregor. I would have enjoyed killing you, when the day and hour came. But you're dead already. This edifice is two hundred and forty seconds away from destruction. Cherish this–'

He tossed me the xenos Necroteuch and I caught it in one gloved hand.

'You've won. Take that consolation to the afterlife.'

He started to run, towards the lip of the roof, and then threw himself out in a perfect dive, arms raised. For a moment, he hung in space, then he forked his body in, executed a precise roll and disappeared into the lake of fire below.

I pulled Bequin to me as Cynewolf, Midas and the other Deathwatch Marine approached. Endor, crumpled in the Astartes' arms, looked dead. I prayed he was, for in a moment this place would dissolve in fire.

'Rosethorn from Aegis, above and... well, above, for Emperor's sake! Damn this Glossia crap! *Move!*'

My gun-cutter swung in over the edifice roof, ramp-jaws open. I could see Fischig at the helm through the cockpit screens, yelling at me. Aemos was at his side.

I watched 56-Izar die from the bridge of the *Saint Scythus* as we left orbit. Petals of flame the size of continents spread out under its milky skin. Sanction Extremis. *Exterminatus.*

After the deluge of fire, the virus bombs. The seething storms of tailored plagues. The nuclear atrocity.

It was a cinder by the time we left. No contact with the saruthi race was ever made again.

And the tainted, glowing light of the Necroteuch was extinguished forever.

EPILOGUE

AT PAMOPHREY

At Pamophrey, we rested.

Forty weeks of voyage through the immaterium had dulled our sense of victory. The fleet dispersed at Thracian Primaris and the last I saw of Sergeant Jeruss was a waving hand across a smoky, beery bar.

I rented a villa out by the Sound at Pamophrey. Midas slept most of the day, and whiled away the night in games of regicide with Aemos and Fischig. Bequin bathed in the sun, and swam in the breakers.

I sat out on the salt-whipped stoop and watched over the beach like a god who has forgotten his creations.

Great labours still awaited us. Reports to be made, interviews and debriefings to be attended. Lord Rorken had called for a tribunal of enquiry, and the High Lords of Terra were awaiting a full account of the matter. Months of paperwork, hearings and evidential audits lay ahead. The identity of the force behind Molitor and his daemonhost remained a mystery, and though Lord Rorken was as anxious as myself to find an answer, I doubted any would readily emerge. The question might fester and stagnate, unanswered, in the slow, unwieldy bureaucracy of the Inquisition for years.

I would not allow that. As soon as I was free to engage upon another case, I would dedicate myself to finding Cherubael's master. The beloved rule of man had come close to great calamity thanks to his scheming.

I would not forget the saruthi. They were an object lesson - if any were truly needed - of how an entire, advanced culture might be consumed by Chaos.

Seabirds looped in the gusting tide wind. The breakers crashed.

The blank-eyed man still haunted my dreams.

After-echoes or ripples of the future?

I would have to wait and see.

MISSING IN ACTION

I lost my left hand on Sameter. This is how it occurred. On the thirteenth day of Sagittar (local calendar), three days before the solstice, in the mid-rise district of the city of Urbitane, an itinerant evangelist called Lazlo Mombril was found shuffling aimlessly around the flat roof of a disused tannery lacking his eyes, his tongue, his nose and both of his hands.

Urbitane is the second city of Sameter, a declining agro-chemical planet in the Helican subsector, and it is no stranger to crimes of cruelty and spite brought on by the vicissitudes of neglect and social deprivation afflicting its tightly packed population. But this act of barbarity stood out for two reasons. First, it was no hot-blooded assault or alcohol-fuelled manslaughter but a deliberate and systematic act of brutal, almost ritual mutilation.

Second, it was the fourth such crime discovered that month.

I had been on Sameter for just three weeks, investigating the links between a bonded trade federation and a secessionist movement on Hesperus at the request of Lord Inquisitor Rorken. The links proved to be nothing – Urbitane's economic slough had forced the federation to chase unwise business with unscrupulous shipmasters, and the real meat of the case lay on Hesperus – but I believe this was the Lord Inquisitor's way of gently easing me back into active duties following the long and arduous affair of the Necroteuch.

By the Imperial calendar it was 241.M41, late in that year. I had just finished several self-imposed months of recuperation, meditation and study on Thracian Primaris. The eyes of the daemonhost Cherubael still woke me some nights, and I wore permanent scars from torture at the hands of the sadist Gorgone Locke. His strousine neural scourge had damaged my nervous system and paralysed my face. I would not smile again for the rest of my life. But the battle wounds sustained on KCX-1288 and 56-Izar had healed, and I was now itching to renew my work.

This idle task on Sameter had suited me, so I had taken it and closed the dossier after a swift and efficient investigation. But latterly, as I prepared to leave, officials of the Munitorum unexpectedly requested an audience.

I was staying with my associates in a suite of rooms in the Urbitane Excelsior, a shabby but well-appointed establishment in the high-rise district of the city. Through soot-stained, armoured roundels of glass twenty metres across, the suite looked out across the filthy grey towers of the city to the brackish waters of the polluted bay twenty kilometres away. Ornithopters and biplanes buzzed between the massive city structures, and the running lights of freighters and orbitals glowed in the smog as they swung down towards the landing port. Out on the isthmus, through a haze of yellow, stagnant air, promethium refineries belched brown smoke into the perpetual twilight.

'They're here,' said Bequin, entering the suite's lounge from the outer lobby. She had dressed in a demure gown of blue damask and a silk pashmeena, perfectly in keeping with my instruction that we should present a muted but powerful image.

I myself was clad in a suit of soft black linen with a waistcoat of grey velvet and a hip length black leather storm-coat.

'Do you need me for this?' asked Midas Betancore, my pilot and confidant.

I shook my head. 'I don't intend to be delayed here. I just have to be polite. Go on to the landing port and make sure the gun-cutter's readied for departure.'

He nodded and left. Bequin showed the visitors in.

I had felt it necessary to be polite because Eskeen Hansaard, Urbitane's Minister of Security, had come to see me himself. He was a massive man in a double-breasted brown tunic, his big frame offset oddly by his finely featured, boyish face. He was escorted by two bodyguards in grey, armour-ribbed uniforms and a short but handsome, black-haired woman in a dark blue bodyglove.

I had made sure I was sitting in an armchair when Bequin showed them in so I could rise in a measured, respectful way. I wanted them to be in no doubt who was really in charge here.

'Minister Hansaard,' I said, shaking his hand. 'I am Inquisitor Gregor Eisenhorn of the Ordo Xenos. These are my associates Alizebeth Bequin, Arbites Chastener Godwyn Fischig and savant Uber Aemos. How may I help you?'

'I have no wish to waste your time, inquisitor,' he said, apparently nervous in my presence. That was good, just as I had intended it. 'A case has been brought to my attention that I believe is beyond the immediate purview of the city Arbites. Frankly, it smacks of warp-corruption, and cries out for the attention of the Inquisition.'

He was direct. That impressed me. A ranking official of the Imperium, anxious to be seen to be doing the right thing. Nevertheless, I still expected his business might be a mere nothing, like the affair of the trade federation, a local crime requiring only my nod of approval that it was fine for him to continue and close. Men like Hansaard are often over-careful, in my experience.

'There have been four deaths in the city during the last month that we believe to be linked. I would appreciate your advice on them. They are connected by merit of the ritual mutilation involved.'

'Show me,' I said.

'Captain?' he responded.

Arbites Captain Hurlie Wrex was the handsome woman with the short black hair. She stepped forward, nodded respectfully, and gave me a data-slate with the gold crest of the Adeptus Arbites on it.

'I have prepared a digested summary of the facts,' she said.

I began to speed-read the slate, already preparing the gentle knock-back I was expecting to give to his case. Then I stopped, slowed, read back.

I felt a curious mix of elation and frustration. Even from this cursorial glance, there was no doubt this case required the immediate attention of the Imperial Inquisition. I could feel my instincts stiffen and my appetites whetten, for the first time in months. In bothering me with this, Minister Hansaard was not being over careful at all. At the same time, my heart sank with the realisation that my departure from this miserable city would be delayed.

All four victims had been blinded and had their noses, tongues and hands removed. At the very least.

The evangelist, Mombril, had been the only one found alive. He had died from his injuries eight minutes after arriving at Urbitane Mid-rise Sector Infirmary. It seemed to me likely that he had escaped his ritual tormentors somehow before they could finish their work.

The other three were a different story.

Poul Grevan, a machinesmith; Luthar Hewall, a rug-maker; Idilane Fasple, a mid-wife.

Hewall had been found a week before by city sanitation servitors during routine maintenance to a soil stack in the mid-rise district. Someone had attempted to burn his remains and then flush them into the city's ancient waste system, but the human body is remarkably durable. The post could not prove his missing body parts had not simply succumbed to decay and been flushed away, but the damage to the ends of the forearm bones seemed to speak convincingly of a saw or chain-blade.

When Idilane Fasple's body was recovered from a crawlspace under the roof of a mid-rise tenement hab, it threw more light on the extent of Hewall's injuries. Not only had Fasple been mutilated in the manner of the evangelist Mombril, but her brain, brainstem and heart had been excised. The injuries were hideous. One of the roof workers who discovered her had subsequently committed suicide. Her bloodless, almost dessicated body, dried out – smoked, if you will – by the tenement's heating vents, had been wrapped in a dark green cloth similar to the material of an Imperial Guard-issue bed-roll and stapled to the underside of the rafters with an industrial nail gun.

Cross-reference between her and Hewall convinced the Arbites that the rug-maker had very probably suffered the removal of his brain stem and heart too. Until that point, they had ascribed the identifiable lack of those soft organs to the almost toxic levels of organic decay in the liquiescent filth of the soil stack.

Graven, actually the first victim found, had been dredged from the waters of the bay by salvage ship. He had been presumed to be a suicide dismembered by the screws of a passing boat until Wrex's careful cross-checking had flagged up too many points of similarity.

Because of the peculiar circumstances of their various post mortem locations, it was pathologically impossible to determine any exact date or time of death. But Wrex could be certain of a window. Graven had been last seen on the nineteenth of Aquiarae, three days before his body had been dredged up. Hewall had delivered a finished rug to a high-rise customer on the twenty-fourth, and had dined that same evening with friends at a charcute in mid-rise. Fasple had failed to report for work on the fifth of Sagittar, although the night before she had seemed happy and looking forward to her next shift, according to friends.

'I thought at first we might have a serial predator loose in mid-rise,' said Wrex. 'But the pattern of mutilation seems to me more extreme than that. This is not feral murder, or even psychopathic, post-slaying depravity. This is specific, purposeful ritual.'

'How do you arrive at that?' asked my colleague, Fischig. Fischig was a senior Arbites from Hubris, with plenty of experience in murder cases. Indeed, it was his fluency with procedure and familiarity with modus operandi that had convinced me to make him a part of my band. That, and his ferocious strength in a fight.

Wrex looked sidelong at him, as if he was questioning her ability.

'Because of the nature of the dismemberment. Because of the way the remains were disposed of.' She looked at me. 'In my experience, inquisitor, a serial killer secretly wants to be found, and certainly wants to be known. It will display its kills with wanton openness, declaring its power over the community. It thrives on the terror and fear it generates. Great efforts were made to hide these bodies. That suggest to me the killer was far more interested in the deaths themselves than in the reaction to the deaths.'

'Well put, captain,' I said. 'That has been my experience too. Cult killings are often hidden so that the cult can continue its work without fear of discovery.'

'Suggesting that there are other victims still to find...' said Bequin casually, a chilling prophecy as it now seems to me.

'Cult killings?' said the minister. 'I brought this to your attention because I feared as much, but do you really think–'

'On Alphex, the warp-cult removed their victims' hands and tongues because they were organs of communication,' Aemos began. 'On Brettaria, the brains were scooped out in order for the cult to ingest the spiritual matter – the anima, as you might say – of their prey. A number of other worlds have suffered cult predations where the eyes have been forfeit... Gulinglas, Pentari, Hesperus, Messina... windows of the soul, you see. The Heretics of Saint Scarif, in fact, severed their ritual victims' hands and then made them write out their last confessions using ink quills rammed into the stumps of–'

'Enough information, Aemos,' I said. The minister was looking pale.

'These are clearly cult killings, sir,' I said. 'There is a noxious cell of Chaos at liberty in your city. And I will find it.'

I went at once to the mid-rise district. Grevan, Hewall and Fasple had all been residents of that part of Urbitane, and Mombril, though a visitor to the metropolis, had been found there too. Aemos went to the Munitorum records spire in high-rise to search the local archives. I was particularly interested in historical cult activity on Sameter, and on date significance. Fischig, Bequin and Wrex accompanied me.

The genius loci of a place can often say much about the crimes committed therein. So far, my stay on Sameter had only introduced me to the cleaner, high-altitude regions of Urbitane's high-rise, up above the smog-cover.

Mid-rise was a dismal, wretched place of neglect and poverty. A tarry resin of pollution coated every surface, and acid rain poured down unremittingly. Raw-engined traffic crawled nose to tail down the poorly lit streets, and the very stone of the buildings seemed to be rotting. The smoggy darkness of mid-rise had a red, firelit quality, the backwash of the flares from giant gas processors. It reminded me of picture-slate engravings of the Inferno.

We stepped from Wrex's armoured speeder at the corner of Shearing Street and Pentecost. The captain pulled on her Arbites helmet and a quilted flak-coat. I began to wish for a hat of my own, or a rebreather mask. The rain stank like urine. Every thirty seconds or so an express flashed past on the elevated trackway, shaking the street.

'In here,' Wrex called, and led us through a shutter off the thoroughfare into the dank hallway of a tenement hab. Everything was stained with centuries of grime. The heating had been set too high, perhaps to combat the murky wetness outside, but the result was simply an overwhelming humidity and a smell like the fur of a mangy canine.

This was Idilane Fasple's last resting place. She'd been found in the roof.

'Where did she live?' asked Fischig.

'Two streets away. She had a parlour on one of the old court-habs.'

'Hewall?'

'His hab about a kilometre west. His remains were found five blocks east.'

I looked at the data-slate. The tannery where Mombril had been found was less than thirty minutes' walk from here, and Graven's home a short tram ride. The only thing that broke the geographical focus of these lives and deaths was the fact that Graven had been dumped in the bay.

'I hasn't escaped my notice that they all inhabited a remarkably specific area,' Wrex smiled.

'I never thought it had. But "remarkably" is the word. It isn't just the same quarter or district. It's a intensely close network of streets, a neighbourhood.'

'Suggesting?' asked Bequin.

'The killer or killers are local too,' said Fischig.

'Or someone from elsewhere has a particular hatred of this neighbourhood and comes into it to do his or her killing,' said Wrex.

'Like a hunting ground?' noted Fischig.

I nodded. Both possibilities had merit.

'Look around,' I told Fischig and Bequin, well aware that Wrex's officers had already been all over the building. But she said nothing. Our expert appraisal might turn up something different.

I found a small office at the end of the entrance hall. It was clearly the cubbyhole of the habitat's superintendent. Sheaves of paper were pinned to the flak-board wall: rental dockets, maintenances rosters, notes of resident complaints. There was a box-tray of lost property, a partially disassembled mini-servitor in a tub of oil, a stale stink of cheap liquor. A faded ribbon and paper rosette from an Imperial shrine was pinned over the door with a regimental rank stud.

'What you doing in here?'

I looked round. The superintendent was a middle-aged man in a dirty overall suit. Details. I always look for details. The gold signet ring with the wheatear symbol. The row of permanent metal sutures closing the scar on his scalp where the hair had never grown back. The prematurely weathered skin. The guarded look in his eyes.

I told him who I was and he didn't seem impressed. Then I asked him who he was and he said 'The super. What you doing in here?'

I use my will sparingly. The psychic gift sometimes closes as many doors as it opens. But there was something about this man. He needed a jolt. 'What is your name?' I asked, modulating my voice to carry the full weight of the psychic probe.

He rocked backwards, and his pupils dilated in surprise.

'Quater Traves,' he mumbled.

'Did you know the midwife Fasple?'

'I sin her around.'

'To speak to?'

He shook his head. His eyes never left mine.

'Did she have friends?'

He shrugged.

'What about strangers? Anyone been hanging around the hab?'

His eyes narrowed. A sullen, mocking look, as if I hadn't seen the streets outside.

'Who has access to the roofspace where her body was found?'

'Ain't nobody bin up there. Not since the place bin built. Then the heating packs in and the contractors has to break through the roof to get up there. They found her.'

'There isn't a hatch?'

'Shutter. Locked, and no one has a key. Easier to go through the plasterboard.'

Outside, we sheltered from the rain under the elevated railway.

'That's what Traves told me too,' Wrex confirmed. 'No one had been into the roof for years until the contractors broke their way in.'

'Someone had. Someone with the keys to the shutter. The killer.'

The soil stack where Hewall had been found was behind a row of commercial properties built into an ancient skin of scaffolding that cased the outside of a toolfitters' workshop like a cobweb. There was what seemed to be a bar two stages up, where a neon signed flicked between an Imperial aquila and a fleur-de-lys. Fischig and Wrex continued up to the next scaffolding level to peer in through the stained windows of the habs there. Bequin and I went into the bar.

The light was grey inside. At a high bar, four or five drinkers sat on ratchet-stools and ignored us. The scent of obscura smoke was in the air.

There was a woman behind the counter who took exception to us from the moment we came in. She was in her forties, with a powerful, almost masculine build. Her vest was cut off at the armpits and her arms were as muscular as Fischig's. There was the small tattoo of a skull and crossbones on her bicep. The skin of her face was weathered and coarse.

'Help you?' she asked, wiping the counter with a glass-cloth. As she did so I saw that her right arm, from the elbow down, was a prosthetic.

'Information,' I said.

She flicked her cloth at the row of bottles on the shelves behind her.

'Not a brand I know.'

'You know a man called Hewall?'

'No.'

'The guy they found in the waste pipes behind here.'

'Oh. Didn't know he had a name.'

Now I was closer I could see the tattoo on her arm wasn't a skull and crossbones. It was a wheatear.

'We all have names. What's yours?'

'Omin Lund.'

'You live around here?'

'Live is too strong a word.' She turned away to serve someone else.

'Scary bitch,' said Bequin as we went outside. 'Everyone acts like they've got something to hide.'

'Everyone does, even if it's simply how much they hate this town.'

The heart had gone out of Urbitane, out of Sameter itself, about seventy years before. The mill-hives of Thracian Primaris eclipsed Sameter's production, and export profits fell away. In an effort to compete, the authorities freed the refineries to escalate production by stripping away the legal restrictions on atmospheric pollution levels. For hundreds of years, Urbitane had had problems controlling its smog and air-pollutants. For the last few decades, it hadn't bothered any more.

My vox-earplug chimed. It was Aemos.

'What have you found?'

'It's most perturbatory. Sameter has been clear of taint for a goodly while. The last Inquisitorial investigation was thirty-one years ago standard, and that wasn't here in Urbitane but in Aquitane, the capital. A rogue psyker. The planet has its fair share of criminal activity, usually narcotics trafficking and the consequential mob-fighting. But nothing really markedly heretical.'

'Nothing with similarities to the ritual methods?'

'No, and I've gone back two centuries.'

'What about the dates?'

'Sagittar thirteenth is just shy of the solstice, but I can't make any meaning out of that. The Purge of the Sarpetal Hives is usually commemorated by upswings of cult activity in the subsector, but that's six weeks away. The only other thing I can find is that this Sagittar fifth was the twenty-first anniversary of the Battle of Klodeshi Heights.'

'I don't know it.'

'The sixth of seven full-scale engagements during the sixteen month Imperial campaign on Surealis Six.'

'Surealis... that's in the next damn subsector! Aemos, every day of the year is the anniversary of an Imperial action somewhere. What connection are you making?'

'The Ninth Sameter Infantry saw service in the war on Surealis.'

Fischig and Wrex had rejoined us from their prowl around the upper stages of the scaffolding. Wrex was talking on her own vox-set.

She signed off and looked at me, rain drizzling off her visor.

'They've found another one, inquisitor,' she said.

It wasn't one. It was three, and their discovery threw the affair wide open. An old warehouse in the mill zone, ten streets away from Fasple's hab, had been damaged by fire two months before, and now the municipal work-crews had moved in to tear it down and reuse the lot as a site for cheap, prefab habitat blocks. They'd found the bodies behind the wall insulation in a mouldering section untouched by the fire. A woman and two men, systematically mutilated in the manner of the other victims.

But these were much older. I could tell that even at a glance.

I crunched across the debris littering the floorspace of the warehouse shell. Rain streamed in through the roof holes, illuminated as a blizzard of white specks by the cold blue beams of the Arbites' floodlights shining into the place.

Arbites officers were all around, but they hadn't touched the discovery itself.

Mummified and shrivelled, these foetally curled, pitiful husks had been in the wall a long time.

'What's that?' I asked.

Fischig leaned forward for a closer look. 'Adhesive tape, wrapped around them to hold them against the partition. Old. The gum's decayed.'

'That pattern on it. The silver flecks.'

'I think it's military issue stuff. Matt-silver coating, you know the sort? The coating's coming off with age.'

'These bodies are different ages,' I said.

'I thought so too,' said Fischig.

We had to wait six hours for a preliminary report from the district Examiner Medicae, but it confirmed our guess. All three bodies had been in the wall for at least eight years, and then for different lengths of time. Decompositional anomalies showed that one of the males had been in position for as much as twelve years, the other two added subsequently, at different occasions. No identifications had yet been made.

'The warehouse was last used six years ago,' Wrex told me.

'I want a roster of workers employed there before it went out of business.'

Someone using the same m.o. and the same spools of adhesive tape had hidden bodies there over a period of years.

* * *

The disused tannery where poor Mombril had been found stood at the junction between Xerxes Street and a row of slum tenements known as the Pilings. It was a fetid place, with the stink of the lye and coroscutum used in the tanning process still pungent in the air. No amount of acid rain could wash that smell out.

There were no stairs. Fischig, Bequin and I climbed up to the roof via a metal fire-ladder.

'How long does a man survive mutilated like that?'

'From the severed wrists alone, he'd bleed out in twenty minutes, perhaps,' Fischig estimated. 'Clearly, if he had made an escape, he'd have the adrenalin of terror sustaining him a little.'

'So when he was found up here, he can have been no more than twenty minutes from the scene of his brutalisation.'

We looked around. The wretched city looked back at us, close packed and dense. There were hundreds of possibilities. It might take days to search them all.

But we could narrow it down. 'How did he get on the roof?' I asked.

'I was wondering that,' said Fischig.

'The ladder we came up by...' Bequin trailed off as she realised her gaffe.

'Without hands?' Fischig smirked.

'Or sight,' I finished. 'Perhaps he didn't escape. Perhaps his abusers put him here.'

'Or perhaps he fell,' Bequin said, pointing.

The back of a tall warehouse over-shadowed the tannery to the east. Ten metres up there were shattered windows.

'If he was in there somewhere, fled blindly, and fell through onto this roof...'

'Well reasoned, Alizebeth,' I said.

The Arbites had done decent work, but not even Wrex had thought to consider this inconsistency.

We went round to the side entrance of the warehouse. The battered metal shutters were locked. A notice pasted to the wall told would-be intruders to stay out of the property of Hundlemas Agricultural Stowage.

I took out my multi-key and disengaged the padlock. I saw Fischig had drawn his sidearm.

'What's the matter?'

'I had a feeling just then... like we were being watched.'

We went inside. The air was cold and still and smelled of chemicals. Rows of storage vats filled with chemical fertilisers lined the echoing warehall.

The second floor was bare-boarded and hadn't been used in years. Wiremesh had been stapled over a doorway to the next floor, and rainwater dripped down. Fischig pulled at the mesh. It was cosmetic only, and folded aside neatly.

Now I drew my autopistol too.

On the street side of the third floor, which was divided into smaller rooms, we found a chamber ten metres by ten, on the floor of which was spread a sheet of plastic smeared with old blood and other organic deposits. There was a stink of fear.

'This is where they did him,' Fischig said with certainty.

'No sign of cult markings or Chaos symbology,' I mused.

'Maybe not,' said Bequin, crossing the room, being careful not to step on the smeared plastic sheet. For the sake of her shoes, not the crime scene, I was sure. 'What's this? Something was hung here.'

Two rusty hooks in the wall, scraped enough to show something had been hanging there recently. On the floor below was a curious cross drawn in yellow chalk.

'I've seen that before somewhere,' I said. My vox bleeped. It was Wrex.

'I've got that worker roster you asked for.'

'Good. Where are you?'

'Coming to find you at the tannery, if you're still there.'

'We'll meet you on the corner of Xerxes Street. Tell your staff we have a crime scene here in the agricultural warehouse.'

We walked out of the killing room towards the stairwell.

Fischig froze, and brought up his gun.

'Again?' I whispered.

He nodded, and pushed Bequin into the cover of a door jamb.

Silence, apart from the rain and the scurry of vermin. Gun braced, Fischig looked up at the derelict roof. It may have been my imagination, but it seemed as if a shadow had moved across the bare rafters.

I moved forward, scanning the shadows with my pistol.

Something creaked. A floorboard.

Fischig pointed to the stairs. I nodded I understood, but the last thing I wanted was a mistaken shooting. I carefully keyed my vox and whispered, 'Wrex. You're not coming into the warehouse to find us, are you?'

'Negative, inquisitor.'

'Standby.'

Fischig had reached the top of the staircase. He peered down, aiming his weapon.

Las fire erupted through the floorboards next to him and he threw himself flat.

I put a trio of shots into the mouth of the staircase, but my angle was bad.

Two hard round shots spat back up the stairs and then the roar and flash of the las came again, raking the floor.

From above, I realised belatedly. Whoever was on the stairs had a hard-slug side arm, but the las fire was coming down from the roof.

I heard steps running on the floor below. Fischig scrambled up to give chase but another salvo of las fire sent him ducking again.

I raised my aim and fired up into the roof tiles, blowing out holes through which the pale light poked.

Something slithered and scrambled on the roof.

Fischig was on the stairs now, running after the second assailant.

I hurried across the third floor, following the sounds of the man on the roof.

I saw a silhouette against the sky through a hole in the tiles and fired again. Las-fire replied in a bright burst, but then there was a thump and further slithering.

'Cease fire! Give yourself up! Inquisition!' I bellowed, using the will.

There came a much more substantial crash sounding like a whole portion of the roof had come down. Tiles avalanched down and smashed in a room nearby.

I slammed into the doorway, gun aimed, about to yell out a further will command. But there was no one in the room. Piles of shattered roofslates and bricks covered the floor beneath a gaping hole in the roof itself, and a battered lasrifle lay amongst the debris. On the far side of the room were some of the broken windows that Bequin had pointed out as overlooking the tannery roof.

I ran to one. Down below, a powerful figure in dark overalls was running for cover. The killer, escaping from me in just the same way his last victim had escaped him – through the windows onto the tannery roof.

The distance was too far to use the will again with any effect, but my aim and angle were good. I lined up on the back of the head a second before it disappeared, began to apply pressure – and the world exploded behind me.

I came round cradled in Bequin's arms. 'Don't move, Eisenhorn. The medics are coming.'

'What happened?' I asked.

'Booby trap. The gun that guy left behind? It exploded behind you. Powercell overload.'

'Did Fischig get his man?'

'Of course he did.'

He hadn't, in fact. He'd chased the man hard down two flights of stairs and through the main floor of the warehall. At the outer door onto the street, the man had wheeled around and emptied his autopistol's clip at the chastener, forcing him into cover.

Then Captain Wrex, approaching from outside, had gunned the man down in the doorway.

We assembled in Wrex's crowded office in the busy Arbites Mid-Rise Sectorhouse. Aemos joined us, laden down with papers and data-slates, and brought Midas Betancore with him.

'You all right?' Midas asked me. In his jacket of embroidered cerise silk, he was a vivid splash of colour in the muted gloom of mid-rise.

'Minor abrasions. I'm fine.'

'I thought we were leaving, and here you are having all the fun without me.'

'I thought we were leaving too until I saw this case. Review Bequin's notes. I need you up to speed.'

Aemos shuffled his ancient, augmetically assisted bulk over to Wrex's desk and dropped his books and papers in an unceremonious pile.

'I've been busy,' he said.

'Busy with results?' Bequin asked.

He looked at her sourly. 'No, actually. But I have gathered a commendable resource of information. As the discussion advances, I may be able to fill in blanks.'

'No results, Aemos? Most perturbatory,' grinned Midas, his white teeth gleaming against his dark skin. He was mocking the old savant by using Aemos's favourite phrase.

I had before me the work roster of the warehouse where the three bodies had been found, and another for the agricultural store where our fight had occurred. Quick comparison brought up two coincident names.

'Brell Sodakis. Vim Venik. Both worked as warehousemen before the place closed down. Now they're employed by Hundlemas Agricultural Stowage.'

'Backgrounds? Addresses?' I asked Wrex.

'I'll run checks,' she said.

'So... we have a cult here, eh?' Midas asked. 'You've got a series of ritual killings, at least one murder site, and now the names of two possible cultists.'

'Perhaps.' I wasn't convinced. There seemed both more and less to this than had first appeared. Inquisitorial hunch.

The remains of the lasrifle discarded by my assailant lay on an evidence tray. Even with the damage done by the overloading powercell, it was apparent that this was an old model.

'Did the powercell overload because it was dropped? It fell through the roof, didn't it?' Bequin asked.

'They're pretty solid,' Fischig answered.

'Forced overload,' I said. 'An old Imperial Guard trick. I've heard they learn how to set one off. As a last ditch in tight spots. Cornered. About to die anyway.'

'That's not standard,' said Fischig, poking at the trigger guard of the twisted weapon. His knowledge of guns was sometimes unseemly. 'See this modification? It's been machine-tooled to widen the guard around the trigger.'

'Why?' I asked.

Fischig shrugged. 'Access? For an augmetic hand with rudimentary digits?'

We went through to a morgue room down the hall where the man Wrex had gunned down was lying on a slab. He was middle-aged, with a powerful frame going to seed. His skin was weatherbeaten and lined.

'Identity?'

'We're working on it.'

The body had been stripped by the morgue attendants. Fischig scrutinised it, rolling it with Wrex's help to study the back. The man's clothes and effects were in plasteen bags in a tray at his feet. I lifted the bag of effects and held it up to the light.

'Tattoo,' reported Fischig. 'Imperial eagle, left shoulder. Crude, old. Letters underneath it... capital S period, capital I period, capital I, capital X.'

I'd just found the signet ring in the bag. Gold, with a wheatear motif.

'S.I. IX,' said Aemos. 'Sameter Infantry Nine.'

The Ninth Sameter Infantry had been founded in Urbitane twenty-three years before, and had served, as Aemos had already told me, in the brutal liberation war on Surealis Six. According to city records, five hundred and nineteen veterans of that war and that regiment had been repatriated to Sameter after mustering out thirteen years ago, coming back from the horrors of war to an increasingly depressed world beset by the blight of poverty and urban collapse. Their regimental emblem, as befitted a world once dominated by agriculture, was the wheatear.

'They came back thirteen years ago. The oldest victim we have dates from that time,' said Fischig.

'Surealis Six was a hard campaign, wasn't it?' I asked.

Aemos nodded. 'The enemy was dug in. It was ferocious, brutal. Brutalising. And the climate. Two white dwarf suns, no cloud cover. The most punishing heat and light, not to mention ultraviolet burning.'

'Ruins the skin,' I murmured. 'Makes it weatherbeaten and prematurely aged.'

Everyone looked at the taut, lined face of the body on the slab.

'I'll get a list of the veterans,' volunteered Wrex.

'I already have one,' said Aemos.

'I'm betting you find the names Brell Sodakis and Vim Venik on it,' I said.

Aemos paused as he scanned. 'I do,' he agreed.

'What about Quater Traves?'

'Yes, he's here. Master Gunnery Sergeant Quater Traves.'

'What about Omin Lund?'

'Ummm... yes. Sniper first class. Invalided out of service.'

'The Sameter Ninth were a mixed unit, then?' asked Bequin.

'All our Guard foundings are,' Wrex said proudly.

'So, these men... and women...' Midas mused. 'Soldiers, been through hell. Fighting the corruption... your idea is they brought it back here with them? Some taint? You think they were infected by the touch of the warp on Surealis and have been ritually killing as a way of worship back here ever since?'

'No,' I said. 'I think they're still fighting the war.'

It remains a sad truth of the Imperium that no virtually no veteran ever comes back from fighting its wars intact. Combat alone shreds nerves and shatters bodies. But the horrors of the warp, and of foul xenos forms like the tyranid, steal sanity forever, and leave veterans fearing the shadows, and the night and, sometimes, the nature of their friends and neighbours, for the rest of their lives.

The guards of the Ninth Sameter Infantry had come home thirteen years before, broke by a savage war against mankind's arch-enemy and, through their scars and their fear, brought their war back with them.

The Arbites mounted raids at once on the addresses of all the veterans on the list, those that could be traced, those that were still alive. It appeared that skin cancer had taken over two hundred of them in the years since their repatriation. Surealis had claimed them as surely as if they had fallen there in combat.

A number were rounded up. Bewildered drunks, cripples, addicts, a few honest men and women trying diligently to carry on with their lives. For those latter I felt especially sorry.

But about seventy could not be traced. Many may well have disappeared, moved on, or died without it coming to the attention of the authorities.

But some had clearly fled. Lund, Traves, Sodakis, Venik for starters. Their habs were found abandoned, strewn with possessions as if the occupant had left in a hurry. So were the habs of twenty more belonging to names on the list.

The Arbites arrived at the hab of one, ex-corporal Geffin Sancto, in time to catch him in the act of flight. Sancto had been a flamer operator in the guard, and like so many of his kind, had managed to keep his weapon as a memento. Screaming the battlecry of the Sameter Ninth, he torched four Arbites in the stairwell of his building before the tactical squads of the judiciary vaporised him in a hail of gunshots.

'Why are they killing?' Bequin asked me. 'All these years, in secret ritual?'

'I don't know.'

'You do, Eisenhorn. You so do!'

'Very well. I can guess. The fellow worker who jokes at the Emperor's expense and makes your fragile sanity imagine he is tainted with the warp. The rug-maker whose patterns suggest to you the secret encoding of Chaos symbols. The midwife you decide is spawning the offspring of the arch-enemy in the mid-rise maternity hall. The travelling evangelist who seems just too damn fired up to be safe.'

She looked down at the floor of the land speeder. 'They see daemons everywhere.'

'In everything. In every one. And, so help them, they believe they are doing the Emperor's work by killing. They trust no one, so they daren't alert the authorities. They take the eyes, the hands and the tongue... all the organs of communication, any way the arch-enemy might transmit his foul lies. And then they destroy the brain and heart, the organs which common soldier myth declares must harbour daemons.'

'So where are we going now?' she asked.

'Another hunch.'

The Guildhall of the Sameter Agricultural Fraternity was a massive ragstone building on Furnace Street, its facade decaying from the ministrations of smog and acid rain. It had been disused for over two decades.

Its last duty had been to serve as a recruitment post of the Sameter Ninth during the founding. In its long hallways, the men and women of the Ninth had signed their names, collected their starchy new fatigues, and pledged their battle oath to the God-Emperor of mankind.

At certain times, under certain circumstances, when a proper altar to the Emperor is not available, guard officers improvise in order to conduct their ceremonies. An Imperial eagle, an aquila standard, is suspended from a wall, and a sacred spot is marked on the floor beneath in yellow chalk.

The guildhall was not a consecrated building. The founding must have been the first time the young volunteers of Urbitane had seen that done. They'd made their vows to a yellow chalk cross and a dangling aquila.

Wrex was leading three fireteams of armed Arbites, but I went in with Midas and Fischig first, quietly. Bequin and Aemos stayed by our vehicle.

Midas was carrying his matched needle pistols, and Fischig an auto shotgun. I clipped a slab-pattern magazine full of fresh rounds into the precious bolt pistol given to me by Librarian Brytnoth of the Adeptus Astartes Deathwatch chapter.

We pushed open the boarded doors of the decaying structure and edged down the dank corridors. Rainwater pattered from the roof and the marble floor was spotted and eaten by collected acid.

We could hear the singing. A couple of dozen voices voicing up the Battle Hymn of the Golden Throne.

I led my companions forward, hunched low. Through the crazed windows of an inner door we looked through into the main hall. Twenty-three dishevelled veterans in ragged clothes were knelt down in ranks on the filthy floor, their heads bowed to the rusty Imperial eagle hanging on the wall as they sang. There was a yellow chalk cross on the floor under the aquila. Each veteran had a backpack or rucksack and a weapon by their feet.

My heart ached. This was how it had gone over two decades before, when they came to the service, young and fresh and eager. Before the war. Before the horror.

'Let me try... try to give them a chance,' I said.

'Gregor!' Midas hissed.

'Let me try, for their sake. Cover me.'

I slipped into the back of the hall, my gun lowered at my side, and joined in the verse.

One by one, the voices died away and bowed heads turned sideways to look at me. Down the aisle, at the chalk cross of the altar, Lund, Traves and a bearded man I didn't know stood gazing at me.

In the absence of other voices, I finished the hymn.

'It's over,' I said. 'The war is over and you have all done your duty. Above and beyond the call.'

Silence.

'I am Inquisitor Eisenhorn. I'm here to relieve you. The careful war against the blight of Chaos that you have waged through Urbitane in secret is now over. The Inquisition is here to take over. You can stand down.'

Two or three of the hunched veterans began to weep.

'You lie,' said Lund, stepping forward.

'I do not. Surrender your weapons and I promise you will be treated fairly and with respect.'

'Will... will we get medals?' the bearded man asked, in a quavering voice.

'The gratitude of the God-Emperor will be with you always.'

More were weeping now. Out of fear, anxiety or plain relief.

'Don't trust him!' said Traves. 'It's another trick!'

'I saw you in my bar,' said Lund, stepping forward. 'You came in looking.' Her voice was empty, distant.

'I saw you on the tannery roof, Omin Lund. You're still a fine shot, despite the hand.'

She looked down at her prosthetic with a wince of shame.

'Will we get medals?' the bearded man repeated, eagerly.

Traves turned on him. 'Of course we won't, Spake, you cretin! He's here to kill us!'

'I'm not–' I began.

'I want medals!' the bearded man, Spake, screamed suddenly, sliding his laspistol up from his belt with the fluid speed only a trained soldier can manage.

I had no choice.

His shot tore through the shoulder padding of my storm coat. My bolt exploded his head, spraying blood across the rusty metal eagle on the wall.

Pandemonium.

The veterans leapt to their feet firing wildly, scattering, running.

I threw myself flat as shots tore out the wall plaster behind me. At some point Fischig and Midas burst in, weapons blazing. I saw three or four veterans drop, sliced through by silent needles and another six tumble as shotgun rounds blew them apart.

Traves came down the aisle, blasting his old service-issue lasrifle at me. I rolled and fired, but my shot went wide. His face distorted as a needle round punched through it and he fell in a crumpled heap.

Wrex and her fireteams exploded in. Flames from some spilled accelerants billowed up the wall.

I got up, and then was throw back by a las shot that blew off my left hand.

Spinning, falling, I saw Lund, struggling to make her prosthetic fingers work the unmodified trigger of Traves's lasgun.

My bolt round hit her with such force she flew back down the aisle, hit the wall, and tore the Imperial aquila down.

Not a single veteran escaped the Guildhall alive. The firefight raged for two hours. Wrex lost five men to the experienced guns of the Sameter Ninth veterans. They stood to the last. No more can be said of any Imperial Guard unit.

The whole affair left me sour and troubled. I have devoted my life to the service of the Imperium, to protect it against its manifold foes, inside and out.

But not against its servants. However misguided, they were loyal and true. However wrong, they were shaped that way by the service they had endured in the Emperor's name.

Lund cost me my hand. A hand for a hand. They gave me a prosthetic on Sameter. I never used it. For two years, I made do with a fused stump. Surgeons on Messina finally gave me a fully functional graft.

I consider it still a small price to pay for them.

I have never been back to Sameter. Even today, they are still finding the secreted, hidden bodies. So very many, dead in the Emperor's name.

MALLEUS

BY ORDER OF HIS MOST HOLY MAJESTY
THE GOD-EMPEROR OF TERRA

SEQUESTERED INQUISITORIAL DOSSIERS
AUTHORISED PERSONS ONLY

CASE FILE 442:41F:JL3:Kbu

Please enter your authority code > ●●●●●●●●●●●●●●●

Validating…

Thank you, Inquisitor.

You may proceed.

CLASSIFICATION: ***Primary Level Intelligence***
CLEARANCE: ***Obsidian***
ENCRYPTION: ***Cryptox v 2.6***
DATE: ***337.M41***
AUTHOR: ***Inquisitor Javes Thysser, Ordo Xenos***
SUBJECT: ***A matter for your urgent consideration***
RECIPIENT: ***Lord Inquisitor Phlebas Alessandro Rorken, Inquisition High Council Officio, Scarus Sector, Scarus Major***

Salutations, lord!

In the name of the God-Emperor, hallowed be his eternal vigil, and by the High Lords of Terra, I commend myself, your Highness, and hope I may speak plainly, in confidence, of a delicate matter.

To begin generally, my work on Vogel Passionata is now complete and my noble duty to the Great Inquisition of Mankind discharged successfully. My full, documented report will follow in a few days, once my savants have finished compiling it, and I trust that your Highness will find it satisfactory reading. To summarise, for the purpose of this brief missive, I am proud to declare that the malign influence of the so-called wyrd-kin has been expunged from the hive cities of Vogel Passionata, and the inner circle of that obscene xenophile order broken forever and put to cleansing flame. Their self-proclaimed messiah, Gaethon Richter, is himself dead by my hand.

A matter, however, has arisen from this. I am troubled by it, and unsure as to the best course of action. For this reason I am writing to you, Highness, in the hope of receiving guidance.

Richter did not go without a fight, as you might expect. In the final, bloody throes of the battle, as my combined forces stormed his fastness beneath the main hive, he called forth to oppose us a being of dreadful power. It slaughtered nineteen of the Imperial Guardsmen assigned to my purge-team, as well as Inquisitor Bluchas, Interrogators Faruline and Seetmol, and Captain Ellen Ossel, my pilot. It would have slain me too, but for the strangest mischance.

The being was an unholy thing, made like a man, but gleaming with an inner light. Its voice was soft, its touch was fire. I believe it was a daemonhost of unfathomable power, with the most vile propensity for spite and cruelty. My report will recount in detail the particular abominations this being subjected Seetmol and Ossel to before it destroyed them. I will spare you those dreadful facts here.

Having disposed of Bluchas, it cornered me on an upper landing in the fastness as I was penetrating the inner sanctum of the wyrd-kin 'messiah.' My weapons did no harm to it, and it laughed gleefully as it threw me backwards down the length of the staircase with a casual flick of its wrist.

Dazed, I looked up as it descended towards me, unable to conceive of a defence against it. I believe I may have clawed around to find my fallen weapon.

That gesture caused it to speak. I report the words exactly. It said, 'Don't worry now, Gregor. You are far too valuable to waste. Indulge me, just a little scar to make it look authentic.'

Its talons tore across my chest and throat, and ripped away my rebreather mask. The wounds will heal, they tell me, but they were deep and excruciating. The being then paused, as it saw my face properly for the first time, free from the mask set. Dreadful dark anger flared in its eyes. It said – forgive me, Highness, but this is the fact of it – it said, 'You are not Eisenhorn! I have been tricked!'

I believe that it would have killed me there and then, but for the frontal assault of the Adeptes Astartes Aurora Chapter, which tore into the hall at that precise moment. In the mayhem, the being fled, though I cannot even now say how. Whatever the terrifying strength of the Adeptus Astartes, this thing was a hundredfold more powerful.

Later, on his knees, with my weapon to his head, seconds before his execution, Gaethon Richter begged for 'Cherubael' to return. He wailed he could not understand why 'Cherubael' had abandoned him. I believe he was speaking of the daemonhost.

I trust your Highness can see my trouble. Mistaking me for another of our kind – and an unimpeachably worthy example, I might add – this thing spared my life. It seemed to me, indeed, that it did so with pre-arranged connivance.

Inquisitor Gregor Eisenhorn is highly regarded, numerously honoured and justly praised as an example of all that is good, strong and dogmatic about our brotherhood. However, since this circumstance, I have begun to wonder, to fear that–

I feel I cannot say what I wonder or fear. But I thought you should know of this, and know it soon. It is my belief that the Ordo Malleus should be informed, if only as a precaution.

I hope and pray this matter will be found empty of truth and consequence. But, as you taught me, sir, it is always better to be sure.

Sealed as my true word by this, my hand, this 276th day of the year 337.M41.

The Emperor Protects!

Your servant,

Thysser

[Message ends.]

ONE

I DISCOVER I AM DEAD
UNDER DARK FIRE, THE LAIR OF SADIA
TANTALID, UNWELCOME

As I grow older, may the Emperor protect me, I find I measure my history in terms of milestones, those occurrences of such intense moment they will never pass from one's memory: my induction into the blessed Ordos of the Inquisition; my first day as a neophyte assigned to the great Hapshant; my first successful prosecution; the heretic Lemete Syre; my elevation to full Inquisitorial rank at the age of twenty-four standard years; the long-drawn out Nassar case; the affair of the Necroteuch; the P'glao Conspiracy.

Milestones, all of them. Marked indelibly onto the engrams of my memory. And, alongside them, I remember the Darknight that came at the end of the month of Umbris, Imperial year 338.M41, with particular clarity. For that bloody end was the start of it. The great milestone of my life.

I was on Lethe Eleven under instruction from the Ordo Xenos, deep in work, with the accursed xenophile Beldame Sadia almost in my grasp. Ten weeks to find her, ten hours to close the trap. I had been without sleep for three days; without food and water for two. Psychic phantoms triggered by the Darknight eclipse were roiling my mind. I was dying of binary poison. Then Tantalid turned up.

To appraise you, Lethe Eleven is a densely populated world at the leading edge of the Helican sub-sector, its chief industries being metalwork and shield technologies. At the end of every Umbris, Lethe's largest moon matches, by some cosmological coincidence, the path, orbit and comparative size of the local star, and the world is plunged into eclipse for a two week period known as the Darknight.

The effect is quite striking. For the space of fourteen days, the sky goes a cold, dark red, the hue of dried blood, and the moon, Kux, dominates the heavens, a peerlessly black orb surrounded by a crackling corona of writhing amber flame. This event has become – students of Imperial ritual will be unsurprised to learn – the key seasonal holiday for all Letheans. Fires of all shape, size and manner are lit as Darknight begins, and the population stands vigil to ensure that none go out until the eclipse ends. Industry is suspended. Leave is granted. Riotous carnivals and firelit parades spill through the cities. Licentiousness and law-breaking are rife.

Above it all, the dark fire of the eclipsed sun haloes the black moon. There is even a tradition of fortune-casting grown up around the interpretation of the corona's form.

I had hoped to catch the Beldame before Darknight began, but she was one step ahead of me. Her chief poisoner, Pye, who had learned his skills in early life as a prisoner of the renegade dark eldar, so the story went, managed to plant a toxin in my drinking water that would remain inert until I ingested the second component of its binary action.

I was a dead man. The Beldame had killed me.

My savant, Aemos, accidentally discovered the toxin in my body, and was able to prevent me from eating or drinking anything further. But graceless death beckoned me inexorably. My only chance of survival was to capture the Beldame and her vassal Pye and extract the solution to my doom from them.

Out in the dark streets of the city, my followers did their work. I had eighty loyal servants scouring the streets. In my rooms at the Hippodrome, I waited, parched, unsteady, distant.

Ravenor came up trumps. Ravenor, of course. With his promise, it wouldn't be long before he left the rank of interrogator behind and became a full inquisitor in his own right.

He found Beldame Sadia's lair in the catacombs beneath the derelict church of Saint Kiodrus. I hurried to respond to his call.

'You should stay here,' Bequin told me, but I shook her off.

'I have to do this, Alizebeth.'

Alizebeth Bequin was by that time one hundred and twenty-five years old. She was still as beautiful and as active as she had been in her thirties, thanks to discreet augmetic surgery and a regime of juvenat-drugs. Framed by the veil of her starch-silk dress, her handsome face and dark eyes glared at me.

'It will kill you, Gregor,' she said.

'If it does, then it is time for Gregor Eisenhorn to die.'

Bequin looked across the gloomy, candlelit room at Aemos, but he simply shook his ancient, augmented skull sadly. There were times, he knew, when there was simply no reasoning with me.

I went down into the street, where canister fires blazed and masked revellers capered and caroused. I was dressed all in black, with a floor length coat of heavy black leather.

Despite that, despite the flames around me, I was cold. Fatigue, and the lack of nourishment, were eating into my bones.

I looked at the moon. Threads of heat around a cold, black heart. Like me, I thought, like me.

A carriage had been called for. Six painted hippines, snorting and bridled, teamed to a stately landau. Several members of my staff waited nearby, and hurried forward when they saw me emerge onto the street.

I assessed them quickly. Good people all, or they wouldn't have made the cut to be here. With a few wordless gestures I pulled out four to accompany me and then sent the rest back to other duties.

The four chosen mounted the carriage with me. Mescher Qus, an ex-Imperial Guardsman from Vladislav; Arianrhod Esw Sweydyr, the swordswoman from Carthae; and Beronice and Zu Zeng, two females from Bequin's Distaff.

At the last moment, Beronice was ordered out of the carriage and Alizebeth Bequin took her place. Bequin had quit active service with me sixty-eight standard years before in order to develop and run her Distaff, but there were still times she didn't trust her people and insisted on accompanying me herself.

I realised this was just such a time because Bequin didn't expect me to survive and wanted to be with me to the end. In truth, I didn't expect to survive either.

The carriage started off with a whipcrack, and we rumbled through the streets, skirting around ceremonial fires and torchlit processions.

None of us spoke. Qus checked and loaded his autocannon and adjusted his body armour. Arianrhod drew her sabre and tested the cutting edge with one of her own head hairs. Zu Zeng, a native of Vitria, sat with her head down, her long glass robes clinking with the carriage's motion.

Bequin stared at me.

'What?' I asked eventually.

She shook her head and looked away.

The church of Saint Kiodrus lay in the waterfowlers' district, close to the edge of the city and the vast, lizard-haunted salt-licks. The darkness throbbed with insect rhythms.

The carriage stopped in a street of blackly rotting stone pilings, two hundred metres short of the church's wrecked silhouette. The sky was amber darkness. Behind us, the city was alive with bright points of fire. The neighbourhood around us was a dead ruin, slowly submitting to the salty hunger of the marshes.

'Talon wishes Thorn, rapturous beasts within,' Ravenor said over the vox-link.

'Thorn impinging multifarious, the blades of disguise,' I responded. My throat was dry and hoarse.

'Talon observes moment. Torus pathway requested, pattern ebony.'

'Pattern denied. Pattern crucible. Rose thorn wishes hiatus.'

'Confirm.'

We spoke using Glossia, an informal verbal code known only to my staff. Even on an open vox-channel, our communications would be impenetrable to the foe.

I adjusted my vox-unit's channel.

'Thorn wishes aegis, to me, pattern crucible.'

'Aegis arising,' Betancore, my pilot, responded from far away. 'Pattern confirmed.'

My gun-cutter, with its fabulous firepower, was now inbound. I looked to the others in the shadows as I drew my weapon.

'Now is the time,' I told them.

We edged into the gloomy, slime-swathed ruins of the church. There was a heady stink of wet corruption in the air and sheens of salt clung to every surface. Clusters of maggot-like worms ate into the stones, and flinched back as the fierce beams of our flashlights found them.

Qus ran point, his autocannon swinging from side to side, hunting targets with the red laser rangefinder that projected from the corner of his bionically enhanced left eye. He was a stocky man, rippling with muscle under his harness of ceramite armour. He had painted his blunt face in the colours of his old regiment, the 90th Vladislavan.

Arianrhod and I tailed him. She'd dulled her sabre's blade with brick dust but still it hooked the light as she turned it in her hands. Arianrhod Esw Sweydyr was well over two metres tall, quite the tallest human woman I have ever met, though such stature is common amongst the people of far away Carthae. Her long-boned frame was clad in a leather bodysuit embossed with bronze studs, over which she wore a long, tasselled cloak of patchwork hide. Her silver hair was plaited with beads. The sabre was called Barbarisater and had been carried by women of the Esw Sweydyr tribe for nineteen generations. From the braided grip to the tip of the curved, engraved blade, it measured almost a metre and a half. Long, lean, slender, like the woman who wielded it. Already I could sense the vibration of the psychic energies she was feeding into it. Woman and blade had become one living thing.

Arianrhod had served with my staff for five years, and I was still learning the intricacies of her martial prowess. Ordinarily I'd be noting every detail of her combat trance methods, but I was too fatigued, too drawn out with hunger and thirst.

Bequin and Zu Zeng brought up the rear, side by side, Bequin in a long black gown with a ruff of black feathers around the shoulders, and Zu Zeng in her unreflective robes of Vitrian glass. They stayed back far enough so the aura of their psychic blankness would not conflict with the abilities of Arianrhod or myself, yet close enough to move forward in defence if the time came.

The Inquisition – and many other institutions, august or otherwise – has long been aware of the usefulness of untouchables, those rare human souls who simply have no psionic signature whatsoever and thus disrupt or negate even the most strenuous psychic attack. When I met her on Hubris, a century before, Alizebeth Bequin had been the first untouchable I had ever encountered. Despite her unnerving presence – even non-psykers find untouchables difficult to be around – I had added her to my staff and she had proved to be invaluable. After many years of service, she had retired to form the Distaff, a cadre of untouchables recruited from all across the Imperium. The Distaff was my own private resource, although I often loaned their services to others of my order. They numbered around forty members now, trained and managed by Bequin. It is my belief that the Distaff was collectively one of the most potent anti-psyker weapons in the Emperor's domain.

The ruins were festering with shadows and dank salt. Rot-beetles scurried over the flaking mosaic portraits of long-dead worthies that stared out of alcoves. Worms crawled everywhere. The steady chirrup of insects from the salt-licks was like someone shaking a rattle. As we probed deeper, we came upon inner yards and grave-squares where neglect had shaken free placestones and revealed the smeared bones of the long interred in the loamy earth below. In places, rot-browned skulls had been dug out and piled in loose pyramids.

It saddened me to see this holy place so befouled and dreary. Kiodrus had been a great man, had stood and fought at the right hand of the sacred Beati Sabbat during her mighty crusade. But that had been a long time ago and far away, and his cult of worship had faded. It would take another crusade into the distant Sabbat Worlds to rekindle interest in him and his forgotten deeds.

Qus called a halt and pointed towards the steps of an undercroft that led away below ground. I waved him back, indicating the tiny strip of red ribbon placed under a stone on the top step. A marker, left by Ravenor, indicating this was not a suitable entry point. Peering into the staircase gloom, I saw what he had seen: the half buried cables of a tremor-detector and what looked like bundles of tube charges.

We found three more entrances like it, all marked by Ravenor. The Beldame had secured her fastness well.

'Through there, do you think, sir?' Qus whispered, pointing towards the columns of a roofless cloister.

I was about to agree when Arianrhod hissed 'Barbarisater thirsts...'

I looked at her. She was prowling to the left, towards an archway in the base of the main bell-tower. She moved silently, the sabre held upright in a two-handed grip, her tasselled cloak floating out behind her like angelic wings.

I gestured to Qus and the women and we formed in behind her. I drew my prized boltpistol, given to me by Librarian Brytnoth of the Adeptus Astartes Deathwatch Chapter on the eve of the Purge of Izar, almost a century before. It had never failed me.

The Beldame's minions came out of the night. Eight of them, just shadows that disengaged themselves from the surrounding darkness. Qus began to fire, blasting back a shadow that pounced at him. I fired too, raking bolt rounds into the ghostly opposition.

As befitted such a loyalty, she recruited only convicted murderers for her minions. The men who attacked us in that blighted yard were base killers, shrouded in shadow fields she had bought, borrowed or stolen from her inhuman allies.

One swung at me with a long-bladed halberd and I blew off his head. Just. My body was tired and my reactions were damnably slow.

I saw Arianrhod. She was a balletic blur, her beaded hair streaming out above her flying cloak. Barbarisater purred in her hands.

She severed the neck of one shadow with a backward slash, then pirouetted around and chopped another in two from neck to pelvis. The sabre was moving so fast I could barely see it. She stamped hard and reversed her direction of movement, causing a third shadow to sprawl as he overshot her. His head flew off, and the sabre swept on to impale a fourth without breaking its fluid motion. Then Arianrhod swept around, the sword held horizontally over her right shoulder. The steel haft of the fifth shadow's polearm was cut in two and he staggered back. Barbarisater described a figure of eight in the air and another shadow fell, cut into several sections.

The last minion turned and fled. A shot from Bequin's laspistol brought him down.

A pulse was pounding in my temple and I realised I had to sit down before I passed out. Qus grabbed me by the arm and helped me down onto a block of fallen wall stone.

'Gregor?'

'I'm all right, Alizebeth... give me a moment...'

'You shouldn't have come, you old fool! You should have left this to your disciples!'

'Shut up, Alizebeth.'

'I will not, Gregor. It's high time you understood your own limits.'

I looked up at her. 'I have no limits,' I said.

Qus laughed involuntarily.

'I believe him, Mistress Bequin,' said Ravenor, stepping from the shadows. Emperor damn his stealth, even Arianrhod had not seen him coming. She had to force her sabre down to stop it slicing at him.

Gideon Ravenor was a shade shorter than me, but strong and well-made. He was only thirty-four years old. His long black hair was tied back from his sculpted, high cheek-boned face. He wore a grey bodyglove and a long leather storm coat. The psycannon mounted on his left shoulder whirred and clicked around to aim at Arianrhod.

'Careful, swordswoman,' he said. 'My weapon has you squarely.'

'And it will still have me squarely when your head is lying in the dust,' she replied.

They both laughed. I knew they had been lovers for over a year, but still in public they sparred and sported with each other.

Ravenor snapped his fingers and his companion, the festering mutant Gonvax, shambled out of hiding, drool stringing from his thick, malformed lips. He carried a flamer, the fuel-tanks strapped to the hump of his twisted back.

I rose. 'What have you found?' I asked Ravenor.

'The Beldame – and a way in,' he said.

Beldame Sadia's lair was in the sacrarium beneath the main chapel of the ruin. Ravenor had scouted it carefully, and found an entry point in one of the ruptured crypts that perhaps even she didn't know about.

My respect for Ravenor was growing daily. I had never had a disciple like him. He excelled at almost every skill an inquisitor is meant to have. I looked forward to the day when I supported his petition to Inquisitorial status. He deserved it. The Inquisition needed men like him.

Single-file, we entered the crypt behind Ravenor. He drew our attention carefully to every pitfall and loose flag. The stench of salt and old bones was intolerable, and I felt increasingly weak in the close, hot air.

We emerged into a stone gallery that overlooked a wide subterranean chamber. Pitch-lamps sputtered in the darkness and there was a strong smell of dried herbs and fouler unguents.

Beings were worshipping in the chamber. Worshipping is the only word I can use. Naked, daubed in blood, twenty depraved humans were conducting a dark eldar rite around a torture pit in which a battered man was chained and stretched.

The stink of blood and excrement wafted to me. I tried not to throw up, for I knew the effort would make me pass out.

'There, you see him?' Ravenor whispered into my ear as we crawled to the edge of the gallery.

I made out a pale-skinned ghoul in the distant shadows.

'A haemonculus, sent by the Kabal of the Fell Witch to witness the Beldame's practices.'

I tried to make out detail, but the figure was too deep in the shadows.

I registered grinning teeth and some form of blade device around the right hand.

'Where's Pye?' asked Bequin, whispering too.

Ravenor shook his head. Then he seized my arm and squeezed. Even whispers were no longer possible.

The Beldame herself had entered the chamber.

She walked on eight, spider legs, a huge augmetic chassis of hooked arachnid limbs that skittered on the stones. Inquisitor Atelath, Emperor grant him rest, had destroyed her real legs one hundred and fifty years before my birth.

She was veiled in black gauze that looked like cobwebs. I could actually feel her evil like a fever-sweat.

She paused at the edge of the torture pit, raised her veil with withered hands and spat at the victim below. It was venom, squirted from the glands built into her mouth behind her augmetic fangs. The viscous fluid hit the sacrificial victim full in the face and he gurgled in agony as the front of his skull was eaten away.

Sadia began to speak, her voice low and sibilant. She spoke in the language of the dark eldar and her naked brethren writhed and moaned.

'I've seen enough,' I whispered. 'She's mine. Ravenor, can you manage the haemonculus?'

He nodded.

On my signal, we launched our attack, leaping down from the gallery, weapons blazing. Several of the worshippers were punched apart by Qus's heavy fire.

Whooping the battlecry of Carthae, Arianrhod flew at the haemonculus, way ahead of Ravenor.

I realised I had pushed it too far. I was giddy as I landed, and stumbled.

Her metal spider legs striking sparks from the flagstones, Beldame Sadia reared up at me, ululating. She pulled back her veil to spit at me.

Abruptly, she reeled backwards, thunderstruck by the combined force of Bequin and Zu Zeng who flanked her.

I gathered myself and fired at her, blowing one of the augmetic limbs off her spider-frame.

She spat anyway, but missed. The venom sizzled into the cold stone slabs at my feet.

'Imperial Inquisition!' I bellowed. 'In the name of the hallowed God-Emperor, you and your kind are charged with treason and manifest disbelief!'

I raised my weapon. She flew at me.

Her sheer bulk brought me down.

One spider limb stabbed entirely through the meat of my left thigh. Her steel fangs, like curved needles, snarled into my face. I saw her eyes, for an instant, black and without limit or sanity.

She spat.

I wrenched my head around to avoid the corrosive spew, and fired my bolt pistol up into her.

The impact threw her backwards, all four hundred kilos of wizened witch and bionic carriage.

I rolled over.

The haemonculus had met Arianrhod's attack face on, the glaive around his right hand screaming as the xenos-made blades whirled. He was stick-thin and clad in shiny black leather, his grin a perpetual consequence of the way the colourless skin of his face was pinned back around his skull. He wore metal jewellery fashioned from the weapons of the warriors he had slain.

I could hear Ravenor crying out Arianrhod's name.

Barbarisater sliced at the darting eldar monster, but he evaded, his physical speed unbelievable.

She swung again, placing two perfect kill strokes that somehow missed him altogether. He sent her lurching away in a mist of blood. For the first time since I had known her, I heard Arianrhod yelp in pain.

Flames belched across the chamber. Gonvax shambled forward, forever loyal to his master... and his master's lover. He tried to squirt flames at the haemonculus, but it was suddenly somehow behind him. Gonvax shrieked as the glaive eviscerated him.

With a howl, Arianrhod threw herself at the dark eldar. I saw her, for a moment, frozen in mid-air, her sabre descending. Then the two bodies struck each other, and flew apart.

The sabre had taken off the eldar's left arm at the shoulder. But his glaive...

I knew she was dead. No one could survive that, not even a noble swordswoman from far Carthae.

Bequin was pulling me up. 'Gregor! Gregor!'

Beldame Sadia, her spider carriage limping, was fleeing towards the staircase.

Something exploded behind me. I could hear Ravenor bellowing in rage and pain.

I ran after the Beldame.

The upper chapel, above ground, was silent and cold. Darknight flares glimmered through the lines of stained glass windows.

'You can't escape, Sadia!' I shouted, but my voice was thin and hoarse.

I glimpsed her as she skittered between the columns to my left. A shadow in the shadows.

'Sadia! Sadia, old hag, you have killed me! But you will die by my hand!'

To my right now, another skuttling shadow, half-seen. I moved that way.

I was stabbed hard from behind, in between my shoulder blades. I turned as I fell, and saw the manic face of the Beldame's arch-poisoner, Pye. He cackled and giggled, prancing, a spent injector tube clutched in each hand.

'Dead! Dead, dead, dead, dead, dead!' he warbled.

He had injected me with the secondary part of the poison.

I fell over, my muscles already cramping.

'How does it feel, inquisitor?' Pye chuckled, capering towards me.

'Emperor damn you,' I gasped and shot him through the face.

I blacked out.

When I came round, Beldame Sadia had me by the throat and was shaking me with her augmetic mandibles.

'I want you awake!' she hissed, her veil falling back and the toxin sacs in her wizened cheeks bulging. 'I want you awake to feel this!'

Her head exploded in a spray of bone shards and tissue. The spider carriage went into convulsions and threw me across the chapel. It continued to scuttle and dance, her corpse jerking slackly from it, for a full minute before it collapsed.

I was face down on the floor, and I tried to turn, but the advancing effect of the poison was shutting me down.

Shutting me down hard.

Massive feet strode into my field of vision. Armoured feet, plated with ceramite.

I rolled as best I could and looked up.

Witchfinder Tantalid stood over me, holstering the boltgun he had used to kill Beldame Sadia. He was encased in gold-encrusted battle armour, the pennants of the Ministorum suspended over his back plate.

'You are an accursed heretic, Eisenhorn. And I claim your life.'

Not Tantalid, I thought as my consciousness spun away again. Not Tantalid. Not now.

TWO

SOMETHING SO TYPICALLY BETANCORE
MY FALLEN
THE SUMMONS

From the moment I slipped into unconsciousness at the feet of the vicious Witchfinder Tantalid, I knew nothing more until I woke, twenty-nine hours later, aboard my gun-cutter. I remembered nothing about the seven attempts to shock my system back to life, the cardiac massages, the anti-venom shots injected directly into my heart muscle, the fight to make me live again. I learned all about it later, as I slowly recovered. For days, I was as weak as a feline whelp.

Most particularly, I knew nothing about the way Tantalid had been denied. Bequin told me, a day or two after my first awakening. It had been something so typically Betancore.

Alizebeth had been hard on my heels up the stairs from the sacrarium, in time to see Tantalid's arrival. She had known him at once. The Witchfinder is notorious throughout the sub-sector.

He'd been about to kill me, and I was unconscious at his feet, going into anaphylactic shock with the venom bonding and seething in my veins.

She'd cried out, fumbling for her weapon.

Then light – hard, powerful light – had streamed in through the stained glass windows. There was a roaring sound. My gun-cutter, its lamps on full beam, rose to a hover over the ruined chapel, lighting up the night. Guessing what was about to follow, Bequin had thrown herself down.

Betancore's voice had boomed out from the hull tannoy of the hovering gunship.

'Imperial Inquisition! Step away from the inquisitor now!'

Tantalid had squinted up into the glare, his stringy tortoise head turning in the rim of his massive carapace armour.

'Ministorum officer!' he had yelled back, his voice amplified by his suit's vox-unit. 'Back off! Back off now! This heretic is mine!'

Bequin grinned as she told me Betancore's response. 'Never argue with a gun-cutter, you asshole.'

The slaved servitors in the cutter's blunt wingtips opened fire, hosing the chapel with autocannon shells. The stained glass windows had all shattered, statues had been decapitated, flagstones had disintegrated. Hit at least once, Tantalid had fallen backwards into the dust and debris. His body had not been found, so I presumed the bastard had survived. But he had been smart enough to flee.

My prone body had not been touched, even though the chapel around me had been peppered with fire.

Typical Betancore bravado. Typical Betancore finesse.

She was just like her damned father.

'Send her to me,' I told Bequin as I lay back in my cot, half-dead and feeling terrible.

Medea Betancore looked in a few minutes later. Like her father, Midas, she was clad in the red-piped black suit of a Glavian pilot, and she proudly wore his old cerise, embroidered jacket.

Her skin, like Midas's, like all that of all Glavians, was dark. She grinned at me.

'I owe you,' I said.

Medea shook her head. 'Nothing my father wouldn't have done.' She sat on the foot of my cot.

'He'd have killed Tantalid, though,' she decided.

'He was a better shot.'

That grin again, pearl white teeth framed by ebony skin.

'Yeah, he was that.'

'But you'll do,' I smiled.

She saluted and left.

Midas Betancore had been dead for twenty-six years. I missed him still. He was the closest thing to a friend I had ever had. Bequin and Aemos, they were allies, and I trusted them with my life. But Midas…

May the God-Emperor rot Fayde Thuring for taking him. May the God-Emperor lead me to Fayde Thuring one day so that I and Medea may avenge Midas.

Medea had never known her father. She'd been born a month after his death, raised by her mother on Glavia, and had come into my service by chance. I was her godfather, a promise to Midas. Duty bound, I had visited Glavia for her ascension to adulthood, and watched her drive a Glavia long-prow through the vortex rapids of the Stilt Hills during the Rites of Majority. One glimpse of her skills had convinced me.

Arianrhod Esw Sweydyr was dead. So were Gonvax and Qus. The battle in the sacrarium had been fierce. Ravenor had killed the raging haemonculus, but only after it had ripped open his belly and taken off Zu Zeng's left ear.

Gideon Ravenor was in intensive care in the main city infirmary of Lethe. We would collect him once he was out of danger.

I wondered how long that would be. I wondered how he would be. He had loved Arianrhod, loved her dearly. I prayed this loss would not set him back too far.

I mourned Qus and the swordswoman. Qus had been with me for nineteen years. That Darknight in the chapel had robbed me of so much.

Qus was buried with full honours in the Imperial Guard Memorial Cenotaph at Lethe Majeure. Arianrhod was burned on a bare hill west of the salt-licks. I was too weak to attend either service.

Aemos brought the sabre Barbarisater to me after the pyre. I wrapped it in a vizzy-cloth and a silk sheet. I knew I was duty bound to return it to the tribal elders of the Esw Sweydyr on Carthae before long. That would mean a round trip of at least a year. I had no time for it. I put the wrapped sword in my safebox.

It barely fitted.

As I worked my way back to health, I considered Tantalid. Arnaut Tantalid had risen from the rank of confessor militant in the Missionaria Galaxia seventy years before to become one of the Ministorum's most feared and ruthless witch-hunters. Like many of his breed, he followed the doctrines of Sebastian Thor with such unswerving precision it bordered on clinical obsession.

To most of the common folk of the Imperium, there would be blessed little to choose between an Ordo Xenos inquisitor such as myself and an ecclesiarchy witchkiller like Tantalid. We both hunt out the damning darkness that stalks mankind, we are both figures of fear and dread, we are both, so it seems, laws unto ourselves.

Twinned though we may be in so many ways, we could not be more distinct. It is my personal belief that the Adeptus Ministorum, the Imperium's vast organ of faith and worship, should focus its entire attention on the promulgation of the true church of the God-Emperor and leave the persecution of heretics to the Inquisition. Our jurisdictions often clash. There have, to my certain knowledge, been two wars of faith in the last century provoked and sustained by just such rivalry.

Tantalid and I had locked horns twice before. On Bradell's World, five decades earlier, we had faced each other across the marble floor of a synod court, arguing for the right to extradite the psyker Elbone Parsuval. On that occasion, he had triumphed, thanks mainly to the strict Thorian mindset of the Ministorum elders of Bradell's World.

Then, just eight years ago, our paths had crossed again on Kuuma.

Tantalid's fanatical hatred – indeed, I would venture, fear – of the psyker was by then insurmountable. I made no secret of the fact that I employed psychic methods in the pursuit of my work. There were psychic adepts in my staff, and I myself had worked to develop my own psychic abilities over the years. Such is my right, as an authorised bearer of the Inquisition's seal.

In my eyes, he was a blinkered zealot with psychotic streak. In his, I was the spawn of witches and a heretic.

No courtroom argument for us on Kuuma. A little war instead. It lasted an afternoon, and raged through the tiered streets of the oasis town at Unat Akim.

Twenty-eight latent psykers, none older than fourteen, had been rooted out of the population of Kuuma's sprawling capital city during a purge, and sequestered prior to their collection by the Black Ships. They were recruits, a precious resource, untainted and ready to be shaped by the Adeptus Astropathicus into worthy servants of the God-Emperor. Some of them, perhaps, would have the ultimate honour of joining the choir of the Astronomican. They were frightened and confused, but this was their salvation.

Better to be found early and turned to good service than to remain undetected and become tainted, corrupt and a threat to our entire society.

But before the Black Ships could arrive to take them, they were spirited away by renegade slavers working in collusion with corrupt officials in the local Administratum. Vast sums could be made on the black market for unregistered, virgin psychic slaves.

I followed the slavers' trail across the seif dunes to Unat Akim with the intention of liberating the youngsters. Tantalid made his way there to exterminate them all as witches.

By the end of the fight, I had driven the witchfinder and his cohorts, mostly foot soldiers of the Frateris Militia, out of the oasis town. Two of the young psykers had been killed in the crossfire, but the others were safely transferred into the hands of the Astropathicus.

Tantalid, fleeing Kuuma to lick his wounds, had tried to have me declared heretic, but the charges were swiftly overturned. The Ministorum had, at that time, no wish to court conflict with their allies in the Inquisition.

I had expected, known even, that Tantalid would return sometime to plague me. It was a personal matter now, one which his fanatical disposition would fix upon and transform into a holy calling.

But the last I had heard, he had been leading an ecclesiarchy mission into the Ophidian sub-sector in support of the century-long Purge Campaign there.

I wondered what had brought him to Lethe Eleven at so inopportune a moment.

By the time I was back on my feet, two weeks later, the Darknight was over and I knew the answer, in general if not specific terms.

I was hobbling around on a cane in the private mansion I had rented in Lethe Majeure when Aemos brought me the news. The great Ophidian Campaign was over.

'Great success,' he announced. 'The last action took place at Dolsene four months ago, and the Warmaster has declared the sub-sector cleansed. A famous victory, don't you think?'

'Yes. I should hope so. It's taken them long enough.'

'Gregor, Gregor... even with a force as large as the hallowed Battlefleet Scarus, the subjugation of a sub-sector is an immense task! That it took the best part of a century is nothing! The pacification of the Extempus sub-sector took four hundred y–'

He paused.

'You're toying with me, aren't you?'

I nodded. He was very easy to wind up.

Aemos shook his head and eased his ancient body down into one of the leather chairs.

'Martial law still dominates, I understand, and caretaker governments have been established on the key worlds. But the Warmaster himself is returning with the bulk of the fleet in triumph, setting foot in this sub-sector again for the first time in a hundred years.'

I stood by the open windows, looking out from the mansion's first floor across the grey roofs of Lethe Majeure which seemed to coat the hills of the Tito Basin like the scaled hide of some prehistoric reptile. The sky was a magnolia haze, and a light breeze breathed. It was almost impossible now to picture this place beset by the filthy, permanent shadows of the Darknight.

Now, perhaps, I knew why Tantalid had returned. The Ophidian war was over, and his holy mission concluded with it.

'I remember them setting out, don't you?' I asked.

A foolish question. My savant was a data-addict, driven since the age of forty-two standard to collect and retain all manner of information thanks to a meme-virus he had contracted. There was no possibility of him forgetting anything. He scratched the side of his hooked nose where his heavy augmetic eye-pieces touched.

'How could either of us forget that?' he replied. 'The summer of 240. Hunting the Glaw clan on Gudrun during the very Founding itself.'

Indeed, we had played a particular role in delaying the start of the Ophidian Campaign. The Warmaster, or lord militant as he had been back then, had been all but set to launch his purge into Ophidian space when my investigation of the heretic Glaw family had triggered a mass uprising later known as the Helican Schism. To his great surprise and displeasure, the Warmaster had been abruptly forced to redirect his readied forces in a pacification of his very own sub-sector.

Warmaster Honorius. Honorius Magnus they were calling him. I had never met him, nor had I much wish to. A brutal man, as are so many of his kind. It takes a special mindset, a special brutality, to crush planets and populations.

'There is to be a great Jubilation on Thracian Primaris,' Aemos said. 'A Holy Novena congregated by the Synod the High Ecclesiarchy. It is rumoured that the Imperial Lord Commander Helican himself will attend, specifically to bestow upon the Warmaster the rank of Feudal Protector.'

'I'm sure he'll be very pleased. Another heavy medallion to throw at his officers when he's annoyed.'

'You're not tempted to attend?'

I laughed. In truth, I had thought to return to the Helican sub-sector capital before long. Thracian Primaris, the most massive, industrialised and populated world in the sub-sector, had wrested capital planet status from ancient Gudrun after the disgrace and foment of the Schism, finally achieving the preeminence it felt its size and power had long deserved. It was now the chief Imperial planet of this region.

There was work to be done, reports to be filed and presented, and those things could best be achieved by returning to my property on Thracian, my base of operations, near to the Palace of the Inquisition. But I had little love for Thracian Primaris. It was an ugly place, and I only made my headquarters there out of convenience. The thought of pomp and ceremony and festivals filled me with quiet dread.

Perhaps I would go to Messina instead, or to the quiet of Gudrun, where I maintained a small, comfortable estate.

'The Inquisition is to attend in great strength. Lord Rorken himself...'

I waved a hand in Aemos's direction. 'Does it appeal to you?'

'No.'

'Are there not better uses for our time? Pressing matters? Things that would be more easily achieved away from such overblown distractions?'

'Most certainly,' he said.

'Then I think you know my mind.'

'I think I do, Gregor,' he said, rising to his feet and reaching into the pocket of his green robe. 'And therefore I'm fully prepared for the fact that you're going to curse me when I give you this.'

He held out a small data-slate, an encrypted message-tile whose contents had been received and stored by the astropaths.

The official seal of the Inquisition was stamped across its front.

THREE

CAPITAL WORLD
THE OCEAN HOUSE
INTRUDERS, PAST AND PRESENT

Thracian Primaris, capital world of the Helican sub-sector, seat of government, Helican sub-sector, Scarus sector, Segmentum Obscurus. You can read that description in any one of a hundred thousand guidebooks, geographies, Imperial histories, pilgrimage primers, industrial ledgers, trade directories, star maps. It sounds impressive, authoritarian, powerful.

It does no justice at all to the monster it describes.

I have known hellholes and death-planets that from space look serene and wondrous: the watercolours of their atmospheres, the glittering moons and belts they wear like bangles and jewels, the natural wonders that belie the dangers they contain.

Thracian Primaris is no such dissembler. From space, it glowers like an oozing, cataracted eye. It is corpulent, swollen, sheened in grey veils of atmospheric soot through which the billion billion lights of the city hives glimmer like rotting stars. It glares balefully at all ships that approach.

And, oh! But they approach! Shoals of ships, flocks of them, countless craft, drawn to this bloated cesspit by the lure of its vast industrial wealth and mercantile vigour.

It has no moons, no natural moons anyway. Five Ramilies-class star-forts hang above its atmosphere, their crenellated towers and buttressed gun-stations guarding the approaches to and from the capital world. A dedicated guild of forty thousand skilled pilots exists simply to guide traffic in and out of the jostling, crowded high-anchor reaches. It has a planetary defence force, a standing army of eight million men. It has a population of twenty-two billion, plus another billion temporary residents and visitors. Seven-tenths of its surface are now covered by hive structures, including great sections of the world's original oceans. City-sprawl fills and covers the seas, and the waters roll in darkness far beneath.

I loathe the place. I loathe the lightless streets, the noise, the press of bodies. I loathe the stink of its re-circulated air. I loathe its airborne grease-filth adhering to my clothes and skin.

But fate and duty bring me back there, time and again.

The encrypted Inquisitorial missive had been quite clear: I, and a great number of my peers, was summoned to Thracian Primaris to attend the

Holy Novena, and wait upon the pleasure of the Lord Grandmaster Inquisitor Ubertino Orsini. Orsini was the most senior officer of the Inquisition in the entire Helican sub-sector, a status that made him equal in rank and power to any cardinal palatine.

I was not about to decline.

The voyage from Lethe Eleven took a month, and I brought my entire entourage back with me. We arrived just four days shy of the start of the Novena. As a tiny pilot boat led my ship in to anchor through the massed ranks of orbiting starships, I saw the dark formations of Battlefleet Scarus, suckling at a starfort as if they were its young. This was their heroic homecoming. There was a taste of victory in the air. An Imperial triumph on this scale was something to be savoured, something the Ministorum could use to boost the morale of the common citizenry.

'Your itinerary has been prepared,' said Alain von Baigg, a junior interrogator who served as my secretary. We were aboard the gun-cutter, dropping towards the planet.

'Oh, by whom?'

He paused. Von Baigg was a diffident and lustreless young man who I doubted would ever make the rank of inquisitor. I'd accepted him to my staff in the hope that service alongside Ravenor might inspire him. It had not.

'I would have presumed that the preparation of my itinerary might have included my own choices.'

Von Baigg stammered something. I took the data-slate he was holding. The list of appointments was not his handiwork, I saw. It was an official document, processed by the Ministorum's nunciature in collaboration with the Office of the Inquisition. My timetable for all nine days of the Holy Novena was filled with audiences, acts of worship, feasts, presentation ceremonies, unveilings and Ministorum rites. All nine days, plus the days before and after.

I was here, damn it! I had responded to the summons. I would not allow myself to be subjected to this round of junkets too. I took a stylus and quickly marked the events I was prepared to attend: the formal rites, the Inquisitorial audience, the Grand Bestowment.

'That's it,' I said, tossing it back to him. 'The rest I'm skipping.'

Von Baigg looked uncomfortable. 'You are expected at the Post-Apostolic Conclave immediately on arrival.'

'Immediately on arrival,' I told him sternly, 'I'm going home.'

Home, for me, was the Ocean House, a private residence I leased in the most select quarter of Hive Seventy. On many hive worlds, the rich and privileged dwell in districts high up in the top-most city spires, divorced as far as possible from the dirt and crowding of the mid and low-hab levels. But no matter how high you climbed on Thracian Primaris, there was nothing to find but smog and pollution.

Instead, the exclusive habitats were on the underside of the hive portions that extended out over and into the hidden seas. There was at least a tranquillity here.

Medea Betancore flew the gun-cutter down through the traffic-thick atmosphere, threaded her way between the tawdry domes, dingy towers, rusting masts and crumbling spires, and laced into the seething lanes of air vehicles entering a vast feeder tunnel which gave access to the hives' arterial transit network.

Bars of blue-white light set into the walls of the huge tunnel strobed by the ports. In under an hour we had reached a great transit hub, three kilometres down in the city-crust, where she set the cutter down on a massive elevator platform that sedately lowered us and a dozen other craft into the sub-levels of Hive Seventy. The cutter was then berthed in a private lifter-drome and we transferred to a tuberail for the final stretch to the maritime habitats.

I was already weary of Thracian Primaris by the time I reached the Ocean House.

Built from plasma-sealed grandiorite and an adamite frame, the Ocean House was one of a thousand estates built along the submarine wall of Hive Seventy. It was nine kilometres beneath the city crust and another two below sea level. A small palace by the standards of most common Imperial citizens, it was large enough to house my entire retinue, my libraries, armoury and training facilities, not to mention a private chapel, an audience hall and an entire annex for Bequin's Distaff. It was also secure, private and quiet.

Jarat, my housekeeper, was waiting for us in the entrance hall. She was dressed, as ever, in a pale grey gown-robe and a black lace cap draped with a white veil. As the great iron hatch-doors cycled open, and I breathed the cool, purified air of the house, she clapped her plump hands and sent servitors scurrying forward to take our coats and assist with the baggage train.

I stood for a moment on the nashemeek rug and looked around at the austere stone walls and the high arched roof. There were no paintings, no busts or statuary, no crossed weapons or embroidered tapestries, only an Inquisitorial crest on the far wall over the stairs. I am not one for decoration or opulence. I require simple comfort and functionality.

The others bustled around me. Bequin and Aemos went through to the library. Ravenor and von Baigg issued careful instructions to the servitors concerning some baggage items. Medea disappeared to her private room. The others in my retinue melted away into the house.

Jarat greeted them all, and then came to me.

'Welcome, sir,' she said. 'You have long been from us.'

'Sixteen months, Jarat.'

'The house is aired and ready. We made preparations as soon as you signalled your intentions. We were saddened to hear of the losses.'

'Anything to report?'

'Security was of course double-checked prior to your arrival. There are a number of messages.'

'I'll review them shortly.'

'You are hungry, no doubt?'

She was right, though I hadn't realised it.

'The kitchen is preparing dinner. I took the liberty of selecting a menu that I believe you will approve of.'

'As ever, I have faith in your choices, Jarat. I'd like to dine on the sea terrace, with any who would join me.'

'I'll see to it, sir. Welcome home.'

I bathed, put on a robe of grey wool, and sat for a while alone in my private chambers, sipping a glass of amasec and looking through the messages and communiqués by the soft light of the lamp.

There were many, mostly recent postings from old acquaintances – officials, fellow inquisitors, soldiers – alerting me to their arrival on the planet and conveying respects. Few needed more than a form reply from my secretary. To some, I penned courteous, personal responses, expressing the hope of meeting them at some or other of the Novena's many events.

There were three that drew my particular attention. The first was a private, coded missive from Lord Inquisitor Phlebas Alessandro Rorken. Rorken was the head of Ordo Xenos in the Helican sub-sector, my immediate superior and part of the triumvurate of senior inquisitors who answered directly to Grandmaster Orsini. Rorken wanted to see me as soon as I was back on Thracian. I responded immediately that I would come to him at the Palace of the Inquisition the follow morning.

The second was from my old friend and colleague, Titus Endor. It had been a long time since I had set eyes on him. His message, uncoded, read: 'Gregor. My greetings to you. Are you home?'

The brevity was disarming. I sent an affirmative response that was similarly brief. Endor clearly did not want to converse in writing. I awaited his reponse.

The third was also uncoded, or at least lacked electronic encryption. It said, in Glossia: 'Scalpel cuts quickly, eager tongues revealed. At Cadia, by terce. Hound wishes Thorn. Thorn should be sharp.'

The sea terrace was probably the main reason I had leased the Ocean House in the first place. It was a long, ceramite-vaulted hall with one entire wall made of armoured glass looking into the ocean. The industrialisation of Thracian Primaris had killed off a great part of the world's sea-life, but at these depths, hardy survivors such as luminous deep anglers and schools of incandescent jellies could still be glimpsed in the emerald nocturnal glow. The candlelit room was washed by a rippling green half-light.

Jarat's servitors had set the long table for nine and those nine were already taking their seats and chatting over preprandial drinks as I arrived. Like most of them, I had dressed informally, putting on a simple black suit. The kitchen provided steamed fubi dumplings and grilled ketelfish, followed by seared haunches of rare, gamey orkunu, and then pear and berry tarts with a cinnamon jus. A sturdy Gudrunite claret and sweet dessert wine from the vineyards of Messina complemented the food perfectly. I had forgotten the excellent qualities of the house Jarat ran for me, so far away from the hardship of missions in the field.

Around the table with me were Aemos, Bequin, Ravenor, von Baigg, my rubricator and scribe Aldemar Psullus, Jubal Kircher, the head of household security, a trusted field agent called Harlon Nayl, and Thula Surskova, who was Bequin's chief aide with the Distaff. Medea Betancore had chosen not to join us, but I knew the intensity of the piloting chores down through Thracian airspace had undoubtedly worn her out.

I was pleased to see that Ravenor was present. His injuries were healing, the physical ones at least, and though he was quiet and a little withdrawn, I felt he was beginning to come through the shock of Arianrhod's death.

Surskova, a short, ample woman in her forties, was quietly briefing Bequin on the progress of the newer Distaff initiates. Aemos chuntered on to Psullus and Nayl about the events on Lethe Eleven and they listened intently. Psullus, enfeebled and prematurely aged by a wasting disease, never left the Ocean House and devoted his life to the maintenance and preservation of my extensive private libraries. If Aemos hadn't related the story of our last mission to him, I would have made sure I did. Such tales were his only connection to the active process of our business and he loved to hear them. Nayl, an ex-bounty hunter from Loki, had been injured on a mission the year before and had not been able to join us for the Lethe endeavour. He too lapped up Aemos's account, asking occasional questions. I could tell he was itching to get back to work.

Von Baigg and Kircher chatted idly about the preparations for the Novena that were now gripping the hives of Thracian, and the security consequences they brought. Kircher was an able man, ex-Arbites, and dependable if a little unimaginative. As dessert was served, the discussion broadened across the table.

'They say the Bestowment will be the making of the Warmaster,' Nayl said, his loaded spoon poised in front of his mouth.

'He's made already, I'd say,' I retorted.

'Nayl's right, Gregor. I heard that too,' said Ravenor. 'Feudal Protector. That's as good as Imperial Lord Commander Helican admitting the Warmaster is on an equal footing with him.'

'It's a sinecure.'

'Not at all. It makes Honorius the favourite to become warmaster-in-chief in the Acrotara theatre now that Warmaster Hiju is dead, and Hiju was being groomed for a place on the Senatorum Imperialis, perhaps even to sit amongst the High Lords of Terra.'

'Honorius may be "Magnus", but he's not High Lord material,' I ventured.

'After this he might be,' said Nayl. 'Lord Commander Helican must think he has potential, or he wouldn't be giving him such an almighty hand up.'

Politics left me cold, and I seldom empathised with political ambitions. I only studied the subject because my duties often demanded a detailed working knowledge. Imperial Lord Commander Helican, which is to say Jeromya Faurlitz IV of the noble Imperial family Faurlitz, was the supreme secular authority in the Helican sub-sector, for which reason he styled himself with the sub-sector's name in his appellation. On paper, even the cardinals of the Ministorium, the Grandmaster of the Inquisition, the senior luminaries of the Administratum and the Lords Militant had to answer to him, though as with all things in Imperial society, it was never as easy as that. Church, state and military, woven together as one, yet constantly inimical. In favouring Warmaster Honorius with the Bestowment, Lord Helican was throwing his lot in with the military - an overt signal to the other organs of government - and clearly expected the Warmaster to return the favour when he rose to levels of government beyond those of a single sub-sector. It was a dangerous game, and rare for so senior an official to play openly for such an advantage, though the battle-glory that surrounded Honorius made a perfect excuse.

And that made it a dangerous time. Somebody would want to redress that balance. My money would be on the Ecclesiarchy, though it's fair to say I'm biased. However, history has shown the Church to be chronically intolerant of losing power to the military or the state. I said as much.

'There are many other elements,' Aemos chuckled, accepting a refill of dessert wine. 'The Faurlitz line is weak and lacks both support in the Adeptus Terra and a ready ear at the Senatorum Imperialis and the courts of the Golden Throne. Two powerful families, the De Vensii and the Fulvatorae, are seeking to make gains against the Faurlitz, and would take this as an open show of defiance. Then there's the House of Eirswald, who see their own famous son, Lord Militant Strefon, as the only viable replacement for Hiju. And the Augustyn dynasty, let's not forget, who were ousted from power when High Lord of Terra Giann Augustyn died in office forty years ago. They've been trying to get back in with feverish determination these last few years, pushing their candidate, Lord Commander Cosimo, with almost unseemly impudence. If Nayl's right and the Bestowment makes Honorius a certainty as Hiju's successor, he'd become a direct competitor with Cosimo for the High Lord's vacant position.'

Down the table, Bequin yawned and caught my eye.

'Cosimo's never going to make it,' Psullus put in candidly. 'His house is far too unpopular with the Adeptus Mechanicus, and without their consent, however tacit, no one ever makes it to High Lord rank. Besides, the Ministorum would block it. Giann Augustyn made no friends there with his reforms. They say it was a Callidus of the Officio Assassinorum, under orders from the Ecclesiarcy, that took old Giann off, not a stroke at all.'

'Careful what you say, old friend, or they'll be sending one after you,' Ravenor said. Psullus held up his bony hands in a dismissive gesture as laughter rippled around the table.

'It is, still, most perturbatory,' Aemos said. 'This Bestowment could lead to a House war. Quite apart from all the obvious opponents, Lord Helican and the Warmaster could find themselves tasked by Imperial families who are thus far neutral. There are many who are quite comfortable with their situation, and who would strike with astonishing ruthlessness simply to avoid being drawn into an open bloody clash.'

There was silence for a moment.

'Psullus,' said Ravenor quickly, changing the subject with a diplomat's deftness, 'I have a number of works for you that I collected on Lethe, including a palimpsest of the Analecta Phaenomena...'

Psullus engaged the young interrogator eagerly. Aemos, von Baigg and Nayl continued to debate the Imperial intrigue. Bequin and Surskova made their goodnights and withdrew. I took my crystal balloon of amasec to the glass wall and looked out into the oceanic depths. Kircher joined me after a moment. He smoothed the front of his navy blue jacket and put on his black gloves before speaking.

'We had intruders last month,' he said quietly.

I looked round at him. 'When?'

'Three times, in fact,' he said, 'though I didn't realise that until the third occasion. During night cycle about six weeks ago, I had what seemed to be a persistent fault on the alarms covering the seawall vents. There was no further sign, and the servitors replaced that section of the system. Then again, a week later, on the service entrance to the food stores, and the outer doors of the Distaff annex, both on the same night. I suspected a system corruption, and planned an overhaul of the entire alarm net. The following week, I found the security code on the outer locks of the main door had been defaulted to zero. Someone had been in and left again. I scoured the building and found vox-thieves buried in the walls of six rooms, including your inner chambers, and discreet farcoders wired into three communication junction nodes, spliced to vox and pict lines. Someone had also tried, and failed, to force their way into your void-vault, but they didn't know the shield codes.'

'And there were no traces?'

'No prints, no microspores, no follicles. I washed the air itself through the particle scrubber. The in-house pict recorders show nothing... except a beautifully disguised time-jump of thirty-four seconds. The astropaths sensed nothing. In one place, the intruder must have walked across four metres of under-floor pressure pads without setting them off. In retrospect, I realised the two prior incidents, far from being system faults, were experimental tests to probe, gauge and estimate our security net. Trial runs before the actual intrusion. For that, they used a code scrambler on the main doors. If they'd actually been able to crack it, they could have reset the code and I'd never have known they'd been in.'

'You've double-checked everything? No more bugs to be found?'

He shook his head. 'Lord, I can only apologise for–'

I held up a hand. 'No need, Kircher. You've done your job. Show me what they left.'

Kircher unrolled a red felt cloth across the top of a table in the quiet of the inner library. He was nervous, and beads of sweat were trickling down from his crest-like shock of white hair.

I hadn't wanted to alarm anyone, so I had asked only Ravenor and Aemos to join us. The room smelled of teak from the shelves, must from the books, and ozone from the suspension fields sustaining especially frail manuscripts.

The felt was laid out. On it lay nine tiny devices, six vox-thieves and three farcoders, each one set in a pearl of solid plastic.

'Once I'd stripped them out, I sealed them in inert gel to make sure they were dead. None were booby trapped.'

Gideon Ravenor stepped in and picked up one of the sealed vox-thieves, holding it up to the light.

'Imperial,' he said. 'Unmarked, but Imperial. Very high grade and advanced.'

'I thought so too,' said Kircher.

'Military? Secular?' I asked.

Ravenor shrugged. 'We could source them to likely manufacturers, but they likely supply all arms of the Imperium.'

Aemos's augmetic optics clicked and turned as he peered down at the objects on the cloth. 'The farcoders,' he began, 'similarly advanced. It takes singular skill to patch one of these successfully into a comm-node.'

'It takes singular skill to break in like they did,' I countered.

'They have no maker markings, but they're clearly refined models from the Amplox series. Much more refined than the heavy-duty units the military use. It's just conjecture, but I'd say this was beyond the Ministorum too. They're notoriously behind when it comes to tech advancements.'

'Who then?' I asked.

'The Adeptus Mechanicus?' he ventured. I scowled.

He shrugged, smiling. 'Or at least a body with the power and influence to secure such advanced devices from the Adeptus Mechanicus.'

'Like?'

'The Officio Assassinorum?'

'Who would break in to kill, not listen.'

'Noted. Then a powerful Imperial house, one with clout in the Senatorum Imperialis.'

'Possible...' I admitted.

'Or...' he said.

'Or?'

'Or the one Imperial institution that regularly employs such devices and has the prestige and determination to make sure it is using the best available equipment.'

'That being?'

Aemos looked at me as if I was stupid.

'The Inquisition, of course.'

I slept badly, fitfully. Three hours before the end of the night cycle, I sat up in my bed, suddenly, coldly awake.

Dressed only in the sheet I had wrapped around me, I stalked out into the hall, my grip firm on the matt-grey snub pistol that lived in a holster secured behind my headboard.

Dim blue light filtered through the hallway, softening the edges of everything. I crept forward.

I was not mistaken. Someone was moving about down below, in the lower foyer.

I edged down the stairs, gun braced, willing my eyes to accustomise to the gloom.

I thought to hit a vox and alert Kircher and his staff, but if someone was inside, skillful enough to get past the alarms, then I wanted to capture him, not scare him off with a full blown alert. In the few hours since I had arrived back at the Ocean House, a nasty taste of treachery had seeped into my world. It might be largely paranoia, but I wanted an end to it.

A beam of white light stabbed across the foyer floor from the half open kitchen doors. I heard movement again.

I sidled to the doorframe, checked the safety was off, and slid, weapon first, through the gap in the doors.

The outer kitchen, a realm of marble-topped workbays and scrubbed aluminium ranges, was empty. Metal pots and utensils hung silently from ceiling racks. There was a smell of garlic and cooked herbs in the still air. The light was on in the inner pantry, near the cold store, and the illuminated backwash filled the room.

Two steps, three, four. The kitchen's stone floor was numbingly cold under my bare feet. I reached the door to the inner pantry. There was movement inside.

I kicked the door open and leapt inside, aiming the compact sidearm.

Medea Betancore, clad only in a long, ex-military undershirt, roared out in surprise and dropped the tray of leftover ketelfish she had been gorging on. The tray clattered on the tiled floor in front of the open larder.

'Great gods alive, Eisenhorn!' she wailed in outrage, jumping up and down on the spot. 'Don't do that!'

I was angry. I didn't immediately lower my aim. 'What are you doing?'

'Eating? Hello?' She sneered at me. 'Feel like I've been asleep for a week. I'm famished.'

I began to lower the gun. A sense of embarrassment began to filter into my wired state.

'I'm sorry. Sorry. You should... maybe... get dressed before you come down to raid the larder.' It sounded stupid even as I said it. I didn't realise how stupid until a moment later. I was too painfully aware of her long, dark legs and the way the singlet top was curved around the proud swell of her bust.

'You should take your own advice... Gregor,' she said, raising one eyebrow.

I looked down. I had lost the sheet kicking open the door. I was what Midas Betancore used to call 'very naked.'

Except, of course, for the loaded gun.

'Damn. My apologies.' I turned to scrabble for the fallen sheet.

'Don't stand on my account,' she sniggered.

I froze, stooped. The muzzle of a Tronsvasse parabellum was pointing directly at my head from the darkness behind me.

It lowered. Harlon Nayl looked me up and down for a moment in frank dismay and then raised a warning finger to his lips. He was fully clothed, damn him.

I retrieved my sheet.

'What?' I hissed.

'Someone's in. I can feel it,' he whispered. 'The noise you two were making, I thought it was the intruder. Didn't know you were so keen on Medea.'

'Shut up.'

The two of us fanned out back through the outer kitchen. Nayl pulled up the hood of his vulcanised black bodyglove to cover his pale, shaved head. He was a big man, a head taller than me, but he melted away into the darkness. I watched carefully for his signals.

Nayl waved me left down the hall. I trusted his judgment completely. He had stalked the galaxy's most innovative and able scum for three decades. If there were intruders, he'd find them.

I entered the Ocean House's main hall, and saw the front entry was ajar. The code display on the main lock was blinking a default of zeros.

I swung round as a gun roared behind me. I heard Nayl cry out and sprinted back into the inner foyer. Nayl was on the floor, grappling with an unidentifiable man.

'Get up! Get up! I'm armed!' I shouted.

In reply, the unknown intruder smacked Nayl's head back against the floor so hard he knocked him out, and then threw Nayl's heavy sidearm at me.

I fired, once, and blew a hole in the wall. The spinning gun clipped my temple and knocked me over.

I heard a series of fleshy cracks and impacts, a guttural gasp and then Medea Betancore's voice shouting, 'Lights up!'

I rose. She was standing astride the intruder, one hand braced in a fierce fist, the other pulling down her undershirt for modesty.

'I got him,' she said, glancing round at me.

The dazed intruder was clad in black from head to foot. I wrenched off his hood.

It was Titus Endor.

'Gregor,' he lisped through a bloody mouth. 'You did say you were home.'

FOUR

BETWEEN FRIENDS
AN INTERVIEW WITH LORD RORKEN
THE APOTROPAIC CONGRESS

'Grain joiliq, with shaved ice, and a sliver of citrus.'

Seated in my sanctum chamber, Endor took the proffered drink and grinned at me. 'You remembered.'

'Many were the nights, in those fine old days. Titus, I've mixed your drink of choice too many times to count.'

'Hah! I know. What was that place, the one off Zansiple Street? Where the host used to drink the profits?'

'The Thirsty Eagle,' I replied. He knew full well. It was as if he was testing me.

'The Thirsty Eagle, that's it! Many were the nights, as you say.'

He held up his tumbler of clear, iced spirits.

'Raise 'em and sink 'em and let's have another!'

I echoed the old toast and clinked my lead-crystal of vintage amasec against his glass.

For a moment, it was indeed like the fine old days. Both of us, nineteen years old, full of piss and promethium, newly promoted interrogators ready to take on the whole damn galaxy, students of old Inquisitor Hapshant. Five years later, almost simultaneously, we would both be elected full inquisitors, and our individual careers would begin in earnest.

Nineteen years old, drunk on our feet, carousing in an armpit of a bar off Zansiple Street after hours, mocking our illustrious mentor and bonding for life, bonding with that unquestioning exuberance that seems to me now only possible in youth.

It was like regarding a different life, so far away, almost unrecoverable. I was not that Gregor Eisenhorn. And this man, with his long, braided grey hair and scarred face, sitting in my sanctum dressed in a body-heat masking stealth suit, was not that Titus Endor.

'You could have called,' I began.

'I did.'

I shrugged. 'You could have joined us for dinner tonight. Jarat excelled herself again.'

'I know. But then...' he paused, and rattled the ice around in his drink thoughtfully. 'But then, it might have become known that Inquisitor Endor had visited Inquisitor Eisenhorn.'

'It is well known that those two are old friends. Why would that have been a problem?'

Endor set down his drink, unpopped the fasteners around his waistband and pulled the top half of his stealth suit up over his head. He cast the garment aside.

'Too hot,' he remarked. His undershirt was dark with sweat. The jagged saurapt tooth still hung around his neck on a black cord. That tooth. Years ago, I'd dug it out of his leg after he had driven the beast off. Brontotaph, twelve decades ago and more. The pair of us, alongside Hapshant, in the mist-meres.

'I've come for the Novena,' he said. 'I was summoned to attend by Orsini's staff, like you I imagine. I wanted to talk to you, talk to you as far off the record as was possible.'

'So you broke into my house?'

He sighed deeply, finished his drink and walked over to the spirit stand in the corner of the room to fix another.

'You're in trouble,' he said.

'Really? Why is that?'

He looked round, peeling strips of citrus rind off a fruit with a paring knife.

'I don't know. But there are rumblings.'

'There are always rumblings.'

He turned to face me fully. His eyes were suddenly very hard and bright. 'Take this seriously.'

'Very well, I will.'

'You know what the rumour-mill is like. Someone's always got a point to make, a score to settle. There were stories. I dismissed them at first.'

'Stories?'

He sighed again and returned to his seat with his refreshed drink.

'There is talk that you are... unsound.'

'What talk?'

'Damn it, Gregor! I'm not one of your interview suspects! I've come here as a friend.'

'A friend who broke in wearing a stealth suit and–'

'Shut up just for a minute, would you?'

I paused.

'Gladly. If you cut to the chase.'

'The first I heard, someone was bad-mouthing you.'

'Who?'

'It doesn't matter. I waded in and told them just what I thought. Then I heard the story again. Eisenhorn's unsound. He's lost the plot.'

'Really?'

'Then the stories changed. It was no longer "Eisenhorn's unsound", it was, "The people who matter think Eisenhorn's unsound". As if somehow suspicion of you had become official.'

'I've heard nothing,' I said, sitting back.

'Of course you haven't. Who'd say it to your face but a friend... or a convening judge from Internal Prosecution?'

I raised my eyebrows. 'You're really worried, aren't you, Titus?'

'Damn right. Someone's gunning for you. Someone whose got the ear of the upper echelon. Your career and activities are under scrutiny.'

'You get that all from rumours? Come on, Titus. There are plenty of inquisitors I can think of who'd like to score points off me. Orsini's a closet Monodominant, and the puritan idealists are forming a power block around him. They are radicals, in their way. You know that. Us Amalathians are too louche for their tastes.'

I mentioned before how I hated politics. Nothing is more fruitless and wearying than the internal politics of the Inquisition itself. My kind is fractured internally by belief factions and intellectual sectarianism. Endor and myself count ourselves as Amalathian inquisitors, which is to say we hold an optimistic outlook and work to sustain the integrity of the Imperium, believing it to be functioning according to the divine Emperor's scheme. We preserve the status quo. We hunt down recidivist elements: heretics, aliens, psykers, the three key enemies of mankind – these are of course our primary targets – but we will set ourselves against anything that we perceive to be destabilising Imperial society, up to and including factional infighting between the august organs of our culture. It has always struck me as ironic that we had to become a faction in order to fight factionalism.

We profess to be puritans, and certainly are so compared to the extreme radical factions of the Inquisition such as the Istvaanians and the Recongrenators.

But equally alien to us are the extreme right wing of the puritan factions, the Monodominants and the Thorians, some of whom believe even the use of trained psykers to be heretical.

If I was in trouble, it would not be the first time an inquisitor of tempered, moderate beliefs had run foul of either extreme in his own organisation.

'This goes beyond simple faction intrigue,' Titus said quietly. 'This isn't a hardliner deciding to give the moderates a going over. This is particular to you. They have something.'

'What?'

'Something concrete on you.'

'How do you know?'

'Because twenty days ago on Messina, I was detained and questioned by Inquisitor Osma of the Ordo Malleus.'

I suddenly realised I was up out of my seat.

'You were what?'

He waved dismissively. 'I'd just finished a waste-of-time matter, and was preparing to pack up and ship for Thracian. Osma contacted me, polite and friendly, and asked if he could meet with me. I went to see him. It was all very civil. He made no effort to restrain me... but I don't think I could have left before he had finished. He was guarded, but he made it clear that if I decided to walk out... his people would stop me.'

'That's outrageous!'

'No, that's Osma. You've met him surely? One of Orsini's. Bezier's right-hand man. Thorian to the marrow. He makes a point of getting what he's after.'

'And what did he get?'

'From me?' Endor laughed. 'Not a thing, except for a glowing character reference! He allowed me to leave after an hour. The bastard even suggested we might meet and dine together, socially, during the Novena.'

'Osma is a skilled operator. Slippery. So... that begs the question, what did he want?'

'He wanted you. He was interested in our friendship and our history. He asked me about you, like he wanted me to let something personal and damning slip. He didn't give away much of anything, but it was clear he had dirt. Some report had been filed that compromised you, directly or indirectly. By the end of it, I knew that the rumours I had been hearing were just the surface ripples of a secret inquiry. I knew then that I had to warn you... without anyone knowing we'd spoken.'

'It's all lies,' I told him.

'What is?'

'I don't know. Whatever they think. Whatever they fear. I've done nothing that deserves the attention of the Ordo Malleus.'

'I believe you, Gregor,' Endor said, in a way that suggested to me he undoubtedly did not.

We took fresh drinks onto the sea terrace. He looked out at the kalaedoscopic swirls of luminous plankton and said, 'They've only just begun.'

I nodded and looked down at the drink cradled in my hands.

'On Lethe... Tantalid came after me. I supposed at the time it was old scores, but from what you've said tonight, I doubt that now.'

'Be careful,' he murmured. 'Look, Gregor, I should go. This should have been a better reunion of old friends.'

'I want to thank you for the chance you took. The effort you made to bring this to me.'

'You'd do the same.'

'I would. One last thing... how did you get in?'

He looked round at me sharply.

'What?'

'In here? Tonight?'

'I used a code scrambler on the door.'

'You diverted the alarms.'

'I'm not a novice, Gregor. My scrambler was set to trigger a nulling cascade effect through the system.'

'That's quite a piece of kit. May I see it?'

He took a small black pad from his hip-pocket and passed it to me.

'An Amplox model,' I noted. 'Quite advanced.'

'I only use the best.'

'Me too. I've employed these before. They seem... just in my experience... to work best after a few tests.'

'How so?'

'A dry run or two, I mean. To assess the system you're trying to penetrate. A few soft passes to gauge the security and let the scrambler assimilate and learn what it's up against.'

'Yeah, I've done that, when I've had the luxury of time. These suckers learn fast. Still, they do the job on the spot when time is tight.'

'Like tonight?' I handed the device back to him.

'Yes... what do you mean?'

'It got you in tonight from cold? No test runs necessary?'

'No, of course not. This visit was spur of the moment. And until that pretty bitch of yours kicked me in the face, I had thought myself very lucky to have gotten so far.'

'So you haven't been here before? You haven't been in before?'

'No,' he said sharply. Either I had offended him or...

'Go if you have to,' I said.

'Goodnight, Gregor.'

'Goodnight, Titus. I'd offer to show you out, but I think you know the way well enough.'

He grinned, raised his glass and finished it in a single swig.

'Raise 'em and sink 'em and let's have another!'

'I hope so,' I replied.

The Palace of the Inquisition on Thracian Primaris is high in the cloud tiers of Hive Forty-Four. The size of a small city itself, it is the chief office of the Inquisition in the Helican sub-sector, maintaining a permanent staff of sixty thousand. I make no excuses for its black staetite facings, its darkened windows, its protective spines of iron spikes. Critics of the Inquisition may regard its architecture as almost comically overdone, playing directly to the general public's worst fears about the nature of the Inquisition with its deliberate, black menace. That, I would say, is precisely the point. Fear keeps the populace in line, fear of an institution so terrible it will not hesitate to punish them for transgressions.

At the start of the next day cycle, I went to the Palace, escorted by Aemos, von Baigg and Thula Surskova. Ironically, I felt vulnerable with only three companions at my side. I had grown too used to a large retinue these last few decades. I had to remind myself that there had been a time when my entire retinue would have numbered three such people.

The Palace of the Inquisition is not a place for casual or accidental meetings. Inside, it is a dark maze of shadowy halls, void screens and opaquing fields. The staff and visitors move privately behind masking energy fields, their business confidential. On entry to the echoing main hall, my party was issued with a drone cyber-skull that hovered at our shoulders and projected an insulating cone of silence around us. We were offered an astropath adept too to further ensure our privacy, but I declined. Surskova, with her untouchable quality, was all I needed.

The hooded Inquisitorial guards, their burgundy armour threaded with gold leaf and emblazoned with the seal of our Office, led us across the black marble floor, their double-handed powerblades held upright before them. Glinting brown opaquing fields swirled into being on either side, forming a solid, buzzing corridor of energy that divorced us from our surroundings.

Alain von Baigg played with his high collar distractedly as we walked. He was nervous. The oppressive threat of the palace affected even its own servants.

Lord Rorken awaited us in his private chambers. A void shield dissipated to allow us through the circular doorway and flickered back to life once we were inside. The guards did not accompany us. I told my trio to wait for me in the austere vestibule where there were two cast iron benches piled with white satin bolsters.

I went in through the inner door.

I had come wearing black, with a three-quarter cloak of dark brown leather. My Inquisitorial crest was pinned at my throat. My companions were all formally robed too. One did not call on Master of the Ordo Xenos in casual attire.

The reception chamber was dazzlingly bright. The walls were mirrors, framed in ormolu gilt, and the floor was a polished cream marble. Thousands of candles burned all around, on stands, on forked candelabras, or simply placed directly on the floor. The mirrors reflected their glare. It was like standing in a prism that was catching golden sunlight.

I blinked, and raised my hand to shield my eyes. I saw a hundred other men in cloaks do the same. My reflections. Multiplied Gregor Eisenhorns, framed by twinkling candles. I saw I looked edgy.

That would not do.

'None may escape the penetrating glare of the Inquisition's light,' said a voice.

'For to do so means perforce they embrace the outer darkness,' I finished.

Rorken strode towards me. 'You know your Catuldynas, Eisenhorn.'

'His apopthegms please me. I have never much liked his later allegories.'

'Too dry?'

'Too arch. Too mannered. For my taste, Sathescine has a superior voice. Less... bombastic.'

Rorken smiled and took my hand. 'So you rate poetic beauty over content?'

'Beauty is truth, and truth beauty.'

He raised an eyebrow. 'What is that?'

'A pre-Imperial fragment I once read. Anonymous. As to your first question, I would read Sathescine over Catuldynas for pleasure, and insist that my neophytes read Catuldynas repeatedly until they can quote it as well as I.'

Rorken nodded. He was a compact man, his head shaved but for a short goatee, and he wore crimson robes over black clothes and gloves. It was impossible to guess his age, but he must have been at least three hundred years old, for he had held his high office for a century and a half.

Thanks to augmentation and juvenatus processes, he looked like a man in his late forties.

'Can I offer you refreshment?' he asked.

'Thank you, no, sir. The nunciature has organised a busy schedule for me through the Novena, so I would be grateful if we could deal with things directly.'

'The Ministorum's nuncios have set busy schedules for us all. The Lord Commander has charged them with arranging as much pomp as possible for this celebration. And the Gregor Eisenhorn I know won't be sticking to their appointments if he can help it.'

I made no reply. That was a telling remark.

I became wary. Rorken and I had a good working relationship, and I felt he had trusted me ever since the affair with the Necroteuch ninety-eight years before. Since then he had been pleased to lead me, guide me, and oversee my cases personally. But one did not become anything like friends with the Master of the Ordo Xenos Helican.

'Have a seat. You can spare me a little time, I think.'

We sat on high-backed chairs either side of a low table, and he gave me chilled water imported from the chalybeate springs of Gidmos.

'A restorative tonic. I understand the Beldame tested you hard on Lethe Eleven.'

I slid a data-slate out of my cloak.

'A preliminary draft of my full report,' I said, handing it to him. He took it and put it, unread, on the table.

'Do you know why I have asked to see you?'

I paused, and took a calculated gamble.

'Because of the stories that I am unsound.'

He cocked his head in interest. 'You've heard them?'

'They've been brought to my attention. Recently.'

'Your reaction?'

'In all honesty? Puzzlement. I don't know the matter of the stories themselves. I feel someone must have a grudge.'

'Against you?'

'Against me personally.'

He sipped his water. 'Before we go any further, I must ask you... Is there any reason, any reason at all, that you think this story has arisen?'

'As I said, a grudge is the–'

'No,' he said quietly. 'You know what I'm asking you.'

'I've done nothing,' I said.

'I'll take your word for that. If at a later time I discover you're lying, or even hiding something from me, I will... be displeased.'

'I have done nothing,' I repeated.

He steepled his hands and looked out across the sea of candles. 'Here is the way of it. An inquisitor – who, it does not matter – reported to me in confidence a disturbing encounter. A daemonhost made a show of sparing a man's life, because it thought he was you.'

I was fascinated and horrified at the thought.

'I am not able to confirm it, but the daemonhost has been identified as Cherubael.'

Now my blood ran cold. Cherubael.

'You've had no contact with that entity since 56-Izar?'

I shook my head. 'No, sir. And that was almost a century ago.'

'But you've been looking for it ever since?'

'I've made no secret of that, sir. Cherubael is the agency of an invisible enemy, one whose machinations involved even a member of our Office.'

'Molitor.'

'Yes, Konrad Molitor. I have spent a great deal of time and effort trying to uncover the truth about Cherubael and its unseen master, but it has been fruitless. Ten decades, and only the barest few hints.'

'The matter of Cherubael's involvement in the Necroteuch affair was passed to the Ordo Malleus, as you know. They too have failed to turn up a trace of it.'

'Where was this alleged encounter?'

He paused. 'Vogel Passionata.'

'And it thought it was sparing me?'

'The implication was the daemonhost had better things in mind for you. There was a strong suggestion of... a compact between you and it.'

'Nonsense!'

'I hope so–'

'Really, nonsense, sir!'

'I hope so, Eisenhorn. Grandmaster Orsini has no time for radical elements in the Inquisition. Even if he wasn't so hardline, I'd not stand for it. Ordo Xenos Helican has no place for those who consort with Chaos.'

'I understand.'

'Make sure you do.' Rorken's face was dark and stern now. 'Your search for this entity continues?'

'Even now I have agents in the field hunting for it.'

'With any signs of success?'

I thought of the Glossia-coded message I had received the night before. 'No,' I said, my first and only lie in the conversation.

'The inquisitor in question urged me to take the matter to the Ordo Malleus. I'll not throw one of my best men to the mercy of Bezier's dogs. I kept the matter internal to our Ordo.'

'Then why the stories?'

'That's what troubled me too. Word has got out anyway. I thought it prudent to advise you that the Ordo Malleus might be scrutinising you.'

A second warning in twelve hours.

'I'd like to suggest you leave Thracian and get on with other work until the matter blows over,' he said. 'But your presence is required for the Apotropaic Congress.'

Pieces now fell into place. The sheer scale of the triumph celebrations, the magnitude of the Novena, were appropriate enough, but the number of senior inquisitors summoned to attend was heavy handed to say the least. Military and Ecclesiarch luminaries may be ordered around to swell such events, but inquisitors are a different breed, more aloof, more... independent. It is unusual for us to be called together in any great gathering, particularly by such incontestable orders. I had presumed Orsini was throwing his weight around to impress the Lord Commander Helican.

But that was not the case. There was to be an Apotropaic Congress. That is why we had been called here.

Apotropaic studies are conducted all the time by the Inquisition, and usually involve one or perhaps as many as three inquisitors. On a larger scale, they are named Councils, and require a quorum of at least eleven inquisitors. Larger than that, they become a Congress. Such assemblies are extremely rare. I knew for a fact that my late master Hapshant had served on the last such Congress held in the sub-sector. That was two hundred and seventy-nine years in the past.

The purpose of these studies, even at their smallest level, is the acute examination and assessment of unusually valuable captives. Once in the custody of the Inquisition, a rogue psyker, a charismatic heretic, an alien warlord... whatever... undergoes a sometimes lengthy formal examination quite separate from the dissection of his or her actual crimes. They are often already condemned and only waiting for sentence to be carried out. At that stage, the Inquisition wishes to expand its own learning, to understand more precisely the nature of the enemies of mankind. The subjects are dissected, usually intellectually, sometimes psychically and occasionally literally, in order to discover their strengths, weaknesses, beliefs and drives. Vital truths have in this way been discovered by Apotropaic councils, truths that have armoured the servants of the Imperium for later clashes. To illustrate, the Imperial Guard's famous victory over the Ezzel meta-breed was only successful thanks to methods of detecting their presence discovered by the examination of an Ezzel scoutform by the Apotropaic Council of Adiemus Ultima in 883.M40.

The size of the inquiry depends on the number or magnitude of the subject.

'Thirty-three heretic psykers of level alpha or above were captured by the Warmaster at Dolsene, during the final major engagement of the Ophidian Suppression,' Rorken told me, showing me a data-slate. The security clearance on the slate was so high that even I was impressed. 'Trained, somehow, to control and master the warp-spawned filth they channel, they formed the backbone of the Enemy's high command defence, the beating heart of the adversary.'

'How were they taken? Alive, I mean?' It was astonishing. Untrained psykers are terrifying enough, their minds always carrying the horrendous potential to open up a gate into the immaterium, to let its daemons flood through into our universe. But these... these fiends, they had somehow learnt – or been trained – to focus their warp-spawned talents, to contain the daemons within themselves and use their damnable strength. My mind reeled at the threat they had posed, and posed still, though they were our prisoners.

Rorken gestured to the slate in my hands. 'You'll find a summary of the incident there, appended to the main list. In brief, it was luck... luck, and the amazing courage of the Adeptus Astartes, working in conjunction with Inquisitors Heldane, Lyko and Voke.'

'Voke... Commodus Voke.'

'I forgot, you're old friends, aren't you? He was involved with the Glaw affair on Gudrun, just before the Schism.'

'Old friends is probably pushing it. We worked together. We generated a mutual respect. I've seen him infrequently since then. I'm amazed the old dog is still alive.'

'Alive, despite the prognoses of several generations of medicae experts. And still powerful. To achieve this, in his twilight years...'

I nodded. Even a speed-reading of the incident suggested an act of near mythical valour. Voke's service to the Emperor was, as ever, above and beyond any reasonable expectation of duty.

'I know Heldane too. He was Voke's pupil. So he's finally made it to inquisitor rank too?'

'For sixty years now... Eisenhorn, you lead a solitary life, don't you?'

'If you mean I don't keep up with the comings and goings of elections and the businesses of other inquisitors, sir, yes. I do. I focus on my work, and the needs of my staff.'

He smiled, as if indulging me. In truth, my attitude was not uncommon. As I have said, we of the Inquisition are an aloof, independent kind, and have little interest in the affairs of our colleagues. I saw another difference between myself and Rorken. Whatever my seniority, I was still an agent of the field, a worker, an achiever, who might be gone into the distant gulfs of the Halo Stars for months or even years at a time. His rank tied him to his palace, and wrapped him in the intrigues and mechanisms of the Imperial ruling classes in general and the Inquisition in particular.

I remembered Commodus Voke as a poisonous old viper, but a determined ally. During the affair of the Necroteuch, believing himself to be on his deathbed, he had implored me to stand reference for his pupil Heldane. I had promised him that, though when Voke then proceeded to stay alive, I had never followed it through. He had been around to see that Heldane got his rosette.

Heldane... I had never liked him at all.

I'd never met Lyko, the third member of the glorious trio, but I knew him by reputation as an inquisitor whose star was very much in the ascendant. Their spectacular achievement on Dolsene would further all their careers magnificently.

I read through the list of inquisitors summoned to form the Council, a list which included my name. There were sixty in all. Titus Endor was amongst them. So was Osma, and so was Bezier. Some names, like Schongard, Hand and Reiker, leapt out as men I had little wish to be in the same room with. Others – Endor, naturally, and Shilo, Defay and Cuvier – were individuals it would be a pleasure to see again.

Some names I'd barely heard of, or never heard of at all; others were famous or infamous inquisitors who I knew only by reputation. It was quite an assembly, drawn from all over the sector.

'My inclusion on this list?' I began.

'Is no surprise. You are a senior and respected member of our office.'

'Thank you, sir. But I wonder, did Voke request me personally?'

'He was going to,' Rorken told me, 'but you had already been nominated.'

'By whom?'

'Inquisitor Osma,' he replied.

FIVE

THE TRIUMPH
AT THE SPATIAN GATE
THE LINE BREAKS

For all my condemnations of the overzealous pageantry of the Novena, I will admit that the Great Triumph of the first day filled me with a sense of pride and exhilaration.

Across Hive Primaris, the largest and most powerful hive on Thracian, dawn brought a chorus of klaxons and a cacophony of bells. Ministorum services, relayed live from the Monument of the Ecclesiarch, were broadcast on every crackling pict channel and public vox service. The phlegmy intonations of Cardinal Palatine Anderucias rolled across the street levels of the great hive city, overlapping like some gigantic choral round due to the echoes of doppler distortion.

Civilians and pilgrims flooded into the streets of Hive Primaris in their millions, clogging the arterial routes and feeder tunnels, and blackening the sky with their craft. Many were turned back to surrounding hives to watch the proceedings on vast hololithic screens raised in stadiums and amphitheatres for the event.

The Arbites struggled to control the flow of people and keep the route of the Triumph clear.

The day cycle began brightly. In the night, flocks of dirigibles from the Officium Meteorologicus had seeded the smog fields and upper cloud levels with carbon black and other chemical precipitants. Before dawn, sixteen hundred-kilometre wide rainstorms had washed the clouds away and drenched the primary hives, sluicing the dirt and grime away. For the first time in decades, the sky was clear. Not blue exactly, but clear of yellow pollution banks. The sun's light permeated the atmosphere and the steepled ridges and high towers of the hives glowed. I had heard, from informal sources, that this radical act of weather control would have profound ill consequences for the planet's already brutalised climate for decades to come. Reactive hurricane storms were expected in the southern regions before the week was out, and the drainage system of the primary hives was said to be choked to bursting by the singular rainfall.

It was also said that the seas would die quicker, thanks to the overdose of pollutants hosed into them so suddenly by the rain-clearance.

But the Lord Commander Helican had insisted that the sun shone on his victory parade.

I arrived early to take my place, fearing the great flow of traffic into the hive. I brought Ravenor with me. We were both dressed in our finest garb, emblems proudly displayed, and wore ceremonial weapons.

Medea Betancore flew us in, and landed us at a reserved Navy air-station just south of the Imperial armour depot. By the time she'd got us on the ground, the air routes were so thick she had no choice but to stay put there for the day. There was no flying out. She bade us a good day, and strolled away across the pad to chat with the ground crew servicing a Marauder.

A private car, arranged by the Nunciature, took Ravenor and myself to the hive's old Founding Fields at Lempenor Avenue, where the Inquisition was expected to gather to join the march. Outside the windows of the speeding lifter limousine, we saw steam rising from the empty, rain-washed streets. Despite his best efforts, the Lord Commander Helican would have clouds before noon.

I leant forward in the car's passenger bay and straightened Ravenor's interrogator rosette. He looked nervous, a look I didn't associate with him. He also looked the very image of an inquisitor. I realised he didn't look nervous so much as just very young. Like a man hurrying to join his drinking friends in the Thirsty Eagle off Zansiple Street.

'What is it?' he asked, smiling.

I shook my head. 'This will be quite a day, Gideon. Are you ready for it?'

'Absolutely,' he said.

I noticed he had added the tribe badge of clan Esw Sweydyr to the decoration of his uniform.

'An appropriate touch,' I remarked, pointing to it.

'I thought so,' he said.

At ten, the Triumph began. A deafening roar of hooters and sirens blasted across the hive, followed by a mass cheer that quite took my breath away. By then, the streets were packed with close on two billion jubilant citizens.

Two billion voices, raised as one. You cannot imagine it.

In sunlit air vibrating with colossal cheering, the Great Triumph moved out from the Armour depot. It was to follow an eighteen kilometre route straight down the kilometre-wide Avenue of the Victor Bellum, right into the heart of the hive and the Monument of the Ecclesiarch. Millions lined the way, cheering, applauding, waving banners and Imperial flags.

At the front rolled eighty tanks of the Thracian Fifth, pennants quivering from their aerial masts. Behind them, the colours band of the Fiftieth Gudrunite Rifles, pumped out the stately *March of the Primarchs*.

Next, the standard bearers: five hundred men carrying aloft the many regimental guidons and emblems representing the units and regiments that had participated in the Ophidian Suppression. It took an hour for them alone to all pass.

On their heels came the Great Standard of the Emperor, a vast aquila symbol like a clipper's mainsail, so big it took a stocky, lumbering, unbelievably ancient dreadnought of the White Consuls to lift it and stop it being carried away by the wind. The dreadnought was escorted by five Baneblade super-heavy tanks.

Behind that, rolled the dead. Every Imperial corpse recovered from the closing stages of the war, loaded in state into fifteen hundred Rhino carriers painted black for the duty. One hundred mighty Space Marines of the Aurora Chapter marched beside the trundling machines, holding up black-ribboned placards on which the names of the dead were etched in gold leaf.

It was noon by the time the marching ranks of the rest of Aurora Chapter, all in full, polished imperator armour, moved by. The massive cheering had not yet diminished. After the Space Marines came sixty thousand Thracian troops, thirty thousand from Gudrun, eight thousand from Messina, four thousand from Samater. Breastplates and lances glittered in the sun. Then the Navy officers from Battlefleet Scarus in neat echelons. Then the White Consuls, glittering and terrifying.

Then the endless files of the Munitorum and the Administratum, followed by the slow-moving trains of the Astropathicus. A dull psychic discharge, like corposant, slithered and crackled around their carriages and their heads, and left a metallic taste in the air.

The Titans of the Adeptus Mechanicus followed them. Four Warlords, blotting out the sun, eight grinding Warhounds, and a massive Super-Titan called *Imperius Volcanus*. It was as if significant sections of the hive itself had detached and begun walking. The vast crowds hushed as they thumped past; man-shaped mechanisms as tall as a steeple, taller yet in the case of Volcanus. Their massive legs rose and fell in perfect synchronisation. The ground shook. Unperturbed, six hundred tech-priests and magos of the Adeptus paraded casually between their feet.

The tank brigades of the Narmenians and the Scuterans followed the god-machines. Five thousand armour units, rolling forward under a haze of exhaust, barrels raised in salute. Tractors towed Earthshaker cannons behind them, three abreast, and then a seemingly endless flow of Hydra batteries, traversing their multiple barrels from left to right, like sun-following flowers.

The Ecclesiarchy followed, led by Cardinal Rouchefor, who srode ahead of his two thousand hierarchs barefoot. Cardinal Palatine Anderucias awaited us all for the blessing at the monument.

From its muster point at the old Founding Fields, the Inquisition fell in line behind the priesthood, six hundred strong.

We were the only part of the Triumph not to march in ordered ranks. We simply strode behind the Ecclesiarch in a sombre wedge. We were not uniform. All manner of men and women filled our ranks, all manner of appearances and aspects. Individuals walking, dressed in dark robes or leather capes, some with great entourages holding up the trains of gaudy robes, some on lifter thrones, some alone and dignified, some even hidden by personal void shields. Ravenor and I walked together in the press, behind the extravagant ensemble of Inquisitor Eudora.

Lord Orsini, the grandmaster, led us, his long purple vestments trained out behind him and supported by thirty servitors. At his side strode Lord Rorken of the Ordo Xenos, Lord Bezier of the Ordo Malleus and Lord Sakarof of the Ordo Hereticus, Orsini's triumvirate.

Sonic booms sounded over the hives as honour escorts of Thunderhawks flashed down above us. Fireworks banged and fizzed, staining the sky with quick blooms of colour and light.

At our backs came the triumphal procession of the Warmaster himself. Honorius rode with Lord Commander Helican, standing in a howdah built upon the humped back of the largest and most venerable aurochothere warbeast. Ten thousand men from their personal retinues marched together. Two hundred grunting, snuffling behemoths from the aurochothere cavalry. Eight hundred Conqueror tanks. Lifter bikes skimmed alongside their line. The frenzied crowd strewed thousands of flowers in their path.

Behind them all came the prisoners.

Like the honoured dead in the funereal Rhinos, the prisoners were an open show of Imperial heroism in general, and the Warmaster's heroism in particular. Honorius delighted in displaying their torment to the adoring populace. The sight of these great, potent creatures cowed and submissive made his own power manifest.

There were several hundred foot soldiers, chained together at the hands and feet, shambling along in two wretched lines. Veterans of the Thracian Guard marched around them, lashing out with force-poles and neural-whips to drive them on. The crowd booed and howled, and pelted the subjugated foe with bottles and rocks.

Six Trojan tank-tractors, painted in the Warmaster's colours and teamed together like horses pulling a state landau, came behind the chained prisoners, towing a vast flatbed trailer designed to transport a super-heavy tank. On the flatbed, shackled in adamite and encased in individual void shield bubbles, were the thirty-three psykers, the greatest trophies of all. They were dim, contorted shapes, barely human, swimming in the milky green cocoons of the imprisoning shields. Along with the White Consuls guarding the tractor-team, two hundred astrotelepaths strode alongside it, mentally reinforcing the void bubbles that were damping the psychic fury of the captives. Frost coated the metal of the flatbed. More psychic ball-lightning drifted overhead.

Twenty thousand men and five hundred armoured machines of the Thracian Interior Guard formed the tail of the Great Triumph, marching under the dual standard of Thracia and the Warmaster.

After barely fifteen minutes of walking in the immense procession, I was utterly numb. The noise of the crowd alone vibrated me to the very marrow. My diaphragm shook every time the flypast came in low or when the great siege sirens of the Titans blasted. The scale of the occasion was overwhelming, the sensory assault bewildering. Seldom have I been so in awe of the power of my species.

Seldom have I been so forcibly reminded of my place as a tiny cog in the workings of the holy Imperium of Mankind.

Following the mighty Avenue of the Victor Bellum, the Triumph passed under the Spatian Gate, a monolithic structure of glossy white aethercite. The memorial gate was so cyclopean, even the Titans passed under it without difficulty.

It had been raised to commemorate Admiral Lorpal Spatian, who had been killed in the early years of the Ophidian Suppression during the magnificent fleet action that had taken Uritule IV.

The inner part of the arch was painted with majestic murals depicting that event, and rose to a dome so high, a microclimate of clouds regularly formed under the apex. I had known Spatian personally, and like several others in the procession, I paused under the giant gate to pay my respects to the eternal flame.

No, that is not true. I had known Spatian, during the Helican Schism, but not at all well. For reasons I could not explain, I felt compelled to stop. I certainly had no great urge to honour him.

'Sir?' Ravenor asked as I stepped aside.

'Go on, I'll catch up shortly,' I told him.

Ravenor moved on with the procession while I lit a votive candle and set it amongst the thousands of others around Spatian's tomb. The vast tide of the Triumph moved slowly by behind me. Other figures had detached themselves from the procession and stood nearby, paying silent homage to the admiral.

'Eisenhorn?'

I looked round, the voice breaking my reverie. An elderly but powerful Navy officer stood before me, splendidly austere in his white dress jacket.

'Madorthene,' I said, recognising him at once.

We shook hands. It had been a few years since I'd seen Olm Madorthene – Lord Procurator Madorthene, as he was now. We'd first met at Gudrun during the Necroteuch affair when he had been a mid-ranking officer in the Battlefleet Disciplinary Detachment, the Navy's military police. Now he ran that detachment. He'd been a useful and reliable ally over the years.

'Quite an event,' he said, with a reserved smile. Outside, the horns of the immense Titans blared again and the noise from the crowd swelled.

'I find myself sufficiently humbled,' I said. 'The Warmaster must be loving it.'

He nodded. 'Uplifting, good for public morale.'

I agreed, but in truth my heart was not in it. It wasn't just the overwhelming cacophony of it, or my deep-seated reluctance to be here at all. Since Ravenor and I had stepped out to take our place in the Triumph, I had nursed a sense of foreboding that was growing with each passing minute. Was that what had made me pause here, under the great arch?

'There's a look on your face,' said Madorthene. 'This isn't really your thing, is it?'

'I suppose not.'

'What is it, old friend?'

I paused. Something...

I strode back to the south arch of the Spatian Gate and looked back down the huge river of the Triumph. Madorthene was with me. The Warmaster's retinue was just then beginning to pass under the Gate. Cymbals and horns clashed and blared. The noise of the crowd boomed in like a tidal wave surging down.

There were petals in the air. I remember that clearly. A blizzard of loose petals gusting up from the flowers the crowd was strewing.

A formation of twelve Lightnings was swooping in low from the south, coming down the length of the Triumph parade, following the Avenue of the Victor Bellum. Coming towards the Gate. They were in line abreast, the tips of their forward-swept wings almost touching. A display of perfect formation flying from the Battlefleet's best pilots. Sunlight glinted on their canopies and on the raked double-vanes of their tailplanes.

The sense of foreboding I had felt now became oppressively real. It was like heavy clouds had passed in front of the sun.

'Olm, I–'

'Emperor's mercy! He's in trouble, look!' Madorthene cried.

The fighters were half a kilometre from the Gate, moving at a high cruising speed. The left hand wingman suddenly wobbled, bucked...

...and veered.

The flier directly inside of him pulled hard to avoid a collision, and his starboard wing clipped the wingtip of the next Lightning in line. There was a bright puff of impact debris.

One by one, like pearls coming off a necklace, each aircraft was knocked out of the formation. The once-sleek line broke in utter disarray.

Madorthene hurled me to the ground as the jets shrieked overhead, rattling the world with their afterburners.

The two that I had seen strike each other were spinning in the air, somersaulting like discarded toys, splintering trails of metal scrap behind them. In the confusion, it seemed to me as if several others had also accidentally collided.

One Lightning, over ten tonnes of almost supersonic metal, cartwheeled down and went into the crowd on the west side of the Avenue. It bounced at least once, showering human debris into the air. At its final impact, it became a massive fireball that belched up a blazing mushroom cloud a hundred metres into the air. Shock and berserk panic filled the crowd. The stench of flame and heat and promethium washed over me.

There was a flash and the ground shook as a second stricken Lightning spiralled in under the shadow the Gate. Then, almost simultaneously, a third and louder blast came as a third aircraft, sent lurching out of control, sheared off a wing on the top corner of the Spatian Gate itself, right above us, and began tumbling down, end over end.

In the face of this calamitous accident, the soldiers in the Triumph were scattering in all directions. I dragged Madorthene back in under the arch as shattered chunks of the stricken aircraft avalanched down.

A catastrophe. A terrible, terrible catastrophe.

And it was just beginning.

SIX

DOOM COMES TO THRACIAN
CHAOS UNSLIPPED
HEADSHOT

Even at that stage, gripped by horror and outrage, I knew that a great hollow part of me deep in my soul could not, would not believe that this had simply been a tragic accident.

There were fire and explosions all around, mass panic, screaming.

And another sound. An extraordinary low moaning, a swelling, surging susurration that I realised was the sound two billion people make when they are panicking and in fear for their lives.

The crowds had spilled over onto the Avenue, quite beyond the measure of the Arbites to contain them, fleeing both the dreadful crash sites and the fires, and also the imagined risk that to stand still somehow invited more Imperial warcraft to fall upon their heads.

The crowd moved as one, a fluid thing, like water. There was no decision making process, no ringleader. Mass instinct simply compelled the people who swamped the vast street, in awful, trampling tides, overwhelming the ranks of the Triumph, much of which was already breaking up in shocked dismay. There was no sound of music any more, no cheering, no drums or sirens. Just a braying insanity, a world turned on its head.

I saw people die in their hundreds, trampled underfoot or crushed in the sheer press of bodies. In some cases, the dead were so squeezed by their neighbours, they were carried along for many metres before being freed to slither to the ground.

I saw troopers from the retinues, and Arbites, firing into the crowd in terror before they were run down. Barricades collapsed. Standards swayed and toppled. Walkways over the drain canals alongside the Avenue cracked and fell in, spilling hundreds down into the rockcrete trenches.

I'd lost sight of Madorthene in the pandemonium. I tried to push out from the arch into the sunlight, but fleeing bodies slammed into me. The entire approach to the Spatian Gate was a mass of twisted wreckage and fire from the impact high above. Several dozen Guardsmen lay twisted and dead amid the wreckage, killed by falling metal and stone, their dress uniforms dusted white with powdered aethercite or scorched by fire.

Through the sea of screaming humanity, I could see several of the massive aurochotheres stampeding out of control, rearing up, shaking their riders from their backs, trampling into the multitude. Lifeless bodies were tossed high into the air by their swishing tails.

I managed to slide along the outer edge of the gate until I could look north, towards the distant Monument of the Ecclesiarch. Right along the wide Avenue, the scene was repeated. The procession of the Triumph was overrun by the sheer numbers of the terrified public.

There was fire too, great plumes of it, rising from the crowd spaces on either side of the road in three places and on the Avenue of the Victor Bellum itself, about seven hundred metres beyond the Gate. It also seemed to me that fire also rose from other open areas beyond the next spire, off the roadway into the artisans' quarter. By my estimation, at least five more of the stricken Lightnings had fallen from the sky, ripping into the mass of the citizenry teeming in panic on the Avenue.

Soot and ash fogged the air. Distantly, above the milling nightmare of bodies, I could see the vast shapes of the Titans, turning on their metal hips, hesitant, as if utterly confused.

I doubt I saw the other Lightnings before anyone else. But I was transfixed. They were all I could see. There were four more of them, presumably the only survivors of the disastrous flyby. They had turned, and were sweeping back down the Avenue. Their formation was nothing like as precise or pretty as it had been just before the accident.

But they were much lower. And much faster.

And I knew what that meant, for I had seen it before.

An attack run.

Emperor spare me, my heart almost stopped as I saw the insane intention taking shape before me.

I screamed out something, but it was futile. One voice against two billion.

Streams of tracer rounds spat from the heavy cannons under their noses. Wing-mounted lascannons sparkled soundlessly.

Two went low over the crowd, slaughtering thousands. The other two followed the Avenue itself, raking the Great Triumph.

The destruction was extraordinary, as if invisible, white-hot ploughs had been set into the sea of bodies, slicing long, straight, explosive furrows out of the Imperial citizenry below. Or as if some fast-moving, burrowing force was scattering them from below. Stippled lines of explosions sawed through the populace, casting up both human and mechanical wreckage. There was an actual fog of liquefied tissue in the air. I saw tanks struck on the highway, detonating in the mob. Hundreds of Guarsdmen and Space Marines in the ruined cavalcade opened fire into the air, chasing the planes, churning the sky with bright, criss-crossed lines.

A Lightning swept by almost overhead, cutting to the left of the Spatian Gate. Its strafing firepower explosively mangled hundreds of people perilously close to me, showering me and the white stone of the Gate's side face with cooked blood.

Hundreds of batteries in the procession were now firing into the sky, the Hydras blitzing the air. Even tanks were firing – out of anger, I suppose, for they hadn't a hope in hell of hitting the fast-moving aircraft.

Yet something must have struck. A second Lightning tilted as it passed over the Gate, tiny explosions shredding its left wing and tail section. It dove straight down into the Avenue itself. It hit what seemed to me to be the heart of the Warmaster's section of the Triumph. The blast wake blew out across the wide roadway, killing as many with its concussive effects as with the impact fireball itself.

The three remaining Lightnings banked again down over the far end of the Avenue and made for a third pass. I was struck by the way they didn't turn as a pack. They flew individually, as if divorced from the world. Were their pilots possessed, insane? My mind span. Two of them banked into each other and almost hit. One didn't veer, and carried on up the Avenue, hungry for more carnage. The other was forced to swing wide, corrected, and turned over the wailing crowd mass to the west of the Avenue.

The third overshot and almost disappeared. I saw it loop faraway, out over the river haze, its wings glinting in the sun. Then it too came back for us. Like the others, straight back heedlessly into the teeth of the firestorms that the tanks, Hydras and infantry were throwing up at them.

Several hundreds more died in that final run. Loyal citizens whose exciting day out had turned to horror; proud Guardsmen back from the war, thinking only to enjoy this special hour of praise; mysterious Space Marines, who were there only because they had been invited to be there, as an expression of honour, who perhaps greeted this death as just an alternative to their expected fate. Imperial nobles and dignitaries died in their hundreds. Several noble households never recovered from the losses at the Triumph of Thracian.

The last three Lightnings fell in this manner.

One, crossing the Spatian Gate and beyond, was blown apart in an airburst by tracking Hydras on the chaotic street.

A second flew the gauntlet of anti-air salvos without adjusting its height and then, struck by one of the guns almost as an afterthought, turned upside down in a lazy yaw. Streaming smoke, it tilted down towards the ground but exploded against the Monument of the Ecclesiarch.

The third came in, guns chattering, and actually flew under the arch of the Spatian Gate. By then, the Titans themselves had turned to engage, and my guts convulsed with the subsonic roar of their weapons. I could see them, three kilometres away, weapon mounts pumping and flashing, high above the crowd.

Excelcis Gaude, one of the Warlord Titans, caught it dead on, and killed it in the air, but not cleanly enough. The tumbling Lightning, ablaze from end to end, hit the immense Warlord Titan square on and decapitated the colossus as it exploded.

I was lost. I was stupefied. I was speechless.

I felt as if I should fall to my knees amid the tumult and beg the God-Emperor of Mankind for salvation.

But my part in this was only just beginning.

Pellucid blue flame, like a searing wall of acid, suddenly washed through the churning mob behind the Gate. Men, women, soldiers, civilians, were caught in it and shuddered, melting, resolving into skeletons that turned to dust and blew away.

I felt the pain in my sinuses, the throb in my spine. I knew what it was.

Psyker-evil. Raw Chaos, loosed on this world.

The prisoners were loose.

The warriors did not matter. A vast pitched battle was already raging across the Avenue behind Spatian's broken Gate. The Thracian Guard, the Aurora Marines and the Arbites were striving to contain the outbreak of enemy prisoners, many of whom had taken the opportunity to break free and grab weapons. A ferocious, point-blank war had seized the great approach.

But what concerned me were the psykers. The captured heretics. The thirty-three. They had broken free.

I drew my power sword and my boltgun, plunging into the milling bodies, crunching over the calcified bones of those slaughtered by the psychic wave.

An inhuman thing, a Chaos prisoner, leapt at me, and I struck its head off with my blade. I leapt over a dead Space Marine, who was leaking blood onto the rockcrete from splits in his imperator armour, and pushed through the howling civilians.

Four Thracian Guardsmen were directly ahead of me, using the charred corpse of a fallen aurochothere for cover as they blasted into the press.

I was a few steps away from them when the gigantic dead animal reanimated, a psychic puppet, killing them all.

My weapons were useless. I focussed my mind and blew the thing apart with a concussive mental wave.

An Aurora Marine flew through the air over me, ten metres up, his legs missing.

I ran on, scything my blade at the escaped prisoners who menaced me.

The road was covered with the dead. Humans, on fire from head to foot, stumbled past me and collapsed on their faces.

The Trojan tractor team was on fire, its massive trailer slewed around. Three of the enemy pyskers lay dead on the payload space, and four void shields remained intact, their occupants frantic within.

But the others...

Upwards of twenty-five alpha-level enemy psykers had escaped.

I saw the first, a stumbling, emaciated wretch of a man, near the end of the trailer. Corposant flickered around his head and he was trying to eat a screaming astropath novitiate.

My boltgun stopped his daemonic work.

I dropped to my knees, gasping and crying as the second found me. She was a stringy female, clad in a gauzy white veil, her fingernails like talons.

She cowered behind the end of the trailer, sobbing and lashing out at me with her foul power. She had no eyes.

I am not alpha-class. My brain was broiling and bubbling.

A Thracian Guardsman ran at her from the left, and instinctively, she turned her attention to him. His head popped like a blister.

I shot her through the heart and knocked her flat on her back. Her limbs continued to thrash for over a minute.

Electrical discharge spat out at me from nearby in the crowd. People, screaming and burning, tumbled frantically back from a male psyker who was striding, head down, towards the hives. He was a dwarf, with stunted limbs and an enlarged cranium. Ball lightning crackled around his pudgy fingers.

I stabbed at him with my mind, just to get his attention and then exploded his face with a pin-point bolt.

Emperor save me, he kept coming. I had blown the front off his skull, but he kept coming. Blind, his features a gory mess. He stumbled across the ground towards me, his still-active mind boring into mine.

I fired again, almost panicking myself, and blew off one of his arms. Still he came on. My jacket, hair and eyelashes caught fire. My brain was about to explode out of my skull.

A Space Marine in the colours of the Aurora Chapter came at him from behind and shredded him into pulp with his boltgun.

'Inquisitor?' the Space Marine asked me, his voice distorted by his helmet mic. 'Are you all right?'

He helped me up.

'What insanity is this?' he rasped.

'You have a vox-channel? Alert Lord Orsini!'

'Already done, inquisitor,' he crackled.

Behind us, the tractors exploded en masse, flinging fire and debris high into the air.

A scalded child ran past us, shrieking.

The Space Marine grabbed the child in his massive arms.

'This way, this way, out of danger...'

'No,' I said slowly. 'Don't... don't...'

His visored face swung up at me in confusion, the child cradled in his arms.

'Don't what?' he asked.

'Look at the brand! The mark there!' I yelled, pointing to the Malleus rune burned into the child's ankle. The hammer of witches. The brand-mark of the psyker.

The Chaos child looked up at me and grinned.

'What mark?' asked the Space Marine. 'What mark are you talking about?'

'I... I...'

I tried to fight it, please know that. I tried to repel the unholy power of the child's mind as it groped into my head. But this thing, this 'child,' was far beyond my powers to contain.

Kill him, it said.

My hand was shaking, resisting, as I swung the boltgun around and shot the Space Marine through the head. A searing white agony flooded my horrified being.

Now kill yourself, it suggested, chortling.

I put the smoking muzzle of the boltgun against my own temple, my vision filled with the giggling face of the child, perched on the knee of the collapsed, headless Space Marine.

That's it... go on...

My finger tightened on the trigger.

'No... n-no...'

Yes, you stupid fool... yes...

Blood streamed out of my nose. I wanted to fall to my knees, but the monster wouldn't let me. It wanted me to do one thing, and one thing only. It implored me, ripping my consciousness apart.

It was strident and it was undeniable.

I pulled the trigger.

SEVEN

VOKE, AND SPECULATIONS
ESARHADDON
THROUGH THE VOID

But I did not die.

The boltgun, that gift from Librarian Brytnoth, which had never failed me in ten decades of use, failed to fire.

The child-thing shrieked and leapt away into the smoke and flames and struggling shapes around me. The dead Space Marine toppled over. The air frothed with psychic discharge and three figures ran past me in pursuit of the tiny abomination. Inquisitors. All three were inquisitors, or interrogators at least. One, I was sure, was Inquisitor Lyko.

I lowered my shaking hand. Both it, and the boltgun it clutched, were cased in psionic ice, the mechanism jammed and locked out.

I turned and found Commodus Voke standing a few paces behind me. His ancient face was contorted with internal pressure. Crusts of psipathetic frost glittered on his long black gown.

'Point. It. Aside.' His words came out as halting gasps. 'I. Cannot. Hold. It. Much. Longer.'

Swiftly, I turned the boltgun aside and up into the air. With a barking gasp, he convulsively relaxed and the weapon bucked and fired. The deadly round whined away harmlessly into the sky.

Voke was sagging, the gyros in the augmetic exo-skeleton that cradled his frail body straining to manage his balance. I gave him my hand in support.

'Thank you, Commodus.'

'No matter,' he said, his voice a whisper. His strength began to return and he peered up at me with his bird-bright eyes. 'Only a brave man or a fool tangles with a plus-alpha psyker.'

'Then I am both or neither. I was closest to the emergency. I could not just stand by.'

We were assailed by extraordinary noises from the charnel ground behind us. Gunfire, grenades, screams and the popping, surging sounds of minds fracturing reality, compressing matter, boiling atmosphere. I saw a robed man, an inquisitor or an astropath, rising slowly into the sky in a pillar of green fire, burning, shredding inside out. I saw geysers of blood like waterspouts. Squalls of hail and acid rain, localised to this small stretch of the Avenue, blustered across us, triggered by the ferocity of the psychic war.

Figures were rushing in to join that battle. Many from the Ordos with their expert bodyguards, and dozens of the Adeptus Astartes. There was a vibration underfoot, and I saw that one of the towering Warhound Titans was stalking past the Spatian Gate, spitting its turbo lasers at ground targets. A series of withering explosions, mainly psyker-blasts, tore through the habitats and hive structures on the eastern side of the wide - and now infamous - Avenue.

Imperial Marauders flashed low overhead. The sky was black with smoke, all sunlight blotted out. Wisps of ash fell on us like grey snow.

'This is... a great crime,' Voke said to me. 'A black day in the Imperial annals.'

I had forgotten how much Commodus Voke loved understatement.

The greater part of Hive Primaris remained lawless and out of control for five days. Panic, rioting, looting and civil unrest boiled through the streets and hab-levels of the wounded megapolis as the Arbites and the other organs of the Imperium struggled to impose martial law and restore order.

It was a desperate task. The indigenous population alone was vast, but it had been swelled to an unimaginable extent by pilgrims and tourists for the Novena. Sympathetic panic riots broke out in other hives too. For a day or two, it seemed like the entire planet was going to collapse in blood and fire.

Small sections of Hive Primaris had managed to insulate themselves: the elite spire levels; the noble houses, built like fortresses; the impregnable precincts of the Inquisition, the Imperial Guard, the Astropathicus, the various bastions of the Munitorum and the Royal Palace of the Lord Commander. Elsewhere, especially in the common and general hab levels, it was like a war zone.

The Ecclesiarchy suffered particularly gravely. With the Monument of the Ecclesiarch in flames, the common masses regarded the nightmare as some holy curse, and turned in their frenzy on all the churches, temples and sacerdotal orders they could find. We learned within the first few hours that Cardinal Palatine Anderucias had been killed in the destruction of the Monument. He was far from the only great hierarch to perish in the orgy of carnage that followed.

The recapture or extermination of the remaining rogue psykers was the first and most fundamental task facing the authorities. Ten were known to have escaped the initial battle on the Avenue of the Victor Bellum, and these had fled into the hive, sowing carnage as they went, hunted by the forces of the Inquisition and all the Imperial might that could be brought to bear in support.

Two of them made it only a kilometre or two from the route of the procession, hounded every step by Imperial forces from the Avenue battle, and were neutralised by nightfall on that terrible first day. Another went to ground in a vegetable cannery in an eastern sector outhab, and was laid to siege. It cost three days and the lives of eight hundred Imperial Guardsmen, sixty-two astropaths, two Space Marines and six inquisitors to blast it out and burn it. The cannery, and the outhab for three square kilometres around it, was flattened.

There was little or no central control for our forces. Admiral Oetron, who had remained with the orbiting battlefleet as watch commander, managed to move four picket ships into geo-synchronous orbit above Hive Primaris, and for a while succeeded in providing comprehensive vox and astropathic communications for the ground forces. But by nightfall on the first day, psychic storms had blown up across the hive and all relayed reception was lost.

It was a dark and frightening period. Down in the burning streets, we sub-divided as best we could into small units, functioning autonomously. Simply by dint of being with Voke, I became part of a group that made its headquarters in an Arbites section house on Blammerside Street in the mercantile district. Desperate groups of citizens flocked to us, craving aid and mercy and sanctuary, and much larger gangs attacked the section house time and again, driven by fear, by rage against the Imperial machine or simply because we wouldn't let them in.

We couldn't. We were overflowing with injured and dead, far too many for the Arbites surgeons and morgue attendants to manage. There was very little food, medical supplies or ammunition left, and we were also rationing water as the mains supply had been cut.

The power was down too, but the section house had its own generator.

All through the night, bottles and missiles and promethium bombs splintered off the shielded windows, and fists pounded on the doors.

By merit of his seniority, Voke was in command. Aside from myself, there was Inquisitor Roban, Inquisitor Yelena, Inquisitor Essidari, twenty interrogators and junior servants of the Inquisition, sixty troopers from the Interior Guard, several dozen astropaths and four White Consul Space Marines. The Arbites themselves numbered around one hundred and fifty, and the section house was also sheltering about three hundred nobles, ecclesiarchs and dignitaries from the Great Triumph, as well as a few hundred common citizens.

I remember standing alone in a ransacked office of the Arbites commander just after midnight, looking out through shielded windows at the burning streets and the blossoms of psyker storm that were wrenching the sky apart. I had received no word or sign of Ravenor since the catastrophe had begun. I remember my hands were shaking even then.

In truth, I believe I was in shock. From the event itself, naturally, and also from the psychic assaults I had suffered in the course of it. I pride myself on a sharp mind, but there was no sharpness to me then.

Numb, my brain kept returning to the idea that this outrage had been deliberate.

'There is no question,' Voke said from behind me, clearly reading my surface thoughts without my permission. He lifted and straightened a steel chair and sat down on it.

'Accidents happen, warplanes crash!' he cried. 'But these turned and attacked. Their assaults were deliberate.'

I nodded. At least one of the Lightnings had crashed into the Warmaster's entourage and another had come down amongst the files of the Inquisition. No one yet knew how many of my institution had been slain, but Voke had seen enough of it to know that as many as two hundred of our fellow inquisitors had been obliterated.

I remembered the conversation that had turned around my dining table, the speculations about those powerful forces who would oppose Honorius's bestowment.

'Is this the first act in a House war?' I said. 'The Ecclesiarchy, or perhaps great dynasties, trying to thwart Lord Commander Helican's advancement of the Warmaster? His elevation to Feudal Protector would not have been popular with many, powerful factions.'

'No,' he said. 'Though I'm sure that's what many will think. What many will be supposed to think.'

Voke looked at me intently. 'Freeing the psykers was the point,' he said. 'There is no other explanation. The Archenemy struck to cause mayhem and allow the prisoners to escape, and to wound the section of the parade that was most able to contain their escape.'

'I won't argue with that in principle. But was freeing the psykers the point itself, or simply a means to an end?'

'How so?'

'Was it an attempt to liberate the psykers... or was this just an act of extreme violence against the Imperium that the release of dangerous psykers was meant to exacerbate?'

'Until we know what was behind it, we can't answer that.'

'Could the psykers themselves have done it? Manipulated the minds of the pilots?'

He shrugged. 'We can't know that either. Not yet. The Warmaster might have been guilty of bravado in displaying his prisoners, but he would have made certain security around them was seamless. I must suspect an outside hand.'

We said nothing for a moment. Honorius Magnus himself had barely survived the crash-blast and was undergoing emergency surgery aboard a medical frigate at the Navy-yard. No one yet knew if Lord Commander Helican was alive. If he was dead, or if the Warmaster died of his injuries, then Chaos would have won a historic victory.

'I suspect an outside hand too,' I told Voke. 'Perhaps another psyker or psykers, trailing their colleagues here to stage an escape.'

He pursed his lipless mouth. 'The greatest triumph of my life, Gregor, capturing those monsters in the name of the Emperor... and look what it becomes.'

'You can't blame yourself for this, Commodus.'

'Can I not?' He squinted at me. 'In my place, how would you feel?'

I shrugged. 'I will make amends. I will not rest until every one of these wretches is destroyed, and order restored. And then I will not rest until I find who and what was behind it.'

He stared at me for a long time.

'What?' I asked, though I had a feeling I knew what was coming.

'You... you were close to the scene, as you said to me. Closer than many, and shielded from the worst of the destruction by the bulk of the Spatian Gate.'

'And?'

'You know what I want to ask you.'

'You thought you'd start with me. I'm too tired, Voke. I stopped to honour the admiral's tomb.'

He raised one eyebrow, as if he sensed I didn't really believe it myself. But at least he did me the courtesy of not ripping into my mind with his much more powerful psychic abilities to scour out what truth might be there. We had reached an understanding through our encounters over the years, and were now even when it came to owing each other our lives.

He knew me well enough not to press this.

Not now, at least.

An interrogator hurried into the room.

'Sirs,' she said. 'Inquisitor Roban wishes you to know that we have made contact with one of the heretics.'

As far as could be learned, the rogue was an alpha-plus psyker called Esarhaddon, one of the leaders of the coven. Sowing tumult and woe in his wake, he had fled into the hive with a group led by Lyko and Heldane in pursuit. Heldane had managed to contact one of Voke's astropaths with a scrambled summons for help.

Voke, Roban and I headed out into the hive streets with a kill team of sixty that included the four White Consuls. Their squad leader was a particularly large sergeant called Kurvel. We travelled on foot through the debris and smoke. Gangs of citizens jeered and pelted missiles at us, but the sight of four terrible Space Marines kept them at bay.

Esarhaddon, Voke warned me, was a being of dreadful intellect and not to be underestimated. When we saw the monster's choice of bolt-hole, I understood what Voke meant.

The noble family of Lange was prominent in the aristocracy of Thracian Primaris, and kept an ample summer palace in the east sector of Hive Primaris, near to the mercantile quarter where they had made their fortunes.

The palace rose proud of the lowhab streets around it, swathed in its own force bubble.

This had been one of the city areas we had supposed to be secure. With their power and resources, noble houses should have been able to protect themselves for the duration of the unrest.

But not against Esarhaddon. He was inside, with all the resources of the palace to protect him.

We met Heldane on the western approach road to the palace. He had a team of about twenty with him. The street itself was littered with bodies, most of them citizens.

'He's controlling the crowds as if they were puppets,' Heldane said curtly, with no word of greeting. 'Waves of them keep coming at us, preventing us getting to the garden walls and the servants' annex along there.'

As I may have said, I had little time for Inquisitor Heldane. A very tall, grim man, his face an unsightly mass of scar tissue since an encounter with a hungry carnodon back on Gudrun. He'd been Voke's pupil when I had first met him; now he was a full inquisitor, with mental powers, it was said, that exceeded even his old master's. As I saw him there, I shuddered. He had undergone extensive surgery, not to disguise the damage to his face, but to exaggerate it. His skull seemed to have been extended into an almost equine shape, with a snout-like mouth full of blunt teeth, and dark, murky eyes. Fibre-wires and fluid tubes braided his cranium in place of hair. He wore plasteel body armour the colour of blood and carried a segmented power glaive.

'Eisenhorn,' he nodded, noticing me. It was like having a warhorse shake its head in my direction.

'They're coming again!' The cry went up from Heldane's men. Down the street, moving through the fire spills, figures were lurching towards us.

Weapons! Stand ready! Heldane had spoken, but not with his voice. His psychic command shook through our skulls and some of our own troopers looked dismayed.

Missiles rained down on us, and the Interior Guardsmen raised an umbrella of riot shields. Small arms fired at us too, and an Arbites near me fell with his knee buckled the wrong way.

Our attackers, some hundred or more, were hive citizens, blank faced and moving like marionettes. As Heldane had reported, some monumental psychic force was making puppets out of them. The smoky night air ionised with the psionic backwash.

I take no pleasure in actions like the one that followed. The beast Esarhaddon was forcing us to fight innocent civilians just to protect ourselves.

Maybe he thought we'd shrink from the task and leave him alone.

We, however, were the Inquisition.

Kurvel led his White Consuls at the front, banging their weapons against their chest-plates and howling defiance through their helmet speakers. I saw a promethium bomb strike one and shatter, swathing him in liquid flame. He simply strode on.

We fired over the mob's heads, trying to break them, but they had no will of their own. Our firing became kill-shots. In ten minutes, we had reluctantly added a fair number to the planet's rising death toll.

That brought us to the corner of the street, facing the high walls of the garden and the edge of the palace's iridescent force shield itself.

I could hear a low chuckling in my head.

Esarhaddon.

Where's Lyko? I heard Voke ask Heldane psychically.

He took a team around the front to try and disable the force wall.

'You idiot!' I said, out loud, looking over at Heldane. 'This monster can control a crowd that big and you mind-speak this close to him?'

'This monster,' Heldane replied, 'can read every mind in the city and beyond. He knows what we're all doing. There is no point in secrecy. Just effort. Is that beyond you?'

'How long until the next attack?' Kurvel asked, reloading his weapon.

'They've become less frequent since we first arrived,' replied Heldane. 'However long it takes Esarhaddon to mind-search the surrounding habs and recruit another puppet force. He's having to cast his net wider each time.'

'How did he get in there?' Roban asked.

Heldane simply shook his head and shrugged. Roban, a robust inquisitor of middle years dressed in brown and yellow layered robes, was a good man, though I didn't know him well. But he was an outspoken Xanthanite and the ultra-puritan Heldane had little time for him.

Voke and Heldane fell to discussing possible assault plans with Kurvel as the soldiers around us formed a defensive position.

'This is a damned thankless task,' Roban said to me. 'I don't even know why we're here!'

'Cannon fodder,' said his youthful interrogator, Inshabel, bluntly, and it made us both laugh.

'There has to be something...' I said. I took out my pocket scope and tried to read the energy patterns and spectrums.

'You!' I called to one of the Arbites in our party, a grizzled precinct commander in full riot gear.

'Inquisitor?'

'What's your name?'

'Luclus, sir.'

'Dear God-Emperor!' I sighed again and Roban laughed once more.

'Okay, Luckless – this palace must come into your precinct's patrol area.'

'Yes, sir.'

'So street security around it is your responsibility.'

'Again, yes sir.'

'So... just as a matter of procedure, your section house will have on file the shield type and harmonics for the palace, in case of emergencies.' In my experience, it was standard protocol for any Arbites precinct to know such things about key structures within their purview.

'It's classified, sir.'

'Of course it is,' I sighed again. 'But now would be a good time...'

He got on his vox-link and after a lot of effort, managed to get a channel open to the section house.

'You're on to something, aren't you?' Roban asked me.

'Maybe.'

'The wily Inquisitor Eisenhorn–'

'The what?'

'No offence. Your reputation precedes you.'

'Does it now? In a good way?'

Roban grinned and shook his head, like a man who might have heard something, but who had decided to make up his own mind.

'It's an old type-ten conical void,' Arbites Commander Luclus reported presently. 'Tangent eight-seven-eight harmonic wave. We don't have an override code. Lady Lange wouldn't permit it.'

'I bet she wishes she had now,' said Interrogator Inshabel, caustic and to the point once again. I was beginning to like him.

'Thank you, Luckless,' I said.

'It's... Luclus, sir.'

'I know.'

I tried to remember everything Aemos had counselled me about shields over the years. I wished I had his recall. Better still, I wished I had him here.

'We can collapse it,' I said, with fair confidence.

'Collapse a void shield?' Roban asked.

'It's conical... super-surface only. And it's old. Voids shrug off just about anything, but they don't retain their field if you take out one or more of the projectors.

'That buttress there, the one the garden wall is built around, that's got to be one of the projector units, seated down into the ground.'

Roban nodded, apparently impressed. 'I see the logic, but not the practice.'

I walked over to Brother-Sergeant Kurvel, interrupting his conversation with Heldane without apology, and explained what I wanted to do.

Heldane scoffed at once. 'Lyko's already trying that!'

'How?'

'He's located the outer controls at the front gate and is trying to break their coding...'

'Coding and controls that will be dead and locked out thanks to Esarhaddon. Lyko's wasting his time. We can't switch this off. We can't break Esarhaddon's control over its system. But we can undermine the system itself.'

Heldane was about to speak again, but Voke shut him up.

'I think Gregor may be on to something.'

'Why?'

Voke pointed. Close to five hundred citizens were now advancing towards us from streets on all sides.

'Because as you pointed out, Heldane, the monster can hear us, and he clearly doesn't like the sound of this plan.'

It took Kurvel about ten minutes to gouge out the pavement and a section of garden wall with his lightning claw, and all the while we were under attack from the growing mob of puppets.

'Sewer!' Kurvel announced.

I turned to the others as shots and missiles rained down. 'Commodus... you have to hold them off a while longer.'

'Count on it,' he said.

'Roban, get a small squad and follow me.'

Heldane wasn't happy. But by then, Heldane wasn't calling the shots any more. I believe he took his rage out on the enslaved citizens.

I dropped into the sewer hole with Kurvel, Roban, Inshabel and three troopers of the Interior Guard. The defence on the street above could barely spare any of them.

The filthy sewer tube went in under the wall itself before dropping sharply away. Old, patched stone swelled around the base of the buttress. The stone was warm, and foamy clumps of fungus were growing on it.

Inshabel trained a spotbeam in so I could see.

Kurvel could see in the dark. He took out his last two krak grenades and fixed them to the stonework with smears of adhesive paste from a tube he carried in his pack.

'I wish we had more. We could blow the wall right through.'

'We could, brother-sergeant, but this might be better.'

'Why?'

'Because if we can simply make this projector fail, the energies of the shield will short out before they collapse. Rather than blowing outwards, that'll cause an electromagnetic pulse within the field itself. And I think an EM pulse is the last thing Esarhaddon wants right now.'

As if to prove my suspicions right, a stabbing sheet of psychic power lashed at us. Esarhaddon had realised his vulnerability, and was turning his immense power on us now. The puppets had been sport, but now it was time to control or blast out the minds of his hunters before they stopped being playthings and became a danger.

The psyker attack was devastating. Two of the Interior Guardsmen simply died. Another started firing, hitting Kurvel twice and wounding Inshabel. Regretfully, Roban blasted the trooper down with his laspistol.

Our minds were harder to attack, especially given the shield formed by the rock above us and our proximity to the energy flux of the shield.

But Roban, Inshabel, Kurvel and I would be dead or homicidal in seconds.

How I wished for Alizebeth, or any of the Distaff right then.

'Trigger it! Trigger it!' I gasped, the blood vessels in my nose and throat opening yet again that day.

'We're right on top of the–'

'Just do it, brother-sergeant! In the name of the God-Emperor!'

The blast took out the projector. It filled the sewer tunnel with flickering destruction. It would have killed us but for the fact that Brother-Sergeant Kurvel shielded us with his massive armoured body.

It cost him his life.

I have made a point to have his name and memory celebrated by the White Consuls.

With the generating projector killed, the void shield collapsed in on itself, blacking out the palace systems with the thunderclap of electromagnetic rage.

Blacking out Esarhaddon's seething mind too.

My research into untouchables, through Alizebeth and then through the Distaff she created and ran, had indicated to me that perhaps psychic power, no matter how potent, relied in the final analysis on the electrical workings of the human mind, the firing of impulse charges between synapses. Untouchables somehow blanked this, and triggered a disturbing and disarming vacancy in the natural and fundamental processes of the human brain. That, I had initially concluded, was why psykers don't work around untouchables... and why forgetfulness and unease is prevalent in their company. And, ultimately, why they disturb and upset humans so, and psykers doubly so.

I'd turned the old void shield into a brief, bright untouchable event.

And now, Emperor damn him, the heretic psyker Esarhaddon, temporarily rendered deaf, blind and mute, was mine.

EIGHT

ESARHADDON'S LAIR
LYKO THE VICTOR
A VESTIGE

We went into the grounds of the Lange palace over the wall. There was a harsh stink of ozone from the ruptured shield, and the trimmed fruit trees and laraebur hedges of the gardens were singed and smouldering.

With Roban and Inshabel, I ran down a flint-chip path between the servants' wing and the east portico. Flashlights and under-muzzle torches bobbed in the gardens behind us as Heldane led the main force of our troop round to the garden terrace.

The house was dead and dark, all power killed by the pulse. The main doors on the east portico lay splintered on the mosaic floor where the accompanying wave of overpressure from the void collapse had blown them in. All of the windows were smashed holes too.

Photo-receptors and climate controls in the portico's polished bluewood panels were fused and charred. Smoke and the glow of flames issued from deeper in the palace.

We pushed further in, finding dead house staff and inert servitors. A whole suite of state rooms on the first floor was burning where ornate promethium lamps had been knocked over.

We checked the rooms on each side as we progressed. Roban led the way, sweeping his braced laspistol from side to side.

'How long?' Inshabel asked me.

'Until?'

'Until he recovers from the pulse?'

I didn't know. There was no telling how badly we'd hurt Esarhaddon, or how resilient his mind was. We hadn't got long.

On the second floor, a flight of aethercite steps brought us up into a grand banqueting hall. The roof, a turtleback of toughened glass, had fallen in and the psi-storms crackled and surged in the sky far above. Every step crunched glass or disturbed debris.

There were bodies here too, the bodies of nobility and servants intermingled.

I heard movement and sobbing from an adjoining antechamber.

The wretched occupants of the room gasped in terror as our flashlights found them. A handful of survivors from the household, cowering in fear in the dark. Many displayed signs of psychic burns or telekinetic welts.

'Imperial Inquisition,' I said firmly but quietly. 'Stay calm. Where is Esarhaddon?'

Some flinched or moaned at the sound of the name. A regal dowager in a torn pearlescent gown curled up in the corner and began weeping.

'Quickly... there's little time! Where is he?' I thought to use my will to spur them into an answer, but their minds had been tortured enough already that night. Even a mild mental probe might kill some of them.

'W-when the lights went out, he ran... ran towards the west exit,' said a blood-soaked man dressed in what I presumed was the uniform of the House Lange bodyguard.

'Can you show us?'

'My leg's broken...'

'Someone else then! Please!'

'Frewa... you go. Frewa!' The bodyguard gestured to a terrified page boy crouching behind a column.

'Come on, lad, show us the way,' Roban said encouragingly.

The boy got to his feet, his eyes white with fear. I wasn't sure if he was more afraid of Esarhaddon or the inquisitors looming over him.

A communicating hallway ran from the rear of the banquet hall west towards the house's private landing platform. Specks of blood and glass twinkled along its tiled floor.

I felt what seemed to me a breath of wind on my skin. An exit to the outside, perhaps?

Heavy blast shutters were prised open in the entrance to the gloomy loading dock. Past the shadowy shapes of several slumped, dormant cargo servitors, stood a main hatchway through which cold exterior light flickered.

My weapon raised, I waved Roban and Inshabel round to the right. The page boy cowered back in the doorway. The air quality was changing, as if the atmosphere itself was stiffening and drawing tight. Like some great force gathering its breath.

Esarhaddon was recovering, I was certain.

Livid green light suddenly bathed the loading dock, a psychometric flare accompanying a burst of savage psionic power. Roban and I staggered, our lungs squeezed and fingers of telekinesis thrusting at our minds. Inshabel cried out as he was bowled over from behind by the page boy, Frewa. Dull-eyed and frothing at the mouth, the boy had been reduced, in an instant, to a mindless puppet. Inshabel fought, but the boy was feral, and despite the interrogator's superior bulk he was pinned.

The pain in my head was intense, but I knew Esarhaddon must still be way below full strength. I raised the strongest mind shield my abilities were able to conjure and moved forward.

There was a sudden grind of servo-gears. A large steel paw swung at my head and I dived back.

A cargo servitor, its metal carapace caked with verdigris, rose up to its full height of three metres and clanked across the deck towards me on squat hydraulic legs. Plumes of steam squirted from its broad shoulder joints as it pistoned its arms at me again. Hot yellow dots of light burned in the eye sockets of its dented visor.

Despite its mechanical appearance, the cargo drone, like all servitors, was built around human organic components: brain, brain-stem, neural network, glands so Esarhaddon could control it just like a standard human.

It swung at me again, and missed. The slicing limb had cut the air with a distinct whistle.

It was built like a great simian: squat legs, barrel chest, wide shoulders and long, thick arms. Ideal for hefting heavy cargo items into the belly-hold of a liftship.

Ideal for smashing a human body into gory paste.

Roban cried out a warning. A second, larger cargo servitor with a long quadruped body, was also moving. Its body casing was pitted, brown metal and it had a fork-lifter assembly where its head should have been, giving it the appearance of a bull. The greased black forks of the lifter lurched at Roban, who fired six or seven shots that dented or bounced off the machine's chassis.

I ducked two more slow, heavy blows from the ape-servitor. We were losing precious time. With every tick of the clock, Esarhaddon was recovering and becoming more powerful.

I put a bolt round into the thickest part of the servitor's body and rocked it back, the gears and pistons of its legs whining as they compensated for the recoil.

My power sword was out now, the blade burning. Blessed for me by the Provost of Inx, it was my weapon of choice. My swordsmanship had always been good, but Arianrhod had instructed me in the Carthaen *Ewl Wyla Scryi* before her death. *Ewl Wyla Scryi*, literally, 'the genius of sharpness', the Carthaen way of the sword.

I made a figure of eight turn, the *ghan fasl*, and then a back-hand crosscut, the *uin* or reverse form of the *tahn wyla*.

The stroke was good. The energised blade sliced clean through the servitor's left forearm, sending the massive manipulator paw clattering to the deck.

It lurched bodily at me, as if enraged, clawing with its remaining hand and lashing with the fused, smoking end of its recently truncated limb.

I made a head-height horizontal parry called the *uwe sar*, and then left and right block strokes, the *ulsar* and the *uin ulsar*. Sheets of sparks cascaded from each hit against its metal body. I ducked right under the next huge blow, spun round out of the crouch and came up to face it again in time to follow through with the *ura wyla bei*, the devastating diagonal downslash, left to right. My blade edge and tip sawed the servitor's torso plating wide open in an electrical flash.

The exchange had given me long enough to mentally identify the seat of the servitor's brain-stem component, lit up and glowing in my mind's eye with the psionic power that drove it. It lay deep under the carapace between the collar bones.

One more *uwe sar* and then the *ewl caer*, the deathstroke. Tip first, plunging clean through the bodywork, impaling the organic brain. I rested the crackling blade there for a moment while the yellow dot eyes went out and then ripped it clear again, sidestepping as the servitor slammed down onto the flooring.

'Roban!' I called out, leaping over my despatched foe.

But Roban was dead. The servitor's forks had his limp body impaled through the belly and it was shaking it as if trying to dislodge him.

Inshabel was on his feet, tears streaming down his face as he blasted at the servitor with his autogun.

Cursing, I ran forward, raised the power sword with both hands and swung it down over the servitor's back. I doubt the Carthaens, in all their wisdom, have a name in the most hallowed *Ewl Wyla Scryi* for an enraged downstroke that severs the backbone and torso of a servitor.

Inshabel ran to his dead master as the servitor collapsed, trying to pull the corpse clear.

'Later! Later for that!' I said, spiking the command with my will. Inshabel was close to losing his wits to anger and grief, and I needed him.

He snatched up his weapon and ran after me.

'The page boy?' I asked.

'I had to hit him. I hope he's just unconscious.'

We came out into the storm-wracked night on the palace landing pad. Psychic lightning splintered the sky above us and the wind lashed us. There was no one on the pad itself, but a fight was raging on the lawns beyond. I could see eight figures, some robed, some dressed in the body armour of the Interior Guard, closing to surrounding a lone humanoid who crackled and glowed with spectral light. Thorny jags of flame lit out from the cornered figure and dropped one of the Guardsmen as we watched.

Esarhaddon. They had Esarhaddon cornered.

Inshabel and I leapt down from the pad - a three metre drop onto the wet grass - and ran to join the fray.

I could see Esarhaddon clearly now despite the rain. A tall, almost naked man with wild black hair and a lean, stringy body, corposant gleaming and sliding around his capering limbs.

We were just ten metres from the edge of the fight when one of the robed figures raised a bulky weapon and blasted at the rogue psyker.

A plasma gun.

The violet beam, almost too bright to look at, struck Esarhaddon. In his weakened state, he had no defence against it.

He ignited like an incendiary round and burned from head to foot in the middle of the lawn.

Lowering our weapons, Inshabel and I walked to join the ring of figures standing around the white hot pyre. As his robed and hooded acolytes murmured prayers of grace and deliverance, Inquisitor Lyko set down his plasma gun.

'The Emperor will thank you, Lyko,' I said.

He glanced round, seeing me for the first time. 'Eisenhorn.' He nodded. His narrow face was lined and taut and his blue eyes hooded. He was only about fifty years old sidereal, a mere youth by inquisitional standards. Young enough for his promising career to survive the way this day's atrocity would tarnish his achievement on Dolsene.

'I do not serve the Emperor for his gratitude. I do it for the glory of the Imperium.'

'Quite so,' I said. I looked back at the molten heat that had been our quarry. It mattered little to me that I'd made this opportunity for Lyko. He could take the glory. I didn't care. The escape of the psykers had stolen much of the glory he had received of late. Hunting them down was the only way he could make amends.

Planetwide, there was some sense of rejoicing when it was announced that Lord Commander Helican had survived the carnage unscathed, and that Warmaster Honorius would live. That announcement came on the sixth day of unrest, by which time the Imperial authorities had begun to reimpose order on the stricken citizens of Thracian Primaris. But it helped. Common folk who assumed themselves to be lost were calmed into believing law was back in the hands of the great and good. Panics died away. Arbites units unleashed their last few suppression raids against the die-hard recidivist looters in the lowhabs.

My own spirits were not much lifted. For a start I was privy to the confidential fact that Lord Commander Helican had actually died screaming and shitting himself under a crash-diving Imperial Navy Lightning on the Avenue of the Victor Bellum. A double had been arranged by the Ecclesiarchy and the Helican Senatorum, and that double continued to act in his place until, several years later, he 'died naturally of old age' and a successor was established in less-turbulent circumstances.

I can speak of that public deceit now in this private record, but at the time, communicating that secret was a death-crime for even the highest lord of the Imperium. I was not about to break that confidence. I am an inquisitor and I understand how fundamental it is to maintain public order.

In addition to fatigue and the pain of my wounds, what darkened my mood was the news about Gideon Ravenor. Now, of course, we all understand what a priceless and brilliant contribution he was to make to Imperial learning, and how that would never have happened if he had not been confined to a life of mental rumination.

But back then, in that stinking hospice ward off the Street of Prescients, all I saw was a young man, burned and crippled and physically paralysed, a brilliant inquisitor ruined before he could fulfill his potential.

Ravenor, in the eyes of some, had been lucky. He had not been amongst the one hundred and ninety-eight Inquisition personnel killed outright by the crashing fighter that fell into the Great Triumph beyond the Spatian Gate.

He, like fifty others, had been caught on the edge of the explosion and lived.

My pupil was barely recognisable. A blood-wet bundle of charred flesh. One hundred per cent burns. Blind, deaf, mute, his face so melted that an incision had been made in the fused meat where his mouth should have been so he could breathe.

The loss touched me acutely. The waste even more. Gideon Ravenor had been the greatest, most promising pupil I had ever taught. I stood by his plastic-sheeted cot, listening to the suck and drool of his ventilator and fluid drains and remembered what Commodus Voke had said in the Arbites sector house on Blammerside Street.

'I will make amends. I will not rest until every one of these wretches is destroyed and order restored. And then I will not rest until I find who and what was behind it.'

Right then, there, for Ravenor's sake, I made that promise to myself too.

At that time, I had little idea what that would mean or where it would take me.

I returned to the Ocean House at last on what would have been the ninth and final day of the Holy Novena. There was no one to greet me, and the place seemed empty and forlorn.

I stalked into my study, poured a too-large measure of vintage amasec and flopped down into an armchair. It felt like an eternity since I had sat here with Titus Endor, worrying over speculations that seemed now so insignificant and remote.

A door opened. From the instant chill in the air, I knew at once it was Bequin.

'We didn't know you'd returned, Gregor.'

'Well, I have, Alizebeth.'

'So I see. Are you alright?'

I shrugged. 'Where is everybody?'

'When the...' she paused, considering her words. 'When the tragedy occurred, there was a great public commotion. Jarat and Kircher took the staff into the secure bunkers for safety, and I locked myself away with the Distaff in the west wing, waiting, hoping for your call.'

'Channels were out.'

'Yes. For eight days.'

'But everyone is safe?'

'Yes.'

I leaned out of my chair and looked at her. Her face was pale and drawn from too many nights of fear.

'Where's Aemos?'

'Outside, with Betancore, Kircher and Nayl. Von Baigg's around too. Is... is it true what we've heard about Gideon?'

'Alizebeth... it's...'

She crouched down and put her arms around me. It is difficult for a psyker to be hugged by an untouchable, no matter how long and close their personal history. But her intentions were good, and I tolerated the contact for as long as seemed polite. When I gently pushed her back, I said, 'Send them in. In fact, send everyone in here.'

'They won't all fit, Gregor.'

'The sea terrace, then. One last time.'

Sitting or standing around in the lime glow of the sea terrace, the numerous members of my faithful band looked at me expectantly. The place was packed. Jarat had fussed around, bringing out drinks and sweetmeats until I had pressed a glass of amasec into her gnarled hands and forced her down into a chair.

'I'm closing the Ocean House,' I said.

There was a murmur.

'I'm retaining the lease, but I have little wish to live here any more. In fact, I have little wish to be on Thracian any more. Not after this... Holy Novena. There seems no point maintaining a staff here.'

'But, sir, the library?' Psullus said from the back.

I held up a finger.

'I will take up a contract arrangement with one of the hive accommodation bureaux to keep the house in working order with servitors. Who knows, sometime I might have need of a place here again.'

I refilled my glass before turning back.

'But I wish to move my centre of operations. It's compromised, if nothing else.'

At that, Jubal Kircher looked into his cit-juice uncomfortably.

'I wish to relocate the household to the estate on Gudrun. Its environment suits me better than this... hive-hell. Jarat, you and Kircher will supervise the packing and organisation for the move. I would like you to undertake the duties of head of household at the Gudrun estate, if you are willing. I realise you have never been off Thracian.'

She sat forward, her eyebrows raised, considering this sudden change to her life. 'I... I would be honoured to do so, sir,' she said.

'I'm pleased. The country air will do you good. The estate is managed by a caretaker staff, so I'll need a good housekeeper, and a good chief of house security. Jubal... I'd like you to consider that job.'

'Thank you, sir,' said Kircher.

'Psullus... we're going to transplant the library permanently to Gudrun. That task is yours, as is the ongoing duty of being my librarian. Can I entrust you with it?'

'Oh, yes... there will be problems, of course, the handling and care of certain shielded texts and–'

'But I can leave it with you?'

Psullus waved his frail hands at me in a gesture of excitement that made everyone laugh.

'I know this wholesale move will take months to manage and carry out. Alain... I'd like you to supervise and oversee the whole thing.'

Von Baigg looked suddenly awkward. 'Of – of course, inquisitor.'

'This is a weighty task, interrogator. Are you up to it?'

'Yes, sir.'

'Good. I will return to the Gudrun estate no later than ten months from now. I trust it will be the home I expect.'

It was a promise I would fail miserably to keep.

'What of the Distaff, sir?' asked Surskova.

'I want to divide that,' I said. 'I want six of the best Distaff members sent to Gudrun to bide there at my wishes. The future of the Distaff itself I see as separate from my living arrangements. I have a lease on a spire-top residence on Messina. That will be the new official home of the Distaff. Surskova, you will supervise the move and establishment of the untouchable school there.'

She nodded, shocked. Bequin seemed taken aback.

I looked round at the hundred-plus servants, warriors and aides crammed into the room.

'That's it. Until I see you all again, may the God-Emperor protect you.'

I was left alone with Aemos, Bequin, Medea and Nayl.

'Not for us the chores of moving house,' I said.

'I had a hunch not,' smirked Medea.

'For us, two missions.'

'For us?' asked Bequin.

'Yes, Alizebeth. Unless you think you and I are too old for such diversions?'

'No, I– I–'

'I've been too long at the back of things. Too long relying on my capable staff. I yearn for field work.'

'The last field work we were in nearly got you killed,' scolded Bequin darkly.

'Proving that I'm losing my edge, I think.'

'For shame!' muttered Nayl with a smile.

'So we're going to have an adventure, all of us. Just the few of us. Remember what those were like, Aemos?'

'Frankly, I'm still not over them, Gregor, but yes.'

'Alizebeth?'

Bequin crossed her arms ill-humouredly. 'Oh, I'd just love to come and watch you get killed...'

'We're all agreed, then?' I said. I can't help being deadpan. Gorgone Locke made sure of that. But my delivery was good enough to get Nayl and Medea raucous with laughter and Aemos chuckling.

Alizebeth Bequin grinned despite herself.

'Two missions, as I said. After this briefing, I'll allow you to recruit a few personnel from the staff. Nayl – a fighter or two you can count on. Aemos – an astropath we can use without worry. Alizebeth – one or two from the Distaff. A maximum of ten in the party, all told. No more, you understand? Argue it out between yourselves. Don't bring me into it. We leave in two days, and I don't want to even hear about any arguments second hand.'

'So what are the missions?' asked Medea, lounging back in her padded chair and slipping her long legs over the arm. She took a long swig of her weedwine and added, 'You said two, right?'

'Two.'

I pushed a stud on a data wand in my hand and a hololithic screen fogged into life over the table. The words of the message I'd received before the start of the tumult on Thracian were displayed in shimmering letters: 'Scalpel cuts quickly, eager tongues revealed. At Cadia, by terce. Hound wishes Thorn. Thorn should be sharp.'

'Shit!' cried Nayl.

'Is that authentic?' Medea asked, looking at me.

'It is.'

'God-Emperor, he's in trouble, he needs us...' Bequin murmured.

'Very probably. Medea, you have to arrange transit for us to Cadia. That's the first port of call.'

'What's the second?' asked Aemos.

'The second?'

'The second mission?'

I looked at them all. 'We all know how serious the Cadian matter is. But I made a vow to Gideon. I want to find out what was behind the outrage here. I want to find it, hunt it out and punish it.'

You know, it's funny how things turn out.

It was late, and we were devouring a splendid meal Jarat had prepared for us. Nayl was telling a devastatingly crude joke to Aemos, Medea and Bequin and I were talking over the rearrangement of the Distaff and the missions ahead.

I think she was feeling excited. Like me, she'd been taking a back seat for too long.

Kircher came up the terrace, entering the filmy green light.

'Sir, you have a visitor.'

'At this hour, who?'

'He says his name is Inshabel, sir. Interrogator Nathun Inshabel.'

Inshabel was waiting for me in the library.

'Interrogator. Has my staff offered you refreshment?'

'None needed, sir.'

'Very well... so to what do I owe this visit?'

Inshabel, no more than twenty-five, pushed his thick blond hair out of his eyes and looked at me fiercely. 'I... I am masterless. Roban is dead...'

'God-Emperor rest him. He will be missed.'

'Sir, do you ever think what it would be like if you died?'

The notion stopped me in my tracks. I had, in all honesty, never considered it.

'No, Inshabel. I haven't.'

'It's a terrible thing, sir. As Roban's senior acolyte it falls to me to disburse his staff, his fortune, his knowledge. I'm left to tidy up, as it were. I have to make sense of Roban's estate.'

'You will not fail in that duty, interrogator, of that I'm sure.'

He smiled weakly. 'Thank you, sir. I had... I had thought to come to you, and beg you to take me on. I so very much want to be an inquisitor. My master is dead, and I know that your own... your own interrogator is...'

'Indeed. I choose my own staff, of course. I–'

'Inquisitor Eisenhorn. Begging you to take me on as a driftwood student was not why I came here. As I said, I had to close up Roban's estate. That meant filing and authorising the pathologica statement of his death. Inquisitor Roban was killed by a cargo servitor manipulated by a rogue psyker.'

'Yes?'

'So to complete the papers, I had to review the death notice of Esarhaddon so as to establish causal motive.'

'That is the procedure,' I admitted.

'The statement was very brief. Esarhadon's corpse was burnt from the calves upwards and utterly immolated. As in the incidents of spontaneous human combustion, the relics left by the plasma weapon were little more than the flesh and bones of the feet and ankles. Just bare vestiges.'

'And?'

'There was no Malleus brand on the ankle flesh.'

'It– What..?'

'I don't know who Inquisitor Lyko burned on the lawns of the Lange house... but it wasn't the heretic Esarhaddon.'

NINE

EECHAN, SIX WEEKS LATER
A WORD WITH THE PHANT
KNIVES IN THE NIGHT

The bicephalic minder in the squalid doorway of the twist bar regarded us with one of his lice-ridden heads, while the other glazed out, smoking an obscura pipe.

'Not your place, not your kind. Get on.'

The sap rain was falling heavily on our heads through the rotten awning, and I had little wish to stand in it any longer. I nodded a sidelong glance to my companion, who tugged back his hood and showed the minder the cluster of malformed, winking eyes that mottled his cheek and ran down his pallid throat. I raised my own damp cloak and revealed the knot of stunted tentacles that sprouted from an extra sleeve slit under my right armpit.

The minder got off his stool, one head nodding dozily. He was big, broad and tall as an ogryn, and his greasy skin was busy with tattoos.

'Hnh...' he muttered, limping around us as he sized us up. 'Maybe then. You didn't smell like twists. Okay...'

We went inside, down a few dark steps into a nocturnal club room that was fogged with obscura smoke and pulsing with a brand of harsh, discordant music called 'pound.' Panes of red glass had been put over the lights of the lanterns and the place was a hellish swamp, like the damnation paintings of that insane genius Omarmettia.

Mal-forms, deforms, halfbreeds and underscum huddled or gambled or drank or danced. On a raised stage, a naked, heavy-breasted, eyeless girl with a grinning mouth where her navel should have been gyrated to the pound beat.

We reached the bar, a soiled curve of hardwood under a series of hard white lights. The barkeep was a bloated thing with bloodshot eyes and a black snake tongue that flickered between his wet, slit mouth and rotting teeth.

'Hey, twist. What will it be?'

'Two of those,' I said, pointing to clear grain-alcohol shots that a waitress was carrying past on a tray. She would have been beautiful except for the yellow quills stippling her skin.

Twists. We were all twists here. 'Mutant' is a dirty word if you're a mutant. They delight in referring to themselves by the Imperium's glibbest and most detrimental slang, as a badge of honour. It's a pride thing, a common habit with any underclass. Non-telepaths do it when they call themselves 'blunts.' The tall, slender people of low-grav Sylvan do it when they call themselves 'sticks.' A slur's not a slur if you use it on yourself.

Labour laws on Eechan permit twists to work as indentured labourers in the industrial mill-farms and the sap distilleries, provided they abide by the local regime and keep themselves to the licensed shanty towns huddled in the skirts of the bad end of Eechan mainhive.

The barkeep slapped two heavy shotglasses down on the counter and filled them to the brim with grain liquor from a spouted flask.

I tossed a couple of coins down and reached for my drink.

The bloodshot eyes leered at me.

'What's this? 'Perial coins? Come now, twist, you know we ain't allowed to trade in those.'

I paused. A glance down the counter showed me that the rest of the clientele were paying in mill-authorised coupons or nuggets of base metal. And that they were all staring and scowling at us. A basic mistake, right off the bat.

My companion leaned forward and sipped his drink. 'Don't get fret with two thirsty twists who's happened to have lucked into a good black score, eh?'

The barkeep smiled and his black tongue flickered. He scooped up the coins. 'Ain't no fret, twist. You earn 'em, I'll take 'em. Just sayin' you might not want to go flashing 'em, s'all.'

We took our drinks away from the bar, looking for a table. It had taken six weeks to reach Eechan, and I was impatient for a lead.

The beat changed. Another pound number began pumping through the underfloor speakers, which to my untutored ears was simply a variation in auditory assault. But the crowd clapped and roared approval. The naked girl with the grinning stomach began rotating her hips the other way.

'I have a feeling I should be leaving this to you,' I whispered to my companion.

'You're doing fine.'

'"Don't get fret, twist..." for God-Emperor's sake... where did you learn to talk like that?'

'You never hung with twists?'

'Not like this...'

'So I'm guessin' you don't s'love that genejack pound beat, twist?'

'Stop it or I'll shoot you.'

Harlon Nayl grinned and blinked with all his sixteen eyes in mock offence.

'Sup up, twist. If that ain't Phant Mastik, I'll poke my eyes out.'

'Oh, let me,' I hissed, and slugged back my shot. 'Raise 'em and sink 'em and let's have another!' I grimaced to myself as the burning spirit scalded down my oesophagus, and then scooped two more drinks from the tray of the porcupine girl as she sashayed past.

Phant Mastik sat with his cronies in a side booth. Generations of rad-storm mutation had made him an obese thing with wrinkled flesh and enlarged features. His ears were frayed fan-like swathes of veiny skin and his nose was a drooping proboscis. An incongruous tuft of thick red hair decorated his neanderthal brow.

His eyes were deep-set and black.

And sad, I thought. Tremendously sad.

He was drinking from a big tankard by snorting the alcohol up through his dangling nose. His mouth, distorted by tusk-like jags of tooth, was useless. A twist whore, with an unnecessary number of arms, was sipping her drink, smoking an obscura stick, retouching her make-up and doing something to Phant under the table that he was clearly enjoying.

We approached.

Phant's minders got up immediately to block us. A horned brute and a twist whose entire head was a wrinkled skin hood for an outsized eye. They both reached into their robes.

'How you tonight, twists?' puffed Horn-brute.

'We fine. No fret, Just s'gotta talk to the Phant,' said Nayl.

'Ain't not gonna happen,' said Big-eye, his voice muffled by his clothing. God-Emperor knew where his mouth was.

'I s'think so, when we have us such a scalding black score, him to enjoy.' Nayl didn't shrink back.

++Let them through++ Phant said, his voice conveyed by an augmetic carry-sound unit. A vox-implant. Few twists had the money for that. Phant was certainly a player.

The minders stepped aside and allowed us into the booth. We sat.

++Go on++

'Twist, I s'tell ya, we be in the market for section-alpha brainjobs. We s'hear you got one for the begging.'

++Hear? Where?++

'Round and around,' said Nayl.

++Uh huh. And you are?++

'Just two twists s'gonna earn us a deal,' I said.

++That right?++

We sat in silence for a moment as Phant called for more drinks. The girl was now combing and fixing her hair and doing her make-up. One of her many hands was on my knee under the table.

She winked at me.

With an eye growing from the end of her tongue.

++What I got, ain't no section-alpha, twists. S'section-alpha-plus++

'That is s'why we came to you, Phant! S'why! No upper limit for our buy!'

++How you gonna pay?++

Nayl dropped one of the ingots onto the table.

'Pure mellow-yellow. And we got the bars. Much as it takes. So...? S'when-where?'

++I gotta talk to some people++

'Kay.'

++Where can I reach you?++

'The Twist and Sleep.'

++You sleep tight. Maybe I call you++

The audience was over. We took a table of our own near the raised stage and stayed for a couple more rounds, making a show of appreciating the indecent writhings of the girl with the belly mouth.

After an hour or so, we saw Phant and his retinue leave by a side door. 'Let's go,' I said. We finished our drinks and rose. Nayl gave porcupine girl a handful of coins and patted her bottom. Her quills bristled, but she smiled.

The minder didn't spare us a look with either of his heads as we left. Out of sight, round the corner of the dreary barstoop, I handed Nayl one of a pair of brass stimm-injectors and we detoxed quickly to rid our bodies of the alcohol dulling our systems.

It was the dead of night, but there was little darkness. The great curve of Eechan's ring systems glowed with reflecting sunlight and shone like bands of diamond-crusted platinum.

The main street of the shanty was a rutted, water-logged morass, and flaking boardwalk pavements edged the rows of slumping, dingy buildings. Glowing signs and the few street lamps reflected in the street puddles.

Beyond the shanty, to the west, the alpine slopes of the mainhive rose against the stars, like a dark mountain of trash decorated with a million little lights. To the east were the stacked, grubby mushrooms of the mill-farms and the distilleries, venting brown steam and yellow pollutants into the wind.

To the south, in the verdant farm lands, plains of thick, rubbery growth, we could see the running lights of several vast harvesters. They were segmented juggernauts: beetle-like machines the size of small starships, chewing up the greenbelt with massive reaping mandibles and digesting it through vast interior vats and worklines. Flues lined their backs like spines and spewed moisture waste and atomised sap up high into the atmosphere, where it drifted and fell again like rain. Everything in the twist shanty was sticky with sap-fall. The rain was tacky and thick like syrup. The street puddles were viscous. Downpipes glugged and throbbed rather than pouring. Everywhere, there was a stench of decomposing plantfibre and liquefied cellulose.

'Do you think he took the bait?' I asked.

Nayl nodded. 'You could see he was interested. Gold's rare on Eechan. His eyes lit when I showed him that ingot.'

'He'll want to check us, though.'

'Of course. He's a businessman.'

We walked along the street, hoods raised against the sticky rain. There were a few mutants around, all of them dressed in rancid tatters. They shambled along, lurked in doorways around covered braziers, or shared obscura bottle-pipes out of the rain in dim breezeways.

A squirt of sirens warbled down the main street and Nayl pulled me into an alley-end. A black armoured land speeder with blazing grilled lamps crept past.

I saw the crest motif of the mainhive Arbites on the side and an armoured officer sat in the top hatch manipulating a spotlight.

The beam played across us and passed along. Another flute of siren-noise sounded and we heard a vox-amplified voice demand, 'Idents and papers, you five. Now!'

Moaning and grumbling, a pack of twists moved out into the street, lit by the spot-beam, as the officers dismounted to shake them down and run their gene-prints through the system.

Something we couldn't afford to let happen. Not if we wanted to maintain our position as anonymous mutants. One flash of my credentials would speed us past any Arbites red-tape. But it might also alert Lyko.

I'd insisted on full concealment for the mission. No one knew we were here, officially. Aemos had done some surreptitious checking, and there was no official trace of Lyko either. But that was to be expected, and there was no telling how many mainhive officials he might have back-handed to alert him of any Inquisitorial presence.

Nayl and I turned west at the next junction, and followed the maze of alleys and breezeways between the rents and mill-habs to reach the Twist and Sleep by a circuitous route that would keep us off the main thoroughfares and away from Arbites patrols.

And, as it turned out, bring us right into trouble.

It didn't look like trouble at first. A short, flat-browed runt in rags stepped into our path, grinning like a salesman. He held his hands open, as if he was going to curtsy.

'Twists, my twists, my friends... spare a few 'perials for a poor badgene down on his luck.'

I heard Nayl begin to say, 'Not tonight, twist. S'get you to one side.'

But I had already tensed. How had this scabscum known to ask for Imperial coins if he hadn't seen us at the bar and followed us on purpose?

His accomplices came out of the gloom and sap-rain behind us.

I rammed the word *Evade!* hard into Nayl's mind with a 'pathic surge and dropped.

A massive, spiked weapon sailed through the space our heads had just been occupying and connected with nothing but air.

The runt who had waylaid us uttered quite the most obscene series of curses I have ever, ever heard and dived on me. He had a double-headed dagger with a nurled hand-guard.

I caught his upflung wrist as he made to gouge at me, broke his elbow and kicked him through a nearby fence while he was still screaming in pain.

'Boss! Move!' I heard Nayl sing out and I rolled hard aside in the mud as the spiked weapon slammed down into the mire.

It was a thick length of timber with dozens of nails and knife blades hammered through it.

The friendly end of it was held by two amazingly large paws. The paws belonged to a hulk, a two hundred kilo monster covered with blistered fish-scales and bony scutes. It wore only a pair of ragged blue trousers held in place around its midriff, almost comically, by a pair of red braces.

It swung the spike-post at me again, and I had to dive and shoulder-roll to escape it.

Nayl was going toe-to-toe with two others: a snouted female in black leather whose mouth and nose were hideously combined into one drooling, snarling organ, and a tall, thin male with a face peculiarly distorted by bone and gristle.

The female had a reaping sickle in each hand, and the tall male was armed with a mace made out of a reinforced strut toothed with the rusting blades of two wood saws.

Nayl had drawn his serrated shortsword and duelling knife and was fending off thrusts and strikes from both of them.

A power sword, a boltgun, a lascarbine... they would all have finished this unnecessary encounter fast enough. But we had agreed to carry nothing that would mark us out from the twist population. Tech-levels were low in the shanty. A plasma gun might have ended this quickly, but stories would have got round.

The scaly giant was on me again, and I fell through the rotting flakboard of a fence in my efforts to evade his swing. I found myself lying amid the debris in the back yard of one of the loathsome hab-rents. A light went on in an upper window and abuse, stones and the contents of a chamber pot were hurled at me.

The giant came on, swinging his club from side to side. The nails and blades were darkly caked with dried blood.

He backed me towards the rear of the rent dwelling and made to swing again.

No! I commanded, using the will. He stopped dead. The rain of abuse and excrement from above stopped too.

It would take him a moment to reconfigure his mind and find his anger again. I moved right at him, punching a knuckle-curved fist at the place where his nose should have been. There was a crack of bone and a spray of blood.

The giant went down hard on his back, his nasal bone slammed back into his brain.

Nayl seemed to be enjoying his uneven duel. He was jeering at his attackers, deflecting the sickles with his sword and blocking the strenuous attacks of the mace with his knife. I saw him spin and belly-kick the male away, then turn to give the ghastly, snorting female his full attention.

But more figures were emerging from the night.

Ugly, abhuman scum dressed in rags. Three, four of them.

I called a warning out to Nayl and pulled out my blackpowder pistol. It was a clumsy antique I'd acquired from the black market on Front's Planet, but even so I'd dumbed it down to Eechan tech levels by replacing the engraved furniture with a shaped piece of packet-wood.

The flintlock mechanism was in good order, though. It cracked loudly with a fizz and a flash, the recoil punishing my wrist, and the ball went point-blank through the forehead of the nearest twist, exploding the rear of his cranium in a surprisingly messy fountain.

But it was a one-shot piece and there was no time for reloading.

Two of the remaining outlaws came right at me, the other turning to come in on Nayl's flank.

I broke the teeth of the first one to reach me with the rounded butt of the pistol, and ducked the second's poorly judged slice with a rapier.

Backing away, I drew my own blade. Also a rapier. Shorter by a good ten centimetres than my opponent's but balanced and guarded with a hand-net of articulated metal struts.

Our blades clashed. He was good, trained to his skill by a life of slaughter in the underhive. But I... I had me on my side.

I dazzled him with the *ulsar* and the *uin ulsar*, and then drove him back with a four-stroke combination of *pel ighan* and *uin pel ihnarr* before ripping the blade out of his dazed fingers with a swift *tahn asaf wyla*.

Then the *ewl caer*. My blade transfixed his torso. He looked confused for a second and then fell down, sliding dead off my blade.

His broken-faced accomplice, blood spilling from my pistol whipping, flew at me and I span, decapitating him with the edge of my blade. The Carthaens believe side-blade work is lazy, and stress the use of the point.

But what the hell.

Nayl had killed the third attacker with a bodypunch, and as I turned, he locked both of the female's sickles around his twisting knife and ran her through with his main blade.

He turned to me and raised his bloody shortsword to his nose in a salute. I returned it with my rapier.

The siren of an Arbites groundcar was wailing along the alley.

'Time to be gone,' I said to Nayl.

'I thought you were dead!' Bequin cursed as Nayl and I burst in to the room in the Twist and Sleep.

'We had some fun on the way home,' Nayl said. 'Don't worry, Lizzie, I brought the boss back safe.'

I smiled and fixed myself a small amasec from the bureau. Bequin hated to be called 'Lizzie.' Only Nayl had the balls to do it.

Aemos was hovering by the window. Somehow, the rags of his twist disguise suited him.

'Most perturbatory... the Arbites are coming this way.'

'What?'

Nayl moved to the window.

'Aemos is right. Three land cruisers pulled up outside. Officers coming in.'

'Hide yourselves, now!' I ordered.

Aemos hurried through the communicating door into the other bedchamber and threw himself down on the cot. Nayl blundered into the adjoining bathroom and used a tooth mug and loud groans to suggest he was busy throwing up.

Alizebeth looked at me frantically.

'Into bed! Hurry!' I ordered.

The Arbites kicked open the door and played their flashlights over the bed. 'Hive Arbites! Who's in here?'

'What is this?' I asked, dragging the sheets back.

'Streetfight killers... witnesses said they came in here,' said the Arbites sergeant, advancing towards the bed.

'Me, I been here all night. Me and my friends.'

'They gonna vouch for you, twist?' asked the sergeant, raising his weapon.

'Wass goin' on? Too much light!' said Bequin, emerging from the dirty linen on the bed. Somehow she had removed her dress beneath the sheets. Clad in brief underwear, she slithered on top of me.

'Wass you doin'? Stoppin' a girl makin' her way? Shame on you!'

The sergeant ran his flashlight beam up and down the length of her body as it clung to me. I smiled the inane smile of the lucky or well-oiled.

He snapped the light off. 'Sorry to interrupt you, miss.' The door closed and the Arbites thumped away.

I looked down at Bequin with a wink. 'Good improvisation,' I said.

She leapt off me and grabbed her clothes. 'Don't get any funny ideas, Gregor!'

I'd had funny ideas about her for years, truth be told. She was beautiful and sublimely sexy. But she was also an untouchable. It hurt me to be close to her, physically hurt.

I hate that fact. I feel a lot for Bequin and I long to be with her, but it was never going to happen. Never, ever.

That's one of the truly great sadnesses of my life.

And hers too, I hope, in my more self-aggrandising moments.

I lay in bed and watched her drag on her dress again, and I felt the pang of desire.

But there was no way. No way in the galaxy.

She was untouchable. I was a psyker.

That way pain and madness lay.

TEN

RUMINATIONS ON LYKO
THE CHEW-AFTER
THE HIGHEST BIDDER

Tumultuous sap-storms hammered the twist-town in the pre-dawn, blanketing the sky with swirling vapours and shaking the tiles and shutters with the gross weight of their heavy pelting goop. Thunder rolled. In the aftermath, veils of mist swathed the countryside, and the stillness was alive with gurgling and dripping and the swarming scurry of sap-lice and storm-bugs.

Nayl went out early with Aemos and bought paper pails of warm food from the twist-town commissary just down the street, which was already serving the work lines forming for the shift change in the mills. By the time they returned, we had been joined by Inshabel and Husmaan, who had slept through the night's altercation with the Arbites in a shared room down the hall.

I'd yet to formally notify the Ordo that Inshabel had joined my band, but he was now very much part of it. I felt he had the right to be here on this mission, for Roban's sake, and for his own. He had brought the news of Esarhaddon to me, directly and selflessly. Few of my team yet referred to him by his rank – it would be a long while until anyone eclipsed the memory of Interrogator Ravenor – but he had meshed well, with his bright mind and healthy, caustic wit. He was already providing me with more solid service than Alain von Baigg had ever managed.

Duj Husmaan had been a skin-hunter on his homeworld of Windhover when Harlon Nayl had first met him. That was back in Nayl's bounty-chasing days, before he'd joined my cause. I'd recruited Husmaan eight years before on Nayl's recommendation, and he'd proved to be a resourceful, if superstitious, warrior with a great sense for pathfinding. Nayl had personally selected him from the individuals in my retinue as muscle for this venture, and I had no quibble with the choice.

Husmaan was a slender man of medium height with coppery skin and white, sun-scorched hair and goatee. Here on Eechan, like all of us, he'd drabbed down his clothing to ragged black twist robes. He ignored the bundle of disposable wooden forks that Aemos had brought back from the commissary and started to eat the hot food from his paper pail with his fingers.

I picked at my own food idly, wondering how close we were to Lyko.

* * *

Lyko had been a fool and had damned himself. The damaging revelation that it hadn't been Esarhaddon who had been torched on the lawns of the Lange palace could have been circumvented if Lyko had kept his head. He could have claimed it a mistake, another example of the heretic psyker's treachery.

But Lyko had run. Out of fear, or chasing some timetable, I didn't know. But he'd run and, in so doing, incriminated himself.

I'd gone to his residence, a rented hab high in the spires of Hive Ten, the moment Inshabel had alerted me to the deceit. But Lyko had cleared out, taking his people with him. His hab was empty and abandoned, with just a few scatterings of trash left behind in the stripped rooms.

I had set my staff to work tracing him, a tall order given the planet-wide data-access problems in the wake of the rioting. I had decided almost at once to pursue him alone, without informing the Inquisition. You may see this as odd, almost reckless. In a way, it was. But Lyko was an inquisitor of good repute, held in high regard, and with many friends. There was scant chance I could tell the Ordos I was undertaking a hunt for him on the basis he was harbouring a notorious rogue psyker without the fact reaching him, or without his friends making trouble for me.

Those friends of his, of course, included Heldane and Commodus Voke: the stalwart trio that had captured the thirty-three rogues on Dolsene in the first place. How empty that 'heroic' action now seemed to me. I had been so impressed when Lord Rorken had shown me the report. Perhaps the 'capture' had been easy, or even staged, if Lyko was secretly in league with Esarhaddon. Perhaps it had all been part of an elaborate conspiracy to perpetrate the atrocity of Hive Primaris.

I was dogged by grim, unanswerable speculations. I had no way to prove Lyko was corrupt, not even now, though I certainly suspected it. He might have been an unwitting pawn on Dolsene, or at the Lange palace, or he might have been in it all along. It was possible too that his departure from Thracian was a coincidence that I had misinterpreted. It wouldn't have been the first time an inquisitor had moved undercover without announcement.

It was even possible that he too had discovered the deceit after the event, and was moving fast following some lead to make amends for his mistake. Or that he was fleeing the shame... or...

So many possibilities. I had to play the odds the safest way. I was sure Lyko was guilty to a greater or lesser extent, so I would follow him. Even if he was simply chasing Esarhaddon too, it would lead me in the right direction.

And I couldn't inform the Inquisition, or talk to Voke or Heldane. My uncertainty was such that I couldn't even trust them not to be part of it.

A complex trail of almost subliminal clues had put me on his tail. I'll spare you the bulk of the details, for they would merely document the painstaking tedium that is often the better part of an inquisitor's work. Suffice to say, we searched and processed vox logs, and the broadcast archives of the local and planetary astropathic guilds. We watched ship transfers, orbital traffic, departure lists, cargo movements. I had personnel in the streets, watching key locations, asking off-the-record questions in trader bars, calling in favours from friends of friends, acquaintances of acquaintances, even one or too old adversaries. I hired trackers and bloodhounders, and took every scent trace I could from Lyko's apartment. I had pheromone codes programmed into servitor skulls that I released into up-ports and orbital stations.

I had well over a hundred personnel on my staff, many of them trained hunters, researchers or surveillancers, but I swear the sheer load of data would have burned out our brains.

We would have failed without Aemos. My old savant simply rose to the challenge, never put off, never fatigued, his mind soaking in more and more information and making a thousand mental cross checks and comparisons every hour, tasks I couldn't have managed in a day with a codifier engine and a datascope.

He seemed, damn his old bones, to enjoy it.

The clues came in, one by one. A shipment of cargo put into long-term storage in a holding house in Hive Eight and paid for by a debit transfer from one of Lyko's known associates. A two-second pheromone trace in the departure halls of a commercial port down on the coast at Far Hive Beta. A fuzzy image captured from a Munitorum pict-watcher on the streets of Hive Primaris.

A passenger on a manifest listing making an unnecessary number of interconnecting flights between up-ports before moving off planet, as if trying to lose pursuit.

Then the key ones: a cursory excise exam of freight that registered the presence of psi-baffling equipment in an off-world shipment. A series of clumsily disguised and presumably hasty bribes to key longshoremen at the Primaris starport. A rogue trader vessel – the *Princeps Amalgum* – staying a day longer at high-anchor than it had logged permission to do, and then a sudden change in its course plans.

Instead of a long run to the Ursoridae Reef, it was heading spinwards, via Front's World, to the twist farms of Eechan.

There was a knock at the room door just after dawn, and I sent everyone except Nayl into the adjoining room. Bequin and Inshabel had the presence of mind to scoop up all the food pails except two. I went over to the window, and Nayl sat down in a chair, with his arm casually over the back so anyone coming in couldn't see the autopistol in his hand.

I focussed my mind for a moment to make sure our twist disguises were live, and then said, 'Enter.'

The door opened and the porcupine girl from the twist bar came in. She was dressed in a glistening sap-cloak, and she looked at us curiously as she pushed back her hood.

'You take your time, twists,' she said.

'You got something, sweetgene, or you simply s'got to check the good stuff you passed on last night?' Nayl asked with a lascivious smile.

She scowled, and a head crest of spines rose in a threat posture.

'I s'got a message. You know who from.'

'The Phant?'

'I ain't saying, genesmudge. I just bring it.'

'Then s'bring it.'

She reached into her cloak and produced an old, low-tech tracker set, battered and worn. Holding it up briefly, she thumbed it on long enough for us to see the green telltale winking, and then switched it off again and dropped it with a clatter onto the peeling tabletop.

'S'gonna be an auction. Bidder's market, so bring lotsa yellow, he says. Lotsa.'

'Where? When?'

'Today at shift two, in the chew-after. That s'tell you where.'

'That it?' I asked.

'S'all I have. I just bring it.' She hesitated at the door. 'You s'might wanna make my worth while.'

I put my hand into my coat pocket and pulled out a single, large denomination Imperial coin.

'You take these?'

Her eyes lit up. 'I take anything.'

I tossed it over to her and she caught it with one hand.

'Thanks,' she said. She went out through the door and then looked back at us, as if my generous contribution to her immediate happiness had shifted her opinion of us.

Which, sadly, given this miserable place, it probably had.

'S'don't trust him,' she advised, then closed the door and left.

The chew-after was the local name given to the tracts of farmland laid waste after the harvesters had been through. Wrecklands of shredded vegetation that began to regrow within days of a harvest, such was the speed and fecundity of Eechan's floral growth. At any one time, there were several thousand square kilometres of chew-after in the farmlands round the mainhive.

We headed south, into the most recent areas of thresh-wake, following the signal of the tracker.

Noon. That was what she had meant by shift two. The second shift change of the day. We gave ourselves two hours to get there.

On top of all my speculations about Lyko, things still didn't add up. It had been easy enough for Nayl to identify Phant Mastik as the local slaver, with a specialisation in mindjobs, but why was Lyko using him? Why was Lyko selling Esarhaddon at all?

Aemos had suggested it was part of a final trade now that Esarhaddon had completed his part of their pact. That supposed Lyko was in control, which I doubted. And if he was simply cutting the heretic loose now the work was done, why sell him? Why, indeed, come all this way to do that? Inshabel supposed that maybe Lyko was now anxious to get rid of the rogue-psyker because he was afraid of him.

I had my own theory. Lyko had brought Esarhaddon to Eechan for some other purpose, and arranging a mock sale through the Phant was simply bait to draw anyone who might have followed him out into the open.

As it turned out, I was right. I wasn't surprised. It's what I would have done.

The chew-after was a miasmal waste. As far as the eye could see, which wasn't far at all given the clinging sap-mists from the night before, the land was a gouged, punished ruin of ripped shoots, shredded plant-fibre, wrenched-up root balls and pressure-flattened soil. The massive track-marks of the harvesters had left wide ruts the depth of a man's waist, at the bottom of which plant material and soil was layered into a glassy flatness like they had been set in aspic.

The misty air was wet with sap and everything was crawling with lice motes and storm-bugs. They swarmed in the air, settled all over us, and we could feel them in our clothes.

By then, although we maintained our twist disguises, we were all armed and armoured at full strength. One doesn't walk into a likely trap with a blackpowder pistol and a sharp stick. I wore body armour, and carried my power sword and boltpistol. The others were similarly heavy with battle-gear. If we were caught now, maintaining the pretence we were twists would be the last of our problems.

Ten kilometres south, through the swirling, sticky mists, we could hear the chugging, rending sounds of the harvesters as they moved on their way. Every few metres there was another bloody smear or furry pulp, the remains of crop rodents caught in the reaping blades of the factory machines.

'You'd think,' said Inshabel, pausing to wipe the gooey sweat from his face, 'that the wildlife would have got used to the farm-factories by now. Learned to get out of the way.'

'Some things never learn,' Husmaan muttered. 'Some things always come back to the source.'

'He means food. He always means food,' Nayl chuckled to me. 'To Duj, everything comes back to food.'

'According to mill statistics,' said Aemos, 'there are four billion crop-rats in every demitare of field space. Rivers of them flee before the harvesters. We've seen one rat-corpse for every twenty-two metres, which suggests only two-point-two per cent of them were unlucky enough to be caught in the blades. That means the vast percentage fled. They're smarter than you think.'

He paused. Everyone had stopped and was staring at him.

'What?' he asked. 'What? I was only saying...'

'That old geezer fantisises about maths and stats more'n I fantisise about the lay-dies,' Nayl told Bequin as we moved forward again.

'I'm not sure which of you I'm supposed to feel more sorry for,' she said.

Husmaan held up the tracker the Porcupine-girl had given us and shook it. Then he slapped it a couple of times for good measure.

We waded through the plant fibre and came level with him.

'Problem?' I asked.

'Damn thing... too old.'

'Let me see it.'

Husmaan handed it to me. It was a piece of crap, all right. Battered by a lifetime of hard knocks, with a nearly flat powercell. A nice touch that, I thought, noting Lyko's careful planning. An unreliable tracker made this seem so much more genuine. A brand new or well-powered unit would have been as good as a written invitation beginning 'Dear people chasing me, please come here and get killed...'

I shook the device myself and got a good return. Just enough juice to lead us to our deaths.

'That way,' I said.

It was close to noon. The sun was up, but the sap-mists hadn't dissipated. We were bathed in a warm, yellow, filmy glare. According to the tracker, we were about half a kilometre from the auction site.

'They're expecting me and Nayl, so we'll go in with Bequin.' I wanted an untouchable close to me. 'Inshabel, cut east with Aemos. Husmaan, west. Covering positions. Don't move in unless you hear me vox a direct command. Understand?'

The three nodded.

'If you find anything, keep it Glossia and keep it brief. Go.'

Nathun Inshabel armed his lascarbine and moved away to the left with Aemos along a harvester track-bed, leaving tacky footprints in the glassy, crushed residue at the bottom of the huge rut. Husmaan's hempcloth-wrapped long-las was already armed. He darted away to the right, quickly lost in the mist.

'Shall we?' I said to Bequin and Nayl.

'After you,' Nayl grinned.

I made one last command by vox, in Glossia code, and we trudged into the ripped thickets of the chew-after.

The Phant's people had used flamers to clear a wide space in the morass of the chew-over. We could smell the burnt pulp-fibre from several dozen metres away.

The mist was still close, but I could make out several crop-runner trucks, skimmers and land speeders parked in the blackened clearing. People bustled around them.

'What do you see?' I asked Nayl.

He played his magnoculars round again. 'Phant... and his twist cronies. The horned guy, and that eyeball creep. Maybe a dozen, some of whom think they're hidden around the perimeter. Plus the prospective buyers. I make... three... no, four, all hive-types, with minders. Sixteen other bodies, all told.'

I yanked up my hood. 'Come on.'

'There's an alarm strand round the site.'

'We'll trip it. That's what it's there for.'

The alarm strand was an ankle-high wire-cord tied taut between the churned root clumps. Every metre or so, the air-dried shell case of a storm bug was carefully tied to it, forming a little, hollow-sounding bell. They rattled and jangled as we deliberately plucked the wire.

In a moment, ragged-robed twist muscle loomed out of the murdered undergrowth, aiming matchlocks and blades at us.

'We're s'here for the auction,' I told them, holding up Phant's tracker. 'S'invited.'

'Name?' croaked a frog-headed thing with a crossbow and a spittle problem.

'Eye-gor, from off. With his twists.'

Frog-head waved us into the site. The others assembled before the low, flak-board stage on which Phant Mastik stood, looking round at us.

'Eye-gor! Off-world twist, with two others,' Frog-head announced.

Phant nodded his heavy, tusked head and Frog-head and his men backed off, putting up their weapons.

++S'glad you could make it, twist++

'You the Phant. You the twist with the stuff. But... I s'hear my own name loud, not these others.'

++Let's all be known, then the sale can begin++

Phant looked down at the other buyers. One, a stunning female up-spire hiver in a tight bodyglove nodded. 'Frovys Vassik,' she said through a pan-lingual servitor-skull drone that floated at her shoulder.

She was clearly speaking some high-caste dialect cant which the drone was translating. I assayed her and her two male bodyguards quickly: dilettante wealthers, would-be cultist types, well-armed and armoured with all the wargear spire money could afford.

'Merdok,' said the next, a frail, white-suited, elderly man leaning on a cane and wiping perspiration from his brow with a japanagar lace kerchief that had cost more than the lowly Phant's entire outfit. He had four minders, squat females in rubberised war-rena suits, each with an electronic slave-leash collar around her throat.

'Tanselman Fybes,' said the bland-faced man to Merdok's left, stepping forward with a courteous nod. He was dressed in a bright orange cooler-suit, with large, articulated exchanger vanes sprouting from his shoulders. His breath smoked in the personal veil of cold air the suit was generating around him.

He was also alone, which made him instantly more dangerous than the hive retards who had brought muscle.

'You may address me as Erotik,' said the last, a bitch-faced crone who had inadvisably wedged her ancient body into a close-fitting, spiked, black bodyglove, the mark of a death-cultist.

Or would be death-cultist, I thought. She had five masked and harnessed slaves with her, all of them sweating in the misty heat. I saw at once they were out of their depth. They played at death-cult, up in the eyries of the mainhive, maybe cutting their skin and drinking blood once in a while. The closest they had come to a real death-cult was watching some blurry, fake snuff-pict to impress their friends after a banquet.

'S'greet you all. I'm Eye-gor. S'off world, and twisted as they come.'

I bowed. Fybes and Vassik returned the motion. Merdok mopped his brow and Erotik gestured a very ham-fisted sign of the True Death which nearly made Nayl laugh out loud.

'Can we get started, my friend Phant?' Merdok asked, dabbing his kerchief around the sweat runs on his face. 'It's midday and bloody hot out here.'

'And I have murders to do and blood to drink!' Erotik cried. Her plump and unhealthy minders oohed and aahed and tried to get their nipple-spikes and bondage straps comfortable.

'Oh dear God-Emperor... they're never going to make it out alive...' whispered Bequin.

'More fool them...' I whispered back.

Phant's men used force-poles and electrolashes to goad the sale item from the back of a crop-runner truck onto the stage. It was a rangy human, strait-jacketed and bindfolded, with a heavy psychic-damper muzzle buckled around his head.

++Alpha-plus quality. One only. S'bids, now?'++

'Ten bars!' cried Erotik at once.

'Twenty,' said Vassik.

'Twenty-five!' cried Merdok.

Fybes cleared his throat. His cough blew cold steam out from the private atmosphere generated by his suit. 'I think that's established the common level here. I do hate mixing with proles. One thousand bars.'

Erotik and her minders gasped.

Merdok looked pale.

Vassik glanced round at Fybes with a curt look.

'Ahh. At least someone sees the true worth of the item on sale. Good. We can begin serious bidding.' Vassik cleared her throat and her cyber-skull dutifully issued white noise. 'Twelve hundred bars,' she said.

'Thirteen hundred!' Erotik cried out, desperately.

'Fifteen,' said Merdok. 'My best offer. I had no idea this meet would be so hungry... or so rich.'

'Two thousand,' said Vassik's hovering skull.

'Three,' said Fybes.

Merdok was already shaking his head. Erotik was walking away towards the edge of the site, complaining loudly to her pudgy sex-toys, who bustled around her.

'Three five,' said Vassik.

'Four,' said Fybes.

'Anything?' I whispered to Bequin.

'Not even the slightest latent push. But those baffles could be doing their job.'

'So it could be Esarhaddon?'

'Yes. I doubt it. But it could.'

'Nayl?'

Harlon Nayl looked round at me.

'Nothing. The Phant's minders are getting edgy because the old witch and her sad hump-muffins are trying to leave before the auction's finished. But nothing else...'

'Five five,' Vassik's servitor-skull rasped.

'Six,' said Fybes.

Merdok had withdrawn to one side of the site with his minders, and was taking a sustaining puff of obscura from a portable water-pipe one of the war-rena slave fems was holding for him. Erotik and her chubby concubines were arguing with Horn-head and another couple of twists on the other side of the burned acre.

'Eight five!' Vassik was announcing.

'Nine!' returned Fybes.

'Fifty!' I said quietly, tossing a huge pile of ingots down onto the stained soil.

There was a pause. A long, damned pause.

++Fifty bid++

Phant looked down at us all.

Merdok and Erotik and all their people were simply dumbstruck. Vassik turned away, screaming, and her minders had to hold her down as she went into fits of rage.

Fybes just looked at me, his breath coming slow and short in clouds.

'Fifty?' he said.

'S'fifty, count 'em. You got better?'

'What if I have, Eye-gor? And please... stop it with the "s'stupid s'twist" talk. It's getting on my nerves.'

Fybes walked towards me. He reached up and pulled his face off. The flesh disintegrated like gossamer as he pulled it away, revealing his blank, piercing eyes.

'Oh, Gregor. You do so like to make an entrance, don't you?' said Cherubael.

ELEVEN

FACE TO FACE
NO WITNESSES
DEATH ALONG THE LINE

His was the last face I had expected to see here, though it had been in my mind and my nightmares for nearly a hundred years.

'It's been a while, hasn't it, Gregor?' the daemonhost said softly, almost cordially. 'I've thought of you often, fondly. You bested me on 56-Izar. I... held a grudge for a while, I must admit. But when I learned you had survived after all, I was quite delighted. It meant there would be a chance for us to meet again.'

The orange cooler-suit began to burn and collapse off him in molten hanks until he was naked. He rose gently, arms by his side, like a dancer, and hovered on the wind a few metres above the churned soil. He was still tall, and powerfully made, but the aura that shone from him was more sickly green than the gold I remembered.

Unhealthy bulging veins corded his body, and the nub-horns on his brow had grown into short, twisted hooks.

'And so we meet again. Aren't you going to say anything?'

I could feel Bequin shaking in terror beside me.

'Stay calm, stay still,' I told her.

The daemonhost glanced at her and his smile widened. 'The untouchable! How wonderful! An almost exact repeat of our first encounter. How are you, my dear?'

'What do you want?' I asked.

'Want?'

'You always want something. On 56-Izar, it was the Necroteuch. Oh, I forgot. You never want anything, do you? You're just a slave, doing another's bidding.'

Cherubael frowned slightly. 'Don't be uncivil, Gregor. You should treasure the fact that I have taken a personal interest in you. Most things that cross me get destroyed very quickly. I could have hunted you out years ago. But I knew... there was a bond.'

'More of your riddles. More nothings. Tell me something real. Tell me about Vogel Passionata.'

He laughed, an ugly sound. 'Oh, you heard about, that did you?'

'Reports of the incident have made me suspect in the eyes of many.'

'I know. Bless you, that wasn't my intention. It was just a tiny error on my part. I'm sorry if it's inconvenienced you.'

'I have no wish to be seen as a man who would form a compact with daemons.'

'I'm sure you haven't. But that is what's happening, whether you like it or not. Destiny, Gregor. Our destinies are entwined, in ways you cannot even begin to see. Why else would you dream about me?'

'Because it has become a central goal of my life to hunt you down and banish you.'

'Oh, this is a lot more than simple professional obsession. Think, why do you really dream of me? Why do you search for me so diligently, even hiding the extent of that search from your masters?'

'I...' My mind was racing. This thing knew so much.

'And why did I spare you? If it had been you on Vogel Passionata, I would have let you live. I let you live on Thracian.'

'What?'

'You stopped to pay homage at Spatian's tomb, and the Gate shielded you from the disaster. Why did you stop? You don't know. You can't explain it, can you? It was me. Watching over you. Planting the suggestion in your mind. Making you pause for no reason. We've been working together all along.'

'No!'

'You know it, Gregor. You just don't know you know it.'

Cherubael floated away a short distance, and looked around. The auction site was frozen, all eyes on him. No one dared move, not even the most weak-willed twist guard. Even those present who didn't know what he was recognised the extraordinary evil and power he represented.

'What are you waiting for?' a voice yelled from nearby. Several armed men stepped out of their cover in the chew-after tangles and approached. It was Lyko, with six gristly examples of hired muscle.

'Look who I found, Lyko. I sprung this trap, just like you suggested, to discover if anyone was on your tail, and look who it turned out to be.'

'Eisenhorn...' Lyko murmured, fear crossing his face for a second. He looked over at Cherubael.

'I said, what are you waiting for? Kill them and we can be gone.'

It was suddenly clear to me Lyko wasn't the daemonhost's master. Like Konrad Molitor all those years before, Lyko was another pawn, a corrupted agent of someone... something... else.

'Must I?' asked the hovering figure.

'Do it! No witnesses!'

'Please!' cried the elderly Merdok. 'We only meant t–'

Lyko whipped around and incinerated the old man with his plasma gun.

That broke the impasse. Phant's people and the other buyers broke in panic, drawing weapons, shouting. Indiscriminate shooting began. Lyko's gunmen, all ex-military types with autocannons, hosed the staging area and cut down the fleeing twists. I saw Phant Mastik hit by a burst of fire and collapse in rough sections backwards off the platform.

His horn-headed minder ran at Cherubael, firing a grubby old laspistol.

Cherubael hadn't moved. He was simply watching the murder around him. The las-shots sizzled off his skin, and he glanced down at the twist, as if his reverie had been broken.

The daemonhost didn't even move a hand, a finger. There was just a slight nod in the direction of the horned minder, and the miserable twist was somehow filleted where he stood, waves of force stripping off his flesh and popping out his skeleton, parts of it still articulated.

I felt the warp churning around that dismal place as Cherubael went to work. Once he had started, his fury was unstinting. Merdok's war-rena fems disappeared in a sudden vortex and died, fused together. The mud beneath Vassik's feet boiled, and she and her bodyguards sank, screaming and thrashing, into it.

I was frozen, rigid. I felt Bequin pulling at me.

Shots seared past my face. I snapped round, and saw two of Lyko's men charging us. One dropped suddenly, headshot by what could only have been a sniping round from Husmaan out in the torn undergrowth.

Nayl flew past me and gunned the other down with his Tronsvasse parabellum.

'Come on! We've got to get out of here!' he yelled at me.

There was blood and filth and swirling plant-fibre in the air. A warp storm was crackling around us, so dense and dark we could barely see, barely stand against its churning force. But I could make out the glowing shape of Cherubael through it all.

I drew my power sword and ran towards him.

'Gregor! No!' Bequin screamed.

I had no choice. I had waited the best part of a hundred years. I would not let him go again.

He floated around to face me, smiling down.

'Put that away, Gregor. Don't worry. I won't kill you. Lyko has no power over me. I'll deal with his complaints later, and–'

'Who does have power over you? Who is your master? Tell me! You caused the atrocity on Thracian, didn't you! Why? On whose orders?'

'Just go away, Gregor. This is not your concern now. Go away.'

I think he was honestly surprised when I hacked the power sword into his chest.

I don't really know if I had imagined I could do him any harm.

The blessed blade almost disembowelled him before it exploded and hurled me backwards.

He looked down in dismay at the wound across his torso. Warp energies, bright and toxic, were spilling out of it. In a second, the wound closed as if it had never been.

'You little fool,' said Cherubael.

I found myself flying backwards through the air, blood in my mouth.

The impact of landing shook my bones and smashed the breath out of me. My head swam. The daemonhost's power had thrown me a good thirty metres across the site, into the underbrush.

Furious psychic detonations went off all round. Screaming, semi-sentient winds from the deepest warp snaked around the field, destroying the last of the twists and the fleeing buyers.

I tried to rise, but consciousness left me.

When I came to, the chew-after was on fire. There was no sign of Cherubael. Inshabel and Aemos were pulling me to my feet.

'Bequin! Nayl!' I coughed.

'I'll find them,' Inshabel said.

'Where's Lyko?' I asked Aemos, as Inshabel ran off, weapon drawn.

'Fled, with his men, in two of the land speeders.'

'And the daemonhost?'

'I don't know. It seemed to just vanish. Maybe it had a displacer field.'

I started to run back into the site, though my body was burning with pain. Aemos cried out after me.

Most of the vehicles were smashed or overturned, but a couple were still intact.

I scrambled into a small, black speeder; a sleek, up-hive sports model that had presumably belonged to Vassik. I cued the thrusters, lifting off before I'd even strapped on the seat harness.

The craft was powerful and over-responsive. It took a moment to master the lightness of touch needed to accelerate without sudden blurts of speed. I turned it unsteadily in the air as I climbed too fast above the blasted site. Below, I could see Nayl, ragged and bloody, shouting up at me to come back.

Banking out of the cone of smoke at a hundred metres, I got my bearings. On every side, the acreage of the chew-after spread out until it became lush greencover again. There was the mainhive, looming in the distance. Where were they? Where were they?

I saw two dots in the air three kilometres to the west and gunned the machine after them. Heavy land speeders, making towards the bulk of the nearest harvester factory.

I pushed the turbines to their limit, coming in low and fast behind the slower lift-machines. I knew they'd seen me the moment autofire chattered back in my direction, wildly off target.

I began to jink, the way Midas had taught me, before they got their aim in. I thought about shooting back at them, but it took both hands on the stick just to keep the sports speeder level.

We were passing over green crop land now, an emerald sea that raced away below in an alarming blur. More tracer shots howled back past me.

A big shadow passed across the sun.

'Want them splashed?' crackled from the vox.

Downjets flaring, the streamlined bulk of my gun-cutter settled in beside me, matching my speed. It seemed huge compared to my insignificant little speeder; one-fifty tonnes, eighty metres from beak nose to finned tail, landing gear lowered like insect legs. I could see Medea grinning in the cockpit.

I daren't lift my hands from the jarring stick to activate the vox.

Instead, I opened my mind directly to hers.

Only if you have to. Try and get them to land.

'Ow!' answered the vox. 'Warn me next time you're gonna do that.'

The great bulk of the cutter suddenly surged forward, afterburners incandescent and landing gear raising, and banked away to the right. Its thrust wake wobbled me hard. I watched it turn out in a wide semi-circle, low over the crops, furrowing them with its downwash. It looked like a vast bird of prey swooping round for the kill.

With its interplanetary thrust-tunnels, it easily outstripped the racing speeders, and came in towards them, head on.

I felt a surge of psychic power. My enemies had nothing but their minds with which to combat the gun-cutter.

The cutter suddenly broke left, dipped and then righted itself. They'd got to Medea, if only for a moment.

She was angry now. I could tell that simply from the way she flew. With a wail of braking jets, she turned the cutter on a stall-hover as the speeders flashed past.

The chin-turret crackled, and heavy-gauge munitions tore the second of the two speeders into a shower of flames in the air.

Hitting the throttle, I zipped in behind the hovering gun-cutter, chasing down the other speeder.

No more! I sent to Medea. *I want them alive if possible!*

The remaining speeder was close ahead now. I could feel Lyko's mind aboard it.

He was closing on the armoured bulk of the harvester, which now dominated the landscape ahead. It was a giant, six hundred metres long and ninety high at the peak of its humped, beetle-back. It was kicking a vast wake of sap-spray and smoke out behind it. The rattle of its threshing blades was audible above the scream of my speeder's engines.

My quarry dipped, and flew in along the spine of the huge factory machine, heading for a rear-facing docking hangar raised like a wart on the hull's back. Warning hails were beeping at me over the speeder's vox-set, the alarmed challenges of the harvester.

The heavy speeder braked hard and landed badly in the mouth of the docking hangar. Turning in to follow it, I saw figures scrambling out. They disappeared, into the hangar, all except one man, who dropped to his knees on the approach slip and began firing back at me with his autocannon.

Streams of high-velocity rounds whipped past on either side. Then a bunch of them went into my port intake with a clattering roar that shook the speeder and threw shards of casing out in a belch of sparks.

Warning lights lit up across the control board.

I dropped ten metres, put the nose in.

And bailed.

I broke my left wrist and four ribs hitting the topside of the harvester. With hindsight, I was lucky not to have been killed outright, lucky even to have hit the harvester's hull at all. It was a long way down. I managed to grab a stanchion cable as I began to slither down, and wrapped my right arm around it.

My speeder glanced once off the approach slip, and bounced up again, tail up, beginning to tear apart. Trailing debris, the machine cartwheeled in, vapourised the gunman, hit Lyko's parked land speeder, and shunted it right into the hangar, which exploded a second later in a sheet of fire and metal.

I limped along the approach slip, sidestepping chunks of burning wreckage, and climbed over the smashed, smouldering speeders into the hangar. Impact klaxons were rasping out, and automatic fire-fighting sprays were still squirting out dribbles of retardant foam.

At the back of the hangar, a hatch was half open, next to the cages of the service and cargo elevators.

I pushed through the hatch. A metal staircase descended into the factory. At the bottom, it opened out into a companionway that ran the length of the harvester. Stunned work-crews, most of them twists in sap-stained overalls, gazed at me.

I produced my rosette.

'Imperial Inquisition. Where did they go?'

'Who?'

'Where did they go?' I snarled, enforcing my will without restraint.

The effect was so powerful, none of them could speak, and several passed out. All the others pointed down the companionway towards the head of the factory.

Another hatch, another staircase. The noise of the internal threshers was now shudderingly loud. I came down into the vast internal work line, a long chamber that ran the length of the harvester. It was a huge, deafening place, the air thick with sap mist. A massive processing conveyor carried the harvested produce along from the reaping blades at the harvester's mouth, at a rate of several tonnes every second. Twist workers in masks and aprons worked the front part of the line with chaintools and cutting lances which were attached to overhead power systems by thick rubber-trunked hoses. They sorted and cut the larger sections of root and stalk before the crop went through the great vicing rollers and stamping presses into the macerating vats further back down the factory.

With the alarms sounding and warning lights flashing, the line had come to a halt, and the workers were looking around, liquid cellulose and sap dripping off their gauntlets, overalls and work tools.

I blundered through them, overseers shouting at me from gantry stations far above. I could see Lyko, thirty metres away down the line, pushing through with one last gunman and a bound, visored figure that could only be Esarhaddon.

The gunmen turned and fired at me down the length of the line vault. Three workers crumpled, one spilling over onto the belt. The shots spanged sparks off the metal walkways and machinery.

As the other workers dived for cover, I dropped to my knee and reached for my boltgun. It wasn't there. In fact, the entire holster was ripped open. I wasn't sure when I lost it: during Cherubael's assault or slamming off the hull of the harvester, but it was long gone. And my beloved power sword had been disintegrated on contact with the daemonhost.

More shots whizzed down the work-line and dented the metal facings of the belt-drivers. I crawled into cover behind a drum of hydrobac tool-wash.

I pulled my back-up weapon from the ankle-holster built into the side of my boot. It was a compact, short-frame auto with a muzzle so short it barely extended beyond the trigger guard. The handgrip was actually longer than the barrel, and contained a slide-magazine of twenty small-calibre rounds.

Selecting single-fire, I cracked off a couple of shots. The aim was lousy and the power poor. It really was meant to be a close-range last ditch.

The gunman down the line, undeterred by my pathetic display, switched over to full auto and raked the deck area and working space beside the stationary belt. Workers, all pressing themselves into cover, began to scream and yell.

The shooting stopped. I dared a look out. There was a clunk and a whirr and the conveyor started moving again.

The gunman was following his departing master again. Lyko was almost out of sight, pushing his captive ahead of him.

Why was Esarhaddon a captive, I wondered? I still didn't understand the relationship between Lyko, the psyker and Cherubael.

I ran on. The gunman, Lyko and his captive psyker had all disappeared through a bulkhead door. To follow them, I'd have to go in blind. And if I'd been in Lyko's place, I'd have used the bulkhead as a point to turn and wait.

My gut readings of his actions had not been wrong so far.

I leapt up onto the wide conveyor belt, ignoring the shouts of the cowering work crew, and slithered across it through the matted, sticky crop load. The sap and the moving belt made it nigh on impossible to stay upright. For a moment, I thought I might slip and be carried along under the nearest roller press.

I leapt off the far side onto the solid deck, dripping with green mush and vegetal fluid. Now I was following the work-line down the other side of the wide conveyor, which divided the harvester centrally.

There was a bulkhead door on this side, too.

I went through it, low.

The gunman was waiting behind the other door on the far side of the moving belt. He saw me, cursed, and turned with his autocannon. I was firing already. Even at this shorter range, the pathetic stopping power of my auto was evident. His drum-barrelled autocannon was about to roar out my doom.

I dived headlong, thumbing my weapon to auto and ripped off the entire clip of small slugs in a shrill, high-pitched chatter.

What I lacked in power I made up for in numbers. I hit him six or seven times in the left arm and collar and staggered him backwards, his bonded armour torn open. The heavy cannon flew out of his hands and landed on the moving belt between us to be carried out of view.

He was far from dead, though he was bleeding profusely from the multiple small calibre grazes and impacts. He was probably glanding some stimm that kept his edge.

Snarling an oath, he drew a military-issue las-pistol from his webbing, and climbed up on the work-line foot rail on his side of the rolling belt to get a better angle at me. I threw the empty gun at him and made him duck, and then grabbed one of the hose-suspended work lances hanging by the line-edge.

He got off a shot that barely missed my shoulder. I swung the lance at him, the chain-blade tip chittering, reaching out across the belt. But it was hard to manipulate it with one wrist smashed.

So I turned the swing into a throw and launched the long tool like a harpoon.

The chain-tip impaled him and he died still screaming and trying to drag the industrial cutter from his chest. As he went limp, the tension in the rubberised power-hose pulled the lance back towards its rest hook on my side of the line, dragging the body onto the conveyor. The belt carried it along as far as the hose would allow, and then it stuck fast, the belt moving under it.

Piles of wet plant fibre began damming up against it and spilling over onto the floor.

Eisenhorn, a voice said in my mind.

I wheeled round and saw Lyko standing on a grilled gantry that formed a walk-bridge over the belt. The plasma gun he had used to burn the fake Esarhaddon was aimed at me. I could see the battered psyker, his head still masked and visored, lashed to a wall-pipe on the far side of the line.

You should have left well alone, Eisenhorn. You should never have come after me.

I'm doing my job, you bastard. What were you doing?

What had to be done. What needs to be done.

He came down the walk-bridge and stepped towards me. There was a hunted, terrified look in his face.

And what needs to be done?

Silence.

Why, Lyko? The atrocity on Thracian... how could you have allowed that? Been part of it?

I... I didn't know! I didn't know what they were going to do.

Who?

He squashed my cheek with the muzzle of his potent weapon.

'No more,' he said, speaking for the first time.

'If you're going to kill me, just do it. I'm surprised you haven't already.'

'I need to know something first. Who knows? Who knows what you know?'

'About you and your little pact with the daemonscum? About your theft of an alpha-plus class psyker? That you stood by while millions died on Thracian? Hah!' *Everyone.* I added the answer psychically for emphasis. *Everyone. I informed Rorken and Orsini himself before I left on your trail*

'No! There would have been more than just you after me...'

'There is.'

'You're lying! You're alone...'

You're doomed.

He stormed his mind into mine, frantic to tear the truth out of me. I think he was truly realising how far into damnation he had cast himself.

I blocked his feverish mind-assault, and countered, driving an augur of psychic rage into his hind brain. It was in there. I could feel it. His true master. The face, the name...

He realised what I was doing, realised that I outclassed him psychically. He tried to shoot me with his plasma gun, but by then I had shut down his nervous system and blocked all autonomous function. I scoured his mind. He was frozen, helpless, unable to stop me ransacking his memory, despite the blocks and engram locks he had placed there. Or someone had.

There. There. The answer.

He uttered an agonised, oddly modulated scream.

Lyko tumbled away from me.

Cherubael hovered above us, high in the roof space of the factory chamber, casting a glow of filthy warp-light.

Choking, twitching, his limbs limp, Lyko was rising up towards him. Smoke was coming out of his mouth and nostrils.

'Now, now, Gregor,' Cherubael said. 'Nice try, but there are some secrets that must remain.'

With a nod of his head, he tossed Lyko aside. The traitor-inquisitor flew down to the front of the factory space, bounced hard off the inner hull and then fell down into the churning reaper blades in the factory harvester's maw.

His body was utterly disintegrated.

Cherubael hovered lower, grabbed the comatose, bound form of Esarhaddon like a child picking up a doll.

'I won't forget what you did,' said the daemonhost, looking back at me one last time. 'You'll have to make it up to me.'

Then he was gone, and Esarhaddon was gone with him.

TWELVE

AT CADIA, BY TERCE
THE PYLONS
TALKING WITH NEVE

A bitter autumn wind was coming down off the moors, and the turning ribbon-leaves of the axeltrees were beginning to fall. They fluttered past me like dry strands of black kelp, and collected in slowly decomposing drifts on the windward side of the graves and the low stone walls.

Above, the overcast sky was full of racing brown clouds.

I followed the old, overgrown path up the wooded slope, under the hissing axeltrees, and stood for a while alone, looking down at the wide grave field and the little shrine tower that watched over it. There was no sign of life, and, apart from the wind, no movement. Even the air-shay that had brought me here from the landing fields at Kasr Tyrok had departed. I almost missed the driver's grumbles that the place was so far out of town.

Far away, almost out of sight beyond the glowering moors, I saw the nearest of the famed, mysterious pylons, an angular silhouette. Even from this distance, I could hear the strange, moaning note the wind made as it blew through the pylons' geometries, geometries that thousands of years of human scholarship had failed to explain.

This was my first time on the world they called the Gatehouse of the Imperium. So far, it was not endearing itself to me.

'So, Thorn... you were none too sharp, were you?'

I turned slowly. He had arrived behind me, as silent as the void itself.

'Well?' he asked. 'What time do you call this?'

'I consider myself suitably chastened,' I said.

He was impassive, then the scar under his milky eye twitched and he smiled.

'Welcome to Cadia, Eisenhorn,' said Fischig.

Aside from Aemos, Godwyn Fischig was my longest serving companion, though he and Bequin often disputed that record. I'd met them both on Hubris, during my hunt for the Chaos-broker Eyclone, which led in turn to the whole bloody affair of the Necroteuch.

I'd actually encountered Fischig first. He'd then been a chastener in the local Arbites, ordered to keep a watch on me. He became my ally through circumstance. Bequin had crossed my path, if my memory serves, about a day later, but I had co-opted her almost directly into my service, while Fischig had remained, technically, a serving Arbites officer for some considerable time before resigning to join me.

Which is why Bequin claimed the prize, and why they sometimes fell to disputing it when the hour was late and the amasec unstoppered.

His was a big man, of my own age, his cropped blond hair now turning silver. But he was as robust as ever, clad in a coat of black fur, a mail surcoat and steel-fronted boots.

He shook my hand.

'I was beginning to think you wouldn't make it.'

'I was beginning to think so too.'

He cocked his head slightly. 'Trouble?'

'Like you wouldn't believe. Let's walk and I'll tell you.'

We wandered back down the tree-shrouded path together. He knew something of the atrocity on Thracian, which was by then some seven months past, but he had no idea I had been caught up in it.

When I told him the details, especially about Ravenor, his face darkened.

He had admired Gideon – frankly, it had been difficult not to admire Gideon – and I sometimes felt that Gideon was the man Fischig would have liked to have been.

Fischig's great strength was his self-knowledge. He understood his own limitations. His strengths were loyalty, physical power, fine combat skills, observation and a nose for detail. He was not quick witted, and his abhorrence of book-learning meant that even the rank of interrogator was beyond him. Though he would have loved to rise formally through the ranks of the Inquisition, he had never tried, contenting himself with becoming one of the fundamental components of my staff.

To try, he knew, would have meant failure. And Godwyn Fischig hated to fail.

We crossed the narrow funeral lane and went into the grave field by the old lychgate in the low wall. I told him about Lyko, and Esarhaddon. I told him of the warnings from Endor and Lord Rorken. I told him about the bloody, inconclusive mess on Eechan. I told him about Cherubael.

'I would have come as soon as I received your message. But Rorken practically forbade me. And then, as you have heard, matters got out of hand.'

He nodded. 'Don't worry, I'm a patient man.'

We stood for a moment in the middle of the vast field of graves. Several shivering priests in ragged black robes were wandering through the lines of crumbling gravestones, pausing to study each one.

'What are they doing?'

'Reading the names,' he said.

'What for?'

'To see if they can be read.'

'Okay… why?'

'As you might imagine, a martial world like this produces many dead.

Long ago, an edict was made by the planetary government that only certain fields of land could ever be used for burial. So cemetery space is at an optimum. Hence, the Law of Decipherability.'

'Which is?'

'The law states that once the eroding hands of time and the elements have made the last names on a field's gravestones illegible, the anonymous dead may be exhumed, the bones buried in a pit, and the field reused.'

'So they tend the field for years until the names can no longer be read?'

He shrugged. 'It's their way. Once the names have vanished, so has the memory, and so has any need for honour. The time's coming for this place. Another year or two, they tell me.'

That struck me as infinitely melancholic. Cadia was a warrior-world, standing guard in the one navigable approach to the warp-tumult of the infamous Eye of Terror. The region, known as the Cadian Gate, is the route of choice for invasions of Chaos, and Cadia is seen by most as the Imperium's first line of defence. It has bred elite troops since it was first colonised, and billions of its sons and daughters have died bravely protecting our culture.

Died bravely... then left to slowly vanish in the desolate fields of their home world.

It was dismal, but probably entirely in keeping with the stoic martial mindset of the Cadians.

Fischig pushed open the heavy axelwood door of the shrine tower and we went inside out of the wind.

The tower was a single chamber, a drum of stone, with weep-hole window slits high up near the summit. A circle of rough wooden pews was arranged around a central altarpiece, above which a massive iron candelabra in the form of a double-headed eagle was suspended on a chain from the beamed roof.

On this dark autumn day, the light from the votive candles fixed amongst the metal feathers of the aquila's unfurled wings was the only illumination. There was a spare, thin, golden light, an atmosphere of frugality and numinous grace.

And a musty stink of rotting axel leaves.

We sat together on a pew, both of us briefly honouring the altar with the sign of the aquila, our hands splayed together against our hearts.

'It's strange,' sighed Fischig after a long pause. 'You sent me out, over a year ago, on yet another quest for signs of that daemonspawn Cherubael. And just when I find a trace, you run into him again, on the other side of the damn sector.'

'Strange is possibly not the word I'd use.'

'But the coincidence. Is it coincidence?'

'I don't know. It seems so much like it. But... that thing... Cherubael... disarms me so.'

'Naturally, old friend.'

I shook my head. 'Not because of his power. Not that.'

'Then what?'

'The way he speaks to me. The way he says he's using me.'

'Daemon guile!'

'Perhaps. But he knows so much. He knows... ah, damn it! He speaks as if our destinies are irrevocably entwined. Like he matters to me and vice versa.'

'He does matter to you.'

'I know, I know. As my goal. My prey. My nemesis. But he talks like it's more than that. Like he can see the future, or can read it, or has even been there. He talks to me like... he knows what I'm going to do.'

Fischig frowned. 'And... what do you think that might be?'

I rose and stalked to the altar. 'I have no idea! I can't conceive of doing anything that would please or benefit a daemon! I can't ever imagine myself that insane!'

'Trust me, Eisenhorn, if I ever thought you were, I'd shoot you myself.'

I glanced back at him. 'Please do.'

I halted and looked up into the flickering flames of the candles, seeing the many shadows and possible shadows of myself they cast, interlapping and criss-crossing the stone floor. Like the myriad possibilities of the future. I tried not to look into the thicker, blacker shadows.

'The warp-spawned bastard's just playing games with you,' said Fischig. 'That's all it is. Games to put you off the scent and keep you at bay.'

'If that's the case, why does he keep saving my life?'

We went back out into the moorland wind. The moaning of the pylon seemed louder to me now.

'Who's with you?' Fischig asked.

'Aemos, Bequin, Nayl, Medea, Husmaan... and a lad you've not met, Inshabel. We came here directly from Eechan.'

'Long ride?'

'Best part of six months. We got as far as Mordia on a free trader called the *Best of Eagles*, and then came the rest of the way as guests of the Adeptus Mechanicus. The super-heavy barge *Mons Olympus*, no less, carrying virgin Titans to the garrisons of the Cadian Gate.'

'Quite an honour.'

'The inquisitor's rosette carries its benefits. But I tell you, the tech-priests of Mars are damned surly company for a two month voyage. I would have gone mad but for Bequin's regicide tournaments.'

'Nayl getting any better?'

'No. I think by now he owes me... what is it? Hmm. His first born and his soul.'

Fischig laughed.

'Oh, it wasn't all so bad. There was one fellow, a veteran princeps from the Titan Legion. Old guy, centuries old. At the point of retirement, like those men ever retire. He was supervising the transfer of the new war machines. Name of Hekate. We got to drinking some nights. Remind me to tell you some of his war-stories.'

'I will. Come on...'

He had a land speeder parked down off the lane under the swaying axel-trees. We brushed fallen ribbon-leaves off the hood and got in.

'Let me show you what I found. Then we can all meet and greet in a safe place.'

'How safe?'

'The safest.'

We flew over the moorlands, into the biting winds, hugging the terrain. The light was fading. The grim glory of Cadia was spread out below us. This was the merciless, windblown wilderness that raised one of the Imperium's hardiest warrior breeds. Here were the scattered islets in the Caducades Sea where they were left naked as pre-pubescents to survive the ritual Month of Making. Here were the hill-forts where the Cadian Youth armies wintered and toughened and waged mock wars on their neighbour forts. Here were the crags, ice-lakes and axel-forests where they learned the arts of camouflage.

Here were the wide, sundered plains where their live firing exercises were staged.

There is a saying: 'If the ammo ain't live, this ain't no Cadian practice.' Right from the time they are issued with their own las-guns, which is about the same time they are given their first primary readers, the young warrior-caste of Cadia are handling live ammunition. Most can fire, and kill, and perform most infantry field drills before they reach the age of ten standard.

Little wonder that the shock troops of Cadia are among the Imperium's best.

But we weren't here to gawp at the rugged crucible of landscape that had formed the Cadians.

We were here to look at the pylons.

'Cherubael's been here,' said Fischig, jockeying the control stick and eyeing the windspeed gauge. 'Far as I know, nine times in the last forty years.'

'You're sure?'

'It's what you pay me for. Your daemonhost – and whatever he's working for – is fascinated by Cadia.'

'Why have the Inquisition not had a hint of it?'

'Come on, Gregor. The galaxy is big. Aemos once told me that the weight of data generated by the Imperium would fry all the metriculators and codifiers on Terra in a flash if it was input simultaneously. It's a matter of making connections. Sifting the data. The Inquisition – and you – have been looking all over for signs of Cherubael. But some things just don't flag. I got lucky.'

'How?'

'I was doing my job. Old friend of mine, Isak Actte, from the old Arbites day. Used to be my boss, in fact. He rose, got promoted, wound up on Hydraphur as an Arbites general and then got stationed here as watch overseer to the Cadian Interior Guard. I contacted him years ago, and got a message I had to check.'

'You're intriguing me.'

He ran us low over a headland and our speeder made a small, sharp shadow on the glittering ice-lake below.

'Actte said the Arbites had closed down a heretical cell here on Cadia about ten years ago. Called themselves the Sons of Bael. A fairly worthless lot, by all accounts. Harmless. But under interrogation, they'd admitted to following a daemon they called Bael or the Bael. The local inquisitor general spent some time with them and had them all burned.'

'What's his name?'

'Gorfal. But he's dead, three years gone. The current incumbent is a she. Inquisitor General Neve. Anyway, the cell has flared up a few times since then. Nothing a good team of riot-officers couldn't handle. Like I said, the Sons of Bael were pretty harmless, really. They were only interesting in one thing.'

'Which was?'

'Measuring the dimensions of the pylons.'

The pylon had been looming in our windscreen for a while now, and Fischig swept us around it, almost kissing the black stone.

The moaning song of the wind as it laced through the geometries of the pylon was now so loud I could hear it over the racing turbines of the speeder.

The pylon was vast: half a kilometre high and a quarter square. The upper facing of the smooth black stone was machined with delicate craft to form holes and other round-edged orifices no bigger than a man's head. It was through these slim, two hundred and fifty metre tubes that the wind moaned and howled.

And the tubes weren't straight. They wove through the pylon like worm tunnels. Tech-magos had tried running tiny servitor probes through them to map their loops, but generally the probes didn't come back.

As we banked up higher for another pass, I could see the distant shape of the neighbouring pylon, across the moors, sixty kilometres away. Five thousand, eight hundred and ten known pylons dot the surface of Cadia, not counting the two thousand others that remain as partial ruins or buried relics.

No two are identical in design. Each one rises to a precise half kilometre height and is sunk a quarter kilometre into the ground. They predate mankind's arrival in this system, and their manner of manufacture is unknown. They are totally inert, by any auspex measure known to our race, but many believe their presence explains the quieting of the violent warp torrents that makes the Cadia Gate the single, calm, navigable route to the Ocularis Terribus.

'They were trying to measure this thing?'

'Uh huh,' Fischig replied clearly over the speeder's drive as we pulled another hard turn. 'This and several others. They had auspex and geolocators and magnetic plumbs. Finding the exact dimensions... and I do mean exact... was the entire goal of the Sons of Bael.'

'They connect with Cherubael... I mean, beyond the "Bael" part?'

'The interview logs I've read show they name "Bael" fully as a god called

Cherub of Bael, who came amongst them and made demands that they measure the pylons in return for great knowledge and power.'

'And the inquisitor general... this Gorfal? He suppressed this?'

'Not deliberately. I think he was just sloppy.'

'I want to speak with the current inquisitor general... Neve, did you say her name was?'

'Yeah. I thought you might.'

While daylight remained, we flew west to Kasr Derth, the largest castellum in the region and the seat of provincial government for the Caducades. Fischig switched on the speeder's voxponder and broadcast the day's access codes to the sentry turrets as we passed the outer ring-ditch. Even so, Manticore and Hydra batteries traversed and tracked us as we went over.

The voxponder pinged fretfully as it detected multiple target-locks.

'Don't worry,' said Fischig, noticing my look. 'We're safe. I think the Cadians enjoy taking every possible opportunity to practise.'

We ran down the line of a slow moving convoy – drab, armoured twelve-wheeler transports escorted by lurching Sentinel walkers – and followed the highway up towards the ridge of the earthwork. Beyond it, and two more like it, the heavy, grey fortifications and shatrovies of Kasr Derth sulked in the twilight.

Watch-lights on skeleton towers stood on the upper slope of the earthwork. More turret emplacements and pillboxes studded the defence berm like knuckles. Again, the voxponder pinged.

Fischig dropped the speed and altitude, and swung us down towards the eastern barbican, a small fortress in its own right, bristling with Earthshaker platforms. A bas-relief Imperial eagle decorated the upper face of the ashlar-dressed structure.

We ran in through the barbican's gate, over the hydraulic bascule that crossed the inner moat, and into the castellum's deliberately narrow and twisting streets.

Cadia's earliest kasrs had been built in the High Terra style, with the wide streets laid out on a grid system. In early M.32, a Chaos invasion had made wretchedly short work of three of them. The broad, ordered avenues had proved impossible to defend or hold.

Since then, the kasrs had been planned in elaborate geometric patterns, the streets jinking back and forth like the teeth of a key. From the air, Kasr Derth looked like an intricate, angular puzzle. Given the Cadians' mettle and their skills at urban-war, a kasr could be held, street by street, metre by metre, for months if not years.

We slunk along the busy, labyrinthine streets as the caged lamps came on and business began to shut for the night. I was about to remark to Fischig that it looked for all the world like a military camp, until I realised that even the civilian fashion was for camouflaged clothing. It soon became easy to pick out locals from visitors. The jag-white and grey of tundra dress or the panelled green and beige of moor fatigues marked out newcomers and off duty soldiery. The population of Kasr Derth wore grey and brown checkered urban camouflage.

We passed the stilted horreums of the Imperial Cadian Granary, and the tight-packed baileys of the rich and successful. Even the townhouses of the wealthy had armouring on their mansard roofs.

To the left lay the brightly-lit aleatorium, to which night crowds were already flocking to gamble away their pay. To the right, Kasr's senaculum with its gleaming, ceramite-plated shatrovy pyramid. Ahead, lay the minster of the Inquisition. The voxponder pinged again as the gun-walls along the deep approach followed us.

Fischig settled the speeder down on the spicae testicae paving of the minster's inner yard, where sunken guide-lights stitched out a winking cross. Inquisitorial guards in gold-laced burgundy armour approached us as we swung back the speeder's canopy and climbed out.

I showed the nearest one my rosette.

He clipped his heels together and saluted.

'My lord.'

'I wish to see the inquisitor general.'

'I will inform her staff,' he said obediently, and hurried away across the herringbone paving, holding up his baldric so his power sword wouldn't trip him.

'You won't like her,' Fischig said as he came round the parked speeder to join me.

'Why?'

'Ah, trust me. You just won't.'

'It's late. I had finished business for the day,' said Inquisitor General Neve, stabbing her holoquill back into the brass power-well on the desk.

'My apologies, madam.'

'Don't bother. I'm not about to shut my doors to the famous Inquisitor Eisenhorn. We're a long way from the Helican sub, but your fame precedes you.'

'In a good way, I hope.'

The inquisitor general rose from her writing desk and straightened the front of her green flannel robe. She was a short, sturdy woman in her late one tens, if my eye was any judge, with salt and pepper hair plied back tightly into a bourse. She had the typical pale, tight flesh and violet eyes of a Cadian.

'Whatever,' she snapped.

We stood in her sanctum, an octastyle chamber with a black and white cosmati floor and aethercite walls inscribed with a waterleaf design. It was lit with rushlights and the flame glow accented the carved lotus motif.

Inquisitor General Neve clumped around her desk to face us, leaning on an ornate silver crutch.

'You'll want to be reviewing the Bael records, I suppose?'

'How did you guess?' I asked.

She favoured her weight on her sound foot and pointed the rubber-capped toe of the crutch at Fischig.

'Him, I know. He's been here before. One of yours, I suppose, inquisitor.'

'One of my best.'

She arched her spare, plucked eyebrows. 'Hah. Much that says about you. Come on. The archivum.'

A dim screw-stair led down to the basement archivum. The turning steps of the spiral were hard for her to manage, but she shooed me away curtly when I offered to assist her.

'I meant no insult, inquisitor general,' I said.

'Your kind never do,' she snapped. I felt it wasn't the moment to inquire what kind that might be.

The archivum was a long, panelled chamber lit only by the lamps of the double-faced desk-row that ran down its middle.

'Light buoy!' Neve snarled, and a servitor-skull drifted down from the coffered ceiling, hovering at her shoulder and igniting its halogen eyebeams.

'Bael, Sons of. Find,' she told it, and it coursed away, turning and dipping, sweeping the racks of the catalogue with its twin spears of light.

It stopped, eight sections down, and began to buzz around a shelf groaning with data-slates, file tubes and dusty paper books.

Fischig and I followed Neve as she hobbled over to join it.

'Sons of... Sons of... Sons of Teuth, Sons of Macharius, sons of bitches...' She glanced round at me. 'That passes for humour here, Eisenhorn.'

'I'm sure it does, madam.'

Her fingers went back to the stacks, running along the fraying spines and tagged slate-sleeves, following the skull-buoy's light beams.

'Sons of Barabus... Sons of Balkar... Here! Here it is. Sons of Bael.'

She pulled a file case off the shelf, blew the dust off it into my face and handed it to me. 'Put it back where you found it when you've finished,' she said. She turned to go.

'Your pardon, wait,' I said.

Two emphatic thumps of her crutch swung her around to face me again. 'What?'

'Your predecessor... um...'

'Gorfal,' whispered Fischig.

'Gorfal. He burned the members of this cult without examination. Have you never reviewed the case?'

She smiled at me. It wasn't encouraging.

'You know, Eisenhorn... I always imagined roving inquisitors like you had adventurous, exciting lives. All so very exhilarating, all that celebrity and heroism and notoriety. To think I used to dream of being like you. You have no idea, do you?'

'With respect, inquisitor general... of what?'

She gestured at the file case I was clutching. 'The crap. The nonsense. The bric-a-brac. The Sons of Bael? Why the hell should I review that case? It's dead, dead and nothing. A bunch of fools who were pulled off the Westmoorland pylon in the middle of the night for playing around with geo-locators. Whoooo! I'm so scared! Imagine that, they're measuring us! Do you have any idea what this wardship is like?'

'Inquisitor general, I–'

'Do you? This is Cadia, you silly fool! Cadia! Right on the doorway of Chaos! Right in the heart of everything! The seepage of evil is so great, I have a hundred active cults to subdue every month! A hundred! The place breeds recidivists like a pond breeds scum. I sleep three or four hours a night if I'm lucky. My vox chimes and I'm up, called out to another nest of poison that the Arbites have uncovered. Firefights in the street, Eisenhorn! Running battles with the foot soldiers of the archenemy! I can barely keep up with the day-to-day banishments, forget the past cases my crap-witted predecessor filed. This is Cadia! This is the Gate of the Eye! This is where the bloody work of the Inquisition is done! Don't distract me with stories of some engineering club gone bad.'

'My apologies.'

'Taken. See yourselves out.' She limped away.

'Neve?'

She turned. I dropped the file case on to the reading table.

'They might have been idiots,' I said, 'but they're the only solid link I have to a daemonhost that could destroy us all.'

'A daemonhost?' she said.

'That's right. And the beast that controls it. A beast that, if I'm right... is one of ours.'

She lurched back down the archivum.

'Convince me,' she said.

THIRTEEN

A REUNION
WAR-BELLS
THE LONG, SLOW TASK BEGINS

I don't know if I did convince the inquisitor general. I don't know if I could. But she heard me out and stayed around for another two hours, helping to locate the files of connected cases and other materials. Past nine, she was called away to a disturbance on an island community in the Caducades. Before she left, she offered accommodation for me and my staff in the minster, which I politely declined, and made it clear that I had her permission to continue my investigation in Kasr Derth, provided I kept her informed.

'I've heard stories about your... adventures, Eisenhorn. I don't want anything like that happening on my turf. Do we understand each other?'

'We do.'

'Good night, then. And good hunting.'

Fischig and I were left alone in the archivum.

'You were wrong,' I told him.

'How's that?'

'I did like her.'

'Hah! That hard-nosed bitch?'

'Actually, I liked her *because* she was a hard-nosed bitch.'

I always took pleasure in meeting a fellow inquisitor who conducted their work fairly and seriously, even if their methods differed from mine. Neve was a thoroughbred puritan, and lacked patience. She was abrupt to the point of rudeness. She was over-worked. But she called things as she saw them, despised sloppiness, and took the threats to our society and way of life completely seriously.

In my opinion, there was no other way for an inquisitor to behave.

We worked on until midnight, studying and collating the contents of hundreds of case-files.

By then, the gun-cutter had arrived from the landing fields at Kasr Tyrok, in response to my vox-summons. Fischig found one of Neve's rubricators and charged him with making data-slate copies of the most promising files ready for our return in the morning. Then we got back into the speeder and flew through the castellum's zig-zag streets to the town field.

The stars were out, and it was cool. Noctule moths fluttered around the landing lights of the waiting cutter.

There was a mauve smudge in the night sky, down low over the eastern horizon. The rising nebula of the Eye of Terror. Even from this great distance, just a blur in the heavens, it put a chill into me. If the two-headed eagle symbolises all that is good and noble and right about the Imperium of Mankind, that rancid blur symbolised all that was abominable about our eternal foe.

Laughter and warm voices greeted Fischig as we went aboard. Aemos shook him repeatedly by the hand and Bequin planted a quick kiss on his cheek that made him blush. He exchanged a few playful put-downs with Nayl and Medea, and asked Husmaan if he was hungry.

'Why?' the scout-hunter asked, his eyes widening in anticipation.

'Because it's supper time,' said Fischig. 'Betancore, get this crate into the air.'

We were going to that safe place he had mentioned.

I had not been aboard the sprint trader *Essene* for some five years. A classic Isolde-pattern bulk clipper, the ship was like a space-going cathedral, three kilometres long, and looked as majestic holding low anchor above Cadia as it had when I first saw it, nearly one hundred years before, in the cold orbit of Hubris.

Medea coasted us in towards the cargo hatch of the gigantic craft.

'A rogue trader?' asked Inshabel cautiously, looking over my shoulder at the ship ahead.

'An old friend,' I reassured him.

Shipmaster Tobias Maxilla was, I suppose, my most unlikely ally. He'd made his living shipping luxury goods officially, and unofficially, along the space lanes of the Helican sub-sector. He still did. He was a merchant, he maintained, to any that asked.

But he had a pirate's taste for adventure, a yearning for the halcyon days of early space-faring. I had hired his ship during the affair of the Necroteuch, to provide nothing more than transport for my team, but he had got involved, with increasing glee, and he'd stayed involved ever since. Every few years over the last century, I had hired him to run passage for me or some of my staff, or he had contacted me to ask if his services were needed. Just because he was bored. Just because he was 'in the neighbourhood.'

Maxilla was an educated, erudite man with a subtle wit and a taste for the finest things in life. He was also a charming host and a good companion and I liked him immensely. He was in no way a formal part of my staff. But he was, I suppose, after all this time and all those shared adventures, a vital part.

The year before, when it had been decided that Fischig would embark on this long chase after the Cadian leads, I had asked Maxilla to provide him with transportation, for as long as it was needed. He had agreed at once, and not because of the generous fee I was offering. To him, it sounded like a true adventure. Besides, it promised a chance to give the old *Essene* a proper long run out, beyond its normal route of the Helican stars.

A genuine voyage. An odyssey. That was what Tobias Maxilla lived for.

He was waiting in the cargo hold to greet us even before the extractor vents had finished dumping out the cutter's thruster fumes. He had dressed for the occasion, as was his way: a blue velvet balmacaan with huge sleeves and a jabot collar, a peascod doublet of japanagar silk, patent leather sabattons with gold buckles, and a stupendous fantail hat perched on his powdered periwig. His face was skin-dyed white and set with an emerald beauty spot. His cologne was stronger than the thruster fumes.

'My dear, dear Gregor!' he cried, striding forward and taking my proffered hands with both of his. 'A signal joy to have you back aboard our humble craft.'

'Tobias. A pleasure, as always.'

'And dear Alizebeth! Looking younger and more fragrant than ever!' He clasped her hand and kissed her cheek.

'Steady now, you'll smudge... your make up.'

'Wise Aemos! Welcome, savant!'

Aemos just chuckled as his hand was shaken. I don't think he ever knew quite what to make of Maxilla.

'Mr Nayl!'

'Maxilla.'

'And Medea! Ravishing! Quite ravishing!'

'You certainly are,' Medea said playfully, allowing one of her circuit-inlaid hands to be kissed.

'You knew we were coming, Maxilla. You might have smartened up a bit,' said Fischig. Amid laughter, they shook hands. I realised their relationship had changed. They had been together for a year on this mission. Fischig had never really connected with Maxilla: their backgrounds and lives were too divergent. But clearly, a year in each other's company had brokered a true friendship at last.

That pleased me too. An inquisitor's band works better when it is close knit.

Maxilla turned to Husmaan and Inshabel.

'You two I don't know. But I will, as that's what dinners are for. Welcome to the *Essene*.'

Maxilla's sculptural gold servitors, each one a work of art, had prepared a late supper for us in the grand dining lounge. A paté zephir of crab, fresh from the Caducades that morning, ontol flowers poivrade in their husks, fillets of Cadian boar hongroise, followed by an ebonfruit talmouse with cream and Intian syrup. The gilded sommelier served petillant Samatan rosé, heavy-bodied Cadian claret, a sweet and sticky Tokay from a lowland clos on Hydraphur, and stinging shots of Mordian schnapps.

Our humours were good, and the impromptu supper gave us time to step back from the work at hand and relax. None of us spoke of the case, or the demands that it was likely to make of us. To rest the mind often clears it.

I was going to need clarity now.

We returned to Kasr Derth the next morning in the gun-cutter. The steel dawn over the wide island group of the Caducades was cut by the rising edge of a burning, red sun. As we swept in over the craggy mainland, the peaks and edges of the moors were caught with a pink alpenglow.

Despite the fact that we were broadcasting the correct clearances, we were challenged six times in the half-hour descent. At one point, a pair of Cadian Marauders rolled in and flanked us as they checked us over.

Military security dominated the Cadian way of life. Every non-military transport, shuttle and starship was placed under acute observation, especially those that behaved suspiciously or wandered from the authorised flight routes. Aemos told me that a pinnace carrying the Deacon of Arnush, visiting Cadia for a promulgation seminar, had been shot down over the Sea of Kansk six months earlier, simply because it failed to give the correct codes. It made me wonder how our unknown foe had got his minions on and off Cadia.

Unless, like us, he had an identity and a rank that easily turned aside routine security checks.

We were diverted sixty kilometres west of Kasr Derth because a war was going on. The dawn light was filled with the flashes and light streaks of a mass rocket attack.

Eight regiments of Cadian Shock, just a few days away from shipping out to a tour of duty on one of the inner fortress worlds of the Cadian Gate, were staging a live firing exercise.

We finally set down on the minster's launch pad over an hour late. The war-bells in every tower and shatrovy in the Kasr were ringing to signal that the roar of battle from the nearby plains and moors was just a practice.

We divided our efforts. Fischig took Aemos to the Minster's archivum to study the records we had ordered copied the night before and do further research. Bequin, escorted by Husmaan, went to search the stacks of the Ecclesiarchy's records in the apostolaeum. Inshabel and Nayl visited the Administratum's catalogue of records.

I went with Medea to the Ministry of Interior Defence.

There are no Arbites on Cadia. A permanent state of martial law governs the world, and as a result, all civil policing duties are overseen by the Interior Guard, a sub-office of the Cadian Imperial Guard itself. In Kasr Derth, the region's administrative capital, their headquarters is the Ministry of Interior Defence, a grey-stone donjon adjoining the fortress of the martial governor, right at the heart of Kasr Derth.

Members of the Interior Guard are chosen at random. Worldwide, one in every ten soldiers recruited into the Cadian forces is transferred into the Interior force at the end of basic and preparatory, whatever their achievements and promise. As a result, some of the most able troopers ever raised on this planet of warriors serve out their time on the home world itself, and Cadia boasts one of the most effective and skilled planetary defence forces of any Imperial world.

We were seen by a Colonel Ibbet, a powerful, lean man in his forties who looked like he should have been leading the charge into the Eye of Terror. He was courteous, but mistrustful.

'We have no files on illegal or suspect immigration.'

'Why is that, colonel?'

'Because it doesn't happen. The system does not permit it.'

'Surely there are unfortunate exceptions?'

Ibbet, his grey and white camoed uniformed starched and pressed so sharply you could have cut yourself on the creases, steepled his fingers.

'All right, then,' I said, changing tack. 'What if someone wanted to get onto the planet anonymously? How could that be managed?'

'It couldn't,' he said. He wasn't giving at all. 'Every identity and visit-purpose is logged and filed and any infractions quickly dealt with.'

'Then I'll start with the files annotating those infractions.'

Resignedly, Ibbet showed us into a codifier room and assigned us a military clerk to take us through the records. We sorted and checked for about three hours, slowly becoming bored with the interminable lists of orbital boardings, air-space interceptions and ground-based raids. I could tell that a thorough review of these records alone was going to take weeks.

So that's what we did. We spent ten and a half weeks scouring the archives and catalogues of Kasr Derth, working in shifts and living out of the quarters on the gun-cutter. Every few days, we returned to the *Essene* for a little rest and reflection.

It was the dead of winter by the time we were finished.

FOURTEEN

WINTER BRINGS A CHANCE
THE DAMNED HAS A NAME
THE PYLON AT KASR GESH

Wintertide on Cadia.

There had been glinting ice-floes in the gun-metal waters of the Caducades that morning, and light snow had fallen on the moors. At that time of year, the foul corona of the Eye of Terror was visible even during the fleeting hours of daylight. The unholy mauve radiance of the nights became a violet fuzz in the cold daylight, like a badly-blotted ink stain on white paper.

It made us feel like we were under surveillance all the time. The Eye, bloodshot, angry, peering down at us.

Worst of all were the moor winds, cold and sharp as a Cadian's bayonet, blowing down from arctic latitudes. The high lakes were all frozen now, and lethal pogonip fogs haunted the bitter heaths and uplands. In the Kasr itself, it seemed like the locals had a morbid fear of heaters or window insulation.

Chilly gales breathed down the hallways of the minster and the Administratum building. Water froze in the pipes.

Despite it all, the war-bells sounded every few days, and the moors rolled with the sounds of winter manoeuvres. I began to imagine that the Cadians were simply shooting at each other to keep warm.

Ten and a half long, increasingly cold weeks after we had begun our systematic search of the Kasr's records, I was making my now habitual morning walk from the minster of the Inquisition to the headquarters of the Interior Guard. I wore a thick fur coat against the cold, and spike-soled boots to combat the sheet ice on the roads. I was miserable. The search had left us all pale and edgy, too many fruitless hours spent in dark rooms.

There had been so many promising leads. Links and traces of the Sons of Bael, unauthorised starship traffic, suspicious excise logs.

They had all dwindled away into nothing. As far as we could make out, no living member of the Sons of Bael, or any living associate or family member, remained. There had been no pylon-related cult activity, not even registered xeno-archaeological work. I had interviewed specialist professors at the universitary, and certain tech-priests from the Mechanicus who were shown in the records as having expert knowledge of the pylons.

Nothing.

With Inshabel, Nayl or Fischig, I had travelled the region, as far afield as

Kasr Tyrok and Kasr Bellan. A worker in the gunshops of Kasr Bellan, who had been identified as a Bael cult member, turned out to simply have the same name, misfiled. A wasted ten hour round trip by speeder.

Aemos had constructed a codifier model by which we checked record anomalies against the timetable of past cult activity.

There seemed to be no correlation at all.

I walked up the steps of the Ministry of Interior Defence, and submitted myself to the clearance check in the postern guardhouse. It should have been a formality. I had been arriving at the same time almost every day for the last seventy-five. I even recognised some of the Guardsmen by sight.

But still, it was like the first time I had ever been there. Papers were not only stamped, but read thoroughly and run through an anti-counterfeit auspex. My rosette was scrutinised and tagged. The duty officer voxed my details through to the main building to get authorisation.

'Doesn't this ever bore you?' I asked one of the desk officers as I waited, folding my papers back into my leather wallet.

'Doesn't what bore me, sir?' he asked.

I hadn't seen Ibbet since the first week. I'd been rotated between a number of supervisors. One told me it was because of shift changes, but I knew it was because none of them liked to deal with an inquisitor. Especially a persistent one.

That morning, it was Major Revll who escorted me in. Revll, a surly young man, was new to me.

'How can I assist you, sir?' he asked curtly.

I sighed.

Open log books and data-slates were piled around the workstation where I had abandoned them the night before. Revll was already calling for a clerk to tidy them away and make space for me before I could explain that I'd made the mess in the first place.

He looked at me warily. 'You've been here before?'

I sighed again.

I had two hours. At eleven, I was due to meet Inshabel and Bequin and fly out to a village on one of the islands in the Caducades to investigate a rumour that a man there knew something about smuggling. Another waste of time, I was sure.

I started in on the air-traffic day-book, reading through the lists of orbital transfers for a summer day two years earlier. Halfway down the slate was an entry showing a shuttle transfer from an orbiting ship to a landing field near Kasr Gesh. Gesh was near to one of the pylons frequented by the Sons of Bael. Moreover, on checking, I realised the date put it three days before the last incident of cult activity at the pylon.

I stoked up the data-engine, and requested further information on the entry. I was immediately denied. I used a higher decrypt key, and was shown a report that withheld both the name of the ship and the source of its authority. I began to get excited, and scrolled down. Even the purpose of the visit was restricted.

Now I typed in the teeth of my highest decrypt key. The terminal throbbed and chattered, sorting through files and authorisations.

The name came up. My elation peaked, and plunged away.

Neve. The mysterious entry had been a record of a classified mission by the inquisitor general. Back to square one.

The island was cold and bare. A small fishing community clung to the rim of the western bay. Inshabel swung the speeder down onto the cobbled tideway where spread nets had gone stiff with ice.

'How much longer, Gregor?' Bequin asked me, winding her scarf around her throat.

'How much longer what?'

'Until we give up and leave? I'm so sick of this fate-forsaken world.'

I shrugged. 'Another week. Until Candlemas. If we haven't found anything by then, I promise we'll say goodbye to Cadia.'

The three of us trudged up the icy walk to a grim tavern overlooking the sea wall. Anchor fish, as tall as men, were hung outside, salted and drying in the winter air.

The barman didn't want to know us, but his steward brought us drinks and led us through to a back parlour. He admitted that he had sent the message about the smuggler. The smuggler was here to meet us, he said.

We entered the back parlour. A man sat by the roaring grate, warming his jewelled fingers at its flames. I smelled cologne.

'Good morning, Gregor,' said Tobias Maxilla.

Despite the shouting coming from the back parlour, the steward brought us herb omelettes and bowls of steaming zar-fin broth, along with a bottle of fortified wine.

'Are you going to explain?' asked Inshabel tersely.

'Of course, dear Nathun, of course,' Maxilla replied, pouring a careful measure of wine into each glass.

'Be patient.'

'Now, Tobias!' I snapped.

'Oh,' he said, seeing my look. He sat back. 'I confess I have become despondent these last few weeks. You've been so busy and I've just been waiting up there on the *Essene*... well, anyway, you've said a number of times that the answer you're searching for depended on one key thing. It depended on you establishing a way of getting past this dire planet's obsessively tight security. Anonymously. And I said to myself... "Tobias, that's what you do, even though Gregor doesn't like to think about it. Smuggling, Tobias, is your forte." So I decided to see if I could smuggle myself down here. And guess what?'

He sat back, sipping his glass, looking disgustingly pleased with himself.

'You smuggled yourself onto the planet to prove it could be done?' asked Bequin slowly.

He nodded. 'My shuttle's hidden in the spinneys behind the village. It's amazing how many zipped mouths and blind eyes you can buy with a purse of hard cash round here.'

'I don't know what to say,' I said.

He made an open-handed gesture. 'You told me weeks ago that the Interior Guard recognised no illegal or suspect immigration. Well, I'm here today – literally – to prove that claim wrong. Cadia's a tough nut to crack, I'll admit. One of the toughest I've faced in a long and naughty career. But not impossible, as you see.'

I sank my wine in a single gulp. 'I should sever my links with you for this, Tobias. You know that.'

'Oh, pooh, Gregor! Because I've shown up the Cadian Interior Guard as a bunch of fools?'

'Because you've broken the law!'

'Ah ah ah! No, I haven't. Bent it, possibly, but not broken it. My presence here is entirely legal, under both Cadian local and Imperial general law.'

'What?'

'Come on, my old friend! Why do you think my shuttle wasn't blasted out of the heavens this morning by eager Cadian lightning jockeys? That was a rhetorical question by the way. Answer... because when the interceptors came scrambling up to meet me, I broadcast the right security clearance, and that contented them.'

'But the day codes are privileged! The counter-checks are triple! They are issued only to those with appropriately high credentials. What authority could you possibly have used to get them?'

'Well, Gregor... yours, of course.'

It had been staring me in the face, and it took the grandstanding flamboyance of Maxilla, in his very worst showing-off mode, to reveal it. The reason the Interior Guard had no file on illegal or suspect immigration was because there was nothing of that nature to file. Those that tried to run the strict gauntlet of Cadian security and failed, died. The ones that got through were never noticed.

Because they were using high-level security clearances, masquerading as the sort of official visitor who would not be stopped.

People like me. People like Neve.

'I never made this trip,' Neve said, staring steadily at the data-slate I was showing her. 'Or this.'

'Of course not. But someone borrowed your authority code. Used it to gain trans-orbital access. That's how they were getting in. Look here, your code again, and again. And before that, the code headers of your predecessor, Gonfal. It goes back forty years. Each and every flurry of activity from the Sons of Bael... and other cults... can be matched by space-to-surface transfers cleared as genuine Inquisition flights.'

'Emperor protect me!' Neve looked up. She put down the data-slate and called hoarsely for a servitor to bring more lights into her octastyle sanctum.

'But my authority code is protected. How was it stolen? Eisenhorn, yours was used to prove this. How was that stolen?'

I paused. 'It wasn't, not exactly. One of my associates borrowed it to prove the point.'

'Why doesn't that surprise me? Oh, no matter! Eisenhorn, there's a great deal of difference between you and me. You may have rogue elements in your band who act behind your back in unorthodox, unilateral ways. I do not. My code could not have been abused so.'

'I accept your point, but it could. Who has access to your code?'

'No one! No one below me!'

'But above you?'

'What?'

'I said this could be one of ours. A senior inquisitor, a grandmaster even. Certainly a wily veteran with enough clout to pull the right strings.'

'That would require a direct override at the highest levels.

'Exactly. Let's look.'

In the end, that was my adversary's downfall. All the blood and fury and combat we had gone through was as nothing to this prosaic clue that revealed his identity. To steal Neve's authority code, and the authority codes of her predecessors, my adversary had been forced to use the clout of his own identity get into the files.

The record of that operation was encrypted, of course. Sitting side by side at the codifier in her sanctum's annex, Neve and I quickly found it. It wasn't even hidden. He never thought anyone would look.

But still, it was encrypted.

The cryptology was beyond both me and Neve. But together, combining our ranks, we could request, via the Astropathicus, permission to use the Inquisition's most powerful decryption keys.

It took five hours to approve our joint rating.

Just after midnight, a scribe from the Officio Astropathicus brought us the message slate. Midwinter winds shook the sanctum's casements.

I was alone with Neve. We had felt it inappropriate to have company. This was a matter of the gravest import. We had talked, of this and that, to pass the time, though both of us were restless and edgy. She poured generous glasses of Cadian glayva, which took the edge off the cold.

Her aide announced the scribe, and he entered, bowing low, his augmetic chassis grinding beneath his robes. He held out a slate to her clutched in the mechadendrites that served as his hand. Neve took it and dismissed him.

I rose, and put down my barely touched glass of spirits.

Neve limped over to me, leant on her silver crutch, and held up the slate.

'Shall we?' she asked.

We went into the annex and loaded the slate into the ancient codifier. The limpid green display shifted feverishly with runes. She opened the file we were after and set the key to work.

It took a moment or two.

Then the identity of the veteran who had used his power to manipulate Neve's code was revealed on the small, green-washed screen. At last, the damned had a name.

It shocked even me.

'Glory from above,' breathed Inquisitor General Neve. '*Quixos*.'

Aemos was arguing with Neve's chief savant, Cutch.

'Quixos is dead, long dead!' Cutch maintained. 'This is clearly a case of someone using his authority...'

'Quixos is still registered as living by the annals of the Inquisition.'

'As an oversight! No body has ever been retrieved. No proof of death–'

'Precisely...'

'But still! There has been no sign or word from Quixos for over a hundred years.'

'None that we've seen,' I said.

'Eisenhorn's right,' Neve said. 'Inquisitor Utlen was presumed dead for over seventy years. Then he reappeared overnight to bring down the tyrants of Esquestor II.'

'It's most perturbatory,' Aemos muttered.

Quixos. Quixos the Great. Quixos the Bright. One of the most revered inquisitors ever to roam the Imperium. His early texts had been required reading for all of us. He was a legend. At the age of just twenty-one he had burned the daemons out of Artum. Then he had purged the Endorian sub-sector of its false goat-gods. He had transcribed the *Book of Eibon*. He had broken the wretched sub-cult of Nurgle that had tainted one of the palaces of Terra itself. He had tracked down and killed the Chaos Marine Baneglos. He had silenced the Whisperers of Domactoni. He had crucified the Witch-king of Sarpeth on the battlements above his incinerated hive.

But there had always been an odour about Quixos. A hint that he was too close to the evil he prosecuted. He was a radical, certainly. Some amongst the Ordos said he was a rogue. Others said, in low, private voices, much worse.

To me, he was a great man who had perhaps gone too far. I simply honoured his memory and his achievements.

Because, as far as I had been concerned, he was long dead.

'Could he still be alive?' Neve asked.

'Madam, not at all...' Cutch began.

'I don't know why you employ him,' I said, pointing dismissively at the Cadian savant. 'His advice isn't sound.'

'Well really!' Cutch huffed.

'Shut up and go away,' Neve told him.

She stalked across to me and took my empty glass from me. 'Go on, then. Your opinion.'

'You want it? From an adventurer like me? Are you sure, inquisitor general?'

She thrust a topped-up glass of glayva into my hand so hard it sloshed. 'Just give me your damned opinion!'

I sipped. Aemos was staring over at me nervously from the settle by the door.

'Quixos could be very much alive. He'd be... what, now, Aemos?'

'Three hundred and forty-two, sir.'

'Right. Well, that's no age, is it? Not given augmetics, or rejuvanat drugs... or sorcery.'

'Dammit!' Neve said.

'He's an incredibly gifted individual, as his career testifies. He has a reputation, however unwarranted, for straying too far to the radical side. He has... dabbled with the warp. We can say that much. Just because we've heard nothing of him these last hundred or more years, doesn't mean he isn't still active.'

'And that activity?' Neve smacked the tip of her crutch down twice on the tiled floor. 'What? What? Utilising daemonhosts? Perverting inquisitors? Hunting for abominated texts like your Necroteuch? Triggering the dreadful atrocity of Thracian?'

'Perhaps? Why not?'

'Because that would make him a monster! The exact antithesis of everything our order is about!'

'Well, yes it would. It's happened before. A powerful man who gets so close to the evil he is sworn to combat he gets dragged into it. Inquisitor Ruberu, for example.'

'Yes, yes! Ruberu, I know...'

'Grandmaster Derkon?'

'Granted. I remember...'

'Cardinal Palfro of Mimiga? Saint Boniface, also called the Deathshead of a Thousand Tears?' intoned Aemos.

'For the Emperor's sake!'

'High Lord Vandire?' I suggested.

'All right, all right–'

'Horus?' Aemos dared to whisper.

There was a long silence.

'Great Quixos,' Neve murmured, slowly turning to face me. 'Will he be added to that unholy list? Is one of our greatest to be condemned so?'

'If he must be,' I replied.

'What do we do?' she asked.

'We find him. We find out if the passing centuries have truly changed him into the being we fear he is. And if they have, Emperor pardon me, we declare him Heretic and Extremis Diabolus, and we destroy him for his crimes.'

Neve sat down hard, staring into her glass. There was a knock at the sanctum's door, which Aemos answered.

It was Fischig.

'Sir... madam...' he said, acknowledging Neve.

'Well, Fischig?'

'Further to your discoveries today, we have been monitoring inter-orbit traffic. Two hours ago, a craft made planetfall at Kasr Gesh. It cleared Cadian airspace using the inquisitor general's authority code.'

Gesh was the site of the last known cult activity.

I gathered up my coat. 'With your permission, inquisitor general?'

Neve rose with me, her face set hard. 'With *your* permission, Inquisitor Eisenhorn. I'd like to come with you.'

Kasr Gesh was three hours flight from Kasr Derth. Cruel winter had blown in from the upland heaths, and the gun-cutter was vibrating its way against powerful ice storms.

My band was all aboard, preparing weapons. So was Inquisitor General Neve and a six-man squad of Cadian Elite Shock, impassive troopers in winter camo armour, prepping matt-white lasrifles and stubbers in the crew-bay.

'God-throne, they're tough-ass bastards,' Nayl muttered to me as I passed him coming out of the bay.

'Impressed?'

'Scared is more like it. Regular Cadian is soldier enough for me. These are elite. The elite of the elite. The Kasrkin.'

'The what?' It wasn't like an experienced fighter to show deference to other fighting men.

'The Kasrkin. The Cadian best, and you can imagine what that means. Holy Terra, they're stone-killers!'

'How do you know?'

'Oh, please... look at their necks. The Caducades sea-eagle brand. Come to that, just look at their necks. I've seen slimmer trees!'

'Good thing they're on our side,' I said.

'I bloody hope so,' Nayl returned, and moved forward.

The deck lurched again. I walked back down the bay, steadying myself on the overhead handloops, and approached Neve.

She was dressed in Cadian mesh armour, and was adjusting her winter hood. I saw she had exchanged her silver crutch for a lift-assisted cane fitted with a compact cylindrical grenade launcher.

In my fur coat and bodyglove armour, I felt underdressed.

'Your usual attire?' I asked.

'Necessary clothing. You should come out with me sometime, cult-hunting in the islands after dark.'

'My staff are... worried. These men are Kasrkin?'

'Yes.'

'Their reputation precedes them.'

'So did yours.'

'Good point. But, anyway...'

Neve looked round at the row of Cadian elite. 'Captain Echbar!' she shouted, raising her voice above the roar of the buffet and the thrusters.

'Inquisitor general ma'am!' said the warrior on the end.

'Inquisitor Eisenhorn wants reassurance that you are the best of the best and will be careful to watch the backsides of him and his band.'

Six snow-visored faces turned to look at me.

'We've logged the bio-spoors of you and your company into our sighting auspexes, sir,' Echbar announced to me. 'We couldn't shoot them now even if we wanted to.'

'Make sure you don't. My staff and I will be leading the way in. The situation may not call for firepower. If it does, the vox or psyker command is "Rosethorn". Vox-channel is gamma-nine-eight. Are you prepared for a psychic summons?'

'We're prepared for anything.' Echbar told me.

The gun-cutter stopped shaking.

'We've come out of the storm,' Medea voxed me.

A moment later, she crackled, 'I see approach lights. Kasr Gesh landing field in two.'

The pylon stood three kilometres outside the earthworks of Kasr Gesh. The night was clear and glassy, with a heaven full of stars. The Eye of Terror throbbed dimly at the top of the sky. It seemed to me more lurid and brighter than ever before.

Somewhere up there, I knew, orbital detachments of the Cadian Interior Guard were hunting the hidden starship from which the visitors to Kasr Gesh had come. Neve had scrambled them before we left, with strict orders not to move until we had engaged on the ground.

We didn't want our visitors tipped off.

My team moved in up through the frost-caked scrub of the moorland slope. The pylon was simply a black, oblong, absence of stars. I could hear it moaning.

I slid out my main weapon: a storm-bolter which I had sprayed green in memory of the prize sidearm I had lost somewhere on Eechan, may Librarian Brytnoth forgive me. This storm-gun was slightly larger and more powerful, but nothing like so well engineered as the boltpistol I had treasured.

On my hip I wore a Cadian hanger, a short, curved twin-edged sabre that replaced my beloved power sword. It was just a simple piece of sharp steel, but I'd had the hierarchs at the Ministorum of Kasr Derth make some modifications.

Still, in truth, I felt vulnerable going up that slope.

Nayl was to my left, fielding a combat-cannon. Husmaan to my right with his trustworthy long-las. Inshabel was to his right, armed with a brace of antique laspistols that had belonged to Inquisitor Roban. Fischig, hefting an old and trusted Arbites-issue riot-gun, had gone wide to the far left.

Bequin, a long-barrelled autopistol in her gloved hand, was right beside me.

Behind us, Neve and her Kasrkin lurked, waiting for my signal.

Aemos was aboard the gun-cutter with Medea, hovering above the drop point, lights killed. They, rather than Neve and her elite, were my reassurance.

'What do you see?' I voxed.

'Nothing,' replied Husmaan and Nayl.

'I've got an angle into the seat of the pylon,' said Inshabel. 'I see lights.'

'Confirm that,' crackled Fischig, wide to the left. 'There are men down there. I count eight, no ten. Twelve. Portable lights. They've got machines.'

'Machines?'

'Handheld. Auspexes.'

'Measuring again,' Neve whispered over the link.

'I'm sure,' I said. Then I said, in Glossia: 'Thorn eyes flesh, rapturous beasts at hand. Aegis to arms, crucible. All points cowled. Razor torus pathway, pattern ebony.'

My storm-gun made a loud click as I racked it.

The robed men working in the floodlights around the foot of the pylon froze and slowly turned from their work to look at me.

I walked down from the moor, through the ice-stiffened bracken, bracing my gun in a pose that could kill any one of them.

Bequin followed me a few steps behind, her pistol held loosely, ready to swing up.

I knew we were covered by Husmaan, Inshabel, Nayl and Fischig.

'Who is the leader here?' I asked, panning my weapon around.

'I am,' said one of the robed figures.

'Step forward and identify yourself,' I said.

'To whom?'

I raised the rosette plainly in my left hand. 'Imperial Inquisition.' Some of the robed men moaned with dismay.

The leader did not. He stepped forward. I could suddenly smell a cold, metallic scent, one that was not new to me.

A warning that came too late.

The leader slowly drew back his cowl. His angular, cruel head was hairless and a cold blue light shone out through his skin. Sharpened, steel-tipped horns sprouted from his brow. His eyes were white slits.

A daemonhost!

'Cherubael?' I said, foolishly, stupidly.

'Your witless ally is not here, Eisenhorn,' said the being, baring his teeth and gleaming with light.

'My name is Prophaniti.'

FIFTEEN

ROSETHORN
WHAT CADIANS ARE BORN FOR
THE LAST THING I EXPECTED

There were two ways for this to go. The first was for me to continue talking, and still be talking when the daemonhost killed me and tossed my smoking corpse on the piled bodies of my comrades. The second was for me to say 'Rosethorn' and place my trust in the mettle of my supporters and the ever-vigilant gaze of the holy God-Emperor.

I said 'Rosethorn.'

The thing, Prophaniti, was stepping towards me. I shot at it with my storm-gun, watching in horrid fascination as it caught the white hot bolt rounds out of the air in its outstretched hands, like a man idly catching slow-tossed racquet balls.

The bolts dulled to an ember-red in its palms, and it tossed them aside.

But its entire attention was on me.

Its mistake.

Husmaan's first hot-shot round cracked into the side of its head, and snapped its skull around. As it was reeling, its robes were ripped across by double laspistol fire from Inshabel. Then Fischig's riot-gun roared and knocked it down in the brittle bracken. Fischig liked to spend his free time hand-moulding the shot for his riot-gun's cartridges. Every pellet was silver, and stamped with a sacred sigil of warding that I had taught him long ago.

Prophaniti writhed in agony, the blessed buck-shot burning into its flesh. It started to rise, wrathful and frenzied, but a grinding whir rose from my left, a sound like a circular saw running up to speed.

Nayl's cycling drum-cannon raked the daemonhost and the earth around it, doing hideous damage. The blizzard of shots twisted it, ripping off one of its legs at the knee and the fingers off its left hand.

Eldritch power, white-cold like frost, spurted from its wounds like lava, and burned the soil.

The other cultists were moving now, pulling weapons and firing wildly into the night. The place lit up with shooting.

Las-fire came from behind us, startlingly close, whipping past our elbows and shoulders. Two of the cultists crumpled, one of them smashing over some of the erected floodlights.

Echbar and his Kasrkin charged in past us to engage.

In truth, I may say now that they were somehow more terrifying than the daemonhost. For Prophaniti was a supernatural thing, and one expected it to be horrifying.

The Kasrkin were just men. It made their actions all the more astonishing. Six white blurs, they fell upon the cultists, lasguns barking at close range. They wasted no shots. One shot, one kill. A cultist fled past me, and a Kasrkin swung to bring him down. His weapon refused to fire as its sight-auspex detected my bio-spoor in the range-field. A second later, I was no longer blocking the shot and the weapon spat.

The fleeing cultist tumbled over headlong in the brush.

More cultists had emerged from the other side of the pylon, and I could hear rapid exchanges of gunfire in that direction. Nayl's combat-cannon was making its distinctive metallic whir between bursts of fire. Inshabel's las-cracks overlapped themselves.

'Fischig!' I yelled. 'Lead off round the back of the pylon. See what you can find. Maybe take a damn prisoner before the Kasrkin slay them all!'

I turned back to deal with the ruined daemonhost. We had punished it badly, but I had no illusions as to its resilience.

Or rather... I had thought I hadn't.

Prophaniti was already gone, the ground still smoking and congealing where it had lain.

'Damn! Damn!'

Neve limped down the slope to me. 'Eisenhorn?'

'The daemonhost! Did you see it?'

She shook her head. A loud explosion rolled from the far side of the pylon.

'You killed it, didn't you?'

'Not even slightly,' I replied.

'Gregor!' Bequin shrieked.

Prophaniti was behind me, hanging in the air, incandescent with power. It was naked, and wore the terrible wounds we had inflicted like medals. The right leg, frayed at the knee, dribbled glowing white ichor. Entry wounds and burns bubbled and smoked across its chest. Its head hung slack on a neck broken by Husmaan's hot-shot. It spread its arms and a hand that was just a thumb and a mangled palm sprayed lightning into the midnight grass.

'Nice... try...' the slack head gurgled.

With its robe gone, I could see its body was strung with chains, padlocks and bindings. Stitching needles and other iron awls were pierced into its luminous flesh. Various amulets hung from the chains, or from the barbed wire looped around its neck.

'Run,' I said to Neve and Bequin. 'Run!'

Neve raised her silver cane and triggered the launcher.

The grenade hit Prophaniti in the lower torso and blew it back a few metres with a flash of fyceline.

It rushed back towards us, moaning and chattering in a warp-cursed language.

Bequin grabbed both me and Neve. Her untouchable quality was our only defence now, and she knew it.

Prophaniti stopped short of us, just a metre or so away, hovering in the air and shining like a star. I could smell the rank stench of eternal murder about it.

Its broken neck made a sound like snapping twigs as it slowly turned its lolling head to look at us. The light of dead suns billowed from its eyes and mouth.

Bequin's fingers bit into my arm. The three of us looked up at it, hair ruffled by the warp-winds it generated.

'Tenacious,' it said. 'No wonder Cherubael likes you. He said you employed untouchables. A wise move. You can't hurt me with your guns, but with her around, I can't touch you with my mind.'

'Fortunately, I don't have to,' it added.

It lashed out suddenly with its maimed hand. Neve shrieked as she was hurled aside. There was blood on Prophaniti's thumb talon.

Alizebeth's psychic deadness blocked its psychic rage. But not its physical assault.

It lashed out again, and I leapt back, dragging Bequin.

Prophaniti cackled.

'Alizebeth!' I yelled, and grabbed her by the hand. 'Stay with me!'

I drew my hanger. The short curved blade shone in Prophaniti's glare. The runes inscribed on the blade by the Ministorum glittered.

I swung hard, skillessly and frantic, the blade of the hunting sword biting into its rib-meat. It howled and flew back, smoke issuing from the gash.

I circled, hanger in my right hand, Bequin clinging to my left.

'You've done your homework. Pentagrammatic runes on your blade. A nice touch. They hurt!'

It lunged at me.

'But nothing like the hurt you will feel!'

Alizebeth screamed. She fell, and I struggled to hold on to her hand. If our contact broke, I would feel the full force of the daemonhost's power.

I blocked with my falcate blade, shredding the flesh off the left part of its chest, exposing the ribs.

Its talons ripped into my left shoulder and down my flank, ripping my body-armour into tatters.

Blood cascaded down inside my clothes.

I swung again, trying for an *uin ulsar*. It gripped my blade fast, in its one good hand. Smoke rose from the clamping fist around the blade.

It clenched its teeth in pain. 'The wards... hurt... but they are no... stronger... than the weapon... you should learn to... make your weapons sounder... next time...'

'Not that there will be... a next time...' it added. The hanger had become so hot, I let it go with a howl. Prophaniti tossed the buckled, molten steel aside. It had burned its hand terribly, but it didn't seem to notice.

'Now comes death,' it said, reaching for me.

The next few seconds are burned in my memory. I will never see such heroism again, I am sure. Captain Echbar and two of his Kasrkin troopers assaulted Prophaniti from the rear. Their lasguns wouldn't fire because Bequin and I were in their range-field.

Echbar body-tackled the daemonhost, smashing it away from us. Prophaniti hurled him aside, and then incinerated the second Kasrkin mid-leap with its eyes. The third jammed his Cadian bayonet up to the hilt in Prophaniti's breastbone. Fire exploded back from the wound, down the trooper's arm and engulfed him.

He fell back screaming as Echbar came in again, a ragged hole in his cheek and throat. His knife, clenched double-handed, split Prophaniti open down the back bone. The warp-energies that boiled out blew Echbar apart.

Screaming, Prophaniti writhed away through the air.

I knew it wasn't dead. I knew it couldn't really die.

But the Cadian elite had given me an opening by sacrificing their lives. They had fallen in the service of the God-Emperor, which is what every Cadian is born to do.

'Aegis! By scarlet inferno! Thorn redux!'

I screamed the words into my vox, clinging on to Bequin's hand.

Prophaniti came hurtling towards us.

Lights blazing, the gun-cutter surged in overhead in a killing run. The down-draft blasted the icy bracken flat and threw us over. Medea was low, so low...

The gun-servitors trained wing and chin turrets on the charging daemonhost.

When they opened up, their firepower was so monumental, they vapourised it.

The light went out.

I pulled Bequin to me as the drizzle of liquidised host-form rained on us out of the cold night.

I could hear Fischig calling my name.

'Help her,' I said to Fischig as I rose, and he scooped Bequin up.

I looked around. The place was littered with dead, most of them cultists. Inshabel had found Neve, lacerated but alive, twenty metres up the slope, and was calling for a medic.

The aft thrusters of the gun-cutter winked hot-white in the night sky as Medea banked around out of her run to come down again.

Nayl, who had taken a flesh wound to the arm, leaned against the pylon and shut off his whirring cannon-drum.

'We... we need to regroup,' I said.

'Agreed,' said Fischig.

'You have no idea what you're up against, do you?' asked Husmaan.

We all turned. The old skin-hunter from Windhover was stalking down the moor slope towards us, his long-las slung over one crooked arm. Fierce graupel had begun to fleck down from the clouding sky.

'Do you?' he hissed again. I felt Bequin tense.

It wasn't Husmaan.

Husmaan looked at me. White light shone from his eyes. His voice was Prophaniti's.

'Not the slightest clue,' he said. 'You can destroy my physical host, but you cannot break the links to the master.'

'Husmaan!' Inshabel cried.

'Not here any more. He was the most open mind, so I took him. He will serve for a while.'

I took a step forward. Husmaan raised a hand. 'Don't bother, Eisenhorn,' said Prophaniti. 'I could kill you all here, now... but what's about to happen is far more interesting.'

Husmaan, his arms held out from his body and his head back, suddenly rose into the air, dropping his prized long-las. Steadily, he floated away into the sky until he had vanished over the moors into the dawn's counter glow.

'What did he mean?' asked Bequin.

'I don't–'

Floodlights mobbed over the rise and we suddenly heard the clank of armoured tracks.

Twenty Cadian APCs crested the brow, their floods beaming down at us. Cadian shock troops scrambled down the slope, covering us with their guns.

'What the hell?' Nayl cried.

I was stunned. This was the last thing I had expected.

'Inquisitor Eisenhorn,' boomed a vox-amped voice from the lead APC. 'For crimes against the Imperium, for the atrocity at Thracian, for consorting with daemonhosts, you are hereby arrested and condemned to death.'

I recognised the voice.

It was Osma.

SIXTEEN

THE HAMMER OF WITCHES
THREE MONTHS IN THE CARNIFICINA
FLIGHT FROM CADIA

Flanked by six robed interrogators reading aloud from the Books of Pain and the Chapters of Punishment, Inquisitor Leonid Osma came down the moorland slope towards me. Pink dawn light was beginning to spear lengthways across the bleak heath, and the gorse and bracken was stirred by the early morning breeze. Distantly, heath grouse and ptarcerns were whooping and calling to the midwinter sun.

Osma was a well-built, broad-shouldered man in his one fifties. He wore brass power armour that glowed almost orange in the ruddy dawn. Ornate Malleus crests decorated his armour's besagews and poleyns and six purity seals were threaded around his bevor like a floral wreath. A long cloak of white fur played out behind him, brushing the tops of the heather and gorse.

His face was blunt and pugnacious. His eyes were glinting dots set in puffy lids, fringed by heavy, grey eyebrows. His bowl-cut hair was the colour of sword-metal. Some years before, he had lost his lower jaw during a fight with a Khornate berserker. The augmetic replacement was a jutting chin of chrome, linked into his skull by feed tubes and micro-servos. The emblem of the Inquisition rose above his head on a standard mounted between his shoulder blades. In one hand he carried a power hammer, the mark of his Ordo.

In the other, a sealed ebony scroll tube. I recognised it at once. A carta extremis.

'This is insanity!' Fischig growled. The Cadians around us stiffened and jabbed with their weapons.

'Enough!' I warned Fischig. I turned to my companions. They looked so lost, so miserable, so dismayed.

'We will not fight our own,' I told them. 'Surrender your weapons. I will soon have this laughable error resolved.'

Bequin and Inshabel handed their weapons to the Cadian guards. Fischig reluctantly allowed the storm troopers to divorce him from his riot-gun. Nayl unclipped his drum-cannon's ammo feed, slid out the magazine box and passed that to the waiting troops, leaving the disabled heavy weapon strapped around his torso on its harness.

I nodded, satisfied. 'Thorn bids Aegis, by cool water, soft,' I whispered into my vox and then turned to meet Osma.

He raised his power hammer in a brief gesture and the mumbling interrogators fell silent and closed their books. 'Gregor Eisenhorn,' he said in precisely enunciated High Formal Gothic, 'In fealty to the God-Emperor, our undying lord, and by the grace of the Golden Throne, in the name of the Ordo Malleus and the Inquisition, I call thee diabolus, and in the testimony of thy crimes, I submit this carta. May Imperial justice account in all balance. The Emperor protects.'

I slid my storm-gun out of its holster, ejected the clip and handed it to him grip first.

'I hear full well thy charge and thy words, and make my submission,' I responded in the ancient form. 'May Imperial justice account in all balance. The Emperor protects.'

'Dost thou accept this carta from my hand?'

'I accept it into mine, for that I may prove it thrice false.'

'Dost thou state thy innocence now, at the going off?'

'I state it true and clear. May it be so writ down.'

Vox-drones idling by the shoulders of the interrogators had been recording all this, but the youngest interrogator was transcribing it all with a holoquill into a dispositional slate suspended before him on a grav plate. I noted this detail with some satisfaction.

Preposterous though the charges were, Osma was prosecuting with total and precise formality.

'I ask of thee thy badge of office,' Osma said.

'I deny thy asking. By the code of prejudice, I declare my right to retain my rank until due process is concluded.'

He nodded. His language changed from High Formal to Low Gothic. 'I expected as much. Thank you for avoiding unpleasantness.'

'I don't think I've avoided any unpleasantness, Osma. What I have avoided is bloodshed. This is ridiculous.'

'They all say that,' he muttered snidely, turning away.

'No,' I said levelly, stopping him dead. 'The guilty and the polluted fight. They deny. They struggle. In my lifetime, I have brought down nine marked diabolus. None went quietly. Mark that fact in your record,' I said to the scribing interrogator. 'If I was guilty, I would not be submitting to your process so politely.'

'Mark it so!' Osma told his hesitating scribe.

He looked back at me. 'Read the carta, Eisenhorn. You're guilty as sin. This show of understanding and co-operation is exactly what I would have expected from a being as canny and clever as you.'

'A compliment, Osma?'

He spat into the bracken. 'You were one of the best, Eisenhorn. Lord Rorken actually pleaded for you. I acknowledge your past triumphs. But you have been turned. You are Malleus. You are an abomination. And you will pay.'

'This is insane...' Neve muttered, limping towards us.

'And none of your business, inquisitor general,' Osma replied.

Neve faced him, her torn armour wet with her own blood.

'This is my province, inquisitor. Eisenhorn has proved himself to me. This charade is interfering with Inquisition business.'

'Read the carta, inquisitor general,' Osma told her. 'And shut up. Eisenhorn is clever and convincing. He has fooled you, lady. Be thankful that you're not implicated.'

My companions were arraigned at Kasr Derth, under Neve's recognizance. No such luxury for me. I was flown south aboard a Cadian military lighter, through the dawn, to the furthest islet of the Caducades group, to the infamous Cadian prison, the Carnificina.

They had fettered my hands and feet. I sat on a bracket-bench dropped from the wall of the lighter's armoured hold, surrounded by Cadian guards, and read the carta by the shifting light that sheared in through the window slits.

I could scarcely believe what I was reading.

'Well?' grunted Fischig from his seat in the corner. I had been allowed one spokesman, and I had selected Fischig, with his legal background.

'Read it,' I said, holding the carta out to him.

One of the impassive Cadians took it from me and passed it to the scowling Hubrusian.

After a few moments spent reviewing the scroll, Fischig blurted out an incredulous profanity.

'Just what I thought,' I said.

The Carnificina jutted up from the thrashing sea like the molar of a massive herbivore, the gum eaten away.

It had not been built so much as hollowed out of the upthrust crag. There wasn't a wall on the prison isle thinner than five metres.

Vicious plungers broke in white spray around its granite base and the western aspects were open to the worst of the pelagic abuse from the oceans beyond. Icebergs from the calving glaciers at Cadu Sound and the distant Caducades Isthmus jostled and splintered in the open water between the prison isle and the barren atolls opposing it.

Kelp and hardy, lean axel trees decorated its lower slopes.

The lighter swung in over the eastern ramparts and settled on a pad cut from the stone. I was marched under guard out into the cold sunlight, and then into the dank hallways of the rock. The white-washed walls sweated and stank of seawater. Rusting chains ran down from the ceiling to the hatches of forgotten oubliettes.

I could hear the shouts and screams of prisoners. The demented and infected of the Cadians lived here, mostly ex-servicemen who had been driven mad in the wars of the Eye.

The Cadian troops handed me over to a squad of red-uniformed prison guards who reeked of unwashed flesh and carried pain-flails and leather whips.

They opened up a fifty centimetre-thick hatch cover riven with studs, and pushed me into a cell.

It was four paces by four, cut from stone, with no window. It stank of piss. The previous incumbent had died here... and never been removed.

I pushed aside his dry bones and sat on the wooden bunk. I knew nothing. I had no idea if the Cadian Interior had captured that rogue starship, or if anyone had managed to track the flight of the thing that had been poor Husmaan.

The path to Quixos, the path we had been so lucky to strike at last, was disappearing by the second as we played these games. And there was nothing I could do about it.

'When did you first decide to consort with daemons?' asked Interrogator Riggre.

'I have never done so, or decided to do so.'

'But the daemonhost Cherubael knows you by name,' said Interrogator Palfir.

'Is that a question?'

'It–' Palfir stammered.

'What is your relationship with the daemonhost Cherubael?' cut in Interrogator Moyag sternly.

'I have no relationship with any daemonhost,' I replied.

I was chained to a wooden chair in the great hall of the Carnificina, winter sunlight shafting down from the high windows. Osma's three interrogators stalked around me like caged beasts, their robes swirling in the draft.

'It knows your name,' Moyag said testily.

'I know yours, Moyag. Does that give me power over you?'

'How did you orchestrate the atrocity at Thracian Hive Primaris?' asked Palfir.

'I didn't. Next question.'

'Do you know who did?' asked Riggre.

'Not precisely. But I believe it was the being you have referred to. Cherubael.'

'He has been in your life before.'

'I have thwarted him before. One hundred years ago, at 56-Izar. You must have the records.'

Riggre glanced at his colleagues before replying. 'We do. But you have been searching for him ever since.'

'Yes. As a matter of duty. Cherubael is a repellent abomination. Do you wonder that I would seek him out?'

'Not all your contacts with him have been recorded.'

'What?'

'We know some contacts have remained secret,' Moyag rephrased.

'How?'

'The sworn testimony of an Alain von Baigg. He states that you sent an operative code-named Hound out to make contact with Cherubael, one year ago, and that you refrained from telling your Ordo master about it.'

'I didn't think to bother Lord Rorken with the matter.'

'So, you don't deny it?'

'Deny what? Hunting for Chaos? No, I don't.'

'In secret?'

'What inquisitor doesn't work in secret?'

'Who is Hound?' asked Palfir.

I had no wish to make Fischig's life more difficult just then. I said, 'I don't know his real name. He works clandestinely.'

I thought they would press me, but instead Moyag said, 'Why did you survive the Thracian horror?'

'I was lucky.'

Palfir walked a circle around me, his polished boots squeaking on the worn floor. 'Let me make it clear. We are just beginning here. In respect to your rank and career, we are employing interrogation of the First Action. The First Action is–'

I cut him short. 'I have been an inquisitor for many years, Palfir. I know what the First Action is. Verbal interview without duress.'

'Then you know of the Third and Fifth Actions?' sneered Riggre.

'Light physical torture and psychic interrogation. And by the way, you just utilised the Second Action – verbal threat of and/or description of Actions that may follow.'

'Have you ever been tortured, Eisenhorn?' asked Moyag.

'Yes, by less squeamish men than you. And I have interrogated too. Second Action methods really won't work on me.'

'Inquisitor Osma has authorised us to use any methods up to and including Ninth Action,' spat Palfir.

'Again, a threat. Second Action. It won't work on me. I told you that. I am trying to be co-operative.'

'Who is Hound?' asked Riggre.

Ah, there it was, the follow-up, designed to wrong-foot by coming out of sequence. For a moment, I began to admire their interrogation skills.

'I don't know his real name. He works clandestinely.'

'Is it not Godwyn Fischig? The man you chose as your second here. The man who waits outside this chamber?'

There are times when the injuries Gorgone Locke did to my face on Gudrun have their benefits. My face simply couldn't show the reaction they were hoping to see. But inside, I balked. Their intelligence was good, good enough to have cracked Glossia, if only partially. I was sure of the source. They had already mentioned that weasel von Baigg. Months before, on Thracian right before the atrocity, I had begun to suspect von Baigg. At that time, I merely assumed he was Lord Rorken's plant to watch over me. Now I realised he was happy to talk to anyone. I had recognised von Baigg's weakness and stalled his career. Clearly he had decided to seek advancement from other inquisitors by selling me out.

'If you are telling me Fischig is the operative I know as Hound, I am truly surprised,' I replied levelly, choosing my words with extreme care.

'We will talk to him in time,' said Palfir.

'Not while he is my recognised second. That would break the code of prejudice. If you wish to interview him, I must be allowed a new second. Of my choosing.'

'We will get to that,' said Riggre.

'Why did you survive the Thracian horror?' asked Moyag.

'I was lucky.'

'Explain lucky?'

'I had stopped to honour the tomb of the admiral. The Spatian Gate protected me from the air strikes.' After the lies Cherubael had told me on Eechan, I dreaded this question coming up again under psychic interview. The lies, or at least my attempts to screen them, would be picked up.

'The atrocity was simply cover to allow you to liberate and remove from Thracian the heretic psyker Esarhaddon.'

'I would normally address that notion with scorn. If the entire event had been staged simply to "launder" the psyker, then it was inhumanly wasteful. However, I believe in some regards you are right. That's what the atrocity was engineered to do. But not by me.'

Moyag licked his yellowing teeth eagerly. 'You maintain that it was in fact Interrogator Lyko who executed the event?'

'In collaboration with the daemonhost.'

'But Lyko cannot answer those charges, can he? Because you killed him on Eechan.'

'I executed Lyko on Eechan as a traitor-enemy of the Imperium.'

'I submit to you that you killed him because he was on to you. You killed him to silence him.'

'Do I really have to be here? You're doing a fine job of making up your own answers.'

'Where is Esarhaddon?'

'Wherever Cherubael took him.'

'And where is that?' asked Palfir.

I shrugged. 'To his master. Quixos.'

All three of them laughed. 'Quixos is dead. He died long ago!' Moyag chuckled.

'Then why did the inquisitor general and I find that he had been manipulating her codes to gain access to Cadian airspace?'

'Because that's how you made it look. You say Quixos used his power to steal her authority code. If that's true, then it's a crime any deviant inquisitor of renown could manage. You could manage it. And using a dead man's code means no one is going to object.'

'Quixos isn't dead.' I cleared my throat. 'Quixos is Hereticus and Extremis Diabolus. He has perverted inquisitors such as Lyko and Molitor into his service. He uses daemonhosts. He triggers holocausts to cover his theft of alpha-plus class psykers.'

The three interrogators fell silent for a moment.

'We are wasting time here,' I said. 'I am not the man you want.'

But the time-wasting continued. A week, passed, then a second. Every day, I was taken to the great hall and subjected to anything from two to six hours of First Action interview. The questions were repeated so many times, I became sick of hearing them. None of the interrogators seemed to listen to my statements. As far as I knew, no part of my story was being checked out.

They were clearly wary of escalating to physical or psychic means of extraction. Because I was a psyker, I could at least make things difficult enough so that they'd never know how much of what they were getting out of me was true. Osma had evidently decided to wear me down with endless cycles of verbal cross-examination.

For fifteen minutes each evening, with the ocean light fading, I was allowed to speak with Fischig. These conversations were pointless. The cell areas were undoubtedly laced with vox-thieves and listening devices, and as far as we knew, Glossia was compromised.

Fischig could tell me little, although I was able to learn that Medea, Aemos and the gun-cutter were not in Osma's hands, and neither was the *Essene*.

There had been no further sighting of Prophaniti-Husmaan, and Fischig was certain that the mystery starship that had delivered Prophaniti to Cadia had not been intercepted that fateful night.

Through Fischig's agency, I sent petitions to Osma, to Rorken and to Neve, protesting my arrest and urging them to take further action regarding Quixos. No word came back.

Candlemas was long past. Three more weeks went by. I realised that the year had turned. Outside the thick, bleak walls of the Carnificina, it was 340.M41.

At the end of my third month of detention and interrogation, I was led into the great hall for my daily interview and found Osma waiting for me instead of the usual interrogators.

'Sit,' he said, gesturing to the chair in the centre of the stark room.

It was dark and cold. Bitter, late winter storms were pushing in from the east, and though it was day, no light came from the high windows. They were muffled with snow. My breath steamed in the air, and I shivered. Osma had arranged six lamps around the edges of the room.

I sat down, pushing my hands into the pockets of my coat against the chill. I didn't want Osma to see my distress. He stood, warm and insulated in his burnished power armour, reviewing a data-slate.

I could see myself, reflected in the polished panels of his backplate. My clothes were ragged and filthy. My skin pale. I had dropped a good seven kilos, and now sported a thick beard as unruly as my hair. The only item in my possession was the Inquisitorial rosette in my coat pocket. It comforted me.

Osma turned to face me. 'In three months, your story has not changed.'

'That should tell you something.'

'It tells me you have great reserves of strength and a careful mind.'

'Or that I'm not lying.'

He put the slate down on one of the lamp tables.

'Let me explain to you what is going to happen. Lord Rorken has persuaded Grandmaster Orsini to have you extradited to Thracian Primaris. There you will stand trial for the charges in the carta extremis before a Magistery

Tribunal of the Ordo Malleus and the Officio of Internal Prosecution. Rorken isn't happy, but it is all Orsini would allow. Rorken, I have heard, feels that your innocence – or guilt – can be ascertained once and for all in a formal trial.'

'The result of that trial may embarrass you and your master, Lord Bezier.'

He laughed. 'In truth, I would welcome such embarrassment if it meant the exoneration of a valuable inquisitor like you, Eisenhorn. But I don't think it will. You will burn on Thracian for this, Eisenhorn, as surely as you would have done here.'

'I'll take my chances, Osma.'

He nodded. 'So will I. The Black Ships will arrive in three days time to conduct you to Thracian Primaris. That gives me three days to break you before the matter is taken out of my hands.'

'Be careful, Osma.'

'I'm always careful. Tomorrow, my staff will begin Ninth Action examination of you. There will be no respite until the Black Ships arrive or you tell me what I want to hear.'

'Two days of Ninth Action methods will probably guarantee I won't be alive when the Black Ships come.'

'Probably. A shame, and questions will be asked. But this is a lonely prison and I am in charge. That is why, today, I'm just talking to you. Just you and me. A last chance. Tell me the whole truth now, Eisenhorn, man to man. Make this easy on us both. Confess your crimes before the pain begins tomorrow, spare us the trial on Thracian, and I'll do everything in my power to ensure your execution is quick and painless.'

'I'll gladly tell you the truth.'

His eyes brightened.

'It's all there, on that slate you were reading. Exactly as I have been saying these last three months.'

When the guards took me back to my frigid cell, down stone hallways where the ocean gales moaned, Fischig was waiting for me. Our daily fifteen minutes.

He had brought a lamp, and a tray with my night meal: thin, tepid fish-broth and stale hunks of rusk bread with a glass of watered rum.

I sat down on the crude bunk.

'I'm to be extradited for trial,' I told him.

He nodded. 'But I understand tomorrow the painwork begins. I've filed a protest, but I'm sure it'll be accidentally lost in the trash.'

'I'm sure it will.'

'You should eat,' he said.

'I'm not hungry.'

'Just eat. You'll need your strength and from the look of you, you've precious little of that.'

I shook my head.

'Gregor,' he said, dropping his voice. 'I have a question to ask you. You won't like it much, but it's important.'

'Important?'

'To me. And to your friends.'

'Ask it.'

'Do you remember – God-Emperor, but it seems so long ago! – last year, when we met up again, at that grave field outside Kasr Tyrok?'

'Of course.'

'In the shrine tower, you said to me that you couldn't conceive of doing anything that would please or benefit a daemon. You said, "I can't ever imagine myself that insane."'

'I remember it clearly. You said that if you ever thought I was, you'd shoot me yourself.'

He nodded, with a sour chuckle. There was a moment of silence, broken only by the crackling of the lamp and the boom of the sea outside the prison ramparts.

'You want to be sure, don't you, Godwyn?' I asked.

He looked at me, reproachfully.

'I can understand that. I expect total loyalty from you and all my staff. You have the right to be assured of the same from me.'

'Then you know my question.'

I fixed him with my eyes. 'You want to ask if I'm lying. If there's any truth to the charges. If you have been working for a man who consorts with daemons.'

'It's a stupid question, I know. If you are those things, you won't hesitate to lie again now.'

'I'm too tired for anything but the truth, Godwyn. I swear, by the Golden Throne, I am not what Osma says I am. I am a true servant of the Emperor and the Inquisition. Find me an eagle and I'll swear on that too. I don't know what else I can do to convince you.'

He got to his feet. 'That's enough for me. I just wanted to be sure. Your word has always been enough, and after all the years we've been together, I was sure that you'd tell me if... even if it was...'

'Know this, old friend. I would. Even if I was the scum Osma believes me to be, and even if I could hide it from him... I couldn't lie to a direct question from you. Not you, Chastener Fischig.'

The guard rapped on the cell door.

'One minute more!' Fischig shouted. 'Eat your supper,' he said to me.

'Did Osma put you up to this?' I asked.

'Hell, no!' he snarled, offended.

'It's all right. I didn't think so.'

The guard hammered again.

'All right, damn your eyes!' Fischig growled.

'I'll see you tomorrow,' I said.

'Yeah,' he replied. 'Do one thing for me.'

'Name it.'

'Eat your supper.'

The cramps began just after what I guessed was midnight. They woke me from a bad sleep. Pain surged through my body and my mind was numb.

I hadn't felt this bad since Pye's handiwork on Lethe Eleven, during the Darknight almost two whole years before.

I tried to rise, and fell off the bunk. Spasms wracked me, and I cried out. I vomited up the dregs of the dire supper. Bouts of fever-heat and death-chill twitched through me.

I don't know how long it took for me to crawl to the cell door, or how long I lay there beating my fists against it until it opened. Hours, possibly.

Consciousness ebbed and flowed with the cramping and the rising agony.

'Holy Emperor!' the guard exclaimed as he opened the door and saw me by the light of his rush-lamp.

He called out and feet came beating down the cell way.

'He's sick,' I heard the guard say.

'Leave him till morning,' said another.

'He'll be dead,' the first guard answered nervously.

'Please...' I stammered, reaching out my hand. It was frozen in a claw-shape, paralysed and ugly.

Others were arriving. I heard Fischig's voice.

'He needs a doctor. Trained medicae help,' Fischig said.

'It's not allowed,' complained a guard.

'Look at him, man! He's dying! An attack of some sort.'

'Let me through,' said another voice.

It was the prison medic, accompanied by Interrogator Riggre, who looked as if he had been roused from his bed.

'He's faking it, leave him!' Riggre said contemptuously.

'Shut up!' Fischig snarled. 'Look at him! That's no act!'

'He's a master of deception,' Riggre returned. 'Maybe he's been licking the lead-paint off the door to aid his act, more fool him. This is a sham. Leave him.'

'He's dying,' said Fischig.

'He looks bloody sick,' said a guard uncomfortably.

More cramping spasms twisted me involuntarily.

The doctor was hunched over me. I could hear the beeping of the medicae auspex he'd taken from his pharmacopoeia.

'This is no act,' he muttered. 'His body's in seizure. You can't fake muscle binding like that. Blood-oxygen is down to thirty per cent and his heart is defibrillating. He'll be dead in less than an hour.'

'Give him a shot. Fix him!' Riggre yelled.

'I can't, sir. Not here. We haven't got the facilities. Ahh! Emperor, look! He's bleeding out now, from the eyes and nose.'

'Do something!' Riggre screamed.

'We have to get him to an infirmary. Kasr Derth is the nearest. We have to get him there quickly or he's dead!'

'That's ridiculous, doctor!' said Riggre. 'You must be able to do something...'

'Not here.'

'Call up a flight, Riggre,' Fischig said.

'He's a primary level prisoner of the Inquisition! We can't just take him out of here!'

'Then get Osma–'

'He's gone back to the mainland for the night.'

Fischig's voice was low. 'Are you going to be the one to tell Osma you let his prize captive die on the floor of his cell?'

'N-no...'

'I'll tell him, then. I'll tell Osma that his man Riggre cheated him of the greatest prosecution of his career because he couldn't be bothered to authorise transport and thus let Eisenhorn die of toxic shock in this prison stack!'

'Call up transport!' Riggre shouted at the guards. 'Now!'

They carried me up to the stone-cut landing pad on a stretcher. Voices yelled and argued in the biting wind and blizzard-filled darkness. The medic had fixed up an intravenous drip and was trying to slow my symptoms with a few drugs from his kit.

The pad lights flickered on, cold and white, and backlit the swirling snow into black dots.

A Cadian shuttle came in low, its attitude thrusters shaking the pad and swirling the snowfall in random directions.

They carried me into the green-lit interior, and the worst of the cold and weather was stolen away as the hatch shut. I felt the sudden yaw of the ship as we lifted up and turned away towards the mainland. Fischig loomed over me, adjusting the restraining straps that held me into the shuttle's cot. Over the roar of the engines, I could hear Riggre shouting at the pilot.

Covertly, Fischig slid an injector vial from his coat and fixed it into the intravenous rig in place of the prison doctor's injector.

I began to feel better almost at once.

'Stay still, and breathe slowly,' Fischig whispered. 'And hold on tight. Things are about to get... bumpy.'

'Contact! Three kilometres and coming in hard!' I heard the co-pilot blurt.

'What the hell is that?' Riggre demanded.

There was a pinging sound from the shuttle's transponder.

'Throne of Earth! They've got a target-lock on us!' exclaimed the pilot.

'Attention, shuttle,' a voice crackled over the open vox. 'Set down on the islet west five-two by three-six. Now, or I will shoot you out of the air!'

My vision was settling now. I looked across the green-lit cabin and saw Riggre pull a laspistol.

'What treachery is this?' he asked, looking at Fischig.

'I think you should do as you were asked and set down right now,' said Fischig calmly.

Riggre made to fire the pistol, but there was a searing flash of light. Fischig burned Riggre with a blast from the digi-weapon built into the jokaero-made ring on his right index finger. An item of Maxilla's jewellery, I realised.

Fischig fired another shot that vaporised the vox-system.

'Down!' he ordered the pilot, pointing the ring at him.

The shuttle made emergency groundfall in a snowstorm on the rocky beach of the uninhabited islet.

'Hands on your heads!' Fischig ordered the crewmen as he bundled me out of the hatch and into the blizzard.

I could barely walk and he had to support me.

'You poisoned me,' I gasped.

'I had to make it convincing. Aemos prepared a dose that would reactivate the binary poison in your body. Pye's poison.'

'You bastards!'

'Hah! A man who can curse is far from dead. Come on!'

He half-carried me across the shingle into the oceanic gale, snowflakes stinging our faces. Lights swooped down ahead of us as the gun-cutter came in, executing a perfect, Betancore-style landing on the icy shingle.

Fischig bundled me up the landing ramp into the arms of Bequin and Inshabel.

'Dear lord, have you thought this through?' I wheezed.

'Of course we have!' Bequin snapped. 'Nathun! Get a booster shot of antivenin!'

For the second time in under two years, I was dead. From binary poison at the hands of Beldame Sadia's henchmen on Lethe, and now, dead in a shuttle-crash, brought down in a winter-storm over the Caducades on Cadia.

The gun-cutter lofted from the beach, ran the length of it, and then came back towards the downed shuttle.

May the Emperor forgive me and my staff for the deaths of Riggre and the two flight crew. Their deaths were the only way I could maintain my security.

'Fire,' I heard Nayl tell Medea.

The gun-cutter's ordnance strafed the Cadian shuttle and blew it apart. By dawn, the jetsam along the remote islet's shore would suggest nothing but a tragic crash caused by the hellish storms.

We banked up through the cover of the storms towards orbital space. Though no one told me, I knew our flight plan was covered by someone else's authority code.

Neve's was my guess. Probably with her permission.

The *Essene* was waiting for us.

'Now what?' I asked Fischig hoarsely.

'Dammit, I've risked everything I count dear to get you this far,' he replied. 'I was kind of hoping you'd know what to do now.'

'Cinchare,' I said. 'Tell Maxilla to get us to Cinchare.'

There are some secrets that are worth keeping.

'What's at Cinchare?' Bequin asked.

'An old friend,' I said.

'Not a friend, exactly,' added Aemos.

'No. Aemos is right. An old associate.'

'Two old associates, to be specific,' Aemos added.

Bequin pulled a particularly angry face. 'You pair and your old intimacies. Why don't you ever give a straight answer?'

'Because the less you know, the less the Inquisition can harm you if we're caught,' I said.

'The new lean you,' syruped Maxilla as I walked onto the *Essene*'s bridge.

I had shaved away my beard, had my ragged hair clipped back, and dressed in a suit of black linen after my shower. I was still terribly weak on my feet and in no mind for Maxilla's foolery.

'Course is set for Cinchare,' Maxilla said stiffly, apparently recognising my mood. His gold-masked servitors chimed in agreement. His hooded Navigator, all senses fixed on some different, quite other place, said nothing.

'I have a question,' said Inshabel. He was seated at secondary navigation position, reviewing the star-maps. 'Why Cinchare? A mining world out in the edges of the Segmentum, almost a Halo Star. I thought we'd be trying to find Quixos.'

'There's no point.'

'What?' Maxilla and Inshabel asked, almost in unison.

I sat down on a padded leather seat. 'Why make the endeavour to find Quixos when he would surely kill us at a stroke? We've barely survived individual encounters with two of his daemonhosts. We haven't the strength to fight him.'

'So?' asked Inshabel.

'So the first thing we do is find the strength. Prepare. Arm ourselves. Make ourselves ready to take down one of the most powerful evils in the Imperium.'

'And for that we need to go to Cinchare?' Inshabel whispered.

'Cinchare's the start, Nathun,' I said. 'Trust me.'

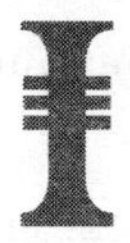

SEVENTEEN

ROGUE STAR
DOCTOR SAVINE, CORA AND MR HORN IN THE ANNEX

Even at full warp, it took the *Essene* thirty weeks to reach Cinchare.

True, we took a circuitous route, avoiding all possible encounters with the forces of the Imperium. I hated that. For once, I hated the subterfuge.

We learned, indirectly, a few weeks into the voyage, that my escape from Cadia had been discovered. The Inquisition – and other agencies – were hunting me. I had been formally declared Heretic and Extremis Diabolus. Lord Rorken had finally counter-signed Osma's carta.

I was now something I had never been before.

A fugitive. A renegade. And in aiding me, my band of comrades had made themselves fugitives too.

We had a few scrapes. Refuelling at Mallid, we were discovered and pursued by an unidentified warship which we lost in the empyrean. At Avignor, a squadron of Ecclesiarchy battle-boats, standing picket watch along the border of the diocese, tried to run us to ground. We only escaped that one thanks to a combination of Maxilla's shipcraft and Medea's fighting nous.

On Trexia Beta, Nayl and Fischig ran across a band of Arbites hunters while they were trying to hire an astropath. They never told me how many they had been forced to kill, but it sat badly with them for weeks.

On Anemae Gulfward, Bequin succeeded in obtaining the services of an astropath, a sickly female called Tasaera Ungish. When Ungish found out who I was, she begged to be returned to her backwater world. It took a long time to convince her that she was in no danger from me. I had to open my mind to her in the end.

At Oet's Star, we were discovered by an Inquisitor Frontalle during a resupply layover. As it was with Riggre and the Cadian pilots, I will always be haunted by those necessary deaths. I tried to reason with Frontalle. I tried very hard. A young man, he believed that taking me down was the key to a famous career. Eisenhorn the Heretic, he kept calling me. They were the last words on his lips when I pitched him into the geothermal heating exchanger.

From Trexia Beta onwards, there was an almost permanent rumour that a kill-team of the Grey Knights was hunting us. And the Deathwatch Chapter too.

I prayed to my God-Emperor that I could complete this task before the forces of righteousness overtook me. And I prayed to him that my friends might be spared.

Between those escapades, there were only the long, slow weeks of transit in the deep warp. I filled my time with study, and with weapons practice with Nayl, Fischig or Medea. I battled to get myself healthy again. The Carnificina had wasted me, both in body and spirit. The weight I had lost would simply not go back on, despite Maxilla's generous banquets.

And I felt slow. Slow with a blade, slow on my feet. Slow and clumsy with a gun.

Even my mind was slow. I began to fear that Osma had broken me.

Tasaera Ungish was a semi-paralysed woman in her fifties. The arduous rituals of the warp had left her broken and all but burned out, consigned to a life as a junior telepath in the class-chambers of Anemae Gulfward. Her raddled body was supported by an augmetic exo-skeleton. I believe she might have been beautiful once, but her face was now hollow and her hair thin where the implant plugs of her calling had been sited.

'That time again, heretic?' she asked as I walked into her quarters. This was about the twentieth week of the voyage.

'I wish you wouldn't call me that,' I said.

'Coping strategy,' she purred. 'Your woman Bequin connived me out of a safe life on Anemae Gulfward, and made me party to a heretic's private crusade.'

'A safe life, Ungish? A bad end. You'd have been dead in another six months, the strain of the traffic they were making you process.'

She tutted, her augmetic chassis whirring as she poured us two glasses of amasec. Hers was laced with fitobarrier enhancers, and her room stank of lho-leaf. I knew the rigours of her life had left her in constant pain, and she fought that pain off with everything she could lay her hands on.

'Dead and buried on Anemae Gulfward in six... or dead in agony in your service.'

'It's not like that,' I said, nodding as I took the glass she proffered.

'Is it not?'

'No. I've let you see my mind. You know the purity of my cause.'

She frowned. 'Maybe.' She was having difficulty manipulating her own glass. The mechadendrites that governed her right hand were old and slow. She waved me off when I tried to help.

'Maybe?' I asked.

She took a big swig of her drink and then poked a lho-stick between her crinkled lips.

'I've seen your mind, heretic. You're not as clean as you like to think you are.'

I sat down on the chaise. 'Am I not?'

She lit the lho-stick and exhaled a deep lungful of its narcotic smoke with a sigh.

'Ah, don't mind me. A ruined worn-out psyker who talks too much.'

'I'm interested. What do you see?'

Her exo-skeleton made soft whines as it walked her over to the other couch and the hydraulics hissed as they settled her into the seat. She took another deep puff.

'I'm sorry,' she said. 'Would you like one?'

I shook my head.

'I have served the Astropathicus all my life, such as it is, on guild tenure and as a freelance, as now. When your woman came to me with a job offer and real money, I took it. But, oh me, oh my...'

'Astropaths are supposed to be neutral,' I countered.

'Astropaths are supposed to serve the Emperor, heretic,' she said.

'What have you seen in my mind?' I asked, bluntly.

'Too, too much,' she responded, blowing a magnificent smoke-ring.

'Tell me.'

She shook her head, or that's what I supposed the hissing action of her head-cage was supposed to convey.

'I suppose I should be grateful. You took me from a dead life to this... an adventure.'

'I don't need you to be grateful,' I said.

'Dead and buried on Anemae Gulfward in six... or dead in agony in your service,' she repeated.

'It won't be like that.'

She blew another smoke ring. 'Oh, it will. I've seen it. Clear as day.'

'You have?'

'Many times. I'm going to die because of you, heretic.'

Ungish was stubborn and defeatist. I knew she had seen things she wouldn't talk about. Eventually, I stopped asking. We met every few days, and she psychometrically captured images from my mind. The Cadian pylons. Cherubael. Prophaniti, and the ornaments he wore.

By the time we reached Cinchare, I had a sheaf of psychometric pictures and, thanks to the crippled astropath, a grim sense of the future.

Cinchare. A mineral rock orbiting a rogue star.

Plagued by gravitic storms, the Cinchare system wanders sloppily through the fringes of the Halo Stars at the edge of Imperial space. Ten thousand years ago it had been a neighbour of 3458 Dornal, and had nine planets and an asteroid belt. When we finally found it, it was lurching through the Pymbyle systems, major and minor, and had suffered two serious cosmological collisions. Now it had six planets and radiating sheets of asteroid belts. Cinchare's rogue star was locked in a drunken dance with Pymbyle Minor, a flirtatious encounter of gravities that would take another million years to resolve.

Cinchare itself, or more properly Cinchare rogue system/planet four X181B, was a blue nugget of rock swaggering along an almost figure-eight far orbit around the clashing stars, following the vagaries of their impacting gravity wells.

Rich in ultra-rare metals including ancylitum and phorydnum, it had been a miner's plunder-haven for as long as it had been identified.

'No watch ships. Precious little in the way of guidance buoys,' Maxilla said as he steered the *Essene* in-system. 'I've got a habitation hot-spot. The mining colony, I'll bet.'

'Park us in orbit,' I told him. 'Medea, fire up the cutter for landfall. Aemos, you're with me.'

'Whoo!' whispered Medea, tightening the grip of her circuit-inlaid hands around the bio-sensors of the cutter's steering yoke. Another hard buffet had shaken the craft.

'The gravity-tides are all over the place. I keep hitting eddies and anti-trojan points.'

'Small wonder,' Aemos muttered, easing himself into a deck-seat and connecting the restraint harness across his lap. 'The rogue star and its planet-herd have made a disaster area of this system.'

'Hmmm...' said Medea, showing no concern as she rolled the cutter up and over on its back to avoid a jagged black asteroid that tumbled across our path. The close approach to Cinchare was a debris field, full of rock matter and collision slag, all swirling around in complex and exotic orbits. Parts of this field had formed into thin ring systems around Cinchare, but even the rings were buckled and warped by gravity-clashes. The space around us was a bright misty gold where starlight was catching the banks of dust and micro-litter. The cutter's shields could handle most of the larger rocks that swirled through it, but some were giants and required evasive manoeuvres.

Through the gold dust-light, we began to see Cinchare more clearly: an irregular, glittered blue object, spinning fast along a stricken axis. It was half in shadow, and the peaks of its mineral mountains made pre-dawn flashes as they caught the early light coming up over the daylight terminator.

'The closer we get to the body, the worse the gravitic disturbances will become, of course,' Aemos mused aloud. Medea didn't need the advice. Even I knew that an irregular body – and especially an irregular body composed of varying densities – would have a near-space lousy with abnormal gravity effects. I think Aemos was just chatting to keep his mind off things.

Medea banked us around the searing trails of three bolides, and into what felt like a chute of high gravity. Cinchare's surface, a revolving, pitted cold expanse, rushed up to meet us and filled the main ports. The descent and proximity alarms started to sound, and Medea killed them both with an impatient sideways stab of her hand. We levelled out a little.

'The mining facility beacons just woke up,' Medea cleared her throat. 'I've got a pre-lock telemetry handshake. They're requesting ident.'

'Give it.'

Medea activated the cutter's transponder and broadcast our craft's identifying pulse. It was one of the disguise templates we stored in the codifier for covert work, a delicate piece of fakery designed by Medea and Maxilla. According to its signature, we were a research team from the Royal Scholam Geologicus on Mendalin.

'They've cleared us to touch,' Medea reported, easing us past another buffet of gravity turbulence. 'They've activated the guide pathway.'

'Any vox contact?'

She shook her head. 'It could all be mechanical.'

'Take us in.'

Cinchare Minehead was a cluster of old industrial structures plugging the cone of an upthrust impact event. Flight approach was down a rille in the crater edge. The buildings seemed at first sight to be rude and unfinished, rough-hewn from the blue rock, but I quickly realised they were standard Imperial modular structures caked with accretions of blue dust and gypnate. As far as records showed, Cinchare Minehead had been here for nine hundred years.

We set down on a cleared hardpan surrounded by serially winking marker lamps. The braking jets kicked up a swirling halo of eluviam into the air-less sky. After a short wait, two monotask servitors, heavy-grade units on caterpillar tracks, emerged into the hard starlight from the shadows of a docking barn, attached clamps to our front end and silently towed us back into the barn.

It was a grim place of dirty bare metal and lifting gear. Two battered prospector pods sat in berthing bays, and in the gloom at the far end was a cargo shuttle that had seen better days.

The barn doors closed behind us, and flashing hazard lamps in the berthing dock moved from amber to green as the atmosphere was cycled back in. Apart from the servitors, there was no sign of life.

'Cutter's systems show green on outside conditions,' said Medea, swinging out of her seat.

'Are we ready?' I asked.

'Sure,' said Medea. She had switched her regular Glavian pilot's gear, with its distinctive cerise jacket, for a much more anonymous set of grubby flight overalls. Heavy, tan and baggy, they were actually the quilted liner of an armoured void-suit. The surface was covered in eyelets, laces and stud-connectors where the armour segments would lock on and there were umbilical sockets in the chest. Medea had removed the helmet ring and allowed the heavy collar to hang open. She wore workgloves and steel-capped military boots, and tucked her hair up under a billed cap with the Imperial eagle on the front.

Aemos had adjusted the hydraulic settings of his augmetic exo-skeleton to hold him in the stiffest, most upright stance possible. With a long tunic-cloak of black bagheera, a white skull cap and an engraved data-cane, he looked every centimetre a distinguished scholam academic.

I lacked any trace of my usual Inquisitorial garb. I wore leather breeches and high, buckled boots, an old flak-armour jerkin with dirty ceramite over-plates, and a full-face filter mask with tinted eyeslits that resembled nothing so much as a snarling skull. Nayl had lent me a motion tracker unit from his personal kit, which I had strapped over my right shoulder, and a heavy, snub-nosed laspistol that hung in an armpit rig under my jerkin. A combat shotgun rested in a scabbard between my shoulder blades, and I had a belt of shells for it around my waist. I looked and felt like hired thug-muscle... which was precisely the point.

Medea popped the hatch and we descended into the barn.

It was cold, and the air was parched from too many automatic scrubbings. Odd mechanical noises sounded sporadically in the distance. Squat, short-base servitors were busy tinkering with the old shuttle's exposed engine-guts.

We clanged up the grille stairs to the interior hatch. It was marked with a bas-relief symbol of the Adeptus Mechanicus, and an enamelled sign below it announced that the tech-priesthood was the supreme authority at Cinchare Minehead.

The heavy hatch whirred back into its wall-slot revealing a gloomy prep-tunnel lined with empty void-suits that swung on their hooks in the breeze. Beyond that, there was a dank scrub-room, a darkened office with a padlock on the door, and an empty survey suite with a deactivated chart table.

'Where is everybody?' Medea asked.

We followed the echoing hallways through the complex. Grubby mining equipment was scattered or piled in corners. A small first-aid station had been stripped of surgical equipment and stacked with crates of pickled fish. A side room was empty except for hundreds of broken wine bottles. A disused walk-in freezer store exuded the stink of spoiled meat through its open door. Water spattered from the dark, lofty ceilings of some vaults. Chains swung from overhead hoists. Cold, dry breezes gusted down the halls.

When the wall-speakers boomed, we all started.

'Allied Imperial Minerals! Duty rotation in fifteen minutes!'

The voice was an automatic recording. Nothing stirred in response.

'This is most perturbatory,' murmured Aemos. 'According to Imperial records, Cinchare Minehead is an active concern. Allied Imperial has a workforce of nineteen hundred running their deep-cast mines, and Ortog Promethium another seven hundred at their gypnate quarries. Not to mention independent prospectors, ancilliary service workers, security and the personnel of the Adeptus. Minehead is meant to have a population of nearly three thousand.'

We had reached a main concourse, a wide thoroughfare lit by overhead lamps, many of which were smashed. Abandoned merchant shops and bars lined either side.

'Let's look around,' I said. We fanned out. I walked to the north end of the trash-littered concourse and found steps leading down into a wide plaza full of more empty shops and businesses.

I heard the whine of an electric motor from down to the left, and followed it. Round the corner of a boarded-up canteen, a fat-tyred open buggy was pulled up outside the unkempt entrance of a claims registry. I went inside. The floor was covered in spilled, yellowing papers and dented data-slates. A snowdrift of used and mouldering ration cartons filled a side door into a filing room.

Nayl's motion detector clicked and whirred. It projected its display on the inside of my mask's right lens. Motion, the rear office, eight metres.

I edged to the door and peered in, my hand on the grip of the holstered las.

A long-limbed man in filthy overalls was crouching with his back to me, rummaging through a foot locker.

'Hello?' I said.

He jumped out of his skin, turning and rising in the same frantic motion, then crashed backwards against a row of metal cabinets. His long, gawky face was pale with fear. His hands were raised.

'Oh crap! Oh dear God-Emperor! Oh, please... please...'

'Calm down,' I said.

'Who are you? Oh, crap, don't hurt me!'

'I'm not going to. My name is Horn. Who are you?'

'Bandelbi... Fyn Bandelbi... Mining superintendant second class, Ortog Promethium... Crap, don't hurt me!'

'I'm not going to,' I repeated firmly. At least the frayed nametag on his dungarees agreed with him: 'BANDELBI, F. SUPER 2nd O.P.'

'Put your hands down,' I said. 'Why did you think I was going to hurt you?'

He lowered his hands and shrugged. 'I didn't... sort of... I don't know...'

He regained a little composure and squinted at me. 'Where did you come from?' he asked. He was an ugly, lantern-jawed fellow with unkempt greasy hair and stubble. There was the hint of a raw pink birthmark on the side of his throat.

'Off rock. Just got here. I was wondering why there was no one around.'

'Everyone's gone.'

'Gone?'

'Gone. Shipped out. Left. Because of the Gravs.'

'The Gravs?'

I don't know if he was going to answer. My motion tracker suddenly flashed an alert up on my lens and I wheeled around to find a man standing in the registry's entrance. He was a big man with dark skin and a white stubble of hair and beard. The autopistol in his right hand was aimed at my face.

'Nice and slow,' he said. 'Lose the guns. And the mask.'

'What's going on? Who's in charge here?' demanded a voice from outside. It was Aemos.

The man with the gun glanced outside and then waved me ahead of him. Aemos, looking very haughty and dignified, stood in the streetway behind the parked buggy.

'Well? I am Doctor Savine, from the Royal Scholam Geologicus on Mendalin. Is this the way Cinchare Minehead greets its guests?' I was impressed. There was a querulous tone of piqued authority. Aemos had acting talents I had never imagined.

'You got papers?' asked the man with the gun, still covering me. Bandelbi had emerged and was watching the exchange.

'Of course!' Aemos snapped. 'And I'll show them to someone in authority.'

The man with the gun reached his free hand down into the neck of his mesh-reinforced coat and pulled out a polished silver badge on a neck chain. 'Enforcer Kaleil, Cinchare Minehead Security Service. I'm the only authority you'll find round here.'

Aemos tutted and rapped the tip of his data-cane down on the rockcrete ground. The cane-head clicked around and cast a small hologram into the air above it: identity details, the seal of the Royal Scholam Geographicus, and a slowly revolving 3-D scan of Aemos's head.

'Okay, doctor,' nodded Kaleil. He gestured to me with the gun. 'What about this goon?'

'You think I'd travel out to this misbegotten rock without a bodyguard? This goon is Mr Horn.'

'This goon was putting the squeeze on my friend Bandelbi.'

Aemos looked at me sternly. 'I've warned you about that, Horn! Dammit! You're not in the Mordian gang-wars now!'

Aemos turned back to Kaleil. 'He is somewhat enthusiastic. One testosterone-stimm too many, somewhere along the line. But I needed muscle, not brains, and he was cheaper than a cyber-mastiff.'

Be thankful you can't see my face behind this mask, old friend, I thought.

'Okay. But keep him on a leash,' said Kaleil, holstering his weapon. 'Let's go to the security station and you can tell me what the hell you're doing here.'

'And you can tell me where the hell everyone is,' replied Aemos. Kaleil nodded and gestured for us to lead the way down the street.

'So you don't need me to detonate anyone's skull, Doctor Savine?' said a voice.

Kaleil and Bandelbi froze. Medea slunk from cover in a shutterway across the street, a Glavian needle pistol held in an unwavering two-handed grip and aimed at Kaleil's head.

'Crap!' Bandelbi gasped.

'My pilot,' Aemos said, deadpan. He flapped a hand sidelong at Medea. 'No, Cora. We're all friends here now.'

Medea grinned and winked at Kaleil, sliding her weapon away inside her flight suit.

'Had you cold, Enforcer Kaleil.'

Kaleil gave her a murderous glare and led us towards the security station.

The station was on the second floor of a round building on the corner of the deserted plaza. A guard-rail ran at hip-height around the office, and beyond that, inwardly-raked windows permitted a wide view down into the plaza area. Kaleil thumbed a wall-control that reduced the tinting in the glass and made the room a little brighter.

Seats were arranged around a central, circular workstation, above which glowed a holo-display. Empty ration pouches and ale bottles cluttered the surfaces of the workstation, and handwritten notes and memos had been taped along the edges of the console. Around the room were couch seats with splitting upholstery, and piles of junk. A door in the rear led through to an armoury and a ready room. The air was humid and smelled of sweat and unwashed clothes.

Kaleil took off his mesh jacket and tossed it onto a couch. He wore a grubby vest that showed off his physique and the Imperial Guard tattoos on his upper arms.

His badge of office hung down over his chest like an athlete's medal.

'Get 'em refreshment,' he told Bandelbi. The miner began swishing each of the ale bottles standing on the cowling of the workstation to find one with some contents left.

'Fresh ones,' Kaleil scolded. 'And I'm sure the doctor would prefer something softer... or harder.'

'Amasec, if you have it,' said Aemos.

'Ale's fine,' smiled Medea, flopping onto a couch and folding her legs up under her.

I shook my head. 'Nothing.'

Bandelbi disappeared.

Kaleil sat down backwards on one of the workstation chairs so he could fold his arms on the top of the backrest.

'Okay, doctor. What's the story?'

'I am the head of the metallurgy department at the Royal Scholam. Do you know Mendalin?'

Kaleil shook his head. 'Never been there.'

'A fine world, a noble world. Famed for its academia.' Aemos carefully took a seat next to Medea.

I stood back, by the windows. I could tell Kaleil had one eye on me.

'We are engaged in a twenty year program, commissioned by Archduke Frederik himself, to investigate the inner transition qualities of the rarest metals for... well, the applications are classified, actually. The results may improve the industrial health of Mendalin's engine yards. The archduke is a keen amateur metallurgist. He's the patron of the Royal Scholam, in fact.'

'Do tell,' murmured Kaleil.

'Phorydnum is one of the metals to be covered in our program. And this planetoid is one of the nearest sources of it. The Administratum has kindly issued me with a bond to visit Cinchare and obtain samples, and I have letters from the Lord Director of Imperial Allied to inspect the phorydnum workings. Do you wish to see them?'

Kaleil waved a dismissive hand.

'I also hoped to meet with the tech-priests stationed here in order to discuss their understanding of the properties of this precious substance.'

'You're on a fact-finding trip?'

'A research mission,' said Aemos.

Bandelbi returned with three ales and an enamel cup. He carried them on a dented locker door which he was using as a tray.

'It's not good stuff,' he told Aemos, handing him the cup. 'Just ration issue grade.'

Aemos sipped it without the hint of a shudder. 'Rough, but bracing,' he announced.

Kaleil took his bottle and tugged a swig from the neck.

'You've had a wasted journey, I'm afraid,' he said. 'Emperor knows what

Imperial Allied were playing at when they gave you those letters. They must know their people have pulled out.'

'Explain,' I said. Kaleil shot me a glance.

'This rock's been worked pretty consistently for the last nine centuries. It's hazardous work, but the rewards are great. As you said, Cinchare's a rich source of many metals that are very hard to come by.'

He took another swig.

'These last twenty years, the authorities here have been getting worried about the conditions. The gravity distortions. Cinchare moving ever closer into the grav fields of Pymbyle. Reckoning was that the place would be unviable in another eighty, ninety years. Imperial Allied and Ortog stepped up their work, trying to strip out as much as they could before Cinchare passed into a gravity envelope that would make it untouchable for the next few thousand years. The indie prospectors too... they came flocking. Regular old fashioned ore-rush, the past few years.'

'So what happened?' asked Medea.

'The Gravs,' said Bandelbi. He was clearing a seat for himself on one of the paper-stacked couches. He looked up and saw Medea's quizzically raised eyebrow.

'Gravity sickness,' he said at once in response to her unasked question. He scratched the birthmark on his neck nervously. He'd been keeping a keen eye on her. She was probably the first woman he'd seen in a while. Kaleil was more composed.

'Gravity sickness,' Bandelbi continued, 'weight distemper, lead-head, the Gravs... you know.'

'Chronic Gravitisthesia, also known as Mazbur's Syndrome. A progressive disorder caused by exotic gravitational flux. Symptoms include paranoia, loss of co-ordination, bursts of anxiety or rapture, memory loss, hallucination and sometimes, in extremis, homicidal urges. The condition is usually accompanied by myasthenia gravis, osteochondritis, osteoporosis, scoliosis and leukaemia,' Aemos finished.

Kaleil widened his eyes. 'I thought you were a doctor of metals, doctor, not a medicae.'

'I am. But gravity, that invisible power, is a fundamental part of the life of all elements. So I take an interest in it.'

'Yeah, well... the predictions said Cinchare might become unviable due to gravity in ninety years. But the human body is softer than a hunk of mineral ore. The Gravs first showed up about two years back. Workers getting sick. A few cases of violence and insanity. Then we realised what was going on. Imperial Allied pulled out nine months ago. Ortog seven.'

'It's ironic,' Aemos said. 'Cinchare is mineral rich precisely because of the exotic gravities it has been subjected to in its billion year life. Elements have been transmuted and rearranged here in ways that may be unique. Cinchare is a precious philosopher's stone, my friends, an alchemist's dream! And now mankind cannot benefit from its gifts for precisely the same reason they exist in the first place!'

'Yeah, doc, ironic is what it is,' said Bandelbi, knocking back his ale.

'That doesn't explain why you're still here,' I said.

'Skeleton crew,' said Kaleil in a tone that said it was none of my business. 'The Adeptus Mechanicus pulled out too, about three months ago. But one of theirs stayed behind. Some sort of vital research that had to be finished. And we were ordered to stay behind and keep Cinchare Minehead open until he finished.'

I moved round and looked out of the station windows. The plaza was empty of everything except trash. 'And how many is "we", Enforcer?'

'Service crew of twenty. I'm in charge. All volunteers.'

'The techlords promised us triple pay!' Bandelbi told Medea, clearly trying to impress her.

'Gee whiz,' she smiled.

'Where are the others? The other eighteen?' I pressed.

Kaleil got up off his chair and tossed his empty bottle at an overflowing litter basket in the corner. It bounced off and broke on the floor. 'Around about. This is a big place. What you see is just the tip. Like a... what's it called, those frozen lumps of water they have in the sea on some planets?'

'Iceberg?' Medea suggested.

'Yeah, like one of those. Ninety per cent of Cinchare Minehead is sub-soil. That's a crap of a lot of space to patrol, maintain and keep ticking over.'

'You're in vox contact with the rest of the skeleton crew?'

'We keep in touch. Some I don't see for weeks.'

'This tech-priest, the one who remained?' Aemos said. 'Where is he?'

Kaleil shrugged. 'Gone rockside. Into the karsts and the mines. I've not seen him for two months.'

'When do you expect him back?' Aemos said, as if it didn't matter.

Kaleil shrugged again. 'Never.'

'What was his name?' I asked, turning to look directly into the enforcer's dark eyes.

'Bure,' he said. 'Why?'

'Well, this is all most perturbatory!' Aemos blurted, rising from his seat. 'The archduke will be very put out. It has cost a deal of time and money to venture this mission. Mr Kaleil... since we've come this far, I'd like to do what little I can.'

'Like what, doctor?'

'Obtain some samples, inspect the phorydnum workings, study the minerology ledgers?'

'I don't know... Cinchare Minehead's meant to be closed up now. Officially.'

'Would it really be too much to ask? I'm sure the Lord Director of Imperial Allied would be pleased if you co-operated with me. Pleased enough to proffer a bonus if I made a report to him.'

Kaleil frowned. 'Uh huh. What are we talking about?'

'A day to overview the ledgers and the mineralogy database, perhaps another day to examine the sample archives from the quarries. And... well, how long would it take to arrange a visit to the phorydnum face? The latest one?'

'I call my staff in, maybe two days round trip.'

'So... excellent! Four days total and we'll be gone.'

'I dunno...' said Bandelbi.

'Don't you want me hanging around for a few days?' asked Medea, reading Bandelbi's body language as acutely as any trained inquisitor, and revealing as much latent acting ability as Aemos.

'I shouldn't allow it,' said Kaleil. 'This place is off limits now. Company orders. You didn't ought to stay here.'

'You stay here,' I pointed out.

'I get danger money,' he said.

'And you could get more,' said Aemos. 'I promise you, I'll speak highly of your co-operation to the Lord Director of Imperial Allied... and my old friends at the Adeptus. They would reward well anyone assisting a servant of the archduke.'

'Get me an ale,' Kaleil told Bandelbi. He looked at us, rolling his chin. 'I'll talk to my staff, see what they think.'

'Good, good,' said Aemos. 'I do hope we can reach an arrangement. In the meantime, we'll need quarters. Are there spare beds here?'

'Cinchare's been fulla empty beds since the workforce moved out,' Bandelbi told Medea through a nasty smile.

'Find them a hab,' Kaleil told the miner. 'I'll get on to the crew.'

'Something's not right,' I said, pulling off my mask and tossing it onto the floor.

'These cots are really rather cosy,' Aemos replied, adjusting the tension of his exo-frame and reclining on the mattress.

We were in a dry, stuffy rec-room above the miners' welfare. The artificial lamplight from the plaza outside slanted in through sagging blinds. Bandelbi had provided three metal cots with subsiding mattresses and sleeping bags that smelled like they had been used to sieve motor fuel and cabbage.

'You always worry,' Medea said, uninhibitedly shrugging off her flight suit and kicking it into a corner. She was clad in nothing but her vest and briefs, and her shoulder holster, which she was now unclasping.

Aemos rolled over and looked the other way.

'It's my job to worry. And stop getting undressed. We're not finished.'

Medea looked at me, and rebuckled her gun rig with a dark frown.

'Okay, my lord and master... what? What's not right?'

'I can't quite put my finger on it...' I began.

Medea tutted and flopped down on her cot.

'Yes, you can, Gregor,' Aemos said.

'Maybe I can.'

'Try.'

'This stuff about the Gravs. Even if the corporations were suckered, it's not like the Adeptus Mechanicus to fail in a prediction. Any cosmologist would know if Cinchare was entering a gravitation wilderness that would be harmful to humans. They'd know it years in advance. Emperor protect me, stellar objects move far slower and more predictably than human minds!'

'A good point,' said Aemos.

'And one that you'd already thought of, I'm sure,' I said.

'Yes,' he confirmed. 'Kaleil is clearly lying about something.'

'And you don't think anything's wrong?'

'Of course I do,' Aemos muttered. 'But I'm tired.'

'Get up,' I told him brusquely.

He sat up.

'At least we know Bure's still here,' I said.

'This is the guy we came to find?' Medea asked.

I nodded. 'Magos Bure.'

'So how do you two know him? A tech-priest magos?'

'Old story, my dear,' said Aemos.

'I've got time.'

'He was a loyal ally of my master, Inquisitor Hapshant, Aemos's old boss,' I said, cutting to the chase before Aemos could get going.

'A blast from the past, huh?' she grinned.

'Something like that.'

'Still, it's a lo-o-ong way to come just to catch up with an old friend,' she added.

'Enough, Medea!' I said. 'You don't need to know the particulars yet. Maybe better for you if you don't.'

She blew a raspberry at me and began to pull her flight suit back on.

'You tried to reach the *Essene* recently?' I asked.

'My vox hasn't got the range,' she sulked back, fiddling with the zipper. 'Gravity distortions are too much. We expected that. I could go back to the cutter and use the main 'caster.'

'I need you here. We need to scare up some answers fast. I want you to sneak Aemos down to the Administratum archive, and see if you can coax anything out of the data banks, if they're still functioning.'

'While you...'

'I'm going to the annex of the Adeptus Mechanicus. Meet back here in three hours. We're looking for any clues, but particularly any traces of Bure's whereabouts.'

Aemos nodded. 'What if we're challenged?'

'You couldn't sleep, you went for a walk, and you got lost.'

'And if they don't believe me?'

'That's why Medea's going with you,' I said.

The annex of the tech-priesthood lay in the western sector of Cinchare Minehead's jumbled maze of pressurised habs and processing sheds, about two kilometres from the plaza. At first, I hadn't known where I was going, but the tunnels and transit ways were marked with numbered signs and symbol-coded notices, and after a while I found a large, etched-metal directory map screwed to a pillar beside a bank of dusty public drinking fountains.

A twist of the tap on one of the fountains produced nothing but a dry rasp.

Approaching the annex, the whitewashed tunnel walls were overpainted with dark red stripes, and there were numerous caution signs and warnings that demanded correct papers and identities on pain of death.

Still, the whole place was bare and empty, and thick with dust and litter.

At the end of the red-striped access tunnel, the vast adamantite blast-gates to the annex stood open. There was an eerie silence.

The annex was a colossal tower of hewn rock dressed in red steel, filling a side chimney of the crater that housed Cinchare's minehead. A sealed glass dome covered the paved yard between the blast-gates and the annex, and the building itself rose up beyond the glass to the top of the crater rim. High above, I could see the blue rock and the starlit void beyond. Meteors streaked overhead

The doorway of the annex was a giant portal taller than three men, framed by thick doric columns of black lucullite. Above it leered the graven image of the Machine God, its eyes clearly carved in such a way that they would flare ominously with gas burn-offs piped up from the mines. They were cold and dead now.

And the burnished metal doors of the portal were open.

I stepped inside. Fine sand covered the floor of the grand prothyron. Dust motes glittered in the bars of light spearing into the high hallway through deadlights up near the ribbed roof. Both walls were entirely panelled with banks of codifiers and matriculators, all dormant and powered down. Crescents of dust bearded every single switch and dial.

I knew at once this was a bad sign. The tech-priests treasured machines more than anything else. If they had evacuated as Kaleil described, there was no way they would have left such a wealth of technology here... especially as each unit was clearly designed to slot out of its alcove in the black marble walls.

The chamber beyond the prothyron was a veritable chapel, a cathedral dedicated to the God-Machine, the master of Mars. The floor was creamy travertine slabs, so tightly laid not even a sheet of paper could be slipped between the stones. The chapel itself was triapsidal with walls of smooth, cold lucullite and a roof thirty metres above my head. There was yet more precious technology arranged in six concentric circles of intricate brass workstations around a central plinth. All of it was dead and unpowered.

I crossed the chamber towards the plinth, painfully aware of how loud my footsteps rang back from the emptiness. Chilly starlight shone down through an opaion in the centre of the roof, directly above the massive grandiorite plinth. The huge, severed head of an ancient Warlord Titan hung above the plinth where the starlight shafted down. I realised that nothing supported the head – no cables, no platform, no scaffolding. It simply hung in the air.

As I got close to the plinth, gazing up at the Titan's face, my hair pricked. Static, or something like it, bristled the atmosphere. Some invisible, harnessed force – perhaps gravity or magnetics, certainly something beyond my understanding – was at play here, suspending the multiple tonnes of the machine-skull. It was a silent marvel, characteristic of the tech-priesthood. Even with the power shut down, their miracles endured.

On one workstation console – a brass frame full of intermeshed iron cogs, silvered wires and glass valves – I saw a length of canvas-sleeved neural hose, one end plugged into the display, the other frayed and severed. That was more than just a case of someone leaving in a hurry.

Over the years, my dealings with the Adeptus Mechanicus had been few. They were a law unto themselves, like the Astartes, and only a fool would meddle with their power. Bure – Magos Geard Bure – had been my closest contact with them. Without the Priesthood of Mars, the technologies of the Imperium would wither and perish, and without their ceaseless endeavours, no new wonders would ever be added to mankind's might.

Yet here I stood, unmolested and uninvited, in the middle of one of their inner sanctums.

My vox-link pipped. A voice, Medea's, badly distorted by gravity flux, said 'Aegis wishes Thorn. By halflife d–'

It cut off.

'Thorn attends Aegis,' I said. Nothing.

'Thorn attends Aegis, the whisperless void.'

Still nothing. What little I had caught of Medea's brief message troubled me – 'halflife' was a Glossia code word that could be used in phrases to disclose an important discovery or indicate a grave predicament. But what troubled me far more was the fact she had cut off. My reply, if she had heard it, indicated her transmission had been incomplete or garbled.

I waited a full minute, then another.

Without warning, my vox pipped quickly three times. Medea had test-keyed her transmitter in a non-vocal code form that indicated she couldn't talk and that I should stand by.

I brushed the thin skin of dust off one dead workdesk and gazed at the worn, rune-marked keyboard and the small display screens of thick, convex glass, wondering what secrets I could possibly unlock from it.

Little, I decided. Aemos, who frankly knew more than it was healthy to know, might have a chance. He had worked closely with Bure years before, and I fancied he had more experience of the mysterious tech-priests and their ways than he cared to admit.

My motion-tracker suddenly clicked around, and I tensed, pulling my stub-nose laspistol. The tracker's display on my mask's right lens indicated a movement or contact seventeen paces to my left, but even as I turned, it flashed up more. Multiple contacts, all around, coming so fast that they overlapped and utterly confused the tracker for a moment. The lens display showed a default 'oo:oo:oo' for a second as it struggled to compute the vectors, and then it scrolled a tight column of coordinates in front of my eye.

But by then, I knew what it had sensed.

The sanctum was coming to life.

In swift succession, each workstation chattered into action, cogs whirring, valves glowing, screens lighting, pistons hissing. Pneumatic gas-pumps exhaled and communiqué flasks began to pop and whizz through the network of elegant glass-and-brass message tubes that ran between the consoles and up the walls. Several desks projected small hologram images above their hololith hubs: three dimensional strata maps, spectroscopy graphs, sonar readings and oscillating wave-forms. Powerful underlights ignited on the plinth-top beneath the floating head of the Titan and threw its features into malevolent relief.

I sank down behind one of the stations, which vibrated and chattered against my back. The sudden, inexplicable life was daunting and alarming. Somewhere close by, one particular machine was rattling and repeating like an old machine gun on full auto.

As suddenly as it had started, the life died away. Stations fell silent and their lights went out. The throb of power leaked away into the darkness. The Titan's underlights dimmed and died. One by one, the holograms extinguished and the desks fell dormant. The chirring of cogs and servos and the throb of valves ebbed into stillness.

The last sound to go was that autogun racket. It continued for a good few seconds after everything else had stopped, then it too ceased abruptly.

The chapel was then as dark and quiet as it had been when I first entered.

I got to my feet. There had been no power in this place, no feeding source. What had started and woken the machines? It had to have been some signal from outside.

Using commonsense and guesswork, I went around the circle of stations nearest to me, hunting for the one that had chattered like a stubber. The most likely candidate was a bulky desk that seemed to have external and general gain vox functions. But its keys were dead to my touch.

On a whim, I got down on my knees and peered behind the desk. There were fixings where a basket hopper should have been sitting to catch the print-outs. The hopper was missing. The sheaf of print-out had fallen down into the dust under the desk.

I scooped the sheaf out. It was about nine metres long, punch-cut by the printer's jaws into shorter sections. Clearly this desk had been disgorging print-outs for some time without anyone around to collect them. The sections at the bottom of the spool were beginning to yellow.

I looked them over, but they meant nothing. Tabulated columns of machine code in close, regular bands. Carefully, I laid them out on the travertine floor and rolled them tightly into a thick scroll.

I was nearly finished when my vox pipped.

'Aegis wishes Thorn. By halflight disabused, in Administratum by heart. Scales fall from eyes. Multifarious, the grasp of changelings. Pattern thimble advised.'

'Pattern thimble acknowledged. Thorn arising by heart.'

Medea's words had told me all I needed to know. They had found something in the Administratum, and they needed me back swiftly. There was danger from Chaos all around. I should trust no one.

I holstered my laspistol and tucked the print-out scroll into my waistband.

As I ran out of the annex and down the red-striped tunnel, I tugged my combat shotgun out over my shoulder and racked the slide.

EIGHTEEN

PATTERN THIMBLE
GOING ROCKSIDE
GEARD BURE'S TRANSLITHOPEDE

Glossia's not so hard to understand. It uses subliminal symbols and 'head words.' Don't look for a mystery in it, it isn't there. That's why it works so well as a private code. There is no encryption - at least no mathematical encryption - to be calculated and broken. It is idiomatic and visceral. It is verbal impressionism. It uses the uncalculable, unregulated mechanisms of poetry and intimacy to perform its functions. There have been times in the last - well, the increasing years of my career, let's say - there have been times when an ally or retainer of mine has sent me a Glossia message using terms and words that have never been used before. And still, I have understood them.

It's a knack. It's knowing how to use, and improvise, a shared cant. There are basic rules of construction and metaphor, of course, but Glossia's strength lies in its nebulous vagueness. Its idioms. Its resonance. It is akin to the gut-slang of the Ermenoes, who have replaced language with subtleties of skin-colour.

Pattern thimble, for example.

'Pattern' indicates a course of action or behaviour. 'Thimble' is a qualifier, disclosing the manner or mode of said action. A thimble is a small tin cap that you might use to protect your finger from the short, sharp stabs of a needle during darning. It wouldn't fend off, say, an atomic strike or a horde of genestealers. But, in the idiom of Glossia, it would seal you against sudden, spearing, close attacks. It is also quiet and unremarkable.

And so, quietly, unremarkably, I slipped down the tunnel ways of Cinchare Minehead towards the officium of the Administratum. I was stealthy and secretive, and my motion tracker and shotgun were my thimble.

Pattern thimble. Gideon Ravenor had coined that particular phrase, adding it to the vocabulary of my Glossia.

I thought of Ravenor, alone in his plastic-sheeted cot on Thracian. My anger, dimmed these last few months, welled.

My motion tracker warned me into cover at a junction of transit tunnels about half a kilometre from the plaza. Hidden behind a stack of empty promethium drums, I watched as two electric buggies buzzed past, heading towards the concourse area. Bandelbi was driving the lead one. There were two miners with him, and three more in the buggy behind. They all looked grimy and slovenly.

There were more buggies in the plaza, parked out in front of the security office. I saw a couple of labourer-types lounging in the building doorway, smoking lho-sticks.

I slipped into the miner's welfare through the back. Medea and Aemos were waiting for me in the shabby rec-room billet.

'Well?'

'We nosed around the Administratum,' said Aemos. 'It wasn't even locked.'

'Then the place started to crawl with Kaleil's people and we skedaddled,' said Medea. Both of them looked tense and pensive.

'They see you?'

She shook her head. 'But there is a damn sight more than twenty of them. I counted thirty, thirty-five at least.'

'What did you find?'

'Recent archives are non-existent, or they've been erased,' said Aemos. 'Nothing for the last two and a half months, not even a caretaking log, the sort of thing you'd expect Kaleil to have been obliged to keep.'

'He could be recording it at the security office.'

'If he was following official protocol, it would have been automatically copied to the central archives. You know how anal the Administratum is about keeping full records.'

'What else?'

'Well, it was a cursory examination – we didn't have much time. But Kaleil told us Imperial Allied pulled out nine months ago and Ortog Promethium followed them two months later. According to the archive, both corporations were active, working and fully crewed as recently as three months ago. There's no record of any "Grav" cases, nor any filed reports or memos about the possibility of such a problem.'

'Kaleil was lying?'

'In all respects.'

'So where is everyone?'

Aemos shrugged.

'Do we leave now?' Medea asked.

'I'm determined to find Bure,' I replied, 'and there's something afoot here that really ought to–'

'Gregor,' Aemos murmured. 'I hate to be the one to point this out, but this isn't your concern. Although I know full well you are as loyal to the Golden Throne now as you ever were, in most respects that matter, you're no longer an inquisitor. Your authority is no longer recognised by the Imperium. You're a rogue... a rogue with more than enough problems of your own to sort out without involving yourself in this.'

I think he expected me to be angry. I wasn't.

'You're right... but I can't just stop being a servant of the Emperor, not just like that, no matter what the rest of mankind believes me to be. If I can do any good here, I will. I don't care about recognition, or official sanction.'

'I told you he'd say that,' Medea sneered at Aemos.

'Yes, you did. She did,' he said, looking back at me.

'Sorry to be so predictable.'

'Moral constancy is nothing to apologise for,' said Aemos.

I took the scroll of paper I'd recovered from the annex and showed it to my old savant.

'What do you make of this?' I told them what had happened in the sanctum of the Machine-God.

He studied the curling sheaf for a few minutes, checking back and forth. 'There are elements of this machine code that I can't make out. Adeptus encryption. But... well, look at the text breaks. These are the filed records of regular transmissions from outside the minehead. Every... six hours, to the second.'

'And the sanctum's dormant systems would wake up the moment an external transmission came in?'

'In order to record it, yes. How long were the machines in life?'

I shook my head. 'Two, maybe two and half minutes.'

'Two minutes forty-eight seconds?' he asked.

'Could be.'

He ran his finger along a line of header text above the last code-burst. 'That's exactly how long the latest transmission lasted.'

'So someone's out there? Outside the minehead on Cinchare somewhere, sending regular transmissions back to the Adeptus annex?'

'Not just someone... it's Bure. This is the Adeptus code-form for his name.' Aemos leafed back through the sheets and studied the yellowest and oldest. 'He's been broadcasting for... eleven weeks.'

'What is he saying?'

'I've no idea. The main text is too deeply codified. Mechanilingua-A or C or possibly some modern revision of one of the hexadecimal servitoware scripts. Possibly Impulse Analog version nine. I can't–'

'You can't read it. That's enough for me.'

'All right. But I know where he is.'

I paused. 'You do?'

Aemos smiled and adjusted his heavy augmetic eyewear. 'Well, no. I don't actually know where he is. But I can find him.'

'How?'

He pointed to a vertical strip of coloured bars that ran down the side of each transmission burst. 'Each broadcast is routinely accompanied by a spectrographic report on the location of the transmitter. These colours are a condensed expression of the type, mix and density of the rock surrounding him. It's like a fingerprint. If I had a good quality strata map of Cinchare, and a geologicae auspex, I could track him down.'

I smiled. 'I knew there was a reason I kept you around.'

'So we're going after him?' asked Medea.

'Yes, we are. We'll need transport. A prospecting pod, maybe. Can you handle one of those?'

'Piece of cake. Where do we get one?'

'Imperial Allied has an excursion terminal full of them,' Aemos said. 'I saw a schematic guide of the minehead screwed to a wall.' I had seen just the same sort of thing, but I didn't recall a detail like that. It reminded me of thc extraordinary photo-memory Aemos possessed.

'What about the chart and auspex you said you'll need?' Medea asked.

'Any prospector machine will have an on-board mineralogicae or geologicae scanner,' said Aemos. 'That will suffice. A comprehensive chart, though, that'll be less of a certainty. We'd better make sure we have one before we set off.'

He sat down on his cot and began to adjust the settings of his wrist-mounted data-slate.

'What are you doing?' I asked, sitting down next to him.

'Downloading a chart from the security office's cogitorum.'

'Can you do that?' Medea asked.

'It's simple enough. Despite the gravitics, my slate's vox-link has enough range to communicate with the office's codifier. I can make a text-bridge and ask it to send its chart files.'

'Yeah, yeah, but can you do that without knowing the system's user-code?' Medea asked.

'No,' said Aemos. 'But fortunately, I do know it.'

'How come?'

'It was on a note taped to the edge of the central control desk. Didn't you see it?'

Both Medea and I shook our heads and smiled. Just sitting there with Kaleil, talking and sipping fifth-rate amasec, Aemos had soaked up and memorised every detail of the place.

'One question,' Medea said. 'We don't know what's going on here, but it's probably a safe bet your friend is no friend of Kaleil and his pals. If we can find him using this, why haven't they?'

'I doubt even an experienced miner could make much sense of this spectroscopy expression. It's an Adeptus code,' Aemos said, proudly.

'It's simpler than that,' I said. 'They haven't found it. The annex was covered in dust, undisturbed. I don't think Kaleil or any of his people have been into the annex. Fear of the Adeptus Mechanicus is a strong disincentive. They don't know what we know.'

In the night, they came to kill us.

Once Aemos had downloaded the chart – and several other files of data besides – we resolved to get a few hours' sleep before making our move.

I had been asleep for about a hour when I woke in the dark to find Medea's fingers stroking my cheek.

As soon as I stirred, she pinched my lips shut tight.

'Spectres, invasive, spiral vine,' she whispered.

My eyes became accustomed to the half-light. Aemos was snoring.

I rose off my cot and heard what Medea had heard: the stairs outside the rec-room creaking. Medea was pulling on her flight suit, but keeping her needle pistol aimed at the door.

I pulled my laspistol from its holster on the floor and then leant over to Aemos, putting my hand over his mouth.

His eyes flicked open.

'Keep snoring but get ready to move,' I whispered into his ear.

Aemos struggled up, snorting out fake snores as he collected up his robe and cane.

I had stripped down to my vest. My jacket and motion tracker were on the floor at the foot of the cot. There was no time to reach for them.

Someone kicked the door in. The bright blue lances of two laser sights stabbed into the rec-room, and a tight burst of stubber fire blew holes in my vacated cot and puffed padding fibres up from the wounds in the mattress.

Medea and I returned fire, bracketing the doorway with about a dozen shots between us. Two dark shapes toppled backwards. Someone screamed in pain.

A flurry of gunfire from ground level outside slammed up in through the windows, blowing one of them right out of its mounting in a shower of glascite. Ruined slat-blinds rippled and jiggled with the impacts.

'Back!' I cried, firing twice at a shape in the doorway. A triple pulse of answering las-fire scorched past my head.

But light flooded in behind us as a rear door crashed open. Medea swung around, lithe and long-limbed, and broke in the face of the first intruder with a high kick that sent him reeling back.

Figures charged in from the doors before and behind us. I shot two, but then was carried over onto my back by two more who struggled frantically to rip the laspistol out of my hand. I kneed one in the groin and shot him through the neck as he coiled away.

The other one had his hands on my throat.

I speared my mind right into his and triggered a massive cerebral haemorrhage that burst his eyeballs and sent him slack.

The smell of blood and cordite and the miners' unwashed bodies was intense. Medea danced back, and delivered a forearm slam to the face of another assassin that made him stumble and gasp.

She flexed and delivered a spin-kick which hit him so hard he smashed back out of the window.

Another was coming at her from behind. I saw a knife blade flash in the gloom.

Aemos, slow but steady, swung round and broke the knife-man's neck with a single punch. Another thing too easy to underestimate about my old savant was the inhuman strength his augmetic exo-chassis provided.

There was a little more wild gunfire, and then the spitting sound of Medea's Glavian pistol.

I curved my back and sprang back onto my feet in time to gun down a man with a shotgun who was coming in through the door.

Silence. Drifting smoke.

Voices were shouting below on the plaza.

'Grab your things!' I ordered. 'We're going right now!'

* * *

Half-dressed and lugging the rest of our kit, we scrambled down the back stairs. The body of one miner shot by Medea lay crumpled on the steps under the first landing. The front of his Ortog Promethium overalls was soaked with blood.

There was a livid birthmark on the side of his awkwardly twisted neck.

'Look familiar?' asked Aemos.

It did.

'Didn't that creep Bandelbi have a birthmark too?' Medea asked.

'Most certainly,' I replied.

We broke our way through a series of cluttered storerooms and came out in an access alley behind the shops adjoining the welfare. A ginger-haired miner posted as rearguard for the ambush turned in surprise as we emerged, his hands fumbling with the shotgun slung over his shoulder on a leather strap.

Drop it and come here! I said, using my will.

He tossed the weapon down and trotted over to us, his eyes glazed and confused.

Show me your neck! I willed again.

He brushed up his tousled hair with one hand and tugged his worksuit's neckline down with the other. The birthmark was there, centred on his nape.

'We haven't got time for this!' Aemos said. Running footsteps were pounding through the building behind us and we could hear shouts and curses.

'Where did you get this mark?' I willed at the ginger-haired man.

'Kaleil gave it me,' he said slackly.

What does it mean?

Driven by my undeniable will-force, he tried to say something that the rest of his mind and soul simply forbade. It sounded like 'Lith' but it was impossible to say for sure as the effort killed him.

'Dammit, Gregor! We have to go!' Aemos roared.

As if to prove his point, two miners burst out of the doorway we had come through, aiming autorifles. Medea and I whipped around as one and dropped them both, one kill shot each.

Aemos's faultless recall led us through the winding sub-streets of Cinchare Minehead to the massive, dank bulk of Imperial Allied. There was a hue and cry behind us, mixed with the whine of electric buggies.

We ran across the plant's wide, metal drawbridge, through a rockcrete gatehouse festooned with razorwire, and on down through the echoing entrance hall.

Footsteps followed.

The excursion terminal was a semi-circular barn of corrugated steel overlooking the mouth of the main working. Six prospecting pods sat in oily iron cradles under the barn's roof. They were slug-shaped machines, painted in the silver and khaki colours of Imperial Allied. Each one had a rack of flood and spotlights mounted above the cockpit, and several large servo arms and locator dishes arrayed under the chin.

'That one!' Medea yelled, heading for the third in line. She was still trying to fasten her flight suit properly. I carried my jacket and motion tracker. There had been no time to stop and get dressed.

'Why this one?' I yelled, following her.

'The power hoses are all still attached and it's showing green across the board on the telltales! Unclamp the hoses!'

I threw my stuff to Aemos, who hurried aboard behind Medea through the small side hatch, and ran to where three thick power cables were attached to the multi-socket in the flank of the pod. Just as Medea had noticed, all the indicator lights above the socket were green.

I twisted the valves and pulled them free, one by one. The last one was reluctant and needed a moment of brute force.

Las-shots spanked into the hull casing beside me.

I jerked the hose free and then turned, firing back down the length of the barn terminal. The pod's attitude thrusters began to cough and wheeze as Medea brought the craft to life.

Solid and las-shots peppered around me. I ran to the hatch and climbed in. Medea was at the helm in the cramped cockpit.

'Go!' I cried, slamming the hatch shut.

'Come on! Come on!' Medea cursed at the pod's controls. The over-urged engines whined painfully.

'Cradle lock!' Aemos spluttered desperately.

Realising her mistake, Medea swore expertly, eased the power down a tad, and threw a greasy yellow lever on the right-hand bulkhead. There was a jarring clank as the locking cuff that held the pod tight in the cradle disengaged.

'Sorry,' she grinned.

Freed, the pod lifted out of its landing cradle, swayed to the right as gunfire hunted for it, and then accelerated away, into the lightless mouth of the mine tunnels.

The upper workings of the Imperial Allied mines were huge excavations reinforced with rockcrete and filled with abandoned mining machines. Medea kicked in the pod's lamp array and illuminated our path with hard spot-beams of clear white light. At the far end of one reinforced spur, the lamps picked out a sudden, wide gradient where the horizontal incuts of the surface mines began their descent. Running down the steep slope were derelict cable-trams of filthy ore-hoppers and a funicular railway for transporting workcrews to the lower faces.

Aemos sat behind us in the pod's small cabin, reviewing the charts he had obtained from the security office. 'Continue down,' was all he said.

The steep access bore descended for about a kilometre and a half, occasionally flattening into work-shelves with entries to side seams. The view through the front screen seemed to be in black and white: the fierce white light piercing the blackness and revealing only pale grey dust and rock, and the occasional sparkle of druse.

Medea slowed us as we passed over more fragmented and extensive piles of breakdown and then, under Aemos's instruction, manoeuvred us down into the throat of an almost vertical chimney. This chimney – a pitch in mining terms – was a natural formation, possibly an ancient lava tube. Slowly revolving laterally, we hovered down into it. Flowstone caked the walls like swathes of creamy drapery, and quilled bushes of volcanic glass sprouted from outcrops. The space was small, even for a compact pod like the one we had borrowed. Occasionally, Medea would nudge or clip an out thrust of quills and the glass fragments would fall silently, glittering, into the pit below.

About two kilometres down, the pitch opened out into a complex series of curving tubes, sub-caves and sumps. It was like moving out of an oesophagus into the complex chambers of an intestinal tract. The flowstone started to show more colour: steely blues with milky calcite swirls, mottled reds glinting with oolites. Flinty black druse and other clastic litter covered the smoothed folds of the ancient floor.

Medea pointed my attention to the small scanner box mounted below the main petrographic assayer. The little screen was awash with an almost indecipherable graphic of ghosting strata layers and reflecting lithic densities. Three bright yellow cursors showed clearly in the upper quadrant.

'They're coming after us,' she said.

'They seem to know where we are right enough. How are they tracking us?'

'Same way we're getting such a clean return on their position.'

'Are the locators on this crate that powerful?'

Medea shook her head. 'They're fine for the immediate locality, but they've got nowhere near enough gain to penetrate the rock.'

'So?'

'I think all these prospector pods have high-powered beacons, probably built into flight recorders. They'd need them for routine search and recovery.'

'I'll take a look.'

I swung out of my seat and moved back down the pod, stooping, and using the overhead hand-rails to support myself. Aemos was still at work. He'd fired up the pod's mineralogicae auspex, and was running a complex cross-search for the spectographic fingerprints that appeared on the Adeptus Mechanicus transmissions. He didn't even have the scrolls open any more: the complex subtleties of the colour bars had long since been committed to memory.

Every few minutes, he consulted the main chart and called a course-correction to Medea.

At the rear of the pod, between racks holding old rebreathers with perishing rubber visor-seals, I found a small crawl space into the engine bay.

I stuck my head and shoulders inside, and shone around with a lamp-pack I'd unbuckled from one of the rebreather sets. A simple process of elimination directed me to a fat metal drum clamped to the underside of the gravitic assembly and the housing for the kinaesthetic gyroscopes. Adeptus Mechanicus purity seals secured its cover.

I slid back out into the cabin, selected a medium plasma cutter from the tool web, and went back in. The hot blue tongue of the cutter sliced the drum's cover off and fused its pulsing innards.

Back in the cockpit, I saw we were now travelling down a wide cavern that was barbed with oily dripstones and varnished with incandescent blooms of moon-milk and angel's hair.

'They look lost already,' Medea remarked, nodding at the scanner box. She was right. The yellow cursors were moving with nothing like the same confidence. They were milling, trying to reacquire our signal.

We travelled for two more hours, through small flask-chambers gleaming with cavepearls, across vast low seas of chert and lapilli, between massive stalactites that bit tunnels in two like the incisors of prediluvial monsters. Domepits and sumps sheened with brackish alkaline water and the smoke snaking from nests of fumaroles betrayed the fact that there was now a rudimentary atmosphere: methane, sulphur, radon and pockets of carbon monoxide. Venting cases from Cinchare's active heart and the gas-products of chemical and gravito-chemical reactions built and collected here, far below ground, leaking only slowly up to the airless surface. Hull temperature was increasing. We were now about fifteen kilometres down, and beginning to feel the effects of the asthenosphere.

'Hey!' said Medea suddenly.

She slowed the pod, and swung it around, traversing the lights. We were in a gypnate chamber where the chert-covered floor was scalloped by several gours formed by water eons before. Several side spurs led away into tight pinches or were revealed on the chart to pinch out no further than twenty metres in.

'What did you see?' I asked.

'There!'

The spot-lamps framed a black shape that I thought for a moment was just a jagged pile of boulders and stalagmite bosses. But Medea roved us in.

It was a prospecting pod, similar to ours, but bearing the crest of Ortog Promethium. It had been crushed and split like an old can, the stanchions of its cabin protruding from the metal hull like ribs.

'Hell...' Medea murmured.

'Mining's a dangerous job,' I said.

'That's recent,' Aemos said, appearing at our shoulders. 'Look at the tephra.'

'The what?' asked Medea.

'It's a generic term for clastic materials. The dust and shale bed the wreck's lying on. Move the lamp round. There. The tephra's yellowish-white gypnate all around, but it's scorched and fused under the wreck. Mineral smoke from the fumaroles we passed just now vent back down here and cover everything with oxidised dust. I'd wager if it's been there more than a month, the powder would have overlaid the scorching... and coated the wreck.

'Pop the hatch,' I said.

The subterranean atmosphere seemed scalding hot and I began to sweat freely the moment I jumped down from the sill. I could hear nothing except my breath rasping inside my rebreather mask. I trudged round to the front of the hovering pod into the cones of its lights, and saw Aemos and Medea in the lit cockpit, both hidden behind rebreather masks of their own.

I waved once and crunched off over the dusty sill, my bootcaps catching the occasional geode which scattered and flashed in the light.

There was no mistaking the blast holes in the wreck's hull. Sustained fire from a multi-laser had split the pod wide open. I shone my hand torch in through the rents and saw a blackened cabin space, burned out.

The three crew members were still in there, at their posts, reduced to grimacing mummies by the acidic air, and by the hundreds of glistening white worms that writhed and burrowed as my light hit them. It figured that with its hot, wet, gaseous interior, Cinchare was a far from dead world.

More troglobyte things scurried and squirmed around my feet. Long-legged metallic beetles and inflated, jelly-like molluscs, all drawn to this unexpected source of rich nutrients.

Something moved beside me and slammed into my left hip. I fell hard against the broken hull, cursing that I hadn't been wearing my motion tracker. It came in again, and this time I felt a sharp pain in my left thigh. I kicked out with a mask-muffled curse.

It was about the size of a large dog, but longer and lower, moving on lean hind limbs. Its skin was nearly silver, and its eye-less head was just a vast set of jaws filled with hundreds of transparent fangs. All around the maw, long sensory bristles and tendrils twitched and rippled.

It lunged again, its thin, stiff tail raised high as a counterbalance. This thing, I guessed, was top of the food chain in Cinchare's lightless cavities. Too big to force its way inside the wreck to get at the corpses, it had been lurking outside, feeding on the carrion worms and molluscs that had congregated on the crash.

With a twist of its head, it had a good grip on my left ankle. I could feel the tips of its teeth biting through the heavy leather of my boot.

I managed to tug my shotgun from the scabbard on my back and shoot it through the torso at point black range. Viscous tissues and filmy flesh scattered in all directions and the thing flopped over. By the time I had prised its jaws off my boot with my knife, the carrion-eaters had begun to swarm over it and feed.

We moved off again, down a gour-lined spur and into a cavern breathtakingly encrusted with glass-silk and billions of cavepearls.

'There's been fighting down here,' I told Aemos and Medea, raising my voice to be heard over the re-cycling cabin air as we pumped the last of the coarse Cinchare gas-soup out.

'Who's fighting who?'

I shrugged, and sat back to tug one of the predator's broken fangs out of my boot leather.

'Well,' said Aemos, 'you'll be interested to know that the cavern with the wreck in it matched one of the spectroscope traces from the Mechanicus transmissions exactly.'

'How long ago?'

'About two weeks.'

'So... Bure could have been the one who did the shooting.'

'Bure... or whoever's sending transmissions back to the annex.'

'But why would he take out a prospector pod?' I wondered aloud.

'Rather depends on what the prospector pod was trying to do to him,' said Medea.

Aemos raised his tufty eyebrows. 'Most perturbatory.'

Another three hours, another two kilometres down. It was damn hot, and the air outside was thick with venting steams and gases. Fumaroles, some large, some in scabby clusters, belched black smoke into the caves, riddling some areas like honeycomb. Several caverns and domepits were home to luminous acidic lakes, where the geothermals steadily simmered the water. Gorges and the occasional pitch showed flares of red light from lava rivers and asthenospheric cauldrons of molten rock.

We no longer had to rely on the lamps. The cave systems were lit by streams of glowing magma, flaming lakes of pitch and promethium and thick, sticky curtains and rafts of bio-luminescent fungi that thrived in the heated ducts. The pod's air-scrubbers were no longer able to remove the scent of sulphur from the cabin air, and the cooling system was inadequate. We were all sweating, and so were the interior walls of the cabin. Condensation dribbled down the bare metal of the hull's inner skin.

'Dead stop, please,' Aemos said.

Medea cut the thrusters and let us coast slowly over a seething lake of lava that radiated a glare of almost neon brilliance from beneath its blackened crust.

Aemos checked the chart against the spectroscope readings that the mineralogicae assayer was sending to a small repeater screen in the cabin bay.

'This is it. The source location for the last transmission.'

'You're sure?' I asked.

He gave me a withering look. 'Of course.'

'Swing us around, slowly,' I told Medea. We craned to look out of the pod's front ports, playing the lamp array up and down to make sense of the stark shadows in the cavern walls.

'What are those? Tube tunnels?'

'Auspex says they pinch out in a few hundred metres. God-Emperor, it looks pretty primordial out there!' Medea wiped a trickle of perspiration out of her eyes.

'What's that the lights are catching there?'

Aemos peered to where I was pointing. 'Amygdules,' he said. 'Cavities filled with quartzes or other secondary minerals.'

'Okay,' said Medea, unscrewing the stopper of a water-flask. 'Seeing as how you know everything... what's that?'

'Well, I... most perturbatory.'

It was a hole, perfectly circular, thirty metres in diameter, cut into the far rock wall.

'Edge closer,' I said. 'That's not a natural formation. It's too... precise.'

'What the hell made a hole like that?' Medea murmured, nudging us in.

'An industrial mining drill could–'

'This far down? This far from any mine infrastructure?' I cut Aemos short. 'Look at this place. Only sealed units like this pod can function at this depth.'

'Barely,' Medea commented, ominously. She was keeping a weather eye on the hull-integrity read-out. Amber runes were twitching on and off.

'It's deep,' I said. I looked at the display for the forward scanners. 'Goes off as far as we can read and maintains its shape and size.'

'But it's cut sheer through igneous rock... through the side of a forty kilometre square batholyth! That's solid anthragate!' There was a note of confusion in Aemos's frail old voice.

'I've got tremors,' said Medea suddenly. The needles on the rolling seismograph had been scratching away for a good hour or more, such was the background instability this deep down. But now they were skritching back and forth wildly.

'There's a pattern to them,' Aemos said. 'That's not tectonic. That's too regular... mechanical almost.'

I paused for a moment, considering our options. 'Take us into the shaft,' I said.

Medea looked at me, as if she was hoping she'd misheard me.

'Let's go.'

The cut shaft was so perfectly circular it was scary. As we sped down, we could see that the inner surface of the tube was fused like flowstone, with radiating patterns of furrows scooped into it.

'This was plasma-cut,' said Aemos. 'And whatever cut it, left an impression of its motivators in the rock before it cooled and hardened.'

The tube snaked occasionally, whilst maintaining its form. The bends were long and slow, but Medea took them cautiously. The seismograph was still jiggling.

I took out a holoquill and wrote a phrase down on the back of a chart-pad.

'Can you convert this into simple machine code?' I asked Aemos.

He looked at it. 'Hmmm... "Vade elquum alatoratha semptus"... you have a good memory.'

'Can you do it?'

'Of course.'

'What is that?' asked Medea. 'Some kind of sorcery?'

'No,' I smiled as Aemos got to work. 'It's like Glossia. A private language, one that hasn't been used in a long time.'

'There,' said Aemos.

'Punch it into the voxponder and set it to continuous repeat,' I said.

'I hope this works,' said Aemos. 'I hope you're right.'

'So do I,' I said.

Instrumentation pinged. 'We're approaching the end of the bore-hole!' Medea called. 'Another kilometre, and then we're out into a huge cavity!'

'Get that signal going!' I urged my elderly savant.

* * *

We were on it almost before we were ready. A massive tube of machined metal, thirty metres in diameter and seventy long, with a huge plasma cutting-screw at the front end and rows of claw-like impellers that cycled down its flanks like the active teeth of a gigantic chainsword. It had cut its way from the tube and was grumbling across the clastic silt of the chamber floor away from us, pumping thick clouds of vapourised rock and steam out behind it.

'Emperor protect me! It's huge!' Aemos exclaimed.

'What in the name of the Golden Throne is that?' gasped Medea.

'Slow down! Slow down!' I cried, but she was already braking us back behind the leviathan.

'Oh crap!' said Medea. Recessed hardpoints along the giant's flank had swivelled and opened, and multi-laser batteries had popped out to target us.

I grabbed the vox-set's hand-mic.

'Vade elquum alatoratha semptus!' I yelled into the mic. 'Vade elquum alatoratha semptus!'

The weapons – which could have obliterated us in a single salvo – did not fire. They remained trained on us, however. Then heavy shutter doors on the back end of the enormous machine opened slowly, revealing a small, well-lit hangar space.

'We won't get another invitation!' I told Medea.

With a worried shrug, she steered us inside.

I led the pair of them out of the pod into the arched dock-bay. The shutters had locked shut behind us, and pungent sulphurous fog pooled around our feet as it was pulled out of the bay by chugging air processors.

The bay was of a grand design, fluted with brass fittings and brushed steel. There was a brand new prospector pod, painted oxide-red, in the docking cradle next to the one that had received our singed specimen. Three other cradles, new and black with oil, lay vacant. All the light came from phosphorescent gas filaments in caged glass hoods around the room, and the effect was a flickering, lambent glow. An iron screwstair with padded leather rails led up to a boarding platform above us.

'That's a good sign,' I said. The bas-relief roundel of the Adeptus Mechanicus was visible above the inner door lock on the platform.

We all started as long servitor arms whirred out from compartments in the walls. In a second, six were trained on us: two with auspex sensors, sniffing us, and four with weapon mounts.

'I suggest we don't move,' I whispered.

The inner lock clanked and opened. A hooded figure in long orange robes seemed to hover out onto the platform. It grasped the handrail with both hands and looked down at us.

'Vade smeritus valsara esm,' it growled.

'Vade elquum alatoratha semptus,' I replied. 'Valsarum esoque quonda tasabae.'

The figure pulled back its hood, revealing a mechanical skull finished in oil-smudged chrome. Its lens-like eyes glowed bright green. Fat black cables under its jaw pulsed and the vox-caster screwed into its throat spoke.

'Gregor... Uber... It's been a long time.'

NINETEEN

WALKING THROUGH STONE
LITH
THE INMATE

'This is Medea Betancore,' I said, once Geard Bure's strong mechanical grip had finally released my hand.

'Miss Betancore,' Bure bowed slightly. 'The Adeptus Mechanicus of Mars, holy servants of the God-Machine, bids you take sanctuary in this, its worthy device.'

I was about to hiss at Medea and explain that she had been greeted formally, but, typically, she needed no prompting.

She deftly made the machine-fist salute of the Mechanicus and bowed in return. 'May your devices and desires serve the God-Emperor until time runs its course, magos.'

Bure chuckled – an eerie sound when it came from a prosthetic voice-box – and turned his unblinking green eye-lights to me.

'You've trained this one well, Eisenhorn.'

'I–'

'He has, magos,' said Medea quickly. 'But that response I learned from study of the Divine Primer.'

'You've read the Primer?' Bure asked.

'It was basic study in air school on my home world,' she replied.

'Medea has a... considerable aptitude for machines,' Aemos said. 'She is our pilot.'

'Indeed...' Bure walked around her and uninhibitedly caressed her body with his metal fingers. Medea temporarily humoured him.

'She is machine-wise, yet she has no augmentation?' Bure questioned me.

Medea stripped off her gloves and showed him the intricate circuits inlaid into her hands.

'I beg to differ, magos.'

He took her hands in his and gazed in hungry wonder. Drool-like ropes of clear lubricant oil trickled out between his chrome teeth like spittle.

'A Glavian! Your enhancements are... so... beautiful...'

'Thank you, sir.'

'You've never thought to permit any other augmentation? Limbs? Organs? It is quite liberating.'

'I... get by with what I've got,' smiled Medea.

'I'm sure you do,' Bure said, suddenly swinging round to face me. 'Welcome to my translithopede, Eisenhorn. You too, Aemos, my old friend. I must admit I can't conceive what brought you here. Is it the Lith? Has the Inquisition sent you to deal with the Lith?'

News of my disgrace clearly hadn't reached him, and for that, I was thankful.

'No, magos,' I said. 'A stranger quirk has brought us here.'

'Has it? How odd. When I first detected your signal - in dear Hapshant's old private code - I couldn't believe it. I nearly shot you down.'

'I took a chance,' I said.

'Well, that chance has led you to me and I'm glad. Come, this way.'

His skeletal silver hands ushered us towards the door lock.

Bure had no lower limbs. He floated on anti-gravity suspensors, the hem of his orange robe hanging a few centimetres above the plated deck. We fell in step behind him and walked the length of a long, oval companionway lined with brass bulkheads and more gas filament lamps.

'This burrowing machine is a wonder,' Aemos said.

'All machines are wonders,' Bure replied. 'This is a necessity, the primary tool of my work here on Cinchare. There were, of course, a number of lesser prototypes before I made the necessary refinements. This translithopede was engineered from my designs by the Adeptus fabricatory on Rysa and shipped here for my use three standard years ago. With it, I can go where I please in this rock, and unlock the secret lore of Cinchare's metals.'

Magos Bure had been a metallurgy specialist for two hundred years, his knowledge and discoveries almost worshipped by his brethren in the tech-priesthood. Before that, he had been a fabricator-architect in the Titan forges of Triplex Phall. To my certain knowledge, he was almost seven hundred years old. Hapshant had occasionally hinted that Bure was far older than that.

Not a shred of the magos's flesh remained. The vestigial organic parts of Geard Bure the human being - his brain and neural systems - were sealed inside his gleaming mechanoid body. I had never learned if this was a matter of design or necessity. Perhaps, as is the case with so many, disease or grievous injury had forced such extreme augmentation upon him. Or perhaps, like Tobias Maxilla, he had deliberately discarded the weakness of flesh in favour of machine perfection. Knowing the technophiliac disposition of the Mechanicus priesthood, the latter seemed more likely to me.

My late mentor, Inquisitor Hapshant, had encountered Magos Bure in the early part of his career, during the celebrated mission to secure the STC Lectionary from the ashrams of Ullidor the Techsmith. As I have remarked, the Inquisition - indeed most august bodies of the Imperium - find dealings with the Cult Mechanicus problematic at best. Its power is legendary and its insularity notorious. The cult is a closed order which guards the secrets of its technologies jealously. But Bure and Hapshant developed a beneficial working relationship based on mutual esteem. On several occasions, Bure's specialist wisdom assisted my mentor in the prosecution of important cases, and on several others, the favour was returned.

That is why, a century before, I entrusted an item of particular importance to his expert custody.

The control chamber of the wheezing translithopede was a split-level chapel where a raised command podium, like a giant brass pulpit, overlooked two semi-circular rows of busy control stations. The riveted iron walls were painted matt red and etched with the various aspects and runes of the Machine God. The forward wall was shrouded in long drapes of red velvet.

Six oil-streaked servitors worked at the chattering control stations, their hands and faces plugged directly into the systems via thick, metal-sleeved cables or striped flexes marked with purity seals and parchment labels. Glass valves and dials flickered and glowed, and the air was heady with the scent of oils and sacred unguents.

Two relatively human tech-adepts in orange robes were overseeing the activity. One was linked directly into the vehicle's mind-impulse unit through a trio of neural plugs, and he murmured aloud the rites and scriptures of the Adeptus. The other turned and bowed as we came onto the podium.

He had a wire-mesh speaker where his mouth should have been. When he spoke, it was in a pulse of binary machine code.

Bure responded in kind, and for a few moments they exchanged tight bursts of condensed data. Then Bure floated over to a brass lectern built into the podium's rail and opened his robe. Two probing neural cables extended from his chrome sternum like sucker-worms hunting for prey and connected swiftly with the polished sockets on the lectern.

Now Bure was also conjoined with the translithopede's mind-impulse unit.

'We make good speed,' he told us. He twitched, and the velvet drapes at the far end of the chamber drew aside automatically, revealing a large holographic display. Secondary images overlaid the main one, showing three-dimensional charts and power/speed graphics. The main image was just a dark rushing blur laced with crackles of blue energy.

This was the view directly ahead of us, the rock disintegrating before the awesome destructive force of the plasma cutting-screw. We were travelling straight through solid rock.

'Perhaps it's time we discussed what's going on here,' I said.

'We hunt,' sad Bure.

'You've been hunting for a long time, magos,' said Aemos. 'Eleven weeks now. What are you hunting for?'

'And why is Cinchare minehead derelict?' I added.

Bure paused as he selected the correct electrograft memory. He was almost lost in the euphoria of mind-impulse union.

'Ninety-two days ago, as far as I am able to reason it, an independent prospector called Farluke, working under license for Ortog Promethium, returned from a long tour of assay rock side and presented his masters with a unique discovery. They tried to keep it secret for a while, hoping, I believe, to exploit it for their own ends. That error in judgment was costly. By the time they realised their mistake, and shared their data with the Adeptus, it was already too late.'

'What had Farluke found?' asked Aemos.

'It is called the Lith. I have not seen it, but I have studied extracts recovered from the bodies of tainted men.'

'Recovered?' breathed Medea, unnerved.

'Posthumously. The Lith is a hyper-dense geode of approximately seven hundred tonnes. It is, as I understand it, a perfect decahedron four metres in diameter. Its mineral composition is exotic and inexplicable. And it is alive.'

'What? Magos! Alive?'

'Sentient, at least. It is infused with the wretched filth of Chaos. How long it has lain undiscovered in the depths of this world, I do not know. Perhaps it has always been here, or perhaps it was hidden in pre-Imperial times by unknown hands to keep it safe... or to dispose of it. Perhaps, indeed, it is the reason Cinchare has broken from the order of its stellar dance and drifted, rogue and wild, through the stars. I had hoped, initially, to find it and recover it. Its composition alone promised a wealth of precious knowledge. But now I hunt for it... simply to destroy it.'

'It has corrupted this world, hasn't it?' I said.

'Completely. As soon as it came in contact with men, it began to twist their minds with its malign power. It subjugated them. The Ortog work teams sent down to examine it were the first. What is, to all intents and purposes, a cult sprang up spontaneously. Each initiate had a splinter of rock shaved from the Lith buried beneath his skin in a simple, brutal ritual.'

'We've seen the marks.'

'Disorder spread through Cinchare minehead as the cult grew. The Lith couldn't be moved, but splinters were brought up and used to infect more and more of the workforce. Once tainted, the workers began to disappear, setting off on pilgrimages down into the mines to make worship to the Lith. Many never made it. Most have simply vanished. I've tried to follow their tracks, sometimes encountering hostile cult elements bent on protecting their deity. But Farluke's original data is unreliable. I cannot find the Lith's true location. I fear it is just a matter of time before the cult manages to extend its reach beyond Cinchare. Or...'

'Or?'

'Or they will complete some arcane task instructed by the Lith and awaken its power in full... or allow it to connect with its own kind.'

We considered this grim possibility for a moment. Aemos quietly pulled up an entry on the screen of his data-slate, unclipped the device from his wrist, and handed it to Bure.

'Does this help?' he asked.

Bure stared at the slate. His green eyebeams dilated into hard, bright points.

'How in the name of the Warpsmiths did you–'

'What is it?' I asked, stepped forward.

'The location of the Lith,' said Aemos proudly.

'How did you get this?' Bure cried, his vox undercut by excited binary chatter.

'The cult needs to know where it is. The reference was clearly marked in the charts I downloaded from the security office. I didn't realise its significance until now.'

'You just downloaded this?' Bure said.

'I believe they thought they had no reason to hide it. It wasn't encrypted.'

Bure threw back his chrome skull and laughed, a screeching, mocking cackle. 'Eleven weeks! Eleven weeks I have scoured and searched and fought my way through the bowels of this rock, hunting for clues, and the answer was up there all the time! In plain sight!'

He turned to Aemos and laid a steel hand on the savant's stooped shoulder. 'I have always admired your wisdom, Uber, and recognised why Hapshant valued you so... but now I realise that great wisdom comes from simplicity.'

'It was luck, nothing more.'

'It was bold simplicity, savant! A moment of direct, clear thought that quite dwarfs my labours down here.'

'You're too kind...' Aemos mumbled.

'Kind? No, I am not kind.' Bure's eye-lights swelled and flashed. 'I will cut my way to the heart of the Lith, and then its spawn will see how unkind my soul can be.'

Two hours later, after Bure's servitors had taken us to a sparely furnished cabin and provided us with flavourless, odourless nutrient broth and hard cakes of fibre bread, we were summoned back to the control chamber.

Outside, a small war was going on.

I had already sensed we had decelerated from tunnelling speed by the reduced throb of the impellers, and now I saw why. We had bored out of the rock into a towering vault lit by spurting pools of magma and flaming spouts of gas. On the chamber's holographic screen, I could see distorted, jarring images of the cavern outside. Silent laser fire was jabbing at us.

Bure was linked to the podium's lectern.

'We've found their nest,' he said. 'They resist.'

As I watched, two soot-stained prospector pods powered in towards us, firing small arms from their open hatches.

Bure nodded to one of his tech-adepts, and the shriek of multi-laser blasts rang through the hull. One pod exploded in a ball of light, the other tumbled away, shredded and burning.

I realised there were men on the ground too: miners in armoured work-suits scurrying forward and firing at the translithopede.

Bure increased magnification, and we saw that some of them carried pallets of mining charges, hoping to get close enough to breach our hull.

'Stalkers,' Bure said. It was evidently an order. There was a clank and a thud as hatches opened somewhere below us, and then new shapes began to move into view on the screen.

They were combat servitors. Heavyweight and burnished silver, they strode on powerful, backward-jointed legs, puffing black exhaust from their upthrust smoke stacks. Cannons in their upper limbs jerked with pneumatic recoil as they systematically targeted and cut down the cultists.

'Stalker 453, left and target,' Bure murmured. They were all slaved to his direct control.

One of the stalkers retrained its weapons and gunned four more cultists down. The charge-load they had been hefting exploded in a bright flash that blacked out the display for a second. When the holo-image returned, the stalker was already pacing on after new targets.

'Stalker 130 and Stalker 252, fan right. Opposition in cover behind that stalactite mass.'

'Oh great Emperor,' said Aemos suddenly. 'Some of them are unarmoured.'

It was true. A good many of the men assaulting us wore no shielding or environment armour. Their clothes were charred to black rags and their flesh was blistered and raw. Some force was keeping them active and functioning in this great infernal depth where no living thing should have been able to survive unprotected. Not the pressure, the extreme heat, not even the toxic, corrosive atmosphere was stopping them. The taint of the Lith had transmuted them into denizens of this underworld.

The wave of stalkers strode forward inexorably, and the translithopede followed them slowly, its impelling lines of adamantium cilia dragging it across the cavern rock. The multi-lasers fired again, destroying another vehicle – a large ore transporter that had been attempting to crash itself into our machine.

The mighty plasma screw churned again and ruptured apart a curtain of massive dripstones. Drizzles of dust obscured our picture for a few seconds.

When it cleared, we saw the true horror, and realised the ultimate, blasphemous fate of Cinchare minehead's population.

The blasphemy was huge, a writhing mound of baked, raw flesh and cooking bone. One by one, the tainted workers of Cinchare, even Bure's corrupted brethren from the Adeptus, had come down here to willingly contribute their organic matter to this mass.

As the translithopede came into view, it rose up, forming a great, rearing worm of red ooze and blackened meat fifty metres high. A ghastly mouth, big enough to swallow a prospecting pod, gaped wide in its cresting head, and it belched a vast ball of flaming gases at us.

The translithopede shook, warning hooters sounded, and the picture was lost. One control station below exploded, throwing its servitor to the deck. Smoke billowed through the chamber.

'Such power,' Bure marvelled, emotionless. The whole machine lurched again, more violently, and we stumbled, despite the internal gravity systems and inertial dampers.

The screen image restored, jumping, for a brief moment, enough to see that the blasphemy seemed to be coiling itself around us. The hull creaked and protested. Minor explosions rang out from lower decks. Plated seams bulged and several rivets flew out like bullets.

'Bure!'

'I will break it! I will cast it out!'

'Bure! In the name of the Emperor!'

He wasn't listening. All his efforts were focussed on the mind-impulse link driving the translithopede, on the orchestration of his stalkers as they rallied to counter-attack the monstrosity. His confidence in the supremacy of the Machine over all things was blinding him to the very real possibility that the formidable Cult Mechanicus had just met its match.

I turned to Medea and Aemos.

'Come on!' I cried.

We were halfway down the translithopede's main companionway, heading towards the rear of the great machine, when a still more violent impact shook it. Without warning, the inertial dampers failed and we tumbled as the burrower was rolled onto its side. The glass mantles of the gas lights smashed, and weak flame sputtered and danced along the walls. There was a further series of terrific impacts.

We got to our feet, now forced to use the curving wall as a floor. The pulsing shriek of the multi-lasers was by then a constant noise outside.

Red warning lights were flashing in the arched dock-bay. Our pod had been torn from its cradle by the latest impact and lay crumpled on its side, reclining against part of the roof arching. But the oxide-red pod was still safely locked in place.

Medea and I jumped down from the dock's inner hatch onto the ceiling, but Aemos called after us.

'I can't make that jump,' he protested. I knew he was right.

'Then seal the hatch and get back to help Bure!'

'The Emperor protect you both!' he shouted as the hatch closed.

Power cables that had once lain on the deck now dangled like ropes. Grabbing one each, we began to rappel up towards the pod in its cradle. We were halfway there when the world seemed to shudder again and the translithopede righted itself violently. Medea and I went sprawling, loose debris skittering all around us. I had barely enough time to dive and heave Medea aside before our own wrecked pod came crunching back down the wall, slamming sideways onto the floor.

Another lurch and the deck tipped the other way, out of true by about twenty degrees. The unanchored pod began sliding across the deck towards us.

'Get in!' Medea yelled. 'Get in!' She had the side hatch of the red pod open and dragged me halfway inside. A moment later, and the translithopede rocked back thirty degrees in the other direction.

The loose pod immediately squealed back across the deck and crashed into the wall bulkheads. I was dangling by my hands from the open hatch.

'Crap! Get in! Get the hell in!' Medea wailed, fighting to hold on to me. I grunted and swung my legs up so that my toe caps caught the door sill. With a further effort, I managed to pull myself up, and Medea slammed the hatch.

There was still more shaking and rocking. We clambered in to the seats of the pilot station in the low cockpit, and strapped on the harnesses. Medea was keying the pod's drive ignition when the translithopede inverted again and left us hanging in our seats by the safety straps. The pod was now locked in its cradle on the roof.

'This'll be fun,' Medea laughed aggressively. She had sent a remote command to open the dock-bay's shutter doors. Then she powered the pod's engines to full thrust and disengaged the cradle lock.

For a dizzying second, we dropped, upside down, like a rock. Then she hit the thrusters and looped us. We missed the dock-bay roof by a handsbreadth and flew out through the opening shutters even as the entire translithopede rolled over again.

The blasphemy had wrapped itself around Bure's great subterranean burrower with constricting coils. It thrashed and shook the machine, and I could clearly see the armoured hull beginning to buckle and crumple. There were smoking sockets where some of the multi-laser batteries had been ripped away. The stalkers were converging on the wrestling giants, strafing the Chaos worm with furious barrages. The remains of several lay crushed where the translithopede had rolled on them.

Medea banked us around, trying to speed-familiarise herself with the control layout.

'What do we do? I take it you've got a plan?'

I shook my head. 'I'm working on it.' Bure's pod was unarmed – I know this because I checked feverishly the moment we were airborne – and there was nothing that might be turned into an offensive weapon apart from a mining laser under the chin of the cockpit. A mining laser with fierce cutting power and a range of about five metres.

'Take us deeper into the cavern,' I said, consulting the display on the pod's geologicae auspex.

'Away from the fight?'

'We can't engage that thing... so we find the Lith instead. And that return has got to be it.'

There was a pulsing cursor on the screen: big, unmistakable.

Cultists on the cave floor blasted at us as we zipped over them and headed off down the long, volcanic cavern. Spumes of pyroclastic wrath detonated up from the lava lakes and threatened to envelop us.

Then we saw the Lith.

It had been buried in a plug of obsidian jutting from the cavern wall, but serious excavation work had been done to reveal it.

Heavy mining pods and anti-grav drill platforms sat on the ash slopes below it, and the ground was covered in fragments of obsidian.

It was, as Bure had described, a perfect decahedron four metres across, dark green and glassy like water-ice. It glowed with an inner light. Even from a distance, it felt malevolent. I sensed an unnerving tickling at the edge of my psychic range. Medea looked sick.

'I don't want to get any closer,' she said suddenly.

'We have to.'

'And do what?'

I wondered if we could cut it with the mining laser. I wondered indeed if that would do any good. I doubted we would make much of dent in it even if we power-dived the pod at it.

Yet, the cultists had shaved splinters from it to promulgate their evil. It was vulnerable... unless it had somehow allowed the splinters to be removed.

We certainly couldn't move it.

I could feel it now, whispering in my head. There were no words, just a murmur that chilled my spine. Insidious, slow... slow like eons of geological time, slow like a glacier or a tectonic plate. It spoke softly and without haste, gently unfolding its seductive message. It had no need to rush. It had all the time in the galaxy...

The pod yawed wildly. I started and looked around. Medea had lost partial control because she had turned to be violently sick over the side of her seat. Her skin was blanched and she was panting and sweating.

'I... I can't...' she gasped. 'Don't make me go any closer...'

She had reached her limits. I leaned over and put my hand against the side of her head. 'Sleep,' I said softly, using the will.

She sank into merciful unconsciousness.

I took the controls.

I was no flier like Medea Betancore, and for a moment, I thought I was going to dive us nose-first into the lake of bubbling magma as I fumbled with the actuators.

But Medea's late father had trained me well enough. I swooped low over the pool of molten rock, creating a shockwave vortex in the brimstone, and banked around a massive anthragate column that rose up into the jagged roof. There was just a last wide lake of fire between me and the ash shore where the Lith was exposed.

It was whispering again, but I shook it off. I had trained my mind hard to resist the ministrations of Chaos and its psychic wiles. This was how it turned weak minds. This was how it had polluted and tainted the population of Cinchare minehead. The whispering... the formless, shapeless words of power that drew mankind into the embrace of the warp...

An idea struck me. I like to think it was an idea born out of the same pure simplicity that Bure had celebrated in Aemos. A perfect, simple possibility.

I shrugged from my mind my fears for the life of Aemos and the magos. The blasphemy might already have torn the translithopede apart in the cavern far behind me. If they were not beyond hope, then this was the best I could do for them.

Risking a free hand, I reached sideways and activated the pod's voxponder, setting it to record. Then, concentrating on my steering once more, I began to speak, clearly and loudly, dredging words up from my memory. Long ago, on my birth planet, DeKere's World, as a child, standing in the long hall of the primary scholam with the other pupils, reciting together...

A collision warning blared, and I veered to the left in time to glimpse a prospecting pod that filled my cockpit windows for a moment before racing past.

Two bright yellow cursors had appeared on my auspex display. The beacon locators of prospecting pods, like the ones that had chased us into the mine system.

The one that had tried to collide with me was turning wide over the lava lake. The other was coming in on an intercept course. I swung round to face it and then gulled away at the last minute. The pass was close, close enough to see the Ortog Promethium symbols on its flank. Close enough to see Enforcer Kaleil's face through the cockpit ports.

The first pod, an Imperial Allied symbol just visible through the heat-flaked paint, came in and blocked my route to the shore and the Lith. Its driver, unidentifiable, had smashed the window lights out and was firing a lascarbine out from the cockpit. Despite our comparative speeds, I felt several shots land home, banging into the pod's fuselage. I steered away, trying desperately not to break my recitation as I concentrated on the air duel.

I began to chant the words like a mantra.

As I turned from the Imperial Allied pod, I met Kaleil's vessel head on. I rolled hard to evade, but still we clipped and the whole pod shook. Warning lights lit up across the control console. I had thruster damage and reduced manoeuvring ability. The lava lake flashed up to consume me but I climbed hard, away from the ash beach.

All the while, my recitation continued.

The Imperial Allied pod was on my tail, streaking the air with las-shots. We whipped hard around the anthragate pillar, but I couldn't shake him. I tried to think what Medea would do. What Midas would have done. For a moment, my words faltered as I planned and executed my frantic response.

The pod was right behind me. I braked hard, and managed to spin the anti-grav machine in place using the attitude jets, dropping my nose as if curtseying to my attacker. And I ignited my mining laser.

The Imperial Allied pod was far too close to my rear to effect a turn or a brake. I think he was trying for a collision, but I was just too high for him. He ran in under my hull at full thrust, so close he tore the lighting array and the auspex antennae off the underside of my pod.

He also ran straight through the incandescent spear of my mining laser. It sliced the Imperial Allied pod lengthways and sent the disintegrating halves spinning away into the white hot magma below.

My pod was half crippled now from the pair of impacts. I continued my recitation, hoping the brief lapse wouldn't matter.

With its antennae gone, the auspex was blind, but I could see Kaleil anyway. He was gunning across the lake straight for me.

I hovered in place. There was a time for action and, as I had already gambled, a time for words. I switched off the voxponder and keyed the open channel.

'Kaleil?'

'Horn!'

'Not Horn... Inquisitor Eisenhorn.'

Silence. He was two hundred metres and closing at a speed that would wipe us both out.

I pressed the vox-mic close to my mouth and used every shred of my will.

'Don't,' I said.

The Ortog Promethium pod veered and then dived straight down into the lava lake. A halo of fire broke up from the slow, undulating splash it made in the liquid rock.

I limped my pod over to the ash beach and set down about twenty metres short of the Lith. Medea moaned in her sleep. I dreaded the dreams that might be boiling through her subconscious.

'Get out of my head!' I snarled aloud at the Lith's persistent whispering.

It took me a moment to rewind the voxponder recording and set it to a continuous loop. Then I diverted its signal into the echo-sounding sonar system that the pod used to supplement its auspex in assay and location work. I twiddled the dials until the powerful sonar was aimed directly at the malevolent decahedron.

Conveyed in fierce ultrasonic pulses, my recording blasted the Lith. The Emperor's Prayer of Abrogation Against the Warp, learned by rote by every good schoolchild of the Imperium. An innocent blessing against the darkness, a banishment of Chaos. I doubted it had ever been used so actively. I doubted my scholam tutors had ever conceived of such a use for that simple, sing-song declaration.

'Words,' I murmured. 'Your corrupt whispers against my words of power. How do you like that?'

I pushed the sonar gain to maximum. In terms of sonics alone, the pulses would have stunned a man to unconsciousness and snapped his bones.

For a good minute or more, I feared it was having no effect.

Then the whispering ceased. It became a subsonic moaning of rage and anguish, and finally agony.

The Lith's surface became discoloured, as if mottled by mould. It shuddered, cracking the obsidian around it.

Then its inner luminescence sputtered and went out, and it became indistinguishable from the black volcanic glass that surrounded it.

When the Lith died, so did its servants, and so did the blasphemy. Checking that Medea was now just sleeping soundly, I nursed the damaged pod back down the cavern in time to see the last stringy remnants of the foul worm combusting and sliding off the translithopede's buckled hull. The air was thick with dirty cinders and the smoke of burning fat.

The burning corpses of cultists littered the chamber floor. Motionless stalkers stood in their midst, cycling on pause, waiting for the next command.

Broken and twisted, the great burrower was at least intact. When I brought the pod into the dock-bay, Bure's own tech-adepts themselves emerged to take care of Medea's unconscious body.

The companionway floor was raked over at an angle. Bure's engineer priests were still trying to repair the inertial dampers.

Acrid smoke filled the air, unpleasantly scented by the fat-fires outside. Aemos met me in the doorway of the control chamber and hugged me briefly in a rare display of affection. Bure had shed his orange robe. A sinister, stark, inhuman silhouette, he watched our very human exchange from the edge of the podium, backlit by fires raging in the workstations below.

'We're fine now, old friend,' I said to Aemos.

He broke the embrace, as if guilty. 'You did well, Gregor. Marvellously! I... I didn't mean any disrespect...'

It was at times like that I wished I could still smile. I am too used to my face being the impassive mask Gorgone Locke gave me.

Using my will gently, so he might understand the truth of my words, I said, 'No disrespect taken, old friend.'

Aemos smiled sheepishly and turned away.

His suspensors hissing, Bure glided over to me. To my surprise, he hugged me too. It was brief and clumsy, his servo arms conveying no warmth. I felt terrible sorrow for him then. His human core had been moved by the events and he had seen and copied Aemos's impromptu display of affection. Just then, I believe, he passionately wanted to be human again. Just for a moment. But his vicing arms had no more emotion in them than the tight handshake with which he had first greeted me.

He swung away, his arms to his sides. His green eye-lights flicked back and forth over the repair teams as they worked to contain the damage.

'I have never said,' he began, his voxed voice toneless and cold, though it tried to be neither of those things. 'Hapshant. He thought the world of you, Eisenhorn. He told me once that he believed you would eclipse his career with your own. I think he was right.'

'Thank you, magos.'

He turned around to look at me. His eye were tiny spots of emerald fire.

'You never did say what brought you here.'

'Recent matters somewhat overtook us, magos.'

'Yes. But still, you never did say...'

'I have to explain the... circumstances that have changed in my life, magos. I will explain them carefully, in the hope that you will understand and not think badly of me. But first... I gave you something to safeguard and study, a century ago. I'd like to see it again.'

It was ironic, as if some karmic balance was at work. Of course, I didn't believe in such things. Bure had burrowed and tunnelled his way fruitlessly through the heart of Cinchare for eleven weeks, only to have Aemos casually present him with the Lith's location. And we had gone deep into the mines to find Bure only to learn that what I had come to Cinchare for had been safely locked away in the annex of the Adeptus Mechanicus all along, had I but looked for it.

It took thirty hours for the ailing translithopede to make its way back to the surface. Once we'd broken through the blue gypnate crust at the Imperial Allied mineworks, I sent Aemos and Medea back to the cutter to check in with Bequin and the others, still waiting aboard the *Essene* at high orbit.

I hoped they hadn't done anything foolish in my absence.

Bure took me to the annex. His encoded touch brought the sanctum to life, and lit long hallways to either side of the Mechanicus chapel. He led me down one of these, the illumination plates still flickering as they warmed up after such a prolonged period of disuse.

The magos linked his thoracic neural cables to a wall socket and disengaged a lock. A heavy, armoured door slid open. Then another, inside the first, then a third, a sturdy iris valve that withdrew segmentally into the wall frame with a noise like swords sheathing.

'This is what you want,' said Bure. 'He has been most informative, over the years.'

'I'll review your reports later, magos,' I said. 'Leave me with him now.'

Bure withdrew.

I stepped through the iris valve and down three grilled steps into the cell, feeling the nauseating static prickle of the psychic dampening fields. Every surface was dusted with ice-crystals. There was a crackle of synaptic energy.

'Hello, Eisenhorn,' said a hollow, vox-projected voice. It came from a casket that squatted on a basalt block in the centre of the room. Both casket and stone were caked in ice. Tiny lights darted and blinked inside the casket's open lid.

I prepared myself. Then I replied.

'Pontius Glaw. We meet again.'

TWENTY

INTERVIEW WITH THE DAMNED
BURE, WARSMITH
ORBUL INFANTA

'Let me make sure I understand you, Eisenhorn,' said the disembodied voice of Pontius Glaw, slowly and contemptuously. 'You think I'm going to help you?'

I cleared my throat. 'Yes.'

Pontius laughed. Synapse leads connected to the gold circuits of his engram sphere flashed in series. 'I didn't think a man of such studied dullness and sobriety as you would have the ability to surprise me, Eisenhorn. My mistake.'

'You *will* help me,' I said, quietly but emphatically.

I brushed frost from the grilled steps and sat down facing his casket. It was claw-footed, rectangular, compact and filled with complex technology designed for one purpose: the support and operation of the engram sphere, a rough-cut nugget the size of a clenched fist in which resided the intellect – and perhaps the soul – of one of the most notorious heretics in the Imperium.

Pontius Glaw, dead in body for nigh on three hundred years, had been in his physical life one of the more unwholesome products of the powerful Glaw dynasty. That family line, part of the high nobility of Gudrun, had whelped many heretics in its time, the last of whom had been instrumental in the affair of the Necroteuch. Supported by the considerable efforts of Imperial Navy Security, I had all but crushed their poisonous lineage, and in the process had captured the engram sphere of Pontius Glaw. His family and their minions had attempted to sacrifice thousands of innocents in order to restore him to physicality. That, too, I had denied.

Once the affair had ended, I had been left with this casket full of heretical spite. In terms of technology alone, it was a wonder, and there was no telling what secrets the Pontius might have in it. So instead of destroying it, I had passed it into the safekeeping of Magos Geard Bure. Bure, I knew, would have the time and skill enough to unlock its technical marvels at least. And he was trustworthy.

But from time to time in that past hundred years, I had questioned the validity of that decision. In all honesty, I should have surrendered the Pontius to the Ordo Hereticus for examination and disposal. The fact that

I hadn't sometimes played on my conscience, for it suggested deceit and unwholesome subterfuge on my part. In the light of events in the past year, I found myself fighting back the notion that perhaps my accusers were right. Had it been the act of an unsound man to secret away such a radical entity?

Aemos had consoled my spirits, reminding me that the casket utilised mind-impulse technology undoubtedly stolen from the Cult Mechanicus. There was, he said, no question that such a device should be in the custody of the Adeptus priesthood.

'Go on then,' Pontius said. 'Make your case. Why would I help you?'

'I require specialist information that I'm certain you have. Certain lore.'

'You are an inquisitor, Eisenhorn. All the resources of the Imperium are at your disposal. Am I to understand that, well, that your scope has become somewhat limited?'

I was damned if I was going to tell this monster of the straits I was in. And even though he was right in a way, there was no Imperial archive I knew of that could answer my questions.

'What I need might be regarded as... proscribed knowledge.'

'Ahhhhh...'

'What? "Ah" what?'

Even without features or body language to read, Pontius seemed insufferably pleased with himself. 'So you've finally reached that place. How wonderful.'

'What place?' I felt uncomfortable. I had been planning this interview for months, and now control was slipping entirely to Glaw.

'The place where you cross the line.'

'I hav–'

'All inquisitors cross the line eventually.'

'I tell y–'

'All of them. It's an occupational hazard.'

'Listen to me, you worthless–'

'Methinks Inquisitor Eisenhorn protests too much. The line, Gregor. The line! The line between order and chaos, between right and wrong, between mankind and man-unkind. I know it, because I've crossed it. Willingly, of course. Gladly. Skipping and dancing and delighting. For the likes of you, it is a more painful process.'

I rose. 'I don't think this conversation is going anywhere, Glaw. I'm leaving.'

'So soon?'

'Perhaps I'll be back in another century or two.'

'It was on Quenthus Eight, in the spring of 019.M41.'

I paused at the cell hatchway. 'What was?'

'The moment I crossed the line. Would you like to hear about it?'

I was rattled, but I returned to my seat on the steps. I knew what he was doing. Imprisoned in his casket without touch or smell or taste, without any sensory stimulation, Pontius Glaw craved company and conversation. I had learned that much during my long interrogations of him aboard the *Essene* ten decades before during the voyage to the remote system KCX-1288. Now he was simply feeding me morsels to make me stay and talk to him.

However, in a hundred years of captivity, he had never come close to revealing such intimate details of his personal history.

'019.M41. A busy year. The buttress worlds of the far eastern rim were resisting a holy waaagh! by the greenskins, and two of the High Lords of Terra had been assassinated in as many months by disaffected Imperial families. There was talk of civil war. The sub-sector's trader markets had crashed. Trade was bad. What a year. Saint Drache was martyred on Korynth. Billions starved in the Beznos famine.'

'I have access to history texts, Pontius,' I said dryly.

'I was on Quenthus VIII, buying fighters for my pit-games. They're a good breed, the Quenthi, long in the hams and quite belligerent. I was, perhaps, twenty-five. I forget exactly. I was in my prime, beautiful.'

There was a long silence while he considered this reflection. Light-sparks pulsed along his wires.

'One of the pit-marshals at the amphitheatre I was visiting advised me to see a fighter who had been bought in from the very edges of the Ultima Segmentum. A great, tanned fellow from a feral world called Borea. His name was Aaa, which meant, in his tongue, "sword-cuts-meat-for-women-prizes". Isn't that lovely? If I had ever sired a son, a human one, I mean, I would have called him Aaa. Aaa Glaw. Quite a ring to it, eh?'

'I'm still on the verge of leaving, Glaw.'

The voice from the casket chuckled. 'This Aaa was a piece of work. His teeth were filed into points and his fingertips had been bound and treated with traditional unguents since his birth so that they had grown into claws. Claws, Eisenhorn! Fused, calcified hooks of keratin and callouses. I once saw him rip through chainmail with them. Anyway, he was a true find. They kept him shackled permanently. The pit-marshal told me that he'd torn a fellow prisoner's arm off during transit, and scalped a careless stadium guard. With his teeth.'

'Charming.'

'I bought him, of course. I think he liked me. He had no real language, naturally, and his table manners! He slept in his own soil and rutted like a canine.'

'No wonder he liked you.'

The frost crackled around the casket. 'Cruel boy. I am a cultured man. Ha. I *was* a cultured man. Now I am an erudite and dangerous box. But don't forget my learning and upbringing, Eisenhorn. You'd be amazed how easy it is for a well-raised and schooled son of the Imperium to slide across that line I mentioned.'

'Go on. I'm sure you had a point to make.'

'Aaa served me well. I won several fortunes on his pit-fights. I won't pretend we ever became friends... one doesn't become friends with a favourite carnodon now, does one? And one certainly never makes friends with a commodity. But we built an understanding over the years. I would visit him in his cell, unguarded, and he never touched me. He would halt out old myths of his home world, Borea. Vicious tales of barbary and murder. But I'm getting ahead of myself. The moment, the moment was there on

Quenthus, in the amphitheatre, under the spring sun. The pit-marshal showed me Aaa, and tempted me to purchase him. Aaa looked at me, and I think he saw a kindred soul... which is probably why we bonded once he was mine. In his simple, broken speech, he implored me to buy him, telling me graphically what sport I would have of him. And to seal the deal, he offered me his torc.'

'His torc?'

'That's right. The slaves were allowed to keep certain familiar items provided they weren't potential weapons. Aaa wore a golden torc around his neck, the mark of his tribe. It was the most valuable thing he possessed. Actually, it was the only thing he possessed. But no matter... he offered it to me in return for me becoming his master. I took it, and, as I said, I bought him.'

'And that was the line?' I sat back, unimpressed.

'Wait, wait... later, later that same day, I examined the torc. It was inlaid with astonishing technology. Borea might have been a beast-world by then, but millennia back, it had clearly been an advanced outpost of mankind. It had fallen into a feral dark age because Chaos had touched it, and that torc was a relic of the decline. Its forbidden, forgotten technology focussed the stuff of the Darkness into the wearer's mind. No wonder Borea, where every adult male wore one, was a savage waste. I was intrigued. I put the torc on.'

'You put it on?'

'I was young and reckless, what can I say? I put it on. Within a few hours, the tendrils of the warp had suffused my receptive mind. And do you know what?'

'What?'

'It was wonderful! Liberating! I was alive to the real universe at last! I had crossed the line, and it was bliss. Suddenly I saw everything as it actually was, not as the Ministorum and the rot-hearted Emperor wanted to see it. Engulfing eternity! The fragility of the human race! The glories of the warp! The fleeting treasure of flesh! The incomparable sweetness of death! All of it!'

'And you ceased to be Pontius Glaw, the seventh son of a respectable Imperial House, and became Pontius Glaw, the sadistic idolator and abomination?'

'A boy's got to have a hobby.'

'Thank you for sharing this with me, Pontius. It has been revealing.'

'I'm just getting started...'

'Goodbye.'

'Eisenhorn! Eisenhorn, wait! Please! I–'

The cell hatches clanged shut after me.

I waited two days before I returned to see him. He was sullen and moody this time.

I entered the cell and set down the tray I was carrying.

'Don't expect me to talk to you,' he said.

'Why?'

'I opened my soul to you the other day and you... walked out.'

'I'm back now.'

'Yes, you are. Closer to that line yet?'

'You tell me.' I leaned over and poured myself a large glass of amasec from the decanter on the tray. I rocked the glass a few times and then took a deep sip.

'Amasec.'

'Yes.'

'Vintage?'

'Fifty year old Gathalamor vintage, aged in burwood barrels.'

'Is it... good?'

'No.'

'No?'

'It is perfect.'

The casket sighed.

'You were saying. About that line?' I asked.

'I... I was saying I was most annoyed with you,' Pontius returned, stubbornly.

'Oh.' I casually slid a lho-stick from the paste-board tub I had backhanded from Tasaera Ungish's stateroom. I lit it and took a deep drag, exhaling the smoke towards the infernal casket. Nayl had injected me with powerful anti-intoxicants and counter-opiate drugs just half an hour earlier, but I sat back and openly seemed to relish the smoke.

'Is that a lho-stick?'

'Yes, Pontius.'

'Hmmm...'

'You were saying?'

'Is it good?'

'You were saying?'

'I... I've told you of my slip. My crossing of the line. What else do you want of me?'

'The rest. You think I've crossed the line too, don't you?'

'Yes. It's in your bearing. You seem like a man who has understood the wider significance of the warp.'

'Why is that?'

'I told you it happens to all inquisitors sooner or later. I can imagine you as a young man, stiff and puritanical, in the scholam. It must have seemed so simple to you back then. The light and the dark.'

'Not so obvious these days.'

'Of course not. Because the warp is in everything. It is there even in the most ordered things you do. Life would be brittle and flavourless without it.'

'Like your life is now?' I suggested, and took another sip.

'Damn you!'

'According to you, I'm already damned.'

'Everyone is damned. Mankind is damned. The whole human species. Chaos and death are the only real truths of reality. To believe otherwise is ignorance. And the Inquisition... so proud and dutiful and full of its own importance, so certain that it is fighting against Chaos... is the most ignorant thing of all. Your daily work brings you closer and closer to the warp, increases your understanding of orderless powers. Gradually, without noticing it, even the most puritanical and rod-stiff inquisitor becomes seduced.'

'I don't agree.'

Pontius's mood seemed to have brightened now we were engaged in debate again. 'The first step is the knowledge. An inquisitor must understand the basic traits of Chaos in order to fight it. In a few years, he knows more about the warp than most untutored cultists. Then the second step: the moment he breaks the rules and allows some aspect of Chaos to survive or remain so that he can study it and learn from it. I wouldn't even bother trying to deny that one, Eisenhorn. I'm right here, aren't I?'

'You are. But understanding is essential. Even a puritan will tell you that! Without it, the Inquisition's struggle is hopeless.'

'Don't get me started on that,' he chuckled. Then paused. 'Describe the taste of that amasec in your mouth. The quality, the scent.'

'Why?'

'It is three hundred years since I have tasted anything. Smelt anything. Touched anything.'

I had feared my gambit with the amasec and the opiate too obvious, but it had drawn him in. 'It feels like oil on my tongue, soft, body-heat. The aroma precedes the taste, like peat and pepper, spiced. The taste is a burn in the throat that lights a fire behind my heart.'

The casket made a long, mournful sound of tantalised regret.

'The third step?' I prompted.

'The third step... the third step is the line itself. When the inquisitor becomes a radical. When he chooses to use Chaos against Chaos. When he employs the agencies of the warp. When he asks the heretical for help.'

'I see.'

'I'm sure you do. So... are you going to ask me to help you?'

'Yes. Will you give me that help?'

'It depends,' the casket murmured. 'What's in it for me?'

I stubbed out the lho-stick. 'Given what you've just said, I assume your reward would be the satisfaction of seeing me cross that line and damn myself.'

'Ha ha! Very clever! I'm enjoying that part already. What else?'

I turned the glass in my hand, swilling the amber spirit around. 'Magos Bure is a talented man. A master of machinery. Though I would never release you from imprisonment, I could perhaps ask him for a favour.'

'A favour?' Pontius echoed with trembling anticipation.

'A body for you. A servitor chassis. The ability to walk, reach, hold, see. Perhaps even the finessing extras of sense actuators: rudimentary touch, smell, taste. That would be child's play for him.'

'Gods of the warp!' he whispered.

'Well?'

'Ask. Ask me. Ask me, Eisenhorn.'

'Let us talk for a while... on the subject of daemonhosts.'

'Do you know what you're doing?' Fischig said to me.

'Of course,' I said. We had taken over the security office in Cinchare minehead as our base. Bequin and Aemos had set the place straight and got it running properly, and Medea, Inshabel, Nayl and Fischig patrolled the area regularly. Bure had provided servitor-stalkers as additional guards, and a vox-uplink had been established with the orbiting *Essene* to forewarn us of any arriving space traffic.

It was late one afternoon in the third week of our visit to the mining rock. I had just returned from my daily visit to Glaw's cell in the Mechanicus annex and I stood with Fischig by the windows of the office, looking down into the plaza.

'Really sure?' he pressed.

'I seem to remember him asking us the same thing when we sprang him from the Carnificina,' said Bequin, coming over to join us. 'Thanks to Osma and his ridiculous witch-hunt, we've been forced into a corner. If we can come through this successfully, we will redeem ourselves.'

Fischig snorted. 'I just don't like it. Not dealing with that butcher. Not promising him anything. I feel like we've crossed the line–'

'What?' I asked sharply. I had told them only the very sparest details of my conversations.

'I said I felt like we'd crossed the line. What's the matter?'

I shook my head. 'Nothing. How are the rest of the preparations going?'

I sensed Fischig wanted to have it out, but it was really too late for that. I deflected him with the subject change.

'Your magos friend is working. Nayl took him the blade yesterday and showed him your notes and diagrams,' he said.

'The communiqués are all written, encrypted and sealed, ready to be sent,' said Bequin. 'Just give the word, and Ungish will transmit them. And I have the declaration here.' She handed me a data-slate.

It was a carta extremis formally declaring Quixos Heretic and Extremis Diabolus, naming his crimes and given in my authority. It was dated the twentieth day of the tenth month, 340.M41. There was no location of issue, but Aemos had made certain all the other particulars were phrased precisely according to High Imperial Law and the statutes of the Inquisition.

'Good. We'll send that in a few days.' I knew that the moment the carta was published, my agenda would be known. Thc scheme I was embarking on might take years to complete, and all that time I would be hunted. I really didn't want to stir things up so soon.

'How much longer will we be here?' Bequin asked.

'I don't know. Another week? A month? Longer? It depends on how forthcoming Glaw decides to be.'

'But you've got things from him already?' asked Fischig.

'Yes.' Not too much, I hoped.

I walked through the empty streets of the minehead for an hour or two that evening to clear my mind. I knew damn well that I was choosing a dangerous path. I had to remain focussed or I risked losing control.

Once I'd got the upper hand with Glaw, I'd been playing with him during those early conversations. His talk of the line, his three-step description of the corruption that awaited an imprudent inquisitor... that was nothing new to me. I had indulged him so that he might feel superior and smug. Any inquisitor worth the rosette knew the perils and temptations that surrounded him.

But it didn't stop his words from cutting me. Every puritanical Commodus Voke was a potential Quixos. When Glaw said that the line was often crossed without it being recognised, he was right. I'd met enough radicals to know that.

I had always, always prided myself on my puritanical stance, moderate and Amalathian though it might be. I deplored the radical heresies. That's why I wanted Quixos.

But I worried still. I considered what I was doing to be risky, of course, but also pragmatic given my difficult situation. To destroy Quixos, I had to get past his daemonhosts, and that required power, knowledge and expertise. And I could no longer turn to the Holy Inquisition for support. But had I crossed the line? Was I becoming guilty of sins that could so easily escalate into radical abomination? Was I so obsessed with bringing Quixos to justice that I was abandoning my own principles?

I was sure I was not. I knew what I was doing, and I was taking every precaution I could to manage the more dangerous elements I was employing. I was pure and true, even now.

And if I wasn't, how could I tell?

I climbed an observation mast that rose above the mine settlement and lingered for a while in the caged glass blister at the top, looking out across the town's skyline to the ragged blue landscape of Cinchare, and the gliding stars beyond it. Shoals of meteors burned bright lines down the sky.

There was a noise on the stairs behind me. It was Nayl.

He put away his sidearm. 'It's you,' he said, joining me in the blister. 'I was patrolling and I saw the tower door open. Everything all right?'

I nodded. 'You fight dirty sometimes, don't you, Harlon?'

He looked at me quizzically and scratched his shaved scalp. 'Not sure I know what you mean, boss,' he said.

'All those years, bounty hunting... and I've seen you fight, remember? Sometimes you have to break the rules to win.'

'I suppose so. When all's said and done, you use whatever works. I'm not proud of some of my more... ruthless moments. But they're necessary. I've always been of the opinion that fairplay is overrated. The bastard trying to skin you won't be playing fair, that's for sure. You do what you have to do.'

'The end justifies the means?'

He raised his eyebrows and laughed. 'Now that's different. That kind of thinking gets a man into trouble. There are some means that no end will ever justify. But fighting dirty, occasionally, is no bad thing. Neither's breaking the rules. Provided you remember one thing.'

'Which is?'

'You have to understand the rules in the first place if you're going to break them.'

* * *

Apart from my daily visits to Glaw in the annex, I also spent time with Bure. He was labouring in his workshops, assisted by servitors and his tech-adepts. He had thrown himself totally into the tasks I had set him. Though he never said, I think he saw it as returning with interest my efforts in the battle with the Lith.

He had also listened without alarm when Aemos and I had related the history of the recent past. It felt like a confession. I explained the carta out against me, my rogue status. He had accepted my innocence without question. As he put it, 'Hapshant wouldn't have raised a radical. It's the rest of the galaxy that's wrong.'

That was good enough for him. I was quietly moved.

One day in the sixth week of our increasingly prolonged stay, he called me to his workshop.

It lay beneath the main chapel of the annex and was two storeys deep, a veritable smithy alive with engineering machines and apparatus the purposes of which baffled me. Steam-presses hammered and banged, and screw-guns wailed. Quite apart from my own projects, there was much work to do repairing the annex and the translithopede. I walked down through the swathes of steam and found Bure supervising two servitors who were machining symbols into a two-metre long pole of composite steel.

'Eisenhorn,' he said, raising his bright green eye-lights to look at me.

'How goes the work?'

'I feel like a warsmith, back in the foundries of the forge worlds, when I was flesh. The specifications you have asked for are difficult, but not impossible. I enjoy a challenge.'

I took several sheets of paper from my coat pocket and handed them to him. 'More notes, taken during my last interview with Glaw. I've underlined the key remarks. Here, he suggests electrum for the cap piece.'

'I was going to use iron, or an iron alloy. Electrum. That makes sense.' He took my notes over to a raised planning table that was littered with scrolls, holoquills, measuring tools and data-slates. Pages of notes that I had already provided him with were piled up, along with the psychometrically captured images Ungish had drawn from my mind of the Cadian pylons, Cherubael, Prophaniti, and the ornaments he had worn.

'I'm also pondering the lodestone for the cap. I considered pyraline or one of the other tele-empathic crystallines like epidotrichite, but I doubt any of them would have the durability for your purposes. Certainly not for more than one or two uses. I also thought of tabular zanthroclase.'

'What's that?'

'A silicate we use in mind-impulse devices. But I'm not convinced. I have a few other possibilities in mind.' It was a measure of the trust Bure showed me that he felt he could mention such Cult Mechanicus secrets so freely. I felt honoured.

'Here's the haft,' he said, showing me to the etching bench where the two servitors were machining the decoration of the long pole.

'Steel?'

'Superficially. There's a titanium core surrounded by an adamantium sleeve under the steel jacket. The titanium is drilled with channels that carry the conductive lapidorontium wires.'

'It looks perfect,' I said.

'It is perfect. Virtually perfect. It's machined to within a nanometre of your measurements. Let me show you the sword.'

I followed him to a workbench at the far end of the smithy where the sword lay on a rest under a dust sheet.

'What do you think?' he asked, drawing the cloth back.

Barbarisater was as beautiful as I remembered it. I admired the fresh pentagrammatic wards that had been etched in the blade since I had last seen it, ten on each side.

'It is a remarkable artifact. I was almost unwilling to make the alterations you requested. As it was, I wore out eight adamantium drill bits on this side alone. The hardened steel skin of the blade around the solid core has been folded and beaten nine hundred times. It is beyond anything we can manufacture today.'

I would owe Clan Esw Sweydyr for this weapon, as I already owed them for Arianrhod's life. I should have returned it to their care, for it was part of their clan legacy and *usuril*, or 'living story'. It was mine to safeguard, not to take, and certainly not to deface this way. But face to face with Prophaniti at Kasr Gesh I had learned two things. Indeed, that monstrous thing had told them to me. Pentagrammatic wards worked against daemonhosts, but they were no stronger than the weapon that bore them.

To my certain knowledge, there were few finer, stronger blades in human space. I would make my peace and apologies to the clans of Carthae in time, fates permitting.

I went to touch it, but Bure stopped me. 'It is still resting. We must respect its anima. In a few days, you can take it. Train with it well. You must know it intimately before you use it in combat.'

He accompanied me to the door of the forge. 'Both weapons must be blessed and consecrated before use. I cannot do that, though I can ceremonially dedicate their manufacture to the Machine God.'

'I have already planned for their consecration,' I said. 'But I would welcome your ceremony. When I go against Quixos, I can think of no more potent a patron god to be looking down over me than your Machine Lord.'

'We will be leaving in a few days,' I told him.

The casket was silent for a while. 'I will miss our conversations, Eisenhorn.'

'Nevertheless, I have to go.'

'You think you're ready?'

'I think this part of my readiness is complete. Is there anything else you can tell me?'

'I have been wondering that. I cannot think of anything. Except...'

'Except what?'

The lights around the engram sphere twinkled. 'Except this. Apart from everything you've learned from me, the secrets, the lore, the mysteries, you must know that going after this foe is... dangerous.'

I laughed involuntarily. 'I think I've worked that much out already, Pontius!'

'No, you don't know what I mean. You have the determination, I know, the ambition, I know that too - you have the knowledge, we assume, and the weapons too, we hope - but unless your mind is prepared, you will perish. Instantly, and no ward or staff or blade or rune will save you.'

'You sound like... you care if I lose.'

'Do I? Then consider this, Gregor Eisenhorn. You may deem me a monster beneath contempt, but if I do care, what does that say about me? Or you?'

'Goodbye, Pontius Glaw,' I said, and closed the cell hatches behind me for the last time.

I will record this thought now, because I feel I must. For all that Pontius Glaw was... and for all that came later, I cannot shake my bond to him, though I try. There, in the cell on Cinchare, and a century before in the dim hold of the *Essene*, we had spoken together for hundreds of hours. I had no doubt that he was an unforgivably evil thing, and that he would have killed me in a second during those times had he been allowed the chance. But he was a being of extraordinary intellect, wit and learning. Admirable in so many, strange ways. But for that torc, Aaa's torc, back on that spring day on Quenthus, his life may have been different.

And if it had been different, and we had met, we would have been the greatest of friends.

We had stayed on Cinchare for three months. Too long, in my opinion, but there had been no way to speed the preparatory work.

We celebrated Candlemas in the little chapel of the Ministorum off the plaza, lighting candles to welcome the new Imperial year, and lighting others to commemorate the town's dead. Aemos and Bequin read the lessons, for all of the Ecclesiarchs were amongst the remembered dead. Bure and his tech-adepts worshipped with us, and he hovered to the choir rail under the great statue of the God-Emperor to lead us in the devotional prayers.

I was fretful and edgy. Partly because I was anxious to get underway now, but also because of the lore in my head, the mysteries to which Glaw had introduced me. So much, so much of it dark. I knew I was a changed man, and that change was permanent.

But I considered that a year before - just a year, though it felt much, much longer - I had been a helpless prisoner in the bleak Carnificina, and Candlemas had passed me by before I had realised it.

I was not that man any more either, and that change had been nothing to do with Pontius Glaw's whispered secrets. For all the darkness swilling in my head, it was better to be here, strong and ready, fortified, in the company of friends and allies.

There was no choirmaster to play the organ, so Medea had brought her father's Glavian lyre, and played the Holy Triumph of the Golden Throne so that we could all sing.

* * *

That night, we feasted in the refectory of the Cult Mechanicus to honour the start of 341.M41. Maxilla, who remained on duty aboard the *Essene*, sent a banquet to us on a shuttle, along with servitors to wait upon us. One of them reported that a vast storm of meteors had swarmed across the sky at the stroke of midnight, lighting the night side of Cinchare with their fires. Nayl growled that this was a bad omen, but Inshabel insisted it was a good one.

I suppose it rather depended which part of the vast spread of the Imperium you came from.

The others spent the next two days packing up and making ready to leave, but Aemos and I attended the dedication ceremony in the cimeliarch of the Adeptus Mechanicus annex.

Machine Cult servitors chanted in a modulated binary code and beat upon kettledrums. Magos Bure was clad in his orange robes with a white stole over his shoulders.

He blessed the weapons he had made in turn, taking one then the other from the two tech-adepts who stood in attendance.

Barbarisater, the pentagrammatic power sword, lifted to the light that speared down from the eyes of the Machine God's altar. Then the rune-staff, Bure's masterpiece.

He had fashioned a cap-piece for the rune-etched steel pole out of electrum in the form of a sun-flare corona. In the centre of it was a human skull, marked with the thirteenth sign of castigation. The skull was the lodestone, carved by Bure himself into a perfect facsimile of my own skull, as measured by radiative scans. He had tried and rejected over twenty different tele-empathic crystals before finding one he trusted would be up to the task.

'It's beautiful,' I said, taking it from him. 'What crystal did you use in the end?'

'What else?' he said. 'I carved that copy of your skull from the Lith itself.'

He came to see us off, to the docking barn where the gun-cutter had sat for so long. Nayl and Fischig were carrying the last things aboard. We had broken astropathic silence at last the night before, and informed Imperial Allied, Ortog Promethium, the Adeptus Mechanicus and the Imperial authorities of the fate that had befallen Cinchare minehead. We would be long gone before any of them arrived to begin recovery work.

Bure said farewell to Aemos, who shuffled away to the cutter.

'There's nothing adequate I can say,' I told the magos.

'Nor I to you, Eisenhorn. What of... the inmate?'

'I'd like you to do what I asked you. Give him mobility at least. But nothing more. He must remain a prisoner, now and always.'

'Very well. I expect to hear all about your victory, Eisenhorn. I will be waiting.'

'May the Holy Machine God and the Emperor himself protect your systems, Geard.'

'Thank you,' he said. Then he added something that quite took me aback, given his total belief and reliance on technology.

'Good luck.'

I walked to the cutter. He watched me for a moment, then disappeared, closing the inner hatch after him.

That was the last time I ever saw him.

From Cinchare, the *Essene* ran back, fast and impatient, into the great territories of the Segmentum Obscurus, a three-month voyage that we broke twice.

At Ymshalus, we stopped to transmit the prepared communiqués, all twenty of them. Inshabel and Fischig left us too at that point; Inshabel to secure passage to Elvara Cardinal to begin his work there, and Fischig for the long haul back to Cadia. It would be months, if not years, before we saw them again. That was a sorrowful farewell.

At Palobara, that crossroads on the border, busy with trading vessels and obscura caravans guarded by mercenary gunships, we stopped and transmitted the carta declaration. There was no going back now. Here, I parted company with Bequin, Nayl and Aemos, all of whom were heading back to the Helican sub-sector by a variety of means. Bequin's goal was Messina, and Aemos, with Nayl to watch over him, was bound for Gudrun. Another hard parting.

The *Essene* continued on for Orbul Infanta. This was now a lonely, waiting time. Each night, the remains of my company gathered in Maxilla's dining room and ate together: myself, Medea, Maxilla and Ungish. Ungish was no company, and even Medea and Maxilla had lost their sparkle. They missed the others, and I think they knew how dark and tough the time ahead would be.

I spent my days reading in the cabin library of the cutter, or playing regicide with Medea. I practised with Barbarisater in the hold spaces, slowly mastering the tricks of its weight and balance. I would never match a Carthae-born master, but I had always been good enough with a sword. Barbarisater was an extraordinary piece. I came to know it and it came to know me. Within a week, it was responding to my will, channelling it so hard that the rune marks glowed with manifesting psychic power. It had a will of its own, and once it was in my hands, ready, swinging, it was difficult to stop it pulling and slicing where it pleased. It hungered for blood... or if not blood, then at least the joy of battle. On two separate occasions, Medea came into the hold to see if I was bored enough for another round of regicide, and I had to restrain the steel from lunging at her.

Its sheer length was a problem: I had never used a blade so long. I worried that I would do my own extremities harm. But practice gave me the gift of it: long-armed, flowing moves, sweeping strokes, a tight field of severing. Within a fortnight, I had mastered the knack of spinning it over in my hand, my open palm and the pommel circling around each other like the discs of a gyroscope. I was proud of that move. I think Barbarisater taught it to me.

I worked with the rune staff too, to get used to its feel and balance. Though my aim was appalling, especially over distances further than three or four metres, I became able to channel my will, through my hands, into its haft and then project it from the crystal skull in the form of electrical bolts that dented deck plating.

There was, of course, no way I could test it for its primary use.

We reached the shrine world of Orbul Infanta at the end of the twelfth week. I had three tasks to perform here, and the first was the consecration of the sword and the staff.

With Ungish and Medea, I travelled down to the surface in one of the *Essene*'s unremarkable little launches rather than the gun-cutter. We went to Ezropolis, one of Orbul Infanta's ten thousand shrine cities, in the baking heartland of the western continent.

Orbul Infanta is an Ecclesiarchy governed world, famously blessed with a myriad shrines, each one dedicated to a different Imperial saint, and each one the heart of a city state. The Ecclesiarch chose it as a shrine world because it lay on a direct line between Terra and Avignor. The most popular and thriving shrine cities lay on the coast of the eastern continent, and billions of the faithful flocked to them each year. Ezropolis was far away from such bustle.

Saint Ezra, who had been martyred in 670.M40, was the patron saint of undertaking and setting forth, which I took to be appropriate. His city was a shimmering growth of steel, glass and stone rising from the sun-cooked plains of the mid-west. According to the guide slates, all water was pumped in from the western coast along vast pipelines two thousand kilometres long.

We made planetfall at Ezra Plain, the principal landing facility, and joined the queues of pilgrims climbing the looping stairs into the citadel. Most were clad in yellow, the saint's colour, or had tags or swathes of yellow cloth adorning them. All carried lit candles or oil lamps, despite the unforgiving light. Ezra had promised to light a flame in the darkness to mark all those setting forth, and consequently his hagial colour was flame yellow.

We had done the necessary research. I wore a suit of black linen with a sash of yellow silk and carried a burning votive candle. Ungish was draped in a pale yellow robe the colour of the sun at dawn, and clutched a plaster figurine of the saint. Medea wore a dark red bodyglove under a tabard on which was sewn a yellow aquila symbol. She pushed the small grav-cart on which Barbarisater and the staff lay, wrapped in yellow velvet. It was common for pilgrims to cart their worldly goods to the shrine of Ezra, in order that they might be blessed before any kind of undertaking or setting forth could properly get underway. We blended easily with the teaming lines of sweating, anxious devotees.

At the top of the stairs, we entered the blessed cool of the streets, where the shadows of the buildings fell across us. It was nearly midday, and Ecclesiarchy choirs were singing from the platforms that topped the high, slender towers. Bells were chiming, and yellow sapfinches were being released by the thousand from basket cages in the three city squares. The thrumming ochre clouds of birds swirled up above us, around us, singing in bewilderment. They were brought in each day, a million at a time, from gene-farm aviaries on the coast, where they were bred in industrial quantities. They were not native to this part of Orbul Infanta, and would perish within hours of release into the parched desert. It was reported that the plains around Ezropolis were ankle-deep with the residue of their white bones and bright feathers.

But still, they were the symbol of undertaking and setting forth, and so they were set loose by the million to certain death every midday. There is a terrible irony to this which I have often thought of bringing to the attention of the Ecclesiarchy.

We went to the Cathedral of Saint Ezra Outlooking, a significant temple on the western side of the city. On every eave and wall top we passed, sapfinches perched and twittered with what seemed to me to be indignation.

The cathedral itself was admittedly splendid, a Low Gothic minster raised in the last thirty years and paid for by subscriptions generated by the city fathers and priesthood. Every visitor who entered the city walls was obliged to deposit two high denomination coins into the take boxes at either side of the head of the approach stairs. A yellow robed adept of the priesthood was there to see it was done. The box on the left was the collection for the maintenance and construction of the city temples. The one on the right was the sapfinch fund.

We went inside Saint Ezra Outlooking, into the cool of the marble nave where the faithful were bent in prayer and the hard sunlight made coloured patterns on everything as it slanted through the huge, stained glass windows. The cool air was sweetened by the smoke of sweetwood burners, and livened by the jaunty singing from the cantoria.

I left Medea and Ungish in the arched doorway beside a tomb on which lay the graven image of a Space Marine of the Raven Guard Chapter, his hands arranged so as to indicate which holy crusade he had perished in.

I found the provost of the cathedral, and explained to him what I wanted. He looked at me blankly, fidgeting with his yellow robes, but I soon made him understand by depositing six large coins into his alms chest, and another two into his hand.

He ushered me into a baptism chancel, and I beckoned my colleagues to follow. Once all of us were inside, he drew shut the curtains and opened his breviary. As he began the rite, Medea unwrapped the devices and laid them on the edge of the benitier. The provost mumbled on and, keeping his eyes fixed on the open book so he wouldn't lose his place, raised and unscrewed a flask of chrism with which he anointed both the staff and the sword.

'In blessing and consecrating these items, I worship the Emperor who is my god, and charge those who bring these items forth that they do so without taint of concupiscence. Do you make that pledge?'

I realised he was looking at me. I raised my head from the kneeling bow I had adopted. Concupiscence. A desire for the forbidden. Did I dare make that vow, knowing what I knew?

'Well?'

'I am without taint, puritus,' I replied.

He nodded and continued with the consecration.

* * *

The first part of my business was done. We went out into the courtyard in front of the cathedral.

'Take these back to the launch and stow them safely,' I told Medea, indicating the swaddled weapons on the cart.

'What's concupiscence?' she asked.

'Don't worry about it,' I said.

'Did you just lie, Gregor?'

'Shut up and go on with you.'

Medea wheeled the cart away through the pilgrim crowds.

'She's a sharp girl, heretic,' Ungish whispered.

'Actually, you can shut up too,' I said.

'I damn well won't,' she snapped. 'This is it.'

'What? "It"?'

'In my dreams, I saw you foreswear in front of an Imperial altar. I saw it happen, and my death followed.'

I watched the sapfinches spiralling in the air above the yard.

'Deja vu.'

'I know deja vu from a dream,' said Ungish sourly. 'I know deja vu from my backside.'

'The God-Emperor watches over us,' I reassured her.

'Yes, I know he does,' she said. 'I just think he doesn't like what he sees.'

We waited until evening in the yard, buying hot loaves, wraps of diced salad and treacly black caffeine from street vendors. Ungish didn't eat much. Long shadows fell across the yard in the late afternoon light. I voxed Medea. She was safely back aboard the launch, waiting for us.

I was waiting to complete the second of my tasks. This was the appointed day, and the appointed hour was fast approaching. This would be the first test of the twenty communiqués I had sent out. One had been to Inquisitor Gladus, a man I admired, and had worked with effectively thirty years before during the P'glao Conspiracy. Orbul Infanta was within his canon. I had written to him, laying out my case and asking for his support. Asking him to meet me here, at this place, at this hour.

It was, like all the messages, a matter of trust. I had only written to men or women I felt were beyond reproach, and who, no matter what they thought of me, might do me the grace of meeting with me to discuss the matter of Quixos. If they rejected me or my intent, that was fine. I didn't expect any of them to turn me in or attempt to capture me.

We waited. I was impatient, edgy... edgy still with the dark mysteries Pontius Glaw had planted in my head. I hadn't slept well in four months. My temper was short.

I expected Gladus to come, or at least send some kind of message. He might be detained or delayed, or caught up in his own noble business. But I didn't think he'd ignore me. I searched the evening crowds for some trace of his long-haired, bearded form, his grey robes, his barb-capped staff.

* * *

'He's not coming,' said Ungish.

'Oh, give it a rest.'

'Please, inquisitor, I want to go. My dream...'

'Why don't you trust me, Ungish? I will protect you,' I said. I opened my black linen coat so she could see the laspistol holstered under my left arm.

'Why?' she fretted. 'Because you're playing with fire. You've crossed the line.'

I balked. 'Why did you say that?' I asked, hearing Pontius's words loud in my head.

'Because you have, damn you! Heretic! Bloody heretic!'

'Stop it!'

She got to her feet from the courtyard bench unsteadily. Pilgrims were turning to look at the sound of her outburst.

'Heretic!'

'Stop it, Tasaera! Sit down! No one's going to hurt you!'

'Says you, heretic! You've damned us all with your ways! And I'm the one who's going to pay! I saw it in my dream... this place, this hour... your lie at the altar, the circling birds...'

'I didn't lie,' I said, tugging her back down onto the bench.

'He's coming,' she whispered.

'Who? Gladus?'

She shook her head. 'Not Gladus. He's never coming. None of them are coming. They've all read your pretty, begging letters and erased them. You're a heretic and they won't begin to deal with you.'

'I know the people I've written to, Ungish. None of them would dismiss me so.'

She looked round into my face, her head-cage hissing as it adjusted. Her eyes were full of tears.

'I'm so afraid, Eisenhorn. He's coming.'

'Who is?'

'The hunter. That's all my dream showed. A hunter, blank and invisible.'

'You worry too much. Come with me.'

We went back into the Cathedral of Saint Ezra Outlooking, and took seats in the front of the ranks of carrels. Evening sunlight raked sidelong through the windows. The statue of the saint, raised behind the rood screen, looked majestic.

'Better now?' I asked.

'Yes,' she snivelled.

I kept glancing around, hoping that Gladus would appear. Straggles of pilgrims were arriving for the evening devotion.

Maybe he wasn't coming. Maybe Ungish was right. Maybe I was more of a pariah than I imagined, even to old friends and colleagues.

Maybe Gladus had read my humble communiqué and discarded it with a curse. Maybe he had sent it to the Arbites... or the Ecclesiarchy... or the Inquisition's Officio of Internal Prosecution.

'Two more minutes,' I assured her. 'Then we'll go.' It was long past the hour I had asked Gladus to meet me.

I looked about again. Pilgrims were by now flooding into the cathedral through the main doors.

There was a gap in the flow, a space where a man should have been. It was quite noticeable, with the pilgrims jostling around it but never entering it.

My eyes widened. In the gap was a glint of energy, like a side-flash from a mirror shield.

'Ungish,' I hissed, reaching for my weapon.

Bolt rounds came screaming down the nave towards me from the gap. Pilgrims shrieked in panic and fled in all directions.

'The hunter!' Ungish wailed. 'Blank and invisible!'

He was that. With his mirror shield activated, he was just a heat-haze blur, marked only by the bright flare of his weapon.

Mass panic had seized the cathedral. Pilgrims were trampling other pilgrims in their race to flee.

The backs of the carrels exploded with wicked punctures as the bolt rounds blew through them.

I fired back, down the aisle, with tidy bursts of las-fire.

'Thorn wishes Aegis, craven hounds at the hindmost!'

That was all I was able to send before a bolt round glanced sidelong into my neck and threw me backwards, destroying my vox headset in the process.

I rolled on the marble floor, bleeding all over the place.

'Eisenhorn! Eisenhorn!' Ungish bawled and then screamed in agony.

I saw her thrown back through the panelled wood of the box pews, demolishing them. A bolt round had hit her square in the stomach. Bleeding out, she writhed on the floor amid the wood splinters, wailing and crying.

I tried to crawl across to her as further, heedless bolt-fire fractured the rest of the front pews.

I looked up. Witchfinder Arnaut Tantalid disengaged his mirror shield and gazed down at me.

'You are an accursed heretic, Eisenhorn, and that fact is now proven beyond doubt by the carta issued for you. In the name of the Ministorum of Mankind, I claim your life.'

TWENTY-ONE

DEATH AT ST EZRA'S
THE LONG HUNT
THE CELL OF FIVE

Precisely how he had found me was a mystery, but I believe he had been on my tail for a long time, since before Cinchare. The fact that he had come to Saint Ezra Outlooking at that hour and that day convinced me that he had intercepted my communiqué to Gladus. And he might have triumphed over me, right there, right then, if he'd but pressed the advantage and finished the job with his boltgun.

Instead, Tantalid holstered his bolt pistol and drew his ancient chainsword, Theophantus, intent on delivering formal execution with the holy weapon.

I fired my laspistol, powering shot after shot at him, driving him backwards. His gold-chased battle suit, which gave his shrivelled frame the bulk and proportions of a Space Marine, absorbed or deflected the impacts, but the sheer force knocked him back several paces.

I jumped up, firing again, and retreating down the epistle side of the cathedral, towards the feretory. Bystanders and church servants were still fleeing. Its iron teeth singing, Theophantus swung at me. Tantalid was barking out the Accusal of Heresy, verse after verse.

Be quiet! I yelled, enforcing my will.

The psychic sting shocked him into silence, but he was generally protected by psi-dampers and ignored my next will-driven order to 'desist' completely.

The chainsword revved around and I threw myself aside as it cleft a bench pew in two. The backswing nearly caught me, but I dodged behind a pier column that took the force of the blow in a splintering shower of sparks and stone chippings.

Ungish was still crying out in pain. The sound chilled and infuriated me. I fired my laspistol again, but the last few shots fizzed and spluttered, underpowered. The power cell was exhausted. I dived again, feinting past his slow-moving bulk, and grappled with him from behind. It was a desperate ploy. Unarmoured as I was, I stood little chance of overwhelming his brute force or hurting him. He got a steel-gloved paw round behind himself, grabbed me by the coat and tore me off him.

My coat ripped. I bounced hard off a pillar and crashed awkwardly through the delicate fretwork of a confessional screen. I had barely pulled myself out of the flimsy wooden wreckage when the chainsword swooped in again and chewed a deep gouge in the cathedral floor.

I ran from him then, across the south aisle towards the feretory. Two men of the cathedral's Frateris Militia, clearly seeking advancement by coming to the aid of the fearsome Ministorum witch-hunter, closed in to block my escape. They were both clad in Ezra's yellow and carried short stave-maces in one hand and temple lanterns in the other.

I think they both quickly regretted their enthusiastic involvement.

I didn't even bother with the will. I think my rage was too great to have used it cleanly anyway. I side-stepped the first mace, caught and broke the wrist that wielded it, and kicked the man down. The mace turned in the air as it flew from the sprawling oaf's useless hand, and I caught it and turned it cross-wise in time to block the down-stroke of the other man's club. As he bounced back with the recoil of his own, negated strike, I smacked him in the side of the knee with my captured weapon. He fell over with sharp wail of pain, losing hold of his own mace and trying to beat me with his temple lamp instead. I took the lamp away from him and kicked him in the belly so he doubled up on his side, sobbing and trying to remember how to breathe.

The first man was back up, running at me. I spun and smashed the temple lamp in his face, sideways. Both its light and his went out.

The paving shook as Tantalid hove down on me. I used the captured mace like a sword, double-handed, to deflect his first strokes. It was iron-banded hardwood, and tough, but no match for a chainsword. After three or so clashes, the mace was chewed and mangled. I threw it aside and tore a church standard down from the wall beside the feretory door. Theophantus immediately shredded the old embroidered cloth and wood-frame titulus from the end, but that left me with three metres of cast-iron pole.

I held it like a quarterstaff, striking Tantalid hard on the side of the head with one end and then square on the opposite hip with the other. Then I stabbed the end at him viciously, like a spear-thrust, and managed to dent the chest-plate of his armour.

In response – and frothing mad with anger himself now – he put up Theophantus and shortened my pole by about half a metre. I wrenched the remaining pole around one-handed and struck him on the other side of the head. Blood was spilling from his ears. He howled and made an attack that almost took my arm off.

My third attempt to clip his miserable head missed. He was wise to it now, and blocked with his chainsword. The chain teeth caught in the pole and plucked it from my hands, throwing it up ten metres into the air. It landed behind some pews with a loud, echoing clang.

I rocked back from the follow up, but the murderous saw caught my right shoulder and gashed me deeply. Clutching the wound, I ducked again, and Theophantus decapitated a statue of Saint Ezra's pardoner.

No matter what I did, it was going his way. He had the weapons and the armour on his side. And now I was bleeding badly, which meant I would progressively slow and weaken, and it was just a matter for him to keep pressing the onslaught and he would triumph.

I became aware of another commotion near the main doors of the great church. Many startled worshippers and hierarchs had retreated and gathered there to watch the holy combat. Now they were spilling aside, their huddle breaking. A figure stormed through them.

Medea.

She ran down the main aisle, calling to me, firing her needle pistol over the tops of the pews at Tantalid. The lethal rounds pinged and clicked off his armour, and he turned in annoyance.

Tantalid dragged out his boltpistol and fired at this new attack. Medea hurled the object she had been carrying in her other hand and then disappeared from view as she dived to evade the hammer blows of the bolt rounds. At least, I prayed it was a deliberate dive. If he had hit her...

The object she had thrown bounced off a pew near me and landed on the floor, spilling from its yellow cloth.

Barbarisater.

Risking dismemberment from the chainsword, I hurled myself at the Carthaen blade. My hands found its long grip and I rolled twice to avoid the next downstrike of Theophantus.

Barbarisater purred in my grip as I came up. The runes blazed with vengeful light.

Tantalid realised that the nature of the battle had suddenly changed. I saw it in his eyes.

My first swing severed his wrist, cutting clean through the power-armoured cuff, dropping his hand to the floor, still clutching the smoking boltgun.

My second met Theophantus and destroyed it, spraying disintegrating chain-teeth and machine parts into the air.

My third cut Witchfinder Tantalid in two from the left shoulder to the groin. Neither half of him made a sound as they fell apart onto the cathedral floor.

Barbarisater was still seething with power, and twitched as Medea emerged unhurt from behind a choir stall. I forced the hungry blade down.

'Come on!' she said.

Ungish was dead. There was nothing I could do for her. And there was so much I should have done. She had been right. Right about this. Right about her fate. I dreaded to think how much more of what she had said might prove to be true too.

Hearing my frantic Glossia call when Tantalid first attacked, Medea had taken the launch up from Ezra Plain outside the city, despite all official warnings for her to abort, and flown it right in, setting down in the courtyard outside Saint Ezra Outlooking.

As we ran out now, into the evening, through crowds of stunned onlookers who leapt out of our path, the city Arbites and the Frateris Militia were rising in alarmed response. There was no point waiting to face them.

The launch shot us skywards, back towards the *Essene*, to leave Orbul Infanta as fast as we could.

It was a mess, and I was terribly disheartened. The confidence with which we had all set out from Cinchare seemed to have dissolved. Orbul Infanta had been just the first part of a long stratagem, and thanks to Tantalid, it had ended badly. I'd failed to contact Gladus, and discovered that as careful as I had been, my communiqués were not secure. The third task I had planned to undertake on Orbul Infanta, a search of the Imperial archivum for certain information relating to Quixos, hadn't even been started.

At least the weapons were consecrated. And Barbarisater had more than proved itself in combat.

Frigates of the Frateris Militia, along with several Imperial Navy guard boats, attempted to block the *Essene*, but Maxilla's Navigator got us out of the system and real space before they could even close range. Some ships pursued us into the warp, and we were chased for eight days, finally losing our pursuers through a series of real-space decelerations and redirections.

We went to ground. A month at a low-tech depot on a farming world, another two at the automated station at Kwyle. I was jumping at shadows by then, expecting enemies and rivals to loom out of every doorway. But it was quiet and we were unmolested. Maxilla had made a career out of passing unnoticed and avoiding attention. He lent that practiced art to our cause now, and reassured me into the bargain.

Three months after leaving Orbul Infanta in such haste, we risked a run to Gloricent, an outlying but prosperous trade world in the Antimar sub-sector, another division of the Scarus Sector, just two sub-sectors over from the Helican sub itself. Though worlds like Gudrun and Thracian Primaris were a good four months away by starship, it felt a little like being home. Disguised, Medea and I visited the sea-lashed stone piles of one of the main trade-hives, and procured a pair of astropaths, hiring their services from the local commercial guild on an open-ended lease.

Their names were Adgur and Ueli, both young males, both psychically capable but dull-witted and emotionless. Their young heads were shaved and their plugs shiny and new, and they spoke to me in overly formal ways that sounded like the parrot-learned etiquette it sadly was. But their eyes were ringed with darkness and their flesh was losing its youthful lustre. The rigour of the astropathic life was already taking its toll.

Using them, I sent fresh communiqués that superceded the original ones and revised certain aspects of my scheme. None of the messages now suggested the sort of trial meetings I had attempted with Gladus. I would not give so much away now.

After a week, and no reponses, we left Gloricent and went, via Mimonon to Sarum, the capital world of the Antimar sub-sector. I managed to do some useful work in its libraries, but backed off when a sour little confessor on a research sabbatical took to following me as if he recognised me.

While at anchor off Sarum, I got my first responses, all coded: from Bequin on Messina, and from Aemos on Gudrun. Both reported that their parts of the plan were going much more smoothly than mine had. Two days later, a partially scrambled astropathic message came from Inshabel on Elvara

Cardinal. What parts I got of it seemed to indicate some success. I was impatient to know more.

The week before we left Sarum, I received two more, both anonymous, one from Thracian Primaris, the other from a cluster of slave-worlds that owed fealty to the Salies Province of the Ophidian sub-sector. From the careful code and language of both, I recognised their senders.

My spirits lifted.

After that improvement, things again seemed to slow and stagnate. There was no progress, and no further communications. We were forced to quit Lorwen, our next stop after Sarum, with unseemly haste, when a flotilla of warships from Battlefleet Reaver arrived. I know now that the Battlefleet manoeuvres at Lorwen – and incidentally at Sarum and Femis Major too – were part of a major precautionary deployment against a pair of space hulks that had suddenly roamed into the sub-sector. But they caused us over thirteen weeks of anxious hiding amongst the brown and black dwarf stars of an extinguished stellar nursery.

Another Candlemas went by while we were in the empyrean, en route to the Drewlian Group. Medea, Maxilla and I marked it together, just the three of us. The two astropaths and the Navigator were not invited to attend. I raised a glass to toast the continued success of our mission. I don't think I would have been so hearty if I had known it would be another full year before the final act of the plan would play out.

I spent the first four months of 342 fruitlessly engaged in a search for the celebrated precog-hermit Lukas Cassian in the stinking marshes of Drewlia Two, only to learn that he had been murdered by a Monodominant cult four years earlier. During that quest, I terminated the activities of a plague-daemon sect infesting the marshlands. That was quite an undertaking in its own right, but my full account of it is filed in the Inquisition archives separately, and it has no bearing on this record. Besides, I still regard it bitterly as an interruption and waste of time. Neither will I set down here the full story of Nathan Inshabel's ventures on Elvara Cardinal, or Harlon Nayl's frankly extraordinary experiences on Bimus Tertius, though both tales connect to this record. Inshabel has written his own, refreshingly witty account of his exploits, which may be accessed by those with the appropriate clearance, something I recommend as illuminating and rewarding. Nayl asked me not to include his story, and has never committed it to record. It may be learned only by those with the temerity to ask him and the money to pay for a long night's serious drinking.

All this while, I remained an Imperial outlaw, wanted by the Inquisition for my heresies. It is interesting to note that at no time during this period did the Inquisition formally refute or overturn the carta I had declared on Quixos.

The year 343.M41 was half gone already by the time the *Essene* took me to Thessalon, a feudal world near Hesperus in the Helican sub-sector. It had been chosen by Nayl as the point for our secret congregation. Commanding a twenty-man field team selected from my staff on Gudrun, he arrived a week before the rest of us to secure the location and make sure we were not compromised. His preparations were thorough and ingenious. No one entered the area without him knowing it, nor could anyone have done so. At the slightest sign of outside interruption or official interference, we would have ample time to withdraw and flee.

As a final precaution, I was the last to arrive.

Thessalon is a tough little world whose population lives in a dark age and knows nothing of the Imperium or the galaxy beyond its skies.

The meeting place was a ruined keep in the north of the second continent, two thousand kilometres from the nearest indigenous community. A few lonely animal herders and subsistence farmers undoubtedly saw the lights of our ships in their heavens, but to them they were just the portents of the gods and the bright eyes of fabulous beasts.

Medea deposited me at the edge of a conifer forest at nightfall, and then took the gun-cutter back to stand off as air-cover, ready to redeploy at a moment's notice. For the first time in over two standard years, I was dressed as an inquisitor in black leather, storm coat and proudly displayed rosette. I also wore my faith-harness with the engraving *Puritus*. Damn anyone who believed I wasn't worthy of it.

Nayl, in combat armour, with a laser carbine cradled over one arm, appeared out of the trees and greeted me. We shook hands. It was good to see him again. His men, who were all around I was sure, were invisible in the gathering darkness.

Nayl led me through the black woods into a break in the trees where the pine tops framed a perfect oval of starfilled mauve. The keep, a jumbled pile of grey stone, stood in the clearing, with hooded lamps glowing from the lower slit windows.

Nayl walked me past and around the alarm-sensors, the tripwires and the beams of motion detectors that webbed the structure. Servitor-skulls from my personal arsenal hovered in the shadows, alert and armed.

Bequin and Aemos met me under the broken entrance arch. Aemos looked pale and worried, but his face broke into a warm smile as he saw me. Bequin hugged me.

'How many?' I asked her.

'Four,' she said.

Not bad. Not great, but not bad. It rather depended who those four were.

'And everything else?'

'All the preparations are now set. We can begin this undertaking at any time,' Aemos said.

'We have a target?'

'We do. You'll learn how when we brief everyone.'

'Good.' I paused. 'Anything else I should know?'

All three of them shook their heads.

'Let's do it then,' I said.

Despite all the precautions, I was taking my life in my hands. I was presenting myself, voluntarily, to four members of the Inquisition. I was trusting that my previous friendships and allegiances with them would count for more than the accusations Osma had laid at my door. These four were the only four who had responded out of the original twenty communiqués. Nayl had vetted each one, but there was still a very real chance that any or all of them had attended simply to execute the declared heretic Gregor Eisenhorn.

I would soon know.

As I stepped into the main, candlelit chamber, a hush killed the small talk and six men turned to face me. Fischig, imposing in black body armour, nodded me a half-smile. Interrogator Inshabel, in a bodyglove and lightweight cloak, bowed his head and smiled nervously.

The other four stared at me levelly.

I walked into their midst solemnly.

The first lowered the hood of his maroon cape. It was Titus Endor. 'Hello, Gregor,' he said.

'Well met, old friend.' Endor had been one of the first two to contact me anonymously the previous year, from the Salies slave-worlds. The other, who had written from Thracian Primaris, stood next to him.

'Commodus Voke. You honour me with your presence.'

The wizened old wretch sneered at me. 'For the sake of our history, and damn-his-eyes Lyko, and other matters, I am here, Eisenhorn, though the Emperor knows I am very suspicious of this. I will hear you out, and if I don't like what you have to say, I will withdraw... without breaking the confidence of this meeting!' he added sternly with a raised finger. 'I will not betray this congress, but I reserve the right to leave and quit if I find it worthless.'

'That right is yours, Commodus.'

To his left stood a tall, confident man I didn't recognise. He wore brown leather flak armour under a long blue coat of cavalry twill and his silver rosette was fixed on the left breast. His domed head was shaved, but there was a violet glint in his eyes that told me he was a Cadian.

'Inquisitor Raum Grumman,' said Fischig, stepping forward. Grumman took my proffered hand with a curt nod.

'Inquisitor General Neve acknowledges your communiqué to her, and asks me to express her true sadness that she could not join you here. She personally requested me to take her place, and render you the service I freely render her.'

'I am grateful for it, Grumman. But right from the start, I want to be sure that you know what we're about here. Just being here because your provincial chief requested it isn't enough.'

The Cadian smiled. 'Actually, it is. But to reassure you, I have reviewed the matter carefully with Neve herself and your man Fischig. I have no illusions about the danger of being here and siding with you. Given the evidence, I would have been here anyway.'

'Good. Excellent. Welcome, Grumman.'

The identity of the fourth and final guest took me aback. He was clad in polished battleware plating that looked custom-made and exorbitantly expensive. With gauntleted hands, he lifted the scowling houndskull helmet off his head. Inquisitor Massimo Ricci, of the Helican Ordo Xenos. He was hardly an old friend, but I knew him well.

'Ricci?'

His handsome, haughty face displayed a wide smile.

'Like Grumman, I am here to extend apologies from another. For numerous reasons that I'm sure you can appreciate, Lord Rorken cannot answer your request in person. It would be political suicide for him to participate in this matter. But my lord has faith in you still, Eisenhorn. He has sent me to act as his proxy.'

Ricci was one of Lord Rorken's most valued and admired inquisitors. Many said he was a likely successor for the post as a Master of the Ordo Xenos. For him to be here was an enormous compliment, both from Lord Rorken, who had seen fit to send one of his most illustrious men, and from Ricci himself, who was risking a high-profile career just by being here. Clearly both of them had taken my proposal and cause very seriously.

'Gentlemen,' I said. 'I am pleased, and honoured, to see you all. Let us discuss this matter, freely and openly, and see where we stand.'

The Thessalonian night winds moaned through the ruined cavities of the keep as I briefed them. Inshabel and Nayl had carried chairs in, and erected a heavy trestle table. Bequin and Aemos provided data-slates, charts, papers and other pieces of evidence as I called for them.

I talked for about two hours, taking them through the entire matter of Quixos as it was known to me. Much of what I said had been laid out in the initial communiqués, but I filled in all the details, and answered questions as they arose. Endor seemed satisfied, and hardly spoke. It was good to have a true friend here, one who simply trusted my word and purpose. Grumman was also generally non-committal. Voke and Ricci asked plenty of questions, and required clarification on the smallest points.

All three Ordos were represented around that table: Voke was Ordo Malleus – though thankfully not a tight member of Bezier's inner circle – Ricci and I were Ordo Xenos, and Grumman and Endor were Ordo Hereticus. All of us apart from Grumman were assigned servants of the Ordos Inquisitorae Helican. Only Titus Endor, who I knew to be famously demure, wasn't wearing his rosette openly.

I believe I spoke eloquently and well.

We broke after two hours to stretch our legs, ruminate and take refreshment. I went outside, taking in the cold night air, listening to the wind swish the conifers. Fischig joined me and brought me a glass of wine.

'It's bad with Neve,' he said, just getting right into it. He had travelled back to Cadia from Cinchare to collect more data and to specifically recruit the inquisitor general.

'Because of me?'

He nodded. 'Because of everything. Osma made big trouble after we sprung you from the Carnificina. He had the combined clout of Bezier and Orsini behind him, after all. That made Neve's superior, Grandmaster Nunthum of the Ordos Cadia, sit up and take notice, I can tell you. They were after her for her job. But they couldn't prove a thing. Neve's very good at being slippery. And she fought your corner like a she-bear too, believe you me.'

'She's safe?'

'Yeah. Thanks to a massive incursion of the Enemy eight months ago. The Cadian Gate's on a war footing and utterly in turmoil. Last thing anyone's worrying about is what part Neve may have played in the Eisenhorn Conspiracy.'

'That's what they're calling it?'

'That's what they're calling it.'

I sipped the wine, expecting something rough and local. It turned out to be a damned good Samatan red. From my own cellars, I guessed.

Bequin would have taken care of such things and chosen the very best to mollify our guests.

'Grumman: what do you make of him?'

'I've got plenty of time for him, Gregor,' Fischig said. 'Smart mind, knows what he's doing. Given the scrutiny she was under, Neve knew she couldn't get away, so she picked Grumman, and I don't think she would have if he wasn't worth his salt.

'The pair go back a long way, and Grumman's doing this out of respect for her. But we spent a long time talking on the voyage back here, and I think he's in it for himself now too.'

'Good. The others?'

'Voke's full of surprises,' he snorted. 'When you said he was going to be on your list of contacts, I thought you were mad. Not as mad as writing to Lord Rorken, of course, but anyway... I never thought the old bastard would show, or even deign to answer you. He's so stiff even the rod up his arse has got a rod up its arse. That's one bet I would have lost. He must like you more than he lets on.'

'We have an understanding,' I said. I'd saved Voke's life on the flagship *Saint Scythus*, but he'd returned that favour on the Avenue of the Victor Bellum. Maybe that was enough.

'He needs convincing,' said Fischig, 'but I think he's in for the long haul.'

'You do?'

'You see that creep Heldane anywhere?'

I knew what Fischig meant. Heldane would have opposed this mission without question, and taken great delight in bringing me in, dead or alive. Voke had clearly come here without his old pupil knowing. Fischig was right. That was a good sign.

'Endor, well, he's safe, isn't he?' said Fischig. 'Given your history, he'd have come anyway.'

'It's good to have him here. What about Ricci?'

Fischig's voice suddenly dropped to a hiss. 'Speaking of whom.'

He withdrew. Clutching a goblet of wine, Ricci walked out of the archway behind us and joined me, gazing up at the staggeringly bright star-field.

'I hope you realise how lucky you are,' Ricci said.

'Every day.'

'You took a risk contacting Lord Rorken. He's always liked you, but given the current climate, liking you is a dangerous habit. He was at loggerheads with Bezier and Orsini over your case.'

'And still he sent you?'

'Let me be direct, Gregor. I think it will help. Lord Rorken, may his fortunes multiply in the face of the God-Emperor, sent me to assist you in the unmasking and destruction of the heretic Quixos. But if, along the way, I should discover anything that confirmed the generally-believed allegations of your own heresy...'

'What?'

'I think you understand.'

'You're his hatchet man. You'll help me... but if I cross the line in your eyes, Rorken has sanctioned you to execute me.'

He raised his glass. 'I think we know where we stand.'

We did. Now it made much more sense that Rorken had sent so senior an agent to my side.

I said nothing. Ricci smiled and went back inside.

We sat down around the table again and debated some more. I found most of the questions – especially those from Voke and Ricci – wilfully small-minded.

At last, after another hour, Grumman voiced a pertinent query.

'Supposing we agree to this. Agree that Eisenhorn is wrongly charged and that Quixos deserves our sternest censure... how do we do that? Do we know where Quixos is?'

'Yes,' I said, though I didn't know the answer myself. My people had enjoyed the best part of two years to do their work, many dozens of agents sifting data from hundreds of worlds.

Unbidden, Bequin stepped forward and took a seat with us at the table.

'About three months ago, our research discerned a pattern in the data surrounding the near-mythical life of Quixos. And that pattern centred on Maginor.'

'Capital of the Niaides sub-sector, Viceroy sector, Ultima segmentum,' announced Voke.

'Your astronomical knowledge is humbling, sir,' Bequin said smoothly. She handed out data-slates.

'As you can see from the file of data marked "alpha", Quixos certainly visited Maginor almost two hundred years ago, and became involved with a cartel of trade interests and noble families known as the Mystic Path. The Path was a network which was already utilising prohibited and forbidden lore and technologies. Quixos should have closed them down and burned them. It is clear he did not. Instead, he fed and supported them. He nurtured them until they became a power base for his invisible empire of dark belief. No longer a cartel but a cult. A cult of Quixos.'

'Why do we think he's still there?' asked Ricci.

'We think he's made his hidden fastness there, sir,' said Bequin. 'The reaches of the Mystic Path now spread throughout the segmentum and beyond. Maginor is its heart. In 239.M41, Inquisitor Lugenbrau and a warrior band numbering some sixty individuals disappeared on Maginor. No trace of them was ever found, though Interrogator Inshabel was able to... ah... recover an incomplete verbal transcript of a pict-recording apparently made during Lugenbrau's raid.'

I speed-read the transcript. It was harrowing. 'You got this from Elvara Cardinal, Inshabel?' I asked.

Inshabel was at the back of the room. He stepped forward, blushing. 'Not directly, sir. It actually came from the Inquisitorial data-library on Fibos Secundus. How is a damn good story, but it's probably wasting valuable time to repeat it just now.'

Inshabel was right, as I have already said. It was a damn good story, and I enjoyed it when he told it to me later. I urge you to access it.

'We believe Lugenbrau was hunting Quixos, although he may not have known it,' continued Bequin. 'He and his entire band were wiped out by Quixos's forces.'

'Lugenbrau,' murmured Voke, setting his slate down and looking off into space. 'I never met him, but he was a trusted pupil of my late comrade, Inquisitor Pavel Uet. When Lugenbrau went missing, Uet took it hard. The loss shortened his life.'

Voke looked at me with his rheumy eyes. 'If I wasn't decided before, Eisenhorn, I am now. Quixos must pay.'

'I agree,' said Endor, tossing his slate onto the table and looking grim. 'At the very least, the Inquisition demands vengeance for this.'

'Maginor, then?' Grumman asked.

'It's still his base of operations, sir, we are sure of that,' said Bequin. 'And until a week ago, we were all set to prepare for a strike against Maginor. Then we received this.' She held up an astropathic transcript.

'I will read it, if I may.' She carefully put on her half-moon glasses. They suited her, but I knew her vanity made her hate them. It said a lot about the situation that she was willing to wear them in front of these men.

'It begins... "Gregor, my friend. I have been kept up to date with the data concerning your quarry. It gives me something to do, these winter afternoons. I agree that Maginor may be the seat of the evil, and certainly requires the attention of the Inquisition. But, if you'll pardon me, I suggest that Maginor be left to the Ordos Niaides. Using pointers Aemos gave me, I have assessed the following. My full findings are on the data-files attached below, but in short, I think you should be looking at Farness Beta. Quixos's fascination with the pylons of Cadia made me think, you see.

'"See below, that I have traced massive stonecutting orders to the limit-world of Serebos, which lies galactically south of Terra. The masonic guilds of Serebos are famously secretive about their contracts. They provide an inert, obsidian-like black glass-stone called serebite, a beautiful substance that is in high demand right across the Imperium. Serebite is, as far as reckoning goes, as close to the material used on Cadia for the pylons as it is possible to get. As I have said, the masonic guilds are close about their contracts, but there is little hiding the transportation of a massive copy of one of those pylons by shipping guild bulk-lifter. Three-quarters of a kilometre long and a quarter square! Quixos has ordered the manufacture of a perfect copy of the Cadian pylons, and has had it shipped to Farness Beta."'

Bequin paused and looked up at us.

'"If you've ever trusted my advice, trust this now,"' she continued. '"Quixos is on Farness. And if you're going to stop him, it must be now. Your devoted friend and pupil. Gideon."'

Gideon. Gideon Ravenor. Crippled as he was, he had found this insight, which totally altered our plan of attack. I was speechless. I felt almost tearful.

'There is a postscript,' said Bequin. 'He writes, "The daemonhosts will be your foullest problem. I know you are prepared, but I send you these. One for each of the twenty you have summoned."'

Bequin took off her half-moon glasses and rose. Nayl brought in a crate and set it down on the table. Inside were twenty scrolls of daemonic protection, each sealed inside a blessed tube of green marble, and twenty consecrated gold amulets of the God-Emperor as a skeletal relic. It was so typical of Ravenor to attend to such details. Nayl handed them out, a heavy scroll tube and an amulet to each of us.

'I'm convinced,' Ricci said, getting to his feet and hanging the amulet around his neck so that it hung between the purity seals of his armour.

'I am glad. Grumman?'

'I'm with you,' said the Cadian.

'A toast,' I said, raising my glass. 'To this cell of five. And to the others who have assisted in getting us this far.' Bequin, Aemos, Nayl, Fischig and Inshabel also saluted with their glasses.

'To Farness Beta. To the end of Quixos.'

The five inquisitors in the drafty keep clinked glasses.

'Farness Beta,' said Ricci. 'Remind me. Where is that?'

'In the throat of the Cadian Gate,' said Grumman. 'Right on the edge of the Eye of Terror.'

TWENTY-TWO

FARNESS BETA
CHERUBAEL AND PROPHANITI
QUIXOS

It was early in 343.M41 before we reached Farness Beta. By then, war was bifurcating the Cadia sub-sector, and armies of sheer horror were spewing out of the Eye of Terror. Like a whirlpool of fire, the Eye dominated the skies of most gate-worlds, distended and angry, flaring more savagely than at any time in living memory. Every flash and pulse of its maelstrom was another warp hole opening, another flotilla of death unleashed. That spring was known as the Staunch Holding of the Cadian Gate, and entered the history books, as every scholar knows.

During the first months of 343, the Cadians saw off the greatest incursion of Chaos suffered in three hundred years.

It was almost as if the Archenemy knew something.

The *Essene* brought me to Farness champing and eager to get on. We were escorted through the immaterium by two other ships: Ricci's stately steeple of a cruiser and Voke's ancient porcupine of a warship. Endor and Grumman, along with their retinue bands, travelled aboard the Essene with me. It had been a long time since the Essene had carried so many people.

The Imperial Navy taskforce, a ten-ship squadron seconded from Battlefleet Scarus for special operations under the remit of the Battlefleet Disciplinary Detachment, was waiting for us.

The taskforce had already been on station for a fortnight, and its reconnaissance and intelligence operations had comprehensively prepared the ground for us.

'We have a confirmed location for Pariah,' Lord Procurator Olm Madorthene told me over a vox-pict link from his own ship.

Pariah was the operational word we had set for Quixos. 'Or at least his seat of activity, anyway. I'm relaying the data to you now. Site A is what you're looking for.'

I turned from my seat on the *Essene*'s elegant bridge and Maxilla nodded to one of his beautiful servitors. The map display flashed up on the secondary screen of my console.

'I have it,' I said, turning back to look at Madorthene's slightly fuzzy image on the main bridge display.

'It's a table mountain called Ferell Sidor, literally the "altar of the sun", up in one of the remote northern wards of Hengav province. Provincial government has declared the whole ward a Sacred Territory because the area is riddled with Second Dynasty tholos tombs. Access is supposed to be restricted to the Ecclesiarchy, the Farnessi royal families and sanctioned archaeologists. We believe Pariah obtained licenses to excavate on Ferell Sidor about six years ago, in the guise of an archaeological mission from the Universitariate of Avellorn. The local authorities are supposed to monitor such missions, but frankly they have no idea what he's up to there. If you look at the detail map...'

'Yes, got it.'

'You can see the extent of the workings. Pariah's constructed a small town up there, alongside the pit.'

'The excavation is considerable...'

'We think that's where he's buried or sited this facsimile pylon. It's difficult to get a clear view. We didn't want to get too close and tip him off.'

I rose from my bridge throne and stood facing the enormous image of the lord procurator's face. 'You're set?'

'Absolutely. You have a copy of my assault strategy there. Make any amendments you like.'

There was no need. Madorthene's plan was economical and efficient. Officially, this was an operation by the Battlefleet Disciplinary Detachment, prosecuting leads gathered during the inquest into the Thracian Atrocity. Lord Procurator Madorthene had entered into a co-operative pact with Commodus Voke to execute the plan. In reality, his pact was secretly with me. Olm was the only non-inquisitor I had written to.

We encrypted the call-signs and command authorities for the operation, agreed the zero-hour, and wished each other luck.

'The Emperor protects, Gregor,' he said.

'I hope so, Olm,' I replied.

Two hours before sunrise the next day, five hundred Imperial Guard from the Fifty-First Thracian moved in towards Ferell Sidor – Site A – from covert forward assembly points in the surrounding hills where they had been dropped by troop ships the day before. They advanced, silently, in three prongs, the first securing the single trackway that gave land-vehicle access to the table mountain. When all three were in position, we woke Ferell Sidor up.

The frigates *Zhikov* and *Fury of Spatian* bombarded the mountain for six minutes, raising a ball of fire that lit the landscape as if the sun had come up early. In its afterglow, thirty Marauder bombers overflew Site A at low level and delivered thirty thousand kilos of high explosives.

Another false dawn.

Despite this punishing overture, when the ground troops went in eight minutes after the last bomb, resistance was furious. Madorthene had feared that the best part of Quixos's strength lay underground, wormed inside the mountain, resistant to the worst aerial assaults.

In the blazing ruins of the excavation township, the Thracian troops found themselves engaging fanatical and well-armed cultists. Most wore the insignia and colours of the Mystic Path. Many were mutants. Initial reports estimated over eight hundred enemy warriors. Madorthene committed the taskforce reserve: another seven hundred Thracian assault soldiers.

By then, we were already deploying in the second wave. Medea landed Inshabel and myself on the edge of the strike zone, along with Endor and his two weapon-servitors. Ricci's shielded pinnace settled in close by, kicking up dust and delivering him and Commodus Voke, along with a bodyguard of twenty Inquisitorial troops. Grumman, using a Navy dropship loaned by Madorthene, was the last to make groundfall, but the first to engage. Grumman's ten-man squad were all ex-Kasrkin specialists.

As we hurried forward through the backwashing smoke, our landing ships rising back into the pre-dawn sky behind us, there was a tremor and a palpable upwelling of psychic force. Frighteningly powerful waves of psyker power erupted from the epicentre of Site A, killing over thirty of the forward troops... and then suddenly cut off.

We had all anticipated Quixos would have vast psychic defences – he had, after all, been collecting psykers like Esarhaddon – and it seemed likely that active psychic assaults would be a key element of his resistance, perhaps even more significant than his daemonhosts. I had taken no chances.

In two groups, my entire Distaff of untouchables, some fifty individuals all told, had moved in alongside the first ground-troop advances. Bequin, guarded by Nayl and twelve of my warrior staff, led one group, and Thula Surskova, protected by Fischig and a dozen more fighters, led the other.

The Distaff had never been used on such a scale before, but it proved to be the weapon I had always suspected. The blankness they generated contained and negated the engulfing psychic storm, effectively bottling it inside Site A and preventing it from threatening our closing forces.

With Inshabel, I moved underground, down the rock-cut steps into the inner sectors of Site A. For almost an hour we fought our way through the smoked-swathed surface structures, a metre at a time. Now, with the sun rising, we found our first access point to the lower levels: a stairwell exposed by a bomb crater.

The place was strewn with smouldering debris and a few unidentifiable bodies. In places, power cables were hanging, sparking, from the rockcrete roof. We both wore motion trackers, and switched left and right, gunning down cultists as they appeared. My boltgun was already running short of shells, and Inshabel was on to his second-to-last power cell. The level of resistance was unbelievable.

At a junction in the seemingly random jumble of tunnels, we encountered Endor. He had a couple of Thracian troopers and an Inquisition guardsman with him, but he'd lost both of his slow-moving attack-servitors. I knew what he was thinking just by the look in his eyes. We had come in strong and confident, but perhaps not strong enough. I thought I had anticipated the worst Quixos could throw against us. Maybe I had underestimated him after all.

Ferocious bursts of shooting alerted us to a firefight in a larger chamber to the left. We arrived in time to meet four wounded, terrified Thracian troopers fleeing towards us.

'Back! Go back!' they were screaming.

I pushed past them.

The chamber beyond was massive and half-filled with veiling smoke. Green, unnatural flames were licking up the walls. At the far end, the already huge chamber seemed to open out into something much, much vaster.

But that was not what occupied my eyes.

Surrounded by over fifty bodies, most of them Imperial Guard, Commodus Voke was standing his ground against Prophaniti.

The old inquisitor was shuddering, his robes stiffening with psychic ice. Corposant fire glowed from his mouth and eyes. The daemonhost, its cruel features just recognisable as a distortion of poor, lost Husmaan's face, hovered in front of Voke, struggling at an invisible barrier of telekinetic wrath.

We ran forward, abruptly drawing fire from cultists spreading into the chamber from the right. The Thracian beside me bucked and twitched as he was hit twice, and Inshabel cursed as he was winged.

Endor urged the remaining men to advance on his lead, and took the fight to the cultists, his laspistol blazing and his chainblade swinging.

Voke was close to breaking. I could see him wavering under the immense pressure.

I holstered my boltgun and stumbled across the bodies and debris to aid him, praying that my runestaff would do what it was supposed to.

And a dizzying blast of white light and scourging heat blew me back through the air.

I tried to get up, half-realising that I had been blown clean out of the chamber, through a flakboard partition into some kind of dank chute. Invisible forces lifted me to my feet. Light bathed me.

Cherubael hovered before me.

'Gregor,' it said. 'You've come so far. I knew you had it in you.'

I held the runestaff in front of me. The green marble scroll of daemonic protection that Ravenor had sent had already been reduced to a shattered remnant by the force of Cherubael's opening attack.

'I've waited for this moment for such a long time,' said the daemonhost. 'Remember on Eechan I said you'd have to make things up to me? Well, this is the time. Now. This is the moment that everything's been about. The one I have seen coming since our paths first crossed. Destinies... our destinies, intertwined, remember that?'

'How could I forget?' I spat. 'You claim to have been using me all along! Guiding me! Even protecting me! I watched you kill Lyko on Eechan! So that I would live... for this moment? Why?'

Cherubael smiled. 'When the warp is in you as it is in me, you see time from all angles. You see what will be and what will come, what someone here now will do in a century or two, what someone there has done a thousand years in the past. You see the possibilities.'

'Riddles! That's all you ever speak!'

'No more riddles, Eisenhorn. From the moment I first met you, I saw you were the only one, the only one with the tenacity, the skill and the opportunity to give me what I want. What I want most of all. I saw that if I kept you safe, you would come and give me that most precious thing here, on this world, at this hour.'

'I would never help a daemon like you!'

Cherubael grinned, blank-eyed and utterly serious. 'Then destroy me, if you can.'

It lunged. I raised the runestaff and channelled my will down through the psi-conductive pole into the lodestone. The carved fragment of the Lith blazed with blue light.

Pontius Glaw knew a thing or two about daemonhosts. Their greatest weakness was the strength of the will that had bound them as slaves. The runestaff, so carefully prepared and constructed, so painstakingly etched with the ancient symbols of control, was a lever to topple that binding will by amplifying my own to levels that would overwhelm it.

For a brief moment, I felt how it must feel to be an alpha-plus psyker.

The scintillating spear of energy that shot from the lode-stone struck Cherubael in the chest.

The daemonhost smiled for a second, and then its flesh-vessel ruptured open, billowing a storm of Chaos-fire in all directions. I had cast it out of its binding and banished it back into the warp.

And in the moment as my amplified mind overmastered his, I saw the years of enslavement it had endured at Quixos's hands, the torments of its binding, the great, forbidden text of the *Malus Codicium* whose arcane knowledge Quixos had used to create his daemonhosts.

And I realised that I had given Cherubael exactly what it wanted after all. *Freedom.*

I stumbled back into the main chamber. By then, Voke, whose resistance to Prophaniti had been astonishing, was dead.

I remembered Voke's words after the atrocity on Thracian: 'I will make amends. I will not rest until every one of these wretches is destroyed, and order restored. And then I will not rest until I find who and what was behind it.'

He could rest now. That work was done.

The daemonhost was casting the valiant old man's empty husk of a body aside and gliding towards Endor and Inshabel, who were both already on their knees in agony. Cyan flames washed from Prophaniti's fingertips and wrapped my two friends in tight, burning psychic shackles. They were trapped morsels for it to feed off at its leisure.

Prophaniti froze when I appeared, instinctively knowing I posed a more serious threat. The Lith-stone was still smoking with blood-red light.

The daemonhost surged through the air at me, teeth bared, arms spread, incandescent with light, baying my name. It was like facing the attack run of a supersonic warcraft firing all guns. I know so. It is my misfortune to have experienced that too.

Prophaniti whooped with glee.

'At Kasr Gesh, you told me to make my weapons sounder next time, monster!' I howled, and impaled its charging form on the steel pole of the runestaff. 'Is this sound enough?'

Prophaniti screamed and exploded, blowing me off my feet. I don't think I banished it. I think I obliterated its essence forever.

The runestaff was, miraculously, unscathed, and lay amid the rubble. But Prophaniti's dissipating being had made it white hot from base to cap, and I could not pick it up again.

I ran across to Titus Endor and Inshabel, both of whom lolled weakly on the floor.

Inshabel was dazed but intact. Endor had daemon gashes across his chest and neck. He looked up at me blearily.

'You got them both, Gregor...'

'I pray there are no more,' I replied, trying to staunch his bleeding. His rosette slid out of his coat pocket and I leaned to pick it up.

The Inquisitorial symbol was decorated with the ornate crest of the Ordo Malleus.

'Malleus?' I hissed.

'No...'

'When did you transfer, Endor? Damn you, when did you change Ordos?'

'They forced me...' he wheezed, 'Osma forced me! When he had me on Messina... there were certain matters from a case a few years ago. He'd got his hands on them somehow... He... he promised I would burn if I didn't help him get to you.'

'What matters?'

'Nothing! Nothing, Gregor, I swear! But he had Bezier's backing! He could have made anything look heretical! I transferred orders to stop him breaking me. He said I would be rewarded, advanced. He said Ordo Malleus was a better prospect for me.'

'But you were to keep an eye on me?'

'I told him nothing! I never sold you out. I did just enough to keep Osma satisfied.'

'Like coming here. No wonder you hid your rosette. He wanted you to take me down, didn't he?'

Endor was silent. Inshabel looked on in stark disbelief.

'I... I was to go along with this operation, in the hope that it might be successful. Orsini's under no illusions that Quixos is a menace, and this was an expedient way, perhaps, of eliminating him. If you were still... alive at the end of it, I was told to arrest you on the carta charges. Or, if you resisted...'

'Get him up to ground level,' I told Inshabel quietly. 'Find him a medic. Don't let him out of your sight.'

'Yes sir!'

'Gregor!' Endor gasped as Inshabel lifted him. 'By the God-Emperor, I never meant–'

'Get him out of here!' I growled.

The assault on Ferell Sidor was three hours old when Grumman, Ricci and I entered the undervault of the excavation pit. Madorthene's forces were still locked in a monumental struggle with the renegade's warriors throughout the warren of tunnels and chambers in the table mountain.

Ricci was weak from a blade wound, and all of his bodyguards were dead. Grumman had just two Kasrkin left with him, both of them armed with lasrifles.

The vast undervault was an excavated pit almost a kilometre deep, open to the sky. The serebite copy of the Cadian pylon rested in the base of it, surrounded by adamantite scaffolding. Gibbet cages, hundreds of them, hung from the scaffolding on chains. In each one, trapped and helpless, was a human body.

They were Quixos's carefully collected arsenal of rogue psykers, secretly acquired from all over the Imperium. It must have taken him decades to accumulate so many. One of them, I had no doubt, was Esarhaddon

'What is he doing?' Ricci asked, a touch of awe in his voice.

'Something we have to stop,' said Grumman, with a direct simplicity I appreciated. It was the only answer any of us needed.

We had been living at our nerve ends since the assault began, and were wired with combat sharpness. Even so, despite our combined experience and skill, what happened next took us all totally by surprise.

One moment there was nothing. The next, a robed, armoured form was in amongst us, moving so fast it was simply a blur.

So fast. So accursedly fast.

Instantly, Ricci was split open down the length of his spine. As he was still in the process of falling on his face, choking on his own blood, one of the Kasrkin was severed at the waist, and toppled in halves, his gun firing spasmodically. The other Kasrkin folded up around the impaling thrust of a long, dark blade, spontaneously combusting from the belly out.

Grumman pushed me out of the way as the devastating blur turned again, and fired his laspistol at it three times. Snapping round faster than my eyes could follow, the long, dark blade the blur was wielding deflected each crackling shot.

Grumman's head left his shoulders.

Quixos, the arch-heretic, the renegade, the unforgivable radical, whirled on me before Grumman's butchered body had even started to slump.

I had one fleeting glimpse of the long daemonsword, Kharnagar. It was gnarled and knotted and thick with abominable runes and irregular claw-like serrations.

That's all I saw as it came whistling towards my face.

TWENTY-THREE

THE HERETIC
AFTERWARDS

A bare hand's breadth from my head, the blood-red blade came to a dead stop, blocked by the gleaming steel of Barbarisater.

Time seemed to stand still for a heartbeat. We faced each other, our blades locked together. Quixos had been a speed-distorted phantom until our swords had struck. Now he was frozen, glaring between the crossed blades at me.

The renegade's armour was ragged and filthy, and ornate with warp-signs. His Inquisitorial rosette was displayed, incongruously, on his right shoulder guard. It revolted me to see it worn amongst such corruption.

His ancient face was a misshapen, pustular horror. Rudimentary antlers bulged from his brow. His skin was dark like granite. Wheezing augmetic cables and implants bulged at his throat and under the dirty head-cloth he wore. His eyes were shining balls of blood.

In honesty, he was a disappointing little monster compared to the notion of him that had built up in my mind. But there was no denying his inhuman strength and speed.

Eisenhorn, he said. It was psychic. His twisted mouth didn't open.

Barbarisater felt him move before I did. It lurched in my hands. In the time it takes to draw a breath, we had exchanged a flurry of twenty or more blows. The talon-edged blade of Kharnager rang dully off the Carthaen steel. Barbarisater's pentagrammatic runes flashed and flared with discharging energy. Kharnager groaned softly.

Heretic! Slave of Chaos! his raw, broken mind-voice railed in my brain.

You speak of yourself! I returned. Our blades continued to ring off one another, hunting for a gap, mutually denied.

Why would you try to end my work here if you were not a minion of the warp?

Your work? This thing?

We broke, and then came in again, blades striking so fast the noise became one long ringing tone. I barely made an *ulsar* in time to stop one of his rapid down-stabs. He blocked my response of a *tahn wyla,* and the *uru arav* that I followed it with.

This is just the test, the prototype. Once the trials with it are conducted, then my work will flower!

You carve up a mountain... for a prototype? A prototype of what?

The pylons of Cadia pacify the warp, he spat. *By amplifying them using extreme-level psykers, they could be made into a weapon. A weapon to destroy the warp! A weapon to collapse the Eye of Terror in upon itself!*

He was raving, insane. What patches of truth or sane notions might lurk in his words, I had no idea. There was no way to distinguish them from his lunatic fancy. All I knew was that a pylon, psychically super-charged, might do all manner of things, but its side-effects would be catastrophic. It could lay waste to the continent, the planet.

I think, and here lay the true horror of it, I think Quixos knew that. I think he considered that to be an acceptable price to pay, just as he had considered the atrocity on Thracian a necessary cost to obtain a psyker of such peerless quality as Esarhaddon. What other abominations had he caused in acquiring the others?

As Grumman had said, just before his death, this simply had to be stopped.

I looked at his face.

This was where radicalism led. This was the true face of one who had reached the place and crossed the line. This was the obscene reality behind Pontius Glaw's jaunty glorifications of Chaos.

We rained blows at each other, drawing sparks and little curls of vapour from the blade edges. I tried a low swing, but he leapt over it, and alternated a series of scissoring blows that drove me backwards across the dusty ground. I thought my feet would slip. He was a whirlwind.

I saw my moment. Barbarisater saw it too. A slight underswing on his blade return that opened a gap for a *sar aht uht,* a slice to the heart, just for a microsecond.

I thrust in, putting all my will into the blade. Somehow, dazzlingly, he still managed to turn Kharnager and block me.

Barbarisater struck the daemonsword and broke in half.

And it was the ultimate failure of the ancient Carthaen blade that gave me victory. If it had stayed intact, the block would have stopped it and the fight would have continued.

Breaking around Quixos's sword-edge, the truncated half of Barbarisater in my hand continued on, with all my mustered force behind it, until the broken end plunged through his cloak, his body armour, his augmetic implants and ran him through the torso.

The *ewl caer.*

It took almost equal force to break the suction of his flesh around the blade and rip it out.

Quixos staggered backwards, polluted blood spurting from the wound, his augmetics shorting out and exploding.

Then he fell to the dusty floor of the undervault, and became dust himself, until there was nothing left but rotting augmetic devices and empty armour twisted under his lank cape.

Heretic! his mind screeched out as he died.

Coming from him, the word felt like a compliment.

* * *

Site A was dismantled and destroyed by the taskforce, and the faux pylon smashed by sustained orbital fire. Quixos's psykers, and his surviving servants, were imprisoned, and then turned over to the Black Ships of the Inquisition, six of which arrived a few days later, once we had published news of our achievement. Most of the captives were deemed too dangerous or too tainted to keep, even under the closest guard, and were executed. Esarhaddon was one of those.

Many precious texts and artifacts were recovered from Site A, and many more that were diabolic and abominable. He had accumulated a vast resource of esoteric material, and there was supposed to be a great deal more at his fastness on distant Maginor. A further purge would reveal the truth of that.

As the report has it, no trace was ever found of the *Malus Codicium*, the foul grimoire on which his power had ultimately been based.

By the time I had returned to Gudrun with my followers and allies, the carta issued against me had been abolished. None of Osma's allegations could stand up in the face of the evidence gathered at Farness, or the many statements collected by the Inquisition, statements pleading my innocence made by such individuals as Lord Procurator Madorthene, Inquisitor General Neve, Interrogator Inshabel and, God-Emperor help him, Titus Endor.

I was never offered any sort of official apology, not by Grandmaster Orsini, or by Bezier, and certainly not by Osma. His career didn't suffer one bit. Twenty years later, he was elected Master of the Ordo Malleus Helican after Bezier's sudden, unexpected death.

Grumman's remains, and the remains of his Kasrkin, were buried in one of the lonely field-grave plots on Cadia, to be remembered as long as the Law of Decipherability allowed. Ricci had a library named after him on his home world of Hesperus. Voke was buried with full honours at the Thorian Sacristy adjoining the Great Cathedral of the Ministorum on Thracian Primaris. A small brass plaque commemorating the achievements of his long and dedicated career remains on the sacristy wall to this day.

He and I had never been friends, but I own that in the years after he was gone, I missed his caustic manner from time to time.

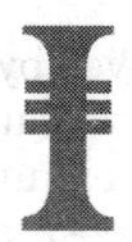

EPILOGUE

WINTER, 345.M41

The voice was like the sound of some eternal glacier – slow, old, cold, heavy.

It asked simply, 'Why?'

'Because I can.'

The silence lasted for a long time. The thousand candle flames flickered and rippled the carefully inscribed stone walls with echoes of their moving glow.

'Why? Why... have you done this... this wretched thing to me?'

'Because I have power over you where once you had power over me. You used me. You orchestrated my life. You moved me like a regicide piece to the place where I best served your desires. Now, that is reversed.'

It thrashed against its chains and shackles, but it was still too weak from the ordeals of the snaring, the entrapment.

'Damn you...' it whispered, falling limp.

'Understand me. I said I would never help a thing like you, but you tricked me into doing so and almost got away with it. That's why I have done this. That's why I have expended the considerable time and effort involved in raising you, snaring you and binding you. This is a lesson. I will never, ever allow my actions or my life to benefit the Archenemy. You said that from the outset, you knew I was the one who would free you from Quixos's service. It's a shame for you that you failed to see what I might do to you instead.'

'Damn you!' the voice was louder.

'There will be a time, Cherubael, daemon-thing, when you will wish with all your putrid soul to be Quixos's plaything again.'

Cherubael threw itself at me as far as it could before the chains went taut and snapped it back. Its scream of rage and malice shook the cell and blew every last one of the candles out.

I sealed the vacuum hatch, engaged the warp dampers and the void shield, and turned the thirteen locks one by one.

From far away in the house, Jarat was ringing the bell for dinner. I was bone-weary from my exertions, but food and wine and good company would refresh me.

I climbed the screwstair from the deep basement stronghold, code-locked the door and wandered to my study. Outside, the snows had come early to

Gudrun. Light flakes were blowing in through the twilight, across the woods and paddocks, and settling across the lawns of my estate.

In the study, I returned the items I had been carrying to their places. I put the bottles of chrism back on the shelf, and the ritual athame, mirror and lamens in the casket. The Imperial amulet went back on its velvet pad in the locking draw, and I slid the tube-scrolls back into their catalogue rack.

Then I placed the runestaff on its hooks in the lit alcove above the glass case containing the broken pieces of proud Barbarisater.

Finally, I opened the void safe in the floor behind my bureau, and gently laid the *Malus Codicium* inside.

Jarat was ringing the bell again.

I sealed the safe and went down to dinner.

BACKCLOTH FOR A CROWN ADDITIONAL

Lord Froigre, much to everyone's dismay including, I'm sure, his own, was dead.

It was a dry, summer morning in 355.M41 and I was taking breakfast with Alizebeth Bequin on the terrace of Spaeton House when I received the news. The sky was a blurry blue, the colour of Sameterware porcelain, and down in the bay the water was a pale lilac, shot through with glittering frills of silver. Sand doves warbled from the drowsy shade of the estate orchards.

Jubal Kircher, my craggy, dependable chief of household security, came out into the day's heat from the garden room, apologised courteously for interrupting our private meal, and handed me a folded square of thin transmission paper.

'Trouble?' asked Bequin, pushing aside her dish of ploin crepes.

'Froigre's dead,' I replied, studying the missive.

'Froigre who?'

'Lord Froigre of House Froigre.'

'You knew him?'

'Very well. I would count him as a friend. Well, how very miserable. Dead at eighty-two. That's no age.'

'Was he ill?' Bequin asked.

'No. Aen Froigre was, if anything, maddeningly robust and healthy. Not a scrap of augmetics about him. You know the sort.' I made this remark pointedly. My career had not been kind to my body. I had been repaired, rebuilt, augmented and generally sewn back together more times than I cared to remember. I was a walking testimonial to Imperial medicae reconstruction surgery. Alizebeth, on the other hand, still looked like a woman in her prime, a beautiful woman at that, and only the barest minimum of juvenat work had preserved her so.

'According to this, he died following a seizure at his home last night. His family are conducting thorough investigations, of course, but...' I drummed my fingers on the table-top.

'Foul play?'

'He was an influential man.'

'Such men have enemies.'

'And friends,' I said. I handed her the communique. 'That's why his widow has requested my assistance.'

But for my friendship with Aen, I'd have turned the matter down. Alizebeth had only just arrived on Gudrun after an absence of almost eighteen months, and would be gone again in a week, so I had resolved to spend as much time with her as possible. The operational demands of the Distaff, based on Messina, kept her away from my side far more than I would have liked.

But this was important, and Lady Froigre's plea too distraught to ignore.

'I'll come with you,' Alizebeth suggested. 'I feel like a jaunt in the country.' She called for a staff car to be brought round from the stable block and we were on our way in under an hour.

Felippe Gabon, one of Kircher's security detail, acted as our driver. He guided the car up from Spaeton on a whisper of thrust and laid in a course for Menizerre. Soon we were cruising south-west over the forest tracts and the verdant cultivated belt outside Dorsay and leaving the Insume headland behind.

In the comfortable, climate-controlled rear cabin of the staff car, I told Alizebeth about Froigre.

'There have been Froigres on Gudrun since the days of the first colonies. Their house is one of the Twenty-Six Venerables, that is to say one of the twenty-six original noble fiefs, and as such has an hereditary seat in the Upper Legislature of the planetary government. Other, newer houses have considerably more power and land these days, but nothing can quite eclipse the prestige of the Venerables. Houses like Froigre, Sangral, Meissian. And Glaw.'

She smiled impishly at my inclusion of that last name.

'So... power, land, prestige... a honeytrap for rivals and enemies. Did your friend have any?'

I shrugged. I'd brought with me several data-slates Psullus had looked out for me from the library. They contained heraldic ledgers, family histories, biographies and memoirs. And very little that seemed pertinent.

'House Froigre vied with House Athensae and House Brudish in the early years of Gudrun, but that's literally ancient history. Besides, House Brudish became extinct after another feud with House Pariti eight hundred years ago. Aen's grandfather famously clashed with Lord Sangral and the then Governor Lord Dougray over the introduction of Founding Levy in the one-nineties, but that was just political, though Dougray never forgave him and later snubbed him by making Richtien chancellor. In recent times, House Froigre has been very much a quiet, solid, traditional seat in the Legislature. No feuds, that I know of. In fact, there hasn't been an inter-house war on Gudrun for seven generations.

'They all play nicely together, these days, do they?' she asked.

'Pretty much. One of the things I like about Gudrun is that it is so damned civilised.'

'Too damned civilised,' she admonished. 'One day, Gregor, one day this place will lull you into such a deep sense of tranquil seclusion that you'll be caught with your pants down.'

'I hardly think so. It's not complacency, before you jump down my throat. Gudrun – Spaeton House itself – is just a safe place. A sanctuary, given my line of work.'

'Your friend's still dead,' she reminded me.

I sat back. 'He liked to live well. Good food, fine wines. He could drink Nayl under the table.'

'No!'

'I'm not joking. Five years ago, at the wedding of Aen's daughter. I was invited and I took Harlon along as... as I don't know what, actually. You weren't around and I didn't want to go alone. Harlon started bending his lordship's ear with tales of bounty hunting and the last I saw of them they were sprinting their way down their fourth bottle of anise at five in the morning. Aen was up at nine the next day to see his daughter off. Nayl was still asleep at nine the following day.'

She grinned. 'So a life of great appetites may have just caught up with him?'

'Perhaps. Though you'd think that would have shown up on the medicae mortus's report.'

'So you do suspect foul play?'

'I can't shake that idea.'

I was silent for a few minutes, and Alizebeth scrolled her way through several of the slates.

'House Froigre's main income was from mercantile dealings. They hold a twelve point stock in Brade ent Cie and a fifteen per cent share in Helican SubSid Shipping. What about trade rivals?'

'We'd have to expand our scope off-planet. I suppose assassination is possible, but that's a strange way to hit back at a trade rival. I'll have to examine their records. If we can turn up signs of a clandestine trade fight, then maybe assassination is the answer.'

'Your friend spoke out against the Ophidian Campaign.'

'So did his father. Neither believed it was appropriate to divert funds and manpower into a war of reconquest in the sub-sector next door when there was so much to put in order on the home front.'

'I was just wondering...' she said.

'Wonder away, but I think that's a dead end. The Ophidian War's long since over and done with and I don't think anyone cares what Aen thought about it.'

'So have you got a theory?'

'Only the obvious ones. None of them with any substantiating data. An internecine feud, targeting Aen from inside the family. A murder driven by some secret affair of the heart. A darker conspiracy that remains quite invisible for now. Or...'

'Or?'

'Too much good living, in which case we'll be home before nightfall.'

* * *

Froigre Hall, the ancestral pile of the noble House Froigre, was a splendid stack of ivy-swathed ouslite and copper tiles overlooking the Vale of Fiegg, ten kilometres south of Menizerre. Water meadows sloped back from the river, becoming wildflower pastures that climbed through spinneys of larch and fintle to hem the magnificent planned gardens of the house; geometric designs of box-hedge, trim lawn, flowering beds and symmetrical ponds. Beyond the sandy drive, darkened woods came right down to skirt the back of the great hall, except for where a near-perfect sulleq lawn had been laid. Aen and I had spent several diverting afternoons there, playing against each other. A kilometre north of the house, the gnarled stone finger of the Folly rose from the ascending woods.

'Where to put down, sir?' Gabon asked over the intercom.

'On the drive in front of the portico, if you'd be so kind.'

'What's been going on here?' Alizebeth asked as we came in lower. She pointed. The lawn areas nearest to the hall were littered with scraps of rubbish – paper waste and glittery bits of foil. Some sections of grass were flat and yellow as if compressed and starved of light.

Tiny stones, whipped up by our downwash, ticked off the car's bodywork as we settled in to land.

'Oh, my dear Gregor!' Lady Freyl Froigre almost fell into my arms. I held her in a comforting embrace for a few patient moments as she sobbed against my chest.

'Forgive me!' she said suddenly, pulling away and dabbing her eyes with a black lace handkerchief. 'This is all so very terrible. So very, very terrible.'

'My deepest sympathies for your loss, lady,' I said, feeling awkward.

A houseman, his arm banded in black, had led us into a stateroom off the main hall where Lady Froigre was waiting. The blinds were drawn, and mourning tapers had been lit, filling the air with a feeble light and a sickly perfume. Freyl Froigre was a stunning woman in her late sixties, her lush red hair, almost flame-pink it was so bright, pulled back and pinned down under a veil coiff of jet scamiscoire. Her grief-gown was slate epinchire, the sleeves ending in delicate interwoven gloves so that not one speck of her flesh was uncovered.

I introduced Alizebeth, who murmured her condolences, and Lady Froigre nodded. Then she suddenly looked flustered.

'Oh, my. Where are my manners? I should have the staff bring refreshments for you and–'

'Hush, lady,' I said, taking her arm and walking her down the long room into the soft shade of the shutters. 'You have enough on your mind. Grief is enough. Tell me what you know and I will do the rest.'

'You're a good man, sir. I knew I could trust you.' She paused and waited while her current wracks subsided.

'Aen died just before midnight last night. A seizure. It was quick, the physician said.'

'What else did he say, lady?'

She drew a data-wand from her sleeve and handed it to me. 'It's all here.'

I plucked out my slate and plugged it in. The display lit up with the stored files.

Death by tremorous palpitations of the heart and mind. A dysfunction of the spirit. According the the medicae's report, Aen Froigre had died because of a spasm in his anima.

'This means...' I paused, '...nothing. Who is your physician?'

'Genorus Notil of Menizerre. He has been the family medicae since the time of Aen's grandfather.'

'His report is rather... non-specific, lady. Could I present the body for a further examination?'

'I've already done that,' she said softly. 'The surgeon at Menizerre General who attended said the same. My husband died of terror.'

'Terror?'

'Yes, inquisitor. Now tell me that isn't the work of the infernal powers?'

There had, she told me, been a celebration. A Grand Fete. Aen's eldest son, Rinton, had returned home two weeks before, having mustered out of his service in the Imperial Guard. Rinton Froigre had been a captain in the Fiftieth Gudrunite and seen six years' service in the Ophidean sub-sector. Such was his father's delight on his return, a fete was called. A carnival feast. Travelling players from all around the canton had attended, along with troupes of musicians, acrobats, armies of stall holders, entertainers, and hundreds of folk from the town. That explained the litter and faded patches on the lawn. Tent pitches. The scars of marques.

'Had he any enemies?' I asked, pacing the shuttered room.

'None that I know of.'

'I would like to review his correspondence. Diaries too, if he kept them.'

'I'll see. I don't believe he kept a diary, but our rubricator will have a list of correspondence.'

On the top of the harpsichord was a framed portrait, a hololith of Aen Froigre, smiling.

I picked it up and studied it.

'The last portrait of him,' she said. 'Taken at the fete. My last connection with him.'

'Where did he die?'

'The Folly,' said Lady Froigre. 'He died in the Folly.'

The woods were damp and dark. Boughs creaked in the late afternoon wind and odd birdsong thrilled from the shadows.

The Folly was a stone drum capped by a slate needle. Inside, it was bare and terribly musty. Sand doves fluttered up in the roof spaces. Cobwebs glazed the bare windows.

'This is where I found him,' said a voice from behind me.

I turned. Rinton Froigre stooped in under the doorframe. He was a well-made boy of twenty-five, with his mother's lush red hair. His eyes had a curious, hooded aspect.

'Rinton.'

'Sir,' he bowed slightly.

'Was he dead when you found him?'

'No, inquisitor. He was laughing and talking. He liked to come up here. He loved the Folly. I came up to thank him for the fete that he had thrown in my honour. We were talking together when suddenly he went into convulsions. Just minutes later, before I could summon help, he was dead.'

I didn't know Rinton Froigre well, though his service record was very respectable, and I knew his father had been proud of him. Aen had never mentioned any animosity from his son, but in any noble house there is always the spectre of succession to consider. Rinton had been alone with his father at the time of death. He was a seasoned soldier, undoubtedly no stranger to the act of killing.

I kept an open mind – literally. Even without any invasive mental probing, it is possible for a psionic of my ability to sense surface thoughts. There was no flavour of deceit about Rinton's person, though I could feel carefully contained loss, and the tingle of trepidation. Small wonder, I considered. Uncommon are the citizens of the Imperium who do not register anxiety at being quizzed by an inquisitor of the Holy Ordos.

There was no point pressing him now. Rinton's story might easily be put to the test with an auto-seance, during which psychometric techniques would simply reveal the truth of his father's last moments to me.

Rinton walked me back to the Hall, and left me to my ponderings in Aen's study. It was as he had left it, I was told.

The room was half-panelled and lined for the most part with glazed shelves of neatly bound books and data-slates. Discreet glow-globes hovered around the edges of the room at head-height, set to a low luminosity, and a selection of scroll-backed couches and over-stuffed chairs were arranged in front of the high-throated ceramic fireplace with its wood-burning fusion stove.

The desk, under the diamond-paned west windows, was a wide crescent of polished duralloy floated a metre off the carpet by passive suspensor pods. The desk was clean and bare.

I sat at it, depressing slightly the hydraulics of the writing chair – I was half a head taller than Aen Froigre. I studied the mirror-smooth, slightly raked surface of the desk. There was no sign of any control panel, but a gentle wave of my hand across it woke up heat-sensitive touch-plates engraved into the duralloy's finish. I touched a few, but they needed Aen's touch – probably a combination of palmprint and genekey – to unlock them.

That, or Inquisition-grade software. I unpinned my Inquisitorial rosette, which I had been wearing on the sternum of a my black leather coat, and slid open the signal port. Holding it low over the desk, I force fed the touch-plates with several magenta-level security override programs. It gave up the fight almost at once, opening systems without even the need for passwords.

Built into the stylish desk – an item of furniture that had clearly cost Aen a lot of money – was a fairly powerful cogitator, a vox-pict uplink, a message archive, two filing archives, and a master control for the simple, limited electronic systems built into the Hall. Separate pages of each file and message could be displayed as a facsimile on the blotter plate and a touch of a finger turned them or put them away. Aen had destroyed all paper records.

I played with it for some time, but the most interesting thing I found was a log of invoices for services provided at the fete, and a list of the invitations. I copied both into my own data-slate.

Alizebeth and Gabon arrived while I was busy with that. Alizebeth had been interviewing the household staff, and Gabon had been out, walking the grounds.

'There were over nine hundred guests here, sir,' he said, 'and maybe another five hundred players, musicians, entertainers and carnival folk.'

'Where from?'

'Menizerre, mostly,' he replied. 'Local entertainers, a few troubadours and some street tumblers from the biweekly textile market. The biggest individual groups were Kalikin's Company, an acclaimed troupe of travelling actors, and Sunsable's Touring Fair, who provided the games and rides and diversions.'

I nodded. Gabon was as thorough as usual. A short, spare man in his one fifties with cropped black hair and a bushy moustache, he had been with the Dorsay Arbites for about seventy years before retiring into private service. He wore a simple, refined dark blue suit that had been ingeniously tailored to hide the fact that he was wearing a handgun in a shoulder rig.

'What about you?' I asked Alizebeth. She sat down on one of the couches.

'Nothing scintillating. The staff seem genuinely shocked and upset at the death. They all react with outrage at the idea your friend might have had any enemies.'

'It seems quite clear to me that he did have some,' I said.

Alizebeth reached into the folds of her gown and fished out a small, hard object. She tossed it across onto the desk top and it landed with a tap. There it extended four, multi-jointed limbs and scurried across onto my palm.

I turned the wriggling poison-snooper over and pressed the recessed stud on its belly. A little ball of hololithic energy coalesced above its head-mounted projector and I read it as slowly scrolled around on its own axis.

'Traces of lho, obscura and several other class II and III narcotics in the garden area and the staff quarters. Penshel seed traces found in the stable block. More lho, as well as listeria and e. coli in small amounts in the kitchen section... hmmm...'

Alizebeth shrugged. 'The usual mix of recreational drugs one might expect, none in large quantities, and the kitchens's as hygienic as anywhere. You'd probably get the same sort of readings from Spaeton House.'

'Probably. Penshel seeds, they're quite unusual.'

'A very mild stimulant,' said Gabon. 'I didn't know anyone still used that stuff. Time was, it was the drug of choice in the artists' quarter of Dorsay, back when I was on the force. The seeds are dried, rolled and smoked in pipes. A little bohemian, an old man's smoke.'

'Most of the outdoor traces can be put down to the visiting entertainers,' I mused, 'plus a little off-duty pleasure from the staff or loose-living guests. What about the stable block? Are any of Froigre's ostlers penshel smokers?'

Alizebeth shook her head. 'They'd cleared large parts of the stable area to provide spaces for the fair stall-holders.'

I put the snooper down on the desk and it wriggled back and forth for a few moments until it got enough purchase to right itself. 'So nothing untoward, in fact. And certainly no significant toxins.'

'None at all,' said Alizebeth.

Damn. Given the description of Aen's death, I had been quite sure poison was the key, perhaps some assassin's sophisticated toxin that had not shown up on the initial medicae report. But Alizebeth's snooper was high-grade and thorough.

'What do we do now?' she asked.

I passed her my data-slate. 'Send the contents of this to Aemos by direct vox-link. See what he can come up with.'

Uber Aemos was my ancient and trusted savant. If anyone could see a pattern or make a connection, it was him.

Evening fell. I went outside, alone. I felt annoyed and frustrated. In fact, I felt thwarted. I'd come there as a favour to my old friend's widow, offering my services, and in most respects I was overqualified. I was an Imperial inquisitor, and this was most likely just a job for the local Arbites. I had expected to have the entire matter sewn up in a few hours, to settle things swiftly in a quick, unofficial investigation, and leave with the thanks of the family for sparing them a long, drawn-out inquest.

But the clues just weren't there. There was no motive, no obvious antagonist, no aggressor, but still it seemed likely that Aen Froigre had been killed. I looked at the medicae report again, hoping to find something that would establish natural causes.

Nothing. Something, someone, had taken my friend's life, but I couldn't tell what or who or why.

The evening skies were dark, stained a deep violet and smeared with chasing milky clouds. An early moon shone, passing behind the running trails of cloud every minute or so. A wind was gathering, and the stands of trees beside the lawn were beginning to sway and swish. The leaves made a cold sound, like rain.

I walked over to my flyer, popped the cargo trunk and took out Barbarisater. I slowly freed it from its silk bindings and drew the long, gleaming blade from its machined scabbard. Barbarisater had been an heirloom sword, a psychically-attuned weapon from the forges of distant Carthae and slaved to the minds of the generations of warrior women who had wielded it. Enhancing its strength with pentagrammic wards, I had used the long sabre in my battle against the heretic Quixos, during which struggle it had been broken below the tip. Master swordsmiths had remade the blade from the broken main portion, creating a shorter, straighter blade by rounding off and edging the break and reducing the hilt. A good deal smaller than its old self, now more a single-handed rapier than a hand-and-a-half sabre, it was still a potent weapon.

Naked, in my hand, it hummed and whined as my mind ran through it and made it resonate. The incised wards glowed and sobbed out faint wisps of smoke. I walked out over the grass under the seething trees, holding the blade out before me like a dowsing rod, sweeping the scene, letting the blade-tip slide along the invisible angles of space. Twice, on my circuit of the lawns, it twitched as if tugged by sprite hands, but I could discern nothing from the locations.

But there was something there. My first hint of a malign focus. My first hint that not only was foul play involved, but that Lady Froigre might be right.

Though they had left only the slightest traces behind them, infernal powers had been at work here.

Alizebeth came into my room at eight the next morning. She woke me by sitting down on the side of my bed and handed me a cup of hot, black caffeine as I roused.

She was already dressed and ready for work. The day was bright. I could hear the household coming to life: pans clattering the kitchen block and the butler calling to his pages in the nearby gallery.

'Bad storm in the night,' she said. 'Brought trees down.'

'Really?' I grumbled, sitting up and sipping the sweet, dark caffeine.

I looked at her. It wasn't like Bequin to be so perky this early.

'Out with it,' I said.

She handed me a data-slate. 'Aemos has been busy. Must've worked all night.'

'Through the storm.'

'There was no storm up his way. It was local.' I didn't really hear that reply. I was caught up in a close reading of the slate.

Failing to cross-match just about every detail I had sent him, Aemos had clearly become bored. The list of guests I had sent him had led to nothing, despite his best efforts to make connections. The caterers and performers had revealed nothing either. No links to the underworld or cult activity, no misdeeds or priors, except for the usual clutch of innocent and minor violations one might expect. One of the travelling actors had been charged with affray twenty years before, and another had done time for grievous wounding, that sort of thing.

The only item that had flagged any sort of connection was the description of Aen Froigre's death. Aemos had only turned to that rather vague clue once he'd exhausted all others.

In the past twenty months, eleven people in the Drunner Region of Gudrun, which is to say the coastal area encompassing Menizerre, Dorsay and Insume all the way to Madua chapeltown, had died of a similar, mystery ailment. Only a tight, deliberate search like the one Aemos had conducted would have shown up such a connection, given the scale of area involved and the size of population. Listed together, the deaths stood out like a sore thumb.

Here, Aemos had come into his own. Another clerk might have sent those findings to me and waited for direction, but Aemos, hungry to answer the questions himself, had pressed on, trying to make a pattern out of them. No simple task. There was nothing to demo-graphically or geographically link the victims. A housewife here, a millkeeper there, a landowner in one small village, a community doctor in another, seventy kilometres away.

The only thing they had in common was the sudden, violent and inexplicable nature of their demises: seizures, abrupt, fatal.

I set down my cup and scrolled on, aware that Alizebeth was grinning at me.

'Get to the last bit,' she advised. 'Aemos strikes again.'

Right at the last, Aemos revealed another connection.

A day or two before each death, the victim's locality had been paid a visit by Sunsable's Touring Fair.

Lady Froigre was most perturbed to see us about to leave. 'There are questions here still...' she began.

'And I'm going to seek the answers,' I said. 'Trust me. I believe my savant has hit upon something.'

She nodded, unhappy. Rinton stepped forward and put his arm around his mother's shoulders.

'Trust me,' I repeated and walked out across the drive to my waiting flyer.

I could hear the sound of chain blades, and turned from the car to walk around the side of the hall. One of the trees brought down in the night's freak storm had crushed part of the stable block and the housemen were working to saw up the huge trunk and clear it.

'Is that where you detected Penshel seed?' I asked Alizebeth when she came to find out what was keeping me.

'Yes,' she said.

'Fetch my blade.'

I called the housemen away from their work, and walked into the collapsed ruin of the stable, crunching over heaps of coarse sawdust. The ivy-clad tree still sprawled through the burst roof.

Alizebeth brought me Barbarisater and I drew it quickly. By then Lady Froigre and Rinton Froigre had emerged to see what I was doing.

Barbarisater hummed in my hand, louder and more throatily than it had done the previous night. As soon as I entered that part of the stable block, the particular stall the tree had smashed, it jumped. The taste of Chaos was here.

'What was this used for?' I asked. 'During the fete, what was this area used for?'

'Storage,' said Lady Froigre. 'The people from the fair wanted to keep equipment and belongings out of sight. Food too, I think. One man had trays of fresh figs he wanted to keep out of the light.'

'And the hololithographer,' said Rinton. 'He used one of those stalls as a darkroom.'

So how do you find a travelling fair in an area the size of the Drunner Region? If you have a copy of their most recent invoice, it's easy. The fair-master, eager to be paid for his services at Froigre Hall, had left as a payment address an inn eighty kilometres away in Seabrud. From the invoice, I saw that Aen had been asked to mail the payment within five days. The fair moved around a great deal, and the travelling folk didn't believe much in the concept of credit accounts.

From Seabrud, we got a fix on the location of Sunsable's Fair.

They had pitched on a meadow outside the village of Brudmarten, a little, rustic community of ket-herds and weavers that was flanked by a lush, deciduous woodland hillside to the east and marshy, cattle-trampled fields below at the river spill to the west.

It was late afternoon on a hot, close day, the air edged with the heavy, fulminous threat of storms. The sky was dark overhead, but the corn was bright and golden down in the meadows, and pollen balls blew in the breeze like thistle-fibres. Grain-crakes whooped in the corn stands, and small warblers of the most intense blue darted across the hedges.

Gabon lowered the limo to rest in a lane behind the village kirk, a pale, Low Gothic temple in need of up-keep. A noble statue of the Emperor Immaculate stood in the overgrown graveyard, a roost for wood doves. I buckled on my sword and covered it with a long leather cloak. Gabon locked the car.

'Stay with me,' I told Alizebeth, and then turned to Gabon. 'Shadow us.'

'Yes, sir.'

We walked down the lane towards the fair.

Even from a distance, we could hear the noise and feel the energy. The arrival of the fair had brought the folk of Brudmarten and the neighbouring hamlets out in force. Pipe organs were trilling and wheezing in the lank air, and there was the pop and whizz of firecrackers. I could hear laughter, the clatter of rides, the ringing of score bells, children screaming, rowdy men carousing, pistons hissing. The smell of warm ale wafted from the tavern tent.

The gate in the meadow's hedge had been turned into an entranceway, arched with a gaudy, handpainted sign that declared Sunsable's Miraculous Fair of Fairs open. A white-eyed twist at the gateway took our coins for admission.

Inside, on the meadow, all manner of bright, vulgar sights greeted us. The carousel, lit up with gas-lamps. The ring-toss. The neat, pink box-tent of the clairvoyant. The churning hoop of the whirligig, spilling out the squeals of children. The colourful shouts of the freak show barker. The burnt-sugar smell of floss makers. The clang of test-your- strength machines.

For a penny, you could ride the shoulders of a Battle Titan – actually an agricultural servitor armoured with painted sections of rusty silage hopper. For another penny, you could shoot greenskins in the las-gallery, or touch the Real and Completely Genuine shin bone of Macharius, or dunk for ploins. For tuppence, you could gaze into the Eye of Terror and have your heroism judged by a hooded man with a stutter who claimed to be an ex-Space Marine. The Eye of Terror in this case was a pit dug in the ground and filled with chemical lamps and coloured glass filters.

Nearby, a small donation allowed you to watch an oiled man struggle free from chains, or a burning sack, or a tin bathtub full of broken glass, or a set of stocks.

'Just a penny, sir, just a penny!' howled a man on stilts with a harlequined face as he capered past me. 'For the young lady!'

I decided not to ask what my penny might buy.

'I want to go look at the freak show,' Alizebeth told me.

'Save your money... it's all around us,' I growled.

We pushed on. Coloured balloons drifted away over the field into the encroaching darkness of the thunderhead. Corn crickets rasped furiously in the trampled stalks all about us. Drunken, painted faces swam at us, some lacking teeth, some with glittering augmetic eyes.

'Over there,' I whispered to Alizebeth.

Past the brazier stand of a woman selling paper cones of sugared nuts, and a large handcart stacked with wire cages full of songbirds, was a small booth tent of heavy red material erected at the side of a brightly painted trailer. A wooden panel raised on bunting-wrapped posts announced 'Hololiths! Most Lifelike! Most Agreeable!' below which a smaller notice said 'A most delightful gift, or a souvenir of the day, captured by the magic art of a master hololithographer.' A frail old man with tufted white hair and small spectacles was seated outside the booth on a folding canvas chair, eating a meat pie that was so hot he had to keep blowing on it.

'Why don't you go and engage his interest?' I suggested.

Alizebeth left my side, pushed through the noisy crowd and stopped by his booth. A sheet of flakboard had been erected beside the booth's entrance, and on it were numerous hololithic pictures mounted for display: some miniatures, some landscapes, some family groups. Alizebeth studied them with feigned interest. The old man immediately leapt up off his chair, stowed the half-eaten pie behind the board and brushed the crumbs off his robes. I moved round to the side, staying in the crowd, watching. I paused to examine the caged birds, though in fact I was looking through their cages at the booth tent.

The old man approached Bequin courteously.

'Madam, good afternoon! I see your attention has been arrested by my display of work. Are they not fairly framed and well-composed?'

'Indeed,' she said.

'You have a good eye, madam,' he said, 'for so often in these country fairs the work of the hololithgrapher is substandard. The composition is frequently poor and the plate quality fades with time. Not so with your humble servant. I have plied this trade of portraiture for thirty years and I fancy I have skill for it. You see this print here? The lakeshore at Entreve?'

'It is a pleasing scene.'

'You are very kind, madam. It is handcoloured, like many of my frames. But this very print was made in the summer of... 329, if my memory serves. And you'll appreciate, there is no fading, no loss of clarity, no discolouration.'

'It has preserved itself well.'

'It has,' he agreed, merrily. 'I have patented my own techniques, and I prepare the chemical compounds for the plates by hand, in my modest studio adjoining.' He gestured to his trailer. 'That is how I can maintain the quality and the perfect grade of the hololiths, and reproduce and print them to order with no marked loss of standard from original to duplicate. My reputation rests upon it. Up and down the byeways of the land, the name Bakunin is a watchword for quality portraiture.'

Alizebeth smiled. 'It's most impressive, Master Bakunin. And how much...?'

'Aha!' he grinned. 'I thought you might be tempted, madam, and may I say it would be a crime for your beauty to remain unrecorded! My services are most affordable.'

I moved round further, edging my way to the side of his booth until he and Alizebeth were out of sight behind the awning. I could hear him still making his pitch to her.

On the side of the trailer, further bold statements and enticements were painted in a flourishing script. A large sign read 'Portraits two crowns, group scenes three crowns, gilded miniatures a half-crown only, offering many a striking and famous backcloth for a crown additional.'

I wandered behind the trailer. It was parked at the edge of the fairground, near to a copse of fintle and yew that screened the meadow from pastures beyond the ditch. It was damp and shaded here, small animals rustling in the thickets. I tried to look in at one small window, but it was shuttered. I touched the side of the trailer and felt Barbarisater twitch against my hip. There was a door near the far end of the trailer. I tried it, but it was locked.

'What's your business?' growled a voice.

Three burly fairground wranglers had approached along the copse-side of the booths. They had been smoking lho-sticks behind their trailer on a break.

'Not yours,' I assured them.

'You had best be leaving Master Bakunin's trailer alone,' one said. All three were built like wrestlers, their bared arms stained with crude tattoos. I had no time for this.

'Go away now,' I said, pitching my will through my voice. They all blinked, not quite sure what had happened to their minds, and then simply walked away as if I wasn't there.

I returned my attention to the door, and quickly forced the lock with my multi-key. To my surprise, the thin wooden door still refused to open. I wondered if it was bolted from inside, but as I put more weight into it, it did shift a little, enough to prove there there was nothing physical holding it. Then it banged back shut as if drawn by immense suction.

My pulse began to race. I could feel the sour tang of warpcraft in the air and Barbarisater was now vibrating in its scabbard. It was time to dispense with subtleties.

I paced around to the front of the booth, but there was no longer any sign of Bequin or the old man. Stooping, I went in under the entrance flap. An inner drop curtain of black cloth stopped exterior light from entering the tent.

I pushed that aside.

'I will be with you shortly, sir,' Bakunin called, 'if you would give me a moment.'

'I'm not a customer,' I said. I looked around. The tent was quite small, and lit by the greenish glow of gas mantles that ran, I supposed, off the trailer supply. Alizebeth was sat at the far side on a ladderback chair with a dropcloth of cream felt behind her. Bakunin was facing her, carefully adjusting his hololithic camera, a brass and teak machine mounted on a wooden tripod.

He looked round at me curiously, his hands still polishing a brass-rimmed lens. Alizebeth rose out of her seat.

'Gregor?' she asked.

'The good lady is just sitting for a portrait, sir. It's all very civilised.' Bakunin peered at me, unsure what to make of me. He smiled and offered his hand. 'I am Bakunin, artist and hololithographer.'

'I am Eisenhorn, Imperial inquisitor.'

'Oh,' he said and took a step backwards. 'I... I...'

'You're wondering why a servant of the Ordos has just walked into your booth,' I finished for him. Bakunin's mind was like an open book. There was, I saw at once, no guile there, except for the natural money-making trickery of a fairground rogue. Whatever else he was, Bakunin was no heretic.

'You took a portrait of Lord Froigre at the fete held on his lands just the other day?' I said, thinking of the picture on the harpsichord back at the hall.

'I did,' he said. 'His lordship was pleased. I made no charge for the work, sir. It was a gift to thank his lordship for his hospitality. I thought perhaps some of his worthy friends might see the work and want the like for themselves, I...'

He doesn't know, I thought. He has no clue what this is about. He's trying to work out how he might have drawn this investigation to himself.

'Lord Froigre is dead,' I told him.

He went pale. 'No, that's... that's...'

'Master Bakunin... do you know if any other of your previous subjects have died? Died soon after your work was complete?'

'I don't, I'm sure. Sir, what are you implying?'

'I have a list of names,' I said, unclipping my data-slate. 'Do you keep records of your work?'

'I keep them all, all the exposed plates, in case that copies or replacements are needed. I have full catalogues of all pictures.'

I showed him the slate. 'Do you recognise any of these names?'

His hands were shaking. He said, 'I'll have to check them against my catalogue,' but I knew for a fact he'd recognised some of them at once.

'Let's do that together,' I said. Alizebeth followed us as we went through the back of the tent into the trailer. It was a dark, confined space, and Bakunin kept apologising. Every scrap of surface, even the untidy flat of his little cot bed, was piled with spares and partly disassembled cameras. There was a musty, chemical stink, mixed with the scent of Penshel seeds. Bakunin's pipe lay in a small bowl. He reached into a crate under the cot and pulled out several dog-eared record books.

'Let me see now,' he began.

There was a door at the end of the little room. 'What's through there?'

'My darkroom, along with the file racks for the exposed plates.'

'It has a door to the outside?'

'Yes,' he said.

'Locked?'

'No...'

'You have an assistant then, someone you ordered to hold the door shut?'

'I have no assistant...' he said, puzzled.

'Open this door,' I told him. He put down the books and went to the communicating door. Just from his body language, I could tell he had been expecting it to open easily.

'I don't understand,' he said. 'It's never jammed before.'

'Stand back,' I said, and drew Barbarisater. The exposed blade filled the little trailer with ozone and Bakunin yelped.

I put the blade through the door with one good swing and ripped it open. There was a loud bang of atmospheric decompression, and fetid air swept over us. A dark, smoky haze drifted out.

'Emperor of Mankind, what is that?'

'Warpcraft,' I said. 'You say you mix your own oxides and solutions?'

'Yes.'

'Where do you get your supplies from?'

'Everywhere, here and there, sometimes from apothecaries, or market traders or...'

Anywhere. Bakunin had experimented with all manner of compounds over the years to create the best, most effective plates for his camera. He'd never been fussy about where the active ingredients came from. Something in his workshop, something in his rack of flasks and bottles, was tainted.

I took a step towards the darkroom. In the half-light, things were flickering, half-formed and pale. The baleful energies lurking in Bakunin's workshop could sense I was a threat, and were trying to protect themselves by sealing the doors tight to keep me out.

I crossed the threshold into the darkroom. Alizebeth's cry of warning was lost in the shrieking of tormented air that suddenly swirled around me. Glass bottles and flasks of mineral tincture vibrated wildly in metal racks above Bakunin's work bench. Jars of liquid chemicals and unguent oils shattered and sprayed their contents into the air. The little gas-jet burner flared and ignited, its rubber tube thrashing like a snake. Glass plates, each a square the size of a data-slate, and each sleeved in a folder of tan card, were jiggling and working themselves out of the wooden racks on the far side of the blacked out room. There were thousands of them, each one the master exposure of one of Bakunin's hololiths. The first yanked clear of the shelf as if tugged by a sucking force, and I expected it to shatter on the floor, but it floated in the air. Quickly others followed suit. Light from sources I couldn't locate played in the air, casting specks and flashes of colour all around. The air itself became dark brown, like tobacco.

I raised my sword. A negative plate came flying at my head and I struck at it. Shards of glass flew in all directions. Another came at me and I smashed that too. More flew from the shelves like a spray of playing cards, whipping through the air towards me. I made a series of quick *uwe sar* and *ulsar* parries, bursting the glass squares as they struck in. I missed one, and it sliced my cheek with its edge before hitting the wall behind me like a throwing knife.

'Get him out of here!' I yelled to Alizebeth. The trailer was shaking. Outside there was a crash of thunder and rain started to hammer on the low roof. The hurtling plates were driving me back, and Barbarisater had become a blur in my hands as it struck out to intercept them all.

Then the ghosts came. Serious men in formal robes. Gentlewomen in long gowns. Solemn children with pale faces. A laughing innkeeper with blotchy cheeks. Two farmhands, with their arms around each other's shoulders. More, still more, shimmering in the dirty air, made of smoke, their skins white, their clothes sepia, their expressions frozen at the moment they had been caught by the camera. They clawed and tugged at me with fingers of ice, pummelled me with psychokinetic fists. Some passed through me like wraiths, chilling my marrow. The malevolence hiding in that little trailer was conjuring up all the images Bakunin had immortalised in his career, ripping them off the negative plates and giving them form.

I staggered back, tears appearing in my cloak. Their touch was as sharp as the edge of the glass plates. Their hollow screaming filled my ears. Then, with a sickening lurch, the world itself distorted and changed. The trailer was gone. For a moment I was standing on a sepia shoreline, then I was an uninvited guest at a country wedding. My sword hacking and flashing, I stumbled on into a baptism, then a colourised view of the Atenate Mountains, then a feast in a guild hall. The ghosts surged at me, frozen hands clawing. The innkeeper with the blotchy cheeks got his icy fists around my throat though his face was still open in laughter. I chopped Barbarisater through him and he billowed like smoke. A sad-faced housemaid pulled at my arm and a fisherman struck at me with his boat hook.

I began to recite the Litany of Salvation, yelling it into the leering faces that beset me. A few crumpled and melted like cellulose exposed to flame.

I heard gunshots. Gabon was to my right, firing his weapon. He was standing on the pier at Dorsay at sunset, in the middle of a inter-village game of knockball, and a harvest festival, all at the same time. The conflicting scenes blurred and merged around him. A bride and her groom, along with five mourners from a funeral and a retiring Arbites constable in full medals, were attacking him.

'Get back!' I yelled. Barbarisater was glowing white-hot. Thunder crashed again, shaking the earth. Gabon shrieked as the bride's fingers ripped through his face, and as he stumbled backwards, whizzing glass plates chopped into him like axe heads.

His blood was in the air, like rain. It flooded into the ghosts and stained their sepia tones crimson and their pale flesh pink. I felt fingers like knives draw across the flesh of my arms and back. There were too many of them.

I couldn't trust my eyes. According to them, I was standing on a riverbank, and also the front steps of an Administratum building. The locations overlaid each other impossibly, and neither was real.

I leapt, and lashed out with my blade. I hit something, tore through and immediately found myself rolling on the rain-sodden turf behind the trailer.

Lightning split the darkness overhead and the rain was torrential. The storm and the bizarre activity around Bakunin's booth had sent the commonfolk fleeing from the meadow. The trailer was still vibrating and shaking, and oily brown smoke was gushing from the hole in the side wall I'd cut to break my way out. Inside, lights crackled and flashed and the phantom screaming continued. The warptaint was berserk.

Bakunin appeared, looking desperate, with Alizebeth close behind him. He put his hands to his mouth in shock at the sight of me torn and bloodied.

'Where is it?' I snarled.

'Third shelf up, above the workbench,' he stammered. 'The green bottle. I needed tincture of mercury, years ago, years ago, and an old woman in one of the villages gave it to me and said it would do as well. I use it all the time now. The emulsions it mixes are perfect. My work has never been better.'

He looked down at the grass, shaking and horrified. 'I should have realised,' he muttered. 'I should have realised. No matter how much I used, the bottle never emptied.'

'Third shelf up?' I confirmed.

'I'll show you,' he said, and sprang to the trailer, clambering in through the hole I had smashed.

'Bakunin! No!'

I followed him inside, tumbling back into the jumble of landscapes and the maelstrom of screaming ghosts. Just for a moment, a brief moment, I saw Aen Froigre amongst them.

Then I was falling through another wedding, a hunting scene, a stockman's meeting, a farrier's smithy, the castle of Elempite by moonlight, a cattle market, a–

I heard Bakunin scream.

I deflected three more deadly hololith plates, and slashed through the thicket of howling ghosts. Spectral, as if it wasn't there, I saw the workbench and the shelves. The green bottle, glowing internally with jade fire.

I raised Barbarisater and smashed the bottle with the edge of the shivering blade.

The explosion shredded the inner partition wall and lurched the trailer onto its side. Dazed, I lay on the splintered wall, sprawled amongst the debris of glass and wood.

The screaming stopped.

Someone had called the local Arbites. They moved in through the crowds of onlookers as the last of the rain fell and the skies began to clear.

I showed them my credentials and told them to keep the crowd back while I finished my work. The trailer was already burning, and Alizebeth and I threw the last few hololith prints into the flames.

The pictures were fading now. Superimposed on each one, every portrait, every landscape, every miniature, was a ghost exposure. An after-image.

Bakunin, screaming his last scream forever.

HERETICUS

BY ORDER OF HIS MOST HOLY MAJESTY
THE GOD-EMPEROR OF TERRA

SEQUESTERED INQUISITORIAL DOSSIERS
AUTHORISED PERSONS ONLY

CASE FILE 442:41F:JL3:Kbu

Please enter your authority code > ••••••••••••••

Validating...

Thank you, inquisitor.

You may proceed.

To Gregor Eisenhorn, a communiqué
Carried by Guild Astropathica (Scarus) via meme-wave 45~a.639 triple intra
Path detail:
Origin: Thracian Primaris, Helican Sub 81281 origin date: 142.386.M41
(relayed: divergent M-12/Ostall VII)
Received: Durer, Ophidian Sub 52981 reception date: 144.386.M41
Transcript carried and logged as per header
(redundant copy filed buffer 4362 key 11)

Author: Lord Inquisitor Phlebas Alessandro Rorken
Master of the Ordo Xenos Helican,
Inquisition High Council Officio, Scarus Sector

My dear Gregor,

In the name of the God-Emperor, and of the Holy Inquisition, greetings.

I trust the elders of Durer have welcomed you in a manner befitting your status. Hierarch Onnopel has been charged by my officio to ensure that you are provided with all requirements for the long task ahead. May I take this opportunity to express my gratitude to you again for agreeing to conduct this Examination in my stead. My health, so it would appear to everyone but me, is still a matter for concern. My physician clucks over me night and day. They have changed my blood a number of times and talk of further surgery, but it is all for naught. I am healthy and sound and would be on the road to recovery but for their coddling. Indeed, I would be on the road to Durer too but for that.

Yet it seems a quack from the Officio Medicae has authority over even one such as I. The work I have done to bring the heretics of Durer to trial must be finished in my absence, and I can think of no surer hand than yours to steer the business.

I write to you for two reasons - apart, that is, for expressing my thanks. Despite my efforts, Sakarof Lord Hereticus has insisted on sending two of his own delegates to the Examination: Koth and Menderef, you know them both. I'm sorry, Gregor, but you must tolerate them. They are a burden I would have spared you from.

Secondly, I am forced to saddle you with Inquisitor Bastian Verveuk. He was an interrogator under Lord Osma, and had come to my staff to finish his preparation. I had promised him a hand in the Examination, primarily because of his good offices in securing the central prosecutions. Please accommodate him in your counsel, for my sake. He is a good man, young and untried, but capable, though he reeks of the puritan. Didn't we all at that age? He will arrive with you on the 151st. Make him as welcome as you can. I know you hate to incorporate unknowns into your camp, but I ask this as a personal favour. Osma will make things very difficult for me if I retard his pupil's progress at this late stage.

I wish you speed, wisdom and success in the closure of this inspection. Sealed and notarised by astropathicae clerk, this 142nd day of 386.M41.

The Emperor protects!

Rorken

[message ends]

To Gregor Eisenhorn, a communiqué
Carried by Guild Astropathica (Scarus) via meme-loop repeat 45~3.5611 secure
Path detail:
Origin: Thracian Primaris, Helican Sub 81281 origin date: 142.386.M41 (relayed: loop navigatus 351/echo Gernale beacon)
Received: Durer, Ophidian Sub 52981 reception date: 144.386.M41
Transcript carried and logged as per header (redundant copy filed buffer 7002 key 34)

Author: Inquisitor Bastian Verveuk, Ordo Xenos
Inquisition High Council Officio, Scarus Sector, Scarus Major

Salutations, sir!

In the name of the God-Emperor, hallowed be his eternal vigil, and by the High Lords of Terra, I commend myself your eminence and trust that this communiqué finds your eminence in good health.

Great was my excitement when my Lord Rorken informed me that I was to take a part, at his side, in the formal Examination of the vile and abominated heretics of Durer. At once, I threw myself into the cataloguing of advance discovery, and assisted in the compilation of the evidentiary archive that would support the particulars of the Examination.

You may then imagine my terrible disappointment when my lord's sudden and lamentable illness seemed to cast the very occurrence of that divine work into doubt. Now, this very hour, my lord has informed me that you are to oversee the matter as his proxy and that you have agreed to find a place for me at your side.

I cannot contain my exhilaration! The chance to work at close hand with one such as you! I have studied your holy work with awe since my earliest days in the preparatory scholams. You are an object lesson in devotion and puritanical duty, an example to us all. I look forward with great eagerness to discussing matters of contra-heretical law with you, and perhaps hearing first hand a few scraps of your dazzling insight. It is my most fervent ambition to pursue the rank of inquisitor in the Ordo Hereticus, and I am sure I would be better armed for such duty if I had the benefit of learning from your own first-hand accounts of such infamous beings as the dread Quixos.

You will find me a devoted and hard-working colleague. I count the days until we can begin this sacred work together.

Hallowed be the Golden Throne!

Your servant,

Bastian Verveuk

[message ends]

To Lord Rorken, a communiqué
Carried by Guild Astropathica (Ophidia) via meme-wave 3Q1~c.122 double intra
Path detail:
Origin: Durer, Ophidian Sub 52981 origin date: 144.386.M41
(relayed: divergent B-3/loop Gernale beacon)
Received: Thracian Primaris, Helican Sub 81281 reception date: 149.386.M41
Transcript carried and logged as per header
(redundant copy deleted from buffer)

Author: Gregor Eisenhorn, Inquisitor

re: Bastian Verveuk

My lord, what foetid corner of the Imperium breeds these fawning idiots?

Now you really owe me.

G. E.

[message ends]

ONE

THE CASE OF UDWIN PRIDDE
SMALL TALK WITH VERVEUK
SOMETHING LIKE VENGEANCE

When the time came, Fayde Thuring was damn near impossible to stop.

I blame myself for that. I had let him run on for too long. For the best part of eight decades he had escaped my attentions, and in that time he had grown immeasurably from the minor warp-dabbler I had once let slip away.

My mistake. But I wasn't the one to pay.

On the 160th day of 386.M41 a nobleman in his late one sixties appeared at the Examination hearings held in the Imperial Minster of Eriale, the legislative capital of the Uvege in the south-west of Durer's third largest landmass.

He was a landowner, widowed young, and he had built his fortune in post-liberation Durer society on a successful agri-combine venture and the inherited wealth of his late wife. In 376, as a mature, successful and highly eligible newcomer amongst the gentry of the Uvege, a prosperous region of verdant farmland, he had made a socially-advancing second marriage. His new bride was Betrice, thirty years his junior, the eldest daughter of the venerable House Samargue. The Samargue family's ancient wealth was at that time seeping away as the efficient land-use policies of Administratum-sponsored combines slowly took control of the Uvege's pastoral economy.

The nobleman's name was Udwin Pridde, and he had been summoned by the hierarch of the See of Eriale to answer charges of recidivism, warp-craft and, above all, heresy.

Facing him across the marble floor of the Minster was a dignified Inquisitorial body of the most august quality. Inquisitor Eskane Koth, an Amalathian, born and bred on Thracian Primaris, one day to be known as the Dove of Avignon. Inquisitor Laslo Menderef, a native of lowland Sancour, Menderef the Grievous as he would become, an Istvaanian with a cold appreciation of warp-crime and poor body hygiene. Inquisitor Poul Rassi, son of the Kilwaddi Steppes, a sound, elderly, even-handed servant of order. The novice Inquisitor Bastian Verveuk.

And myself. Gregor Eisenhorn. Inquisitor and presiding examiner.

Pridde was the first of two hundred and sixty individuals identified by

Lord Rorken's work as possible heretics to be weighed by this Formal Court of Examination. He looked nervous but dignified as he faced us, toying with his lace collar. He had hired a pardoner called Fen of Clincy to speak on his behalf.

It was the third day of the hearings. As the pardoner droned on, describing Pridde in terms that would have made a saint blush for want of virtue, I thumbed half-heartedly through the catalogue of pending cases and sighed at the scale of the work to come. The catalogue – we all had a copy – was thicker than my wrist. This was the third day already and still we had not progressed further than the preamble of the first case. The opening rites had taken a full day and the legal recognition of the authority of the Ordos Helican here on Durer, together with other petty matters of law, yet another. I wondered, may the God-Emperor forgive my lack of charity, if Lord Rorken's illness was genuine or just a handy excuse to avoid this tedium.

Outside, it was a balmy summer day. Wealthy citizens of Eriale were boating on the ornamental lakes, lunching in the hillside trattorias of the Uvege, conducting lucrative business in the caffeine houses of the city's Commercia.

In the echoing, cool vault of the Minster, there was nothing but the whining voice of Fen of Clincy.

Golden sunlight shafted in through the celestory windows and bathed the stalls of the audience gallery. That area was half empty. A few dignitaries, clerks, local hierarchs and archivists of the Planetary Chronicle. They looked drowsy to me and I knew their account of these proceedings would be at odds with the official log recorded by the pict-servitors. Hierarch Onnopel himself was already dozing. The fat idiot. If his grip on the spiritual fibre of his flock had been tighter, these hearings might not have been necessary.

I saw my ancient savant, Uber Aemos, apparently listening intently, though I knew his mind was far away. I saw Alizebeth Bequin, my dear friend and colleague, reading a copy of the court briefing. She looked stately and prim in her long dark gown and half-veil. As she pretended to turn the pages, I glimpsed the data-slate concealed inside its cover. Another volume of poetry, no doubt. The glimpse made me chuckle, and I hastened to stifle the sound.

'My lord? Is there a problem?' the pardoner asked, breaking off in mid-flow.

I waved a hand. 'None. Please continue, sir. And hasten to your summary, perhaps?'

The Minster at Eriale was only a few decades old, rebuilt from war rubble in a triumphant High Gothic style. As little as half a century before, this entire sub-sector – the Ophidian sub-sector – had been in the embrace of the arch-enemy. In fact, it had been my honour to witness the embarkation of the great Imperial taskforce that had liberated it. That had been on Gudrun, the former capital world of the Helican sub-sector, one hundred and fifty years previously. Sometimes I felt very old.

I had lived, by that time, for one hundred and eighty-eight years, so I was in early middle age by the standards of privileged Imperial society. Careful augmetic work and juvenat conditioning had retarded the natural deteriorations of my body and mind, and more significant artifice had repaired wounds and damage my career had cost me. I was robust, healthy and vigorous, but sometimes the sheer profusion of my memories reminded me how long I had been alive. Of course, I was but a youth compared to Aemos.

Sitting there, in a gilt lifter throne at the centre of the high table, dressed in the robes and regalia of a lord chief examiner, I reflected that I had perhaps been too hard on that duffer Onnopel. Any reconquered territory, taken back from the taint of the warp, would perforce be plagued by heresy for some time as Imperial law reinstated itself. Indeed, Ordos dedicated to the Ophidian sub-sector had yet to be founded, so jurisdiction lay with the neighbouring Officio Helican. An Examination such as this was timely. Fifty years of freedom and it was right for the Inquisition to move in and inspect the fabric of the new society. This was necessary tedium, I tried to remind myself, and Rorken had been correct in calling for it. The Ophidian sub-sector, thriving in its recovery, needed the Inquisition to check on its spiritual health just as this rebuilt Minster needed stonemasons to keep an eye on its integrity as it settled.

'My lord inquisitor?' Verveuk whispered to me. I looked up and realised Fen the pardoner had finished at last.

'Your duty is noted, pardoner. You may retire,' I said, scribing a mark on my slate. He bowed.

'I trust the accused has paid you in advance for your time,' said Inquisitor Koth archly. 'His assets may be sequestered, 'ere long.'

'I have been paid for my statement, sir,' confirmed Fen.

'Generously, it seems,' I observed. 'Was it by the word?'

My fellow inquisitors chuckled. Except Verveuk, who barked out a overloud whinny as if I had just made the finest jest this side of the Golden Throne. By the Throne, he was a sycophantic weasel! If ever a windpipe cried out for a brisk half-hitch, his was it.

At least his snorting had woken Onnopel up. The hierarch roused with a start and growled 'hear, hear!' with a faux-knowing nod of his many chinned head as if he had been listening intently all along. Then he went bright red and pretended to look for something under his pew.

'If there are no further comments from the Ministorum,' I said dryly, 'perhaps we can move on. Inquisitor Menderef?'

'Thank you, lord chief examiner,' said Menderef politely, rising to his feet.

The pardoner had scurried away, leaving Pridde alone in the open expanse of the wide floor. Pridde was in chains, but his fine garb with its lace trim seemed to discomfort him more than the shackles. Menderef walked around the high table to face him, turning the pages of a manuscript slowly.

He began his cross-examination.

Laslo Menderef was a slender man a century old. His thin brown hair was laquered up over his skull in a hard widow's peak and his face was sallow and taut-skinned. He wore a long, plain velvet robe of selpic blue with his rosette of office and the symbol of the Ordo Hereticus pinned at his breast.

He had a chilling manner that I admired, though I cared not at all for the man's radical philosophy. He was also the most articulate interrogator in Sakarof's officio. His long-fingered, agile hands found a place in the manuscript and stopped there.

'Udwin Pridde?' he said.

'Sir,' Pridde answered.

'On the 42nd day of 380.M41, you called upon the house of an unlicensed practitioner of apothecary in Clude and purchased two phials of umbilical blood, a hank of hair from the head of an executed murderer and a fertility doll carved from a human finger bone.'

'I did not, sir.'

'Oh,' said Menderef amiably, 'then I am mistaken.' He turned back and nodded to me. 'It appears we are done here, lord examiner,' he said. He paused just long enough for Pridde to sag with relief and then wheeled round again. Glory, but his technique was superb.

'You're a liar,' he said. Pridde recoiled, suddenly alert once more.

'S-sir–'

'The apothecary was executed for her practices by the Eriale Arbites in the winter of 382. She kept annotated records of her dealings which, I presume, she foolishly thought might serve as some kind of bargaining tool in the event of her apprehension. Your name is there. The matter of your purchases is there. Would you like to see it?'

'It is a fabrication, sir.'

'A fabrication... uhm...' Menderef paced slowly around the defendant. Pridde tried to keep his eyes on him but didn't dare turn from his spot. Once Menderef was behind him, Pridde started to shake.

'You've never been to Clude?'

'I go there sometimes, sir.'

'Sometimes?'

'Once, maybe twice every year.'

'For what purpose?'

'There is a feed merchant in Clude who–'

'Yes, there is. Aarn Wisse. We have spoken with him. Though he admits to knowing you and doing business with you, he says he never saw you at all in 380 or the year after. He has no receipt of purchase for you in his ledger.'

'He is mistaken, sir.'

'Is he? Or are you?'

'Sir?'

'Pridde... your pardoner has already taken up too much of the day extolling – and magnifying – your multiple virtues. Do not waste any more of our time. We know you visited the apothecary. We know what you purchased. Make us like you more by collaborating with this line of questioning.'

Pridde shuddered. In a small voice, he said, 'I did make those purchases, sir. Yes.'

'Louder, for the court, please. I see amber lights winking on the vox-recorders. They're not picking up your voice. The lights have to glow green, you see. Like they are now, hearing me. Green means they hear you.'

'Sir, I did make those purchases!'

Menderef nodded and looked back at his manuscript. 'Two phials of umbilical blood, a hank of hair from the head of an executed murderer and fertility doll carved from a human finger bone. Are those the purchases you mean?'

'Yes, sir...'

'Green lights, Pridde, green lights!'

'Yes, sir!'

Menderef closed the manuscript and stalked round in front of Pridde again. 'Would you like to explain why?'

Pridde looked at him and swallowed hard. 'For the stock.'

'The stock?'

'My breeding stock of cattle, sir.'

'Your cattle asked you to make these purchases?'

Koth and Verveuk laughed.

'No, no, sir... I had purchased fifty head of breeding stock from a farm in the South Uvege two years before. Cosican Red-flank. Do you know the breed, sir?'

Menderef looked back at us, playing to the gallery with raised eyebrows. Verveuk laughed again. 'I am not on first name terms with cattle, Pridde.'

'They're good stock, the best. Certificated by the Administratum Officio Agricultae. I was hoping to breed from them and establish a commercial herd for my combine.'

'I see. And?'

'They sickened, over winter. None would carry to term. The things they whelped were still-born... such things... I had to burn them. I asked the Ministorum for a blessing, but they refused. Said it was a failing in my stockmanship. I was desperate. I had sunk a lot of capital into the herd, sir. Then this apothecary told me...'

'Told you what?'

'That it was the warp. Said the warp was in the feed and the land, the very meadows. She said I could cure the trouble if I followed her guidance.'

'She suggested you used rural warpcraft to mend your ailing cattle?'

'She did.'

'And you thought that was a good idea?'

'As I said, I was desperate, sir.'

'I know you were. But it wasn't for the cattle, was it? Your wife had asked you to make the purchases, hadn't she?'

'No, sir!'

'Yes, sir! Your wife, of the Samargue bloodline, desperate to restore power and vigour to its ailing fortunes!'

'Y-yes...'

'Green light, Pridde!'

'Yes!'

From the documentation and my preparation, I already knew that House Samargue was the biggest game we were after on Durer. To his credit, Verveuk had suggested we begin with Pridde, a minor player, no more than an accomplice really, and use him as a lever to open up the noble family. On the basis of his testimony, the corruption of the ancient House would be easy to force out into the open.

Menderef continued his questioning for over an hour and, to tell the truth, it made for captivating theatre. When the Minster bell sounded nones, he cast a subtle glance at me to indicate there was no point pressing Pridde further for the time being. A break, with opportunity for the defendant to pace and worry, would serve us well for the day's second session.

'We will suspend the hearing for a brief term,' I declared. 'Bailiffs, conduct the accused to the cells. We will resume at the chime, an hour from now.'

I was hungry and stiff. Lunch offered a decent respite, even if I would have to tolerate Verveuk.

Bastian Verveuk was thirty-two standard years old and had been an inquisitor for seven months. He was a fresh-faced boy, he seemed to me, of medium height with a centre-parted bowl of heavy blond hair and slightly hooded, earnest eyes. He looked like he was yearning all the time. Yearning and swept up in some spiritual rapture.

He had a brilliantly ordered mind and had doubtlessly served Osma well as an interrogator. But now his hour had come and he was pushing up the ranks with immodest ambition. His transfer to Rorken's staff – for 'supplementary schooling' – had probably been the result of Osma losing patience with him. Osma was like that. Osma was still the same Osma who had plagued me fifty years before. Except that now he was set to inherit Orsini's role as Grand Master of the Inquisition, Helican sub-sector. Grand Master Orsini was dying and Osma was his chosen heir. It was just a matter of time.

Rorken was dying too, if the rumours were true. Soon, I would be friendless in the high ranks of the Ordos Helican.

Thanks to Rorken's infirmity, I had acquired Verveuk. He was simply a burden I had to carry. His manner, his yearning, his bright eagerness; his damned questions.

I stood in the Minster's warm sacristy, sipping wine and eating thick seedbread, smoked fish and a strong, waxy cheese locally produced in the Uvege. I was chatting with Rassi, a pale, quiet senior inquisitor from the Ordo Malleus who had become a firm friend in recent years despite his association with the caustic Osma.

'A month, you think, Gregor?'

'For this, Poul? Two, maybe three.'

He sighed, toying his fork around his plate, his silver-headed cane tucked under his arm to free his hands. 'Maybe six if they each bring a bloody pardoner, eh?'

We laughed. Koth slid past us to refill his glass and cast us a nod.

'Don't look now,' Rassi murmured, 'but your fan club is here.'

'Oh, crap. Don't leave me with him!' I hissed, but Rassi had already moved away. Verveuk slid up beside me. He was balancing a dish of game terrine, pickles and salted spry that he clearly had no intention of eating.

'It goes well, I think!' he started.

'Oh, very well.'

'Of course, you must have great experience of these sessions, so you know better than I. But a good start, would you not say?'

'Yes, a good start.'

'Pridde is the key, he'll turn the lock of House Samargue.'

'I'm quite sure of it.'

'Menderef's work was something, wasn't it? The cross-exam? So deft, so well-judged. The way he broke Pridde.'

'I – uh – expected no less.'

'Quite something, yes indeed.'

I felt I had to say something. 'Your choice of Pridde. As the first accused. Well judged, well... well, a good decision, anyway.'

He looked at me as if I was his one true love and I'd just promised to do something significant.

'Lord, I am truly honoured that you say so. I only did what I thought best. Really lord, to hear that from you, fills my heart with–'

'Stewed fish?' I asked, offering him the bowl.

'No, thank you, lord.'

'It's very good,' I said, slathering my bread with it. 'Though like so many fine things in life, you can quite quickly have too much of it.'

He didn't take the hint. The hint would most likely have to be embossed on the tip of a hi-ex bolter round and fired up his nose before he'd notice it.

'I feel, lord,' he said, setting his untouched dish aside, 'that I can learn so much from you. This is an opportunity that few of my status get.'

'I can't fathom why,' I said.

He smiled. 'I almost feel I should thank the miserable tumors eating at my Lord Rorken for this chance.'

'I feel I owe some sort of payback to them too,' I muttered.

'It's so rare that a – if I may say – veteran inquisitor such as yourself... a field inquisitor, I mean, not a desk-bound lord... participates in a process like this and mingles with lesser officers such as me. Lord Rorken has always spoken so highly of you. There is much I want to ask you, so many things. I have read up on all your works. The P'Glao Conspiracy, for example. I have reviewed that from end to end, and I have so many queries. And other matters–'

Here it comes, I thought.

And there it came.

'The daemonhosts. And Quixos. There is, oh, so much in that that demands the attention of a scholar such as myself. Can you give me personal insight? Perhaps not now... later... we could dine together and talk...'

'Well, perhaps.'

'The records are so incomplete – or rather, restricted. I yearn to know how you dealt with Prophaniti. And Cherubael.'

I was waiting for the name. Still, hearing it, I winced.

Cherubael. That's what they all asked. Every last neophyte inquisitor I met. That's what they all wanted to know. Damn their interest. It was over and done with.

Cherubael.

For one hundred and fifty years, the daemon had plagued my dreams and made each one a nightmare. For a century and a half, it had been in my head, a shadow at the horizon of sanity, a softly breathing shape in the dark recesses of my consciousness.

I had done with Cherubael. I had vanquished it.

But still the neophytes asked, and swirled up the memories again for me.

I would never tell them the truth. How could I?

'Lord?'

'I'm sorry, Verveuk, my mind wandered. What did you say?'

'I said, isn't that one of your men?'

Godwin Fischig, dressed in a long black coat, still powerful and imposing after all these years, had entered the sacristy by the rear door and was looking around for me.

I handed my plate and glass to the startled Verveuk and went directly across to him.

'I didn't expect to see you here,' I whispered, drawing him aside.

'Not really my thing, but you'll thank me for busting in.'

'What is it?'

'Paydirt, Gregor. You'll never guess in a hundred centuries who we've turned up.'

'Presuming we don't have a million years, Fischig, tell me.'

'Thuring,' he said. 'We've found Thuring.'

Vengeance, in my opinion, is never an adequate motive for an inquisitor's work. I had sworn to make Thuring pay for the death of my old friend Midas Betancore, of course, but the eighty years since Midas's murder had been filled to distraction with more weighty and more pressing cases. There had not been time or opportunity to spare the months – perhaps years – required to hunt Thuring down. He was... not worth the effort.

At least, that is what Lord Rorken always counselled me when I brought the matter up. Fayde Thuring. An inconsequential player in the shadow-world of heresy that lurks within Imperial society. A nothing who would run foul of justice soon enough all by himself. Undeserving of my attention. Not worth the effort.

Indeed, for a long time, I had believed him dead. My agents and informants had kept me appraised of his activities, and early in 352.M41 I had learned he had fallen in with an out-world fraternity of Chaos called the Hearthood, or sometimes the Chimes of the World Clock. They practised a stylised worship of the Blood God, in the form of a local tribe's minor swine-deity called Eolkit or Yulquet or Uulcet (the name differed in every source consulted) and for some months had plagued the crop-world Hasarna. Their cult-priest took the ceremonial guise of the swine-butcher or culler who, in older times, had travelled between the communities of Hasarna at the end of each autumn, slaughtering the livestock ready for the cold months. It was an old tradition, one that mixed ritual blood-letting with the dying of the calendar year, and is common throughout the Imperium. Pre-Imperial Terra had just such a myth once, called the Hallows, or the Eve of Hallowing.

The cult leader was Amel Sanx, the Corruptor of Lyx, reappearing for the first time after a century of hiding to spread his poisons. Sanx was so notorious a heretic that once it became known he was involved, the initial Inquisitorial efforts to prosecute the Hearthood multiplied a hundredfold and a kill-team of the Adepta Sororitas led by Inquisitor Aedelorn obliterated them in a raid on Hasarna's northern capital.

In the aftermath, it was discovered that Sanx had already sacrificed most of his minor followers as part of a ritual that Aedelorn's raid had interrupted. Thuring was one of his second tier of trusted acolytes in the Hearthood. His body was listed as amongst the ritual victims.

Midas's killer was dead. Or so I had thought until that moment in the sacristy of Eriale's Minster.

'Are you sure of this?'

Fischig looked at me with a shrug as if I should have trouble doubting his words.

'Where is he?'

'That's the part you've going to love. He's here.'

They had taken their places already in the main vault of the Minster by the time I joined them. House Samargue had brought out a militant advocate to answer for them and already he was strenuously trying to establish the fragility of Udwin Pridde's testimony.

I slammed my fist on the table to shut him up.

'Enough! This Examination is suspended!'

My fellow inquisitors swung round to look at me.

'It's what?' asked Menderef.

'Until further notice!' I added.

'But–' Koth began.

'Gregor–?' asked Rassi. 'What are you doing?'

'This is highly irregular–' Verveuk said.

'I know!' I told him, right into his face. He flinched.

'My lord chief examiner,' asked the Samargue's advocate, stepping towards the bench nervously, 'may I presume to ask when this hearing might recommence?'

'When I'm ready,' I snarled. 'When I'm good and ready.'

TWO

BETANCORE, BLOOD UP
FISCHIG'S BRIEFING
ARMING FOR BATTLE

It caused quite a stir. What am I saying? Of course it caused quite a stir. Crowds quickly gathered outside the Minster in the bright afternoon sunshine. The archivists and pamphleteers who had been dozing in the public gallery scampered off to promulgate the news. Even the confessors and preachers who had been wandering the streets, lambasting the commonfolk with bilious sermons against heresy, followed the crowds to the Minster square.

'You can't just suspend a Court of Examination!' Menderef raged at me. I shoved him aside and strode on down the long aisle towards the main doors of the Minster. Bequin and Fischig were in step with me, and Aemos scurried to catch up.

'You say "here", what do you mean?' I asked Fischig, dragging off my fur-trimmed cloak and my chain of office and tossing them onto a pew.

'Miquol,' he said. 'It's an island in the northern polar circle. About two hours' transit time.'

'Eisenhorn! Eisenhorn!' Menderef yelled behind me, a twitter of agitated voices around him.

'You sure it's him?'

'I've reviewed Godwin's findings,' snapped Bequin. 'It's Thuring, all right. I'd put money on it.'

We reached the end of the Minster's nave and were crossing towards the entrance arch and daylight. A hand caught my sleeve.

I turned. It was Rassi.

'What are you doing, Gregor? This is holy work you're abandoning.'

'I'm not abandoning anything, Poul. Didn't you hear me? I'm suspending it. This Examination is all about feeble little recidivists and their ungodly habits. I'm set on a true heretic.'

'Really?'

'Come along if you don't believe me.'

'Very well.'

As I pressed on through the great doorway, Rassi turned and intercepted Koth and Menderef. He shouted down their objections. 'I'm going with him,' I heard him say to them. 'I trust Eisenhorn's judgment. If he was wrong to break the court here, I'll testify to that when I return.'

We were out in the daylight. Mobs of civilians gazed at us, some shielding their eyes from the sun's glare where the blossom-heavy trees of the square failed to shade them.

'Medea?' I asked Fischig.

'Already called in. I presumed; I hope that's all right.'

'Does she know?'

Fischig glanced at Bequin and Aemos. 'Yes. I couldn't hide it from her.'

Almost on cue, Medea's voice crackled over my vox-link. 'Aegis descending, the Armour of God, by two,' she reported in Glossia code, her voice hard-edged and bitter.

'Damn it!' I said. 'Clear the square!'

Fischig and Bequin ran forward into the crowd. 'Clear the area!' Bequin yelled.

'Come on, move! Move now!' Fischig bellowed.

No one obeyed.

Fischig pulled out his handgun and fired into the air. Shrieking, the crowd surged back and streamed away down the approach streets.

Just in time.

My gun-cutter, all four hundred and fifty tonnes of it, swung in over the roof of the Eriale Municipal Library and descended on wailing thrusters into the Minster square. The downwash blew the blossom off the trees and filled with air with petals like confetti.

I felt the ground shake as the vessel set down hard. Flagstones cracked under the steel pads of the extended landing struts. Casements around the square shattered. The trees in the square billowed furiously in the outrush of the jets. The nose ramp whined open.

I hurried up the ramp with Aemos and Bequin, pausing to beckon Rassi aboard. Leaning on his cane, he walked more slowly than us. Fischig waited at the foot of the ramp, sternly ushering in the other members of my retinue who had been stationed in the vicinity of the Minster. Kara Swole, who had been monitoring the crowd from a caffeine house opposite the library. Duclane Haar, whose sniper-variant long-las had been tracking the traffic around the Minster's main door from the roof of the Administratum's tithe barn. Bex Begundi, who had been posing as a homeless mutant begging for alms in the porch of Saint Becwal's Chapel, his pistols concealed under his pauper's bowl.

Fischig pulled them all in and then ran up the ramp, hauling on the lever that slammed the ramp shut.

Almost immediately, the gun-cutter rose again, puffing out a cloud of blossom.

In the entry bay, I took a quick head count.

'Verveuk! What are you doing here?'

'As my Lord Rorken instructed,' he said, 'I go where you go, lord.'

We gained altitude, climbing into the stratosphere for the transit north. My own people knew their places and tasks, but I pulled Kara Swole aside and told her to make sure Rassi and Verveuk were comfortable. 'Inquisitor

Rassi deserves every courtesy, but don't give Verveuk a millimetre. Don't let him get in the way.'

Kara Swole was a well-muscled acrobat-dancer from Bonaventure who had assisted one of my investigations three years before and had enjoyed the experience so much she'd asked to join my retinue permanently. She was small and lithe, with very short red hair, and her muscular frame made her look almost stocky, but she was nimbler and more agile than just about anyone I had ever met and had a genuine flair for surveillance. She'd become a valued member of my team and she'd told me more than once that the employment I offered her was infinitely preferable to her previous life in the circus arenas of her homeworld.

Kara glanced in Verveuk's direction. 'He looks like a ninker to me,' she murmured. 'Ninker' was her insult of choice, a slang term from the circus creole. I'd never had the heart to ask her what it meant.

'I believe you're right about that,' I whispered back. 'Keep an eye on him... and make sure Rassi's happy. When we get to the destination, I want you and Haar guarding them with your lives.'

'Understood.'

I gathered Fischig, Bequin, Aemos, Haar and Begundi around the chart table for a briefing, and also summoned Dahault, my astropath.

'All right... how did you find him?'

Fischig smiled. He was obviously pleased with himself. 'The audit turned him up. At least, it turned up some appetising clues that made me look harder and find him. He'd been operating in three of the northern seaports, and also in the capital. I couldn't believe it at first. I mean, we thought he was dead. But it's him.'

An audit was part of my standard operating practice, and I'd set one going the moment Lord Rorken prevailed on me to conduct the Examination, four months earlier. Under Fischig's leadership, a large part of my support staff – over thirty specialists – had gone ahead to Durer to carry it out. The purpose of an audit was twofold. First, to review and recheck the cases to be presented for Examination to make sure we weren't wasting our time and that we were in possession of all the relevant data. It wasn't that I didn't trust Lord Rorken's preparation, I just like to be certain about what I'm prosecuting. Secondly, it was to investigate the possible existence of heretical cases that might have been overlooked by the Examination. I was going to be devoting a lot of my time and resources to this clean up of Durer, and I wanted to make sure I was being thorough. If there was other recidivism here, I wanted to root it out at the same time.

Fischig and the audit team had made a virtual fingertip search of the planetary records, cross-checking even minor anomalies against my database. It proved that Rorken's preparatory work had been excellent, for very little turned up.

Except Fayde Thuring. Fischig had first discovered some off-world financial transactions that flagged because they linked to merchant accounts on Thracian Primaris that Thuring had been associated with twenty years earlier. Fischig had backtracked painstakingly through shipping registers and accommodation listings and had lucked upon some footage recorded by a mercantile company's security pict. The man captured digitally by the pict-recorder bore a striking similarity to Fayde Thuring.

'As far as we can make out,' said Fischig, 'Thuring's been on Durer for about a year. Arrived aboard a free trader last summer and took up residence in Haynstown on an eighteen month merchant's visa. Uses the name Illiam Vowis and claims to be a dealer in aeronautical engineering. Not short of cash or connections. Most of the business seems legit, though he's been buying up a lot of machine parts and tooling units and hiring on a fair number of local tech-adepts. From the outside, it looks like he's setting up a repair and servicing outfit. What he's actually doing is not yet clear.'

'Has he purchased or rented any workspace property?' asked Begundi.

'No. That's one of the discrepancies.' Fischig looked up at me. 'He keeps moving around. Difficult to track. But four days ago, I got a good lead that he was in the northern seaport, Finyard. So I sent Nayl to get a proper look.'

Harlon Nayl, a long serving member of my cadre and an ex-bounty hunter, was one of my finest. 'What did he find?'

'He was too late to catch Thuring. He'd already gone, but Nayl got into the hotel suite he had been using before their housekeeping could clean it up, and got enough hair and tissue fibres to run a gene-scan against the samples we hold on file. Perfect match. Illiam Vowis is Fayde Thuring.'

'And you say he's now on a polar island?'

Fischig nodded. 'Nayl took off after Thuring, found out he had arranged passage to this place Miquol. Used to be a PDF listening station there, years ago, but it's uninhabited now. We don't know what he's doing there, or even if he's been there before. Nayl should have reached the island himself by now. He hasn't checked in, but the magnetosphere is wild as hell up near the pole, so comms are out. Long-range, anyway.'

'This is excellent work, old friend,' I told Fischig, and he smiled appreciatively. Godwin Fischig, once a chastener in the Arbites of Hubris and a law enforcer of considerable ability, was one of my real veterans. He'd served at my side for fifteen decades now, for as long as Alizebeth Bequin. Only Aemos had been with me longer. The three of them were my rock, my foundation, the cornerstones of my entire operation. And they were my friends. Aemos provided wisdom and an unimaginably vast resource of knowledge. Bequin was an untouchable, and ran an academy of similarly gifted individuals called the Distaff. They were my greatest weapon, a corps of psychically blank individuals who could be used to block even the most powerful psykers. Bequin was also my emotional rudder. I confided in her more than the others and looked to her for support when I was troubled.

Fischig was my conscience. He was an imposing man with an age-grizzled face that was now quite jowly. A thin down of grey hair covered his scalp where once he had been blond. The scar under his milky eye had gone pink and glossy over time. Fischig was a formidable warrior and had gone through some of the worst times at my side. But there was none more single-minded than he, none so pure... puritanical, if you will. Good and evil, Law and Chaos, humanity and the warp... they were simple, black and white distinctions for him. I admired that so. Time, experience and incident had greyed my attitudes somewhat. I depended on Fischig to be my moral compass.

It was a role he seemed happy to perform. I think that's why he had stayed with me so long, when by now he could have become a commissioner of Arbites, a divisional prefect, maybe even a planetary governor. Being the conscience of one of the sub-sector's most senior inquisitors was a calling that gave him satisfaction.

I wondered sometimes if Fischig regretted the fact that I had never sought higher office in the Inquisition. I suppose, given my track record and reputation, I could have become the lord of an Ordo by now, or at least been well on my way. Lord Rorken, who had become something of a mentor to me, had often expressed his disappointment that I had not taken up the opportunities he had offered to become his heir. He had been grooming me for a while as successor to the control of the Ordo Xenos, Helican sub. But I had never fancied that kind of life. I was happiest in the field, not behind a desk.

Of all of them, Fischig would have benefitted most if I had followed that kind of course. I could well imagine him as the commander-in-chief of the Inquisitorial Guard Helican. But he had never expressed any hint of unhappiness in that regard. Like me, he liked the challenge of field work.

We made a good team, for a long time. I'll never forget that, and despite what fate was to bring, I'll always thank the God-Emperor of mankind for the honour of working alongside him for as long as I did.

'Aemos,' I said, 'perhaps you'd like to review Fischig's data and see if you can make any further deductions. I'm interested in this island. Punch up the data, maps, archives. Tell me what you find.'

'Of course, Gregor,' Aemos said. His voice was very thin and reedy, and he was more hunched and wizened than ever. But knowledge still absorbed him, and I think it nourished him in the way that food or wealth or duty or even love kept other men going way past their prime.

'Fischig will assist you,' I said. 'And perhaps Inquisitor Rassi too. I want a workable plan of operations in–' I checked my chronometer '–sixty minutes. I need to know everything it is possible or pertinent to know before we hit the ground. And I want a positive, uncomplicated plan of what we do when we get there. Alizebeth?'

'Gregor?'

'Get in contact with as many of our specialists here on Durer as you can find and get them moving in to support us. Distaff especially. I don't care how long it takes or what it costs. I want to know we have solid backup following us.'

She nodded graciously. She was a brilliant man-manager. Bequin was still as demure and beautiful as the day I had met her, a century and a half before, a spectacular testament of the way Imperial science can counter the effects of aging. Only the faintest creases in the corners of her eyes and lips betrayed the fact that she was not a stunning woman in her late thirties. Lately, she had taken to walking rather regally with a shoulder-high ebony cane for support, claiming that her bones were old, but I believed that to be an affectation designed to reinforce her very senior and matriarchal role.

Only when I looked into her eyes could I see the distances of age. Her life had been hard and she had witnessed many terrible things. There was a sort of wistful pain in the depths of her gaze, a profound sadness. I knew she loved me, and I loved her as much as any being I had ever known. But long ago, mutually, we had set that aside. I was a psyker and she was an untouchable. Whatever the sadness we both felt because of our denied love, being together would have been so much more agonising.

'Dahault...'

'Sir?' the astropath answered smartly. He had been with me for twenty years, by far the longest stretch any astropath had managed in my employ. They wear out so quickly, in my experience. Dahault was a vital, burly man with a spectacular waxed moustache that I believe he grew to compensate for his shaved head. He was certainly powerful and able, and had taken to my regime of work well. Only in the past few years had he started to show the signs of psychic exhaustion – the shallow, drawn skin, the hunted look, the aphasia. I dearly hoped I would be able to retire him on a pension before his calling burned out his mind.

'Check ahead,' I told him. 'Fischig says the magnetosphere is blocking vox traffic, but Thuring may be using astropaths. See what you hear.'

He nodded and shuffled away to his compact, screened cabin under the bridge to connect his skull-plugs to the astro-communication network.

I turned last to Bex Begundi and Duclane Haar. Haar was an ex-Imperial Guard marksman from the 50th Gudrunite Rifles, a regiment I had an old association with. Of medium build, he wore a matt anti-flect bodyglove, the cap-pin of his old outfit dangling round his neck on a cord. He had lost a leg in action on Wichard, and been invalided out of service. But he was as good a shot with the sniper-variant long-las as Duj Husmaan, now long gone and in a manner I sorely regretted.

Haar was clean shaven and his brown hair was as neatly trimmed as it had been in the days of parade ground drill. He wore an optic target enhancer that clamped around the side of his skull, looping over his ear, and could drop the articulate arm of the foresight down over his right eye for aiming. He preferred the enhancer to a conventional rifle-mounted scope, and with his tally of clean hits, I wasn't about to argue.

Bex Begundi was a rogue, in the strictest sense of the term. A desperado, old Commodus Voke would have called him. An outlaw, scammer, con-artist and low-life, born in the slums of Sameter, a world I had no love for as I'd once left a hand there. He was one of Harlon Nayl's recruits – possibly one of his intended bounties who had been offered a life or death choice – and had joined my team six years before. Begundi was unspeakably cocky and prodigiously skilled with handguns.

Tall, no more than thirty-five years old, he was not exactly handsome but oozed a devastating charisma. He was dark haired, a jet-black goatee perfectly trimmed around his petulant smile, with hard cheekbones, and corpse-white skin dye contrasting with the wipes of black kohl under his dangerously twinkling eyes, as was the gang-custom of the slums. He was dressed in a leather armour body jacket embroidered with rich silk thread and preposterous panels of sequins. But there was nothing remotely comical about the paired Hecuter autopistols holstered under his arms in a custom-made, easy-draw rig.

'We're in for a fight when we get down, make no mistake,' I told them.

'Rockin' good news,' said Begundi with a hungry smile.

'Just point me at the target, sir,' said Haar.

I nodded, pleased. 'No showboating, you hear me? No grandstanding.'

Begundi looked hurt. 'As if!' he complained.

'Actually, I was thinking of you, Haar,' I replied. Haar blushed. He had proved to be extremely... eager. A killer's instinct.

'You can trust me, sir,' he said.

'This is important. I know it's always important, but this is... personal. No screw ups.'

'We're after the guy who popped Dee's dad, right?' asked Begundi.

Dee. That's what they called Medea Betancore, my pilot.

'Yes, we are. For her sake, stay alert.'

I went up into the cockpit. The high-altitude cloudscape was sliding past outside. Medea was flying like a daemon.

She was just over seventy-five years old, just a youngster still. Stunning, volatile, brilliant, sexy, she had inherited her late father's pilot skills as surely as she had inherited his dark Glavian skin and fine looks.

She was wearing Midas's cerise flying jacket.

'You need to stay focused, Medea,' I said.

'I will,' she replied, not looking up from the controls.

'I mean it. This is just a job.'

'I know. I'm fine.'

'If you need to stand down, it can be arranged.'

'Stand down?' She snapped the words and looked round at me sharply, her large, brown eyes wet with angry tears. 'This is my father's killer we're going for! All my life I've waited for this! Literally! I'm not going to stand down, boss!'

She had never known her father. Fayde Thuring had murdered Midas Betancore a month before her birth.

'Fine. I want you with me. I'd like you with me. But I will not allow emotion to cloud this.'

'It won't.'

'I'm glad to hear it.'

There was a long silence. I turned to go.

'Gregor?' she said softly.

'Yes, Medea?'

'Kill the bastard. Please.'

In my cabin, I made my preparations. The soft robes I had been wearing as lord chief examiner went in favour of an armoured bodyglove, steel-reinforced knee boots, a leather jacket and a heavy storm coat with armoured shoulder panels. I pinned my badges of office on my chest, my Inquisitorial rosette at my throat.

I selected my three primary weapons from the safe: a large calibre bolt pistol, the runestaff handmade for me by Magos Bure of the Adeptus Mechanicus, and the curved, pentagram-engraved force sword that I had commissioned to be forged from the broken half of the Carthaen warblade, Barbarisater.

I blessed each one.

I thought of Midas Betancore, dead nearly a century now. Barbarisater purred in my hands.

THREE

MIQUOL
DURER PDF LISTENING STATION 272
THE TURNABOUT

Miquol was a vast volcanic slab jutting from the black waters of the polar ocean, sixteen kilometres long and nine wide. From the air, it looked bleak and lifeless. Sheer cliffs a hundred metres high edged its shape but its interior was a ragged desert of crags and rock litter.

'Life signs?' I asked.

Medea shrugged. We weren't picking anything up, but it was obvious from the jumping, hiccuping displays that the magnetics were playing hell with our instruments.

'Shall I set down topside?' she asked.

'Maybe,' I said. 'Bring us around for another pass to the south first.'

We banked. Cloud cover was low, and banks of chill fog swathed the island's gloomy sprawl.

Fischig joined us in the cockpit.

'You said there was an old facility here?' I said.

He nodded. 'A listening station, used by the Planetary Defence Force in the early years after the liberation. Been out of use for a couple of decades now. It's high up in the interior. I've got a chart-ref.'

'What's that?' Medea asked, pointing down at the southern cliffs. Down below, we could make out some derelict jetties, landing docks and prehab sheds clustered on a sea-level crag at the foot of the cliff. Some kind of vertical trackway, a row of rusting pylons, ran from the back of some of the larger sheds up the face of the cliff.

'That's the landing facility,' said Fischig. 'Used to serve the island when there were still PDF staffers stationed here.'

'There's a sea-craft down there,' I said. 'Fairly large.'

I looked across at Medea. 'Put down there. The crag there beside the sheds. The cliffs will keep the cutter out of sight too.'

It was bitingly cold, and the air was dank with fog and sea-spray. Aemos and Dahault stayed with Medea aboard the cutter and the rest of us ventured out. On the ramp, I turned to Verveuk. 'You stay aboard too, Bastian.'

He looked dismayed. That damned yearning look again.

'I'd like to feel I have someone I can count on watching the cutter,' I lied smoothly.

His expression changed immediately: pride, self-importance.

'But of course, lord!'

We crossed the crag in the lee of the high cliffs towards the prefabs. They were old-pattern Imperial modulars, shipped in and bolted together. Time and weather had much decayed them. Windows were boarded and the fibre-ply walls were rotten and patched. Rain and spray had scrubbed away most of the surface paint and varnish, but in places you could just make out the faded crest of the Durer PDF.

Haar and Fischig led the way. Haar had his long-las raised to his shoulder, his fore-sight dropped into place, hunting for targets as he paced forward. Fischig carried a las-rifle in one hand. A motion tracker unit was buckled over his left shoulder, whirring and ticking as it subjected Fischig's immediate vicinity to invisible waves of vigilance. Rassi and I were close behind them, with Alizebeth, Kara and Begundi at the rear.

Fischig pointed to the vertical trackway we had seen from the air. 'Looks like a cable-carriage or a funicular railway. Runs up to the cliff top.'

'Functional?' Rassi inquired.

'I doubt it, sir,' said Fischig. 'It's old and hasn't been maintained. I don't like the look of those cables.' The main lifting lines were heavy-gauge hawsers, but they swung slackly in the wind between the pylons and showed signs of fraying. 'There are stairs, though,' Fischig added. 'Right up the cliff alongside the track.'

We crossed to the jetties. They too were badly decayed. Rusting chains slapped and clanked with the sea-swell. The craft moored there was a modern, ocean-going ekranoplane, twenty metres long and sleekly grey. Stencils on the hull told us it was a licensed charter vessel from Finyard, presumably the vessel Thuring had hired to bring him here.

There was no sign of crew, and the hatches were locked down. There wasn't even a hint of standby automation.

'Want me to force entry?' asked Kara.

'Maybe–' I was interrupted by a shout from Haar. He was standing in the entrance of the nearest prefab, a docking shed that stood over the water on stilt legs. Haar gestured inside as I joined him. In the half-light, I could see four bodies slumped on the duckboards of the dry well. Fischig was kneeling beside them.

'Local mariners. Their papers are still in their pockets. Registered operators from Finyard.'

'Dead how long?'

Fischig shrugged. 'Maybe a day? Single shot to the back of the head in each case.'

'The crew from the sea-craft.'

He rose. 'Makes sense to me.'

'Why didn't they dump the bodies at sea?' Haar wondered.

'Because an ekranoplane is a specialist vehicle and they needed the crew alive to get them here,' I suggested.

'But if they killed them once they were here–' Haar began.

I was way ahead of him. 'Then they're not planning on leaving the island. Not the way they arrived, at any rate.'

I had Kara Swole break into the ekranoplane. There was nothing useful inside, just a few items of equipment and personal clutter belonging to the murdered crew. The passengers had taken everything else with them.

The only thing we learned was that Thuring might have as many as twenty men with him on Miquol, given the ekranoplane's load capacity and the number of emergency life jackets.

'They've gone inland,' I decided. 'And that's where we're going too.'

'Shall I get Dee to fire up the cutter?' Begundi asked.

'No,' I said. 'We'll go in on foot. I want to get as close to Thuring as possible before he makes us. We can call in the cutter if we need it.'

'Medea won't like that, Gregor,' said Bequin.

I knew that damn well.

I believed Medea deserved every chance to avenge her father. Vengeance might not be an appropriate motive for an inquisitor, but as far as I was concerned it was perfectly fine for a headstrong, passionate combat-pilot.

However, her passion could become a liability. I wanted Thuring taken cleanly and I didn't relish the prospect of Medea going off in a blind fury.

Bequin was right, though. Medea really didn't like it.

'I'm coming!'

'No.'

'I'm coming with you!'

'No!' I caught her by the arms and stared into her face. 'You are not. Not yet.'

'Gregor!' she wailed.

'Listen! Think about this logic–'

'Logically? That bastard killed my father an–'

'Listen! I don't want the cutter giving us away too early. That means leaving it here. But I do want the cutter ready to respond at a moment's notice, and that means you have to stay here on standby! Medea, you're the only one who can fly it!'

She shook off my grip and turned away, gazing at the rolling surge of the ocean.

'Medea?'

'Okay. But I want to be there when–'

'You will. I promise.'

'You swear it?'

'I swear it.'

Slowly, she turned look at me. Her eyes were still bright with hurt. 'Swear it on your secrets,' she said.

'What?'

'Do it the Glavian way. Swear it on your secrets.'

I remembered this now. The Glavian custom. They considered an oath most binding if it was sworn against private, personal secrets. In the old days, I suppose, that meant one Glavian pilot swearing to exchange valuable technical or navigational secrets with another as an act of faith and honour. Midas had made me do it once, years before. He'd made me swear to a three-month sabbatical at a time when I was working too hard. It hadn't been possible, because of one case or another, and I'd ended up having to tell him that I adored Alizebeth and wished with every scrap of my being that we could be together.

That was the deepest, darkest secret I had been carrying at the time. How things change.

'I swear it on my secrets,' I told her.

'On your gravest secret.'

'On my gravest secret.'

She spat on the ground and then quickly licked her palm and held out her hand. I mirrored her gestures and clasped her hand.

We left her with Aemos, Dahault and Verveuk at the gun-cutter and made our way up the cliff stairs.

It was raining by the time we reached the top, and the last few flights were treacherously wet. Salty wind flapped in from the sea, gusting into our coats and clothes.

I was worried about Poul Rassi. Though he didn't look it, he was over a century older than me, and the climb left him pale and breathless. He was relying on his cane more than before.

'I'm all right,' he said. 'Don't fuss.'

'Are you sure, Poul?'

He smiled. 'I've been in the courts and privy chambers for too many of the last few years, Gregor. This is almost an adventure. I'd forgotten how much I liked this.' Rassi raised his cane and flourished it ahead of us like a sabre. 'Shall we?'

We advanced into the hinterland of Miquol. Fischig had an auspex locked off on the old PDF base, so we headed for that as a place to start.

The sky was the luminous, hazy white of a blown valve-screen. Stripes of fog clung to the ground like walls of smoke. The rain was constant. The landscape was a mix of jagged upthrust outcrops and steep, shadowy valleys littered with scree. Boulders were scattered all around, some the size of skulls, some the size of battle tanks. The rock was dark, almost the colour of anthracite, and occasionally it was splintered out in cascades of volcanic glass. A forbidding, grey place. A monochrome world.

After two hours, we passed a rust-eaten tower of girders capped by sagging, corroded alloy petals that had once been a communications dish. One of the peripheral receivers of the listening station.

'We're close,' said Fischig, consulting his auspex. 'The PDF base is over the next headland.'

Durer PDF listening station 272 had been established shortly after the planet's liberation by the newly formed Planetary Defence Force as part of a global overwatch program. Through it, and around three hundred facilities like it, the Durer PDF had been able to maintain a round-the-clock watch of orbital traffic, local shipping lane activity and even general warp space movements, providing the planet with an early warning network and gathering vital tactical intelligence for this part of the sub-sector in general. Over a period of twenty years following the annexation of the territory, the network had gradually been run down, eventually supplanted by a string of scanner beacons in high orbit and a slaved sub-net of sensor buoys seeded throughout the Durer system.

The PDF had finally vacated the obsolete station some three decades before, undoubtedly grateful that they would never have to tolerate a tour of duty on this harsh rock again.

The station lay on the shore of a long polar lake, framed by ragged infant mountains to the north. It was an exposed place, bitten by the sub-zero winds. The lake, smudged with mist, was a flat, gleaming mirror of oil-dark water, its glassy surface occasionally disturbed by a flurry of wind ripples.

On the grey shore there were eighteen longhouses arranged in a grid around a drum-like generator building, a hangar large enough to shelter several troop carriers or orbital interceptors, a cluster of store barns, a number of machine shops, a small Ecclesiarchy chapel, a central command post with adjoining modules arranged in a radial hub and the main dish array.

All of it had succumbed to the feral ministry of the environment. The modules and prefabs were aged and dilapidated, windows covered with boards. The roadways between the prefabs were littered with rusting trash: old fuel drums, the carcasses of trucks, piles of flaking storm shutters. The vast main dish, angled towards the west, was a skeleton of its former self, just a hemisphere described by bare girders and dangling struts. In the black mirror of the lake, its reflection seemed like that of a giant, bleached ribcage. But it looked to me more like the ruins of an orrery, just the shattered remains of the central solar ball, permanently peering in the direction it had last been turned.

Hugging cover, we made our way onto the cold shore and crossed the short distance to the nearest longhouse. We all had weapons drawn by now, except Begundi. Fischig's auspex and motion tracker both indicated life-signs close by, but how close they weren't telling. Thanks to the damn magnetic interference we were forewarned but as good as blind.

We were non-verbal by now. I gestured and sent Haar ahead down the left side of the street, Fischig down the right. I'd have liked to deploy Kara too, but she was keeping to my orders and sticking close to Rassi, her assault weapon tight in her gloved hands. Rassi, his sombre, fur-trimmed robes flapping in the wind, had produced a multi-barrel pepperpot handgun of exotic manufacture.

Bequin hung back from me so that her psychic deadness wouldn't conflict with my mind. For the trek across Miquol she had changed her formal gown for a quilted body suit and stout boots, with a hooded cloak of dark green, embroidered velvet wrapped around her. I noticed she had also left her long walking cane aboard the cutter. She had drawn a slim, long-nosed micro-las that I had given her on her hundred and fiftieth birthday. It had pearl-inlaid grips and was a custom masterpiece, an antique made by Magos Nwel of Gehenna.

The pistol suited her. It was slender and elegant and devastatingly potent.

Up ahead, I saw Fischig signal to Haar. Haar knelt down and gave the big man some cover as he crossed to the back door of the next longhouse. I sent Begundi forward in support. Begundi still hadn't drawn his hand cannons from their shoulder rig, and ran with an easy, loping gait.

Once Begundi had reached him, Fischig slipped inside the longhouse. There was a pause, and then Begundi went in too.

We waited.

Begundi appeared in the doorway and beckoned to us.

It was good to be out of the damp, though the dark, rot-stinking interior of the old prefab barrack wasn't much better. We got inside, and Haar and Kara stood guard at the doorway, with Begundi covering the front.

Fischig had found something.

Fischig had found someone.

It was an old man. Filthy, wizened, lice-ridden and diseased. He cowered in the corner, whining each time the beam of Fischig's hand-lamp probed at him. If I'd passed him on the streets of Eriale, I'd have taken him for a beggar and not given him a second look. Out here, though, it was different.

'Give me the lamp,' I said. The old man, who seemed more animal than human, shrank back as I turned the hard white light on him. He was caked in filth, starving and gripped by fear.

But despite the dirt, I could recognise his robes.

'Father? Father hierarch?'

He moaned.

'Father, we're friends.' I unclasped my rosette and held it out to show him. 'I am Inquisitor Gregor Eisenhorn, Ordo Xenos Helican. We are here in an official capacity. Don't be afraid.'

He looked at me, blinking and slowly reached out a dirt-blackened hand towards the rosette. I let him take it. He looked at it for a long time, his hands trembling. Then he started to weep.

I waved Fischig and the others back and knelt down beside him.

'What's your name?'

'D-Dronicus.'

'Dronicus?'

'Pater Hershel Dronicus, hierarch of the parish of Miquol, blessed be the God-Emperor of Mankind.'

'The God-Emperor protects us all,' I answered. 'Can you tell me how you come to be here, father?'

'I've always been here,' he replied. 'The soldiers may have gone, but while there is a chapel here, there is a parish, and so long as there is a parish then there is a priest.'

By the Golden Throne, this old fellow had lived here alone for thirty years, maintaining the chapel.

'They never deconsecrated the ground?'

'No, sir. And I am thankful. My duty to the parish has given me time to think.'

'Go mad, more like,' Haar muttered.

'Enough!' I snapped over my shoulder.

'Let me see if I understand this right,' I said to Dronicus. 'You served here as a priest and when the PDF abandoned the site, you stayed on and looked after the chapel?'

'Yes, sir, that is the sum of it.'

'What did you live on?' asked Fischig. That detective brain, looking for holes in the story.

'Fish,' he said. From his astonishingly foul breath, I believed that.

'Fish... I went down to the landing point once a week and fished, smoking and storing the catch in the hangar. Besides, the soldiers left a lot of canned produce. Why? Are you hungry?'

'No,' said Fischig, unprepared for the generosity of the question.

'Why are you hiding in here?' Bequin asked softly.

Dronicus looked at me as if needing my permission to answer.

'Go ahead,' I nodded.

'They drove me out,' he said. 'Out of my hangar. They were mean. They tried to kill me, but I can run, you know!'

'I have no doubt.'

'Why did they drive you out?' Fischig asked.

'They wanted the hangar. I think they wanted my fish.'

'I'm sure they did. Smoked fish, that's worth something out here. But they wanted something else, didn't they?'

He nodded, a bleak look on his face. 'They wanted the space.'

'What for?'

'For their work.'

'What work?'

'They are mending their god.'

I glanced sidelong at Fischig.

'Their god? What god is that?'

'Not mine, that's for sure!' Dronicus exclaimed. Then he suddenly looked reflective. 'But it's a god, nevertheless.'

'Why do you say that?' I asked.

'It's big. Gods are big. Aren't they?'

'Usually.'

'You said "they",' said Rassi, crouching down next to me. 'Who do you mean? How many of them are there?'

Rassi's tone was admirably calm and reassuring, and I could feel the gentle bow-wake of the psychic influence he was cautiously bringing to bear. No wonder he had such a great reputation. I almost felt stupid for not asking such obvious questions.

'The god-smiths,' the old priest replied. 'I do not know their names. There are nine of them. And also the other nine. And the fourteen others. And the other five.'

'Thirty-seven?' breathed Fischig.

Dronicus screwed up his face. 'Oh, there's a lot more than that. Nine and nine and fourteen and five and ten and three and sixteen...'

Rassi looked at me. 'Dementia,' he whispered. 'He's able to account for them only in the groups he's seen them. He's not capable of identifying a whole. They are just numbers of people that he's seen at various times.'

'I'm not stupid,' cut in Dronicus simply.

'I never said you were, father,' Rassi replied.

'I'm not mad either.'

'Of course.'

The old man smiled and nodded and then, very directly, asked, 'Do you have any fish?'

'Boss!' Haar hissed suddenly. I rose quickly.

'What is it?'

'Movement... thirty metres...' His fore-sight was twitching as it downloaded the data. He knelt in the doorway and eased his rifle up to a firing position.

'What do you see?'

'Trouble. Eight men, armed, moving like an infantry formation. Coming this way.'

'We must have tripped something on the way in,' said Begundi.

'I don't want a fight. Not yet.' I looked at the others. 'Let's exit that way and regroup.'

'We have to take him,' said Rassi, indicating the old priest.

'Agreed. Let's go.'

Begundi opened the far door of the hut and led the way out. Bequin followed him, then Fischig. Rassi reached out to help the old priest up.

'Come on, father,' he said.

Seeing the hand coming for him, Dronicus yelped.

'Shit! We're rumbled!' said Haar. 'They're coming!'

Las-fire, bright and furious, suddenly hammered at the doorway and blew holes through the rotten fibre-ply.

Kara dived down for cover. Haar kept his place and I heard his long-las crack.

'One down,' he said.

Rassi and I hauled the old priest to his feet and bundled him towards the back exit. Behind us, the long-las cracked again, and was joined by the chatter of Kara Swole's assault weapon. Return fire hammered into the side of the longhouse, perforating the wall.

'Get him out,' I told Rassi and ran to the door.

Standing over Kara as she fired, I shot several bolt rounds through the gaping window. Las-shots seared down the street and burst against the side of the hut. I got a glimpse of figures in bulky grey combat fatigues scurrying closer and pausing to unload their lasrifles in our direction.

A sudden thought, true and clear, lanced into my brain. I grabbed Kara and Haar. 'Move!' I howled.

We had made it to the rear door when the grenade took the front off the hut. The entire doorway area where Haar had been crouching erupted in a flash of flame and shredded fibre-ply.

The blast-rush blew us out into the street.

Fischig hauled me up.

'Go! Go!'

Kara was bleeding from a shrapnel wound on her temple and Haar was dazed. But we ran, dragging them with us, up the muddy roadway towards the main dish.

Three men in insulated combat armour raced into the street ahead of us, raising lasrifles.

Begundi's Hecuter pistols were in his hands faster than any of us could raise the weapons we already held. He blazed out twin streams of shots, the shell cases spraying out from the slide-slots of his weapons. All three men ahead of us lurched back and sprawled.

Begundi ran ahead, chopping down another two as they emerged, his handguns roaring. Then he dropped suddenly onto his back, rolled round and blasted another assailant off the roof where he had suddenly appeared.

Five more loomed behind us, breaking out of the rear door we had escaped through.

Fischig and Kara turned, firing. They dropped three of them. Bequin brought down the fourth with a single well-placed head-shot. A round from my bolt pistol knocked the fifth five metres back down the road.

'Thorn? Desiring Aegis? Pattern oath?' my vox suddenly squawked. Medea was monitoring the activity over the vox-link.

'Negative! Thorn wishes Aegis repose under wing!' I replied, using Glossia, the informal private code I shared with my staff.

'Aegis stirred. The flower of blood.'

'Aegis repose, by the thrice ignited. As a statue, to the end of Earth.'

'Gregor! Let me come!'

'No, Medea! No!'

We were in a serious firefight now. Las-shots and hard rounds whipped in all directions. Fischig and Haar laid down heavy cover fire. Kara and Bequin selected targets more particularly and hit most of them. Begundi blazed away with his matched handguns. I fired carefully, cautiously, keeping the old priest behind me. Rassi's fission-lock pepperpot banged and sparked and hailed lead balls at the enemy. Every few seconds, he raised his cane and sent forth a drizzle of psycho-thermic flame from the silver tip.

'Brace yourselves,' I yelled. 'You especially, Poul.'

He nodded.

Reveal yourselves! I urged, using the will at full force.

Such a raw outburst would usually have floored all those around me, but Haar, Begundi and Kara had all been mentally conditioned during rigorous training to black out my psy-streams. Bequin was untouchable and Fischig wore a torc that protected him.

Rassi, forewarned, put up a mental wall. The old priest screamed, stood up and wet himself.

He wasn't the only one to stand up. Our attackers rose into view, each one clutching a smoking weapon, each one blinking in dumb confusion.

Begundi, Fischig and I cut them all down in a few, lethal seconds.

Victory.

For a moment.

Suddenly, Dronicus was running away down the street and Rassi was doubled up by convulsions. I felt it too. A sudden jolt in the background psionic resonance. Like a painfully bright flash of light.

I staggered back and slammed into the side of the nearest hut. Blood spurted out of my nose. Begundi and Kara fell to their knees. Haar sat down hard, sobbing. Even Fischig, protected by his torc, felt it and staggered.

Alizebeth, the only one unmoved, glanced around at us and yelled, 'What? What is it?'

I knew where it had come from. The hangar. I struggled upright in time to see the hangar roof quiver and buckle as something broke through it from inside.

Something huge that smashed entire roof panels out of the way as it got to its feet.

It must have been lying down in the hangar, I realised. Now it was rising and activated. What we had felt had simply been the backwash of its mind-link going live.

With dreadful certainty, I realised that Fayde Thuring was going to be damn near impossible to stop.

I had made an unbelievable, unforgivable mistake. I had underestimated him and his resources. He was nothing like the minor warp-dabbler I had once let slip away.

He had a Titan, Emperor damn him.

He had a Battle Titan.

FOUR

CRUOR VULT
FLEEING THE GIANT
A TERRIBLE LONG SHOT

Its name was *Cruor Vult.* It weighed two and half thousand tonnes and stood sixty metres tall. Like all the great Warlord-class Battle Titans, it was a biped, almost humanoid in its proportions. Hooved with immense three-toed feet of articulated metal, its massive legs supported a colossal pelvic mount and the great, riveted torso that housed its throbbing atomic furnaces. Broad shoulders provided ample space for turbo-laser batteries. Beneath the shoulder armour, the Titan's arms elevated the machine's primary weapons: a gatling blaster as the right fist, a plasma cannon as the left. The head was comparatively small, though I knew it was large enough to contain the entire command deck. It was set low down between the shoulders, making the monster ogrish and hunched.

I have seen Titans before. They are always a terrifying sight. Even the Imperial Battle Titans are awful to behold. The Adeptus Mechanicus, who forge and maintain the war machines for the benefit of mankind, regard them as gods. They are perhaps the greatest mechanical artefacts the human race has ever manufactured. We have made more powerful things – the starships that can cross the void, negotiate warp space and reduce continents to ashes with their ordnance – and we have made more technically sophisticated things – the latest generations of fluid-core autonomous cogitators. But we have made nothing as sublime as the Titan.

They are built for war and war alone. They are created only to destroy. They carry the most potent armaments of any land-based fighting vehicle anywhere. Only fleet warships can bring greater firepower to bear. Their image, bulk, their sheer size, is intended to do nothing except terrify and demoralise a foe.

And they are alive. Not as you or I would understand it, perhaps, but there is an intellect burning inside the mind-impulse link that connects the drivers and crew to the Titan's function. Some say they have a soul. Only the Priests of Mars, the adepts and tech-mages of the Cult Mechanicus, truly understand their secrets and they guard that lore ruthlessly.

Perhaps the only thing more terrifying than a Battle Titan is a Chaos Battle Titan, the infamous metal leviathans of the arch-enemy. Some are manufactured in the smithies and forges of the warp, their designs copied and parodied from the Imperial originals, sacrilegious perversions of the

Martian god-machines. Others are ancient Imperial Titans corrupted during the Great Heresy, traitor legions that have lurked in the Eye of Terror for ten thousand years in defiance of the Emperor's will.

Which this was, frankly I cared little. It looked deformed, blistered with rust, draped with razorwire and covered with blade-studs that sprouted like thorns. What I first took to be strings of yellow beads hanging from its shoulders and blade-studs were actually chains of human skulls, thousands of them. Its metal was a dull, dirty black and inscribed with the unutterable runes of Chaos. Its head was a leering skull plated in glinting chrome. Its name was wrought in brass on a placard across its gigantic chest.

It stepped forward. The ground shook. The ruptured roof panels of the hangar squealed as they tore and caved in around its swinging thighs. It strode through the fabric of the hangar like a man wading through a stream. The building's front burst out and fell away with a tremendous crash as the Titan broke its way through.

And then it howled.

Great vox-horns fixed to the sides of its skull blared out the berserk war-cry of the monster. It was so painfully loud, so deep in the infrasonic register, that it reflexively triggered primal fear and panic in us. The earth shook even more than it had done under the weight of its footsteps.

It was coming our way. Now it was clear of the hangar, I could see the long segmented tail it dragged and whipped behind it.

Move! I said, directing my will at my colleagues in the hope of snapping them into some sort of rational response. Every few seconds, the rock under our feet vibrated as it took another step.

We started to run through the streets of the deserted station, trying to keep as much of the buildings as possible between us and it. Our one advantage was our size. We could evade it by staying hidden.

With a metallic screech of badly lubricated joints, it slowly turned its head and waist to look in our direction and then stomped heavily round to follow us. It walked straight through a longhouse, shattering it like matchwood.

'It knows where we are!' Rassi cried, desperately.

'How can it?' Haar whined.

Military grade sensors. Heavy-duty auspex. Devices so powerful that they could overcome the island's magnetic distortions. This beast had been made to fight in horrifically inhospitable theatres, resisting toxins, radiations, vacuums, bombardments. It needed to be able to see and hear and smell and target in the middle of hell. The local magnetics that had bested our civilian instruments were nothing to it.

'It's so... big...' Bequin stammered.

Another crash. Another longhouse kicked over and splintered. A squeak of protesting metal as a derelict troop truck was pulverised underfoot.

We turned back, running back almost the other way now, passing south of the chapel and the command centre. Again, with an echoing grind of engaging joints, it came about and renewed its inexorable pursuit.

I felt a spasm, a pulse on a psychic level. I was feeling the surge and flicker of its mind-impulse link.

'Get down!' I yelled.

The gatling blaster opened fire. The sound was a single blur of noise. A huge cone of flaming gases flickered and twitched around the blaster muzzles.

A storm of destruction rained around us. Hundreds of high-explosive shells hosed the street, blitzing the fronts of the buildings, pulping them. Firestorms sucked and rushed down the street. Billions of cinders and debris scarps sprayed all around. The stench of fyceline was chokingly strong.

I got up in a blizzard of ash and settling sparks. We were all still alive, if chronically dazed by the concussive force. Either the Titan's targeting systems were off-set, or the crew were still getting used to its operation. The sensors might be capable of tracking our movement, but the Titan still had to get its eye in. Perhaps it could only sense us in a general way.

'We can't fight that!' said Fischig.

He was right. We couldn't. We had nothing. This was so one-sided it wasn't even tragic. But we couldn't run, either. Once we left the cover of the station's buildings, we would be in the open and easy targets.

'What about the gun-cutter?' blurted Alizebeth.

'No... no,' I said. 'Even the cutter hasn't got enough kill-power. It might make a dent, but it wouldn't stand a chance. That thing would shoot it out of the sky before it even got close.'

'But–'

'No! It's not an option!'

'What is then?' she wanted to know. 'Dying? Is that an option?'

We were running again, away from the burning zone of devastation. With another overwhelming blurt of decibels, the blaster cut loose again. A longhouse and part of the command centre to our right disintegrated in a volcanic flurry of spinning wreckage and fire. There were walls of flame everywhere, gusting yellow and bright into the grey gloom.

Begundi led us down a side street between the ends of longhouses, Fischig and Kara Swole almost carrying the exhausted Rassi. We ducked down in the shadows against the rotting side wall.

Hiding, we could no longer see the Titan. There was silence, interrupted only by the crackle of blazing fibre-ply and the creak of prefab frames slowly slumping.

But I could feel it. I could feel its abhuman mind seething malevolently through the deepest harmonics of the psyk-range. It was north of us, on the other side of the chapel and the store barns, waiting, listening.

A vibrating thump. It was moving again. The rate of the footsteps increased as it picked up speed until the ground no longer had time to stop shaking between thumps. Pebbles skittered on the ground and loose glass dislodged from the broken windows of the nearby longhouses.

'Go!' growled Fischig. He broke and started to run east across the main street. The others began to follow his lead.

'Fischig! Not that way!' I leapt after him, grabbing him in the middle of the roadway. There was a groan of tortured metal and the Titan itself appeared at the end of the street, traversing its mighty upper body to face us.

Fischig froze in terror. I threw us both forward behind the rusted hulk of an old PDF troop carrier.

Blaster fire ripped down the street, kicking up a wild row of individual impacts that pitted the rocky ground, demolished the edge of a barn and filled the air with greasy flame, smoke and powdered rock.

A flurry of shots sliced through the shell of the troop carrier, splitting its fatigued armour wide open and hurling rusty shrapnel in all directions. The force of the hits actually lifted the carrier's mouldering bulk and spun it around, end to end. I dragged Fischig behind a longhouse and just prevented us from being crushed under the lurching metal shape. The carrier came to rest against the side wall of the prefab, stoving in the wall panels.

The earthshaking footsteps resumed. The Titan was advancing down the street. I looked at Fischig. He was dazed and pale. A ragged chunk of shrapnel had embedded itself in his left shoulder. It would have decapitated him if it hadn't been for the motion tracker unit strapped there. As it was, the tracker was a smouldering wreck and blood poured from the hunk of metal projecting from his trapezius.

'Holy Throne,' he murmured.

I hoisted him up and glanced back across the street. Begundi and Swole had managed to get everyone else back into cover before the barrage. I could see them through the smoke, huddled in the shadows.

I raised my free hand and made gestures that were as clear as possible. I wanted them to back off and regroup. We would have to split up. There was nowhere we dared cross the open street in either direction.

Fischig and I blundered off in the opposite direction, coming out in a drain gully behind the row of longhouses where a stream emptied down through the station to the lake. We crossed it using a small wire-caged footbridge and then fell into cover on the far side of a machine shop.

'Where is it?' Fischig wheezed in pain.

I checked. I could see the huge machine towering above the prefabs two hundred metres back, shrouded in the black smoke that was roiling up from its last onslaught. It had reached the old troop carrier and was standing there. It looked for all the worlds as if the giant war-engine was sniffing the air.

It turned again suddenly, filling the air with the sound of whirring gears and clanking joints, and smashed through the longhouse as it moved off after us.

'It's coming this way,' I told Fischig. We started to run again, across the levelled rockcrete apron of the machine shop and then down the gently sloped street towards the command centre.

Fischig had slowed right down. It was gaining on us.

There was a distant, booming roar that echoed around the entire lake basin. A ball of flame rose into the air from the very western end of the station area.

'What the hell was that?' Fischig growled.

The Titan clearly wanted to know too. It adjusted its path and moved away from us, striding towards the site of the unexplained blast, oblivious to the collateral damage it was leaving in its wake.

'That,' said a voice behind us, 'was the best diversion I could come up with.'

We looked around and there was Harlon Nayl.

Nayl was a good friend and a respected member of my team. I hadn't seen the old bounty hunter since he had set off for Durer with Fischig's party to conduct the audit. He was a big man, dressed as always in a black combat-armoured bodyglove. With his heavy skull shaved and polished and his grizzled face, he looked a fierce brute, but there was a grace to his movements and a nobility to his stature that always set me in mind of Vownus, the rogue hero of Catuldynus's epic verse allegory *The Once-Pure Hive.*

He held a vox-trigger detonator in his hand.

We followed Nayl into the shelter of a storebarn and the bounty hunter immediately began to field dress Fischig's wound. The Battle Titan was still prowling around west of us, investigating the mysterious blast.

'I tried to raise you on the vox, but the channels were screwed,' Nayl said.

'Magnetics,' I said. 'How long have you been here?'

'Since first light. I rented a speeder to follow Thuring. It's hidden up in the hills on the far side of the lake.'

'What have you found?' Fischig asked, wincing as Nayl sprayed his wound with antisept.

'Apart from the obvious, you mean?'

'Yes,' I said.

'Thuring's got backing. Serious capital support. Maybe a powerful local cult we don't know about, more likely an off-world cabal. He's got manpower, resources, equipment. When I first arrived, I poked around, got a glimpse of what was in the hangar... that took my breath away, I can tell you. Then I "borrowed" one of his men and asked some questions.'

'Did you get any answers?'

'A few. He was... trained to resist.'

I knew Nayl's interrogation techniques were fairly basic.

'How long did he last?'

'About ten minutes.'

'And he told you–'

'Thuring has known for some time that the Titan was here. Probably information received from his backers. It seems no one knew that Miquol was used by the arch-enemy as a Titan pen during the occupation. The bloody PDF were stationed here for years and never realised what was hidden just up there in the mountains.'

I peered out of the barn door. The Titan had come about and was plodding back in our direction. I could taste its bitter psychic anger and feel the earth quivering under my feet.

'Harlon!'

He leapt up and came to join me. 'Damn,' he hissed, viewing the Titan.

He took out his detonator again, selected a fresh channel and thumbed the trigger.

There was a flash, a rolling report, and another mass of fire blossomed from the western shore of the lake. The Titan turned immediately and stomped towards the fresh blast.

'It's not going to fall for that many more times,' said Nayl.

'So there was a Titan... that damn thing... abandoned and dormant in the mountains?'

'That's about the size of it. Left behind in the mass retreat, never found by Imperial liberators. Sealed in a shielded cavern... along with two more like it.'

'Three Titans?' snarled Fischig.

'They've taken this long to get just that one working,' said Nayl. 'Thuring's aboard that thing, commanding it personally. He's delighted with his new toy, even though it's not up to optimum. You'll notice it's only used its solid munition weapon. I don't think its reactors are generating enough juice yet to power up its energy batteries.'

'Lucky us,' I said.

'What I can't tell you is why Thuring is restoring a monster like that.'

There could be many reasons, I thought. He could be doing it on the behest of his rich sponsors, which seemed likely. He could be intending to sell it to the highest bidder. There were cult groups in the Ophidian sub-sector that would love to own that sort of power. He could even be working for some higher power, perhaps enlisted by the actual legions of the arch-enemy.

Or he could be doing this for himself. That idea chilled me. Thuring was evidently a more significant player than I had estimated. He could have designs of his own, and with a Battle Titan at his command those designs could be very bloody. He could hold cities to ransom, here on Durer or elsewhere. He could raze population centres, slaughter millions, particularly once the turbines of *Cruor Vult* were operating at full power.

Whatever the truth, the dismal fate of the ekranoplane's crew told me he wasn't intending to leave the island the way he had come in. A bulk lifter could easily land here, pick up the Titan and be away before the frankly paltry watch forces of Durer could react. Thuring was planning to leave here with the Titan. I knew that as a certainty. It didn't matter where he was going after that. Imperial blood would be spilled as a result. We had to stop him.

Which brought me back to my original problem.

How the hell were we going to fight that?

Frantically, with the Titan now turning back from the second diversion, I considered the tools at our disposal. It was hard to concentrate, because the angry flutter of the Titan's mind link was interfering with my mind. I suppose that's what gave me the idea. The desperate idea.

I reached to key my vox link and then paused. The behemoth would detect vox transmissions effortlessly. Instead, I stretched out with my mind, trying to find Rassi.

'Nayl?' I asked. 'What's the most secure structure here?'

'The chapel,' he said. 'It's reinforced stone.'

I opened my mind fully. *Thorn enfolds kin, within a seal, the worshipful place.* If Rassi could hear me, he wouldn't understand Glossia, but I figured he'd have the sense to consult the others.

After a long pause, the answer came.

Kin come to Thorn, in sealed worship, abrupt.

'Let's move!' I told Nayl and Fischig.

We reached the chapel first. The dread Titan had begun to stride our way again by then, but Nayl fired the last of his diversions and distracted it east.

We tumbled into the ancient church. It was generally stripped bare and full of slimy black mold. A few remaining wooden pews were sagging with damp corruption. The double-headed eagle from the altar lay trampled on the floor. I noticed that its dented wings were polished brightly. Dronicus had tended this place fervently until Thuring's men had arrived and smashed up his diligently maintained shrine. It was a heartbreaking sight.

I bowed to the altar and made the sign of the eagle across my chest with both hands.

The others arrived in a hurry, weapons drawn, slamming the door shut behind them: Bequin, Haar, Begundi, Swole and Rassi.

Rassi was panting hard. Bequin was pale. Both Haar and Swole had cuts and contusions from near misses.

'You have a plan?' asked Rassi, almost immediately.

I nodded. 'It's a terrible long shot, but I don't know what else to do.'

'Let's hear it,' said Fischig.

I do not pretend, as I have already reflected, to have any specific understanding of the workings of a Battle Titan. No man does, unless he be a priest of Mars or, like Thuring, the owner of illicitly transmitted lore. Aemos probably knew a thing or two. I knew for certain he had seen Adeptus Mechanicus mind-impulse units firsthand, for he'd told me as much, long before, in the cryogenerator chamber of the tomb-vault Processional Two Twelve on Hubris.

But he was not with me in that chilly, ransacked chapel, nor was a decent conversation with him viable.

However, I knew enough to understand that the function of a Titan depended on the connection between man and machine, between the human brain and the mechanical sentience. That was achieved – miraculously – through the psychic interface of the mind-impulse unit.

Which meant, in very simple terms, that the root of our problem was essentially a psychic one. If we could disrupt or, better still, destroy, the mind link...

'This runestaff was made for me by Magos Geard Bure of the Adeptus Mechanicus,' I told Rassi, letting him feel the weight of the weapon. It was a long, runic steel pole with a cap-piece in the form of a sun's corona, fashioned in electrum. The lodestone at the cap's centre was a skull, a perfect copy of my own, marked with the thirteenth sign of castigation, that had been worked from a hyper-dense geode of tele-empathic mineral called the Lith that Bure had found on Cinchare. It was a psionic amplifier of quite devastating power.

'We use it to boost our collaborating minds. Force a way into the machine's consciousness.'

'Indeed. And then?'

I glanced over at Alizebeth. 'Then Madam Bequin takes hold of the runestaff and delivers her untouchable blankness into the heart of it.'

'Will that work?' Kara Swole asked.

There was a long pause.

Bequin looked at me and then at Rassi. 'I don't know. Will it?'

'I don't know either,' I said. 'But I think it's the best chance we have.'

Rassi breathed deeply. 'So be it. I don't see another hope, not even a remote one. Let's get on with it.'

Poul Rassi and I took the runestaff between us, our hands clamped around the long haft.

He closed his eyes.

I tried to relax, but the instinctual barriers of self protection that exist in every mind kept mine from letting go. I didn't want to get inside that thing. Even from a distance, it stank of putrid power. It reeked of the warp.

'Come on, Gregor,' Rassi whispered.

I concentrated. I closed my eyes. I knew the Titan was treading nearer, because I could feel the chapel floor shaking.

I tried to let myself go.

It was like clinging to a precious handhold when you are dangling over a pit of corrosive sludge. I couldn't bear to submit and slide away. What waited for me down there was cosmic horror, a broiling mass of filth and poison that would dissolve my mind, my sanity, my soul.

Chaos beckoned, and I was trying to find the courage to jump into its arms.

I could feel the sweat dribbling down my brow. I could smell the rotten odour of the derelict chapel. I could feel the cold steel in my hands.

I let go.

It was worse than anything I could have imagined.

Drowning. I was drowning, face down, in black ooze. The sticky, foetid stuff was filling my nostrils and my ears, trying to pour like treacle down into my mouth and choke me. There was no up, no down, no world.

There was just viscous blackness and the unforgettable smell of the warp.

A hand grasped me by the back of the jacket and yanked me up. Air. I spluttered, puking out filmy strings of phlegm stained black by the ooze.

'Gregor! Gregor!'

It was Rassi. He stood beside me, knee deep in the warp mud. God-Emperor, but his mind was strong. I'd have been dead already but for him.

He looked drawn and weak. Warp-induced pustules were spotting his face and crusting his neck. Blowflies billowed around us, their buzzing incessant in our ears.

'Come on,' he said. 'We've come this far.' His words came broken up as he was repeatedly forced to spit out flies that mobbed around his dry lips.

I looked around. The sea of black ooze went on forever. The sky over our heads was thickly dark, but I realised that the billowing clouds were impossibly vast swarms of flies, blocking out the light.

Firelights, distant, flashing, reflected across the slime.

We were in the outer reaches of the Chaos Titan's mind-link.

Swathed in films of ectoplasmic ooze, we struggled forward, holding each other for support. Rassi was moaning. His psychic self had brought no cane to support him.

Flames underlit the horizon and the sea of sludge rolled nauseatingly. I had not encountered a mental landscape this abominable since my first dreams of Cherubael, years before.

Cherubael.

Just the thought of him in my mind brought the flies rushing around me. The slime reacted too, popping and bubbling about my knees. I felt a keening, a sharp need, that filled the polluted air around me.

Cherubael. Cherubael.

'Stop it!' wailed Rassi.

'Stop what?'

'Whatever you're thinking about, stop it. The whole world is reacting.'

'I'm sorry...' I suppressed the notion of Cherubael in my mind with every ounce of my will. The tremors subsided.

'Throne, Gregor. I don't know what you've got in your head, I don't want to know...' said Rassi. 'But... I pity you.'

We trudged forward, first one of us slipping over, then the other, then one bringing the other down. The deep slime licked at us, hungry.

Thousands of kilometres ahead of us, a source of power throbbed. I could dimly make out the silhouette of a man. But it wasn't a man. It was *Cruor Vult*. 'Blood wills it,' that would be the simplest Low Gothic translation. The Titan stood there, distant, the master of this psychic realm.

Daemonic forms ghosted around us. Their spectral, screaming faces were madness to behold. They were like smoke, like shadowplay. They snarled at us.

Another few hundred metres and images began to flash into my mind. We were breaking into the edges of the Titan's memory sphere.

I saw such things.

May the God-Emperor spare me, I saw such things then.

I stood on the brink and peered into the abyss of the Titan's memories. I saw cities die in flames. I saw legions of the Imperial Guard incinerated. I saw Space Marines die in their hundreds, scurrying around my feet like ants.

I saw planets catch fire and burn to ashes. I saw Imperial Titans, proud warlords, burst apart and die under the onslaught of my hands.

I saw the gates of the Imperial Palace on Terra through a blizzard of fire. I saw down through many thousands of years.

I saw Horus, vile and screaming out his wrath.

I saw the whole Heresy played out in front of my eyes.

I saw the Age of Strife, and witnessed first hand the Dark Age of Technology that preceded it.

I fell, plummeting through history, through the stored memory of *Cruor Vult*.

I saw too much. I started to scream.

Rassi slapped me hard around the face.

'Gregor! Come on now, we are almost there!'

We were at the heart of it all now, frail as whispers. We were in the bridge of the Titan, seeing the multiple, overlapping spectres of the men who had commanded it, all sat in the princeps's throne, all dead.

Daemons crouched on my back, writhed on my shoulders, gnawed at my ears and cheeks.

I saw horror. Absolute horror.

Beside me, Rassi reached out and touched the mind-impulse unit built into the floor of the bridge.

'Now, I think...' he said.

'Alizebeth!' I yelled.

In the rank confines of the chapel, Bequin leapt forward and grabbed the runestaff from the hands of two inquisitors who were quivering with power, stress and terror, our eyes rolled up blankly so that only the whites showed.

She gripped the runestaff, focused her untouchable force and–

FIVE

MY PLAN FAILS
DAMN VERVEUK ALL TO HELL
THE UNTHINKABLE

She was killed.

Not at once, of course. The backrip of the Titan's terrible sentience tore into her, overwhelmed her untouchable quality by dint of its sheer force, and broke her mind.

Electrical discharge crackled down the haft of my runestaff, throwing Rassi and myself away and blasting Alizebeth back across the chapel. The scorch marks are still visible on the uncorruptible steel: the perfectly etched fingerprints of Poul Rassi, Gregor Eisenhorn and Alizebeth Bequin.

Nayl told me afterwards that the psychic recoil had tossed Rassi and myself to either side like dolls, but the main force had been directed at Bequin. She had flown through the air a dozen metres, her cloak fluttering out and cracked off the back wall of the chapel with a sound that Nayl knew meant snapping bones.

He ran to her, calling her name. Fischig lurched forward too. Rassi and I lay on the ground, weeping and gasping. The runestaff, steaming, had landed on the stone floor between us with a clang.

My plan had failed dismally and completely.

Blood trickling from my nose, I got up, Swole and Haar helping me. I had little idea where I was. Images of the Age of Strife still permeated my mind.

'Rassi?' I gasped.

'Alive!' said Begundi, crouching next to the sprawled inquisitor. 'But he's weak...'

'Alizebeth?' I asked softly, looking to where she lay. Fischig and Nayl were huddled over her. Nayl looked back at me, and shook his head.

'No...' I said, pushing Kara Swole away as I stepped forward. Not Alizebeth. Not her, after all this time.

'She's hurt bad, boss,' Nayl said. 'I'll try to make her comfortable, but...'

The tread of *Cruor Vult* echoed outside.

I staggered towards Bequin. She looked so still. So broken.

'Oh sweet Emperor, please, no–'

'Inquisitor...' said Haar. 'We're dead now, aren't we, for sure?'

I realised slowly that the Titan was right outside.

'What are you doing?' Begundi yelled at me.

I had no idea. I was only partially conscious. I had Barbarisater in my fist and was running for the door. I think I meant to go out and face the Titan with my sword. That's how far gone I was.

One man with a sword, intent on facing down a Battle Titan.

Before I could reach the door, I heard the scream of down-jets and the chatter of cannon-fire.

I didn't have to look out to know it was my gun-cutter. Damn Medea.

'Thorn to Aegis, the spite of justice! Belay! Belay!'

'Thorn requires Aegis, the shades of Eternity, Razor Delphus Pathway! Pattern Ivory!'

'Thorn denies! The cover of stillness! Belay!

'Aegis responds to Verveuk. The matter, quite done.'

'No!' I bellowed. 'Nooo!' Medea's response had told me that she was following Bastian Verveuk's orders now. He had commanded her to take the gun-cutter up. He had ordered her to attack the Titan.

I honestly believe that he thought he was helping me. That he could do some good.

Damn Verveuk. Damn Verveuk all to hell.

I ran outside in time to see the majestic raptor-shape of my gun-cutter burning in low across the PDF station, blazing its guns at the slowly turning Titan. The streams of hi-calibre shells were just pinging off the giant's thick, armoured skin.

Cruor Vult turned with a scrape of metal against metal, raised its right fist and fired. The conical flame-flash of its muzzle gases, white-hot to the point of incandescence, twitched and flickered around the gatling blaster.

The cutter bucked and lurched as the first rounds struck it. It tried to evade, but the air was air was too thick with pelting bolts.

The ferocious salvo ripped the belly out of my beloved gun-cutter and tore off a tail-wing. Spewing flames and smoke, the cutter veered off, debris cascading away from its shredded hull. It tried to climb.

Its main engines stalled out.

Leaving a wide streak of smoke behind it in the air, the cutter banked violently to the left, ripped a wing strut through the edge of the ancient, rusted dish, and dropped. It hit the shore of the lake, burying itself in the beach mud and shingle, leaving a smouldering groove thirty metres long behind it.

I stumbled forward, trying to see, but the main bulk of the downed cutter was obscured by buildings. It was ablaze, I could tell that much. *Cruor Vult* began to pace slowly towards the beach.

I had a sudden mental image of a hunter walking to his wounded quarry, preparing to fire a final, point-blank kill-shot.

Around the corner of the next longhouse, I could see down the glinting shingle of the icy lakeshore. The Titan was crunching away from me, its vast treads leaving perfect indentations of pulverised pebbles behind it. The cutter was half on its side, a mangled, truncated wreck, driven down into the scree and hard, cold mud of the shoreline. Wretched black fumes were boiling out of its innards, and curls of steam were rising where the lake water was in contact with flaming debris.

There was a little, tinny bang, and an exit hatch blew out of the cutter's flank, fired off by explosive bolts. A figure, clearly injured, fell out of the hatch, and began to struggle up the beach.

It looked like Verveuk.

The Titan was only about fifty metres from the crashed vessel now, its feet lifting sprays of water as it strode through the beachline shallows.

I became aware of movement beside me. It was Haar, his long-las raised and aimed at the Titan, a defiant gesture so full of courage it quite eclipsed its own basic stupidity. Kara Swole was close behind him, anxiously accompanying Rassi, who had dragged himself out to join me. He looked half-dead from his trials in the mind-link, his eyes sunken and dark, his lips tight and bloodless.

I wonder how the hell I looked.

Begundi followed after them. He'd holstered his pistols again. He knew firepower like that was pointless. Fischig and Nayl had stayed by Alizebeth's side in the chapel.

Rassi had my runestaff, and was using it to stay upright.

'Get back,' I said to them all. 'Just get back... there's nothing we can do.'

'We fight...' gasped Rassi. 'We fight... the arch-enemy... in the name of the God-Emperor of Mankind... until we drop...'

He raised my runestaff and used it to amplify his weary mind. Psychothermic energy, manifesting far more powerfully than it had done through his cane, spat at the towering back of the great Titan. I don't know if he hoped to hurt it. I don't know if he was so far gone by that stage to believe he could. I think he was simply trying to distract it from the cutter.

Rassi's scorching arc of flame seemed so devastating as it swirled out of the runestaff beside me, so bright it hurt my eyes, so hot it singed my hair. But by the time it struck the Titan, its true scale was woefully revealed. It flared uselessly off the Titan's rear torso cowling.

But still he kept it going. The psychothermic fire turned green and then blue white. Haar started to fire his weapon. I think Kara did too.

Like kisses into the whirlwind, my old master Hapshant would have said.

Cruor Vult raked the cutter's wreck with blaster rounds. The first few instants of the merciless blitz ruptured the hull, twisting it, deforming it, dashing shards of metal up across the shore and out over the lake, peppering it with splash ripples.

The cutter seemed to writhe, as if it was trying to escape the bombardment. In truth, it was simply being shifted and jolted as the hurricane of shots hammered it from end to end and shredded it.

Then it exploded. A big, bright flash, a cudgelling boom and a rush of shockwave. The blast ripped a hole in the beach and sent a significant tidal wave back across the lake towards the far side.

Where the cutter had been – where Medea, Aemos and Dahault had been – was just a pit of leaping flame. Debris, water and pebbles rained down painfully like an apocalyptic cloudburst. The Titan virtually disappeared in a sudden outrush of steam.

Verveuk had been fifty metres from the wreck, stumbling inland, the last I had seen him. When I dared raise my head from the rain of shingle, there was no sign of him.

Its murder done, the Battle Titan turned on us.

I was knocked flat, and I struck my head so hard on a prefab wall I blacked out for a second. I discovered later that Begundi had taken me down into what little cover was available with a desperate flying tackle.

Cruor Vult had improved its aim.

The cold island air was full of mineral dust from the pebbles and rock that had been atomised by its blaster fire. Rassi and Haar simply didn't exist any more. They had been vaporised by the mega-grade military weapon. My runestaff, blackened but intact, lay on a wide patch of ground that had been transmuted to furrowed glass by the hideous alchemy of blaster fire. The only other trace of them was a small, broken section of Haar's lasrifle.

Kara Swole lay twenty metres away where the blast had thrown her. She was covered in blood, and I was sure she was dead.

And I was sure we were dead too. Thuring had won. He had killed my friends and allies in front of my eyes and now he had won.

I had nothing to left to fight him with. I had nothing that could take on the power of a Titan. I'd had nothing when this one-sided duel began, and I sure as hell had nothing left now.

I...

An idea came upon me, insidious and foul, wrenched into the light by the extremity of my position. I shook it off. It was unthinkable. The notion was revolting, inexcusable.

But it was also true. I did have something.

I had something more powerful than a Titan.

If I dared use it. If I had the audacity to unleash it.

Unthinkable. Unthinkable.

Cruor Vult thundered towards me through the ebbing steam.

I could hear the whine of the autoloaders in its massive gatling assembly connecting up fresh munition hoppers. I could see the beach pebbles at my feet, thousands of them, skipping slightly with every step it took.

'Bex...'

'Sir?'

'Get Kara and run. Go for the chapel.'

'Sir, I–'

Do it now, I willed and he sprang up, running fast.

I crawled over to the runestaff and grabbed its haft. It was hot to the touch, and sticky with blood.

Duclane Haar and Poul Rassi would have to serve as the sacrifice, I realised pragmatically, already disgusted with myself. There was no time, no opportunity to do anything more elaborate. As it was, I had scarcely any of the tools, devices, unguents, charms or wards that I would normally have believed necessary to undertake an action like this.

I caught myself. Until that very moment, I had never even considered undertaking an action like this, no matter the preparations.

Kneeling on the vitrified ground in the path of an oncoming Chaos Battle Titan, holding upright in both hands a runestaff slick with the blood residue of two beloved friends, I began the incantations.

It was hard. Hard to remember word-perfect the pertinent verses of the *Malus Codicium*, a work I had studied on and off for years in secret. These were writings I had been eager to learn and understand, but which filled me with dread all the same. After my first sabbatical to study the *Codicium*, just a few months after the execution of its previous owner Quixos, I had been forced into retreat to recover, and required counselling from the abbots of the Sacred Heart monastery on Alsor.

Now I was trying to remember the same passages. Driving myself. Struggling to repeat writings I had once struggled to erase from my mind.

If I got even a word wrong, a phrasing, a point of vocabulary, we would all be dead at the hands of an evil far worse than *Cruor Vult*.

SIX

CHAOS AGAINST CHAOS
THE PRICE
THE CONSEQUENCE

A moment. A freezing classroom many years before. Titus Endor and myself, shivering in our seats at ebonwood desks eroded by the scratchings and carvings of a thousand previous pupils. We were merely eighteen days into our initial training as junior interrogators. Inquisitor Hapshant had stormed in, slammed the door, cast his stack of grimoires down on the main lectern – which made us both jump – and declared: 'A servant of the Inquisition who makes Chaos his tool against Chaos is a greater enemy of mankind than Chaos itself! Chaos knows the bounds of its own evil and accepts it. A servant of the Inquisition who uses Chaos is fooling himself, denies the truth, and damns us all by his delusion!'

On the lakeshore at Miquol, I was not fooling myself. I knew how desperate this gamble was.

Commodus Voke, dead fifty years by then, had once said to me... and I paraphrase for I did not record it word for word at the time – '"Know your enemy" is the greatest lie we own. Never submit to it. The radical path has its attractions, and I admit I have been tempted over the years of my life. But it is littered with lies. Once you look to the warp for answers, for knowledge to use against the arch-enemy, you are using Chaos. That makes you a practitioner. And you know what happens to practitioners, don't you, Eisenhorn? The Inquisition comes for them.'

On that desolate beach, I felt sure I could sort truth from lies. Voke had simply misunderstood the fineness of the line.

Midas Betancore had once, during a late night of drinking and Glavian rules regicide, said, 'Why do they do it? The radicals, I mean. Don't they understand that even getting close to the warp is suicide?'

With the runestaff in my hands, on that frozen island on Durer, I knew it wasn't suicide. It was the opposite.

* * *

Godwin Fischig, in a grave-field shrine on Cadia, had once warned me to stay away from any hint of radical sympathy. 'Trust me, Eisenhorn, if I ever thought you were, I'd shoot you myself.'

It wasn't that simple. Emperor damn me, it just wasn't that simple! I thought of Quixos, such a brilliant man, such a stalwart servant of the Imperium, so totally polluted by treasonous evil because he had tried to understand the very filth he fought against. I had declared him heretic and executed him with my own hand.

I understood the dangers.

Cruor Vult thundered towards me. I uttered the last of the potent syllables and dipped my mind into the warp. Not the simmering warp-scape of the Titan's mind-link, but the true warp. Channelled by the runestaff and warded by the prayers I had ritually intoned, I flowed into a vaster, darker void. I reached across the fabric of space towards Gudrun, far away, an entire sub-sector away, towards a private estate on the Insume Headland.

I reached into it, into a secret oubliette that had been vacuum sealed, warp-damped, void-shielded and locked with thirteen locks. Only I knew the codes to break down those barriers, for I had set them myself.

It was crumpled in the middle of the floor, wrapped in chains.

I woke it up. I set it free.

I jerked out of my trance. The runestaff bucked in my hands as the unleashed daemon energy flared through it.

I fought to retain my grip and to enunciate precisely the words of command and the specific instructions.

Like a small sun dawning, the enslaved daemon poured out of the head of the runestaff. Its radiance lit up the dismal shore and cast a long shadow out behind the Titan.

'Cherubael?' I whispered.

'Yessss...?'

'Kill it.'

Lightning crackled. A freak storm suddenly erupted over the lake, swirling the heavens and driving rain down in sheets, accompanied by fierce winds and catastrophic electrical displays.

A ghastly white thing, moving so rapidly it could only be registered as an afterimage on the retina, surged out of my staff and went straight into the black bulk of *Cruor Vult*.

The Titan hesitated, mid-step, one foot raised. It shuddered. Its great arms flailed for a moment. Then its chrome skull-face cracked, crazed and shattered, blowing out in a burst of sickly green light.

Cruor Vult swayed, the rainstorm drenching off its creaking bulk.

A halo of light lit up the lake shore and the old PDF base. *Cruor Vult*, ancient enemy of mankind, exploded from the waist up in a globe of furious white heat. Nothing of its head, torso or arms survived the immolation.

The legs, one foot still raised, tottered and swayed and then collapsed, falling sideways like an avalanche and destroying the ruined remains of the station's dish.

Cruor Vult was dead. Feyde Thuring was dead.

And I was unconscious, hurled back by the death-blast.

And that meant Cherubael was free.

If it had fled then, it would have escaped. Indeed, it might have fled deep enough into the miasmic warp to evade me forever, even if I exhausted what was left of my life trying to summon it back. It was wary of me now, and knew my tricks.

Certainly, it might have escaped far enough to avoid my clutches for many years to come, and in that time have cost the Imperium dearly.

But it did not. The daemon was too consumed by rancor for that.

It came back to kill me.

I woke with a start, and realised instantly that Cherubael was free thanks to my loss of control. I looked around, but it seemed like I was alone on the beach. The sky was still swollen with storm clouds, and lightning formed crackling golden crowns around the peaks of the mountains.

The rain was easing, pattering across the glossy, wet pebbles and the steaming ruin of *Cruor Vult*. My skin prickled. I knew it was still here.

I had done the unthinkable, and now I had to undo it. Cherubael had to be bound again. It could not be allowed to remain free.

I picked up the runestaff. The rain was washing the filmy blood off its hard, polished form. I held it firmly in my left hand and drew Barbarisater. The blade twitched, tasting the daemon in the air.

'Gracious Emperor of Mankind, hallowed be your majesty, bright be your light everlasting, vouchsafe your servant in this hour of peril–'

'That won't save you,' said a voice. I switched around, but there was no sign of a speaker.

'Bright be your light everlasting, vouchsafe your servant in this hour of peril, so that I may continue to serve you, great lord, and purify your dominion of '

'It won't, Gregor. The Benediction of Terra? It's just words, Gregor. Just words.'

'...continue to serve you, great lord, and purify your dominion of man, casting out all daemons and changelings of warpcraft–'

'But I have more than words for you, Gregor. I liked you, Gregor, of all men, you had a spirit I admired. I worked for you, I spared you more than once... consider that. All I asked in return was that you honour our compact and release me. And what did you do? You tricked me. You trapped me. You *used* me.'

The words seemed to echo all around me, but no matter how fast I turned, I could not see it. Its voice was in my head. I struggled to continue the repetitions, struggled to keep hold of the sense of the benediction, but it was hard. I wanted to answer its taunts. I wanted to rage at it that it had tricked me first. There had been no compact between us! It had used me to fashion its own escape from the enslaving charms Quixos had wrought around it.

I dared not. I focused on the repeats. Barbarisater shivered from hilt to tip, resonating with the psychic power that washed around me.

'...vouchsafe your servant in this hour of peril, so that I may continue to serve you, great lord–'

A star came out, over the lake. A hazy ring of white around a brilliant, gleaming centre. Almost fluttering, like a leaf on the wind, it eddied down towards me and settled a few metres away.

The pebbles beneath it turned to glass. The light was almost too bright to look at. Cherubael hovered in the centre of the glare. He was at his most deadly now, non-corporeal, a daemon spirit, raw and bare, unfettered by a fleshly host. I could not resolve any real details in the light. In truth, I had no wish to gaze upon the daemon's true form. It was not even man-shaped any more. I had always presumed white light to be pure and somehow chaste, to be noble and good. But this whiteness was unutterably evil, chilling, its purity an abomination.

'...hallowed be your majesty, bright be your light everlasting...'

'Shut up, Gregor. Shut up so I can hear myself kill you.'

My weapons, staff and sword, were useless physically. Cherubael had no host body to destroy. But they were strong psychically. I had banished Cherubael with the runestaff once before, and as far as I know obliterated his daemon kin Prophaniti. But my mind had been stronger in those battles, and psychic weapons are only as powerful as the will that directs them. Cherubael knew how tired and ill-focused I was. I could feel it trying to weaken me by teasing out the agonies I felt inside... Bequin, Medea, Aemos, Rassi, Haar... It wanted me to think about the deaths of those dear friends so that I would be weakened still further by grief.

But it was weak too. It had just expended huge reserves of power vanquishing a Titan.

The light surged forward, to test me, I think. I swung Barbarisater to deflect it and felt the electrical impact down my arm. It surged again and I swept the staff around, driving it back.

It circled me. I'd stung it. It knew it was in for a fight.

If that's what it wanted...

I lunged at it, Barbarisater keening. Cherubael blocked with a bar of luminous energy and convulsed out a pulse of pale radiance that blew me off my feet into the air.

I landed hard on the shingle, but sprang up fast, remembering every close combat move I'd been taught over the years by the likes of Harlon Nayl, Kara Swole, Arianrhod Esw Sweydyr, Midas, Medea...

It was coming right onto me, blinding bright. It was like fighting a star. I smashed at it with the head of my staff and then somersaulted out of its path, landing on my feet and sprinting away.

I ran under the smouldering arches of *Cruor Vult*'s fallen legs and then back up the tough slog of the beach towards the station. I could distinctly hear the air rush as it burned after me.

I feinted left, but it had guessed as much. The daemon-star was right on me. I swung my sword, leapt to the right, and vaulted over its next blade of light using the staff as a pole.

Cherubael laughed. Its cackling voice followed me as I sprinted up between two longhouses. The daemon-star chased after me, its psychic force scattering the beach stones behind it in a wake.

I heard a groaning, crashing sound and realised the walls were closing in. Cherubael was lifting both longhouses off their blocks and crushing them together with me in between.

I tore through the wall of the left hand prefab with Barbarisater and leapt through as the juddering huts slammed into each other. Cherubael burned through the fibre-ply wall to get at me, and was greeted by my counter-attack of stabbing blade and staff.

I could drive it back, but I couldn't do any more than that. My mental reserves were just not strong enough.

My only chance was to bind him again. But how?

Dronicus came out of nowhere. I believe, or at least it is a notion I cling on to for the sake of my sanity, that the Emperor of Mankind provides help for his true servants in their hour of need, even in the strangest forms. Dronicus, old, insane Dronicus, had clearly been observing the day's dreadful events from hiding, and now he emerged because he had made a gravely mistaken apprehension. He had seen the white light of the daemon destroy the Titan. To him, therefore, the white light was a friend because it had vanquished a foe.

To him, the potent white light was the Emperor returned to save him.

He ran out of the shadows, calling the Emperor's name, praising him, piteously expressing his gratitude. He was an ancient, emaciated man dressed in dirt and rags. He should have offered no threat to the daemon whatsoever.

Except that, in the Emperor's honour, he had retrieved the fallen aquila altarpiece from the chapel and was holding it up in front of him.

Cherubael howled and backed away, tumbling like thistledown along the dirt track between the longhouses. Perplexed, Dronicus ran after it, offering words of worship to the Emperor that must have driven holy spikes into Cherubael's rotten soul.

I had a moment's respite from the assault.

I looked around. I knew I had to think fast.

Bastian Verveuk was still alive. He was a bloody, broken mess, his clothes and hair virtually burned off him from the cutter's death-blast. Though I loathed him for what he had done, I felt pity as I saw him. His eyes were still yearning. They seemed to light up with joy as they saw me approach. He reached out a bloody hand.

He thought I was coming to rescue him.

I confess here, now, that I hate myself for what I did. That I despised Verveuk does not excuse it. He was an odious wretch who had cost me more dearly than I could say, but he was still a servant of the Inquisition. And, damn him, he worshipped and trusted me.

But there was no alternative. I made the right decision. I had released Cherubael because *Cruor Vult* simply had to be stopped for the good of mankind. Now Cherubael had to be stopped, and I was forced to make a similarly hard choice. I will pay. In time. In the hereafter, when I come before the Golden Throne.

I knelt beside him. His yearning face looked up at me. Damn that yearning, puppy look!

'M-master...'

'Bastian, are you a true servant of the Emperor?'

'I... I am...'

'And you will so serve him in any way you can?'

'I will, master.'

'And are you pure?' Foolish question! Verveuk's damned purity had led to all his mistakes. His puritanical piety had made him a liability in the first place.

But he was pure. As pure as any man could be.

I placed my hand on his chest and made my fingers wet with his blood. Then I daubed certain runes and markings on his forehead and face, on his neck and his heart, muttering seldom heard imprecations from the *Malus Codicium*.

'W-what are you doing?' he wavered. Damned questions, even now!

'What must be done. You are doing the Emperor's work, Bastian.'

A scream howled out of the station and Dronicus appeared, running terrified towards the lake. His hands were on fire, dripping with white-hot, molten metal.

Cherubael had finally found the strength to melt the aquila.

Still screaming, the poor old man plunged into the icy lake, the water steaming and spitting around his agonised hands.

Cherubael's deadly star came shimmering down the beach towards me.

'Forgive me, Verveuk,' I said.

'O-of course, master,' he mumbled.

'F-for what?' he added, suddenly.

Bellowing the incantations of binding, the litany of servitus, the wards of entrapment, I met Cherubael head on, the runestaff glittering with power.

'*In servitutem abduco*, I bind thee fast forever into this host!'

'What in the name of hell happened here?' Fischig bellowed, his gun raised as he ran down towards me.

'Everything. Nothing. It's over, Fischig.'

'But... what is that?' he asked.

The daemonhost floated a few centimetres off the ground next to me. I had fashioned a leash from my belt, tied off around Verveuk's scorched, distended throat.

'I have trapped a daemon, Godwin. He is bound and cannot harm us now.'

'But... Verveuk?'

'Dead. We must honour him. He has given his all to the Emperor.'

Fischig looked at me warily. 'How did you know the means to bind a daemon, Eisenhorn?' he asked.

'I have learned much. It is an inquisitor's job to know these things.'

Fischig took a step back. 'Verveuk...' he began. 'He was dead before you used his body, wasn't he?'

I didn't answer. Three shuttles were powering in across the lake, preparing for landing. The reinforcements summoned by Alizebeth had finally arrived.

SEVEN

TAKING LEAVE OF MIQUOL
GUDRUN, SANCTUARY
HER HEART'S DESIRE

I wanted nothing more than to be gone from the place. It had exhausted me and cost me.

My followers, well-drilled specialists all, deployed from the shuttles and took control of the area, rounding up the last of Thuring's dismayed accomplices. I was told that Menderef and Koth were on their way too, bringing with them units of militia and Inquisitorial guard.

I wasn't going to wait around for them.

There were things I wanted as few people as possible to see.

I issued instructions that would bite great holes out of my personal coffers. But I didn't care.

I sent Bequin away on a shuttle as fast as possible, with Nayl and Begundi guarding her.

Nayl was told to get her condition stabilised at the nearest general infirmary and then arrange passage for her off-world, to the Distaff's headquarters on Messina. They took Kara Swole with them too. Kara was alive, but seriously wounded.

I gave Fischig strict instructions to remain behind as my proxy. His heart didn't seem in it. I knew the daemonhost was troubling him more than he dared to say.

His brief was simple. Secure the island until the main Inquisitorial party arrived. See to it that a full statement was made and that the cache of dormant Chaos Titans was destroyed. Then formally close the Examination until further notice.

It didn't seem unreasonable. A senior inquisitor had just risked all and lost much stopping a Battle Titan. His withdrawal from the Durer Examination for recovery seemed utterly justified.

I would contact him later, and take it from there.

I was about to leave on another of the shuttles, with the silent, shrouded daemonhost, when the first piece of good news that day came to my attention.

Medea and Aemos had survived.

They were cut and battered, but she had dragged Aemos from the cutter crash and got him to cover before Verveuk had ejected. They had lain in cover, dazed and breathless.

They had seen everything.

I embraced them both. 'You're both coming with me,' I said.

'Gregor... what did you do?' Medea asked.

'Just get on the shuttle.'

'What did she mean?' Fischig asked.

I didn't answer him directly. I was too tired. Too afraid that my stumbling explanation would not satisfy him. 'See that things here are done properly. I will contact you in a month with instructions.'

I gave him my rosette badge of office so that his authority would be unquestioned.

It was gesture of the frankest trust, but it seemed to disturb him. Then I held out my hand, and he grasped it with a half-hearted grip.

'I'll do my job,' he said. 'Have I ever let you down?'

He hadn't, and I supposed that was his point. Fischig had never let me down, but perhaps now the reverse was not so true.

Two days later, we were ensconced in a suite of cabins aboard the far trader *Pulchritude*, en route to Gudrun in the Helican sub. A three-week passage, Emperor willing.

I slept for long periods during the voyage, the deep and thankfully dreamless sleep of the soul-weary, but my fatigue lingered. The work on Miquol had been draining, mentally and emotionally. Each time I woke, feeling rested, there was a moment of precious calm before I remembered what I had done. Then the anxieties returned.

Every day of the voyage, I made two visits. The first was to the ship's chapel, where I said my observances more dutifully and strictly than I had done in a hundred years. I felt unclean, violated, though the violation was self-inflicted, I know. I longed for a confessor. In better days, I would have turned to Alizebeth, but that was not possible now.

Instead, I prayed for her survival. I prayed for Swole's health to be restored. I made offerings and lit candles for the souls of Poul Rassi, Duclane Haar and poor Dahault, who had perished in the cutter crash.

I prayed for Bastian Verveuk's soul and craved absolution.

I prayed for Fischig's understanding.

In my service to the God-Emperor, I have always considered myself a dutiful and faithful soul, but it is strange how the everyday customs of worship become so easily neglected. During that voyage, having stumbled closer to the path of heresy than at any time in my life, I felt, ironically, as if my faith was renewed. Perhaps it takes a glimpse over the lip of the abyss to truly appreciate the pure heavens above. I felt chastened and virtuous, as if I had survived an ordeal and emerged a better man.

During the moments of self-doubt and anxiety, and they were numerous, I wondered if that sense of spiritual improvement was simply subconscious denial. Had the events of Miquol really been an overdue wake-up call to steer me smartly back onto the puritan path, or was I deluding myself? Deluding myself like Quixos and all the others who had fallen into the abyss without even realising it.

The second daily visit was to the armoured hold where the daemonhost was secured.

The *Pulchritude*'s captain, a stern Ingeranian called Gelb Startis, had almost refused point blank to accept the daemonhost aboard his ship. Of course, he didn't know it was a daemonhost. Very few individuals in the Imperium would know how to recognise one, and besides I had draped the silent figure in hooded robes. But there was a tangible air of evil and decay around the shrouded monster.

I'd been in no mood to bargain with Startis. I'd simply established my credentials with my signet ring, given him my personal guarantee that the 'guest' would be properly monitored, and paid him three times the going rate for our passage.

That had made the whole venture more appealing for him.

I'd chained the daemonhost in the hold, and spent ten hours inscribing the area with the correct sigils of containment. Cherubael was still zombie-like and dumb, as if entranced. The severe trauma of its binding was still lingering, and for the while it was docile.

On each visit, I triple-checked the sigils and, where necessary, refreshed them. I used a quill and ink dye to permanently mark in the runes I had painted on its flesh in blood.

That was chilling work. Verveuk's body had healed and was now glossy and healthy. His eyes were closed, but his face was still that of the young inquisitor, though the boy's forehead was beginning to bulge with the vestigial nub-horns that were sprouting from the bone.

On the ninth day, it opened Verveuk's eyes. The blank wrath of Cherubael shone out. It had finally come through the terrible rigours of binding, rigours made worse by the crude and rudimentary way I had performed the rite.

'He wants you dead,' were the first words it spoke.

'Am I speaking to Bastian or Cherubael?'

'Both,' it said.

I nodded. 'Nice try, Cherubael. I know Verveuk is gone from that body.'

'He hates you though. I tasted his soul as he passed out of this body and I passed in. He knows what you did and he's taken that dread knowledge to the afterlife with him.'

'The Emperor protects.'

'The Emperor craps himself at the sound of my name,' it responded.

I slapped its face hard. 'You are bound, lord daemon prince, and you will be respectful.'

Floating off the dirty hold floor, wrenching at its securing chains, Cherubael began to scream obscenities at me. I left.

On each return visit, it tried a different tack.

On the tenth day, it was pleading, remorseful.

On the eleventh, sullen and promising grievous harm to me.

On the thirteenth, silent and uncooperative.

On the sixteenth, sly.

'The truth of it, Gregor,' it said, 'is that I've missed you. Our times together have always been exhilarating. Quixos was a cruel master, but you understand me. On that island, you called on me for help. Oh, we've had our differences. And you're a tricky so-and-so. But I like that. I think my existence could be an awful lot worse than being in your thrall. So, tell me... what do you have planned? What glorious work will you and I do together? You'll find me willing, ready. In time, you'll be able to trust me. Like a friend. I've always wanted one of those. You and me, Gregor, friends, working together. How would that be?'

'That would be impossible.'

'Oh, Gregor...' it chided.

'Silence!' I said. I couldn't stomach its silky bonhomie. 'I am an Imperial inquisitor serving the light of the Golden Throne of Terra, and you are a thing of filth and darkness, serving only yourself. You are everything I stand against.'

It licked its lips. Verveuk's canines were becoming ice-white fangs. 'So why did you ever decide to bind me, Eisenhorn?'

'I regularly ask myself the same question,' I said.

'Release me, then,' it whispered. 'Cut me free from these pentagrammic bindings and let me go. We'll call it even. I'll go, and we'll never bother each other again. I promise. Let me go and that will be the matter done.'

'Just how stupid do you think I am?' I asked.

He floated up a little higher, cocked his head on one side, and smiled. 'It was worth a try.'

I was at the door when he called my name again.

'I'm content, you know. Being bound to you.'

'Really?' I replied with disinterest.

It nodded gleefully. 'It gives me ample opportunity to corrupt you entirely.'

On the nineteenth day, it nearly got me. When I entered the hold, it was sobbing on the floor. I tried to ignore it, checking the sigils, but it looked up.

'Master!' it said.

'Verveuk?'

'Yes! Please, master! It's gone away for a moment, and I have control again. Please, cut me free! Banish it!'

'Bastian, I–'

'I forgive you, master! I know you only did what you had to do and I'm more grateful than you could know that you chose me as worthy for this desperate work! But please, please! While I have control! Banish it and release me from this torture!'

I approached it, gripping my runestaff. 'I can't, Bastian.'

'You can, master! Now, while there's a moment clear! Oh, the agony! To be locked in here with that monster! To share the same flesh! It is gnawing away at my soul, and showing me things to drive me insane! Give mercy, master!'

I reached out and pointed to a complex rune inscribed on his chest. 'You see this?'

'Yes?'

'That is the rune of voiding. It is an essential part of the binding transaction. It empties the host of any previous soul so that the daemon can be contained. In effect, it kills the original host. You are not Bastian Verveuk because Bastian is dead and departed from this flesh. I killed him. You mimick his voice well, as I would expect, because you have his larynx and palate, but you are Cherubael.'

It sighed, nodded and floated up again to the limit its chains would permit.

'You can't blame me for trying.'

I slapped its face again hard. 'No, but I can punish you.'

It didn't react.

'Understand this, daemon. Binding you, using you, that has cost me dearly. I hate myself for doing it. But there was no choice. Now I have you enslaved again, I am going to take no chances. The correct containment of you will now become my life's primary devotion. The history texts will not remember me as a man so driven to accomplish things he got lazy and slack. There is no escape from me now. I will not allow it. You are mine and you will stay mine.'

'I see.'

'Do you understand?'

'I understand you are a man of the highest piety and resolve.'

'Good.'

'Just one thing: how does it feel to be a murderer?'

Earlier, I remarked that very few citizens of the Imperium of Man would recognise a daemonhost or understand what one was. That is true. It is also true that the select group who would know included several of my followers. Those that had been with me on 56-Izar, Eechen, Cadia, Farness Beta.

Aemos and Medea certainly understood the concept of daemonhosting. I had briefed them myself. I felt that Medea, like Fischig, only vaguely understood what I had brought onto the *Pulchritude* with me, though they regarded it with shuddering suspicion.

Aemos knew, though. He knew damn well. As far as I could tell, he knew everything that it was possible to know without going mad. But he had been with me longer than any of them. We had been friends and companions for more years than I dared count. I knew I had his trust and that I'd have to err wildly before he questioned my methods.

I realised after a day or two of the voyage that he wasn't even going to mention it.

I couldn't have that. I wanted openness. So I brought the matter up myself.

It was late one night, perhaps the fifth night of the voyage. We were playing double regicide (two boards in parallel, one played backwards using militants as crowning pieces, the other played long with sentries wild and a freedom to regent-up on white-square takes after the third sequence of play... this was the only formation of the ancient strategy game that even began to test his mind) and sipping the best amasec Startis could provide.

'Our passenger,' I began, picking up a squire piece and then putting it down again as I contemplated my next move, 'what are your thoughts? You've been very quiet.'

'I didn't believe it was my place to remark,' he said.

I moved the squire to militant three and immediately regretted it. 'Uber, how long have we been friends?'

I could tell he was actually about to calculate. 'I believe we first met in the seventh month of–'

'I mean roughly.'

'Well, to say friends, perhaps several years after our first meeting, which would make it–'

'Could we agree that a rough estimate would be... a very long time?'

He thought about it. 'We could,' he said, sounding unconvinced.

'And we are friends, aren't we?'

'Oh, of course! Well, I hope so,' he said, promptly taking my dexter basilisk and securing a ruthless toe-hold into my second line. 'Aren't we?'

'Yes. Yes, we are. I look to you for answers.'

'You do.'

'Sometimes, I think those answers could come without me having to ask the questions first.'

'Hmmm,' he said. He was about to move his yale. He raised the bone-carved piece and studied it closely. 'I have always wondered about the yale,' he said. 'A heraldic beast, obviously, tracing its origins back into the ages before the Great Strife. But what does it represent? The analogies of the other pieces, given historic traditions and the structure of Imperial culture, are obvious. But the yale... of all pieces in regicide, that one puzzles me...'

'You're doing it again.'

'Doing what?'

'Procrastinating. Avoiding the issue.'

'Am I?'

'You are.'

'I'm sorry.' He put the piece down again, taking one of my raptors in a move I simply hadn't seen coming. Now hc had my militant in a vice.

'Well?'

'Well?'

'What do you think?'

He frowned. 'The yale. Most perturbatory.'

I rallied and took his yale abruptly. It was a foolish move, but it got his attention.

'About the other matter. The passenger.'

'It's a daemonhost.'

'Yes, it is.' I said, almost relieved.

'You bound it into Verveuk's body on Miquol.'

'I did. I think you watched me do it.'

'I was concussed, drowsy. But, yes. I saw it.'

'What do you think about that?'

He made a guard piece a regent and crossed into my sinister field. The game would be over in another half dozen moves.

'I try not to, for what it's worth. I try not to imagine how a man I have followed and believed in for so long suddenly has the means and power to unleash a daemon, channel it and bind it again. I try not to think about the possibility that Bastian Verveuk was alive when the binding occurred. I try to believe that my beloved inquisitor hasn't crossed a line from where there is no crossing back.'

'Checkmate,' he added.

I conceded both boards and sat back. 'I'm sorry,' I said.

'For what?'

'For putting you through this.'

'Your questions are–'

'No. I don't mean that. In the course of my hunt for Quixos, I learned several dark things. Chief of those was the means to control a daemon. It is knowledge that I would have chosen never to use. But the Titan was too much. It couldn't be allowed to survive. I had nothing left in my arsenal except dark lore.'

'I understand, Gregor. Truly. This conversation wasn't even necessary. You did what you had to do. We survived... most of us anyway. Chaos was denied. That's the job, isn't it? No one ever said it would be easy. Sacrifices have to be made or the God-Emperor's work will never be done.'

He leaned forward, his augmetic eyes glittering in the firelight. 'Honestly, Gregor... if I thought you had become some demented radical, would I be sitting here playing regicide with you?'

'Thank you, Uber,' I said.

Aemos had given me a harder time than I had expected. Medea, on the other hand, I was braced for, and her reaction surprised me too.

'Daemon-what? I don't care.'

'You don't?'

'Not really. Thuring is all I care about, and you used everything you had to to get him.'

'I did.'

'Well, good for you.'

We were sitting in amongst the plush cushions of the *Pulchritude*'s observation deck.

She peered at me, frowning. 'Oh, I get it. You're afraid that all of us will think that you've become some heretical psycho crazy.'

By 'all of us' she meant my staff.

'Do you?'

'Hell, no! Get over it, boss! If I could do what you can do, I'd have done the same! Screw Thuring any way you can!'

I sighed. 'I didn't do it for your father, Medea.'

'What?'

'I mean I did, but I didn't. I wanted to avenge Midas, of course, but I only unleashed the daemon because Thuring and his damned Titan threatened more than just us.'

'That planet, you mean?'

'That planet... and others.'

'Right.'

'What's the matter?'

She stroked her hair back off her face and reached for her drink. 'You're telling me that if the planet hadn't been in danger, you wouldn't have done the whole daemon thing?'

'No. I want you to understand this. I wanted Thuring dead. I wanted him to pay for your father's death. But I didn't release Cherubael in vengeance. That would have been petty and small-minded. I could never have justified that, not even to myself. I released the daemon because Fayde Thuring had become more than just a personal enemy. He'd become an enemy of the Imperium. I had to stop him then, and I was out of options. What I mean is, it was a totally pragmatic decision in the end. Not a weak, emotional one.'

'Whatever. Thuring suffered, didn't he? He burned? That's all I care about. But you owe me, though?'

'I do?'

'You swore it. On your secrets. That I'd be there when–'

'You were!'

'No thanks to you! And not so I could play a part and make Thuring suffer. So you owe me. And I want that secret. Now.'

'What secret?'

'You choose. But it's got to be the darkest one you have. Since you brought it up, what about this... this Cherubael?'

And that was how I came to tell her everything about the daemonhost. Everything. I did it because of the honour of our oath. I also did it, I believe now, because I wished to unburden myself to a confessor and Bequin wasn't there. I did it and didn't even pause to think what might result from it.

God-Emperor forgive me.

I have always loved Gudrun, the old capital world of the Helican sub-sector. For a long time, I had made my main home on Thracian Primaris, a world crusted by cities, riddled with crime, lamed by overpopulation. But I had only lived there for the sake of convenience. It was the capital world after all, and the Palace of the Inquisition was sited there. I visit it as little as possible, for it depresses me.

But after the vile events of the Holy Novena, five decades before, I had transferred my chief residence to the more relaxing climes of Gudrun. Returning there, I felt somehow safe.

We bade Startis farewell and offloaded our luggage onto a privately chartered shuttle. I had prepared a cargo pod for Cherubael, fully inscribed and warded, the accomplishment of which took many hours. I said the appropriate rites and chained it inside, adding a charm that would render it docile. The pod was loaded by mute servitors into the shuttle's hold.

We dropped planetwards.

From the ports of the passenger bay, I looked down at the green expanses of the world. The great stretches of wild land and forest, the blue seas, the tight order of the ancient cities. For many years it had been the sub-sector capital, until the bloated giant Thracian Primaris had commandeered that role. I knew from experience that evil and corruption lurked here as much as it did on any Imperial world. But this was the epitome of Imperial life, for all its vices and flaws, a singular example of the very culture I had devoted my life to safeguard.

We made a detour on the descent. I felt it prudent to secure Cherubael somewhere other than my residence, though I had previously stored it in the secret oubliette below the foundations. If there were any official consequences to the incident on Durer, my estate could be subject to all manner of unwelcome scrutiny.

I covertly owned a number of premises on Gudrun. They were not held in my name, so that they could be used as safehouses or private retreats. One was a semi-ruined watchtower in the wilds, three hundred kilometres south of my home, a lonely, remote spot that I had found conducive to meditation over the years.

Using the shuttle's servitors, I placed the warded cargo pod containing the daemonhost in the tower's crypt, made the necessary rituals of holding, and activated the simple but efficient alarm perimeter I had installed in the tower when I first purchased it.

It would do for the while. Later, I would be very thankful I had made that decision.

My home was a dignified estate out on the Insume headland, twenty minutes' flight time from the venerable lagoon city of Dorsay. Called Spaeton after the feudal family that had built it, it was an H-plan villa constructed of grey ouslite stone with a green copper-tile roof. There were adjoining garages and stables, an aviary, a drone-hive, a famous landscaped garden and maze laid out mathematically by Utility Krauss, a water dock down on the private inlet and a perfect sulleq lawn. It was surrounded to the north and east by untenanted woods, fruit orchards and ample paddocks, and from the terrace it had clear views over the Bay of Bisheen.

Jarat, my housekeeper, welcomed us back. It was late evening and the residence was warm, clean and ready for occupation. Plump and dressed in her trademark grey gown-robe and white-veiled black cap, Jarat was very old by then. Alongside her were Jubal Kircher, my head of security, and Aldemar Psullus, my rubricator and librarian. Beside them, Eleena Koi of the Distaff and the astropath Jekud Vance. The rest of the house staff, thirty of them, maids, ostlers, gardeners, cooks, sommeliers, eltuaniers and launderers, were lined up in fresh-pressed white uniforms behind them, along with the five black-armoured officers of the security detail. I greeted each one personally. Jarat and Kircher had employed several newcomers since I had last been there, and I made a point of talking to them and learning their names: Litu, a perky junior chambermaid; Kronsky, a new member of the security detail; Altwald, a new head groundsman inheriting his job from his father, who had retired.

I wondered when Jarat would retire. Or Kircher, come to that. In the case of Jarat, probably never, I decided.

My first act was to open the stronghold oubliette in the basement. I shut down the shields and deactivated the locks, and then spent a long time obliterating all traces of what the oubliette had been used for. I used a flamer to scour the walls and burn away the runic inscriptions. The grisly remains of Cherubael's previous host form, now an empty husk, lay amid the slack chains, and I cremated that too. The host form had been a vat-grown organic vessel I had privately commissioned for use in the original summoning. At the time, it had been a hard enough decision just to use a synthetic body.

I thought of Verveuk and shivered. I burned everything.

Then I bathed, and stayed a long time in the hot water.

Two weeks I spent, recuperating at Spaeton. I had tried to rest, or at least recover, during the voyage home, but there is a tension in travel itself and my concerns about the daemonhost's rudimentary confinement had prevented me from relaxing.

Now, I could rest at last.

I took long walks around the headland's paths, or stood on the point watching the waves crash into the rocks at the fringe of the inlet. I sat reading in the gardens during the warm evenings. I helped junior staff members collect early windfalls into wicker drowsies in the orchards.

I went nowhere near the library, the maze or my office. Alizebeth was never far from my thoughts.

Aemos served as secretary during that period, a job that Bequin would previously have undertaken. Around breakfast time every morning, he would inform me of the number of communiqués received overnight, and I would tell him to handle them. He responded to general letters, filed private ones for my later attention, and stalled anything official. He knew there were only a few kinds of communiqué that I would permit myself to be troubled with if they arrived: word of Bequin, a direct communication from the Ordos, or anything from Fischig.

On a bright morning early in my third week there, with dawn mist fuming off the lawns where the early sun caught it, I was sparring with Jubal Kircher in the pugnaseum.

It was the third morning we had done so. Realising how out of condition I felt, I had commenced a regime of light combat work to tone myself up. We were dressed in bodygloves with quilted shield-sleeves, and circled each other on the mat with scorae, basket-hilted practice weapons from Carthae.

Jubal was a weapons master but he was getting a little old, and on peak form I had no trouble besting him. Where he truly excelled me was in combat-lore and the techniques of military science, which he had studied all his life. He used those that morning, preying on my softness and slowness, overwhelming my superior strength and speed with patient expertise.

Three quarters of an hour, five rounds, five touches to him. His old lined face was glowing with perspiration, but he was five times the winner I was.

'Enough for today, sir?' he asked.

'You're going easy on me, Jubal.'

'Beating you five love straight is going easy?'

I hung my scorae over my belt and adjusted the straps of my sleeve-shield. 'If I was one of your security detail in training, I'd have five bruises now to go with my five losses.'

Kircher smiled and nodded. 'You would. But an ex-Guard bravo or a slumboy trying to make my grade needs the bruises to remind him that work here isn't some well-paid retirement. I don't believe you need to learn that sort of lesson.'

'None of us are too wise to learn.' We both looked and saw Medea entering the pugnaseum. She wandered around the edge of the mat, one moment in the shadows of the wall panels, the next in the glaring yellow oblongs cast by the skylights. She looked at me.

'Just repeating one of your many aphorisms.'

I could tell something was up with her. Kircher shifted uncomfortably.

'Let me spar with him,' she said. I nodded to Jubal, who saluted, Carthaen style, with his scora and left the circular room.

Medea took off her father's cerise jacket and hung it on a window knob.

'What'll it be?' I asked, taking a sip of water from a beaker on the decanter stand.

She walked over to the armoury terminal and keyed on the screen, jump-cutting rapidly through the graphic templates the monitor displayed. She was dressed in a tight, semi-armoured bodyglove and her feet were clad in training slippers. She had prepared for this, I realised.

'Blades and power-bucklers,' she announced, stopping the menu and keying the authority stud.

There was a distant rattle and whirr as automated systems in the armoury under the floor processed the selected weapons from their racks and elevated them up into the ready rack in the wall next to the terminal. Two buckler modules. Two swords, matching, each the length of an adult human femur, single-edged and slightly curved with a knuckle-bar around the grip. She tossed one to me and I caught it neatly.

I walked over to join her, placing my scorae in the rack that would return it to storage. Then I took my buckler. It strapped around the left forearm, supporting a round, machined emitter the size of a pocket watch. Engaged, it projected a disc of shield energy the size of a banquet plate above the back of my hand and forearm.

'Attention, you have selected weapons of lethal force. Attention, you have selected weapons of lethal force...' The terminal issued the notice in soft but urgent repeats.

I shut it off with a key-press.

'We can use full body shields, if you're worried,' she said.

'Why would I be worried? This is just sparring.'

We engaged our power-bucklers and faced each other across the centre of the mat, slightly side on, shield towards shield, our blades held low in our right hands.

'Signal cue,' I said.

'Three,' said the terminal speaker, 'two, one… commence.'

Medea had been practising.

She swept round with her blade, and simultaneously parried my first approach with her buckler which squealed and sparked off mine as their fields met and repulsed.

I undercut defensively, gathering her blade in towards our shields so that for a moment all four weapons were locked in a protesting knot of spitting electrical energy.

We broke, and circled.

She came in again, leading with her sword. I fended it away with my buckler, then again, and then for a third time as we continued to go around.

She was canny. Sword and buckler work was as old as all the worlds, and the trick to staying alive was to use the shield more than the sword. The trick to winning, however, was to use the sword more than the shield.

I kept my buckler to the front but, by seeming to be unguarded with her own force shield lagging back as if casually forgotten, she was inviting me to overstep or make a badly judged lunge.

I left my blade well alone, keeping it where she could see it, and using my shield as Harlon Nayl had schooled me. The buckler was a weapon. Not only could it block, it could lock or even break a blade. I had heard of some duels where the small shield's solid-energy edge had actually delivered the killing stroke to an unprotected windpipe.

Medea rotated suddenly, driving my buckler aside with a swipe of her own, and lashed in with her blade, dancing across the mat. I was forced to parry with my sword, and then rally hard as she kept up the pressure.

Her blade sliced to within a handsbreath of my face and I cross-guarded desperately with both blade and buckler.

She drove her own shield in under my guard and her own locked sword and doubled me up with a punished strike to my midriff.

I fell onto the mat.

'Enough?' she asked.

I got up. 'We'll go again.'

She came at me again, leading with the blade as I had expected. I ducked, swung round and feinted in time for her buckler to swing in to parry my blade.

The spitting electrical dish tore the sword from my hand, stinging my fingers.

Just as I had intended.

Her eyes were on my sword, distracted as it flew aside. With my now free right hand, I grabbed her buckler arm above the elbow and pulled it down so that her own power shield locked with her sword as she brought it up. She stumbled. I smashed her across the extended shoulder with the flat of my buckler and knocked her down.

I could have used the edge. I could have aimed for her exposed face. But we were sparring.

'Enough?' I asked.

She said nothing.

'Medea?'

She extinguished her buckler and pulled the strapping off.

'What's on your mind?'

Medea looked up at me. 'I never wanted revenge,' she said.

'You told me you did.'

'I know. And I suppose I did. Part of me. Revenge... it doesn't feel...'

'Satisfying?'

'Like anything at all. Just empty. Stupid and empty.'

'Well... I could have told you that. In fact, I think I did.'

I helped her up. We didn't speak for a minute or two as we put the weapons back in the rack and returned them to the underfloor store bay.

Then we took beakers of water from the stand, opened the pugnaseum's side doors and went out onto the sunlit terrace.

It was going to be a hot day. The sky was cloudless and the light white. The shade of the woods seemed gloriously dark and inviting. The distant inlet was hazy with glare and the sea glinted like diamonds.

'Ever since I was old enough to understand what Fayde Thuring did,' she said, 'I've wanted something. I've always presumed it was revenge.'

'Revenge is a disguise for other, more valid emotional responses,' I said.

She looked at me sourly. 'Stop trying to be my father, Eisenhorn.'

She might has well have slapped me across the face. I had never thought of it that way.

'I only meant–' I began.

'You're a very wise man,' she said. 'Very clever. Learned. You give people the most profound advice.'

'I try.'

'But you don't *feel*.'

'Feel, Medea?'

'You know things but you don't feel them.'

Birds twittered in the edges of the woods and the orchards. Two of the junior groundstaff were pressing the lower lawns with a heavy roller. I wasn't quite sure I knew what she meant.

'I feel–'

'No. You don't feel the content of your advice, most of the time. They're just wisdoms, without heart.'

'I'm sorry you think that way.'

'It isn't a criticism. Well, not really. You are just so driven to do what is... right, that you forget to wonder why it's right. I mean–'

'What?'

'I don't know.'

'Try.'

She sipped her water. 'You fight the way Kircher tells you to fight because he says that's the best way to do it.'

'It usually is.'

'Of course. He's an expert. That's why you defeated me. But why is it the best way to fight? Using those weapons, for example?'

'Because–'

'Because he told you? He's right. But why is he right? You never wonder about that sort of thing. You never wonder what mistakes or decisions were made to arrive at that right way.'

'I'm still not sure I follow you...'

She smiled and shook her head. 'Of course you don't. That's my point. You've spent your whole life learning the best way to do everything. Learning the best way to fight. The best way to investigate. The best way to learn, even. Did you ever wonder why those are the best ways?'

I put my glass down on the low wall at the edge of the terrace. 'Life's too short.'

'My father's life was too short.'

I said nothing.

'My father died and I wanted something, and you told me that it wasn't revenge. And you were right. Revenge is trash. Worthless. But why? What was it I needed instead?'

I shook my head. 'I was only trying to spare you the effort. Revenge is a waste of time and–'

'No,' she said, looking at me directly. 'It's a displacement activity. It's something you can lock on to and do because you can't do the thing you really want to do.'

I had grown impatient. 'And what might that be, Medea? Do you know?' I asked.

'I do now,' she said. 'Thuring killed my father. I needed something, and it wasn't payback. It was what he took from me. I needed to know my father. If I'd ever had that, then I'd never have given Thuring another thought.'

She was right. It was so obvious, it chilled me. I wondered how many other, similar, obvious mistakes I had made in my life with my head so full of certain knowledge and my heart so numb.

I looked back at the pugnaseum, and saw Midas's cerise jacket handing where she had left it, draped against the inside of one of the windows like a trapped butterfly.

'I can give you what you want,' I said, 'in part, at least. If you really want it.'

I summoned my astropath, Vance, and requested that he made the prepa rations. He suggested that evening might be a good time, when things were quieter, and so I asked Jarat to serve a light dinner early to leave the evening clear, and to leave out a cold supper in case we were hungry once we were done.

At seven, Medea and I went to the reading room above the house's main library. I gave Kircher specific instructions that we were not to be disturbed. Most of the household had retired early to private study or relaxation in any case.

Psullus, the rubricator, was in the library, repairing some bindings that were fraying at the spines.

'Give us a while,' I said to him.

He looked unnerved. Infirm with a progressive wasting disease, he virtually lived in the library. It was his private world and I felt cruel ousting him from it.

'What should I do?' he asked cautiously.

'Go sit in the study, watch the stars come out. Take a good book.'

He looked around and sniggered.

My library was at the heart of Spaeton House, and occupied two floors. The lower level was divided by alcoves of shelves and the upper gallery was supported by those alcoves, giving access to further shelving stacks lining the gallery walls. Soft glow-lamps hung from slender ceiling chains and cast a warm, golden light all around, and the panelled reading lecterns along the centre of the ground floor were fitted with individual reading lamps that generated little pockets of brighter blue luminescence.

The place was comfortably warm, its atmosphere carefully controlled to guard against any excess humidity that might damage the stored books. There was a smell of wood polish, chemical preservatives, and the ozone whiff of the stasis fields that protected the oldest and most fragile specimens.

Once Psullus had gone, taking with him a copy of Boydenstyre's *Lives*, I led Medea up the brass staircase to the upper gallery and along to the heavy door of the private reading room at the far end.

At the door, Medea paused and took a Glavian needle pistol from her pocket.

'I brought this,' she said. 'It was also my father's, one of the pair made for him.'

I knew that well enough. Medea still carried the matched pistols in combat.

'Leave it outside,' I told her. 'It's never a good idea to attempt connection through weapons. Even friendly heirlooms like that. The sting of death attaches itself to them and you'd find that unpleasant. The jacket will be fine.'

She nodded and left the gun on a bookshelf near the reading room door. We went inside and found Vance waiting for us. The small chamber was candle lit, with three chairs arranged around a cloth-covered table. The last rays of sunset were glimmering in through the stained glass skylight.

We took our seats. Vance, a tall, stooping man with kindly, tired eyes, spread Midas's cerise jacket on the tablecloth. He had already been meditating enough to put him near to the trance state, and I gently guided Medea to a receptive calmness.

The auto-seance began. It is a simple enough psychic procedure, and one which I have used many times for investigation and research. Vance was the conduit, channelling the power of the warp. I focused my own mind-strength to keep us centred. From the point of transition, the room took on a cold, frosty light. Solids became transluscent and fizzy. The dimensions of the little reading room stretched and shifted impatiently.

Midas's jacket, now a wisp of turquoise smoke, was swathed in the aura it had accumulated over time, the echoes of its contact with human hands, human minds.

'Take it,' I said. 'Touch it.'

Medea reached out her hand warily and brushed her fingers against the edge of the aura, which bloomed and fluffed up at her touch.

'Oh,' she said.

We teased apart the psychic memories clinging to that garment until we found her father. Midas Betancore, pilot, warrior, my friend. We coaxed his phantom out of hiding.

It was no ghost, just the after-image he had left behind. An impression of him, his looks, his voice, his emotions. A distant hint of his rich chuckle. The faint odour of the lho-sticks he liked to smoke and the cologne he chose to wear. We saw him young, little more than a boy. We saw him in virile middle age, just a few years from his untimely death. There, at the helm of the gun-cutter, itself now just a ghost too, the Glavian circuitry inlaid into his hands marrying him profoundly to the craft's controls. There, steering a long-prow. There, watching the suns rise over the Stilt Hills of Glavia.

We tasted his grief at the death of Lores Vibben, but I had Vance pass along quickly to spare us the empathic pain. We clung to him through several exhilarating dogfights, sharing the joy of virtuoso manoeuvres and expert kills. We watched as he saved my life, or the lives of my companions, over and again.

We listened at a dinner table while he made the company roar and clap with an outrageous tale well told. It made all three of us laugh out loud. We saw him, in silence, studying a regicide board and trying to fathom out how Bequin had managed to beat him again. We watched him, through a blizzard of coloured streamers, take his bride to the altar of the High Church at Glavia Glavis. I glimpsed myself, alongside Fischig, Alizebeth and Aemos, in the front pew, cheering and ringing our ceremonial bells with the rest of the congregation.

'That's my mother!' Medea whispered. The veiled woman on Midas's arm was stunning, exquisite. Jarana Shayna Betancore. Midas always did have such good taste. Jarana lived still, far away on Glavia, a distinguished widow and director of a shipwrighting firm. 'She looks so young,' Medea added. There was a note of sadness in her voice. She hadn't been back to Glavia to visit her mother for many years.

Then, almost as if we were intruding, we saw Midas and Jarana embracing on the shores of Taywhie Lake. Midas was beside himself with happiness and excitement.

'Really? Really?' he kept asking.

'Yes, Midas. Really. I'm really pregnant.'

I looked at Medea, saw the tears in her eyes.

'We should stop now, I think,' I said.

'No, I want to see more,' she said.

'We should,' I advised. I could tell that Vance was getting tired. And I knew it wouldn't be long before we stumbled into memories of Fayde Thuring and the last hours. 'We should stop. We–'

I was cut off by the sudden shrilling of my communicator. I cursed loudly. Kircher had been told: no interruptions.

The sound shattered the seance at once. The blue light flashed and vanished, and the room returned to normal with a sudden lurch that blew out the candles and cast us painfully out of the warp. Vance slumped forward, breathing hard, in distress. My head ached with a sudden piercing pain. Medea pulled the jacket towards her across the table and buried her head into its silk folds, sobbing. The walls were sweating.

Damn Kircher. Seances shouldn't be broken like that. Any one of us could have been badly damaged by the abrupt termination. As it was, we were all emotionally dazed.

I got up. 'Stay here,' I said to them both. 'Take a moment to recover.' Vance nodded feebly. Medea was lost in her own storm of feelings.

I went outside and pulled the door closed, breathing hard. Yanking the little hand vox from my pocket, I keyed the 'respond' rune.

'This had better be good, Jubal,' I said hoarsely.

Static crackled back.

'Jubal? Jubal? This is Eisenhorn.'

Nothing. Then a quick blurt of frantic words I couldn't make out. Then static again.

'Jubal?'

From somewhere distant, on the other side of the house, I heard a trio of muffled cracks.

Las-fire.

I snatched up Midas's needle pistol from the shelf where Medea had left it and ran for the library door.

EIGHT

THE FALL OF SPAETON HOUSE
FOR OUR LIVES
SASTRE, LOYAL SASTRE

The halls of the house were quiet, with the lights dimmed, but I could smell burning. I hurried down a carpeted crosswalk, arming the needle pistol. Thirty rounds and a fully charged cell. I had no reload.

Tiny red lights were winking on the security monitor dials recessed into the walls at regular intervals. I went to the nearest one, opened the cover and was about to press my signet ring into the reader when I heard movement.

I raised the gun.

Two maids and a houseman ran into view and yelped when they saw me.

'Steady, steady!' I cried out, lowering the gun. 'This way, come on!'

They ran up to me and cowered behind some ornamental plant stands.

'What's going on?'

They were too scared to answer at first. I saw that the youngest of them was the new girl, Litu. She looked up at me with terrified, tear-pink eyes.

'Litu? What's going on?'

'Raiders,' she said, her voice breathy with panic. 'Raiders, sir. Just minutes ago, there was suddenly this great big bang from upstairs, and then shooting. Men running around, with guns. I saw a man dead. I think it was Urben. I think.'

Rocef Urben. One of my security detail.

'He had all blood coming out of his face,' she stammered.

'The raiders, Litu. From which direction?'

'From the west, sir,' said the houseman, Colyon. 'From the main gate, I think. I heard Master Kircher say they were coming from the stable block too.'

'You saw Kircher?'

'It was a bit mad, sir. I heard him as he ran past.'

I looked around. The smell of burning was getting stronger and I could hear more shots.

'Colyon,' I said, 'do you have your house keys?'

'I'm never without them, sir,' he said.

'Good man. Go along here to the east porch and then get yourself and these women into the gardens. Head for the orchards. Hide. Got a comm?'

'Yes, sir.'

'If you don't hear from me in the next twenty minutes, try and get all three of you off the property. Look after them, Colyon.'

'I will, sir.'

They ran off. I fitted my ring into the monitor and authorised access. The little wall unit lit the air with a small diagnostic hologram. Incredibly, it stated that all security systems, all detectors, all perimeter shields, were shut down. They'd been shut down at source, using an authorised command code.

How in the name of hell?

'Jubal?' I tried the vox again. 'Anybody? This is Eisenhorn. Respond.'

The hand vox answered this time. A man's voice, hard like stone. 'Eisenhorn. You are dead, Eisenhorn.'

I went down through the staff quarters. It seemed like everyone had fled. Doors were open and a few chairs were overturned. Half drunk cups of caffeine, still steaming. A half-finished game of regicide in the butler's pantry. A pict-unit still playing a live broadcast from the arena at Dorsay. A fallen lho-stick burning a patch in the carpet.

I stamped out the embers.

Through a door into the west landing I found Urben. He was dead all right. He was sprawled with his back arched in the doorway. Laser fire had blasted him open.

I was bent over him when I heard footsteps.

Three men came in through the other side of the landing, but I only saw two of them. They were moving fast, with the fluid confidence of trained killers. They were wearing combat armour made of rubberised mesh, their faces hidden behind grotesque papier-maché masks, the kind you can buy in Dorsay's market for the carnivals. They had cut-down lasrifles.

They fired as soon as they saw me, their shots striking the doorframe. I barely had time to dive into cover. I heard the pip and chatter of their microbead communicators.

One, sporting a gilded carnodon mask, moved in, running low, as another in a mermaid mask gave cover.

From the doorway, I fired the needle pistol twice and put two tiny holes through the carnodon leer. The raider folded up and crashed to the floor, his knees buckling under him.

The mermaid fired again, repeatedly, and I switched to the other side of the doorway.

Cease! I commanded, using my will. No reaction. They were psy-shielded.

Someone had prepared.

I crouched and fired up at the chandelier. When it came crashing down, the mermaid dived to the side and I caught him squarely with three needles, any of which would have been a kill shot. The mermaid thumped backwards heavily and brought a console table over as he fell.

I moved through the door, not realising the third one was there. His shots grazed my shoulder and knocked me down hard.

There was a very loud bang.

I looked up.

'Gregor?'

It was Aemos.

'Gregor, I think I've jammed your bloody gun,' he said.

I got up. Aemos was standing in a nearby doorway, fiddling with my bolt pistol. The third, unseen raider had made a clotted dent in the plasterwork.

'Give it to me,' I said, snatching the bolt pistol and freeing the slide.

'Thank you, Aemos,' I added.

He shrugged. 'It's most perturbatory,' he said. 'Guns and me, we don't seem to get on and I always–'

'Aemos, hush! What the hell's going on?'

'We're under attack,' he said.

'I need a little more than that, old friend.'

'Well, I know little more, Gregor. Boom, we're under attack. No warning, no nothing. Men everywhere. Lots of running around and shooting. We thought you were dead.'

'Me?'

'They hit the study first. A grenade or something.'

'Damn! Come with me. Stay close.'

We went upstairs. Skeins of smoke drifted through the air. I had the needle pistol in one hand and the boltgun in the other. At the top of the stairs we found two members of my house staff. They had been shot against a wall.

'Oh, that's terrible...' Aemos murmured.

It was. Someone would pay dearly for this outrage.

The door to my study was open and the smoke was issuing from inside.

'Stay back,' I whispered to Aemos and lunged in through the door.

The room was a mess. A missile or ram-grenade fired from the lawns had blown out the main windows and turned the desk and chair into kindling. Cold night air breezed in through the shattered casement and wafted the smoke from the burning rug and shelving into the house.

There were three more raiders inside, ransacking the bookshelves and trying to force open the file store. A man with a clown mask was raking precious manuscripts, slates and scrolls out of a climate-controlled case into a sack. Another in a serpent mask was repeatedly kicking the display case in which Barbarisater was stored, trying to rupture it. A third, sporting a grinning sun, was attacking the armoured sleeve of my file bureau with a crowbar.

They all turned, reaching for their weapons.

Throne, they were fast! I had the drop, but they moved like lightning. The serpent actually managed to loose a burst at me that went over my diving head before I felled him with a bolt-round. His body hit the armour glass cover of the sword case and left a streak of gore down it as it slid off. The clown was slower, and his torso was punctured by needle rounds before he'd dropped the sack. He just fell over, his mask crumpling as it struck first one shelf edge, then another, then another on its way down to the floor.

The sun face threw the crowbar aside, and dived behind the ruins of the desk even as I was rolling out of the end of the dive and re-aiming.

His blurt of las-fire met my hail of bolts and needles. I swear that at least two of my bolt rounds were exploded in mid-air by his laser shots. But the needles went clean through the desk and clean through him. He lolled back, dead.

I got up and walked towards the destroyed end of my study.

That's where I found Psullus. I'd sent him here just a few hours before. The burning pages of Boydenstyre's *Lives* were littered around. He'd been sitting at my desk when the missile had taken out the window bay.

'Dear Emperor... Aldemar...' Aemos was bitterly shocked at the ghastly sight.

I was simply furious by then. I pushed the needle gun, now virtually spent, into my pocket and grabbed more bolt clips from the shelf by the window.

'We have to get out of here, Aemos,' I said.

He nodded dumbly. I picked up the sack that the clown had been filling and handed it to Aemos. 'Fill it,' I said. 'You know what's valuable.'

He hurried to obey.

I typed security codes into the cases containing Barbarisater and the runestaff. The armour glass covers purred open.

Outside, there was a shrill whining noise and the beams of searchlights crossed the lawns and the orchards. My attackers had air cover.

One final necessity. I opened my encoded void-safe and took out the ancient, wretched copy of the *Malus Codicium*. I tucked it into my coat, but Aemos had seen it.

'Come on!' I said.

'One moment,' Aemos replied, tugging a last few scroll cases into the sack and then hoisting it onto his back.

'Now, I'm ready,' he said.

I went to the door, boltgun in one hand and Barbarisater in the other. The staff was slung across my back. I could hear a fierce bout of shooting from below, a serious firefight.

My loyal friend Jubal Kircher wasn't going without a fight.

'Follow me,' I told Aemos.

It had only been a few minutes since the comm-alarm that had disrupted the auto-seance. Already that tranquil encounter with the shade of Midas Betancore seemed like ancient history.

The house was on fire. From the east wing, flames leapt up into the cool night and filled the air with fluttering ashes and cinders. We cowered behind a wall in the yard outside the kitchen, and got a look out across the back lawn. Three heavy speeders had landed there, crouching like glossy black insects on their extending landing claws. Their side hatches were open and cabins empty. A fourth, and then a fifth, passed low overhead, searchlights sweeping down as they riddled the back of the house with cannon fire.

Five fliers. Each one was capable of carrying a dozen armed men. That meant a small army was assaulting Spaeton House. Someone wanted me and my staff eradicated. Someone wanted my precious secrets and trinkets looted. And someone had enough money and influence to make those things happen.

In truth, the house's auto-defences should have easily held off the attack, even an attack of this magnitude. Inquisitors make enemies. A fortified residence is an occupational necessity.

But Spaeton House had been broken wide open. Its screens, void shutters, lock-outs, motion detectors, sentry servitors, gun-pods... everything had been inert when the attackers arrived.

They were mercenaries, I was sure of that. Highly trained, highly motivated, utterly ruthless. But who had bank-rolled them, and why?

Answers later, I decided, as another series of explosions rippled across the estate and lit the sky.

The stable block, which I used as a hangar and garage, had just gone up.

'What about one of their vehicles?' Aemos whispered, gesturing the fliers on the lawn.

It was too risky. We'd be out in the open and the speeders were likely to be guarded. I shook my head.

'The water dock then?' he suggested. 'Maybe they haven't got to the boats?'

'No, they had everything else covered. They knew the layout, knew to hit the stables. They were briefed about this place inside and out.'

We went back inside, through the kitchen and across the little walled herb garden into the scullery behind the dining hall. Smoke fumes strung the air like silk hangings. I had one last means of escape, one I believed they didn't - couldn't - know about.

Barbarisater twitched and I knew someone was coming. I pushed Aemos back behind me.

Two figures came into view. One was Eleena Koi, the untouchable assigned to the house. She was supporting Xel Sastre, one of Kircher's men. He had been wounded in the arm and shoulder.

'Eleena!' I hissed.

'Lord! Thank the Emperor! We thought you were dead!' Her narrow face was taut with panic and Sastre's blood was all over her brushed epinchire gown.

I took a quick look at Sastre's wounds. They were bad, but he'd live if we could get him to an infirmary.

'Have you seen any others? Kircher? Have you seen him?'

'I saw him die,' said Sastre. 'They were driving us back, and he stayed to hold the main hall. Took on twenty of the bastards.'

'You sure he's–'

'They blew him apart. But not before he'd finished a good half dozen. He told me... told me Kronsky let them in.'

'What?'

'Kronsky. The new guy hired last month. He betrayed the whole house. Shut down the defence system.'

An inside job, as I had feared. Kircher had employed this Kronsky in good faith, and no doubt scrupulously vetted his background and subjected him to a mind-search. And I had welcomed Kronsky to my house. My respect for the resources, skill and preparation of my unknown enemy grew.

A speeder howled by close outside, and the sound of its sporadic fire shook the windows in their frames.

'Can you keep up?' I asked Sastre and Eleena. They nodded. 'Where are we going?' asked Eleena.

'Out through the dining hall, then quickly across the lawn of the rose garden into the orchard behind the maze. After that, we swing south, make our way to the front fence and then over the main road into the woods.'

I was describing a journey of over two kilometres, but no one balked. Staying put was suicide.

I wanted to try my vox again and try to raise Medea, but knew it was pointless. The raiders had all channels covered. Instead, I reached out with my mind.

Medea... Medea...

To my amazement, I was answered almost at once. It was Vance.

We're just outside the pugnaseum. Medea's going to try and take one of their fliers.

No! Stop her, Jekud. They're too well guarded. Tell Medea 'The Storm Oak.' She'll know what it means. If we get there first, I'll wait as long as I can.

The dining hall was in darkness and the buffed wood floor was littered with glass. The windows had been blown in and the drapes rustled in the night breeze.

We made our way across to the windows. Outside, the rose garden was quiet and gloomy. The light of the fires cast long shadows across the immaculate lawn.

We ducked back inside as a flier flew over. It paused above the lawn, engines wailing, its downjets rippling the surface of the lawn. It was so close I could hear the crackle and sputter of the cockpit intervox. The searchlamp swung towards us, suddenly blinding, jabbing beams of frosty white light into the dining hall. The glass litter glittered like a constellation.

Then the speeder moved off again, thundering around towards the back of the house.

'Go!' I hissed.

We ran across the lawn. Aemos was surprisingly spry, but Eleena struggled with Sastre. I dropped back and helped her with him. He kept apologising, telling us to leave him.

He was a good man.

We reached the edge of the orchard and lost ourselves in the shadows of the arbors, following the back of the maze. The air was richly scented with the maze's pungent privet and the sweet, acid smell of the ripening fruit. Moths and nocturnal insects fluttered in the half light.

Well into the orchard, seventy metres from the house, we stopped for breath. Weapons fire and shouting still echoed from the residence. I looked around, trying not to look at the brilliant blaze of the buildings so I could adjust to the gloom under the trees. They were low, graceful apple, tumin and ploin, planted in orderly rows. The white bark of the tumin trees shone like snow in the dimness, and some of the early ploin clusters had been carefully bagged against scavenging birds. Scant days before, I had been out here with the junior staff, joking as we gathered up the first tumin crop. Altwald had been with us, taping the bags around the dark, swelling ploins. That night, Jarat had served a glorious tumin tart as dessert.

Jarat. I wondered what had become of her in all this.

I never did find out.

Sastre stiffened and brought up his laspistol at a movement nearby, but it was just a garden servitor, moving along the aisle of fruit trees, spraying pesticide. Oblivious to the carnage nearby, it was simply obeying its nightly programming.

We started forward again, but when I looked back, I saw several figures coming out of the dining hall windows and spreading out across the rose garden.

I bade the other three move ahead and crept back, staying as concealed as possible, in case they had night-vision lenses or motion detectors.

I came upon the slow-moving servitor from behind, opened a back panel as it trudged monotonously forward, and keyed in new instructions. It moved off towards the rose garden, adjusting its route only to avoid trees. I had increased its pace.

I was already on my way back to rejoin the others when I heard the first few shots: the raiders, surprised by the sudden appearance of the servitor. With any luck, it would delay or distract them. If they had been following our movement, then maybe the servitor would convince them that was all they had detected.

We kept going until we were well clear of the maze and had left the orchard behind. We crossed dark, overgrown paddocks, fumbling blindly. The only light came from the haze in the sky behind us where Spaeton House blazed.

We turned south, or a rough estimation of south. This was still my estate - indeed the land I held title for stretched for several kilometres in all directions - but this was uncultivated wood and scrubland. I could hear the sea, tantalisingly out of reach beyond the headland behind us.

I wondered how far we could get before the raiders finished their quartering of the house and realised I had slipped through their fingers.

We hurried on for another twenty minutes, passing through glades of scrawny beech and wiry fintle. The ground was lush with nettles. We reached a waterlogged irrigation ditch, and it took us several minutes to manhandle Sastre across.

I could see the perimeter fence and the road beyond. On the far side of that, the rising mass of the wild woodland, the heritage forests that still covered two thirds of Gudrun, untouched and unmolested since the first colonies were built there.

'We're almost there,' I whispered. 'Come on.'

Tempting fate, as always, Eisenhorn. Tempting fate.

Las-bolts slashed the air over our heads. A few at first, then more, from at least four sources. They lowered their aim and the bright orange shots ripped into the nettles, kicking up mists of sap and pulp. Two young larches by the fence ditch were splintered. Dry gorse and fintle shuddered and burst into flames.

A flare went up, bursting like a star, and damning us all with its invasive light.

'The fence! Come on!' I cursed.

Behind us, by the light of the flare, I could see dark figures wading through the nettles and emerging from the trees. Every few moments, one of the figures would halt and raise his weapon, spitting dazzling pulses at us.

Further away, back at the bright pyre of Spaeton House, I saw two white blobs of light rise and disengage themselves from the fireglow. Speeders, called in, heading this way, chasing their beams across the paddocks and woods.

We were at the fence. I channeled my fury into Barbarisater and slashed open a hole two metres wide.

'Get through!' I yelled. Aemos went through the gap. Sastre stumbled and fell, losing his grip on Eleena's arm. I pushed her through the gap too and went back for the wounded man.

Sastre had trained his pistol at the advancing killers, and was firing. He was sitting down, leaning his back against the fence. He made two kills as I remember, cutting down figures struggling forward in the weeds and undergrowth fifty metres away.

'Go, sir!' he said.

'Not without you!'

'Go, damn it! You won't get far unless someone slows them down!'

A rain of las-fire fell around us, puncturing the fence and throwing up wet clods of earth. I was forced to turn and use Barbarisater to deflect several shots. The blade hummed as it twitched and soaked up the power.

'Go!' Sastre repeated. I realised he had been hit again and was trying to hide it. He coughed blood.

'I can't leave you like this–'

'Of course you can't!' he snapped. 'Give me a bloody weapon! This damn las-cell is nearly spent.'

I crouched beside him and handed him my boltgun and my spare clips.

'The Emperor will remember you, even if I don't live to,' I told him.

'You damn well better had, sir, or I'm wasting my efforts.'

There was no time for anything further, no time even to take his hand. As I clambered through the fence, I heard the first roaring blasts of the boltgun.

Eleena and Aemos were waiting for me on the far side of the road in the fringes of the wild woods. I gathered them up and we ran into the darkness, stumbling over gnarled roots, clambering up loamy slopes, surrounded by the midnight blackness of the primordial forest.

The boltgun continued to fire for some time. Then it fell silent.

May the God-Emperor rest Xel Sastre and show him peace.

NINE

THE STORM OAK
GOING BACK
MAKING MIDAS PROUD

For almost an hour, we plunged into the great darkness of the forest, blind and desperate. In what seemed an alarmingly short time, we lost all sight of the great conflagration we had left behind. The woodland, dense and ancient, blocked it out.

'Are we lost?' Eleena mumbled in a faltering voice.

'No,' I assured her. Kircher, Medea and I had spent many hours hunting and tracking in the wild woodlands, and I knew these fringes well enough, though in darkness, there was an unhelpful depth of mystery and unfamiliarity.

Once in a while, I noticed a landmark: a jutting tooth of stone, an old tree, a turn in the terrain. Usually, I recognised such things once we were right on them, and took a moment to adjust our bearings.

Twice, speeders passed overhead, their stablights backlighting the dense foliage. If they'd possessed heat trackers, we would have been dead. But they were hunting by searchlight alone. At last, I privately rejoiced, the enemy has made an error.

We reached the oak.

Medea had named it the Storm Oak. It had been hundreds of years old when lightning had killed it and left it a splintered, leafless giant, like a shattered castle turret. The bark was peeling from its dead wood, and the area around it was crawling with grubs and rot-beetles. It had grown in a hollow, sprouting from the dark soil overhang of a scarp twenty metres high. The oak itself was fifty metres tall from its vast, partly exposed root mass to its shattered crown, and fifteen metres across the trunk.

I scrambled down into the hollow beneath its roots. When the lightning had struck it, ages past, it had partially ripped the massive tree from the ground, creating a cavern under its mighty foundations. The dank hole was like a natural chapel, with roots serving as the crossmembers for the ceiling. The previous owners of Spaeton House had, I had been told, used it as a chancel for private ceremonies.

Medea and I had decided to use it as a hangar.

No one else knew about this, except Kircher. We had all agreed it was a dark, secret place to stow a light aircraft. A bolt hole. I don't think we ever really imagined a doom falling on Spaeton House like the one that overwhelmed it that night, but we had played along with the idea it might be wise to keep one transport tucked out of sight.

The transport in question was a monocoque turbofan flier, handmade on Urdesh. Light, fast, ultra-manoeuvrable. Medea had purchased it ten years before when she was bored, and had stored it in the main hangar at Spaeton until one notorious night while we were away on a case when several junior staff members had decided to take it for a spin, it being so much more racey than the house shuttles and bulk speeders.

They'd had the damage repaired by the time we got home, but Medea had noticed. Reprimands had followed.

Weeks later, when we found the Storm Oak during a hunting trip, and devised the notion of a last ditch transport, Medea had moved the craft here. We never actually thought we'd have to use it for escape. It was just an excuse to park it away from the envious juniors.

I stripped off the tarp and popped open the hatch. The cabin interior smelled of leather and the faint dampness of the forest.

Six metres long and finished in slate grey, the craft had a wedge-shaped cabin that tapered to a short, V-vaned tail. There were three turbofan units, one fixed behind the cabin under the tail for main thrust, the other two mounted on stubby wings that projected from the cabin roof on either side. The wing units were gimbal-mounted for lift and attitude control. The cabin was snug, with three rows of seats: a single pilot's seat in the nose, with two high-backed passenger seats behind it and a more functional bench seat behind them against the cabin's rear partition.

I strapped myself into the pilot's seat and ran a pre-flight to wake the systems up as Eleena and Aemos installed themselves in the pair of seats behind me. The instrument panel lit up green and there was a low sigh as the fans began to turn.

Eleena closed the hatch. The leaf-litter in the root cave began to twitch and flutter.

We'd heard nothing from Vance since we entered the wild woodland. I reached out with my mind, urging them to hurry up. There was no answer.

The plane's power cells showed about seventy-five per cent capacity. There were no alert or disfunction runes on the diagnostic panel. I went through a final check. The craft was armed with a light las-lance, fitted discreetly under the nose in a fixed-forward mount. We'd never used it, and the instruments showed it was off-line. I entered a code to activate it, and the screen told me it was stowed for safety and non-functional.

With the fans still idling, I got back out and went round to the flier's nose, crouching down to look beneath. The lance, little more than a slender tube, was capped with a rubberised sleeve to muzzle the weapon and keep dirt out of the emitter. I fumbled with the sleeve and removed it. Pulling the safety sleeve off broke a wire clasp that allowed a small pin to be yanked out. The lance was enabled.

I climbed back into the cabin, slammed the hatch and checked the instruments. The weapon was now showing as on-line and I activated the power-up function to charge its firing cells.

I'd just about finished when I felt it.

'Sir, what's wrong?' Eleena cried out as I gasped and lurched forward.

'Gregor?' said Aemos, alarmed.

'I'm okay... it was Vance...' A quick, terrible psychic shriek from the direction of the estate. A psyker in pain.

I tried to raise him again, but there was nothing except a blurry wall of background anguish. Then I heard, for a second, his mind urging Medea, urging her to run, run and not to look back.

Again I gasped as a second jolt of agony rippled through the mental spectrum.

'God-Emperor damn it!' I cursed and threw the plane forward. The fans wailed. We were instantly surrounded by a maelstrom of leaves and dead twigs which rattled and pinged off the fuselage and windows. I nursed out just a few centimetres of lift to clear the ground, with the wing fans angled straight down, and we edged forward out of the Storm Oak's root cave on minimum thrust.

I kept one eye on the proximity scanner, which was throbbing red as it detected the structure enclosing us. As soon as it signaled that the tail boom had cleared the overhang of the root ball, I keyed in more lift and we rose, swirling the leaves of the clearing around us in a whirling eddy.

We hovered and turned slowly, once, twice, as I let the auspex's terrain tracker scan the area. Then I lined up.

'Uhm, Gregor?' Aemos said, leaning forward and pointing over my left arm at the illuminated compass ball. 'We're heading north.'

'Yes.'

'It, uhm, goes without saying north is the direction we came from.'

'Yes. Sorry. We're going back.'

I put the nose down, the wing jets whirred round to an aft three-quarter thrust in their socket mounts, and the craft raced off into the darkness.

I swept us through the forest at something like twenty knots, lights off. Visibility was virtually zero, so I flew using a combination of the auspex and the proximity scanner, reading the green and amber phantoms of tree boles and branches as they loomed, steering around and under. Every now and then I cut it too fine, and the collision alert sounded as something swept across the screen in vivid red. There were plenty of near misses, but only once did I hit something - a small branch that snapped away, thankfully. Aemos and Eleena both cried out involuntarily.

'Relax,' I urged them.

We'd have made better - and safer - progress above the forest canopy, but I wanted to stay concealed for as long as possible.

In vain, I reached out to find Vance's mind.

Barely avoiding a massive low branch, we came down a long slope under the trees, and the auspex showed me that we'd reached the edge of the woodland. The road was just ahead.

Through the tree-line, I could see light, pulsing white. Another flare. I cut the forward thrust, and crept forward on down-angled jets, just a drifting hover.

I could see out over the road and the fence into the paddocks and scrub south of Spaeton House we had toiled through on foot to make our escape. The whole area was bathed in a cold, grey luminosity, a wobbling flicker cast by the dying flare. Black shapes, dozens of them, scrambled through the grasses and weeds, spread in a line, searching.

Medea, I willed. She couldn't answer. She was a blunt. But I prayed she could hear.

Medea, I'm close.

There was a sudden surge of activity to the north-east, around a spinney of fintle trees. The flash of las-fire. Two fresh flares banged up, making everything harsh black and white. The raiders were moving towards the spinney.

They had someone cornered, pinned down. I knew in my gut it was Medea.

With my lights still off, I gunned the flier forward, going low over the road and fence and across the paddock reaches. The downwash sliced a wake in the grasses. Figures turned as we swept over them. By the flarelight, I glimpsed carnival faces.

I hugged the ground, scattering some of the raiders, and powered towards the spinney. Las flashes were coming my way now.

My thumb flipped the safety cover off the control stick's firing stud. There was no aiming mechanism for the fixed lance except the craft itself. If the flier was pointing at something, then the lance was too.

I squeezed the stud.

The lance fired a continuous beam for as long as I held down the trigger. It had no pulse or burst option. A line of bright yellow light, pencil thin, sliced out from under the nose and ripped into the scrub by the spinney. I saw mud and plant debris spray up from the furrow it cut. The plane's nose was dipped. I was falling short. I nudged the flier's snout up and fired again.

Two raiders collapsed, sliced through by the beam. Several saplings and a mature fintle at the edge of the spinney came down in a shower of leaves. With the plane moving, it was damn hard to aim at all.

Twenty metres short of the trees, I pulled up in a shallow hover. Serious fusillades were zipping at us now. The craft wobbled as shots struck the lower hull.

I fired for a third time, holding the flier level and gently rotating her right to left as I held the trigger down. Raiders threw themselves flat to avoid the lethal beam of light passing over them. Several didn't make it. The lance simply sectioned them, clean through flesh, bone and armour. I must have hit a power pack or a grenade, because one exploded in a sheet of flame.

More shots thumped into the fuselage from the rear. I surged forward again, sweeping around the west side of the trees.

I saw Medea on the auspex. She was running clear of the spinney at the north end, breaking cover. It took me a moment to find her by eye. Just a dot in the long weeds. A bright dot. She was wearing her father's cerise jacket. I realised she must have come out into the open to give me a chance to set down and reach her. The thin trees in the spinney were far too tightly packed.

Las-bolts chased her. She turned and fired back with a handgun, still running.

You're clear! Get down!

I saw her turn, seeing where I was. Then she was hurled face first into the grass by a las-shot.

'Medea!' I accelerated hard, pushing us back into our seats. 'Aemos! Get ready with the side hatch!'

I got as close in to the patch of weeds where she had fallen as I dared. The down-thrust of the plane could cause serious injuries. We jolted hard as I set down, throwing the throttles to idle. Aemos was opening the hatch, but he was old and slow and scared. Eleena couldn't reach over because he was blocking her.

I leapt out, pushing Aemos back into his seat, and thumped down into the wet nettles and burry fex-grass. The night air was sudden and cold. Another flare bloomed above us, and I realised the echoing spit I could hear was the enemy guns discharging in my direction.

I ran forward, searching for her.

'Medea! Medea!'

Now I was on the ground, it was nigh on impossible to tell where in the thigh-high grass she'd fallen.

'Medea!'

A las-round stung the air to my left. The closest of the raiders, running across the paddock, was only a few dozen metres away.

I realised I was unarmed. I'd given my boltgun to Sastre, and Barbarisater and the staff were stowed in the flier behind me.

No, I had Medea's Glavian needle pistol. It was still in my coat pocket. I dragged it out and fired, aiming it with both hands.

My first shot hit the nearest raider and he fell over into the grass. My second shot winged another and he too disappeared into the rough scrub.

I glanced at the needler's mechanical dial. Two rounds left.

Bending low, I searched the grass with increasing frenzy as shots whined in close.

'Medea!'

And there she was, face down in the thick scrub. There was a bloody, burned hole in the back of her silk jacket.

I dragged her up and threw her limp body over my shoulder. The autopistol she had been using slipped heavily from her slack hand.

I stooped and grabbed it. The clip was half-full.

I swung round, trying to keep her from falling, and fired the autopistol wildly at the advancing enemy, relishing the satisfying roar and recoil of the hefty solid-slug weapon. Needle guns were elegant and deadly, but you barely knew you'd fired them.

This thing, chrome and square-nosed, kicked like a yurf, and spent brass cases rang as they flew from the pumping slide.

I started to run back to the plane, expecting a shot in the back any moment. I heard las fire, but it wasn't coming from behind me. Eleena Koi was braced in the open side hatch of the flier, laying down covering fire with a laspistol

I hadn't realised she was carrying. Aemos had got into the back, onto the bench seat, giving Eleena access to the door.

Aemos reached out and gathered Medea in his arms. Eleena seized her too and the three of us bundled the girl into the rear beside Aemos.

I was wishing so hard she wasn't dead.

Eleena fired one last time and fell back into the passenger seats. I jumped in, yelling at her to slam the hatch.

There was no time to strap in. Multiple shots slammed against the aircraft's flank. A window panel burst. Dents appeared in the inner skin, spalling fragments off the hull.

I hoisted us off the ground, and spun us to face the charging raiders.

I think, although I can't be sure, I said something singularly unedifying as I pressed the trigger. Something like: 'eat this, you bastards.'

I don't believe I actually hit any of them but, by the Golden Throne, they took cover.

'Sir!' Eleena yelled over the scream of the turbofans.

A ball of light was approaching from the other side of the spinney. I couldn't see the speeder, just its stablight shining like a white dwarf against the night sky.

Time to go.

I kept it low, but pulled away south across the paddock at full thrust, accelerating all the time. We were doing forty, forty-five knots by the time we reached the road. The woods loomed.

In an instant, I weighed my options. Go high, over the trees, and be a clear target for any pursuer. Go through, lights off, and drop speed dramatically to avoid collision. Go through, lights on.

I picked the third way.

The flier's lamps kicked on, lighting a cone of space ahead of us. Even with the lights, and the auspex and the proximity alarm, this course was borderline suicide. Within a few seconds, having only just avoided a head-on smash with a mature spruce, I had to drop the speed to thirty.

'You're... you're gonna get us killed!' Eleena wailed.

'Be quiet!' The black shapes of tree trunks whipped past on either side, forcing me to turn and bank hard, repeatedly, jagging left, then right, then left again. Branches, some as massive as trees in their own right, swept over us like arches or under us like bridges. Several times, we exploded through sprays of canopy, the engine-out alarm pipping as the fans fought to clear away the leaf debris choking them. The phantoms on the scanner screen were almost constantly red.

Eleena started to say an Imperial prayer.

'Say one for us all,' I barked. 'Aemos! What's Medea's condition?'

'She's alive, thank the stars. But her breathing's not right. Perhaps a collapsed lung, or internal cauterisation. She needs a medic, Gregor.'

'She'll get one. Make her as comfortable as you can. There's a medi-pack in the locker behind you. Patch her wound.'

Apart from being an insane death wish, flying at speed through dense, ancient forest at night was baffling. Simply avoiding collision required such concentration, I kept losing my bearings. A few forced turns to the left, say, pointed us east. Correcting that, and evading an oak to the right, and we were turned west. We were zig-zagging through the wild woodland, and a zig-zag is not the fastest route of escape.

At least four of the five speeders I had seen during the raid were after us. Two were following us directly through the trees, about five hundred metres behind us. The other two had gone up and over the tree cover, making much better time, chasing hard to pass over us and get ahead.

They were ex-military models; I'd seen that much from the glimpse I'd got of them parked on the lawns. Bigger power plants than this nimble Urdeshi turbofan; bigger, and better armoured. And their cannons, mounted on racks in the doorframes, meant they could, essentially, fire in any direction. They didn't have to be pointing at their target.

The auspex started to chime and I saw hard light flash down through the leaf cover above us, breaking through in shafts like a sun breaking through low cloud. One of the fliers above the forest was matching us for speed.

I jinked and evaded, not so much to lose him as to avoid instant obliteration against the bole of a tree. I saw the forest floor convulse and ripple as the door gunner fired down at us.

So I banked hard, one wing down, right around a colossal fanewood, and shot off in a westerly direction. The overhead lights disappeared for a moment, but then reappeared, travelling fast, parallel to us, to the left. A tree, flashing past to my right, lost its bark in a blitz of diagonal crossfire.

Damn them. I was fairly certain they had no heat or motion tracking instruments. They were following the glow of my lamps underlighting the canopy.

I killed the lights but unfortunately didn't kill my speed. The proximity alarm squealed, and though I yanked on the stick, we struck a trunk a grazing blow.

We wobbled hard. The engine-out alert shrilled a continuous note. The starboard fan had stalled.

I went to hover, and pressed restart on the starboard unit, hoping that it had simply been jolted dead by the impact. If the casing or the fan itself were buckled, restarting might be very messy indeed for all of us.

The dead fan turned over and coughed. I tried again. Another mewling wheeze. Twenty metres behind us, the forest was coming to pieces in a deluge of wood pulp, bark scraps and pulverised foliage as the flier high above tried to smoke us out with a sustained salvo.

The starboard fan whipped into life on the third attempt. Staying at hover, I played the stick back and forth and side to side, pitching and yawing the craft, dropping its nose and then its tail, dipping the stubby wings, just to make sure I hadn't lost any attitude control. It seemed alright.

I looked over my shoulder and saw Eleena staring at me, her face corpse-pale. Aemos was cradling Medea.

'Are we all right, Gregor?' he whispered.

'Yes. I'm sorry about that.'

The glade to our left suddenly lit up with vertical shafts of light and was pummelled by cannon fire. They were still searching blindly.

I had a sudden moment of recall. A void duel. Seriously outnumbered. Midas flying by the seat of his well-tailored pants. I remember him glancing at me from the controls of the gun-cutter, and saying: 'Mouse becomes cat.'

Mouse becomes cat.

Still hovering, I rotated the flier towards the blitzed glade and then raised the nose slowly, pointing it at the light source above the trees. Aiming it at the light source.

I squeezed the toggle, just for a second.

The lance beam seared up into the backlit canopy. There was a brief flash and then a nine tonne metal fireball that had once been a speeder simply dropped down into the clearing, smashing through the branches, ripping apart and hurling flaming debris in all directions.

'Scratch one,' I said, smugly. Well, it's what Midas would have said.

There were lights behind us, zooming closer through the forest. Keeping the lamps off, I nudged us away from the wreckage inferno and turned in behind a twisted antlerbark that had slumped sideways in old age. Curtains of moss draped from its weary branches.

I watched the lights approach, easing the nose around to follow the nearest one. They had slowed down, hunting for signs of us. The nearest lights were tantalisingly close, but obscured by a line of fat oaks.

The other one zipped in towards the blazing crash site.

I swung us up, leading the flier's nose towards the coasting speeder.

It came into view, stablights sweeping the woodland floor.

I fired again.

The shot was pretty good. It sheared the tail boom off the speeder. With its rear end discharging blue electrical arcs, it spun out of control, end over end. It made a mess of a giant fanewood, and vice versa.

The other speeder came out from the cover of the oaks, firing right at us. The shots rent aside the curtains of moss.

I realised someone had had the sense to bring night vision goggles. They could see us.

I tried one shot, missed and then turned tail, kicking in the floods and raising the speed as high as I dared. The proximity alert screen was just an overlapping red blur now, and we were all thrown around by the violent turns I was forced to make.

The pilot of the speeder chasing us was good. Distressingly good. Like the merc foot troops, he was clearly the best of his kind money could buy.

He stuck to my tail like a leech.

Pushing thirty-eight knots, I caroomed through the dense trees, pulling gees sometimes when the turns demanded it. He raced after me, following my lead and enjoying the gain of my turbowash slip stream

The chase was verging on balletic. We snaked and criss-crossed between trees, banked and looped like dancing partners. Several times I stood on a wingtip coming round one side of a big tree and he mirrored the move coming round the other. Fans screaming, I pulled a hard turn to the north, and then rolled, reversing, turning south. He overshot, but was back a moment later, accelerating fast onto my tail. Tracer rounds winked past me.

Two hard jolts came in quick succession, and the instruments confirmed what I suspected. We'd been hit. I was losing power: not much, but enough to suggest a battery had been ruptured or disconnected. He was firing again. Stitching lines of tracer shells spat past the cockpit. Now I had distress runes lighting up on my control panels.

Something drastic was needed, or we'd be his latest cockpit stripe. I thought about cutting the fans and dropping to make him overshoot, but at the speed we were going, we'd crash and burn.

'Hold on!' I yelled.

'Oh shit,' said Eleena Koi.

I killed the thrust and went vertical.

We exploded up through the canopy into the sky, shredding branches around us. The speeder shot by underneath. Astonished, he tried to bank round to re-engage, but my manoeuvre had flummoxed him. Just for a moment, but long enough.

He didn't trim his thrust as he tried to make the turn. A tree took one stabiliser wing clean off and that was the last I saw of him except for the series of impact explosions he made under the trees below us.

I was shaking, my hands numb. Exhaustion punched into me. The concentration had been so terribly intense.

But Midas, I was sure, would have been proud of me. He'd forever been trying to teach me his skills, and he'd declared on more than one occasion that I'd never make a combat pilot.

In his opinion, I had the essential reflexes and strength, but I never saw the big picture. And it was always that last, overlooked detail that got you killed.

That last, overlooked detail came in from the north, across the treetops, autocannons flashing.

TEN

DOWN
DOCTOR BERSCHILDE OF RAVELLO
KHANJAR THE SHARP

It was the fourth speeder that had been hunting us. Before I could even let out a curse, its streaming cannon fire had severed our tail boom and mangled the aft fan, shredding off its cover and twisting the still-spinning props.

We started to rotate violently. The cabin vibrated like a seizure victim. Eleena screamed.

I wrestled with the controls, fighting the bucking stick. I cranked the wing fans to vertical and throttled up to break the drop. The flier crunched down through upper branches, glanced off a main bough, and nose dived.

I stood on the rudder and yanked back the stick.

'Brace!' I yelled. That was all I had time to say.

We side-swiped a fanewood's trunk, a collision that ripped off the port fan and stripped the monocoque's hull paint down to the bare metal and bounced once off a peaty ridge of moss and leaf mould. Then we rose again, yawing to the left as the remaining turbofan screamed to the edge of its tolerance trying to gain some sort of lift. The engine-out alarm shrilled as the fan stalled, overcome by the pressure. We fell then, sideways, survived a headlong impact with an oak that crazed the windshield and slammed into the loamy earth, slithering a good fifty metres before we rocked to a halt on our side.

I didn't black out but the long silence following the crash made it feel like I had. I blinked, lying on my shoulder against the side hatch. Eleena moaned and Aemos started coughing. The only other sound was the tinkling patter of the shattered windscreen scads gradually collapsing into the cabin.

I got up and clambered over the seats.

'Eleena? Are you hurt?'

'No, sir... I don't think so...'

'We have to get out. Help me.'

Together we dragged the coughing Aemos clear and went back for Medea who was still, mercifully, unconscious.

The searchlights of the speeder lanced down through the hole we had made in the canopy, poking around.

Any moment now...

Eleena and I dragged the other two into the shelter of a hollow a good distance from the downed aircraft.

'Stay here,' I whispered to her. 'Give me your weapon.'

Silently, she offered me her stubby laspistol.

'Stay down,' I advised and ran back to the wreck, retrieving my staff and my sword. I tossed the runestaff into the undergrowth to keep it out of sight and drew Barbarisater.

The speeder was coming down through the upper branches, trying to pick out the flier with its stablight. I tucked the sword and pistol into my belt and lunged up into the lower branches of the gros beech that overlooked our crash site.

The tree was huge and gnarled. Grunting, I swung myself up into the main boughs and then further up into the web of thinner branches.

The speeder hovered into view, crawling slowly towards the smoking wreck, its searchlight playing back and forth. I could see the masked side-gunner in the open door, one hand on the yoke of the pintle-mounted autocannon, the other on the bracket of the lamp.

The speeder descended. I climbed higher, up into the lofty reaches of the beech, until I could climb no further and the hovering speeder was directly below me.

The pilot said something. I distinctly heard the crackle of his intervox. The door gunner replied and let go of the lamp, setting both hands on the cannon's grips, turning it to aim down at the crumpled flier.

The glade below me filled with flashes and booms as he riddled the airplane with his cannon fire. The valiant little Urdeshi craft shredded like tinfoil.

The door gunner stopped shooting and called down to his pilot.

Now or never.

I let go of the branches and dropped straight onto the roof of the speeder. It rocked slightly beneath me. I steadied myself, crouched down, gripped the upper frame of the door hatch and swung in, boots first.

The gunner was bent over with his back to the hatch, getting a fresh ammunition box from the wall rack. My boots connected with his lower back and shunted him face-first against the cabin wall. I landed beside him as he staggered backwards, his hands clutching at his broken face, grabbed him by the arm and propelled him backwards out of the hatch. We were ten metres up.

The pilot gave a muffled grunt as he looked round and saw me. A second later, the muzzle of the laspistol was pressed against the corner of his jaw.

'Set down. Now,' I said.

I prayed I was dealing with a mercenary and not a cultist. A merc would know when to cut his losses, and bargain to live for another day and another paycheck. A cultist would fly us into the nearest tree, gun or no gun.

Making his motions very slow and clear so I could be sure to read them, the pilot cut the speeder's main thruster, and sank us to the forest floor.

'Shut us down,' I said.

He obeyed, and the lift units hummed to a halt. The dashboard went blank apart from a few orange standby lights.

'Unstrap. Get out.'

He unbuckled his harness and slowly pulled himself up out of the pilot's seat as I covered him with the pistol. He was a short but well-built man in ablative armour and a grey flight helmet with a breathing visor.

He jumped down from the speeder's side hatch and stood with his hands raised.

I got down next to him. 'Take off the helmet and toss it back into the speeder.'

The pilot did as he was told. His skin was pale and freckled, his thinning hair shaved close. He regarded me with edgy blue eyes.

'Unzip the suit.'

He frowned.

'To the waist.'

Keeping one hand raised, he drew the zipper of the ablat-suit down, revealing an undervest and shoulders marked with old, blurry tattoos. The psi-shield was a small, disc-shaped device hung round his neck on a plastic cord. I snapped it off and tossed it into the undergrowth. Then I used my will.

'Name?'

'Nhh...' he growled, grimacing.

'Name!'

'Eino Goran.'

I nudged my mind against his. It was like rubbing up against something sheathed in plastic.

'Right, we both know that's an emplated identity. A rush job from the feel of it. Real name?'

He shook his head, his teeth clenched. Emplate IDs were cheap enough to buy on the black market, especially a fairly poor quality one like this. They were fake personalities, usually sold with matching papers, psi-woven over the subject's persona like a fitted dust cover on a piece of furniture. Nothing fancy. If you had the money, you could buy fingerprints and retinas to match. If you really had the money, a new face too.

This one was like a false wall erected in a hurry to ward off casual minds. It lacked any sort of real history, not even vague biographical engrams. A mind mask as cheap and unrealistic as the carnival faces his comrades had worn.

But, though poor, it had been put in place with great force. I tried to shift it, but it wouldn't budge. That was frustrating. It was obviously false, but I couldn't get past it.

There was no time to worry at it now.

Out! I willed, and he collapsed unconscious.

'Eleena! Aemos! Come on!' I shouted, dragging the limp man back into the speeder. I checked him for weapons – there were none – and then lashed his hands behind his back with a length of cable from the speeder's pulley spool. By the time Eleena and Aemos reached me, carefully bearing Medea, I had the pilot gagged and blind-folded, and tied to one of the speeder's internal cross-members.

We got everything aboard – the items we had rescued from my study, the runestaff, all of it – and secured Medea in a pull-down cot in the aft of the speeder's crew bay. Then I got into the pilot's seat and, once I'd made sense of the control layout, got us airborne.

I edged up just above the treetops, running unlit. The moon was up and the night was clear, apart from a brown smudge against the stars away to the north. The smoke from my burning estate, I had no doubt. There was no sign of anything else in the air. Hugging the tips of the trees, I turned us south.

Once we were underway, I checked out the cockpit. It was clearly an ex-military flier, bought for the purpose in my opinion. Insignia mouldings had been chiselled off, service numbers erased with acid swabs. Apart from the basic controls, the cabin was provided with several socket racks where optional instrument modules could be bolted in. Only a vox-set had been fitted. There were gaps where an auspex, a terrain-reader and night vision displays might have gone, and also slots for a navigation codifier and a remote fire control system that would have slaved the door weapon to the pilot and done away with the necessity of a separate gunner. Whoever had supplied the mercenaries with their vehicles had provided only the most basic package. An armed troop-lifter with an old model vox-caster comm. No automated systems. No clue to origin or source.

But it had decent power and range - over a thousand kilometres left in it before it would need a recharge. Something to get them in, lay down cover and get them out again.

The forest flickered by beneath us. The vox burbled intermittently, but I had no idea of the codes or cant they were using, and little desire to let anyone know the flier was still operational.

After a while, it shut off. I unplugged it, pulled it out of its rack and told Eleena to toss it overboard.

'Why?' she asked.

'I don't want to risk it having a tracker or transponder built into it.'

She nodded.

I tried to get our bearings manually, using the basic instrumentation, working to reconstruct a map of the area in my head. It was pretty much guesswork. Dorsay, the nearest main city, was perhaps a hour west of us now, but given the scale of the operation mounted against me, I felt going there would be like flying into a carnodon's den.

There were small fishing communities and harbour towns on the east side of the Insume headland, the closest now more than two hours away. Madua, a chapel town in the south-east, was in range. So was Entreve, a market city on the fringe of the wild woodland. So were the Atenate Mountains.

I thought about calling the Arbites on the vox, but decided against it. The attack on Spaeton House must surely have been noted by sentries at Dorsay, especially once the main fires started, but no emergency support units had come. Had the Arbites been paid to turn a blind eye? Had they been more complicit still in the raid?

Until I understood who and what my enemies were, I could trust no one, and that included the authorities and even the Inquisition itself.

Not for the first time in my life, I was effectively alone.
I headed for the mountains. For Ravello.

Ravello is a hill town in the flanks of the western Atenates, situated at the foot of the Insa Pass, on the shores of a long freshwater lake that forms the headwaters of the great Drunner. It has a small but distinguished universitariate specialising in medicine and philology, a brewery that exports its lake-water ale all over Gudrun, and a fine chapel dedicated to Saint Calwun, which houses to my mind some of the best religious frescoes in the sub-sector.

It is a quiet place, steep and densely packed, its old buildings lining narrow hill streets so tightly their green copper roofs overlap like plate armour. From the air, it looked like a patch of dark moss clinging to the blue slopes of the Itervalle.

The sun was rising as we approached from the north. The air was clear, a baking blue. We had left the wild woodland in the first touches of dawn, and climbed up into the foothills, following the line of the Atenate Minors up into the higher altitudes. The Itervalle was high enough to have cloud cover round its peak, but across the lake, the first of the great giants rose: Esembo, ragged like a tooth; Mons Fulco, a violet triangle stabbing the sky; snow-capped Corvachio, the sport and bane of recreational climbers.

We were nearly out of power and the speeder was getting sluggish. I dropped us to road level and came in through the western gate. There were no traffic and no pedestrians. It was still early in the morning.

The streets were paved with the same blue-grey ouslite that the buildings were constructed from, bright in the sunlight, dank in the shadows of the narrow streets. We passed through a square where a student lay sleeping off a night's drinking on the lip of a small fountain, along a wider avenue where ground cars and civilian fliers were parked in a herringbone, and then turned up a narrow street and climbed the hill out of the glare of the sun. I opened the speeder's windows and breathed in the fresh, clear air. The muted sounds of the flier's engines washed back at me, reflected oddly by the tall, shuttered faces of the dwellings on either side of the steep, paved lane.

It had been a long time, but I still knew my way around.

We parked in a cul-de-sac alley just off the lane, little more than a blunt courtyard where a mountain spurra struggled to grow against the face of a wall. The spurra, or at least its little yellow spring flowers, was the emblem of Saint Calwun, and votive bottles and coins littered the little stone basin the tree was growing from.

A first floor shutter twitched at the sound of our engines, and I was glad I had asked Aemos to stow the door gun during our flight. At least we resembled a private transport.

'Stay here,' I told Eleena and Aemos. 'Stay here and wait.'

I walked back down the street in the quiet morning. I was still wearing the boots, breeches, shirt and leather coat I had put on before the auto-seance the night before, but Aemos had lent me his drab-green cloak. I made sure

I was displaying no insignia or badge of office, except my signet ring, which would pass notice. Medea's autopistol, reloaded with shells from a box magazine we found on the speeder, was tucked into the back of my belt.

A stray dog, coming up from the town centre towards me, paused to sniff my cloak hem and then trotted on its way, uninterested.

The house was as I remembered it, halfway down the lane. We had passed it on the way up, and now I made certain. Four storeys, with a terrace balcony at the top under the eaves of the copper-tiled roof. The windows were shuttered and the main entrance, a pair of heavy panelled wooden doors painted glossy red, were bolted shut.

There was no bell. I remembered that. I knocked once and waited.

I waited a long time.

Finally, I heard a thump behind the doors and an eyeslit opened.

'What is your business so early?' asked an old man's voice.

'I want to see Doctor Berschilde.'

'Who is calling?'

'Please let me in and I will discuss it with the doctor.'

'It is early!' the voice protested.

I raised my hand and held my signet ring out so its design was visible through the eyeslit.

'Please,' I repeated.

The slit shut, there was a rattle of keys and then one of the doors opened into the street. Inside was just shadow.

I stepped into the delicious cool of the hall, my eyes growing accustomed to the gloom. A hunched old man in black closed the door behind me.

'Wait here, sir,' he said and shuffled away.

The floor was polished marble mosaic that sparkled where scraps of exterior light caught it. The wall patterns had been hand-painted by craftsmen. Exquisite, antiquarian anatomical sketches lined the walls in simple gilt frames. The house smelled of warm stone, the cold afterscents of a fine evening meal, smoke.

'Hello?' a voice filtered down from the stairs above me.

I went up a flight, onto a landing where shutters had been opened to let thc daylight stream in.

'I'm sorry to intrude,' I said.

'Gregor? Gregor Eisenhorn?' Doctor Berschilde of Ravello took a step towards me, registering sleepy astonishment.

She was still a very fine figure of a woman.

I think she was about to hug me, or plant a kiss on my cheek, but she halted and her face darkened.

'This isn't social, is it?' she said.

I went back to the speeder and flew it round to the private walled courtyard behind her residence where it was screened from view. The doctor's old manservant, Phabes, had opened the ground floor sundoors, and stood ready with a gurney for Medea. Eleena, Aemos and I followed them inside. I left the pilot, still in his will-induced fugue state, tied up in the flier.

Crezia Berschilde had put on a surgical apron by then, and met us in the ground floor hall. She said little as she examined Medea and checked her vitals.

'Take her through,' she told her man, then looked at me. 'Anybody else injured?'

'No,' I said. 'How is Medea?'

'Dying,' she said. All humour had gone from her voice. She was angry and I didn't blame her. 'I'll do what I can.'

'I'm grateful, Crezia. I'm sorry I've troubled you with this.'

'She ought to go to the town infirmary!' she snapped.

'Can we avoid that?'

'Can we make this unofficial, you mean? Damn you, Eisenhorn. I don't need this!'

'I know you don't.'

She pursed her lips. 'I'll do what I can,' she repeated. 'Go through into the drawing room. I'll have Phabes bring some refreshment.'

She turned on her heel and disappeared into the house after Medea.

'So,' said Aemos quietly, 'who is this again?'

Doctor Crezia Berschilde was one of the finest anatomists on the planet. Her treatises and monographs were widely published throughout the Helican sub-sector. After years of practice in Dorsay and, for a period, off-world on Messina, she had taken up the post of Professor of Anatomy here at Ravello.

And, a long time ago, I had nearly married her.

One hundred and forty-five years earlier, in 241 to be exact, I had lost my left hand during a firefight on Sameter. The details of the case are unimportant, and besides, they are recorded elsewhere. I was fitted with a prosthetic, but I hated it and never used it. After two years, during a stay on Messina, I had surgeons equip me with a fully functioning graft.

Crezia had been the chief surgeon during that procedure. Becoming involved with a woman who has just sewn a vat-grown clone hand onto your wrist is hardly a way to meet a wife, I realise.

But she was quick-witted, learned, vivacious and not put off by my calling. For years we were involved, on and off, first on Messina, then at a distance, and then on Gudrun once she had moved back to Ravello to take up her doctorate and I had based myself at Spaeton House.

I had been very fond of her. I still was. It is difficult to know if I should use a word stronger than 'fond.' We never did to each other, but there are times I would have done.

I had not seen her for the best part of twenty-five years. That had been my doing.

We sat in the drawing room for over an hour. Phabes had opened the windows and the day's brilliance blasted in, turning the tulle window nets into hanging oblongs of radiant white. I could smell the clean, fresh chill of mountains.

The drawing room was furnished with fine old pieces of furniture, and filled with rare books, surgical curios and display cases full of immaculately restored antique medical apparatus. Aemos was quickly lost in close study of the items on display, murmuring to himself. Eleena sat quietly on a tub chair and composed herself. I was fairly sure she was inwardly reciting the mind-soothing exercises of the Distaff. Every few minutes she would absently brush a few strands of brown hair off her slender face.

The doctor's man returned with a silver serving cart. Yeast bread, fruit, oily butter and piping hot black caffeine.

'Do you need anything stronger?' he asked.

'No, thank you.'

He pointed to a weighted silk rope by the door. 'Ring if there's anything you need.'

I poured caffeine for us all, and Aemos helped himself to a hunk of bread and a ripe ploin.

Eleena tonged half a dozen lumps of amber sugar crystal into her little cup. 'Who did it?' she asked at length.

'Eleena?'

'Who... who raided us, sir?'

'The simple answer? I have no idea. I'm working on possibilities. It may take us a while to find out, and first we have to be secure.'

'Are we safe here?'

'Yes, for the time being.'

'They were mercenaries,' said Aemos, dabbing crumbs from his wrinkled lips. 'That is beyond question.'

'I thought as much.'

'The pilot you captured. You saw the tattoos on his torso.'

'I did. But I couldn't read them.'

Aemos sipped his hot, sweet drink. 'Base Futu, the language of the Vessorine janissaries.'

'Really? Are you sure?'

'Reasonably so,' he said. 'The man has a repatriation bond written on his skin.'

I considered this news. Vessor was a feral world on the rimward borders of the Antimar sub-sector that bred a small but hardy population famous for its vicious fighters. Attempts had been made to form a Guard regiment there, but the Vessorine were hard to control. It wasn't that they lacked discipline, but they found loyalty to Terra too cerebral a concept. They were bonded into clan families, understanding simply the material wealth of land, property, homestead and weapons. As mercenaries, therefore, they excelled. They would fight, peerlessly, savagely and to the death, in the Emperor's name, provided that name was stamped on high denomination coinage.

No wonder the attack on Spaeton House had been so direct and efficient. In hindsight it was remarkable any of us had got out alive. I was glad I hadn't known who they were at the time. If I'd been told I was facing Vessorine janissaries, I might have frozen up... instead of charging them head on to rescue Medea.

I took off the cloak Aemos had lent me, and also my leather coat, and rolled up the sleeves of my shirt. The sun was warming the drawing room.

I had just taken the pistol out of my belt to check it when Crezia came into the room. She was peeling off surgical gloves and when she saw the gun in my hands, her already sour look became fiercer. She pointed sharply at me and then gestured outside.

'Now,' she said, curtly.

I pushed the weapon into the folds of the cloak on the table and followed her out, across the hall into a sitting room hung with oil paintings and hololithic prints. The shutters in here were still shut and she made no attempt to open them. She turned up the lamp instead.

'Shut the door,' she instructed.

I pushed the door shut. 'Crezia–' I began.

She held up a strong, warning finger. 'Don't start, Eisenhorn. Just don't. I'm this damn close to throwing you out! How dare you c–'

'Medea,' I interrupted firmly. 'How is she?'

'Stable. Just about. She was shot in the back with a laser weapon and the wound was left untreated for several hours. How do you think she is?'

'She'll survive?'

'Unless there are complications. She's on life support in the basement suite.'

'Thank you, Crezia. I'm in your debt.'

'Yes, you damn well are. You're unbelievable, Eisenhorn. Twenty-five years. Twenty-five years! I don't see you, I don't hear from you and then you turn up, unannounced, uninvited, armed and on the run, so it would appear, with one of your party shot. And you expect me just to take this in my stride?'

'Not really, I know it's a terrible imposition. But the Crezia Berschilde I knew could cope with an emergency now and then. And she always had time for a friend in need.'

'A friend?'

'Yes. You're the only person I can turn to, Crezia.'

She snorted scornfully and tugged off her apron. 'All those years, I was happy to be the one you could turn to, Gregor. And you never did. You kept me at arm's length. You never wanted me involved in your business. And now...' She let the words trail off and shrugged unhappily.

'I'm sorry.'

'You bring guns into my house–' she hissed.

'I probably shouldn't tell you about the mercenary tied up in my speeder then,' I said.

She snapped round to look at me, incredulous, and then shook her head with a grim smile. 'Unbelievable. Twenty-five years and you roll up at dawn, bringing trouble with you.'

'No. No one knows I'm here. That's one of the reasons I came.'

'Are you sure?'

I nodded. 'Someone raided my residence last night. Razed it. Murdered my staff.'

'I don't want to hear this!'

'We barely got out alive. I needed sanctuary and medical help for Medea. I needed to find somewhere I knew would be safe.'

'I don't want to hear any more!' she snarled. 'I don't want to be tangled up in your battles. I don't want to be involved! I have a nice life here and–'

'You do need to hear it. You need to know what's going on.'

'Why? I'm not going to get involved! Why the hell didn't you go to the Arbites?'

'I can't trust anyone. Not even the authorities, right now.'

'Damnation, Eisenhorn! Why me? Why here?'

'Because I trust you. Because my enemies may have every known associate of mine on the planet under observation, every Arbites precinct, every office of the Ministorum and the Imperial Administratum. But our relationship is secret. Even my closest friends don't know we were ever associated.'

'Associated? Associated? You know how to flatter, you pig!'

'Please, Crezia. There a few things I need to do. A few things I need to arrange. A little help I need to ask of you. Then we'll be gone and you'll never have to worry about this again.'

She sat down on a chaise and rubbed her hands together anxiously.

'What do you need?'

'To begin with, your forbearance. After that... access to a private vox-link. I'll need you to summon an astropath, if that's in any way possible, and also have your man purchase clothes and other items for us.'

'The town tailors will be closed today.'

'I can wait.'

'There may be clothes here.'

'Very well.'

'There's a vox-link in my study.'

I went to look in on Medea, who was sleeping peacefully in the scrubbed medical suite built into the basement of Crezia's town house, and then retired to the room Phabes had prepared for me. Eleena and Aemos were in adjoining rooms, resting.

I bathed and shaved, doing both activities on automatic as my mind worked things through. I discovered my body had acquired several new bruises since the day before and a las-graze across the thigh I hadn't even noticed. My clothes were dirty, torn and smoke-damaged, and the breeches were covered in burrs and sticky grass seeds.

Phabes had laid some clothes out in my room, several changes of male attire. I recognised they were my own. I'd kept clothes here over the years, mostly soft, informal wear to change into when I visited. Crezia had stored them. I didn't know whether to be delighted or alarmed. All these years, and she hadn't thrown out the possessions I'd left in her territory. They were fresh too, as if aired or laundered regularly. I realised that Crezia Berschilde had always expected me to return one day.

Perhaps it was the manner of my return that had upset her – that I came back for her help and not simply for her. I couldn't blame her for that. I wouldn't be pleased to see me now, considering the trouble I was in. And not if I had broken all links of friendship two and a half decades before.

The chapel bells were ringing in the town below, calling the faithful for worship. Lakeside inns were opening up, and the smells of roasting and herbs were carried on the breeze.

I chose a dark blue cotton shirt with a thin collar, a pair of black twill trousers and a short flat-fronted summer jacket of black suede. The boots I had been wearing the night before would have to make do, but I scrubbed them clean with a cloth. I wanted to tuck the pistol into my jacket, but I knew how Crezia felt about guns, so I left it, with Barbarisater and the runestaff, under the mattress of my bed. The sacks of scrolls and manuscripts Aemos and I had rescued from Spaeton were with him in his room.

I had little else with me: my signet ring, a short-range hand vox, some coins and my warrant of office – a metal seal in a leather wallet. It was the first time since Durer that I missed my rosette. Fischig still had that, wherever he was.

As I hung my leather coat up in the wardrobe, I felt a weight in it and remembered I did have something else.

The *Malus Codicium*.

It was an infernal book, thrice damned. I knew of no other copy in existence. One half of the Inquisition would kill me to get their hands on it, the other half would burn me for having it in my possession.

Quixos, the corrupt veteran inquisitor I had finally brought to account on Farness Beta, had built his power upon it. I should have destroyed it when I destroyed him or at least surrendered it to the Ordo. I had done neither. Using it, secretly studying it, I had increased my abilities. I had captured and bound Cherubael using its lore. I had broken open several cult conspiracies thanks to the insight it had given me.

It was only a small thing, fat, soft-covered in simple black hide, the edges of its pages rough and hand-cut. Innocuous.

I sat down on the corner of the bed and weighed it in my hands. Splendid mid-morning sunlight shone in through the casement, the sky was blue, the slopes of the Itervalle visible from the rear of the house a soft lilac. But I felt cold and plunged into darkness.

I'd never really thought about why I had saved that hideous work for my own ends. Knowledge, I suppose. Curiosity. I had encountered prohibited artefacts many times in my life, the most notorious being the accursed Necroteuch. That loathsome thing had possessed a life of its own. It stung to the touch. It lured you in and coerced you into opening it. Just to be near it was to poison the mind.

But the *Codicium* was silent. It always had been. It had never seemed alive, like the other toxic, rustling volumes I have encountered. It had always been just a book. The contents were disturbing, but the book itself...

I wondered now. The moment it had come into my possession, things had started to change. Starting with Cherubael and on, on to the bleak events on Durer.

Maybe it was poisoning me. Maybe it was twisting my mind. Maybe I had crossed far too far over the line without realising it, thanks to its baleful influence.

Perhaps that was a measure of how evil it was. That it was painless.

Invisible. Insidious. The moment you touched the Necroteuch, you knew it was a vile thing, you knew you had to resist its seductive corruption. You knew you were fighting it.

But the *Malus Codicium*... so infinitely evil, so subtle, seeping slowly into a man's soul before he even knew it.

Was that how a servant of the Emperor as great as Quixos had become a monster? I had always wondered why he had never seen what he was becoming. Why he was so blind to his own degeneration.

I opened the drawer of my night stand and put the book inside. As soon as we were clear of Ravello, I would have to deal with it.

I went down to Crezia's study and found the vox-link. There was a hololithic pict unit too, and I tuned that in. Morning broadcasts, weather, planetary news. I watched for some time but there was no mention of any incident in the Dorsay region. I had anticipated as much, but it was still unnerving.

I used the vox and listened in to the Imperial channels, eavesdropping on Arbites frequencies, PDF transmissions, Ministorum links. Nothing. Either no one knew what had happened the night before at Spaeton House, or they were staying ominously silent.

I needed an astropath. If I was going to contact anyone, it would be off-world. I had no choice.

I really couldn't trust anybody on the planet.

The flier was still parked in the back courtyard. Phabes had been good enough to run a power cable from the house and the craft's batteries were recharging.

It was hot in the yard. Insects buzzed in the thick spill of flowering bucanthus that covered the side wall.

The mercenary was awake. He twisted his head from side to side as he heard me approach, blind and dumb.

I tore the tape from his mouth and then filled a dish-cup with water from a bottle I had borrowed from the kitchen. I held it up to his mouth.

'It's just water. Drink it.' He pursed his lips and turned his head away.

'You'll dehydrate in this heat. Drink.'

He refused again.

'Look, if you dehydrate, you'll become weak and far more vulnerable to my questions and mind probes.'

He paused and swallowed, but then shied away from the cup again as I brought it up.

'Have it your way,' I said and put the dish down. The Vessorine were famously hardy. It was said they could go without food or water for days when battle demanded it. If he wanted to show off, it was fine by me.

I rose and went over the body of the speeder carefully. I had borrowed a scanner wand from Crezia's study, and set it to detect high and low band signals... transponders, beacons, codes. I found nothing. For good measure. I swept the Vessorine too. Both flier and prisoner were clean. If the mercenaries were looking for us, they wouldn't find us because of the craft or pilot.

It had taken me half an hour to sweep the vessel. I went back to the pilot. The mid-morning sun was now high enough to throw sunlight in through the flier's side hatch, and he was obviously feeling the heat because he'd drawn his legs up into what shade remained.

I offered the water again. No response.

'Tell me your name,' I said.

His jaw clenched.

'Tell me your name,' I repeated, using the will now.

He shuddered. 'Eino Goran.' His voice was dry and slurry.

'And before it was Eino Goran, your name was what?'

'Nngh...'

His resolve was strong. The Vessorine were a blunt race, with a high frequency of untouchables. Part of their martial training was to learn methods of resisting interrogation, and at first I thought he might have some well-developed mind-trick to wall out psychic impulsions.

But as I questioned him further, I began to suspect it was more to do with the emplated identity he was wearing. I'd tried to pick it away, but it still wouldn't budge. Crude and simple it may have been, but it was psychically riveted into place. Part of that profound fixture, I was sure, was acting as a screen. It wasn't that he wouldn't answer. He couldn't.

'Gregor?'

I looked out of the hatch and saw that Crezia had come out into the yard. 'Gregor, what the hell are you doing?'

I got out of the flier and drew her back towards the garden doors. The Vessorine had undoubtedly heard her use my name. It couldn't be helped.

'That man's tied up like damn cygnid!' she said.

'That man would kill me given the chance. He's tied up for all our sakes. I have to ask him questions.'

She glared at me. She had changed into a long gown of blue satin with an epinchire trim. Her straw-blonde hair was tightly braided behind her head and held up by two golden pins. She was beautiful and haughty, just as I remembered her. Crezia had high cheekbones, a generous mouth, and pale brown eyes given to expressions of passion and intelligence. The only passion I had seen in them since my arrival had been fury.

'Like a cygnid,' she repeated. 'I won't have it. Not in my house.'

'Then what do you suggest? Have you a secure room, one that can be locked from outside?'

'Provide you with a cell for him? Pah!' she scoffed.

'It's that or the flier.'

She thought about it. 'I'll have Phabes clear out a box room upstairs.'

'No windows.'

'They all have damn windows! But the room I'm thinking of has just a small vane-light. Not big enough for anyone to get through.'

'Thank you.'

'I want to check him over.'

It was no good arguing. She inspected the man carefully.

'Don't be alarmed. I'm Doctor Cr–'

'He really doesn't need to know your name. Or mine. Think about it.'

She drew a deep breath. 'I am a doctor. I'm only going to check on your health. Do you have a name?'

He shook his head.

'He's using the name Eino Goran.'

'I see. Eino, this situation is unpleasant, but if you co-operate with me, and with Gr... with my associate here, it will work out for the best. Soon.'

Associate. I could feel the spiteful relish she put into that word.

Crezia looked at me disapprovingly. 'He needs to drink and eat. Drink particularly, in this heat.'

'Tell him, not me.'

'You need to drink, Eino. If you don't drink, I'll have to put you on a fluid drip.'

He allowed her to feed him the dish, and sipped slowly.

'Very good,' she said. Then to me, 'His bonds are far too tight.'

'That's not going to change.'

'Then get him up and walk him round a little. Tie his hands the other way.'

'Later perhaps. If you knew what he was, what he has done, you wouldn't be so humane.'

'I'm a officer of the Medicae Imperialis. It never matters what they've done.'

We went back into the drawing room.

'His identity is emplated. I need to get past the barriers.'

'To find out who he really is?'

'To find out who he's working for.'

'I see.' She sat down and bit at a fingernail. She always did that when she was troubled.

'You have medical stocks here. Zendocaine? Vulgate oxybarbital?'

'You're joking?'

I shook my head and sat down opposite her. 'Deadly serious. I need a psychoactive or at least an opiate or barbiturate to loosen his will power.'

'No. Absolutely no way.'

'Crezia...'

'I will not be party to torture!'

'It is not torture. I'm not going to hurt him. I just need to open his mind.'

'No.'

'Crezia, I am going to do it. I have the mandate of the Holy Inquisition to perform interrogation, and these circumstances permit me an even greater latitude of emergency powers. Wouldn't you rather it be done under your expert supervision?'

In the latter part of the afternoon, we brought the Vessorine inside, and put him in the box-room Phabes had cleared. There was nothing in the room but a bedframe and mattress. I removed his blindfold and then covered him with the autopistol as Aemos removed his bindings.

Crezia looked on, pointedly saying nothing about the weapon.

'Unfasten your tunic again,' I said.

Crezia started to say something but I cut her off. 'You'll need to get at his arm, won't you, doctor?'

There was another reason for getting him to disrobe. Aemos carefully studied the man's tattoos, making notes. The Vessorine just stood there, stripped to the waist, sullen. He refused to make eye contact.

I noticed he was slender but whipcord tough. The marks of old scars dotted his torso. I'd taken him to be a reasonably young man, but either he was older than he looked, or his short life had been barbarically tough.

Aemos finished. 'I'll get it translated properly. But it's what I thought it was.' He turned to go downstairs. I stopped him and passed him the pistol.

'Cover him, please.'

Aemos waited while I re-tied the merc's hands. I tied them in front of his body now, and then lashed his ankles together and tied off the end of that cord to the bedstead.

'Sit down,' I told him. He sat. I took the weapon back from Aemos, tucked it into my belt and sent him on his way.

'If you will, doctor?'

She looked at me. 'Just like that? Don't you want to give him the chance to volunteer first?'

There was no point, but I wanted to keep Crezia on side.

'Tell me your name,' I said.

'Eino Goran.'

'Tell me your real name.'

'Eino Goran.'

I shot a warning look at Crezia and used the will. I focused it in the Vessorine's direction so she would be spared, but it still made her shiver.

He gurgled a non-verbal response.

'Now, please.'

Crezia quickly injected twenty millilitres of zendocaine into the man's upper arm and drew back. Zendocaine is a psychoactive, a synaptic enhancer that causes a flurry of cortex activity disguised by a soothing opiate. The man coughed, and after a few moments his eyes took on a glassy sheen.

Crezia checked his blood pressure.

'Fine,' she said.

I placed my hand on the man's temple, and eased my mind into his. He was relaxed and offered no resistance, but his mind was lively. An ideal balance if I was going to prise off his emplated identity.

I tried a few test questions, both verbally and mentally. His answers were slurred.

'What is your name?'

'Eino Goran.'

'What is your age?'

'Forty sstannard.'

'What is your height?'

'Two anna third kwen.' That was a good sign. I had no idea what a 'kwen' was, but I'd take a bet it was a Vessorine measure.

'Where are we?' I continued.

'Inna room.'

'Where is the room?'

'Inna house. Dunno.'

'On what world?'

'Gudrun.'

'What colour is the sky?'

'Hnn, this sky?'

'Yes. What colour is this sky?'

'Blue.'

'What other sky might I have meant?'

'Dunno.'

'What is my name?'

'Gregor.'

'How do you know that?' I asked, without reacting.

'She call it you.'

Crezia glanced at me nervously.

'Who does that make me?'

'Dunno.'

'Who might I be? Who do you suppose?'

'Eisssnhorn.'

'Why do you know that name?'

'Job.'

'What job?'

'Be merc work. Pay job.'

'Tell me more about that.'

'Dunno more.'

'What is your name?' I asked the mercenary again.

'Tol' you. Eino Goran.'

'Where are you from?'

'Hesperus.'

'What colour is the sky?'

'Blue. Defn'ly.'

'What is your name?'

'Eino. Goran. Eino Goran. Eino Goran.'

The words came out like a mountain stream, overlapping, light, without any meaning.

'Where are you from?' I went on.

'Hesperus... uh. Dunno.'

'What does the tattoo on your upper body signify?'

'Bond.'

'In what language?'

'Dunno.'

'Is it a repatriation bond?'

'Uh huh.'

'That's a mercenary custom, isn't it?'

'Uhm.'

'It states, for any captor to see, that if you are returned to your home world, or an agency of your home world unharmed, a bond will be paid. Is that correct?'

'Yeah.'

'Are you a mercenary?'

'Yessss.'

'What colour is the sky?'

'Blue. No, yes... blue.'

'What is your name?'

'Uh...'

'I asked you, what is your name?'

'Wait... I know this. Be hard to think...' His eyes rolled in their sockets.

'What is your name?'

'Dunno.'

'Are you a mercenary?'

'Yeah...'

'Was I your target last night?'

'Yeah.'

'Who was your target last night?'

'Eisenhorn.'

'Am I Eisenhorn?'

'Yes.' He looked at me, but his eyes remained glassy, unfocussed.

'What were your orders?'

'Chill 'em all. Burn the place.'

'Where did the orders come from?'

'Clansire Etrik.'

'Is clansire a rank?'

'Yeah.'

'Is Clansire Etrik a Vessorine janissary?'

'Yes.'

'Are you a Vessorine janissary?'

'Yes.'

'What is your name, janissary?'

'Sire! Vammeko Tarl, sire!'

He paused and blinked, not sure what he had just said. Crezia was staring at me.

'You're doing very well, Tarl,' I said.

'Uh huh.'

The emplate was shredding away from his mind like damp paper now. I went in for the kill with my full willpower now his mind was open.

'Where were you hired?'

'Twenty weeks ago. Nnngh. Twenty weeks.'

'Where was that?'

'Heveron.'

'What were you doing there?'

'Looking for work.'

'Before that?'

'Gnnh... be hired for a border war. Local governor hired us. But the war fizzled out.'

'And you found a new client?'

'The Clansire did. Good pay, for a long-term hire. Off-world, transit paid.'

'To do what?'

'They didn't tell us. Shipped us off to someplace.'

'Where?'

'Gudrun?'

'Was it Gudrun?'

'Yeah...' A shudder went through him.

'And the job, in outline?'

'Hardware and fliers provided by client. Told to hit this place on a headland. Chill everyone.'

'Whose place was this?'

'Be someone called Eisenhorn.'

'How many men were hired?'

'All of us. The entire clan.'

'And how many men is that?'

'Eight hundred.'

I paused. Eight hundred?

'All for this job on Gudrun?'

'No. Be seventy of us for that. The rest for other jobs.'

'What other jobs?'

'Wasn't told. Gah... my head aches.'

Crezia touched my sleeve. 'You must stop,' she whispered. 'He's beginning to hyperventilate.'

'Just a few more questions,' I hissed back.

I looked at Tarl. He was sweating and rocking slightly in his seat as his breaths came quick and fast.

'Where did you stage before the raid?'

'Nnh... Piterro.' A small island in the Bay of Bisheen. Interesting.

'What was the name of the ship that brought you here?'

'The *Beltrand*.'

'What was the name of your client?'

'Dunno.'

'Did you ever meet him?'

'No.'

'Did you ever meet any of his agents?'

'Yeah... uhhnn! It hurts!'

'Gregor!'

'Not yet! Tarl, who was the agent?'

'Woman. Psyker. She came to emplate us the night before the raid.'

'She personally fixed your identity veils?'

'Yes.'

'What was her name?'

'Call herself Marla. Marla Tarray.'

'Picture her in your mind, Tarl,' I ordered. I got a brief but vivid flash of a sharp featured woman with long, straight black hair. Her eyes were what I remembered most. Kohl-edged, large and green like jade. She seemed to look into my head. I snatched back.

'Are you all right?' Crezia asked.

'Yes, I'm fine.'

'We're going to stop now,' she told me straight. 'Right now.'

'Right now?'

'That's what I said.'

The janissary had sunk back on the bed, his skin puffy and damp. He closed his eyes and moaned.

'He's coming down. Now he's feeling the disruptions of your mind probe.' I could see she was shaking slightly. She'd felt them too, second hand.

'One last question.'

'I said we were stopping now and I meant it. I have to stabilise him.'

I held up my hand. 'One more. While he's still open. We come back later or tomorrow and he'll have closed up. And you don't want to do this again, do you?'

'No,' she relented.

'Tarl? Tarl?'

'Go 'way.'

'What was the name of your client? What was the name of Marla Tarray's boss?'

The Vessorine murmured something.

'What was that?' whispered Crezia. 'I didn't catch it.'

I had. Not verbally, but in my mind. Something blocked out, something he hadn't been able to say even before if he'd wanted to. As he collapsed into psi-fugue, the last shreds of his emplated veil melted away and the final name tumbled out.

'He said Khanjar,' I told her. 'Khanjar the Sharp.'

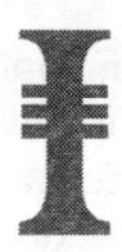

ELEVEN

ADEPT CIELO
DEATH NOTICES
DANGEROUS KINDNESS

I woke before dawn. It was still twilight outside, and the curtains of my room swayed in the cold breeze.

I got dressed, and went downstairs. On the way, I checked on Tarl. He was profoundly asleep, curled on his bed. Crezia had made sure he was alright, given him a secondary, mild opiate to reduce his trauma and covered him with a blanket. He'd been out for the best part of fourteen hours. Crezia had almost flipped out with fear when she discovered the captive in her box room was a Vessorine janissary.

I checked Tarl's bindings, and he groaned softly as I disturbed the blanket.

Aemos was already up. Drinking caffeine he had brewed himself, he sat in Crezia's study, listening to the early morning vox broadcasts.

'Couldn't you sleep?' I asked.

'I slept fine, Gregor. But I never sleep for long.'

I fetched another cup and poured caffeine from his pot.

'There's nothing about us,' he said, gesturing to the vox.

'Nothing?'

'It's most perturbatory. Not a word, not even on the Arbites band.'

'Someone managed to hire eight hundred Vessorine killers, Uber. They have clout. The news has been withheld. Or censored.'

'The others will know.'

'How do you mean?'

'Fischig, Nayl. The moment they don't get a response from Spaeton House, they'll know something is up.'

'I hope so. What did you make of our friend's tattoos?'

'Base Futu, just as I supposed. I cross-checked it using the doctor's cogitator.' He took out a note-slate and adjusted his eye-glasses. 'This mark bears witness that Vammeko Tarl, a janissary, is owned by the Clan Etrik, and a bond of ten thousand zkell will be paid for his repatriation. He is of flesh made and his flesh speaks for him.'

Aemos looked up at me. 'Strange practice.'

'Totally in keeping with the Vessorine mindset. Janissaries are objects. Material items. You might as well keep a cannon or a tank as a prisoner of war. They have no political affiliation, no loyalties within the particular frame of whatever conflict they're involved with. No use as a hostage. Putting that little incentive on each one makes things clear and simple. Puts a simple price on the matter and dissuades a captor from simply killing them.'

'How much is ten thousand zkell, then?'

'Enough, I should think.'

'What do we do with him when we leave?'

Now there was a question.

I went into the kitchen to brew more caffeine and hunt for bread, and found Crezia juicing ploins and mountain tarberries in a chrome press. Her hair was loose and she was wearing a short, cream silk houserobe.

'Oh!' she said as I walked in.

'I'm sorry,' I said, retreating.

'Oh, don't bother, Gregor. You've seen me in a lot less.'

'Yes, I have.'

'Yes, you have. Fruit juice?

'I was looking for caffeine, actually.'

'How could I forget? Breakfasts on the terrace... me with my fruit and grain-cakes, you with your caffeine and eggs and salt-pork.'

I filled a pan from the sink pump and lit the stove. Then I rinsed out the pot. 'I suppose now's your opportunity to tell me "I told you so", ' I said.

'What do you mean?'

'You always said fruit and grain-loaf was the path to a healthy life, remember? You used to go on about diet and fibre and all sorts. Told me my intake of caffeine and alcohol and red meat would kill me.'

'I take it back.'

'Really?'

'It won't be your diet that kills you, Gregor,' she said, suddenly biting at a fingernail.

'You were right, of course. Look at you.'

'I'd rather not,' she said, crushing a ploin with excessive force.

'You're as lovely as the day I first met you.'

'The day you first met me, Gregor Eisenhorn, you were half-comatose with anaesthetic and I was wearing a scrub mask.'

'Ah. How could I forget?'

She looked at me witheringly.

'Still,' I said. 'I'm not lying. I treated you badly. I'm still treating you badly. Someone like you doesn't deserve that.'

She tasted her pulpy juice drink. 'I won't argue with any of that. But... it's nice to hear you admit it.'

'It's the truth. So's the fact you're still lovely.'

She sighed. 'Juvenat programs are all easy to administer. I look this way thanks to Imperial science, not fruit juice.'

'I still believe in fruit juice.'

She grinned. 'You don't look so bad yourself, red meat and caffeine considered.'

The pan began to boil. 'I feel about a thousand years old next to you. Life has not treated me kindly.'

'Oh, I don't know. There's a nobility about your scars. Something very masculine about the way you wear your age well.'

I started to look in cupboards for the ground beans.

'That canister there,' she said. 'The chicory blend you always used. I've never lost the taste for it.'

I took the tin canister and spooned out several measures into the pot. 'Crezia,' I said, 'you should have let go of me a long time ago. I was never any good for you. I was never any good for anyone, truth be told.'

'I know,' she said. 'But I can't. That's just the way of things.'

I poured the boiling water into the pot and let it stand.

'How's Alizebeth?' she asked suddenly.

I had been sort of waiting for that. I had broken my long relationship with Crezia Berschilde in the end because of Bequin. Even though I knew Alizebeth and I could never be together in any way except friends, I knew I would never get past my love for her. It was too much in the way, and that could never be fair on Crezia.

Twenty-five years before, in that very house, I had told her as much. And walked away.

'She's dying,' I said.

Crezia put her glass down suddenly. 'Dying?'

'Or already dead.' I told her what had happened on Durer.

'Oh, God-Emperor,' she said. 'You should go to her.'

'What could I do?'

'Be there,' she said firmly. 'Be there and tell her before it's too late.'

'How do you know I haven't already told her?'

'Because I know you, Gregor. Too well.'

'I... well...'

'The two of you never... I mean?'

'No. She's an untouchable. I'm a psyker. That's the way it works.'

'And you never told her?'

'She knows.'

'Of course she knows! But you never told her?'

'No.'

She embraced me. I pulled her close. I thought of all the things I had never done, or never started, or never finished. Then I remembered all the things I had done and could never undo.

'The last thing you want is me, Crezia,' I whispered into her hair.

'I'll be the judge of that.'

The kitchen door burst open and Aemos limped in. Crezia and I let each other go.

We could have been doing anything for all Aemos cared. 'You have to come and hear this, Gregor,' he said.

He had been listening to the Sub-sector Service on the vox, news from all around the Helican sub, some of it days or weeks old. By the time we were standing around the old set, the news had moved on to stock reports and shipping forecasts.

'Well?' I asked.

'A report from Messina, Gregor. The upper levels of spire eleven of Messina Prime were destroyed twenty-four hours ago by what was cited as a recidivist blast.'

I went cold. Spire eleven, Messina Prime. That was the location of the residence I had leased for the use of the Distaff. Nayl and Begundi had taken Alizebeth and Kara there. For safety.

'The report said that over ten thousand lives had been lost,' Aemos murmured. 'The Messina Arbites are hunting for suspects, but it's been attributed to a radical free Messina outfit.'

I sat down, trembling. Crezia crouched beside me, hugging me. The Distaff... gone? Bequin... Nayl... Kara Swole... Begundi?

It was too much.

I realised why Khanjar the Sharp had hired so many Vessorine janissaries. Multiple strikes, multiple worlds. What else had this Khanjar hit? What other pain had he already caused me?

Who else had he killed?

'What's going on?' Eleena asked, coming in, rubbing her sleepy eyes.

I paced the house and the courtyard garden. Two or three times, I started up towards the box room, the autopistol in my hand. Damn the bond! I would have vengeance!

Each time, I turned back. I'd counselled Medea against vengeance, and so I should listen to my own good advice. Killing Tarl would be like breaking a sword. What was it Medea had said? *It's a displacement activity. It's something you can lock on to and do because you can't do the thing you really want to do. I needed something, and it wasn't payback.*

So what was it? I needed to get back in the game. I needed to round up my allies. I needed to discover who Khanjar the Sharp was.

And then, damn the advice I had given Medea, I needed to destroy him.

At nine sharp, Adept Cielo arrived with his clerk, having been summoned the day before. Both were hooded and cloaked, which I suppose was their idea of subtlety.

I met with them in the drawing room, with Crezia in attendance. She had dressed in a trouser suit of beige murray.

Adept Cielo was an elderly, experienced astropath, one of the best the Guild House in Ravello had to offer.

'I take it, sir, this is a private matter?'

'It is.'

'Are you purchasing my services in cash?'

'No, adept, by direct fund transfer. I have a confidential message service which I wish to use. I expect the utmost discretion.'

'You have the guarantee of the Guild, sir,' said Cielo. His clerk opened a data-slate and offered me the thumb-print scanner.

I pressed my thumb against it and then entered my code.

'Ah,' said Cielo, as the slate chimed and displayed a readout. 'That's all sorted out. Your accounts have released the funds. Everything's in order, Mr Eising. Let us proceed.'

Of course, I wasn't using any accounts that were connected with the person of Gregor Eisenhorn. I had good reason to suspect my finances were under observation, if not frozen. But I wasn't even going to try, because that would let my enemy know that someone with the authority to access Gregor Eisenhorn's accounts was still alive, and it would be comparatively simple to trace that access.

As with the various properties I owned, I had resources under other identities. 'Gorton Eising' had several holdings with the Imperial Thracian treasury, with enough funds for my current needs.

I had set up the confidential message service many years before so that I could send and receive messages without using my real identity. It was essentially an automatically maintained mailbox account that I could access, using an astropath, from any location. I could send messages through it, and read any communiqués that had been posted to it. The service was registered under the name 'Aegis.'

When Cielo accessed the Aegis account, there were no communiqués waiting to be read. Composing the contents in Glossia, I had Cielo send warning messages to Fischig on Durer, to Messina, to agents of my organisation on Thracian Primaris, Hesperus, Sarum and Cartol. I used the signature 'Rosethorn.' I also sent a private, coded, anonymous transmission to a friend outside the Helican sub-sector. It was a single word message that read 'Sanctum.'

I would wait for responses before I contacted my Lord Rorken. I wanted to take things one step at a time. Not for the first time in my career, I wanted to stay out of sight, except to friends.

Of course, even sending communiqués in another name was risky. Many or all of the people I was trying to contact might be under surveillance themselves – if they hadn't already been eliminated. But Glossia was a private code. Even if my messages were intercepted, they would be impossible to decipher.

The first responses arrived by noon the next day. Cielo's clerk came up from the Guild House to deliver them.

One was a message from Fischig, in Glossia, that essentially told me he was already en route from Durer and would arrive at Gudrun in about twenty days. I dispatched a reply that emphasised caution and told him to contact me when he was close.

The message 'Sanctum' had been answered with the words 'Sanctum arising, in fifteen.' There was no ident on the communiqué, and the source was deep space.

The clerk then passed me a data-slate. 'The communiqués to Messina, Thracian Primaris, Hesperus and Cartol have all been returned as undeliverable.

That is strange. The message from Hesperus has a statement from the local Arbites attached, recommending you get in touch with them directly. There has been no response from Sarum.'

After the clerk had left, I discussed it with Aemos. He was as alarmed as I was. 'Undeliverable? Most perturbatory. And the interest of the Arbites is disturbing.'

'What progress with the names?' I asked. He had been at work on Crezia's codifier all morning.

'Nothing. No listing for a Marla Tarray and nothing on any Khanjar the Sharp. A khanjar is a blade weapon, of course. A curved dagger from ancient Terra. The word is occurs in several Imperium cultures.'

'Can you resource further?'

'Not using this machine. But your doctor friend is going to walk me to the universitariate this afternoon and get me access to their main data engines.'

He was gone for hours, until late in the evening. Crezia had teaching duties to perform, and Phabes was all but invisible. I was left alone with Eleena.

I checked the prisoner. He was awake but unresponsive. Crezia had left him a tray of food and some water before leaving, but it was untouched. I tried a few questions but he didn't stir. He was zoned out in a post-interrogation stupor.

Medea was still sleeping, but her life signs was good and there was no trace of post-operative infection. I kissed her forehead gently and went back to the kitchen.

Eleena was seated at the refectory table, one third down a bottle of fine Hesperean claret. Without asking, she fetched me a glass and poured me some.

I sat down with her. The kitchen doors were open, affording us a cool evening breeze and a fine view out over the courtyard to the Itervalle. The mountain was ochre in the setting sun, and even as we watched it gently shifted colour, becoming russet, then almost scarlet, then ultramarine.

'Have you eaten?' Eleena asked.

'No. Have you?'

'I'm not very hungry,' she replied, and drank a mouthful of wine.

'I'm sorry, Eleena,' I said.

'Sorry, sir? Why?'

'Sorry that you should be in the middle of all this. It's an unpleasant business and costing us all dear.'

She smiled. 'You got me out of Spaeton alive, sir. For that I'm thankful.'

'I only wish I could have got everyone out alive.'

She shrugged. I could tell she was haunted by the killing she had seen. Sastre's brave sacrifice in particular had scarred her. Eleena Koi was only about twenty-five, just a girl, and a new recruit to the Distaff. She'd not seen any active service in the field yet. She'd been posted to Spaeton as resident untouchable – something the Distaff regarded as an easy job – to get her acclimatised to the work. Some acclimatisation.

'If you'd like to leave, I think that would be all right. I could arrange some adequate papers, some money. You could get off-world, to safety.'

Eleena looked almost offended. 'I am a contracted untouchable in the pay of the Distaff, sir. Perhaps, Emperor bless me, the last one alive. I knew service to an inquisitor would be dangerous when I started. I'm under no illusions.'

'Even so–'

'No, sir. I'm strong enough for this. It may be extreme, but it's what I was hired to do. Besides...'

'Besides what?'

'Well, for one thing, we know that the enemy has at least one powerful psyker in his pay. That means you'll need an untouchable.'

'True.'

'And... I think I'd feel safer sticking with you, sir. If I went off on my own, I'd be looking over my shoulder for the rest of my life.'

'Thank you, Eleena. You could stop calling me "sir" now, though. If what we've been through these last few days can't be counted as a bonding process, I don't know what can.'

'Right,' she smiled. It was a change to see a smile on her face. She was tall and overly thin, in my opinion, always seeming edgy and nervous. The smile suited her.

Neither of us said anything for a few moments.

'So, what should I call you?' she asked eventually.

We chatted idly for a while longer, until the Itervalle had become black and the sky Imperial blue. The stars were out.

'Do we have a plan?' she asked.

'Theoretically, we find out who is set so murderously against us and hunt him down. Practically, that means staying here, out of sight, for a while at least, then getting off planet.'

'How long for that, do you think?'

'My preferred means of planet exit will be available in fifteen days.'

She refilled our glasses. 'I like that. I like it when you sound like everything's under control.'

'So do I,' I chuckled.

'So... once we're off-planet, what then? Practically speaking?'

'It depends on a few things. What we manage to turn up in the next two weeks. Whether I dare correspond with the Ordos.'

'You don't think the Inquisition is involved, do you?'

'Not at all,' I replied. It wasn't a lie, because I was sure we weren't in conflict with any external agency, but it wasn't entirely the truth either. I had been in the job long enough to know that nothing is out of the question. But there was no point alarming her. 'It's simply that I think our enemy is so well co-ordinated, so well provided, that he's watching everything. If I contact the Inquisition, it could betray us.'

I took up my glass and drank a good measure of the fine red wine. 'So, if nothing turns up, when we leave here... it's open. There are places we could run to find security, friends I could call upon. Our best bet might be to disappear and stay hidden until our plans are formalised. But I'm torn. I'd like to head to Messina. If there's a chance any of them are alive...'

Apart from roaming field agents engaged on diverse tasks, the Distaff headquarters on Messina represented my only other base of operations. If it was gone, and Spaeton House too, I was cut adrift.

'I had many friends at the Distaff Hall. I hope they're all right.' She looked at the table and fiddled with her glass. 'I suppose you're most concerned about Madam Bequin.'

'Well–' I began.

'She being such an old friend and colleague of yours, I mean. And that she was badly hurt on Durer. And everyone knows...' She stopped suddenly.

'Knows what, Eleena?'

'Well, that you love her.'

'Everyone knows, do they?'

'You can't hide something like that. I've seen you together. You adore each other.'

'But–'

'You're a psyker and she's one of us. I know, I know. That doesn't mean you don't love her, all the same.'

She looked at me and blushed. 'This wine!' she said. 'I've said far too much, haven't I?'

'No, Eleena,' said Crezia. Neither of us had heard her come in. 'Talk some sense into him, will you? He has to go back and see her. It's the right thing.'

Crezia was dressed in her formal tutorial robes. She took a glass from the rack, came to the table and, finding the bottle was empty, set about opening another.

'How was your day?' I asked, trying to change the subject.

'I spent four hours lecturing the sophomore class on the principles of thoracic palpation. I've never seen such a crowd of ill-prepared dolts. When I got one fellow up for a practical, he took hold of the volunteer subject's thigh. How do you think my day was?'

She sat down with us at the table. 'I looked in on our guest. I'm concerned about his condition. He hasn't taken any food or drink, and he's only marginally responsive. I think you may have damaged him with your mental probings.'

'Either that,' I said, 'or he's having an adverse reaction to the drugs.'

'Possibly. If he's the same in the morning, I'll run some bloodwork on him. Whatever, he's not well and he's not comfortable. There's severe lividity in his hands and feet. You tied those bonds so damn tight.'

'As tight as they needed to be, Crezia. He's a Vessorine janissary paid to murder me, don't forget.'

'Shut up and pour me a drink.'

The moment Aemos came in, past ten o'clock, I could tell something was wrong. He was carrying a small pile of data-slates and accepted a drink from Eleena without question, which was unusual for him.

His hand was trembling as he raised the glass to sip. Even Crezia could see this was not like him.

'Well, old friend?' I asked.

'I spent hours resourcing those names, Gregor. Still nothing on this Khanjar, though I assembled a list of planets that still use the word.' He slid a slate across to me.

'Marla Tarray... a little more success there. A Marla Tari was arrested by the Arbites on Hallowcan five years ago for participating in cult activity. She was pending trial when she escaped custody. She turned up twice more: on Felthon, where she was a known associate of the cult leader, Berrikin Paswold; and on Sanseeta, where she was wanted in connection with the murder of Hierarch Sansum and five Ministorum clerics. The Inquisition also has a warrant out for her restraint as a suspected rogue psyker.'

'So, an active participant in cult activity, then?' I looked at the extracts Aemos had put on a slate. They didn't tell me much more. If I contacted the Inquisition, they'd have a more complete file. Despite the risks, I felt inclined to get in touch with Rorken.

'If it's the same woman,' he replied.

There was no picture, but the physical description matched my mind's retrieved image.

'What's her background?'

'There's nothing on that... except that when questioned during her detention on Hallowcan, she claimed to be thirty-seven and stated her birthworld was Gudrun.'

'Interesting...' I said. 'We should check her details against the planetary census and–'

'I believe you pay me to be thorough, Gregor,' said Aemos, churlishly. 'I've already done that. There is no record of her here. In fact, there is no one on Gudrun with the surname Tarray or Tari. The surname does, however, occur on other worlds. Too many, in fact, to be of any help.'

'So, savant,' said Crezia, 'what's really troubling you?'

Aemos took another glug of wine and pushed a slate into the centre of the table. 'I was running out of options with the names, so I turned to something else. I inspected the news registers from across the sub-sector, hunting for key words. You won't like it.'

I read down the slate, my heart turning to cold stone. It showed me bulletin reports of incidents from several planets in the sub. Just little items, most of which wouldn't even have made column space beyond the regional news wires. Certainly, the events reported wouldn't have been planetary news, and definitely not interplanetary. Aemos had only found them because he had been specifically looking, and trawling the Imperium's news wire data compendium.

The first report was of the explosion on Messina. Messina Prime, the main hive, spire eleven. The blast had occurred at ten fifty, local. That was chilling. By my estimation, the raid on Spaeton had commenced at precisely the same time, given sidereal adjustments. The explosion had incinerated the uppermost ten levels of the spire. The death toll was put at eleven thousand six hundred. The Lord Governor had declared a state of emergency.

There was a long appended list of properties and business destroyed.

Amongst them halfway down the second page, was the Thorn Institute, the name by which the Distaff had been publically known.

No survivors. I supposed it could have been a coincidence, but I didn't believe in them. Which meant that my foe, this Khanjar the Sharp, had not hesitated to exterminate thousands of civilians just to take out the Distaff.

The news file stated that a proscribed movement calling itself the Scions of Messina had claimed responsibility. That group, it said, struck for Messina's independence from the Imperium.

Which was frankly rubbish. Messina was as Imperial as a planet-culture got.

The second report listed on the slate was filed from Cartol. A family touring Kona Province on vacation had been found murdered by unknown gunmen. Two men and three women. Identities were to follow as soon as they had been established. Authorities on Cartol estimated the time of death at between ten and midnight, two days back.

I had sent my agent Leres Phinton, along with Biron Fakal, Loys Naran and two untouchables, to Cartol five months earlier, to gather evidence concerning a death cult in the Kona region. They had reported back regularly. Dear God-Emperor...

I scrolled to the next item. From Thracian Primaris. A private residence in Hive Sixty-Two had been firebombed just before midnight. Eight dead, unidentified. The location was listed as Sixty-two, Up-Hive, level 114, 871... which was the address of the subsidiary office I maintained on the capital world of the Helican sub-sector. Barned Ferrikal, who had been with me for thirty years, ran that place with a staff of seven.

The next. Hesperus. Two men killed in a firefight with juve-gangs. Just before midnight a week ago. They had wandered into the wrong part of town, an Arbites spokeman said.

Lutor Witte and Gan Blaek, two of the most capable undercover agents I ran, had been operating on Hesperus for a year, seeking to uncover a Tzeentchian cult that was preying on the juve population of the underhives.

Next, Sarum, capital world of the Antimar sub. One of my most promising pupils, Interrogator Devra Shiborr, had gone there under my instruction eight months prior to infiltrate and expose a chaotifiliac ring in the central university. She had posed as Doctor Zeyza Bajj, a historian from Punzel.

The news item recorded the death, apparently by suicide, of the promising academic Bajj. Her body, dead for about eight hours, had been discovered in her bathroom at choir bell this same morning.

And then the last, the most shocking. From the Sameter Global News Wire, posted a week ago. The residential home of Inquisitor Nathun Inshabel had been attacked by an unidentified enemy and obliterated. Inshabel was listed amongst the dead.

I sat back. They were all looking at me. Aemos was leaning his chin on his hands and the two women were staring with anxious patience.

'They're all dead,' I said. 'Everyone. Every thread of my staff operation. My home here, the Distaff headquarters, and all the agents I had on active work in the field. Every one, everything. All hit at effectively the same hour on the same day of the week.'

My voice tailed off. I was too deeply shocked. Crezia poured me a glass of amasec and took one herself.

All of it, gone. The operation I had spent decades building up, the friends and allies I had drawn together... destroyed in one night. All my visible resources had been identified, targeted and eliminated. Apart from dear Fischig, slogging his way back to meet us, we were all that was left.

I felt disconnected more than anything else. The network of intelligence and active personnel I had built up since the start of my career had been brutally taken from me.

I was alone.

I wanted nothing... nothing more than to see this Khanjar the Sharp face to face and make a reckoning.

I went to bed, the amasec untouched, and slept fitfully. In the small hours, I woke painfully from a dream I couldn't quite remember at first. As I lay in the darkness, the details slowly returned to me. I had been dreaming about the escape from Spaeton. Medea and Jekud Vance had been calling out to me, begging to be rescued. I remembered the sensation of taking Medea's hand, and clutching out at Vance, who couldn't quite reach me. The janissaries shot him down, cutting his body apart with las-fire. His psychic death scream had cut into my mind like a hot wire, and that's what had woken me.

Hadn't it?

I woke again at four. The night was quiet except for the click of the mountain crickets.

Something was wrong. I got up, slid the autopistol out from under the mattress and crept out into the landing.

I could hear Aemos snoring in his room, and the distant sighs of Crezia in slumber.

Eleena's door was open.

I looked in. The bed was empty and the quilt cast off onto the floor.

I edged down the corridor with my back to the wall and my weapon raised in both hands, almost as if I was praying. There was a light shafting out from under the next door. The bathroom.

I heard water gurgle and light suddenly flooded me as the door opened.

I aimed the gun.

'Oh god! Golden Throne, sir! What the hell are you d–'

I slapped my hand across Eleena's startled mouth and pulled her into the shadows.

'You scared the hell out of me,' she whispered once I relaxed my grip.

'Sorry.'

'I was just going to the bathroom.'

'Sorry. Something's wrong.'

'Gregor? What's the noise?' Crezia's voice floated down the landing.

'Get back in your room!' I hissed.

In a typically Crezia Berschilde manner, she did the opposite. She was pulling on her silk robe as she padded down to join us.

'What is damn well going on?'

'For once, just shut up, Crezia,' I snapped.

'Well, excuse me all to hell.'

I pushed them both behind me and crept down towards the door of the box room.

'Nice rump,' said Crezia. I was only wearing a wrap.

'Will you be serious just for a minute?' I snarled back.

'Please, doctor,' urged Eleena. 'This is serious.'

The box room door was shut and dark.

'See?' said Crezia. 'No problem.'

I felt the doorknob and realised it was loose. Crezia jumped as I kicked the door in, and aimed my gun at the bed.

The empty bed.

Eleena turned on the light. The wispy, fraying strands of Tarl's bindings were still tied to the bedstead. He'd bitten through them or tugged them off.

'Golden Throne, he's gone!'

'Oh no...' Crezia murmured. 'I only loosened his bonds a little.'

'You did what?'

'I told you! I told you I was worried about the constriction. The lividity in his hands and his–'

'You didn't tell me you'd slackened them off!' I raged.

'I thought you'd understood what I meant!'

I ran downstairs. The unlit hall was pale with moonlight that slanted in through the half-open front doors.

'He can't have gone far! What does it matter any way?' Crezia called after me.

I stepped out into the street. There was no sign of any one or anything. The cool shadows of the night spread fluidly across the flagstones.

Tarl, I was sure, was long gone.

I went back inside and Crezia turned on the hall lights.

And screamed.

Phabes was bent over in the corner, like a man who has fallen asleep sitting up. But he was very dead. His throat had been slashed. A wide pool of blood was leaking outwards slowly from his hunched form.

'Do you see now, Crezia? Do you?' I yelled up at her.

Tarl was loose. He knew who I was and where I was. We had to leave.

Fast.

TWELVE

INTO THE NIGHT, INTO THE MOUNTAINS
THE TRANS-ATENATE EXPRESS
A PROMPT FROM THE DEAD

'No,' said Crezia. 'No. No way. No.'

'This isn't up for debate, Crezia. It's not a suggestion, it's a... an instruction.'

'How dare you order me around like one of your staff lackeys, Eisenhorn. I am not leaving!'

I opened my mouth, then closed it again. The brutal murder of her man Phabes was causing her great distress. Getting through to her would be hard.

I turned to Aemos and Eleena. 'Get dressed. Collect up everything and stow it in the flier. I want to be away from here in under half an hour.' They both hurried away.

It was difficult to know how long the janissary had been gone. Phabes, whose body Aemos had covered with a sheet, was still quite warm, so I reckoned Tarl only had an hour's head start, ninety minutes worst case. Given his Vessorine pragmatism, I figured he had headed straight for a vox-station to report our location to his brethren. That's what I'd have done in his position. He could have tried to kill me himself, but by then he knew not to underestimate my abilities. There was a decent chance I'd have taken him down, in which case the secret of my location would never have got out.

No, he'd gone to find means of sending the message. It was impossible to know how close elements of his party were, but if we were still here in sixty minutes' time, I didn't much rate our chances.

It also occurred to me that once he'd got his message off safely, he'd be clear to come back and have a try at me himself.

I took Crezia by the hand and led her back upstairs. Her eyes were puffy and red, and she was a little vacant with shock. She sat on the end of my bed as I got dressed.

'If I could just go, Crezia, I would,' I said softly, finding a fresh shirt. 'If it was just a matter of walking away and removing all my crap from your life, that's what I'd do. But that's not what's going to happen. Mercenaries will be heading this way. They will be arriving soon, probably before dawn. They will question and kill anyone they find. You won't be able to tell them you don't know where I've gone. They will... well, they're Vessorine janissaries and they're being paid well. I can't leave you here.'

'I don't want to go. This is my home, Gregor. My damn home, and look what you've done.'

'I'm sorry.'

'Look what you've damn well done to my life!'

'I'm sorry. I'll make amends.'

She got up, the anger coming back and eclipsing her sorrow. 'How? How the hell can you make up for this? How the hell can you make up for all the pain you've ever caused me?'

'I have no idea. But I will. And you have to stay alive so I can. I've got the ruination of your nice comfortable existence on my conscience, Crezia. I will not add your death to that.'

'Fine words. I'm not coming. I'm going back to bed.'

I grabbed her by the arm and stopped her. I had to find a different tack. As a medic, she was almost professionally selfless. Appealing to her sense of self preservation was futile.

'I need you to come. That's the truth of it. I've got to take Medea with me. I can't leave her here, and I don't think she's in a position to travel.'

'Of course she isn't!'

'So she'll die?'

'If you move her now? In her state?'

'Better she travelled with a doctor then, don't you think?'

She shook off my hand. 'I will not allow you to jeopardise the health of my patient, Eisenhorn,' she warned.

'Then consider the prognosis, doctor. If she stays here, she'll be dead by morning. They will kill her when they find her. If she comes with me without you, she'll likely die too. I think what's really in question here is your medicae oath to preserve life.'

I hated being so manipulative... well, with her anyway. She regarded me with venom, knowing that I'd cornered her.

'You bastard. You clever, clever bastard. I don't know why I ever loved you.'

'I don't know why either. But I know why I loved you. You always cared. You always did the right thing.'

She turned and walked out of my room.

I finished dressing, and tucked spare clothes and Barbarisater into a leather grip I found on top of the wardrobe. Then I picked up the rune staff and–

–stopped in the doorway.

The *Malus Codicium* was still in the drawer of the nightstand. I wrapped it in a pillow case and tucked it into the grip. How could I have nearly forgotten it?

The first answer that occurred to me was strange and unnerving. Perhaps it wanted to be forgotten.

The flier's interior lights illuminated a patch of the little courtyard. Aemos and Eleena had stowed everything – clothes for each of them, and the manuscripts and books we had rescued from Spaeton House. I put my own stuff aboard and ran a pre-flight. The flier was charged to optimum.

'Help me, damn you all!' Crezia said.

She was dressed in a dark green utility suit and a quilted coat, and had two travel bags with her. Medea lay on a grav-gurney, strapped in place with a resuscitrex unit and a narthecium full of supplies magnetically anchored to the underside of the gurney. Crezia had slaved two med-skulls to our patient, and they hovered in the air behind the stretcher.

We got Medea aboard and then clambered in ourselves. Crezia sat beside Medea, saying nothing. She didn't even look back at the house as we rose into the night and powered away.

We flew south, towards the main Atenate range, a massif of gigantic peaks that split the centre of the continent for three and a half thousand kilometres. The Itervalle and its neighbours were just foothills compared to this great geological structure.

I didn't want to stay in the air for too long. Tarl knew we had a flier and would have informed his comrades. This was just a short hop to get us going. I studied a chart-slate and began to compose a route.

By dawn, we were about ninety kilometres to the south-west and several hundred metres higher, in the base valleys of the ragged-edged Esembo. It was a soaring black shape in the early light, with a glinting wig of ice. Its mighty neighbours lurked behind it.

We set down at a town called Tiroyere, a small place that thrived as a logging centre and a waystation for travellers heading to the resorts at the top of the Esembo Pass. I parked the flier on the edge of the town under a brake of firs that would shield it from aerial observers.

No one had said much. The air was briskly cold and I turned the cabin heater to maximum for Medea's benefit.

'We should eat,' Eleena said. 'I'd go and get something... but...'

None of us had any money.

Crezia pulled off her gloves and produced a wallet from her coat. 'Am I the only person who thinks practically?' she commented sourly.

Eleena took a credit bar from Crezia and walked down through the trees into the town. She came back fifteen minutes later carrying a styrene box in which were four tall, sweet caffeits in disposable flasks, hot pastries in waxed paper wraps, a loaf stick and some vacuum-sealed sausage meats.

She'd also bought a mini data-slate loaded with a touring guide of the region. 'I thought it might be useful,' she said.

'Great,' said Crezia. 'Now we can pick the best spots to ski.'

While Eleena had been gone, I had spent considerable time and effort freeing the flier's side hatch. It had been bolted open in military style for the permanent gunner position. With the weapon stowed and a fragile human cargo, I wanted the cabin sealed. It would pull to but the latch wouldn't engage. I tried brute force, but I don't think it had ever been closed in its entire service life.

We ate and drank in silence, and the med-skulls administered sustenance for Medea via the fluid drips.

I watched the sky and the long arc of the road into the town. There wasn't much traffic. A few utility vehicles and mobile dromes, the occasional fast speeder. All tourists heading for the resorts.

While I ate, I scrolled through the guide Eleena had bought.

We left Tiroyere at nine thirty, and spent the rest of the day flying further west, around the shoulders of the Esembo, over the mirrors of the high lakes and on towards the northern resort of Gruj. For a long time, I was convinced we were being followed by a small, yellow speeder. I became so concerned that I diverted east, around a tract of mountain pasture and steep forest.

I lost sight of the yellow craft, but about thirty minutes later picked up a black one that shadowed us steadily at a distance of five kilometres. My anxieties returned again.

In the late afternoon, as we flew in towards Gruj, the black flier turned south on a route that would take it to the spa resort of Firiol on the southern face of Mons Fulco.

I had been jumping at phantoms.

At Gruj, I landed the speeder in the cover of some pines south-west of the old city wall. I took Crezia's credit bar and walked into the town alone.

Gruj was an old town with a meandering plan like Ravello, but it was far less picturesque. Slot bars and dance parlours occupied the main thoroughfares and there was a busy stream of young, vacationing Gudrunites on every street.

I found the local chambers of the Adeptus Astra Telepathica, a tall, black windowed structure on the corner of the main square, and went inside.

A careworn female adept called Nicint debited my credit bar and provided me with access to the Aegis account. I wanted to check if anything had come in during the last day or so.

I was in for a surprise.

There was a communiqué from Harlon Nayl.

He had survived.

His message was quite long, and written in Glossia. The gist of it was that he had left Messina two weeks earlier, suspecting, for reasons that he didn't go into, that something bad was afoot. That didn't surprise me. Nayl had a nose for trouble. That he, of all my poor, lost agents, had been forewarned of the danger was easy to believe. He was, at the time of sending, just three days shy of Gudrun.

I had the adept send a reply, also in Glossia, telling Nayl to head for the southern capital New Gevae and, once there, to arrange passage off planet. I asked him to confirm and told him I would send again when I was close. Four days was my estimate. Four days and we would be with Nayl at New Gevae and heading off-world.

The snow-trak was essentially a luxury recreational vehicle. A well upholstered cockpit and adjoining cabin housed in a sleek grey hull and carried on a main track power unit with thick forward wheels for steering.

The rental agent was in full flow, singing the machine's praises, when I cut him off.

'I'll take it.'

'A sound choice, sir.'

'Two weeks' rental. I'm driving to Ontre, and I'll be leaving it there.'

'That's fine, sir. Deliver it to our offices in Ontre. There's a little paperwork to fill out. You have means of identity?'

Crezia's credit bar soaked up the cost of the deposit. I wanted to keep the transaction fairly anonymous.

I used the rental agent's palm reader to rouse another of my slumbering fake identities. Torin Gregori, a vacationing Thracian businessman with ample funds. The dealer seemed satisfied.

The snow-trak was a hefty brute with a surprising kick in its heels. I drove it back out of the town towards the flier, stopping on the way to stock up from a grocery market.

My friends at the flier regarded my approach with caution. I discovered later that Eleena had had her laspistol drawn and ready.

I leaned out of the cab and waved at them. 'Get yourselves aboard. We're switching vehicles.'

We left the empty speeder under the trees, and as soon as Medea was safely positioned in the plush, leather-padded cabin, I headed out towards the pass road.

I didn't tell the others about Nayl. I didn't want to get their hopes up.

By nightfall, we were powering up the snow-dusted highway over the pass towards Ontre. Gruj fell away behind us. I thought I saw a small yellow flier approaching the town as we left, but it was too far away to be sure.

We drove through the night, taking turns at the wheel. The weather was clear, and the cockpit vox was tuned to the climate-casts to catch snow advisories.

Crawling up the northern hem of Mons Fulco, we ran through steady squalls of snow, and had to drop speed and use the main lamps. Crezia was driving at that point. She'd lived in the mountains for long enough to know what to do.

I napped in the cabin, resting out on the long bench seat opposite the still sleeping Medea. I dreamed about her again, dreamed about saving her. Jekud Vance was in my dream too, desperate for my help. He screamed, bawling out a spear of sound and psi-pain that woke me.

I blinked over at Medea, but she was still stable. Eleena was asleep nearby.

The cabin rocked and vibrated with road noise and snow ghosts fluttered past the windows.

'Are you all right, Gregor?' Aemos asked.

He was sitting on the bench seat at the back of the cabin, surrounded by data-slates.

'A dream, that's all, Uber. It woke me last night too.'

I paused and sat up. The previous night I had assumed I had been woken by the sounds of Tarl's escape. But now it had happened again. The dream had woken me. Woken me both times. Jekud Vance's terrible death-scream of pain and rage and frustration.

We rumbled into Ontre in mid-afternoon the following afternoon. Heavy snow had slowed us down, and ice caked the copper roofs of the famous resort. But heavy snow had also brought the winter sports crowd into town in great numbers. The place was buzzing with activity, the roads sluggish with vehicles, the skies flecked with arriving speeders.

I drove the snow-trak into the parking lot of the Ontre Transcontinental Station, and found a place. Aemos and I went up to the concourse building where Torin Gregori purchased tickets for three connecting sleep berths. The express was due in an hour we were told.

Just as the mighty Atenate Range creases the centre of Gudrun's largest continent, so the Trans-Atenate Express runs like an artery along it. The railway is famously romantic. Most who ride it do so because of the ride, vacationers who would rather travel than arrive. The young flock to centres like Gruj and Ontre to use them as a base for skiing and ice-surfing, but the wealthy choose the Trans-Atenate, where they can sit in coddled luxury and watch Gudrun's most spectacular scenery slip by outside the window.

The great, chrome, promethium-fuelled locomotive pulled into Ontre at five, pulling a string of ten double-decked carriages. Porters helped us to manoeuvre Medea aboard.

Our cabins, on the top deck of car three, a wagon-lit, were first class and spacious. We put Medea in one of them, with Eleena to one side of her and Crezia to the other. Uber and I shared a fourth. There were communicating doors between the suites and everything was finished in polished maple.

The express hooted its siren and panted out of Ontre, muscularly taking the gradient into the Fonette Pass. The huge silvery beast could reach one hundred and seventy kilometres an hour on flat sections.

I regarded the timetable. Overnight to Fonette, then a short stretch to Locastre, followed by a high speed, uninterrupted run all the way down through the Atenate Majors, across the Southern Plateau to the coast.

We would be in New Gevae in just under three days.

There was barely any sense of motion: a slight, rolling vibration that one swiftly became oblivious to. The cars were robust, thick skinned, heated and insulated against the Atenate chill, but the side effect of this was to virtually eliminate exterior sound. The massive engine, deafening from the vantage of the platform concourse at Ontre, was virtually inaudible. Only when the express hammered down a cutting or a gorge and the engine noise was compressed and channeled backwards by the steep sides, did we catch a whisper of it at all.

With the cabin blind down, I might have been at home in a comfortable parlour.

While daylight remained, I kept the blind up and was afforded panoramic views of the pass, the snowfields, pink and soft in the sunset, the hard-shadowed scarps of rising ice broken at the folds by knuckles of black rock. Once in a while, beige smoke from the engine streamed past the windows and obscured the view.

On slow turns, it was possible to lean across to the window port itself and see the foreshortened flanks of the cars and train ahead, segmented like a great snake, the chrome and blue-and-white livery catching the last of the sun. Twice, a long, jumping shadow of the train ran along side us across the snows.

Night fell and the views outside vanished. I drew the blind. Aemos was snoozing, so I thought I might walk the length of the train and get to know the layout.

The communicating door opened and Crezia came in. She was dressed in a grey satin robe with tightly laced pleating that ran from the high throat right down to the top of the gathered skirt. A fur wrap was draped over one arm, and she had put her hair up.

I rose from my seat almost automatically.

'Well?' she enquired.

'You look... stunning.'

'I meant "well" as in, isn't it time you escorted me to dinner?'

'Dinner?'

'Main meal of the day? Usually found somewhere between lunch and a nightcap?'

'I am familiar with the concept.'

'Good. Shall we?'

'We are fleeing for our lives. Do you think this is the time?'

'I can think of no better time. We are fleeing for our lives, Gregor, on the most exclusive and opulent mode of travel Gudrun has to offer. I suggest we flee for our lives in style.'

I went into the bathroom and changed into the most presentable clothes I had with me. Then I linked arms with her and we strolled back along the companion way to the dining van three cars back.

'Did you bring these clothes with you?' I asked quietly as we wandered down the softly lit, carpeted hallway, encountering other well-dressed passengers walking to and from the dining van.

'Of coursc.'

'We left in haste, and you packed a gown like that?'

'I thought I should be ready for anything.'

The dining salon was on the upper deck of the sixth car. Crystal chandeliers hung from the arched roof, and the roof itself was made of armourglas. It doubled as an observation lounge, though just then it simply provided a ceiling of starry blackness.

A string quartet was playing unobtrusively at one end, and the place was filling up. The air was filled with gentle music, clinking silverware and low voices. Discreete poison snoopers hovered like fireflies over each place setting. A uniformed steward showed us to a table by the portside windows.

We studied the menus. I realised how hungry I was.

'How many times, do you suppose?' she asked.

'How many times what?'

'Years ago, when we were together. You would come to visit me in Ravello, secretive as is your manner. How many times did I suggest we took the express through the mountains?'

'You mentioned it, yes.'

'We never did, though.'

'No, we didn't. I regret that.'

'So do I. It seems so sad we're doing it now out of necessity. Although I might have guessed I'd only get you on a romantic trip like this if you had to do it.'

'Whatever the reason, we're here now.'

'I should have put a gun to your head years ago.'

We ordered potage velours, followed by sirloin of lowland runka, roulade with a macedoine of herbs and forest mushrooms affriole, and a Chateau Xandier from Sameter that I remembered was a favourite of hers.

The soup, served with mouthwatering chapon and a swirl of smitane in wide-lipped white dishes delicately embossed with the crest of the Trans-Continental company livery, was velvety and damn near perfect. The runka, simply pan-seared in amasec, was saignant and irreproachable. The Xandier, astringent and then musty in its finish, made her smile with fond memories.

We talked. We had decades to fill in. She told me about her work and her life, the interest in xeno-anatomy she had developed, the monographs she had composed, a new procedure for muscle grafting she had pioneered. She had taken up the spinet, as a means of relaxation, and had now mastered all but two of Guzella's Studies. She had written a book, a treatise on the comparative analysis of skeletal dimorphism in early human biotypes.

'I almost sent you a copy, but I was afraid how that might be misconstrued.'

'I own a first edition,' I confessed.

'How loyal! But have you read it?'

'Twice. Your deconstruction of Terksson's work on the Dimmamar-A sites is convincing and quite damning. I might take issue with your chapters on Tallarnopithicene, but then you and I always did argue over the "Out of Terra" hypothesis.'

'Ah yes. You always were a heretic in that regard.'

I felt I had so much less to give back. There was so much about my life in the last few years I couldn't or shouldn't tell her. So I told her about Nayl instead.

'This man is trustworthy?'

'Completely.'

'And you're sure it's him?'

'Yes. He's using Glossia. The beauty of that code is that it's individually idiomatic. It can't be broken, used or understood by outsiders. You'd have to be in my employ for a long time to grasp the fundamentals of its mechanism.'

'That bodyguard. The one who betrayed your household.'

'Kronsky?'

'Yes. He was in your employ.'

'Not for long. Even with the basics he'd grasped, he couldn't dupe me for long using Glossia.'

'So we're going to be rescued?'

'I'm confident we'll be able to get off-planet.'

'Well, Gregor, I think that good news calls for an indulgent dessert.'

The steward brought us ribaude nappé, sticky and sweet, followed by rich black Hesperine caffeine and digestifs, an oaky amasec for me and a thimble of pasha for her.

We were laughing together by then.

It was a fine dinner and a good night spent in delightful company. I have not known its like to this day.

I was woken by the jar and a thump of a halt just after dawn. Outside, a whistle blew, muffled by the car's hull, and there came the distant mutter of men's voices.

Slowly, I slid out of bed, doing my best not to disturb Crezia. She was still deeply asleep, though she rolled over and reached, murmuring, into the cooling space I had just vacated.

I tried to find some clothes. They were strewn on the floor, and with the blind down, it was a matter of touch.

I prised back the edge of the blind with one finger and peeked out. It was already light, frosty and colourless. There was a station outside, and people milling on the snowy platform.

We had reached Fonette.

I got dressed, shivering. Now the train was halted and idling, the wall vents issued a cooler wash of air.

I opened the door and slipped out, casting one last look behind me. In her sleep, Crezia had curled up into a ball, cocooning herself in the bedsheets, shutting out the cold and the world.

Outside, it was near-freezing and very bright. The wide platform was busy with passengers leaving or joining the express, and servitor units conveying pyramids of baggage.

Snow was lightly falling. I hugged myself and stamped my feet. Several other travellers had got down from the train to stretch their legs.

Fonette station occupied an elevated area above the town, shadowed to the north by Mons Fulco and to the south by the Uttcs, Minor and Major, and then the weather-veiled bulk of the Central Atens.

'How long do we stop?' I asked a passing porter.

'Twenty minutes, sir,' he replied. 'Just long enough for change over and for the tender to take on water.'

Not long enough to run down into the town, I figured. I stayed on the platform until the boarding whistle sounded and then stood in the carriage hallway leaning out of the doorway window as we slowly pulled out of town.

The station building slid by, revealing a view of the town below that had not been visible from the platform. Steep roofs iced with snow, a Ministorum chapel, a sturdy Arbites blockhouse. A landing field, just below the station causeway, filled with berthed and refuelling fliers.

One of them was small and yellow.

* * *

I went back to Crezia's cabin, took off my coat and boots and lay beside her until she woke. She rolled over and kissed my mouth.

'What are you doing?' she asked, sleepily.

'Checking the timetable.'

'I don't think there are any changes on this line.'

'No,' I agreed. 'We'll be at Locastre in about four hours. There's a longer halt there. Forty-five minutes. Then the long run to New Gevae.'

She sat up, rubbing her eyes. Drowsy, unguarded, she was more beautiful than ever.

'So what?' she asked.

'I'll check the astropathic account there. There'll be time.'

There was a knock at the door. It was the cabin-service steward with a laden trolley. The last thing we had done the night before was to order a full, cooked breakfast.

Well, not quite the last thing.

Eleena and Aemos were up, taking breakfast together. Crezia pulled on her robe and checked on Medea, who was still stable and sleeping deeply.

'The signs are good,' she told me on her return. 'Tomorrow, perhaps the day after, she should be back with us.'

We ate together in her cabin, picking up our conversations from the night before. It was all familiar and relaxed, as if we had adjusted our clocks by twenty-five years. I realised how much I had missed her company and vitality.

'What's the matter?' she asked. 'You seem preoccupied.'

I thought about the yellow speeder.

'Nothing,' I said.

During the long, slow climb up through the Uttes to Locastre, I went through the data-slates of material Aemos had compiled since the attack on Spaeton House. I paid particular attention the name Khanjar the Sharp. Aemos had compiled a list of planet cultures where the word 'khanjar' was still in parlance. Ninety-five hundred worlds, and I went down the list systematically, even though I knew Aemos, with his greater knowledge of trivia, had already done so. Any one of them might hold the key. A khanjar was a ceremonial oathing dagger on Benefax, Luwes and Craiton. It was the slang term for a gang-lord on distant Mekanique. It was the common word for a pruning knife on five worlds in the Scarus sector alone. It was a hive-argot adjective for sharp practice on Morimunda. On three thousand worlds, it was simply the word for knife.

A knife cutting me to the quick. Who was Khanjar the Sharp? Why was he diligently seeking my destruction and the destruction of my entire operation?

I turned to consider the slate listing the injuries he had dealt against me, the deaths he had, I'm sure, ordered. They were all still shocking to me. The sheer scope of his murderous efforts astounded me. So many targets, so many worlds... and all struck at the same sidereal moment.

I found that I kept coming back to the notice of Inshabel's death. It was, simply, the odd one out. Every other victim or location target had been a specific part of my personal organisation. But Nathun Inshabel was not. He was – had been – an inquisitor in his own right. During my campaign against the heretic Quixos, almost fifty years earlier, Inshabel, then holding the rank of interrogator, had been part of my team. He had joined my fold after the death of his master, Inquisitor Roban, during the atrocity on Thracian Primaris, and had continued to aid me devotedly until after the purge of Quixos's stronghold on Farness Beta. After that, with my sponsorship, he became an inquisitor and began his own work.

Since then, we had been in contact only a few times and, apart from our old friendship, there was no connection between us. Why had he been marked out for destruction too? Coincidence was not a good enough answer.

What connected us? Who connected us? The obvious name was Quixos, but that led nowhere. I had eliminated Quixos myself.

I ran through the list of worlds again, trying to discern a link.

One of the planets named on the list was Quenthus Eight.

That name snagged me like a protruding claw. Quenthus Eight. A margin world. I had never been there. But I'd once been told about it.

Running on instinct, I cross-checked Quenthus Eight with the vast list of worlds on which Tarray or Tari was a registered surname. Aemos had already cross-referenced the lists of worlds using 'khanjar' with worlds owning the surname 'Tarray', and had come up with seven hundred possibles. Now I was able to add sense to one of them.

There it was. 'Khanjar' was the word for a war knife on Quenthus Eight, and Tarray was a clan name from that world. Nearly three hundred and fifty years before, one of the most vile sociopaths in the Imperium had started his career on Quenthus Eight. Marla Tarray's reported claims to have been born on Gudrun had been discounted by Aemos, who had checked the census and found no sign of the name.

He hadn't gone back far enough. He hadn't gone back three and a half hundred years. I did, and found that Tarry had been a peasant name on Gudrun until that time. The family tree ended right there.

I knew who it was. I knew who my enemy was.

THIRTEEN

LOCASTRE
FULL STOP
END OF THE LINE

We arrived at Locastre over an hour behind schedule. Unseasonal blizzards had swept up from the east into the Uttes, and the express had been forced to reduce speed to a crawl. On steep gradients through the passes, there was a danger of back-slip, and we could feel the frequent jerks as the car bogies hunted over the ice-caked rails. There was a ten minute stop on a straight section on the west of Utte Major as the train's engineer gangs got out and winched the locomotive's nose plough into place. The blizzard was around us then and everything outside the windows was a colourless swirl.

I went down to the end of the car and peered out through the van windows. Black blobs were moving in the white haze, some lit by fizzling flares of green and red. I felt several jolts and metallic clunks shiver through the deck beneath me.

The intercar tannoy softly informed us that we would be on our way soon, reassured us that the weather was no hazard, and soothed us with the news that complimentary hot punch was now being served in the dining salon. Unnecessarily muffled in furs or expensive mountainwear, other passengers came to peer out of the mush-flecked ports, grumbling and what if-ing.

I returned to the cabin I shared with Aemos, locked the doors and sat down with him. I ran through my theory.

'Pontius Glaw...' his old lips spat the name. 'Pontius Glaw...'

'It fits, doesn't it?'

'From what you tell me, Gregor. Though of course, I know little of what passed between you and that monster on Cinchare.'

We had first tackled the villainy of Pontius Glaw and his poisonous brood right there on Gudrun back in 240, an age ago as it seemed. At the time, Glaw himself, a notorious heretic, had been dead for two centuries, his obscene activities curtailed by Inquisitor Angevin.

But Glaw's intellect and engrammed personality had been preserved in a psipathetic crystal by his noble family. We thwarted the attempts of House Glaw to restore him to corporeal life, and afterwards I had the crystal placed for safekeeping with my old ally, Magos Geard Bure of the Adeptus Mechanicus.

A century later, in 340, I had revisited Bure's remote fastness on the mining world Cinchare during the Quixos affair, in order to obtain arcane information concerning daemonhosts from his prisoner. Without Pontius Glaw's dark advice, I would never have been able to vanquish Quixos or his slaved daemons Prophaniti and Cherubael.

But I had been forced to deal with Glaw. Make it worth his while. The lure I dangled was that in return for his help, I would commission Bure to manufacture a body for him to inhabit.

And, because I was an honourable man, I kept my word, believing that even if Glaw was given mobility, he would never escape Geard Bure's clutches.

It seemed I had been wrong about that.

During those private interviews on Cinchare, Glaw had confessed to me the event that had driven him, the accomplished scion of one of Gudrun's most respected noble houses, into the worship of the warp.

It had happened on Quenthus Eight in 019. Glaw had been visiting the Quenthi amphitheatres, purchasing gladiators for his pit-fighting hobby. Even before his fall, he was a cruel man. He bought one brute, a warrior from a remote feral world... Borea, I seem to recall. Anxious to please his new master, the warrior had given Glaw his torc. It was an ancestral relic from the feral world, and neither the warrior nor Glaw realised it was tainted with the foulest Chaos. Glaw had put it on and immediately had fallen into its clutches. That one simple act had sealed his fate and transformed him into the idolatrous fiend who had plagued the Helican sub-sector for nearly two decades.

I gave Aemos the gist of this.

'The matter seems to fit together. You believe, I take it, that Pontius Glaw has escaped from his prison on Cinchare, built up his forces, and is now targetting you for revenge?'

'Revenge? No... well, indirectly, perhaps. He certainly would want to have his revenge on me, but the scale of his attack, the effort, the comprehensive scope... every element of my operation, and Inshabel too.'

Aemos shrugged. 'Inshabel was with us at Cinchare.'

'That's my point. Pontius is trying to destroy everyone who might know he exists. Most of the Imperium believes he is long dead. We pose a threat to him just by knowing about him.'

I could tell Aemos had something on his mind that he didn't want to say.

'Aemos?'

'Nothing, Gregor.'

'Old friend?'

He shook his head.

'Say it. Pontius Glaw's existence is only a secret because I never informed the Ordos that he was still sentient. Because I never delivered his engram sphere into the custody of the Ordo Hereticus as I should have. And he's only free now because I had a body built for him.'

'No.' He got to his feet and squinted out of the car window, trying to see something, anything, in the blizzard. 'We've had this conversation before, or at least one like it. About Cherubael.'

He turned to look at me. He was so very old. 'You are an inquisitor of the Glorious Imperium of Mankind. You are dedicated to the destruction of evil in any facet of its three classic forms: Xenos, Malleus, Hereticus. You face unimaginable hazards. Yours is the most arduous task undertaken by any Imperial servant. You must use every weapon at your disposal to protect our culture. Even the arsenal of the enemy. And you know full well that sometimes such uses have consequences. We may now regret your actions with Pontius Glaw, but without those, Quixos would not have been brought down. We can play the "if only" game all day. The simple truth is that victory comes at a price, and we are paying that price now. The true measure of your character is what you do about it.'

'I correct my mistakes. I bring down Pontius Glaw.'

'I have no doubt of that.'

'Thank you, Aemos.'

He sat down again. 'This Tarray woman. How does she fit in?'

I showed him the census record. 'The Tarrays were a low caste family on Gudrun during Glaw's organic lifetime. Then the line stops abruptly, but reappears on Quenthus. I think the Tarrays, or at least a Tarray, was amongst Glaw's retinue, and he took them to Quenthus. I need you to look into that at Locastre.'

'Locastre? But we're only going to be stopping there for forty-five minutes.'

I gestured to the window. 'It'll probably be longer given the weather, but you'll have to move fast. I'm going to use the time to access the Aegis account.'

The handle of the locked connecting door ratcheted back and forth.

'Gregor?' It was Crezia.

'What are you doing locked in there?' she called through the door.

'Just discussing things with Aemos.'

'They're serving hot punch in the salon. I thought we might mingle.'

'In a minute,' I called out in reply. There was a lurch and the train started to move again.

I looked at Aemos. 'The things we've spoken about... they don't go any further. Not yet. Crezia doesn't need to know, neither does Eleena, come to that.'

'My lips are sealed,' he said.

We came out of the blizzard and down a comfortable gradient into Locastre. It was nearly midday. The bad weather lurked like a grey wall behind us, veiling the Uttes, but reports suggested it was moving into the valley.

At Locastre, the porters announced a ninety minute stop.

I told Eleena to make sure the express didn't leave until Aemos and I were safely back.

Locastre occupies a cleft valley gouged by glaciers. The old buildings are dark grey – granite stands in for the traditional Gudrun ouslite used in the lowlands – and the altitude and climate is such that pressurised, heated tunnels of armourglas sheath the streets. I hired a servitor litter and had it scurry me through the warm, damp street tunnels, as ominous squalls of snow peppered the transparent roof above.

Outside the office of the Astropathic Guild, I told it to wait and left my credit bar locked into its fare-meter as good faith. It settled low on its spider-limbed chassis, venting steam from its hydraulics.

There was a message from Nayl waiting for me in the Aegis account. He had made good time, and was already in New Gevae. Passage off-world had been arranged with a freighter called the *Caucus*. He was eager to see me.

Nayl's communiqué was in Glossia and I phrased my reply the same way. Weather permitting, we would be in New Gevae in two days. On arrival, I would arrange a meeting with him.

'Is that all, sir?' asked the adept attending me.

I remembered Crezia's comments over dinner about Nayl being trustworthy. I added another line, suggesting that the situation reminded me of the tight spot we'd been in on Eechan, years before, facing Beldame Sadia.

'Send it, please,' I said.

Up at the station, the express sounded its horn.

The express rumbled up into the Central Atens, chased by the weather. Despite the fact that we were now scaling some of the steepest and longest gradients in the route, the locomotive was running at full power, trying to outpace the snows for as long as it could.

The main range of the Atens, through which we now travelled, included the greatest mountains on Gudrun: Scarno, Dorpaline, The Heledgae, Vesper, Mount Atena. Each one dwarfed the peaks like Mons Fulco that we had encountered earlier. They seemed as dark and cyclopean as tilted continents.

They were also beautiful. Peerless tracts of blue-white ice, unblemished leagues of snow, sharp sunshine that almost twinkled like starlight in a vacuum.

Until, before nightfall, it all vanished. Freezing fog and vapour descended like a stage curtain, sealing out the light and dropping visibility to a few dozen metres. Then snow began to flutter again and our speed decreased. The weather had caught up with us.

'Gregor?' I had been watching the snowstorm. 'Come in here.'

Crezia beckoned me through the connecting door. Medea was awake.

The cyberskulls hovered back to give me room as I sat down beside her cot. She looked tired and drawn, faded almost. But her eyes were half open and she managed a thin smile as she saw me.

'Everything's okay. You're in safe hands.'

Her mouth moved, but no sound came out.

'Don't try to speak,' Crezia whispered.

I saw curiosity in Medea's eyes as she focused on Crezia.

'This is Doctor Berschilde. A good friend. She saved your life.'

'...long...'

'What?'

'How long been sleep?'

'The best part of a week. You were wounded in the back.'

'Ribs sore.'

'That will pass,' said Crezia.

'They... they get us?'

'No, they didn't get us,' I said. 'And they're not going to get us either.'

Shrouded by the bitter blizzards and maintaining no more than sixty kilometres an hour, we journeyed on across the roof of the world. I ventured out into the public areas and even to the salon a few times, and found that diverting entertainments had been laid on: buffet meals, music, card schools, a regicide tournament, screenings of popular hololithic extravaganzas. Uniformed Trans-Continental personnel were out in force, keeping everybody happy and volubly disseminating the notion that being caught in an Atenate icestorm was all part of the romance of the famous rail line.

And not a potentially lethal misfortune.

If the locomotive derailed, or the power plant malfunctioned, and the train became stranded in the midst of a blizzard that lasted more than a couple of days, we'd freeze to death and they'd have to wait until spring to dig us out.

Of course, in the nine hundred and ninety years of the Trans-Atenate Express's operation, that had never happened. The train had always got through. It was a remarkably secure form of transport, given the terrain it crossed.

But there is a first time for anything, as people can be forgiven for thinking. Years of experience warned the train staff to start reassuring and distracting the passengers the moment weather closed in, or they'd have a panic on their hands. The idle rich can be such worriers.

We came to a halt four times before dawn the next day. The first time was at about ten in the evening. The tannoy informed us that we were waiting for wind speeds to ease before crossing the Scarno Gorge Bridge and that there was no cause for concern. Less than five minutes later, we were on our way again.

I was still awake at one when we gently coasted to a stop again. I felt uneasy, and after fifteen minutes, tucked the autopistol into my belt, strapped Barbarisater to my hip and covered them both with Aemos's long green over-robe.

The hallway was dark, the lights dimmed to an auxiliary amber. Little green cue lights glowed on the staff-only monitor display that was set in the panelled wall at the end of the car.

I heard someone coming up the spiral stairs from the car's lower deck and turned to see a steward who regarded me quizzically.

'Is everything all right, sir?' he asked.

'That was my question. I was wondering why we'd stopped.'

'It's just routine, sir. We're just coming over the Scarno Gradient and the Master Engineman has ordered a check of the braking elements in case of excess icing.'

'I see. Just routine.'

'Everything's perfectly safe, sir,' he said with well-rehearsed assurance.

As if to prove him right, the lights flickered and we were moving again. He smiled. 'There we are, sir.'

I went back to my cabin. I barely marked the two further stops we made that night. But I kept my weapons to hand.

The second full day of travel passed without incident. The weather alternated between long, furious blizzards and quick, glorious episodes of sunlit calm. We stopped five more times before supper. Five more routine hesitations. The tannoy whispered that though we were behind schedule, we were likely to make up time once we were clear of the mountains and crossing the Southern Plateau in the latter part of the following day.

I was growing impatient. I found myself pacing the train a lot, end to end. I even took Crezia to the salon for lunch and stayed long enough to play a board or two of regicide with her.

Medea was gaining strength. By the afternoon, she was sitting up and eating for herself. The cyber-skulls disconnected all her drips except the vital monitor. We took turns to sit with her. I let Eleena tell her the details of what had happened since the attack on Spaeton House. Medea listened intently, increasingly dismayed.

When it was my turn to spend an hour at her side, she said, 'You came back for me.'

'Yes.'

'You might have been killed.'

'You would have been.'

'They killed Jekud,' she said after a pause. 'We were running across the paddocks and they cut him down.'

'I know. I felt it.'

'I couldn't help him.'

'I know.'

'I felt terrible. After all he had done to show me my father. And I couldn't save him.'

'It was probably quick. The Vessorine are ruthless killers.'

'I thought I heard him call out, after he had fallen. I was going to turn back for him, but they were everywhere.'

'It's alright.'

She took a beaker from the bedstand and sipped. 'Eleena says they killed everyone.'

'I'm afraid they might have.'

'I mean, not just here. The Distaff. Nayl. Inshabel.'

I nodded. 'Someone was very thorough that night. But here's a thought to cheer you: Nayl's alive, and so's Fischig. We're going to meet up with both of them.'

That made her smile. 'How did Nayl get away?'

'I don't know. He hasn't given me any details. It would seem he got wind of something and left Messina before the attack. I'm looking forward to finding out what he knows.'

'Like who's behind this, you mean?'

I winked. 'That, Medea, I already know.'

Her eyes widened. 'Who?'

'I'll tell you when I've confirmed my suspicions. I don't want you worrying unnecessarily.'

'Now that's just cruel,' she scolded. 'I won't be able to think about anything else now.'

'Then see what you come up with,' I suggested. Medea was privy to most of my operation, and I thought it might be interesting to see if she arrived at any conclusion herself.

The jolt made me strike my head against the side panel of the bed and woke me up in time to feel two more hard judders before the train came to a complete stop.

It was nearly three in the morning and pitch black. I could hear the ice flakes pattering like small arms fire off the window of the cabin.

Every halt we had made so far had been smooth and gentle. Not like this.

Aemos had woken too, and sat up as I turned on the sidelight and strapped on Barbarisater.

'What is it?' he asked.

'Nothing, I hope.' The inter-cabin door opened and Eleena looked in.

'Did you feel that?' she asked sleepily.

'Find your pistol,' I told her.

We woke Crezia and got all three of them into Medea's cabin. Crezia looked befuddled and worried. Eleena was wide awake by then and checking the cell of her weapon.

I pulled on Aemos's over-robe to conceal my own armaments.

'Stay here and be vigilant,' I said and then left the connecting suite via the door to my cabin.

In the gloomy hall, I could hear movement in the other cabins, low voices and the occasional pip of a summoning alarm as worried passengers tried to call the stewards.

I went back down the car to the monitor display the moment I saw the two red lights shining amongst the green ones.

I slid open the display's glass cover and fitted my signet ring to the optical reader. The potent Inquisitorial authority codes loaded into my signet ring rapidly overcame Trans-Continental Line's confidence software and gave me access to the express's master system.

The monitor's little screen woke up, and flickered with user-friendly graphics and bars of data. I requested clarification of the red warning lights.

Alert code 88 decimal 508 – a systematic trigger of active brake units, cars seven through ten, forcing main brake arrest.

Alert code 521 decimal 6911 – irregular breach of door seal, door 34, car eight, lower.

I hurried along the upper deck of the train, heading for the rear. Some cabin doors opened and anxious faces looked out. 'No need for concern!' I called in my best Trans-Continental tone, backing it up with a gentle surge of will that slammed doors after me like a drum roll.

At car six, I had to go down to the lower deck because of the dining salon. Passing into car seven, I saw three train staffers hurrying down the companionway in the direction of car eight.

The lower hallway of car eight was bitterly cold and a gale was blowing down it. I saw six or seven rail employees pulling on foul weather gear and lighting flares as they jumped down out of the open wagon door into the night. Several more were grouped around the monitor display and one, a steward, saw me approach.

'Please go back to your cabin, sir. Everything's fine.'

'What seems to be the problem?'

'Just hurry back, sir. What is your cabin number? I'll bring along complimentary liqueurs in a few minutes.'

'The rear brakes have just thrown and door 34 is open,' I said.

He blinked. 'How did you–'

'What's going on?'

'Sir, I want to guarantee your comfort, so if you'd just like to–'

I didn't have time for a debate. 'What's going on, Inex?' I asked, reading his name off his brass lapel badge and juicing my words with just a touch of will. A name always helped to enhance the mental coercion.

He blinked. 'The brake systems in the rear four wagons have engaged, which triggered an overall braking incident,' he said, quickly and obediently.

'Did someone pull the emergency rope?'

'No, sir. We'd have a source for that, and anyway the train's entire brake system would have fired simultaneously. We believe it's ice in the aft units.'

'That would cause a partial brake lock?'

'Yes, sir.'

'What about the door?'

'It opened just after we stopped. The chief steward thinks it was one of the engineers, opening the door to get out and check the brakes without informing the system he was unlocking the door.'

'It wasn't forced?'

'It was opened from inside. With a key.' The effects of my will were ebbing and his jocular tone returned. 'We've got personnel out lineside now, sir, checking the brakes.'

'Including this engineer who supposedly opened the door in his eagerness to find the fault?'

'I'm sure, sir.'

'Find out,' I said, using the will more forcefully.

He ran back to the monitor panel, and his colleagues stood back, puzzled, as he operated the device.

'Who has access to door keys?'

'Who the hell are you?' one of the others asked.

'A concerned member of the public,' I said, blanketing them all with will power. 'Who has keys?'

'Only engineers of level two and higher, class one stewards and the guards,' said another, stammering in his desperation to tell me.

'How many people is that?'

'Twenty-three.'

'Are they all accounted for?'

'I don't know,' said Inex.

'Stand aside,' I ordered, and used my ring on the monitor. The train had a staff and crew of eighty-four. Each one had a sub-dermal tracker implant so that the train master could account for the location of his people at all times. The display showed a graphic map of the train, but the screen was so small I had to scroll along it, looking at the schematic bit by bit. Master personnel were shown in red, engineers in amber, stewards in green and guards in blue. Ancilliary staff like chefs, waiters, porters and cleaners were pink.

Red and amber dots clustered in the locomotive section, and blue and green ones were speckled throughout the wagons. The upper deck of car nine, the crew quarters, was full of pink lights. I saw a cluster of green and blue cursors that represented the men grouped around me at the back of car eight's lower deck, near door 34. A sub-menu listed the amber and blue lights that had left the train to inspect the running gear.

There was one green light amongst the pink ones in car nine. I called up more information. The green light belonged to Steward Class One Rebert Awins. He was in his quarters.

The express had made an emergency stop and all the staff apart from the ancilliaries were moving to secure the train. Except Awins.

'Awins is class one. He'd have keys.'

'Yes, sir,' said Inex.

'Why isn't he assisting?'

They all looked at each other.

'When did you last see him?'

'He was on the morning shift today,' said one of them.

'I saw him in the rec room at shift change having his lunch,' added another.

'Since then?'

They shook their heads.

'He should have come on again at nine,' said Inex. 'Shall I check on him.'

No, I was going to say. Because he's dead. But there was no point scaring them.

I changed my mind. 'Do that, Inex.' I reached over and took the intercom headset off the man nearest me. He didn't protest. He didn't even notice.

'Go to his room and tell me what you find. Vox channel...' I studied the headset's small ear piece and adjusted the responder. '...six.'

'Yes sir,' said Inex. As he turned to go, I reached out and touched him briefly on the forehead. He shuddered. My psi-imprint would stay with him for a good thirty minutes now, even once he was out of my vicinity.

Inex ran off.

I looked at the car door. It had been pulled to, but the 'unsecure' light was still blinking. There were thawing cakes of dirty ice on the metal deck inside the door.

'How many people went out?' I asked.

One of them checked the display. 'Twenty, sir.'

'How many have come back inside since you got here?'

'None,' they all said.

They would be looking for me. For us. They knew we were on the train, and they'd got someone aboard at Fonette or Locastre. Someone who had befriended Rebert Awins, killed him and taken his pass keys. Someone with the technical expertise to trigger a partial brake lock, stop the train and then use Awin's keys to open an exterior door and let his associates aboard.

Someone who, by now, surely knew which cabins we were occupying.

I ran back down the train towards car three, using the lower deck hallways. I slid Barbarisater from its nedskin scabbard. It seemed so incongruous to be hurrying down a train's companionway brandishing a sword. But the cabins around me were full of innocent Imperial citizens and I didn't dare use my pistol.

I also didn't dare use the intercom.

I reached out psychically. Eleena was an untouchable blank, so I called to Aemos, Crezia and Medea.

Be ready. Trouble coming.

I passed several train staff in the hall as I made my way past and they jumped back in alarm as they saw the blade.

Forget! I willed at each one as I passed, and they just went on their way.

I reached the front end of car four and prepared to go up. A Trans-Continental steward lay face down on the stairs, his neck snapped.

Just then, the frantic voice of Inex wailed into my earpiece. 'He's dead! Oh God-Emperor! He's dead! Rebert's dead! Sound the alarm!'

The distress klaxon started to warble and recessed light plates in the wall began to blink orange. I saw a third red light had lit up on the car-end monitor panel.

I jammed my signet ring against the reader and cued information.

Alert code 946 decimal 2452 – irregular breach of window seal, window 146, car three, upper.

I clambered over the steward's corpse and made my way up the stairs.

The upper hallway of car three was even colder than the chill of car eight. The end window on the port side, beside the intercarriage articulation, was wide open and freezing air and snow was whirling in. The window had been cut out of its frame with a powerblade or melta torch.

The light was bad. Gloomy, half-dimmed lamps aggravated by the fretful blink of the alarm lights. The klaxons still whooped.

I realised there were three dark shapes halfway down the hall ahead of me, skulking low. They hadn't heard me arrive over the howl of the blizzard and the shrill of the alarms.

I hugged the panelled wall. Barbarisater throbbed, hungry. Even passively, I could sense the three men were psi-shielded. They made big silhouettes. Combat armour. I saw the ugly shadow of an assault weapon as the point man waved his partners forward.

Forward towards the doors of our compartments.

I edged closer.

The point man, oozing professionalism as he visually checked his rear, saw me.

And all hell broke loose.

FOURTEEN

BARBARISATER VERSUS THE JANISSARIES
ETRIK, BLADE TO BLADE
LUNCHTIME DRINKS IN NEW GEVAE

The two killers nearest me turned and opened fire with blunt, large calibre autoguns. I suppose the sword in my hand was a damn give away, but they'd have killed me anyway, even if they had mistaken me for a wayward bystander.

They were professional killers, Vessorine janissaries. They had a job to do, a contract to fulfill, and anyone in their way was a target.

The fact that they were using solid-round weapons confirmed they were Vessorine. The ultimate military pragmatists. They'd tailed the train in a poorly-insulated speeder and deployed through a blizzard. In those conditions, standard las-weapons might have died, their cell-power drained by the cold. But a well-lubricated autogun would fire below freezing. It had only to rely on its percussive hammer action.

Vessorine janissaries. I had faced them before without knowing what they were. Now I knew, and their formidable reputation almost gave me pause. Vessorines, three of them. Plated in combat armour and firing heavyweight man-stopper ammunition. Frankly, I'd rather have squared off with angry Kasrkin.

But Barbarisater was in my hand, alert and alive. I had been using my will openly for some time, and that had quickened its strength. I made a *ghan fasl*, the figure-eight stroke and smashed the first three shots away, impact sparks sheeting from the energised sword blade. Then I struck an *uwe sar*, an *ulsar* and a *ura wyla bei* in rapid series, deflecting squashed rounds into the panelling around me. Wood splintered.

I dived sideways as further shots punched into the hallway carpet and exploded on the inter-wagon doors. People were screaming in the cabins all around.

I rolled and came up on my feet as the first Vessorine rounded the car-end corner and fired half a dozen times. His ejecting shell-cases pattered off his torso in a fog of blue smoke and his gun muzzle lit up like a blowtorch. Point blank.

Except I was behind him.

His gunfire shredded the wagon wall and ruptured the window frame. Barbarisater removed his head.

The second one was charging and firing too. He let out a mask-muffled bellow as he saw his comrade collapse in pieces.

I threw an *ura geh* sequence that diverted the white blurs of his bullets, then followed in with a *uin tahn wyla* that chopped the barrel off his weapon, a reverse *tahn* stroke that severed his forearms, and then the *ewl caer*. The death stroke.

Hot red blood was already spurting from his arm stumps and steaming in the freezing air as Barbarisater plunged through his ceramite chest armour and burst his heart. The gunshot walls were painted with instantly frozen dribbles of bloody ice.

A bullet creased the corner of my jaw with enough force to rip open the flesh of my chin and knock me to the carpet. I tried to rise, but the third Vessorine was right over me. I heard his weapon rack.

He screamed. I smelled a burning in the cold air.

I looked up.

The Vessorine was trying to shield himself, as if from a swarm of stinging insects. Crezia's cyber skulls were flitting around him, stabbing repeatedly with their surgical lasers.

His yelps were cut off by the double crack of a las-weapon.

The janissary collapsed like a deadweight at my feet.

I looked down the hall and saw Eleena Koi in the doorway of my room, holding her pistol in a defiant two-handed grip.

'Eleena!' I yelled. 'Get the others out of the compartment! Get them out into the hall and move them this way!'

'But Medea–' she began.

'Do it!'

I ran to the cut-out car window and hauled myself out into the vicious chill. I had to sheath Barbarisater and it didn't like it. Outside, it was bone-achingly cold and the blizzard pummelled me with hail hard as stones. There was precious little in the way of handholds and the exterior of the car was iced up.

I found something to cling to... solid runnels of ice, I think. My fingers went numb.

I hauled myself up onto the roof of car three, the vast snow-peppered blackness of the Atenate night above me.

The blizzard ensured I couldn't see far. I could barely stand up. The convex aluminium roof of the wagon was iced smooth as a skating rink.

A few steps along and my legs went out. I fell smack on my front, dazed and winded. Blood filled my mouth; I had bitten my tongue.

Spitting blood and made angry by the pain, I dragged myself forward through the elemental deluge. I saw shapes ahead of me in the white-on-black maelstrom. Three more armoured figures on the edge of the roof.

They had lowered a directional detonator onto the window of the cabin I had shared with Aemos. As I watched, they triggered it and blasted the window inwards in a hail of glass and fire. The first janissary began to rope down to swing in through the blown window. His comrades were hunched on the rooftop, anchoring his lines.

I leapt up and Barbarisater flew out, crackling in the wet air.

The augmented Carthean warblade came down, splitting the lines in two and cutting deeply into the wagon roof. The descending killer shrieked as he fell away down the side of the two storey carriage.

The other two jerked round like lightning, one going for his sidearm, the other leaping at me with clawing hands. A *tahn wyla* met him and bisected his head like a ripe gummice fruit.

The corpse rolled off the car top into the darkness. I stood ready, Barbarisater twitching in my hands. The remaining Vessorine backed away, aiming a large calibre autopistol at me. The two of us could barely stand, such was the blizzard's windshear.

He fired once. An *ulsar* flicked the round away. He fired again, his feet slipping, and I made an *uin ulsar* that spat the bullet off into the darkness.

'My name is Gregor Eisenhorn. I am the man you have been paid to kill. Identify yourself.'

He hesitated. 'My nomclat be Etrik, badge of Clansire. Clan Szober.'

'Clansire Etrik. I've heard so much about you.' I had to raise my voice over the storm. 'Vammeko Tarl mentioned your name.'

'Tarl? He be–'

'The one who let you aboard?' I finished for him. 'I thought so. I had a feeling he'd been tailing me.'

'Be it he you just slew.'

'Is that so? Tough. Give yourself up.'

'I will not.'

'Uh huh. Tell me this, then... how much is Pontius paying your clan for this work?'

'Who be Pontius?'

'Khanjar, then. Khanjar the Sharp.'

'Enough.'

He fired again and then lunged at me, swinging a power sword up in his left hand. Barbarisater knocked the whizzing slug away and then formed an *uwe sar* to block the downswing of the glittering blade. There was a bark of clashing energies.

I switched to a double-handed grip and ripped Barbarisater in a cross-wise stroke as Etrik tried to use his pistol again. The tip of the blade cut through the gun's body and left him with only a handgrip. But the Clansire's sword, a short yet robust falchion of antique design, darted in and sliced through the meat of my right shoulder. I howled.

I snarled into a *leht suf* that rebounded his thrust and swung reversing *ulsars* that parried two more fast cuts and put me on the front foot. Etrik was a big man, with a considerable reach and alarming strength. That meant even his most nimble and extended strikes were delivered with punishing force. I did not recognise the blade technique he was using, although I was aware that the warriors of Vessor considered sword skill one of the three primary battle arts, devoting as much time to it during their training as to gun lore and open hand. The very fact he was the owner of an heirloom power weapon identified him as an expert.

My skills were a heterodox blend of methods that I had mastered over the years, but at the core of them was the *Ewl Wyla Scryi* or 'the genius of sharpness', the ancient Carthean swordmastery system.

On top of the Trans-Atenate Express, any blade methods had to be semi-improvised. Neither of us were steady on our feet, our boots sliding on the iced metal, and the gale dragged at us hard.

He kept attacking high, aiming for the throat, I imagine, and I was driven into a variety of *tahn feh sar* parries with a tightly vertical blade that defend the head and ear. My own attacks were lower, *fon uls* and *fon uin* strokes that targeted the heart, belly and swordarm.

His defence was excellent, especially a sliding backdrag that fouled every *fon bei* I struck in an attempt to push his blade down laterally and open his guard. His attack strokes were inventively arrhythmic, preventing all but the most last moment anticipations. He was hideously skilful.

I wondered if that was why Pontius Glaw had hired these Vessorines. He was such a connoisseur of martial skills and warrior breeds. He didn't just want killers. He wanted masters of the killing art.

In Clansire Etrik, he'd got his money's worth.

I realised that the mercenary, with a combination of cross parries and driving thrust strokes, was pressing me back towards the gap between carriages three and four. I was cornered with my back to the drop, my combat options restricted. I didn't dare risk a backwards jump without looking, and I couldn't take my eyes off his sword for a moment. I knew he would be building up to a sharp frontal attack that would either catch me with no room to dodge or topple me off the edge.

Carthean sword-craft teaches that when an imminent attack is unavoidable, the only practical response is to limit or force it. The technique, which has many forms, is called the *gej kul asf*, which means 'the bridled steed'. It imagines the adversary is an unbroken mount who is going to charge no matter what you do, and that your blade is a long-reined bridle that will control that charge on your terms. Etrik was going to lunge, so I needed to reduce the lunging options. I went into an *ehn kulsar*, where the sword is raised, two-handed, with the hilt above shoulder height and the blade tipped down in a thirty-five degree angle from the horizontal. Sharp, lateral blade turns robbed him of any sideways or upper body opportunities. His only option was to come in low, parrying up, to get in underneath my guard. I was forcing him to target my lower body, an area his swordplay had shown he didn't favour. It also required him to extend in a low, ill-balanced way.

Etrik made the lunge, shoulder down and sword rising from a hip-height grip. My 'bridle' entirely determined the height and direction of the thrust.

Instead of backing or attempting to knock his rising blade aside with a diagonal stroke, I sidestepped, like a bull-dancer evading a head-down aurox in the karnivale pits of Mankareal. Now he was running his sword into empty space.

He tried to pull in, but he'd committed his weight behind it. His left foot kicked out on the roof ice and his right one went skidding sideways. Etrik grunted out a curse and did the only thing he could. He turned his lunge into a leap.

He just made the roof of the next wagon, his chest and arms slamming into it, his legs wheeling over the drop. His falchion had a pommel spike and he slammed it down into the roof to anchor himself, his boots trying to get a grip on the weatherproof plastic sides of the intercarriage articulation.

I had seconds to turn my temporary advantage into a permanent upper hand.

But my hasty sidestep had left me with no more purchase on the iced roof than Etrik. My legs suddenly flew out from under me and I crashed down on my back. I rolled as fast as I could and fumbled for a handhold, but it cost me Barbarisater. The precious sword squealed as it tumbled over the edge of the roof.

I was holding on, barely. Etrik's pommel spike shrieked across the roof metal as he put his weight onto it and dug in. With a few scrabbling kicks, he hoisted himself up onto the roof of car four and looked back at me. He chuckled an ugly jeer as he saw me worse off than he was.

Still chuckling, he gingerly took one step out onto the top of the intercarriage articulation, and then another, balancing as he crossed back to car three to finish me off.

Another two steps, and he would be within stabbing range.

I decided which of my handholds was most secure and let go with the other, fumbling round behind myself.

Etrik came off the articulation, took the last step, his sword raised to rip at me, and found himself looking down the barrel of my autopistol.

It was contrary to all the noble rules of the *Ewl Wyla Scryi* to start a sword duel and finish it with a gun. The Carthean masters would have been ashamed of me. But I wasn't feeling particularly noble by then.

I fired just once. The shot hit him in the sternum and slammed him backwards. With a cheated look on his face, Etrik disappeared off the far side of the roof.

I was exhausted, and drained from the extreme cold, by the time I got back inside the car. The upper hallway was full of people. Stewards were ushering terrified and distraught passengers into other cars. Master personnel were gazing in perplexed dismay at the fight damage and the trio of Vessorine corpses. Eleena was arguing heatedly with one of the master crewmen.

Everyone looked round and someone screamed as I slithered back in through the window. I must have looked a sight: caked in frost and frozen blood from the wounds to my arm and chin.

Crezia and Aemos pushed through the onlookers and reached my side.

'I'm alright.'

'Let me look at that... Golden Throne!' gasped Crezia, twisting my head to study the gash in my chin.

'Don't fuss.'

'You need–'

'Now's not the time. Is Medea all right?'

'Yes,' said Aemos.

'So you're all unscathed?'

'You're wounded enough for all of us,' Crezia said.

'I've had worse,' I said.

'He has,' agreed Aemos. 'He's had worse.'

Eleena was still shouting at the train master, who was shouting right back at her. He was a tall, distinguished man in an ornate, brocaded version of the Trans-Continental uniform topped with a Navy-style cap. Clearly very old, his eyes, nose and ears had been replaced with augmetic implants: primitive, functional devices finished in boiler-metal black that probably had been handcrafted for him by the locomotive's devoted engineers. Even his teeth, framed by a spectacular white tile beard, were cast iron. His name was Alivander Suko, and I later discovered that he had been master of the Trans-Atenate Express for three hundred and seventy-eight years. He looked like a bearded locomotive in human form.

I pulled Eleena back and faced him.

'I demand an explanation,' Suko growled, his voice reverberating from a mechanical larynx, 'for this... outrage. Nothing like this has ever happened aboard the Trans-Atenate. This vulgar violence and impropriety–'

'Impropriety?' I echoed.

'Are you responsible for this?' he asked.

'I would not have chosen for this to occur, but... yes.'

'Detain him now!' Suko yelled. A pair of burly train guards who had withdrawn laspistols from the express's emergency locker the moment the alarms had started sounding, stepped forward.

'There are three dead here, three more outside,' I said softly, looking into the train master's electric-shuttered eyes and pointedly ignoring the guards. 'All armoured, all armed... combat warriors. Do you really think it's a good idea to mess with the man who killed them?'

Silence fell on the corridor, colder and harsher than the ice storm still gusting in through the shattered window. All eyes were on us, including, to Suko's discomfort, the last of the gawping passengers still being herded out.

'Shall we continue this in private?' I suggested.

We went into one of the vacated cabins. I opened the hinged wooden cover of the suite's little cogitator, switched it to hololithic mode and pressed my signet ring against the data-reader. The little desk projected a hologram of the Inquisitorial seal, overlaid by credential details, followed by a slowly turning three dimensional scan of my head.

'I am Inquisitor Gregor Eisenhorn of the Ordos Helican.' Suko and his guards were speechless.

'Do you accept that, or would you like me to rotate slowly in front of you until you're convinced?'

The train master looked at me, so taken aback he barely knew what to say. 'I'm sorry, my lord,' he began. 'How can Trans-Continental assist the work of the mighty Ordos?'

'Well, sir, you can get this train moving again for a start.'

'But–'

I'd had enough. 'I have been travelling incognito, sir. But not any more. And if I'm going to reveal myself as an inquisitor, I'm damn well going to behave like one. This train is now under my control.'

We remained halted long enough for the engineers to service the brakes and secure the exploded windows. And long enough for the train guards, under my direct supervision, to search the entire vehicle for any other passengers without tickets.

Wrapped in crew-issue foul-weather gear, I went outside and retrieved Barbarisater, which complained fractiously about being left in the blizzard. I sheathed the whining blade and went to check on the three janissaries who lay sprawled and stiffening in the snow.

The express resumed progress at five and there were no more interruptions. We thundered out of the night and into a more temperate dawn where the land was thick with snow but the ice storms had abated.

Suko raced the locomotive right up to the safety margins to make up time. The express cut down through the southern extremities of the Atenate Range, descending through hill country and rocky glacial plains. If I'd been awake, I would have seen hard pasture and scree slowly blooming into forest and deciduous woodland, and then the first little hamlets of the vast Southern Plateau, sunlit in the morning air.

But I was deep asleep, my wounds dressed, Barbarisater slumbering fitfully at my side and Crezia watching over me.

I woke after five, with the express still making excellent time. We were due in at New Gevae at midnight. I'd given Suko strict instructions to send no word ahead of our plight.

It was likely that Pontius would try again at New Gevae. I studied the route map and thought about getting Suko to make an unscheduled stop at one of the satellite stations in the towns north of New Gevae. We could disembark and hire air transport, and the train could run on to the city.

I thought my implacable and attentive enemy might anticipate this move. And I also considered that arriving in plain view at a major city terminal might be the safer plan.

I lay on my cabin's cot, meditating as the lowland scenery of the plateau zipped by outside. Medea was up and around by then, hobbling painfully and using, of all things, my runestaff as a crutch. Only she would have the wit to dare such disrespect.

She limped into my cabin and flopped down on the edge of my cot, nursing her sore back. Crezia was asleep in the opposite berth.

'Never a dull moment, eh?' said Medea.

'Never.'

She nodded over at Crezia. 'She didn't leave your side, Gregor. All day.'

'I know.'

'She's more than just an old friend, isn't she?'

'Yes, Medea.'

'You and your secrets.'

'I know.'

'You never told me.'

'I never told anyone. Crezia Berschilde deserved the privacy.'

She glanced at me. 'Gregor Eisenhorn deserved the privacy too, don't you think? You may be a great and terrible inquisitor and everything, but you're a human being too. You have a life outside this awful work.'

I thought about that. Sadly, I didn't agree.

'But you're together again, then. You and the good doctor.'

'I have renewed a friendship I should never have allowed to lapse.'

'Yeah, right. Renewed.' She made a surprisingly coarse and graphic gesture.

I couldn't help but smile. 'Was there something else, or did you just come in to demonstrate the vulgar extremes of your miming ability?'

'Yeah, there was something else. What do we do when we get there?'

New Gevae was a cluster of monolithic hive pyramids covering the delta of the Sanas river. We could see its twinkling lights in the distance over an hour before we arrived. The Trans-Atenate Express rattled and hissed into the main terminal at two minutes to midnight. I got out ahead of the crowds and strode across the wide concourse under the arched glass roof to the Astropathic Guild's office near the freight cargo pens.

I accessed the Aegis account and read the reply from Nayl. He agreed that it was like the trouble on Eechan, and cursed Sadia's name. He said the *Caucus* was ready to ship out, and that he would be at a bar called Entipaul's Lounge at noon the next day. The bar was in hive four, level sixty.

I looked at the communiqué sadly and then glanced at the waiting adept. 'Two-word reply. "Rosethorn attends". Send it.'

I walked into Entipaul's Lounge the next day at a minute before noon. It was a cage of aluminium tubes and spray-painted flakboard panels artfully wired up so that the ropes of lights pulsed in time to the pound music the place pumped through the caster system. The place wanted to seem tough and underhive and dangerous, but it was all for show. This was a lunchtime and after-work watering hole for mid-hive clerks and Administratum graders, a place for assignations with winsome girls from the logosticator pool, the celebrations that accompanied promotions or retirements, or rowdy birthday drinks. I'd been into real twist bars and heard genuine pound. This place was just sham, theatre.

I was shrouded in Aemos's over-robe, the hood pulled up, wearing a rebreather mask I'd borrowed from the express. I wanted to look like some tech-adept on his lunch break, or a warewright stealing off for a tryst with his girl.

The place was largely empty. A bored-looking steward polished glasses behind the narrow sweep of the bar, and two uniformed waitresses chatted in the rear doorway, holding their glass trays like riot shields. Half a dozen men sat in the booths that radiated off the bar's central hub, and a hooded figure was sitting, drinking alone, with its back to the door.

I sat at one of the hub tables. One of the waitresses approached. She smelled of obscura and her pencilled eyebrows framed wildly dilated eyes.

'Choice?'

'Tunderey clear-grain, double, in a chill-sleeve.'

'Dokey-doke,' she returned as she stalked away.

The music continued to blast. She returned with a single shot glass on her suspensor tray. The glass was actually a cup of pressure-moulded ice. She tonged it onto my table and caught the coin I flipped at her.

'Keep the change,' I murmured.

'Big spender,' she mocked and paced off, wiggling a backside that had no business being wiggled.

I didn't touch the drink. Gradually, the ice melted and the oily liquid began to seep out over the table top.

The hooded figure got up and wandered over to me.

'Rosethorn?'

I looked up. 'That's me.'

She dropped the hooded cloak away from her shoulders. She had sharp features and long, straight black hair. Her kohl-edged eyes glinted like jade.

Not Harlon Nayl at all. Marla Tarray.

She sat down opposite me and knocked back my drink, licking the ice-water off her long fingers.

'You knew we'd get you sooner or later.'

'I guess so. Who's we?'

The other drinkers in the bar had got up and formed a circle around us, sitting at adjacent tables. Marla Tarray clicked her fingers and they all drew back coats or cloaks to reveal the handguns they carried. She clicked again and the weapons disappeared.

'So this is a trap?'

'Of course.'

'The astrograms weren't from Nayl?'

'Evidently.'

'You've broken Glossia?'

'How clever are we?'

I sat back. 'How did you do that?'

'Wouldn't you like to know, Mr Eisenhorn?'

I shrugged. 'Seeing as you've got me cold, yes. These men are more of your damned Vessorine, aren't they? I'm dead in my seat. I can't see the harm.'

'I imagine you've guessed already.' she said. She smiled. I could feel her powerful mind trying to delve into mine.

'Jekud Vance.'

'That's right, Mr Eisenhorn. Your astropath proved to be very useful. With the right persuasion. And the Janissaries excel at persuasion. Vance sent the communiqués, pretending to be Nayl. He knew Glossia.'

She probed at my mind again.

'You're using shielding techniques,' she said, her face darkening.

'Of course I am. You would be too if the situation was reversed. I have to say though, I'm disappointed. I was hoping that Pontius might be here himself. This is a trap after all. Eisenhorn's last stand. He might have been civil enough to come and watch me die.'

'Pontius is busy elsewhere,' she snapped, and then realised what she'd said.

'Thank you for that confirmation,' I said.

'You bastard!' she snapped. 'You're dead! What good will it do you? This is a trap!'

'Yes, it is. A trap.'

She hesitated. The janissaries had all risen, guns out, aiming at me. The bar staff were fleeing, terrified.

Marla Tarray slowly reached out and took the rebreather mask off my face.

'Etrik?' she stammered, her jade eyes wide.

'Yes,' I said, three kilometres away in a locked lodging house room, sweating and straining as I channeled my will via the runestaff and animated the body of Clansire Etrik.

Tarray leapt back from the table, knocking over her chair. 'Damnation!' she shrieked. 'He's got us! He's got us! How the hell did he know?'

'You could talk like Nayl and use Glossia thanks to Jekud, but Jekud didn't know what Nayl knew. We fought Sadia on Lethe Eleven, not Eechan,' I had Etrik say.

Marla Tarray drew a plasma pistol and shot Etrik through the chest. The Vessorines all around opened fire with their autoguns and las-carbines.

As my puppet was torn apart, I let go of the warp vortex that had been spinning in my mind ever since I had summoned it.

It surged out of Etrik's collapsing body and expanded, annihilating the janissaries, Entipaul's Lounge and the entire level sixty deck of hive four in a radius of fifty metres.

Marla Tarray was atomised. In the last milliseconds of her life, her mental shields collapsed in terror and I got a precious snapshot into her powerful psyker mind. Not everything, but enough.

Enough to know that I had just annihilated Pontius Glaw's daughter.

FIFTEEN

SANCTUM, CATHARSIS AND FISCHIG
TEHT UIN SAH
PROMODY

Fifteen days later, we were a long, long way from New Gevae, a long way from Gudrun itself. I had, for the time being, evaded the clutches of Khanjar the Sharp.

The morning before my meeting – or my puppet's meeting, I should say – with Marla Tarray in the mid-hive bar, Aemos and I had arranged passage on a packet lighter called the *Spirit of Wysten*, and by the evening, we were leaving the planet. Five and a half days out from Gudrun, in the vicinity of Cyto, we rendezvoused with the *Essene*.

My old friend Tobias Maxilla, eccentric master of the sprint trader *Essene*, had come in response to the Glossia code word 'Sanctum' without hesitation, breaking off from his merchant runs in the Helican spinwards and laying course for Gudrun. He had never been a formal part of my operation, but he was an ally of long standing, and had provided the services of his ship on many occasions.

He always claimed to do this for financial reward – I regularly made sure the Ordos remunerated him handsomely – and to keep on the good side of the Imperial Inquisition. Privately, I believe his allegiance to me was the product of an adventurous streak. Getting involved in my business offered more diverting occupation than a trade voyage down the Helican worlds.

There was no ship, and no ship's master, that I trusted more than Tobias Maxilla and the *Essene*. With my life shattered, my back to the wall and an enemy after my blood, he was the one I turned to for rescue and escape.

One could also always rely on Maxilla to lift a company's spirits. In truth, the mood in my little group had been uncomfortable since New Gevae. And that was largely my own fault.

As soon as I had realised that 'Nayl' was just another of Glaw's deceits, a ruse to lure me into a trap, I had set my trap in return. Certain sections of the *Malus Codicium* concerned the creation and remote animation of thralls – human beings psionically controlled as puppets. I had never tried the technique, for it seemed ghoulish. The *Codicium* suggested the process worked best with a freshly killed cadaver. But on the other hand, it was simply an elaborate extension of my use of will, and it suited my purpose.

I didn't go into detail about what I was going to do, but Medea, Eleena,

Crezia and Aemos knew something unorthodox was afoot, and they were all concerned when I had Etrik's body covertly taken from the train to a lodging we had rented in hive four. Crezia mumbled something about body snatching, and Medea was dubious. Back aboard the *Pulchritude*, she'd shrugged off as a joke the idea that I was dabbling too far. She seemed to have accepted the whole business with Cherubael.

Now she seemed less confident about esoteric psyker tricks.

Even Aemos seemed reserved. He had not said a word about the *Malus Codicium* since he'd seen me remove it from the safe in my study. And he'd made it clear on several occasions that he trusted my judgement.

But there had still been a feeling in the air.

I kept them out of the room while I performed the rituals, and that may have been a mistake too. Except for Eleena, who was spared the sensations, they all felt the unnerving, creeping backwash of the act.

I had also never used a warp vortex before, but it seemed the only weapon I could equip my thrall with that would trap the trappers. In hindsight, I wonder if the *Malus Codicium* had planted the idea in my head.

The vortex worked. It destroyed the enemies who had tried to snare me. I doubt I will use one again. The feedback left me unconscious, and I was ill and weak for two days afterwards. My friends had to break down the door of the room to get at me, and they must have been shaken by the sight that greeted them. The burnt circle on the floor, the psy-plasmic residue trickling off the walls, the symbols I had painted. I think they felt for the first time that I had attempted something I wasn't quite in control of.

Perhaps they were right.

None of them had wanted to talk about it. Aemos had found the *Malus Codicium* on the floor beside me and slipped it into his pocket before the others could see it. Later, aboard the *Spirit of Wysten*, he'd handed it back to me privately.

'I don't want to touch it again,' he said. 'I don't think I want to see it again.'

I was unhappy at his reaction. His life was devoted to the acquisition of knowledge – it was an actual clinical compulsion in his case – but there he was rejecting a source of secret data, albeit dark, that could be found almost nowhere else in the galaxy. I thought he alone might appreciate its worth.

'It's the *Malus Codicium*, isn't it?'

'Yes.'

'They never found it. On Farness Beta, after Quixos fell, the Ordos searched for it and never found it.'

'That's true.'

'Because you took it for yourself and never told them.'

'Yes. It was my decision.'

'I see. And that's how you learned to control daemonhosts too, isn't it?'

'Yes.'

'I'm disappointed in you, Gregor.'

Maxilla was, as ever, the perfect host, and the general spirit did pick up a little once we were in his company. He met us at the *Essene*'s fore starboard airgate, dressed in a chequered sedril gown-coat, a blue silk cravat pinned with a golden star pin and a purple suede calotte with a silver tassel. His skin dye was gloss white with black hearts over his eyes, and a fine platinum chain ran between the diamond earring in his left lobe to the sapphire stud in his nose. Behind him, gold-plated servitors waited with salvers of refreshments. He greeted us all, flirting with Medea and making a particular fuss of Crezia and Eleena, two females he had not met before.

'Where to?' was his first question to me.

'Let me use your astropath, and set course for the place we first met.'

I sent word, in Glossia, to Fischig, telling him to alter his route to avoid Gudrun and meet me at a new rendezvous point. 'Thorn wishes Hound, at Hound's cradle, by sext.' Maxilla's cadaverous, nameless Navigator performed his hyper-mathematical feats of divination, and set the *Essene* thundering into warp space as fast as its potent drive could carry it.

As always, I was unable to rest easily while travelling in the hellish netherworld of the warp, so instead I retired with Maxilla to his stateroom. He was a terrible gossip and always relished a few hours catching up whenever we were reunited. Surrounded as he was by a crew that was more servitor than human, he did so crave company.

But I had been looking forward to a private talk. I'd never confided in him particularly before, but now I felt he might be the only man in the Imperium who would give me a fair hearing. And if not fair, then at least one free of harsh judgment. Maxilla was a rogue. He made no excuses about it. His entire life had been devoted to testing the ductile qualities of rules and regulations. I wanted, I suppose, to find out what he thought of me.

His stateroom was a double-storey cabin behind the *Essene*'s cathedral-like main bridge. A ten-seat banquet table of polished duralloy that I had dined at many times before occupied a mezzanine area at the far end under a domed section of roof that could peel back shielding at the wave of a control wand to become an observation blister.

Curved stairways, with tefrawood balustrades that Maxilla claimed had been salvaged from a twenty mast sunjammer on Nautilia, ran down from either end of the mezzanine onto the main deck area, a wide hall with a floor of inlaid marble. Works of art – paintings, statues, antiques, hololiths – were displayed all round the room between the crystelephantine wall pillars. Some were protected by softly glowing stasis fields, others hung weightlessly in invisible repulsor beams.

Elegant scroll-armed couches and chairs, some draped with throws of Sampanese light-cloth, were arranged on a large rectangle of exquisite Olitari rugwork in the centre of the room. The rug alone was worth a small fortune. The room was illuminated by six shimmering chandeliers from the glassworks of Vitria, each one suspended by a small antigrav plate so they floated below the dished ceiling.

I sat down on a couch and accepted the balloon of amasec Maxilla handed to me.

'You look like a man who wishes to unburden himself, Gregor,' he said, taking a seat opposite.

'Am I so transparent?'

'No, I fear it is rather more a case that I am hopeful. It's been a boring few months. I crave excitement. And when the only man I know who makes a habit of getting involved in the most ridiculously perilous ventures anyone ever heard of calls to me for help, I perk up.'

He fitted a lho-stick into a long silver holder, lit it with a tiny flick of his digital ring weapon and sat back, exhaling spiced smoke, rolling the amasec in his glass around with an experienced hand.

'I...' I tried to begin, but I didn't really know where to start.

He put his glass down and made a gesture with his control wand like a theatrical conjuror. The air became close and slightly muffled.

'Speak freely,' he told me. 'I've activated the suite's privacy field.'

'Actually,' I admitted, 'my hesitation was more to do with not knowing what to say.'

'I deal in routes and journeys, Gregor. In my experience, the best place to start is always–'

'The beginning? I know.'

I told him, first in general terms and then with increasing detail, about the events as they had unfolded. Durer. Thuring. The battles with *Cruor Vult* and Cherubael. His dyed face became tragic, like a clown's, as I told him about Alizebeth. He had always had a soft spot for her.

Though I felt I had taken his advice and started from the beginning, I realised more and more that I had not. I kept going back, filling in details. To explain Cherubael, I had to go back to Farness Beta and the struggle against Quixos, and that in turn required mention of the mission to Cinchare. I told him about the assault on Spaeton House and our desperate flight across Gudrun. I recounted the murders that had taken place across the sub-sector. He'd known Harlon Nayl and Nathun Inshabel, not to mention several other members of my team. My account of Pontius Glaw's revenge was a litany of bad tidings.

Once I had begun, I couldn't stop. I spared nothing. It felt liberating to confess everything at last and unburden myself. I told him about the *Malus Codicium*, and how I might have compromised myself by keeping it. I told him about my dabbling with daemonhosts. And thralls. And warp vortices. I owned up to the deal I had struck with Glaw on Cinchare and how that had empowered him and turned him into the threat that now pursued me.

'Everyone, Tobias, everyone in my operation – my family, if you will – everyone except you, Fischig and the handful I brought aboard here with me, has died because of what I did on Cinchare. Something in the order of... well, I haven't made an exact count. Two hundred servants of the Imperium. Two hundred people who had devoted themselves to my cause in the firm belief that I was doing good work... are dead. I'm not even counting the likes of Poul Rassi, Duclane Haar and that poor bastard Verveuk who perished in what turns out to be the overture to this bloodbath. Or Magos Bure, who must have been killed by Glaw for him to have escaped.'

'Might I correct you, Gregor?' he asked.

'By all means.'

'You called it *your* cause. That they were devoted to your cause. But it isn't, is it?'

'What do you mean?'

'You still, passionately, believe that you are doing the Emperor's work?'

'Damn right I do!'

'Then they died in the service of the Emperor. They died for His cause. No Imperial citizen can ask for anything more.'

'I don't think you were listening, Maxilla–'

He got to his feet. 'No, I don't think you were, inquisitor. Not even to yourself. I'm pressing this point because it's so basic you seem to have overlooked it.'

He walked across the stateroom and stood looking up at a hololithic portrait of an Imperial warrior. It was very old. I didn't want to think where he might have got it from.

'Do you know who this is?'

'No.'

'Warmaster Terfuek. Commanded the Imperial forces in the Pacificus War, almost fifty centuries ago. Ancient history now. Most of us couldn't say what the damn war was about any more. At the Battle of Corossa, Terfeuk committed four million Imperial Guardsman to the field. Four million, Gregor. They don't do battles like that any more, thank the Throne. It was of course the age of High Imperialism, the era of the notable warmaster, the cult of personality. Anyway, Terfeuk got his victory. Not even his advisors thought he could win at Corossa, but he did. And of those four million men, only ninety thousand left the field alive.'

Maxilla turned and looked at me. 'Do you know what he said? Terfeuk? Do you know what he said of that terrible cost?'

I shook my head.

'He said it was the greatest honour of his life to have served the Emperor so well.'

'I'm happy for him.'

'You don't understand, Gregor. Terfeuk was no butcher. No glory hound. By all accounts he was humane, and beloved by his men as fair and generous. But when the time came, he did not regret for a moment the cost of serving the Emperor and preserving the Imperium against all odds.'

Maxilla sat down again. 'I think that's all you're guilty of. Making hard choices to serve the Emperor the best you can, to serve him where maybe others would not be strong enough and fail. Doing your duty and living with the consequences. I'm sure dear Terfeuk had sleepless nights for years after Corossa. But he dealt with that pain. He didn't have any regrets.'

'Committing men to battle is not quite the same as–'

'I beg to differ. Imperial society is your battleground. The people you have lost were your soldiers. And soldiers are only martial resources. They are there to be used. You used your own resources to win your battles. This book you speak of. This daemonhost. He sounds fascinating. I'd love to meet him.'

'You wouldn't, I assure you. And it's an "it" not a "he".'

Maxilla shrugged. 'I fancy you wanted to talk to me about this because you thought you might get a sympathetic ear. Me being an old rogue and everything.' There were times, I swear, I believed Maxilla could read my mind.

'Let me tell you something, Gregor. I love you like a brother, but we're nothing alike. I am a rogue. A gambler. A liar. A reprobate. My vices are many and unmentionable. I never bend the rules; I break them. Snap them. Shatter them. However and wherever I may. In that regard alone, I am a kindred spirit. You are bending the rules of the Imperium, of the Inquisition. You are, undoubtedly, what they call a radical. But that's where the similarity ends. I break the rules for my own gain. To get what I want, to amplify my wealth and status. To make things better for me. Me. Just me. But you're not doing it for yourself. You're doing it for the system you believe in and the God-Emperor you worship and by damn, that means your conscience can be clean.'

I was taken aback by the passion of his speech. I was also taken aback by the suggestion – one that no one had dared make before – that I had become a radical. When had that happened? My actions may have been radical but did that make me a radical to the marrow?

Sitting there, in that opulent room, I realised Maxilla had hit on the truth, a truth I had been denying. I had changed without recognising that change in myself. I would always be grateful to Tobias Maxilla for that bruising realisation. I felt better for it.

'I suppose you can't turn to your superiors for help?'

'No,' I said, still reeling from the fresh viewpoint.

'Because you'd have to tell them things you don't want them to hear?'

'Of course. To get any kind of official help, I'd have to make a full report. And that report would fall apart under the lightest scrutiny if it omitted the *Codicium*, Cherubael. By the Throne, the list goes back! I even hid Pontius Glaw from them. What could I say? Pontius Glaw is exterminating my forces. Where did he come from, my lord grand master? Well, to be honest, I've known of his existence for centuries, but I kept him hidden from you. And he's only up and around now because I decided to give him a body.'

He chuckled. 'I see your point. What will you tell Fischig? Dear Godwyn is as straight up and down as any man I know.'

'I'll deal with Fischig.'

'So what is your next move? You mentioned this daughter of his, the psyker. You saw things when you killed her, didn't you?'

I had indeed. Marla Tarray's entire mental shield had crumbled just before the vortex annihilated her. The picture I had obtained was far from complete, but it was plentiful.

'Marla Tarray was much older than she looked or claimed. She was the bastard offspring of Pontius Glaw and a serving girl from Gudrun that Glaw had taken with him to Quenthus Eight. Marla was born in 020, corrupted from conception by the tainted torc Pontius wore. Several notorious heretics who have evaded the Inquisition in the last three hundred years were actually her under different guises. Many cases could be closed now she is dead.'

'Pontius won't be too pleased.'

'I imagine Pontius Glaw now wants me dead even more than before. But they were after the *Malus Codicium*, you see. I learned that from her undefended mind. Glaw knew Quixos must have it and, once Quixos was dead, realised it must be in my possession. He wants that book so much.'

'Do you know why?'

'I saw images of an arid world just before Marla Tarray died. A dried out husk where primaeval cities lay buried under layers of ash. Glaw's after something there, and he needs the *Codicium* to help him.'

'What?'

'I don't know.'

'Where?'

'I don't know that either. There was a name, a word in her mind. *Ghül.* But I don't know what it means or what it refers to. Her mind was in collapse. Very little made sense.'

'I'll consult my charts and my navigator. Who knows?' He sat forward and looked at me. 'This book. This *Malus Codicium*. May I see it?'

'Why?'

'Because I appreciate unique and priceless objects.'

I took it from my jacket and passed it to him. He studied it with reverence, a smile on his face.

'Not much to look at, but beautiful for what it is. Thank you for the opportunity to hold it.' He handed it back to me.

'I can't believe I'm going to say this,' he added, 'me of all people. But... I'd destroy it, if I were you.'

'I think you're right. I believe I will.'

I put down my empty glass and walked to the doors. Maxilla evaporated the privacy field.

'Thank you for your time and hospitality, Tobias. I think I'll turn in now.'

'Sleep well.'

'One last thing,' I said, turning back in the doorway. 'You said you break the rules to get what you want. That you serve no one but yourself and everything you do is for your own ends.'

'I did.'

'Then why do you help me so often?'

He smiled. 'Good night, Gregor.'

The *Essene* put in at Hubris four days later. Hubris was an outlying world in the Helican sub-sector and Fischig, Bequin, Maxilla and I had all met there for the first time in 240.

Indirectly, that's where we'd first stumbled across Pontius Glaw too. Everything was turning full circle in the strangest way.

I had rerouted Fischig here as a convenient and out of the way meeting place, but it seemed apt. He'd been a chastener in the local Arbites when he'd first crossed my path. It was his homeworld.

For eleven out of every twenty-nine months, Hubris orbits so far beyond its star that the population are forced to hibernate in massive cryogenic tombs to survive the blackness and the cold. Those winters of eternal night are called Dormant and I had experienced one on that last visit.

But now we arrived at the start of Thaw, the middle season between Dormant and Vital.

The tombs had emptied and the great cities were waking under a pale sun. The population was engaged in a frenzied jubilee of feasting and dancing and general excess that lasted three weeks and was supposed to celebrate the society's rebirth, but which probably had deep rooted origins in the traditional methods of recovery from extended cryogenic suspension such as forced physical activity and high-calorie intake.

I offered to travel to the surface to meet him, partly because I thought Crezia, Eleena and Medea could do with the relaxation of a festival and Maxilla had never been one to turn down a party.

But Fischig answered he would as soon come up to the *Essene*, and he arrived, piloting his own shuttle, a few hours later.

I could tell he was tense from the moment he stepped aboard. He was polite, and seemed pleased to see Medea, Aemos and Maxilla. But with me he was reserved.

I told him it was good to see him, and that I was relieved he had escaped Glaw's purge.

'Glaw, eh?' he said. He had heard all about the fall of the Distaff and our other holdings. 'I had wondered who it was.'

'We need to talk,' I said.

'Yes,' he said. 'But not here.'

Maxilla lent us his stateroom and I turned on the privacy field.

'There's nothing you couldn't say in front of the others, Godwyn,' I said.

'No? Glaw's killed everyone except us few. Because–'

'Because?'

'You should have destroyed that monster years ago, Eisenhorn. That, or handed him over to the Ordos. What the hell were you thinking?'

'Same as I'm thinking now. I did what was best.'

'Nayl? Inshabel? Bure? Suskova? The whole damn Distaff? That was best?' His tone was venomous.

'Yes, Fischig. And I never heard you contradict my decisions.'

'Like you'd have listened!'

'To you? Yes. Not once did I hear you say we should turn Glaw over to the Ordos.'

'Because you always make it sound so logical! Like you know best!'

I shrugged. 'This is beneath you, Godwyn. It sounds like sour grapes. Things didn't turn out the way I would have wished and you're making out it's all my fault. I took tough decisions that I thought were right. If you'd ever – *ever* – objected, I'd have considered your opinion.'

'Too easy, too damn easy. I was only ever your lackey, your minion. If I'd said we vapourise Glaw, you'd have said yes and then hidden him anyway.'

'Do you really think I'm that underhand? You, of all my counsel, I respect the most!'

'Yeah?' He tossed his gloves onto a couch and helped himself to a schooner of Maxilla's clawblood. 'Who told Bure to build Glaw a body without telling any of us? Who suddenly knows how to conjure daemons like an expert? You cover your secrets with such an almighty righteous air we all thank the stars and the Emperor Himself you chose us to help you in your work. But you're a liar! A conspirator! And maybe worse!'

'And you're too much a puritan idealist for your own good. And mine,' I hissed. 'I dearly wanted your help, Godwyn. You are one of the few men I really trust and one of the few humans in space with the stalwart spirit to keep me on the level. I needed you now, in my fight to destroy Glaw. I can't believe you're turning against me like this.'

He stared down at the contents of his glass. 'I always did warn you I would if you crossed the line.'

'I've crossed no line. But if you feel that way... go. Get off this ship and leave me to my work. You'll always have my gratitude for the service you put in. But I won't have this bitterness.'

'That's what you think?'

'Yes.'

He hesitated. 'I gave my life to you, Gregor. I admired you. I always believed you were... right.'

'I still am. I serve the Emperor. Just like you. Get rid of your rancor and we can work together again.'

'Let me think about it.'

'Two days, and we're leaving orbit.'

'Two days then.'

Apparently, his ruminations only took him a day.

I had just received, via the *Essene*'s astropath bank, a rather fascinating communiqué, and I went looked for Fischig. I found Crezia playing regicide with Maxilla in a mid-deck suite. He'd taken quite a shine to Doctor Berschilde.

She got up as I entered the room, and excitedly displayed the stunning funz-silk gown she was wearing. 'Tobias had his servitors make it for me! Isn't it gorgeous?'

'It is,' I agreed.

'The poor woman had virtually no wardrobe at all, Gregor. Just a few travel bags. It was the least I could do. You wait until you see the epinchire dress they're embroidering for her.'

'Have you seen Fischig?' I asked.

Crezia looked at Maxilla sharply and the ship master suddenly became occupied with his study of the game board.

'What?' I asked.

Crezia took me by the arm and walked me over to the cabin windows. 'He's gone, Gregor.'

'Gone?'

'Early this morning. He left in his shuttle. Dreadful man.'

'He was my friend, Crezia.'

'Not any more, I think.'

'Did he say anything?'

'No. Not to me. Or to Tobias, except a quick goodbye. He was up late last night though, talking to Medea and Aemos.'

'About what?'

'I don't know. I wasn't included. Tobias took Eleena and me on a guided tour of his art collection. He has some extraordinary p–'

'They talked and this morning he just left?'

'I like Medea, but I think she may be a little careless. I'd never have told that Fischig man about the things you did in New Gevae.'

'And she did?'

'I'm just saying. She might have.'

I had servitors summon Aemos and Medea. They arrived in my stateroom at about the same moment. Both of them looked awkward.

'Well?'

'Well what?' snapped Medea.

'What the hell did you say to him?'

She looked away. Aemos toyed with the hem of his cloak.

'I simply tried to make him understand, Gregor. About what you were doing... what you had done. I thought if he knew it all he might see it like I see it.'

'Really? It didn't cross your mind he was a puritanical son of a bitch on a hair trigger? Just like he's always been?'

'I felt honesty was the best policy,' Aemos muttered. Medea said something under her breath.

'Oh, say it so we can all hear!' I snarled.

'Honesty is the best policy,' Medea said. 'I was appreciating the irony.'

'How so?'

'The stuff you never told us. The honesty you withheld.'

'That's rich coming from you, Medea Betancore. In point of fact, I believe I told you everything. Shared everything. Sworn on my secrets.'

'Yeah, well...' she looked away.

'Oh Throne, you told him, didn't you? You told him about Cherubael and the *Codicium* and Glaw and everything!'

She turned on me, tears in her anguished eyes. 'I thought he would understand if everything was out in the open...'

'No wonder he left,' I said, sitting down.

'Medea was only doing the same as me,' Aemos said. 'We were defending you to him, trying to make him understand and see things the way we saw them. We thought–'

'What?'

'We thought he might change his mind and trust you again if he knew it all.'

'I thought you both had more sense,' I said as I strode past them and out of the room.

* * *

There were several craft cradled in the *Essene*'s hangar. Two ferry pods, a bulk pinnace, three standard shuttles and a number of small fliers.

I was busy directing the deck servitors to make a two man speeder flight ready when Medea came in, red-eyed and dressed for the surface in a fleece jacket.

'I'll fly you down,' she said.

'Don't bother. You've done enough.'

'It's my job, Gregor! I'm your pilot!'

'Forget about it.'

I clambered into the tight cockpit of the bright red speeder, pulled the canopy shut and fired up the single, in-line thruster.

The launch chute opened and I shot away from the *Essene* at full throttle.

I tracked his flight path to Catharsis, the capital city of Hubris. Festival flares and fireworks were spitting up above the slanted roofs of the vast inland metropolis. The jubilee was in full swing. Once I had parked the sprightly little flier at Catharsis downport, I found myself weaving through a dense river of jumping, whooping people that clogged the winding streets. All of them showed the grey pallor of recent cold-sleep. All of them were drunk.

Bottles were pressed into my hands and young women and men alike planted kisses on my face. I was jostled and shoved and scattered with petals and confetti. The smell of the cryogenic chemicals sweating out of them permeated the entire town.

It took all afternoon to find him. He was alone in an upstairs suite in a crumbling but characterful hotel overlooking the Processional Tombs.

'Get out,' he said as I opened the door.

'Godwyn...'

'Get the hell out!' he yelled, smashing a shot glass against the far wall. He'd been drinking hard, which was unlike him, although everyone else on Hubris except me must have been in the same state.

Fireworks coughed and whizzed in the square under his windows.

Fischig glowered at me for a long time, and then disappeared into the suite's bathroom. He emerged with two more shot glasses and a dish of ice.

I stood in the doorway and watched as he slowly and carefully prepared two drinks. Anise, poured over smashed ice.

He placed one in front of himself and slid the other one towards the chair opposite.

To me, that was an act of diplomacy.

I sat down facing him and lifted the glass.

'To all we've been together,' I said. We knocked back the shots.

I slid the glass back across the table top towards him and he made two more.

He passed the second one back to me and caught my eyes for the first time. I stared into his face, saw the eye-fogging scar that had already marked him by the time we met, saw the faint mauve scar tissues where the side of his face had been rebuilt after our clash with the saruthi on the warped world orbiting KCX-1288.

'I never meant to run out on you,' he said.

'I didn't ever suppose so. When did Godwyn Fischig last run out on a fight?'

He laughed bitterly. We sank the second drink and he fixed a third.

'Whatever Medea told you. Whatever Aemos told you... it's true. But it's not what you think.'

'Yeah?'

'I'm no heretic, Godwyn.'

'No?'

'I think I might have become what you'd call a radical. But I'm no heretic.'

'Isn't that what a heretic would say?'

'Yes. I guess so. If you'd let me into your mind, you'd see...'

'No thanks!' he shuddered, shoving his chair back with a squeak.

'Okay.' I sipped my glass. 'It won't be the same without you.'

'I know. You and me. Bastards! The Eye of Terror itself was shy of us!'

'Yes it was.'

'We could do it again,' he said.

'We could?'

'We could work side by side like old times and hunt out the darkness.'

'Yes, we could. I'd like that.'

'That's why I'm sorry I ran out like that. I should have stayed.'

I nodded. 'Yes.'

'I owe you that much. I should have tried harder. You're not gone. Not all the way. You're just slipping.'

'Slipping?'

'Into the pit. The radical pit. The pit no one comes back from. But I can pull you out.'

'Pull me out?'

'Yes. It's not too late.'

'Too late for what, Godwyn?'

'Salvation,' he said.

The crowds outside were screaming and clapping. Barrages of fireworks were being launched into the early evening air, scattering new stars in their wake like fireflies.

'What does "salvation" mean?' I asked.

'It's why I'm here, why the Emperor put me at your side. To keep you centred. It's destiny.'

'Is it? And what does destiny entail?'

'Renounce it all. All of it. Give over the *Malus Codicium* to me... the daemonhost, your runestaff. Let me take you back to the Ordos head-quarters on Thracian. You can do penance there. I'll plead for you, plead for leniency. They wouldn't be too hard on you. You'd be active again before too long.'

'You actually believe that you could take me back to the Ordos, tell them what I've done, and they'd let me practise again?'

'They'd understand!'

'Fischig, you don't understand!'

He looked at me, disappointed. 'You won't then?'

'I think this is where I say goodbye. I admire your efforts, but I can't be saved, Godwyn.'

'You can!'

'No,' I shook my head. 'You know why? I don't need saving.'

'Then this is where I say goodbye too,' he said, pouring another drink.

'Remember what we did,' I said.

'Yes.'

I shut the door behind me and left.

It took me three hours to get back to the landing field through the solid mob of revellers. I powered the quick-heeled red speeder back up to the *Essene*.

They were all waiting for me in the hangar as I docked. Maxilla. Crezia. Eleena. Aemos. Medea.

I tugged the rumpled copy of the astropathic communiqué I had received earlier out of my pocket and tossed it at Maxilla. 'We're breaking orbit. New destination: Promody.'

'What about Fischig?' asked Eleena.

'He isn't coming.'

There is a move in Carthean blade work called the *teht uin sah*. The phrase literally describes a position of the feet, but the philosophy is deeper. It means the moment in a duel when you gain the advantage and begin to win home. It is the turning point, the little fulcrum on which a life or death fight turns. The moment your fortunes change and you realise victory can be yours if you rally hard enough.

I felt that the astropathic communiqué from Promody was the equivalent of the *teht uin sah*. It had been sent to me, uncoded, by a trusted friend I hadn't seen in a long time.

It read simply 'Khanjar must be stopped.'

It took the *Essene* ten weeks to reach Promody, a jungle world on the trailing hem of the Scarus sector, specifically the Antimar sub-sector.

I went planetside alone, using the little red speeder, in case it turned out to be a trap.

They were waiting for me on a tropical hillside, below a break of pink-lobed punz trees. The evening was warm and fragrant. Insects fidgeted in the gathering dark. The air was humid.

I got out of the steaming speeder.

My old pupil, Gideon Ravenor, sustained by his force chair, rolled forward across the mossy ground to greet me. To his left, he was flanked by Kara Swole. To his right, Harlon Nayl.

SIXTEEN

SURVIVING MESSINA
GIDEON'S OMEN
NOTHING LASTS FOREVER

Harlon gave me a great bearhug and Kara timidly kissed my cheek on tiptoe. I gazed at them both, hardly believing it.

'You have a habit of coming back from the dead,' I said to Harlon. 'I'm just glad it's real this time.'

He frowned. 'What do you mean?'

'I'll explain later. I refuse to explain anything more until you tell me how this is possible.'

'Why don't we go inside?' Ravenor suggested. He led us back up the path through the punz trees and across glades where the light was stained gold by the fleshy orange leaves that formed the canopy. Brilliantly feathered lizards flitted from branch to branch and diaphanous insects the size of man's open palm fluttered like seedcases in the humid breeze.

Ravenor's force chair hissed over the ground a few centimetres in the air, surrounded and suspended by a spherical field generated by the slowly revolving and tilting antigravity hoop that encircled it.

Beyond the wooded slope, the ground was flooded. A vast lake of yellow liquid stretched out under the jungle canopy that sprouted up from the water in lurid clumps. Fronds, rushes and fibrously rooted trees formed hammock islets in the lake, along with batteries of puffy mauve or orange zutaes with giant leaves and tangles of saprophitic vines.

Antigrav walkboards bridged out across the resinous water, linking the dryland to Ravenor's camp by way of several of the hammocks.

The camp had been raised on a duralloy raft twenty metres square, held above the water by locked, cycling repulsor lift-pods. Angular, geometric, the structure the raft supported looked like a large tent, but I realised from its gentle shimmer that it was formed from intersecting fields of opaque force energy.

We went in through the one-way field membrane that formed the door and entered a cool, climate-controlled chamber lit by glow-globes. Equipment was stacked up in metal containers and there were several items of collapsible furniture. Further screens denoted adjoining rooms, veiled off. A grey-haired man in a linen robe was working at a small camp table, reviewing data on a portable codifier.

Kara unfolded three more of the stacked camp chairs while Harlon fetched bottles of chilled fruit-water and some shrink-wrapped ration packs. A young woman came in from one of the other rooms and conferred quietly with the man at the codifier.

'You're busy here, I see?' I said.

'Yes,' said Ravenor. 'The view should be good.'

I didn't quite understand what he meant but I let it pass. There were other things on my mind.

Harlon thumb-popped the cap of a bottle and passed it to me before taking his seat.

'Here's to us all, still alive despite the odds.' He clinked his bottle against mine and Kara toasted with hers.

'Well?' I said.

'A bunch of hard-arse merc bastards smoked the Distaff. Took the whole spire out. Killed the lot of them,' Harlon said, matter of factly, but there was still an edge of rage in his voice.

'And you?'

'Madam Bequin saved us,' said Kara.

'What?'

'We got her back to Messina okay, stable,' said Kara. 'The medicae facility at the Distaff hall made her comfortable. They got me back on my feet in about a week. Then Madam Bequin suddenly took a turn for the worse.'

'She stroked out,' growled Harlon. 'A really bad whassit called–'

'Cerebrovascular ischemia,' Ravenor said quietly.

'It was beyond the abilities or resources of the hall's medicae, so we rushed her to Sandus Sedar Municipal General for surgery,' said Kara. 'We knew you wouldn't want us to leave her there alone, so we stayed with her in shifts. I took one watch, and alternated with Nayl. On the night the hall was raided, I had just started my shift.'

'And I was on my way back to spire eleven in an air cab,' finished Harlon.

'So neither of you were there?'

'No.'

'You two... and Alizebeth... all survived?'

'Lucky us, eh?' said Harlon.

'Where is she?' I asked. 'And how is she?'

'Never regained consciousness. She's on vital support in my ship's infirmary,' Ravenor replied. 'My personal physician is tending her.' I knew Doctor Antribus, Gideon's medicae. Bequin couldn't be in more experienced hands.

I looked back at Harlon and Kara. I could tell the Loki-born ex-bounty hunter was enjoying stringing this tale out. He'd probably been rehearsing it for weeks.

'So... go on.'

'We went to ground. Me and Kara. We couldn't move Madam B, so we signed her in under a fake identity so she couldn't be linked to your operation. Then me and Kara went hunting. We caught up with the hit squad at a shanty town lift-port down in the suburbs. Thirty of them. Vessorine janissaries, no less. Never tangled with those brothers before, though I'd heard of them, of course. Now, could they fight like bastards.'

'I've seen them up close.'

'Then you'll appreciate that two against thirty, even with the drop to us, was hard ball. I smoked three of them–'

'Two,' corrected Kara. 'It was two.'

'Okay, two definites and a probable. Kara, may the Emperor bless her, took out six of the pigs. Blam blam blam!'

'We can split a bottle of amasec while you give me a play by play later, Nayl. Stick to the meat.'

'My family motto, chief,' Harlon grinned. 'Well, as it turned out, me and Kara had probably bitten off a sight more than we could chew, and we ended up cornered in a freight yard next to the lift-port. Backs to the wall time. Last stand. A change of underwear moment. And then, just like that,' he clicked his fingers, 'salvation arrived.' He looked over at Inquisitor Ravenor.

'Just glad I was able to help.' Ravenor demurred.

'Help? Him and his kill team kicked arse! Far as I could tell, only eight of the mercs got out alive. Jumped their ship and ran off-world.'

I set my empty bottle down on the duralloy floor and sat forward with my elbows on my knees. 'So, Gideon,' I said, 'how in the name of Terra did you come to be there on Messina at the right time?'

'I wasn't,' he said. 'I was there at the wrong time. If I'd reached Messina a day earlier, I'd have been there at the right time. But my ship was delayed by a warp storm that also shut down my communications.'

'That's the second time since I arrived you've been enigmatic,' I said. 'Is that any way to treat your old master?'

Gideon Ravenor had been my interrogator and pupil back in the late 330s, the most promising Inquisitorial candidate I have ever met. A level delta latent psyker with a P.Q. of 171, he had also possessed a genius intellect rounded out with a fine education, and an athlete's physique. During the Holy Novena on Thracian Primaris, he had been caught up in the infamous Atrocity and his body had been woefully crippled. Since that time, he had lived within the cocoon of his force chair, a brilliant mind sustained within a paralysed, useless frame.

But that had not stopped him from becoming one of the Inquisition's finest agents. I myself had sponsored his promotion to full inquisitor status in 346. Since then he had successfully prosecuted hundreds of cases, the most notable being the Gomek Violation and, of course, the Cervan-Holman Affair on Sarum. He had also penned several works of considerable insight: the celebrated essays *Towards an Imperial Utopia, Reflections on the Hive State* and *Terra Redux: A History of the early Inquisition*, a study of warp craft that was fast becoming a standard primer, and a work called *The Mirror of Smoke* that dealt with man's interaction with the warp-state with such conspicuous perception and poetry that I believed it would survive as much as art as it was instruction.

Ravenor was all but invisible within the dim globe of his chair's field, just a shapeless shadow suspended in the fizzling gloom. His body was utterly redundant and everything he did was performed by psi-force alone. His mind had grown stronger in his infirmity, compensating for the things denied him. I was sure he was now much more than a level delta psionic.

'My work in the last few years has required me to develop an understanding of divination and prophecy,' Gideon said slowly. 'Things have been... revealed to me. Things of great significance.'

I could tell he was being very careful about what he said. It was as if he wished to tell me more but didn't dare. I decided I should respect his caution, and allow him to tell me only what he felt he could.

'One of those revelations – a vision, if you like – forecast that a violent fate would befall the Distaff on Messina. The event was predicted to the precise hour. But I couldn't get there in time to prevent it.'

'The destruction of the Distaff was predicted?' I said.

'With distressing accuracy,' he replied.

I suddenly realised I was hearing his voice, by which I mean the voice Ravenor had used before his terrible injuries, a voice produced by a man whose mouth and larynx had not been melted by burning promethium. I had become so used to the monotone synthetic speech of his chair's psi-activated voxsponder.

'My work has also allowed me perfect stronger psionic abilities,' he said, and one of them was clearly reading my surface thoughts. 'I ditched the voxsponder about a year ago. I have developed enough psionic control to broadcast my speech naturally.'

'I'm hearing you in my head?'

'Yes, Gregor. Hearing the voice you're used to. It doesn't work with untouchables or psychically shielded individuals of course – THAT'S WHY I KEEP THE OLD VOXSPONDER ON STANDBY.'

He uttered the last part of his sentence mechanically via the toneless voice box built into his chair and the grating, emotion-free electronic words made us all laugh with surprise.

'Though I was too late to save the Distaff, I got Kara, Harlon and Alizebeth to safety off-world.'

'For that, you have my gratitude. But why summon me so far off the beaten track to meet with you?'

'Promody has secrets that we need,' he said.

'What manner of secrets?'

'I have been allowed to see the future, Gregor,' Ravenor said. 'And it isn't pretty.'

'Imperial culture has never set much store by divination,' Gideon told me. 'I have come to suspect that is a great weakness.'

It was much later. Night had fallen over the swampy bayou and the air was dancing with bioluminescent flies. Ravenor and I had taken a stroll along the grav walks behind his camp.

'A weakness? Surely it is a greater weakness to take it seriously? If we believed the rantings of every dribbling marketplace seer, of every demented Ecclesiarchy prophet who claimed to have been granted divine revelations–'

'We would be mad, true. Most of it is rubbish, lies, mischief, the delusions of broken minds. Sometimes prophetic insights are genuine, but they are usually made by psykers who have either done it by accident or who are insane. In either case, the visions are untrustworthy or too confused to be interpreted in any practical, useful way. But just because mankind isn't very good at it doesn't mean it can't be done.'

'It is my understanding that other races are reputed to excel at it,' I said.

'That has certainly been my experience,' he replied. 'Serving the Ordo Xenos has been enlightening. The more I have studied alien races in order to discern their weaknesses, the more I have learned their strengths.'

'We are talking about the eldar, aren't we?' I risked the question. He didn't reply immediately. His last words had been close to heresy. The force sphere around him flickered slightly with anxiety.

'They are a strange breed. They are able to read the invisible geography of space-time and unravel probability with great precision. But they are mercurial. Sometimes they use their insight as a lever to change the outcome of events. Sometimes they stand idle and watch as prophecies play out. I believe there is no human alive who could explain why they make the choices they do. We just don't see things the way they do.'

'Their greater lifespan gives them greater perspective...'

'It's partly that. Although orthodox thinking would say that greater perspective is their curse. The Ministorum believes the eldar are too resigned to destiny. That they are indolent and almost cruel, or else brutally manipulative.'

'You don't think so?'

'I'll admit only a selfish fascination, Gregor. They interact with the fundamental structure of the universe. As you might well appreciate, any talent for living or perceiving beyond one's physical body is attractive to me. My work has–'

He broke off.

'Gideon?'

'I wanted to learn something of the way their minds witness reality independent of their bodies. Their farseers, for example, have a kinaesthetic sensibility that operates regardless of the restraints of time and space–'

We paused at the edge of a walkway and looked out across the misty nocturnal swamp. Glowing insects and airborne spores drifted in the air, their paths occasionally punctuated by the sudden swoops of aerial night hunters. Sinuous things moved through the glistening water below the floating walkways, barely disturbing the oily surface.

'I've said too much,' he murmured.

'You do not need to be guarded with me, Gideon. I will not judge you for seeking knowledge. I'm... not the puritan you once knew.'

'I know. I would tell you if I could. But in order to learn certain things, I have been forced to make promises.'

'To the eldar?'

'I cannot even confirm that. I am not proud of the promises, but I will honour them.'

'Then what can you tell me? You said that things had been revealed to you.'

'One of their kind has foreseen a great darkness ahead of us all. It is so abrupt and acute that it has twisted and altered the skeins of probability that the eldar read. It was revealed to him in a sequence of connected visions.

One of those was the destruction of the Distaff. When that came true, I was shaken. It proved the visions were not fanciful.'

'What else has he seen?' I asked.

'A living blade, a man-machine, bestriding a long-dead world and preparing to strike a blow that will spill human and eldar blood alike,' he said. 'After that... nothing.'

I looked down at him. 'Nothing?'

'Nothing. That vision is the most distant thing he is now able to see. It's no more than six months from now. Beyond that, he has been unable to glimpse anything at all.'

'Why?'

'Because there is no future left to see.'

SEVENTEEN

PSYCHOARCHAEOLOGY
GHÜL
THE BARQUE OF THE DAEMON

Gideon's message to me proved that he already knew the name Khanjar the Sharp, but as we talked, I discovered he knew very little besides the name.

'Nayl and I tracked the janissaries after they fled Messina in an effort to discover who had hired them. It was well hidden. The Vessorine take great pains to protect the identity of their clients. There were false trails, payments from bogus accounts and via holding companies. But we wormed it out eventually. Khanjar the Sharp.'

'Which meant what to you?'

'Nothing... except that he was the individual who had ordered the systematic destruction of your operation... and that his name featured prominently in a number of the farseer's visions. We believe Khanjar and the man-machine from the climactic revelation are one and the same.'

'Khanjar the Sharp is Pontius Glaw,' I said.

He was astonished and excited. The revelations had said nothing of Glaw. The Khanjar guise had masked his true identity from the eldar.

'Why target you?' he asked.

'Self-preservation. I am one of the few people who knows he still exists. In fact, I'm sorry to say, he exists *because* of me. He was also searching for something that he believes I possess.'

'Like what?'

I had no choice but to tell him everything. My dealings with Glaw, Marla Tarray, the *Malus Codicium*...

'You weren't joking when you said you weren't the puritan I once knew,' he said.

'Are you shocked?'

'No, Gregor, I'm not. I believe radicalism is inevitable. We all become radicals eventually as we appreciate that we must know our enemy in order to defeat him. The real dangers come from extreme puritans. Puritanism is fuelled by ignorance, and ignorance is the greatest peril of all. That's not to suggest the path of the radical is easy. Eventually even the most careful and responsible radical will be overwhelmed by the warp. The real judge of character is what good a man can do for the Imperium before he is drawn too far.'

'There is one other thing. In the mind of his daughter there was an image of a desiccated world that closely matches the one you describe from the eldar revelations. There was a name connected with it: *Ghül.*'

'Let me investigate that further,' he said, and turned his force chair back down the walkway towards the camp.

Ravenor had brought me to that remote jungle world because Promody had featured in another of the eldar visions. Khanjar the Sharp had been there recently, perhaps as little as six weeks before. Ravenor intended to find out why.

Ravenor's field team numbered about ten individuals – several technicians, six astropaths and an archaeologist called Kenzer, the grey-haired man I had seen earlier.

'But there are no ruins on Promody,' I remarked shortly after I had been introduced to him.

'Not any more, sir,' he agreed. 'But there is compelling theory that Promody was once one of several worlds inhabited by an ancient culture.'

'How ancient?'

He glanced at me nervously. 'Pre-Dawn,' he said.

A culture from before the rise of man. That was breathtaking.

'So this compelling theory,' I pressed, 'this comes from the eldar?'

He didn't want to answer but my rank gave him little option.

'Yes, sir. But this culture predates even them. And was quite dead long before even they came to the stars.'

Ravenor's technicians had spent their time since reaching Promody conducting a survey with the assistance of the astropaths. They had studied the surface and atmosphere of the planet for signs of Khanjar's visit, looking for traces of landing sites, the residual pollution of vehicle exhausts, the echoes of human minds. They were certain now that the campsite on the bayou was close to the place where Khanjar made planetfall. Now the astropaths were preparing for an auto-seance on a scale greater than any I had ever attempted.

Gideon called me to the force tent.

'Ghül is the name of a planet,' he said.

'The dead world in the vision?'

'Quite probably.'

'And where is it?'

'We don't know.'

'Who's we? Where did this information come from?'

He sighed. 'Lord seer?' he called.

One of the inner screens drew aside and a slim, very tall figure in a long, hooded robe stepped through from the privacy of the inner rooms. The robe was made of a gleaming blue material that flashed like shot-silk but seemed heavier and more fluid. There was a strange, unpleasantly sweet scent, like burnt sugar. I knew that hood would never be drawn back in my presence. I was not fit to see the face beneath.

'This is Eisenhorn,' the figure said. It wasn't a question. The words flowed melodically with a strange cadence that no human could ever approximate.

'Who am I addressing?' I said.

'The book is in his coat,' the figure said to Ravenor, ignoring me. 'An insult that he carries it so casually.'

'Gregor?'

I took the *Malus Codicium* from my pocket. The figure made a warding gesture with its gloved right hand.

'It's an insult that your friend will have to tolerate, I'm afraid,' I said. 'This isn't leaving my person.'

'It has contaminated him. It smoulders in his blood. It has yoked him to daemons.'

'And more besides, no doubt,' I countered. 'But take one look into my mind and tell me I'm not dedicated to the salvation of all of us.'

I dropped my psi-shield provocatively, but though I could sense the eldar's temptation to look, he did not touch my mind.

'Ravenor vouches for you,' the hooded figure said after a moment. 'I will content myself with that. But do not come any closer.'

'So what do I call you?'

'You won't have any need to,' the eldar replied bluntly.

'Please,' Gideon cut in. He was clearly very uncomfortable. 'Gregor, you may refer to my guest as "lord seer". My lord, perhaps you could tell Gregor about Ghül?'

'In the First Days, a race came from the maelstrom and raised settlements in this space. Seven worlds they made, and the greatest of these was Ghül. Then they were overturned and left no trace behind.'

'From the maelstrom? From the warp? You mean a daemon race?'

The lord seer said nothing.

'Are you saying daemons once colonised seven worlds in our reality?'

'They fled a war. Their king was dead and they carried his body for burial. On his tomb they raised the first city, and then made six worlds around it to honour his rest forever.'

'Ghül is the tomb of a daemon king?'

There was no response.

'What? Are you just going to answer every other question? Is Ghül the tomb-world? Is that what Glaw is after? The tomb of a daemon?'

'I have not seen the answer,' said the eldar.

'Then take a wild guess!'

'The daemon king is dead. Khanjar cannot hope to raise him.'

'Unless he has the *Malus Codicium*,' I said.

'Not even then.'

'So what, then?' I snapped.

'Traditionally,' Gideon put in, 'in human culture, anyway, a king is buried with great treasures and artefacts beside him.'

'So there's something in this tomb. Something so valuable that the *Malus Codicium* is just a key to get it. Where is Ghül?'

'We don't know,' said Ravenor.

'Does Glaw know?'

'I think that's why he was here.'

The eldar withdrew and I was glad to be out of his presence. I found it hard to know how Ravenor tolerated him.

Outside, the final preparations were being made. All of Ravenor's people except Kenzer and the six astropaths were withdrawing to his ship. Nayl and Kara were going to the *Essene*.

'A message from Maxilla,' Nayl said to me. 'You've had a communiqué from Fischig.'

'Fischig? Really?'

'It seems he's changed his mind. That he regrets his clash with you and wants to come back.'

'I think it's too late for that, Harlon.'

Nayl shrugged. 'Cut him some slack, I say, boss. You know how hardline he is. He's had time to think about things. Get his head around stuff. Let him come back. From what Gideon's been saying, we could probably use him.'

'No. Later maybe. Not now. I don't think I can trust him.'

'He probably thinks the same thing about you,' grinned Nayl. 'Joke!' he added, raising his hands to pacify me. 'Good luck,' he finished, then walked off to the shuttle where Kara Swole was waiting.

It was just dawn. Before their departure, the technicians had extended the antigrav walkways to form a circular path across the bayou fifty metres in diameter. The astropaths spread out around the suspended walkways under the thick, steaming vegetation. I stood with Gideon and Kenzer on one of the central sections. The evenly spaced astropaths began to murmur as they sank into their trances and the air became charged with psypathic energy.

Instead of focusing on a single object, as Jecud Vance and I had done with Midas's jacket, the astropaths were opening the entire area up, conjuring its psychic traces. A cold, blue glow began to spread around us, quite at odds with the light of the rising sun. Things became filmy and misty.

'I see something...' Kenzer said.

So did I. Shapes, like clouds, writhing and forming above the water at the centre of the circle. Nothing distinct.

I felt Ravenor reach out with his mind and fine tune the coherence of the image. Just standing there beside him, I could feel how strong his mind had grown. My old pupil was frighteningly powerful.

Suddenly the image resolved. Three figures, wading through the bayou's knee-deep water. One, a massive ogryn with a blaster cannon, followed in the splashing wake of a sturdy male human dressed in beige combat armour, his face hidden by a rebreather. This human was scanning the area with a hand-held auspex. The third figure was beside him. It was tall, broad, and moved with a strange stiffness, its body partially draped with what looked at first like a cape of feathers.

They weren't feathers. They were blades. Tongues of polished, sharpened metal interlaced into an armoured garment. Beneath it, I could glimpse a body of burnished chrome, duralloy and steel, a mechanical humanoid body of marvellous design.

The work of Magos Geard Bure, I had no doubt. The late Geard Bure.

This was Khanjar the Sharp. The man-machine… the 'living blade' from the eldar vision. Pontius Glaw.

I could see his face. It was the face of a beautiful young man with a mane of curled hair, but the hair didn't move and the expression didn't alter from a curling smirk. It was a mask worked from gold, like the head of a noble gilded statue. I had seen the face before, in old records that showed Pontius Glaw in his prime.

There was no sound, but Glaw said something to his point man. Then he turned and seemed to address someone or something we couldn't see.

There was a long pause as they waited and then the ogryn shuffled back, as if alarmed by something. The point man set his auspex to close focus. Glaw stood still as if awestruck for a moment, then clapped his metal hands in delight.

'I can't see what they're doing…' Kenzer said.

'There's nothing there to see,' Gideon snapped in disappointment. That seemed to be the case. There was a faint visual distortion where the psychic ghost of the location failed to match its real counterpart exactly. But nothing else.

'No,' I said suddenly. 'I think there is. Get your astropaths to widen the field of the seance.'

'What?' Gideon asked.

'Just do it.'

With a little effort, Ravenor's telepaths managed to increase the diameter of the conjured scene. Almost at once, were able to make out shadowy figures lurking around the edge.

'Psykers!' said Gideon.

'Exactly,' I said. 'The reason we can't see what he's up to is because he did what we're doing!'

'An auto-seance.'

'That's right.'

'How did you guess, Gregor?'

'Mr Kenzer here said there were no ancient remains on Promody. Glaw has to be looking for the past by other means.'

'But we can't resolve what it is he's seeing…'

'Go back,' said a voice behind us. Silently, the eldar seer had joined us on the walkway.

'Go back,' he said again.

It took a few minutes for the astropaths to compose themselves and re-establish the image. Now I could feel the eldar's mental strength supporting them.

We watched as the scene replayed. The three figures approached us just as before. Glaw conversed with his point man and then called back to his psykers.

The world changed.

There was no jungle. No water. Great, smooth cliffs of rock blocked out the sky. Stone columns like giant fir trees towered over us. We were seeing what Glaw's psykers had allowed him to see. The surface of Promody as it had been eons before the age of man. A cyclopean city of glassy black rock that had long since vanished so completely only its psychic phantom remained.

'God-Emperor!' Kenzer gasped and collapsed in a faint. It was terrifying. Mesmeric. The scale was so big. We felt like microbes or motes of dust on the streets of an Imperial hive.

I stared, fascinated. Now when the ogryn shuffled back in fear and Glaw stood awestruck, I could see why. Glaw clapped his hands in delight and the point man began scanning a wide section of the ghostly wall with his auspex.

'There's an inscription!' Ravenor cried.

I leapt off the walkway and waded through the oily water until I was beside the images of Glaw and his men. 'We need to get this before it fades!' I shouted. Ravenor flew his chair in over the water to join me. Recording sensors in his chair began to whir and store the images.

They were written in a language I had never seen before. It made me sick to look at it. There was no linear form. It simply spiralled and meandered up across the massive wall face, looping and circling.

I felt dizzy. Glaw was capering and dancing like a lunatic, his machine body lurching and awkward.

The light around us began to wink and flicker.

'We're losing it,' said Ravenor.

'Probably time we did...' I said, stumbling back towards the walkway.

The colossal city melted away. Then Glaw and his companions vanished and blue light ebbed away.

Ravenor's telepaths were slumped on the walkways, exhausted. The eldar stood, head bowed.

'It looked like a chart.'

'It was a chart,' said the eldar. 'A plan of the seven worlds. And on it was the location of Ghül.'

Pontius Glaw knew where he was going. He'd known for some weeks. He might already have arrived.

It took Ravenor and the lord seer about a day to make sense of the findings. Allowing for procession and sidereal shifts as best they could considering the vast passage of time involved, they determined that the world known before the time of man as Ghül was in an uncharted system designated 5213X, three months outside Imperial space and twenty weeks from our current location.

We made preparation to break orbit the following night. Ravenor explained to me that the eldar had requested to be taken to a secret location en route, where he could access something called a warp tunnel. Ravenor was beholden to him.

We agreed to rendezvous at Jeganda, three weeks short of 5213X, prior to the final leg of our chase.

'Do we inform the Ordos?' Ravenor asked.

'No. What strength they could lend us would be outweighed by problems they'd cause. I will prepare a full documented account of everything we know to be transmitted back in the event that we...'

'We?'

'Fail,' I finished.

Before we departed, I dared to visit Ravenor's ship, the *Hinterlight*. I took Crezia and Harlon Nayl with me. Medicae Antribus showed us to the low-lit chamber off the starship's infirmary where Alizebeth lay inside a softly glowing stasis field.

Crezia and Harlon hung back by the hatchway.

Alizebeth looked like she was asleep. Her skin was as pale as the snows of the high Atenates.

'Is she alive?' I asked Antribus.

'Yes, sir.'

'I mean... without these vital supports, the stasis field–?'

'If we shut them down, she may remain the way she is. But she might also fade. It is never easy to tell in cases of such significant injury.'

'Will she recover?' I asked.

'No,' he said, caring enough to look me in the eyes. 'Except for some miracle. She will never regain consciousness or mobility.'

'So she's dead to us? Has she any quality of life?'

'Who can say, sir? She's not in any pain. I believe she is dreaming an endless, tranquil dream. If you consider that to be cruel, we can disconnect the machines and let nature take its course.'

He withdrew. Crezia appeared at my side.

'What are you going to do, Gregor?' she asked.

'I won't turn the machines off. Not yet. My mind's too full of that bastard Glaw. I'll make a decision afterwards.' If there is afterwards, I thought. 'I'd like you and Nayl to stay with her. Look after her. Will you do that?'

'Of course,' she said. I realised this was the first time she'd ever set eyes on Alizebeth Bequin.

'Really? It's a big thing to ask of you.'

'I'm a doctor, and your friend, Gregor. It's not a big thing.'

I turned to go.

'She can probably hear you,' she said suddenly.

'Do you think so?'

Crezia shrugged and smiled. 'I don't know. There's every chance she can. And if she can't, does it matter?'

'Does what matter?'

'Tell her, Gregor. Now, before you go. Tell her, for goodness sake. Do the right thing by one of us at least.'

She left me alone and I sat down beside Alizebeth's cot.

And then, though I don't know to this day if she ever heard or understood, I told her all the things I should have told her years before.

* * *

I said goodbye to Ravenor and promised to wait for him at Jeganda. I kissed Crezia goodbye and went to the *Hinterlight*'s hangar to cross back to the *Essene*. Nayl came to see me off.

I shook his hand. 'Keep an eye on Gideon,' I said.

He frowned. 'You don't trust him?' he asked.

'With my life. But I don't trust his friends.'

As the *Essene* pulled away from Promody, gathering speed as it headed for the immaterium translation point Maxilla's Navigator had calculated, I went to find Aemos.

He was in his suite of rooms, puzzling his way through a deep stack of books he'd borrowed from Maxilla's library.

'Something else to divert you,' I said, handing him a pile of data-slates and record tiles. Before we had parted company, Ravenor had copied for me everything he had been permitted to copy, including a pict-file of the inscription as his force chair's sensors had recorded it.

'Gideon has marked some key passages in his notes to get you up to speed, but the inscription, which is a chart, is what really interests me. Gideon's... associate... told me what it means, or the part of it that applies to Ghül, anyway. I'd like to know a little more, in literal terms.'

'You want me to decipher an alien text that was long dead before man appeared?'

Put like that it was a tall order. 'There are some other samples of the same script that Ravenor obtained from other sites. I don't know. Do what you can with it. Anything you can turn up will be useful.'

The voyage to Jeganda was not the longest I have ever undertaken, but it felt like it. I was fretful and ill at ease, impatient to arrive. My mind would not stop thinking about Glaw's head start, or how close the farseer's nothingness loomed.

To fill the time, I meditated and exercised, burrowed my way through Maxilla's library in search of anything pertaining to the eldar and their legends. Kara worked to get Medea up to fitness and, after two weeks, the three of us were running through demanding combat training each day. Sometimes Eleena joined us for the lighter sessions to keep in shape. I was glad I had an untouchable with me, given our destination and Glaw's abilities.

Except for Alizebeth, who didn't really count under the circumstances, Eleena was the last living member of the Distaff. I wondered if I would ever recruit and build it again.

I wondered if I would even get the chance.

During the third week, Aemos called me to his suite to discuss his findings so far. I wondered why he hadn't simply told me over dinner. We all met for a meal each evening anyway.

He told me he was making progress. The ancient culture which had built Ghül appeared indirectly in several old sources. It seems that early Imperial explorers had known myths of a dead, precursor race from some of their first contacts with xenos species, though Aemos was concerned that some of the references could be to other dead cultures, or to species that had migrated or transplanted themselves.

One theme emerged. The race of Ghül were marked as 'others' or 'outsiders' because they had not originated in our galaxy. The name 'Ghül' itself didn't appear anywhere.

'One minor culture, the Doy of Mitas, have a legend concerning the "xol-xonxoy", daemons who ruled once and would return. The word meant "warped ones".'

'A good enough description as any. The eldar seemed convinced that the culture was a colony of daemons from the warp. Not even a race in its own right, more a host, an army... a nation. An exiled daemon-king and his followers, perhaps.'

'There are a few more bits and pieces, not much. I'm getting nowhere with the inscription, though it is extraordinary, and Gideon's footage of that seance most perturbatory. I'd like to borrow your book.'

'You what?'

'Your damned book. I use the adjective advisedly.'

'You said you never wanted to see it again,' I reminded him.

'I don't, Gregor. It chills me to know it is even on board. But what chills me more is what we're going out there to find. And you've asked me to do a job. And that's the only tool available to me that I haven't used.'

I took the *Malus Codicium* from my pocket. For a moment I couldn't bring myself to pass it to him.

'Be careful,' I hissed.

'I know the procedures,' he said grumpily. 'You've had me study prohibited texts before.'

'Not like this one.'

I kept an eye on Aemos after that, visiting him regularly and making sure he came to meals. He became tired and short-tempered. I wanted to take the book away from him, but he said he was nearly done.

We were a week from Jeganda when he finished his work.

'It's incomplete,' he warned, 'but the main elements are there.'

He seemed even more fatigued than before and had developed a slight shake on his left side. His suite was a mess of papers and slates, notes and scrawlings, scattered books. In places, where he had apparently run out of paper, he had continued his notes on tabletops or even walls.

Uber Aemos had performed his greatest work of service for me, the hardest task I had ever set him. And it had cost him. It had damaged his health and, I was afraid, his sanity.

'The daemon-king,' he said, spreading out a large sheet of scribbled-on vellum across the litter on his desk, 'who is represented by this glyph here...' he pointed with a palsied finger, '...and by this triple formation of symbols here was called Y-Y-Y–'

'Aemos?'

'Yssarile!' He all but had to spit the word out of his mouth to make the sound. The gilded clock on the table beside his unmade bed chimed twice suddenly for no reason.

'It keeps doing that,' Aemos growled crossly. His finger stabbed another mark on the paper for me to look at and then traced down a curling line of script. His notes, I realised, had taken the form of the chart itself. 'Here, look. There was a war. The daemon-king Y-Y-'

'Just call him the daemon-king.'

'The daemon-king fought a war of staggering enmity with a rival. The rival's name is not given, but from the marking here, I would guess it was one of what we tentatively understand to be the four primary powers of Chaos, although it seems there were only three at that time. I wonder why?'

I couldn't answer that. I wondered if the farseer could.

'The rival is described as a foul sorcerer,' Aemos continued. 'I don't pretend or want to know the hierarchies of the warp, but in simple terms, Y-Y-damnit! Yssarile! was a lieutenant, a warlord, a prince... whatever you want to call it, who tried to usurp the place of this primary power.'

Aemos unrolled another crumpled sheet and wiped pencil shavings off it. 'The war lasted... a billion years. As we would understand it. The daemon-king was destroyed by his rival. Killed outright. His host fled in terror at this crushing defeat, and sought sanctuary in the material universe. Our universe. There they established a capital and six kindred colonies. The capital, Ghül, was built upon the daemon-king's mausoleum, which was itself constructed around his barque.'

'His barque?'

'I suppose they mean his ship. The word is closer to "chariot" or "galley" in literal terms. And I think this may be the key point. The barque was his war machine, the craft that he rode into battle. It is described - here, and also here - as being of such power and might that the warped ones who wrote this were themselves staggered by it.'

He looked at me. 'The barque of the daemon-king. A weapon of inconceivable power that lies entombed in the mausoleum of Ghül. That prize, so I am told, is what Glaw is after.'

'Told?'

He started, shaking his head. 'I'm tired. I meant that's what I've learned. From this. My work.'

'You said "told".'

'I did not.'

'Distinctly.'

'Yes, well I did. Because I used the wrong word. Learned. That's what I have learned.'

I put my hand on his shoulder, reassuringly, but he flinched. 'Aemos, you've done an extraordinary job with this. I've asked a lot of you.'

'Yes, you have.'

'Too much.'

'I serve you, sir. It is never too much.'

'I'll have Maxilla prepare another room for you. You can't sleep in here.'

'I'm used to the clutter,' he said.

'It's not the clutter I'm worried about.'

He shuffled away, muttering.

'I need to take the book back now,' I said.

'It's here somewhere,' he said, off-hand. 'I'll bring it to you later.'

'I'll take it now.'

He glared at me.

'Now, please,' I repeated.

He pulled the *Malus Codicium* from under a pile of notes that fluttered onto the carpet, and held it out. I took hold, but he would not let go.

'Aemos...'

I managed to yank the book away. The clock mischimed again.

'I think you should consider your options, Gregor,' he said.

'What do you mean?'

'The powers we face are great. Too great, perhaps. We are woefully under-strength. I think we should be stronger.'

'How do you propose we do that?'

'Summon the daemonhost.'

'What?'

He took off his heavy augmetic eyeglasses and polished the lenses with the corner of his robe.

His hands were shaking badly now.

'I didn't approve before, on Durer. But I think I grasp things a little better now. I understand the choices you've made. The rules you've bent. All for the good, and I apologise for ever doubting you. With the daemonhost, we might stand a chance. Summon it here.'

'How?'

He became agitated with me. 'Like you did on Miquol!'

'That was sheer desperation,' I reproved.

'We're desperate now!'

'And we have no host to summon it into...'

'You didn't then!'

'And it nearly killed us with its raw power before I could trap it.'

'Then use one of Maxilla's astropaths as a host!'

I stared at him levelly. 'I won't kill a man just to provide a host.'

'You did on Miquol,' he hissed softly.

'What did you just say?'

'You did on Miquol. Verveuk wasn't dead. You sacrificed him for the good of us all. Why would you flinch from doing it again?'

'Why would I do again something I wish had never happened?'

'Are we not playing for the highest stakes? One life, sir. What is that compared to the millions that may die if Glaw succeeds? Summon the daemonhost. Summon Cherubael to help us.'

I walked slowly to the door. 'Get some rest,' I said with forced lightness. 'You'll feel better for it. You'll have changed your mind.'

'Whatever,' he said, turning away dismissively.

He was entirely unprepared for the will I unleashed at him.

'What did it say to you?' I commanded.

Aemos cried out and his legs gave way. He crashed to the deck and half overturned a table in his efforts to stay upright.

His papers avalanched onto the floor.

'It told you, didn't it? It told you! You damn fool, Uber, what did you do?'

'I couldn't crack the code!' he wailed. 'The language was beyond me! But there was so much more in that book! That beautiful book! I realised I could do more!'

'You spoke to the daemonhost.'

'Nooo!'

'Then how else would you know its name, because I sure as hell never told you!'

He shrieked out and staggered back to his feet, his face locked in a grimace of pain and shame and fear.

'It was there in the pages!' he cried. 'Close like a whisper in my ear! So soft! It said it could help! It said it would tell me everything I needed if I could only arrange its release!'

'Oh, God-Emperor! Everything you've told me today you learned from that bastard thing Cherubael!'

'It was true!' he screamed. 'True! Yssarile! Yssarrrrilllle!'

The clock began to chime furiously. A glass pitcher and three tumblers on the bureau shattered. One lens of Aemos's eyeglasses cracked clean across.

He collapsed onto the floor.

I summoned servitors and took him to the sickbay. For safety, we locked him in an isolation bay. His safety, and ours.

The damn clock was still chiming when I went back to his room to burn the papers.

EIGHTEEN

MEETING AT JEGANDA
MISPLACED LOYALTIES
TO THE LAST, TO THE DEATH

Aemos. All that last week of travel, he was my primary concern. I kept a watch on him in the infirmary, but he was generally unresponsive. He woke a few hours after the confrontation, and then said nothing. He refused to eat at first, and remained awake, day and night, staring at the locked door of the isolation chamber.

I dearly wished I hadn't had to lock it.

After a day he took food and drink, but remained silent. We all attempted to get some reaction from him. Both Medea and Maxilla tried for hours at a time.

By the time we reached Jeganda, a day ahead of schedule, our mood was low.

I had never realised before then how central to our team spirit Aemos had been. We all missed him. We all hated what had happened.

I hated myself for allowing it.

Aemos had been careless where I should have been able to trust him, but even so... it was my doing. I hated myself.

And I hated Cherubael, whose baleful influence had been cursing my life for too long. I wondered if I would ever - could ever - be free of it.

I made a resolution. If I lived, if I vanquished Glaw, I would destroy the *Malus Codicium* and then return to Gudrun and destroy Cherubael. I would take my runestaff and annihilate it, just as I had annihilated its kin Prophaniti on Farness Beta.

Jeganda system is dominated by a huge, ringed gas giant. In orbit above it is an semi-automated waystation established and maintained by a consortium of trade guilds and Navigator houses as a stop-over and service facility.

The *Essene* coasted in. There was no sign of any other vessels. Maxilla made contact with the station master and a drone tug led us into one of the wide docking gantries that extended from the rim of the dish-shaped station.

I crossed via the airgate with Maxilla and Medea and we were met by the master, a hirsute, sluggish man called Okeen. He ran the place with a staff of four. It was a twenty-month contract, he explained, and then they stood down in favour of a fresh crew. They didn't get many visitors, he told us.

They'd be happy to resupply the *Essene*'s technical needs, for a competitive price, he told us.

He told us plenty. Isolation does terrible things to men's minds.

We couldn't shut him up. I finally left him with Maxilla. Maxilla could talk too.

Medea and I went to the station's central hub to see if the resident astropath had received any messages for us from Gideon. It was a dismal place of rotting and poorly maintained hallways and dark hangars. There was a background smell that I decided was spoiled meat and Medea maintained was stale lactose.

It turned out that, despite Okeen's non-stop chatter, there was one thing he hadn't told us.

Someone was waiting for us in the recreation lounge.

'Gregor.' Fischig rose to his feet from a threadbare couch. He was dressed in black with a waist-length shipboard cape of dark red, wire-shot fully that was secured at his throat with a small, silver Inquisitorial crest.

I faced him across the room. 'What are you doing here, Godwyn?'

'Waiting for you, Gregor. Waiting for a chance to make things right.'

'And how do you propose doing that?'

He shrugged. It was an open, relaxed, almost apologetic gesture. 'I said things I shouldn't have. Judged you too quickly. I always was a hard-nosed idiot. You'd think my years of service with you might have taught me the error.'

'You'd think,' quipped Medea.

I held up a warning finger to silence her. 'You made your feelings perfectly clear on Hubris, Fischig. I'm not sure we can work together any more. There's a mutual lack of trust.'

'Which I want to do away with,' he said. I'd never heard him so calm or sincere.

'Godwyn, you questioned my purity, branded some of my actions heretical and then offered to redeem me.'

'I was drunk for that last part,' he said, with a tiny flash of smile.

'Yes, you were. And what are you now?'

'Here. Willing. Reconciled.'

'Well,' I said. 'Let's start with the "here" part. How the hell did you know I'd be here?'

He paused. I looked round slowly at Medea who was studying the deck.

'You told him where I'd be, didn't you?'

'Uhm...'

'Didn't you?'

She snapped round to face me, every bit as haughty and rebellious as her dear, damned father. 'All right, I did! Okay? We need Fischig–'

'Maybe we don't, girl.'

'Don't "girl" me, you bastard! He's one of us. One of the band. He kept sending to the ship. Sending and sending. You wouldn't listen to him, so I replied.'

'Nayl told me he'd sent one message.'

'Yeah,' she said snidely. 'And Nayl told me what you'd sent back. The big brush-off. To a man who's devoted his life to you. A man who got a bit angry with you and then thought about it and regretted it. Fischig wants to make amends. He wants to be with us again. Haven't you ever regretted anything?'

'More than you can possibly imagine, Medea. But you should have told me.'

'I asked her not to,' Fischig said. 'I imagined how you'd react. I'm grateful Medea thought so highly of me. Could you not find it in you to trust me again? Trust me like she does?'

'Quite possibly. But I wanted to do it on my terms, when I was ready. There's too much going on just now.'

'Oh, come on,' implored Medea.

'How did you get here?' I asked Fischig sharply.

'I got passage on a tramp trader. It dropped me off here a week ago.'

I'd asked the question so I could test his reply and get a measure of his veracity. As he answered, and I probed delicately out with my mind, I found the last thing I was expecting.

'Why are you psi-shielded?' I asked.

'Just a precaution,' he said.

'Against what?' I demanded.

'Against this moment,' Fischig said. There was true anguish in his eyes. He drew the compact bolt pistol out from under his cape.

'Fischig!' Medea howled in horror.

Barbarisater was already in my hands, humming. 'Don't be a fool,' I said.

He'd only be a fool if he was doing this alone.

The words were not vocal. They were burning wires of psychic venom wrapped around a monstrous cudgel of mental force that smashed into the back of my skull. I stumbled forward, half-blind. Medea fell over hard, totally unconscious.

I saw figures emerging from the doorways off the lounge space all around. Five, six, more. Men dressed in the hooded, burgundy armour of an inquisitor's personal retinue, their chest plates decorated with gold leaf in the form of the Inquisition's crest. Two of them grabbed me and ripped the force sword from my slack fingers. The others aimed their weapons at me.

'Don't hurt him! Don't hurt him!' Fischig cried.

The guards dragged me round to face an individual emerging from the lounge's greasy kitchenette area. I saw a tall man in black armour and robes, with a monstrous face that had been surgically deformed to inspire fear and loathing. It was equine, snouted, with a mouth full of blunt teeth and dark pools for eyes. Fibre-wire and fluid-tubes formed gleaming ropes across the back of his skull.

He'd once been the pupil and interrogator of my old, long-dead ally Commodus Voke. Now he was an inquisitor in his own right.

'Eisenhorn. How simply vile to see you again,' said Golesh Constantine Pheppos Heldane.

* * *

The guards dragged Medea and me back on board the *Essene*. I was still dazed. I could hear Fischig begging Heldane to order his men to be more careful with us.

Oh, what a mistake Fischig had made.

As we were bundled through the stations docking gantries, I saw the sleek black shape of an Inquisitorial cruiser now occupying the dock station next to the *Essene*. Heldane's ship. It had probably lain concealed in the atmosphere of the gas giant until the trap was sprung.

They took us into the main stateroom. Heldane's men, and I guessed there must have been a full detachment, had secured the *Essene*.

'How many travellers with you?' Heldane snapped at me.

I made no answer.

'How many?' he repeated, following his words with a blade of psi-pain that made me cry out. I needed to concentrate. I needed to rebuild my mental defences.

Feigning injury, I looked around and took stock. Maxilla stood nearby, surrounded by guards, glowering. Eleena was sitting bolt upright and pale on a couch. Medea was sprawled on the floor, just waking up. There was no sign of Aemos or Kara.

'Four!' said Maxilla. 'These four. The rest are my crew, servitors all of them, slaved into my ship.' He was playing the part of the innocent ship-master, outraged at the invasion of his vessel, distancing himself from his troublesome passengers. But I knew he was frightened.

'You're lying. I can tell,' said Heldane, pacing round Maxilla. 'Your defences are good, I'll grant you that, shipmaster. Don't lie to me.'

'I'm not–' Maxilla began and then cried out in pain.

'Don't lie to me!'

'Leave him alone!' Fischig boomed. 'He's just the captain. The shipmaster, like you said. He's not part of this.'

Heldane looked round at Fischig with a withering stare. 'You made this happen, chastener. You came to the Ordos and begged us to save your dear, heretical master from damnation. Well, that's what I'm doing. So shut your mouth and let me get on with it. Or would you rather I probed the minds of these delicious young ladies?'

'No.'

'Good. Because the shipmaster is rather interesting. He's not altogether human, is he? Are you, Tobias Maxilla? Your defences are admirable, but only because your brain isn't entirely organic. You're so much a machine, sir, you hardly deserve the title "man", do you?'

'Look who's talking,' Maxilla said bravely.

I felt the psi-surge from across the room and it made me wince. Heldane's inhuman features folded into an angry, animal roar and Maxilla stumbled, cried out and fell to his knees, showers of sparks exploding from burned-out servos in his neck, right shoulder and right wrist.

'Now will you answer, metal man,' Heldane leered at Maxilla, 'or shall I burn out another part of your blasphemous body?'

'There are five,' I said loudly. 'Five of us.'

'Aha... the heretic speaks.' Heldane switched round to face me, his attention drawn from Maxilla, at least for a moment.

'The other member of my party is my savant, Aemos. I'm sure you remember him. He's in the infirmary.'

'How very obliging of you, Gregor,' Heldane said. I prayed that I had outwitted him. Heldane could undoubtedly feel from our minds that someone was missing. If I showed him Aemos, I hoped he would be satisfied and miss Kara entirely.

'I would advise you to leave him there.'

'Why?'

'He... there was an accident,' I said. 'He is damaged.'

'Warp damaged?'

'No. He will recover.'

'But he is infirm because of contact with the warp?'

'No!'

Heldane turned to a couple of his men. 'Go to the infirmary. Locate this man. Kill him and incinerate his remains.'

'God-Emperor, no!' I cried.

I tried to get up, tried to reach out with my mind to wrest Barbarisater from Heldane's hands. I was too weak and he was too strong. Another psychic assault smashed me to the floor.

'Is everything all right?' a new voice asked. 'There was a lot of unseemly shouting just then.'

'Everything's fine, my lord. Welcome aboard,' I heard Heldane say.

I rolled over and saw the newcomer enter the *Essene*'s stateroom. He was resplendant in his brass power-armour, his augmetic jaw as stubbornly set as the last time I had seen him. 'Osma...' I whispered.

'Grand Master Osma of the Ordos Helican, if you don't mind,' he said sourly.

He had been elevated. Orsini was dead and Leonid Osma had finally achieved the rank he had spent his life chasing. So much had happened in the Helican sub-sector since I had become preoccupied with running and staying alive. Osma, my nemesis, the man who had once tried to have me declared extremis diabolus and who had imprisoned me, tortured and hunted me, had now become the master of the Ordos Helican and my supreme overlord.

The guards dragged me up onto the mezzanine area of the *Essene*'s stateroom and sat me in one of the chairs facing the long banquet table. They stood back, and Osma and Heldane approached. Osma was holding Barbarisater and studying the intricate workings of the blade. His own huge power hammer was anchored to his belt.

Heldane sat down facing me.

'There's no love lost between us, Eisenhorn. I won't insult you by pretending there is. Make things easy for all of us. Confess.'

'Confess what?'

'Your heresy,' said Osma.

'I am not a heretic. And this is not a tribunal of my peers. I cannot be judged so.'

I knew damn well I could. Grand master or no grand master, Osma could deal with me however the hell he wanted.

'Confess,' he said again, sitting down in the seat next to Heldane with a whine of armour servos. He really was fascinated by Barbarisater, turning it over in his gauntleted hands.

'Confess what?'

'We have a list of charges,' Heldane said, producing a data-slate from his cloak. 'Your man Fischig was very specific about his concerns. You have consorted with daemons and conjured one of them as a daemonhost on more than one occasion. You have hidden proscribed texts from the Inquisition. You have shielded a known heretic from the Inquisition and allowed him to roam free.'

I fixed Heldane with a hard stare. 'You mean Pontius Glaw? I'll admit nothing, but I'll tell you this much. If you detain me here, you'll pay a much greater price than you can ever imagine. I am sworn to stop Pontius Glaw and you are preventing me from performing my holy duties.'

'Your days of performing holy duties are long gone,' said Osma.

'Where is the *Malus Codicium*?' Heldane asked.

I toughened my mind shield, hoping against hope that the simple surface truth would not get out. In my pocket. In my damn pocket. Your men searched me for weapons but they didn't bother about a battered old book in my coat.

Heldane didn't read it.' 'He's still wonderfully resilient,' he told Osma.

They were assuming the *Codicium* would be in a secure place. A void safe, a strong box, under my damn mattress! They had no idea it would be right there in front of them, covered only by a layer of leather coat. I had to keep that simple, stupid fact from them.

'Millions will die. Tens of millions perhaps. If you don't let me finish my work.'

'That's what they all say,' said Osma. He rose and leaned over at me, his blunt, grizzled face looming close. 'You're going to burn, Eisenhorn. Burn and suffer. I am only grand master today because I have never suffered heretics like you. You are the worst kind of fool.'

'Tell us about the daemonhost,' said Heldane. 'Where is it secured? How can we find it? What are its command words?'

'Command words?' I replied. 'Why would you need those? Do you intend to control the daemonhost yourself?'

Heldane sat back and glanced at Osma.

'Of course they don't!' said Fischig, who had been lurking on the mezzanine steps. 'They're not heretics like you... they wouldn't–'

He looked round at Osma and Heldane.

'You don't want the daemonhost, do you, masters?'

'It must be contained and dealt with,' said Osma. 'Leave this business to your superiors, please. You interrupt too much.'

'But the daemonhost? You talk like you want it for yourselves.'

Osma glanced at the long-snouted inquisitor. 'Heldane? Tell this man to go away. He's served his purpose.'

'Go, Fischig!' Heldane snapped, and my former friend descended the stairs and sat down on one of the couches, gazing at Eleena and Medea, who were trying to make Maxilla comfortable.

'The daemonhost!' Heldane rasped. 'Give it to us!'

'And you call me a heretic...'

Heldane's psychic slap rocked me back in my seat.

A guard approached Osma. 'We have searched the infirmary, lord. There is no one there.'

Thank the Emperor, I thought. Kara has freed Aemos.

'Kara?' said Heldane suddenly. 'Who is Kara?'

No one, I willed.

'There is a sixth person aboard,' Heldane told Osma. 'Probably now working with the savant.'

'Find them!' Osma snapped, and half of his guard unit hurried from the stateroom. 'Bring more squads across from our ship if you have to.'

There was jolt, followed by a terrible raking squeal of metal on metal from somewhere outside.

'What was that?' Heldane demanded.

He got up and hurried down the steps towards the entrance to the main bridge. The *Essene* jolted again.

Osma rose and pointed the tip of Barbarisater at me. 'Move!' he ordered. 'Watch the rest of them,' he told the guard captain.

We followed Heldane onto the bridge. Fischig joined us, along with Maxilla, who was being held upright by a guard.

We were listing badly. On the main screen, we could see a forward view of the waystation.

The *Essene* had disengaged from its moorings, and was slowly tearing backwards away from the dock. Docking gantries were grinding and buckling against the ship's hull.

'What have you done?' Osma said to me.

'This is none of my doing,' I replied.

A series of minor explosions ripped through the control stations on the right hand side of the huge bridge area, showing the marble floor with sparks and machine-part debris.

Another blast rocked the starboard chapel annex that contained the astropathic vault and buckled the hatch. A helm servitor combusted and toppled over, smashing open its sculptural golden casing.

'Sabotage!' said Osma.

Heldane turned on Maxilla. 'Your handiwork!'

'Mine?' said Maxilla. 'Why the hell would I risk damage to my precious ship just to help these criminals? They mean nothing to me!'

'You're lying, you metal freak!' Heldane barked and grabbed Maxilla by the throat, lifting him off the ground. 'Tell us what you've done! Put it right! Get your crew to stabilise the ship!'

'I've done nothing...' Maxilla choked.

Heldane hurled him across the chamber. The inquisitor was strong by any standards, but he supplemented his physical strength with telekinesis. Maxilla hit the wall with a terrible splintering impact, and Heldane held him there with his powers for an awful moment, squashing him against the duralloy with his mind. There were several loud cracks of bone and metal.

Then he let him go and the limp, broken body of Tobias Maxilla fell to the marble deck and lay still.

'Why did you do that?' Fischig cried.

'Shut the hell up, you idiot,' Heldane answered. 'We need to get this vessel locked down.'

Fischig and one of the guards took a few steps forward towards the main bridge consoles. Fischig knew the *Essene*. He probably thought he could access the thrusters and level us out before the dock gantries did any more damage to the hull.

The astropathic vault blew out in a sheet of white flame that atomised two of the helm stations and threw Fischig and the guard off their feet.

Screaming and writhing, incandescent with green tongues of fire that washed across its naked contorting body, a figure levitated out of the burning vault.

But it wasn't screaming. It was laughing.

It was Cherubael.

It was shining so brightly it hurt to behold it, but I could see enough to realise it was wearing the body of one of the *Essene*'s astropaths. Plug sockets still decorated its gleaming flesh, some still trailing wires. All clothing had burned away, but the astropath's extensive bionic augmentation was clear. The body had no legs, just a dangling assembly of cables and machined connectors where the astropath, like most of Maxilla's crew, had plugged directly and permanently into a vault socket.

Heldane and two of the guards ran towards it, the guards shouting prayers against the warp as they opened fire. Heldane drew a force sword from his waist. I felt the backwash as he assaulted the daemonhost with the full force of his psychic powers.

Osma was staring at the daemonhost in astonishment. It suddenly occurred to me that despite his rank and authority, he probably had very little first hand experience of abominations like Cherubael.

'You wanted the daemonhost, grand master,' I said. 'Looks like you've got him.'

My words snapped him into activity and he looked round, but Barbarisater was already hissing through the air directly into my extended hand.

'Heretic!' he screamed. His power hammer swung up in his plated fists, crackling with energy and he came at me. He had significant advantage. He was psi-shielded and heavily armoured against an adversary with no armour whatsoever.

Our weapons crashed together. We broke and swung again. There was massive strength behind his blows and I was still weak from the psychic mauling Heldane had given me.

'There's no time for this, you fool!' I yelled. 'I didn't unleash the daemonhost, but I'm the only chance you have to stop it!'

Behind us, Cherubael giggled hysterically as it torched the guards firing at it. It skimmed down and locked in combat with the furious Heldane.

Osma was defiant. He would not break off. He deflected my sword stroke with a hammerblow so powerful I was rocked back, my guard open. His follow-through came right at my face and I threw my body back to evade it. It missed. Barely. The hammer's energy scorched my cheek.

But I had lost my footing.

I crashed over onto the marble deck and rolled sideways as the hammer came down and cracked the stone flags. Osma's weapon, the Malleus symbol of his Ordo, rushed up again for the deathstroke.

There was a shriek of energy and the air above me was split by a blinding turquoise beam. It struck Osma full in the face and vapourised his head in a splash of light, bone shards and adipose tissue. His body hit the floor with a metallic crash and the fused remains of his heavy augmetic jaw bounced away across the deck.

I rose.

Maxilla, still sprawled and wretchedly twisted where Heldane had dropped him, slowly lowered his hand. The digital ring weapon on his elegantly gloved finger was glowing.

I turned back to the fight. Medea and Eleena had entered the room along with the remaining guards, looking on in horror. Some of the guards fled.

Heldane was being driven back across the bridge by the radiant, cackling daemonhost. He was throwing everything he had at Cherubael, and the daemon was just laughing, teeth backlit into silhouette by the light of the warp streaming out of its gaping maw.

Heldane's robes were beginning to smoulder.

'Eleena!' I shouted and she ran to me. None of the awestruck guards even tried to stop her.

'There's no time to do this cleanly. I need you next to me. You may be able to block some of its power.'

She nodded and grabbed my coat with both hands. She was terrified out of her wits. But she did not falter.

I pulled the *Malus Codicium* from my coat and leafed desperately through the pages. I couldn't find what I was looking for. I damn well couldn't find what I was looking for!

The marble deck of the bridge cracked and parted underneath Heldane like solid ground split by an earth tremor. One of his feet slipped into the crack and he swayed.

Cherubael snorted with glee and clapped its hands. The deck quaked and the crack closed again, like a vice.

Heldane screamed. He screamed the terrible howl of the damned. He was pinned into the deck by his crushed leg. Cherubael advanced.

Heldane slashed with his sword in terror. The blade melted. The inquisitor's clothes caught fire. Ablaze from head to foot with green flames, he screamed again. On fire, upright, fixed to the spot, he looked just like a heretic burning at the stake.

Cherubael looked away from his prey, bored with it now it was dying. It surged forward and floated towards me. Eleena let out a sobbing whimper.

'Stay close!' I told her.

'Hello, Gregor,' said Cherubael. Its voice was hoarse and impaired. The astropath it inhabited hadn't spoken for many years and the voice organs had partially atrophied.

'Don't we have fun together, Gregor?' it went on, its blank eyes fixed on me. It was smiling, but there was nothing warm in those vacant orbs. Nothing at all, in fact, except evil.

'It's always such a delight to play these games with you. But this game must be a bit of surprise, eh? Didn't expect to see me, did you? It wasn't you that called me this time.'

It came closer. I could feel, not heat, but burning cold emanating from it. I was still ripping through the pages of the book to find what I was looking for.

'Here's another surprise for you,' it added, dropping its voice to a whisper. 'This is the last time we play. I've had enough of the way you make up all the games. You see what I did to that horse-faced idiot? I won't do that to you, old friend. I'll do something that really, really hurts.'

It lunged forward but then backed off slightly, as if stung. It had touched the psychic deadzone around Eleena. Cherubael turned his attention down towards her.

'Hello. Aren't you a sweet little thing? What a pretty face! Shame I'm going to ruin it.'

'Mmmh!' Eleena sobbed.

'You're a clever old stick, Gregor. Always careful enough to have an untouchable at your side when you meet with me. This isn't the regular one, though, is it? What happened to her?'

I wrenched the book open.

'She won't save you, mind,' said Cherubael, reaching out with hands that were sprouting thick, ugly talons.

I thrust the book up and held it in front of his eyes with both hands, clamping the pages open so that the daemonhost could clearly see.

It was diagrams of the four chief runes of banishment. They wouldn't banish Cherubael, because they hadn't been properly invoked. But I was pretty sure just reading them would hurt.

Cherubael squealed and tumbled back. I stepped forward a pace, keeping the book raised and open.

Wracked with agony, the daemonhost soared back across the bridge, crashed through the main screen and shattered the hololithic plates in a shower of crystal and sparks. It bounced twice off the ceiling like a maddened hornet fighting a window pane, the colour of its flame-halo turning yellow and then furnace orange.

Cherubael dropped, hit the floor and burned through it leaving a circular, smouldering hole.

'Oh dear Emperor–' Eleena gasped.

'Come on!' I said. 'It won't be long before it comes back for another try. Move!'

Medea ran forward. The last few guards were busy beating out the flames swathing Heldane with their capes. He was still screaming.

'Get her out of here!' I told Medea, pushing Eleena towards her. 'Hangar deck! Go!'

They hurried towards the exit. Deep, bass detonations from somewhere deep in the *Essene* rocked the floor. Multiple alarms were sounding. Sparks cascaded from the buckled ceiling of the bridge.

I went over to Maxilla. His eyes flickered and he looked up at me. 'I didn't mean it...' he said in a tiny voice.

'Mean what?'

'I told that brute none of you meant anything to me. But I didn't mean it.'

'I know.'

'Thank you,' he said, and died.

I ran from the bridge into one of the main longitudinal corridors. Smoke was boiling along it from untold damage below. On the floor, I saw weapons and cloaks dropped by Osma's guards in their panic to leave.

I'd taken about a dozen steps when a loud voice told me to halt.

Fischig was coming after me, aiming his bolt pistol with a straight, firm arm. He was bloodied and bruised by the explosion that had knocked him down, but there was an utterly determined set to his face. I'd seen that look before, but I'd never been on the receiving end of it.

'Stop where you are,' he said.

'Come on! We have to get clear. The ship is dying.'

'Stop where you are,' he repeated.

'Come with me. I'll explain everything and you'll see why it's vital for us to–'

'Shut up,' he said. 'It's all lies. It's always been lies. You know you nearly fooled me back then. I was almost convinced I'd made a terrible mistake going to Osma. But then you showed your true colours. Brought that daemon back and proved that everything I feared about you was true.'

'This isn't the time or place, Godwyn. I'm leaving now. Come with me if you want.'

I turned my back on him and walked away.

'Gregor, please–'

I kept walking. I was sure he wouldn't shoot. We went back too far. When it came down to it, he wouldn't be able to stop me.

The boltgun roared. The shot exploded my left knee. I cried out and fell, leaning on Barbarisater. There was blood everywhere. I couldn't believe he'd found the will to do it.

With a yelp of pain I hauled myself up on the sword. He fired again and now my right leg went out from under me, also mangled at the knee.

I lay on my back. I could feel the death throes of the *Essene* quaking and thundering through the deck beneath me. Fischig stood over me.

'Stop this...' I gasped. 'Get me to the hangar.'

He drew back the slide of the bolt pistol. He was shaking with distress, wracked by grief and disappointment and duty and belief.

'Please,' he said. 'Renounce it all. Repent your sins and accept the Emperor for the good of your soul. It's not too late.'

'You're still trying to save me.' I managed to get the words out through the pain. 'Glory be, Fischig... you actually shot me so you could try and save my soul?'

'Renounce the warp!' he stammered. 'Please! I can save you! You're my friend and I can still save you from yourself!

'I don't need saving,' I said.

He aimed the gun at my head. His finger tightened on the trigger. 'May the Emperor protect you, Gregor Eisenhorn,' he said.

He twitched. Once. Twice. He swayed. The bolt pistol wandered in his lolling hand and fired, harmlessly, against the corridor wall. He dropped to his knees and then fell forward onto his face as if he was praying.

I struggled to pull myself up so I could lean my back against the wall. My legs were crippled, bloody and useless.

Medea crouched down next to me. Tears were streaming down her cheeks. She let go of the needle pistol and let it clatter onto the deck.

Kara appeared behind us, a las-carbine in her hands, with Eleena and Aemos at her heels. They all looked in horror at the sight of me and Fischig.

Aemos was deathly pale, and leaning on my runestaff like a penitent pilgrim.

'Help me up,' I said, from between clenched teeth. Kara and Medea hoisted me up between them.

I looked at Aemos. 'You summoned Cherubael? It was you, wasn't it? You summoned him into one of the *Essene*'s poor bloody astropaths?'

'They were going to burn us as heretics,' he said softly, 'and then we'd never be able to stop Glaw.'

'But how did you perform the rituals, Uber? You didn't even have the book any more.'

'That book,' he sighed. 'That damn book. It's all in here now.' He tapped his wrinkled forehead with a scrawny finger.

He'd memorised it. During those weeks of study he'd memorised the *Malus Codicium*. Thanks to a mcmc-virus, he was a data addict. That's what made him such a fine savant. And now his addiction had taken him to overdose.

'You memorised the whole thing?'

'Word,' he swallowed and then finished, 'perfect.'

There was another juddering boom and a rush of hot air gusted down the corridor.

'Are we gonna stand around like ninkers all day or are we gonna get off this ship?' Kara snapped, bracing against me.

'I think that might be wise,' I agreed.

But the way was blocked. Cherubael had come back for me.

Its malicious rampage had crippled the *Essene*. It was still seething with the pain I had inflicted. It wasn't even talking any more.

It surged down the corridor towards us. I couldn't reach the *Malus Codicium* now. I was having enough trouble just standing up.

Eleena cried out in terror. I cursed, helpless, useless.

Aemos hobbled forward and place himself between us and the charging warp-spawn. He braced the runestaff against the floor and lowered the tip towards Cherubael. He knew what to do. May the God-Emperor show him mercy, he knew better than I.

There was a release of power and light so powerful that it was beyond sound. The host body disintegrated, showering us with a hail of burned flesh, charred bone and blackened augmetic debris.

Aemos and the runestaff shuddered and jerked as they both lit up with corposant that crackled and flashed up and down them.

The last few electrical arcs sizzled away into the deck. Aemos remained standing where he was with the staff still upraised. A tiny plume of smoke licked off the headpiece.

'Aemos? Aemos!'

'I've... dispossessed it... for a moment...' Aemos said without turning round. His voice was low and his words were emerging only by huge effort. 'So it's weak... and confused... but that won't... last... we need... a proper host vessel... for it to... occupy...'

He turned to face us. The destruction of the astropath's host body had singed his clothes and knocked his eyeglasses off.

'What did you do with it?' I asked.

He didn't answer. The effort would have been too great. Aemos would only ever say two more words to me.

'Aemos, what did you do with it?' I repeated.

He opened his eyes. They were blank. Completely blank.

It took us ten minutes to make the daemonhost safe, ten minutes we really didn't have. I was encumbered by the fact I couldn't move unaided. Eleena had to hold the *Malus Codicium* for me as I did the work, making the marks and runes and wardings with blood from my own wounds. I recalled the same hasty rituals I had performed on the beach at Miquol.

'Come on!' Kara urged.

'There! It's done! Aemos, can you hear me? It's done!'

His old hands were shaking. He lowered the staff. I could see his mouth trying to form the words, but he couldn't manage it.

But I knew this part. The incantation, the litany, the abduration against evil. The final sealing words.

'*In servitutem abduco,* I bind thee fast forever into this host!'

Medea nearly burned out the lift-jets of Maxilla's bulk pinnace getting us clear of the hangar deck. Everything shook. It didn't have anything like the kick of the old gun-cutter, but she nursed every last ounce of thrust she could out of it.

We managed to get about sixteen kilometres from the *Essene* when the first of the real spasms shook it. The majestic sprint-trader, Isolde-pattern, pride of its master, looked like a black shell to us, lit from within by raging atomic fires, spilling trails of debris behind it as it slowly tumbled into the embrace of the gas giant.

There was a small bright flash and then two more, almost simultaneous, like a flicker. Then a white dot appeared where the *Essene* had been, and grew bigger, and then became a white line that got brighter and longer and closer, until we could see it was the flaming edge of a huge expanding disk of nuclear energy.

The pinnace vibrated frantically like a bead rattle in the hand of an excited child as the shockwave seared past and around us.

Then it was quiet, and still again.

And the *Essene* was gone.

Aemos was crumpled in one of the high-backed acceleration seats in the pinnace's passenger space. His eyes were closed and his breathing was shallow and ragged.

Kara helped me to the seat next to him. She was saying something urgent about improving the tourniquets and field dressings on my legs but I didn't really hear her.

'Uber?'

As if I had disturbed him in his sleep, he opened his eyes. They were his eyes again. Bloodshot, old, blinking to focus without his eyeglasses.

His breath sounds were getting worse.

'You hold on,' I said. 'There's a portable medicae unit in the cargo section, Eleena's trying to get it working.'

He grunted something and swallowed.

'What?' I said.

He surprised me by suddenly taking my blood-stained hand and gripping it tightly. He turned his head slowly and squinted at the daemonhost we had made together. It sat, strapped into its seat, on the other side of the aisle, head bowed and dormant.

'Most...' he whispered. 'Most perturbatory...'

I was going to reply, but his grip had slackened, his breathing had stopped. My oldest friend had gone.

I sat back, gazing at the cabin roof. The sensations that I had been blocking swept in and overwhelmed me.

I felt frail, as if I was made of paper. I knew I had lost a huge quantity of blood.

The pain in my legs was like fire, but it was nothing compared to the pain in my heart.

I heard Kara calling my name. She called it again. I heard Eleena asking me to say something.

But the void had come up like a wall, and they were too far away to hear.

NINETEEN

IN THE HALLS OF YSSARILE
LEAVES OF DARKNESS
IN THE NAME OF THE HOLY GOD-EMPEROR

Someone, somewhere close by, was using one of those damned shuriken catapults. I could hear the *jhut! jhut! jhut!* of the launcher mechanism and the thin, brittle sounds of the impacts.

There was blood in my mouth, I noticed. I'd worry about it later. Crezia would fuss no doubt. 'You should not be doing this,' she had warned me fiercely in the infirmary of the *Hinterlight*.

Well, that's where she was wrong. This was the Emperor's work. This was my work.

'Moving up,' Nayl said over the intervox. 'Twenty paces.'

'Understood,' I replied. I stepped forward. It was still an effort, and still very much a surprise to feel my body so wretchedly slow. The crude augmetic braces around my legs and torso weighed me down and forced me to plod, like an ogre from the old myths.

Or like a Battle Titan, I considered, ruefully. One heavy footstep after the next, lumbering to my destiny.

It was the best work Crezia and Antribus had been able to manage given the time and the resources available. Crezia had passionately wanted me confined to vital support until I could be delivered to a top level Imperial facility.

I'd insisted on being mobile.

'If we throw together repairs now,' she had said, 'it'll be worse in the long term. To get you walking we'll have to do things that no amount of later work can repair, no matter how excellent.'

'Just do it,' I'd said. For the opportunity to reach Pontius Glaw, I'd happily sacrifice prosthetic sophistication. All I needed was function.

Barbarisater trembled in my right fist as it sensed a bio-aura, but I relaxed. It was Kara Swole.

She jogged back down the chasm towards me, dressed in a tight, green armoured bodyglove and a thick, quilted flak coat. She had a dust visor on, and a fat-nosed compact handcannon slung over her shoulder.

'All right, boss?' she said

'I'm doing fine.'

'You look...'

'What?'

'Pissed off.'

'Thank you, Kara. I'm probably annoyed because you and Nayl are having all the fun taking point.'

'Well, Nayl thinks we should tighten up anyway.'

I voxed back to the second element of our force. In less than two minutes, Eleena and Medea had joined us. Along side them came Lief Gustine and Korl Kraine, two men from Gideon's band who had subbed as reinforcements, as well as Gideon's mercenary archaeologist, Kenzer.

'Moving up,' I told them.

'You managing okay, sir?' Eleena asked.

'I'm fine. Fine. I just wish you'd...' I stopped. 'I'm fine, thank you, Eleena.'

They were all still worried about me. It had only been three and half weeks since the carnage at Jeganda. I'd only been walking for five days. They all quietly agreed with Crezia's advice that I should still be in the infirmary and leaving this to Ravenor.

Well, that was the perk of being the boss. I made the damn decisions. But I shouldn't be angry with them for worrying. But for Kara and Eleena's frantic emergency work on the pinnace, I'd be dead. I'd crashed twice. Eleena, the only one whose blood-type matched mine, had even made last minute donations.

Pulled apart at the seams, my band was pulling together tighter than ever.

'Let's pick up the pace,' I said. 'We don't want Nayl and Ravenor to have all the glory.'

'After you, Ironhoof,' Medea said. Kara sniggered, but pretended she was having trouble with her filter mask.

'I can't imagine why you think you can get away with that nickname,' I said.

We heard the shuriken catapult buzzing again. It was close, the sound rolling back to us around the maze of the gorge.

'Someone's having a party,' said Gustine. Bearded, probably to help disguise the terrible scarring that seemed to cover his entire skin, Gustine was an ex-Guardsman turned ex-pit fighter turned ex-bounty hunter turned Inquisition soldier. He said he came from Raas Bisor in the Segmentum Tempestus, but I didn't know where that was. Apart from that it was in the Segmentum Tempestus. Gustine wore heavyweight grey ablative armour and carried an old, much-repaired standard Imperial Guard lasrifle.

He'd been with Ravenor for a good many years, so I trusted him.

The whizzing sounds echoed again, overlapping with laser discharges.

'Ravenor's friends,' Medea said. None of us were comfortable about the eldar. Six of them had arrived on Gideon's ship as a bodyguard for the farseer. Tall, too tall, inhumanly slender, silent, keeping themselves to the part of the ship assigned them. Aspect warriors, Gideon had called them, whatever that meant. The plumed crests on their great, curved helmets had made them seem even taller once they were in armour.

They'd deployed to the surface with Ravenor, the seer lord and three more of Ravenor's band.

A third strike team of six under Ravenor's senior lieutenant Rav Skynner, was advanced about a kilometre to our west.

Ghül, or 5213X to give it its Carto-Imperialis code, was nothing like I had imagined it. It didn't at all resemble the arid world I had glimpsed in Marla Tarray's mind, the dried-out husk where primaeval cities lay buried under layers of ash. I suppose that was because all I'd seen was her own imagined view of the place. She'd never seen it. She hadn't lived long enough to get the chance.

I wondered if Ghül matched the farseer's vision. Probably. The eldar seemed unnecessarily precise bastards to me.

We'd approached the world in a wide, stealthy orbit. The *Hinterlight* was equipped with disguise fields that Ravenor was reluctant to explain to me but which I felt were partly created by his own, terrifyingly strong will. High band sensors had located a starship in tight orbit, a rogue trader of some considerable size that didn't appear to realise we were there.

Ghül itself was invisible. Or nearly invisible. I have never seen a world that seemed so much to be not there. It was a shadow against the starfield, a faintly discernable echo of matter. Even on the sunward side, it lacked any real form. It appeared to soak up light and give nothing back.

When Cynia Preest, Ravenor's ship-mistress, had brought us the first surface scans to study, we thought she was showing us close up pictures of a child's toy.

'It's a maze,' I remember saying.

'A puzzle... like an interlock,' Ravenor decided.

'No, a carved fruit pit,' Medea had said.

We had all looked at her. 'The works of the Lord on the heart of a stone?' she asked. 'Anybody?'

'Perhaps you'd explain?' I'd said.

So she had. A some length, until we grasped the idea. The hermits of Glavia, so it seems, thought no greater expression of their divine love for the Emperor could be made than to inscribe the entire Imperial Prayer onto the pits of sekerries. A sekerry, we learned, was a soft, sweet summer fruit that tasted of quince and nougat. A bit like a shirnapple, we were reliably informed. The pits were the size of pearls.

Thankfully, no one had made the mistake of asking what a shirnapple was.

'I don't know how they do it,' Medea had gone on. 'They do it by eye, with a needle, They can't even see, I don't think. But they used to show us liths of the carved pits, magnified, in scholam. You could read every word! Every last word! The works of the Lord on the heart of a stone. All laced together, tight and compact, using every corner of the space. We were taught that the prayer pits were one of the Nineteen Wonders of Glavia and that we should be proud.'

'Nineteen Wonders?' Cynia had asked.

'Golden Throne, woman, don't get her started!' I had cried out. But there had indeed been something in Medea's comparison. The surface of Ghül had been engraved, that's what it looked like. A perfect black sphere, engraved across its entire surface with tight, deep, interlocking lines. In reality, each of those lines was a smooth sided gorge, two hundred metres wide and nine hundred metres deep.

I wondered about Medea's description. I remembered the chart we had witnessed during the auto-seance on Promody, and the way dear Aemos's notes had taken on the same scrolling forms of the chart as he struggled to decipher it.

Ghül could very well be engraved, I decided. The warped ones' entire culture, certainly their language, had been built upon expressions of location and place. I imagined that the inscribed wall we had seen during the auto-seance had been part of just such a maze of lines, from a time when Promody had looked like Ghül, the capital world.

Cynia Preest's sensors had located heat and motion traces on the surface. We'd assembled the teams, and prepared for planetfall. The *Hinterlight*'s ship-mistress had been told to line up on the enemy's ship and stand ready to take it out.

Our three vessels, my pinnace and two shuttles from Ravenor's stable, had sunk low into the thin atmosphere and skimmed across the perfect, geometric surface, their shadows flitting across the flat black sections and the deep chasms.

We'd put down in adjacent gorges near the target zone.

The first surprise had been that the air was breathable. We'd all brought vacuum suits and rebreathers.

'How is that possible?' Eleena had asked.

'I don't know.'

'But it's so unlikely... I mean it's unfeasible,' she had stammered.

'Yes, it is.'

The second surprise had been the discovery that Medea was right.

Kenzer had knelt down with his auspex at the side of the gorge, studying microscopically the relationship between chasm floor and chasm wall.

I didn't need him to tell me they were perfect. Smooth. Exact. Machined. Engraved.

'The angle between floor and wall is ninety degrees to a margin of accuracy that... well, it is so precise, it goes off my auspex's scale. Who... who could do a thing like this?' Kenzer had gasped.

'The hermits of Glavia?' Medea had cracked.

'If they had fusion beams, starships, a spare planet and unlimited power supplies,' I had said. 'Besides, tell me this: who polished the planet smooth before they started?'

We moved down the gorge. It curved gently to the west, like an old river, deep cut in its banks. Long before on KCX-1288, facing the saruthi, I had been disconcerted by the lack of angular geometry. Now I was disturbed by the reverse. Everything was so damned precise, squared off, unmarked and unblemished. Only a faint sooty deposit in the wide floor of the trench suggested any antiquity at all.

We caught up with Nayl.

'They know we're here,' he said, referring to the sounds of battle in the nearby gorge.

'Any idea of numbers?' I asked.

'Not a thing, but Skynner's mob has found trouble too. Vessorines, so he reckon, wrapped up in carapace suits and loaded for bear.'

'We'd best be careful then.'

I tried Ravenor, using my mind instead of my intervox.

Status?

THE ASPECTS HAVE–

Whoa, whoa, whoa... quieter, Gideon.

Sorry. I forget sometimes you–

I what?

You're hurt, I meant to say. The aspect warriors have engaged. It's quite busy here.

I could feel the sub-surface twinges of power as he channelled his mind into his force chair's psi-cannons.

Opposition? I sent.

Vessorine janissaries and some other heterodox mercs. We–

He broke off. There was a grinding wash of distortion for a moment.

Sorry, he sent. *Some sort of fusion weapon. They certainly don't want us in here.*

In where?

He broadcast a sequence of map co-ordinates and I took the map-slate out of Nayl's hands and punched them in.

A structure, Ravenor sent. *Ahead of us, south-west of you. It's built into the end pier of one of the gorge junctions. Although I can't see how. There are no doors. The Vessorine are coming out of somewhere, though. There must be a hidden entrance.*

More distortion. Then he floated back to me.

The Vessorine are fighting like maniacs. My lord seer says they have already earned the respect of the aspects.

Your lord seer?

Send again. I didn't make that out.

Nothing, Gideon. We're going to try and come round on your flank, around the north-east intersection of the gorge.

Understood.

Come on! I urged. The others all jumped, all except Eleena, and I realised I was still using my psyche. Sloppy. I was tired and in pain. Still no excuse.

'My apologies,' I said, vocal again. 'We're moving forward. This chasm turns south-west and intersects with two others. Target site's at the junction, so Gideon reckons.'

We hurried forward, moving through the steep shadow of the gorge.

'Glory be!' exclaimed Kenzer suddenly. He was looking up.

Bright flashes lit up the starry sky framed by the sides of the chasm. They washed back and forth like spills of milk in ink. Alerted to our presence, Glaw's starship had presented for combat and the *Hinterlight* was answering. Vast blinks of light lit up the sky like a strobe.

'I wouldn't wanna be up there,' said Korl Kraine. Kraine was a hiver who'd never served in any formal militia. His allegiance was to Ravenor first and to the underclan of Tanhive Nine, Tansetch, second and last. He was a short, pale man wearing patched and cut-off flak-canvas. His skin was dyed with clan colours and his eyes were cheap augments. He wore a string of human teeth around his neck, which was ironic as his own teeth were all made of ceramite.

Kraine raised his night-sighted Tronsvasse autorifle to his shoulder and scurried forward. He'd lived in a lightless warren of city all his life until Ravenor recruited him. This gloom suited him.

The sound of catapults grew louder. There were several of them at work now, buzzing out a duet with heavyweight lasguns. I heard the gritty thump of a grenade.

Kenzer, the archaeologist, was lagging. He wasn't part of Ravenor's official troop, merely an expert paid to help out on Promody. I didn't like him much. He had no fibre and no real commitment.

I didn't need to read his mind to see that he was only here for the potential fortune a few exclusive academic papers about the Ghül discovery could make him.

'Hurry up!' I yelled at him. My back was getting tired and the blood in my mouth was back again.

Kenzer was hunched down at the base of the chasm side, fidgeting with his hand-scanner.

I called a halt and stomped back to him, my heavy boots, reinforced with the brace's metal frame, kicking up soot. Ironhoof, indeed!

I believed my greatest annoyance wasn't the brace-frame or its weight or the lumpen gait I was forced to adopt, not even the non-specific haemorrhage that was seeping into my mouth.

No, the worst thing was my cold scalp.

I really couldn't get used to it. Crezia had been obliged to shave my head in order to implant the cluster of neural and synaptic cables that would drive the augmetic frame around my legs. She had been upset all through the implant procedure. It really was terribly crude, even by basic Imperial standards. But out in the middle of nowhere at all, it had been the best she and Antribus could cobble together.

Needs must, as they say.

I was bald, and the back of my skull was raw, sore and clotted with the multiple implant jacks of the sub-spine feeds my faithful medicaes had installed to make my leg frame work. The steel-jacketed cables sprouted from my scalp and ran down my back into the lumbar servo of the walking brace. The bunched cables were flesh-stapled to my back, like a neat, augmetic ponytail.

I would get used to it, in time. If there was time. If there wasn't, what the hell did it matter?

I stopped beside Kenzer, throwing a hard shadow over him.

'What are you doing?'

'Making a recording, sir,' he gabbled. 'There's a marking here. The carved walls we've seen so far have been blank.'

I peered down. It was difficult to bend.

'Where?'

He pulled a puffer-brush out of his kit-pack and blew the soot away.

'There!'

A small spiral. Cut into the smooth face of the rock.

It looked like a tiny version of the chart we'd seen on Promody, or a really tiny version of the mazed surface of this planet.

'Record it quickly and move on,' I told him. I turned away. 'Let's go,' I called over my shoulder curtly.

Kenzer screamed. There was a flurry of las-fire.

I wheeled back immediately. Kenzer was sprawled on the floor of the gorge, ripped apart by laser shots. He was only partially articulated, such had been the point-blank ferocity of the shots. The wide puddle of blood seeping from his carcass was soaking into the soot.

There was no sign of any attacker.

'What the hell?' Barbarisater was in my hand and had been purring, but now it was dull.

Nayl dropped close to me, his matt-black hellgun sweeping the area of the corpse.

'How in the name of Terra did that happen?' he asked. 'Lief? Korl? Upside?'

I looked back. Gustine and Kraine were walking backwards slowly, scoping up at the cliff tops of the gorge.

'Nothing. No shooters above,' Gustine reported.

I slapped my palm against the cold stone face of the gorge above the marking Kenzer had found. It was unyielding.

We moved forward, following the sweep of the chasm. Kraine was covering our backs. After we'd gone about fifty metres, he suddenly cried out.

I turned in time to see him in a face-to-face gunfight with two Vessorine janissaries in full carapace-wear. Kraine staggered backwards as he was hit repeatedly in the torso, but managed to keep firing. He put a burst of rounds through the face plate of one of the Vessorines before the other one made the kill shot and dropped him into the soot.

Nayl and Medea were already firing. The remaining Vessorine swung his aim and squeezed off another salvo, winging both Eleena and Nayl.

Then he walloped over onto his back as Kara's cannon ripped him apart.

'See to them!' I ordered, pointing Medea at Nayl and Eleena. Nayl had been skinned across the left arm and Eleena had a flesh wound on her left shin. Both kept insisting they were fine. Medea opened his kitbag for field dressings.

I looked at the corpses, Kraine and the Vessorines. Gustine appeared beside me. 'Where the jesh did they come from?' he asked.

I didn't answer. I drew my runestaff over my head out of its leather boot, and gripped it tightly as I focused my force at the gorge wall. Soot and the debris of eons puffed out, and I saw another spiral mark in the wall like the one Kenzer had found.

'Charts,' I said.

'What, sir?' asked Lief.

I bent down, spitting on my fingers then rubbing my hand across the spiral marks. I tried to ignore the fact that there was a smear of blood in the spittle.

'No wonder Ravenor couldn't find a door. We're not seeing this in the right dimension.'

'Pardon me, but what the craphole are you talking about?' asked Lief. I liked him. Always honest.

'The warped ones understood location and moment in way we can't imagine. They were, after all, warped. We see this as a geometric network of mathematically precise chasms, a maze. But it's not. It's four dimensional...'

'Four?' Gustine began, uncertainly

'Oh, four, six, eight... who knows? Think of it this way, like a... a woven garment!

'A woven garment, sir?'

'Yes, all those thick, intertwined threads, such a complex pattern.'

'All right...'

'Now imagine the knitting needles that made it. Just the needles. Big and hard and simple.'

'Okay...' said Medea, joining us.

'This planet is simply the knitting needles. Hard, rigid, simple. The reality of Ghül is the garment woven from it, something we can't see, something complex and soft, interlaced round the needles.'

'I'm sorry, sir, you've lost me,' Lief Gustine said.

'Lost,' I said. 'That's damn right. These marks on the wall. They're like mini charts, explaining how the overall reality can be accessed and exited.'

Ghustine nodded as if he understood. 'Right... so, going back, where the jesh did the janissaries come from?' he asked.

I slapped the hard wall.

'There. Right there.'

'But it's solid rock!'

'Only to us,' I said.

As we moved on again, down the gorge, we formed a pack that covered all sides, like phalanx of spearmen from the old ages of warfare. The sounds of Ravenor's battle had become frenetic. Nayl reported grimly that he couldn't raise Skynner or any of his force any more.

We all hunted the walls for further carvings

'Here, sir! Here!' Kara sang out.

I ran over to the spiral cut she had found. 'Wait,' I ordered.

Like an eye blinking, the smooth rock opened. Suddenly it just wasn't there. A Vessorine janissary in combat carapace pushed out, weapon raised.

Nayl had him cold, felling him with a single shot. But there were more behind the first.

Medea started shooting. Two more mercs had blinked out of the gorge wall on the far side of us.

There was no cover. No damn cover at all.

In a moment, we were fired on from a third angle.

I had already drawn the big Hecuter autopistol I had borrowed from the

Hinterlight's arsenal. Gustine's old las was cracking away beside me and Eleena was emptying her pistol's extended clip on semi-automatic.

They'd just been poaching us up until now. This was a full scale ambush. I counted at least fifteen janissaries, as well as an ogryn with a heavy weapon. Nayl went down, hit in the thigh, but he kept blasting. A las round sparked bluntly against the heavy brace on my left leg.

Time to reset the odds.

'Cherubael!' I commanded.

It had been drifting high above the gorge, trailing us like a kite, but now it descended, gathering speed, beginning to shine.

I had been much more careful in my design of this daemonhost. Elaborating on the basic and hasty ritual construction Aemos and I had wrought in those last few minutes aboard the Essene, I had supplemented the wards and rune markings on its flesh to reinforce its obedience. This daemonhost would not be permitted to have any of the capricious guile of the previous versions. It would not rebel. It would not be a maverick that had to be watched at all times. It was bound and locked with triple wards, totally subservient. I liked to think I could learn from my mistakes, at least sometimes.

Of course, there was a price to pay for such security. This Cherubael could manifest much less power, a direct consequence of its reinforced bindings. But it had enough. More than enough.

It swept down the gorge, warp-flame trailing from its upright body, and demolished one group of attackers in a blurry storm of aether. To their credit, the Vessorines didn't scream. But they broke and started to fall back.

The ogryn fired his heavy weapon at the incoming host. The impact fluttered off Cherubael like petals. It punched its talons into the squealing abhuman's chest and lifted the big brute off the ground.

And then threw him. The ogryn went up. Just simply went up and kept going.

Cherubael changed direction and skimmed across the gorge towards the retreating mercs. Our guns had whittled their numbers down by then and we were in pursuit, though Eleena had stayed with the sprawled, cursing Nayl.

I noticed something else about this new Cherubael. It didn't laugh any more. Ever. Its face was set in an implacable frown. It showed no signs of taking any pleasure in its slaughter.

I was pleased about that. The laughter really did used to get on my nerves.

It was going to take a while to get used to Cherubael's new face, though. Once installed within the flesh host, the daemon had made its usual alterations – the sprouting nub horns, the talons, the smooth, glossy skin, the blank eyes.

But it had not entirely erased the features of Godwyn Fischig.

It killed the last of the ambushers, all save one who reached the gorge wall and accessed the dimension trap they had emerged from.

'Hold it!' I ordered. 'Hold it open!'

Cherubael obeyed. It atomised the last merc as the trap blinked open and then braced its arms wide, preventing the trap from closing. Even for Cherubael, this was an effort.

'Hurry. Up,' it said, as if annoyed with me.

I reached the trap.

There wasn't time to get us all through. Gustine hurled himself in, headlong, and I followed, shouting to the others to stay back and stay together.

The last thing I heard was a loud, liquid impact that must have been the ogryn finally obeying the law of gravity.

The trap blinked shut.

I felt a sickening twist of translation. I landed on top of the sprawled Gustine in a dim, boxy space that smelled musty.

'Ow!' he complained.

I got to my feet. That in itself was ridiculously hard. I was sweating freely by the time I was vertical.

'You okay?' Gustine asked.

'Yes,' I snapped. I wasn't really. My head was throbbing, and the pain in my legs was beginning to overcome the power of the drugs that were self-administering from a dispenser Crezia had fitted to my hip.

'You had better not expect me to carry you,' Cherubael whispered behind me.

'Don't worry. Your dignity isn't in danger.'

I drew Barbarisater, holding it in my right hand, and gripped my runestaff in my left.

I stomped forward. Darkness. A wall. I turned. Another wall.

'Gustine?'

He'd switched on a lamp pack, but it was showing him nothing but black walls. There was no sign of a ceiling.

'How far can you see?' I asked Cherubael.

'Forever,' it said, floating alongside me.

'Fine. In practical terms, how far can you see?'

'Not far in here. I can see that the wall ends there. There is a gap beyond it.'

'Very well,' I plodded ahead. My back really hurt now where the implants went in and my nose was bleeding. Gustine clipped the lamp pack to the bayonet lug of his las.

He tried to reach Nayl on the vox. Dead and silent.

I made an effort to reach Ravenor with my mind. Nothing.

Heavy footed, I moved through the darkness with my odd companions. The runestaff was trembling, sniffing some focus of power.

'You feel that?' I asked the daemon.

It nodded.

I decided we would follow it.

'Have you noticed we can breathe in here too?' Gustine remarked a few minutes later.

'Gosh, I wouldn't have picked up on that.'

He frowned at me, put-upon. 'I mean, the air's right, inside and out.'

'It's so the enemy can breathe,' Cherubael said.

'What's that supposed to mean?'

'They got here first. They got inside. Ghül made the atmosphere appropriate for them as soon as Ghül sensed they were there.'

'You're talking like Ghül is alive.'

'Ghül has never been alive,' it said.

'It's never been dead, either,' it added a moment later.

I was about to ask it to expand a little on that alarming notion, but Cherubael suddenly surged forward in the blackness ahead of us. I saw the flash of its light, a laser discharge.

It came back, blood steaming off its talons.

'They're hunting for us,' it said.

I have seen wonders in my life. Horrors too. I have witnessed vistas and spectacles that have cowed my mind and dwarfed my imagination.

None of them compared to the mausoleum under Ghül.

I cannot say anything about its size except to use inadequate words like vast, huge...

There was nothing to give any scale. We came out of the black tunnels into a black abyss that was to all intents much the same except that the blackness that had been walls was now immaterial. Tiny, scattered specks of light, dozens of them, illuminated small parts of the face of some impossible structure, as dark and cyclopean as the eternal wall ancient philosophers used to believe surrounded creation. The edge of the universe. The side of the casket an ancient god had wrought to keep reality in.

Which god, I wouldn't like to say.

It was warm and still. Not even the air moved. The dots of light showed small parts of a vast design etched onto the face of the mausoleum. Hints of spirals, lines and swirling runes.

This was where the warped ones had laid their dead king to rest.

This was the tomb of Yssarile, over which Ghül had been raised in the strange eons before man.

The sight even stunned Cherubael to silence. I hoped its lack of comment was down to awe. I had a nasty feeling it had more to do with reverence.

Or dread.

Gustine lost it for a while. His mind refused to deal with what his eyes were seeing. He began to weep inconsolably, and fell to his knees. It was a dismal sight to see such a robust, fearless man reduced in such a way.

I let him be as long as I dared, but the sounds of his weeping carried in the dark and seemed alarmingly loud. Some of the tiny lights on the face of the mausoleum began to move, as if descending.

I took hold of the sobbing fighter and tried to use my will to calm him.

It didn't work. No persuasion could anchor the edges of his sanity where it had come adrift.

I had to be harsher. I numbed his mind with a deep psychic probe, blocking his terror out and freezing his thoughts but for the most basic instincts and biological functions.

* * *

We approached the mausoleum across a plain of lightless stone. The further we got, the further away I realised the structure actually was. It was evidently even bigger than I had first realised.

I had Gustine switch off his lamp pack. We simply followed the dots of light up ahead. I suggested that Cherubael might like to warn us if the darkness around us became anything other than a flat table of stone. A chasm, for example.

The only advantage in the mindless scale of the place as I could see it was that the enemy would have a hard job finding us. There was so much space to search.

After what seemed like an hour, we were still a very long way from the tomb. I checked my chronometer to determine precisely how long it had been since we accessed the interior of Ghül, but it had stopped. Stopped isn't right exactly. It was still running and beating seconds, but the time was not recording in any way.

I recalled the clock in Aemos's suite, chiming to mark out times that had no meaning.

As we closed on our destination, I was able to make more sense of the lights. Tiny dots, they had seemed, casting little fields of light.

They were massive lamps, high power, of the sort used to light landing fields or military camps. Mounted on suspensor platforms, they floated at various points in front of the face of the mausoleum, lighting up surface details in patches of glare the size of amphitheatres. There were forty-three of the platforms, each with its own lamp. I counted them.

There were men on the platforms, human figures. Glaw's men, I was sure, some of them mercenary guards, most of them adepts of arcane lore enlisted to his cause.

As we watched, some of the platforms drifted slowly or adjusted the sweep of their light.

They were reading the wall.

By whatever catalogue of means, Glaw had learned of this place, found it and made his way inside to plunder its vile treasures. But its innermost secrets clearly still eluded him.

That was why he had wanted the *Malus Codicium* so badly.

To turn the final lock, to get him through the final barrier.

One of the platforms began to climb vertically, its lamplight flickering across the passing relief of the tomb face. It climbed and then halted far up above at what seemed to be the top of the wall. Its beam picked out an open square, an entrance, perhaps, though who would put an entrance at the top of a wall without steps?

I scolded myself for asking. The warped ones.

'Glaw is up there,' Cherubael said.

It was right. I could smell the monster's mind.

We hurried the last distance to the foot of the mausoleum wall. Several cargo fliers and two bulk speeders were parked down here, alongside metal crates of equipment and spares for the lamp platforms. Their base camp.

We waited. I considered our options.

Almost at the same time, two of the platforms descended the wall to ground level, dimming their huge lamps. There were about six men on each one.

One settled in and two men jumped down, hurrying towards one of the cargo fliers. I could hear them, exchanging words with the crew on the platform. A moment later the other came down softly beside it.

I could see the men. They were dressed in light fatigues or environment robes. Some carried data-slates.

The men who had gone to the flier returned, carrying an equipment crate between them. They loaded it onto the platform and it immediately began to climb back up the wall, its lamp powering back to full beam to resume its work.

'Come on,' I said quietly.

More men were loading more crates onto the other platform. There were six in all – four in robes and two armoured mercs operating the platform controls.

Barbarisater took the three loaders out with two quick strokes. Gustine dragged a man backwards over the platform rail and snapped his neck. Cherubael embraced the two mercs from behind and they turned to ash and sifted away.

We got on board.

'Get ready with the lamp,' I told Gustine. I studied the platform control panel quickly, and then activated the lift. The attitude controls were a simple brass lever.

We rose. The tomb face whispered by. As we lifted past the lowermost of the working platforms, Gustine powered up the lamp and angled it towards the wall.

I couldn't remember quite how far up the platform had been before it had descended for spares. How long before we passed our designated spot and were noticed by the others?

I hoped they were all too engrossed in their work.

We were about two-thirds of the way up when we heard shots from another platform and a lamp swung our way. Almost immediately, so did several others, tracking our ascent. Las-fire pinged across at us. Gustine dropped down by the rail and returned fire. I kept us rising.

'Do you want me to...?' Cherubael asked.

'No, stay put.'

Gustine's next salvo took out the lamp of a platform rising after us. A huge shower of sparks erupted out and drizzled down the tomb face. I felt multiple jolts as shots impacted against the underside of our rig.

Almost there.

We rose up next to the entrance. It was square, maybe forty metres across. A platform was already floating outside it and, clumsy with the controls, I slammed us against it. The men aboard began firing. There were others inside the dim mouth of the entrance. Gustine blasted back. I saw one topple back onto the deck of the other platform, and then another pitch clean off and drop like a stone.

Las-fire and solid rounds raked our vehicle, tearing strips and nuggets out of the deck plating and the rail. Shot through, the lamp died.

I hauled on the control stick and slammed us sideways into the other platform, deliberately this time. We ground against them and drove them into the tomb face. The edge of their hull shrieked out sparks as it tore against the stone. I did it again. They were screaming and firing.

'Let's move!' Gustine yelled.

He heaved a grenade into the mouth of the entrance to clear us a path.

There was a dull bang and a flash, and two figures came flailing out into the air.

Gustine tossed a second onto the other platform and then leapt over the rail into the tomb entrance, blasting into the wafting smoke haze with his lasrifle.

I followed him, Cherubael drifting at my heels. It was damn hard to step wide enough and span the gap between the platform and the entrance's stone lip.

Gustine's second grenade ripped a hole through the deck of the other platform. It sagged and then dropped, like a descending elevator, trailing flames.

Far below us, it tore through two other platforms and spilled men and debris into the air.

The jolt of the blast had come at the wrong moment for me. Our platform shuddered and yawed out like a boat at a dock, and I was still halfway across, forcing my stiff, heavy limbs to carry me.

I was going to fall. The brace around my body felt as heavy as an anchor, pulling me down.

Cherubael grabbed me under the arms and hoisted me neatly into the entrance.

I was grateful, but I couldn't find it in me to thank it. Thank Cherubael? The idea was toxic. Then again, just as unlikely was the notion of Cherubael voluntarily saving my life...

Gustine was fighting his way forward down the entrance, which we saw now was a long tunnel that matched the dimensions of the opening. Crates of equipment were piled up in the mouth, and floating glow-globes had been set at intervals along the wall. They looked like they went on for a long way.

Four or five mercs and servants of our adversary were dead on the tunnel floor and half a dozen more were backed down the throat of it, firing to drive us out.

Cherubael swept forward and obliterated them. We came after him. I so dearly wished I could run.

The tunnel opened on the other side of the tomb face. We set eyes on the interior. By now, I had become numb to the inhuman scale of things. The tomb was a vault in which one might comfortably store a continent. The inner walls and the high, stone-beamed roof were lavishly decorated with swirls of script and emblems that I swore I would never allow to be seen by other eyes. This was the crypt where Yssarile lay in death, and the walls screamed his praise and worship.

I could make out little of the dark gulf below, but there was something there. Something the size of a great Imperial hive city. I discerned a black, geometric shape that was fashioned from neither stone nor metal nor even bone, but, it seemed, all of those things at once. It was repellent. Dead, but alive. Dormant, but filled with the slumbering power of a million stars.

The barque of the daemon-king. Yssarile's chariot of unholy battle, his instrument of apocalypse, with which he had scoured the warped fortresses and habitations of his own reality in wars too dreadful to imagine.

Glaw's prize.

From the globe-lit tunnel, we could make our way out onto a massive plinth of dark onyx that extended from the edge of the inner wall. There was a block raised there, a polished tooth of dark green mineral forty metres tall, set deep into the plinth. It was wound with carved spirals.

Glow-globes floated around it and tools and instruments lay at its foot. Pontius Glaw had been studying this discovery himself. But the noise of our violent entry had alerted him. He was waiting for us.

He emerged from behind the standing block, calm, almost indifferent. His tall, gleaming machine body was as I had remembered it from the auto-seance. The cloak of blades clinked as he moved. The ever-smirking golden mask smirked.

'Gregor Eisenhorn,' he said softly. 'The galaxy's most persistent bastard. Only you could scrabble and slash and claw and crawl your way to me. Which, of course, is why I admire you so.'

I stomped forward.

'Careful!' Gustine hissed, but I had long passed the point where being careful was a high priority.

I faced Glaw. He was broader than me and a good deal taller. His blade-cloak jangled as he stroked a perfectly articulated duralloy hand across the surface of the green block. Then he raised the same hand and held it up for inspection.

'Magos Bure did a fine job, didn't he? Such a craftsman. I can never thank you enough for arranging his services. This is the hand I killed him with.'

'There's more than his blood on your hands, Glaw. Do you answer to that name now, or do you prefer to hide behind the title Khanjar?'

'Either will do.'

'Your daughter didn't take either of your names.'

He was silent. If I could get him angry, I could perhaps force an error.

'Marla,' he said, 'so headstrong. Another reason to kill you, apart from the obvious.'

He was about to say something else, but I had waited long enough. I blasted my will through the runestaff, and lunged forward, swinging my blade.

The psychic blast knocked him back, and he half-turned, his cloak whirling out and turning Barbarisater aside with its multiple edges. His turn became a full spin and I lurched back to avoid the lethal hem of his blade-cloak.

Gustine moved in, firing bolts of light that simply reflected off Glaw's gleaming form.

Cherubael came in from the other side. Its searing attack scorched Glaw's metal, and I heard him curse. He slashed at Cherubael with his open hand, extending hook blades from slots in the fingertips.

The hooks ripped into Cherubael's flesh but it made no cry. It grappled with Pontius Glaw, psychic power boiling the space between them and flaring out in spasming tendrils of light. The very air crisped and ionised. Glaw's dancing metal feet chipped flakes of onyx off the plinth beneath him. I tried to get in, to land a blow in support of the daemonhost, but it was like approaching a furnace.

Gustine simply looked on, open-mouthed. He was so far out of his league it wasn't funny.

Glaw tore out a savage blow that spun Cherubael away for a second and followed it up with a lance of mental fury that actually made the daemonhost tumble out of the air. Cherubael got up slowly, like a thrown rider, and rose up off the ground again.

In that short break, I rejoined the struggle, driving at Glaw with alternate blows of staff and sword, keeping the most powerful mind wall I could erect between us.

Glaw smashed the wall into invisible pieces, struck me hard and tore the staff out of my hand. His blades lacerated my arm and ripped my cloak.

I exerted all the force I had and rallied with Barbarisater, cutting in with rotating *ulsars* and heavy *sae hehts* that chimed against his rippling cloak armour. The runestaff had fallen out of reach.

I ducked to avoid a high sweep of his razor-hem, but I had forced myself too hard. I felt cranial plugs pop and servos tear out of my back. Pain knifed up my spine. I barely got clear of his next strike. My sword work became a frantic series of *tahn feh sar* parries, as I tried to back away and fend off his hooks and cloak-blades.

Cherubael charged back at Glaw, but something intercepted it in mid-air. Out of the corner of my eye, I saw Cherubael locked in aerial combat with an incandescent figure. They tumbled away, off the plinth, out over the gulf of the tomb.

'You don't think you're the only one to have a pet, do you?' Glaw jeered. 'And my daemonhost is not restricted in its power like yours. Poor Cherubael. You've treated him so badly.'

'It's an "it", not a "him",' I snarled and placed a high stroke that actually notched his golden mask.

'Bastard!' he squealed and swept his cloak around under my guard. The thick metal of my body-brace deflected the worst of it, but I felt blood welling from cuts to my ribs.

I staggered back. The agony in my spine was the worst thing, and I was certain my already limited motion was now badly impaired. My left leg felt dead and heavy.

Ironhoof. Ironhoof.

He thrust at me with his talons and nearly shredded my face. I blocked his hand at the last second, setting Barbarisater between his splayed fingers and locking out his strike.

He threw me back. I was off-step, out-balanced by my slow, heavy mechanical legs.

Laser shots danced across Glaw's face and chest as Gustine tried vainly to help out. Glaw pirouetted – a move that seemed impossibly nimble for such a giant – and his cloak whirred out almost horizontally with the centrifugal force.

Hundreds of fast moving, razor-sharp blades whistled through Gustine, so fast, so completely, that he didn't realise what had happened to him.

A mist of blood puffed in the air. Ghustine collapsed. Literally.

Glaw turned on me again. I'd lost sight of Cherubael. I was on my own.

And only now did I admit to myself that I was out-matched.

Glaw was almost impervious to damage. Fast, armoured, deadly. Even on a good day, he would have been hard to defeat in single combat.

And this wasn't a good day.

He was going to kill me.

He knew it too. As he pressed his assault, he started to laugh.

That cut me deeper than any of his blades. I thought of Fischig, Aemos and Bequin. I thought of all the allies and friends who had perished because of him. I thought of what his spite had done to me and what it had cost me to get this far.

I thought of Cherubael. The laughter reminded me of Cherubael.

I came back at him so hard and so furiously that Barbarisater's blade became notched and chipped. I struck blows that snapped blade-scales off his clinking cape. I struck at him until he wasn't laughing any more.

His answer was a psychic blast that smashed me backwards ten paces. Blood spurted from my nose and filled my mouth. I didn't fall. I would not give him that pleasure. But Barbarisater flew, screaming, from my dislodged grip.

I was hunched over. My hands on my thighs, panting like a dog. My head was swimming. I could hear him crunching over the onyx towards me.

'You'd have won by now if you'd had the book,' I said, coughing the blood from my mouth.

'What?'

'The book. The damned book. The *Malus Codicium*. That's what you were really after when you sent your hired murderers against me. That's why you tore my operation apart and killed everyone you could reach. You wanted the book.'

'Of course I did,' he snarled.

I looked up at him. 'It would have unlocked the prize already. Done away with this endless, fruitless study. You'd simply have opened the tomb and taken the daemon's chariot. Long before we could ever get here.'

'Savour that little triumph, Gregor,' he said. 'Your little pyrrhic victory. By keeping that book from me you have added extra months... years, to my work. Yssarile's weapon will be mine, but you've made its acquisition so much harder.'

'Good,' I said.

He chuckled. 'You're a brave man, Gregor Eisenhorn. Come on, now – I'll make it quick.'

His blades clinked.

'I suppose, then,' I added, 'I'd have been mad to bring it with me.'

He froze.

With a shaking, bloody hand, I reached into my coat and took out the *Malus Codicium*. I think he gasped. I held it out, half open, so he could see, and riffled the pages through with my fingers.

'You foolish, foolish man,' he said, smiling.

'That's what I thought,' I said. With one brutal jerk, I ripped the pages out of the cover.

'No!' he cried.

I wasn't listening. I fixed my mind on the loose bundle of sheets in my hands and subjected them to the most ferocious mental blast I could manage. The pages caught fire.

I threw them up into the air.

Glaw screamed with despair and rage. A blizzard of burning pages fluttered around us. He tried to grab at them. He moved like an idiot, like a child, snatching what he could out of the air, trying to preserve anything, anything at all.

The pages burned. Leaves of darkness, billowing across the plinth, consumed by fire.

He snatched a handful, tried for more, stamping out those half-burned sheets that landed on the ground.

He wasn't paying any attention to me at all.

Barbarisater tore into him so hard it almost severed his head. Electricity crackled from the rent metal. He rasped and staggered. The Carthean blade sang in my hands as I ripped it across his chest and shattered part of his cloak.

He fell backwards, right at the edge of the plinth, his finger hooks shrieking as they fought to get a purchase on the smooth onyx. I swung again, an upswing that ripped off his golden mask and sent it spinning out over the gulf. The interior of his head was revealed. The circuits, the crackling, fusing cables, the crystal that contained his consciousness and being, set in its cradle of links and wires.

'In the name of the Holy God-Emperor of Terra,' I said quietly, 'I call thee diabolus and here deliver thy sentence.'

My own blood was dripping off Barbarisater's hilt between my doubled handed grip. I raised the blade.

And made the *ewl caer*.

The blade split his head and shattered the crystal into flecks of glass.

Pontius Glaw's metal body convulsed, jerked back and fell off the edge of the plinth, down into the gulf, into the blackness of the daemon-king's tomb, its cloak-blades chiming.

I was sitting on the plinth, with my back against the tomb wall, blood slowly pooling around me, when a flight flashed out in the darkness of the vault.

It came closer.

At last, Cherubael floated down and hovered over me. Its face, limbs and body were hideously marked with weals, burns and gashes.

I looked up at it. It was hard to move, hard to concentrate. There was blood in my mouth, in my eyes.

'Glaw's daemonhost?'

'Gone.'

'He claimed it was more powerful than you.'

'You don't know how nasty I can be,' it said.

I thought about that. The last of the diabolic book's pages were mere tufts of black ash, scattered across the plinth.

'Are we finished here?' it asked.

'Yes,' I said.

It frowned.

'I'm going to have to carry you after all, aren't I?' it sighed.

DOSSIER ADDENDUM
NOTES CONCERNING THE KEY INDIVIDUALS IN THIS ACCOUNT

Inquisitor Gideon Ravenor supervised the annulment of 5213X, also known in some records as Ghül. Despite long debates amongst the Sector Ordos, no attempt to recover an artefact and material from 5213X was ever permitted. Under orders from Battlefleet Scarus, under the command of Lord Admiral Olm Madorthene, annihilated the planet in 392.M41. Ravenor continued to serve the Inquisition for several centuries, performing many notable acts, including the destruction of the Heretic Thonius Slyte, but his posthumous fame results more from the quality of his writings, especially the peerless work The Spheres of Longing.

Inquisitor Golesh Heldane survived the destruction of the Essene *at Jeganda. His bodyguards were forced to sever his leg to free him and carried him to his ship. He spent many years recovering from his horrific injuries, which required still more severe augmetic reconstruction than he had already undergone. He returned to active service, but his career was blighted by his reputation. He was killed, following injury, on Menazoid Epsilon in 765.M41.*

Harlon Nayl continued in the service of the Inquisition for many years and, along with Kara Swole and Eleena Koi, joined the staff of Inquisitor Ravenor. Their individual fates are not recorded in the Imperial archive, though it is believed that Nayl died circa 450.M41.

Crezia Berschilde returned to Gudrun, where she served as Chief Medicae (anatomica) at the Universitariate of New Gevae until her retirement due to failing health in 602.M41. Several of her treatises on augmetic surgery have become standard authority texts.

Medea Betancore returned to Glavia and became the director of her family shipwright business, a post she held for seventy years. She disappeared en route to Sarum in 479.M41, although several later reports suggest she survived that date.

* * *

Lord Inquisitor Phlebas Alessandro Rorken recovered from his ill-health and became Grand Master of the Ordos Helican after the disappearance of Leonid Osma. He held the post for three hundred and fifteen years.

Inquisitor Gregor Eisenhorn is believed to have continued in the service of the Ordos after the events on 5213X, though recorded details of his life and work after that date are conjectural at best. His eventual fate is not recorded in the Imperial archives.

There is no archived mention of the being known as 'Cherubael.'

THE KEELER IMAGE

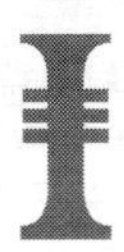

Medonae the Eater, so called because of his appetites, had declared an auction, and word of this sale brought dealers and speculators from across the subsector, despite the isolation of his home.

An item in the catalogue drew my attention. I sent an agent in advance to confirm the provenance, and when word came back to me that it seemed authentic, I made arrangements to attend the sale in person.

Medonae the Eater dwelt on a war-burned rock called Pallik. Its orbit and revolutions blessed Pallik with a complex and irregular pattern of days and nights, some long, some short, some bright, some dim, which had led to the publication of various thick zodiacs and ephemeris tracts. I was not much bothered with learning the names and durations of the day-night cycle. All I knew was that I should avoid the long and formidable 'burnday', a periodic event when all three suns rose together.

Many of those attending the auction arrived by cutter and orbital boat, setting down in the bleak flats of the desert outside the sloping walls of Medonae's palace. Others came into the local city, Baryt Prime, and then hired caravans to trek out to the palace, six hundred kilometres beyond the city gates. Caravans made the trip almost daily, laden with goods from the city's produce markets, such was Medonae's appetite.

I set down on a mesa five kilometres from the palace, and made the way on foot. It was a lowday, when only the second sun made an appearance in the heavens, and then only for a brief interval of six and a half standard hours.

It was cold and dry. Through my glare shields, the sky was a deep, rich blue and the sun a white ball that cast lens flare when I turned my head. Light glinted on the hulls of shuttles and cutters parked on their landing frames on the desert floor. I saw the thin dust plume of a caravan procession fifteen kilometres out.

The palace was of fair size. It was all that remained of a city that had been levelled by war. Portions of it sloped away into the desert sands in litters of rubble, suggesting that a great deal more of the ancient habitation lay below ground or was, at least, buried in the bosom of history.

Sentinels at the gatehouse watched me approach.

'You come to Medonae?' asked one, his voice a vox-hiss through his rebreather mask. Both of them were dressed in plate and bodygear that had once been Astra Militarum issue, now repainted in the bright colours of a circus.

'I do,' I replied.

'Your name?'

'Gregor Eisenhorn,' I replied. I saw no reason to lie.

'And your standing?'

I showed them my Inquisitorial rosette.

Neither blanched.

'Have you come to purge us, sir?' one of them laughed.

'I don't know,' I answered. 'Has anyone here denied the sanctity of the Throne?'

'Not us,' chuckled the other. 'We are all obedient to Holy Terra here, all of us.'

'Then my business is purely to bid and buy,' I said.

I was admitted.

The entry halls of the palace were busy with visitors. Each one, it seemed, had brought an ample entourage. Medonae's servitors were conveying trays of food and drink from the kitchens, each new dish announced by a liveried chamberlain who declared the name of the delicacy as though it were another guest at the proceedings. I was offered a flask of water – a ritual gift for any traveller arriving out of the desert – which I took, and a beaker of wine that I did not. Various lots from the forthcoming sale had been set on display throughout the halls so that they could be viewed. I saw prayer-wheels from the Long Graves of Thracian, diadems from the Slave Worlds, a fine bust of Saint Kiodrus still in its satin-lined box, and a good oil of Guilliman, done by Manxis of Eustis Majoris, or so the ticket stated. The composition was well enough, but the brushwork lacked the finesse of Manxis himself. I thought that, most likely, it was a copy or the work of his school.

I was admiring it when a voice at my shoulder said, 'I know why you're here.'

I turned.

'I am Medonae,' the man said. He was tall, slender, smiling, dressed in a green bodyglove and half-cloak. He wore what might be described as too much jewellery, including a tiara of pearl and crystal.

'You are Medonae?'

'I am, in fact, his mouth,' the man said. His smile was alarmingly broad. 'He speaks through me, and I conduct his business.'

'You are his proxy, or an avatar?' I asked.

'An avatar,' he replied. The tiara and the rings, I realised, were part of a more extensive suite of telekine systems that allowed Medonae to puppet the man and operate through him.

'You are Gregor Eisenhorn,' he said, 'of the Ordos.'

'I am.'

'Your reputation precedes you. There can be only one item in this sale that would attract an individual such as yourself. Would you like to see it?'

He led me to a side chapel. The lowday sun fell pale through the bars of the tall windows. The object stood on a pedestal, protected by light screens. It was a vitreous plate milled in plastek, about a third of a metre square.

'Magnificent, isn't it, sir?' Medonae's mouth said.

It was the most appalling thing I had ever seen.

'Exquisite.'

'I'll leave you to enjoy it,' he said.

I wasn't alone in the room. Several other visitors were viewing the piece. One was a hard-set man with extensive augmetic optics sutured into his skull.

'Quite a thing,' he mused.

'Indeed,' I replied.

'Genuine,' he added. His optics whirred. 'I can gauge the age of the glass, the plastek sheath. The format of the plate matches the kind she was known to use. A miracle beyond measure that something so fragile could have survived so long, when so much else perished.'

'Truly,' I agreed.

'But even more,' he went on, 'the image itself. The composition. She had an extraordinary eye as a remembrancer. I doubt any soul in the Imperium has ever matched her skill at the capture of picts.'

'This they say of her,' I said. 'An exceptional gift. Which is why she was chosen, of course, for the expedition.'

'To think,' he sighed, 'that someone had that kind of superlative talent, beyond any before or since, and yet that is *still* not the thing she is most famous for.'

He looked at me. His optics clicked and buzzed.

'What do you think?' he asked. 'Do you think the most incredible thing about it is that it is an original pict, made ten thousand years ago, by the hallowed founder of the Imperial Truth? Or that it is a pict of Horus Lupercal?'

'I think the most incredible thing about it,' I replied, 'is that it is sitting on sale here and not sequestered in a vault on far-off Terra.'

Euphrati Keeler was a remembrancer. In the last years of the Great Crusade, armed with a good eye and a picter, she had been appointed to the 63rd Expeditionary Force, to observe and record the operation of the Luna Wolves. Her work was remarkable. Her fame spread. The Warmaster himself regarded her with favour. In that distant age, the God-Emperor had decreed that the operation of the Imperium should be documented by artists and historians to make a chronicle of the foundation of the Age of Man. Such had been the mindset then: that the great work of engineering a civilisation should be honestly, freely and independently recorded.

That does not sound like the Emperor I know.

Such freedom ended, of course, in the atrocities that followed, in the years of bloodshed we now call the Heresy War. Keeler was present on the ground at the start of it. She was a witness to the first acts of bloodshed. She stood in time at the zero point where history turned a corner, and she did so with a picter in her hand, capturing that transformation.

Her story did not end there. She so easily might have been one of the trillions extinguished in the fires that followed. Her name is not commonly known today... except that it *is*, as Saint Euphrati. She was blessed with divine grace and gifts, and from her – and those few close to her in those bleak years – the essence of the Imperial Creed was born. She was one of the first saints. From her, and those disciples around her, arose the tenets of the Lectitio Divinitatus, the truth of us all, that the Emperor of Mankind is not a man, but a god. It is through her that the truth was recognised. It was in her that our faith was born.

The man with the optics was called Sejan Karyl. We returned to the main halls and sat together, talking of what we had seen.

'The pict itself isn't the prize, you know?' he said.

'It is beyond value,' I said. 'An image of Lupercal, in life, before he fell. The beauty and strength of his visage speak to the depth of the catastrophe that occurred.'

'Some might say that none should look upon it, ever,' he said.

'Who might say that?'

'The Inquisition,' he replied, 'of which, I hear, you are a part.'

'I believe it should be seen,' I said. 'As a warning – to show how even the greatest perfection can be blackened... To refresh our determination to guard against the dark.'

He shrugged.

'If,' he said, 'it is Horus *before* he fell.'

'You think it after?'

'Would that not be a stranger lesson? If that was his face *after* Chaos stole him? Chaos hides its nature well.'

'You say it's not the prize,' I said, changing the subject.

'According to the catalogue,' he said, 'it comes with notes. Some frail documents written in her hand, describing the image and the circumstances of its capture.'

'You've seen them?'

Karyl shook his head.

'They are reserved for the successful buyer alone. But I have heard of their contents.'

I had too, naturally. That was partly why I had come. It was said the notes were revelatory. That they showed, in Keeler's own, authenticated script, that she considered Horus a man, not a transformed, daemonic being. Further, they related that it had been commonly known at the time that the Emperor denied His divinity. He had formally declared that He was not a god, and sought to suppress the notion that He was. The Lectitio Divinitatus was already growing back then. The notes showed that the Emperor wanted it proscribed and forbidden.

They showed that the Emperor did not believe Himself to be a god. Keeler and her companion saints had created the foundation of Imperial faith *against* the Emperor's express wishes.

That was a different kind of heresy, and I wasn't sure if the heretic was Keeler or, somehow, the Emperor Himself.

'There's no way to know the truth,' I said.

'The truth is in the writing,' said Karyl.

'The *danger*,' I corrected him, 'for truth is arbitrary – it's what people will do with it. If one, shall we say, stood against the Imperial Truth, one might use a pict and manuscript from such an august and exceptional source as the basis for a new creed.'

'To undermine the faith and deny the Emperor's divinity?'

'It is not reaching to imagine so.'

'And that, I presume, is why the Inquisition is here... To seize the image and remove that possibility.'

'I never said why I was here,' I replied.

'Not you.'

He nodded gently in the direction of a woman on the far side of the hall. She was talking with other guests.

'Halanor Kurtecz,' said Karyl. 'Ordo Hereticus. So I am told.'

'If the Ordo Hereticus wanted the Keeler image,' I replied, 'they would have stormed the palace, taken it, put all within to the sword, and levelled the site from orbit.'

'Maybe,' he said. 'Unless they wanted to find out who was interested first, to observe the individuals a relic of this kind brings out of the woodwork.'

He was right. I had thought as much. The sale was private, but it was still bait of the first magnitude. From my seat, I could see at least six persons of interest from the Ordo watch-lists: renegades, recidivists and heretics, lured into the open by the mouth-watering promise of a truly blasphemous artefact. If I had been in control of Ordo Hereticus operations, I would have stayed my hand, planted agents in the palace, and waited for the sale. Then, in one stroke, I would have taken possession of the heretical image, and also ended a dozen key enemies of the Imperium, possibly obtaining enough information, via torture and interrogation, to bring down most of the cult networks in the subsector.

In a way, that was why I had come. I didn't want the Keeler image. I wanted to see it, but I had no desire to own it. It was too dangerous to exist. I had come to see who the offering of it might bring out.

One *in particular*.

And I was sure I had found her. Karyl, with his sharp, augmetic eyes, had spotted her already. Halanor Kurtecz. She was no inquisitor. Sensor templating and psionic pattern recognition had registered enough positives: disguise, masking, juvenat treatments... They could all hide a lot.

But I was reasonably sure that Halanor Kurtecz was in fact the arch-heretic Lilean Chase.

The Cognitae, the oldest, greatest and most pernicious cult of Chaos in history, was present in the person of their legendary and elusive leader. Only something like the Keeler image of Horus Lupercal had the power to draw her out of hiding.

My long and bloody work was about to be completed.

Half an hour before the start of the sale, I was summoned to see Medonae.

He was in a private chamber. His mouth, all smiles as before, greeted me at the door and led me in.

Medonae the Eater had stopped being a functional human being many years ago. His appetite had got the better of him. His pallid, physical bulk, a pyramid of flesh that weighed over nine tons, was supported in a frame of suspensor pods and lifter bars. He no longer had discernible limbs. Gangs of slaves worked to massage oils into his flesh to keep it supple, a never-ending process, while trains of servitors carried in a ceaseless procession of foodstuffs that were fed to him by hovering cyberdrones high in the framework rigging.

It was hard to make out his actual face: just a small dot near the summit of the mountain of meat.

'My dear Inquisitor Eisenhorn,' he said, using his mouth. 'I wanted a word. I have a feeling that today will not end well. I want your assurance that you will not seek to prosecute me.'

'You have staged a sale, Medonae,' I replied. 'I know of no laws you have broken.'

'Your assurance, please, sir.'

'You have it. May I say, Medonae, that if you feel this auction will go badly, you should not have orchestrated it.'

'I would not have,' his mouth said, smiling. 'I worked to arrange a private sale for the image. A private sale. But it was not to be.'

'What do you mean?' I asked. My psychic powers detected a slight tremor. Fear, perhaps, or trepidation. The infinitesimal artificial delay between Medonae's thought process and its delivery by his mouth avatar gave me a window into his mind.

'I decided an auction would be best,' his mouth was saying.

I was forced to arrange this sale against my will, his mind was thinking.

I threw myself to the left.

Las-beams, bright as a sun's heart, scorched the ground where I had been standing.

Medonae had been coerced into this face-to-face meeting too. I cursed myself for not realising sooner that a man like Medonae the Eater, so ashamed of his physical state that he used an avatar for personal interaction, would never request to see anyone in person.

I rolled hard, incidentally knocking the mouth off his feet. The teeth of the trap were two cyberskulls, sweeping down from the high roofspace, their las kill-systems cycling for a second shot. A beam scored the floor behind me. Another struck the mouth as he rose, cutting him clean through. He dropped again with a gasp, face down, spattering the tiles with the gore and internal organs released by his bisection.

High above, in the rigging, Medonae's real mouth wailed with pain from the psychic feedback.

I cut loose, unleashing my mind at the grinning cyberskulls that whizzed towards me. One fierce mental jab, and I blew out the auto-control mechanisms, freeing them from the psionic impulse that directed them. One plunged like a meteor into the ground and exploded. The other whistled over my shoulder at high speed, out of control, and smashed against the chamber wall.

Sparks showered down from Medonae the Eater's rigging. My jab had burned out Medonae's telekine array too.

Three men burst into the chamber. I recognised them as members of Halanor Kurtecz's entourage. They were heavyset, powerful, fast.

And psyk-shielded.

I went for my sidearm, but the first was on me. He had a hooked dagger, which I blocked. I rolled backwards, hurling him over me onto the floor. I was back on my feet before he was, and swept his legs out from under him.

Turning, I drew my Tronsvasse handgun, and cut down the other two. The impact of the shots smashed both of them down hard.

The first man landed on my shoulders, his arm around my throat, bending me backwards. Only the wrist of my gun hand was stopping his dagger from plunging into my face. I threw an elbow, but it didn't connect. The man's strength was augmetically amplified. He was an engineered killer, a lifeward or a Cognitae murderform.

I have been crippled for decades. My feet, legs and lower back are sheathed in a heavy scaffold of metal calipers to allow me movement. I stamped backwards with one iron-shod boot, and crushed the arch of the killer's left foot.

He snorted in agony. His grip slackened slightly, and I tried the elbow again.

As he reeled backwards, I swung around and struck him across the head with my Tronsvasse. He fell sideways, his skull cracked, blood squirting from his ear.

Shots tore past me. More members of the Kurtecz crew had rushed into the chamber. They were firing hard-round autopistols and las-snubs.

I fired back as I ran for cover, smashing through a row of startled onlookers: bemused servitors with their trays of fine food who had come to a standstill, order systems shut, and were watching the pandemonium unfold. I knocked two clean over, and they fell, spilling their trays. Ambush fire from my would-be killers ripped into the line, dropping more of the confused slave-units. Plates smashed. Trays of gourmet food crashed to the ground.

My attackers fanned out across the room. My shots – snapped off between the milling, bewildered servitors – were driving Chase's men into cover on the far side of Medonae's mass. One of them had holstered his pistol, and was deploying a rotator cannon from the pack on his back.

I ducked.

The raking fire ripped across the floor, chewed through the servitors, and demolished the tiled decoration of the wall. Chips of enamelled ceramics and glass from the ornate windows showered in all directions. I heard the cannon's motor whining as the gunman changed munitions packs.

Shots screamed in from another angle. This was fire from a hellgun. The shots, placed with indecent accuracy, exploded brackets on the rigging that supported Medonae's mass.

There was a long, ugly shriek of metal giving way, then the whole nine-ton bulk of Medonae the Eater rolled sideways, hurling servitors and squealing slaves into the air.

Medonae rolled like a landslip, and crushed the killers where they crouched in ambush.

One survived, broke free, and ran. Another hellgun shot detonated his head.

I rose, cautiously. The air smelled of smoke, blood, food and skin oil. Slaves were wailing, weeping, nursing broken limbs.

Harlon Nayl padded into view, his hellgun up to his cheek and ready to fire.

'All right?' he asked me.

'Fine,' I replied.

Nayl had been my advance agent.

'I was wondering where you were,' I said.

'Keeping out of sight, like you told me,' he said.

I looked at the tumbled mass of Medonae the Eater. He was alive, helpless, mewling. Slaves were struggling to right him before his own bodyweight compressed his organs into failure. The blood of Chase's men seeped out from under him.

'I gave him an assurance,' I said.

'I didn't,' said Nayl with a grin. He knelt beside his final kill, rolled the body over, and fished something out of the man's jacket. He showed me.

An Inquisitorial badge. Nayl raised his eyebrows significantly.

'Cognitae, Harlon,' I said, 'posing as Ordo Hereticus.'

He shrugged.

'We have to find Chase.'

'You mean Kurtecz?' he asked.

'That's the name she's using.'

'It's really her?'

'Seems so,' I said. 'I can't believe we've finally got this close.'

'Well, it's been a jolly journey getting here,' said Nayl. 'The fun, the friendship. The journey's more important than the destination, isn't that what they say?'

I looked at him.

He sighed.

'Just trying to lighten the mood,' he said.

'Chase will want the Keeler image,' I said. 'Come on.'

Death, gunfire and word that the Ordo Hereticus was cutting loose, had caused panic in the palace. Guests and prospective buyers were fleeing with their entourages. Nayl and I pushed through the press of bodies, and made for the side chapel where the image had been put on display.

Sejan Karyl was lifting the Keeler image off its stand. His hands were gloved. An armoured carry-casket lay open at his feet, ready to receive it.

'Helping yourself?' I asked. I aimed my Tronsvasse at him.

Karyl smiled ruefully.

'I think the sale is off,' he said, 'and this is something I am anxious to obtain.'

He laid the glass plate gently in the casket, and turned back to the display stand. Under the velvet cushion was a small packet. Keeler's writings, the real prize.

'I can't let you take that,' I said. 'Halanor Kurtecz... Have you seen her?'

'No,' said Karyl. He was busy with the packet, opening the seal.

'Leave that,' I said. 'Think carefully, Karyl. When did you last see Kurtecz?'

'She fled, I think,' he said. He smiled. 'It's funny... I never thought I'd be grateful to the Ordo Hereticus, but thanks to them, this is now mine.'

Nayl took a step towards him, his hellgun aimed.

'My boss said put it down, so put it down. You've got some front. There are two guns trained on you and you *still* think you're going to walk out of here with that?'

I glanced around. Karyl was confident in something. But what?

'I should thank you too, I suppose,' Karyl said to me. 'But for you, the Ordo would not have driven this operation, and Kurtecz–'

'She isn't Ordo Hereticus. She isn't Halanor Kurtecz,' I said. 'Her name is Lilean Chase.'

Karyl looked at me. An expression of delight filled his face.

'Oh,' he said, laughing. 'I had thought so *highly* of you, but now I find you're a dolt like all the rest. Lilean Chase? You're so wrong, it's hysterical.'

He opened the packet and began to read.

'Delightful,' he murmured. 'Keeler is quite explicit. The Emperor is not a god. He disavows any effort to name Him so. You see, here? She states that it was her encounter with daemons in the presence of Horus Lupercal that drove her to extremes of belief. If daemons exist, then to her a god must exist too. The universe could not be so cruel, otherwise. The existence of a god was necessary to counterbalance the horror of the warp. The Lectitio Divinitatus is based on a lie. Imperial faith is based upon fear. The "saint" admits it.'

'Hand that to me,' I said. 'It is a deeply heretical text. It's going nowhere.'

'This?' Karyl smiled, gesturing with the papers. 'This is just the bonus prize, our reward for being patient today. It will make a nice addition to our library. It doesn't tell us anything we didn't already know.'

'You are Cognitae,' I said.

'Yes, Gregor. Lilean sends her regards. She had hoped to meet you in person one day, given the years you've been searching for her. But she's busy elsewhere. She sent me to collect this. *Your* road ends here.'

Nayl raised his hellgun, and aimed it at the man's head.

'I don't think you're in much of a position to issue threats like that,' he said.

'I'm not,' said Karyl. 'Today... this sale, it was a sting operation. The Ordo Hereticus learned that Medonae had the image. They knew it would be an irresistible lure to heretic groups. They coerced him into announcing an auction rather than trying to sell it privately. They knew the Cognitae would send an agent to get it.'

He grinned.

'That's *me*, by the way.'

'Halanor Kurtecz–' I began.

'Is an inquisitor,' he replied. 'Ordo Hereticus. She's running this operation. This sale was bait for the prize *she's* after.'

'The Cognitae–'

'Gods, *no*! A far *greater* heretic. The renegade psyker, the diabolus... Gregor Eisenhorn. This was all for your benefit, Gregor. *You* are the wanted man here. Your ex-masters, the Ordo Hereticus, want you ended.'

From the halls behind me, I heard screams, and the sound of weapons-fire. With Nayl covering Karyl, I went back to the chamber door to look.

Ordo Hereticus kill-teams were sweeping into Medonae's palace, slaughtering every living thing they could find. They had co-opted Tempestus Scions to do the bloodwork. I saw Inquisitor Kurtecz among the storm troops, ordering them on, relaying messages to find me and detain me at all costs.

I had believed I was setting a trap for Chase and the wretched Cognitae, but in truth it was a trap set for me. I was impressed at the skill and flair with which Kurtecz and her colleagues had lured me out of hiding.

I was horrified to see, now more clearly than ever, how much of an outcast I had become. To the Ordo Hereticus, I was as abominable as the Cognitae.

Today, the Cognitae were but a footnote, and Chase had used her opportunist cunning to lift a great treasure while the Ordo and I kept each other busy.

I had been outplayed by both sides: the Cognitae *and* my former masters.

I felt sick. The Ordos were blind if they could not distinguish between me and a threat as malevolent as the Cognitae cult. I had been right to cut my ties and continue my work alone. That knowledge gave me some small comfort.

Harlon cried out. I turned to find him knocked to the ground. Karyl had the sealed carry-casket in his hand, and was aiming a lasgun at Nayl.

Impressive. It took a lot to outsmart Harlon Nayl, especially when he had a gun to your head.

'I'll be leaving now, Gregor,' said Karyl.

I shot at him. My blasts withered in mid-air. Karyl – or whatever his true name was – was a high-function psyker. That's how he'd floored Nayl, and why he had seemed so confident. He'd hidden the power earlier, but now it was boiling out of him. I took the brunt of it, and it hurled me back into the wall.

I felt several ribs break.

But, at last, someone had underestimated me. I was a high-function psyker *too*. Karyl had power, but Chase should have sent someone with considerably more. Staying in the dark places had its advantages. People didn't know what I was truly capable of. Chase did not appreciate who she was dealing with.

My power had been blocked earlier by the Inquisition's mind-shields. Now it was free, and it was fuelled by my anger and frustration.

I yelled a single word of power.

The force of it, like a flaming shockwave in the air, struck Sejan Karyl, and threw him not just into the chamber's back wall but *through* it. Stonework ruptured. A terrible, blinding light shone in through the demolished hole.

I pulled down my glare shields, and helped Nayl to his feet. He pulled on his goggles too, and we drew up the heavy hoods of our coats.

Outside, the desert was too bright to look at. The heat was immense. While we had been inside the palace, lowday had ended, a brief night had flickered past, and burnday had begun.

Karyl lay on his back on a heap of rubble. Every bone in his body was shattered, but he was still alive. Blood from his wounds was cooking off him, and his exposed flesh was frying. He held the packet of Euphrati Keeler's ancient manuscript in one blackened claw of a hand, but the paper was already burning.

He was trying to put it out, but he was on fire too.

I watched his body burn, the papers with it.

'Get Medea on the vox,' I said to Nayl. 'Tell her to bring the gun-cutter in. We need rapid extraction.'

He nodded, and I heard him speaking Glossia into his vox-headset.

I opened my mind.

+Cherubael? Can you hear me?+

+Of course, Gregor.+

+I need your assistance.+

+My, my, Gregor. Do you need me to come and kill lots and lots of people for you?+

I hesitated. I thought for a moment of the Tempestus Scions and Inquisition teams ploughing through the palace at our heels, just minutes away from finding us.

'Yes,' I said, with great reluctance.

+I didn't quite hear that, Gregor.+

+Yes.+

Nayl and I took the armoured carry-casket, and set off into the burning desert. Medea was en route, less than a minute away.

We got a fair distance clear of the palace, and I turned to look back, in time to see a light come down from the sky that was brighter and more dreadful than the burnday glare of the three suns.

Medonae's palace began to die with volcanic finality.

I looked away.

From somewhere, I heard a deep, satisfied laugh.

It was probably the daemonhost, delighting in his slaughter, but just for a moment, I thought it had come, echoing, from the casket in my hand.

From the smiling, noble image that Euphrati Keeler had made so long before.

THE MAGOS

I wake and feel the fell of dark, not day.
What hours, O what black hours we have spent
This night! what sights you, heart, saw; ways you went!
And more must, in yet longer light's delay.

With witness I speak this. But where I say
Hours I mean years, mean life.
Bones built in me, flesh filled, blood brimmed the curse.

– Religious verse, Terran, M2

ONE

THE BONE COAST

Sometimes, at night, the lights would wake him.

It didn't happen often. These days, there wasn't much traffic on the Bone Coast Highway. Cargo convoys, now and then; the occasional freight tanker, once in a while; perhaps a fast transit, purring up the coast road to Delci, or down to Tycho. By day, he'd glimpse the dirty sunlight winking off their hulls as they rattled past. He'd hear their engines and the thok-thok! of their heavy wheels on the highway's broken rockcrete. The sounds of other lives with places to go, rushing past him, Doppler-distorted.

At night, sometimes, passing lights backlit his window blinds and drifted across the ceiling of his little bedroom.

Very rarely, the passing lights slowed down, perhaps hoping his little roadside property was a tavern or machine shop. They'd speed up again as soon as they saw their mistake.

Rarest of all, they'd stop. If they knocked at his door to ask directions, Drusher would answer them as politely and helpfully as he could. He didn't know much. He hadn't had much direction of his own for a very long time.

Some didn't knock. He'd hear them outside, prowling around, trying doors and windows, boots crunching on the chalky gravel. Reavers, that was his guess, road-mobs. There were more of those these days, chancers and migrants from the lawless zones of the north. He'd hide in the back room, one hand on his gun, until they went away. He'd heard stories. He knew that, one day, they'd do more than just try the door.

They'd kick it down. They'd come in.

That night, he woke to lights on the tatty blinds. They drifted above him, right to left, across the water-stained ceiling. Something southbound.

It slowed, then was gone.

Drusher lay back on his lumpy pillow and sighed. He stared up at the blank darkness and found it no less fathomable than his life. He'd been dreaming of something, something better than this. He wondered whether, if he closed his eyes and willed it, he could find his place in the dream again and pick up where he left off.

The lights came back, left to right this time. They stopped. The same vehicle, reversing. He recognised the throbbing engine tone.

He got out of bed. He put on his old spectacles with shaking hands. He didn't know what to reach for first, his jacket or his anxiety meds. Then he remembered he'd been out of anxiety meds for three months. He pulled his jacket on over his nightshirt and pushed his feet into unlaced boots.

The lights went out. The engine died. That decided it for him. Anyone who pulled over to ask directions out here left their engine running.

There were no lights on inside his property. He fumbled in the blue gloom and found his way to the hall. He heard boots on the gravel outside: someone moving around, to the left of the front door, then the right, casing the place.

This was not how he wanted to die. In all honesty, he would have been pushed to make a list of ways he *did* want to die, but being beaten to a pulp in his own property by a foraging road-mob certainly wouldn't have been on it.

Drusher crept into the back room. He tried to remember where he'd left his gun. He didn't like guns, never had. It had sat on the dresser for a while, a paperweight for some ageing migration reports. But it had kept looking at him, so he'd put it in a drawer.

That was it, a drawer. Which drawer?

As quietly as he could, he looked in one, then another. He was on the third drawer when someone came to the door. He could see the front door from the back room. The shadow against the window lights was distressingly big.

The owner of the shadow knocked. Hard. The sound made Drusher jump. It took a big hard fist to make a big hard noise like that. He couldn't help but fancy he was hearing, for the first time, the very fist that would eventually beat the life out of him.

Idiot, he told himself. *That's it. Paralyse yourself with fear. With fancy.* Valentin Drusher's imagination was his worst enemy. He tried to remind himself of that. He could imagine far worse and more horrible things than his imagination, but that kind of proved the point.

He found the gun. It was under a bundle of expired ration stamps, a broken clock and a coil of fishing wire. Of course it was. The ideal place. It was a small, chunky automatic, a Regit Arms .40 that Macks had given to him years ago. He had never, ever fired it.

Was it even loaded? She'd given him ammunition. Had he loaded it? If he hadn't, where was the box of ammunition? If he had, were the bullets still good? Did they... go off? Was that a thing?

He probably should have cleaned the weapon too, the way she'd taught him. It was probably so corroded it had seized solid.

Much like his life.

The shadow knocked a second time. Drusher started again. He steeled himself and decided to do the bravest thing he could think of.

He put the gun in his pocket and ran out of the back door.

The property was a pre-fab shack set back, a hundred metres or so, from the ragged coast highway. Drusher had lived in it for seven years. It was weather-worn and set on waste gravel, shrouded by bleached undergrowth and gnarled saltwood trees. From the front porch, by day, he could see the ocean, but that wasn't necessarily a good thing. To the rear, where the property backed into the dust dunes and the ridges of silt, were the coops and pens and outhouses. Everything got covered in a fine white dust blown in by the sea wind.

At night, it seemed a ghostly place, the white dunes silver against the low black sky. The air was still. It was a warm night, breathlessly warm. Even in winter, the Bone Coast was a thirsty place.

Drusher scuttled towards the outbuildings. Sweat was already dripping off him. He considered making a run for it, but there was nothing around for kilometres. The war, twenty or so years earlier, had scoured the Peninsula. The area around his home was a Throne-forsaken waste of bone-dry dunes, dotted ruins, inshore refineries, long since closed down, and the rusted carcasses of ATV carriers. The remoteness, and lack of amenities, were key reasons why the place had appealed to Drusher, and also key reasons why he'd been able to rent it for a manageable sum. He remembered the landlord, a property dealer in Tycho City, actually smiling with relief when Drusher had signed the lease and forked over the first quarter rent.

He decided to hide in the outbuildings, among the clutter. Most of the stuff had been there when he arrived. He'd added to it over time. Scavenging on the shore and inland had provided him with materials to use in various projects, the coops and pens for instance. Steel poles and wooden posts for frames, chain-link and mesh fencing to make the cages. Fuel cans hacksawed in half to make water troughs. There was some old sacking he used for windbreaks and lagging. He imagined himself under it, being very still.

He froze when he saw movement. A man appeared, walking around from the front of the property. He had a stablight in his hand and was playing it around. Drusher's eyes had adjusted to the darkness. He made the man to be young, slight of frame, fair-haired. Then the stab-beam pointed his way, and the glare ruined his night vision.

He ducked down, wincing, and crawled behind a pile of rotting cargo pallets. They had been going to be a lookout tower, a blind from which he could observe the winter migrations. But he'd never worked out how to engineer the old pallets into a platform that wouldn't collapse under him.

He heard the man call out. He heard footsteps on the chalky gravel. He dashed towards the pens and let himself in.

It was musty and dry inside. The air stank of birdlime, and there were feathers matted into the cage wire. His menagerie fluttered and warbled at his arrival. There were two *Tarkoni tarkonil* in the cage nearest the door, ailing creatures that he had found on his walks, one with a broken wing, the other matted with promethium. He was nursing them back to health, though he doubted either would ever be fit for release. Beside them, in the row of smaller cages, were various seabirds that had been grounded by a storm the previous winter, and seemed to have lost their migratory instincts. He'd fed them, and they'd stayed, pecking around the property, showing no signs of resuming their endogenous journeys. In his journal, he had written up each case, theorising that the electromagnetic fury of the storm had screwed up the magnetoceptive faculties that regulated their migratory behaviour. Either that, or it had caused some malfunction of the trigeminal system. They had lost the motivation to go on, and had forgotten why they were supposed to.

Sympathising acutely, he had taken them in.

In the end cage, beside the feed store, was the foul-tempered sea raptor, *Gortus gortus gershomi*. It hadn't been foul tempered when he found it. It had been dead, hanging like a broken umbrella from a stretch of chain on the beach. It had tangled a foot in the wire, exhausted itself trying to flap free and died upside down, of thirst and starvation.

He'd taken it as a specimen, intending to mount the long wing feathers on an armature for study and reduce the carcass to bones for anatomical comparisons. Only when he had brought it back to his shack, and laid it on his work table, had he realised that a flicker of life remained. He had cleaned it and fed it by hand, using a pipette that, now he came to think of it, was definitely part of the cleaning kit Macks had given him for the gun.

As it regained strength, it did not express gratitude of any sort. Drusher had been disappointed, but not surprised. He was a magos biologis and knew from long experience that wild things remained wild, and would peck if he got too close. Setting aside his brief, foolish dream of a wise and saturnine companion who would perch around his home and watch him with cold eyes as he shuffled into old age, he had confined it to the cage, intending to release it when it was strong enough.

It was still there after six months. He had yet to work out a way of opening the cage to let it out without losing several fingers and his eyes.

Drusher stood in the pens, breathing hard. He heard the *tarkonils* chatter and flap, the seabirds yik with agitation, and the damn raptor clack its scissor beak with undisguised contempt.

He was as trapped as they were.

The man approached the pens. Drusher edged towards the feed store. The raptor bashed at the wire, snapping at him.

'Please be quiet,' he whispered to it, putting a shushing finger against his lips.

It glared at him with fathomless, jet-dot eyes and resumed its assault on the wire.

A light shone in. The door opened. Drusher saw the man silhouetted against the night.

'Show yourself!' the man called out. The stab-beam swung. 'Throne's sake! Are you in there? Are you hiding?'

The man took a step forwards. Drusher shrank back, his shoulders against the door of the feed store.

'Take w-what you want!' he cried. 'I don't have much, but just take it!'

He'd heard that if you allowed the road-mobs to pick you clean without arguing, sometimes they let you live.

'I don't want anything,' the man replied. He sounded surprised. The stab-beam found Drusher's cowering, flinching face. 'I've come for you.'

Well, that was it, then. He was done for. Might as well just string him up from a fence by one foot like a broken umbrella.

At least he knew, now. At least he knew all hope was gone. It gave him an odd sort of strength, a resolve that he'd only managed to summon a couple of times before in his entire life. There was nowhere left to go. His back was against the wall. Well, literally, the door of the feed store, but metaphorically a wall, unyielding. He was cornered, trapped.

As on those previous occasions, the sudden resolve unlocked something in him. A will to live, an anger towards the world that thwarted and frustrated him at every last damn turn.

He wrenched open the clasp of the end cage. The sea raptor came out like a summoned fury in a blizzard of feathers. Keening, it went for the light and the open door.

The man in the doorway yelled out in alarm. The raptor hit him, pecking and raking. He yelped, covered his face and tried to fight it off. Its wings slammed at him. He lost his footing and fell sideways, the back of his head bouncing off the doorframe.

The raptor burst past, up into the night air, wings wide.

A second later, Valentin Drusher followed it out of the pens with equal determination, leaping over the body of the man sprawled in the doorway. He saw the raptor high above, its powerful white-fletched wings beating as it banked towards the sea. He felt as if he were flying too, flying free, leaving the horror of the world behind and soaring high into–

Something hit him across the mouth and clothes-lined him onto his back. The impact knocked his spectacles off. He was stunned for a moment, his head spinning, his mouth full of blood.

Another man was standing over him. He was very big, the owner of the shadow at the door. Drusher groped around, found his spectacles and jammed them back on. They were bent, but he could see the man. He was wearing a jack-armoured coat. His head was shaved, rounded and solid like the tip of a large-calibre bullet. He had a goatee.

He looked down at Drusher, baffled.

'The hell you playing at?' he asked.

'Don't kill me!' Drusher gurgled.

'I'm not going to,' the man replied.

Drusher wrenched out the pistol and aimed it at the man's face.

'Do not kill me!' he cried.

The man looked at the gun in annoyance.

'Well, *now* I want to,' he said.

Stab-beams bobbed behind him. More people, running over.

'Have you found him?' a voice asked.

'I found someone,' said the bald man, frowning at Drusher. 'He's got a gun.'

'And I'll use it!' Drusher yelled, lying on his back and brandishing the weapon wildly.

The bald man sighed and, in some manner that Drusher couldn't quite understand but which clearly involved terrifying reflexes, took the gun out of Drusher's hand.

'Now he hasn't,' the bald man called out.

The other figures arrived. They shone their stablights at him.

'Is that him?' the bald man asked.

'Yes,' said one of the figures. A woman. 'Valentin Drusher. Magos biologis.'

'He doesn't look like a magos biologis,' said the bald man. 'Just some old loon. Why isn't he wearing any trousers?'

'I was in bed!' Drusher wailed.

'With your boots on?' the bald man asked.

'That was after!' cried Drusher.

The woman bent down beside Drusher.

'Get up and stop making a fuss, Valentin,' she said. 'These nice people have come a long way to find you.'

Drusher knew her voice. After fifteen years, he still knew the smell of her too. Body heat, leather, a faint fragrance called *True Heart* that had cost him too much money in a Tycho city perfumery twenty years before.

'Macks?'

'Hello, Drusher,' said Germaine Macks. 'It's been a while.'

TWO

A SPECIFIC AREA OF TECHNICAL EXPERTISE

There were four of them. Macks and three others, two men and a woman.

'I made you this,' the other woman said. She put a tin mug down on the table beside Drusher.

She was a finely made woman with very dark skin, her hair tight-pinned around her head. Drusher could not guess her age. Thirty, perhaps? She wore gloves and an embroidered cerise jacket.

'What is it?' Drusher asked, dabbing at his split lip.

'Caffeine,' she said.

'I don't have any caffeine,' he replied.

The woman frowned and gestured towards the kitchen. 'Brown powder. Silver tin. Second shelf. Marked "Caffeine".'

'A sample of desiccated treefox droppings, for analysis,' said Drusher.

She nodded thoughtfully, then shrugged.

'Probably better not drink it, then,' she advised.

They had brought him inside and allowed him to get dressed. The bald man had not given him back his gun. Drusher's mouth, jaw and neck hurt from the blow that had knocked him down. He was fiddling with his spectacles, but the frames were still bent. No one had even said sorry.

Macks came in, pulled out the other chair and sat facing Drusher. He hadn't seen her in fifteen years. Her short hair was just beginning to lose its depth of colour, but she still looked good. He could see the tiny zigzag scar above the left-hand side of her mouth, and the trace of the other scar on her forehead. Both were old now, faded, like memories. She wore the uniform of a Magistratum marshal. Beside her, he felt ancient.

'I heard you retired,' he said.

'Didn't suit me,' she said. 'The division was understaffed so I took reassignment.'

'Tycho City?'

She shook her head.

'Unkara Province. Up north.'

He nodded, as if that meant something.

'Still a silly bastard, I see,' she said. 'When someone knocks on your door, you don't run away and attack them with eagles.'

'You do out here,' said Drusher.

She raised her eyebrows. 'Why are you living like this, Valentin? In this dump. Alone.'

'Well, odd as it may sound, there is very little in the way of paid work available for a highly qualified magos biologis on Gershom,' he said. 'A fact that I have wrestled with for, let me see now, *thirty-four years*, and a detail I wish I had been aware of when, as a young man with splendid prospects, I took the commission to do a survey of the planet's indigenous fauna, and ended up stuck here for the rest of my–'

'Don't start,' she said.

He opened his mouth to carry on, but saw the look on her face. It was a self-pitying rant she'd heard from him too many times. He cleared his throat.

'It also appears from experience,' he said, less emphatically, 'that I do not make for sparkling company, and so an isolated existence is better for everyone. Someone once told me I'd be happier alone. Or that I'd make others happier if I was alone. I don't recall precisely. There was a lot of shouting and door-slamming.'

Macks sighed and looked away.

'Did you train that eagle?'

Drusher glanced around. The younger, blond man was sitting on a bench in the corner. He was holding a dressing to the gashes on his cheek and neck.

'It was a sea raptor,' said Drusher.

'What?' asked the blond man.

'A sea raptor. Not an eagle. *Gortus gortus gershomi*.'

'Uh-huh,' said the man. 'I asked if you trained it.'

'No.'

'Then... a control implant of some kind?'

'No.'

'Is he psykana?' asked the bald man. He was suddenly standing in the doorway behind Drusher.

'No, he's not,' said Macks.

'Good,' said the bald man, 'because, you know–'

'I let a wild thing out, and you were in the way,' said Drusher to the younger, blond man.

'Ah, but you *knew* Voriet was in the way,' said the bald man, 'and you knew what would happen.'

'Yes,' said Drusher. He hesitated, then looked over at the blond man.

'I'm sorry,' he said.

Voriet shrugged.

'It's fine,' he replied. 'It was smart thinking, actually.'

'Yeah,' growled the bald man. 'If we'd been a road-mob, you'd have eagled the *crap* out of us.'

'What is this about?' Drusher asked. He was looking directly at Macks, the only person in the room he felt he could consider a friend, and even then, not much of one. 'Who are these people?'

The blond man got to his feet. With his free hand, he took out a rosette and showed it to Drusher.

'Interrogator Darra Voriet, Ordo Hereticus,' he said. 'These are my associates Medea Betancore and Harlon Nayl.'

Valentin Drusher didn't hear much beyond the word 'Ordo.' It felt as though a trapdoor had opened under him and plunged him into a world where there would never, ever be enough anxiety meds.

'We have need of assistance,' said Nayl, the big bald man. 'A specific area of technical expertise. You came highly recommended.'

'By the marshal, I presume?' asked Drusher, wiping his lips. Macks had produced a hip flask of amasec and let Drusher take a swig to steady his nerves.

'Yes,' said Voriet.

'I don't do consultations,' said Drusher.

'What are you, retired?' sneered Nayl. 'Living in your beachfront property, training eagles?'

'N-no–'

'I think I just heard you complaining there were piss-all opportunities for employment here on Gershom,' said Nayl.

'Does this pay?' asked Drusher.

'Yes,' said Nayl, 'in the form of deep satisfaction, and pride at having served the Emperor of Mankind and His Inquisition.'

'I thought so,' said Drusher.

'There's a stipend, and expenses,' said Voriet.

'Is there?'

'Maybe,' said Nayl. 'Name a fee. Bear in mind you're labouring under the false impression that you have any choice in this. The Inquisition needs your help. It's not a yes/no option.'

Drusher looked across the table at Macks. Panic was beginning to set in.

'Why did you bring these people here?' he hissed. 'What have you got me into? Why are you doing this to me *again?*'

'They need a magos biologis, Valentin,' she said.

'Well, they can find someone else,' said Drusher. 'I'm not going to get dragged into another one of your insane adventures.'

'Come on, Valentin. Outer Udar was fun. And Tycho City? We went to the zoo.'

'So you have history?' asked Medea Betancore.

'We do,' said Macks. 'Which is why I brought you to him.'

'A history of "insane adventures"?' said Betancore. 'In, what was it... Outer Udar and–'

'It's possible he was referring to the three years we were married,' said Macks.

Nayl snorted.

'It's not funny,' said Drusher.

'I am absolutely certain it wasn't,' said Nayl, 'for her.'

Drusher got up and tried to appear dignified.

'Look, sir,' he said. 'I am a magos biologis. I study flora and fauna. Make taxonomies. I have been here on Gershom for more than thirty years. I wish

I hadn't been, but there you go. It's not much of a life, however it's what I do. Twice, in the past, Marshal Macks has co-opted my assistance in certain matters. The last time was twenty years ago. They were dangerous experiences, very much outside my wheelhouse. I do not wish to repeat them. Ever. So I suggest you look for somebody more qualified to help with... whatever it is you're doing.'

'Thing is,' said Nayl, 'there's *no one* more qualified. Not in this system. No one else even *qualified*, period. You're the only magos biologis. Marshal Macks didn't recommend you because she thought you were particularly good. She recommended you because you were the only magos biologis she knew.'

Drusher sat down again.

Macks looked at Nayl sharply.

'You really didn't have to tell him that,' she said.

Nayl shrugged.

'I know what he's like,' Macks went on. 'He'll mope now. Sulk. We'll never get him to cooperate.'

'Wow,' murmured Drusher. 'You're making it better *all* the time.'

'I'll make him cooperate,' said Nayl.

Betancore raised a gloved hand.

'First of all,' she said, 'we're on a clock. He's waiting for us. I don't want to keep him waiting much longer, do you? And I'd rather we brought this gentleman along in a cooperative frame of mind than drag him unwillingly. So there must be something he wants, something that will make it worthwhile for him.'

'He wants to get off this planet,' said Macks.

Drusher looked at her. She was serious.

'He's wanted nothing more since the day I met him. One-way passage.'

'Where do you want to go?' asked Voriet.

Drusher swallowed hard.

'Anywhere,' he said quietly. 'Anywhere that isn't here.'

Voriet looked at Betancore. 'We can do that. Get him somewhere. Gudrun. Thracian Primaris...'

'You'd... pay for a travel bond?' asked Drusher.

'We've got a ship,' said Betancore.

Drusher began packing some belongings in an old Munitorum kitbag. His house was full of clutter, but when it came down to it, there were very few items he felt he had to take: his journals, the manuscript of his taxonomy, his sketchbooks. He wasn't sure any of that even mattered, but he felt obliged to take them; something to show he hadn't entirely wasted the previous thirty-four years.

'What is the issue?' he asked Nayl.

'Wildlife problem. Up north. Unkara Province.'

'And the work involves?'

'Insane adventures. You won't like it.'

'I will be resolved. I *can* be resolved, you know.'

'When the offer is right,' said Nayl.

Drusher stiffened.

'I'm not a mercenary,' he said.

Nayl shrugged.

'I am,' he replied.

He looked at Drusher.

'Just to be fair,' he said, 'you say you've had insane adventures.'

'I have.'

'I'm sure. I'm also sure that whatever escapades you and the marshal have enjoyed in the past... they're nothing. Nothing compared to what we do.'

'You underestimate what–'

'No,' said Nayl.

'Then you're boasting.'

'Not that either. I'm just trying to tell it to you straight. In all fairness. This isn't going to be like anything you've known before.'

'It must be like something I've known, sir,' said Drusher, 'or you wouldn't need my expertise.'

Nayl thought about that.

'Well, you know animals,' he admitted. 'You know how to let a wild thing out of a cage, and what will happen when you do. This is going to be like that, only in reverse.'

'Putting something back in a cage?'

'Mmm-hmm. We'll do the heavy graft. We just need expertise. Identification. Insight. That sort of thing.'

Drusher fastened the kitbag.

'Ready?' Nayl asked.

'Yes,' said Drusher. He paused. 'No, wait. Cages. You reminded me. I'll be right back. Two minutes.'

He went outside, to the back of the property. It was nearly dawn. The sky had turned mauve over the white dunes. It almost looked beautiful. *Typical*, Drusher thought. *Now that I'm finally leaving...*

He went to the pens and opened the cages one by one, shooing out the *tarkonils* and the seabirds. He couldn't leave them caged up and not come back. He threw down some feed for them, and they started to peck, strutting around the little yard warily.

They'd have to fend for themselves. It wasn't kind, but it was kinder than leaving them penned up to starve.

He looked at the property. He wasn't coming back. He wouldn't miss it.

He realised he was being watched.

The sea raptor was perched on a fence strut at the top of the dunes. It should have been down the coast by now, or out to sea, but there it was, watching him.

Drusher took off his spectacles, cleaned the lenses on the hem of his shirt so he could see better, and put them back on.

The sea raptor ruffled its wings, then spread them and powered down in one long swoop, landing on the ridge of the pens above him. It clacked its proud beak.

Drusher smiled.

'So all those months of being a bastard,' he said to it softly, 'and you wanted to stay after all? You could have sat on the back of my chair at night, watched me work... Go on, now. You're free.'

The raptor tilted its head and studied him.

'Go on,' he said. 'I'm going. You can go too. But thanks for seeing me off and everything.'

The raptor tilted its head the other way and opened its beak. He could see the sharp spear of its tongue. Such a majestic creature, so–

It stooped from the roof ridge into the yard, killed one of the pecking *tarkonils* outright, and took off with it in its talons. He watched it fly away into the dawn sky, lugging the limp prey with hefty beats of its wings.

A few *tarkonil* feathers drifted in the air around Drusher like snowflakes.

'Typical,' Drusher said.

'Who are you talking to?' asked Macks, stepping through the back door.

'Myself,' said Drusher.

'Ready?'

'I'm supposed to be a magos biologis, Germaine, but every day I realise I know nothing about anything. You sure you want me for this?'

'Not really,' she said, 'but we're going anyway.'

THREE

HELTER FORTRESS

Several roads converged in Unkara Town – the highways from the Peninsula to the south and the western routes through to Ottun and the ocean – and the least of them, a track, wound north into the hills for ten kilometres until it found the fortress.

The hills were not hills. They had earned that insufficient title in ages past, because they were a four hundred kilometre spur of the Tartred Range, and all peaks on Gershom were hills compared to those monsters.

They towered in their own right: younger mountains, sharp-edged, clothed in evergreen forests below their shoulders, sweeping up into spires of naked dark granite. They were called the Unkaran Hills, known too as the Karanines, and they formed the northern and eastern limits of the province. Their older, glowering cousins, the Tartreds, could be seen, from high ground on a clear day, as a blue shadow two hundred kilometres away, like the front wave of a great deluge, frozen solid and forever about to roll in and sweep the province away.

The history of the territory had been fraught. It had evaded Gershom's recent conflicts, including the long and complex civil war that had ravaged the Peninsula, spared by its outlying state and lack of significance. But the fortresses that clung to the long spur of the hills spoke of older disputes. Outer Udar lay to the east of the Tartreds' flanks, and in the early days of settlement, its territories had bred fierce nomadic peoples with an expansionist mindset. Long, ungainly wars of invasion and repulsion had haunted the Karanine belt.

No one studied them any more. The deeds and efforts of those wars were remembered only by the pages of history texts that slept on the library shelves of Unkara Town, and were never opened. The sites of skirmishes and battles were lost in the woodland slopes and valleys, so overgrown and misplaced that even their particular significances and causes had vanished. Occasionally, a farmer, grazing high pasture, or a woodsman in the deeper forest, would stumble on a rusted buckle or spear tip, or a piece of bone that was not an animal's, and realise that something had once happened in that empty place.

Only the fortresses remained as any kind of memorial to an age of conflict.

Raised in the dark granite of the Karanines, they had taken longer to fade into nature. Most were gone: heaps of stone scattered on lonely hillsides; stumps of wall, furred with moss, lingering in forest twilight.

Some had endured. Talla Keep, far to the west of Unkara Town, was a ruin, but its architecture was so cyclopean and its prospects so magnificent, it had enjoyed a romantic afterlife as a site for visitors, hunters, recreational walkers and a few amateur historians. Korlok Fort, another ruin, was less accessible, but it had survived in a local children's rhyme, and in the name of two hostelries in the town.

Helter Fortress was the most complete. It was the closest of all the fortresses to the town, and for the two centuries following its duties as a stronghold, it had served as the home of the Karanine Proctors, then as the summer retreat of the provincial governor, and finally as the estate of a local dignitary called Esic Fargul, who had retired there to enjoy the rewards of a successful career in the timber industry.

Fargul's wealth had run out five years before his health. Helter sank into neglect, and the old man died there, alone, in a draughty bedchamber on the fifth floor of the tower.

Helter Fortress was shut up at his passing. Its windows were boarded over, its gates chained, and weeds took up residence. No one had lived there, or even visited, for thirty years.

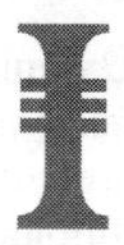

FOUR

HEURISTIC AMPLIFICATION DISCIPLINES

Garofar found Audla Jaff where he had left her in the old man's library. She was still reading, but he noticed it was a different book from the one she had been intent on an hour earlier.

An early rain had come up after dawn. Garofar could hear it pattering at the plastek sheeting they'd taped across Helter's broken windows, and tapping at what glass remained. There were wooden shutters, but Jaff had opened them for light, despite the glow-globes she had set around her perch on the ratty old chaise.

It had been two weeks since he'd met her, and he still didn't know what to make of her: elfin, with a frame like a boy, and a high forehead that made the curve of her brow seem huge, and very young, younger than him. She was smart, he knew that. Big eyes, like new coins, a tiny pinched mouth. He understood she was some kind of expert retained by the visitor. With the visitor absent, she was in charge.

He stood for a moment, feeling awkward, rain dripping off the leather-jack of his deputy's uniform.

'I've done a sweep,' he said.

'Are your colleagues on station?' she asked. She didn't look up. She turned a page.

'Yes, mam,' he said. He thought of Cronyl, sheltering from the rain in the gatehouse, and Edde, walking the west wall with her riotgun under her slicker.

'Any... any word from him?' he asked.

She closed the book and picked up another from a pile beside her.

'No,' she said.

'You don't think... something might have...'

'No,' she said. She was intent on the book. 'It's possible that something has, of course, but I doubt it. He knows what he's doing. Is there any sign of the others?'

He shook his head.

'Did you check the cold store?' she asked.

'Yes,' he said.

She raised her head and looked at him. The slightest hint of a question.

'You're reading, mam,' he said, changing the subject.

'I am,' she said, looking right at him.

'A book.'

Jaff looked down at the book in her hands and reacted as if surprised to see it there. Garofar had noticed her sense of humour before. It was at odds with her serene, cerebral manner. It seemed older than she was.

'I am,' she said.

'Anything in particular?' he asked.

'This?' she asked, gesturing with the book, a slim volume. '*Folk Verse of the Karanine Passes* by Nettial Farell, second edition, published by the Red Grange Press in Delci seventy-eight years ago, some water-marking, foxing and shelfwear, inscribed on the flyleaf "To my dear nephew Esic, your beloved aunt".'

She rolled off the details rapidly without even consulting the book.

'Good, is it?' he asked.

Jaff rose to her feet, unfolding her legs from under her. She was significantly shorter than him.

'You have a tell, Deputy Garofar.'

'A tell?'

'Several. In this case, a slight twitch of the masseteric ligament on the left side. A micro-expression that indicates annoyance or aggravation. You wonder why I am reading and not working. You ask if the book is good, when what you want to ask is why it's you who has to do the patrol sweep in the rain. The answer to your un-vocalised question is that I am researching. I am not reading for recreation. I am investigating Esic Fargul's library, or at least those parts of it that have not been reduced to pulp by damp and insect activity.'

Garofar glanced around the library. It had to hold upwards of ten thousand books.

'You... pick books at random?'

'No, I am working methodically.'

Garofar couldn't hide a laugh.

'You're reading them all? The entire library?'

'Yes.'

'Good luck with that, mam,' he smiled. 'I guess you'll be here a few years after we've all gone.'

'Why?'

'Well, to read all the books... I mean...'

'I have one hundred and seventeen more to go,' she said.

'You're joking,' he said.

'I must be,' she said with a flash of raised eyebrows.

'You can't have read... I mean... We've been here a couple of weeks.'

She put the book down.

'You really don't know what a savant is, do you, deputy?'

Garofar thought he did, but clearly he didn't.

'You could explain,' he suggested.

'Do you know what the Heuristic Amplification Disciplines of the Neo-Distaff Institute are?' she asked.

'I do not, mam.'

'Then a direct explanation will be ineffective. Do you know what a sponge is?'

'Yes,' he replied tightly.

'Then I am a sponge, and data is water.'

'I see,' he said.

'Do you know what a metaphor is, deputy?'

'I do, mam.'

'And according to your masseteric ligament, you know what condescension is too. So I apologise for that. Now, let's discuss your lateral cheek septum.'

'My...?'

'Your other tell, deputy,' said Jaff. 'A micro-twitch. When I mentioned the cold store, you lied. You didn't check it.'

Garofar sighed.

'No, mam. I... I know I should have. But it's a waste of time. All those bodies. I mean, they're not going anywhere...'

'Can you say that with certainty, deputy?' she asked.

Garofar didn't reply. He heard the rain pattering on the plastek sheeting. He felt cold, colder than he should have, even in the damp, draughty room, half open to the Karanine weather. It had sounded like a pretty interesting assignment when Macks had put him on it. A major case: murders, killings, the talk of Unkara Town, the idea that external investigators had arrived. No one had outrightly said so, but Garofar was pretty sure they were connected to the Ordos – big stuff, the sort of thing that didn't happen in a backwater province, the sort of thing that could get an ambitious junior officer noticed, and maybe lead to advancement, because opportunities in the Karanines were scarce, especially when the marshal showed zero signs of ever wanting to retire, like she should have done years ago, and make way for new blood...

But it had turned out to be much less comfortable. Cold, wet, tedious, yet with a constant undercurrent of something Garofar felt was malevolent, like a storm waiting to break. It wasn't the bodies. He'd seen plenty of bodies: accidents, bar fights, farming mishaps, plus a brief tour in the local militia during the last years of the civil war, before he joined law enforcement. Bodies didn't faze him, though the number and the manner of death in this case was unusual. What unsettled him was something he couldn't put his finger on, like they were poking at something that shouldn't be poked, or opening a cage that had been locked for a damn good reason. And that lead investigator was a piece of work. Scary as hell in his own right. If it had been up to Garofar, the lead investigator would have made it onto the list of suspects, just turning up in town like that, with his cruel manner and his band of disreputable henchmen.

But it wasn't up to Garofar. Hadeed Garofar was just a deputy with an assistant investigator's ticket. He was local enforcement. He was muscle. He did as he was told.

'Let's check the cold store together,' said Jaff. 'I want to take some ambient measurements anyway.'

'Yes, mam. Good,' he said. 'Measurements of ambient what?'

'Just ambient,' she replied. She buttoned her coat. Then she looked at him. 'I hear an engine,' she said, 'approaching.'

'The others must be back, mam,' he replied.

'Hmm. If they are, they've changed vehicle.'

'How can you tell?' he asked.

'It sounds different,' she said.

Deputy Cronyl had opened the gates to let the transporter enter the yard. He stood watching, his riotgun hooked over the crook of his arm as it came to a halt. Deputy Edde had appeared on the top wall to add cover.

The transporter was a cargo-4, an all-terrain variant, spattered in mud from the forest track. It pulled up beside the green ATV and the heavy, bronze Marshal Division transporter already parked there.

Garofar followed Audla Jaff into the yard.

The hatches popped on the cargo 4, and five people got out. Garofar's boss, Macks, and three of the investigator's team: the suave Voriet, the big thug Nayl and Mamzel Betancore, whose beauty stopped Garofar in his tracks every time he saw her.

It looked like someone had taken a swing at Voriet. There was a dressing strapped around his face. That pleased Garofar no end. Voriet was an arrogant bastard. He was of a type Garofar knew too well: privately schooled cadet officers in the Territorial Guard, petulant aristos, privileged rich kids from the cities, who rolled into Unkara every summer season to hunt and drink and sail the lakes, and generally harass any female they could find. They had rich fathers who retained expensive lawyers who, in turn, could disappear any indiscretions.

The fifth man looked like a vagrant. He was old and pale, and thin to the point of being haggard. His hair was grey, and he wore a shabby chequered suit and an overcoat that had outlived several previous owners. Little wire-frame spectacles perched on his face. The frames were bent, and they gave him a cock-eyed appearance. This was the expert they'd gone off to locate?

'Morning, chief,' Garofar called to Macks.

She nodded back. She was handing down a kitbag that was apparently the extent of the expert's luggage. The expert was standing nearby, adjusting his spectacles and looking around as if he'd never seen daylight or old high walls before.

'Garofar, this is Magos Biologis Drusher,' Macks said.

'Sir,' Garofar nodded curtly.

'Find him a room and give him a hand with his bag. We'll brief in twenty minutes.'

'Yes, mam,' said Garofar. He picked up the kitbag. 'Fifth floor is free,' he said.

Macks shook her head.

'Stick him on the fourth, near to me. If you put him on the fifth, someone will tell a ghost story about the old man dying up there and we'll never hear the bloody end of it.'

The expert, Drusher, scowled at her.

'I'm not a child, Macks,' he said. 'I don't believe in ghosts. An old building where someone once died? So what?'

'I know what you can get like, Valentin,' she replied.

'I presume the bedding has been changed since this old man died in it?' he asked.

She nodded.

'Stick him on the fifth, then, deputy,' she said.

'You were gone a long time,' Jaff said to Voriet.

'Delayed,' Voriet replied. 'The transporter broke down outside Ottofan. Transaxle. We had to rent another ride.'

Jaff looked at Garofar and flashed her eyebrows again. Scary bitch. How could she tell that just from a distant noise?

'Brief in twenty,' Macks repeated. 'Is he here?'

'No,' said Jaff.

'You could have briefed me on the road,' said Drusher. 'It was a long enough journey.'

'Some things you need to see for yourself before they make sense,' said Nayl.

Garofar led Drusher up to the fifth floor.

'Old place,' Drusher remarked.

'Yes.'

'Unoccupied?'

'Before us, yeah, for years.'

'Nice views,' said Drusher, pausing to look out of one of the window slits.

'I suppose.'

'I bet you get a lot of hill-browns up here. Pine finch. Crosshammers. Goldhawks. And lots of charhoops in autumn.'

'I couldn't say,' said Garofar.

Drusher shrugged and continued climbing the stairs after him.

'What happened to Voriet's face?' Garofar asked.

'I attacked him with an eagle,' said Drusher.

Garofar stopped.

'Really?' he asked.

'Not really,' Drusher replied, 'but that appears to have become the narrative, despite my attempts to correct it, so I'm just going along with it.'

The flaking stone steps led up to a landing where the floor was boarded with wood. It had once been polished, a fine surface, but water damage from the leaking roof had stained it, making it patchy and rough. Buckets and other open vessels had been set at strategic points to catch drips. Some were so full, puddles were spreading around them.

'Along here,' said the deputy. 'Mind your step.'

'They haven't told me much,' said Drusher.

'About what?'

'About anything. This matter. This case. This investigation.'

Garofar looked at him.

'I get the feeling a lot of it's classified, sir,' he said.

'You don't know?' asked Drusher.

'I'm just local law, sir,' he said. 'Staffing, support, you know.'

'So it's classified by the Ordos, then?' asked Drusher, more to himself.

Deputy Garofar's manner suddenly became keen. He looked Drusher in the eye.

'So they *are* from the Ordos?' he asked. 'Inquisition?'

Drusher nodded.

'Yes. I saw a badge. Voriet identified himself. Didn't you know?'

'No,' replied Garofar. 'They don't say much about anything. The marshal was already investigating this case when they sort of turned up and took over. She's cooperating. It's not like her to just roll over. It feels like they have something on her.'

'Not Macks,' said Drusher.

'You know her?'

'From way back.'

'Well, I suppose if they are from the Ordos, that would explain her compliance,' said Garofar, 'her eagerness to assist. I mean, that's how it works, doesn't it? The Inquisition has authority everywhere.'

'As I understand it. What was the case?'

'Sir?'

'The case Marshal Macks was investigating?' asked Drusher.

Garofar hesitated.

'Oh, come on, Deputy... Garofar,' said Drusher, pausing slightly to squint and read the officer's name badge. 'I let slip they were from the Ordos. It's your turn. Like you said, they're playing it close. Even my old friend Macks.'

Garofar shrugged.

'There was a death. Last winter. A farmer found the body. Open and closed, really, or should have been. Ursid kill.'

'*Ursa minora gershomi?*' said Drusher. 'Or *majora,* I suppose? Or even a cave ursid, though those are rare these days?'

'Sir?'

'A banded ursid, or a big grey?'

'Yeah, we get both kinds up here. The king greys once in a while. So, we thought, some poor idiot left the wood path, got taken. Never got an identification on the victim, though. No papers. We ran genetic samples through the system, and even shared them with other networks. Then in the spring, there were two more. Same deal.'

'Found together?'

'No,' said Garofar. 'Kilometres apart. Within days, another, then another a month after.'

'Five. All male?'

'No. Four male, one female.'

'All unidentified?'

'Yeah, which is odd. We get a lot of visitors up here in season. Hunters and the like. Plus, nice views, like you said. So people from outside the province aren't unusual. But five unknowns? That's starting to feel off.'

'Was there feeding? They were all ursid kills.'

'Oh, yeah,' said Garofar. 'All the meat was gone. All the organs. Funny, that's the first question the marshal asked.'

Drusher smiled.

'She remembered the basics,' he said.

'She wanted it squared away, certainly. I mean, we get the odd animal attack. But five felt like there might be a rogue beast. Plus, the identification thing. Macks, she ordered up some expensive facial reconstruction on three of the bodies, then we ran the results around every hostelry, tavern and guest house in the area. I mean, it was possible we had five dead visitors who all happened not to have papers on them, or who had their papers eaten along with them.'

'Unlikely,' said Drusher.

'But possible. No point seeing patterns where there aren't any. But nothing. No one recognised them. So the reconstructs went out on the wire too.'

'And that brought the Ordos in?'

'Yes,' said Garofar. 'But before they got here, we found the rest.'

'The rest of what?'

'The rest of the bodies, sir. It was spring, like I said. The thaw. Warmest spring in a decade. There was meltwater flooding in this valley and the next along. It brought bodies down. People who'd been dead since last year that we hadn't found because they'd been frozen up. The tech-adepts say some of them might even be from the year before. Or as long ago as eight years.'

'All ursid kills?'

'The exact same specs, sir. Ursid kill, unidentified subjects. Two more of them female.'

'How many bodies?' asked Drusher.

'I don't know, sir,' said Garofar.

'Oh, come on, deputy. You're on the case. How many bodies?'

'I mean to say, I don't know what the total's going to be. We've got eighteen so far. They're still digging up more.'

Drusher opened his mouth to speak. Nothing much was forthcoming.

'We've got all the bodies downstairs. In the cold store,' said Garofar.

'Here?'

'Yes. Orders of the lead investigator. He wanted all the bodies in one place for examination, so they set up a facility in the cellars where it's cold.'

'That's ridiculous,' said Drusher. 'You need a proper morgue and laboratory to conduct–'

'Orders of the lead investigator,' Garofar repeated.

'Well, he sounds like an idiot,' said Drusher.

'Oh, he's not,' said Garofar. 'I don't know what he is, apart from damn scary, but he's not an idiot.'

'I disagree, and I'll tell him so to his face,' said Drusher. 'I've only ever assisted law enforcement cases, but I know well enough there's a proper procedure for this kind of thing.'

They had reached a door.

'This the haunted bedroom, deputy?' Drusher asked.

'Well, the old man died here years ago,' replied Garofar.

'Which old man?'

'Fargul. Last person to own this place. I don't think he's still here, so you'll be all right.'

He opened the door, and they went in. It had once been a grand bedroom, but the plaster was crumbling, and the boards were bare. Large windows, the shutters open, overlooked the valley below. It smelled damp.

Drusher and Garofar halted in their tracks. There was a man standing by one of the windows, his back to them. He was staring out. He was tall, broad and solid, his bulk covered in a long, black coat.

'Throne, but you scared me!' exclaimed Garofar. 'I didn't know you were back, sir.'

The man turned to look at them. It was impossible to discern his age. His craggy face was grizzled and badly scarred. Augmetic plugs and leads trailed back from pinch points and sockets in his hairless scalp, and disappeared down under his high collar. His expression was impenetrable.

'That will be all, deputy,' he said.

'Shall I tell the others that you're–'

'That will be all,' the man said. 'Unless you'd like to stay and discuss the unguarded sharing of confidential matters with outsiders.'

Garofar put the bag down, shot a look at Drusher and left.

'You're Drusher?' the man asked, staring at Drusher. 'The one Macks recommended?'

'I am,' said Drusher.

'My name is Eisenhorn,' the man said. 'I believe there was something you wanted to tell me to my face.'

FIVE

CLASSIFIED

Drusher followed the inquisitor back downstairs. The rain had come up again, and he could hear it pelting against the thick walls.

'I didn't mean anything by it,' he said.

'I don't really care,' replied Eisenhorn.

It was a slow descent. The inquisitor lumbered. His legs and lower body were braced inside some kind of augmetic exo-support. Every step was a heavy effort, every movement marked by the puff of hydraulic servos. Drusher had often thought himself old and in bad shape, but he was nimble beside the other man. How did a body even keep going after what must have been years of damage and injury? Surely there came a point at which enough was enough? There was an ugly stink of obsession coming off Eisenhorn, the stench of a man driven beyond reason to accomplish something. When was enough enough? Only in death? Drusher had heard that phrase often enough over the years, the noble mantra of the military. It was nonsense, obviously. Only an idiot thought that, or an idiot who pretended to be a hero. An idiot either way.

Drusher's initial evaluation of the inquisitor had not changed, though he decided to keep that to himself. No point making his bad start worse. Sure, this Eisenhorn fellow was intimidating. He had the badge and the terrifying authority that came with it. But he was just another idiot of which the galaxy had so many: a man with delusions of grandeur; a man who felt he could make some kind of difference in the grand scheme of things; a man who believed his work mattered.

Try making a complete taxonomy, and tell me *that* matters, Drusher thought. Try doing *that* for seven years, and tell me it wasn't hard work.

'Perhaps you can tell me more about this investigation?' said Drusher.

'Isn't that why you're here? To tell me more about it?'

'Well, I'll need something to go on,' said Drusher.

'I think Deputy Garofar told you plenty.'

'I just asked him, casually. He wasn't really sharing classified information or anything–'

Eisenhorn paused and glanced at him.

'In this situation, I decide what is classified, magos.'

Holy Throne, you're an arsehole, thought Drusher. I get it. You're tough as anything, and years of privileged authority have gone to your head. You're not impressing me at all with this 'get a load of me' act. Given the shape you're in – mental, I'm guessing, as much as physical – you should have retired *years* ago.

'Maybe, now you're here, you can share some details?' said Drusher curtly. 'You want a magos biologis with specific expertise in the fauna of this planet.'

'And you want passage off this world,' replied Eisenhorn, 'so that seems a reasonable basis for cooperation.'

'So... I just do what you tell me to do?' asked Drusher.

'That would be adequate,' Eisenhorn replied. He continued down the stairs.

Drusher pulled a face then hurried to catch up.

'A reasonable basis for cooperation would be an exchange of data,' he said. 'I have questions.'

'Proceed.'

'Why have you taken this case away from local enforcement?'

'That's classified. Ordo business.'

'Great. Have you always operated in such an unorthodox manner?'

'Also essentially classified, but for the sake of this discussion, yes.'

'Would it kill you to tell me more about this?'

'Yes.'

'I didn't mean literally,' said Drusher.

'I did,' said Eisenhorn.

'Do you find that people who meet you end up regarding you as an arrogant son of a bitch?' snapped Drusher.

Eisenhorn stopped. He did not look around.

'I mean, come now, sir,' said Drusher. 'I'm trying to assist. Could you ease off with this hard-nosed act?'

'It's not an act, magos.'

'Terra's sake,' Drusher sneered. 'Did someone once hurt you really, *really* badly?'

Eisenhorn slowly turned around to look at Drusher.

Drusher took a step back.

'The list of people in this galaxy who have not hurt me is very, very short, magos,' he said.

Drusher adjusted his spectacles, pursed his lips and nodded.

'You've asked some questions,' said Eisenhorn. 'My turn. What is the average bite radius of *Ursa minora gershomi?*'

'Twelve centimetres.'

'*Majora?*'

'A range up to seventeen,' said Drusher. 'Nineteen for the arctic form. The cave ursid–'

'Is an ultra-rare, prehistoric form,' said Eisenhorn. 'It has probably been extinct for some centuries. If it exists at all, it is restricted to the northernmost area of Outer Udar.'

'Oh, it exists,' said Drusher. 'Or, at least, it did thirty years ago. I have examples and evidence in my taxonomy. And you're wrong about its locale. There were still some in the Tartred Mountains.'

'Are there any other apex predators on this planet whose kills would resemble those of the banded or grey ursids?'

'Not to an expert. You can't rule out introduced exotics, of course.'

'You've seen that here?'

'More than once. Marshal Macks will corroborate that.'

'Why do you want to leave Gershom?' asked Eisenhorn.

The question took Drusher aback slightly.

'My... my work is complete,' he replied. 'It has been for years. A complete taxonomy. It's simply a case that there is nothing left to be done. But, unfortunately, economic circumstances prevent–'

'You could have retired,' said Eisenhorn. 'I hear that's nice.'

'I... sort of had, sir. Forced to by circumstances. I had a property down on the Bone Coast and – ahmm – worked with maritime ornithological efforts.'

'You kept birds in a cage in a shack on the beach, magos,' said Eisenhorn. 'Your retirement was enforced, by your own admission. If you had been able to leave Gershom, at any point in the last three decades, you would have done so.'

'Yes.'

'Because, somewhere, there were still things to be done, things to be found, secrets to be learned?'

'Yes.'

'So it's fair to say that you would *not* have retired, given the choice, because there is still so much work to be done?'

'I suppose so,' said Drusher.

'Work that you really want to do, and which you would prefer not to leave in the hands of others to finish?'

'Yes,' said Drusher. Rain beat against the walls.

'I think we are beginning to find an accommodation, magos,' said Eisenhorn. 'You have let your light go out. I'm sorry for that. I have not let mine die yet. There is work still to be done on Gershom. Work I do not wish to leave to others. You can assist me, for it intersects with your area of specialty. And perhaps, in assisting, you may discover that there is still, and always will be, work of your type for you to commit your life to. As, I think, you always intended.'

'Show me the bodies, sir,' said Drusher.

'You have a copy of your taxonomy?'

'I do,' said Drusher.

'I ask that you show it to my savant, Audla Jaff. She will only need it for half an hour.'

He resumed walking. Drusher stood and watched him plod away painfully down the steps. A thought clarified.

'Hey! Sir!' Drusher called after him. 'How did you know I was even *thinking* about issues of retirement?'

Eisenhorn did not look back or reply.

Drusher hurried down the stairs after him.

'How did you *know* that?' he called. 'And how did you know I wanted to call you an idiot?'

In the cold main hall of Helter Fortress, the gathered team looked up as they heard raised voices.

Eisenhorn appeared, striding from the stair arch towards the basement doors.

'Sir–' Voriet began.

Eisenhorn held up a hand stiffly, not breaking stride.

'I'm going to the cold store,' he announced. 'Harlon, Audla, Marshal Macks, with me, please.'

Drusher appeared, out of breath, red-faced, annoyed. He trotted after the inquisitor.

'You've met him, then?' asked Macks, grinning.

'Shut up, Germaine,' he replied.

SIX

THE COLD STORE

Nayl drew back the bolts on the door and opened the cold store. It had been a root cellar, Drusher decided, serving the fortress kitchens through the winter when there had still been a garrison to feed.

The walls were whitewashed. There were eighteen steel gurneys arranged in rows, green plastek sheeting bagging the bodies. More gurneys were folded and stacked along the wall as if other visitors were presently expected.

Monitoring equipment was set up between the gurneys, radiating fields of prickly blue light.

'It's not cold enough,' Drusher said immediately. 'It's not cold enough, and it's too damp. This is no place for the preservation of organic remains.'

'Correct,' said Eisenhorn. 'Hence the stasis field generators.'

'And if generator power fails?' asked Drusher.

'Then the fortress is going to start to stink,' said Nayl.

'And your evidence will be lost,' said Drusher.

'Evaluation, please, magos,' said Eisenhorn. 'I understand it will be preliminary.'

'Preliminary. Very well,' Drusher said, nodding. He took off his spectacles, wiped the lenses and put them back on, but did not move.

'These people were not the victims of ursid attacks,' he said.

There was a pause.

Nayl looked at him.

'You haven't even opened a bag yet, magos,' he said, gesturing towards the rows of gurneys.

'Nevertheless,' said Drusher.

'Let him continue,' said Eisenhorn. 'Magos? *Not* ursid attacks?'

'No, sir.'

'But there was evidence of feeding, Valentin,' said Macks, bewildered. 'I mean *gross* evidence. You always told me to look for–'

'I think ursids may have fed on them, but they didn't kill them.'

'Expand,' said Eisenhorn.

'Ursids kill people,' said Drusher, 'especially the smaller, more aggressive *Ursa minora*. But they don't hunt them for food. An ursid kills a man because they meet by accident. The ursid reacts in surprise, or in defence of young. It kills, swiftly.'

'Yeah, then it feeds,' said Macks.

'Sometimes,' Drusher replied. 'Ursids are omnivorous. They will eat flesh, meat of any sort, actually, even human. One might encounter a man, kill him, then feed. Or it might feed on a body if it finds one. But human flesh is not a regular part of its diet. It does not seek it out.'

'But a rogue animal,' said Macks. 'One that's got a taste for it. I mean, a taste for human flesh. That happens, doesn't it? You once told me that.'

'It does,' said Drusher. 'It's very rare. The man-eater syndrome. Often a diseased or wounded animal. One whose aggression is compounded. Multiplied.'

'So a rogue animal did this?' asked Nayl.

'Again, no,' said Drusher.

'You can tell that without even looking?' asked Nayl.

'You can compare bite prints or something,' suggested Macks.

'I can tell it by *counting*,' said Drusher. 'Eighteen bodies. Fifteen male, three female. Perhaps more to come. In a period of a year or two. How many ursids are there in the Karanines?'

Nayl and Macks looked at each other.

'I'll tell you–' Drusher began.

'Population sparse,' said Audla Jaff suddenly. 'As with all major carnivores or apex predators. An ursid's average feeding ground is three hundred square kilometres. Slightly more for *minora*. When young are present, the range increases. Thus we might calculate the distributed population of the region, by taking the overall size of the area and dividing by an averaged figure of three hundred. Thus, about one hundred and thirty.'

'Very good,' said Drusher.

'One hundred and thirty ursids in these woods?' said Nayl.

'In this province,' corrected Drusher.

'Actually, I was allowing for the entire run of the Karanine belt,' said Jaff.

'I don't get it,' said Macks. 'One hundred and thirty. That's a lot of ursids.'

Drusher looked at Jaff.

'How much does an adult ursid consume in a year, mam?'

'As much as it can,' she replied. 'But conservatively, three times its body weight.'

'You see?' said Drusher. 'One ursid would not have killed and eaten eighteen plus human beings.'

'Hang on,' said Nayl, 'you just said one hundred and thirty of them.'

'As a total, distributed population,' said Drusher. 'We might attribute one or perhaps two deaths in a five-year period to accidental encounter and misadventure. Or we might explain multiple deaths to the action of a rogue animal, a man-eater, which, as I mentioned, is an extremely rare phenomenon. So a man-eater might have – and I *stress* it's unlikely – killed eighteen poor souls... but it would not have eaten them all. That's simply too much food, even for a large and aggressive ursid.'

Eisenhorn looked at him, steadily.

'Interesting,' he said.

'Preliminary,' said Drusher.

'Then go beyond preliminary. What do you think killed them?'

'Something else,' said Drusher. 'If examination reveals ursid feeding patterns, and I confidently expect it will be indicative of a non-frenzied pattern, then we might surmise that the local ursid population devoured found corpses. But they did not make the kills.'

'Well surely,' said Macks, 'other ursids could have found and fed upon kills made by the rogue animal? You said it couldn't eat them all itself?'

'That's possible, but again unlikely,' said Drusher. 'It's a matter of territory. *Minora* are fiercely territorial. But let's take a look.'

He walked over to the nearest gurney.

'Do you have any–'

'Oil of osscil?' asked Macks, holding out a small pot.

'I was going to say *True Heart*,' he replied.

'Don't be smart,' she said, but grinned. 'Osscil or nothing.'

He took the pot, smeared some under his nose and unzipped the bag.

He stared for a moment.

'Gonna throw up?' Macks asked.

'No,' he said. He took off his spectacles and began to fiddle with them. 'I just want to be able to see straight.'

Audla Jaff casually took the spectacles out of his hands and performed three quick, deft twists.

She reached up and put them back on his nose gently. They sat perfectly straight.

Drusher blinked.

'Goodness me,' he said.

'Keep going, magos,' Jaff whispered as she stepped back. 'You're impressing him.'

Drusher plucked a pair of surgical gloves from a carton, put them on and picked up a stainless steel probe from a tray. He hunched down and began to examine the exposed corpse. It was little more than a skeleton, blackened with old blood and tatters of congealed tissue.

'There is some indication of an ursid feeding pattern. Tooth marks on the ribs here. If I can get a cast, I can confirm. Do you have an electromacroscope?'

'Yes,' said Eisenhorn.

'Then I can provide a comparative for you in a couple of hours. A side by side of bite marks and dental impressions. I think it will confirm the feeding patterns of several individual ursids. It's not frenzied, just as I expected. They were scavenging.'

He looked up.

'Was there feeding residue at the sites?' he asked.

'Feeding what?' asked Macks.

'Residue. Ursids are not clean eaters. They will tear chunks off. Scatter bones. Ribs, the bones of extremities.'

'Some of the bodies were washed down by meltwater,' said Eisenhorn. 'So we have no idea where they were killed.'

'But the ones that were found in situ? Where you presume they were slain?'

'No,' said Macks. 'No residue.'

'That's odd,' said Drusher.

'Expand,' said Eisenhorn.

'It suggests those locations were not the scenes of the crimes, so to speak. It suggests the killing and perhaps even the feeding happened elsewhere.'

'They were dump sites?' asked Macks.

'They were dump sites,' Drusher nodded.

'That's criminal pathology,' said Eisenhorn.

'It is,' agreed Drusher. 'Ursids may have grazed the kills and destroyed evidence. That might have been intentional. But the victims were killed elsewhere, then dumped. Add to that, the extremely unlikely coincidence that all the victims cannot be identified on any local or planetary database. Even rogue ursid man-eaters do not select their prey on the basis of identity profiling. Which means, you're looking for human actors, inquisitor. Men did this. This is serial execution or serial murder.'

He looked at Eisenhorn.

'But you knew that already, didn't you?' Drusher asked.

Eisenhorn didn't reply.

'Then tell me, if you want me to work at optimum efficiency,' said Drusher, 'what brought the Inquisition into this?'

'Eighteen deaths,' said Nayl flatly.

'No,' said Drusher, still looking straight at Eisenhorn. 'That's a dreadful tally, but serial murder is still within the purview of the Marshal Division. There's something else. You have positively identified at least one of these bodies, haven't you? Long before you even got here.'

SEVEN

SPIRITS OF PLACE

Drusher put on his coat, slung his satchel over his shoulder and went for a walk. The rain had eased back, and the sky over the valley was a hazy blue.

There was a woman at the fortress gate, a glum woman in Magistratum gear. Her name badge read 'Edde', and she carried a riotgun.

'Where are you going, sir?' she asked.

'I need to examine a few things,' Drusher replied. It seemed to him a better answer than 'I have to get away from these people for a while.'

'Have you been given permission to exit?' she asked.

'Of course I have,' he lied. No one had said anything to him about anything. After his assessment of the bodies in the cold store, Drusher felt as though he might have crossed a line. Eisenhorn had said nothing, except to send them all out of the room. Drusher wasn't sure if he'd revealed truths that had given the inquisitor new things to ponder, or if he'd exposed some secrets Eisenhorn had been keeping to himself. Had he impressed Eisenhorn into silence, or aggravated him? Eisenhorn was impossible to read. He didn't appear to express any nuance of reaction except a grim glare.

Deputy Edde looked at Drusher for a moment, then sighed and unlocked the gates.

From the fortress gates, the forest track ran down the valley through a thick break of trees. Drusher followed it for a while, then left the path and followed the slope of the valley deeper into the forest.

He began to relax. The air was clear and cool, and the scent of pine resin gave it a menthol tang. Sunlight shone through the tall, close-packed evergreens. The rolling forest bed was flax weed, deep green halibor, thistle, eye-wort and banks of antopies that brushed around his shins. Climbing tracedy hung in gauze mantles around lower branches. He saw the meaty combs of blaxiform fungi sprouting from rotting bark, the white cushions of bellecap toadstools in the weeds, processions of senate ants marching vertically up tree trunks, leaves and fat white grubs carried aloft in their jaws like trophies and banners. The air smelled of wet loam, camphor and flower scent. Fat pollinator insects buzzed past. Invisible beetles clicked and chirred in the undergrowth. He heard the cooing warble of the wood dove, *Astra verdus,* and watched tiny brown seed finches dart and snap through the lower branches.

By the time he reached the stream, the fortress long since out of sight behind him, he had his notebook out and his old spotting magnoculars around his neck. He'd seen and noted redbeaks, four different types of arboreal warbler, two root-hens, still dowdy in the last of their winter plumage as they stalked nervously through the ground cover, and a mountain hawk. The hawk had been quite distant. He'd glimpsed it in a patch of sky, framed through the emerald canopy, turning silently on the thermals over the lower valley. *Destrus aquilus gershomi,* the little hill-hawk. He'd noted another sixteen avian species just from call and song.

The gurgling stream was a meltwater rill that followed the contour of the slope, breaking and sharply plunging over clefts and mossy boulders. He followed its course, and the deeper sound of splashing as it fast-fed a pool somewhere ahead. He watched for tracks in the mud, for ursid spore, but the heavy rain had been too recent.

He reached the pool. It was overhung on the rising side by huge blocks of tumbledown stone, swathed in moss. Three different streams fed the pool, the sparkling rush of their flow producing constant, intersecting ripple patterns across its surface. The skin of the water was also wiggling with hookfly larvae. Drusher climbed onto the overlooking stones and sat down to watch tiny, fawn darters skim and hunt the larvae.

There was a decent view. He could look out across the forest banks below, the dense stands of evergreens, and see the dark, sharp mass of the Karanine peaks that formed the opposite side of the high valley, forty kilometres away through the early afternoon haze.

He sketched the pool for a while, then the view. He sat patiently still for five minutes, with no sound except birdsong and the burble of the streams, as a timid crophorn deer came to drink.

He noticed that, despite extensive weathering, the stone blocks he was perching on had traces of hard edges. They had been worked: the remains of some building or wall, perhaps a watchtower guarding the lower approaches to Helter Fortress.

A cold breeze rustled through the forest, and he felt the temperature drop. The sunlight diminished as clouds passed over. More rain coming, he surmised. He wasn't bothered. He was shaded by trees, the cool air was a welcome relief from the bright heat of the day, and it wasn't the first time he'd sat out in a downpour.

Rain was honest. Drusher reflected that perhaps, more than anything else, that was why he had become a magos biologis, to spend as much of his life as he could outside, in nature – whatever nature happened to be – with its simple cause-and-effect systems. It kept him away from the company of people, with their lies and secrets and agendas and games.

That, or he simply wasn't very good at those sorts of interactions.

The thoughtful smile faded slightly from his lips. He was no longer alone. There was a man sitting by the edge of the pool below him. Drusher had no idea how long the man had been there, but he doubted it was more than five minutes. Drusher had been lost in his own thoughts and the tranquility of the place, but he was surprised he hadn't noticed the man arrive.

'Good afternoon,' he called down.

The man looked up and smiled. He looked pleasant enough. He had a round face, and wore a good walking coat and laced boots. He was sketching in a large, green-covered book.

'I didn't see you there, sir,' the man said.

Drusher clambered down. He got a glimpse of the man's sketch. It was a view of the valley, very finely done.

'I don't mean to disturb,' said Drusher.

'Not at all. I was just out, ambling around,' the man said. He continued to sketch.

'Are you a visitor?' Drusher asked.

'Oh no, I live nearby,' the man replied. 'You?'

'A visitor,' said Drusher.

'Ah well, it's that season,' the man said. He paused to put a point back on his graphite stick with a little pocket knife. 'And this area is very pleasant. The Karanines in early summer – wonderful air. Good for the spirit. I sometimes wonder if, when our ancestors first came to this world, they stopped here because it was so agreeable.'

'It is indeed agreeable.'

'And fought over it, of course.'

Drusher frowned. 'Fought, sir?'

'You know, back in the past. The old tribes of Outer Udar, coveting this region because it was so bounteous compared to their sparse homelands. There were wars in these mountains for centuries. All forgotten now.'

'I confess I don't know much about war, sir,' said Drusher, perching on a rock near to where the man sat. 'Or history. I am a student of science and nature. A magos biologis.'

The man looked at him with interest.

'Is that right? Sir, I envy you. That's a fine calling. As a boy, I wanted to become a naturalist too. I won a place at Delci, the scholam there, to study the sciences of living worlds. But duty, you know. My family is in timber. My dear father, he needed a son with business acumen who could take over the trade, so I transferred to the universitariate at Tycho. Had that not been fate's path, I might have been a magos biologis myself.'

'But you still dabble?' asked Drusher.

'Oh yes,' the man said. 'When I can get out of the office, and away from invoices and shipment manifests and audits and labour disputes with the logging gangs. Any spare moment, you'll find me out here, away from it all.'

'You have a good hand,' said Drusher, gesturing towards the sketch.

The man looked down at his work, and propped the sketch up in its green card cover to consider it.

'Kind of you to say so, sir,' he replied. 'I'm sure I lack your skills of observation and execution. Tell me, are you staying nearby?'

'Very close by,' said Drusher.

'You're not a friend of Sark's are you?'

'Sark?'

'Draven Sark.'

'No, I don't know him.'

The man smiled and shrugged. Drusher found it hard to tell how old he was. He looked Drusher's age, but that meant little. So many people had juvenat treatment these days, those who could afford it. The man might have been a hundred years old and not look a day over forty. Drusher had heard that recipients of juvenat work lived to ages of a hundred and seventy sometimes.

'Old Sark's a friend of mine,' the man said, returning to his sketch. 'A neighbour. I only ask because you're the sort of interesting fellow he has as a guest. In the summer months, they come from all over. Sometimes off-world. I'll tell you, the people I've met at his dinners over the years. Scientists, scholars, merchants, artists, fleet officers...'

'What does this Master Sark do?' Drusher asked.

The man frowned.

'Why, I've known him thirty years. Must be at least that. He was one of my father's friends to begin with. Thirty years, and I confess I don't know exactly what it is he does. His background is science. Medical science. The old Materia Medica, but I think he's in investment now. Bulk cargo shipping, mining... that sort of thing. I refer to him as my "very wealthy neighbour". He lives in the old fortress.'

'You mean... Helter?' asked Drusher.

The man looked at him as if he'd made a joke.

'No, no,' he said, gesturing vaguely. 'Keshtre. Further down towards the pass. Much older than Helter.'

'As I said,' remarked Drusher with a smile, 'I don't know the history.'

'Oh, the Karanines are full of hill forts. Ancient places. Many are lost now, of course. Some of them are very grand. Palaces. From the Pre-Udarin Age. Keshtre's one of those.'

Drusher nodded.

'Out here alone,' he said, 'are you not concerned about coming to harm?'

'From what?' the man asked.

'Ursid.'

'Oh, I see them from time to time. They don't bother you unless you're stupid. I'm sure you know that, being a student of nature. You don't seem to be afraid to be out here on your own.'

'As you say,' said Drusher. 'I know what to do if I run across an ursid. I just wondered. There have been some deaths recently. Ursid kills.'

'Really?' asked the man. 'I hadn't heard that.'

'Yes, of late.'

'Well, thanks for the advice. I'll keep an eye out. You know, though, one summer... it must be four or five years ago now, I was out sketching. Now, you were kind enough to compliment my work, but I'm very slow. Like today, I can sit for hours before I produce anything halfway decent. So I'd been sitting for three hours, lost in it, and I looked up and – Throne take me – there was a king grey sitting right there. As close to me as you are now.

Just minding his business. Huge, he was. So I just kept sketching. You know, no sudden movements. And he sat there for a while longer, then grunted and wandered off into the trees. Funniest thing.'

'You... you've been here awhile today, then?' Drusher asked.

The man squinted up at the sun.

'Oh, two hours at least before you came along.'

Drusher hesitated. He was about to speak when he heard someone calling his name in the forests above them.

'Someone's looking for me,' he said.

The man put his sketchbook down and got up. He offered Drusher his hand.

'Well, it was a pleasure to meet you, magos,' he said. He listened for a second to the voice calling out from the trees. 'Magos... Drusher, I believe?'

'Valentin,' said Drusher, shaking the man's hand.

'I'm Esic,' the man said. 'Mind how you go and watch out for those ursids, eh?'

Drusher wandered up the slope from the pool, and saw Nayl coming through the trees towards him. Nayl looked aggravated. He was lugging a large, matt-black lasrifle.

'What's the matter?' Drusher asked.

Nayl slithered to a halt on the mossy slope, and glared at Drusher. He activated the vox-set fixed to his collar.

'I've found him,' he said. 'Stand down.'

'What's the problem?' Drusher asked.

'You left the fortress.'

'So?'

'You don't go out alone. Or without permission.'

'Why?' asked Drusher.

'That's what Eisenhorn instructed,' Nayl snapped. 'Besides, you must have realised it's not safe out here.'

'Safe from what?' asked Drusher.

'Don't be difficult,' said Nayl. 'Come on. Follow me back.'

'There's a man down here,' Drusher said. 'It's odd, actually, he–'

'What man?' asked Nayl.

Drusher turned to point.

Down by the pool, there was no one at all.

EIGHT

AFTER LIFE

I just don't understand,' Drusher kept saying.

'Then stop trying,' said Macks. They were in the old kitchen of Helter Fortress, and she was brewing caffeine in a copper pot.

'I suppose he could have wandered away when my back was turned,' said Drusher. 'But he said he'd been there for hours, and that can't have been the case, because...'

His voice trailed off. He realised he was chafing his upper arms with his hand, and was still wearing his coat.

'It's so cold in here,' he said.

'It is,' she agreed.

He walked over to the sink. His breath was making steam in the air.

'There's ice in the sink. Frost on the... on the *inside* of the windows. Macks?'

'We've been told to ignore it,' she said.

'Macks, it's a warm day outside–'

'Is it?' she asked wearily. She put two tin cups of caffeine on the old table. 'Drink,' she said.

Drusher peered up through the window. The sky was very dark and unsettled. It looked like evening setting in, but it was still mid-afternoon.

'Is there a storm coming?' he asked.

'I guess there must be,' said Macks.

He sat down, facing her.

'What the hell's going on, Germaine? I walked out of the gates not two hours ago, and it was sunny and clear. Now I come back and it's like... midwinter.'

She shrugged. She looked uneasy, and Germaine Macks seldom appeared uneasy.

'There's stuff going on, and we're instructed not to ask questions,' she said.

'That's not really good enough,' he replied.

'It has to be for me,' she said. 'This is my job. I'm assigned to assist.'

'Well, I'm not,' he said. 'I think I've had enough of this. I think I might go.'

She looked at him.

'Don't screw things up, Valentin,' she said. 'They're offering you an off-world ticket. The thing you've always wanted.'

'Well...' he began. 'I've done my part. I've done what I can.'

'Tell me about this man you met,' she said.

'It was just a man. Out for a walk.'

'And he vanished.'

'No, of course he didn't. He must have walked off. It was nothing.'

'What did you talk about?' she asked.

'I don't know. The countryside. He was a local man. I think he said he was in the logging industry.'

'Did he have a name?'

Before he could answer, the kitchen door opened, and Voriet and Betancore walked in.

'We'd like to have a word with the magos,' Voriet said to Macks. She nodded, then realised it meant they were asking her to leave.

Macks got up, shot a look at Drusher and walked out.

Voriet sat down facing Drusher. Betancore stood, leaning against the larder cupboards.

'Let's start with instructions,' said Voriet. 'You follow them, magos. You don't come and go as you please.'

'I didn't know that,' said Drusher.

'You do now,' said Voriet. 'So that won't happen again, will it? Not now you know.'

'It's for your safety, Valentin,' said Betancore.

Drusher shrugged grudgingly.

'All right,' he said. 'But I don't like this very much at all.'

'Now, about this man you met,' said Voriet, ignoring the remark. 'Tell me about him.'

'I just went over this with Macks,' Drusher said. 'He was just a... a... He said he lived locally. He knew the area. The way he talked, he knew the history. He ran a timber business. Or his father did. I get the feeling he'd taken it over. That was it, really.'

'But you thought it was odd,' said Betancore.

Drusher turned to look at her.

'Just in hindsight, really, mam,' he said. 'I didn't see him approach in the first place. I just looked up, and there he was. And I didn't see him leave. But I'm sure that was just me.'

'You're a very observant man,' said Voriet. He put Drusher's notebook on the table and opened it. 'You're a magos biologis. It's part of the training. These notes you took today, they are testament to an acute level of observation. Details of plant and bird and insect that I would have missed.'

'I'm not very good with people,' said Drusher. 'If he'd been a little hill-hawk, I could have probably told you which direction he flew off in, how fast and where his roost was.'

'Did he tell you his name?' asked Betancore.

'Uh, yes. I think he said it was Esic.'

Voriet and Betancore exchanged glances. Betancore stepped forwards and put a data-slate on the table in front of Drusher.

'Is this him?' she asked.

'No. No, that's a much older man. Much older.'

She adjusted the display.

'How about this?'

Drusher pushed his spectacles down his nose and squinted at the pict.

'Yes,' he said. 'Yes. That's him. Who is he? Is he a suspect? Is he a criminal?'

'His name is Esic Fargul,' said Voriet.

'So... related to the man who died here?' asked Drusher.

'Both images are Esic Fargul,' said Voriet, 'taken forty years apart. He *is* the man who died here. In the fifth floor bedroom, thirty years ago.'

There was a long silence.

'Well, that,' said Drusher, 'I mean... *that*... that's patently ridiculous. I mean, I spoke to him. I shook his hand.'

'Quite possibly,' said Voriet. 'That doesn't change the fact that he's dead.'

'I shook his hand...' said Drusher quietly.

'Take a deep breath,' said Betancore softly. 'Sometimes these things are difficult to process.'

'No, not really, mam,' said Drusher. 'Groxshit, however, is difficult to process. Your data is wrong, Master Voriet. He clearly isn't dead.'

'He died of age-related illness and poor circumstance,' said Voriet. 'He was ninety-seven.'

'Then the body was misidentified.'

'Magos Drusher, please try to accept this information,' said Voriet. 'Even if Fargul was somehow still alive, you admit the man you saw was much younger.'

'Well, juvenat work,' said Drusher. 'It reverses the ageing process, doesn't it? That's what I've heard. I've never had it myself.'

'I have,' said Medea Betancore. 'I am one hundred and sixty-four standard years old.'

Drusher's eyes widened.

'Inquisitor Eisenhorn is at least a century older,' she continued. 'Magos, juvenat work arrests ageing. It seldom reverses it. If Fargul was alive, he would not look fifty or sixty years younger than he did in later life.'

'So, you're telling me,' said Drusher, 'a more reasonable explanation is that I met a ghost?'

'The term is inexact,' said Voriet.

'And shook his damned hand?'

'Let's talk about what you discussed with him,' said Voriet.

'No,' said Drusher firmly. 'No, that's not going to happen. Two things are going to happen first. I want some anxiety meds. Strong ones. And I want an explanation that entirely lacks groxshit. And that's not an either/or thing. I want both. Now. Or I'm going to pack my bag and leave.'

'Don't be awkward, magos,' said Voriet.

'We need to tell him,' said Betancore. 'At least the basics.'

Drusher thought she was talking to Voriet, but he saw she was looking up into space almost blankly. There was a soft pop, as though Drusher had yawned and cleared his ears. He distinctly heard a voice say +Proceed.+

'What was that?' he asked.

'I think it would be better coming from you,' she said. Again, she was not speaking to Drusher or Voriet. 'I know you're tired, but I think–'

+Wait.+

Betancore looked at Drusher.

'Wait a moment, magos,' she said.

Drusher wiggled the tip of his finger in his ear. His head felt blocked and oddly pressurised.

+Main room.+

'What was that?' asked Drusher.

'We're going to the main room,' said Betancore.

Eisenhorn was waiting for them. He was sitting in a high-backed chair, and he looked as if he were enduring some silent torment. Drusher felt that Eisenhorn was not so much sitting in the chair, as the chair was preventing him from falling into the centre of the world. His breathing was laboured.

Audla Jaff was lighting candles to draw back the gloom in the great hall. It was still cold, and the chill seemed to radiate from the inquisitor. Outside, a storm had begun to grumble.

'Have a seat, magos,' Eisenhorn said.

Drusher sat down facing Eisenhorn. Voriet and Betancore withdrew to sit on a bench at the back of the hall. Jaff lit the last of the candles and joined them. There was no one else around.

'I have psykana abilities, magos,' said Eisenhorn. 'Do you know what that means?'

'I suppose so. I've never met someone who–'

'You probably have. We don't tend to advertise our talents. Mine are considerable. You had an encounter today. When you left the site without permission–'

'I'm sorry about that–' Drusher began.

Eisenhorn raised a hand to hush him.

'I have no interest in rebuking you, magos. To be honest, I am exhausted. I don't have the time or patience to bring you into line. If you wish for a rebuke, say so, and I will leave it to Voriet and Nayl.'

'By all means do continue,' said Drusher.

'Your encounter today was with a psykana echo. An unanticipated side effect of work I was doing in the cold store.'

'A psykana echo, sir?'

'You referred to it as a ghost,' said Eisenhorn. 'That is a surprisingly accurate term.'

'It was a ghost?'

'Yes.'

'I... well...' Drusher hesitated. 'That's very curious. I don't know what to think about that. I may cry a little bit.'

'Don't,' said Eisenhorn.

'Do my best,' mumbled Drusher.

'Magos, your assessment of the bodies was interesting to me. It confirmed things that I had thought of, ideas I had begun to form. It was remarkably incisive. It revealed secrets that I have not shared.'

'Thank you. Did it?'

'The Inquisition is interested in this case for precisely the reasons you suggested,' said Eisenhorn. 'Marshal Macks circulated the facial reconstructs on all networks. One came to my attention. A person I knew. That's what brought me here.'

'You knew one of the victims?'

'Personally. She worked for me. A field agent. Her name was Thea Inshabel. An interrogator. The daughter of a very old and dear friend, who had joined me to continue her late father's work. She came to this system nine years ago to follow leads relating to a larger case I have been pursuing. She came at my request. Such investigations, magos, they take time. Years. I had not heard from her for some while. Her reports had become intermittent. I was concerned, but sometimes Ordo agents in deep-cover operation are forced to go dark, for their own safety. Interrogator Inshabel was a very experienced and able operator. I was confident that she...'

He paused.

'I should have sent someone to find her,' he said. 'I should not have waited so long. I owed that to her father. To watch out for his daughter...'

'I'm sorry, sir,' said Drusher.

'Now she's dead,' said Eisenhorn. 'Her bones lying, unclaimed and unidentified, in Marshal Macks' morgue. Her reconstruction of Thea's face brought me to Gershom. To find out what she had found out.'

Drusher tilted his head to the side, questioning.

'It's very difficult to get answers from the dead,' said Eisenhorn.

'I can imagine,' said Drusher.

'But there are means,' said Eisenhorn. Thunder rumbled on the far side of a neighbouring mountain, and the first drops of rain began to strike the hall's windows. 'A process of divination, of psychometric assay. It is a testing and complex craft, and should be attempted only by those who are well trained, or those who are prepared to face the consequences.'

'I'm not sure I know what you're describing, sir,' said Drusher.

'In layman's terms, magos, a séance.'

'Oh,' said Drusher.

'The term we use is auto-séance,' said Eisenhorn. 'Thea left nothing except her bones. No clothing, no effects, no trace of where she had been for nine years, where she had lived. So, when I first arrived, I conducted a psychic audience with the remains. It was... unpleasant and unrewarding.'

'I...' Drusher began, but didn't really know what to say.

'Thea had been dead for too long,' said Eisenhorn. 'Her psionic essence was too far detached from her mortal relics. Also, I have reason to believe the means and process of her death were so reductive, so annihilating, that nothing sensible remained. I reached out and touched something, but it was not coherent.'

Eisenhorn shifted in his seat and took a sip from a glass of amasec that had been placed by his side. His hand was shaking.

'I extracted only one thing,' he went on. 'A brief, fragmentary impression of an old fortress. It was not a clear mental image, but research had shown that there were several old structures in the Karanine region. Old fortresses from the settlement era. This place, Helter, resembled the vision. It was the only such structure that remained intact within the vicinity of the bodies that were found in situ. So, I transferred my party here to begin an investigation, a thorough search of the surrounding area.'

'And you brought the bodies too,' said Drusher.

'Yes,' replied Eisenhorn, 'so I could repeat the auto-séance process with each one. It was a gruelling process. Some were utterly inert. From the rest, I obtained nothing but incoherent pain. So, I widened my search and conducted similar divinations at the sites where bodies were found, as well as other locations in the forest. Again, nothing. As you have demonstrated, convincingly, they were dump sites. No psychometric echo of the victims' lives or the moments of their deaths would have lingered there anyway.'

The rain was beating hard now. Lightning blinked in the high windows.

'About today,' said Drusher. 'In the woods–'

Eisenhorn cleared his throat.

'After you made your report,' he said, 'I felt an urge to try again. To restage the divination with poor Thea's body. It was a grim and thankless effort that has left me drained. But I believe it had an unexpected consequence. While I was here, in the cold store, trying to reach Thea Inshabel, the considerable psykanic backwash rippled out into the surrounding forest. It stirred up ghosts, Magos Drusher. Ghosts I was not aware of. Which is how you came to meet Esic Fargul in the woods today. A man thirty years dead. I was conducting my séance in his home, magos, the place where he had lived and the place where he died. It is hardly surprising that it might raise him up into the sunlight.'

'Not to you, perhaps,' said Drusher. 'I have to say, sir, that I am half out of my mind just now. Fear, sir. At what you are telling me. At *you*. Fear and incredulity. I spoke to the man for ten minutes. He was real. He was solid. I could see him and hear him and smell his hair oil and the sweat of a body that has walked briskly in the sun for a whole afternoon. I... I shook his hand.'

'We have used the word *ghost* carelessly, magos,' said Eisenhorn. 'A psionic manifestation can be very real. Utterly convincing, especially to one who does not realise that it is what it is.'

'Or that something like it could even exist,' said Drusher. 'May I...? May I have an amasec?'

Eisenhorn made a small nod, and Audla Jaff came over. She handed Drusher a fine old glass filled with amasec.

'If it eases your mind at all,' said Eisenhorn, 'I doubt the phantom of Esic Fargul knew he was a ghost either.'

'With respect, it doesn't really,' said Drusher. He knocked back the drink in one. Jaff, waiting patiently nearby, stepped in and refilled the glass.

'What did you speak of, magos?' asked Eisenhorn.

Drusher shrugged feebly.

'We talked as two men of similar interests might if they met by chance,' he replied. 'Of nature. Of the country and its various species. He had a leaning to natural history. He... he asked if I was a visitor, if I was staying nearby. He told me he was a local man, with a timber business and–'

'When he asked you that,' Eisenhorn interrupted, 'what did you say?'

'I told him yes,' said Drusher. 'That I was staying in the area. I didn't say where. So he asked me if I was a guest of his neighbour.'

'His neighbour?'

'A friend. A local man of some influence who entertained famously.'

'His name?'

'His name?' Drusher echoed. He frowned. 'I can't recall. Straker? No, Draker? Something like that. Draven something. Draven Sirk? Stark?'

'Sark?' said Eisenhorn. 'Was that the name?'

'I think it was. I can't be sure, but... Sark. Draven Sark. I feel that's what he said.'

'So did Thea,' said Eisenhorn quietly.

Voriet rose to his feet.

'My lord,' he said. 'You said you got nothing today.'

'I didn't think I had, interrogator,' said Eisenhorn. 'Just sounds. Noises. The wailing psionic roar of the warp. But one sound repeated, and now the magos says the name, I know that's what it was. A name. Sark. Thea Inshabel was screaming it.'

'I will begin a search for the name,' said Jaff. She looked at Drusher. 'Do you know the spelling?'

'Of course I don't,' said Drusher.

Eisenhorn slowly rose to his feet, almost clawing at the edge of the table for support.

'Throne,' he murmured. 'All along, Inshabel was trying to tell me something. It was the last remaining fragment of her, the only thing she had strength of will to hold on to. One word. One name. And I didn't realise...'

Medea Betancore had come to his side to steady him.

'You should rest, Gregor,' she said.

'I should work.'

'Leave it to us, for now,' she said, shaking her head. 'Let us do the research. Rest and regain your strength. You're no good to us otherwise.'

'I know where he lived,' said Drusher. Everyone looked at him.

'This Draven Sark,' said Drusher. 'The ghost told me. He said Sark was a neighbour. He lived in another old fortress close by. Down towards the pass, he said, and older than this place. Pre-Udarin he called it. Its name is Keshtre.'

NINE

THAT WHICH IS NOT THERE

Come with me,' said Voriet.

Audla Jaff had gone off to begin her research. Drusher wasn't sure what that meant, and he didn't like to imagine. Medea Betancore had begun the slow process of leading Eisenhorn up the stairs to his chamber. Full night had closed in and with it a thunderstorm of monstrous proportions. Lightning strobed at the fortress windows. The shutters rattled, and the stone hallways resounded with the drumming of rain outside and the frantic dripping within, as water drained through the ragged roof and dribbled into pots and buckets.

Voriet led Drusher to a small parlour behind the kitchen where the others were waiting. A fire had been lit, and it was verging on cosy. Macks looked up as they entered. Nayl was by the hearth, chatting to the three deputies. The storm had driven Cronyl and Edde indoors. Their boots were off, and they were trying to dry their socks against the fire.

'Has something happened?' asked Garofar, lowering a mug of caffeine.

'We may have a lead,' said Voriet. 'Can I borrow you, marshal?'

'Of course,' said Macks, rising to her feet.

'We need some local data,' said Voriet. 'You have maps. I'll need your link to the Magistratum database.'

'No problem,' said Macks. 'That is, if the up-link is still working. The storm's playing blessed hell with vox connections. Look, if it's local information you need, ask my deputies. I'm not from the area, but they were all born in Unkara.'

'Keshtre,' said Voriet. He looked at the deputies. 'Mean anything to any of you?'

'Not me,' said Edde. Cronyl shook his head.

'The bad place?' asked Garofar.

'What?' asked Voriet.

'Like in the bedtime story...' Garofar's voice trailed off. He blushed. 'Sorry. I wasn't trying to be funny.'

'Go on, Hadeed,' said Macks.

'I don't know, mam,' said Garofar. 'It was just a story. A faerie story. The bad place up in the hills. Keshtre. Where the monsters lived. We had to go to bed when we were told and behave and stuff, or the monsters would creep down in the night and steal us away.'

'Where is it?' asked Drusher.

'Begging your pardon, sir,' said Garofar, 'it's not anywhere. It was just a made-up thing.'

'It's a fortress, apparently,' Voriet said to Macks. 'Near here. Towards the pass. That's right, isn't it, magos?'

'That's what the ghost told me,' said Drusher. He knew he could have phrased it better, but he quite enjoyed the look his comment got from everybody.

'There's no other fortresses near here, sir,' said Cronyl. 'Not between here and the pass. The closest is Angmire, but that's forty kilometres north.'

'No, Korlok is closer,' said Edde. 'That's near town. Over west.'

'Oh yeah, Korlok,' said Cronyl, 'but that's just a ruin.'

'Well, they're all ruins,' said Edde, 'apart from Helter. And this place isn't much better than a ruin.'

'Yeah, but Korlok and Angmire aren't *ruined* ruined,' said Cronyl. 'I don't mean fallen stones and traces. The woods are full of that kind of rubble. I thought we were talking places that are still standing.'

'This place would be intact,' Drusher said to Voriet. 'At least, in recent memory. There was somebody living in it maybe fifty or sixty years ago.'

The deputies shook their heads.

'Nowhere like that, sir,' said Edde.

'You sure you mean Keshtre?' asked Garofar.

'What about the name Draven Sark?' asked Drusher.

The deputies looked blank.

'Let's go check it,' said Macks. 'All the research material is in the library. Garofar, you come along.'

'Do you need me?' Nayl asked Voriet.

'Get your things together, Harlon,' said Voriet. 'Take Cronyl and Edde, and do a sweep. Make sure we're locked down.'

Drusher and Macks followed Voriet up the stairs to the library. Garofar hurried along behind them, buttoning his service jacket.

Drusher hadn't seen the library before. It smelled of damp. Rain battered at the shutters and rustled the plastek sheeting. The room was lit by glow-globes and candles. The wind was fluttering the candle flames and stirring loose papers stacked with the piles of old books.

Audla Jaff was sitting on the chaise, working methodically through a pile of tomes.

'Anything?' asked Voriet.

'The name Keshtre appears in three folk tales,' she replied. 'It's not a location. It's just a myth. An imaginary place.'

'Why would he have told me a lie?' asked Drusher.

'Who?' asked Macks.

Drusher shook his head.

'The word is not Unkaran dialect,' said Jaff. 'All the fortresses have names of Karanine origin. Even those of the Pre-Udaran Era. "Keshtre" is a derivative of the Fent language of Outer Udar. Possibly a pre-Gothic proto-root. It means "speaking place" or "meeting place". A moot or court, perhaps, but there is a sinister aspect to it. Literally, "forbidden speaking place", or "place of unholy speech". I repeat, it's not a physical location. It's not on the maps. It's not in the histories.'

'It could be an old name for somewhere else,' said Drusher.

'Not that I've found,' said Jaff. She looked somewhat annoyed.

'Keep looking through the old man's books,' said Voriet.

'There are only a few I haven't reviewed,' Jaff replied.

'Then go back over the rest,' Voriet snapped.

'I retain everything I read, interrogator,' Jaff protested.

'Just do it,' said Voriet. 'I'm not doubting your abilities, savant. We now have key words to look for. Names. Keshtre and Draven Sark. We have an approximate location. You may make a connection that you didn't make before.'

She sniffed.

'Of course,' she said, and turned back to the books.

'We'll look over the area maps again,' said Voriet. Garofar and Macks were already rolling out the Magistratum charts on a side table. They had territorial surveys dating back nine decades.

'She doesn't like you much,' Drusher whispered to Voriet.

'Audla is very precise,' replied Voriet quietly. 'Inhuman levels of retention, processing and data comparison. She is offended when I question her efforts.'

They began to study the maps. Voriet uncased a portable cogitator and plugged its cables into a vox-caster signal amplifier that stood on the floor nearby. He began to type.

'Damn,' he muttered. 'The link keeps going down.'

'We could drive back to Unkara Town,' said Macks. 'Use the hardwired system in the Magistratum building.'

Voriet looked doubtful.

'I'll keep trying for now,' he said. 'This storm's got to ease back at some point.'

'There's nothing on the maps,' said Garofar.

Drusher was peering over the deputy's shoulder. He had quickly identified the symbols for ruin (standing) and ruin (site). Most of the latter represented sites that he doubted would be apparent to anything except ground-penetrating auspex, geophysical detectors or the high-gain scanning of fleet survey vessels. You could visit them in person, walk around and see nothing that suggested a structure had ever been there. He found Helter Fortress marked and saw there were several ruins (standing) and ruins (site) to the south and west within a hundred kilometres. But nothing to the north and east, where the spur of the range ran.

'That must be the pass,' he said, tapping the map with his fingertip to indicate a significant pass through the Karanine range that lay north of Helter Fortress.

'The Karad Pass,' agreed Garofar.

Down towards the pass... that's what the ghost had said.

'So he must have meant this area here,' Drusher mused. He circled the tract of mountain country between their current location and the dramatic formation of the pass at Karad.

'Who?' asked Macks.

'My source,' said Drusher carefully.

'Look,' said Macks, 'if it's not a place, like Hadeed says. Not an actual *place*...'

'It's just a story,' said Garofar. 'Honestly.'

'What? We're wasting our time?' asked Drusher.

Macks shook her head.

'No,' she said. 'Like you said just now, it could be an old name for something else. Or a fanciful name someone gave to somewhere else. I mean, not official. Look, imagine Fargul had moved into this place and decided to call it Fargul's Palace instead of Helter Fortress. That wouldn't necessarily be recorded on a map or the title register. Likewise, he could have called it Elysium or Vaartuk. You know, ironically?'

'Vaar-what?' asked Drusher.

'Vaartuk,' said Macks. 'It's a local dialect word for heaven or paradise. Udaric, right, Garofar?'

'I think that's right,' said the deputy.

'You mean, he calls it that because it's a nice place to retire to?' Drusher asked.

Macks looked at him patiently. It was a look he knew well.

'You're getting hung up on my example, Valentin,' she said. 'I'm making it up as an illustration. This Draven Sark... you said he was a rich man. Influential. He had a grand country seat. He could have cheerfully trashed any name it used to have and given it a new one. Something his friends and acquaintances would know it as, but it wouldn't be official.'

'So it could mean anywhere,' said Garofar. 'Any old site in the province?'

'Potentially,' said Macks.

Drusher sighed.

'I don't think so. Near to Helter, but towards the pass. I know that's not specific enough, but it's still specific. That's the area.'

'Well, you've seen for yourself,' said Macks. 'There's nothing in that area at all. It's wilderness.'

'We could try older maps,' said Garofar. 'What about the settlement-era territory surveys? They might be on file at the Administratum annex. Or even in the museum?'

'No,' said Drusher. 'We're not looking for some site so ancient it had vanished before we started making modern maps. It was an occupied dwelling less than a century ago. It can't have completely vanished in that time.'

'Unless, you know, it's a shade hall,' said Garofar.

Macks and Drusher looked at him. The deputy gestured, embarrassed, to brush his remark aside.

'Ignore me,' he said. 'It was supposed to be a joke.'

'I'll ignore you, Garofar,' said Macks, 'once you explain what a shade hall is.'

'Well, that's what they said about Keshtre in the old stories,' he replied reluctantly. 'In the faerie stories. That it was only there some of the time. It appeared at night, so the monsters that lived inside could roam, then it faded away at dawn, back into the realm of shades.'

Macks glared at him.

'I shouldn't joke,' said Garofar. 'I know this is serious, mam. I'm sorry.'

'The shade hall or faerie mound is an ancient trope,' said Audla Jaff, looking up from her work. 'A liminal location, a threshold place, that exists between the material world and the otherworld. It's a concept that recurs in works of folklore right back to Old Terra.'

'Don't try and make excuses for him, mam,' Macks said to her. 'We're not looking for a faerie mound.'

She turned her attention back to the deputy.

'Garofar? Why don't you go see if Master Nayl needs help with the sweep?'

'Yes, mam,' said Garofar sheepishly, and hurried from the room.

'Anything?' Macks asked Voriet. He was still at work on the cogitator.

'I might have found a reference to the name Sark,' said Voriet. 'But the link is damn slow. I keep having to resend and start over.'

Drusher wandered over to the bookshelves. He ran his finger along the old, decaying spines. There were a lot of books of natural history. Esic Fargul had liked his ornithology. Drusher saw old treatises on migration and nesting patterns, guides to birdsong, feeding grounds. He saw a slim volume at the end of the shelf called *Folk Verse of the Karanine Passes* and took it down. Damp had got to it. It was very much the worse for wear.

'There's nothing in that, sir,' said Jaff, not even looking up.

Drusher frowned at her dubiously.

'She knows, magos,' said Voriet. 'Trust me on that.'

Drusher opened the old book anyway. The pages, rotted away, flaked out in a puff of damp fibres, unintelligible.

'Literally nothing, in this case,' he said. Macks sniggered.

Drusher looked at the book for a moment longer, the empty, discoloured cover, the mulch of paper fibres clinging to the binding. Something that had been but was no longer.

Valentin Drusher's worst enemy was his own imagination. It was a fact he had recognised and accepted many times in the past.

'What if...' he began.

'Valentin?'

'Macks, what if the deputy was right?' he said.

'Meaning what?' asked Macks, coming over.

'That this Keshtre place only partly shares our physical reality? That it's not... not there all the time? Just like the scary bedtime stories say?'

Macks put her hands on her hips and gave him a withering look.

'I know,' he smiled. 'The version of me that got here this morning would have looked at me exactly the same way. But... Germaine, the things I've seen today. The *impossibilities*... I have always been able to codify the living world, according to its rules and its laws and its constants. I look for that. My work is about that. It's reassuring. It's comforting when things make sense. But now I'm not sure of anything. I think *anything* is possible. The rules of sense be damned.'

TEN

RESTLESS

The storm continued into the small hours. After midnight, the thunder diminished into a background grumble, but the downpour increased, beating at the walls and roof like tympani. It felt as though the whole mountainside would wash away in a deluge of mud and take Helter Fortress with it.

'I'm going to do a sweep,' said Macks. In truth, she needed to clear her head. She was beginning to fall asleep over the charts. A circuit would clear her drowsiness.

Voriet and Jaff barely looked up from their work to acknowledge her comment. Drusher had already retired – to his bed, Macks presumed. She buckled on her uniform jacket, picked up her riotgun and a plastek slicker, and left the library.

The fortress was silent, except for the drumming rain and the constant spattering chime of the roof leaks spilling down into pans and buckets. Everything smelled damp. Only a few lamps and candles had been left along the galleries and staircases, so Macks fished out her stablight. On the second floor, she saw Medea Betancore on a bench outside the chamber reserved for Eisenhorn. Betancore was working through a data-slate. She looked tired.

'Anything, marshal?' she asked as Macks approached. Macks shook her head.

'He's sleeping at last,' said Betancore, tilting her head towards the chamber door. 'He needs it.'

'You need it too, mam,' said Macks.

'In a while, perhaps,' replied Betancore. 'I'll stay here for now, in case he needs me. The dreams... wake him.'

Macks nodded. Betancore returned to her data-slate, and Macks made her way back to the stairs.

She went down to the main entrance, pulling on her slicker. Nayl had set up lighting rigs in the yard on their arrival, and she could see their white glow backlighting the small windows above the door.

She dragged the door open.

The yard was bathed in harsh white light from the rigs. Where the heavy rain caught in their stark glare, it made dark stripes like vertical interference bands on a pict-feed. Macks could hear the chatter of the portable generator running the rigs, a murmur behind the constant snake-hiss of the downpour.

She saw Nayl across the yard by the gate. Edde was with him, and they had the main gate dragged open a yard or two, so they could look out into the night. Macks hurried across to them, the rain pattering off her plastek shroud. The air was cold and fresh. She already had water running down the back of her neck.

'Anything?' she asked.

Nayl glanced at her, water dripping off his solid chin.

'Something tripped the outer sensors about half an hour ago,' he said. 'Probably just an animal, but Garofar and Cronyl are checking.'

'Should I get everyone up?' she asked.

He shook his head.

'Probably just an animal,' he repeated.

'Keep me advised,' she said. 'I'll sweep the house.'

Macks returned to the main building. She heaved the heavy door shut and shook off her slicker. She checked the kitchen, then the small back parlour. The fire there was still burning, making it the most comfortable room in the place. Drusher was asleep in an armchair. He hadn't gone to bed after all. He'd brought books down from the library, and one had fallen open across his chest as sleep claimed him. A book on migration habits in the Karanines. Macks saw delicate line drawings of wildfowl. She closed the book and set it aside, drew Drusher's old coat across him as a blanket, and, as an afterthought, bent down and kissed him on the forehead.

He stirred slightly, mumbled and went back to sleep.

Macks had just entered the main hall when she heard the voice. It sounded like a cry. Not a cry of pain, but an urgent call, like someone far away shouting an order.

She halted, listening. The hall was empty, and the candles had burned out. She heard the odd call again, in the distance, muffled by the rain. This time, when it came, her vox-set squawked simultaneously, as if echoing the cry.

Macks adjusted the collar-mounted set. It emitted a quick squeal, then a harsh flood of static.

'Mister Nayl?' she said, tipping her head to talk into the mic. 'Mister Nayl, this is Marshal Macks. Do you copy?'

Static fizzled.

'Nayl, come back. This is Macks.'

There was a burble of audio noise, and then she heard Nayl's voice.

'Reading you, Macks.'

'What was that?' asked Macks.

'That noise?'

'Affirmative.'

'Not sure,' Nayl's voice crackled back. 'Garofar and Cronyl just got back to the gate. Cronyl thinks it was an animal cry.'

'Your vox go weird?' asked Macks.

'Yeah, just for a second,' Nayl replied. 'I think it's atmospherics. We've just got rain here now, but I can see some fierce electrical displays further down the valley.'

Macks wasn't convinced, but she knew how the storm had played hell with Voriet's up-link before midnight.

'Stay in contact,' she said. 'I'm going down to the cold store, then I'll walk the west wall.'

'Channel open,' Nayl responded.

Macks opened the cellar door and followed the stone steps down into the undercroft. There was no light except for her powerful stab-beam.

Then her eyes began to detect a faint blue glow.

The door to the cold store was ajar. The glow of the stasis fields was shining out into the hall.

'Nayl?' she said into her mic. 'The door to the cold store is open. Has anyone been down here?'

Static burbled back.

'Nayl, respond.'

Just more, oddly modulated interference.

Macks waited for a moment. She wanted to move in with backup, but she didn't want to leave the door open, and she'd have to if she was going to go and fetch Nayl and the deputies. She locked her stablight onto the under-rail of her riotgun and moved forwards, aiming the light beam with her weapon.

The door hadn't been forced. The bolts were on the outside, and they had been drawn back.

Slowly, she eased the door open a little wider with the muzzle of her gun and peered in. The whitewashed chamber was lit by the blue ghost-light of the field units. The gurneys sat in rows, green plastek sheets over the remains.

Over *seventeen* of the gurneys...

One, in the middle of the rows, was empty. The plastek sheet was crumpled on the stone floor beside its wheels.

One of the bodies was gone.

Macks cursed under her breath. She edged forwards and slowly settled down into a crouch so she could peer under the rows of gurneys and play her stablight around. Nothing. No heap of bones on the floor.

And how did a bundle of bones fall off a gurney anyway?

Macks rose again slowly, her weapon raised and ready. She realised she was breathing hard, and she forced her herself to slow the rate. She backed gently to the doors and stepped out into the corridor.

'Nayl?' she whispered into the mic on her collar.

Still nothing. She braced her weapon with one hand and pushed the cold store door shut, re-setting the bolts.

Something beside her screamed.

Macks jumped in shock and wheeled around, her weapon levelled. Her heart was racing. There was nothing there. She circled, hunting the length of the corridor both ways with her powerful beam. Nothing.

The scream came again.

'Throne!' she spat. It was her vox. Her damn vox. It was squalling and yelping, uttering shrill bursts of audio-wash.

'Nayl!' she snapped, gripping the collar unit with one hand. 'Nayl, respond!'

She headed back towards the stairs to the main hall.

'Nayl? Someone's been into the cold store. There's a set of remains missing. Nayl!'

Static fluttered.

She half heard her name, scrambled by the interference.

'Nayl, do you copy?'

'Marshal? Say again–'

'Nayl, the cold store's been opened. A body's gone.'

'Copy that.' Nayl's reply was masked with noise.

'Meet me at the entrance,' she barked.

Silence.

'Nayl?'

She reached the main hall and closed the cellar door. For a moment, she thought she saw someone standing at the far end of the hall, a figure in the shadows. But as soon as she turned her stablight that way, it was gone. Just her imagination. She'd got herself spooked. Her mind was playing tricks.

She headed for the front entrance, but changed her mind and switched down the side passage to the parlour first. Drusher was still sound asleep in front of the hearth.

'Valentin?'

She shook him.

'Valentin!'

He woke up, bleary.

'What? Is it... What?'

'Something's going on,' she said. 'Get up.'

'What?' he asked, blinking. 'What sort of something?'

'I don't know. Something.'

He got to his feet, his limbs stiff.

'You looked scared,' he said.

'Just get your coat on,' she replied.

'Germaine, why are you scared?' Drusher asked.

'Shut up, and get your coat on, magos,' she said. 'We're going outside.'

He struggled into his coat. She could see that she'd alarmed him. He wasn't properly awake, and everything was an effort.

'One of the bodies has gone,' she said.

He looked at her.

'Gone? In what way?'

'In a "not there any more" way, Drusher. I just checked the cold store. A body has gone.'

'Taken?' he asked.

'Well, of course. How else would a body disappear? Someone's in the house.'

'You've seen–'

'I haven't seen anything, but someone must have come in. Hurry up.'

He followed her to the door, and they went out together into the kitchen passageway.

There was someone at the far end, by the hall door.

'Mister Nayl?' Macks called out. She raised the stab-beam.

She'd found the missing body.

It was standing up, a twisted skeletal figure, caked in dirt and black organic tatters. It began to limp towards them.

Certain things had trailed Valentin Drusher around his whole life. Poverty was one, frustration was another. A lack of confidence. A wounded sense of being overlooked. All of those things had visited him on an intermittent basis.

But fear had been, pretty much, a constant companion.

Drusher's fear took many forms. Sometimes it was abstract, like his fear of failure and its ugly, contrary twin, his fear of success. He was afraid of authority and afraid of being forgotten. Mostly, his fear manifested as a simple fear of pain. He was a nervous, timid man, who lived in dread of a midnight knock at the door from a predatory road-mob, or of getting in a fight when he was minding his own business, or of being dragged away and beaten by law enforcement if his papers weren't up to date. He was afraid of heights and of drowning. He was afraid of being hurt.

A lingering early memory was the fear of the aggressive canine his father had kept, a creature that never seemed to tolerate Drusher. During his long years of training and education, he had lived in perpetual anxiety about being bitten or stung or clawed by the lab animals and wild specimens he was examining. Even as a magos, that fear had persisted, making him tentative in his work and his studies. He knew a lot about animal behaviour, and, for the most part, he knew how to avoid the risks and handle potentially dangerous life forms, but the most basic rule of all was that even a magos biologis never knew everything, and that an animal, especially one trapped or surprised, could do the unexpected. The damn sea raptor had remained in its cage for months because he'd been too afraid to get near to it.

Twice in his life, he had faced things that were truly fearful: the unholy xenos specimen that he and Macks had cornered in a mill in Outer Udar years before, and the psychotic killing-thing he had hunted in Tycho City.

Those fears lived with him and woke him at night, even though the dangers had long passed. They were hard-edged fears, and they tasted bitter, like dirty iron pressing on his tongue. They made his pulse skip and his skin go clammy. They made him dull and stupid, as if fear were a weight that pressed common sense and logical response out of his head. Both of those truly fearful experiences had happened when he was in the company of Germaine Macks. She was like a damned jinx that made bad things happen to him. Not insane adventures. That was a euphemistic, jolly term that suggested thrills and excitement. Just bad things. Things that had put him in the path of genuine, violent extermination. Things he didn't wish to repeat or even remember. The closest he'd ever come to death.

But there in the kitchen passageway of Helter Fortress, with Macks' stablight – yes, Macks there yet again, the common denominator of his misfortune – with her stablight illuminating the ghastly and impossible as it hobbled towards them, he oddly felt no fear at all.

The figure was simply unbelievable. Old human bones, mottled and stained by loam and mildew and decay, roughly assembled in anatomical order, scabbed and crusted with mould and dried-black blood and residual masses of dead sinew and tissue. The empty eye sockets were dark pits of shadow.

For a moment, time seemed to dawdle, as if waiting for Drusher's mind to catch up. He became aware of how *not frightened* he was. Perhaps he was simply denying what was in front of him, refusing to accept it. Perhaps it was just so extraordinary it had taken him beyond the limits of any fear he could register.

Perhaps the day had already been too strange. He had been forced to accept things that his scientific background did not allow for. The workings of the psykanic mind, the notion of speaking to the dead, the post-mortal apparition of an old man. He had, for Throne's sake, shaken hands with a ghost. Perhaps the strange day spent in the company of Eisenhorn and his curious band of assistants had acted as a crash course, a steep learning curve into the truths of the unknown. Perhaps the day had been like a baptism, annealing his soul and his fear so that it was ready for this moment.

Or perhaps... perhaps it was just too *fascinating*. Drusher's curiosity, the appetite for wonder and discovery that had steered him into his profession, had eclipsed all fears. Even the xenos thing he had faced in the windmill all those years ago, that had been definable. He'd been able to know it, to describe it in accurate terms. He'd been afraid of it simply because it had been going to kill him.

But this... this was beyond his considerable framework of knowledge. He wanted to know what it was. He wanted to understand *how* it could be, how it could exist. It was just organic waste, the skeletal relic of a dead human being. It had no life. It was a broken frame that had once supported life, but that was all. Even on a basic level of organic engineering, the greater part of the mechanism was missing. There were no muscles or tendons left to support or move the bones, no blood supply to feed those muscles, no nerves to stimulate motion and control balance, no heart to pump the blood, no organs to fuel the process, no brain in that cranium to make walking a desire, no eyes to see them with.

But it saw them. And it walked, a precarious, slow walk like a frail old man. It saw Valentin Drusher and Germaine Macks, and it walked towards them.

'That,' Drusher said, almost brightly, 'that is highly unlikely.'

Macks mumbled something that wasn't properly a word. The approaching figure appeared to shudder slightly. Drusher realised that the powerful stab-beam transfixing it was quivering. Macks' hands were trembling wildly. He could hear her sobbing and hyperventilating.

He knew, under any other circumstances, he would be doing the same thing. His mind would have closed down in the choking paralysis of fear.

'Germaine?' he said gently. 'Germaine?'

He put his arm around her shoulder. She was shaking so badly it felt like she was vibrating. She was making an odd, mewling sound. She couldn't *not* look at it.

Drusher couldn't look away either. But he reached out with his free hand

and took the riotgun from her, keeping the stablight aimed at the walking thing. He squeezed his arm tight around her quaking shoulders.

'Germaine? Come on,' he said. 'Come with me. Take a step backwards. That's it. And another.'

He edged them towards the parlour door. She shook against him. Drusher could smell the thing advancing towards them. He could smell rot: not the gross, gagging stink of putrescence, but the faded, dry fragrance of end-stage decomposition.

'Germaine? Another step.'

They had reached the parlour door. He pushed Macks into the room, and she almost fell through the doorway.

Drusher turned back to face the walking thing.

'What are you?' he asked. 'Can you speak? You shouldn't be able to, but then you shouldn't be able to walk either. Can you tell me what you are? Can you tell me how you are possible?'

The figure could not. It simply continued its inexorable trudge towards Drusher. Its right arm began to rise, as if it were reaching out to touch him.

'I'd like an answer,' said Drusher. 'If you won't answer or you can't, I'd like you to go.'

By the light of the torch fastened under the barrel of Macks' heavy weapon, Drusher saw that some kind of energy discharge was crackling over the walking bones, like a faint bioluminescence. It was an electric-green, which reminded him of deep-sea leachfish, or the cave worms, Nematodus cryptus, that he had catalogued in Southern Gersha. The glow came and went, never totally present. For a moment, it shimmered around arm bones, and he saw the brief, ghostly traceries of veins and capillaries. He saw phantom tendons and intercostals come and go across stained ribs. He saw spectral organs pulse in the abdominal void. Some kind of energetic pattern, a light-echo of the lost soft organics. Green pinpricks lit in the empty orbits of the skull sockets, the ghosts of eyes.

'If you don't answer, then we're done,' said Drusher. 'This will be good night. I won't allow you to come any closer. I have a gun. It will shatter what little is left of you.'

The skeletal thing took another wavering step closer.

'I warned you,' said Drusher. Very calmly, he thumbed off the weapon's safety, braced it in a low grip because he knew it would kick, and fired.

In the tight confines of the passageway, the boom was deafening. The blast hit the figure in the sternum.

The explosive force dissipated like steam. Drusher heard flecks of shot patter onto the stone floor, all force spent. The figure kept coming, as though nothing had happened.

'Throne,' said Drusher. He charged the pump grip and fired again, then repeated quickly. Each shot blew out like vapour as it reached the advancing thing.

Only now did fear begin to register in Valentin Drusher. He felt it creep into his joints like frost, numbing him. He got the first taste of bitter metal on his tongue.

He fired one more shot, then ran into the parlour and slammed the door.

ELEVEN

AT THE THRESHOLD

He locked the door behind him. As an afterthought, he dragged one of the old armchairs over and shoved it against the door.

Macks was staring at him. Her eyes were red, and she wiped at her dripping nose with her sleeve.

'We, um,' he began.

'Did you see it?' she whispered. 'You saw it too?'

He nodded.

'I shot it,' he said. 'Several times.'

'Did you...' she asked, her voice very small, 'did you kill it?'

'Not... no,' he said. 'Not really at all. I don't think it can die, because it's not alive. Something odd happened with your gun. Is it loaded... I mean, did you put some kind of blanks in it?'

'What are you even saying?' she gasped at him, incredulous.

'Blanks, you know... *poooffff!*' he said. 'The shots didn't do any damage. Like they were just dummy rounds.'

Macks swallowed hard. She took a step forwards and snatched the gun from his hands.

'Breacher rounds,' she said, popping the slide open to show him the red Munitorum stencil on the yellow sleeve of the ready shell. 'It will blow a hole in a bloody door. Knock a man down, even in armour.'

'Do they... do they go off?' he asked. 'I mean, do they spoil. If you don't use them?'

'You're an idiot,' she snapped, staring at him with wide eyes. 'What are you going on about?'

'It doesn't matter,' he said, trying to sound calm even though a degree of panic was now rising in him, as if he were wading slowly and steadily deeper into an ice bath. 'I shut the door. I locked it.'

'Oh good,' she said sarcastically. She sat down in the other armchair, then immediately got up again. 'You saw it, right?' she asked him. 'You saw... *that?*'

'I did,' he said.

'I've never...' she murmured, pacing. 'I swear by the Throne, I've never been so scared. That was... impossible. I mean, completely and utterly bloody impossible.'

'In the most literal and scientific way,' he agreed.

'Is it still outside?' she asked.

Drusher looked at the locked door and the chair wedged up against it.

'Probably,' he said. 'I'd prefer not to check.'

Macks looked nervously around the small room. There were no other doors and no windows.

'We can't get out,' she said. 'If it's outside the door...'

'It can't get in,' he replied. 'It will go away...'

She looked at him.

'You didn't freeze up,' she said. 'Why didn't you freeze up? You always freeze up.'

Drusher shrugged.

'I don't know. Scientific curiosity,' he said.

'Groxshit,' she said. 'You kept it together somehow.'

'I've rapidly developed a high threshold for strange,' he said. After a moment, he added, 'I think it's beginning to hit me now, though.'

There was a soft noise. They both looked at the door sharply.

It was a scratching sound, like a hound pawing to be let in: the coarse, dry scrape of unfleshed distal phalanges clawing at the old wood of the door.

Macks cursed. They both backed away from the door.

'It can't get in,' he said. 'I locked it. It can't get in.'

He felt that if he repeated it enough, it would become true.

Something started to happen to the door. It shivered slightly, then a dark patch began to appear at shoulder height, as though a blowtorch were being applied to the other side. The patch grew and spread. The wood began to flake and fall away. It looked for all the worlds of man as if the wood were simply and rapidly decomposing.

Macks swore again.

The decay spread, eating the wood away. Flecks of pulp billowed out from the collapsing surface, as though invisible swarms of boring insects were desiccating the wood and devouring it. Macks and Drusher could smell burned sawdust and mildew.

A portion of the upper panel fell away. The decay spread was accelerating. A powerful corrosive sprayed on the door could not have gnawed the fabric away so fast. A bone hand reached in through the gap, flaking the wood, clasping and unclasping at the open air.

'Oh Holy Throne...' Macks murmured.

The door began to collapse in its frame. Parts of it became smoke that boiled with electric-green sparks, motes of dust that tumbled as they burned out. Larger sections fell out whole, bursting into dust as they bounced off the armchair and hit the ground. The figure began to push its way in. They saw the green light of its stare burning from its hollow sockets. They heard the squat legs of the old, heavy chair scrape on the flagstones as it was slowly shoved out of the doorway.

Macks fumbled for her vox.

'Nayl! Nayl!' she yelled. 'For Throne's sake! Help us! The parlour! The parlour behind the kitchen! It's going to kill us!'

The vox-channel warbled back, wordlessly.

Drusher looked around frantically. No other doors, no windows... He ran over to the hearth. The firebox was mounted in the stone chimney place, a later addition to replace the original open fire. Black iron pipework vented the flue up into the chimney itself. The chimney was blocked around the main flue with a sooty metal plate.

He tried to move the firebox, but withdrew his hands instantly with a yelp. Though the fire was dying, the metal was still hot. He kicked instead, savagely and repeatedly, trying to dislodge the firebox from the fireplace. It gradually began to shift. The chimney plate came loose at one side, spilling out clouds of choking soot, and the flue split.

Macks glanced at him.

'What are you doing?' she yelled.

'The chimney,' Drusher replied as he kept kicking furiously. He said it as if that were explanation enough. She understood his meaning.

'We won't fit up the chimney!' she yelled.

'Yes, we will!'

'We can't climb–'

'Yes, we can! Help me!'

'It won't work, Valentin!' she shouted.

He paused, breathing hard from the exertion.

'The alternative is staying in this room,' he said.

He started kicking again. The firebox shifted with a shriek of metal on stone, and sooty clouds spilled out of it.

Macks looked back at the door. The thing was nearly through. Only the chair stood in its way, blocking it.

'Nayl!' she yelled. 'Assist now, for the love of Terra!'

She hoisted the riotgun and began to shoot, methodically pumping shot after shot at the thing. One round blew out part of the door frame. Another punched through the headrest of the arm chair, filling the air with clouds of white kapok. Each shot that hit the thing itself fizzled into nothing.

It strained on relentlessly past the obstacle. Bone hands clawed at the chair, and decay began to spread out from its touch. The upholstery started to wither and perish, exposing yellowed stuffing, springs and wooden frame, then those too began to disintegrate. The chair gradually decomposed from the seat-back down, dissolving into dust. One arm slumped aside as the back-frame powdered. Hungry green sparks writhed on the remaining upholstery.

Macks turned to Drusher and began to kick with him. The firebox dislodged entirely and fell heavily onto its front. They pulled at the broken vent and the chimney plate, ignoring the burns they got from the metal. Accumulated black filth poured out of the flue, decades of dust and soot. They were both coughing and choking.

The plate fell out with a clang.

Drusher looked over his shoulder. The chair was all but gone. The thing was in the room.

'Get up there!' he yelled at her.

'You first!'

'Just get up the chimney, Germaine! I'll boost you!'

She tossed the riotgun and wriggled down into the hot cavity of the chimney place, groping for handholds on the stone. Drusher bent down and made a stirrup from his hands, cradling her right foot to hoist her.

'Climb!' he yelled. 'Climb, Germaine!'

He didn't dare look behind him.

He didn't want to see it when it happened.

Macks' head and upper body were inside the flue. He could hear her scrabbling for grip.

'It's too small!' he heard her yelling, muffled. 'It's too tight! I can't!'

Old, heat-cracked stone inside the chimney gave way. Macks lost her grip and came crashing back out, chunks of stone falling with her. She almost landed on Drusher. They both went over in the hearth.

'Magos! Stay down!'

Drusher heard the commanding voice. He saw Nayl in the doorway behind the walking thing. Garofar and the other deputies were crowding in behind Nayl, staring in utter dismay at the sight in front of them.

But Nayl's face was grim, as if he'd seen the impossible far too many times before. He raised his lasrifle.

Drusher grabbed Macks and pulled her as flat as he could, covering her head and shoulders with his own arms and body.

Nayl fired a sustained burst. Shrieking bolts of light ripped into the parlour, striking the figure from behind, doing nothing but making it jerk a little. Stray bolts tore past it, blowing holes in the far wall over Drusher and Macks. Several shots crippled the old wooden dresser pushed against the wall. It shook, sagged and toppled over on its front.

The figure swayed then slowly turned to face Nayl and the deputies behind him.

'Oh, Holy Terra...' Garofar gasped.

The figure took its first lurching step towards Nayl. It raised its right hand to stroke his face.

Nayl fired again. The las-bolts pummelled at its ribcage, but their heat and light vaporised on contact, becoming a lambent crackle that radiated out across the skeletal form, and vanished.

Nayl cursed. He stood his ground in the doorway and let go of the lasrifle, so that it dropped hard onto its sling, swinging at his waist. He drew a heavy autopistol from a chest holster, ejected the clip, racked the weapon open and took a single round from his breast pocket. He fitted it into the open receiver, slammed the slide shut and took aim with both hands.

The thing was just an arm's length from him.

Nayl fired.

The shot struck the figure in the forehead. The skull burst like a smashed vase. Bone shards sprayed in all directions.

Headless, the figure wavered for a moment. Electric-green energy patterns coursed and flickered around its frame.

Then they winked out.

The dead bones abruptly disarticulated and collapsed like rubbish tipped out of a bucket. They fell in a heap on the parlour floor where the figure had been standing. Thin smoke curled up from the mound of bones.

Nayl lowered the pistol.

'Get Eisenhorn,' he said.

TWELVE

THE HOUSE OF SARK

Early morning light speared in through the slit windows of the washroom on the second floor of the fortress. It was a grey day outside, but the storm had cleared, and the rain had eased back to drizzle.

Drusher was clean, but shivering. There had been no hot water to fill the tin tub, and it had taken a long time to scrub the fireplace soot out of his skin. He had a clean shirt, but his jacket and trousers were the only ones he'd brought along, and he had been forced to put them back on despite the dirt that had rubbed into the fabric.

Macks came in. She'd washed earlier, and her uniform looked clean, but her face was drawn and pale.

'I brought you these,' she said and held out a box of dressings for the burns on his hands.

'Are you all right?' he asked.

She looked away, then took a breath and busied herself applying salve to his palms and fingers. He held his hands out obediently. He wanted to say something, something about what had happened. And not just the horror that had overtaken them in the parlour. About everything. About their chance meeting twenty-seven years before, about their insane adventures, which, to him, included three oddly sweet years in Tycho City that had finally ended in a lot of shouting and slamming of doors.

As usual, and as then, his interpersonal skills failed him.

'The Archenemy of mankind,' she said eventually.

'The what?'

'That's what it was,' she said. 'What they preach about, what they tell us to watch for. I never really thought... I never really thought it was real. But that, *that* was real.'

'I've never thought about it much myself,' he replied. 'I know the edicts, the directives, but I've always found life quite challenging enough without believing in... in supernatural forces. I guess I'm like you. I never thought it was real.'

'It's what the Ordos deal with,' she said, unwrapping some dressings.

'I always thought the Ordos were autonomous secret police,' he said. 'You know, enforcing order, maintaining the Imperial Truth. All that talk of daemonic forces, just propaganda to keep us all scared and in line.'

'Well, the Inquisition is here,' she said, 'so I suppose we're dumb for not taking it seriously.'

'Is it?' he asked.

'What do you mean?' she asked.

Drusher shrugged his shoulders.

'I've been thinking about things,' he said. 'About all of this. You said they needed me because I was the only magos biologis on Gershom. Not that I was the *best*, just that I was the only one–'

'Oh don't start over,' she sighed.

'No, hear me out,' he replied. 'This isn't self-pity. I may *well* be the only magos biologis here. Good *or* bad. But think about the case. This Eisenhorn has a ship. A crew. Significant resources. Technical specialists like that Jaff woman. He hears about the case here from off-world. He knows one of the victims is this woman he claims to know. He comes here. That's shift travel. A commitment of time and expense. But before he set out for Gershom, he knew the victim – *all* the victims – had been mauled by animals. That was an established part of the case. He knew he'd need an expert. So, I'm wondering, why didn't he bring one?'

She didn't answer.

'I mean, the Ordo must have plenty of specialists on staff,' he went on. 'Consultants they can call on at the drop of hat. But he didn't bring one.'

'Well, he thought he'd find one here.'

'Yeah, a crappy one like me? If he got here and realised he needed specialist help, why didn't he signal to the Ordos to send someone? Someone really good?'

'Like you said, Drusher, time. Time and expense.'

He shook his head.

'I don't buy it,' he said. 'He comes unprepared, and he makes do with a has-been like me. Don't look at me like that. I know I'm no great shakes, Germaine. I'm not that deluded. But he makes do.'

'The hell are you suggesting, Valentin?' she asked.

'I'm saying, maybe he's not as connected as he wants us to think,' said Drusher. 'He and Voriet can flash all the badges they like, and pretend to be all sorts of important things, but what if this isn't legitimate at all?'

'You mean... you don't think they're from the Ordos?'

'I'm saying that's possible. Or this whole thing is deeply unofficial. A... How do you people phrase it? A rogue operation. Sending for a high-level magos biologis would have raised flags. I don't know if Master Eisenhorn is a real inquisitor or not, but I think what he's doing here is strictly off the record.'

'I think you're paranoid,' she replied.

'After last night, aren't you?'

She snapped the aid-box shut.

'Well, it's moot anyway,' she replied. 'The storm's cleared. The up-link is re-established. I'm going to contact the area governor this morning. Establish an emergency situation and ask him to mobilise the Territorial Guard. If the Archenemy is here in Unkara, it needs to be contained, and this little group of ours isn't up to the task.'

'I don't think Eisenhorn's going to like that,' said Drusher.

'He can stick it up his arse for all I care,' said Macks. 'I'm Magistratum, and I have a duty.'

He smiled at her.

'That's what I always loved about you, Germaine.'

'What?' she asked.

'You, being you. Never backing down.'

She grinned.

'I did last night,' she said.

'Last night was different,' he said.

'Very,' she replied. 'You were very different. You faced that thing down. You saved me.'

'I think that was Nayl.'

'No, you kept it at bay. You didn't stop trying. Not like you at all.'

'Must be the mountain air.'

She suddenly hugged him tight and planted a long, loud kiss on his cheek.

'Thank you,' she said.

She walked to the door.

'Oh,' she added, turning to look back. 'Nayl's cleaning out the mess in the parlour. The bones and stuff, they'll have to be quarantined. But there were some books you'd brought down from the library. I told Nayl not to move them without checking with you. I didn't know if they were important.'

Drusher went down to the parlour. He felt uneasy returning to the scene of the horror. Daylight made everything seem very ordinary, but he could still smell burned sawdust and cold decay.

Nayl, wearing surgical gloves, was scooping the brown bones into a hazard waste sack.

'Books,' he said when he saw Drusher. He pointed to a side table in the corner. 'Do you need them?'

'I might,' said Drusher. He walked over to the books and began to gather them up.

'How did you kill it?' he asked.

'Head shot,' said Nayl.

'You made it look easy,' said Drusher.

'Nothing easy about it.'

'I fired the riotgun at it multiple times. So did Macks. No effect. It somehow neutralised the force of the shots.'

'Yeah, I heard you gave it a go. Good for you, magos.'

'And that combat weapon of yours. You dumped some serious las into it.'

'I did.'

'With no effect. Yet a single bullet...'

Nayl looked up at him.

'That thing, magos,' Nayl said. 'It was an animation process. An energy form that had simply inhabited the dead bones. It was using them as a framework to move around in, to interact with the physical world.'

'I saw a shimmer on it,' said Drusher. 'An aura. Like an afterimage.'

'Right. So that energy form, it can just soak up kinetic damage from a pump gun, or the high-yield las expended from my weapon.'

'And manipulate that energy to eat through doors. And people.'

'Correct.'

'But a single bullet somehow...?'

'It wasn't the bullet,' said Nayl. 'It's what was *written* on it. Eisenhorn etched it himself and gave me a stash of them. A charm, if you like. Like an amulet. The charm broke the energy field and let the bullet do its damage.'

'Well, I'll take your word for that, Master Nayl. It sounds a lot like hocus-pocus nonsense to me.'

'Me too,' said Nayl. 'But if hocus-pocus nonsense works, you go with it.'

'It sounds like this thing was created,' said Drusher. 'I mean artificially manufactured. And let out.'

Nayl rose to his feet.

'You figured that out, did you?' he asked.

'The cold store door was unbolted,' said Drusher. 'Macks said so. The thing didn't eat its way out, and that's the only way it could have opened the door. So it follows that someone made it and let it out for a reason.'

'There's the makings of an investigator in you yet, sir,' said Nayl.

'What was the reason?' asked Drusher.

'To kill us all,' said Nayl. 'That's my bet. Because maybe we're getting too close to something. What happened last night could have happened any night in the weeks since we arrived. But it happened *last* night. So something happened yesterday that took us all a step too close to the truth. And you know what happened yesterday, magos?'

'No, what?'

'You got here,' said Nayl.

'That's not a very cheery notion,' said Drusher.

'Shall I tell you why I think there's more to you than meets the eye?' asked Nayl. 'Why I think you've got that something that marks a good investigator? You don't ask the stupid questions.'

'What would they be?' asked Drusher.

'Well, since we've been talking, you haven't once asked what it was.'

'I presumed there wasn't a word for it,' said Drusher. 'Or if there was, it would be part of a concept that was meaningless to me as a man of science.'

'That's pretty smart,' said Nayl. 'And you haven't asked who let it out.'

'Because I think you'd have told me if you knew,' said Drusher. 'Or it's classified, and there's no point asking in the first place.'

Drusher carried the small clutch of books back up the stairs to the library. They weren't significant, just essays on wildflowers and ornithology. He'd borrowed them to ease his mind, to refresh his thoughts with something familiar and reassuring. But they belonged in the library, so he was going to put them back there. You didn't borrow a fellow naturalist's books and not return them. Even if that fellow naturalist was thirty years dead.

He heard hammering from the basement. Macks' deputies had been ordered to seal the cold store.

The library was empty. The plastek sheeting on the windows rustled in the breeze. He started to slot the borrowed books back onto the shelves. The last one was the book of migration patterns in the Karanine area. It had been the most interesting, clearly one of Fargul's favourites. The old man had filled the margins with pencilled annotations, remarks drawn from his observations of the seasonal influxes and exoduses. Those little jottings had been what Drusher had found most comforting. The marks of a man who had happily spent years wandering the hills in all weathers, witnessing the patterns of nature, noting unusual sightings, rare specimens and the most likely sites for the observation of particular species. The handwritten notes gave Drusher a sense of kinship.

He flipped through the pages one last time, before putting the book away, relishing the constant delight expressed in Fargul's notes. How the crosshammers always congregated along the same stretch of river each year before beginning migration, gathering in such numbers the trees were bowed with them. How the forests rang with call-and-response in spring when the exhausted redbeaks searched for their life-mates to reunite after the arduous voyage back. How the returning charhoops flocked at the pass in early summer, swarming and mobbing in huge clouds before continuing on up into the hills...

Drusher paused. He read the note again. Surely...

He flipped through the pages and speed-read some of the other annotations. The same thing, several times. Could it be *that* simple?

He put the book down and began to skim along the spines of the shelves. Geographic history... The origin of place-names...

He pulled out a volume or two and put them aside when they proved useless. He lighted on another and tried that instead. There it was. The text confirmed his idea.

'Holy Throne,' he murmured.

He took the geographic text and the annotated book, and turned to hurry out. He stopped.

He'd just noticed another book, tucked away at the end of the shelves.

'I'm sorry, that's simply not appropriate, marshal,' Eisenhorn was saying. He was sitting at the table in the main hall and looked more robust than he had the night before. Sleep had restored him, at least in part.

Voriet and Jaff sat with him. They had been reviewing data-slates together. Nayl and Betancore stood nearby. All of them were looking at Macks, who was standing at the far end of the long table, Garofar at her side.

'Well, tough,' said Macks.

'Marshal, I'd watch your tone,' said Voriet.

'I think what I'll watch, interrogator,' replied Macks, 'is the welfare of the Imperial citizens in this province. The Archenemy is abroad. I saw its handiwork with my own eyes. I am going to contact the governor and declare an emergency, and I'm going to ask him for military support to–'

'We can deal with this, marshal,' said Voriet. 'That's why we're here. This is our specialty. Leave it to us to make the decisions. Don't hinder us by complicating the situation.'

'I have authority in this province,' said Macks.

'An authority superseded by the Ordos,' replied Jaff.

'Let's allow the governor to make that distinction,' said Macks. 'He can overrule me. He may urge a Territorial mobilisation anyway, to support your work. And, of course, he has the authority to request immediate clarification and authorisation from the Office of the Inquisition on Brallant.'

'I can't allow that,' said Eisenhorn. 'This matter is complex and sensitive. What you're suggesting will delay things and potentially place more people in harm's way.'

'Are you asking me not to?' asked Macks. 'Or telling me not to? Or are you going to actually stop me doing it?'

'Cooperation would be the ideal remedy here,' said Eisenhorn.

'I think that's good advice,' said Drusher as he walked in. He dumped the three books on the table. 'I think it's *very* good advice, and I think we should all take it.'

'Magos, please,' said Voriet. 'This is a private briefing. The marshal's already interrupted and she was just about to leave–'

'You recruited me to serve as an expert advisor,' said Drusher, pulling out a chair and sitting down at the table. 'Well, I have some expertise to share. I think if you're really interested in the most efficient resolution of this matter, we could all start to cooperate. You're keeping Macks and me in the dark, and I don't want any more crap about things being classified. Let's start sharing, shall we?'

Voriet and Jaff glanced at Eisenhorn. As ever, he was unreadable.

'What do you have, magos?' Eisenhorn asked quietly.

Drusher waggled his finger.

'No, no,' he said. 'You show me yours and I'll show you mine.'

Garofar snorted. Macks elbowed him.

Eisenhorn sat back. He drummed his fingertips on the tabletop thoughtfully.

'Want me to clear the room, sir?' asked Nayl.

'No, Harlon,' said Eisenhorn. 'Take a seat, marshal. You too, deputy Garofar. My interrogator was just delivering new material. Now the storm's passed, the up-link is re-established. Voriet?'

Voriet looked at him anxiously.

'Sir, are you sure that–'

'Your report, please, interrogator.'

Voriet cleared his throat and activated his data-slate.

'Draven Sark,' he said reluctantly. 'The local annals have no listings for anyone of that name, so it appears that Draven Sark was never a resident of, or visitor to, Gershom. However, he is in the Subsector Census. Current age two hundred and fifty-one standard, whereabouts unknown. A very high-ranking and respected magos medicae in his day. His grandfather is an interesting figure, a senior recollector in the Administratum. His name was Lemual Sark, and he secured his footnote in history four centuries ago through his research on Symbol Iota, which led to a breakthrough in the battle against a virulent pestilence known as Uhlren's Pox.'

'Also known as blood-froth, or the Torment,' said Jaff. 'It was a pandemic. Sark's work was crucial in containing–'

'I am familiar with the case,' said Eisenhorn. 'Sark was able to confirm that Uhlren's Pox was not a natural contagion or a xenos plague, but in fact a weapon deliberately bio-engineered by a servant of the Archenemy.'

'Really?' asked Macks.

Eisenhorn looked at her. 'That detail has been classified and withheld from the general population, marshal. I have just *un*-classified it. So Draven Sark is a descendant?'

'That's the case, sir,' said Voriet. 'The whole Sark family line has been engaged with Materia Medica for many generations, either as medicae experts or medicae specialists serving the Administratum. In Draven Sark's case, the former. He retired decades ago.'

'Whereabouts unknown?' asked Eisenhorn.

'Yes,' said Voriet. 'But it appears he continued to practise on a private basis. In retirement, he assumed several identities. Sadrane Carnac, Philipo Bosk, Emment Pelet...'

'Why does a respected medicae take on assumed names?' asked Macks.

Voriet smiled.

'The circumstances of his retirement are sealed,' he said. 'One may presume malpractice, and a quiet effort to avoid scandal. Draven Sark and his various alter egos have been persons of interest to both the Arbites and the Ordos at different times over the last century. He has a history of unfortunate associations. Nothing that could lead to prosecutions, but enough to convince me he walks in the shadows of lawlessness.'

Voriet scrolled through his slate.

'Some seventy years ago,' he said, 'Philipo Bosk was listed as a resident of Gershom, specifically of Unkara Province. He owned property here, paid his tithes, was listed as "retired".'

'Where were his properties?' asked Eisenhorn.

'Unknown,' said Voriet. 'A great number of municipal records were lost during the civil war. All trace of Philipo Bosk vanishes about twenty years ago. But we have picts of him, and comparative recognition cogitation confirms within an error margin of decimal zero-zero-two per cent that Bosk and Sark are the same man.'

'So, he disguises his identity, but not well,' said Betancore. 'A simple verification reveals the truth. That seems clumsy.'

'Or suggests that Bosk, or Sark, or whatever he wanted to call himself, felt secure,' replied Eisenhorn. 'That he was confident he could not be found, even if someone was looking.'

'If he lived here,' said Drusher, 'then he was happy to be known to his neighbours – neighbours like Esic Fargul – by his real name.'

'Which reinforces my point,' said Eisenhorn. 'His neighbours knew his real name. He entertained and was not a recluse. He had influence and an influential circle of friends. The name of his property was known. Keshtre. Yet neither it nor he can be located. His disguise was casual, Medea, because he was clearly able to hide very well.'

'You should look at his list of known associates, sir,' said Voriet, sliding the data-slate towards his senior. 'An influential circle of friends indeed – artists,

Administratum officials, men of science, senior military officers, at least one ex-governor of Gershom...'

'You see my urge for confidence now, marshal?' Eisenhorn asked Macks.

'That name in the third column, there, sir,' said Voriet, pointing to the slate. 'That was the one that caught my eye.'

'Goran Gobleka,' said Eisenhorn.

'Who's that?' asked Drusher.

'A recidivist,' said Eisenhorn. 'A man pursued for years by the Ordo Hereticus. A suspected member of the Cognitae. And the man that Thea Inshabel was looking for when she came here.'

'What is the Cognitae?' asked Macks.

'Some things must remain classified,' said Eisenhorn. 'The point is, we have a connection. A link between the elements. Sark resided in the Karanines. Thea's remains, and the others,' were discovered in the area. Sark knew the man Thea was hunting. He may have offered sanctuary to his friend Gobleka, especially if his home was somehow impossible to detect.'

'Perhaps not so impossible,' said Drusher.

Eisenhorn stared at him. Jaff and Voriet looked taken aback.

'My turn,' said Drusher. 'When I encountered Esic Fargul in the woods yesterday, *however* I encountered him, he said that Keshtre was a fortress near here, but down towards the pass.'

'So you said,' said Voriet.

'We presumed he meant the Karad Pass, north of here, so that's the area we've been looking at,' said Drusher.

'And there's nothing here,' said Macks.

Drusher opened the old man's annotated text.

'Fargul was a keen observer,' he said. 'See, how he made notes? The little things he noticed? He also knew a good deal about local history. His family had lived here for a long time. In these margin comments, he uses the phrase "the pass" several times. I didn't notice it at first, because I assumed he meant Karad. But here, if you look, he refers to flocks massing at the pass before moving up into the hills.'

'So?' asked Jaff.

'If they were massing at the pass,' said Drusher, 'they would already *be* in the hills. Karad is north of us, deep in the range. He meant somewhere else. To Esic Fargul, "the pass" was something else.'

Drusher pushed the annotated text aside and opened the geographical history.

'In fact,' he said, 'it's so obvious it's a little embarrassing. Here... "Unkara" is derived from the Old Fent word for crossroads. Unkara Town is a crossroads... because it was founded on the best navigational transit point south of the Karanines. It is a major pass between the Karanine foothills and the southern uplands. A more significant pass than Karad, in fact. We don't think of it that way, because there's a town there now, but to an older local man like Fargul, that would be "the pass" and would require no further clarification.'

'So, we've been looking in the wrong area?' asked Voriet.

Drusher nodded. 'I believe we have. Keshtre is not north of us towards Karad, it's south of us towards Unkara Town.'

Audla Jaff sniffed.

'Interesting,' she said. 'But if that's what you have to share, magos, it's comparatively minor. You have used a paltry scrap of expertise to leverage far more information from us.'

'Well,' said Drusher, 'that's what good investigators do, isn't it, Master Nayl?'

'I think,' said Nayl, covering his amusement, 'we should go back to the maps and see what's south of us.'

'There's nothing south of us either,' said Jaff, annoyed.

'Actually, I think there is,' said Drusher. 'I hadn't finished, Mamzel Jaff. I happened upon this too.'

He put the third book in front of him. It was an old volume of a larger format, its green card cover faded by the years.

'This was in the library,' said Drusher. 'It's Esic Fargul's sketchbook. He was carrying it the day I met him.'

'Yesterday,' Nayl reminded him.

'Whatever day yesterday was, Master Nayl,' said Drusher. He opened the book. Its pages were age-spotted and frail. Many loose leaves and sheets of paper had been stuffed into it, held between the covers by the tie ribbon. Drusher turned over drawings of the deep valley, of trees, of pools and tumbled stones, overgrown.

'He liked this country,' said Drusher. 'He drew it a lot. Sometimes, the same location over and over. He liked the river. He also liked the old fortresses. He made many studies of them. Especially the ruined ones. Look at this.'

He pushed one sketch onto the table so they could all see it. It showed two broken stones in a woodland clearing.

'The note at the bottom says "Ballion Fortress". It's clearly nothing more than a few stones. But to Fargul, it was a fortress still. Ballion is not on any of the maps, but it is listed in the indices of several histories as a Karanine fort. So, Fargul, with his love of local lore, knew the old sites even when published history had forgotten them. Now look at this one.'

Drusher spread the sketchbook open. It was a fine graphite sketch of a mountain pool, fed by three brooks and overhung on the rising side by huge blocks of tumbledown stone swathed in moss.

'I watched him draw this,' said Drusher. 'It's where I met him.'

Eisenhorn got up and limped around the table to Drusher's side. He hunched over, one hand on the tabletop, and studied the sketch.

'Your auto-séance, sir,' said Drusher. 'It did not conjure the old man from his grave at random. It conjured him to tell me something important. I just didn't know what until now. See what he wrote beneath the drawing?'

'*Ruins beside pool*,' Eisenhorn read out. '*Keshtre watch gate*.'

'I thought the old stones were a southern watchtower for Helter,' said Drusher, tapping the picture. 'But they are, in fact, a northern watchtower of Keshtre.'

'This was in the library all along?' asked Eisenhorn.

'Yes,' said Drusher. 'Sark really was Fargul's neighbour.'

Eisenhorn straightened up. For a second, he placed his hand on Drusher's shoulder. Drusher wasn't sure if the inquisitor was simply seeking support as he rose, or if he was fleetingly expressing some form of appreciation.

'This was in the library all along?' he repeated. He was looking at Audla Jaff.

'I thought you'd been through every book in the library, Mam Jaff?' asked Garofar.

'I hadn't got to every single volume,' said Jaff sharply. She restrained herself. 'I was working methodically. There were still a hundred or so volumes to be assessed. I clearly hadn't got to that one yet.'

She looked at Eisenhorn.

'My sincere apologies, sir,' she said. 'You know my work to be thorough and–'

Eisenhorn raised his hand.

'Never mind,' he said. 'Let's find the house this ruined gate belongs to.'

THIRTEEN

GATES OF KESHTRE

Drusher buttoned up his old coat and wandered into the yard to join the others. It was late morning, and the sun was out. Most of the party were checking their walking gear or their weapons. Eisenhorn stood apart, talking to Betancore.

As he approached, Drusher overheard the end of their conversation.

'I still say you need to rest and leave this to Voriet,' Betancore was saying.

'Not an option, Medea.'

'Then at least give me a few hours to find a decent ATV to–'

'I can walk. The ground is too steep and the forest too dense for a vehicle.'

'Then I'll walk with you every step of the way–'

'No,' Eisenhorn said. 'I want you at the landing zone, prepped. We may have need of heavier support.'

'Gregor, we don't have the sort of heavy support that–'

'I know we don't have him, Medea. Throne knows I wanted to bring him, but these days he's too wayward. It would have taken all my effort just to keep him in line. We'll have to manage without.'

Medea Betancore glared at her master uncertainly, then noticed Drusher approaching.

'Magos,' she nodded. She looked back at Eisenhorn.

'I'll see you later,' she said.

They left the gatehouse and walked down-range into the forest. The sun had raised a mist from the forest floor, and it fumed like smoke through the glades. Macks and her deputies led the way in a loose line, followed by Nayl and Voriet, with Eisenhorn, Jaff and Drusher bringing up the rear. The progress was leisurely, mainly held back by the speed of the inquisitor's progress.

'You didn't have to accompany us, magos,' said Jaff.

'Well, I feel I've come this far,' replied Drusher lightly. 'I'd like to see the rest.'

'Do you know what the rest is?' she asked.

'No, mam, which is why I want to see it.'

'A man should sometimes be careful about what he wants,' said Jaff.

* * *

Jaff moved on ahead, leaving Drusher to keep pace with Eisenhorn.

'She's right,' Eisenhorn said. 'You may regret this, magos.'

'Because it's going to be dangerous, sir?'

'Yes,' said Eisenhorn. 'There is a chance you won't survive the experience. Or worse–'

'There's a worse?'

'Always. That you may survive it and wish you hadn't. That the memories will haunt you for the rest of your days.'

A redbeak trilled in a nearby tree.

'Tell me about the case,' said Drusher.

'The case?'

'Goran Gobleka. The Cognitae. I may as well know as much as possible, so I can be of as much use as possible. I'm hardly a security risk if I'm going to be dead or insane by the end of the day.'

'The Cognitae are a secret order,' said Eisenhorn. 'You might think of them as a cult, or coven. Their organisation is very old. It may even predate the founding of the Imperium. Certainly, in the last few centuries, it has enjoyed a resurgence in these subsectors. The Cognitae are a pernicious threat to the very foundations of our society. They are ruthless, and they employ dangerous levels of intellectual rigour.'

'What do they want?' asked Drusher.

'What does anybody want?' replied Eisenhorn. 'Power. Mastery. Control. They believe that the domination of our culture, and indeed the liberation of our species, lies in the use of forbidden knowledge. Lore that is heretical in nature and too dangerous for man to know. The secrets of the Archenemy, and the wisdom of the warp.'

'Do you mean... magic?'

'That is a misleading term, but, like "ghost", it will serve as far as you're concerned. The Archenemy of man has the means to unlock and control the very fabric of reality. The Cognitae wish to acquire that ability for themselves.'

'And you're hunting them?'

'One way or another, for most of my life, I have worked to eradicate their evil,' said Eisenhorn. 'In the last two decades, I have begun to unravel what I believe is a significant initiative on behalf of the Cognitae. An endeavour to achieve something of great magnitude.'

'What?'

'I don't know, magos. They hide well. They work in secret. They recruit very effectively. They establish secret scholams on many worlds, institutions where they raise and train prospective members, radicalising them in the process. I have uncovered several, and learned scraps. I piece those scraps together. Whatever they are working towards, it is momentous. Lilean Chase–'

'Who's she?'

'A key member of the Cognitae. One of their adepts, brilliant and misguided. Perhaps their leader in this quadrant. My hunt is for her in particular. A heretic of the most toxic kind. My intelligence suggests she works towards, or perhaps for, something called the Yellow King. This may be a person, or an entity, or simply a condition... A state of power and enlightenment. She must be found and stopped.'

'And this Goran man?'

'One of the scraps, magos,' said Eisenhorn. 'Part of the Cognitae network. He seemed lower priority, which is why I assigned Thea Inshabel to follow his trail. I fear she found something more. I fear Goran Gobleka was *not* low priority at all.'

'This magic stuff...' Drusher began.

'Don't dwell on it, Drusher.'

'It is beyond my remit anyway, sir,' replied Drusher, 'but your man Nayl, he spoke of... uh... words of power. Words that can somehow break it.'

'Words may break it, but they also form it,' said Eisenhorn. 'One of the Cognitae's most cherished goals is to unlock and rediscover Enuncia. This is a language of power, a pre-human language, that can literally manipulate reality. Apart from a few words and letters, no one knows it entirely. Lilean Chase has spent most of her life trying to decode it and build a working lexicon.'

'But you use it?'

'We use our enemies' weapons against them,' said Eisenhorn.

'So you're not above heretical knowledge yourself?'

'It is the curse of the Ordos, magos. We need to know the Archenemy so we can prevail against him. That is why we stand in the shadows, why we walk alongside mankind and not as part of it. We are tainted by the knowledge we must use. It drives most of us to our dooms, eventually.'

'To your graves?'

'Or worse,' said Eisenhorn.

'Why do you do it?' asked Drusher. 'And don't say "because someone must" or anything like that.'

'Why are you a magos biologis, Drusher, when that calling has apparently given you a life you resent?'

'Because I'm good at it,' said Drusher.

'Yes,' said Eisenhorn. 'It's sad, isn't it?'

They reached the pool. But for the low blanket of mist in the surrounding area, it was much as Drusher remembered it from the previous day. Nayl, Voriet and the deputies went ahead to scout, leaving Macks and Audla Jaff with Eisenhorn and Drusher.

Eisenhorn limped to the old, mossy stones and began to examine them. He took off his gloves to run his bare hands across their surfaces.

Drusher watched the birds in the nearby trees for a while and counted off eight species. Then he wandered over to join Eisenhorn.

'Do they know you're hunting for them?' he asked.

'Who?'

'The Cognitae? This Chase woman?'

'Yes, magos.'

'And it would seem, from the fate of your poor associate Thea, they knew you had come close here.'

'It would.'

'Are you familiar with the white tile spider?' asked Drusher.

'Pretend I'm not,' replied Eisenhorn.

'It's small, but venomous. An arachnid. Black, but with a small white square on its abdomen, hence the name. Elusive. It is preyed upon by a number of small lizard species. It has a habit of killing greenback beetles, which the lizards consider to be a delicacy. It does not eat the beetles. It leaves them dead, near its lair. This attracts the lizards, who feed on the beetles and slowly become paralysed by the venom the white tile has injected into their bodies. Once the lizards are helplessly inert, the white tile emerges and kills them. It kills and feeds upon its own mortal enemy, creatures many times larger and more powerful than itself.'

'That was an analogy, wasn't it?' said Eisenhorn.

'The bodies you've found here in the Karanines,' said Drusher. 'That appears to me to be the oddest fact of all. Whatever's afoot here, whatever secret endeavour, why leave them where they can be found? Why draw attention where no attention was being paid?'

'You think this is a trap, magos?'

'I think if you were hunting me, I'd want to find a way to stop that. You say the Cognitae are clever and devious. That thing that attacked us in Helter. Animated by a word of power, I have no doubt...'

'It was.'

'It seems to me that it was animated once we were all here together. You had been absent for days, and several of your staff were away recruiting me. Only when we all returned did it strike. Because we were there to be killed. Brought there by the mystery of the bodies.'

'Drusher,' said Eisenhorn, 'I am not worried that this is a trap. I am absolutely *certain* it is one. An effort I cannot ignore, too delicious to resist, intended to bring me to this place and end me forever.'

Voriet clambered back up the slope to join them at the edge of the pool.

'Sir, we've found the house,' he said. 'What's left of it.'

FOURTEEN

SHADE HALL

The hunting party moved through the forest from the pool.

'What did you find?' Drusher asked Nayl.

'A ruin,' said Nayl. 'Deep in the undergrowth. From the scale of it, it may have been a fortress, but nothing's stood there for a long time.'

'How long?'

'Very long. Hundreds of years.'

'That doesn't fit the data we have,' said Drusher.

'That happens a lot in my line of work,' Nayl replied. 'Unless you're prepared to scare yourself silly and believe it does fit the data. Just not the bits of the data you're comfortable thinking about.'

'Garofar's shade hall?' Drusher laughed, nervously.

'I've seen worse things,' said Nayl. He paused and reached into his backpack. He held out a small handgun to Drusher.

'It's the one I took off you,' he said. 'I took the liberty of cleaning it and loading it.'

'Wasn't it loaded already?'

'These are better bullets,' said Nayl. 'Customised. From my special stash. I thought you might need something.'

'I'm not really a gun person,' said Drusher.

'Do me a favour and take it anyway, magos,' said Nayl.

The stones that had once been a fortress lay tumbled together under the trees, swathed in moss and climbing creepers. The mist hung heavy and still.

It had been a place of significant size. Some of the stone blocks were massive and suggested a heavy outer wall. But even these slabs, their edges worn smooth by years of erosion, were half-buried in the loam. There was no longer even a sense of any ground plan that could be recognised.

'If this is Keshtre,' said Audla Jaff, 'then Keshtre is not the site we are looking for. This isn't just derelict. It has been vacant for hundreds if not thousands of years.'

'Audla's very pragmatic,' Nayl said to Drusher, sidelong. 'She likes to deal in facts. She's not very taken with other possibilities.'

His grin suggested he was sharing a joke with Drusher, but Drusher didn't find that reassuring. The idea that their speculation was correct, and some kind of supernatural truth lay beneath their immediate physical reality, was not reassuring.

'I heard your comment, Harlon,' Jaff said. 'The information provided by Magos Drusher asserted that Keshtre had been occupied by Draven Sark and in use as recently as a few decades ago. But this intelligence was imparted as a by-product of an auto-séance. The warp lies and deceives. Its whispers cannot be trusted, or at least, cannot be understood on face value. The magos' encounter with the ghost of Esic Fargul is open to many interpretations, not least that it was utter, ungrounded fancy.'

She walked through the undergrowth to a nearby tree and ran her hand across its bark, 'This is a Southern Spur Pine, is it not, magos?'

Drusher nodded.

'A mature specimen,' said Jaff. 'To reach this size, it would take... what? Three hundred years standard?'

'At least,' Drusher admitted.

'Yet it – and others like it – are growing within the bounds of the site,' said Jaff. 'Keshtre didn't collapse and perish in the last few decades. It has been gone long enough for three hundred-year-old trees to grow up through its bones.'

Eisenhorn glanced at Voriet, who was scanning the area with a portable auspex of a type Drusher hadn't seen before.

'Nothing residual, sir,' Voriet said. 'Nothing electromagnetic or ectomagnetic. No background psionics. Of course, this device isn't as sensitive as you...'

The inquisitor nodded. He limped through the ruin a little way until he was standing a short distance from them. Then he stopped and closed his eyes.

Drusher and the others waited. Birdsong in the neighbouring glades died away to silence. The breeze stilled, and there was a palpable drop in air temperature.

'Remain calm,' Voriet whispered to Drusher, Macks and the deputies.

Macks looked deeply uncomfortable.

'I'm going to circle the perimeter,' she said. Voriet nodded, and Macks moved away quietly with Cronyl and Edde in tow. Drusher got the feeling she was simply finding an excuse not to be present.

It certainly wasn't comfortable. Though the sun continued to wink through the tree canopy above, light in the glade had somehow dimmed to an eerie dusk. Drusher realised his breath was steaming slightly in the cold air. He saw frost dusting the tree trunks and the ground-cover leaves like powdered sugar. He looked up at the sun, twinkling beyond the leaves, to steady his nerves.

The light slowly returned, the temperature rose and birdsong resumed.

Eisenhorn sighed.

'Nothing,' he said.

'Well,' said Jaff. 'I propose we return to Helter and make a new plan.'

'There are no birds singing,' said Drusher quietly.

'What, sir?' asked Garofar.

'Around this site,' said Drusher. 'No birdsong. You can hear it in the nearby areas, but not here.'

He gestured towards a stand of trees outside the limits of the old ruin.

'I can see redbeaks,' he said. 'And little-tailed skeens. There, up in the branches there. See? But nothing comes this way. We've been here ten minutes, and I haven't seen a single bird enter or cross this area.'

'What does that mean?' asked Voriet.

Drusher shrugged and looked up at the sun again.

There was movement in the undergrowth, and Macks returned with the other two deputies.

'There's a track,' she said. 'A hundred metres that way. Looks like it runs all the way down from the mountain trail. It's been in use. Wheeled vehicles, ATVs, I'd guess. Someone's been visiting this place, often and recently.'

'But the track runs out,' said Edde, 'ten metres short of the ruin. It just stops, then thick undergrowth.'

'Well then,' said Jaff, 'the visitors – hunters, I imagine – came that close and no closer.'

'There's no turning circle,' said Macks. 'No crush marks or compressed vegetation at the end of the trail where a heavy vehicle turned around. I don't know about you, Mamzel Jaff, but I don't drive an ATV several kilometres down a very rough track and then just reverse back the way I came.'

'Perhaps we put a watch on the head of the track?' suggested Voriet. 'See if these visitors come back?'

'You're very quiet, Drusher,' said Eisenhorn.

Drusher was still looking up at the trees.

'The trees are growing wrong,' he said.

'Expand,' said Eisenhorn.

'All the trees growing within the ruin site,' he said. 'They're the same species as in the surrounding woods. But they have a slight inclination. You see it if you look. Growth patterning. It's to do with the elements. Prevailing wind directions, angle to the sun in different seasons, soil, rainfall. Like the hair on a man's scalp, growing in a natural pattern.'

'I don't really see it,' said Eisenhorn.

'It's the sort of thing I'm trained to notice,' said Drusher. 'Trust me. The thing is, the trees on this site are all growing to a slightly different pattern. It's subtle, but distinct.'

'And what would cause that?' asked Eisenhorn.

Drusher frowned.

'It's like...' he began. 'It's like they are growing in a different environment. Responding to a different sun.'

Eisenhorn looked over at Garofar.

'In the old stories for children, deputy,' he asked, 'how did an outsider find a shade hall? How did an outsider enter one?'

Garofar looked puzzled.

'Well, sir, they just appeared,' he replied. 'You could enter them when they were there. Or you were taken there by the... the monsters who dwelt inside.'

'Nothing else? No folk tale rhyme or incantation?'

'I don't know,' Garofar said. 'There was one story about a fellow who called one up. I suppose like an incantation. But I don't know what words you'd use.'

'Words...' murmured Eisenhorn.

'Do you mean that language thing?' Drusher asked.

'I think experimentation would be ill-advised,' said Jaff.

'Your objection is noted,' said Eisenhorn. 'Sark's home was well hidden. Unnaturally well hidden. It was a place of retreat. Of escape. It was, in literal terms, occulted. This may be a false trail, or it may be that we are standing on the threshold of Sark's hall. I'm not leaving until we have exhausted all possibilities of making a definitive determination.'

'Sir, it is a considerable risk,' said Jaff.

'You said it yourself, Audla,' replied Eisenhorn. 'The word Keshtre. You said the name translated as a "forbidden speaking place", or "place of unholy speech". If the Cognitae are hiding in the Karanines, they have built a place of seclusion and retreat, and proofed it against discovery using their darkest skills.'

'I also stated that it's not a physical location, sir,' said Jaff.

'Not at the moment,' said Eisenhorn. 'Not all the time, perhaps. I'd like everyone to prepare themselves. If this works, even in part, there may be some discomfort and disorientation.'

Nayl gripped Drusher firmly and securely by the upper arm. Drusher looked at his hand in surprise.

'What–' he started to say.

'Stick with me,' Nayl said.

Jaff was objecting again. Eisenhorn ignored her, raised his hands and said something.

It was a word, or at least it seemed to be. Drusher didn't know it or understand it. He'd never heard it before in his life.

And he never wanted to hear it again.

FIFTEEN

SIMULTANEOUS REALITY OVERLAYS

Stick with me,' said Nayl.

Drusher was clawing at his head with his fingers. There was a migraine-sharp knot of pain behind his eyes. He could smell blood in his throat. Nausea wallowed through him.

'What?' he said. 'What? *What?*'

He heard Nayl again, saying his name. Nayl's voice was obscured by the sound of a drum. Drusher realised it was the blood pounding in his ears.

'What?' he repeated frantically. 'What did it mean? What did he say?'

He retched hard and fell, dry-heaving, onto the cold stone floor. His stomach was in spasm.

Nayl crouched beside him and patted him on the back.

'Take it slow,' he said. 'You'll level out in a moment.'

Drusher nodded. He couldn't talk.

'You all right?' Nayl asked.

Drusher rocked back onto his heels and knelt, panting.

'I don't know what...' he gasped, wiping his mouth. 'That word. That sound. I don't understand what he said. I don't understand what the word was.'

'Stay calm,' said Nayl. 'Take a few deep breaths.'

'Why are you whispering?' Drusher asked.

'Just stay calm.'

Drusher shifted position, because the hard stone floor was digging into his knees...

Hard stone floor.

Drusher looked down and jumped to his feet with a startled cry.

'Take it easy,' said Nayl.

Drusher slowly looked around. The room was some kind of vaulted chamber of unusual height. The walls and arched ceiling were made of fashioned white stone. The floor was dark green marble. There were tall lancet windows of stained glass. Exterior light shafted into the room through the windows, covering the floor with a multicoloured pattern.

He looked at Nayl.

'We were right,' said Nayl.

Drusher shook his head.

'Please tell me,' he said, 'that I passed out or something, and you took me back to Helter–'

'No,' said Nayl.

'But we were in the woods,' said Drusher.

'And now we're not,' replied Nayl. 'Except I think we are. We're in the woods *and* inside Keshtre.'

'Where are the others?' asked Drusher.

'Not sure,' said Nayl. 'But if we've appeared inside the hall, or it's manifested around us... *whatever*... then...'

He gestured to the wall.

'Macks and Jaff were over there. The others just beyond them. So... that wall appeared between us.'

'I really can't tell you how much I don't like this,' said Drusher.

'I hear you,' said Nayl. 'Stay right here, and don't touch anything.'

Nayl unslung his lasrifle and stalked towards the door.

Drusher clenched his fists to stop his hands trembling. He looked around. The air was cool, and there was a lingering background scent of promethium or some similar industrial petrochemical. The room was unfurnished, apart from an unmade wooden cot, a small chair and a blanket box. He walked over to the windows. There was light outside. The glow of it was dyed in greens and reds and golds by the stained glass. He had to stand on tiptoe to peer out.

He swallowed hard.

'Nayl?' he whispered. 'We're not in the woods.'

Germaine Macks closed her eyes and opened them again.

But it was all still there. She was standing on a metal walkway, suspended over fathomless darkness. Around her, in the gloom, huge mechanisms turned and whirred. Brass cogs many metres in diameter locked teeth with others of their kind, and turned in smooth and uniform perfection. Smaller flywheels rotated rapidly, humming as they whirled. Iron pistons hissed pneumatic sighs, and copper valves opened and closed with automated regularity. The place smelled of oil and hot metal, like a vast machine shop.

'This is real, isn't it?' she whispered.

'I'm afraid so,' replied Jaff. She was standing on the walkway beside Macks. She had drawn a small pistol.

'We were in the woods...' Macks began.

'And now we are not, marshal,' said Jaff. 'I am as surprised as you are, but we must not give in to shock or disorientation. My master was right. We have been translated.'

'Into what?' Macks asked.

'Into *where*,' replied Jaff. 'A sideways shift. The site of Keshtre evidently represents a bend in the geometry of dimensional reality, and we have stepped around that blind corner.'

'This is...' Macks started to say, but thought better of it. 'What do we do?'

'Keep our wits and find Eisenhorn,' replied Jaff. 'It is likely we are neither alone nor safe here.'

She moved along the walkway, her weapon ready. Metal steps led down to a lower gantry that ran beneath a section of huge, whirring cogs.

'What is this machine?' asked Macks, following her. She had her riot-gun ready.

'I'm not able to evaluate that at this time,' replied Jaff. She held up her hand, suddenly, a signal for quiet.

Macks had heard it too. Voices, ahead of them. Macks and Jaff picked their way down the steps quietly. The lower gantry was quite broad. The mechanism purred both above and below it. At the far end, near a further set of steps, they saw Garofar and Edde.

'Garofar!' Macks hissed as loudly as she dared.

The two deputies turned at the sound of her voice, their weapons raised. They lowered them as soon as they saw Macks and Jaff, and came hurrying along the gantry towards them.

'Thank the Throne!' gasped Edde. She was clearly shaken, her mind unable to cope. There was shock in Garofar's eyes too, but he was holding it together.

'This is the shade hall, isn't it?' he said to Jaff.

'It seems there was some basis to the myth, deputy,' she replied.

'Did we open a door?' he asked. 'How could this place be in the woods and we not see a trace of it?'

'I want to go now,' said Edde. 'I want to go away from here, right now.'

'We are still in the Karanine woods,' Jaff said to Garofar, 'and yet we are simultaneously *not*.'

'What does that even *mean*?' he spat back.

'I could explain at great length about simultaneous reality overlays,' said Jaff. 'About areas of binary dimension. I imagine I would be wasting my time. Put simply, this is an extremely rare cosmic phenomenon. An extimate location. Two places occupying the same point of space at the same time, one overlaid on the other and only one of them ever visible at a time, depending on the position of the observer. This is the woodland ruins and it is this structure. We were in one, now we are in the other. Our location hasn't changed. Our position of observation has. Does that help?'

'No,' said Garofar.

'Then we have been taken through a faerie ring into your shade hall, deputy,' Jaff said with contempt.

'What do we do?' Garofar asked Macks.

'We get out of here,' Edde replied, her voice rising in panic. 'We get the hell out–'

'Rein it in, Edde,' said Macks. She got hold of the trembling deputy and almost shook her by the shoulders. 'Edde? Edde! Look at me. Look at me now. I'm going to sort this out. I need you to keep a lid on, all right? Edde? Can you do that?'

Edde nodded, swallowing hard.

'Y-es. Yes, mam.'

'We need to find the others,' said Jaff. 'Eisenhorn, Nayl, Voriet, Magos Drusher and your other deputy. They may be nearby.'

'We haven't seen anybody except you,' said Garofar.

Macks adjusted her collar vox.

'Nayl, this is Macks? Do you copy? Cronyl? Are you reading me? This is Macks.'

She looked at Jaff.

'The vox is dead,' she said.

'The frequency spectrum may be different here,' said Jaff.

'How do you know that?' asked Garofar.

'I don't,' said Jaff. 'It's just an educated guess.'

She turned and looked down the next set of metal steps. It descended to another platform. Other walkways branched off it. Steps led up to higher platforms, obscured by the humming machinery.

She looked at Macks.

'Stay here,' she said. 'I'll scout along here.'

'We should stay together,' said Macks.

'I'll be quick,' said Jaff. 'Stay here, and take a moment to get yourselves together. I'm going to need you to be able to focus.'

She turned and hurried silently down the metal steps. They watched her cross the lower platform then disappear from view behind slowly circling brass gears the size of banquet tables.

'How long do we wait?' asked Garofar.

'Until she comes back,' replied Macks.

'What if she doesn't?' he said.

'Let's not get pessimistic,' said Macks. She tilted her head towards Edde, who was twitching with unease, unable to stand still. Macks knew how the deputy felt. She wasn't far off a panic attack herself. Her hands were shaking badly.

Garofar took the hint.

'Come on, Edde,' he said, trying to sound reassuring. 'We're going to be all right.' He went to put his arm around her shoulders.

There was a sharp, wet pop, like a water bottle bursting. Garofar's face was suddenly speckled with liquid. Edde sagged into him, heavy and limp.

He tried to hold her up. Her head lolled back, and a huge quantity of blood welled out of a hole in her throat.

'Shooter!' he yelled.

The second shot hit him in the ribs, knocking him aside. Garofar and Edde crashed over onto the platform together.

Macks dropped to her knees, her riotgun raised. There was no way in hell to tell where the shots had come from.

'Drop it!' a voice boomed.

'Magistratum!' Macks yelled, her weapon up to her cheek, hunting. 'Go screw yourself!'

'Drop it,' the voice repeated. 'The male is only wounded. He could be saved. But not if you resist.'

Macks glanced frantically at Garofar. He was sprawled on his back, blood bubbles popping as he opened and closed his mouth in silent shock.

Breathing hard, Macks slowly lowered the riotgun. She put it on the metal deck and raised her hands to show they were empty. Then she moved quickly to Garofar's side, and clamped her palms over the chest wound. There was blood everywhere. It was running through the platform mesh underneath Garofar, catching the light as it spattered away into the darkness.

Two people appeared, moving up the lower gantry towards Macks. One was a heavyset, bearded male in a chain-mesh combat jacket. The other was a slighter figure, a woman with tightly cropped red hair. Both were covering Macks with suppressed autorifles. Two more, both male, approached from the other direction. One was overweight and jowly, with thin grey hair. He carried an assault lasrifle with a modified scope and combat grips. The other was a very tall, thin man with neck and cheek tattoos. He covered Macks with a pair of laspistols.

The bearded man came up the steps to Macks as the other three kept back, covering her. He was swarthy, with jet-black hair. His piercing eyes were an odd, violet colour. He looked down at Macks.

'For Throne's sake! Help him!' Macks yelled, her hands locked flat over the wound in Garofar's torso.

'He's done for,' called the overweight man, edging closer, his weapon aimed. 'You can see that. But she's intact enough.'

'You said you'd help him,' Macks pleaded.

'I say all sorts of things,' replied the bearded man. 'Blayg is right. He's done for.'

'No! Get a bloody med kit!' cried Macks.

The man with the violet eyes sighed. He brought up his autorifle and puffed two noise-limited shots into Garofar's head.

Macks screamed and launched herself at the bearded man, clawing with blood-soaked hands.

He snapped his autorifle around like a club and met her face with the stock.

Nayl opened the door and looked out.

'You think you can be quiet now, magos?' he whispered over his shoulder.

'Yes,' said Drusher. He'd calmed down a little.

'Follow me,' said Nayl. 'Stick with me. Do as I tell you.'

Drusher nodded.

Nayl looked at him, eyes narrowed.

'Say it, quietly but clearly,' he said. 'I need to know where you are. I won't be looking at you.'

'I understand,' said Drusher. 'Yes.'

Nayl looked at Drusher for a moment, as if gauging how far he could trust him to behave. Then he appeared to make his mind up.

'Follow,' he whispered.

With the rifle up against his cheek, Nayl opened the door wider. Then, he switched his hand to the foregrip and edged out, panning the powerful assault weapon from side to side. Drusher followed him.

The door led into a long, high hallway. The walls were the same, seamless white stone as the room, the floor the same green marble. It was gloomy, and there was a constant, distant humming noise. Murky light seeped in through high window lights. The proportions of the hallway were odd. It was wide enough for three men to walk together, side by side, but the ceiling was so high, it felt narrow and confined. Drusher guessed the ceiling was five or six metres up. It seemed a curious choice, so much wasted space above head height. Despite the open air above him, he felt claustrophobic, oppressed by the blank, chalk-white walls.

Why build a corridor that shape? Was its grand architecture supposed to impress and intimidate? Then why so plain and austere? He was frankly glad the window lights were too high for him to see out of them.

His old adversary, imagination, decided to make mischief. The thought came to him that this was a very narrow corridor. A single-file passageway for very tall people. People so tall, they could see out of the high windows, because they would be at head height. And those tall people therefore wouldn't be people at all...

'All right?' Nayl asked.

'Yes,' whispered Drusher.

'You started breathing funny again,' Nayl noted. He wasn't looking at Drusher. He was prowling along the hallway, hunched, weapon aimed ready to fire. Drusher wondered why Nayl had chosen to go right instead of left. Both directions looked identical: the slender hallway advancing away as far as he could see.

'Magos?' Nayl prompted.

'Yes,' said Drusher. 'I'm fine.'

He wanted to ask about the window. He wanted to ask Nayl about what he had seen through it. But it clearly wasn't the time.

Nayl had looked through the window too. He had made no comment, as if the view had been what he had expected to see, or as if he'd seen it before. Drusher doubted both options. During their brief acquaintance, Drusher had come to know Nayl as a man who rarely registered any kind of reaction.

There was another door a few metres down on the right. Like the first, it was made of some kind of dense, pale wood, polished until it gleamed. The handle was silver.

'Stay with me,' said Nayl.

'Yes,' said Drusher.

'First priority is to find the others,' said Nayl. 'I think they'll be close. I think our positions will be relative to the ones we were in when we...'

He paused, thinking of the right word. Drusher was guessing 'left.'

'...were still in the woods,' Nayl finished.

'And if they aren't?' he asked.

'Then I've got even less to go on than I hoped,' said Nayl.

He reached the door. He listened at it for a moment, then turned the handle and let it swing open with a prod of his toe. He stepped in.

Drusher followed.

The room was identical to the one they had first found themselves in. A light Drusher now knew was not the sun, shone through stained glass-lancets. There was no cot, just four wooden chairs, arranged in a square with their backs together. There were marks made in blue chalk around the feet of the chairs, meaningless scribbles that were somehow unpleasant to look at.

Drusher found himself staring at them. One of the chairs was slightly out of alignment with the others and, driven by an obsessive compulsive urge, he reached out to straighten it.

Nayl's big hand clamped around his wrist.

'Don't touch anything,' he said firmly. 'No matter how much you want to.'

'Yes,' said Drusher clearly. He had no idea why he'd felt so compelled.

He glanced fitfully at the stained-glass windows. Like the ones in the previous room, their pattern appeared random, purely decorative. Surely the point of stained glass was to make a picture? The coloured panes were used to assemble an image: a saint, perhaps, or something symbolic. This was just a patchwork of green and red and gold shapes, fixed together with leading.

Except it wasn't. He stared. There were recognisable forms there. Figures. Elongated figures, swaying, with long intertwined limbs that–

'Don't look at the windows either,' said Nayl.

'Yes,' said Drusher, looking at the plain white wall instead.

'They're not here,' said Nayl. 'They should have been on the other side of this wall if...'

He sighed, as though it were too much effort to finish, or too distressing to explain the context.

'What does that mean, Nayl?' Drusher asked.

'It means we didn't bi-locate together,' said Nayl. 'Or we did, and we didn't arrive in our relative positions. Or we're not time synchronised. Or–'

He glanced at Drusher.

'I'm just upsetting you now, aren't I?' he asked.

'No, I'm fine,' said Drusher.

'You sure? You made a noise. A sort of groan.'

'No, I didn't,' said Drusher.

'I think you did.'

'I think I'd know.'

'I don't think you would.'

'Nayl–'

'All right,' said Nayl. 'This is a difficult experience, and your mind's not really focused yet. I can see the lost look in your eyes. That's all right. You'll get your bearings. But it's possible you groaned without knowing it, because this is all too much to take in.'

'Are you finding it a difficult experience?' asked Drusher.

'Yeah,' said Nayl.

'Then you're hiding that well. Has this happened to you before?'

'Not this exactly, no.'

'Then something like it?'

'I've had experiences,' said Nayl. 'Things like this that would scare you bloodless. But not this exactly.'

'How do you deal with it?'

'I've been dealing with it for years,' said Nayl. 'One thing I've learned, if you don't deal with these kinds of situations quickly, you're no good to anyone, including yourself.'

'Insane adventures...' murmured Drusher.

'Exactly, magos.'

'You weren't lying.'

'No,' said Nayl. He flashed a quick smile that Drusher took as an attempt to be supportive. 'For your sake, Drusher, I wish I had been.'

'What do we do, Nayl?' Drusher asked.

'We keep looking. We keep looking for the others. It's about all we can do.'

'What about... Can you not say the word again? The word Eisenhorn said? Can't you take us back?'

'I'm sorry,' said Nayl. 'I don't know what he said either. Enuncia is beyond my pay-grade.'

Drusher breathed heavily and nodded. He walked over to the windows.

'What are you doing? Magos?'

Drusher stood on tiptoe and looked through the stained glass. Nayl pulled him back.

'Don't do that,' he said. 'It made you cry last time.'

'That's why I have to,' said Drusher. 'You're right. I'm lost. My mind's all over the place. I'm not really coping. Which means I'm no use to you at all. The sooner I face up to reality and get it together, the better. Think of this as... aversion therapy.'

Nayl frowned, then let go of him. Drusher stood back up on his toes.

He saw the world outside through the coloured glass of the old window. No sunlit woodland, no forest glade, no blue skies, no cobalt edge of the Karanine ridge in the afternoon haze. No Gershom.

Outside was a grey desert. Dunes of dust stretched away as far as he could see, broken by outcrops of rock that looked like the calcified vertebrae of long-dead, leviathan creatures. A thin wind lifted powder from the crests of the dunes, winnowing it into the air like sea spray.

The sky was black and starless. A bone-white curve, like an immense tusk of light, rose from the horizon into the sky. It was a moon, or a close neighbour planet, rising in the sky in three-quarter shadow, impossibly close.

The black void sky had one feature: a blue-white whorl that radiated the light he'd first taken to be the sun's rays. The whorl was immense. A nebula, or some kind of stellar vortex, gleaming fiercely like the negative image of a black hole. Trailing arms of frosty light and energy clouds radiated from the heart of it.

It looked to Drusher like a vast eye gazing back at him.

Drusher let it look. He held its stare and returned it, unblinking.

Then he lowered himself onto his heels and turned away from the window.

'All right,' he said to Nayl. 'I have a little perspective now. I've got my head together.'

'You sure?'

'Positive, Nayl. Lead on. Let's find the others.'

Nayl hesitated.

'I only ask because... you groaned again.'

'I didn't,' said Drusher.

'I'm sorry, but you did. Involuntary I'm sure, but–'

Drusher held up his hand sharply.

Nayl had heard it too. A soft, stifled moan.

'I told you it wasn't me,' Drusher said.

'It came from the hallway,' said Nayl. 'Come on.'

'Just calm the hell down and let me think,' said Voriet.

Deputy Cronyl glared at him. His face was flushed, and he looked set to throw a punch at the interrogator.

'Please,' said Voriet softly. 'I know this is very distressing. I am fighting to process it myself.'

'But how can we be *here* all of a sudden?' Cronyl snarled.

'Just give me a moment,' said Voriet. 'Just a moment...'

He looked at the ancient machinery spinning in the twilight around them. Such an extraordinary device. Could it be? Could the rumours, the uncorroborated intelligence... Could they all have been true?

The heretic scum actually possessed this thing, and it was *working?*

This, he decided with a wince of grief, *this* secret was why Thea had died.

'Here's what we're going to do,' he said, turning to Cronyl.

Something slammed into Cronyl and flipped him. The deputy landed on the metal deck with a yowl of pain. A savage spin-kick connected with Voriet's jaw, snapping him off his feet.

The attacker was a woman with severely cropped, red hair. Cronyl tried to rise, but she jerked down with a snarl and put a punch dagger through his spine. The deputy collapsed on his face, his body twitching, his last exhalation a long, slow, choking wheeze.

Voriet rolled, dragging out his Tronsvasse automatic. The woman kicked and deflected his aim. His shot went wide, the report echoing around in the darkness.

Voriet scrambled backwards on his rear, trying to re-aim. She lunged in and clamped his wrist with her left hand, twisting the pistol aside. He kicked out and took her legs away. She rolled as she fell, jerking his clamped wrist into over-rotation. Voriet gasped in pain. She locked her other hand around the bicep of his pinned arm and pivoted, hauling him head first over her and breaking his arm at the same time.

Voriet howled. The woman sprang up and stamped on his outstretched hand, breaking his fingers around the grip of the pistol. She kicked the gun clear of his useless hand.

He swung at her with his left fist, trying to ignore the overload of pain. She blocked the blow and drove a beak fist into his throat.

Voriet fell back, choking, eyes wide, unable to breathe, unable to rise.

The red-haired woman straddled his chest and stared down at him. She rested her beak fist against his brow.

'Submit,' she whispered, 'and the remains of your life will have a purpose.'

Voriet couldn't speak. He spat instead. Blood and spittle hit her cheek.

She hammer-tapped her beak fist against his forehead and bounced the back of his skull off the metal deck.

They followed the hallway to its far end. Nayl ignored other doors as they passed them. The sound was coming from up ahead.

As they approached, it grew louder. The constant background hum grew louder too. It wasn't a moaning. It wasn't someone in pain or distress. It sounded more like a voice unable to articulate. A voice that wanted to speak, and was trying to speak, but which had never learned any words.

Drusher thought of Macks, and the way she had been reduced to inarticulate gasps by the thing in the kitchen passage. Fear had done that to her. She had briefly been reduced to wordless terror by something that defied her mind's ability to process it. But Germaine Macks was clever and sharp-witted, and she had a considerable and sometimes salty vocabulary.

This sound had a quite different quality. It was a human voice. It wasn't groping in fear, trying to find some words, the way Macks had been. It was vocalising in despair trying to *make* words.

Drusher took a moment to steady himself. Just thinking about Macks had made him upset. He wondered where she was. He wondered if he would see her again. He imagined her, wherever she was, being as scared now as she had been in the passageway.

It was a thought he could scarcely bear.

'Magos?'

He looked up. Nayl was beckoning to him.

There was a hatch at the end of the hallway. It was clearly Imperial tech, a heavy duty hatch like a shift-ship's air-gate. It looked incongruous, as if it had been retrofitted into the old, eerie architecture of the building.

Why would you put something that massive and secure into a place where polished wooden doors with silver handles were otherwise sufficient?

And if the answer to that question was security, what did you keep on the other side?

And why would you then leave the hatch wide open?

Drusher joined Nayl, and they peered in through the hatch.

The chamber beyond was vast and cylindrical. Drusher guessed it was the interior of one of the fortress' main towers. All the original floors and stairways had been removed. The curved walls soared up into darkness above them and dropped away into darkness far below.

The walls had been etched with lines. It was script. Hundreds of thousands of lines of writing, covering every centimetre of the interior walls, in perfect, uniform rows. It must have taken decades for skilled artisans to inscribe it all. Drusher wondered what it said. He was too far away to be able to read any of it.

The hatch led out onto a railed, metal landing inside the hall. The landing hung like a balcony under the hatch. Open metal steps led down to other platform stages below and several further above them. The platforms and connecting steps were all standard template units, Imperial build, the kind seen in manufactories and promethium plants and all manner of workspaces in human habitations across the Imperium. There was something oddly reassuring about their familiarity, but, like the hatch, they seemed uncomfortably out of place in the setting.

Around them, filling the main space of the tower, was vast technology of another sort. This was the source of the constant humming. To Drusher, it looked as if someone had taken all the complex inner mechanisms of an antique mechanical timepiece, enlarged them, then slotted them carefully into the drum of the tower. Cogs, gears, springs and winders whirred and moved in perfect, oiled precision. The crude STC platform sections and steps had been suspended inside the vast brass mechanism, allowing access to it at different levels. On some platforms, powerful cogitator units and workstations had been bolted in place, connected by sheaves of cables and data wires to the Great Machine. Drusher saw their screens and displays flickering with bright lines of changing data: monitor positions from which to study and perhaps even operate the strange and ancient mechanism. The air was dry and smelled of metal filings, oil and warm power systems.

There was a large platform directly below them, a circular gantry fixed in the centre of the tower's interior. In the middle of it was a square iron cage, crudely heavy and filthy black.

Inside the cage was a man.

He was naked. His skin was dirty, scarred and blistered. His hair was long and ragged, and hung over his face and shoulders. He was kneeling on the floor of the cage, hunched over, trembling.

The guttural, moaning sounds were coming from him.

Nayl glanced at Drusher then led the way out onto the landing. His weapon was up and ready at his cheek. As they moved, he covered each angle and turn.

They edged down the metal steps onto the circular gantry. Drusher could smell the rank stench of the man in the cage. The sounds he was making made Drusher's skin crawl.

The man heard them approach, or smelled them. It felt to Drusher like an animal response. He looked up at them in terror. Drusher saw his wild eyes staring through the matted fringe of his hair. He murmured something and backed away into the far corner of the cage.

Drusher peered at him.

'Any idea who that is?' he whispered to Nayl.

Nayl was watching the hatch and the other platforms for signs of movement.

'No,' he replied. 'Not a clue. But it looks like the poor bastard's been in there for a while, magos.'

'Magos?'

They both looked around. The man in the cage was timidly rising to his feet, hunched, pawing the lank hair out of his eyes so he could stare at them. They saw a dirty, broken face that had been ravaged by years of pain and anguish.

'M-magos?' the man said. His mouth moved oddly as he spoke, as if he was working very hard to articulate. A man speaking a language that he had just learned, or which he had forgotten years before.

'M-magos?' he said.

'You can speak?' said Drusher.

'Watch yourself,' Nayl warned.

'Magos,' the man said. He edged towards them. 'Magos,' he repeated. 'I am. I am. That is me. I am the magos. You know me?'

'Do you have a name?' asked Drusher.

'Magos,' the man replied with an anxious nod. 'I... I am the magos. M-magos Sark.'

Nayl and Drusher glanced at each other quickly.

'Are you Draven Sark?' Nayl asked sternly. 'Answer me. Are you Magos Draven Sark?'

The man nodded furiously. He was panting. Drusher saw a weird expression on his face. He was baring his teeth like a dog.

He was trying to smile.

'W-w-w-will you let me out?' he asked. 'P-please. I am Dr-draven Sark. Magos Draven Sark, a-and I would like to c-come out of here now.'

'It depends,' replied Nayl. 'Who put you in there?'

'*He* put himself in there,' said Jaff.

Nayl and Drusher turned around sharply. She was standing on the gantry beside them. She looked scared.

'The hell did you come from?' Nayl exclaimed.

Jaff gestured to the chamber around them.

'I found this place. I've been looking around.'

'Where are the others?' asked Nayl.

'I'm not sure,' she said.

'What do you mean *he* put himself in there?' asked Drusher.

'I've been trying to access data from the terminals in this chamber,' she said. 'It's definitely a Cognitae facility, and it's been here a very long time.'

'How long?' asked Drusher.

'Never mind that,' snapped Nayl. 'Tell us about Sark.'

'He didn't build this place,' replied Jaff. 'But he's run it for the Cognitae for the last century or so. Running its program.'

'Program for what?' asked Drusher.

'I don't know that yet,' she replied. 'But from the notes I found, it seems that Magos Sark was so desperate to get a result, he placed himself in that cage.'

'Yes, because that's what scientists do,' said Drusher.

'He made himself his own laboratory test subject,' said Jaff witheringly. 'He is clearly damaged and obsessive. That cage is a psychometric monitor, and Sark is his own lab rat.'

'We need to know a lot more than that,' said Nayl.

'Well, I was working on it,' said Jaff. 'Then I saw you.'

Nayl lowered his rifle and looked around. He walked to the gantry rail.

'Which terminal were you using, Audla?' he asked. 'Where did you get this information from?'

Audla Jaff raised her hand as if to point. But she was holding a compact, snub-nose laspistol.

She fired. The shot hit Nayl in the back. He lurched forwards, toppled over the rail and fell.

Drusher stared, his mouth wide open.

Jaff turned the weapon on him.

'He was too dangerous to live,' she said. 'But you are containable. And new test subjects are always useful.'

SIXTEEN

THE BAD PLACE

Jaff took a step towards Drusher and placed the muzzle of her sidearm against his forehead. Expressionless, she reached forwards with her other hand, and began patting the pockets of his old coat. She stopped, reached in and fished out the gun Nayl had given him.

She stepped back, keeping her weapon trained on him, and put the confiscated gun in the hip pocket of her jacket. Sark had hunched down in the cage, in fear, and was grunting and moaning again.

Over her shoulder, she called out 'clear' in a strong, loud voice. Her aim never wavered.

'How long?' Drusher asked her.

'How long what?'

'Have you been working against the Ordos?'

'Since the day I was born, magos,' she said. 'I am the product of a Cognitae breeding school. I was engineered as a savant... Precisely the sort of exceptional individual a man like Gregor Eisenhorn finds appealing and useful. The sort of person he recruits.'

'I suppose that explains why you've been so unhelpful every step of the way,' said Drusher. 'Someone like you should have worked out Keshtre's location in a matter of hours. But you already knew where it was. You were trying to stop us finding it.'

She smiled.

'Your face is an open book, Magos Drusher,' she said. 'Micro-spasms in your platysma, zygomaticus and levator labii superioris. Involuntary dilation of the pupils. You are terrified. Your composure is a front. Bravado.'

'My levator labii superioris is doing just fine,' replied Drusher. 'Of course I'm terrified. You just killed a man, and you're aiming a gun at me. You realise your fate will be appalling. I don't know what it will be precisely, but I doubt the Inquisition treats heretics with much mercy.'

'It does not,' she agreed. 'But then, you're not with the Inquisition. The Rot-God-King's Holy Ordos have no inkling of this affair. Eisenhorn is a rogue, magos. He is extreme and dangerous, even by their standards. They declared him hereticus many years ago, and they hunt him as keenly as they hunt the Cognitae. There – the platysma *again*. You didn't know that.'

'I guessed,' said Drusher. 'This whole operation lacked legitimacy. I don't know him well, but I believe he is determined–'

'Oh, Eisenhorn believes his cause is just. In his arrogance.'

'And he hunts for you?'

'Bringing down the Cognitae is his life's work,' she said. 'The ruthless zeal with which he pursues us is the main reason he was disowned by his Ordo masters. Be clear, Magos Drusher. No one is waiting to hear from him. No one is coming to save you. No one knows you're here. He's done. You're all done.'

'You say that confidently, Mamzel Jaff, but you're not certain, are you? A twitch of the masseter, a little tremble of the corrugator supercilii. Doubt, plain as day.'

Jaff frowned and shot her free hand to her face, involuntarily.

'You're a little shit,' she said, glaring at him.

Drusher smiled back. He was no reader of micro-expressions. He'd made it up just to rattle her.

He heard footsteps. A man was coming up the metal steps onto the gantry. He was tall and heavyset, with piercing violet eyes that contrasted strangely with his olive skin, jet-black hair and full beard. He wore a leather-jack suit with a mesh-armour jacket. A large autorifle hung across his shoulder. Three people followed him: a hard-faced woman with cropped red hair, a tall, heavily tattooed man and an overweight man with hooded eyes.

'Why is he alive, Jaff?' the bearded man asked. His voice was extraordinarily deep.

'A useable subject, Gobleka,' she replied. 'High intelligence quotient.'

The man looked at Drusher as if he were an annoying stain on good carpet. *Gobleka.* Drusher recognised the name. The heretic Eisenhorn's interrogator had been hunting on Gershom.

'Have you questioned him?' Gobleka asked Jaff.

'He knows nothing.'

'Establish that as a fact,' hissed Gobleka. 'Thanks to your poor work, the agents of the damn Ordos are *inside* the hall. I want them all found and extinguished, so we'd better know everything they know.'

Drusher saw the look on Jaff's face. That was a micro-expression he understood. Jaff was terrified of Gobleka. Drusher had no doubt this stemmed from Gobleka's imposing physicality and charming manners, but he was also sure Jaff had something to prove. She hadn't sprung the trap and killed them all cleanly at Helter. She'd let them get inside Keshtre. She was clearly keen to demonstrate her competence and make up for the error. Drusher doubted the Cognitae offered much in the way of second chances to those in their service.

'Where's Eisenhorn?' Jaff asked, her weapon still aimed.

'I don't know,' said Drusher.

'True?' asked Gobleka.

'Yes,' said Jaff. 'He couldn't cloak a response to that question.'

Gobleka nodded.

'Take him down to the cellar cages,' said Gobleka.

Jaff hesitated.

'What?' Gobleka asked.

'Can't Blayg or Streekal do it?' she asked.

'Do it your bloody self, Jaff,' sneered the overweight man.

'I want to get back out,' said Jaff to Gobleka. 'Betancore is outside. The remaining loose end. I need to deal with her, and I'm the best choice to get close to her.'

'Put him away. Then you can go,' said Gobleka.

Jaff looked at Drusher and gestured with her gun.

He went where she told him to go. Jaff walked behind him, covering him with her weapon. They descended from the gantry and followed a route down the tower, crossing platforms and walking down suspended staircases, the brass wheels and gears of the Great Machine whirring around them. Drusher tried not to feel alarm at the immense drop below them: his good old fear of heights. A gun at his back served to focus his mind.

'What does it do?' he asked.

'Shut up,' she said.

'You're making something. This machine, it's very old, isn't it?'

'Drusher, you're not *that* useful. Shut up.'

Drusher felt an odd tingling sensation in the base of his skull. He stopped walking and leaned on a handrail.

'Keep walking,' she said.

'Just a minute,' Drusher said. 'I feel faint.'

He looked out at the machinery, at the other platforms and walkways. He looked at the shadows, hoping...

The tingle throbbed in the back of his head.

He straightened up.

'All right,' he said. 'I feel better now.'

He looked at Jaff and gestured at the Great Machine.

'Come on, how old?' he asked.

She jabbed the gun in his ribs.

'Walk,' she hissed.

'You can't blame me for being fascinated, mamzel. It's my job to enquire. My life's work.'

'As of now, you have no life.'

He looked around, thoughtfully.

'These... *tests*. What is my fate going to be, Audla?'

She frowned at him.

'Painful,' she said.

'Oh,' he shrugged. 'That's a shame. I really don't do pain well. What sort of pain?'

'Walk,' she snapped.

'Seriously, so I can brace myself...'

She put the gun against his forehead again.

'Be obedient,' she said. 'Shut up and walk. You are very annoying.'

'So I've been told,' said Drusher. 'You know, I don't think I *will* walk any more. I think, on balance, I'd rather die than submit to these tests you mentioned. I'm not good with pain. I'd rather it was quick.'

He closed his eyes.

There was a sharp crack.

Drusher opened his eyes again. Audla Jaff's limp body lay at his feet.

'You took your time,' Drusher said. 'I didn't know how much more crap I could come out with to keep her distracted.'

'You did just fine,' said Eisenhorn.

'Have you killed her?' Drusher said.

Eisenhorn hunched over her body.

'Not yet,' he said.

'She killed Nayl,' said Drusher.

'She has betrayed me on every level,' replied Eisenhorn. He searched Jaff's pockets, found Drusher's gun and held it out to him.

'I was actually quite pleased to see the back of that,' Drusher said.

'Take it, magos. You need to be armed. I think we're the only two left.'

Drusher took the gun reluctantly.

'I heard you whisper in my head,' he said. He rubbed the back of his skull. 'Right in the back there. It was unpleasant.'

'I had to signal to you without her hearing,' said Eisenhorn. 'I had to get you to stop so I could get close. I didn't want to risk a shot. It wasn't easy.'

'Why?' asked Drusher. 'What do you mean?'

Eisenhorn let out a long, slow breath. Drusher could see that his flesh was pallid, and he was perspiring.

'This place,' he confessed, 'this... machine. It's interfering with my mind. It's radiating a latent power that's conflicting with my psykana gifts. It's taking more effort than usual to use them. And when I do, I can manage short range only.'

'Then don't,' said Drusher. 'You'll exhaust yourself.'

'I'll use what I have to, magos,' Eisenhorn replied, '*when* I have to. For as long as I can. My gifts are about the only edge we have over the Cognitae.'

'What is this machine, inquisitor?'

'I'm not certain,' replied Eisenhorn, 'but I think it's a device called an Immaterium Loom.'

'Which is?'

'It spins things out of the warp,' said Eisenhorn. 'It binds the etheric with the physical. There have been rumours for centuries that the Cognitae were trying to build one. I didn't give those rumours much credence, but yet again the Cognitae dismay me.'

He hoisted Jaff's limp body upright and glanced at Drusher.

'Can you support her? It'll only be for a moment.'

Drusher moved forwards to help.

'Immaterium Looms are volatile things,' said Eisenhorn. 'No one's ever made one before, though many have tried over the millennia. Heretics and Imperial adepts alike. All prototypes have built up interference patterns with the fabric of reality and imploded.'

'But this place... it isn't reality?' asked Drusher, propping Jaff upright.

'As usual, you're sharp,' said Eisenhorn. 'This place, Keshtre, is a weak point in the fabric between our reality and the warp. I think it always has been... a liminal place of monsters, feared by the ancient Udaric tribes who gave it its ominous name, becoming part of folklore, as all such bad places do. The Cognitae have exploited this weakness in real space fabric and built this place in the in-between.'

'To hide?'

'Yes, and now I know they can do it, I realise they may have other such boltholes across the Imperium, in *other* bad places. Which is why they have always been so damned elusive. But here, there is a secondary purpose.'

'Because we're in the warp?' asked Drusher.

'We're in an interstitial space between reality and the warp,' Eisenhorn replied. 'It's called an extimate zone. But yes. It is a laboratory-perfect environment in which to build an Immaterium Loom and set it running without risk of real space contamination interfering with its function.'

'That's all speculation, I take it?' asked Drusher.

'For now. Let's ask Jaff about it,' said Eisenhorn. 'Hold her.'

He stepped back.

+Audla.+

Drusher shivered. He felt the woman quiver in his arms. Her head snapped upright.

'Should you be doing that?' he asked nervously. 'I mean, if your powers are limited and–'

'I need information,' said Eisenhorn. 'Let her go and step away.'

Drusher moved to Eisenhorn's side. Audla Jaff was standing upright, clenched stiffly and awkwardly. Her eyes were open, but she was looking at nothing.

'Please...' she whispered.

+I trusted you.+

Frost crystals began to form on the metal decking around her feet.

+You brought us into a trap.+

'You brought yourself, Eisenhorn,' she whispered. 'Inshabel sniffed out the traces of our work here on Gershom. It was an ideal opportunity to entice you here and remove your persistent opposition.'

+A trap. To silence me.+

'And your retinue,' she said. 'All loose ends.'

+You never expected us to get inside this place, though, did you? You meant to kill me... all of us... at Helter.+

Jaff's eyes narrowed.

'You got further than expected,' she said. 'Thanks to Drusher. I animated the revenant at Helter, but it was not sufficient. I was regrouping to make another attempt. You pushed on despite my efforts to divert you. You opened Keshtre's doors. But we have adjusted. We improvise well.'

'Is this the truth?' Drusher whispered to Eisenhorn.

Eisenhorn was concentrating hard. He looked sick. His cheeks were flushed, and there was sweat on his forehead.

'She can't lie,' he grunted. 'Not given the psionic coercion I am using.'

'Is Macks alive?' Drusher asked Jaff. 'Have you killed her? Have you killed the others?'

'Don't interrupt,' snapped Eisenhorn. He was struggling to focus.

+Is this an Immaterium Loom?+

'Yes.' Jaff shivered, every word tight and unwilling.

+How long has it been here?+

'Sixteen centuries, since it was built. Watched over by a succession of magi.'

+Of which Draven Sark is the latest?+

'The greatest. He found his grandfather's samples. The Torment. The Chaos disease. From it, he refined an inoculation. A viral enhancement that would render test subjects immune to etheric corruption. Thus they might withstand the first stages of transformation by the Loom.'

+Has this worked?+

'There is a high wastage of test subjects,' said Jaff. Drusher could see the horrified look in her eyes. She was fighting not to say these things, and they were coming out anyway. 'A high wastage. But the process has now worked. It worked on Sark. Such devotion. Such self-sacrifice. Such perfection. He has made it work. He has made it work the way Lilean wanted it to.'

+To do what?+

'To construct vessels,' gasped Jaff. Blood was beginning to seep from her left nostril. 'Flesh is weak. What we wish to accomplish surpasses the limits of the human form. We are building *better* vessels. Vessels that can survive the stresses involved. We call them graels. They are precious, but hard to make.'

+I have met a grael before. Grael Ochre.+

Jaff shook as if the name hurt her.

+It said it was the Yellow King. Or that it served the Yellow King.+

'It does,' whined Jaff.

+And Orpheus? Is that this King's name?+

'Please stop this!' she wailed. Drusher glanced at Eisenhorn in alarm. Eisenhorn was trembling. His lips had peeled back to reveal his clenched teeth. He looked to be in as much pain as Jaff.

+Tell me.+

'Lilean is making the grael vessels to serve the King in Yellow,' she moaned.

+And they are vessels for what?+

'To contain the truth of the warp. To be strong enough to speak not one word of Enuncia, but all the words. A fluency in the first language that would shatter human form.'

+Like daemonhosts? But in reverse? A human soul wrapped in an etheric body, rather than an etheric force bound in human flesh?+

'Exactly. They are eudaemonic beings.'

+'Good daemons'? I would take issue with your terminology.+

Jaff snorted, amused. Blood bubbled at her nostrils.

'They are the future and they are hope,' she said. 'Through the graels, the truth may be whispered in the ear of the Rot-God-King and end His domination.'

'Well, that makes so much sense now she puts it like that,' said Drusher.

'Please be quiet,' said Eisenhorn with considerable effort. Jaff was starting to tremble. Blood dripped from her nose, and the drops froze in the ice around her feet.

+How many has he made? How many of these graels has he built?+

'The f-first eight. Th-they have gone to the Yellow King to be deployed.'

+Where?+

Jaff coughed. Blood frothed over her lip. Blood was dribbling from her nose and running from her tear ducts.

'Please stop...' she spluttered.

+WHERE?+

'Qu-queen Mab.'

+Where is that?+

'S-sancour, i-in Angelus.'

+Where is Lilean Chase?+

Jaff began to choke.

+Where is she?+

Jaff was quivering wildly. She vomited blood down her front.

+What is the King in Yellow?+

'P-p-please...' Jaff gurgled.

Her left eyeball burst.

'Is Macks alive?' Drusher yelled.

She shrieked the word 'yes' as she died.

SEVENTEEN

ONE WORD

Drusher turned away. He leant on the platform's rail and stared at the slowly turning cog systems of the Great Machine. He didn't want to be sick. He was afraid that if he started he wouldn't be able to stop.

'That was barbaric,' he said quietly.

'It was necessary,' replied Eisenhorn, his breathing ragged and rapid. 'And Jaff was a heretic. A murderer. A traitor to me.'

Drusher turned around slowly. Eisenhorn was crouching over Jaff's steaming remains.

'No one deserves that,' Drusher said.

'You have lived a very sheltered life, magos,' said Eisenhorn. 'This galaxy is more cruel and dangerous than you can imagine. When you fight against it, you cannot afford to be sentimental or squeamish.'

'I know about you,' said Drusher.

'I resent your interruption,' said Eisenhorn. 'I was interrogating, at great cost to myself. There were a few seconds left. You jumped in with your question–'

'I needed to know about Germaine–'

'You are fond of the marshal,' said Eisenhorn. 'I understand. You must understand she is an insignificant part of this. So are you, and so am I. Your sentiment betrays you. A life or two, a hundred, a thousand, they are collateral in this war.'

'I am quite content to remain a creature of sentiment for the rest of my life,' replied Drusher. 'I am very glad I am *not* like you. I told you, I *know* about you. You chose to ignore the remark.'

Eisenhorn rose to face him. He looked drawn and deathly pale.

'What is it you think you know, magos?'

'You are no inquisitor,' said Drusher. 'Perhaps once, but not now. You are a rogue, disavowed by your own kind. Whatever war you are waging, whatever quest you're on, it's yours alone. You are not sanctioned. There is no official support.'

'There is truth in that,' said Eisenhorn. 'But it only serves to demonstrate that the Holy Ordos don't appreciate the extremity or scale of this threat. I have warned them. They have ignored the warning. Therefore, I must act alone, or no one will stand against it.'

'But it bothers you,' said Drusher. 'You lied. You and Voriet, you maintain the pretence that you are of the Ordos. That you still have that authority. You used that lie to recruit me and to drum up the support of Macks and her deputies.'

'The rosette of the Inquisition has clout,' said Eisenhorn. 'It has influence. You would not have assisted me otherwise... or it would have taken a great deal more persuasion. The guise of inquisitor is expedient in my work.'

'So it's a useful lie? That's all you have to say on the matter?'

'No, actually.' Eisenhorn looked at him. There was a fierce gleam in his eyes. 'I am an inquisitor. It has been my life. I know I am true in the defence of the Golden Throne. If the echelons of the Inquisition, and the other august institutions of the Imperium choose – in their ignorance – to deem me otherwise, then it is *they* who are wrong, not me.'

'One might describe that as a terrifying level of self-delusion, sir,' said Drusher.

'You can describe it however you like, magos,' Eisenhorn replied.

He glanced over his shoulder.

'Someone's coming,' he whispered. 'A psykanic event like this... and Jaff's screams... will not have gone unnoticed.'

Drusher followed Eisenhorn across the platform. He didn't really want to, but he wanted to stay put even less. He glanced back at Jaff's remains.

'Do we just leave her there?'

'Hurry,' Eisenhorn replied.

They moved down some steps to the next platform stage and hid in the shadows of one of the great cogs. From concealment, they could see the stage they had just left. Eisenhorn reached into his coat and drew a large and ornate autopistol. It looked the size of a standard carbine to Drusher.

'What do we–' Drusher began.

+Remain silent.+

A man appeared on the platform above. It was the tall man with florid tattoos that Drusher had seen before. He hurried to Jaff's body, recoiled in disgust, then anxiously began to look around, a laspistol raised.

'Blayg!' he called.

The heavy man appeared a moment later, out of breath.

'What did you find? What was that cry?' he asked.

'Jaff's done for.'

'Damn,' the fat man gasped, seeing the corpse.

'Eisenhorn's handiwork,' replied the tattooed man. 'He's here, and he's loose.'

'What did he do to her?' the fat man asked, tilting his head in ghastly fascination as he stared at Jaff's body.

'Who cares, Blayg? We have to find him before he does worse.'

'Streekal's already hunting,' said Blayg, running a pudgy hand through his thin grey hair. He hefted up the heavy combat las he was carrying.

'Streekal's efficient, but she'll need help,' replied the tattooed man. 'This bastard is as dangerous as his reputation suggests. Go up to the cage. Tell Gobleka what's happened.'

'He'll be furious, Davinch.'

'Of course he will. So tell him gently.'

Davinch, the tattooed man, glanced at his portly colleague.

'Go on!'

'Where are you going?' Blayg asked.

'I'll check down from here,' said Davinch. 'Right down to the cellar. I want to see if Jaff put that magos fool in a cage before this happened to her. Otherwise, we've got *two* interlopers loose. And tell Gobleka someone needs to get outside. There's the other loose end, the Betancore woman. She needs to be tidied up too.'

Blayg nodded. He walked away and began to climb the steps.

'Hurry!' Davinch shouted after him. 'Gobleka may even want to request an outside assist to get this squared away.'

Blayg disappeared out of sight. Davinch had drawn both pistols. He circled the platform and began to move towards the steps close to Eisenhorn and Drusher.

Eisenhorn placed a hand on Drusher's arm.

Drusher felt an uncomfortable psykanic tap. The tattooed man suddenly looked around as if he'd heard someone call his name. He made off in the opposite direction and quickly vanished behind the gears of the Great Machine.

'You could have shot him,' said Drusher quietly.

'I could,' said Eisenhorn, 'but I don't want to bring the whole place down on us. We are the last two, Drusher. Silence and shadows are our friends.'

'Our friends while we do *what* exactly?'

'He mentioned Sark. And Gobleka.'

'I've seen them both,' said Drusher. 'A long way above us, there's a cage on a gantry. A psychometric monitor. Is that the right term? Magos Sark is in it. Caged like an animal. He's become the... I don't know... focus of this machine. He's part of it. It's working because of him.'

'So Jaff said.'

'But his mind is gone,' said Drusher. 'He's very damaged. This Gobleka fellow, he seems to be the one running the operation now.'

'Goran Gobleka is an expert fixer. The Cognitae value his skills. But Sark is the primary target. We have to stop him. Stop this Loom manufacturing any more graels for the King in Yellow.'

'I didn't understand any of what Jaff told you,' said Drusher. 'What are they trying to achieve?'

'I don't expect you to understand, magos,' Eisenhorn replied. 'Frankly, I don't want you to understand. But so you grasp the vital nature of this, the Cognitae – through the King in Yellow – are working to bring down the Imperium. I believe their goal is no less than the assassination of the Emperor. So when we are done here, I will go to the Angelus Subsector, to Sancour, and I will find this place called Queen Mab, and, there, I will hunt down and destroy the King in Yellow. But first, this place must be ended so it can construct no more monsters to serve his scheme.'

Drusher nodded. 'Then let's get Macks and–'

'She's not a priority,' said Eisenhorn.

'She's alive, Eisenhorn.'

'And I'm sorry for that. But she is not the priority here, magos.'

'We can't just leave her–'

'We can.'

'No,' said Drusher. 'I can't.'

'Magos, do you still not understand the importance of–'

'I do,' interrupted Drusher firmly. 'But as you took pains to point out, I am a creature of sentiment. I won't leave my friend to die. You can help me, or you can get on with waging your private war. I'm going to the cellars. I think that's where she may be. If you come, we can get it done quickly, then we can *both* help you deal with Sark.'

'There isn't time,' said Eisenhorn.

'Then off you go, and good luck to you,' said Drusher.

Eisenhorn glared at him.

'Don't try and pull rank,' said Drusher. 'You're not an inquisitor, and I'm not one of your lackeys.'

'You are a very aggravating man, magos,' said Eisenhorn.

'One of my few real skills. Tell me, did you suspect Jaff?'

'I suspect everyone,' said Eisenhorn.

'Hence the levels of secrecy and confidence you exhibited at Helter. Telling no one anything. Sharing nothing. You don't trust anyone do you?'

'I can't afford to, magos.'

'I pity you,' said Drusher.

'I trust those I've known a long time,' said Eisenhorn quietly. 'Medea... Nayl...'

He fell silent as he spoke the name. Then he glanced back at Drusher.

'I was sure there was a spy in my company,' he said, 'even before I arrived on Gershom. That is why I kept things classified. I thought it was Voriet.'

'Voriet? Really?'

'He was interrogator to Inquisitor Cyriaque. He is genuinely an officer of the Ordos. He came to me two years ago, saying that he wished to join me, that he believed in my cause and felt that the Ordos were blind to the real threat. In effect, he went rogue and joined me.'

'But you didn't trust him?'

'Voriet is very able and was a decent addition to my party. But no, I never trusted him. I believed him to be a double-agent, claiming to be a renegade, but sent by the Ordos to infiltrate my operation.'

'Yet you kept him close?' asked Drusher. 'You didn't kill him *just in case?*'

'Voriet was useful, and he's a good man,' replied Eisenhorn. 'I was aware of his true loyalties, so I treated him warily. But I hoped... I hoped that if I let him work with me, he might see the truth. He might become convinced of the danger. That the threat was genuine.'

'And side with you for real?' Drusher paused. 'No, you wanted more than that, didn't you? You hoped that he would report to his masters in the Ordos and convince them your cause was true. Convince them that you were no rogue. He was your way back *in*. Your chance to be accepted back into the folds of the Inquisition.'

'You are astute.'

'It's so ironic, sir,' said Drusher. 'Ironic to the point of comedy. You suspect everyone. You believe there's a spy in your midst. You think it's Voriet, perhaps correctly, but you use him for your own ends, to rebuild the bridges you burned with the Inquisition. And then the *real* spy turns out to be Jaff. Not just an agent of your ex-masters but, worse, an agent of your true enemy.'

'She hid it well. That's what the Cognitae do.'

'You hate that the Ordos cast you out, don't you?' asked Drusher. 'You hate the fact they declared you a heretic?'

'I hate the fact that the Ordos are blind and stubborn,' replied Eisenhorn. 'I could achieve a great deal more, a great deal faster, if I had their blessing, their cooperation and their not inconsiderable support.'

'Or... you have no friends and you don't like it,' said Drusher.

'Pure sentiment,' Eisenhorn responded.

'Well, I have a friend, and I'm going to help her.'

'This is a dangerous location, magos, and you are no combatant. You don't have the skill-set to do her any good.'

'So *help* me,' said Drusher.

'No,' said Eisenhorn. 'Macks is not a priority.'

'That there, sir, is *why* you don't have any friends,' said Drusher. He turned away. 'I'll go do whatever I can. You go do what you need to do. I hope this isn't goodbye, but I think it probably is, and so I wish you well in your efforts.'

He walked down the platform and began to descend the stairs. Eisenhorn stood and watched him for a while. Then turned, limping painfully, and disappeared in the opposite direction.

Drusher stopped and looked back. Eisenhorn was gone.

'Throne,' he muttered to himself. He had been quite sure Eisenhorn was going to change his mind and come after him. The old bastard really was as cold as stone.

And now Drusher was alone. He had no clue what he was going to do or how he could achieve it. Eisenhorn had been right. Valentin Drusher was no fighter. He wasn't going to last a second against any of Gobleka's ruthless minions.

He was way out of his depth. He had been since the moment Harlon Nayl had hammered on his front door.

He continued down the steps. For what little good it might do, he took the gun out of his coat pocket and clutched it tightly.

It took a while to reach the base levels of the tower. Longer, in fact, than Drusher fancied it should have taken, as if the tower were much taller than any real tower could be, as if its dimensions stretched down into impossible depths.

He moved slowly, hugging the shadows, flinching every time a metal step or platform panel creaked under him. The constant movement and whirring of the huge Loom's gears around him kept making him start. He jumped at every shifting machine part, imagining each motion to be the movement of some Cognitae henchman stalking him.

Finally, he climbed down through the huge, wrought-iron girder frame that supported the weight of the Loom. The frame was as substantial as a major road bridge, and its fabric was built into the walls of the tower. Further high-tension steel cables were cross-anchored around the frame to support the immense weight.

Looking down from a catwalk that ran under the heavy frame, Drusher saw a platform built out from the tower wall in the void beneath. It was large, ragged and uneven, a patchwork of steel plates and flakboarding. It looked like part of the hull-skin of an old ship that had been peeled away and repurposed as flooring. Where it extended out over the void, it sagged and became more frayed, its feathered edge dangling above the darkness below.

Below it, the tower walls continued down into the dark still further, but Drusher could see a glint in the blackness that suggested the very base of the tower was filled with promethium, or some other dark, viscous fluid. Beneath the level of the great iron frame, everything was slightly sheened with oil, every surface tacky with a fine, brown stain. The Loom had run, so Jaff had said, for centuries. Precision engineering required lubricant to keep it moving smoothly. Drusher imagined the constant tending and attention the Loom above him had received over the years, the regular application of lubricant and grease to the gears and cogs. Movement and gravity combined to gently remove the lubricant from the Great Machine, and this is where the residue ended up, draining into a sump in the tower's base, a deep well of pooling waste oil.

There was a row of cages on the ragged platform. They looked like the metal box cage that had contained Sark: six cages, placed against the tower wall. Nearby was a small laboratory station, an old auto-medicae unit and some metal storage bins. The whole area was gloomy, lit only by dozens of fat candles ranged around the platform and the work area. It looked uncomfortably like a shrine, like a place of unwholesome ritual.

By the flickering yellow light of the candles, Drusher could see that two of the cages were occupied. He moved around for a better look. A rough metal staircase ran down from the catwalk to the edge of the platform. The hunched figure in one of the cages was Germaine Macks. A crumpled body lay in the cage beside her. The floors of the other cages were littered with blackened human bones.

Drusher crept to the head of the stairs. There appeared to be no one else around. His heart racing, he climbed down the stairs.

Macks looked up and saw him as he stepped onto the platform. She lurched to the front bars of the cage and peered out at him.

'Valentin? Oh Holy Throne! Valentin!'

He smiled at her and put his finger to his lips. The pistol was still in his hand. He put it in his pocket and shushed her properly.

'Keep your voice down, Germaine,' he hissed.

He hurried over to her cage. She looked up at him with wild eyes. She was filthy, and the side of her face was swollen and badly bruised. He knelt down and looked in at her. She grabbed his hand through the bars.

'What did they do to you?' he asked.

'Hit me,' she said. 'Clubbed me with a rifle stock. I'm all right. Don't look so worried, Valentin. Just get me out of here.'

He let go of her hand and started to examine the cage. There was plainly a door, but there was no lock, no keyhole. He tried to pull the door open.

'I've tried that,' she said sarcastically.

'I'm sure you have.'

'He closed it with a word,' she said.

'Who did?'

'The one who clubbed me. Big bastard. Black hair. Freaky violet eyes.'

'Gobleka,' said Drusher.

'Well, when I get out of here, he's a dead man,' she said. 'He killed Garofar and Edde.'

'Both of them?' asked Drusher.

'Cold blood. I had surrendered, and he just...'

Her voice trailed off.

'Hadeed deserved a better end than that,' she said miserably. 'They both did.'

'What do you mean he closed it with a word?' asked Drusher, trying the cage door again.

'I came to as he was putting me in here,' she said. 'He swung the door shut, then said a word, and it was locked fast.'

'Enuncia,' said a hoarse voice from the next cage. Drusher looked up. The other prisoner was Voriet. He was a mess. His throat and forehead were black with bruises, and his eyes were halfway swollen shut. The interrogator tried to struggle into a sitting position, but he was clearly in agony.

'They used Enuncia,' Voriet said. It sounded like his throat was full of blood.

'Do you remember the word he used?' Drusher asked Macks.

She shook her head.

'It wasn't really a word,' she said. 'I didn't understand it.'

'Do you know anything of Enuncia that might help us, Voriet?' Drusher asked.

'I would have used it already if I did,' Voriet replied. 'Eisenhorn keeps that knowledge to himself.'

'How are you hurt?'

'Broken arm, smashed hand,' replied Voriet. He gestured to his face and throat with his left hand. 'And this.'

'Where is everyone else?' Macks asked Drusher urgently.

'Nayl's dead,' said Drusher. 'Jaff too. She was the one who betrayed us.'

'Jaff?' Voriet said.

Drusher looked over at Voriet.

'She was one of them, sir,' Drusher said. 'A Cognitae spy in your midst. She was the one who sicced that thing on us in Helter fortress.'

'I can't believe it...' Macks whispered, rocking back in amazement.

Voriet was clearly shaken by the idea.

'Audla?' he whispered, uncomprehending.

'She was Cognitae,' said Drusher.

'But she... We trusted her,' said Voriet.

'Trust seems to be a real issue with you people,' said Drusher. 'Anyway, she's gone now. Eisenhorn... He dealt with her.'

'Eisenhorn's alive?' asked Voriet.

'Yes.'

'Why isn't he with you?' asked Macks.

'He had better things to do,' said Drusher. He ran his fingers along the door edge again.

'What do you mean?' she asked.

Drusher glanced at Voriet.

'Priorities. Isn't that right, interrogator?' Drusher asked. 'Stopping Sark, stopping all of this, it's what matters to him. We're all expendable.'

'Screw him,' snapped Macks.

'It's unfortunate,' said Voriet. 'But I understand. This heresy must be brought to an end. We are of less consequence.'

'Ah yes,' said Drusher sarcastically. 'Duty.'

'We are sworn to our duty, sir,' said Voriet.

'Even renegades and rogues?' asked Drusher. 'I know all about him, Voriet. And he knows all about you.'

'What do you mean, magos?' asked Voriet.

'That you joined his rogue band to watch him. That you affect sympathy to his cause, yet all the while you operate at the bidding of your Ordo masters. He's suspected you from the start.'

'That's not true,' said Voriet.

'By all means, deny it, Voriet. It's probably safer. But he knows what you are. And he keeps you close because he hopes you will learn and see for yourself the legitimacy of his work. And vouch for him to your masters.'

'You're talking rubbish,' growled Voriet.

'Look where you are, Voriet,' said Drusher. 'In a cage, in a Cognitae stronghold in... What's the word? Extimate space. The Immaterium Loom hums, sir, making weapons called graels to form an army that the Cognitae's King in Yellow will unleash against Terra. Look at the evidence, and tell me this is not a battle that the Holy Ordos should be fighting. They should listen to Eisenhorn. They should help him, support him. Not declare him a heretic.'

Voriet didn't reply.

'Where are you getting this from, Valentin?' Macks asked, wide-eyed.

Drusher shrugged.

'From the lips of Eisenhorn himself,' he replied. 'And from the mouth of the traitor Jaff. But it doesn't matter, Germaine. It's not business for ordinary people like you and me. It is way above us. It's part of a greater, darker cosmos that we are barely aware of in our day-to-day lives. So, I'm just going to get you out of here, and then we can go somewhere far away and forget all about it.'

'How?' she asked.

'How what?'

'How are you going to get me out of here?' she asked.

'That,' he conceded, 'is a problem. This damn door won't budge. And I don't know any magic word to open it.'

Drusher sat back and thought. He got up and wandered across to the workstation. It was cluttered with dirty surgical equipment and glass sample tubes he was quite certain he didn't want to touch. He looked around for a tool or instrument he could use to lever the door open. As he searched, his movement wafted the flames of the fat candles dotted around the work space. There was nothing useable in any of the drawers. He checked the storage bins. Surely some tools, a crowbar...

Nothing. Just junk and more old medicae supplies.

'Wait,' he said suddenly. 'Wait, wait, wait.'

'What?' asked Macks. She and Voriet stared at Drusher as he hurried back to them. Drusher pulled the gun out of his pocket and looked at it.

'Custom bullets,' he said. 'That's what poor Nayl said. Custom bullets, like the one he used to finish that undead thing. Etched by Eisenhorn himself. Like amulets to break this magic.'

He aimed the weapon at the door frame.

'Whoa, whoa!' Macks cried in alarm.

'What?' asked Drusher. 'I know I'm not very good with guns, but...'

'I don't care what that thing's loaded with,' said Macks. 'You're aiming point-blank at cast iron, Valentin! It'll ricochet... or you'll miss the bars and hit me.'

'The marshal's right,' said Voriet. 'That's not going to work.'

'I suppose not,' said Drusher. He laughed sadly. 'I was almost feeling heroic for a second there.'

He paused, then turned the gun around in his hand and fumbled with it until he managed to eject the clip.

'What are you doing?' asked Macks.

Drusher slid the top bullet out into his palm. He tucked the gun and the clip away in his coat pocket and held the bullet up to the light.

'There's a word etched on it all right,' he said, squinting at it. 'Throne knows what it is. I've never seen anything like it.'

'So?' asked Macks.

'I need to...' Drusher said, thinking. 'I need to make a cast, or...'

Clutching the bullet, he went back to the workstation and carefully picked up one of the candles. Its flame guttered and twitched. Wax dripped off its base and dribbled down his fingers. He used an old, glass specimen slide to scrape up hot, soft wax from the desktop.

He went back to the cages quickly and began to shape a lump of soft wax on the door frame, roughly where a lock would have been.

'What are you doing?' asked Macks.

'Concentrating,' said Drusher as he worked. 'Damn, this stuff is surprisingly hard to work with. There...'

'Now what?' asked Macks.

'Just let it cool for a second,' he said. 'Talk to me.'

'What?'

'While we wait,' he said, smiling. 'I'm scared out of my wits here, Germaine. Talk to me. Tell me something.'

'Like what?'

'I don't know. Something. Something from the old days that was good. I still think about the old days, you know? I think about you. I was a useless husband.'

'I knew exactly what you were when I married you,' she said.

'So you should have known better?' he laughed.

She managed a smile.

'We both should, Valentin,' she said. 'You are an extraordinary man, Valentin. A magos biologis. Your life is driven by your work. As is mine. We *both* should have known better. We shouldn't have been such damn optimists.'

'Optimists or romantics?' he asked.

'Both,' she admitted.

'When did we stop being optimists, Germaine?' he asked.

'About fifteen years ago in Tycho City,' she said, smiling.

'It's a shame,' he said. 'I think… I think I should have made more of a life. Made time for things. Been more than a magos. I think we should be optimists again.'

'Do you?' she asked.

'Yes,' he nodded, 'because then there's a better chance of this working.'

He bent down and tested the wax blob.

'Let's see now,' he said. He took out the bullet, lined up the word etched on its case and gently pressed it into the wax. When he took the bullet away, a mirror print of the inhuman word was impressed in the blob.

'Now what?' Macks asked.

Drusher tried the cage door. It was still locked fast.

'We wait,' he said. 'It may take a moment for the charm to take effect.'

'You're just making this up as you go along, aren't you?' said Macks.

'Story of my life,' he replied. 'All made up as it goes along. Preposterous and unlikely. Like one of poor Hadeed Garofar's faerie tales. Everything's felt like that, especially since you came to the Bone Coast to find me. Fantastical and unnatural and following a set of rules no one has bothered to explain to me.'

'It could work,' said Voriet. He had pulled himself up close to the bars of his cage to watch. 'The charm marking… It could break the word-lock. Enuncia conflicting with Enuncia.'

'Let's hope so,' said Drusher.

Macks rattled the cage door.

'It doesn't seem to be,' she said. He could hear her rising tension.

'Just be patient, Germaine. Give it a moment.'

'Easy for you to say,' she snapped. 'You're not in here.'

'Tell me about *True Heart*,' he said, trying to distract her.

'What?'

'Did you wear it specially, or do you always wear it?' Drusher asked. 'I bought you that bottle years ago. If you used it regularly, it wouldn't have lasted. Did you keep buying it?'

'To remind myself of you? You wish.'

'So you wore it specially?'

She shrugged.

'It was in a drawer. I just thought–'

'It would help you convince me,' said Drusher quietly, 'if you smelled the way I remembered you. It would make me feel like you still cared. Make me believe it was more than an official visit.'

Macks sighed.

'I'm sorry,' she said.

'Don't be. It was clever. You were just doing your job. Subliminal persuasion.'

'No,' she said, 'I'm sorry I put it on. I mean, that's why I put it on. To put you at ease. To remind you of a time when we were close. But I'm sorry I did it.'

'Why?' he asked.

She looked at him through the bars.

'Because it reminded me of a time when we were close too,' she said.

Drusher reached his hand in through the bars, and she took it.

'It's going to be all right, Germaine,' he said. 'You and me, side by side, insane adventures.'

'Which you always hated.'

'I think of them fondly in hindsight,' he said. 'They were high jinks compared to this.'

'It isn't working,' she said.

'The reassurance?'

'The wax charm,' she replied. She let go of his hand and shook at the cage door again.

'Just be patient,' he said.

'There's no time for patience, magos,' said Voriet sharply.

Drusher looked around. The woman with the cropped, red hair was coming down the steps onto the platform. She stared at him, smiled and drew her sidearm.

EIGHTEEN

DEAD OR ALIVE

Drusher ripped the pistol from his pocket and aimed it at her.

'Don't,' he said. 'Not another step.'

The woman's smile broadened.

'That's the bitch who hurt me,' said Voriet.

'Her name is Streekal,' said Drusher. 'Streekal, right?'

'Yes,' the woman said.

'Here's what's going to happen, Mamzel Streekal,' said Drusher. He kept the gun aimed and tried not to let on how badly he was shaking. 'Stop where you are, and toss your weapon now.'

'Or what?' she asked.

'Or I shoot you between the eyes,' he said. 'I am a very good shot. Marshal Macks gave me this gun many years ago. She showed me how to use it. I have practised with it every day. I can knock a moving *Gortus gortus gershomi* out of the sky at one hundred metres.'

'A what?' asked Streekal sarcastically.

'A sea raptor,' growled Voriet from his cage.

'See? You do learn,' Drusher said sidelong. He glared at Streekal.

'Toss the weapon now,' he said.

'Be careful,' warned Voriet. 'She is very, very fast. Don't let her get close.'

Drusher thumbed back the hammer.

'Lose the gun now, mamzel,' he said.

Streekal stopped in her tracks. Her eyes narrowed, and her smile dissolved. She raised her sidearm, a compact laspistol, keeping her fingers open to show she had no real grip on it, then threw it aside. It hit the workstation and bounced onto the floor.

'You won't get out of here alive,' she said.

'Don't think about shouting for help,' said Drusher.

'I won't. You won't get out of here alive, because I'm going to kill you.'

'Let's see how you do when you're bound and gagged,' said Drusher.

Streekal raised her hands.

'Go on, then,' she said.

'Don't get close to her!' Voriet hissed.

'Valentin, what are you even going to tie her up with?' demanded Macks, shaking the cage door again. 'Valentin, just shoot her!'

'I'd prefer not to kill people unless I absolutely have to,' said Drusher.

'Then give me the gun and I'll do it!' snapped Macks.

Her hands still raised, Streekal took a step closer. She moved with slow poise, like a ballet dancer.

'Come on then, magos,' she said. 'Tie me up. Make it tight.'

'Stay where you are,' Drusher warned.

She took another step.

'For Throne's sake,' growled Voriet. 'Kill her, magos! She is lethal!'

'He's right,' said Streekal, taking another step.

'Please stop coming closer,' said Drusher. His hand was really trembling. 'I'd really be very upset if I had to kill you.'

Streekal took another pace forwards.

'Throne forgive me,' said Drusher. 'I'm sorry.'

He pulled the trigger.

The gun clicked.

Drusher stared at it in disbelief. He remembered taking the clip out to remove the bullet. The clip was still in his pocket.

'Valentin!' Macks screamed.

Streekal leapt forwards, grinning. She was faster than any human being he'd ever seen. She slammed into him and kicked him in the chest. Drusher flew back against the bars of Macks' cage. He could hear Macks shrieking his name. He was winded. His chest burned. The world was spinning.

Streekal grabbed him by the front of his coat and hauled him to his feet. He tried to hit her with the useless gun. She blocked and sent it spinning out of his grasp.

'You're so dead,' she said. She shoved him backwards. He staggered and grabbed the bars of Voriet's cage to steady himself. The platform surface was uneven and sticky with oil residue. Voriet and Macks were yelling at him. Macks had started to kick furiously at the door of her cage. It reminded Drusher of the way they had kicked the firebox out of the parlour grate: desperate and frantic. Macks was putting every ounce of her strength into kicking the iron door.

A door that would not open.

Drusher had no idea what he was going to do. He didn't know how to fight. He hadn't the first clue how to throw a punch.

Streekal was on him. She was smiling broadly. She had drawn a wicked-looking punch dagger. The blade glinted in the candlelight.

Drusher scrambled. He had to dodge somehow–

Streekal lunged. Drusher tried to evade. He felt so clumsy. So slow.

He lost his footing. His boots slid on the oil-slicked decking, and he went down hard on his backside. Streekal's dagger-punch missed him by a hair's breadth and struck the bars of Voriet's cage instead.

She barked in pain at the abrupt impact and started to turn. A hand grabbed her wrist through the bars of the cage. Wincing in agony, Voriet had seized her with his good hand. He wrenched her back with his full bodyweight and slammed her into the bars of the cage, pulling her arm and the punch dagger into the cage with him.

She fought back. She reached into the cage with her left hand and struck at Voriet as he clung on. Macks was still kicking at her cage door and shouting Drusher's name.

Drusher hauled himself upright. He knew he needed a weapon. There was nothing to hand. He launched himself at Streekal, and pummelled his fists at her. With her arm pinned between the bars by Voriet, she couldn't turn properly. One of Drusher's blows connected. He caught the back of her head so hard it felt like he had broken his fingers. The impact bounced Streekal's face off the bars.

She snarled in pain. Drusher staggered back, clutching his hand. He was still dizzy, and his feet were slipping. His chest burned so badly he couldn't catch his breath. He could hear the constant crash of Macks' boot against the unyielding cage door, her voice screaming his name.

Streekal plunged her left arm through the bars again. She got hold of Voriet's useless right arm and twisted. Broken bone-ends ground against each other. Voriet shrieked in abject pain and fell backwards, his grip on her right wrist lost.

Streekal pulled her arms out of the cage. She turned to Drusher and raised the punch dagger. The collision with the cage bars had broken her nose and split her lip. Blood was running down her chin. She wiped it away with her left wrist.

'You are going to know such pain,' she hissed as she came for him.

Drusher leapt backwards. He slipped again and fell on his back. She landed on him, flattened her left forearm across his neck to keep him pinned and raised the blade of the punch dagger to his cheek.

'Such pain,' she promised, and started to cut.

The door of Macks' cage crashed wide so hard it opened one hundred and eighty degrees on its hinges and slammed against the metal bars. Macks flew out, bellowing.

She landed on them both and wrenched Streekal backwards, clawing at her. The pair of them rolled off Drusher, locked together. Streekal tried to push the punch-dagger low to stab Macks in the ribs. Macks grabbed her wrist and pinned it high. She rolled again, getting Streekal on her back and tried to slam her hand against the deck to make her drop the blade.

Streekal growled like an animal and went for Macks' throat with her teeth. Macks called her the filthiest word Drusher had ever heard her call anybody, and headbutted Streekal in the face.

Streekal's skull slammed back into the deck. She groaned, dazed. Macks slammed her hand against the deck again, and the dagger spun away. Streekal tried to squirm. Macks punched her in the jaw.

'Stay down!' Macks shouted.

Streekal did not obey. Macks knew how to fight. She was a trained marshal. But Streekal's combat training was far superior to the Magistratum's.

She lifted her shoulders, arched her back and hoisted Macks off the ground. Macks lost her balance and started to slide and roll. Streekal bent her legs, got both feet under Macks' belly and kicked hard.

Macks went flying backwards. Streekal leapt up and landed on her. Now she was on top. Her hands closed around Macks' throat and began to squeeze. Macks fought back, but she couldn't shift the woman's weight off her. She began to choke.

Drusher grabbed Streekal and tried to drag her off Macks. Streekal jerked backwards with an elbow that left Drusher bent over on his knees, all the air knocked out of him.

He wheezed helplessly, trying to refill his lungs, tears running down his face.

Streekal got off Macks and straightened up. Macks lay on her back, gasping, unable to breathe or move. Calmly, Streekal walked over to the workstation and retrieved her laspistol.

She came back and stood over Drusher and Macks. She aimed the weapon at Macks' face.

'Heretic-bitch!' Voriet yelled from his cage in hopeless pain. 'You'll burn in eternity for this!'

'I *do* hope so,' said Streekal.

A shot cracked out.

Streekal took a step backwards. She looked puzzled. She swayed.

Another shot hit her, and a ribbon of blood and tissue spurted from her back. She staggered. She looked down at the two bloody holes in her torso, trying to make sense of them. Then she looked up.

Harlon Nayl limped across the platform towards her. He was battered, dried blood caking the side of his face. He was aiming his large automatic pistol at her.

'That's two,' he said. 'Do you know how to die, or do you need another lesson?'

Swaying drunkenly, Streekal raised her pistol to aim at him.

Nayl fired again.

Streekal dropped her gun. Her arm flopped back against her side. She took a couple of awkward, wobbling steps then fell down. The slope of the sagging platform rolled her body over a couple of times, then she simply began to slide on the tarry surface.

Her corpse dropped off the platform lip. They heard it hit the deep, ancient pool of promethium far below.

NINETEEN

THE ENGINE WAKES

Where's Streekal?' asked Gobleka. His intimidating violet stare fixed on Davinch and Blayg.

'She's hunting for him,' said Blayg.

'And Jaff's prisoner might be loose too?' asked Gobleka.

'It's possible,' said Davinch.

'Didn't you check the cellar?'

Davinch hesitated.

'I was going to,' he replied. 'I was on my way down. Then I heard you call my name, so–'

'I didn't call your name, you idiot,' snapped Gobleka. 'I've been up here all the time. You wouldn't have heard me.'

'But–' Davinch began.

'He was playing with you,' sneered Gobleka. 'Psykana tricks, you idiot. He's trying to game us.'

He turned slowly, surveying the expanse of the Loom visible from the main gantry. In the cage behind him, Sark shivered and whimpered.

'He's a monster,' mumbled Blayg. 'You should have seen it, Gobleka. What he did to Jaff.'

'She deserved anything she got,' replied Gobleka. 'She let them get *in* here. She let them walk right in.'

'Wasn't that the point?' asked Davinch. 'To bring them here? To silence them?'

'Not *inside* the hall, you idiot,' said Gobleka.

'Well, maybe not that,' replied Davinch. 'But it makes it easier. They're trapped. They're confused. This place messes with your head, especially when you're not used to it.'

'Davinch, if I'd wanted to bring them *inside* to kill them,' said Gobleka, 'I'd have called in reinforcements. Proactive specialists. A kill-team from the scholam on Gudrun. Maybe negotiate some cooperation from the Traitor Hosts. Or even petition the King to lend us a grael. This is a mess. There's no time for any of that now. An outside assist would take days or weeks to arrive.'

'Yeah, but–' Davinch began.

'*Weeks*, Davinch,' said Gobleka firmly. 'We don't have weeks.'

'But we've killed four of them,' said Blayg. 'And two more caged up. Maybe three, if Jaff got that magos shut away before she died. That just leaves the old bastard himself...'

'The others don't matter, you arsehole,' said Gobleka. 'They're just foot-soldiers, ten-a-penny. The old bastard is the old bastard for a *reason*. We've got an alpha-class psyker with a grudge loose in here. Either of you combat psykers? Didn't frigging think so. I've got to blank him. I've got to use Sark.'

He turned and looked at the cage.

'I've got to use *you* now, haven't I, magos?' he called.

'Magos! M-magos!' the naked wretch in the cage gurgled back.

'Blayg, get the kit,' said Gobleka.

'Wait, Goran,' said Davinch, stepping forwards. 'That's not a good idea. Chase will have your guts. The instructions were clear. Sark is a creative asset. We use what strength he has to *manufacture*. He's not a proactive weapon, and we don't waste his power using him that way.'

'The frigging rules were changed when Jaff ballsed it up, Davinch,' said Gobleka. 'Chase might not like it. The King might not like it. But they'll see it was necessary.'

'But if you damage him–'

'We'll keep him sound,' said Gobleka.

'Gobleka, Sark's burning out,' said Davinch. 'He's still exhausted from the last weaving. He needs time to recover. And if you start him up, and use his power, we don't know how many more constructs we'll get out of him. We may not meet our quota. Or at the very least, we could fall months behind.'

Gobleka walked across the platform until he was nose-to-nose with the tall, tattooed man. Davinch pulled back a little.

'Yes,' said Gobleka. 'Chase will be furious. Imagine how much *more* furious she'll be if we allow Eisenhorn to shut this place down? She'd bring us back from the dead just to kill us all *over* again. Protecting this place is our first responsibility. The Cognitae cannot lose the Loom. It's not an option. He must be found and finished before he can do any damage to it. So we've got to use Sark.'

Davinch nodded reluctantly.

'Besides,' Gobleka added. 'The other one's out there. What's her name?'

'Betancore,' said Blayg.

'Right. She needs to be wiped too. We can't risk any word of this getting off-world. So, Sark can handle that as well. Blayg, get the kit.'

The portly man nodded and hurried off the gantry to a lower platform. Gobleka put his assault weapon down on the deck and went over to the cage. He crouched down.

'Magos?' he called softly. 'Draven? You stay calm now, you hear me?'

The man in the cage moaned and curled up in a tight ball. Gobleka put his hand on the frame of the cage door and said a single word that made Davinch cringe.

The cage door swung open. Sark whined and curled up even tighter.

Blayg returned, carrying a medicae pack. He opened the case, prepped an injector and handed it to Gobleka.

'Full dose?' asked Gobleka.

Blayg nodded.

Gobleka crawled into the cage. Sark shrank back from him, becoming agitated. Gobleka grabbed him, pinned him with one arm and jabbed the injector into the meat of his left buttock. Sark squealed.

Gobleka let him go, slid out of the cage and sealed it again with an unword. Sark began to twitch, and then the twitching grew to a violent thrashing. He contorted and twisted, veins bulging, his limbs spasming.

'Hell's teeth,' murmured Davinch as he watched. 'It takes him longer to come back every time.'

'There will come a time when he won't come back at all,' said Blayg.

'Then we'll find a replacement,' said Gobleka. 'We always knew that day would come...'

His voice trailed off.

'What?' asked Blayg.

'The old bastard,' said Gobleka.

Davinch and Blayg turned in terror, expecting to see Eisenhorn behind them.

'Idiots,' Gobleka laughed. 'Think about it. Think about it, we could turn this mess into a huge victory. Turn it right around. End the threat of Eisenhorn *and* replace the one failing component of this system.'

'Eisenhorn?' asked Blayg.

'He's perfect. He's strong. Mentally, physically. The psykana aspect is a huge advantage. He's already attuned.'

'Yeah, but his *mindset*,' said Davinch. 'He wouldn't cooperate. He wouldn't be willing.'

'You think that animal is willing?' asked Gobleka, pointing at the man writhing and gasping in the cage.

'He was to begin with,' said Blayg.

'The viral shots will destroy the old bastard's resistance,' said Gobleka. 'They'll negate his will, his self, and rewire his brain and his soul. We'll break him and reshape him. I don't think it'll be hard, either. Eisenhorn's been on the edge for too long. Decades. He's been declared a damn heretic, for Terra's sake! It won't be a stretch for him. He's seen the warp. He knows its allure. We'll just tip him over the threshold so he sees the real truth. He'll realise where he should have been from the very start. He'll embrace it like a long-lost love.'

Gobleka grinned broadly at the two men beside him.

'And Chase and the King,' he said, 'they will relish the sheer poetry of their greatest adversary becoming their most valuable asset.'

'Goran?' a weak voice called from inside the cage. 'Goran? Are you there?'

Gobleka looked at his colleagues.

'Get moving, both of you,' he said. 'Find Streekal. Kill anyone else you find. Anyone, caged or not. If you encounter Eisenhorn, try and drive him this way.'

'If he fights?' asked Davinch.

'Then kill him if you have to. But only if you have to. Intact, or alive enough to work with, that's preferable. Get on with it.'

Davinch and Blayg looked at each other then turned and left the gantry. Gobleka walked back to the cage.

'Sark? Magos?'

Inside the cage, Draven Sark slowly stood up. He looked around, blinking at the light, his naked, emaciated body suddenly upright and straight-backed.

'Have I been asleep?' he asked. His voice was thin and dry, but it had lost its deranged flutter.

'Yes, for a while,' said Gobleka.

'Can I come out, Goran? Can I come out of the cage now, please?'

'Not yet, magos,' said Gobleka.

'Have I been asleep?'

'Yes,' said Gobleka.

'The dreams are bad,' said Sark. 'I don't like them.'

'I know, magos, but they will be over soon.'

'You promised that last time, Goran,' Sark said, looking reproachfully at Gobleka. 'You promised I could come out.'

'The work is important, you know that,' said Gobleka. 'But I mean it this time.'

'Is it time to weave again?' asked Sark. He put his hand to his forehead and kneaded his brow. 'I don't think I'm strong enough. I feel like everything is slipping away. Everything is dark at the edges, Goran. Closing in on me. When I weave, I walk out into the darkness, Goran. Into dark places. It's very lonely. I don't want to go back out there any more.'

'You always say that...' Gobleka said soothingly.

Sark looked at him sharply through the bars. Anger spiked in him.

'Because it's true!' he cried. 'How many years have I spent in the dark now? Eh? It feels like centuries. These brief moments of light and wakefulness are too rare. I have sacrificed my life for the King, Gobleka. My life.'

'Then you won't want that sacrifice to be in vain, will you?' asked Gobleka.

'What do you mean by that?' asked Sark.

'I haven't roused you to weave, magos,' said Gobleka. 'There's more weaving to be done, but not today. The hall is under threat.'

'Threat?'

'The Inquisition has found us,' said Gobleka.

'How the hell could they have done?' asked Sark, horrified. 'Keshtre is extimate. It is hidden from all, unless I invite them in. I have taken great pains–'

'And now you must take greater ones,' said Gobleka. 'Gregor Eisenhorn is here. In this tower. He will undo all you have done. Your life's work. You must start the Loom. You must find him and speak out the means to nullify him.'

'Eisenhorn,' said Sark quietly. 'Really here?'

'Yes.'

'I never thought he'd have the guile to get this close,' said Sark. He glanced at Gobleka. 'You're right, of course, Goran. He must be purged. Are there materials to hand?'

'Some,' said Gobleka. 'A few bodies in storage. Failed test subjects, ones we haven't disposed of yet. Some other corpses too. You'll find them once you start.'

'Go open up storage, Goran,' Sark said. He knelt down and looked at Gobleka through the bars.

'Do you want him dead, Goran?' he asked. 'Or do you want him to suffer first?'

'Oh, I want him to suffer, magos,' said Gobleka, 'but I don't want him dead. I want him helpless. Deprived of his abilities.'

'He's too dangerous to toy with, Goran.'

'Think how we can use him,' said Gobleka.

'Use him?'

'You want the dreams to end, don't you?' Gobleka asked. 'You want to be free of that cage? This is how.'

A sad smile crossed the magos' face.

'Goran,' he said. 'You should have led with that. This will be a pleasure.'

He closed his eyes and raised his hands. Quietly at first, the words started to issue from his mouth. Half-words, un-words, formless words. He began to speak them faster and more loudly.

Gobleka watched for a while, until the discomfort became too great. He picked up his assault weapon, left the gantry and walked up two flights of stairs to an upper platform. Below him, the words echoed around the tower.

On the platform, there was a modular container, a metal cargo pod from a commercial shift-ship. It was battered and rusty. He disengaged the lock and swung the door open. The smell of decay that wafted out was sickening.

Gobleka backed away, his hand clamped over his nose and mouth. Organic waste fluid trickled out over the container's sill. He left the door wide open.

He waited. Then he turned his back on the container and sat down on the platform edge beside the head of the stairs.

Below him, the words grew louder. A light began to glow from the gantry below. It throbbed and grew steadily brighter. The machine hum in the tower grew louder.

After a while, he heard a knock and a scrape as things stirred inside the battered cargo pod. He did not look around.

Nor did he look around, a few minutes later, when the first dragging, shuffling footsteps moved past him towards the stairs.

'So,' said Drusher, 'not that I'm saying I'm unhappy about it or anything, but how come you're not dead?'

Nayl was leading them up the staircase towards the massive girder frame under the Loom. He glanced back.

'I got shot, magos, I fell,' he said. 'I survived both.'

'Simple as that?'

'Luck is never simple,' replied Nayl. 'Jaff got me in the back with a las-shot. My jack armour stopped the worst of it, but the thing with jack armour is that it dissipates the force so it can't penetrate. The impact knocked me right over the rail.'

'That's luck?' asked Drusher.

'I fell,' said Nayl. 'Quite a long way. But, as you may have noticed, there's a lot of machinery in this place. I bounced off some gigantic flywheel. Banged up my head and my shoulder. Then I got hooked up. By the strap of my rifle. Wound up just hanging there from a cog, throttled by my own gun-strap.'

'And *that's* luck?'

'Well, it broke my fall,' said Nayl. 'If it hadn't been for the cog, I'd have gone straight down to the bottom. I waited as long as I could, waited for the cog to cycle around, then cut the strap and climbed down some gears onto a platform.'

'It's very interesting what you call "lucky",' said Drusher.

'I'm still alive, aren't I?' asked Nayl. 'That's the lucky part.'

Drusher was fairly sure Nayl was downplaying the cost of his escape. From the way he was limping, the way he was holding himself, it was clear he was carrying some considerable injuries.

They all were. Once they'd got Voriet out of his cage using another of Drusher's patent 'wax charms,' they'd patched him up as best they could, using the old medical supplies in the storage bins. His smashed arm was slung and bound around his torso, the most effective temporary splinting they could muster. He was very pale and very slow, and his pain was constant. Drusher was worried about the damage to Voriet's throat too. He and Macks were taking turns to support the interrogator so he could manage the steps.

Macks seemed robust enough, but the brawl with Streekal had left her bruised and sore. For his part, Drusher felt like he had been run over by a tank. His hand throbbed, and his chest, back and belly ached so much it made him wince. Macks had put a dressing over the slice Streekal had cut in his cheek.

'You're a silly bastard,' she'd told him gently while she did it.

'You need to learn some new moves, magos,' Voriet had said, smiling through his pain. 'That's twice you've tried to get out of trouble by opening a cage and letting something wild out.'

As they climbed, Drusher told Nayl about Jaff and Eisenhorn. He related everything he could think of.

'Have you seen Eisenhorn?' he asked.

'No,' said Nayl. 'I haven't seen anybody. Not until I found you lot.'

'Do we have a plan?' asked Macks.

'Find a way out,' said Nayl. 'Maybe try to use your wax charm trick on a door or something. You're all beaten up. I think Voriet needs serious attention. This is one of those times when we need to escort casualties out of the front line.'

'No,' said Drusher. 'Eisenhorn's gone up to deal with Sark and Gobleka. He'll need help. He's... struggling. Something about this place hurts him.'

'Oh, screw him,' said Macks.

'I told him, once I'd got you out, I'd come back and help him,' said Drusher.

'He didn't come and help you,' said Macks.

'No,' said Drusher. 'But then, he never said he was going to. In fact, he said he definitely wasn't going to. I, on the other hand, said I would help him when I could.'

'So, what, you're a man of your word now?' asked Macks.

'Always have been,' said Drusher.

'With respect,' said Nayl, stopping so he could turn and look back at them, 'I admire your spirit, magos, but I don't know what sort of help you're going to be. Your expertise is not... not combat-oriented.'

Drusher stared at him.

Nayl looked away, awkwardly.

'You know what?' he said. 'I'm sorry I said that. I take it back. It takes balls for a man to go into a fight when he knows how to fight. It takes a damn sight more to go in when he doesn't. Not to have a clue, but to go for it anyway. Balls of steel.'

'That's what we'll call him from now on,' said Macks. 'Balls of steel.'

'Head full of stupid, mind,' she added.

Nayl smiled.

'This is a very big deal, isn't it, Nayl?' asked Drusher, gesturing at the machine above them. 'What's happening here is, uh...'

'The biggest,' said Nayl.

'So then,' said Drusher with a shrug. 'Eisenhorn was right, really. We're all expendable. In the face of this. This isn't Eisenhorn's private war. The outcome affects everything we know, everything we are. Right?'

'Right,' said Nayl.

'So we should help Eisenhorn in any way we can,' said Drusher. 'I mean, we may not be any use at all, but we should try. How did you put it? "To not have a clue, but to go for it anyway"?'

'Something along those lines,' said Nayl.

'I agree with the magos,' said Voriet.

'Shut up,' said Macks. 'You can barely stand.'

'Doesn't stop me agreeing, marshal,' said Voriet.

'All right,' said Nayl. 'We go up. We take a look. If it's out of our league, we get the hell out. Find a way out of this place. Least we can do is get to Medea and get a signal sent.'

'To the Ordos?' asked Macks.

'Yes,' said Nayl.

'The Ordos?' asked Voriet.

'I think we're way past hiding now, Darra,' Nayl said. 'I think Eisenhorn would reckon so too. We've got solid intelligence on the Cognitae here. Old... differences, they don't matter now. If we can't help Eisenhorn, we scream for help and bring the Holy frigging Inquisition down on this place, guns blazing.'

'Even if that means... spending the rest of your life incarcerated?' asked Drusher. 'Or being burned as a heretic? They still do that, right?'

'Even if,' said Nayl.

'Well, I agree with that last part,' said Macks. 'Call in the Ordos. The Magistratum. The Territorial Guard. Anything and everything. But as for the rest of that big-talk pissing contest, I utterly despair of men, sometimes.'

'Me too,' said Nayl. 'We're hardly packing much kill-power.'

Between them, Nayl had his big Tronsvasse auto, Drusher had his Regit compact, which Macks had recovered and reunited with the clip in Drusher's pocket, and Macks had Streekal's laspistol.

'Let's go then,' said Nayl. He turned and started climbing the gantry stairs again. Drusher took a turn supporting Voriet, and Macks went ahead of them, behind Nayl.

'Thank you,' said Voriet quietly as Drusher helped him up the stairs. Every step made him wince and sigh.

'For what?'

'Not telling Nayl what you know,' said Voriet. 'About me, I mean. About what Eisenhorn said about me.'

'Not my business,' said Drusher.

'You blurted it out well enough down at the cages,' said Voriet.

'Yeah, well, we're beyond that now,' said Drusher. 'And there's more than enough trouble to go around as it is.'

They hobbled on together, Drusher's arm around Voriet's back.

'You should tell them, though,' said Drusher.

'Who?'

'The Ordos. Your masters,' said Drusher. 'If you get out of here, you should go to them and tell them what you know. What you've seen. What you believe.'

Voriet nodded.

'That's not good,' said Macks from up ahead. She was looking at the Great Machine above them.

High above, at the very top of the tower, a strange glow was filling the air. It expanded, growing brighter and brighter.

A breeze started to rise. The humming all around them increased.

With a sudden but steady motion that startled them all, the huge wheels and cogs and gears of the Loom began to turn faster, until they were spinning and rattling and whizzing. The slowly cycling machine had suddenly burst into frantic, industrial life.

'Yeah,' Nayl yelled back over the clattering roar of the spinning cogs. 'Not good at all.'

TWENTY

MINDLESS

Eisenhorn stopped for a moment and crouched in the shadows. The sudden and furious din of the Loom around him was making it hard to focus.

Harder than before. The mere background hum of the cycling machine had worn him down and deadened his mind. It had taken him much longer than he had hoped to clamber up to the high levels of the tower. He was painfully aware of how old and unreliable his body had become. It was held together with augmetics and metal bracing. The slow climb had left him tired and short of breath.

Now his mind, the part of him he'd always been able to trust, seemed as faulty as his body. He felt muffled, swathed in a darkness that limited his gifts. A migraine pain stabbed behind his eyes.

The noise of the suddenly active Loom was intense. It was like being at the heart of a Mechanicus factory plant. Sark, or Gobleka, or both, had begun something. There were various possibilities, but the most obvious was that they were moving against him.

He had considered simply sabotaging the Loom. He carried two automatic pistols: the big Hecuter .45, loaded with standard munitions, which was in his hand, and a smaller Scipio compact, loaded with custom rounds, which was strapped in his chest rig. A few shots with the engraved rounds of the Scipio might damage the Loom, possibly even destroy it. They were notoriously volatile devices. And he still had what scraps of his psykana talent remained, and his small but potent vocabulary of Enuncia.

But if he managed to cripple and destroy the Loom, what then? They were in extimate space. He'd die along with it. The Cognitae's precious Gershom facility would be lost, but so would the vital things he had learned from Jaff about the King in Yellow, Sancour and the Angelus Subsector.

A key threat would be stopped, but the greater threat would remain.

Not for the first time, he focused his mind and tried to reach Betancore outside in the Karanines. It was futile. Either the fold in space would not let his messages through, or his abilities were virtually gone. He feared the latter. The pain in his head was intense. He could barely form a thought, let alone try to send it.

So what were his options? He could push on to face Gobleka and Sark. Or he could get out. A word of Enuncia had unfolded reality, bringing him and the group into Keshtre. Surely another word would allow him to step out?

But the Loom would still be running, and Sark and Gobleka would still be alive. And there was no guarantee that if he got out, he could ever get back in again.

By his reckoning, the cage gantry was not far above him. The light was bright up there, a gold amber radiance that turned all the engine mechanisms above him into silhouettes, and all the shadows below him into stark, hard edges.

He had to go on. He wondered if he could. The etheric dissonance field generated by the Loom had increased considerably when the machine started to run at full rate. It was no longer just dulling him and making him sick, it was actively tearing at his psycho-sensitive mind. He thought ruefully about Medea's last words to him. She'd been right. He should have brought Cherubael, despite all the handling problems that would have caused. He needed something that hit hard, like the monstrous daemonhost. He was alone and woefully weakened.

He got up and began to move again, limping for the next metal stairwell.

The first shots hit the platform deck beside him. Bright las-bolts buckled the grille and punched through it.

Eisenhorn threw himself flat. There was very little cover. He tried to gauge the angle the shots had come from by the holes they had cut in the platform, but his facility for psychometric reading and prediction was as good as gone. The damn Loom. It was neutering his mind.

Another flurry of shots came in. One punched clean through the metal handrail above him. This time, he glimpsed them in the air, glowing bolts, arcing down at him. He had some sense of an angle. He rose on one knee and banged off a series of shots with the heavy Hecuter, spent cases pinging out of the ejector. He saw the shots spark and flash as they struck metalwork above him.

He saw a figure dart for cover along a catwalk: the tattooed man, Davinch, his twin laspistols in his hands.

Eisenhorn fired again. In partial cover behind a flywheel, Davinch blasted back. The las-fire went wide of Eisenhorn, to the left this time. The Cognitae fool was a poor shot. He'd had three decent tries at Eisenhorn and missed by a margin each time.

Eisenhorn crawled back, until he was half-shielded by a spinning cog. He took careful, considered aim on the flywheel above, waiting for Davinch to poke his head out again.

Eisenhorn focused his will.

+Davinch!+

It hurt, like a hot spike between the eyes. Eisenhorn tried again. A mental goad like that, particularly when you knew a man's name, was usually enough to jerk him out into the open. He got into the hindbrain and gave it a flick the target couldn't resist. Under optimal circumstances, he could psyke into a man's head and make him jump to his death or shoot himself, a look of horror on his face as his body turned against him.

But these circumstances were far from optimal. The Loom's dissonance field was both snuffing out his psionic ability and reflecting what little he could broadcast.

Eisenhorn began to move again, keeping low as he headed along the platform. Another burst of fire chopped at him. Hard rounds this time, an assault weapon from the rate. The metal slugs ripped across the platform and sparked off a brass bearing behind him.

Different weapon. This was someone else. Blayg, or Gobleka, perhaps. Again, the aim had been wide. Were they *all* terrible shots?

No, they weren't. The evidence was plain. Keshtre was a vital facility, but the Cognitae had only staffed it with a handful of operatives. Just enough to keep it running. So they had to be good, the very best. Elite cult soldiers, hand-picked for their skills. Eisenhorn knew from the case file that Gobleka was a fine marksman. He'd cut down Interrogator Arfon Kadle on Gudrun with a single headshot at three thousand metres.

These men weren't trying to kill him. They were trying to drive him.

He kept low and scanned for movement. He glimpsed Blayg, the short, jowly one, switching positions. Eisenhorn got off a single shot. Blayg dropped out of sight. A moment later, he reappeared and hammered the deck beside Eisenhorn with autofire.

Eisenhorn fought back the pain clouding his head and made a decision. He had to change tactics. He had to use whatever edge, whatever chance, however desperate, to seize back some advantage. They were trying to drive him. They wanted him alive. If he was their prisoner, he might be taken closer to the very place he was struggling to reach. But it had to be convincing.

He rose to his feet, clearly visible.

'You want to drive me, do you?' he yelled. 'Herd me?'

He fired two shots in Blayg's direction.

'I won't play your game!' he shouted. Another fierce burst of autofire rattled into the decking beside him. Eisenhorn remained standing. He didn't even flinch.

Blayg reappeared, peeking down, his combat autorifle aimed at Eisenhorn.

'Comply now, or we drop you!' Blayg shouted.

'What the hell makes you think I'll cooperate?' Eisenhorn yelled back.

'Look down!' Blayg called back, his aim fixed.

Eisenhorn glanced down. He saw the gently wavering red dot of Blayg's targeter floating on the centre of his chest.

'We'd like you alive,' Blayg called, 'but it's not essential. Take the stairs up. Do it! Or I take the shot!'

'Go to hell,' said Eisenhorn.

Blayg had pushed it as far as he wanted to. He had no illusions about Gregor Eisenhorn's brutal and relentless reputation. He'd heard all the stories. He'd seen Jaff's body. The man was inhumanly dangerous.

Damn Gobleka's preferences. Enough chances. Enough playing with fire.

Blayg squeezed the trigger, ripping out a tight burst from his autorifle.

The rounds hit Eisenhorn precisely where the marker had painted him, full in the chest. Eisenhorn reeled backwards in a puff of red vapour, hit the back rail of the platform and slumped down.

Blayg slowly rose to his feet.

'Davinch!' he shouted. 'He's down!'

Sprawled on his back against the rail, Eisenhorn lifted his head and his Hecuter.

'That's right, show yourself, idiot,' he murmured, and fired.

The large-calibre round burst the top of Blayg's skull. He swayed, then folded up in a heap.

Eisenhorn slowly heaved himself to his feet. It was hard to breathe. His chest plating had stopped most of the burst, but his ribs were cracked, and his chest felt as if it had been crushed. One of the high-velocity rounds had punctured through the plate and done some soft tissue damage.

Another had gone low under the plate, punching clean through him below his ribs. Blood was weeping down the front of his coat. He could feel more soaking his back. He concentrated and tried to use his will to block the pain, and seal the bleeding.

His will was gone. The Loom had taken it from him.

Davinch was standing behind him.

Eisenhorn started to turn, but he was far too slow. Davinch whirled a spin-kick that knocked Eisenhorn sideways, then another that flicked away the Hecuter. A third kick, straight to the sternum, put Eisenhorn on his back. Agony from the gunshot trauma flooded him.

The tattooed man stood over him, looking down, both laspistols aimed at Eisenhorn's face.

'Look at you,' Davinch sneered. 'The famous Gregor Eisenhorn, scourge of heretics. It's over, you old bastard. What are you, without that famous psykana gift of yours? Eh? Frigging nothing. Just an old, worn-out shell. A ruin. A nothing.'

Davinch peered closer. He grinned.

'And you're shot too. Dear old Blayg plugged you. That'll be a through-and-through. You're going to bleed out like a pig. That is, if I let you.'

Davinch's smile grew broader.

'And you're going to wish,' he whispered, 'that I had.'

They climbed to the next platform and stopped to let Voriet rest. Nayl kept watch. Drusher and Macks eyed the hurtling gears of the Great Machine all around them with both fear and wonder.

Macks said something.

'What?' asked Drusher. It was hard to hear over the clattering roar of the machine.

'I said it's giving me a headache,' said Macks, raising her voice.

Drusher nodded.

'The noise,' he said.

'And the light, and the heat,' she grimaced. The light shining down from above was brighter than before. It looked sickly and unclean, like the glow of something toxic and contaminating. It made Drusher remember a day, years before, before he had first met Macks, when he'd been caught out in the middle of the steppes of Lower Udar. He had hiked north from a grim livestock town called Kellikow, hoping to find a grazing station the men at Kellikow had mentioned. The station was long gone and derelict, and he'd been looking for alternative shelter when the thunderstorm came in. The light, the whole sky, had turned an extraordinary shade of yellow, a fulminous twilight to herald the fury.

The light filling the tower looked the way the light had done that day. Threatening and unnatural. He'd managed to trudge back to Kellikow, soaked, and spent a week in the infirmary, fighting off pneumonia.

Drusher missed those simpler times.

'It's not just that,' said Voriet from nearby. He was leaning heavily against the metal handrail. 'The mechanism's generating an interference pattern. Background psionics. It's messing with us.'

Macks wasn't listening. 'What the hell's that?' she asked suddenly. 'Nayl? Nayl!'

She pointed. There was a figure on a parallel catwalk some distance away. They could just see it, moving out of sight behind part of the Loom mechanism. It was a human figure, walking quite fast, determinedly, arms at its sides.

'I don't know,' said Nayl, moving along the platform to get a better look, gun in hand.

'Cognitae?' asked Macks.

The look on Nayl's face was doubtful.

'Another one!' Voriet called out. A second figure had appeared on a platform several stages below them. This one was limping, almost shuffling, but though slower than the first, it seemed equally determined.

'Get behind me,' said Nayl.

They turned. A third figure had appeared. It was coming up the steps towards them. It had once been human. It had taken considerable damage to the left side of its body and head. Its flesh was beginning to rot and discolour. Its good eye fixed them with an eager glare. What was left of its face was expressionless.

It was moving fast, striding up the steps and onto the platform.

'Throne's sakes!' Macks exclaimed.

'Back up!' Nayl shouted at the advancing thing. He aimed his gun. The figure did not slow down.

Nayl fired. Centre mass. The heavy round had no effect. Drusher saw a telltale green shimmer around the figure, a pinprick green light in its empty socket. A crackle like electricity.

'Nayl!' he yelled. He pulled the gun out of his pocket and aimed. One shot.

The autosnub jerked in his hand. Drusher discovered it was surprisingly hard to hit a target, even one as big as a human being coming right at him, just a few metres away. His shot simply clipped the figure's right shoulder.

He was about to curse at himself when the figure went down. It went from walking to falling without an interruption. Suddenly slack, as dead as it looked, it crumbled, bounced off the handrail and lay still.

'An animation,' said Drusher.

'Yeah,' agreed Nayl. He was taking the clip out of his gun and opening his pocket to fish out custom rounds.

'Like before,' said Drusher.

'Indeed so, magos,' said Nayl. 'Don't let them touch you!' he yelled to Macks and Voriet.

'Nayl!' Macks called. Another figure was mounting the staircase at the other end of their platform. Before death it had been a stern, older woman. Corruption had bloated and blackened her flesh. Green electric sparks floated in her dead eyes and fizzled around her bared teeth. She too was moving rapidly, coming right at them without hesitation.

Macks squeezed off two las-bolts at her. They were solid shots, but the energy just radiated away.

'Don't waste it!' Nayl told her. 'It won't have an effect.' He had slammed a specialised round into the chamber of his Tronsvasse. He stepped in front of Macks and Voriet, aimed at the woman as she reached the head of the stairs and shot her between the eyes.

There was an ugly puff of matter. The woman's head snapped back, and she toppled down the stairs. She ended up at the foot of the steps, on her back, her legs tangled in the side rails.

'They've sent these things to get us, haven't they?' Drusher asked Nayl.

'Yes,' he replied. He was loading another round. '*Raised* them. That might be why the Loom's working.'

'But we can stop them,' said Drusher.

Nayl nodded.

'But it depends how many of them there are,' he said. 'We've only got a few custom rounds between us.'

'How... how many could they have made?' Drusher asked.

'Depends how many people the Cognitae have killed,' said Voriet. 'How many bodies they have.'

'Let's move,' said Nayl. 'Only shoot if you have to.'

They hurried to the steps where the first figure had appeared. Macks and Drusher helped Voriet between them. They moved down, but another figure had appeared, striding towards them. It was hard to tell if this one had been male or female in life. Its death appeared to have involved being flayed.

'Up! Up!' Nayl urged them, guiding them to the side and up a link staircase to a higher catwalk. He waited as the flayed thing drew closer, then dropped it with a single shot.

He hurried after the other three, up the steps and onto the higher catwalk.

'Be wary,' he advised. 'These devils are much faster than the thing that came for us in Helter.'

'Because they're more intact,' said Drusher.

'What?' asked Macks.

'The thing in Helter was just old bones. This force animates them, but it can only use the structure it's got to work with. Simple mechanics, really. It can make disarticulated bones rise and shuffle along. But these poor creatures are intact–'

'More or bloody less,' said Macks.

'They're articulated,' said Drusher. 'They have tendons, sinews, muscle mass. The force can use that framework to move them faster.'

'I think he's right,' said Nayl.

'I think he's writing a frigging paper on them,' growled Macks.

'Keep moving,' said Nayl.

They followed the catwalk over a massive, spinning drum of brass, then ascended another staircase to the next gantry. Voriet was struggling to keep pace. Twice, he slipped and cried out as his broken arm struck the handrail.

Another figure was waiting for them on the gantry. It was just dry, white bones. Green swirls of light imaged the organs missing from its torso. It shuffled towards them, feet dragging.

Drusher raised his sidearm.

'Don't waste a round,' said Nayl, grabbing his arm. 'We can outrun this one.'

They left it behind, hustling Voriet along, and took another flight of stairs up to a wide catwalk that circled the base of a huge, burnished gyroscope.

'Oh Terra!' Macks exclaimed.

Another figure was pacing inexorably towards them. Its face had been blown away by point-blank shots.

But it was Hadeed Garofar.

TWENTY-ONE

A VERY SUITABLE CANDIDATE

In his cage, on his knees, his head tipped back, Magos Sark crooned un-words into the gulfs of the empyrean, and the words echoed back like the chirring of a trillion insects. The light flooding the tower was coming from inside him, so bright his skin was translucent, and Gobleka was sure he could see the shadow of the magos' skeleton.

Gobleka stood at the edge of the platform for a while, watching. The un-words stirred something primordial in him, as if some deep and vestigial part of his lizard brain was responding. It was the language of infinity, the prehuman, inhuman instructions for creation and negation. He tried to mouth the un-words he heard, to copy and repeat them, to learn them, but they were coming too fast.

They always did. He had tried before, almost every time Sark had started the Loom and begun to weave. Gobleka had never managed to learn any un-words that way. He'd always ended up with a nosebleed or a savage tension headache. The futile effort to learn had, over time, only done one thing. It had changed the colour of his eyes.

The few words Goran Gobleka did know, the few commands of power, had been taught to him by Lilean Chase, and each syllable had taken many painful weeks to master.

Gobleka realised he had been standing on the gantry for too long. The skin of his cheeks and brow was tingling and sore, as though he had been out in a strong sun. He'd been looking at the light for longer than he should have. He knew from experience that word-burn could be more painful than sunburn.

He picked up his autorifle and went down a small curved staircase to the monitor station, set up on a platform below and to the side of the main gantry. He checked the displays of the cogitators. Sark's psychometrics and vitals were off the chart, the former too high and the latter too low, but that was fairly standard when an act of weaving was in progress. Other cogitators were trying to map and decipher the sounds coming from the magos, but their readings were void. Again, that was normal. The Cognitae had procured the most powerful cogitators possible, some taken by force from a Mechanicus facility in the Thracian System, but even these could not cope with the energy and raw data they had been set up to process.

Gobleka wondered how long Sark would last. No human body should have survived the extremes he had endured over the years. Indeed, none had prior to Sark. As a junior adept at Keshtre in the early days, Gobleka had often been tasked with hosing out the cage after a failed trial.

Sark should have died the first time he tried to harness the Loom. He certainly shouldn't have been able to survive the many weavings he had conducted. But then, Gobleka was certain that the process had altered Sark in fundamental ways. Sark had ceased to be remotely human a long time ago.

What did that make him? A god? A daemon? A eudaemonic spirit? Gobleka was sometimes convinced that Sark's soul had burned out years before, and something else, some etheric sentience, had taken up residence inside him, wearing Sark's flesh like a borrowed coat. During the brief moments he became lucid, Sark always begged to be let out of the cage. Gobleka wasn't sure it was Sark talking. It wasn't the magos pleading to be let out of the metal cage, it was the thing inside him whining to be let out of the coat of flesh it was clothed in.

Now, even the coat was wearing out. They needed a viable replacement, especially if they were going to honour the King's request to increase productivity.

Gobleka heard footsteps on the metal stairs behind him, despite the roar of the Loom.

Davinch was ascending to the control platform, half dragging a heavyset man in a black coat. The man's hands were cuffed in front of him, and he was hunched over in pain. Davinch was all but having to force him to walk.

But Davinch had a supremely satisfied look on his scrawny, tattooed face.

'I got him,' he said.

Gobleka walked over. The man in the black coat was standing with his shoulders down and his head bent forwards. He was breathing hard as if he had just run a marathon. Gobleka saw blood dripping from his hands and from the chain of his cuffs.

Gobleka reached out, grabbed the man by the jaw and forced his head up so he could look him in the eyes.

Eisenhorn. The great and mighty Gregor Eisenhorn. His eyes were dead and lifeless. His skin was pale and blotchy, and blood ran from his nose. He was having trouble breathing. Gobleka looked him up and down, and saw the years of scar tissue, the old augmetics under the coat, the leg braces and strapped servo-reinforcement. The man was withered and broken, and had been long before Davinch had got his murderous hands on him.

'I've looked forward to this moment,' said Gobleka. 'Imagined it, you know. What I'd say, what you'd say. All that. But you're a lot less than I expected. Damaged and weak. And old. Bit of a disappointment, really.'

'Imagine,' replied Eisenhorn, grunting the words out between rasping breaths, 'imagine how little I care.'

'Ooh!' grinned Gobleka, play-acting scared. 'Still got it, have you? Still got the old edge, eh? Or that's what you'd like to think. Give me some more, so I can tell people afterwards that breaking you was noble labour, not a piece of piss.'

Eisenhorn didn't reply.

'Where's the blood coming from?' Gobleka asked Davinch.

'Blayg plugged him,' Davinch replied. 'Body shot.'

'Did you patch it?'

'I didn't have a med-pack with me,' said Davinch.

'Well, get one, now,' said Gobleka. 'And get the kit too.'

Davinch nodded and moved to the lockers at the end of the bank of cogitators.

'Where is Blayg?' Gobleka called out as he stood studying Eisenhorn.

'Head shot,' replied Davinch, sorting through supplies.

'Have you seen Streekal?'

'Not a sign,' Davinch replied. He came back with a trauma pack. Gobleka opened it, took out a tube of wound sealant and rammed the applicator nozzle into the glistening hole in Eisenhorn's abdomen. Eisenhorn winced, but remained on his feet.

Gobleka pressed the activator and pumped sealant into the wound. Then he walked around Eisenhorn, yanked up his old, black coat and did the same to the exit wound.

He tossed the tube back to Davinch.

'I said get the kit, Davinch,' he snapped. 'So, get the kit.'

Davinch hurried back to the lockers. Gobleka peered into Eisenhorn's eyes. Eisenhorn just glared into the distance and ignored the eerie violet eyes fixing him.

'Did you search him?' Gobleka asked.

'Of course,' Davinch called back. 'A few bits and pieces. A back-up gun in his chest rig. I took that.'

'Now, what's going to happen,' Gobleka said to Eisenhorn, standing so close they were nose-to-nose, 'is that I'm going to help you. That's a surprise, isn't it? I'm going to keep you alive. I'm going to take the pain away. *All* the pain, physical and mental. That frigged-up psyker mind of yours must be ready to burst by now, right?'

Eisenhorn said nothing.

'This is a big day for you, you know?' said Gobleka. 'Think of it like... think of it like this is what your entire life has been about. Everything you are, everything you've ever done, leading up to this moment. Right here.'

'I think he was trying to trick us,' said Davinch, returning with the kit. 'You know? Like... get caught. He knew he couldn't get past us, so I think he figured he'd let us take him so he could pull some stunt once he was here.'

'Is that it?' Gobleka asked Eisenhorn sidelong as he prepped an injector. 'That didn't work out so well, did it? If that was your plan, it turned into all kinds of shit, didn't it? And there's no one to bail you out, either. They're all dead. You understand that, don't you? They're all dead, all your followers and associates. And if they're not, they will be soon. The magos is hunting them down, any that are left. His instruments are loose in the tower. Your friends, Gregor Eisenhorn, you've brought them to a very, very bad end, you know that? If there are any left alive, which I very much frigging doubt, their deaths will be the most awful thing you can imagine. I bet they wish they'd never signed on. I bet they wish they'd never followed you, and never trusted that you knew what you were doing. You know, I bet their last living thought is hate. Hate for you. Hate for getting them into this mess. Your friends will die *hating* you for–'

'They're not my friends,' said Eisenhorn.

Gobleka grinned, and checked the dose-load of the injector. 'Oh, I don't think that's true. You've got to be a man's friend to follow him into hell.'

Eisenhorn turned his head, slowly, and looked at Davinch.

'He follows you,' he said.

'Davinch?' Gobleka laughed. 'He's paid to. Paid very well. Besides, he sees the bigger picture. The great reward awaiting all those who participate.'

'So do the people who follow me,' said Eisenhorn.

'Do they?' asked Gobleka. 'Do they really? Did you ever tell them, your friends, that you lied to them? That you're mad and outlawed and obsessed? That the path you walk is one of pain, and it's untrue? That your cause is doomed, and everyone knows it? Even the Rot-God-King. Your side is the *losing* side. You follow the False Emperor, Eisenhorn. You pledged your life to Him. You backed the wrong side in this struggle. And that's just a fact.'

'We'll agree to disagree,' growled Eisenhorn.

'No,' said Gobleka. 'From day one, since before the Emperor was the Emperor, it was always going to go this way. Ordained, predicted, projected, prophesied. Chaos will always prevail. It's a universal law. Order does not endure. Chaos overwhelms. Entropy, Eisenhorn. All systems break down eventually. Everything wears out, everything falls apart. The universe returns to its preordained natural state, and that's Chaos, forever and always.'

Eisenhorn remained silent.

'You don't have to take my word for it,' said Gobleka. 'I'm going to show you. That's part of my gift to you today. I'm going to share the truth with you, the truth that's always been, so you can see it and know it for yourself. The scales will fall from your eyes, man, and you will think yourself such a fool to have believed otherwise.'

'You don't know me very well, do you?' asked Eisenhorn.

'See this?' asked Gobleka, raising the injector. 'Sark's masterpiece. An engineered viral inoculant. A miraculous thing. He isolated it from samples collected by his grandfather–'

'The Torment,' said Eisenhorn.

Gobleka grinned. 'A man of learning! Yes, the Torment. Uhlren's Pox. It had so many wonderful names. A gift of the warp, a pestilence like no other. This is inert, of course. An antigenic Sark engineered from the original pathogen. It won't kill you. Well, it probably won't. It will transform you... what you are... how you think. It will remake you in wonderful ways. The way Sark remade himself so he could operate the Loom.'

'Why?' asked Eisenhorn.

'Why what?'

'Why are you giving it to me?'

'Well,' said Gobleka, 'for one it will transfigure you and allow you to see the truth, and–'

'Make me, what? Join you?' asked Eisenhorn.

'Pretty much,' laughed Davinch.

'That won't work,' said Eisenhorn.

'Ah,' said Gobleka. 'Of course. Because of your infamous willpower. Your will, so firm and unshakeable that no temptation or malice can topple it. Eisenhorn, listen... I may have mocked you, but I'm not an idiot. I know you're a man of considerable talents and abilities. Your career shows that. You have particular strengths and skills that could make you very useful to us. To Lilean. Not in your present state, of course. I know you'd never join us. I respect that, even. But this isn't a choice you're going to make.'

Eisenhorn glared at him.

'Seriously,' said Gobleka. 'The Torment antigenic is horrible. This will hurt. Most subjects do not survive. Only Magos Sark has ever lived through more than one shot of it. But I think you will, simply because you're so strong. And the inoculant, once it's scorching through your system, will have plenty to work with. That psyker mind of yours, for example. You have walked in the dark for too many years, exposed your psi-active mind to the warp. It's left its imprint on you. You are an... etheric sensitive, far closer in nature to the creatures you hunt than you'd ever care to admit. You are ripe and ready. A very suitable candidate.'

'Where do you want it?' Davinch asked.

'Throat,' replied Gobleka. He looked back at Eisenhorn.

'Forget your will,' he said. 'Forget resisting. It's not a matter of that. The Torment antigenic will modify you, alter your entire state of being. You will see the warp and *be* the warp, and that will be all. It won't be a matter of accepting it. It will simply be true.'

'You're very certain of these things you keep describing as facts,' said Eisenhorn.

'It's my job,' said Gobleka. 'My service to Orpheus, the King in Yellow. He trusts me to get it right.'

He glanced at Davinch.

'Hold him steady,' he ordered.

Davinch closed in, reaching up to drag Eisenhorn's collar down and expose his throat. Gobleka stepped forwards with the injector.

Eisenhorn's hands were cuffed with military-issue binders. He couldn't pull them apart, so he clenched them together instead, fingers intertwined. As Davinch closed in to seize him, he swung his fists like a club into the tattooed man's gut.

He was not as tired and weak as they had presumed.

Davinch barked out air and doubled up. Eisenhorn brought his hands down, now separated, so that the cuff-chain hooked around the back of Davinch's neck. He slammed down, driving Davinch's face into the metal bracing of his rising kneecap.

Bone cracked. Davinch fell away, moaning and choking. Gobleka was lunging in with the injector.

Every movement hurt. Eisenhorn's gut wound was severe, and just moving abruptly, raising his knee to take down Davinch, had torn the traumatised wound and broken the sealant packing. He felt blood suddenly spill down his back.

He raised both arms and blocked Gobleka. Gobleka was bigger than him and much stronger. He elbowed Eisenhorn's block aside and punched him in the jaw. Eisenhorn staggered a few steps, inadvertently stepping on Davinch's splayed fingers. Davinch was down on his hands and knees, trying to recover. He yelled in pain as Eisenhorn's iron-shod boot crunched across his hand.

Eisenhorn turned and kicked Davinch in the rump, throwing him flat on the deck in Gobleka's path. Gobleka vaulted the fallen man deftly and came at Eisenhorn again. With his hands cuffed, Eisenhorn could only upper-block to one side or the other. Gobleka feinted a punch from the left then kicked hard with his right foot. The kick hit Eisenhorn in the hip, but his bracing armature took most of the force. Eisenhorn swung his fists at Gobleka, but the man leaned out of the swing, then lunged in and caught the chain of Eisenhorn's cuffs with his left hand. He wrenched Eisenhorn's hands and arms down and to the side. Eisenhorn had no choice but to twist away, exposing his neck to the injector Gobleka was stabbing in with his other hand.

There was no point fighting Gobleka's haul on the cuff-chain. Eisenhorn went with it instead, allowing himself to be dragged down. He ducked into the stabbing motion and rammed his shoulder into Gobleka's chest.

Gobleka stumbled backwards, cursing. He had dropped the injector. He reached for it. Eisenhorn kicked it further along the deck.

'Is this it?' Gobleka taunted him angrily. 'Is this the trick you were going to pull? The stunt you were waiting to play?'

'Seems to be working,' growled Eisenhorn.

Gobleka sprang at him. Eisenhorn blocked again with both forearms, then swung his fists together hard. He caught Gobleka's bearded jaw and knocked him sideways across the platform. Gobleka crashed into the bank of cogitators. A screen smashed. Data-slates tumbled to the deck.

'Frigging help me, you idiot!' Gobleka yelled at Davinch.

Davinch was getting up. His nose and lips were a mangled mask of blood. He spat, drawing one of his laspistols.

'Don't kill him,' Gobleka ordered.

The tattooed man cursed aloud and went for Eisenhorn. He twisted the laspistol in his grip and began to beat at Eisenhorn with the weapon's butt. Eisenhorn tried to evade. He raised his chained fists to deflect the blows. Davinch kept hitting. Eisenhorn ducked low and hooked the cuff-chain around Davinch's elbow. Eisenhorn locked his fingers and swung, throwing Davinch off his feet.

He landed hard. Eisenhorn kicked him to keep him down and unlaced his fingers, freeing his cuffed hands from the man's arm. But Gobleka had grabbed him from behind. He had the injector again.

Eisenhorn tried to tear himself away. Gobleka stabbed in with the needle. Eisenhorn got his hands up, trying to block. The injector's needle wedged in the taut loops of the cuff-chain, centimetres from Eisenhorn's throat.

Eisenhorn twisted his wrists, and the cuffs plucked the injector out of Gobleka's hands. It went flying down the platform.

Gobleka broke off and turned to run for it. Eisenhorn moved after him, but was tackled from the side by Davinch. Together, they slammed into the cogitator bank. They grappled. Teeth gritted, hissing blood, Davinch clamped his hand around the back of Eisenhorn's head and rammed his face into the edge of a cogitator's casing. Eisenhorn stamped back into Davinch's shin. As the man screamed in pain, Eisenhorn rotated, grabbed him by the front of his jacket and heaved him into the bank of screens. Another shattered, billowing sparks.

Eisenhorn had his weight on him. Davinch couldn't pivot. He reached up and clawed at Eisenhorn's throat. He got a grip and began to throttle, his fingers biting into Eisenhorn's neck. Eisenhorn let himself be pulled down. He let go of the tattooed man's jacket and allowed his hands to slide up the man's chest, until he had a hand on either side of the man's neck. The cuff-chain bit down into Davinch's throat. Davinch started to splutter and choke, spitting gobs of blood. His legs milled wildly. He let go of Eisenhorn's neck and began to pummel frantically.

Eisenhorn knew he didn't have time to finish the kill. Gobleka was coming in again from behind. He grabbed Davinch by the shoulders, pulled the thrashing man around and smashed his head backwards through a cogitator screen.

Davinch slithered out of the unit in a shower of broken glass and tubing valves, and fell sideways onto the deck.

Eisenhorn turned to meet Gobleka. Gobleka circled, head low, tossing the injector from hand to hand like a knife, daring Eisenhorn with each hand. He dummied, then lunged, the injector in his right hand. Eisenhorn sidestepped and tried to sweep Gobleka into an over-extension with his cuffed hands. But Gobleka was surefooted, and he shoulder-barged Eisenhorn in the belly. He carried him backwards and drove his spine into the platform's handrail.

Searing pain flared from the exit wound as it hit the rail. Eisenhorn gasped. Gobleka drove him again, then threw a low punch into his gut to agonise the entry wound as well. Eisenhorn stumbled sideways, flailing with his cuffed hands, trying to keep Gobleka at bay.

'We're done, you old bastard,' said Gobleka, panting, and wiping his mouth with the back of his hand. He hawked and spat on the deck. 'All done now.'

Eisenhorn swayed, leaning on the handrail to stay upright. He clawed with his cuffed hands and found the injector sticking out of his neck. He tried to pull it out. His fingers were numb and wouldn't work properly.

He fell to one knee, gasping. He finally managed to yank the injector out, but he could see it was empty.

He looked up at Gobleka. Davinch hobbled into view, dripping blood. He clutched Gobleka's shoulder for support.

'You get him?' he asked through swollen lips.

'I got him,' said Gobleka.

TWENTY-TWO

SARK'S INSTRUMENTS

Look away,' said Drusher simply. He grabbed Macks, pushed her face into his shoulder, and fired. The shot went through Hadeed Garofar's chest. The pinpricks of emerald light in what had once been the deputy's eyes went out. His body fell back hard on the catwalk decking.

Macks looked up at Drusher. Her eyes were streaming with tears.

'Those bastards,' she whispered. 'I am going to kill *all* of them.'

'Keep moving! Keep moving!' Voriet yelled.

More animations were approaching around the curved catwalk. One was a rotting thing, the others, two skeletal horrors that looked like they had been burned and fused. All crackled with green electricity. They all advanced slowly, one halting step at a time, but a fourth appeared behind them. It was Deputy Edde. Her eyes were blank, and her throat was a black mess of clotted blood.

She pushed past the skeletal things, advancing swiftly, with expressionless determination.

'Go!' shouted Nayl. He knocked Edde down with a single shot, then turned to run after the others. Drusher and Macks were almost carrying Voriet. He was murmuring in pain from the vigorous motion. There was no time to be gentle about it.

They came around the curve of the catwalk. There were two more animations right in front of them. One, the closest, was a stained brown skeleton draped in tatters of skin and disintegrating clothes. The other, a woman, was a mangled nightmare that looked like it had been systematically pulped with a hammer.

She was moving faster, blood leaking from her ruptured flesh. Drusher fired, but he was hasty, and his shot went wide. He fired again, and the mangled thing dropped bonelessly onto the deck.

But the skeletal animation was right on them. Macks yelled and shoved Drusher and Voriet out of the way. Voriet fell hard, jolting his arm and shrieking. The skeletal thing reached for Macks, clawing, but she evaded and turned her dive into a tumble that took her out from under its swinging arm. It turned instead on the helpless Voriet. Soil-caked finger bones grasped at him, flickering with the lambent ghosts of the flesh and tendons that had once been there. Voriet tried to crawl out of its path, dragging urgently with his working arm.

Drusher shot it point-blank through the back of the skull. The cranium exploded in a shower of bone shards and old loam, and the entire skeleton disarticulated, falling in an avalanche of disjointed pieces.

Nayl hauled Voriet to his feet.

'The stairs!' he barked. There was a long ascending flight to the next platform level further down the curve of the catwalk. Macks grabbed Drusher by the hand, and they started to run. Ahead and behind them, they could see more animations: slow plodding things of bone and faster, striding things that still had some or all of their soft tissue. The closest was a grim cadaver with an arm missing. Ghostly green light flickered an afterimage of where the limb had been.

Drusher shot it in the chest. He turned his aim towards the other advancing animations.

'No, magos. We can make it,' Nayl advised. He had Voriet hoisted over his shoulder. 'Don't waste any more rounds.'

'All right,' Drusher agreed.

'How many have you got left?' asked Nayl.

'I don't know. How many fit into one of these?'

'Eight,' snapped Nayl. 'How many did you fire?'

'I have no idea! Stop asking me questions!' Drusher replied.

'How many have you got left, Nayl?' asked Macks.

They had reached the foot of the stairs. The nearest animations were rushing to block them, marching briskly, like passengers late for a transit. One was a woman with part of her face missing. The other was a man who had no head at all.

Nayl put a careful shot into each of them. They toppled.

'How many *shots*, Nayl?' Macks roared.

'Now?' Nayl replied. 'None.'

They ran up the stairs. It was a long flight, straight up to the next level. Drusher and Macks led the way, with Nayl lagging behind supporting Voriet. Animations were closing in at the stair foot.

From somewhere very high above, somewhere up in the sickly light, they heard a scream. The sound of a man in unbearable anguish. It rang out for several moments above the din of the working Loom, then faded.

'That was him,' said Nayl, a look of horror on his face.

'Eisenhorn?' asked Macks, looking back at him.

Voriet nodded.

'I think Harlon's right,' he said.

'We keep going anyway,' insisted Drusher. He took another couple of steps, looked up and saw a hunched, stained skeleton looking down at him from the top of the steps. Jade light glinted in its vacant orbits. It began to step towards them.

'Back?' he said.

'They're already on the stairs,' Nayl shouted.

Drusher raised his pistol and fired. The shot clipped the animation's head, above the left eye, splintering bone, and almost swung the skull around through a hundred and eighty degrees. The animating force in it broke and died, and the bones collapsed and tumbled down the steps. Some dropped over the edge through the rails. Macks and Drusher flinched to avoid the ones that bounced past their feet.

'Get moving!' Nayl shouted from behind them. They started to run. Drusher wondered what else might be waiting for them at the top.

'What does it mean when a gun does this?' he asked, showing the pistol to Macks as they took the steps two at a time. The slide was jammed and locked all the way back.

'It means it's empty,' she replied.

She looked back at Nayl.

'Nayl, we're all out of specials,' she cried.

'Damn,' said Nayl.

'Nayl!' she cried. She'd seen something behind him.

The animations were already ascending after them, the slower ones hobbling one step at a time. But one was moving fast, much faster than the others. It was pushing past them, scrambling after the four fleeing humans.

It was lithe, jet-black and gleaming. Macks realised that its strange appearance was simply because it was covered, head to foot, in promethium residue.

It was Streekal. The oil filming her staring eyes was backlit by the green glow inside her head, like the rangefinder in a battlesuit's visor. Her mouth was open and slack, and viscous ropes of promethium drooled out of it.

'Move! Move! Move!' yelled Nayl. He wasn't sure if he and Voriet could reach the top of the stairs before Streekal reached them. But he knew for sure that even if they did, they no longer had any way of stopping her.

They ran for the top of the stairs. Nayl picked up Voriet again. Drusher and Macks reached the top. They looked around. There was nothing on the platform, no horrors looming to grab at them.

They turned.

'Nayl! Run!' Drusher yelled. He unlocked the slide and fired his pistol at Streekal, hoping Macks was wrong. The snub simply clicked dry.

'Come on! Come on!' he yelled.

'Just get clear!' Nayl roared back, straining at his limit to run and carry the interrogator. Streekal was only twenty steps behind them, ploughing up the stairs tirelessly, the light gleaming off her oil-swathed form.

Macks drew her laspistol.

'That won't do any good,' Drusher yelled at her. 'Haven't you got the hang of this yet? Normal fire won't–'

'Shut up!' she cried. She was fiddling frantically with the weapon, unlocking and resetting the powercell. With a snap of her wrist, she pulled a connector loose then rammed the energy clip back in.

Nayl and Voriet reached the top of the stairs. Drusher grabbed them and hauled them onto the platform so violently, all three fell sprawling together.

Macks turned to face the oncoming Streekal. The glistening black figure was only a few metres away. She could see the oil welling out of Streekal's open mouth and spattering down her chest.

Macks dropped the laspistol onto the top step.

'Everybody down!' she yelled, throwing herself clear.

Drusher heard a high-pitched whine. It got fiercer and louder. A warning signal. Macks had rigged the pistol's energy clip to overload and discharge.

Streekal reached the top five steps. The pistol detonated like a small bomb, releasing all of its significant charge in one bright flash of energy. The blinding explosion blew the weapon apart and took the upper three steps of the staircase with it. Metal shattered. Handrails buckled and spun away. The expanding ball of heat and light enveloped Streekal.

It didn't harm her at all. But the promethium vapour fuming around her ignited. She was engulfed in a sheet of flame, becoming a burning effigy of a human figure.

She kept moving, but the top of the staircase, wrecked by the blast, was shearing away from the platform. The entire stair structure broke away from the top, dipping slowly and catastrophically into space, spilling the animations, fast and slow alike, off its collapsing length. They dropped away into the darkness below, some glancing and bouncing off the gears and struts of the whirring machine.

The staircase broke off at the base, wrenching away from the catwalk supports, and tumbled after the things it had shrugged off into the air. It fell, grinding and screeching, bending and crumpling.

Streekal fell, arms and legs moving uselessly.

Like a comet, trailing fire, she dropped into the depths. The flames of her descent were visible long after all the other plummeting animations had vanished from view.

Then her light vanished too. She had gone back where she had come from, down to the very base of Keshtre's tower.

'Holy Throne,' breathed Drusher, looking down.

Far below, the darkness winked and flickered. There was a sudden glow, red and dull, that swiftly grew brighter and more fierce.

The promethium sump at the base of the tower had ignited.

TWENTY-THREE

THE TORMENT

The fire had been burning for a while. At first, it was far away, down in the darkness where no one could see it, just a dull red glow, roiling in the blackness. It looked as though it would never be serious, never really catch hold, that it would burn itself out and grow cold.

But fire has been deceiving man since it was first given to him by the gods. Or since he first stole it from them. Stories differ. The only truth that matters is that fire likes to betray. It has burned man's hand since first he took possession of it. When he thinks it is extinguished, it leaps back into life and reveals itself in fury, suddenly overwhelming, all-consuming and too strong to fight.

So with this fire. From the dullest glow to a seething inferno, from nothing to everything in the beat of a heart, taking hold, devouring all, leaving nothing but ashes.

Its heat was upon him, stifling him. Its light was in his eyes. His skin was blistering and flaking. His bones were beginning to fuse and melt.

He heard the constant rattling of the Loom, spinning towards eternity, despite the conflagration that enveloped it. But the noise of the Loom and the roaring rush of the fire were both drowned out by the chirring in the air. The clicking whispers. The sound of a trillion invisible insects stridulating in the back of his mind.

He could bear the heat no longer. He was being burned away. The door to the dark room was open, and hard sunlight shafted in from outside. Despite its glare, the light looked cool compared to the flames that lit him from head to toe.

He got up to reach for it. He pulled his burning body from the rough cot to claw at the light.

'Stay still,' the robed man said gently.

'I burn...' he gasped.

'It is the Torment,' the man told him. 'I'm sorry, this is what it does. We have tried many things to ease the pain. Stasis fields. Ice baths. Opiates. Induced coma. Other victims have told me that it burns like hell's fury even in their dreams.'

'Is this a dream?' he asked. His voice was small, without substance, like burning paper lifting into the air as it crisped away.

'I'm sorry, no,' said the robed man. 'Lie back. You are too weak.'

'I will get up,' he insisted. He hauled himself up. The robed man reached to steady him. Why aren't you burning, he thought. I am on fire, you touch me, your hands are on me. Why aren't you burning too?

He shuffled to the open door. The robed man supported him.

'I don't know your name,' the robed man said. 'You were brought to us in.... in this condition. You carried no identity. These are the first words you have spoken.'

'I... My name... is Gregor. Gregor Eisenhorn.'

'I will do all I can to help you, Gregor Eisenhorn,' the robed man said softly.

They stepped out into the light. The air was humid. He could see the deep blue sky above. He could smell the sea. Beyond the old stone walls of the garden, lush green vegetation rose, the skirts of a rainforest that blanketed the sheer flanks of the volcanic flue that stood in the distance, a ghost in the heat-haze.

The chirring of the insects was louder. Uncountable insects chirping in the jungle thickets beyond the ancient walls.

'Where is this?' Eisenhorn asked, squinting in the bright sunlight. 'Is this some other part of Keshtre?'

'I don't know where that is,' said the robed man. His robes were pure white. His skin was very dark. 'I haven't heard of it. Is it where you were?'

'Then... have I folded again?' Eisenhorn asked. 'Is this another extimate overlap?'

'I'm sorry, my friend,' the robed man said. 'I do not understand the terms you use. Gregor, your fever is so high it cannot be measured. You are hallucinating, I think. Hallucinating and confused. You have contracted a pestilence. It is called Uhlren's Pox. It is severe, I'm sorry to say. Your confusion is part of the illness. I should return you to your bed.'

Eisenhorn looked at him.

'Are you one of Gobleka's people?' he asked.

'I don't know the name, Gregor.'

'Are you a doctor? A medicae?'

'I care for those who come here,' the robed man said. 'I am Baptrice.'

Eisenhorn looked around the garden. His raised voice had attracted attention. Three sisters in stark-white robes and starched bicorn wimples observed him with concern. A grizzled old man sat on a garden seat beside the wall. He was naked except for an old ammunition belt, and his left arm was nothing but a mass of old scar tissue. He was putting brass shell-cases into the loops of the bandolier and then taking them out again, counting each time. '...six, seven, *eight*... six, seven, *eight*.'

'What is this place?' Eisenhorn asked.

'The Hospice of Saint Bastian,' the robed man said.

'On... Symbal Iota?' Eisenhorn asked.

'Yes,' said Baptrice. 'You know where you are, then?'

'What... year? What year is it, sir?'

'Gregor, it is the third year of the Genovingian Campaign and–'

Eisenhorn broke free of his hands and walked out onto the lawn. The insects were so loud.

'Gregor?' called Baptrice. 'You are lucid. I have never seen such lucidity in a patient so tight in the grip of the Torment. I would like you to speak with someone, if you are able. He might learn a great deal from you.'

'Who?' asked Eisenhorn.

'His name is Sark,' said Baptrice.

'Draven Sark?'

'No, sir,' said Baptrice, frowning. 'Lemual Sark. Higher Administrator Medica Lemual Sark. He is visiting us. His speciality is Materia Medica, and–'

'I want to leave now,' said Eisenhorn.

'That cannot be permitted,' said Baptrice sadly.

'Why are you showing me this?' Eisenhorn asked.

'Showing you... what?' asked Baptrice.

Eisenhorn wasn't talking to him. He was staring down at his own hands. Old hands marked with old scars, hands that were dirty with soot and machine oil. Hands that were covered in yellow blisters from the fire that was eating him away.

'Why are you showing me this?' he asked the fire in his blood. 'This is... this is your place of birth. Where you... where the truth of you crossed Sark's path and the connection was made. Where the infection began. Carried not as a disease but as an idea, from father to son to grandson...'

'Sisters!' Baptrice called. There was worry in his voice. 'Help me conduct this poor soul back to his confinement. He is delusional and very sick. I fear for his safety out here.'

The sisters approached. Their robes were ice-white, and their horned cowls trembled as they walked. There were more of them than before. Ten, fifteen...

'Come, Gregor,' said Baptrice. 'Let me take you back. Let the fever run its course. There is hope yet.'

'There was no patient with the Torment housed in this place,' said Eisenhorn. 'No outbreak occurred here at the hospice. It was an asylum. There was only a survivor. One man, an inmate who had survived the pandemic. I have read the reports. This is a lie. You are a lie.'

'Help me with him,' Baptrice smiled. The sisters closed around, their white bicorn wimples like tusks in the sunlight. More of them now, forty, fifty...

'I want to leave,' said Eisenhorn.

'Restrain him gently,' Baptrice said. 'He knows not what he says.'

The sisters surrounded him. There were more of them now than there were chirring insects in the jungle outside. Eisenhorn staggered through them, brushing aside their phantom hands and their snow-white robes. He started to walk, pushing them aside. Somewhere, a cloister bell began to ring. He reached the iron gate in the old garden wall. Beyond, the green darkness of the jungle swarmed with the fricative words of insects.

The flames swirled around him. He opened the gate and stumbled through.

'I suppose you get a lot of cases like mine,' sniffed the small man waiting for him on the other side of the desk.

'Cases?' asked Eisenhorn. The room was cool and grey, as if it were raining outside, or the place were always starved of light. There was a large, ornamental fireplace that clearly had not seen a fire in centuries, a rug on the wooden floor and two plain chairs on either side of the desk. The old man sat in one. A gilt clock stood on the mantle, ticking like an insect in a jungle thicket, steady and slow.

'You may take a seat,' the small man offered. 'Of your own volition. You might as well be comfortable. We're here to talk.'

Eisenhorn sat. The old man was shrivelled and bent, lost in the folds of his hand-me-down robes.

'You get a lot of cases like mine,' he sniffed.

'I don't understand,' said Eisenhorn.

'Oh, you understand. You *understand*, sir. You just don't care. And because you don't care, you don't remember.'

'What am I supposed to remember?' asked Eisenhorn.

'The people you have ruined,' said the man. 'How many is it? Lost count? I'm sure you remember the truly great ones. Pontius Glaw, you'd remember him. Stopping him was the making of you. Or was it the breaking? What about the others? The nondescript ones? The minor cases? The insignificant ones? The innocent? Do you remember them? Or are they just faces that passed you by? Do you remember me?'

'I remember this room,' said Eisenhorn. 'I remember that clock, ticking like–'

'Oh, you remember the *room* do you? That's nice,' said the man. 'Of course you remember this room. It's where you brought them to. All of them. This room and a thousand like it. A room in which to talk. A room in which to slowly dismantle a man's life. How many lives is it now? How many have you brought here? Not the notorious, vile ones, I mean the ones like me. The unfortunates. The ones who walked in off the street, troubled by some minor transgression, only to find they were going to be rendered down. Their pride. Their hopes. Their dreams. Their lives. Their livelihoods. Their possessions. Did you pause to care for any of them?'

'I don't remember *you*,' said Eisenhorn.

'Rather my point, interrogator,' the man said. 'Is it interrogator still? It was then. I'm sure it isn't any more. What are you now?'

'Nothing,' said Eisenhorn.

'Then we are turned about, sir,' said the small man. 'For last we met, I was nothing to you. My name is Imus. Does that stir anything?'

'No.'

'No, of course not. You have always been very good at your job, sir. Very good. You have excelled in your duties. Shall I tell you why?'

'I feel you're going to, Master Imus,' said Eisenhorn.

'Because you never care,' said Imus. 'You are without compunction. This allows you to perform your duty with intense purpose. No sentiment gets in the way.'

'Drusher said that,' murmured Eisenhorn.

'Drusher?' asked Imus. 'Friend of yours?'

'No.'

Imus grinned.

'I knew the answer would be no, you see,' he said, 'because you have no friends. No one comes close to you. You do not allow them to. A connection with another soul would be weakness. Which is why a hundred thousand people have passed through this room, and you have disassembled them all, and you cannot even remember their names. Now, this heartless bearing of yours explains why you are very good at what you do. But it begs the question... why do it at all?'

'Why do it?' Eisenhorn asked.

'Yes, yes! Keep up. Why devote your life to the protection of mankind, when you cannot abide the close connection of another human being?'

'Ordo service is hard,' said Eisenhorn. 'One must put aside certain things. One must stand apart and keep to the shadows. It–'

'Poppycock,' said Imus. He drummed his bony fingers on the desktop. 'The Ruinous Powers, sir, in your expert opinion, are they a contaminant?'

'Yes,' said Eisenhorn.

'Like an infection? A disease? Once contracted, even from the briefest contact with a carrier, never cured?'

'Yes,' said Eisenhorn. The insect-tick of the clock was scratching at his mind. 'It is the great horror of the warp. It never leaves a man once it has stained his hands. Corruption is inevitable.'

'Yet you have touched it, sir.'

'An obligation of my work,' said Eisenhorn.

'True,' said Imus. 'Also true, and a fact you know well... All inquisitors end. They are, by necessity, finite. The work they do... How can I put it? It *tarnishes* them. They are carriers. Infected with the torment of their duty. No matter how noble and dedicated, it gets them all in the end. Doesn't it?'

'The Inquisition has safeguards–'

'Indeed it does,' said Imus. 'Retirement from active service. Restraint. Incarceration. The Inquisition watches itself. When one of its own goes too far, becomes too lost, he is declared heretic as quickly and undeniably as any Archenemy rogue.'

'That's how it must be.'

'But you consider yourself an exception?' asked Imus.

'No, I...' Eisenhorn paused.

'You always knew the path you were walking. You knew the cost. You knew the inevitable–'

'I always accepted that.'

'But now you deny it,' said Imus. 'For so many years, sir, they tried to get you to stop. To retire before it was too late. Your friends – forgive me, I misspoke. The people you *described* as your friends, they all tried, didn't they? And you ignored them. Because you knew better. You overruled them. You cast them aside. They stopped being the people you described as friends. Some died, and you never cared. Some battled you to halt your progress, and you crushed them for it. And now you're here in this room. Even the Holy Ordos, which you claim to serve so dutifully, have declared you a heretic.

Diabolus extremis. And yet, *they* are wrong. Because you know better. You will disregard their authority and carry on anyway, alone and friendless – though you always *were* – claiming to serve the Inquisition even though it no longer wants your service.'

'I know things that–'

Imus held up a hand so small and scrawny it looked like a bird's claw.

'No one's listening any more, sir,' he said. 'Not even you. Look at yourself – broken beyond measure, obsessed. Serving on for decades, beyond any point that is wise or healthy. Always driving forward because *you* know best. You serve mankind, but you have only contempt for the people who cross your path. You use people. You neglect any bonds that might be considered friendship and which constitute the foundation of humanity. You forget the faces and the names of those whose lives you change. People die for you, and you care not.'

Imus pushed back his chair and rose to his feet.

'You should think about it, interrogator,' he said, 'why you do what you do.'

'I know why,' said Eisenhorn.

'The thing is, you poor fellow, you don't. And it's right there in front of you. The truth, staring you in the face. You're so good at finding the truth, yet you fail dismally to find it in yourself.'

'And what is the truth, Master Imus?' Eisenhorn snapped.

'Look at yourself, sir, and tell me what *you* would call a man like you,' said Imus.

Eisenhorn shifted in his seat uncomfortably. He looked at his hands and saw how badly they were seared. Blisters, contracture, third-degree burns, perhaps fourth.

From the fire inside him.

'Sir?' Imus called out. 'Are you quite well? You look rather ill at ease.'

'I'm... I'm burning,' whispered Eisenhorn.

'Like last time?' asked Imus.

'What?'

'When last we sat together in this room, you caught fire. Head to foot. I was most terrified. The fire, it burned your skin and roasted the flesh off your bones until nothing was left, except a torched skull staring back at me.'

'That wasn't real,' mumbled Eisenhorn.

'No, it wasn't,' said Imus. 'It was a trick. A wretched trick of your psyker mind. You did it to scare me, to make me quail. It worked, by Throne it worked. The most terrible thing, and I have never forgotten it, or forgiven you for scaring me like that. Do you remember why you did it?'

'To elicit a response–'

'To elicit a response!' cried Imus. He smiled and opened the glass front of the clock on the mantle. 'That's it exactly. You did it to scare the crap out of me, pardon my language. It was intimidation. Bullying. You've done that your whole life. You did it to get at the truth. Do you remember what you said about that?'

'N-no,' said Eisenhorn, wracked with pain.

'You said that fear simplifies the mind,' said Imus. 'You said it is so strong and pure, it empties the head and removes all barriers and falsehoods. You scared me so you could read the truth inside me, the honest part of me that I could not dissemble.'

'It was a technique,' replied Eisenhorn, fighting to remain conscious. He rose to his feet, found he was too unsteady and sat down again. 'A standard Ordo technique. Just a mind-trick. The fire burning me is real.'

Imus craned his reedy neck and peered at the face of the clock. He began to adjust the hands.

'Real?' he asked, as if only half listening. 'What's real? Look at us, here, in this room. What's real about that? It's just another technique. Another mind-trick. Another phantom fire to burn through to the truth. To... How did you put it? Empty your head and remove all barriers and falsehoods. Fear, sir, to simplify the mind.'

'No,' said Eisenhorn. He took a deep breath. A shadow seemed to have passed over what little daylight existed outside, and the room was darker than ever. 'It is the Torment. The antigenic at work. It's a hallucination. Sark designed the inoculant to condition the mind. To strip away the will. To brainwash–'

'No, he didn't,' said Imus mildly. 'That's not really what it does. It doesn't make you think differently, sir. It makes you think *truly*. It burns away all the psychological armour and rationalisations and excuses a man has accumulated through his life, and shows him the truth that's always lurked underneath it all. Like fear, it simplifies the mind.'

Eisenhorn rested his face in his hands, his elbows on the edge of the desk, and concentrated to control his breathing and moderate the agony.

'I'm weary,' he said, quietly, 'of people telling me that I've... I've crossed some arbitrary line. It's not the truth, and this... this delusion won't convince me otherwise. You're just an old memory, being used as a puppet by the Torment antigenic to get me to confess to something that isn't true.'

'Of course it isn't true,' said Imus. 'You haven't become a heretic. You are quite right to be resolute about that. Why, that absolute certainty is what helps you remain so defiant against accusations. You can conscientiously insist you have not become a heretic, no matter what your old masters say.'

Eisenhorn looked at the old man.

'The real truth,' said Imus, with a smile, 'the thing we've met in this room to winkle out of you, is far more simple. Will you admit it to me?'

'I don't know what–'

'Then I will say it,' said Imus. 'The warp has always been in you. Right from the start. It has called to you, and you have followed it. You wear the robes of an inquisitor to get close to it, and you finish any who dare compete with you for its affections. You are not a heretic because the Inquisition has *proclaimed* you one. You have not slowly *become* a heretic after years of stalking the dark. You have *always* been one.'

Imus grinned at Eisenhorn.

'You must know that's the case,' Imus said. 'Well, you must get a lot of cases like yours. You came to this place of your own volition. You know what happens in this room. You have always been a heretic, Gregor Eisenhorn.

You simply haven't ever had the clarity to recognise the fact. You do now. The barriers are burned down. Fear has simplified your mind. You cannot dissemble.'

'No,' said Eisenhorn. He rose to his feet.

'Come now, don't threaten me,' said Imus. He finished adjusting the clock and closed its case. 'I've been dead for two hundred years. You, you have never lived. You do not walk in darkness. You are darkness. It's always been too late to turn back. It's in your blood. Like a fire that won't go out. You should accept it. That's what you told me and a hundred thousand like me. Accept your transgression and you will find relief. A burden lifted. Embrace it. The warp is your only friend, and it's been waiting for you for a long time.'

Eisenhorn felt the flames rise up, eating at him eagerly.

'This is trickery,' he insisted. 'Fever–'

'No,' replied Imus. 'It's the truth, which is always the most painful thing of all. End your torment, sir. Accept what you are. Acknowledge what you have always been. The pain will be brief. Beyond the pain, why... it is so very beautiful.'

Eisenhorn shook his head. Fire was gnawing his bones away.

'You think the warp is your enemy,' said Imus. 'But it's the only true thing there is. The one constant. Your only friend. Species rise and fall, Imperiums come and go. The warp remains. Bow down and let it take you. It's what you've always secretly wanted.'

The door banged open.

'Will this take much longer, Gregor?' asked Titus Endor. 'I've got things planned.'

Imus sniffed and looked at the clock.

'About time,' he murmured. 'I was getting bored of this.'

Endor drew his autosnub and shot four rounds into the old man. Imus fell into the fireplace and smashed into a hundred thousand fragments of old Sameterware pottery.

'Come on,' said Endor, grinning. 'There's still time to get out. There's always time to get out.'

He took Eisenhorn by the arm and bustled him out of the gloomy room.

'You'll burn yourself,' Eisenhorn said, looking down at Endor's hand gripping him.

'Anything for a friend,' laughed Endor. 'You and me, through thick and thin. You knew I'd always come back, if you needed help.'

'From the dead?'

Endor halted and turned to face Eisenhorn. He put his hands on Eisenhorn's shivering shoulders and looked into his eyes, serious and sober.

'Is this about the thing?' Endor asked. 'The... business? It turned things bad between us, I know. Tell me you've forgiven me. You *must* have forgiven me by now. It wasn't my fault, you know? Just circumstances.'

Eisenhorn looked away. He couldn't meet Endor's urgent gaze any more. There were things in Endor's eyes, writhing worm-things like larvae that pressed against the glossy windows of Endor's eyeballs.

He looked around instead. A huge full moon, the colour of flame, was rising over the desert flats. The vast sky was woad-blue, speckled with stars. The endless sands were turmeric-yellow. There wasn't a building around for a hundred kilometres.

'Is this another stage of the fever?' he asked.

'The what?' asked Endor. He began to walk, his boots kicking up fine dust from the soft yellow sand.

'Another part of–'

'Look, forget it, Gregor, will you?' Endor said. 'I let you down. I shouldn't have. I'm sorry. Can we leave that business behind us? Come on, I've come to get you out of there.'

'You shouldn't consort with me,' said Eisenhorn. 'I will destroy you.'

'I don't need you for that,' snorted Endor.

'I am disavowed and declared heretic.'

'Well, you've always been a bit of a rogue–'

'I mean it, Titus. The Ordos have cast me out.'

'They got rid of me too, you know,' said Endor. 'Said I was, you know, unreliable. Took my rosette. Put me out to pasture. What does it matter? I've known you a long time, Gregor. I know what you are.'

'And what is that?' asked Eisenhorn. A sweet desert breeze rose, and dust swirled between them like smoke.

'A friend,' replied Endor, with a smile and shrug.

'I was never much of a friend to you,' said Eisenhorn.

'Ah, I got used to you and your ways,' said Endor.

'I let you die,' said Eisenhorn. 'I think... I think I knew you were sick. I suspected. I knew I couldn't cure you, but I could have come to find you. Made your last years more comfortable.'

'You could have done,' said Endor. 'But let's face it, that's not you, is it?'

'And what *is* me?'

'Throne alive,' laughed Endor. 'You're maudlin already, and we haven't even started drinking yet.'

'What?'

'Come on,' said Endor. 'I can see you're thirsty. Let's put that fire out, eh?'

Figures had gathered ahead of them, a small group seated on rugs and blankets, around a crackling bonfire, under the wide starlit purple of the desert evening. Eisenhorn could hear talking and laughter.

'Look who I found!' Endor announced. The figures looked up. Some laughed. One handed Endor a bottle.

'About time you got here,' said Midas Betancore. He was poking the fire with a stick. The campfire was built in a circle of broken stones, its flames and sparks roaring up into the night. The crackle of the wood was like the chirring click of insects. Betancore's cerise jacket looked like blood in the flame-light.

'Another hour or two and there'd be no bottles left,' said Harlon Nayl. He was lying back on an old Selgioni travel rug, his shoulders propped against a boulder.

'I'm sorry,' Eisenhorn said to him.

'I was joking, boss,' Nayl replied. 'We brought plenty.'

'No, I'm sorry...' said Eisenhorn. 'You were always so loyal, Harlon, and I got you killed. A crass mistake on my part–'

'Just circumstances,' Endor said encouragingly.

'Listen to me,' Eisenhorn said to Nayl. 'I shouldn't have trusted Jaff. That was a stupid error. But even before that, before the actual *fact* of your death, I placed you in danger so many times. I could have got you killed a thousand times over before I actually did–'

'Give him a drink, for Throne's sake!' Midas called out.

'He's maudlin tonight,' agreed Endor. 'Very maudlin. Up in his head, all brooding, as usual. I told him to lighten up.'

'Did that work?' asked Midas.

'Does it ever?' snorted Nayl.

'Here you go,' said Kara Swole. She handed Eisenhorn a glass of amasec.

'Kara,' he said. He was so tired. His resistance was ebbing. They all looked so young.

'Good to see you again,' she replied.

He took the glass. The heat of the fire inside him ignited the vapour of the amasec. Tiny blue flames danced across the surface of his drink.

'Are you dead too?' Eisenhorn asked her.

'As good as,' she said. 'I have walked in your footsteps. Your path only ever leads to one place.'

'Kara–'

'I'm joking! Throne! What's the matter with you tonight?'

'Some die outright,' said a figure on the other side of the fire. 'Some just end up damaged. Their lives ended, to all intents and purposes. It amounts to the same thing.'

Gideon Ravenor gazed through the roaring flames of the campfire at him. He seemed much further away than the rest of them. He was young and handsome, his hair tied back in a long horse tail. He raised his glass.

'Your health,' he said, nodding.

Eisenhorn tried to move around the campfire to approach Ravenor. The fire somehow contrived to remain between them, keeping Ravenor on its far side, constantly watching Eisenhorn through flames.

'Most perturbatory,' said Aemos, at Eisenhorn's side. 'The way the fire moves like that. As if it is sentient, keeping one thing screened from another.'

He glanced up at Eisenhorn and sipped his drink.

'Wouldn't you say so, Gregor?' he asked.

'Strange indeed,' said Eisenhorn. He looked at the old savant.

'Do you recall the Torment?' he asked.

'Which one?' asked Aemos. 'There have been so many.'

'The Torment, Aemos. Uhlren's Pox–'

'Hmmm! Yes. Sequestered Ordo dossier 1767563 triple seraph. Docket 991. Entered by Rubricator Edrick Callik on–'

'Just the details, Aemos.'

'The first outbreak was recorded on Pirody,' said Aemos, 'some thirty-four years before a second pestilence occurred during the third year of the Genovingian Campaign. Ingenious research by the scholars of Materia Medica revealed the plagues to be related forms of the same pathogen. It was untreatable, and the death toll across many infected worlds was immense. Thanks to the work of a recollector called Lemual Sark, it was eventually identified to be a virus engineered by the Ruinous Powers. Indeed, its efficacy had been enhanced by Subjunctus Valis, an Apothecary of the Doom Eagles Chapter, Adeptus Astartes, who had himself succumbed and was under its malign influence. It would seem, you see, the pox had some self-possession, Gregor. A sentience. Ha ha, like the fire! Is that why you asked?'

'Just... go on, Aemos,' said Eisenhorn.

'The Torment took hold of Valis' mind, the poor devil,' said the old man, pondering the facts as he accessed them from his memory. 'It acted through him, guiding his work so as to protect itself and propagate its curse.'

Aemos looked up at Eisenhorn.

'Hardly the subject of light conversation at a gathering of friends,' he smiled.

'The Torment, Aemos, might it also be an infectious idea? Carried and transmitted by thought as well as body?'

'Well, I suppose, at a stretch...' Aemos shrugged.

'And if it was engineered into an inoculant, Aemos? An antigenic. To transmit the idea alone, without the physical malady? To infect thought, not matter?'

'Gregor,' said Aemos, 'I have no idea who in the Holy Imperium would have the talent or means to perform such a feat. Not even the most gifted magos of Materia Medica.'

'Unless the Torment itself willed it?' asked Eisenhorn. 'Took, let's say, a gifted magos of Materia Medica, and showed him how the feat could be achieved? Transformed his mind to devise the technique required?'

'I would think,' said Aemos, 'it would need to also transform his mind to make him even want to do it.'

'A given,' Eisenhorn agreed. 'So, in such circumstances, how could a man fight the antigenic? How could he stop it corrupting his system?'

'I don't suspect he could,' said Aemos, 'if the Torment could overcome the will and physiology of an Adeptus Astartes...'

'It gets to what is already there,' said Ravenor, through the flames. 'It burns through will to whatever lies beneath. The truth, I suppose you'd call it prosaically. It doesn't turn a man into a heretic. It merely burns back everything to reveal the heretic that's always been there.'

Endor had taken Kara in his arms, and they were laughing and dancing a tight and playful zendov across the old travel rugs spread out around the fire. There was no music. They were dancing in time to the crackle of the flames, the steady chirring beat of invisible insects, the tick of an old clock, the hum of words unsounded. Midas was clapping along. Nayl was opening a bottle. Eisenhorn watched as Nayl got up, walked around the campfire and refilled Ravenor's glass. Ravenor looked up at Nayl, smiled. They laughed at some remark.

'Loyalty's a funny thing,' said Nathan Inshabel, perched on a rock nearby.

The firelight flickered across his face. He looked at Eisenhorn. 'Don't you think so?' he asked.

'I do,' replied Eisenhorn.

'It is strong, yet it is fluid,' said Inshabel. 'Strong enough to drag a man to his death, yet fluid enough to flow from one man to another. And it's heritable too. Passed down through the genes, I suppose, like a living idea that will not perish. Thus, it can survive a man's death and pass, say, to his son or daughter, so she might know that loyalty too, and be dragged down in her turn.'

'Not quite like that, papa,' said Thea, sitting on the sand by his feet. 'You can give your life to a cause, an ideal. You serve what you believe in, that's what you taught me.'

'That's what he taught me,' Nathan said, gesturing towards Eisenhorn with his glass.

Thea Inshabel looked at Eisenhorn with violet eyes. 'But that's true, isn't it, sir?'

'I have always thought so,' said Eisenhorn softly.

'I died for you,' said Nathan. 'I became a target because you were a target and, by association, any who stood with you were in the line of fire. In fact, I was bait. All your staff were. Murdered to draw you out. Oh, don't look at me like that. I don't care. I don't blame you. The work we do is not easy. I haven't come here tonight to twist your guilt.'

'Does he have any?' Endor laughed as he whirled past with Kara.

Nathan chuckled. He looked down and rested his hand on his daughter's head.

'I was so proud when she followed me into the service,' he said. 'Proud of a legacy. My child, in sworn service to the Ordos. And to serve you, as I did...'

He looked at Eisenhorn.

'Like father, like daughter,' he said. 'She became bait in turn. Gobleka knew what he was doing, didn't he? He knew how to draw you out. How to play upon what little sentiment you have.'

'Come off it, Nathan!' roared Endor, as he and Kara danced past in the other direction. 'He has none of that either!'

'Or was it the other way around?' asked Nathan.

'What do you mean?' asked Eisenhorn.

Inshabel shrugged. 'You sent her after Gobleka. You knew he would find out about her. Find out who she was. The family tie, the legacy link. Father and daughter, sworn allies of the old bastard. He wouldn't be able to *resist* killing her and using her as bait. Which means he'd show himself. What a cunning way for you to get Goran Gobleka of the Cognitae to give away his location.'

'It wasn't like that,' said Eisenhorn.

'No, it wasn't, papa!' Thea cried.

'He killed her with an ursid,' said Nathan, staring straight at Eisenhorn. 'In a cage. Threw her in alive. Oh, but not before he had tried the antigenic on her, and watched for days as she screamed through the Torment. Another failed test subject. So into the ursid cage with her.'

'Nathan–' Eisenhorn began.

'My child, Gregor, my child. Used as an instrument to advance your obsession. Used and thrown away.'

'As are we all!' cried Nayl, toasting. Everyone raised their glasses, and shouted the words.

'What kind of man uses his friends that way?' asked Lores Vibben, standing at the edge of the firelight, staring at the flames.

'No one uses his *friends* that way, Vibben,' said Midas.

'You had a daughter too,' Vibben said to him.

'I'm sure she'll be here any moment,' said Midas. He took a sip of his drink. 'Won't she, Gregor? My sweet little Medea. It can't be much longer before she joins the party too.'

Eisenhorn turned from the firelight. Its raging heat was still inside him. He walked away from the little camp into the vast blue gloom of the desert night. The moon glared down at him. He heard laughter and voices behind him.

'Gregor!' Endor ran to catch up with him. 'Gregor, where are you going?'

'I'm not part of that,' said Eisenhorn.

'Don't be daft. You're the reason it's happening,' said Endor.

'This is the Torment,' said Eisenhorn. 'This is the deep-stage corruption of the antigenic, breaking down my mind. Delusion. Collapsing memories. Psychic decay. Annihilation of will.'

'Hey, we all have bad days,' said Endor. 'It's not your fault, just circumstances.'

'Titus?'

'Yes, Gregor?'

'Old Hapshant...'

'Him? Throne rest his bones,' said Endor. He took a swig from the bottle of joiliq he was carrying.

'Why did he choose us?' Eisenhorn asked. 'To be his interrogators, all those years ago?'

'Because we were the very best!' Endor exclaimed. He raised his arms and did a little capering jig in a circle around Eisenhorn.

'Seriously, Titus.'

Endor shrugged.

'He saw something in us,' he replied.

'You know how he died,' said Eisenhorn. 'Throne, *you* know too well how he died. The cerebral worms, they destroyed his mind. His judgement. His cognitive function. The doctors said, after he died, that it was hard to tell how long they had been there. Possibly for years, impairing his critical faculties. He had served for far longer than he was fit. Long past the point when the Ordos would have demanded an inquisitor's retirement.'

'What are you saying? That we were recruited by a madman?'

'What if we were?' asked Eisenhorn.

'I think you'll find the selection screening for Ordo service is a little more rigorous than that,' said Endor.

'But he saw something in us,' said Eisenhorn. 'In his madness, long before the outward signs were obvious... in that collapsing mind of his.'

'Yeah? Like what?'

'The spark of something he'd been hunting all his life. The likeness of the Archenemy he had pursued for so long and so far into madness, he could no longer distinguish between light and dark.'

Endor frowned at him.

'I'm no heretic, you arse,' he snapped.

'No,' said Eisenhorn. 'At worst, I think you're a hedonist who never took anything in his life seriously enough. You liked the power of the rosette, the authority, the opportunities. Then, of course, your own madness came upon you.'

He looked at Endor's hurt expression. He could still see the worms moving in Endor's eyes.

'What does that make you, then?' asked Endor coldly.

'I think that's what I'm being asked to consider,' said Eisenhorn. 'I thought this was brainwashing, but it's not. The Torment, the antigenic, it has no agenda. It simply lays a man bare. It reduces him to his base elements so he can see himself. That is how it breaks will.'

'You're kind of babbling, you know that?' said Endor.

'I am on fire, Titus,' said Eisenhorn. 'You can't see it. Maybe you can with those eyes. I am in agony. I burn to the marrow from head to foot with a blood-froth. It is so intense now, I can scarcely feel it.'

'Have a drink,' Endor suggested.

'No, thank you,' Eisenhorn replied. 'Titus, I've always hunted for the truth. My whole life. And now I think I may have found it, and it terrifies me. To see what I am. To see what... I may have always been. Gobleka and the Cognitae, all of them, they're fools. They want to destroy and torture. They want to annihilate. Their motives were simply to hurt me. But there is, I fear, a truth in their philosophy. Gobleka has shown it to me. It's more than he knew. He dug into me to find something to break me, but he didn't have the first clue what he was going to find.'

'What's that, then?' asked Endor.

'A man just like him,' said Eisenhorn. 'No, that's wrong. More than him. Goran Gobleka is a hired killer with aspirations above his abilities. He found someone like the people he serves. Lilean Chase. The King in Yellow.'

He looked at Endor.

'Could yellow mean flames, do you think?' he asked. 'A figure burning from head to foot? On fire entirely? A symbolic name for someone who has burned through and been transmuted? All that they thought they were, torched away, and only the truth left standing?'

'Gregor,' said Endor. 'I want to say, just me to you, I have no bloody *idea* what you're on about.'

Eisenhorn looked at him, hopelessly. He tried to put it into words, easy words, but no words would come out. Only strangled un-word noises. Endor looked puzzled for a moment, then his eyes slowly gave way, and small worms started to writhe and slide down his cheeks. He stood where he was, frozen.

The chirring of the insects grew into a roar, a strident loud, slow click beating time to their din, the mechanism of a clock beating out the seconds.

'It's almost time,' said Ravenor.

Eisenhorn looked up. He was standing in shadow. The huge arch of the Spatian Gate was above him. The chirring of the insects was the roar of the crowds lining the eighteen-kilometre route of the Avenue Victor Bellum. Two billion cheering voices. He could hear the marching bands of the procession approaching, the grumble of the war machines, the thump-step of the Titan engines. He could feel the monumental noise vibrating his diaphragm.

This was Thracian, Hive Primaris. The Day of the Great Triumph. Ravenor was dressed in his finest raiment, his Inquisitorial rosette on his breast, just above the small tribe badge of Clan Esw Sweydyr.

The Spatian Gate was made of gleaming white ethercite, and it was so tall the great Titans could march beneath its span. Ravenor looked up at it. He seemed so young and invulnerable.

'This is it,' he said, smiling. 'Just seconds now. The moment of transformation.'

He looked at Eisenhorn.

'Mine,' he said, 'most particularly. But yours too. This moment changes you. You were always driven Gregor, but what happens here today – what happens to me – it propels you on from this point. With a fury, a rage you never lose. It sets you on the path into the dark places, and from here, there is no turning back for you.

'Even though I try,' he added. 'I try my damnedest. You know what they will make me do, don't you?'

'Hunt for me.'

'Hunt for you. Hunt you down as a heretic. It will take years, Gregor. It will cost us both. And then, at last, we will stand face-to-face in the King's City of Dust, and it will end.'

'How will it end, Gideon?' Eisenhorn asked.

'Oh, how do you think?' replied Ravenor. 'The pupil always outstrips the master.'

'You... you see the future then?'

'Farseeing,' said Ravenor. 'My personal heresy. My vice in the eyes of the Ordos. That's the walk into dark places that I'm going to take, because of this. Trapped in that box, struggling to free my mind and see into... into anything. It will damn me, and the Ordos will have the leverage they need to make me track you down and finish you.'

'If you see the future,' said Eisenhorn. 'Tell me this... Who is the King in Yellow?'

Ravenor smiled.

'Haven't you figured that out for yourself yet?' he asked. 'He's been there all the time. Since the earliest days of everything.'

'I feared he was me,' said Eisenhorn. 'What I would become somehow.'

'Oh, he's that too,' said Ravenor. 'Come on now, you know what you are. Forget the future, Gregor. No man ever really prospered knowing that. The past is much more interesting. Think hard. There are only seconds left. Think hard and see yourself. Consider the possibility that Master Imus was right.'

'No, he–'

'Just recognise what you've always been,' said Ravenor. 'It'll make it easier for you. No more doubts, no more struggles. Your way will be clear. And it will make it far easier on me too, when the time comes.'

He looked up. They could both hear the screaming note of aircraft engines as they began their low pass along the avenue. Lightnings, twelve of them. There were petals in the air.

'Here it comes,' he said. He held out his hand.

Eisenhorn reached out to take it, but his hand met metal. He was looking at the armoured box of Ravenor's support chair.

'Transformation,' the chair's voxponders crackled. 'Fire. Rebirth.'

Eisenhorn felt the flash. It was so bright he could see nothing but searing white.

Then the flames came. The flames and the wind and the shockwave. His clothes burned away, blowing like ash from his body. His skin blistered, peeled back and shredded. Muscle and sinew disintegrated. His bones, black with heat, buckled and flew like twigs in the wind.

She was holding his hand.

'That was all a long time ago,' she said.

Alizebeth.

The sky was white. Old trees shivered in the cold wind. They swayed, their leaves rustling like the chorus of insects. She led him across the wild fell towards the dark valley below.

'Do you not suppose,' she said, 'it's ironic? The only woman... the only person... you ever loved was a pariah? Untouchable and cast out, anathema to human contact?'

'The thought had crossed my mind,' he said.

'The fire will end soon,' she promised.

'Too late,' he replied. 'It has unmade me. I have raked through my own ashes and I understand.'

'So use that,' she said. 'You have never been able to save anyone, not really. Not me, not Gideon, not Midas... not even yourself. You are doomed and always have been, and so are all who know you.'

'I should have stopped years ago,' he murmured. 'The magos was right...'

'Sark?' she asked.

'No, Drusher.'

'Him, I don't know,' she said.

'He's no one,' Eisenhorn said. 'Just a failed man, clutching at the scraps of life, bemoaning his lot. But he said to me that I had gone on far too long. That I had never worked out when to stop. He was very perceptive. He had given up, you see, far too early and far too easily. But he intuitively saw in me a man who had failed in completely the opposite way. A man who just kept going past any point of reason, his friends begging him to halt, then falling at the wayside as he left them in his wake.'

'I didn't think you had any friends?' she mocked.

'Not any more,' said Eisenhorn.

'So, you see, nothing holds you now,' she said. 'You can walk the last few kilometres without any burden. Nothing matters to you any more. Can you use that freedom for me?'

'To save you?' he asked.

She shook her head.

'Far too late for that,' she replied. She smiled. 'But a part of me. I have... I *will* have... It's hard to explain. A daughter, that's the easiest word but it's not accurate. She is of me, but she is also me. And another pariah. You've done enough, Gregor. Forget Chase and the King. If you keep going, determined to stop them, you will fail. You will never have the will, despite the uncommon will I *know* you have... You'll never have the will to finish this alone. So do something simpler, for me. Save her. Save her from the King before the King claims her. Let me have some afterlife in her.'

'Where is she?' he asked.

'She'll be born two years from now,' said Bequin. 'Deep in the Maze, in the shadow of the City of Dust. She will walk the streets of Queen Mab.'

'On Sancour?'

'Yes, like the Jaff woman said. That's where you'll find her.'

'Your daughter?'

'She's me, Gregor,' said Alizebeth Bequin. 'Beta to my alpha. Think of her that way, and find her.'

'If it's the last thing I do,' he said.

'It will be,' she replied. 'Stop hunting the Great Foe. You've done enough. You've changed the fate of the Imperium in significant ways. End your days with something smaller. One life.'

'Will the torment end then?' he asked her. 'Will the fire go out then?'

'Between you and me, it will never go out,' she said. 'But the pain will cease. Do you remember the Sameter Ninth?'

'The Guard company?'

'The veterans, yes. Their emblem was a wheatear. Do you remember how they kept fighting, years after the fight was done? They were loyal to the Throne, Gregor, utterly loyal, but their war had traumatised them so, they saw enemies everywhere. They fought against the notion of the dark, against every shadow, beyond all bounds of sense or reason.'

'I remember,' he said. 'One of the saddest things I ever witnessed. One of the hardest tasks of my life. To stop men and women from being loyal.'

'Imagine how I feel,' she said.

'You mean me?' he asked.

'I do,' she said. Her smile was everything he remembered.

'There,' she said, 'that's the only time I'll ever get to say those words to you.'

'I do too,' he whispered.

'You've done enough big things in your life,' she said. She faced him and brushed the soot and grit from his old coat. 'Forget them. Do a small thing.'

'Don't go,' he said.

'I'm not the one going,' she said. 'This is where I stop. You go on. You always have. One last walk.'

'I have to finish this first,' he said. 'Sark. Gobleka. Keshtre.'

'You don't,' she replied.

'To reach Sancour, I must be alive,' he said. 'To find this girl, this daughter of yours. I need to end Keshtre and get out so I can make my way to Sancour.'

'You don't,' she repeated.

The rustle of the leaves had become the stirring of insects, and the stirring of insects had become a fizzling noise. The chuckle of an electrocorporeal storm. He hadn't heard its eerie sound since Ignix, long ago.

'The Cackle,' he said.

'You know what that means,' she said.

The regia occulta had opened before them. Lightning writhed and fluoresced around its mouth. Corposant crackled. The wind rose.

Eisenhorn couldn't look at it. He glanced around.

'I know this place,' he said.

'Of course you do,' she said. 'I've never been here myself, but you have. The high fells above Antieth. DeKere's world. You used to tell me about it.'

'Where I was born,' he said.

'Exactly,' she said. 'Where you were born the first time. It felt like the right place to bring you so you could be born all over again.'

She raised her hand to his chin, and he flinched, afraid he would burn her. But she was simply, gently, turning his head, making him look at the gleaming, spitting gateway of the regia occulta.

'This can take you there,' she said. 'One step. Forget the rest, forget it all. Go on now. Before it closes again.'

She kissed him on the cheek.

'Take the pathway,' she said. 'It is straight and true, and the only one you need.'

He turned, but she was gone.

He stepped into the light.

It twists around him and carries him forward. The world falls away, then stars begin to tumble past him like snow. Faster. A blizzard of stars covering the world, raising deep and silent drifts of stellar motes. A heartbeat. A long winter. Centuries snap and pile into one another, like the cars of a runaway train that has left the rails. He sees the Karanines in early summer, the banners flying from the new guardian fortresses. There are armies on the pass, advancing after the spring thaw, bodies released from the lock of winter to move again. The Udaric hordes, clad in leather and bronze, carrying the skulls of cave ursids on their tribal standards, and bearing too their dreams of finding Vaartuk and deliverance. Their chieftain rides at their head, his warhelm crested with the feathers of a sea raptor. In the woods below, the fortress garrisons muster, sounding the call on brass trumpets that loop around their bodies in a circle. The Karanine Guard, forming tight ranks and shield walls in the mouth of the pass, ready to deploy steel blades and precision discipline against the barbarian invaders, and defend their dreams of stable colonisation.

Iron discipline against feral chaos.

Trumpets calling in the woods. Rams horns blaring from the pass.

Redbeaks still trilling in the trees, oblivious, all those years ago.

An old man beside a pool, sketching.

The low summer sun. An eagle flying. A quiver of extimate spaces overlapping.

A room. A hundred thousand rooms. The people in them. Someone crying. A flame-yellow moon. A bonfire. A Selgioni rug. Laughter.

A sea that was not a sea. An immaterial ocean, waves rising higher than all the worlds of ever. Glimpsed behemoths sounding deep beneath the raging surface. Laughter, again. Perpetual laughter. A cackle. Whispers. Words that make. Words that build and un-build. An Old Night, its endless dark filled with insects in their trillions. Chirring words that predate the mouths that spoke them. Words that predate all organic mouths. Words etched on white stone.

An eye that is not an eye. An eye wounded by worms. A wound in space that is not an eye. An influx. An outpouring. A lie. A truth. A father and his eighteen sons. A transgression. A father and his daughter. A dead girl. Another not yet born. Years crumple like paper, overlapped like shuffled cards, out of order.

A golden throne. A figure on it, too bright to see, too dark to name. A figure in a box. A box that is a golden throne. A golden throne that is just a box. A man that is no longer a man. Something once human kept alive by the throne that surrounds him, seeing all, knowing all, reading the future and trying to forget the past. A mind isolated. A dark place. An old pict, the image of a son who was everything and nothing, and no way of knowing if the image was made before or after, because he looked the same before and after, and because time was crumpling like paper, and perhaps the before had been the after all along.

A wheatear. A birthplace.

Something untouchable. Someone too afraid to ever touch.

A man limping away into blackness, utterly alone, his back turned, carrying on, step after step, for a reason he can no longer remember.

A fire.

An ancient city on the edge of a desert. Everything golden with the haze of dust. A shadow city beyond it, a twin. One place that was two, two that were one. An extimate metropolis.

A city of learning. A city of knowledge. A place of Cognitae.

A City of Dust.

Another king. Another throne. All in yellow. Fire and dust.

Eight waiting. Eight points. Eight shots.

Blood. Inheritance.

The King beckons. Cyclopean daemons, too vast to comprehend, kneel at his throne in chains and fealty, whispering un-words.

Chirring like insects.

Like ticking clocks.

Like cackling light.

Like crackling fire.

'You're here now.'

A voice.

'Isn't this where you want to be? Where you've been walking to your entire life? This *is* what you wanted, isn't it?'

Eisenhorn opened his eyes. Dust fogged his vision. His mouth was full of sand.

He was face down.

He hauled himself up, spitting and coughing, trying to clear the dust from his throat. The light around him was golden and fogged with powder. A haze.

'The city's right here,' said the voice. 'You're at the gates.'

'W-which city?' Eisenhorn could barely speak.

'The City of Dust,' said the voice. 'That's right, isn't it?'

'Who are you?'

'I'm right here too,' said the voice.

Eisenhorn looked up. The figure looked down at him.

'Hello, little thing,' said Cherubael.

'Why are you here?' asked Eisenhorn. 'How–'

'You called me,' said Cherubael. 'I came because you called me.'

Eisenhorn tried to stand. The daemonhost reached down to help him.

'Don't touch me!'

Cherubael looked hurt.

'But... you called me,' he said. 'To help you. That's what you always do. That's why you made me. In the end, you see, I'm the only friend you've got. Which says a lot, I think you'll agree.'

'I didn't call you,' said Eisenhorn. He got to his feet. He looked at the city shimmering in the distance beyond the veil of golden dust.

'Oh, but you see, you did,' said Cherubael. The daemonhost hovered in front of Eisenhorn, his broken chain dragging in the dust. 'From the hidden way.'

'The regia occulta?'

'*That's* the thing,' said Cherubael. 'I knew there was a proper name for it. The re-gi-a o-ccul-ta. You called to me as you walked along it.'

'And you came?'

'It's what a friend does,' grinned Cherubael.

Eisenhorn shook his head. The fire had gone out. The pain had gone. *All* the pain had gone, in fact.

'I can't have,' he began. 'I don't control you like that. I have *never* been able to. It takes months to bring you out, constant effort to bind you and keep you contained. The very limit of my mind and my will just to get you to stay calm. I didn't call you. And even if I did, in my madness, I couldn't keep you tame.'

'You can now, Gregor,' said Cherubael.

'No.'

'Indeed, yes,' Cherubael laughed. 'I like it, actually. The fight is gone. The constant struggle, me and you, all that pain and heartache. Blanked out. You call me and I come. That's how it works now. I cannot even *begin* to resist you. I prefer it this way.'

'This is an illusion,' Eisenhorn said to himself. 'It's just... another stage of the Torment. Another mind-trick...'

Cherubael glanced around. His chain rattled.

'Who are you talking to?' he asked.

Eisenhorn looked at him.

'This isn't real,' he said to the daemonhost. 'You're not here. I'm not here. I didn't call you, and I know for damn sure I couldn't control you. My psykana's burned out. I must be close to death. The end-stage delusions of the Torment.'

'No, you're not dead,' said Cherubael. 'Not dying. Not hallucinating. You've simply arrived. This is the place you were always going to, and you've got here. I'm impressed. Honestly. I don't say that to people very often.'

'The place?' asked Eisenhorn.

'Physically,' said Cherubael, '*and* metaphysically. I suppose you get to decide which matters more. The physical place is the City of Dust, inside the City of Queen Mab, on Sancour, in the Angelus Subsector. The year is 500. Give or take a year. *Metaphysically*, well... that's up to you.'

'Sancour?'

'Yes, yes. Absolutely dreadful place, between you and me, but not my choice. You call the shots, now. You did... you did *want* to be here, didn't you?'

'Yes,' said Eisenhorn. 'I... I don't know.'

'It's where she asked you to go,' said Cherubael. 'That untouchable of yours, you know, whatsername...'

'Alizebeth.'

'Yes, A-liz-e-beth. She asked you nicely.'

'It was just the Torment in her form.'

'She asked you nicely anyway. She asked you a favour. A last favour. Save her daughter. I suppose that's what you're going to do. You'd do anything for her.'

The daemonhost saw Eisenhorn looking at the spectral city.

'Or have you changed your mind, Gregor?' he asked. 'Are you still tempted? One final push to bring the Archenemy down?'

'I don't know. I don't know if any of it was true.'

'Seems to me you have a choice. Do the right thing, or do the right thing. I know that doesn't sound like a choice. You know what I mean. Do the big thing that matters, or the small thing that counts.'

'Can't I do both?' asked Eisenhorn.

'I don't know?' asked Cherubael. 'Can you?'

Eisenhorn didn't reply.

'I suppose,' said Cherubael, 'it comes down to what matters most. To you. Obligation to... you know... I don't like to say His name. Let's call Him the Rot-God-King. Or obligation to those who counted on you. Personally, I mean. Let's call them... and here's another word I don't like to use... friends.'

'I don't have any friends,' said Eisenhorn.

'No, you don't, and I've always liked that about you,' said Cherubael. 'But... How can I put it? Friends have *you*. People have befriended you, to their cost. They have stuck to you. They have stayed with you. They have been loyal through everything. You've just never really been loyal back. Which is odd, because loyalty is your big thing.'

'The two things have always conflicted,' said Eisenhorn.

'But?'

'I want to do the right thing,' said Eisenhorn. 'I have always wanted to do the right thing. I'm damned because of it.'

'So?'

'I choose both. And choosing both means I don't start here.'

Cherubael sighed.

'We're not staying then?' he asked.

'I'm not. I have something to finish. I have to... retrace my steps.'

'Have I got to carry you?'

'I don't think you do.'

'Well,' said Cherubael. 'I'll be waiting for you then.'

'You will?'

'Like a good boy. That's what you want. So that's what I'll do. I'll wait right here until you get back. See you in... oh... about twenty years.'

Eisenhorn looked at the daemonhost and shook his head.

'Off you go,' said Cherubael. He gave a little wave. 'Good luck and all that. That is what friends say, isn't it?'

'Why...' said Eisenhorn. 'Why are you being so nice to me?'

'Well, because, quite frankly,' said Cherubael, 'and please don't tell anyone, but right now you scare the absolute shit out of me.'

Eisenhorn smiled.

'Hang on,' said Cherubael. 'I didn't think you could do that any more.'

'Neither did I,' said Eisenhorn.

He raised his hand.

The fire leapt up.

TWENTY-FOUR

WHATEVER DAY YESTERDAY WAS

Davinch clutched Gobleka's shoulder for support.

'You get him?' he asked through swollen lips.

'I got him,' said Gobleka.

They stared down at Eisenhorn's body. It was crumpled against the handrail, propped up in a half-sprawled, half-kneeling position. His eyes were closed, and the empty injector was slipping from his limp fingers.

'Nothing's happening,' said Davinch.

'I thought I heard him scream,' said Gobleka.

'Yeah, me too,' said Davinch. 'It came from his mind, not his mouth. Goran, why isn't he–'

'Just wait,' said Gobleka.

'For what?' asked Davinch. They looked at each other. They both knew the symptomatic progression. They'd documented it in enough test subjects. After the antigenic was administered, a subject lapsed into violent, thrashing seizures that could last hours or days. The skin blistered and peeled. Sometimes it fell off completely. Even for them, it was hard to watch.

After the frenzied agony, every test subject had become still, a few moments of calm that preceded death. None had survived except Sark, and Sark's first exposure had resulted in a six-hour ordeal of fits, screaming and haemorrhaging.

But Eisenhorn had just become comatose. Twenty-five seconds had passed since Gobleka had stabbed the injector into his neck, and he was silent and still.

'It didn't work,' Davinch said. 'I think we killed him.'

Gobleka crouched down and put his ear close to Eisenhorn's mouth.

'He's still breathing,' he said.

Davinch shook his head.

'Not for long,' he said. 'You hit him with a full dose. He was already weak–'

'Strong up here,' said Gobleka, tapping his temple with his index finger.

Davinch continued to look dubious.

'Well, I think that's the problem,' he said. He walked over to the med kit and started to sponge the blood off his face with a sterile dressing. Each wipe made him grimace. 'That's the thing they always said about him. Iron will. He probably tried to fight back. Resist, you know. You don't resist the antigen. Resisting makes it worse. You've fried him. Brain-dead. That's probably just an autonomic response you're seeing. His body spinning down.'

Davinch suddenly recoiled and cried out in alarm.

Eisenhorn had lurched forwards without warning. He was on his hands and knees, his eyes closed, sweat dripping from his face. He was trying to rise, but the cuffs around his wrists were hindering him.

'Get him up,' Gobleka ordered.

They battled to raise Eisenhorn to his feet. As Davinch held him upright, Gobleka slapped Eisenhorn around the face a couple of times.

'Wake up! Can you hear me?'

Eisenhorn's eyelids fluttered.

'Eisenhorn?' whispered Gobleka. He dragged Eisenhorn's right eyelid up with his thumb, expecting to see a blood-blown iris, or worse.

'Great spirits of the dark...' he whispered in wonder. He started to laugh.

'What?' asked Davinch. 'What is it? Gobleka, what?'

Gobleka turned Eisenhorn's face so Davinch could see.

'Damn,' Davinch said.

Eisenhorn's eyes were shining with violet light.

'Voriet needs to rest,' said Drusher.

'No time,' replied Nayl.

'He needs to rest,' Drusher insisted.

'I know he does, magos,' said Nayl. 'But there is no time for that.'

Macks leaned over the rail and looked down.

'That fire's bad,' she said. The air around them was already hazed with smoke. It was dirty and black, and making them cough. Far below, the sump was a blazing sea of flames, a furious petrochemical fire that was beginning to choke the tower with murky, toxic smog.

'On the plus side,' she said, 'I guess it will take out the Loom.'

'There's that,' said Nayl. 'But we have to find an exit. Another ten minutes, and it won't be possible to breathe in here. Besides, that fire's going to climb.'

'I can go on,' said Voriet. Drusher could tell he was lying. Every time Voriet coughed because of the rising smoke, it aggravated the pain of his broken bones. He looked dead on his feet.

Nayl put his arm around Voriet to support him and began to climb the next staircase. Macks and Drusher looked at each other then followed. They could feel the intense heat from below. They followed the stairs up to another inspection catwalk, traced that to its end and took the next set of metal steps up. The Loom's whirring mechanisms were wafting strange circles and hoops in the slow smoke, like ripples in water.

'Do you think he's dead?' Macks asked Drusher.

'Eisenhorn?'

'Yeah.'

'You heard that scream,' said Drusher.

'I felt it,' she replied. 'I don't want to think what they might have done to him to make him scream like that.'

Nayl paused to look up. The eerie light was still glowing above them, but the smoke in the air had made it foggy.

'Just a few more levels,' Nayl said. 'At the main gantry, there was an exit into the rest of the fortress. That's how me and the magos got in. I think that's the only way out. Can you do that, Darra?'

Voriet nodded. His face was pinched and pale, and beaded with dirty perspiration. His clothes were sticking to him.

'Let's go then,' said Nayl.

Voriet reached out with his good hand and caught Nayl's arm. Nayl stopped. 'Back up,' he hissed to the others.

There was an animation on the platform ahead of them, a skeleton that had been bleached white. Odd symbols had been scratched into its bones. It limped towards them, fixing them with the tiny green pinpricks of light that served as its eyes.

They moved back along the platform, hustling Voriet along, and found a short flight of steps down onto an access catwalk. It felt wholly wrong to be going down rather than up.

'More steps ahead,' said Nayl. 'A different way up.'

They approached the steps. These rose from a junction platform between catwalk spans. The steps ran up between two huge whizzing flywheels to another platform gantry that they could barely see in the smoke.

Drusher spotted movement beyond the steps. Two more animations. One was a hunched, decayed thing. The other was Deputy Cronyl. They were closing in.

'Just get to the steps and get up,' said Nayl.

The four began to ascend as fast as they could. Drusher didn't want to look back. Cronyl had been moving quite fast, at a brisk stride.

Voriet slipped. They caught him, and Macks and Nayl began to carry him between them.

'Move, move!' Drusher urged. He glanced behind him. Cronyl was on the steps, the other two animations not far behind him.

'Leave me,' gasped Voriet.

'Shut the hell up,' Macks told him.

They reached the upper platform. It was a broad area of deck, with two exits, one at each end, both staircases leading up.

An animation was coming towards them from the right-hand flight of stairs. It was the Cognitae agent Blayg. The top of his head was missing, and his portly face was drenched in dried blood. A combat assault rifle was hanging around his shoulders on a sling, bobbing against him as he walked. It was just dead weight he was dragging along with him.

'Other way,' said Nayl. They turned.

Audla Jaff was coming towards them from the other flight of steps. The psykana shockwave that had destroyed her seemed to have broken everything inside her. She moved like a damp sheet hung from a wire, loose and heavy, one shoulder drooping, her head tilted askew. Her clothes were soaked in blood.

There was no way past either of them. Cronyl and the other two animations were almost at the top of the stairs behind them.

They were cornered, all exits blocked. Drusher wondered if he should stand his ground and wait for the hands of the animations to reach him, or admit defeat and take a running jump off the platform. He tried to decide which would be a worse way to die: the eradicating horror of the animations' touch, or a long, conscious plunge into a lake of flame.

He put himself in front of Macks.

Nayl knew it was useless, but he pulled out his Tronsvasse. He fired multiple times at Blayg. Fizzling green light ate his shots. One round cut the sling of the autorifle, and it clattered onto the deck. Blayg stepped over it. Nayl turned and shot at Jaff.

The electric aura around her turned his shots to vapour.

The animations raised their hands.

'What do we do?' asked Davinch.

Gobleka was gazing at Eisenhorn. Eisenhorn simply stood there, staring ahead at nothing with his shining eyes.

'Let's get him into the palace,' he said. 'Run some tests, perception exams, psychometrics, you know.'

Davinch grinned at him.

'Chase will adore you for this,' he said. 'This changes everything. With two successful subjects, we can keep the Loom operating full-time. No more shutdowns to let Sark rest.'

Gobleka nodded.

'We'll need to prepare a message,' he said. 'We're going to need more staff here to manage the operation. Maybe Chase herself will come.'

'You can tell her how you turned him,' said Davinch.

'Actually,' said Gobleka. 'I don't think I had to turn him at all. Just give him a little push. I think this is where he was going all along. He just needed to tip over. That's why there was no fight, no convulsions. He was basically already there.'

'Gods below,' said Davinch in awe. 'To think... to think this man was Ordo. That they used him and trusted him. Gave him authority. Damn, Goran, I thought their selection programme was rigorous and–'

'I think that proves the King is winning,' said Gobleka. 'The warp's everywhere, in everything. Even in the very heart of the Holy Inquisition, the very bastards who are supposed to be bulwarks of the fight against it. We're close, Davinch. Months, maybe a year or two. So close. I knew the Rot-God's kingdom was shaky, but it's already disintegrating. It's not even going to be a struggle to topple it. It's rotten to the core. One touch from us and it'll all come crashing down.'

He started to laugh again, but it trailed off. He frowned and sniffed the air.

'Do you smell that?'

'No,' replied Davinch.

'Smoke,' said Gobleka. 'Something's on fire.'

'I don't smell it,' said Davinch. He had gone back to cleaning and patching his face with the contents of the med kit.

'Of course you don't,' snapped Gobleka, 'your nose is mushed across your dumb face.'

He went to the top of the steps and looked over the rail.
'I can see light down there. Way down.' He glanced at Davinch. 'Shit,' he said. 'I think the sump's on fire. The sump well.'
Davinch lowered the crumpled, bloody dressing in his hand.
'Are you serious?' he asked.
'Yes, I'm frigging serious!'
'What do we do?' asked Davinch.
'Put it out. Fast.'
'But how? We don't have any–'
Gobleka looked up towards the main gantry.
'Sark'll have to do it. Trap it. Snuff it.'
'He's been running on full for a while,' said Davinch anxiously. 'What if he isn't strong enough? I mean, what if he's about to crash? He needs so long to recuperate–'
'Help me with Eisenhorn,' said Gobleka.
'What?'
'Just do it, Davinch!' Gobleka fixed him with a savage look. 'Do you want to tell the King how we let the Loom burn?' he asked.
Davinch shook his head.
'Then help me get this frigger up there,' said Gobleka. He paused. 'Wait... Show me his gun.'
'What?'
'You said you took his piece. Show it to me.'
Davinch pulled Eisenhorn's Scipio from the pocket of his jacket and handed it to Gobleka.
Gobleka popped out the clip and examined the uppermost round.
'Enuncia,' he said. 'Look, he's marked the rounds with Enuncia.'
He pushed several bullets out into his palm and showed one to Davinch.
Davinch swallowed hard.
'Is that what it looks like?' he asked.
'You said this was his back-up piece?' asked Gobleka, reloading the clip. 'Right. For special targets. I think these custom loads were the trick you reckoned he was hoping to pull.'
'So what?' asked Davinch.
Gobleka slid the clip back into the Scipio's grip.
'If we're going to put the old bastard in the cage, we're going to have to take Sark out,' he said. 'I want to make sure we're covered.'
'Against what?' asked Davinch.
'I don't trust Sark,' said Gobleka. 'I don't think he really is Sark any more. I don't know exactly what we're going to be letting out of that cage.'

They took Eisenhorn by the shoulders and began to escort him up to the gantry. He was slow and unresponsive, like a sleepwalker.
'This is a bad idea,' Davinch murmured.
'Then have a better one,' Gobleka snarled. Gobleka had been trained to improvise, even in the deepest crisis, and he wasn't about to let any possibility go.

They struggled with Eisenhorn up the steps onto the main gantry. In the cage, the magos was sitting cross-legged like an ancient shaman, radiating light and muttering un-words. Gobleka and Davinch could see at once that Sark was close to the end of his strength. The glow coming from him was beginning to falter, like a dodgy filament. Plasmic residue was slick on his skin, oozing like glue. He was starting to blister.

'Hold him,' Gobleka ordered. He left Davinch watching the silent, lobotomised Eisenhorn and walked over to the cage.

'Magos? Magos Sark?' he called out.

The glow flickered.

'I... I want to stop, Goran,' Sark murmured. 'Can I stop now?'

'There's a fire, magos.'

'It's in me, Goran.'

'No, sir. A fire. Down below. The sump. Can you snuff it out?'

Sark opened his eyes and looked at Gobleka. Beads of blood trickled from his tear ducts.

'I'm so tired,' he mumbled.

'All right,' said Gobleka. 'Magos? Magos, listen to me. You stop now. I promised you, didn't I? It's time to rest. We have another subject.'

'You do? I can rest? Really?'

'Just like I promised, magos.'

'It worked again?' asked Sark. 'You got it to work again?'

'We did.'

'Who?' asked Sark. Gobleka gestured at the figures waiting behind him. Sark peered through the bars, trying to focus his eyes.

'Eisenhorn?' he asked. 'You made it work with him?'

Gobleka nodded.

'Let's get you out of there,' he said.

'Oh please,' said Sark. 'I want to get out. I want to get out.'

Gobleka crouched in front of the cage door. He put his hand on the grip of the Scipio tucked in his waistband.

'Power down, magos,' he said. 'Just bring the Loom back to idling. I'll get you out, and you can rest.'

Sark nodded. He muttered something that wasn't words. The light radiating from him diminished, as if it were sucking back into him, light running the wrong way and draining into nothing. The great gears and wheels of the Loom began to chug and clatter as they decelerated. The industrial roar faded back to a hum.

Panting, Sark looked out at Gobleka.

'Let me out, please, Goran,' he said. 'I so long to be let out. This cage is crushing me.'

Gobleka said an un-word Chase had taught him. The cage door clicked unsealed. Gobleka swung it open.

Sark began to crawl out. He clearly needed help, but Gobleka didn't want to touch him. He wanted to watch him closely and draw Eisenhorn's gun fast if he had to. Outside the bounds of the psychometric cage, anything was possible. Anything could be coming out. Anything could be crawling free.

Sark pawed his way out onto the deck and flopped on his side like an exhausted dog, the plasmic residue dripping off him and pooling around him. Some of it was drying to a crust on his shrivelled skin.

Slowly, he began to rise.

'H-help me,' he called out.

'You can do it,' Gobleka replied, his hand still resting on the pistol.

Sark stood up. He raised his head and looked at the light of the lamps in the rigs around the gantry.

'How long?' he asked, his voice thin and frail. 'How long have I been in there?'

'A long time,' said Gobleka.

'A week?'

'Longer.'

'How long, Goran?'

'Seventeen years, I think,' said Gobleka.

Sark didn't reply. He looked down at himself, at the wreck of his body.

'I won't go back in,' he said at last. 'I have earned my reward. I have earned my place at the King's right hand. I have served. You will not force me back in there again.'

Gobleka saw that Davinch was looking at him, anxious. Gobleka shook his head quietly. They'd deal with Sark in due course. If they could keep him contained and happy, they'd find a way to get him back in when it was time for another weaving.

'I'm going to rest, now,' Sark said. 'Make arrangements, Goran. I want passage to Sancour by the end of the week. A fast ship, a crew that can be trusted. I will make my report to the King personally.'

'I'm going to need to run some tests on you,' said Gobleka.

Sark looked at him sharply. A ripple of violet light flickered in his eyes.

'Just to make sure you're fit to travel,' said Gobleka.

'And to obtain more data, magos,' said Davinch. 'To assist in the preparation of further successful candidates.'

Sark nodded. He walked over to Davinch and faced Eisenhorn.

'You have had some success at least,' said Sark. 'A replication to build on.'

He looked more closely into Eisenhorn's blank face.

'I pity you,' Sark said. 'I hate all you stand for and all the setbacks you have caused the Cognitae over the years, but even so, I pity you for what you are about to endure.'

Eisenhorn didn't reply.

Sark turned and limped up the steps towards the hatch into the palace.

'Should we follow?' Davinch whispered to Gobleka.

'I don't want to leave him alone for long,' Gobleka replied. 'He seems safe, but I really don't know what he is any more. First, let's deal with this.'

He looked at Eisenhorn.

'Let's get him in the cage,' he said.

Nayl took a step towards Blayg.

'Get ready to move,' he told the others. 'I'm going to knock him down. Get ready to run when I do.'

Drusher could see that Nayl meant to tackle the animation and grapple it out of their way.

'You'll die!' he exclaimed.

'We're dying right now,' replied Nayl.

There was a chattering, rattling thump, and the light above them dimmed considerably. The gears and mechanisms of the Loom suddenly spun down and slowed.

The animations collapsed to the deck as though the invisible wires that had been supporting them had suddenly snapped. They heard the separating bones of the skeletal one clattering and bouncing away down the steps.

'What does that mean?' asked Macks.

'Don't question it, Germaine,' said Drusher. 'Move, before they get up again.'

They hurried Voriet past Blayg's body, towards the steps he had approached from. Nayl paused, squatted and picked up Blayg's autorifle. Gingerly, he poked at Blayg with the weapon's stock. No electric crackle. He reached on and took some spare clips from the corpse's pockets.

'Hurry up!' said Drusher.

'I'm coming,' Nayl growled. Hefting the combat weapon, he turned and ran after them.

Gobleka shut the cage door with the locking un-word. Smoke threaded the air, hanging like gauze under the lighting rigs.

Inside the cage, Eisenhorn was on his knees, staring dumbly at his cuffed hands. He slowly raised his head and looked at Gobleka.

'You know what to do,' said Gobleka.

Eisenhorn didn't reply.

'I know this is all unfamiliar,' said Gobleka. He crouched down to peer through the bars. 'You're not used to your mind working this way. Don't fear it. It's just revelation. True understanding is always terrifying. You're seeing the way things are. You've come home to the place that created us all. It's been calling to you since before you were born, and you've been too scared... too indoctrinated by lies... to answer. You can now. It's very freeing.'

'The warp...' Eisenhorn whispered.

'That's right,' Gobleka smiled. 'You don't need to know anything any more. The warp is in you, and it will show you everything. How to live. How to think. How to master this world, and every world. It'll show you how to work the Loom. It will teach you the language you need. The words that you must speak. Just open your mind and they'll flow to you.'

Eisenhorn's lips began to move. No sounds came out. He looked like a child learning to read.

'Make the Loom turn,' said Gobleka. 'Make it spin. I need you to harness its power and extinguish the fire. We must make the Loom safe. That's our first priority. Secure Keshtre, and save the Loom. Let the words come. It'll be an easy task for a man like you.'

Eisenhorn's lips were moving faster. He was starting to murmur. Gobleka heard the first syllables sounding, and it felt like a jolt in his sternum. More, fully formed un-words began to flow from Eisenhorn's mouth.

Davinch had already backed away to the edge of the gantry and was looking on with great concern. He'd scooped up Gobleka's suppressed autorifle, and was clutching it tightly. Gobleka rose and retreated too. Eisenhorn was speaking quite clearly now. The un-words were coming out of him fast and precise. Each one stung at Gobleka's flesh.

He'd never heard the litany of Enuncia vocalised so clearly. The magos had mastered it and harnessed its power, but it had always appeared a struggle for him, a constant effort to maintain mastery. Sark had often stumbled or muttered, his weavings interrupted by inarticulate screams or yelps. Eisenhorn was confident and unhalting. He was almost instantly fluent.

In the cage, Eisenhorn closed his eyes and tilted back his head.

Crusts of rime crackled as they formed around the bars of the psychometric cage. Snakes of green electrical discharge danced around the metal grille of the gantry deck around its base, leaping up to bite at the bars or coil around them like climbing tracedy. One struck upwards and hit a lighting rig, blowing out a set of lamps in a loud burst of sparks.

'Look at him,' breathed Davinch over the sound of the un-words and the fizzle of the discharge.

'Almost immediate command,' replied Gobleka. 'Gods, that speaks to considerable preconditioning. Just as I suspected, he wasn't just suitable, he was ripe. He's been one of us for a very long time. A heretic long before the Ordos declared him such.'

The agony hit Eisenhorn. He shook, and his body stiffened into a savage rictus, his back arched, his wrists pulling uselessly at the chain of the cuffs.

He did not stop speaking.

Something lit inside him. A harsh radiance began to swell, spearing out from his core. Within seconds, he was shining like a lamp, a figure made of light not flesh, his old black clothes a vague silhouette in the glare.

There was a thump and a series of rattling clanks. A chattering sound, a chirring, a cackling, ticking hum. The gears of the Loom around them began to turn. The cogs began to spin.

The Loom roared back to life.

TWENTY-FIVE

CHAOPTERAE METALEPTA

They had stopped to let Voriet rest again when the Great Machine resumed function. The sudden clattering roar and movement made them all flinch.

'If this has restarted...' Voriet began.

'...the animations might restart too,' finished Drusher.

Nayl nodded. He checked the autorifle he'd taken from Blayg's corpse and took out his Tronsvasse.

'Which do you want?' he asked Macks.

'You got clips for both?' she replied.

He nodded.

Macks pointed to the combat rifle, and Nayl handed it over.

'Don't I get a gun?' asked Drusher.

Nayl and Macks looked at him.

'We've only got two,' said Nayl.

'It was sort of a joke,' said Drusher. 'I'm tired.'

'We're all tired,' Nayl agreed. 'One last push. One last ascent. I think we can make it up to the gantry and get to the tower exit. Just a bit of a climb left.'

He looked at Voriet. The interrogator, deathly pale, nodded affirmatively.

'We may have to fight our way past the Cognitae,' said Nayl.

Macks was putting the last of the spare clips in her jacket pockets.

'I don't have any problems with that,' she said.

'Or rescue Eisenhorn,' said Drusher.

'If he's alive,' said Macks. Drusher could hear the doubt in her voice.

'Well, let's do it like we mean it,' said Nayl.

'That's odd,' said Drusher. They looked at him.

He was peering at an insect that was crawling along the platform's metal handrail. It was small, less than two centimetres long, a locustform specimen.

'I haven't seen any insects in here,' said Drusher.

'So?' asked Macks.

'I'm just saying,' said Drusher. He picked the insect up and let it scurry over his hands, examining it.

'*Chaopterae metalepta,*' he said. 'Short horned plains-hopper. Family *Acrididae*. Not native.'

'To where?' asked Macks sourly.

'To Gershom,' said Drusher. 'And from what I saw out of the window, not here either.'

'What window?' asked Voriet, slowly getting to his feet.

'Just a window,' replied Drusher.

'What did you see?' asked Macks.

'Doesn't matter,' said Drusher. He picked up the insect by its wing cases and held it up. Its legs writhed. 'How is this here? See the red banding on the thorax? That's swarm-phase colouring. These things live in huge colonies. When overcrowding becomes an issue, it stimulates the release of serotonin, and the insects shift from statary to migratory morphs. They change colour, and then they begin an upsurge.'

'So?' asked Macks again.

'Well, you wouldn't see just one coloured like this,' said Drusher. 'By definition, an upsurge morph is never seen alone.'

Macks stared at him levelly.

'I'm very glad you find the insect fascinating,' she said. 'Can we get on now?'

'Yes, of course,' he said. He shook the insect off his hand, and it fluttered away. They started up the next flight of stairs, Nayl leading, then Macks, then Drusher helping Voriet.

'There's another one,' said Voriet. Another locustform had settled on the steps.

'Why don't we turn this into a nature ramble?' Macks hissed back at them.

'There's quite a few of them, actually,' said Drusher. Two more insects fluttered past. Several more were crawling on the steps and the rail.

'Where are they coming from?' asked Macks.

'Uhm, my original point,' said Drusher.

More insects began to billow around them.

'Ugh,' said Macks, brushing one away, 'they *are* swarming.'

Drusher peered over the rail. By the light of the sump fire far below, he could see thousands of tiny motes swirling in the spaces between the gears of the Loom. Hundreds of thousands.

'Yes, they are,' he said. 'A major upsurge outbreak.'

'Could it be the heat?' asked Nayl. 'The heat of the fire?'

'Oh, Throne!' exclaimed Macks. 'Yes, let's all stop and study nature!'

An insect landed on Nayl's cheek. He flicked it away.

'She's right,' he said. 'Keep moving.'

They made their way up three more platform sections. From a curved catwalk, they could clearly see the main gantry above them, bathed in noxious light. The air was full of churning insect clouds. The locustforms were settling everywhere: on the catwalk deck, on the rail, on their clothes. The chirring drone of their stridulation was as loud as the din of the furious Loom.

'They're making my damn skin crawl,' yelped Macks, flicking one off her earlobe.

'Focus,' snapped Nayl, brushing more insects off his scalp. 'Look...'

He pointed.

'This walkway curves all the way around to that staircase on the far side of the tower. See? If we can get around there, we can go up. The main hatch is up there.'

'What about Eisenhorn?' asked Drusher. He spat instinctively as an insect nearly flew into his mouth.

'You three go around,' said Nayl. 'I'm going to sneak up this way and see if I can get a look at the gantry.'

He pointed to a narrow service ladder nearby that connected their catwalk to a platform six metres above.

'We stay together,' said Voriet.

'This is probably going to come down to shooting,' said Nayl. 'Be good if we had two angles on them.'

Macks nodded.

'Don't be an idiot, Nayl,' she said.

'Too late to change my approach to life now, marshal,' he replied. 'Just shepherd Voriet and Balls of Steel around to the hatch, all right?'

Nayl started to climb the ladder. Macks hoisted her autorifle, flapped locustforms off her nose and mouth, and began to lead Drusher and Voriet around the catwalk ring.

Nayl reached the top of the ladder. It connected to a control platform immediately below the main gantry. There were banks of cogitator units, several of which had been smashed or damaged. On the deck, he saw traces of blood, some discarded and bloody medical dressings, and a broken injector unit.

Keeping low, he clambered over the rail onto the deck. Swarming insects billowed around him.

'Where are they all coming from?' Davinch asked in disgust, looking at the insects that were streaming in the air and swirling under the lighting rigs.

'I don't know,' replied Gobleka. He was more fascinated by the cage and the man inside it.

'Is this a manifestation?' asked Davinch. 'Is the Loom backwash doing this?'

'I hardly care...'

'This has never happened before, Gobleka,' Davinch snapped. 'We've had a few apports and some light displays... never this!'

He turned and looked down from the gantry rail.

'Maybe they're coming from below,' he said. 'Down in the sump, maybe. The fire...'

He trailed off. There was a man on the control platform below them. He was moving forwards, his head down.

'Gobleka!' Davinch yelled. He snatched out his twin laspistols and began blasting.

'What the hell?' Gobleka cried, turning.

'There's someone down there,' yelled Davinch. 'I think it's one of the old bastard's men!'

He fired again. The man he'd spotted had ducked out of sight. Davinch edged along the rail, trying to get a better angle.

He glimpsed the man again, and fired with both guns. Below, a cogitator unit blew out in a cascade of sparks.

'Get round! Get round!' he yelled to Gobleka.

Gobleka snatched up his autorifle, and began to move around the edge of the gantry, aiming down.

'Where?' he called.

'Control deck,' Davinch answered. He fired again. 'Just below us!'

Shots from a large-calibre pistol cracked back up at him. One hit the gantry rim, another buckled the handrail. Davinch jerked back.

'If you can't plug him, push him my way!' Gobleka shouted, aiming over the rail at the platform below.

Davinch swung back to the rail and rattled off shots with his weapons. He blew out a desk, hacked divots from the decking, overturned a wheeled stool and sent a stack of paper fluttering into the air.

Gobleka saw the target through his scope. A big, bald man, trying to keep low, pushed out of cover and back along the control deck by the fury of Davinch's double-fire. He tracked, settled to fire–

The target vanished. Gobleka's scope went blank, and his suppressed burst went wide. He realised a damn insect had landed on the lens of his scope. He shook the weapon to dislodge it and tried to find the target again.

Suddenly, shots were coming at him. From a different angle. They struck the gantry decking, drawing sparks as they gouged the metal. A second shooter.

Gobleka rolled aside. Where the hell was that coming from? Several more shots thukked into the gantry under him.

Below. The shooter was below him.

He slid forwards to line up.

Macks lowered her autorifle for a second.

'Come on!' Drusher yelled at her. 'Germaine!'

'I see him,' she growled. 'That bastard who killed Hadeed!'

She fired off another suppressed burst. Shots came back at her, plinking off the catwalk frame, shivering hundreds of settled insects into the air in an agitated flurry.

'Move,' she yelled at Drusher and Voriet. 'Get to the stairs!'

Drusher looked at her and knew she wasn't going to shift position until she'd taken her target out. He got his arm around Voriet and began to scurry around the catwalk circuit towards the stairs.

Macks kicked off another burst. She'd lost sight of the bearded man. Over the din of the machine, she could hear overlapping gunshots: Nayl's Tronsvasse, answered by cracking bursts of las-fire.

Further volleys of heavy fire ripped across the gulf at her, rattling and scoring the catwalk. A support cable snapped with a whip-crack.

She looked around. There had to be a better angle. Blayg's autorifle had a broken strap, so she gripped it carefully, slid under the handrail on her belly, and jumped.

She landed a metre lower on the cast-iron casing of a Loom section. She teetered. The surface was slippery with machine oil. There was nothing to hold on to. She began to edge along. Locusts got in her face. Her foot slipped. She remained upright. If she followed the casing, she'd be within grabbing range of a service ladder.

Shots whined past her at a steep angle. Two pinged off the casing behind her. Macks moved fast and took a running jump off the end of the casing. She hit the ladder, and clung on with her free hand, desperate not to lose her hold on the rifle.

She started to climb.

Gobleka tried to track the woman. He saw her take a huge risk and jump from the catwalk. Now she was virtually beneath him. The damn insects were everywhere, fogging air that was already clouded with smoke.

He had to get lower. The bald man was still off to his right on the control deck beneath him, trading shots with Davinch. If he jumped down, he could probably get the drop on the bald man from behind, then take up a better angle on the elusive woman.

He took a last glance at Eisenhorn, glowing like a tiny sun in the cage, and crawled over the edge of the gantry.

He dropped and landed in a crouch on the control platform. There was no immediate sign of the bald man, but both he and Davinch would be out of sight around the curve of the deck. Gobleka stepped forwards. If Davinch was keeping the Ordo thug busy, then he could come up on him from behind...

He saw movement and turned sharply. The woman was clambering up through a deck hole not three metres from him. He could see her hand on the rim, struggling to haul herself up the service ladder and retain a grip on her weapon.

Pathetic. Too easy. He raised his autorifle to hose the deck hole, the moment the woman's head appeared, and send her plunging down the long drop below.

Then he paused. The fact that any of Eisenhorn's people were still alive had come as a surprise. It was time to regain complete control of the situation.

The sound of his own movement masked by the din of the Loom, he crept forwards until he was right over the deck hole. The woman, the female marshal he'd captured earlier in the day, was climbing up with her back to him, breathing hard.

He waited, then snatched out his hand, grabbed her by the back of her jacket collar and slammed her against the rim of the hatch. She cried out in pain. He slammed again two or three more times, driving her back into the hard metal frame of the hatch. She lost her grip on her weapon, and it plummeted away.

Gobleka dragged her out of the deck hole and threw her down. She lay gasping on the deck. He rolled her onto her back, put his boot on her chest and aimed his autorifle at her face.

'How many more of you?' he asked.

She coughed and growled something. A curse.

'How. Many. More?' he snarled.

Nayl curled up tight under the cogitator bank as yet another blitz of las-fire raked the platform. The shooter was close, he had a raised angle and was wielding a pair of high-power laspistols. The onslaught was huge.

The shooter had another advantage too. His last salvo had almost killed Nayl. Nayl had only just made it to cover. He'd taken glancing shots to his right forearm and shoulder, scorching his jack armour. What would probably have been a lethal shot had been deflected by his Tronsvasse. The las-bolt had exploded off his handgun, instead of going through his face.

But the Tronsvasse was scrap. It looked fairly intact, but the impact had fused the slide and the trigger mechanism. It was basically an ugly paperweight.

The shooting had stopped. Nayl kept low, peering out. He watched the shadows. The air was thick with swarming insects and the black smoke from down below. But the strongest light source was coming from the gantry above and behind him. He could see the shadow cast by the handrail of the short access steps that linked the control deck to the platform. They were close by, just four or five metres ahead of him.

He saw another shadow. Movement.

There. The distinct shadow of two long guns held ready, panning.

The shooter was edging down the steps. He was keeping low, almost crouching against the handrail, weapons ready to fire at any movement.

Just you come closer, Nayl thought.

But it was an idle wish. There was no way the shooter wouldn't see Nayl crouching under the cogitator station, the moment he reached the control deck level. Then it would all end in a flurry of las-fire.

It was die, or bluff. Bluffing was a fool's game, but it was preferable to just dying. Nayl waited as long as he dared. He waited for the shadow to edge down further. He waited to detect the sound of a footstep on the deck.

Come on, come on...

He could see the man's shadow moving clear from the shadow of the handrail.

Now or never.

'Don't move!' Nayl yelled.

The shadow froze.

Drusher hauled the exhausted Voriet up the last few rungs of the ladder, and they sat panting on the platform in front of the tower's entry hatch. The shooting had stopped. Drusher wondered who was still alive.

Voriet sat back, eyes closed, far gone with pain and fatigue. Drusher slowly got to his feet, keeping low, and looked across the gantry.

The upper levels of the tower were heavy with black smoke. The swarming insects were everywhere, blizzarding through the dirty air. The Loom was thundering, racing at full power. A fierce light shone from the iron cage in the centre of the gantry.

There was a figure inside it.

A man, cuffed, kneeling, his back arched. A man in agony. Terrible sounds were coming out of him, terrible words that were not words. The sound of them made Drusher feel sick.

'Eisenhorn,' he murmured.

Voriet didn't reply.

'Voriet,' Drusher cried, shaking him. 'It's Eisenhorn!'

'What?' Voriet blinked at him, confused.

'That's Eisenhorn. Down there. In the cage.'

'It can't be...'

'I'm telling you it is.'

'Where are you going? Magos?'

'I'm going to get him,' said Drusher, keeping low and heading down the short flight of steps onto the gantry. 'I'm going to help him.'

'Magos!' Voriet shouted. 'Magos? Drusher... come back!'

TWENTY-SIX

THE CAGE

Drusher crept onto the gantry. The light from the cage was blinding. It burned his skin. The sound of the voice burned his mind.

There was no one around. No sign of anyone. He scurried over to the cage. He could feel the awful heat of it.

Eisenhorn was rigid. He was kneeling, and the light was shining through his skin and from his eyes. Every muscle of his body was locked and seized. The chain of the cuffs binding his wrists was pulled tight.

Only his mouth was moving. Un-words dribbled from it like blood from an open wound.

'Eisenhorn!' Drusher called. He banged on the bars of the cage. 'Inquisitor! Can you hear me?'

He tried the cage door. It was locked shut. Of *course* it was.

'Eisenhorn! Talk to me! How do I get you out of here?'

Drusher felt an odd, bubbling sensation in his head.

+Leave. Me.+

'Eisenhorn?'

+Leave me here.+

Eisenhorn's mouth was continuing to speak un-words in a non-stop stream. But his mind was speaking separately.

'I'm not leaving you,' replied Drusher. He paused to spit out a locust that had flown into his mouth. 'I said I wouldn't, so I won't. How do I get you out of here?'

+You don't.+

It was a cage. A cage sealed with an un-word, just like the ones he had released Macks and Voriet from. He'd figured out how to do that. If only he had a bullet left...

'Can you open it? Eisenhorn? Eisenhorn! Listen to me. Can you open the cage door? Use one of your words and open it.'

+Can't.+

'Why can't you?'

+Busy.+

'Don't talk nonsense! Busy doing what?'

+Weaving. Building up power. To put out the fire.+

'The fire?' asked Drusher. He brushed away the locustforms flying around his face.

+Gobleka said snuff the fire. Save the Loom.+

'What? You're following *his* orders now? Eisenhorn!'

+It's almost done.+

'Why? Why bother? This thing should burn. It's a heretic engine, right? Right? Eisenhorn?'

+A heretic engine.+

'Then why are you trying to save it? Stop. Unlock the cage!'

'What's happening?'

Drusher glanced up. Voriet was standing beside him, swaying with effort.

'He won't come out,' said Drusher. 'He's... he's trying to put out the fire. Save the Loom.'

'What?' replied Voriet. He knelt down beside the cage. 'Sir! Inquisitor! It's Darra Voriet. What are you doing?'

+Saving the Loom.+

'Why?' asked Voriet.

+Because... I have mastered it. The Cognitae, they... they have shown me how. They have shown me... everything. Darra, I can use this.+

'Use it? Sir, what are you saying?'

+I need to save the Loom.+

'He's gone mad,' said Drusher.

+I need to save the Loom. I have control. I can use it to annihilate the Archenemy. Finally and forever.+

Voriet looked at Drusher.

'He's not mad,' said Voriet. 'That's too small a word. He's completely insane.'

Nayl slowly got out from under the cogitator bank. He kept his useless Tronsvasse aimed at Davinch.

Davinch had frozen side-on to him, his laspistols raised. He was staring at Nayl out of the corner of his eye.

'Really don't move,' said Nayl.

'Just shoot me then,' replied Davinch.

'Drop the guns. Do it. Toss them over the rail.'

'I don't think so.'

'Do it,' snapped Nayl.

'Why didn't you shoot?' asked Davinch, not moving.

'Toss the guns.'

'You had the drop. A clear shot,' said Davinch. 'But you didn't take it. No way you want me as a prisoner. Taking me back for trial and punishment? I don't think so. So why didn't you shoot?'

Nayl moved closer.

'Drop the guns over the rail, now,' he said. 'This conversation is beginning to bore me.'

'You can end it any time,' said Davinch. 'One shot. Except you didn't take the shot. You know what I think?'

'I don't care what you think.'

'I don't think you can,' said Davinch. 'You'd have done it by now if you could. I think your gun's out.'

Nayl edged a little closer. Another step and he'd be able to lunge and finish the business with his hands. He thumbed back the hammer.

'Toss the guns,' he said again.

'A hammer works even on an empty gun,' said Davinch. Nayl saw him starting to smile slightly. That confident look he'd seen so many times in his bruising life. A barely imperceptible micro-expression. That tell that gave away the fact a man was about to make a move.

Davinch snapped around to shoot. Nayl was already diving. He slammed into Davinch and body-tackled him against the rail. Both laspistols discharged, sending bolts streaming into the air.

Nayl slammed Davinch's right wrist into the edge of the rail, and the laspistol tumbled away into space. Davinch tried to bring the left-hand pistol around. He fired again, and two shots scorched into the deck. Nayl put his full strength into keeping the man's left arm back.

Nayl shoulder-barged Davinch in the chest, pinned him against the rail and drove the heel of his right fist into Davinch's left thumb.

Davinch screamed in pain. His remaining laspistol went flying down the deck. It bounced and slid to a halt four metres away.

Davinch caught Nayl under the left ear with a jab. Nayl stumbled back, clutching his head. Davinch seized him by the front of his jacket with both hands, and threw him into the cogitator banks. Nayl landed badly, fragile cogitators shattering under his weight. Davinch came in fast, driving punches to Nayl's face and chest. Nayl raised hasty forearm blocks, stopped two and took a fist in the side of his mouth. He swung hard for Davinch, but missed.

Davinch turned and ran for the fallen gun. Nayl pounced and brought him down hard on the deck. They grappled. Nayl had mass on his side, but Davinch was quick with his legs. He hooked his right leg and flipped Nayl off him. Nayl got up, only to take another glancing kick to the face. He stumbled sideways.

Davinch bounced his rangy body onto its feet. Like a dancer, he threw a high spin-kick that hit Nayl in the chest and staggered him backwards. Davinch reversed his spin and threw another kick from the opposite direction. Nayl barely blocked it.

Davinch stayed on his toes. He spun around with another kick, almost in pirouette.

Nayl blundered backwards.

Try that shit again, he thought.

Davinch tilted his balance slightly and whirled into another spin-kick.

Nayl caught him squarely by the kicking ankle.

He locked it, twisted his grip and threw with full force. Utterly overbalanced, Davinch sailed backwards with a scream and went over the rail.

Somehow, he held on. White-knuckled, legs swinging, he clung to the cross struts of the handrail and began to haul himself back onto the platform.

He was half over the rail when he saw Nayl facing him, aiming the fallen laspistol.

'This one isn't out,' said Nayl.

He put four las-bolts through Davinch's head and torso.

Davinch swung backwards, stiffly, like a falling drawbridge, and plunged into the darkness.

Gobleka dragged Macks to her feet. He'd slung his autorifle across his back and drawn Eisenhorn's Scipio. He pulled her against him, his arm around her throat, and put the muzzle of the pistol against her head.

'How many more?' he asked.

'Go screw yourself,' she replied. He tightened his grip and made her choke.

'Let's walk,' he said, shoving her along. A shield was useful. 'You've got a friend up here. A bald guy. He'll be pleased to see you.'

His dry laugh died away.

Ahead of them, an animation was stepping off the connecting staircase and turning to walk along the control deck towards them. It was Blayg. Green light shimmered around his dead flesh. Two more followed it, Cronyl and a halting, slower skeleton.

Gobleka froze.

'I'm a friend!' he yelled. 'Back away!'

They kept coming.

'Back away!' Gobleka ordered. He shouted an un-word order of command that stung at Macks' ear.

The animations did not falter.

Gobleka switched aim from Macks' head to Blayg. He fired, and the shot dropped Blayg in his tracks.

Macks seized the moment as soon as the gun moved away from her head. She elbowed hard into Gobleka's gut then lashed out, clamping the top of Gobleka's right wrist with her left hand and driving her right hand up into his tricep. The force almost bent his elbow the wrong way. Gobleka shrieked, the Scipio flying out of his hand.

Macks tore free from his grip. The Scipio bounced once. She dived for it. It bounced a second time. She grabbed at it, and missed it by a hair's breadth.

It disappeared over the edge of the deck.

She knew she was done. The animations were right on her. She curled into a ball, her legs tucked under her, her hands over her head, and waited for the horror to end her.

Nothing happened.

She looked up. Cronyl and the lurching skeleton had moved past her, ignoring her. They were making straight for Gobleka.

He stared at them in horror, eyes wide.

'Back off! Back off!' he yelled. He tried more un-words as he wrestled to get his rifle off his shoulder.

Macks got down as flat as she could. Still yelling un-words, Gobleka hosed Cronyl and the skeleton with bursts of autofire. The furious volley ripped across the control deck stations, but left the advancing animations untouched.

Gobleka turned to run. Macks saw his staring, violet eyes as he broke to flee.

She had never seen terror like it.

'Why not her?' he cried. 'Why not *her?*'

Gobleka ran to evade the reaching hands of Cronyl and the skeleton thing, and found Audla Jaff, slack and loose-limbed like a hanged man, advancing from the opposite direction.

Her ruined, dead face blank and tilted to one side, Jaff embraced him. A moment later, Cronyl and the skeleton reached him too, their hands on his back, on his shoulders.

Gobleka began a scream, but it faltered and broke. Green sparks, like a raging swarm of insects, whirled around him, spreading from each point of contact, each clasping hand. As the sparks spread, Gobleka vanished. His clothes shredded away and became dust. His living skin turned to paper and withered like powder and ash. Beneath, tissue and muscle and fat rendered down, exposing bones that deformed like melting wax.

In less than ten seconds, Goran Gobleka was reduced to a few misshapen bones and a deformed, stained, screaming skull that fell to the deck between the three animations, and lay smouldering and sparking.

The animations stood over the steaming heap for a moment, then moved on without reaction, disappearing down the curve of the platform.

Macks rose to her feet, shaking.

'Marshal?'

She turned. Nayl was limping towards her. He looked like he had been kicked and punched repeatedly. He was carrying a laspistol.

'What happened?' he asked.

She brushed locusts away from her face.

'I think the rules just changed, Nayl,' she replied.

'You have to stop, sir,' Voriet said. 'You have to stop this now.'

He was slumped against the bars of the cage, too tired to do anything except speak, too weary to brush away the locustforms that were settling on him and crawling on his face.

'Listen to him!' Drusher yelled through the bars.

+This is a chance. The Cognitae have handed it to me. I won't waste it.+

'To do what?' asked Drusher. 'Use their machine against them? To achieve what?'

+An ending.+

'To what?'

+The Long War. The primordial fight.+

'Wh-what are you intending to do, sir?' asked Voriet.

+Control the fire. Then... increase the rate of the Loom. Unpick a hole in the warp. Open one space into another. An extimate fold. Between here and... Queen Mab.+

'What is that?' asked Voriet.

+The City of Dust. Another... another extimate space, I think. I'm going to open it wide and engulf the King in Yellow. Unmake him on his own Loom. Uncreate him word by word.+

'Sir, this is a heresy that must end,' said Voriet. 'You are employing devices and powers beyond our understanding–'

+I understand.+

'Do you? Do you really?' yelled Drusher. 'Or is this just the obsession coming out again? The old drive? The old desperation? The old craziness that doesn't recognise when it's time to stop?'

+You are outspoken, Valentin Drusher. You are ignorant.+

Drusher kicked the bars of the cage.

'You're the one locked in a magical frigging cage trying to unpick the fabric of reality,' he yelled. 'I'd rather be ignorant than crazy!'

He looked at Voriet.

'Unpick the fabric of reality, near enough?' he asked.

Voriet managed a shrug. 'I think, pretty much. Yeah.'

Drusher knelt down and stared through the bars.

'I'm not ignorant,' he said. 'I'm very knowledgeable. Educated. I'm smart enough to know my own limits. Do you know yours? Do you know when a good idea stops being a good idea? Do you know what "too far" looks like?'

+Enough, magos.+

'What happens when you do this?' asked Drusher. 'Does Keshtre collapse? Do you die? Do we die?'

+Perhaps.+

'We came back for you!' Drusher snarled.

+I did not ask you to.+

'You did, actually. You asked for my help. I asked for yours, but you refused. That's all right. But I said I'd come and help you. Now you don't want my help.'

+I don't need it.+

'So tell me what happens when you do this?' said Drusher. 'Some kind of cataclysmic cosmic event, I shouldn't wonder. Continental upheaval. Planets imploding. Stars blowing out. Another Long Night. Am I close?'

+The King will die.+

'Fine, what else?' Drusher asked. 'How many people die here on Gershom if you do this? How many people in... What was it called? Queen Mab? How many innocents? How many children?'

Eisenhorn's mind did not reply.

'Who is Beta?' asked Voriet.

'I don't know,' Drusher replied. 'But the name was just in my head too. Did that feel like sadness? Regret?'

Voriet nodded.

'Eisenhorn!' Drusher yelled at the cage. 'What else happens? You can't know everything. What are the consequences of a catastrophe like the one you're trying to create? You're messing with space and reality, splitting them open. Talk about ignorant! No one knows about that stuff. If you damage the universe that badly, does the damage stop? What if it spreads and you can't halt it?'

+The King will be dead.+

'Oh, well as long as the King's dead, that's all right,' said Drusher. 'You know what, Eisenhorn? You know what? I don't think you know anything, or you don't care. You're about to execute a dreadful act of destruction, and you have no clue what the consequences will be. What if you break reality forever? Break it so it can't heal or repair? Rip it open? So what if the King's dead... That will be it. You'll have destroyed the very thing you've spent your life protecting!'

+I know what I am doing.+

'I don't think you do,' said Drusher.

+Magos. Valentin. I... I will open a door. An exit out of Keshtre. You get out. Take Voriet with you. Macks and Nayl too. They live still. I have done my best to protect them. Get out, and I will try to contain the damage I am about to do. I will... contain it. You will live. Please... get them. Get out.+

Drusher rose to his feet. He flicked insects off his face.

'He doesn't understand, does he?' he asked Voriet. 'He doesn't understand people.'

'I don't think it's ever been part of the job description,' said Voriet. 'Do as he says, Drusher. Find Macks and Nayl, and get out while you can. I'm a bit tired. I'll stay here. Sit with him until the end.'

'Not an option,' said Drusher. 'For Throne's sake! But for a bit of wax and a custom bullet I could open that cage. I've still got the bloody gun.'

He produced the empty little Regit snub from his coat.

'See?'

He stuffed it back in his pocket, despairing. His knuckles touched something else in his pocket. He took the gun back out and reached in.

'Voriet?'

'What?'

'I miscounted,' said Drusher. 'I took a bullet out of the gun to open your cages. Macks never put it back in the clip when she reloaded it for me.'

He held out his hand. The bullet lay in his palm.

'Seven shots,' he said. 'Not eight. I miscounted.'

Voriet blinked in surprise.

'We don't have any wax, magos,' he said.

'Balls to that,' said Drusher. He did what he'd seen Nayl do. He drew back the Regit's slide, opened the firing chamber and slipped the bullet in. Then he snapped the slide shut.

'Step back,' he said.

Voriet struggled to his feet.

'Magos? What are you–'

'Step well back, Voriet. I'm not very good with guns.'

Drusher took careful aim.

And fired.

TWENTY-SEVEN

HOW TO LET A WILD THING OUT OF A CAGE, AND WHAT HAPPENS WHEN YOU DO

The gun Macks had given him all those years ago barked, and sparks blinked off the cage frame.

'Holy Throne!' said Voriet. 'I thought you were aiming at Eisenhorn!'

'I was,' said Drusher. He smiled at Voriet. 'Not really, I was aiming for the cage.'

'Oh, well... Good shot.'

'Voriet, it was *ten centimetres* away.'

Drusher bent down.

'I think it worked,' he said.

He pulled at the cage door, and it swung open, groaning on its hinges.

Drusher started to speak, but things began to change rapidly. The light radiating out of Eisenhorn began to diminish. There was a screeching, squealing din as the mechanism of the Loom began to slow down, gears faltering, cogs decelerating. The chirring row of the swarm grew louder. There were insects and smoke everywhere.

Eisenhorn went limp and fell sideways. His mouth stopped moving. The violet glare in his eyes went out. Blood dribbled from the corner of his lips.

'Get him out!' Drusher yelled.

'You'll have to help me,' said Voriet.

Between them, they scrabbled and dragged the big, heavy body clear of the cage.

'Is he dead?' asked Drusher.

'I don't know,' replied Voriet.

'I might as well have shot him,' said Drusher.

He heard someone calling out his name. Nayl and Macks were hurrying across the gantry towards them, waving insects out of their faces.

'What happened?' Nayl asked, crouching beside Voriet.

'Difficult to sum up,' said Voriet. 'The magos had an idea, so–'

'What did you do now?' asked Macks, turning to Drusher.

'I'd like to think something good,' said Drusher. 'But, who knows?'

She looked at him.

'You all right?' she asked.

'Yeah,' he said. 'You?'

'Fine.'

'I've missed you,' he said.

'It's been ten minutes,' she said.

'No,' he said. 'I meant...'

She hugged him tight.

'You silly bastard,' she whispered.

'He's breathing!' said Voriet.

'Well, she clamped on quite tight there,' said Drusher, 'but I'm fine–'

'*Eisenhorn* is breathing,' said Nayl.

They knelt down around him.

'Need to do something about these cuffs,' said Nayl.

'No idea where the key is,' said Macks.

Eisenhorn opened his eyes. They were pale and looked very old.

'You shouldn't have stopped me,' said Eisenhorn quietly. He was staring up at Drusher.

'Well, I think I should,' said Drusher.

'I was close,' said Eisenhorn. 'The King was going to fall.'

'He'll fall one day,' said Drusher. 'Sometimes it's important to do a small thing.'

Eisenhorn sat up slowly.

'Why did you say that?' he asked.

'No reason.'

'Someone said...' Eisenhorn began. 'Someone said something like that to me. I think I was dreaming. My mind is whirling.'

They helped him to his feet.

'Magos Drusher,' said Eisenhorn. 'You may face the censure of the Ordos for your actions today.'

'Yep,' said Drusher. 'And so will you. And I know which set of charges I'd rather be accused of.'

The smoke was getting thicker. Their clothes were heavy with the weight of crawling insects. From far below, they could hear the groan of tortured metal.

'I vote we leave,' said Nayl. 'As fast as we can.'

They headed for the steps, left the gantry and walked towards the hatch. Macks and Drusher helped Voriet between them. Nayl gave his arm to support the limping Eisenhorn.

The hatch was open. They went through into the long, tall hallway of the shade hall. It was cooler there, but smoke was flowing out of the tower and gathering in thick black folds up in the high ceiling. Insects covered every surface, chirring and ticking. They swarmed in the air.

'Did you open a door?' asked Voriet.

'I think so,' said Eisenhorn. 'I don't know.'

'I feel a breeze,' said Macks.

A figure stood in the hallway ahead of them.

It was Draven Sark. He had bathed and shaved off his beard and filthy hair. He wore the long white robes of a magos of Materia Medica.

'You should have finished your work,' he said.

Nayl raised his laspistol.

'Come with us or stand aside, Sark,' said Eisenhorn.

'Goran made such a mistake,' said Sark, gliding forwards. 'He thought you were usable. Transmutable. What a fool. You cannot make a heretic out of someone who is *already* a heretic.'

+Stand aside.+

Sark winced slightly.

'That will of yours,' he said. 'Indomitable. Unbroken, even by the Torment. You were already where the Torment wanted to take you. It just made you stronger.'

He smiled.

'It made you stronger, and yet you still did not have the strength and purpose to finish your work. You could have defeated us, and you failed. Human weakness got in the way.'

'Not *my* weakness,' said Eisenhorn.

Sark shrugged. 'Human weakness. It is why your side will lose, and the Rot-God-King will fall. It is why we will prevail.'

Nayl fired. The las-bolt hit Sark and left nothing but a tiny scorch mark on his white gown.

Sark's eyes lit with a violet glare. A wall of force slammed down the hallway. Nayl, Macks, Drusher and Voriet were hurled off their feet, and went tumbling as if cast by a hurricane wind. Swarming insects billowed everywhere.

Eisenhorn remained standing.

'I will unmake you now,' said Sark. 'Punishment for your abuse of the Loom, and for your obstruction of our work.'

There was another gust of force. Eisenhorn groaned and sank to one knee. The magos advanced upon him.

'We have both known the Torment, Gregor Eisenhorn,' he said. 'It has changed us both. It has made me stronger. I carry it with me.'

'You carry... *something*...' said Eisenhorn, struggling to remain upright.

'I will cast you to the wind,' said the magos, 'and I will save the Loom. The Great Work will continue.'

'Go to hell,' grunted Eisenhorn.

Sark blasted him again. Insects billowed up, moving as one, and covered Eisenhorn from head to foot, writhing and ticking. Eisenhorn bent his head and raised his cuffed fists in front of him, like a man at penance.

'Fall,' said the magos, and unleashed his power again. Eisenhorn slid back along the marble floor.

'The King seeks to tame us,' said Sark. 'Chain us. Harness us with incantation. What little he knows. How small he thinks. Freed from his bounds, loosed in your world, we will do such *wonders*.'

Drusher hauled Macks to her feet, trying to shield them both from the surging wind and boiling clouds of insects. Nayl dragged Voriet upright.

They all staggered backwards as the magos blasted again with invisible power.

Eisenhorn looked up at Sark. Even moving his head took great effort. He raised his cuffed hands in front of his face. He was quaking, like a great oak in a gale, about to splinter.

He spoke an un-word.

The force of it struck Sark full in the face. It also struck the cuff-chain binding Eisenhorn's wrists and exploded it, driving metal fragments into the magos like buckshot.

Sark staggered backwards, blood streaming from a dozen wounds in his face. They bled like stigmata, dripping onto the white cloth of his gown. His left eye was gone.

He screamed at Eisenhorn in rage. The un-word knocked Eisenhorn backwards. His hands now free, he clutched at the hallway wall to stay upright. He answered with an un-word that struck the magos like a sledgehammer.

The insect swarm became frenzied. Their mass clung to the high, white walls, scoring marks in the stone. In long, threading lines, they were inscribing the words of Enuncia that Eisenhorn and Sark were hurling at each other. Drusher realised where the odd script lining the walls of the tower had come from. The ancient, chirring cackle of prehuman times, recorded syllable by syllable in the fabric of the world, marks in stone left by things before man, the swarming plagues of truth and destruction, the litany of the Torment.

Face-to-face, enveloped in a whirlwind of light and hammering air, Eisenhorn and Sark yelled un-words at each other, trying to un-make each other's flesh and souls. Eisenhorn's eyes shone violet, as bright as Sark's remaining pupil.

With fury, Eisenhorn screamed and drove Sark backwards.

'Go! Go!' he yelled to the others. 'Get out! He's not human!'

'And you *are?*' asked Drusher, shielding his eyes.

+Get out!+

They tried to struggle past the two figures, but the wind was too strong, the concussion of the un-words too great. Eisenhorn focused and began to drive the un-words out of him with his mind instead of his mouth. He drove them with the will that impressed Magos Sark so much.

Sark was hurled back against the wall. It cracked behind him. Chirring insects etched words around his form. Pinned, he writhed, screaming. Black dust began to puff out of his skin as it desiccated and shrivelled. The howls coming from his wide-stretched mouth shattered the windows overhead. Glass rained down.

The black dust continued to spray out of him. He was becoming a skeletal thing, wrapped in the white cloth of his robes. He slid slowly down the wall.

'Move!' cried Eisenhorn.

'You broke him,' yelled Voriet.

'No,' said Eisenhorn. 'Not even slightly.'

Locustforms fluttered around them. A door stood open at the end of the hallway. It had not been there before. Daylight shone through it.

'Quickly,' said Eisenhorn. 'Quickly. Don't look back.'

And they were outside. The Karanine glade. Early evening. The old and mossy rocks of Keshtre Fortress lay around them in the undergrowth.

It was a still evening, but a sharp wind was blowing across the glade, swaying the old trees that faced them.

Drusher looked back.

A sliver of darkness stood behind them, a vertical slit in space like the shadow of a half-open door. The wind was spilling out of it, carrying smoke and clouds of locusts. The sliver was just standing there without a frame or any reference to the forest, a wound to another world.

+Thorn wishes Talon. Aegis, uplifting, a door without walls. Pattern Hawk.+

'What was *that?*' asked Macks, holding her head.

'Keep moving,' said Eisenhorn. 'We have to get as far away as possible.'

'From what?' asked Drusher.

'Sark's not dead, is he?' asked Voriet.

'The human part is,' said Eisenhorn. They were stumbling through the trees, locusts buzzing around them. 'The shell is gone. But not the thing that took up residence inside Magos Draven Sark during those long years he spent inside the cage.'

'What kind of thing?' asked Drusher, wishing he hadn't.

'Something of the warp,' said Voriet.

'Let's use the word daemon,' said Eisenhorn.

'Oh, let's *not!*' exclaimed Drusher.

'Can you close the door?' yelled Nayl, trying to help Voriet to keep up. 'Shut it in there?'

'Not any more,' said Eisenhorn.

They ran down the slope, through the ancient woodland. There was a stream ahead. All the birds had fallen silent, as if knowing it was time to be elsewhere.

A wind howled down the high valley from the slit in the world. Trees hushed and swayed. From the Keshtre site two hundred metres behind them, they heard the air popping and tearing, squeaking and splitting as something wrenched it open like a medicae surgeon levering apart a chest with rib-spreaders.

They splashed across the stream to the far bank. Behind them, they heard trees collapsing, torn up from the roots. Voriet could barely stay with them. Nayl and Drusher grabbed him to carry him.

Drusher heard another sound, a different howling. It was high-pitched, and the roar of it shook his insides.

A shadow passed over them. This was Eisenhorn's daemon, surely. He didn't want to look.

He did anyway, in time to see a massive orbital gunship pass overhead. It was moving so low it slammed through the upper branches of the tree canopy, showering down twigs and leaves. Its burners flared as it slowed and turned. The ground shook.

'We need a clearing,' yelled Nayl. 'Medea can't bring that in here.'

'Two hundred metres that way!' shouted Drusher.

'Really?' asked Nayl.

'Well, maybe three hundred,' replied Drusher. 'I remember Fargul's maps!'

They turned the way he had pointed and began to wade through the underbrush. Locusts still purred past their faces.

'Keep going,' cried Eisenhorn.

'This is insane!' yelled Macks.

'Medea is telling me... keep going,' Eisenhorn replied.

Overhead, impossibly huge and low, the gun-cutter swung around hard, attitude jets flaming. Nose down and lifting slightly, it moved back up the slope towards the Keshtre site.

Something was erupting up through the trees, pushing them down and splintering them back. Stone by stone, the walls of Keshtre Fortress were rebuilding themselves, rising up, pale and loam-caked, out of the old earth.

And something was climbing out of the fortress mound.

Something tall and slender, four times the height of any tree in the Karanines, rose up from behind the ragged curtain of stone. Then, a second, a third.

Drusher stared in amazement. He knew what they were. He'd seen them before. Seen them in a microscope field, magnified a thousand times so he could examine the joints, the chitinous cuticle structure, the black strands of hair follicles that sensed movement and vibration.

Spider legs. Some arachnid form, anyway. A xenos variety of *chelicerata*.

But these limbs were not under a microscope. They were two hundred metres long.

'That's not local,' he said.

'It's not an arachnid either,' said Eisenhorn.

'A daemon, is it?'

'A plague daemon,' said Eisenhorn.

The joints flexed, the legs stepping up over the fortress wall, gaining grip to raise the body behind them. Imagination was no longer Valentin Drusher's worst enemy. Imagination was woefully inadequate compared to this.

The world rattled. The gun-cutter had taken station and opened fire, hosing the fortress site with ordnance from its gunpods, chin-turret and underwing racks.

Fire bloomed in huge hemispheres, ripping up soil, splintered wood and fractured stone, five hectares of woodland laid waste.

The gun-cutter swayed slightly and unleashed again. Rapid-rate las-fire ripped from its chin-mount.

'Throne of Earth, that'll flatten the whole world!' cried Drusher.

'No,' said Eisenhorn. 'Medea's just trying to keep it at bay. To hold it back and buy us time.'

'To do what?'

'Reach the clearing.'

Drusher looked back, still running. The huge dark mass was rising up out of the smoke and raging flames that enveloped it.

It lashed out with its long, clawed limbs. Then tendrils whipped out from the half-seen body mass too. They were organic and boneless: tentacles, or pustular cords, or maybe ragged loops of intestine. Drusher could smell the stench of rot and faecal waste.

One of the huge limbs struck the gun-cutter a glancing blow, it veered hard to the right, jets howling to compensate. The engines shrieked.

'She's too low!' Nayl yelled.

The gun-cutter was ploughing sideways, ripping through treetops and pulverising trunks. It was beginning to shake and rotate, unable to pull clear. There was no room to gain lift and energy.

'Oh Throne!' Voriet wailed.

+Medea!+

There was a long, terrible crashing noise of trees uprooting. The gun-cutter vanished behind the treeline.

The thing from the warp pulled itself clear of Keshtre's walls on its vast legs.

TWENTY-EIGHT

UNWOVEN

I think this is probably all my fault,' said Drusher. 'I'm sorry.'

'No,' said Eisenhorn. 'If you hadn't pulled me out of the cage, Sark would have killed me in it. Taken control of the Loom again. And the thing inside him... It is a *greater daemon*, Drusher. And one not bound and trapped by the King in Yellow's conjurations. It has used Sark as a loophole, a door into our space, freed from the proscriptions of summoning and binding. Sark has unwittingly unleashed a greater and far more immediate threat to Imperial space than the damned King in Yellow.'

They had reached the clearing. It was an old patch of hill pasture that sloped down to the woods at the base of the valley.

Drusher looked back. He couldn't see the daemon, but a vast fog of buzzing blackness veiled the sky beyond the nearest trees. A mass swarm. Trillions of insects, bathed in filthy light.

The ground vibrated. Footsteps, thought Drusher. Giant, scuttling footsteps. In the distance, landslips kicked off by the vibrations thundered down the mountains, raising plumes of dust.

Behind them, something in the black fog screamed. A bellow, an exhalation. An *exaltation*. It boomed out across the Karanines, echoing from peak to peak. A deep, wet, clotted pulsing howl like the droning note of a giant Udaric war-horn, but one big enough to swallow the world.

Drusher wondered how to face his death. He wondered how a man did that, and if it mattered. He felt like sinking to his knees, but that was just the exhaustion. He doubted there was a protocol for facing death when your death was an abomination the size of a city.

He decided to stand and face it, whatever it was going to be. He damn well *wasn't* going to cry. It had been a good life, really. Hard work, some insane adventures. A few, sweet, maddening years somewhere in the middle that he wouldn't have given up for anything. *Shouldn't* have given up for anything.

Macks was tugging at his arm.

'What?' he asked.

'What are you doing?'

He shrugged.

'Facing death,' he replied. 'What else is there?'

She sighed.

'Not a lot, now,' she replied.

'You *see* the trouble you get me in?' he said.

'Bet you wished you'd never met me,' she said.

'Not even once,' he replied.

The howling came again. Wind rushed across them.

The gun-cutter rose up behind the trees on the edge of the pasture, jets screaming. Nose down, it swept across the grass, lifting clouds of spinning leaves and stalks into the air. Drusher could see the amber-lit cockpit. Medea, grim-faced, pulling on the controls.

The forward ramp was lowering even before she put the big craft down on its heavy undercarriage.

They ran up the ramp.

'*Are you all in?*' Medea's voice crackled through the intercabin vox.

'Go!' Nayl yelled.

'Handholds!' Eisenhorn ordered.

They grabbed what they could. Eisenhorn pushed Voriet into an acceleration couch and held him down. Macks grabbed an overhead strap, then grabbed Drusher as he staggered past.

The gun-cutter lifted. The ramp wasn't even shut. Drusher could see the ground dropping away, the pasture...

The gun-cutter swung, lifting its nose. Everyone lurched the other way. Now, Drusher could see evening sky through the still-closing ramp. Acceleration pulled at them hard.

'Strap in,' ordered Eisenhorn. 'Medea! Brace for shockwave in three!'

'Shockwave?' asked Macks.

'I can feel it coming,' said Eisenhorn. 'The fire, you see? It was never put out.'

The gun-cutter climbed on maximum thrust, racing into the high altitudes of the great peaks.

Behind it, in the black fog of the valley, there was a blink. A flash of violet light and jade-green electrical discharge.

A two-kilometre square patch of the woodland folded into itself, and vanished.

Then, the shockwave.

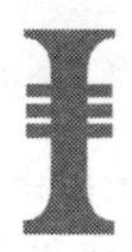

TWENTY-NINE

AT THE CLOSING OF THE WORLD

Caffeine?' asked Medea.

She held out a tin mug to Drusher.

'Thanks,' he said as he took it.

'Took me a while to find you,' she said. 'What are you doing up here?'

'Taking a last look, really,' he said.

From the old walls of Helter, they could see across the valley. It had been raining since before dawn. Rain tapped off the Magistratum slickers they were both wearing. It spotted the lenses of Drusher's old spectacles, but he could see well enough. Less than a kilometre away, the forest was gone, the earth scorched smooth. Great clouds of vapour were still rising off the scar.

'You fly well,' he said.

'There was incentive,' she replied. 'Besides, it's what he pays me to do.'

'You'd do it even if he didn't pay you,' he said.

'There is sadly a great deal of truth in that,' she said. 'Magos, you and Macks... You could use some support after this. He won't mention it or offer it, because, well, you know... but trust me. You don't feel it yet, but you've experienced trauma. Physical trauma. And existential trauma too. There is a confessor I can recommend in Tycho. Better still, off-world specialists on Gudrun, if you're still planning to leave. They have some experience and are discreet. We've used them before. The Houses of the Ordos could offer you some consolation, but I don't recommend it. You'd open yourself to a different world of hurt.'

He nodded.

'By rights,' she said, 'you both would be considered... contaminated by what you've seen. The Ordos would want you restrained from public contact, at the very least. The very least. And even if you speak to the discreet confessors I have recommended, don't say anything stupid.'

'Like?'

'Like mentioning the word *daemon*.'

'All right,' said Drusher.

'But take a recommendation, please,' she said. 'And make Macks do it too. What you've seen this last day or so... No one should ever see that. It will scar you, I'm sorry to say. Change you. Maybe for the rest of your life.'

'I'd be slightly horrified if it *didn't*, Mam Betancore,' he replied. He sipped the caffeine. 'How is Voriet?'

'Nayl and Macks have taken him to the infirmary in Unkara. They voxed just now. He's stable. Young and strong.'

'Good,' said Drusher.

'Eisenhorn wants to see you,' she said. 'He sent me to find you.'

'All right,' said Drusher. 'Will he tell me what happened?'

'Probably not,' she said.

'Will you, then?'

She shrugged.

'As I understand these things,' she said, 'it was the Loom in the end. Damaged by the fire, but a volatile mechanism anyway.'

'Aren't we all?' said Drusher.

'It's not possible to construct them in real space,' she said, 'because of the interference patterns they generate. It was stable only in the extimate fold of the shade hall.'

'And the...' Drusher found he really didn't want to say the word 'daemon'. 'And the thing, it opened that up?'

'Yes,' said Medea. 'Reality was no longer overlapping. It was simultaneous. It was just a matter of time before the fabric of... reality... shredded. Imploded. And took everything with it. Keshtre. A sizeable patch of ground and subsoil.'

'And... the thing itself.'

'Yes.'

'Was he counting on that?' asked Drusher. 'Eisenhorn, I mean? Was he counting on that happening?'

'I believe he was hoping. It was the only possible good outcome. Nothing else on Gershom would have stopped it.'

'Is it still out there?' Drusher asked. 'I mean, is it trapped inside the shade hall?'

'No,' she said. 'That extimate fold is gone. Obliterated. An empyrean gravity compression effect that... Well, I won't bore you with the technical detail.'

'So it's dead?'

She shook her head.

'Things like that can't die. It's been cast back into the warp where it came from. It's still out there... or in there... somewhere. Sorry.'

'No wonder you recommend unburdening,' he said. 'I'm worrying what I will begin to say to the poor confessor I visit.'

He wandered up to the old man's library. Eisenhorn was tossing books from the shelves into a pile on the floor.

'We need to burn this place,' he said. 'The books, the bodies. Everything. I've briefed Macks on how to contain the situation. A cover story. An accident during fleet manoeuvres. Something to keep the governor satisfied. And the Ordos off Macks' back.'

'They'll come looking,' said Drusher.

'Without doubt, but eventually,' said Eisenhorn. 'And when they get here, they'll find very little. And a lot of people who know zero.'

'Is this the part where you reprimand me?' asked Drusher. 'Or, I don't know, burn me along with the books?'

'No, I wanted to thank you,' said Eisenhorn.

'Really?'

'You did more than was asked,' said Eisenhorn. 'And your expertise was invaluable at several key points.'

'Well, you asked for help.'

'I believe I owe you passage off-world,' said Eisenhorn. 'That was the deal. You're a clever man, Drusher, and a great deal of *purpose* still awaits you. A greater career you can accomplish. You should not stay here and waste the rest of your life on a backwater planet that you no longer love.'

'I've found it has more to it than I first imagined,' Drusher replied.

'I can't give you passage,' said Eisenhorn. 'Things are complicated and we must leave shortly. But there's a bag on the chaise there. Take it, with my thanks.'

Drusher walked over to the old chaise, picked up the small leather kitbag and opened it.

'Right,' he said.

'There is an alternative,' said Eisenhorn. 'Don't take the bag. Come with us instead.'

'With you?'

'It will be more insane adventures, I'm afraid.'

'Yes, but *with* you?'

'I have very few friends,' said Eisenhorn. 'Probably none, in fact. And I can't call on many people for help any more. I could use a clever man at my side. I'm running out of allies, and where I'm going...'

'Sancour?'

'Yes.'

'The city of Queen Mab?'

'Indeed.'

'You want me to go with you?'

'As I said, magos, I can count the people who now stand with me on the fingers of one hand. You are a specialist, an expert advisor, and you have shown your mettle.'

'I thought you hated me for pulling you out of that cage,' said Drusher.

'I've had time to reflect,' said Eisenhorn. 'If you hadn't, it would have ended badly.'

'That's what ending *well* looks like?' asked Drusher.

'Often.'

'But you're still going on,' said Drusher, 'to Queen Mab, on Sancour?'

'Yes, magos.'

'Will you ever stop?' asked Drusher. 'I mean, will you ever know *when* to stop? When it's enough... When it is *too much*...'

'I hope so,' said Eisenhorn. 'I hope at least I will have wise people around me to advise me so. To be honest though, magos, I don't think a man like me ever retires. That's not how it works.

'I don't think a man like you retires either,' he added. 'I think that's what you've been trying to tell yourself all along. That there's more to you, more to your life. Come with me, if you'd care to. You have seen things now. You have been tempered by this experience. Everything that follows will be less of a shock.'

'Thank you, sir,' said Drusher. 'But I don't think I will.'

'I thought there was nothing left to keep you here?' Eisenhorn asked.

'So did I,' said Drusher.

Eisenhorn walked over to him and held out his hand.

'Then thank you for your service,' he said. 'We won't meet again, but I have appreciated your company.'

Drusher shook his hand.

'You look well, inquisitor,' he said. 'Better than you did when I first met you. Which, given what we've endured, is quite something. You seem stronger.'

'I am.'

'You've been tempered by this too, then?'

'I think so,' said Eisenhorn. 'I feel stronger than I have in years. Ready to face the endgame.'

'Is that a good thing?' asked Drusher.

'Yes,' said Eisenhorn. He smiled.

'I don't think I've ever seen you smile before,' said Drusher.

'It's not something I've done in a long time,' said Eisenhorn.

THIRTY

THE OLD PLACE

Evening was rolling in, a violet haze off the sea. It was two days after Drusher had stood and watched the fortress of Helter burn.

Macks rolled the Magistratum cruiser to a halt and pulled up on the shingle beside the old highway.

'Really?' she said. 'Back here?'

'It suits me,' he said.

She shrugged. She was trying to appear cheerful, he could tell. But they were both still in their heads. There was a tremor in his hands that wouldn't go away. The universe would never seem the same to either of them.

'Will you come in?' he asked.

'I've got to get back,' she said. 'If I turn around now I can make it to Unkara by dawn. There's a lot of clearing up to do. A lot of paperwork. A whole lot of crap, in fact, including a meeting with the governor tomorrow night.'

'Good luck with that.'

'Oh, well, you know,' she said. 'But I'll come back and visit.'

'Don't leave it too long.'

They looked at each other. He leaned forwards and kissed her. He could smell *True Heart* very faintly. The kiss lingered.

'Get on,' she said. 'I've got to go back.'

He got out of the cruiser and hefted his bag onto his shoulder. She pulled down in a circle and drove back onto the hem of the highway. He raised a hand, a little wave. She stopped and slid down her window.

'*Why* does this place suit you?' she called out.

'Because you'll know where to find me,' he replied.

Macks grinned. She roared away onto the highway.

Drusher watched her lights fade into the twilight. He turned and looked at the old shack. He could hear the rush of the waves on the beach behind him. He could see the sky turning dark like a bruise along the wasteland horizon beyond the dunes.

He walked into the shack. It smelled dry and stale. It was just as he had left it. He put his bag on the table, opened the hall cupboard and cranked on the generator.

He lit a lamp. Outside, the Bone Coast evening was falling fast.

He opened his old bag and unpacked a few bits and pieces. Some food he'd bought in Unkara town. A can of caffeine Medea Betancore had given him. His taxonomy. A folded Magistratum rain slicker, just the thing for wet days. The Regit snub, cleaned and reloaded, with two boxes of shells. Eisenhorn's parting gift, the small leather bag. Esic Fargul's sketchbook with its faded green cover, and an old, annotated book on bird migration.

He went out into the yard behind the shack to watch the last of the day. Seabirds were circling. It *was* sort of beautiful, he thought.

The sea raptor was sitting on the beach fence. It watched him. He smiled at it.

It spread its wings, and flew down, landing at his feet.

'I let you go,' he said. 'You wanted to get out so much.'

It stared at him.

'There's no hope for either of us, is there?' he asked.

He went into the kitchen, opened the wax paper bindings of the provisions he'd bought and brought back a couple of slices of good, cured Karanine ham. He held one out to it.

Its beak snapped as it took it. But Drusher still had all his fingers.

'You old bastard,' he said.

Several nights later, he was working at his table late when lights went by on the highway. He looked up every time a set of lights went past, hoping.

This set, southbound, slowed down and pulled up on the gravel outside. He heard crunching footsteps.

'Don't make a fuss,' he told the raptor perched on the back of the chair facing him. It turned its beady eyes to the front door. 'I'm warning you,' he said. 'I'll put you outside.'

He opened the door before the knock came.

Drusher's smile ebbed slightly. It wasn't her.

'Interrogator Voriet,' he said.

Voriet was patched with dressings, and his arm was in a sling.

'Magos,' he said. 'I apologise for the late hour. Marshal Macks told me where you were.'

'She remembers then,' said Drusher. That was something.

'May I come in?'

'Why not?' replied Drusher, holding the door wide.

Voriet stepped inside. He looked with some alarm at the sea raptor. It had taken up a perch on the top of the dresser and clacked its beak at the interrogator.

'Is that quite safe?' asked Voriet.

'Don't mind him,' said Drusher.

'Are you... keeping it as a pet?'

'Not really. It just won't leave.'

'Have you given it a name?' Voriet asked.

'No,' Drusher lied.

Voriet cleared his throat.

'Speaking of leaving,' he said. 'He's gone.'

'Who?'

'You know very well,' said Voriet. 'Eisenhorn. He and Nayl and Medea. They've gone. Made shift. Left Gershom.'

'And they've left you here?'

'Yes,' said Voriet.

'Are you surprised?' asked Drusher. 'I mean, he knew. Eisenhorn knew all about you. He couldn't trust you, could he?'

'He *could*,' said Voriet. 'After all that. He should have known that he could. I'm disappointed. I thought... Anyway...'

'Caffeine?' asked Drusher.

'Thank you, no,' said Voriet. 'I can't stay. I'm leaving Gershom tomorrow. I'm going to the Ordos, to make a full report.'

'Are you?'

'A full report,' said Voriet. 'I intend to... to... make the case for him. Insist that they revise their ruling. Reconsider his status. Perhaps offer him support and assistance with his undertaking.'

'His *war?*'

'Yes, that.' Voriet looked awkward. 'I want to help him,' he said. 'And I need to offer the Ordos information to establish good faith. Do you know where he's gone?'

'Eisenhorn?'

'Yes. Did he tell you where he was going?'

'He's off on his insane adventures,' said Drusher. 'Off to find the King in Yellow.'

'I know that,' said Voriet.

'Then you know as much as I do, interrogator.'

'He mentioned a place,' said Voriet. 'Queen Mab. The City of Dust. You mentioned it too.'

'It could be anywhere,' said Drusher. '*Literally*,' he added, with a smile.

'You don't know where it is?'

'I don't,' said Drusher. 'I'm sorry. I can't help you.'

'Did he mention anywhere else? Any other names? Anything?'

'No, I'm sorry, he didn't. He's a very closed person, Voriet. *You* know that. He doesn't trust anyone. I was hardly his friend.'

Voriet nodded. 'All right.'

'You sure you won't have some caffeine?'

'No,' said Voriet. 'Thank you, magos. I'm sorry to have intruded.'

The lights faded away. The night highway was empty and quiet. Drusher closed the blinds and sat back down to his work. The raptor clacked its beak.

'Shut up,' said Drusher. 'It wasn't a *big* lie. I just decided something was... classified.'

He sipped his mug of caffeine. He thought for a moment, then got up and took the bag Eisenhorn had given him out of the chest of drawers. He opened it and looked at the fat blocks of pristine currency bonds inside, each bundle mint but non-sequential, wrapped together with treasury ribbons.

A lot of money. Enough for passage off-world, and not steerage class either. Passage to Gudrun, or Sameter, or any number of worlds with extraordinary flora and fauna. Work enough for several more lives, several more taxonomies. And enough cash left over to afford a little juvenat work so he would last those several more lives.

Or, enough currency to buy a nice place in Tycho City or Unkara Town. A really nice place. The sort of place you could retire in and live happily. Especially if you weren't alone.

Walks in the hills. Sketching. Observing. A good supper every night. Long conversations about everything and anything. Anything she ever wanted to talk about, really.

And time to write a decent treatise on non-indigenous fauna, specifically *Chaopterae metalepta,* which Drusher had a feeling would soon be a problem for agriculture in the northern provinces.

Time for anything, in fact. He could wait for it. He could wait for the lights to come back, because he knew they would. Next week, maybe the week after. Soon.

He smiled to himself. He offered the last slice of cured ham to the raptor. It fluttered down from the dresser and stood on the table, taking the offering from his hand almost daintily.

The lamplight caught its dark and bottomless eyes. For a moment, they reflected a violet flash.

It was almost exactly the same shade of violet that Drusher had seen in Eisenhorn's eyes when the inquisitor had smiled at him for the very first and very last time.

CHRONOLOGY

075 (M41)	–	'Pestilence'
198	–	Gregor Eisenhorn born, DeKere's World.
Circa 219	–	Endor and Eisenhorn serve as interrogators under Inquisitor Hapshant.
		'Master Imus' Transgression'
222	–	Eisenhorn appointed full inquisitor.
223	–	'Regia Occulta'
240	–	*Xenos*
241	–	'Missing in Action'
304	–	Gideon Ravenor born.
312	–	Midas Betancore dies. His daughter Medea is an infant.
Circa 345	–	*Malleus*
	–	Ravenor crippled.
346	–	Ravenor appointed full inquisitor.
355	–	'Backcloth For A Crown Additional'
Circa 360	–	'The Strange Demise of Titus Endor'
386	–	*Hereticus*
402	–	*Ravenor*
	–	'Thorn Wishes Talon'
Circa 403	–	*Ravenor Returned*
	–	Valentin Drusher born.
404	–	*Ravenor Rogue*
441	–	*Magos Drusher arrives on Gershom to begin taxonomy.*
448	–	'The Curiosity'
450	–	*Medea Betancore disappears.*
455	–	'Gardens of Tycho'
461	–	*Alizebeth Bequin's stasis-suspended body reported missing.*
Circa 465	–	'The Keeler Image'
Circa 470	–	'Perihelion'
Circa 475	–	*The Magos*
477	–	Beta Bequin "born", Sancour, Angelus Subsector.

Circa 480	–	Eisenhorn arrives on Sancour. Medea begins watching Beta.
Circa 495	–	Ravenor arrives on Sancour.
Circa 500	–	*Pariah*